SIGRID UNDSET was born at Kalundborg, Denmark, on May 20, 1882. From 1899 to 1909, she was a clerk in an office in Christiania. She began publishing stories in 1907, and won resounding success with the novel *Jenny* in 1912, the year of her marriage to Anders C. Svarstad (annulled in 1925). Having undergone a religious crisis, she joined the Roman Catholic Church in 1925. Between 1920 and 1922, Undset published the three volumes (*The Bridal Wreath, The Mistress of Husaby,* and *The Cross*) of her great fourteenth-century historical novel *Kristin Lavransdatter,* which soon made her world famous. This major work was followed (1925–27) by *The Master of Hestviken,* and she was awarded the Nobel Prize for Literature in 1928. She wrote many other novels, as well as essays, poems, tales for young readers, and short stories, a collection of which were published here in 1959 under the title *Four Stories.* Having lived in the United States for some time in the 1940's, she returned to Norway after the Second World War and died at Lillehammer, Norway, on June 10, 1949. What *The Nation* wrote of the second novel of *The Master of Hestviken, The Snake Pit,* can well sum up her remarkable art: "Although she reproduces medieval Norway in all the rich pageantry of color and form, although she spares us neither sounds nor smells, her story also is intensely real. She can transport us eight centuries and several thousand miles more effectively than most writers can take us into the house next door."

The Master of Hestviken

THE

Master of Hestviken

SIGRID UNDSET

THE AXE

THE SNAKE PIT

IN THE WILDERNESS

THE SON AVENGER

A PLUME BOOK

NEW AMERICAN LIBRARY

NEW YORK AND SCARBOROUGH, ONTARIO

Translated from the Norwegian by Arthur G. Chater.

Originally published in two volumes as: Olav Audunssøn I Hestviken
and Olav Audunssøn og Hans Børn. Copyright 1925, 1927 by
H. Ascheboug & Co., Oslo.

This is an authorized reprint of a hardcover edition published by
Alfred A. Knopf, Inc. The hardcover edition was published
simultaneously in Canada by Random House of Canada Limited,
Toronto.

SIGNET, SIGNET CLASSIC, MENTOR, PLUME, MERIDIAN and
NAL BOOKS are published in the United States by New American
Library, 1633 Broadway, New York, New York 10019,
in Canada by The New American Library of Canada Limited,
81 Mack Avenue, Scarborough, Ontario M1L 1M8

First Plume Printing, March, 1978

5   6   7   8   9   10   11   12

The Master of Hestviken

The Master of Hestviken

THE AXE

PART ONE

OLAV AUDUNSSON TAKES A WIFE

OLAV AUDUNSSON TAKES A WIFE

I

THE STEINFINNSSONS was the name folk gave to a kin that flourished in the country about Lake Mjösen at the time the sons of Harald Gille held sway in Norway. In those days men of that stock held manors in every parish that bordered the lake.

In the years of trouble which later came upon the land, the Steinfinnssons thought most of keeping their estates unshorn and their manors unburned, and for the most part they were strong enough to succeed in this, whether the Birchlegs or any of the opposing bands were to the fore in the Upplands. They seemed not to care greatly who in the end might be kings in Norway; but some men of this line had served King Magnus Erlingsson and later Sigurd Markusfostre faithfully and well, and none of them had aided Sverre and his kinsmen more than they could help. Old Tore Steinfinnsson of Hov and his sons joined the cause of King Skule, but when there was once more peace in the land they paid allegiance to King Haakon.[1]

[1] The period preceding that of this story (that is, the late twelfth and early thirteenth centuries) had been one of anarchy in Norway. Harald Gille (or Gilchrist; he came of Norse stock in Ireland) reigned 1130–6. His sons were Inge, Sigurd Mund, and Eystein, who at first reigned conjointly. Inge was the last to be killed (1161), and the crown then went to

Haakon II	1161
Magnus V, Erlingsson	1162
Sverre	1184
Haakon III	1202
Inge Baardsson	1204
Haakon IV, the Old	1217
Magnus VI	1263
Eirik	1280
Haakon V	1299

Sigurd Markusfostre was a son of Sigurd Mund; he was proclaimed King in 1162; in the end he was executed. Sverre was the famous adventurer

But from that time the family began to lose something of its repute. The country was now quieter and law and justice prevailed between man and man; their power was then greatest who held the King's authority or had served in the royal body-guard and won the King's trust. But the Steinfinnssons stayed at home upon their lands and were content to govern their own estates.

They were yet a wealthy kindred. The Steinfinnssons had been the last of the great Uppland lords to own thralls, and they still took the offspring of their freedmen into service or made them tenants on their land. Among the people round about, it was whispered that the Steinfinnssons were a race greedy of power, but they had the wit to choose such liegemen as should be easy to deal with. The men of the kin had no name for being of the wisest; but foolish they could not be called, since they had shown such good sense in the preserving of their estates. And they were not harsh lords toward those of less degree, so long as none offered to raise his voice against them.

Now, two years before King Haakon the Old died, young Tore Toresson of Hov sent his youngest son, Steinfinn, to the royal body-guard. His age was then eighteen; he was a handsome, well-grown man, but it was with him as with his kinsmen: folk knew them by their horses and their clothes, their arms and jewels. But if young Steinfinn had donned a coarse peasant's cloak, many a man would hardly have known him, of those who had called him friend and boon companion over the ale tankards the night before. The Steinfinnssons were goodly men for the most, but, as the saying was, they were lost in the crowd of church folks; and of this Steinfinn his fellows used to say that his wit was none too bad, but that it was as naught to his arrogance.

Now, Steinfinn was in Björgvin,[2] and there he met a maiden, Ingebjörg Jonsdatter, who had her place at the King's court with

whose followers were known as Birchlegs (*Birkebeinar*), from the shifts they were put to for foot-gear and clothing. He won his way to the crown in spite of the fierce opposition of the Church. Skule was the brother of Inge Baardsson, at whose death he claimed the throne. The Birchlegs however supported Sverre's grandson, Haakon Haakonsson, who was proclaimed king at the age of thirteen. Skule continually rebelled against Haakon, who finally defeated him at the Battle of Oslo; after this Skule was captured and slain by the Birchlegs 1240, and the civil wars came to an end.

[2] The modern Bergen.

Queen Ingebjörg. She and Steinfinn took a liking for each other,
and he had his suit preferred with her father; but Jon answered
that his daughter was already promised to Mattias Haraldsson,
a dear friend of young King Magnus and one of his body-guard.
But it seemed Steinfinn could not take his rejection in earnest: he
came again many times, and had men of mark and at last Queen
Ingebjörg herself to plead his cause. It availed nothing, for Jon
Paalsson would not break his word to Mattias.

Steinfinn followed King Haakon in his last warfaring west
oversea. In the fight at Largs he won fair renown for valour.
While the King lay sick at Kirkevaag,[3] Steinfinn often had the
night watch by his side, and at least he himself thought that King
Haakon had shown him great favour.

The next summer Steinfinn was again in Björgvin. And one
fine morning just after John's Mass,[4] as some of the Queen's maidens were coming from Nonneseter toward the King's house, they
met Steinfinn and his body-servant riding through the street. They
were leading a fine horse which Steinfinn said he had bought that
morning, as they saw it, with bridle and woman's saddle. He
greeted the damsels with courtesy and blithe jesting and would
have them try this horse of his. They then went all together to a
meadow and diverted themselves awhile. But when Ingebjörg
Jonsdatter was in the saddle, Steinfinn said that she must have the
loan of the horse to ride back to the King's court, and he would
go with her.—The next that was heard of these two was that they
had passed through Vors and taken to the hills. At last they
reached Hov; Tore seemed at first ill pleased at his son's misdeed,
but afterwards he gave him a homestead, Frettastein, which lay remote in the forest tracts. There he lived with Ingebjörg Jonsdatter
as though they had been lawfully wedded, and he held a christening ale with the most lavish hospitality when she bore him a
daughter next spring.

Nothing was done to him, either for the rape of the woman or
for his flight from the body-guard. Folk said he could thank
Queen Ingebjörg for that. And at last the Queen made a recon-

---

[3] After being defeated at Largs in Ayrshire by Alexander III of Scotland (in 1263) King Haakon retired to Kirkwall (Kirkevaag) in Orkney,
where he died in the Bishop's palace, some remains of which are still to be
seen close by the newly restored cathedral.

[4] June 21.

ciliation between the young couple and Jon Paalsson; he gave
Steinfinn his daughter in marriage and held their wedding at the
King's court in Oslo, where he was then a courtier.

At that time Ingebjörg was expecting her third child; but neither she nor Steinfinn showed becoming humility toward Jon
or thanked him as they ought for his fatherly kindness. Steinfinn
gave costly gifts to his wife's father and her kinsmen, but in other
ways both he and his wife were very overweening and behaved
as though all their life had been honourable, nor had they any need
to humble themselves in order to retrieve their position. They
brought their elder daughter, Ingunn, to the wedding, and Steinfinn danced with her on his arm and showed her to all who were
there; she was three years old, and her parents were proud beyond measure of this fair child.

But their first son died, whom Ingebjörg bore close upon their
marriage, and after that she had still-born twins, both boys. Then
the two bowed the knee to Jon Paalsson and besought his pardon
with contrite hearts. Thereafter Ingebjörg had two sons who
lived. She grew fairer with every year that passed, she and Steinfinn lived together in affection, maintained a great house, and were
merry and of good cheer.

One man there was of whom none seemed to take thought:
Mattias Haraldsson, Ingebjörg's rightful bridegroom, whom she
had played false. He went into foreign lands at the time Steinfinn's
wedding was held and he stayed away for many years. Mattias was
a little man and ill-favoured, but mettlesome, hardy, and of great
wealth.

Steinfinn and Ingebjörg had been married seven years or thereabouts and their daughters, Ingunn and Tora, were ten and eight
winters old, but the sons were quite small—when Mattias Haraldsson came one night with an armed band to Frettastein. It was at
haymaking, and many of the house-folk were away on the outlying pastures; those who were at home were overpowered as
they lay asleep. Steinfinn did not wake until he was pulled out
of the bed, where he slept with his wife. The summer was warm
that year, so folk lay naked; Steinfinn was bare as his mother
bore him as he stood bound by his own board with three men
holding him.

The lady Ingebjörg defended herself like a wild beast, with
tooth and nail, while Mattias wrapped the coverlet about her,

lifted her out of bed, and set her on his knees. Mattias said to
Steinfinn:

"Now could I take such vengeance as ye two deserve—and you,
Steinfinn, should stand there a bound man with no power to protect your wife, if I had a mind to take her who was promised to
me and never to you. But I have more fear of breaking God's law
and I take more heed of good morals than you. So now I shall
chasten you, Steinfinn, by letting you take back your wife inviolate, by my favour—and you, my Ingebjörg, dwell with your
man and peace be with you both! After this night I trow ye will
remember to thank me each time ye shall embrace in joy and gladness," he said with a loud laugh.

He kissed the lady and laid her in the bed, calling to his men
that now they should ride away.—Then he turned to Steinfinn.

Steinfinn had not uttered a word, and, as he saw he could not
break loose, he stood still; but his face was a deep crimson and
he did not take his eyes off Mattias. The other went close up to
him.

"If you have not the grace, man, then maybe you have the wit
to thank me for the mercy I have shown tonight?" asked Mattias
with a laugh.

"Be sure I shall thank you," quoth Steinfinn. "If God grant me
life."

Now, Mattias was dressed in a kirtle with open, hanging sleeves
and tassels at their points. He took the flap of his sleeve in his
hand and whisked the tassel across Steinfinn's face, laughing yet
louder. And of a sudden he drove his fist into the face of the
bound man, so that the blood flowed from Steinfinn's mouth and
nose.

That done, he went out to his men. Olav Audunsson, Steinfinn's foster-son, a boy of eleven years, ran forward and cut Steinfinn's bonds. The lad, Steinfinn's children, and their foster-
mothers had been dragged into the outer room and held there
while Mattias was speaking to his faithless betrothed and her man
within.

Steinfinn snatched a spear and, naked as he was, ran out after
Mattias and his men as they rode down the steep slope, straight
across the plough-land, laughing scornfully. Steinfinn flung the
spear, but it fell short. Meanwhile the boy Olav ran to the men's
room and the byre and let out the serving-men who had been

barred in, while Steinfinn went back to the house, dressed himself, and took his arms.

But all thought of pursuing Mattias was vain, for there were but three horses left at Frettastein and they were loose in the paddock. Nevertheless Steinfinn rode off at once, to seek his father and brothers. As he dressed, he had spoken in private with his wife. She came out with him when he was ready to set out. And now Steinfinn declared to his house-folk that he would not sleep with his wife until he had repaired the shame, so that no man could say she was his by the favour of Mattias Haraldsson. Then he rode forth, but his lady went into an old outhouse that stood in the courtyard, and locked herself in.

The house-folk, men and women, streamed into the hall, eager to learn what had happened. They close-questioned Olav, who sat half-clad on the edge of the bed that Steinfinn's weeping daughters had crept into; they turned to ask the two little maids and the foster-mother of Steinfinn's youngest son. But none of these could tell them aught, and soon the servants grew tired of questioning and went out.

The boy sat in the dark hall listening to Ingunn's obstinate weeping. Then he climbed up into the bed and lay down by her side.

"Be sure your father will take vengeance. You may well believe he will do that. And I trow I shall be with him, to show that Steinfinn has a son-in-law, though his sons are yet too young to bear arms!"

It was the first time Olav had dared to speak straight out of the betrothal that had been made between him and Ingunn when they were children. In the first years he spent at Frettastein the servants had sometimes chanced to speak of it and tease the children with being betrothed, and it had always made Ingunn wild. Once she had run to her father and complained, and he had been angered and had forbidden his people to speak of such things—so wrathfully that more than one of them had guessed that maybe Steinfinn repented his bargain with Olav's father.

That night Ingunn took Olav's reminder of the plans that had been made for them in such wise that she crept up to the boy and wept upon his arm, till the sleeve of his shirt was drenched with her tears.

. . .

From that night a great change came over the life at Frettastein. Steinfinn's father and brothers counselled him to bring a suit against Mattias Haraldsson, but Steinfinn said that he himself would be the judge of what his honour was worth.

Now, Mattias had gone straight home to the manor in Borgesyssel where he dwelt. And the following spring he went on a pilgrimage in foreign lands. But when this was noised abroad and it was known that Steinfinn's wrath was such that he shunned folk and would not live with his wife any more, then there was much talk of the vengeance that Mattias had taken upon his faithless betrothed. Even though Mattias and his men told no different tale of the raid from what was heard at Frettastein, it turned out that the farther the rumour spread over the country, the more cheaply folk judged that Steinfinn had been held by Mattias. And a ballad was made of these doings as they were thought to have fallen out.

One evening—it was three years later—as Steinfinn sat drinking with his men, he asked if there were any who could sing the ballad that had been made upon him. At first all the house-carls made as though they knew naught of any ballad. But when Steinfinn promised a great gift to him who could sing his dance, it came out that the whole household knew it. Steinfinn heard it to the end; now and then he bared his teeth in a sort of smile. As soon as it was done, he went to bed together with his half-brother Kolbein Toresson, and the folk heard the two talking behind the bed-shutters till near midnight.

This Kolbein was a son of Tore of Hov by a concubine he had had before his marriage; and he had always cared more for his children by her than for those born in wedlock. For Kolbein he had made a good marriage and got him a great farm to the northward on Lake Mjösen. But there was little thrift in Kolbein; he was overbearing, unjust, and of a hasty temper and was ever in lawsuits both with lesser men and with his equals. So he was a man of few friends and there was little love between him and his true-born half-brothers, until, after his misfortune, Steinfinn took up with Kolbein. After that these two brothers were always together and Kolbein charged himself with Steinfinn and all his affairs. But he ordered them as he ordered his own and brought trouble with him even when he acted on his brother's behalf.

Assuredly it was not that Kolbein had a will to harm his

younger brother; he was fond of Steinfinn in his own way, after
that the younger in his perplexity had put himself wholly into his
half-brother's hands. Careless and lazy Steinfinn had been in his
days of prosperity; he had thought more of lordly living than of
taking care for his estate. After the night of the raid he shunned
all men for a time. But afterwards, by Kolbein's advice, he took
a whole band of house-carls into his service—young men well
trained to arms, and by choice such as before had done lord's
service elsewhere. Steinfinn and his men slept in the great hall,
and they followed their master wherever he went, but they neither could nor would do much work on the estate, so that he had
great cost and little gain of the whole band.

Nevertheless the farm work at Frettastein was seen to in a way,
for the old bailiff, Grim, and Dalla, his sister, were children of
one of Steinfinn's grandmother's thralls, and they had no thought
beyond the welfare of their young master. But now, when Steinfinn had need of a return from his outlying farms, he cared neither
to see nor to speak with his own tenants and bailiffs—and Kolbein,
who took charge of all such matters in his stead, brought with
him trouble without end.

Ingebjörg Jonsdatter had been a skilful housewife, and in
former days this had made great amends for her husband's lavish
and indolent ways. But now she hid herself in the little outhouse
with her maids, and the rest of the household scarcely saw her.
She spent her days in pondering and repining, never inquired of
the condition of the house or estate, but rather seemed to be
angered if any disturbed her thoughts. Even with her children,
who lived with their mother in the outhouse, she was silent, caring
little for how they fared or what they did. Yet before, in the
good days, she had been a tender mother, and Steinfinn Toresson
had been a happy and loving father, proud of their strong and
handsome children.

So long as her sons, Hallvard and Jon, were still small, she often
took them in her lap and sat rocking them, with her chin resting
on their fair-haired crowns, while she moped, lost in sorrowful
thought. But the boys were not very old before they grew weary
of staying in the outhouse with their mournful mother and her
women.

Tora, the younger daughter, was a good and pretty child. She
saw full well that her father and mother had suffered a grievous

wrong and were now full of cares and sorrow, and she strove to cheer them, kindly and lovingly. She became the favourite of both. Steinfinn's face would brighten somewhat when he looked at this daughter of his. Tora Steinfinnsdatter was delicate and shapely in body and limbs, she ripened early into womanhood. She had a long, full face, a fair skin, and blue eyes; thick plaits of smooth, corn-yellow hair hung over her shoulders. Her father stroked her cheek: "A good child you are, Tora mine—God bless you. Go to your mother, Tora; sit with her and comfort her."

Tora went, and sat down spinning or sewing beside her sorrowful mother. And she thought herself more than rewarded if Ingebjörg said at the last: "You are good, Tora mine—God preserve you from all evil, my child." Then Tora's tears began to fall—she thought upon her parents' heavy lot, and, full of righteous wrath, she looked at her sister, who had never enough constancy to sit still with their mother and could not come into the outhouse without making her impatient with her continual restlessness—till Ingebjörg bade her go out again. And Ingunn made for the door, carefree and unrepentant, and ran out to play and shout with the other children of the place—Olav and some boys belonging to the serving-folk at Frettastein.

Ingunn was the eldest of all Steinfinn's and Ingebjörg's children. When she was little, she had been marvellously fair; but now she was not half as pretty as her sister, people thought. And she had not so much sense, nor was she very quick-witted; she was neither better nor worse than are most children. But in a way she was as much liked by the people of the place as the quiet and beautiful younger sister. Steinfinn's men looked upon Tora with a sort of reverence, but they were better pleased to have Ingunn among them in the hall.

There were no maids of her own age either at Frettastein or any of the farms and homesteads round about. So it was that Ingunn was always with the boys. She took part in all their games and all their pursuits, practised such sports as they used—she threw the spear and the stone, shot with the bow, struck the ball, set snares in the wood, and fished in the tarn. But she was clumsy at all these things, neither handy nor bold, but weak, quick to give up and take to tears when their play grew rough or the game went against her. For all that, the boys let her go with them every-

where. For one thing, she was Steinfinn's daughter, and then Olav
Audunsson would have it so. And it was always Olav who was the
master of their games.

Olav Audunsson was well liked by all on the estate, both great
and small, and yet none would have called him a winning child.
It seemed that none could come at the heart of this boy, although
he was never unfriendly toward any living soul—rather might it
be said that he was good-natured and helpful in his taciturn and
absent way.

Handsome he was, though he was fair of skin and hair as an
albino almost, but he had not the albino's sidelong glance or bowed
neck. Olav's blue-green eyes were pale in colour, but he looked
the world straight in the face with them, and he carried his head
erect upon his strong, milk-white neck. It was as though sun and
wind had little power upon that skin of his—it seemed strangely
tight and smooth and white—only in summer a few small freckles
appeared over the root of the nose, which was low and broad. This
healthy paleness gave Olav's face even in childhood something of
a cold, impassive look. His features too were somewhat short and
broad, but well formed. The eyes lay rather far apart, but they
were large and frankly open; the eyebrows and lashes were so
fair that they showed but as a golden shadow in the sunlight. His
nose was broad and straight, but a little too short; his mouth was
rather large, but the lips were so finely curved and firm that, had
they not been so pale in the colourless face, they might have been
called handsome. But his hair was of matchless beauty—so fair
that it shone like silver rather than gold, thick and soft and lightly
curled. He wore it trimmed so that it covered his broad, white
forehead, but showed the hollow in his neck between the two
powerful muscles.

Olav was never tall for his age, but he seemed bigger than he
was; of perfect build, sturdy and muscular, with very small hands
and feet, which seemed the stronger because the wrists and ankles
were so round and powerful. And indeed he was very strong and
supple; he excelled in all kinds of sport and in the use of arms—
but there was none who had ever taught him to practise these exercises in the right way. As things stood at Frettastein in his growing
up, Olav was left to his own devices. Steinfinn, who had promised to be a father to him when he took charge of the boy, did

nothing to give him such training as was meet for a young man of good birth, heir to some fortune and destined to be the husband of Ingunn Steinfinnsdatter.

That Steinfinn Toresson was Olav's foster-father had come about in this way:

One summer, while Steinfinn was still in goodly case, it chanced that he had business at the Eidsiva Thing. He went thither with friends and kinsmen and took with him his wife and their daughter Ingunn, who was then six years old. The parents had such joy of the pretty child that they could not be without her.

Here at the Thing Steinfinn met a man, Audun Ingolfsson of Hestviken. Audun and Steinfinn had been bedfellows in the King's body-guard and good friends, though Audun was older than the other and the men were of very unlike humour; for at that time Steinfinn was merry and loved to talk of himself, but Audun was a silent man and never spoke of his own affairs.

In the spring of the same year that King Haakon was away warring in Scotland, Audun was married. He took a Danish wife, Cecilia Björnsdatter, Queen Ingebjörg's playmate, who had been with her at the convent of Rind. When the Bishop of Oslo took young King Magnus's bride by force and carried her to Norway, because the Dane King slighted the compact and refused to send his kinswoman thither, Cecilia went with her. At first the young Queen would fain have kept the damsel always with her; but a year later the Lady Ingebjörg seemed already to have changed her mind and she was eager to have Cecilia married. Some said it was because King Magnus himself liked to talk with the Danish maid more than his wife cared for; others declared that it was young Alf Erlingsson of Tornberg who had won her heart, but his father, Baron Erling Alfsson, would not let his son take a foreign wife who owned neither land nor powerful kinsfolk in Norway. Young Alf was a man of fiery nature and wont to have his will in all things, and he loved Cecilia madly. The Queen therefore took counsel to marry off the maid, lest some misfortune might befall her.

However these things might be, the maid herself was chaste and full of grace; and after Audun, who at first had seemed somewhat unwilling, had spoken two or three times with Cecilia, he himself was eager to take her. Their wedding was held at the

King's court in Björgvin; old King Haakon gave the bride a marriage portion. Audun carried his wife to Hestviken. There she was well secured, whether from King Magnus or from Alf Erlingsson.

In the course of the summer Audun with his ship joined the King in Herdluvaag and followed him westward oversea. And when the King died in the Orkneys before Yule—it was in the winter of 1263—Audun commanded the ship that brought the news to Norway. Then he journeyed on to the east, home to his manor. In the summer he came back to King Magnus's bodyguard. His wife had then died in giving birth to a son, who lived. Audun had grown even more silent than before, but now he uttered one thing and another of his affairs to Steinfinn. At Hestviken dwelt his grandfather; he was old and somewhat self-willed. He had been against his grandson's marriage with a foreign wife without kindred. Besides him there was in the house an old uncle of Audun; he was mad. Most of the time Cecilia had lived at Hestviken she had been left alone with these two old men: "It misgives me she had no happy life there in the east," said Audun. In the great-grandfather's honour Cecilia had named the child after him—it was the Danish custom—but Olav Olavsson was greatly angered thereat: "In Norway no child is called after a living man—save with the thought of putting him out of life," said he. It fell out that Audun was left sole heir to these two old men, but he let it be known that he would not go home to Hestviken for a while; he was minded to bide in Björgvin with King Magnus.

It was a short time after this that Steinfinn carried off Ingebjörg, and since then he had neither heard nor sought tidings of Audun Ingolfsson until he met the man at the Thing. Audun was leading a boy of seven years by the hand and was asking for certain men from Soleyar whom he was to meet there. He looked very sick. Audun was a tall man and had always been very spare and slim, with a narrow face, a thin and sharp hooked nose, and his skin and hair were fair to whiteness. Now he was bent in the back and gaunt as a skeleton, wan-faced and blue about the lips. But the boy was a strong and comely child, broad-shouldered and of good build; he was as fair of hue as his father, but in other ways he bore him no great likeness.

Steinfinn embraced his friend with riotous joy, but it filled him with grief to see that Audun was so sick. He would hear of naught else but that Audun must go with him to the house where Steinfinn and his following lived while the Thing lasted.

On the way thither Audun told him that these men he was to have met were the sons of his grandfather's nephew: "And nearer kinsmen have I none; it will fall to them to be the guardians of Olav here, when I am dead." The two old men at Hestviken were still living, but they were clean decrepit; and for himself he had an inward scathe in his stomach, so that he had no good of meat or drink; he could not live many weeks more. He had been with King Magnus all these years until lately, before Yule; then he went home to Hestviken, being very sick. He had not seen his own house more than once since his wife's death, so it was only this winter that he had come to know his son. But now the child's future lay heavily on his heart—and here these kinsmen from Sole-yar had failed to come, and he scarce had the strength to ride up to them, it gave him such pain to ride—and this was the last day but one of the Thing. "The Fathers of Hovedö [5] would gladly take him—but should the boy have a mind to stay there when he grows up and make himself a monk, then our kin would die out with him."

When Ingebjörg saw the fair child who would soon be both motherless and fatherless, she was fain to kiss the boy. But Olav wrested himself from her and fled to his father, while he stared at the lady with his great blue eyes, full of ill humour and surprise.

"Will you not kiss my wife, Olav?" asked Steinfinn with a mighty laugh.

"No," answered the lad. "For Aslaug kisses Koll—"

Audun smiled somewhat uneasily—these were two old folks who served at Hestviken, he said; and at that all the grown people laughed greatly, and Olav turned red and looked at the ground. Then his father chid him and bade him greet Ingebjörg courteously and properly. So he had to go forward and be kissed by the lady; and when little Ingunn came out and said that she too would kiss the boy, Olav dutifully went up and bent forward so that the little maid could reach his lips. But his face was red as fire, and his eyes were full of tears, so that the men laughed and

[5] The Cistercian monastery on Hovedö, the largest island in the fiord off the town of Oslo.

bantered Olav that he set so little store by the favour of fair
women.

But as the evening wore on, when the folk had supped, and sat
over their drink, Olav seemed to thaw a little. Ingunn ran about
among the benches, and where she found an empty place, she
climbed up and sat for a while swinging her legs; then slipped
down again, ran to another place, and crept up there. This made
the grown ones laugh; they called to her and caught at her, and
the child grew more and more wanton and wild. Then it seemed
that Olav had made a great resolution—he rose up from beside his
father, straightened his new knife-belt, walked across the hall, and
sat down by Ingunn's side. And when she slid down and ran to
another seat, the boy followed her, holding back a little, and
seated himself again beside her. Thus the children played hither
and thither among the benches, with laughter and cries from
Ingunn—while Olav followed, steady and serious; but now and
again he glanced at his father, and a faltering smile came over the
boy's mute and handsome face.

The children were nodding in a corner by the time Steinfinn
and Audun came and led them out to the hearth in the midst of
the hall. The guests formed a ring about them; they were far gone
in drink. Steinfinn himself was unsteady on his legs as he took his
daughter's hand and laid it in Olav's. Then Steinfinn and Audun
clenched the bargain of their children's betrothal with a hand-
clasp, and Audun gave Olav a gold ring and helped him to set it
on Ingunn's little hand and hold up the child's fingers so that all
might see the massive ring dangling there. Ingebjörg Jonsdatter
and the women laughed and cried by turns, for no fairer sight than
this little bridal pair had any of them seen.

Then she handed her daughter a horn and bade her drink to her
betrothed, and the children drank and spilled the liquor over their
clothes. Steinfinn stood holding his friend round the neck; with
tears in his voice he swore solemnly that Audun had no need to
grieve for the child he left behind him; he would foster Olav
himself and stand in his father's stead till the boy was a man and
could bring home his bride, said Steinfinn, and kissed Audun on
both cheeks, while Ingebjörg took the children in her arms and
promised to be a mother to Olav, for the sake of Cecilia Björnsdatter, whom she had loved as her own sister.

Then they told Olav he must kiss his betrothed. And now the

boy went forward right boldly, laid his arms about Ingunn's neck, and kissed her as warmly as he could, while the witnesses laughed and drank the health of the affianced pair.

But it seemed as though Olav had now learned to like the sport— all at once he sprang at his young bride, took her roun 1 the neck again, and gave her three or four smacking kisses. Then all the company roared with laughter and called to him to keep on with it.

Whether it was the laughter that made her ashamed or a whim of the little maid—Ingunn tried to struggle out of the boy's arms, and as he only clasped her the closer, she bit him in the cheek with all her might.

Olav stood staring for a moment, fairly amazed. Then he rubbed his cheek, where drops of blood were oozing out. He looked at his bloody fingers—and then made to fly at Ingunn and strike her. But his father lifted him in his arms and carried him away to the bed where they were to sleep. And then the affianced bride and bridegroom were undressed and put to bed, and soon they fell asleep and forgot the whole company.

Next day, when Steinfinn was sober, he would fain have been quit of his bargain. He dropped some hints that it was all done in jest—if they were to make any compact for their children's future, they must first take counsel about it. But Audun, who had been kept from drinking by his sickness, opposed him in this. He bade the other remember that he had given his promise to a dying man, and that God would assuredly avenge it if he broke his word to a forlorn and fatherless child.

Steinfinn pondered. Audun Ingolfsson came of a good and ancient kindred, though it was now short of men and had little power. But Olav was an only child, and even if he could not look for much heritage beyond his ancestral seat of Hestviken, this was nevertheless a great estate. He himself might yet have many children in his marriage—Olav might well be a fit match for Ingunn, with her daughter's portion after him. So Steinfinn sober took up the word he had spoken in his drink, promised to foster Olav and give him his daughter in marriage when the two children should come to years of discretion. And when he rode home from the Thing, he took Olav Audunsson north with him.

. . .

The same autumn there came tidings to Frettastein that Olav's father was dead, a short time after his grandfather and the mad uncle. The messengers brought with them a part of the child's heritage from his father and mother in chattels—clothing, arms, and a casket of jewels. His estate of Hestviken was left in the charge of an old kinsman of the boy—one they called Olav Half-priest.

Steinfinn took his foster-son's goods in keeping, and he so far bestirred himself that twice he sent messages with folks who had errands in Oslo, to appoint a meeting with Olav Half-priest. But nothing came of it at that time, and afterwards Steinfinn took no further step. It was the way with Steinfinn that he was no very active man even when his own affairs were at stake. Both he and Ingebjörg were kind to Olav, and he was treated as a child of theirs, till the trouble came upon them. And after that their foster-son was haply no more neglected than their own offspring.

In a way Olav had been quick to feel at home at Frettastein. He liked Steinfinn and Ingebjörg well enough, but he was a quiet-mannered, rather reticent child, so he was always something of a stranger to them. He never had any true feeling that he belonged to the house, though he was happier here than where he came from. As far as he could, he left off thinking of his first home, Hestviken; but now and then memories of that time came up in him. And it caught him with a clutch of despondency when he called to mind all the old folks there.—The serving-men were worn out with age, and his great-grandfather was ever plaguing his mad old son, whom folk called Foulbeard—he had to be fed like a child and kept away from fire and water and edged tools. Olav had mostly been left to fend for himself. But he had never known any other ways, and the filth and evil stench that followed Foulbeard had been part of the life of the place as far back as the boy could remember, and he had also grown so used to the mad-man's fits of howling and shrieking that they frightened him not so much. But he shrank from these memories.—Sometimes in his last years his great-grandfather had taken him to church with him, and there he had had a sight of strangers, women and children too; but he never had a thought that he might mix with them or talk with them; they seemed to be a part of the mass. And for many years after he had come to Frettastein it might chance that he would have a sudden feeling of loneliness—as though his life here with these people were unreal or not an everyday thing, like a church Sunday, and he were only waiting to go away, back to the life from which he had come. This was never more than a flash of memory that came and vanished again at once—but he never came to feel wholly rooted at Frettastein, though he had no longing for another home.

But at times memories of another kind arose, which stabbed his heart with a sharp longing. Like the return of an old dream he remembered a bare outcrop of rock in the midst of the yard at Hestviken; there were cracks in the warm rock and he had lain there picking out moss with a splinter of bone. Pictures floated before his eyes of places where he had once wandered alone, filling them with his own fancies, and these memories brought an aftertaste of unutterable sweetness. Behind the cowsheds in the yard, there was a lofty cliff of smooth, dark rock over which water trickled, and in the swampy hollow between the cliff and the outhouses it was always dark and shady, with a growth of tall green rushes.—And there was somewhere a stretch of beach where he trod on seaweed and rattling pebbles, and found snail-shells and bits of rotten wood, water-worn and green with slime. Outside, the water lay glittering into the far distance, and the old housecarl, Koll, used to open mussels and give them to him—Olav's mouth watered when he recalled the fine taste of sea-water and the rich yellow morsel that he sopped up from the open blue shell.

When such memories glimmered within him he grew silent and answered absently if Ingunn spoke to him. But it never came into his head to go away and leave her. He never had a thought of parting company with her, when she came and wanted to be with him, any more than he thought he could part from himself. Thus it was with Olav Audunsson: it seemed his very destiny that he should always be with Ingunn. It was the only sure thing in his life, that he and Ingunn were inseparably joined together. He seldom thought of that evening when they had been betrothed—and it was now many years since any had spoken of the children's affiancing. But amid all his thoughts and feelings it was as firm ground under his feet—that he should always live with Ingunn. The boy had no kinsmen to rely on; he knew that Hestviken was now his own, but with every year that went by, his images of the place grew fainter and fainter—it was but fragments of a dream he remembered. When he thought that one day he would go to live there, the fixed and real part of his thought was that he should take Ingunn with him—together they would face the uncertain future.

He never thought whether she was fair or not. Tora was fair, it seemed to him, perhaps because he had heard it said so often. Ingunn was only Ingunn, near at hand and everyday and always at his side; he never thought of how she might be, otherwise than as one thinks of the weather; that has to be taken as it comes. He grew angry and scolded her when she was contrary or trouble-some—he had beaten her too, when they were smaller. When she was kind and fair-spoken with him and the other boys, their play-mates, he felt happy as in fine weather. And mostly they were good friends, like brother and sister who get on well together—at whiles they might be angry and quarrel, but neither thought the other's nature could be changed from what it was.

And among the band of children at Frettastein, of whom none took any heed, these two, the eldest, kept together, because they knew that, whatever happened, one thing was certain—that they should be together. This was the only sure thing, and it was good to have something sure. The boy, growing up alone in the home of a stranger kin, struck root, without knowing it, in her who was promised to him; and his love for the only one he well knew of all that was to be his grew as he himself grew—without his mark-ing the growth. He cherished her as a habit, until his love took on a colour and brightness that showed him how wholly he was filled thereby.

Things went on this wise until the summer when Olav Auduns-son had ended his sixteenth year. Ingunn was now fifteen winters old.

2

OLAV had inherited from his father a great battle-axe—with pointed barbs, steel edge, and inlays of gold on the cheeks; the shaft had bands of gilt copper. It had a name and was called Kin-fetch.[6]

[6] Norse, *Ættarfylgja:* the fetch or "doubleganger" of his race.

It was a splendid weapon and the boy who owned this treasure thought its match was scarce to be found in Norway, as was like enough. But he had never said this to any but Ingunn, and she believed it and was as proud of the axe as he himself. Olav had always kept it hanging above his sleeping-place in the hall.

But one day this spring Olav saw that the edge was notched, and when he took it down, he found that the steel edge had parted from the iron blade and worked loose in the welding. Olav guessed that it would be vain to try to find out who had used his axe and spoiled it. So he said nothing to any but Ingunn. They took counsel what he should do and agreed that next time Steinfinn was from home Olav must ride to Hamar; there dwelt a famous armourer, and if he could not set it to rights, no man could. And one morning in the week before John's Mass Ingunn came and told Olav that today her father was going north to Kolbein; so it might be a timely occasion for them to go to the town next day.

Olav had not thought to take her with him. It was many years since either of the children had been in the town, and Olav did not rightly know how far it was thither; but he had thought he might be home again to supper if he rode down early in the morning. But Ingunn had no horse of her own, and there was none in the place that he could take for her. If they were to take turns at riding his horse, Elk, they could not reach home again till far on in the night—and then it would be so that she must ride and he walk the whole time; that he knew well from the many times they had gone together to mass in their parish church, in the village below. And they would surely be very angry, Steinfinn and Ingebjörg, if they heard that he had taken Ingunn with him to Hamar. But Olav only made answer that they would have to go down to the shore and row to the town—they must set out betimes in the morning.

It was a good while before sunrise when he stole out of the hall next morning, but it was daylight outside, calm and chilly. The air was cold with dew—good as a bath after the dense fumes of man and dog within. The boy sucked it in as he stood on the threshold looking at the weather.

The wild cherry was white with a foam of blossom between the cornfields—spring had come even here in the hills. Far below, the lake lay glistening, a dead grey with dark stripes where the current ran: it gave promise of showers. The sky had a wan look, and dark shreds of cloud drifted low down—there had been rain-storms in the night. When Olav stepped out on the grass of the yard his high boots of yellow undyed leather were darkened with moisture—little reddish splashes appeared on his boot-legs. He sat down on the doorstone and pulled off his boots, tied the laces to-gether, and slung them over his shoulder to carry them with his folded cloak and the axe.

Barefoot he went across the wet courtyard to the house where Ingunn had slept that night with two of the serving-maids, that she might be able to slip away without being seen. For the journey to town Olav had dressed himself in his best clothes—a long kirtle of light-blue English cloth and hose of the same stuff. But the dress was somewhat outgrown—the kirtle was tight across the chest and short at the wrists and it scarce reached to the middle of his calf. The hose too were very tight, and Ingebjörg had cut off the feet the autumn before; now they ended at the ankle. But the kirtle was fastened at the neck with a fine ring-brooch of gold, and round his waist he wore a belt set with silver roses and Saint Olav's image on the buckle; his dagger bore gilt mounts on hilt and sheath.

Olav went up into the balcony and struck three light blows upon the door. Then he stood waiting.

A bird began trilling and piping—it burst forth like a fountain above the sleepy twittering from the thickets round about. Olav saw the bird as a dot against the sky—it sat on a fir twig against the yellowing northern heaven. He could see how it drew itself in and swelled itself out, like a little heart beating. The hosts of cloud high up began to flush, a flush spread over the hillside with a rosy reflection in the water.—Olav knocked at the door again, much harder—it rang out in the morning stillness so that the boy held his breath and listened for a movement in any of the houses.

Soon after, the door was opened ajar—the girl slipped out. Her hair hung about her, ruffled and lustreless; it was yellow-brown and very curly. She was in her bare smock; the neck, which was of white linen, was worked with green and blue flowers, but be-low, it was of coarse grey stuff, and it was too long for her and trailed about her narrow pink feet. She carried her clothes over her arm and had a wallet in her hand. This she gave to Olav, threw down her bundle of clothes, and shook her hair from her face, which was still flushed with sleep—one cheek redder than the other. She took a waist-band and girt up her smock with it.

She was tall and thin, with slight limbs, a long, slender throat, and a small head. Her face was a triangle, her forehead low and broad, but it was snow-white and finely arched at the temples under the thick folds of hair; the thin cheeks were too much drawn in, making the chin too long and pointed; the straight little nose was too low and short. But for all that her little face had a restless charm of its own: the eyes were very large and dark grey, but the whites were as blue as a little child's, and they lay in deep shadow beneath the straight black lines of her brows and her full, white eyelids; the mouth was narrow, but the lips were red as berries—and with her bright pink and white complexion Ingunn Steinfinnsdatter was fair now in her young girlhood.

"Make haste," said Olav, as she sat on the stair winding her linen hose tightly around her legs; and she took good time about it. "You were best carry hose and shoes till the grass be dry."

"I will not go barefoot on the wet ground in this cold—" the girl shivered a little.

"You will be warmer when once you have made an end of putting on your clothes—you must not be so long about it—'tis rosy morning already, cannot you see?"

Ingunn made no answer, but took off her hose-band and began again to wind it about her leg. Olav hung her clothes over the rail of the balcony.

"You must have a cloak with you—do you not see we shall have showers today?"

"My cloak is down with Mother—I forgot to take it with me last night. It looks now like fine weather—but if there comes a shower, we shall find some place to creep under."

"What if it rains while we are in the boat? You cannot walk in the town without a cloak either. But I see well enough you will borrow my cloak, as is your way."

Ingunn looked up at him over her shoulder. "Why are you so cross today, Olav?"—and she began to be busy with her footgear again.

Olav was ready with an answer; but as she bent down to her shoe, the smock slipped from her shoulders, baring her bosom and upper arm. And instantly a wave of new feelings swept over the boy—he stood still, bashful and confused, and could not take his eyes off this glimpse of her naked body. It was as though he had never seen it before; a new light was thrown on what he knew of old—as with a sudden landslip within him, his feelings for his foster-sister came to rest in a new order. With a burst of fervour he felt a tenderness that had in it both pity and a touch of pride; her shoulders sank so weakly in a slant to the faint rounding of the shoulder-joint; the thin, white upper arms looked soft, as though she had no muscles under the silky skin—the boy's senses were tricked with a vision of corn that is as yet but milky, before it has fully ripened. He had a mind to stoop down and pat her consolingly—such was his sudden sense of the difference between her feeble softness and his own wiry, muscular body. Oft had he looked at her before, in the bath-house, and at himself, his hard, tough, well-rounded chest, his muscles firmly braced over the stomach, and swelling into a knot as he bent his arm. With childish pride he had rejoiced that he was a boy.

Now this self-glorious sense of being strong and well made became strangely shot through with tenderness, because she was so weak—he would know how to protect her. He would gladly have put his arm around that slender back, clasped her little girlish breasts beneath his hand. He called to mind that day last spring when he himself had fallen on his chest over a log—it was where Gunleik's new house was building—he had torn both his clothes and his flesh. With a shudder in which were mingled horror and sweetness he thought that never more would he let Ingunn climb up on the roof with them at Gunleik's farm.

He blushed as she looked at him.

"You are staring? Mother will never know I have borrowed her smock; she never wears it herself."

"Do you not feel the cold?" he asked; and Ingunn's surprise was yet greater, for he spoke as low and shyly as though she had really come to some hurt in their game.

"Oh, not enough to make my nails go blue," she said laughing.

"No, but can you not get your clothes on quickly?" he said anxiously. "You have goose-flesh on your arms."

"If I could but get my smock together—" The edges at the throat were stiff with sewing; she struggled, but could not get the stuff through the tiny ring of her brooch.

Olav laid down the whole load that he had just taken on his back. "I will lend you mine—it has a bigger ring." He took the gold brooch from his bosom and handed it to her. Ingunn looked at him, amazed. She had pestered him to lend her this trinket before now, but that he himself should offer to let her wear it was something new, for it was a costly jewel, of pure gold and fairly big. Along the outer edge were inscribed the Angel's Greeting and *Amor vincit omnia.* Her kinsman Arnvid Finnsson said that in the Norse tongue this meant "Love conquers all things," since the Lady Sancta Maria conquers all the malice of the fiend by her loving supplication.

Ingunn had put on her red holy-day garments and bound her silken girdle about her waist—she combed her tangled hair with her fingers.

"You must even lend me your comb, Olav!"

Although he had but just collected all his things again, he laid them down once more, searched out a comb from his pouch, and gave it to her without impatience.

But as they plodded along the road between the fences down in the village, Olav's dizzy exaltation forsook him little by little. The weather had cleared and the sun was broiling hot—and as time went on, it *was* a load: wallet, axe, cloak, and boots. True, Ingunn had once offered to carry some of it; but that was when they were passing through the forest and it was cool beneath the firs, with a grateful fresh scent of pine-needles and hair-moss and young leaves. The sun barely gilded the tree-tops, and the birds sang with full throat—and then the boy was still swayed by his new-born emotion. She bade him stop, she had to plait her hair anew, for she had forgotten her hair-band—ay, 'twas like her. But her tawny mane waved so finely over her forehead as she loosed the braids, making shady hollows at the temples, where the first short hairs lay close and curly, it softened his heart to look at it. So when she spoke of carrying, he only shook his head; and afterwards he heard no more of it.

Down here on the fiord it was full summer. The children climbed a fence and made straight across an enclosure; the meadow was a slope of flowers, pink clouds of caraway and golden globe-flowers. Where there was a thin patch of soil among the rocks, the violets grew thick as a carpet, and within the shade

of the alder brake red catchflies blazed amid the luxuriant green.
Ingunn stopped again and again to pluck flowers, and Olav grew
more and more impatient; he longed to get down to the boat and
be rid of his burden. He was hungry too—as yet neither of them
had tasted food. But when she said that they could sit down and
eat here in the shade by the brook, he replied shortly that it would
be as he said. When they had got hold of a boat, they could make
a meal before rowing away, but not till then.

"You will always have your way," said Ingunn querulously.

"Ay, if I let you have yours we might reach the town tomorrow
morning. But if you will listen to me, we shall be back to Frettastein by that time."

Then she laughed, flung away her flowers, and ran after him.

All the way down, the children had followed the brook that
ran north of the houses at Frettastein. On nearing the village it
became a little river—on the flat, before it fell into the fiord, it
spread out and ran broad and shallow over a bed of large smooth
stones. The lake here formed a great round bay, with a beach
strewed with sharp grey rocks that had fallen from the mountain-
side. A line of old alder trees grew along the bank of the stream
right out to the lake.

At high-water mark, where beach and greensward met, the path
led by a cairn. The boy and girl stopped, hurried through a Paternoster and an Ave, and then each threw a stone upon the cairn as
a sign that they had done their Christian duty by the dead. It was
said to be one who had slain himself, but it was so long ago that
Olav and Ingunn at any rate had never heard who the poor wretch
might be.

They had to cross the stream in order to reach the point where
Olav had thought he could borrow a boat. This was easy enough
for him, who walked barefoot, but Ingunn had not gone many
steps before she began to whimper—the round pebbles slipped
under her feet and the water was so cold and she was spoiling her
best shoes.

"Do but stand where you are and I will come and fetch you,"
said Olav, and waded back to her.

But when he had taken her up in his arms, he could not see
where he put his feet, and in the middle of the river he fell with
her.

The icy water took away his breath for a moment—the whole world seemed to slew over. As long as he lived, this picture remained burned into him—all that he saw as he lay in the stream with Ingunn in his arms: light and shade dropping in patches through the alder leaves upon the running water, the long, grey curve of the beach beyond, and the blue lake glittering in the sunshine.

Then he got to his feet, dripping wet and ashamed, strangely ashamed with his empty arms—and they waded ashore. Ingunn took it ill, as she swept the water from her sleeves and wrung out first her hair-plaits and then the edge of her dress.

"Oh, hold your mouth now," Olav begged in a low and cheerless voice. "Must you always be whining over great things and small?"

The sky was now blue and cloudless, and the fiord quite smooth, with small patches of glittering white sunshine. Its bright surface reflected the land on the other shore, with tufts of light-green foliage amid the dark pine forest and farms and fields mounting the hillside. It had become very warm—the sweet breath of the summer day was heavy about the two young people. In their wet clothes it felt cold merely to enter the airy shade of the birches on the point.

The fisher-widow's cot was no more than a turf hovel boarded at one end, in which was a door. There was no other house in the place but a byre of stones and turf, with an open shed outside to keep the stacks of hay and dried leaves from the worst of the winter weather. Outside the cabin lay heaps of fish refuse. It stank horribly and swarms of blue flies buzzed up as the children came near. These heaps of offal were alive and crawling with maggots—so as soon as Olav had made known his errand and the widow had answered that they might have the boat and welcome, he took the wallet and went off under the trees. It was an odd thing about Olav that ever since he was a little boy it had given him a quite absurd feeling of disgust to see maggots moving in anything.

But Ingunn had brought with her a piece of bacon for the widow, Aud. She came of the folk of Steinfinn's thralls and now she was eager for news of the manor, so Ingunn was delayed awhile.

The boy had found a dry and sunny spot down by the water; there they could sit and dry themselves as they ate. Soon Ingunn came, carrying in her hands a bowl of fresh milk. And with the prospect of food, and now that it was settled about the boat, Olav was suddenly glad at heart—it was grand after all to be out on his own errand and to be going to Hamar. At heart he was well pleased too that Ingunn was with him; he was used to her following him everywhere, and if at times she was a little troublesome, he was used to that too.

He grew rather sleepy after eating—Steinfinn's house-carls were not used to early rising. So he stretched himself on the ground with his head buried in his arms, letting the sun bake his wet back, and he made no more ado about the need of haste. All at once Ingunn asked if they should bathe in the fiord.

Olav woke and sat up. "The water is too cold—" and all at once he turned red in the face and blushed more and more. He turned his head aside and stared at the ground.

"I am freezing in my wet clothes," said Ingunn. "We shall be so fine and warm after it." She bound her plaits in a ring about her head, sprang up, and loosened her belt.

"I will not," muttered Olav in a hesitating voice. His cheeks and brows pricked with heat. Suddenly he jumped up and, without saying more to her, turned and walked up the point into the grove of firs.

Ingunn looked after him a moment. She was used to his being vexed when she would not do as he said. He would be cross for a while, till he grew kind again of himself. Calmly and caring nothing, she undressed and tottered out over the sharp grey stones, which cut her feet, till she reached a little bank of sand.

Olav walked quickly over the grey moss, which crunched under his feet. It was bone-dry already on these crags that jutted into the lake—the firs stifled it with their vapour. It was not much more than a bowshot to the other side of the point.

A great bare rock ran out into the water. Olav leaped onto it and lay down with his face in his hands.

Then the thought came to him—she could never drown? Perhaps he ought not to have left her. But he *could* not go back—

Down in the water it was as though a golden net quivered above stones and mud—the reflection of sunlight on the surface. He grew giddy from looking down—felt as if he were afloat. The rock he lay on seemed to be moving through the water.

And all the time he could not help thinking of Ingunn and being tormented by the thought. He felt plunged into guilt and shame, and it grieved him. They had been used to bathe from his canoe in the tarn above, swimming side by side in the brown water, into which a yellow dust was shed from the flowering spruces around. But now they could not be together as before—

It was just as when he lay in the stream and saw the familiar world turned upside-down in an instant. He felt as if he had had another fall; humbled and ashamed and terrified, he saw the things he had seen every day from another angle, as he lay on the ground.

It had been so simple and straightforward a thing that he should marry Ingunn when they were grown up. And he had always looked to Steinfinn to decide when it should be. The lad might feel a tingling when Steinfinn's house-carls told tales of their commerce with women. But to him it had been clear that they did these things because they were men without ties, while he, being born to an estate, must keep himself otherwise. It had never disturbed his rest to think that he and Ingunn would live together and have children to take the inheritance after them.

Now he felt he had been the victim of a betrayal—he was changed from what he had been, and Ingunn was changed in his eyes. They were wellnigh grown up, though none had told them this was coming; and these things that Steinfinn's serving men and their womenfolk had to do with—ah, they tempted him too, for all she was his betrothed and he had an estate and she a dowry in her coffer.

He saw her as she lay there face-down on the short, dry grass. She rested on one arm beneath her breast, so that her dress was drawn tight over the gentle rounding of her bosom; her tawny plaits wound snake-like in the heather. When she had said that about bathing, an ugly thought had come over him—together with a meaningless fear, strong as the fear of death; for it seemed to him that they were as two trees, torn up by the spring flood and adrift on a stream—and he was afraid the stream would part them asunder. At that fiery moment he seemed to have full knowledge of what it meant to possess her and what to lose her.

But what was the sense of thinking of such things, when all

who had power and authority over them had ordained that they
should be joined together? There was no man and no thing to
part them. None the less, with a tremor of anxiety he felt his childish security shrivel up and vanish, the certainty that all the future
days of his life were threaded for him like beads upon a string.
He could not banish the thought that *if* Ingunn were taken from
him, he knew nothing of the future. Somewhere deep down
within him murmured the voice of a tempter: he must secure her,
as the rude and simple serving-men secured the coarse womenfolk they had a mind to—and if anyone stretched out a hand toward her that was his, he would be wild, like the he-wolf showing his teeth as he stands over his prey; like the stallion rearing
and snorting with rage to receive the bear and fight to the death
for his mares, while they stand in a ring about the scared and quivering foals.

The boy lay motionless, staring himself dizzy and hot at the
play of light in the gliding water, while he strove with these new
thoughts—both what he knew and what he dimly guessed. When
Ingunn gave a call just behind him, he started up as though waked
from sleep.

"You were foolish not to care for a swim," she said.

"Come now!" Olav jumped down to the beach and walked
quickly before her. "We have stayed here far too long."

After rowing awhile he grew calmer. It felt good to swing his
body in steady strokes. The beat of the oars in the rowlocks, the
wash of the water under the boat, lulled his agitation.

It was broiling hot now and the light from the sky and lake
dazzled and hurt the eyes—the shores were bathed in heat haze.
And when Olav had rowed for wellnigh two hours, it began to
tell on him severely. The boat was heavy, and he had not thought
how unpractised he was at rowing. This was not the same as
poling and splashing about the tarn at home. He had to keep far
out, for the shore wound in bays and inlets; at times he was afraid
he might be clean out of his course. The town might lie hidden
behind one of these headlands, invisible from the boat—perhaps
he had already passed it. Olav saw now that he was in strange
country; he remembered nothing from his last journey in these
parts.

The sun burned his back; the palms of his hands were sore; and his legs were asleep, so long had he sat with his feet against the stretcher. But the back of his neck ached worst of all. The lake gleamed far around the tiny boat—it was a long way to land on every side. Now and again he felt he was rowing against a current. And there was scarce a craft to be seen that day, whether far out or close under the shore. Olav toiled at the oars, glum and morose, fearing he would never reach the town.

Ingunn sat in the stern of the boat facing the sun, so that her red kirtle was ablaze; her face under the shade of her velvet hood was flushed with the reflection. She had thrown Olav's cloak about her, for the air on the water was chill to her, sitting still, she said; and then she had drawn the hood down to shade her eyes. It was a fine cloak of grey-green Flanders cloth with a cowl of black velvet—one of the things Olav had had from Hestviken. Ingunn had a well-dressed look in all the ample folds of her garments. She held one hand in the water—and Olav felt an envy of the senses; how good and cool it must be! The girl looked fresh and unweary; she sat and took her ease.

Then he pulled harder—all the harder for the pain he felt in hands and shoulders and in the small of his back; he clenched his teeth and rowed furiously a short space. It was a great deed he had undertaken for her sake, this rowing; and he knew, with pride and a melancholy sense of injury, that he would never have thanks for it: "there she sits playing with her hand over the side and never has a thought of *my* toiling." The sweat poured off him, and his outgrown kirtle chafed worse and worse at the arm-holes. He had forgotten that it was *his* business that brought them; once more he pursed his lips, swept his arm across his red and sweaty face, and took a few more mighty pulls.

"Now I see the towers over the woods," said Ingunn at last.

Olav turned and looked over his shoulder—it hurt his stiff neck past believing. Across the perfectly hopeless expanse of a fiord he saw the light stone towers of Christ Church above the trees on a point of land. Now he was so tired that he could have given up altogether.

He rounded the point, where the convent of preaching friars lay far out on raised foundations; it was a group of dark timber houses about a stave-church, with roofs of tarred shingles, one

above another, dragon heads on the gables and gilt weathercocks
above the ridge-turret, in which the mass bell hung.

Olav put in to the monks' pier. He washed the worst of the
sweat from him before he climbed up, stiff and spent. Ingunn was
already at the convent gate talking with the lay brother who had
charge of some labourers; they were bearing bales of goods down
to a little trading craft. Brother Vegard was at home, she told Olav
as he came up—now they must ask leave to speak with him; he
could best advise them in this business.

Olav thought they could ill trouble the monk with such a trifle.
Brother Vegard was wont to come twice a year to Frettastein
and he was the children's confessor. He was a wise and kindly
man and always used the opportunity to give them such counsel
and exhortation as the young people of that house lacked all too
often. But Olav had never spoken a word to Brother Vegard unbidden, and to put him to the pains of coming to the parlour for
their sake seemed to him far too bold. They could well inquire
the way to the smith of the brother porter.

But Ingunn would not give in. As Olav himself had hinted, it
was perhaps a hazardous thing to hand over such an heirloom to
a smith of whom they knew nothing. But maybe Brother Vegard
would send a man from the convent with them—ay, it was not impossible he might offer to go with them himself. That Olav did
not believe. But he let Ingunn have her way.

She had a motive for it, which she kept to herself. Once, long
ago, she had visited the convent with her father, and then they
had been given wine, which the monks made from apples and
berries in their garden. So good and sweet a drink she had never
tasted before or since—and she secretly hoped that Brother Vegard
might offer them a cup of it.

The parlour was but a closet in the guest-house; the convent
was a poor one, but the children had never seen another and they
thought it a brave and fine room, with the great crucifix over the
door. In a little while Brother Vegard came in; he was a middle-
aged man of great stature, weatherbeaten, with a wreath of grizzled hair.

He received the children's greeting in friendly fashion, but
seemed pressed for time. With awkward concern Olav came out
with his errand. Brother Vegard told them the way shortly and
plainly: past Christ Church eastward through Green Street, past

the Church of Holy Cross, and down to the left along the fence
of Karl Kjette's garden, down to the field where was a pond; the
smith's house was the biggest of the three that stood on the other
side of the little mere. Then he took leave of the children and
was going: "You will sleep in the guest-house tonight, I ween?"

Olav said they must set out for home after vespers.

"But milk you must have—and you will be here for vespers?"

They had to say yes to this. But Ingunn looked a little disappointed. She had expected to be offered other than milk and
she had looked forward to hearing vespers in the minster; the
boys of the school sang so sweetly. But now they durst not go
elsewhere than to St. Olav's.

The monk was already at the door when he turned sharply,
as something came into his mind: "So that is how it is—Steinfinn
has sent for Jon smith today? Are you charged to bid the armourer come to Frettastein, Olav?" he asked, with a trace of
anxiety.

"No, father. I am but come on my own errand." Olav told him
what it was and showed the axe.

The monk took it and balanced it in both hands.

"A goodly weapon you have there, my Olav," he said, but more
coolly than Olav had ever thought a man could speak of *his* axe.
Brother Vegard looked at the gold inlay on the cheeks. "It is old,
this—they do not make such things nowadays. This is an heirloom, I trow?"

"Yes, father. I had it of my father."

"I have heard of a horned axe like this which they say was at
Dyfrin in old days—when the old barons' kin held the manor.
That must be near a hundred years ago. There was much lore
about that axe; it had a name and was called Wrathful Iron."

"Ay, my kindred came from thence—Olav and Torgils are yet
family names with us. But this axe is called Kinfetch—and I know
not how it came into my father's possession."

"It must be another, then—such horned axes were much used
in old days," said the monk; he passed his hand along the finely
curved blade. "And maybe that is lucky for you, my son—if I
mind me rightly, bad luck followed that axe I spoke of."

He repeated his directions, took a kindly leave of the children,
and went out.

. . .

Then they went off to find the smith. Ingunn strode in front; she looked like a grown maid in her long, trailing dress. Olav tramped behind, tired and downcast. He had looked forward so much to the journey to town—scarce knowing what he looked for in it. Whenever he had been here before, it was in the company of grown men, and it had been a fair-day in the town; to his serious and inquiring eyes all had been excitement and festivity: the bargaining of the men, the booths, the houses, the churches they had been in; they had been offered drink in the houses, and the street had been full of horses and folk. Now he was only a raw youth wandering about with a young girl, and there was no place where he could turn in; he knew no one, had no money; and they had not time to enter the churches. In an hour or two they must set out for home. And he had an unspeakable dread of the endless rowing and then the walk up through the fields—God alone knew what time of night they would reach home! And then they might look for a chiding for having run away!

They found the way to the smith. He looked at the axe well and long, turned it this way and that, and said it would be a hard matter to mend it. These horned axes had gone wellnigh out of use; 'twas not easy to fit an edge on them that would not spring loose with a heavy blow, on a helm, to wit, or even on a tough skull. This came from the shape of the blade, a great half-moon with barbs at either end. Ay, he would do his best, but he could not promise that the gold inlay should come to no harm by his welding and hammering. Olav considered a moment, but could see naught else to be done—he gave the axe to the smith and bargained with him as to the price of the work.

But when Olav told where he came from, the smith looked up and scanned his face: "Then you would have it back in all haste, I trow? So that is the way of it—are they making ready their axes at Frettastein these days?"

Olav said he knew naught of *that*.

"Nay, nay. Has Steinfinn any plan, he is not like to tell his boys of it—"

Olav looked at the smith as though he would say something, but checked himself. He took his leave and departed.

They had passed the pond, and Ingunn wished to turn into a road between fences which led up to Green Street. But Olav took her by the arm: "We can go here."

The houses in Green Street were built on a ridge of high ground. Below them ran a brook of dirty water at the edge of the fields behind the townsmen's outhouses and kale-yards. By the side of the brook was a trodden path.

Ashes, apple trees, and great rosebushes in the gardens shaded the path, so the air felt cool and moist. Blue flies darted like sparks in the green shadows, where nettles and all kinds of coarse weeds grew luxuriantly, for folk threw out their refuse on this side, making great muck-heaps behind the outhouses. The path was slippery with grease that sweated out of the rotting heaps, and the air was charged with smells—fumes of manure, stench of carrion, and the faint odour of angelica that bordered the stream with clouds of greenish-white flowers.

But beyond the brook the fields lay in full afternoon sunshine; the little groves of trees threw long shadows over the grass. The fields stretched right down to the small houses along Strand Street, and beyond them lay the lake, blue with a golden glitter, and the low shore of Holy Isle in the afternoon haze.

The children walked in silence; Olav was now a few paces in front. It was very still here in the shade behind the gardens—nothing but the buzzing of the flies. A cowbell tinkled above on the common. Once the cuckoo called—spectrally clear and far away on a wooded ridge.

Then a woman's scream rang out from one of the houses, followed by the laughter of a man and a woman. In the garden a man had caught a girl from behind; she dropped her pail, full of fishes' heads and offal, and it rolled down to the fence; the couple followed, stumbling and nearly falling. When they caught sight of the two children, the man let go the girl; they stopped laughing, whispered, and followed them with their eyes.

Instinctively Olav had halted for a moment, so that Ingunn came up beside him and he placed himself between her and the fence. A blush crept slowly over his fair features and he looked down at the path as he led Ingunn past. These houses in the town that Steinfinn's house-carls had talked so much about—for the first time it made him hot and gripped his heart to think of them, and he wondered whether this was one of those houses.

The path turned and Olav and Ingunn saw the huge grey mass and pale leaden roof of Christ Church and the stone walls of the Bishop's palace above the trees a little way in front of them. Olav stopped and turned to the girl.

"Tell me, Ingunn—did you hear what Brother Vegard said—and the smith?"

"What mean you?"

"Brother Vegard asked if Steinfinn had sent for the armourer to Frettastein," said Olav slowly. "And Jon smith asked if we made ready our axes now."

"What meant they? Olav—you look so strangely!"

"Nay, I know not. Unless there is news at the Thing—folk are breaking up from the Thing these days, the first of them—"

"What mean you?"

"Nay, I know not. Unless Steinfinn has made some proclamation—"

The girl raised both hands abruptly and laid them on Olav's breast. He laid both his palms upon them and pressed her hands against his bosom. And as they stood thus, there welled up again in Olav more powerfully than before that new feeling that they were adrift—that something which had been was now gone for ever; they were drifting toward the new and unknown. But as he gazed into her tense dark eyes, he saw that she felt the same. And he knew in his whole body and his whole soul that she had turned to him and clutched at him because it was the same with her as with him—she scented the change that was coming over them and their destiny, and so she clung to him instinctively, because they had so grown together throughout their forlorn, neglected childhood that now they were nearer to each other than any beside.

And this knowledge was unutterably sweet. And while they stood motionless looking into each other's face, they seemed to become one flesh, simply through the warm pressure of their hands. The raw chill of the pathway that went through their wet shoes, the sunshine that poured warmly over them, the strong blended smell that they breathed in, the little sounds of the afternoon—they seemed to be aware of them all with the senses of one body.

The pealing of the church bells broke in upon their mute and tranquil rapture—the mighty brazen tones from the minster tower, the busy little bell from Holy Cross Church—and there was a sound of ringing from St. Olav's on the point.

Olav dropped the girl's hands. "We must make haste."

Both felt as though the peal of bells had proclaimed the consummation of a mystery. Instinctively they took hands, as though after a consecration, and they went on hand in hand until they reached the main street.

The monks were in the choir and had already begun to chant vespers as Olav and Ingunn entered the dark little church. No light was burning but the lamp before the tabernacle and the little candles on the monks' desks. Pictures and metal ornaments showed but faintly in the brown dusk, which gathered into gloom under the crossed beams of the roof. There was a strong smell of tar, of which the church had recently received its yearly coat, and a faint, sharp trace of incense left behind from the day's mass.

In their strangely agitated mood they remained on their knees inside the door, side by side, and bowed their heads much lower than usual as they whispered their prayers with unwonted devotion. Then they rose to their feet and stole away to one side and the other.

There were but few people in church. On the men's side sat some old men, and one or two younger knelt in the narrow aisle— they seemed to be the convent's labourers. On the women's side he saw none but Ingunn; she stood leaning against the farthest pillar, trying to make out the pictures painted on the baldachin over the side altar.

Olav took a seat on the bench—now he felt again how fearfully stiff and tired he was all over. The palms of his hands were blistered.

The boy knew nothing of what the monks sang. Of the Psalms of David he had learned no more than the *Miserere* and *De profundis*, and those but fairly well. But he knew the chant—saw it inwardly as a long, low wave that broke with a short, sharp turn and trickled back over the pebbles; and at first, whenever they came to the end of a psalm and sang *"Gloria Patri, et Filio, et Spiritu Sancto,"* he whispered the response: *"Sicut erat in principio et nunc et semper et in sæcula sæculorum. Amen."* The monk who led the singing had a fine deep, dark voice. In drowsy well-being Olav listened to the great male voice that rose alone and to the choir joining in, verse after verse throughout the psalms. After all the varied emotions of the day peace and security fell upon his soul as he sat in the dark church looking at the white-clad singers and the little flames of the candles behind the choir-screen. He would do the right and shun the wrong, he thought—then God's might and compassion would surely aid him and save him in all his difficulties.

Pictures began to swarm before his inner vision: the boat, Ingunn with the velvet hood over her fair face, the glitter on the water behind her, the floor-boards covered with shining fish-scales—the dark, damp path among nettles and angelica—the fence they had climbed and the flowery meadow through which they had run—the golden net over the bottom of the lake—all these scenes succeeded one another behind his closed and burning eyelids.

He awoke as Ingunn took him by the shoulder. "You have been asleep," she said reprovingly.

The church was empty, and just beside him the south door stood open to the green cloister garth in the evening sun. Olav yawned and stretched his stiff limbs. He dreaded the journey home terribly; this made him speak to her a little more masterfully than usual; " 'Twill soon be time to set out, Ingunn."

"Yes." She sighed deeply. "Would we might sleep here to-night!"

"You know we cannot do that."

"Then we could have heard mass in Christ Church in the morning. We never see strange folk, we who must ever bide at home—it makes the time seem long."

"You know that one day it will be otherwise with us."

"But you have been in Oslo too, you have, Olav."

"Ay, but I remember nothing of it."

"When we come to Hestviken, you must promise me this, that you will take me thither some time, to a fair or a gathering."

"That I may well promise you, methinks."

Olav was so hungry his entrails cried out for food. So it was good to get warm groats and whey in the guest-room of the convent. But he could not help thinking all the time of the row home. And then he was uneasy about his axe.

But now they fell into talk with two men who also sat at meat in the guest-house. They came from a small farm that lay by the shore a little to the north of the point where Olav and Ingunn were to land, and they asked to be taken in their boat. But they would fain stay till after complin.

Again Olav sat in the dark church listening to the deep male voices that chanted the great king's song to the King of kings. And again the images of that long, eventful day flickered behind his weary eyelids—he was on the point of falling asleep.

He was awakened by the voices changing to another tune; through the dark little church resounded the hymn:

> *Te lucis ante terminum*
> *Rerum Creator poscimus*
> *Ut pro tua clementia*
> *Sis præsul et custodia.*
>
> *Procul recedant somnia*
> *Et noctium phantasmata;*
> *Hostemque nostrum comprime,*
> *Ne polluantur corpora.*
>
> *Præsta, Pater piissime,*
> *Patrique compar Unice,*
> *Cum Spiritu Paraclito*
> *Regnans per omne sæculum.*[7]

He knew this; Arnvid Finnsson had often sung it to them in the evening, and he knew pretty well what the words meant in Norse. He let himself sink stiffly on his knees at the bench, and with his face hidden in his hands he said his evening prayers.

It had clouded over when they went down to the boat; the sky was flecked with grey high up and the fiord was leaden with dark stripes. The wooded slopes on both sides seemed plunged in darkness.

The strangers offered to row, and so Olav sat in the stern with

[7] Ere daylight be gone, we pray Thee, Creator of the world, that of Thy mercy Thou wilt be our Guide and Guardian.

May the visions and spectres of the night be far from us; hold back our enemy, lest our bodies be defiled.

Hear our prayer, O Father most holy, and Thou, only-begotten Son, equal to the Father, who with the Holy Ghost, the Comforter, reignest for ever and ever.

(Ambrosian hymn, seventh century)

Ingunn. They shot forward at a different pace now, under the long, steady strokes of the two young peasants; but Olav's boyish pride suffered no great injury nevertheless—it was so good to sit and be rowed.

After a while a few drops of rain fell. Ingunn spread out the folds of the heavy cloak and bade him come closer.

So they both sat wrapped in it and he had to put an arm around her waist. She was so slender and warm and supple, good to hold clasped. The boat flew lightly through the water in the blue dusk of the summer night. Lighter shreds of mist with scuds of rain drifted over the lake and the hills around, but they were spared the rain. Soon the two young heads sank against each other, cheek to cheek. The men laughed and bade them lie down upon their empty sacks in the bottom of the boat.

Ingunn nestled close to him and fell asleep at once. Olav sat half up, with his neck against the stern seat; now and again he opened his eyes and looked up at the cloudy sky. Then his weariness seemed to flow over him, strangely sweet and good. He started up as the boat grounded on the sand outside Aud's cabin.

The men laughed. No, why should they have waked him?— 'twas nothing of a row.

It was midnight. Olav guessed that they had rowed it in less than half the time he had taken. He helped the men to shove the boat up on the beach; then they said good-night and went. First they became two queerly black spots losing themselves in the dark rocky shore of the bay, and soon they had wholly disappeared into the murky summer night.

Olav's back was wet with bilge-water and he was stiff from his cramped position, but Ingunn was so tired that she whimpered— she would have it they must rest before setting out to walk home. Olav himself would best have liked to go at once—he felt it would have suppled his limbs so pleasantly to walk in the fresh, cool night, and he was afraid of what Steinfinn would say, if he had come home. But Ingunn was too tired, he saw—and they both dreaded to pass the cairn or to be out at all in the dead of night.

So they shared the last of the food in their wallet and crept into the cabin.

Just inside the door was a little hearth, from which some warmth still came. A narrow passage led in, which divided the earthen floor into two raised halves. On one side they heard Aud snoring; they felt their way among utensils and gear to the couch that they knew was on the other.

But Olav could not fall asleep. The air was thick with smoke even down to the floor and it hurt his chest—and the smell of raw fish and smoked fish and rotten fish was not to be borne. And his worn limbs twinged and tingled.

Ingunn lay uneasily, turning and twisting in the darkness. "I have no room for my head—surely there is an earthen pot just behind me—"

Olav felt for it and tried to push it away. But there was so much gear stowed behind, it felt as if it would all clatter down on them if he moved anything. Ingunn crawled farther down, doubled herself up, and lay with head and arms on his chest. "Do I crush you?" In a moment she was fast asleep.

After a while he slipped from under the warm body, heavy with sleep. Then he got his feet down on the passage, stood up, and stole out.

It was already growing light. A faint, cold air, like a shudder, breathed through the long, limber boughs of the birches and shook down a few icy drops; a pale gust blew over the steel-grey mirror of the lake.

Olav looked inland. It was so inconceivably still—there was as yet no life in the village; the farms were asleep and fields and meadows and groves were asleep, pale in the grey dawn. Scattered over the screes behind the nearest houses stood a few spruce-firs as though lifeless, so still and straight were they. The sky was almost white, with a faint yellow tinge in the north above the black tree-tops. Only high up floated a few dark shreds of the night's clouds.

It was so lonely to be standing here, the only one awake, driven out by this new feeling which chased him incessantly farther and farther away from the easy self-confidence of childhood. It was about this hour yesterday that he had risen—it seemed years ago.

He stood, shy and oppressed at heart, listening to the stillness. Now and again there was the clatter of a wooden bell; the widow's cow was moving in the grove. Then the cuckoo called, unearthly clear and far away somewhere in the dark forests, and some little birds began to wake. Each of the little sounds seemed only to intensify the immense hush of space.

Olav went to the byre and peeped in, but drew his head back at once before the sharp scent of lye that met him. But the ground was good and dry under the lean-to roof; brown and bare, with some wisps from the winter's stacks of hay and leaves. He lay down, rolled up like an animal, and went to sleep in a moment.

He was awakened by Ingunn shaking him. She was on her knees beside him. "Have you lain out here?"

" 'Twas so thick with smoke in the cabin." Olav rose to his knees and shook the wisps and twigs from his clothes.

The sun came out above the ridge, and the tops of the firs seemed to take fire as it rose higher. And now there was a full-throated song of birds all through the woods. Shadows still lay over the land and far out on the deep-blue lake, but on the other side of the water the sunshine flooded the forest and the green hamlets on the upper slopes.

Olav and Ingunn remained on their knees, facing each other, as though in wonder. And without either's saying anything they laid their arms on each other's shoulders and leaned forward.

They let go at the same time and looked at each other with a faint smile of surprise. Then Olav raised his hand and touched the girl's temples. He pushed back the tawny, dishevelled hair. As she let him do it, he put his other arm about her, drew her toward him, and kissed her long and tenderly on the sweet, tempting pit under the roots of the hair.

He looked into her face when he had done it and a warm tingling ran through him—she liked him to do that. Then they kissed each other on the lips, and at last he took courage to kiss her on the white arch of her throat.

But not a word did they say. When they stood up, he took the empty wallet and his cloak and set out. And so they walked in silence, he before and she behind, along the road through the village, while the morning sun shed its light farther and farther down the slopes.

On the higher ground folk were already astir on all the farms. As they went through the last of the woods, it was full daylight. But when they came to the staked gate where the home fields of Frettastein began, they saw no one about. Perhaps they might come well out of their adventure after all.

Behind the bushes by the gate they halted for a moment and looked at each other—the dazed, blissful surprise broke out in their eyes once more. Quickly he touched her hand, then turned to the gate again and pulled up the stakes.

When they entered the courtyard, the door of the byre stood open, but no one was to be seen. Ingunn made for the loft-room where she had slept the night before.

All at once she turned and came running back to Olav. "Your brooch—" she had taken it off and held it out to him.

"You may have it—I will give it you," he said quickly. He took off her little one, which he had worn instead, and put it in her hand that held the gold brooch. "No, you are not to give me yours in exchange. I have brooches enough, I have—"

He turned abruptly, blushing, ran from her grasp, and strode off rapidly toward the hall.

He drew a deep breath, much relieved after all to find that the rooms beyond were empty. One of the dogs got up and came to meet him, wagging its tail; Olav patted it and spoke a friendly word or two.

He stretched himself and yawned with relief on getting off his tight clothes. The coat had chafed him horribly under the arms— he could not possibly wear it again, unless it was altered. Ingunn could do that.

As he was about to fling himself into his sleeping-place, he saw that there was already a man lying there. "Are you all come home now?" asked the other drowsily. Olav knew by the voice it was Arnvid Finnsson.

"No, it is but I. I had an errand in the town," he said as calmly as if there were nothing strange in his going to Hamar on business of his own. Arnvid grunted something. In a moment they were both snoring.

3

When Olav awoke, he saw by the light in the hall that it was long past noon. He raised himself on his elbow and found that Ingunn and Arnvid were sitting on the dais. The look on the girl's face was so strange—at once scared and thoughtful.

She heard him get up and came rapidly to his bed. She wore the same bright-red kirtle as the day before; and with the new vision with which he looked on her, Olav turned hot with joy, for she was fair to see.

"Now methinks we shall soon know what Brother Vegard meant—and the smith—with that they said about the axes," she said, greatly moved. "Arnvid says that Mattias Haraldsson was at the Thing and fared northward to the manor he has at Birid."

"Ah," said Olav. He was bending down to tie his shoestring. Then he straightened himself and gave Arnvid his hand in greeting: "Now we shall see what Steinfinn· will do when he hears this."

"He *has* heard it," replied Arnvid. "It is for that he has ridden north to Kolbein, says Ingebjörg."

"You must go out and fetch me some food, Ingunn," said Olav. As soon as the girl was out of the hall, he asked the other: "Know you what thoughts Steinfinn has now?"

"I know what thoughts Ingebjörg has," replied Arnvid.

"Ay, they are easily guessed."

Olav had always liked Arnvid Finnsson best of all the men he knew—though he had never thought about it. But he felt at ease in Arnvid's company. For all that, it would never have occurred to him to call the other his friend; Arnvid had been grown up and married almost as long as Olav remembered him; and now he had been two years a widower.

But today it was as though the difference in their ages had vanished—Olav felt it so. He felt that he was grown up and the other was a young man like himself; Arnvid was not settled and fixed in his ways like other married men. His marriage had been like a yoke that was laid upon him in his youth, and since then he had striven instinctively to outgrow the marks of it—all this Olav was suddenly aware of, without knowing whence he had it.

And in the same way Arnvid seemed to feel that the two young ones had shot up much nearer to him in age. He spoke to them as to equals. While Olav was eating, Arnvid sat shaving fine slices, no thicker than a leaf, from a wind-dried shoulder of reindeer, which Ingunn was so fond of chewing.

"The worst of it is that Steinfinn has let this insult grow so old," said Arnvid. " 'Tis too late to bring a suit—he must take a dear revenge now, if he would right himself in folks' eyes."

"I cannot see how Steinfinn could do aught ere now. The man

took pilgrim's fancies—fled the country with his tail between his legs. But now that we have gotten two unbreeched children for kings, a man may well use his own right arm and need not let the peasants' Thing be judge of his honour—so I have heard Steinfinn and Kolbein say."

"Ay, I trow there is many a man now who makes ready to do his pleasure without much questioning of the law of the land or the law of God," said Arnvid. "There's many a one is growing restive now, up and down the land."

"And what of you?" asked Olav. "Will you not be with them, if Steinfinn and Kolbein have thoughts of seeking out Mattias and—chastening him?"

Arnvid made no answer. He sat there, tall and high-shouldered, resting his forehead in his slender, shapely hand, so that his small and ugly face was completely shaded.

Arnvid Finnsson was very tall and slight, of handsome build— above all, his hands and feet were shapely. But his shoulders were too broad and high, and his head was quite small, but he was short-necked; this did much to take the eye away from the rest of his handsome form. His face too was strangely ill-featured, as though compressed, with a low forehead and short, broad chin, and black curly hair like the forelock of a bull. In spite of this, Olav now saw for the first time that Arnvid and Ingunn bore a likeness to each other—Arnvid too had a small nose, as though unfinished, but in the man it seemed pressed in under the brow. Arnvid too had large, dark-blue eyes—but in him they were deep-set.

Arnvid did not belong to the Steinfinn stock, but Tore of Hov had married his father's sister. And the likeness between his heavy, dark ugliness and Ingunn's restless charm was not to be mistaken.

"So I see you have little mind to go with your kinsmen in that which is now brewing?" said Olav rather mockingly.

"Be sure I shall not hang back," answered Arnvid.

"What will he say to it, Bishop Torfinn, your ghostly father, if you make common cause with us in what Steinfinn has on foot?" asked Olav with his little mocking smile.

"He is in Björgvin now, so he cannot hear aught of it till the thing be done," said Arnvid shortly. "I can do naught else, I must go with my cousin."

"Ay, and you are not one of his priests either," said Olav as before.

"No, the more the pity," replied Arnvid. "Would I were. This matter between Steinfinn and Mattias—the worst of it is, I ween, that it is grown so old. Steinfinn *must* do something now to win back his honour. But then, you may be sure that all the old talk will be chewed over again, and foully will it stink. I hold myself not more fearful than other men—none the less do I wish I could have held aloof from these doings."

Olav held his peace. Now they were touching again on a matter that was no clearer to Olav than it was to the Steinfinnssons. Arnvid had been put to book-learning in his childhood. But then both his elder brothers had died, and his parents took him home again and married him to the rich bride who had been promised to his brother. But it seemed Arnvid did not count it as good fortune to be called to the headship of his family and to possess the manor in Elfardal, instead of being made a priest.

The wife he got was fair and rich and only five or six years older than he; yet the young couple seemed ill suited to each other. In some measure this may have come from their having little say in the house so long as Arnvid's parents were alive. Then Finn, Arnvid's father, died; but just after that his young wife, Tordis Erlingsdatter, died in childbirth. From that time Arnvid's mother took control, and they said she was somewhat masterful. Arnvid let her have charge both of the estate and of his three little sons and submitted to her in all things.

In former times many men of the Steinfinn kin had been priests, and even if none of them had made a special mark in the service of the Church, they had yet been good priests. But when it became the rule that priests in Norway must live unmarried, as in other Christian lands, the Steinfinnssons sought no more after book-learning. It was by prudent marriages that the kin had always extended its power, and that a man might make his way in the world without support in his marriage they could not believe.

Summer heat had come in earnest the day Olav and Ingunn had stolen away to Hamar.

From the crag above the outlying barn the fiord could be seen far below, beyond the waves of forest and patches of meadow in the hollows. On clear mornings Lake Mjösen lay reflecting the headlands, scored with light stripes, which betokened fine weather. As the day went on, all nature was bathed in heat haze, the land on the other side in blue mist, through which the green paddocks around the farms shimmered brightly. Far to the south on Skrei Fell there was still a glitter of snow high up, gleaming like water and cloud, but the patches of snow grew smaller day by day. Fair-weather clouds were piled up everywhere on the horizon and sailed over forest and lake, casting shadows below. Sometimes they thinned out and spread over the sky, making it a dull white, and the lake turned grey and no longer reflected the land. But the rain came to nothing—it was blown away, and all the trees glittered with leaves flickering in the sunshine, as though the very land panted for heat.

The turf roots began to look scorched and the cornfields yellowed in patches, where the soil was thin; but the weeds flourished and grew high above the light shoots of young corn. The meadows burst into purple with sorrel and monk's-hood and St. Olav's flower.[8]

There was little to do on the farm now, and nothing was done—the few who were left at home spent their days in waiting.

Olav and Ingunn idled among the houses. Separately ·and as though by chance they wandered down to the beck that ran north of the farm. It flowed between high banks worn in the turf; the water rushed over great bedded rocks that stretched from bank to bank, and fell into a pool below with a strangely soothing murmur.

The two found a place under a clump of quivering aspens above the stream. The ground was dry here, with fine, thin grass and no flowers.

"Come and lay your head in my lap," said the girl, "and I will clean it for you."

Olav shifted a little and laid his head on her knees. Ingunn turned his fair, silky hair over and over, till the boy dozed, breathing evenly and audibly. She took the little kerchief that covered the throat of her dress and wiped the sweat from Olav's face; then sat with the kerchief in her hand fanning off the flies and midges.

From the higher ground she heard her mother's sharp, im-

---

[8] A name given to several wild-flowers of the Geranium family.

petuous voice. The lady Ingebjörg and Arnvid Finnsson were
walking on the path at the edge of the corn.

Every day Ingebjörg Jonsdatter went up and sat on the crag
above the manor, gazing out as she talked and talked—of her old
deadly hatred of Mattias Haraldsson and of her and Steinfinn's
long-hatched plans of revenge. It was always Arnvid who had to
go with her and listen and give ever the same answers to the lady's
speech.

Olav slept with his head in Ingunn's lap; she sat with her neck
against the stem of an aspen, staring before her, thoughtlessly
happy, as Arnvid came down, wading through the long grass of
the meadow.

"I saw you two sitting here—"

" 'Tis cool and pleasant here," said Ingunn.

"It seems high time to begin haymaking," said Arnvid; he looked
up the slope as a gust of wind swayed the grass.

Olav awoke and turned over, laying the other cheek in Ingunn's lap. "We shall begin after the holy-day—I spoke to Grim
this morning."

"You do Steinfinn no little service here, Olav?" asked Arnvid,
to draw him.

"Oh—" Olav paused. "But 'tis ever the same here, everything is
left undone; 'tis of little use to take a hand. For all that—*now* there
must come a change; Steinfinn will surely be more minded to look
to his affairs. But this is my last summer here."

"Are you to leave Frettastein now?" asked Arnvid.

"I trow I must go home and see to my own property some
time," said Olav with a wisdom beyond his years. "So when Steinfinn has made an end of this matter, there will be talk of my going home to Hestviken. Steinfinn will be glad enough to have Ingunn and me off his hands."

" 'Tis not so sure that Steinfinn will have peace to settle such
matters at present," said Arnvid below his breath.

Olav shrugged his shoulders, putting on a bold air.

"All the more need for him that I take over the charge of my
own estate. He knows I am no shirker, but will back my foster-
father."

"You two are young yet to take over the charge of a great
manor."

"You were no older, Arnvid, when you were married."

"No, but we had my parents to back us—and yet I was the youngest. But they feared our line should die out, when my brothers were dead."

"Ay, and I am the last man of my race, I too," said Olav.

"That is so," replied Arnvid. "But Ingunn is very young."

All this Olav had thought out since the journey to Hamar.

After that first sweet and frenzied day, when he was plunged from one bewilderment to another with his playmate, he calmed down as soon as they were back at Frettastein. None there had so much as noticed their flight. And this had a strangely cooling effect on his mental tumult. Then there was this too, that change and great events were in the air at the very moment when he himself felt that he was grown up—and this seemed to make it more natural that he too should feel an inward change.

He left off playing with the other boys of the place; and none was surprised at this, for the tension that now prevailed at Frettastein had spread to all their neighbours on the hills.

Thus it seemed now quite natural that he should think seriously of his marriage. And in these long, sunny days of summer that he spent with Ingunn he felt a kind of tangible satisfaction in that he now had a much better understanding of the future that was in store for him than he ever could have had in his more childish years.

Instead of uneasiness and timid shame there was come a joyful and inquiring expectation. Something must happen now. Steinfinn would no doubt seize the opportunity—strike a blow. Of the consequences that might follow if Steinfinn struck his blow, Olav had little thought—instinctively he had absorbed the Steinfinnssons' ideas of their own power and glory; there was none to touch them. But neither had he any other thought than that Steinfinn would at once consent when, after the deed was done, he asked leave to go home and hold his wedding. That would be next autumn or winter. And his new-born desire to possess her became one with his new-born ambition—to be his own master. When he took her in his arms, it was as though he held a pledge of his maturity. When they came to Hestviken, they would sleep together and rule together, indoors and out, and there would be none to

give orders but they two. Then they would come into their full
rights.

It was not often, however, that Olav caressed his betrothed now.
If he no longer was so shy and afraid, nor had gloomy thoughts,
as when he felt the first breath of desire, he now had a clear view
of what was manly and seemly. Only, when they parted for the
night, he would often seek an occasion to bid her good-night
alone, in the manner he deemed proper to two lovers who were
soon to be married.

That Ingunn's eyes betrayed far too much whenever they
chanced to look at each other seemed to Olav a part of the good
fortune fate had prepared for him. He noted how she watched
for a chance of looking at him, and her glance was strange, heavy,
and full of delightful darkness. Then she met his eyes—a little
sparkle was kindled in hers; she looked away, afraid she might
smile. She stole a chance of stroking him with her hand when they
met—was fond of playing with his hair whenever they were left
alone for a moment. She was very eager to do things for him—
offered to mend his clothes, brought in his food if he came to a
meal a little later than the rest of the men. And when he said
good-night to her, she clung to him as though hungry and thirsty
for his caresses. Olav took this to mean that she too longed for
their wedding, and he thought that natural—time must be long
for her too in this house; she must look forward eagerly to being
mistress of her own home. It never occurred to him that there
might be young people who did not care for one another although
they were betrothed.

But the journey to Hamar remained a dream to Olav. He
thought of it most often when he lay down at night, and he lived
it again till he felt the strange, sweet tremor in body and mind.
He recalled how they had knelt at dawn behind the widow's byre,
leaning breast to breast, and he had dared to kiss her on the temple, under the hair that smelt so warm and good. And then this
unaccountable melancholy and dread settled on him. He tried
to think of the future—and for them the path of the future was
a straight one, to the church door and the high seat and the bridal
bed. But his heart seemed to grow weak and faint when in these
night hours he tried to rejoice in all that awaited them—as though,
after all, the future could have nothing in store for them so sweet
as that morning kiss.

"What is it?" asked Arnvid crossly. "Cannot you lie still?"

"I am going out awhile." Olav got up, dressed again, and threw a cloak about him.

There was already less light in the sky at night; the thick foliage of the trees looked darker against the misty blue of the hills beyond. The clouds to the northward were streaked with yellow. A bat flittered past him, black and swift as lightning.

Olav went to the bower where Ingunn slept. The door was left ajar for coolness' sake—and still it was close inside, with a smell of sun-baked timber, of bedding, and of human sweat.

The maid who lay next the wall snored loudly in her sleep. Olav knelt down and bent his face over her who lay outside. With cheek and lips he gently touched Ingunn's breast. For an instant he kept quite still so as to feel the soft, warm bosom that lightly rose and fell as she breathed in sleep—and he heard her heartbeats under it. Then he drew his face up to hers and she awoke.

"Dress yourself," he whispered in her ear. "Come out awhile—"

He waited outside on the balcony. Soon Ingunn appeared in the low doorway and stood awhile, as though surprised at the stillness. She took a few deep breaths—the night was cool and good. They sat down side by side at the top of the stairway.

And now they both felt it so strange that they should be the only ones awake in the whole manor—neither was used to being out at night. So they sat there without moving, scarce venturing to whisper a word now and then. Olav had thought he would wrap his cloak around her and put an arm about her waist. But all he did was to place one of her hands on his knee and stroke her fingers; till Ingunn withdrew her hand, threw her arm about his shoulder, and pressed her face hard against his neck.

"Are not the nights darker already?" she asked in a hushed voice.

"The air is dense tonight," he said.

"Ay, haply there will be rain tomorrow," she wondered.

There was a blue-grey mist over the strip of fiord they could see from where they sat, and the hills were blotted out on the far side. Olav looked vacantly before him, pondering: "That is not so sure—there is an easterly set in the wind. Can you not hear how loud the stream sounds above tonight?"

"We had best go to bed," he whispered a little later. They

kissed each other, a quick and timid little kiss. Then he stole down again and she went in.

Inside the hall it was pitch-dark. Olav undressed and lay down again.

"Have you been out talking to Ingunn?" asked Arnvid, wide awake at his side.

"Yes."

Soon after, Arnvid asked again: "Have you found out, Olav, what are the settlements about your estate and Ingunn's?"

"No, I have not. You know, I was so young when I was betrothed to her. But surely Steinfinn and my father must have made an agreement about that—what we are to bring to each other.—Why do you ask me this?" said Olav, with sudden surprise.

Arnvid did not answer.

Olav said: "Steinfinn will take good care that we get what we are to have according to the settlement."

"Ay—he is my cousin." Arnvid spoke with some hesitation. "But you are soon to be our kinsman by marriage—I may well speak of it to you. They say Steinfinn's fortunes are not so good as they were. I have lain awake thinking of what you spoke of—I believe you are right. You will be wise to hasten the marriage—so that Ingunn may get what comes to her as soon as may be."

"Ay, we have nothing to wait for, either," said Olav.

The next day was a holy-day, and the day after they began to cut the grass at Frettastein. Arnvid and his man helped in the haymaking. Early in the day the sky turned pale and grey, and by afternoon big, dark clouds began to drift up from the south and spread over the hazy sky. Olav looked up as they stood whetting their scythes; the first drop of rain fell on his face.

"Maybe 'twill be but a shower or two tonight," said one of the old house-carls.

"Tomorrow is Midsummer Day," answered Olav. "If the weather change on that day, 'twill rain as many days after as the sun shone before, I have always heard. I trow we shall have no better hay crop this year, Torleif, than we had last."

Arnvid was standing a little farther down the field. Now he laid down his scythe, came up quickly toward the others, and pointed. Far down the hillside rode a long line of armed men across a little glade in the forest.

"It is they," said Arnvid. "It seems they are set upon another kind of mowing. And now, by my troth, I wonder how it will go with the haymaking at Frettastein this year."

Late in the evening the rain came down, with a thick white mist that drifted in patches over the fields and wooded slopes. Olav and Ingunn stood under the balcony of the loft where she slept; the lad stared angrily at the pouring rain.

Arnvid came running across the mud of the courtyard, darted in to the couple, and shook himself.

"How is it you are not in the men's councils?" asked Olav with a sneer.

Olav would have followed them when the men went into Inge-björg's little house—they chose it for their meeting, out of ear-shot of the servants. But Steinfinn had bidden his foster-son stay in the hall with the house-carls. Olav was angry—now that in his own thoughts he reckoned himself Steinfinn's son-in-law, he for-got that the other did not yet know their alliance was about to be welded so fast.

Arnvid stood leaning against the wall, glaring before him mournfully. "I shall not shirk my duty, but shall follow my kins-men as far as Steinfinn may call upon me. But I will have no part in their councils."

Olav looked at his friend—the boy's pale, finely arched lips curled lightly in a scornful smile.

4

On the evening of the second day the men went down to the lake. The rain had held off that day, but it had been cold, with a high wind and much cloud.

Kolbein rode with five of his men, Steinfinn had with him seven house-carls and Olav Audunsson; Arnvid followed with one henchman. Kolbein had provided boats, which lay concealed in a cove of Lake Mjösen a little to the northward.

Ingunn went early to rest in her loft. She did not know how long she had slept when she was awakened by a touch on her chest.

"Is it you?" she whispered, heavy with sleep—expecting only to find Olav's soft locks; but she awoke to see a coifed head. "Mother—" she cried in astonishment.

"I can get no sleep," said Ingebjörg. "I have been walking outside. Put on some clothes and come down."

Ingunn got up obediently and dressed. She was surprised beyond measure.

It was not so late after all, she saw on coming out. The weather had cleared. The moon, nearly full, rose due south above the ridge, pale red like a sunset cloud, giving no light as yet.

The mother's hand was hot as fire as she took her daughter's. Ingebjörg drew the girl along, roving hither and thither beyond the houses, but saying scarcely a word.

At one moment they stayed leaning over the fence of a cornfield. Down in the field was a water-hole surrounded by tall, thick rushes, which were darkly mirrored in it, but in the middle of the smooth little pond the moon shone—it had now risen high enough to give a yellow light.

The mother looked into the distance, where the lake and the farms surrounding it lay in a pale, calm mist.

"Have you the wit to see, I wonder, what we have all at stake?" said Ingebjörg.

Ingunn felt her cheeks go white and cold at her mother's words. She had always known what there was to know of her father and mother; she had known too that great events were now at hand. But here by her mother's side, seeing how she was stirred to the depths of her soul, she guessed for the first time what it all *meant*. A feeble sound came from her lips—like the squeaking of a mouse.

Ingebjörg's ravaged face was drawn sideways in a sort of smile.

"Are you afraid to watch this night with your mother? Tora would not have refused to stay with me, but she is such a child, gentle and quiet. That you are not—and you are the elder, I ween," she concluded hotly.

Ingunn clasped her slender hands together. Again it was as though she had climbed a little higher, had gained a wider view over her world. She had always been clear that her parents were not very old folk. But now she saw that they were young. Their love, of which she had heard as a tale of old days, was ready to be quickened and to burn with a bright flame, as the fire may be revived from the glowing embers beneath the ashes. With wonder and reluctance she suspected that her father and mother loved each other even yet—as she and Olav loved—only so much the more strongly as the river is greater and fuller near its mouth than it is high up in the hills. And although what she guessed made her ashamed, she felt proud withal at the uncommon lot of her parents.

Timidly she held out both hands. "I will gladly watch with you all night, Mother."

Ingebjörg squeezed her daughter's hand. "God can grant Steinfinn no less than that we may wash the shame from us," she said impetuously, clasping the girl and kissing her.

Ingunn put her arms round her mother's neck—it was so long since she had kissed her. She remembered it as part of the life that was brought to an end on the night Mattias came to the house.

Not that Ingunn had felt the want of it—as a child she had not been fond of caresses. Between her and Olav it was like something they had found out for themselves. It had come as the spring comes—one day it is there like a miracle, but no sooner is it come than one feels it must be summer always. Like the bare strip of sod that borders the cornfield—so long as it lies naked with its withered grass after the thaw, it is nothing but a little grey balk amongst the sown; but then there comes a forest of tangled wild growth that makes it wellnigh impassable.

Now the springlike bareness of her child's mind was overgrown with a summer luxuriance. She laid her cool, soft cheek against her mother's wasted face. "I will *gladly* share your watching, Mother!"

The words seemed to sink into herself—for *she* had to watch for Olav. It was as though her thoughts had been astray when he set out with the others in the evening—she had not thought of the dangers the men were to face. A fear thrilled through her—but it was only as a flutter at the root of her heart. She could not fancy in earnest that anything could happen to one of *hers*.

For all that, she asked: "Mother—are *you afraid*?"

Ingebjörg Jonsdatter shook her head: "No. God will give us our right, for right is on our side." When she saw her daughter's look she added, with a smile Ingunn did not like—there was a queer cunning in it: "You see, my girl, it is on this wise—'tis a

lucky chance for us that King Magnus died this spring. We have
kinsmen and friends among those who will now have most power
—so says Kolbein. And there are many of them who would fain
see Mattias—do you mind what manner of man he is? Oh no, you
cannot—he is short of stature, is Mattias; yet there are many who
think he might be shorter by a head. Queen Ingebjörg never liked
him. You must know, but for that, he would not lie at Birid at this
time, when knights and barons are gathering at Björgvin and the
young King is to be crowned."

She went on talking as they walked along the fences. Ingunn
fervently desired to speak to her mother of Olav Audunsson, but
she guessed that she was so wholly lost in her own thoughts that
she would not care to hear of aught else. Yet she could not help
saying: "Was it not an ill chance that Olav could not fetch his
axe in time?"

"Oh, your father will have seen that they are as well armed as
there is need, all the men he has taken with him," said the mistress.
"Steinfinn would not have had the boy with him, but he begged
leave to go—"

"But you are cold," said her mother a moment later. "Put on
your cloak—"

Ingunn's cloak still hung in her mother's room; she had not
fetched it in all these fourteen days, but had worn Olav's fine
mantle when she needed an outer garment. Her mother went in
with her. She stirred the fire on the hearth and lighted the lantern.

"Your father and I were wont to move into the great loft in
summer—had we been sleeping there the night Mattias came, he
could not have taken Steinfinn unawares. It will be safer for us
to sleep there till Steinfinn be made free of the law."

The great loft-room had no outside stairway, for it had been
used for storing household goods of value. From the floor below,
a ladder led up into the loft. It was not often that Ingunn had been
up there; the very smell of the place gave her a solemn feeling.
Bags of strong-smelling spices hung among bedcovers of fur and
leather sacks—there was almost an uncanny look about all the
things that hung from the roof. Against the walls stood great
chests. Ingunn went up to Olav's and let the light fall on it; it was
of pale limewood, and carved.

Ingebjörg opened the door to the balcony. She emptied the bedstead of all that was piled upon it and began searching in chests and coffers, making her daughter hold the light for her; then she dropped on the floor all she had in her hands and went out on the balcony.

The moon was now so far to the westward that its light lay like a golden bridge over the water. It was about to sink into a bank of heavy blue cloud, some shreds of which floated up toward the moon and were gilded.

The mother went in again and turned over more of the chests. She had come upon a woman's gown of silk—green with a woven pattern of yellow flowers—the light of the lantern gave the whole kirtle the tint of a fading aspen.

"This I will give to you now—"

Ingunn curtsied and kissed her mother's hand. A silken gown she had never owned before. From a little casket of walrus ivory her mother took a green velvet ribbon, set all over with silver gilt roses. She put it over the crown of her daughter's head, pushed it a little forward, and brought the ends together at the back of the neck under the hair.

"So. Fair as you looked to be when you were small, you are not—but you have grown fairer again this summer. 'Tis time for you to wear the garland—you are a marriageable maid now, my Ingunn."

"Yes; Olav and I have spoken of that too," Ingunn took courage to say. She strove instinctively to speak as naturally as she could.

Ingebjörg looked up—they were both crouching before a chest.

"Have Olav and you spoken of *that*?"

"Yes." Ingunn spoke as calmly as before, dropping her eyelids meekly. "We are old enough now to expect that you will soon see to the fulfilment of this bargain that was made for us."

"Oh, that bargain was not of a kind that cannot be undone again," said her mother; "if you yourselves have no mind to it. We shall not force you."

"Nay, but we are well pleased with what you have purposed for us," said Ingunn meekly. "We are agreed that it is well as our fathers have disposed."

"So that is the way of it." Ingebjörg stared thoughtfully before her. "Then I doubt not some means will be found— Do you like Olav *well*?" she asked.

"What could I do else? We have known each other so long, and
he has always been good and kind and has shown himself dutiful
toward you."

Her mother nodded thoughtfully.

"We knew not, Steinfinn and I, whether you two remembered
aught of that bargain or thought more of it. Ay, some means must
be found, one way or another. At your age you two cannot be
so closely tied. Handsome he is, Olav. And Audun left wealth behind him—"

Ingunn would fain have said more of Olav. But she saw that her
mother was far away in her own thoughts again.

"We went by desert paths, your father and I, when we crossed
the fells," she said. "From Vors we took to the moors, and then
we passed through the upper dales. There was still much snow
on the fells. In one place we had to stay a whole week in a stone
hut. It stood beside a tarn and a snow-field came down into the
water—we heard the flakes of ice break off and splash into the lake
as we lay at night. Steinfinn offered a gold ring from his finger at
the first church we came to below—it was a holy-day. The poor
folk of the fells stared at us agape—we had ridden from the town
as we stood, in our Sunday clothes. They were much the worse
for wear, but, for all that, no such clothes had ever been seen in
that dale.

"But a weary bride I was, when Steinfinn brought me home to
Hov. And already I bore you under my heart—"

Ingunn stared at her mother as though spellbound. In the faint
light of the lantern that stood on the floor between them she saw
so strange a smile on her mother's face. Ingebjörg stroked her
daughter's head and drew her long plaits through her hand.

"—And now you are already a grown maid."

Her mother rose and gave her the great embroidered bedcover,
bidding her shake it out over the balcony.

"Mother!" the girl cried loudly from outside.

Ingebjörg ran out to her.

It was almost daylight and the sky was pale and clear high up,
but clouds and mist lay over the land. Straight across the lake in
the north-west a great fire was blazing, shedding a ruddy light
on the thick air far around. Black smoke poured out, drifted away,
and mingled with the fog, thickening and darkening it far over
the ridge. Now and again they saw the very flames, when they

rose high, but the burning homestead lay hidden behind a tongue of the woods.

The two women stood for a while gazing at it. The mother said not a word, and the girl dared not speak. Then the mistress turned into the loft—a moment later Ingunn saw her running across the yard to her little house.

Two women servants rushed out in their bare shifts and ran down to the courtyard fence. Then came Tora, with her fair hair fluttering loose, her mother leading her two young sons, and all the women of the place. Their cries and talk reached Ingunn.

But when they began to swarm up into the loft, she stole out. With her head bent and her hands crossed under the cloak that she held tightly about her—she would have wished to be quite invisible—she crept up to her own loft and lay down.

A violent fit of weeping came upon her—she could not make out what it was she wept like that for. It was just that she was too full of all that had crowded in upon her that night. She could not bear others to come near her—it made her tears run over. Tired she was too. It was morning now.

When she awoke, the sun was shining in at the door. Ingunn started up and pulled on her shift—she heard there were horses in the yard.

Four or five of their own strayed about grazing, unsaddled. Olav's dun Elk was among them. And there was a neighing from the paddock. The maids ran between the cook-house and the hall—they were all in festival clothes.

She threw her cloak over her and ran to the eastern bower. The floor was strewed with brier-roses and meadowsweet—it almost took her breath away. She had not seen festivity in her home since she was a little girl. Drinking-bouts in the hall and banquets on high days—but not such as they strewed the rooms with flowers for. Her silken kirtle and the gilt circlet lay on Olav's chest. Ingunn fetched them and ran back.

She had no mirror, but she did not feel the want of it as she stood ready dressed in her bower. She felt the weight of the gilt garland over her flowing hair, looked down at her figure wrapped in the green and yellow silk. The kirtle fell in long folds from her bosom to her feet, held in slightly by the silver belt at her waist. The gown was ample and long, so she had to lift it with

both hands as she stepped over the grass of the courtyard. Full
of delight, she knew that she looked like one of the carven images in a church: tall and slender, low-bosomed and slight of
limb, gleaming with jewels.

At the door of the hall she stopped, overwhelmed. The long
fires were burning on the central hearth, and the sunshine poured
in through the smoke-vent, turning the smoke sky-blue as it
drifted under the rafters. And lighted torches stood on the board
before the high seat, facing the door. There sat her mother by
her father's side, and her mother was dressed in red silk. Instead
of the kerchief that Ingunn was used to seeing on her, she wore
a starched white coif; it rose like a crown above her forehead
and left the back of her head uncovered; her knot of hair gleamed
golden within a net.

The other women were not seated at table; they went to and
fro, bearing meat and drink. Ingunn then took up a tankard; she
carried it in her right hand and held up her gown with her left,
making herself as lithe and supple as she could—she thrust her hips
well forward, dropped her shoulders to make herself look more
narrow-breasted, and bowed her neck, leaning her head to one
side like a flower on its stalk. Thus she moved forward, gliding
as lightly as she could.

But the men were already half-drunken, and maybe tired too
after the night's exploit; none paid any great heed to her. Her
father looked up with a laugh when she filled his beaker. His eyes
were bright and stiff, his face blazed red under his tousled tawny
hair—and now Ingunn saw that one arm was bound up over his
chest. He had on his best cloak over the tight leather jerkin that
he wore under the coat of mail. Most of the men seemed to have
sat down to table just as they came from the saddle.

Her father signed to her to pour out for Kolbein and his two
sons, Einar and Haftor; they sat at Steinfinn's right hand.

On Steinfinn's left sat Arnvid. He was red in the face, and his
dark-blue eyes shone like metal. A tremor passed over his features
as he stared at his young kinswoman. Ingunn could see that he,
at any rate, thought her fair this evening, and she smiled with joy
as she filled his cup.

She came where Olav Audunsson sat on the outer bench, and
squeezed in between him and his neighbour as she poured out for
those sitting on the inner bench. Then the boy caught hold of her

down by the knees and pressed her toward him, screened by the table, making her spill the drink.

Ingunn saw at once that he was drunken. He sat astride the bench with his legs stretched far out, his head supported in one hand, with the elbow on the table among the food. It was so unlike Olav to sit thus that she could not help laughing—they used always to tease him for keeping just as steady and quiet, no matter what he drank. God's gifts did not bite on him, said the others.

But this evening the ale had plainly got the better even of his stiffness. When she was going to pour out for him, he seized her hands, put the tankard to his lips, and drank, spilling the drink over himself, so that the breast of his elkskin jerkin was all befouled.

"Now take a drink yourself," he said, laughing up in her face— but his eyes looked so queer and strange; they gleamed with a wanton wildness. Ingunn was flustered a little, but she filled his beaker and drank; then he clutched her again under the table and came near to making her fall into his arms.

The man by Olav's side took the tankard from them. "Bide awhile, you two—you must leave a drop for the rest of us—"

Ingunn went out to fill the tankard again—and then she saw that her hands trembled. With surprise she found that she was shaking all over. It was almost as if she had been scared by the boy's violence. But she was drawn toward him in a way she had never known before—a sweet and consuming curiosity. She had never seen Olav in this state. But it was so joyous—this evening nothing was as it was wont to be. As she went about filling the cups she could not help trying to brush past Olav, that he might have a chance of stealing those rough and furtive caresses of his. It was as though they drew her on.

None had marked that it was growing dark outside before the rain spurted through the smoke-vent. They had to close the ventil; then Ingebjörg bade bring in more lights. The men rose from the board; some went to their places to sleep, but others sat down again to drink and talk to the women, who now began to think of food.

Arnvid and Einar Kolbeinsson, her cousin, sat down by Ingunn, and Einar was to tell her more of the raid:

They had sailed under the eastern shore right up to the river, and there they went across to Vingarheim, so that they came riding down upon Mattias's manor from the north. This proved unnecessary, however, as Mattias had set no watch.

"He never believed Steinfinn would strike in earnest," said Einar scornfully. "None can wonder at that—after so much prating and waiting he would be apt to think that, could Steinfinn bear his shame in patience for six years, the seventh would not be too great a burden for him."

"Meseems I heard a tale of Mattias—that he fled the country for fear of Steinfinn," said Olav Audunsson, who had joined them. He squeezed in between Arnvid and Ingunn.

"Ay, and Steinfinn is lazy too; he is one to sit under the bush and wait till the bird falls into his hand—"

"You would have had him take to lawsuits and wrangling like your father?"

Arnvid interposed and made them keep the peace. Then Einar took up his story:

They came into the courtyard unopposed and some men were posted to guard those houses in which folk might be sleeping, while Steinfinn and the sons of Kolbein went with Arnvid, Olav, and five of the house-carls to the hall. Kolbein stayed outside. The men within started up from sleep when the door was broken down—some naked and some in their shirts, but all reached for their weapons. There were Mattias and a friend of his, the tenant of the farm and his half-grown son, and two serving-men. There came a short struggle, but the drowsy house-folk were quickly overpowered. And then it was Steinfinn and Mattias.

"This was unlooked for—are *you* abroad thus betimes, Steinfinn?" said Mattias. "I mind me you were once so sound a sleeper, and a fair wife you had to keep you to your bed."

"Ay, and 'twas she who sent me hither with her greeting," said Steinfinn. "You surely won her heart when last you came to us—she cannot put you out of her mind.—But don your clothes," he said; "I have ever thought it a dastard's deed to set on a naked man."

Mattias turned flaming red at those words. But he made light of it and asked: "Will you give me leave to buckle on my coat of mail too, since it seems you would make a show of chivalry?"

"No," cried Steinfinn. "For I have no thought that you shall come off with your life from this our meeting. But I am nothing loath to meet you unharnessed."

While Steinfinn unbuckled his coat of mail, Kolbein came in and he and another man held Mattias. This he liked ill, but Steinfinn said with a laugh: "Methinks you are more ticklish than I was—you cannot bear a man's hand near your skin!" After that Steinfinn let Mattias put on his clothes and take a shield. Then the two set upon each other.

In his youth Steinfinn had been counted most skilful in the use of arms, but of late he had fallen out of practice; it was quickly seen that Mattias, small and slight as he was, would be more than a match for the other. Steinfinn had to give ground, foot by foot; his breath came heavily—then Mattias made a cut at him and disabled his right arm. Steinfinn changed his sword over to his left hand—both men had long since thrown away the wreckage of their shields. But now Steinfinn's men thought it looked badly for their master: on a sign from Kolbein one of his men sprang to Steinfinn's side. Mattias was somewhat dazed at this, and now Steinfinn gave him his death-blow.

"But they fought like two good lads, we all said that," said Arnvid.

Meanwhile, as ill luck would have it, some of the strange men-at-arms whom Steinfinn had with him bethought them of pillage, and others tried to stay them from it. And in the tumult some man set fire to a stack of birchbark which stood in the narrow gangway between the hall and one of the storehouses. It was doubtless that Tjostolv who did it, a man none thought well of, and he must have carried bark into the storehouse too, for it burst into flames on the instant, though timbers and roof were wet from the rain. And then the fire took hold of the hall. They had to bear out Mattias's corpse and loose the other men.

Now folk came up from the neighbouring farms, and a number of these peasants came to blows with them. Some were hurt on both sides, but 'twas unlikely that more were slain.

"Ay, we need not have had the fire and the brawling on our hands," said Einar, "had not Steinfinn been set on showing prowess and chivalry."

Olav had never liked Einar Kolbeinsson. He was three years

older than himself and had always loved to tease the younger
boys with his spite. So Olav answered him, pretty scornfully:
"Nay, no man will charge your father or you brothers with *that*—
none will accuse Kolbein Borghildsson of goading on his half-
brother to ill-timed high-mindedness."

"Have a care of yourself, young sniveller—Father's name has
always stood next to Tore of Hov's. Our stock is just as good as
Aasa's offspring—mind that, Olav; and don't sit there fondling my
kinswomen—take your paw out of her lap, and quick about it!"

Olav jumped up and they were at each other. Ingunn and Arnvid ran to part them. Then it was that Steinfinn rose and called
for silence.

The house-folk, men and women, and the strangers drew toward the table. Steinfinn stood leaning on his wife's shoulder—
he was no longer red in the face, but white and sunken under
the eyes. But he smiled and held himself erect as he spoke: "Now
I will give you thanks, all you who were with me in this deed—
first will I thank you, brother, and your sons, and then my dear
cousin, Arnvid Finnsson, and you others, good kinsmen and
trusty men. If God will, we shall soon have peace and atonement
for these things that have befallen this night, for He is a righteous
God and it is His will that a man shall hold his wife in honour
and protect the good name of women. But I am weary now, good
friends, and now we will go to bed, I and my wife—and you must
forgive me that I say no more—but I am weary, and I have gotten
a small scratch too. But Grim and Dalla will have good care of
you, and now ye may drink as long as ye list, and play and be
merry as is fitting on a joyful day such as this—but now we go
to rest, Ingebjörg and I—and so you must forgive us that we leave
you now—"

Toward the close his speech had become thick and halting; he
swayed slightly on his feet, and Ingebjörg had to support him as
they went out of the hall.

Some of the house-carls had raised a cheer, hammering on the
tables with their knives and drinking-cups. But the noise died
away of itself, and the men stood aside in silence. Not a few of
them guessed that Steinfinn's wound might be worse than he
would have it thought.

All followed them out—stood in silent groups watching the
tall and handsome couple as they went together to the loft-room

in the rain-drenched summer evening. Most of them marked how
Steinfinn stood still and seemed to speak hastily to his wife. It
looked as though she opposed him and tried to hold his hand; but
he tore off the bandage that bound his wounded arm to his breast
and flung it impatiently from him. They heard Steinfinn laugh as
he went on.

The house-folk were still quiet when they came in again,
though Grim and Dalla had more drink brought in and fresh wood
thrown on the fire. The table and benches were cleared out of
the way. But most of the men were tired and seemed most inclined for sleep. Yet some went out into the yard to dance, but
came in again at once; the shower was just overhead and the grass
was too wet.

Ingunn still sat between Arnvid and Olav, and Olav had laid his
hand in her lap. "Silk," he said, stroking her knee; "silk is fine,"
he went on saying again and again.

"You are bemused and know not what you say," said Arnvid
with vexation. "You're half-asleep already—go to bed!"

But Olav shook his head and laughed softly to himself: "I'll go
when I please."

Meanwhile some of the men had taken their swords and stood
up for dancing. Haftor Kolbeinsson came up to Arnvid and
would have him sing for them. But Arnvid declined—he was too
tired, he said. Nor would Olav and Ingunn take part in the dance;
they said they did not know that lay—the *Kraaka-maal*.[9]

Einar headed the chain of dancers with his drawn sword in
his right hand. Tora held his left and had placed her other hand
on the next man's shoulder. Thus they stood in a row, a man with
drawn sword and then a woman, all down the hall. It was a fine
sight with all the blades held high. Einar began the singing:

> *"Swiftly went the sword-play—"*

[9] The reader will find this old lay, with a literal translation, in Vigfusson
and Powell: *Corpus Poeticum Boreale*, Vol. II, p. 339. The song is supposed to be sung by the famous Ragnar Lodbrok (Shaggy-breeks) after he
had been thrown into the snake pit by Ælla, King of Northumberland. The
editors remark: "The *story* of the poem is the one legend which has sur-
vived in Norway of the great movement which led to the conquest and
settlement of half England by the Danes in the ninth century." Skarpa-
skerry is Scarborough.

The chain moved three paces to the right. Then the men stepped to the left, while the women had to take one place to the rear, so that the men stood on a line before them; and then they crossed swords in pairs and marked time with their feet, as the women ran under their weapons and re-formed the chain. Einar sang on:

> *"Swiftly went the sword-play—*
> *Young was I when east in*
> *Öresound I scattered*
> *Food to greedy grey-legs—"*

There was none among the dancers who was quite sure of the steps, it was seen. When the women were to leap forward under the swords, they made a poor shift to keep time with the men's tramping. The place was too narrow and constrained, between the long hearth and the row of posts that held up the roof and divided the sleeping-places from the hall.

The three on the dais at the end had risen to have a better view. And when the game threatened to break up even in the second verse, people shouted again for Arnvid and bade him come in. They knew that he could sing the whole dance, and he had the finest of voices.

So when he took his sword, drew it, and placed himself at the head of the row of dancers, the game at once took better shape. Olav and Ingunn stepped in just below him. Arnvid led as surely and gracefully as anyone could look for who saw his high-shouldered, stooping figure. He took up the song in his full, clear voice, while the women swayed in and out under the play of the swords.

> *"Swiftly went the sword-play—*
> *Hild's game we helped in*
> *When to halls of Odin*
> *Helsing-host we banished.*
> *Keenly did the sword bite*
> *When we lay in Iva—"*

Then all was confusion, for there was no woman between Olav and Einar. The dancers had to stop and Einar declared that Olav must stand out; they quarreled over this, until one of the older house-carls said that he had as lief go out. Then Arnvid set the game going again:

"Swiftly went the sword-play—

. . . .

Cutting-iron in battle
Bit at Skarpa-skerry—"

But all the time the ranks were in confusion. And as they came farther on in the lay, there was none but Arnvid who knew the words—some had a scrap of one verse, some of another. Olav and Einar were bickering the whole time; and there were all too few who sang the tune. Arnvid was tired, and he had got some scratches that began to smart, he said, as soon as he stirred himself.

So the chain broke up. Some went and threw themselves on their sleeping-benches—some stood chatting and would have more to drink—or they still wished to dance, but to one of these new ballads the steps of which were much easier.

Olav stood in the shadow under the roof-posts; he and Ingunn still held each other's hands. Olav thrust his sword into the scabbard: "Come, we will go up to your loft and talk together," he whispered.

Hand in hand they ran through the rain over the dark and empty yard, dashed up the stair, and stopped inside the door, panting with excitement, as though they had done something unlawful. Then they flung their arms about each other.

Ingunn bent the boy's head against her bosom and sniffed at his hair. "There is a smell of burning on you," she murmured. "Oh no, oh no," she begged in fear; he was pressing her against the doorpost.

"No—no—I am going now," he whispered: "I am going now," he kept repeating.

"Yes—" but she clung to him closely, dazed and quivering, afraid he would do as he said and go. She knew they had lost their senses, both of them—but all thoughts of past and present seemed swept away on the stream of the last wild, ungoverned hours—and they two had been flung ashore in this dark loft. Why should they leave each other?—they had but each other.

She felt her gilt circlet pushed up on her crown—Olav was rumpling her loosened hair. The garland fell off, jingling on the floor, and the lad took fistfuls of her hair and pressed them to his face, buried his chin in her shoulder.

Then they heard Reidunn—the serving-maid who slept with Ingunn—calling to someone from the yard below.

They started apart, trembling with guilty conscience. And quick as lightning Olav shot out his arm, pulled the door to, and bolted it.

Reidunn came up into the balcony, knocked, and called to Ingunn. The two children stood in pitch-darkness, shaken by the beating of their hearts.

The maid knocked awhile—thundered on the door. Then she must have thought Ingunn had fallen asleep and soundly. They heard the stairs creak under her heavy tread. Out in the yard she called to another maid—they guessed she had gone off to sleep in another house. And Olav and Ingunn flew to each other's arms, as though they had escaped a great danger.

5

OLAV awoke in pitch-darkness—and in the same instant he remembered. He seemed to sink into the depths as he lay. He felt a chill on his brows—his heart shrank suddenly, as a small defenceless creature makes itself smaller when a hand is groping for it.

Against the wall lay Ingunn, breathing calmly, as a happy, innocent child breathes in its sleep. Wave after wave of terror and shame and sorrow broke over Olav—he lay still, as though the very marrow were blown out of his bones. He had but one burning desire—to fly from Frettastein; he was utterly unequal to facing her accusation, when at last she rose from the happy forgetfulness of sleep. But he knew obscurely within himself that the only way to make this terrible thing yet worse would be to steal away from it now.

Then it struck him that he must contrive to slip out of this loft before anyone was awake. He must find out what time of night it was. But he lay on as though all power were taken from him.

At last he broke out of his torpor with a jerk, crept out of bed, and opened a crack of the door. The clouds above the roofs were tinged with pink—it would be an hour to sunrise.

As he dressed, it came back to him that the last time he had

shared Ingunn's bed was last Yule, and then he had been very
angry that he had to give up his place in the hall to a guest and
crawl in among Steinfinn's daughters. He had pushed Ingunn
roughly when he thought she was taking up too much room, and
had jostled her crossly when in her sleep she dug her sharp elbows
and knees into him. The memory of their former innocence
wrung him as the memory of a lost paradise.

He *dared* not stay here longer, he *must* go now. But when he
bent over her, caught the scent of her hair, faintly descried the
outline of her face and limbs in the darkness, he felt—in spite of
his remorse and shame—that this too was sweet. He bent quite
down, almost touched her shoulder with his forehead—and again
that strange divided feeling ensnared his heart: joy at the frail
daintiness of his bride, and torment at the very thought that anyone could touch her roughly or ungently.

Never, he swore to himself, never again would he do her any
ill. After making this resolve he gained more courage to face her
awake. He touched her face with his hand and softly called her
name.

She started up and sat for a moment, heavy with sleep. Then
she threw her arms about him, so that he fell on his knees, with
head and shoulders in the bed.

She wormed herself about him, drew him up in her slender
arms; and as he knelt thus, burying his face in her strangely soft
and yielding flesh, he had to clench his teeth to keep from bursting into tears. He was so relieved and humiliated that she was so
good and kind and did not raise a lament or reproach him. Full
of tenderness for her and of shame and sorrow and happiness, he
knew not what he should do.

Then there came a howl from the yard below—the long-drawn,
uncanny howl of a dog.

"That is Erp," whispered Olav. "He yelped like that last night
too. I wonder how he has got out again"—and he stole to the door.

"Olav—you are not going from me?" she cried in fear, as she
saw he was dressed and ready to go out.

"I must watch my chance—to slip down unseen," he whispered
back. "That hell-hound will wake the whole place soon."

"Olav, Olav, don't go from me—" she was kneeling in bed. As
he sprang back and bade her hush, she threw her arms about him

and held him fast. Instinctively he turned his head aside as he loosened her hold on his neck; he drew up the coverlet and spread it over her.

"Cannot you see that I must go?" he whispered. " 'Tis bad enough as it is."

Then she burst into a fit of weeping—threw herself down on the bed and wept and wept. Olav spread the clothes over her up to her chin and stood there at his wit's end in the dark, begging her in a whisper not to cry like that. At last he knelt down and put an arm under her neck—that stilled her weeping a little.

The dog out in the yard was howling as though possessed. Olav began to rock the girl backwards and forwards. "Do not weep, my Ingunn—do not weep so sorely—" but his face was hard and stiff with tension.

No dog could howl like that except for a corpse or some disaster. And as he knelt there in the chilly morning with the weeping girl in his arms, growing more and more pitilessly sober the while, one thought after another came into his mind.

He had given no great thought to the price that might be paid for their raid on Mattias Haraldsson's house—nor had any of the others, so far as he could guess. And that was just as well; for Steinfinn had no choice.—But he misliked that cursed howling in the yard. Steinfinn's wounds were not so slight; he knew that, for he had held his arm as Arnvid bound it up. And he recalled Steinfinn's face—once in the boat, as they were coming back—and as they rode up the hillside: Kolbein had to dismount and support his brother, leading his horse. And then last evening, when he bade them good-night.

Now he saw all at once how fond he was of his foster-father. He had taken Steinfinn as part of his everyday life—liked him well enough, but looked down on the man a little too, without knowing it, all these years. Such as Steinfinn was, casual, a dawdler, easy and careless through and through, with the painful burden of sorrow and shame that had been thrust upon him and that seemed so ill suited to the shoulders of this thoughtless lord—his foster-son had felt in his heart a slight contempt for what was so unlike his own nature. And now, when Steinfinn had risen up and shown what manner of man he was in the hour of trial; now that Olav felt in his heart of hearts that he loved Steinfinn after all—now he had done this thing to him. And disgraced him-

self and brought ruin upon Ingunn.—His forehead grew icy cold
again and his heart thumped with a dull throbbing—if indeed the
worst misfortune was already past.

He pressed his forehead against her bosom—and could not that
dog be quiet outside?—A kind of sob went through his soul—of
homesickness for his childhood, which was now inexorably past.
He felt his youth and his loneliness so terribly.—Then Olav
straightened himself, stood erect, and shut his mouth firmly on
his sighing: now he had dealt in such wise that he had taken a
grown man's responsibility upon himself. Useless to whine after
the event. And there must surely be a way out.

At last someone came and scolded the dog, tried to get him in,
he could hear. As far as he could guess, Erp ran up into the paddock. All was quiet outside.

Olav took the girl in a protecting embrace, kissed her forehead
at the roots of the hair before he let her go. Then he grasped his
sword and put the belt over his right shoulder. It seemed to put
heart into him to feel the weapon on his hip. He went to the door
and glanced over the balcony.

"There is no one in the yard—now I must slip away."

Ingunn stopped him with a wail: "Oh no, oh no, don't go—
'twill make me so afraid to be left here alone."

Olav saw at once that it was vain to try to reason with her.

"Get up, then," he whispered, "and dress yourself. If they see
us walking together outside, none will suspect."

He went out, sat down on the stairway, and waited. With both
hands on his sword-hilt, and his chin resting on them, he sat
watching the rosy reflection in the western sky fade away as the
light in the east grew stronger and whiter. The grass of the fields
was grey with dew and rain.

He called to mind all the late evenings and early mornings of
that summer with Ingunn—and the memories of their games and
frolics hurt him now and filled him with bitter disappointment
and wrath. A betrayer he had become—but it was as though he
himself had also been betrayed. They had been playing on a
flowery slope and had not had the wit to see that it ended in a
precipice. They had tumbled over before they knew of it. Well,
well, there they lay, 'twas no use whining over it now, he tried
to console himself.

Once they were married, they would get back their honour as

before, and then they would forget this secret humiliation, which
was what the fall was. But now he had looked forward with such
joy to his wedding—that day when all should make for his and
Ingunn's honour, which should confer full maturity upon them.
Now there must be a secret bitterness at the bottom of the cup—
a sense that they were not worthy the honour.

This thing that he had done was reckoned the mark of the
meanest. 'Twas a hind they had gotten for son-in-law, a man who
would prove no trustier than that, folk would say, when it came
out. For a boat and a horse and a bride a man should pay the
right price before he took and used them—unless he had great
need.

For folk of their condition he had thought three months the
shortest time they could fitly wait from the day when the settlement of their estate was proclaimed here at Frettastein before he
held his wedding at Hestviken. But perhaps, now that Steinfinn
had this case of arson and manslaughter on his hands, it would
not look so unreasonable if he hastened on the marriage—so that
instead of the guardianship of two minors he would have a well-
to-do son-in-law whose help he had a right to claim, in fines and
suchlike.

So when Ingunn came out to him and whispered, not daring
to look at him: "If my father knew this of us, Olav, I ween he
would kill us—" Olav laughed a little and took her hand in his.

"For that he would need be far duller than he is. He will have
enough gear to unravel, Ingunn, without this—he may have more
use for a living son-in-law than for a dead.—But you know well
'twould be the worst mischance," he whispered dejectedly, "if
he—or any—came to know of this."

The sun was just rising, it was icy cold outside and wet everywhere. Olav and Ingunn huddled together on the stairway and
sat there nodding sleepily while the pale yellow light in the east
mounted higher and higher in the sky, and the birds twittered
louder and louder—their singing was almost over for the year.

"There he is again!" Olav started up. The dog had come back
into the yard and posted himself howling before the great house.
They both ran down and Olav called to Erp and tried to entice
him away. The dog had always obeyed him, but now he would
not let himself be caught.

Arnvid Finnsson came out of the hall and tried, but the dog would not come to him either. Each time one of the men came near him, he slipped away, ran a short space, and began howling again.

"But have you two not been out of your clothes tonight?" Arnvid asked presently, looking from one to the other.

Ingunn turned red as fire and turned away hastily. Olav answered: "No—we sat talking up in the loft, and then we fell asleep as we sat, and slept on till this dog waked us."

More people came out now, both men and women, wondering at the dog. Last of all came Kolbein.

All at once there was one who cried: "Look—!"

Up in the balcony of the great bower they saw a glimpse of Steinfinn Toresson's head—his face was so changed that they scarce knew him. He called something—then vanished, as though he had fallen inward.

Kolbein dashed to the house, but the door was barred within. Arnvid sprang to his side and they helped Kolbein onto his shoulders; from there he swung himself onto the balcony. A moment later he bent over the rail—his face was utterly distorted: "He has bled—like a slaughtered ox—some of you must come up. Not his maids—" he said, and a shiver of frost seemed to go through him.

In a moment he had opened the door from inside. Arnvid and some of the house-carls went in, while Tora and the serving-maids ran to get water and wine, linen cloths and unguents.

Arnvid Finnsson appeared in the doorway—and all the dread and horror that had gathered in those waiting outside found relief in a groan when they saw him. Arnvid came forward like a sleep-walker—then his eye fell upon Olav Audunsson and he beckoned him aside: "Ingebjörg—" his lower jaw trembled so that his teeth chattered. "Ingebjörg is dead. God have mercy on us poor sinners!—You must take Ingunn—and Tora and the boys—into the hall. Kolbein says that I must tell them."

He turned and walked on in front.

"What of Steinfinn?" asked Olav in hot haste. "In God's name—it cannot be that he—has he *killed* her?"

"I know not—" Arnvid looked ready to drop. "She lay dead in the bed. Steinfinn's wound has opened—the blood has poured from him in streams. I know no more—"

Olav turned quickly to face Ingunn, who was coming up—put

out his hand as though to stop her, as he repeated Arnvid's words:
"God have mercy on us poor sinners! Ingunn, Ingunn—now you
must try—you must try to trust yourself to me, my dear!"

He took hold of her arm and led her with him—she had begun
to weep, softly and sorely, like a child that fears to let its terror
have full sway.

As the day wore on, Olav sat in the hall with the girls. Arnvid
told them what they had gathered from Steinfinn about his wife's
death, and Olav kept his arm openly on Ingunn's shoulder the
while—he scarce knew himself that he did so.

Steinfinn knew but little of what had happened. Before they
lay down, Ingebjörg had tended his arm. He had slept uneasily
and had been wandering in fever during the night, but he seemed
to remember that his wife had been up now and again; she had
given him to drink. He had been waked by the dog's howling—
and then she lay dead between the wall and him.

Ingebjörg had been troubled by fits of swooning in her last
years. Maybe her joy at the restoration of their honour had been
too much for her, Arnvid thought. Ingunn abandoned herself,
weeping, in Olav's embrace, and he stroked her on the back.
There was this, that he himself, and doubtless the others too, in
their first horror had thought of yet worse things. Though God
alone could know why Steinfinn should have wished his wife
dead. For all that, Arnvid's words released them from a horror-
struck suspense. Beneath it all a thought lay at the bottom of
Olav's mind, striving to come forth; he tried to banish it, 'twas
shameful but— Steinfinn had said he firmly believed he should
follow his wife. However things might go, there was a chance
that neither Steinfinn nor Ingebjörg would ever know that he
had betrayed them. Olav could do naught else than feel relieved
now, strangely exhausted, but safer.

There had been a moment when he thought he must go under.
Just after Ingebjörg was borne out, he had met some women
coming from the loft-room. They stopped, after the fashion of
serving-women, to show him the bloody garments they were
carrying out, making loud lamentation the while. One of them
had swept up the flowers from the floor into a fur rug—the
meadowsweet was smeared all over with blood, and above them
lay the strips Arnvid had cut from his and Olav's shirts to bind

Steinfinn's arm—they were soaked and shining with blood. Against his will all that had happened since yesternight, when they assembled in the meadow below the burning homestead, was crowded within him into one vision. And he had not the strength to bear such a horror as this. The disaster to his foster-parents, and then his sin against them— It was as though he had violated his own sister. The boy's whole world was shattered to pieces about him.

It seemed as though his mind could not contain it—and then it slipped away from him again. And when Steinfinn's children clung to him, since no one else in the place had leisure to bestow on them, he found a kind of refuge for himself in watching over them as an elder brother.

Tora wept much and talked much. She had always been the most intelligent and thoughtful of the children. She said to Olav that it seemed hard her parents had not been allowed to enjoy their happiness together after all these years of undeserved sorrow and shame. Olav thought it would have been much worse if Inge-björg had died before Steinfinn had taken his revenge. That their rehabilitation might be dearly bought in other ways was quite clear to Tora. She was also troubled about the welfare of her mother's soul and the future of herself and her brothers and sister, if this were in Kolbein's hands. She had no great belief in her uncle's judgment.

Olav thought that toward Steinfinn, at any rate, Kolbein had acted the part of a trusty kinsman; Mattias's slaying was not unprovoked, and the burning had been the work of chance. And it must be said that Ingebjörg had lived a pious and Christian life in her last years. She had been given a fair burial. No one told the children what some folk were saying: that had Bishop Torfinn been at home, 'twas doubtful if the lady had been committed to the earth in such great honour, until it had been made clear whether the dead woman had had any say in planning the deed or no.

Olav's best consolation came from Arnvid Finnsson. They shared a bed, and when Arnvid was not watching by his sick kinsman, the two young men lay talking far into the night.

And it sustained Olav, as it comforted all the household, that Steinfinn bore his lot in so noble and manly a way. He had lost much blood; yet his wounds were not such as were like to prove

the death of so strong and big a man. But Steinfinn said he knew
he was to die, and he seemed to waste away and be drifting toward
an early dissolution. And in a way Olav deemed this to be the
fittest ending to all that had befallen at Frettastein. It would indeed have been still stranger if Steinfinn and Ingebjörg had taken
up again the old carefree life of riot and revelry and idleness
that they had once led—after all they had gone through.

And this new shame that had come upon them in their daughter
they would never know. That reckoning he would escape.

So it was chiefly anxiety for Ingunn that tortured him. It was
an everlasting uneasiness—her sorrow was perfectly still and mute.
She sat there silent as a stone, while he and Tora were talking.
Now and again her eyes filled with tears, her lips began to quiver
feebly—her tears ran over, but never a sound was there in her; it
was a picture of despair, so far away and so lonely that he had
not the strength to look at it. Why could she not speak her sorrow and let herself be consoled together with them? Sometimes
he felt that she was looking at him; but when he turned his head
to her, he caught a glimpse of a look so pained and helpless—and
instantly she looked away from him. His ears rang and rang with
one of these new dancing-lays he had heard down by the church
last winter—he tried not to think of it, but it came—"or is it thine
honour thou mournest for so? . . ." Often he was near being
angry with her for not letting him be rid of these dark night-
thoughts that had taken such a hold of his throat in his first
remorse and sorrow over his fall.

But he had a care of himself now, strove to be like a good
brother to her. He had avoided being alone with her ever since
the first morning. And he felt safer and had a better conscience
since he had got Tora to persuade Ingunn to go back and sleep
with her sister in the little house. He thought that in Tora's keeping she would be safe from him too.

6

ONE evening Olav came riding down through the wood; he had
been on an errand to the sæter for Grim. The evening sun was
sinking behind the tops of the pines as he came where the path

skirted the marshy side of the tarn a little to the north of the manor. The forest rose steeply around the little brown lake, so that darkness came early here. Then he saw Ingunn sitting in the heather close to the path.

He pulled up his horse as he came up beside her. "Are you sitting here?" he asked in surprise. It was thought to be unsafe hereabouts after sundown.

She was a sorry sight—she had been eating bilberries and was all blue about the mouth and fingers, and then she had wept till her face was swollen, and dried her tears with her berry-stained hands.

"Is it worse with Steinfinn?" asked Olav earnestly.

Ingunn bent forward and wept much louder than before.

"He is not dead?" asked the lad in the same tone.

Ingunn stammered amid her sobs that her father was better today.

Olav held back Elk, who wanted to go on. He had left off being surprised at her constant fits of weeping, but they annoyed him somewhat. It had been better had she been as Tora, who had now got over her mourning for her mother and spared her tears—soon enough they might have other cause for weeping.

"What is it, then?" he asked, a little impatiently; "what do you want with me?"

Ingunn looked up with her befouled and tear-stained face. When Olav showed no sign of dismounting, she flung her hands before her eyes and wept again.

"What ails you?" he asked as before, but she made no answer. Then he leaped to the ground and went up to her.

"What is it?" he asked in fear, taking her hands from her face. For a long time he could get no answer. He asked again and again: "What is it—why do you weep thus?"

"Should I not weep," she sobbed, breaking down completely, "when you have not a word for me any more?"

"Why should I not have a word for you?" he asked in wonder.

"I have done no other sin than that you would have me do," she complained. "I begged you to be gone, but you would not let me go. And since then you have not counted me worth a word. —Soon I shall have lost both father and mother, and you are hard as flint and iron, turn your back on me, and will not *look* at me—

though we were brought up as brother and sister. For naught
else but that I loved you so well that I forgot honour and honesty
for the nonce—"

"Now I never heard the like! I trow you have lost the little wit
you had—"

"Ay, when you cast me off as you have done! But you know
not, Olav," she shrieked, beside herself. "You cannot tell, Olav,
whether I be not with child to you already!"

"Hush, shriek not so loud," he checked her. "You cannot tell
that either as yet," he said sharply. "I cannot guess what is in
your mind—have *I* not spoken to *you?*—methinks I have done
naught else these last weeks than talk and talk, and never did I
have three words of answer from you, for you did but weep
and weep."

"You spoke to me when you were forced to it," she snapped
between her sobs; "when Tora and the others were by. But me
you shun, as though I were a leper—not once have you sought me
out, that we might talk together alone. Must I not weep—when
I think on this summer—every night you came to me in my
bower—"

Olav had grown very red in the face. "Meseems that would be
unwise now," he said shortly. He spat on the corner of his cloak
and began to wipe her face—it availed but little. "I had most
thought of what was best for you," he whispered.

She looked up at him, questioning, intensely sorrowful. Then
he took her in his arms. "I wish you naught but well, Ingunn."

They both gave a start. Something had stirred in the scree on
the far side of the tarn. Not a soul was to be seen, but the solitary
young birch growing on the scree trembled as though a man had
just pulled its stem. It was still daylight, but the little lake was
shadowed by the forest; a mist was rising from the tarn and from
the marsh at its eastern end.

Olav went to his horse.

"Let us come away from here," he said in a low voice. "You
must get up behind."

"Can you not come out to me in the bower, so that we may
talk?" she implored him as he picked up the reins. "Come after
supper!"

"You may be sure I shall come, if you wish it," he said after a
pause.

She held her arms around him as they rode down to the manor. Olav felt in a way strangely relieved. He guessed that he might fling aside his good resolutions of avoiding fresh temptation—when she took it thus. But it humiliated him none the less that she rejected the sacrifice he had wished to offer her.

That thing she had said—how she had begged him be gone, but he would not let her go—it was not true, he suddenly recalled. But he banished the thought as disloyal. If she said so— He had not been so sober that he could swear he remembered aright.

Next evening Olav went to the bower in which Steinfinn lay. Arnvid opened the trap and let him into the loft. Arnvid was alone with the sick man.

It was dark inside, for Steinfinn had grown so cold that he could not bear them to open the door to the balcony. A few rays of sunlight found their way in through chinks between the logs, cleaving the dust-laden darkness and throwing golden patches of light on the furs that hung from the roof. There was a heavy, stifling smell in the room.

Olav went over to the bed to greet his foster-father—he had not seen him for many days, he grudged coming up here now. But Steinfinn slept, moaning a little in his sleep. Olav could not see his face in the darkness by the wall.

There was no change, either for the worse or for the better, said Arnvid. "Will you stay here awhile? Then I will lie down for a space."

He would do that willingly, said Olav, and Arnvid threw some clothes on the floor and lay down. Then Olav spoke: " 'Tis not easy for me, Arnvid—'twere ill to trouble Steinfinn, sick as he is—yet methinks before he dies, Ingunn and I must hear what is his will concerning our marriage."

Arnvid held his peace.

"Ay, I know the time fits ill," said Olav hotly. "But with the weighty concerns that hang over all our heads, I think 'tis now time to settle all that *can* be settled. Nor do I know whether there be any other than Steinfinn who knows what he and my father agreed about our moneys."

As Arnvid made no answer, Olav said: "To me it is of great moment that I receive Ingunn from her own father's hand."

"Ay, I can guess that," said Arnvid.

Soon after, Olav heard that he had fallen asleep.

The little shafts of sunlight were gone. Olav alone was awake
in the darkness and he felt his anxiety as a pain about his heart.

He *must* retrieve what had gone amiss. He had now learned
that his good resolutions were vain—there was no turning back
from the erring road into which he and Ingunn had strayed. And
he felt himself that this new knowledge had coarsened his soul.
But to stand by Steinfinn's bier as his secret son-in-law was beyond his power. Secret shame was a heavy burden to bear, he
knew now.

Before Steinfinn passed away, he must give him Ingunn. "I can
guess that," Arnvid had said. Olav felt hot all over: what was it
that Arnvid guessed? When he came back at daybreak to his
place in the hall, he did not know whether Arnvid was asleep or
only feigning.

He started up as the trap in the floor was raised. It was the
women with lights and food for the sick man. Vaguely Olav recalled the shadowy visions of his light-headed sleep: he was walking with Ingunn by the swamp above; they followed the beck
that ran out of the tarn—then he was with her in the loft-room.
Memories of fervid caresses in the dark were blended with pictures of the scree in the rugged glen. He lay holding Ingunn in
his arms, and at the same time he thought he was lifting her over
great fallen trees. Last of all he had dreamed they were walking
on the path in the dale, where it opened out to the cultivated
land with the lake far below.

This was surely a foreboding that he and Ingunn would soon
leave the place together, he tried to believe.

Steinfinn pleaded when the women woke him to tend his
wound: it booted not, and he would be left in peace. Dalla
feigned not to hear him; she raised his great body and changed
the bedclothes as though he had been an infant. She asked Olav
to hold the candle for her—Arnvid was sleeping soundly, dead-
tired.

Steinfinn's face was scarcely to be recognized, with some
weeks' growth of reddish beard mounting to his cheek-bones.
He turned his face to the wall, but Olav could see by the straining of his throat that he was struggling not to moan, as Dalla took
off his bandages; they had grown fast to the wound.

The secret disgust that Olav had always felt at the sight and smell of festering wounds came upon him with sickening strength. Proud flesh had formed; the wound no longer looked like a gash; it was full of matter and grey, fungous patches, with raw red holes oozing blood.

Ingunn had appeared at his side—pale, with great eyes full of fear she stared at her father. Olav had to nudge her; she absently forgot to give Dalla the fresh bandage when she held out her hand for it. Again Olav felt his shame and sorrow like a stab at the heart—that they could have forgotten her sick and suffering father as they had done. Ah, but—the dark bower and they two alone, in close embrace—dimly he saw how hard it was to keep in mind charity and loyalty to one who was absent.

"Stay here," he said to her, as the other women were going. "This evening I will speak to your father," he explained. He saw that this made her more frightened than glad, and he liked it not.

Steinfinn lay in a doze, worn out by his pain. Olav asked Ingunn to fetch him a little food meanwhile.

She had filched all the good things she could find, she showed him with a laugh when she came back. Presently, as Olav sat eating, with the bowl between his knees, she blew down his neck. She seemed bursting with wantonness and affection this evening. Once more it cut Olav to the heart—here they sat, scarce out of her sick father's sight—and he knew not whether he liked or disliked her caresses most.

Arnvid stirred—Ingunn started up from Olav's knee and busied herself with his food. Suddenly Steinfinn asked from the bed: "Who is it you have with you, Arnvid and Ingunn?"

"Olav is here, Father," said the girl.

Olav braced his heart within him; he went up to the bed and said: "There is a matter of which I would fain speak with you, Foster-father—it is for that I stayed behind when we had done tending you."

"Were you here then? I saw you not." Steinfinn made a sign for the young man to come nearer. "You may sit awhile and talk to me, Olav foster. You have been drawn into our troubles; now we must talk of what you are to do when I die. You ought to go home to Hestviken, methinks, and seek support among your own kinsmen."

"Yes, Foster-father. It is of that I had thought to ask you. Myself I thought it were best so—and that I get Ingunn ere I go. Thus you kinsfolk will be spared the long journey, now that you have feuds upon you."

Steinfinn's eyes flickered irresolutely.

"It is so, Olav, that I mind me well what was spoken between Audun and me. But you must see yourself, boy—'tis not my doing that my fortunes have shaped themselves otherwise than we then foresaw. Now it will fall to Kolbein and Ivar to marry off my daughters—"

Arnvid had joined them:

"Do you remember, kinsman—I was with you that summer at the Thing, and I stood by in the hall when you and Audun betrothed the children?"

"You were a little boy," said Steinfinn hastily; "—no legal witness!"

"No," said Arnvid. "But listen to me, Steinfinn. It has happened before, in case of need, when called to arms or setting out on a long voyage, that a man has given his daughter to him to whom she had been promised before witnesses, without wedding, but only in such wise that he declared before trustworthy witnesses what had been agreed as to the dowry and the bridegroom's gift, and that it was his will that the betrothal should hold as binding wedlock from that day."

Steinfinn turned his head and looked at the three young people. Arnvid went on, eagerly: "Brother Vegard came hither today— and here am I, your cousin, and the old house-folk of yours who know of the compact between Audun and you. You could declare the marriage, with the monk and me for chief witnesses. Then the young couple could dwell in the little house till such time as may be fitting for Olav to fare south with her. Brother Vegard could bless the bridal cup and the bed for them—draw up writings as to their estate—"

Steinfinn reflected awhile. "No," he said shortly, and seemed very weary at once. "A daughter of mine shall not go to bed with her betrothed unfeasted like cottars' children. And there might arise contentions in after time whether she were a duly wedded wife. I marvel that you can think of such things," he went on hotly, "young as these two children are withal. Olav may have coil enough when he meets these kinsmen whom he knows not—without my sending him from me with such a burden on his neck, an outlawed man's daughter, and she smuggled away with no kinsmen of his or mine to stand by when he took her in marriage. Had but Olav been of age, we might have thought of it; but now I scarce believe it would be lawful marriage, should a child such as he is take a wife to himself—"

"It must be right enough that my father let me plight troth with the maid," said Olav. "And you have been my guardian since—"

"Oh, you know not what you talk of. You begged leave to be in the raid with us, but if Mattias's heirs think to bring that against you, 'twill not avail them much, since your kinsmen can make the defence that you were under age and in my service. Were you a married man, answerable at law and my son-in-law, 'twould be another matter. Nay, I owe it to Audun, my friend, to give you no warrant for such folly—now that perchance I am soon to meet him."

"Listen to me, Steinfinn—I am too old, for all that, to obey others after you are dead—these kinsmen of mine whom I have neither seen nor heard of. Rather will I be married and my own master, and take my hazard of the danger."

"You prate like a little child," said Steinfinn impatiently. "It shall be as I have said. But let me rest now—I can no more to-night."

Before Arnvid and Olav went to bed, the former laid the matter before Brother Vegard. But the monk would by no means take upon himself to speak to Steinfinn and try to alter his decision. He held that Steinfinn had judged rightly and wisely—and he as a priest was not allowed to have a hand in a wedding unless the banns had been proclaimed in the parish church on three mass-days. Here it was even doubtful whether Olav himself could conclude the contract so that it would be lawful marriage, seeing he was under age. And besides, he never liked folk to hold weddings without the blessing of the Church. He would in no wise have anything to do with drawing up writings or the like, but he would depart from Frettastein if they concluded such a bargain on doubtful conditions.

Steinfinn grew worse in the days that followed, and Olav could not bring himself to speak again of his marriage when he was up with his foster-father. Nor did he say more to Arnvid about the matter.

But then Ivar Toresson, Steinfinn's full brother, came to Frettastein, and Kolbein with both his sons; they had had word that Steinfinn was now near his end. The day after the coming of these men Olav asked Arnvid to go out with him, that they might speak in private.

He had not dared to speak to Arnvid before—he was afraid of what the other would say. Several nights in the last week he had been with Ingunn in the loft-room. She too was downcast and disappointed that her father had raised such unlooked-for difficulties to giving them to one another. But she can never have thought this would do more than delay their wedding at Hestviken somewhat. She grieved greatly for her father's misery and her mother's death—and in all her sorrows she clung fast to Olav; it seemed she was quite destroyed with grief when she could not hide herself in his embrace. And after a while Olav gave up all thoughts of holding back; he let himself be drawn deeper and deeper into love's rapture—she was so sweet withal. But his disquietude and qualms of conscience were a constant torment. When she fell asleep, clasped tightly to his breast, he suffered pain; it pained him too that she was so innocent in her love, she seemed utterly without fear or remorse. When he stole from her at early dawn, he was weary and dejected.

He was afraid that it might end in her misfortune; but he could not bring himself to speak of this to the girl. Still less had he the heart to tell her that he feared far worse difficulties. It had never before come into his mind that aught could be said against the validity of their betrothal. But now a new light had suddenly fallen upon his position in Steinfinn's household in all these years. He had never stood otherwise than Steinfinn's own children; but, little care as the parents had bestowed on them in these last years, it was strange nevertheless that they had never said a word of his and Ingunn's marriage, nor had Steinfinn taken any steps to find out how his son-in-law's estate was administered. That Kolbein had never heeded him was perhaps no great matter—Kolbein was arrogant and unfriendly toward most men. The coxcombs his sons Olav had never got on with; but he had always thought that this came simply from their counting themselves grown men and him a child. But now it all struck him as very strange—if they had looked upon him all the time as one who was to be their brother-in-law. "In my service," Steinfinn had said—he had never been paid wages here at Frettastein, so that meant nothing—'twas a means to clear him of the manslaughter that his foster-father had hit upon.

Olav led the way through the fields northward to the woods. On reaching the bare rocks he stopped. From there they looked down upon the houses with the steep-sloping fields below them and the forest around.

"We can sit here," said Olav. "Here we shall be safe from eavesdroppers." But he himself remained standing. Arnvid sat with his eyes on the young man.

Olav stood there contracting his white eyebrows—his fair forelock was now grown so long that it almost reached them; this made his face look yet broader, shorter, and more glum. The firm, pale lips were tightly compressed—morose and quarrelsome he looked, and he was become much older in these last weeks. The frank and childlike innocence that had become him so well—since with it all the boy was fully grown and grave of mien—had vanished like the dew. There was another kind of seriousness now upon his wrathful, tormented face. And his paleness and fairness were not so fresh—he was dark under the eyes and had a tired look.

"You have never told me before that you were there when Ingunn and I were given to each other," said Olav.

"I was but fourteen," replied Arnvid, "so it mattered not that I was there."

"Who were the others?" asked Olav.

"My father and Magnus, my brother, Viking and Magnhild from Berg, Tore Bring of Vik and his wife—I know not who the others were. The hall was full of folk, but I cannot call to mind that there were others I knew."

"Was there none in company with my father?" asked Olav.

"No, Audun Ingolfsson was alone."

Olav was silent awhile. Then he said, as he sat down: "Then there are no others alive to bear witness than Magnhild and Tore of Vik.—But maybe they can show us the way to some more."

"That they surely can."

"If they will—" said Olav in a low voice. "But you, Arnvid? Mayhap your testimony goes for little, since you were a child—

but what is your *judgment*? Were we *affianced* that night, Ingunn and I?"

"Yes," said Arnvid firmly. "That I have always held for sure. Do you not remember, they made you plight her with a ring?"

Olav nodded.

"Steinfinn must have that ring somewhere.—Think you you would know it again? That must be a good proof, I trow?"

"I mind me the ring well. 'Twas my mother's signet-ring, with her name and an image of God's Mother on a green stone. Father had promised it to me—I mind me I was ill pleased to give it to Ingunn." He laughed a little.

They sat in silence for a while. Then Olav asked slowly: "How liked you the answer Steinfinn gave me when I spoke to him of the matter?"

"I know not what I shall say," replied Arnvid.

"I know not what assurance I may have," said Olav still more slowly, "that Steinfinn has spoken in such wise to Kolbein that he holds it for a binding bargain between Steinfinn and my father that I was to have Ingunn."

"Kolbein will not be the only one to dispose of the children," said Arnvid.

Olav shrugged his shoulders, smiling scornfully.

"As I said to you," Arnvid went on, "I have always held it a valid betrothal that was made that night."

"Then the new sponsors cannot set aside the bargain?"

"No. That I remember is what I heard when I was at the school. If two children be betrothed by their fathers, it cannot be broken, except the children themselves, when they come to years of discretion—fourteen winters, I think it is—declare to their parish priest that they will have the bargain undone. But then they must both make oath that she is a virgin undefiled of him."

Both the young men's faces turned red as fire; they avoided each other's eyes.

"But if they cannot swear such an oath?" asked Olav at last, in a very low voice.

Arnvid looked down at his hands. "Then it is *consensus matrimonialis*, as it is called in Latin—in their deeds they have already conformed to the counsels of their parents, and if after that either of them marries another, willingly or by constraint, then it is whoredom."

Olav nodded.

"I wonder whether you could help me," he said after a moment, "to find out what Steinfinn has done with that ring."

Arnvid muttered something. Without saying more they got up and walked back.

"Autumn will be early this year," said Olav after a while. The birches already showed yellow leaves among the green, and the ears of corn were turning white among the tall thistles and ragwort. The blue air was full of drifting down—the floating seed of traveller's-joy.

The evening sun fell right in Olav's face, making him blink; and his eyes shone keen and blue as ice under the white lashes. The thick, fair down on his upper lip had a golden look against the boy's milk-white skin. Arnvid felt a drawing as of pain in his chest that his friend was so fair to look upon—he saw himself, dark, ugly as a troll, high-shouldered, and short-necked, against the other's strong and handsome youth. 'Twas not to be wondered at that Ingunn loved him as she did.

How much of right or wrong there was in those two he left others to judge. He would help them as far as he could. He had always liked Olav—believed him to be steadfast and trusty. And Ingunn was so weak—it must have been for that he had always been so fond of the little maid; she looked as though a hand could break her in two.

The air was so heavy in the loft that night that the holy candle which they burned nightly by the dying man could scarcely live. It gave a faint and drowsy light.

Steinfinn was dozing, utterly worn out. The fever was not so high that night, but he had talked at length with his brothers during the evening, and that had told on him. Afterwards, when his wounds were tended, he had been so overspent that the tears poured down into his beard when Dalla had to go roughly to work to get away some matter.

At last, in the course of the night, Steinfinn seemed to be sleeping more easily. But Arnvid and Olav sat on—till they felt so weary in the heavy air that they could scarce keep awake.

"Ay—" whispered Arnvid at last. "Is it your wish that we seek for that ring?"

"We must do so, I ween." Everything within him shrank from

the act—and he saw it went much against the grain with Arnvid
too, but— Still as a pair of thieves they ransacked Steinfinn's
clothes and emptied his keys out of the pouch of his belt. It
dawned on Olav the while that he who has once left the straight
path of honour soon finds himself in broken ground, where he
may be forced to many a crooked leap. But he could see no other
way.

None the less, as he knelt by Steinfinn's clothes-chest, he
thought he had never felt so ill. Now and again they threw a
glance at the bed. It was like robbing a corpse.

Arnvid found the little casket, bound all over with meshwork
of wrought iron, in which Steinfinn kept his most costly jewels.
Key after key they tried before they found one to fit the lock.

Sitting on their haunches, they rummaged among brooches,
chains, and buttons. "This is it," said Olav, drawing a deep
breath, unspeakably relieved.

Together they looked at the ring against the light. It was of
gold, with a great green stone in it. Arnvid made out the in-
scription around the image of God's Mother and the Child, with
a roof above and a woman kneeling at the side: *Sigillum Ceciliæ
Beornis Filiæ.*

"Will you keep it?" asked Arnvid.

"No. It cannot serve—as proof—except it be found among
Steinfinn's hoard?" Olav thought.

They locked the casket and put all in order again. Arnvid
asked: "Will you sleep now, Olav?"

"No, you may sleep first. I am not tired."

Arnvid lay down on the bench. After a while he said, in a wide-
awake voice: "I could wish we had not been forced to do this—"

"I am with you in that wish," replied Olav with a quiver in his
voice.

A *great* sin it was not—could not be, he thought. But it was
so ugly. And he was afraid of it as of an evil omen—for the life
that lay before him; would a man be forced to do many things
that—that irked him so unspeakably as this?

They watched by turns till morning. It made Olav glad whenever he was able to do some little thing for his foster-father—
give him to drink or arrange the bedclothes. At last, early in the

day, when Steinfinn awoke out of a doze, he asked: "Is it you two who are still here?" His voice was weak, but he was clear in his senses. "Come hither, Olav," he bade.

Both the young men came forward. Steinfinn put out his sound hand to Olav. "You are not so wroth with me, foster, that I would not give you your will in what we spoke of that evening, but that you would watch with me all this night? You have ever been obedient and good, Olav—God keep you all your days. As surely as I need His mercy, I tell you, had I had the ruling of it, I should have kept my word to Audun. Were it granted me to live, I should be well pleased to have you as my son-in-law."

Olav knelt down and kissed his foster-father's hand. He could say nothing—inwardly he besought Steinfinn to speak the words that could rescue him from all his difficulties. But shame and guilt kept his lips closed.

This was the last time he spoke with Steinfinn Toresson. He and Arnvid were still sleeping in the afternoon when Haftor Kolbeinsson came and woke them. Steinfinn's death struggle had begun, and all the people of the house went up to be with him.

7

BROTHER VEGARD had given Steinfinn absolution *in articulo mortis;* so he had a fair burial. Steinfinn's kinsmen and friends spoke big words at the funeral feast; they swore that Mattias Haraldsson should lie unatoned. As yet the dead man's next of kin had made no sign—but they all lived in other parts of the country. There was also trouble in the air—rumours were abroad of great events that were brewing. And Steinfinn's kinsmen boasted that the men who would now have most power in the land, while the King and the Duke were children, were their friends.

Only a small part of Steinfinn's debts and dues were settled at the division of his estate among his under-aged children. The kinsmen made as though there were immense riches—but between man and man many a hint was dropped.

Arnvid Finnsson was to stay at Frettastein with the children until Haftor Kolbeinsson had held his wedding at the New Year.

Then Haftor was to move to the manor and have charge of it for Hallvard, Steinfinn's elder son, till the boy came of age.

Steinfinn's brothers stayed behind at Frettastein some days after the funeral guests had departed. The evening before they were to ride away, the men sat as usual drinking ale after the supper had been cleared away. Then Arnvid stood up, making a sign to Olav that he was to come forward.

"It is so, Ivar and Kolbein, that here is my friend, Olav Audunsson, who has bid me lay a matter before you. Steinfinn declared before he died that Olav ought to go home to his own house and speak with his kinsmen of a portion and a morning-gift for Ingunn, when he now takes her to wife. But now we have thought that, as matters stand, 'twill be easier that we conclude this matter at once and that Olav's wedding be held here—thus both we and his kinsmen will be spared the long road, while winter is at hand and our fortunes are so uncertain. Therefore Olav has bid me tell you that he offers to give surety—and I am willing to be his surety as far as sixteen marks of gold—that he will put to what he gets with Ingunn so much that she shall own the third part of his estate, besides her bedclothes, apparel, and jewels according to their condition. He also offers to give surety that he will make full restitution of its cost to him of you who shall provide his wedding—whether you will have ready money, or that he shall sell you for a fair price Ingunn's share in Hindkleiv and make amends to her of his lands in the south—"

Arnvid spoke on for a while about the terms that Olav offered his wife's kinsfolk, and these were unwontedly good. Olav promised masses for the repose of Steinfinn and Ingebjörg, and he pledged himself that the Steinfinnssons should always find in him a trusty and compliant son-in-law, who would hearken to the counsel of his elders as was fitting for a young man of his age. Finally Arnvid asked the Steinfinnssons to receive this offer as it was put forward—with goodwill and in a loyal spirit.

Steinfinn's brothers listened as though the matter gave them no little trouble. While his friend was speaking, Olav had stood before him, on the outer side of the table. He stood erect, with his calm, pale face turned toward Ingunn's uncles. Now and again he nodded assent to Arnvid's words.

At last Kolbein Toresson made reply: "It is true, Olav, that we know there was once talk between your father and our brother that you should marry one of his daughters. And you must not think we do aught but esteem your goodwill in desiring to order this matter so that we might all have been well pleased. But the thing is whether your kinsmen would *now* be so set upon this marriage of our niece to you that they would consent to your offer. But what weighs most is that we now have greater need to ally ourselves by marriage with men who have power and powerful kinsfolk, and these you have not. We must now seek support rather than riches—we look to you to acknowledge this, since you have shown by your offer that you have foresight far beyond your age. But because of the promise Steinfinn once made to your father that he would help you to a good marriage, we will gladly help you in this matter. For Steinfinn's daughters we have other designs—but you must not be dejected on that account: with God's help we shall find you a match as good in every way and better fitted to your age—for young as you are, Olav, you were ill served with a bride as young; you ought either to take a wife who is older and more discerning, or betroth yourself to a maid who is younger and let your wedding wait till you yourself be fully grown."

Olav had turned red in the face while the other was speaking. Before he could make answer, Arnvid said quickly: "Hereabouts all have held Olav and Ingunn to be betrothed—and I myself stood by when Steinfinn handselled him his daughter—"

"Nay, nay," said Kolbein. "I have heard of that, it was a game they played—afterward they spoke of it, Steinfinn and Audun, saying it might be fitting if they turned the jest to earnest one day. And that might well have been, had not our brother fallen into these misfortunes. But since this betrothal has never been concluded—"

"The ring I pledged her with—Steinfinn has it in his coffer, I know it," Olav broke in hotly.

"You may know it; Steinfinn is not like to have made away with any of your goods, my Olav, but your kinsmen shall witness that not a button is missing when they come to receive them on your behalf."

Olav's breath came quick and short.

Kolbein went on: "You must see plainly, Olav, no man of sound mind gives away his children thus, in his drink—"

"Steinfinn did it— I know not whether he were a man of sound mind—"

"—except all covenants about marriage portions and the like were made beforehand. You must know, had Steinfinn thus bound himself to Audun Ingolfsson, he would have said no straight out when I spoke to him this spring of Ingunn for the son of a friend of mine—"

"What said he then?" asked Olav breathlessly.

"He said neither yes nor no, but promised to listen to the man; we spoke of it again when we conferred about this other matter— that it might profit us greatly if Ingunn were married into that kindred. But I stand by what I have said to you, Olav: gladly will we kinsmen help you to a good match—"

"I have not asked you that; I was promised Ingunn—"

Arnvid interposed: " 'Twas one of the last words Steinfinn spoke, Ivar—on the morning of his death—that had he himself been able to give away Ingunn, he would have chosen Olav for son-in-law."

"Ay, that is likely enough," said Kolbein, rising from his seat and coming forward; "but now it falls out, Arnvid, that Steinfinn *could* not do it. *You* should be old and wise enough to see that we cannot turn away the man who can give us most support in our troubles, because Olav has taken for earnest a game they played with him once when he was a little boy. *You* went unwilling enough to your bridal bed, Arnvid—'tis strange you should make such haste to push your friend into his. Belike Ólav will thank us one day that we did not let him have his will in such childish fancies—"

With that he and Ivar went to the closed bed in which Steinfinn had been used to sleep before the raid; they lay down and shut the door.

Arnvid went up to Olav; the young man had not moved and his eyes were fixed on the floor; his face twitched again and again. Arnvid bade him come and lie down.

" 'Twas lucky you curbed yourself so that it came not to angry words between Kolbein and you," said Arnvid as they undressed in the dark behind the pillars.

A sound like a snort came from Olav.

Arnvid went on: "Else it would have been hard to bring this matter to a good ending—Kolbein could have claimed that you should leave the house at once. Let him not mark that your heart is so set upon getting Ingunn and none other—then 'twill be easier."

Olav said nothing. He was used to sleeping on the outer side, but as they were getting into bed, Arnvid asked: "You must let me sleep outside tonight, friend—that ale tonight was not good; I feel sick from it."

"I had no good of it either," said Olav with a short laugh.

But he lay down on the inside against the wall. Arnvid was just falling asleep when he felt Olav get up and try to step over him.

"Where are you going?" asked his friend, taking hold of him.

"I am thirsty," muttered Olav. Arnvid heard him grope his way over to the tub of whey and water; he ladled some out and drank.

"Now come and lie down," Arnvid bade him.

And indeed Olav soon came pattering back, crept into the bed, and lay down.

"It were much best you say nothing to Ingunn of the answer we have had, till we have taken counsel what course to pursue," whispered Arnvid earnestly.

Olav lay quiet a good while before he answered: "Ay, ay." He sighed deeply. "So be it, then."

Arnvid felt a little easier after that. But he dared not abandon himself to sleep before he heard that the young man was in a deep slumber.

8

THE SNOW was falling thickly when Olav came out into the yard at dusk on St. Catherine's Eve.[1] It was the first snowfall of the year; his footprints showed black on the ground as he ran across to the stable.

He stood for a moment before the stable door, watching the whirling mass of white. His eyes blinked as the snowflakes fell on his long lashes; they felt like a light caress against his skin. The forest below the manor on the north and east, which in the

---

[1] November 24.

autumn nights had been full of gloom and desolation, now seemed near and shone like a white and friendly wall through the driving snow and the gathering darkness. Olav felt glad at the snow.

Someone within the stable was speaking in a loud voice—the door flew open behind him, and a man dashed out as if he had been thrown. He pitched against Olav, and both went to the ground. The other got onto his feet and shouted back to someone standing in the doorway, a vague black figure in the pale gleam of the lantern: "Here is one more for you to show your manhood on, Arnvid"—with which he ran off into the snow and the darkness.

Olav shook himself and dived in under the doorway. "What was that with Gudmund?"—when in the shadow behind Arnvid he caught sight of a girl in tears.

"Out with you, foul slut," Arnvid said to her, furious. The woman slunk crouching past the men and out. Arnvid barred the door behind her.

"What is it?" asked Olav again.

"Oh—no great thing, as you may think," said Arnvid hotly. He picked up the little lantern and hung it on the hook; Olav saw that he was trembling with agitation. "Naught else but that now every whoreson who serves about the place seems to think he dare scorn me because—because— I have said I will not have womenfolk in the stables; 'tis unfitting. Gudmund answered me that I should rather keep a watch on the bowers here and on my kinswomen."

Olav turned away. In the darkness beyond, the horses could be heard crunching their fodder and stamping their feet. The nearest stretched its neck and snorted at Olav, and the flame of the lantern was reflected in its dark eyes.

"Did you hear?" Arnvid insisted.

Olav turned to the horse and did not answer. He felt in agony that he was blushing violently.

"What have you to say to that?" asked Arnvid hotly.

"What would you have me say?" answered Olav in a low voice. "As my case stood—after the answer Kolbein gave me— you cannot well be surprised—that I followed your advice."

"My—advice!"

"The advice you gave me that day we spoke together up in

the woods. You said that when two persons under age have been
betrothed by their lawful guardians, none has the right to part
them, but if they agree to follow the designs of their parents,
there is no need of more; they can come together as married
folk—"

"That I have never said!"

"I mind me not how the words went. But such I guessed to
be your meaning."

"My meaning!" whispered Arnvid, deeply moved. "Nay, Olav
—what I meant—I—I thought you knew—"

"No. What meant you, then?" asked Olav point-blank, turning toward the other. Driven by a sense of utter shame, he hardened himself, looked his friend defiantly in the eyes, while his
face was on fire.

But Arnvid Finnsson dropped his eyes before the younger man
and blushed in his turn. What he had thought he could not say.
And he found it hard to undeceive himself now. Confusion and
shame made him speechless. That he had kept up familiar friendship with a man whom he himself believed to be the seducer of
his kinswoman—how ill it looked he seemed not to have guessed
till now. It was as though he had not seen its ugly, dishonourable
side before—because Olav seemed so honourable all through, he
had been blind to the dishonour—when it was Olav.

Nor could he believe it now—that Olav stood there lying to
him. He had always held Olav to be the most truthful of all men.
And he clutched at it now—Olav's words must be worthy of belief. He himself must have wronged his friend with his suspicion in the summer—so it must be. There had been nothing unseemly between the two, though they had been together at night
in the summer.

"I have ever thought well of you, Olav," he said. "Believed
you jealous of your honour—"

"Then you could not well expect," Olav broke in hotly, still
staring the other in the face, "that I should lie down tamely and
let the Toressons trample on my honour and cheat me of my
right. I will not go home to my own country in such guise that
every man may mock at me and say I let these men defraud me
of the marriage I should have made. You know that they use fraud
against me, Kolbein and those—you remember how I got back
my ring?"

Arnvid nodded. When the property was divided, Kolbein had given back to Olav the chests of movables which Steinfinn had taken charge of for his foster-son. But then Olav's mother's signet-ring was among these goods, threaded on a ribbon together with some other rings. And Olav could not say a word about his having lately seen the ring lying among Steinfinn's own treasures.

"And in *my* eyes it concerns my father's honour too," Olav continued excitedly, "if I am to let strangers set at naught his last will and the promises given to him before he died! And Steinfinn—you heard yourself what he said; but he knew well enough, poor man, that he had not the power to carry it against those overbearing brothers of his. Are Ingunn's father and my father to have so little respect in their graves that they are not to be allowed the right to dispose of their own children's marriage?"

Arnvid reflected, a long time.

"None the less, Olav," he said slowly, "you must not now do such things as—go to her in her bower and meet her secretly so that all the house-folk know of it. God knows, I should not have kept my counsel so long—but it seemed to me an ill thing to speak of. You have not been afraid to show *me* disrespect."

Olav made no answer—and Arnvid felt sorry for him when he looked at him. Arnvid said: "I deem, Olav, since it has come to this between you and her, that *you* must take charge of the manor here."

Olav looked up with a question in his eyes.

"Declare to the house-folk here that you will not give way to the new sponsors, but hold them to the bargain Steinfinn and your father made and take your wife to yourself. Step into the master's bed with Ingunn and declare that now you think that *you* are next of kin to have charge for Hallvard and Jon, so long as you and Ingunn stay here in the north."

Olav stood biting his lip; his cheeks were burning. At first Arnvid's advice tempted him—unspeakably. This was the plain road out of all the furtive dealings by night and by stealth which, he felt, were making him a meaner and weaklier man. Take Ingunn by the hand and boldly lead her to the bed and high seat left by Steinfinn and Ingebjörg. Then let them talk about *that*, all these folk about the place who giggled and muttered behind his back—though as yet they had not dared to come out with it before him.

But then his courage sank when he thought of carrying it out. It was their sneers, their nasty little words. They were so apt at that, the people hereabout—with an innocent look, making it hard for a man to return an answer and defend himself, they dropped a few sly words with a sting in them. Many a time the malice in their speech was hidden so cunningly that it was a little while before he guessed what the men were smiling at, when one of them broke off, with too unconcerned an air, or gave a start.— Without being aware of it he had striven in all his doing at Frettastein so to conduct himself as to give them no occasion to make that sort of game of *him*. Until now he had succeeded in some measure—he knew that his fellow servants liked him well enough, and stood in a sort of awe of him, as happens when a man is sparing of words, but is known not to be a fool; thus he may easily be accounted wiser than he is. As yet none had dared to hint at what all knew of him and Ingunn—no word, at least, had come to his ears.

But he flinched at the thought—the laughter and the jesting would break out sure enough when he himself made no secret of the matter and offered to take over the stewardship of the farm, where he had been reckoned a young lad until this year. Insensibly Olav's view of himself and of his position on Steinfinn's estate had changed—he no longer counted Frettastein as the home to which he had belonged as one of the children of the house. The chance words that had trickled into his mind, the fact that Ingunn's kinsmen disregarded him, the stings of an evil conscience and the sense of shame at all he had done in secret, made him see himself in a meaner light than before.

And then there was this—that he was so young; all the other men of the place were much older than he. He was well used, indeed, to their counting him and Ingunn as not yet fully grown. And he blushed at the thought of having to own that he was living with a woman—when no grown man had led him forward and accepted him in the ranks of husbands. Without that he could not feel that it was *real*.

At length he replied: " 'Tis not to be done, Arnvid. Think you either man or woman here would obey me if I tried to command?

Grim or Josep or Gudmund? Or would Dalla willingly give up her keys to Ingunn?"

"No; Ingunn would have to be content to wear the coif—" Arnvid gave a little laugh—"till you can give her the keys of Hestviken."

"Nay, Arnvid; they go in fear of Kolbein, every mother's child here—what you counsel is impossible."

"Then I know of only one other way—and this counsel I should have given you long ago, God forgive me. Go to Hamar and put your case in the Bishop's hands."

"In Bishop Torfinn's? I trow not *I* can look for much mercy of *him*," said Olav slowly.

"Your right you may look for," replied Arnvid. "In this question it is only Holy Church that can judge. You two *can* only be married to each other."

"Who knows if the pious father will not order us to be monk and nun, send us to the cloister to expiate our sin?"

"He will assuredly make you do penance to the Church for going to your bride without banns or wedding. But if you can bring forward witnesses that the betrothal is valid—and that I think we can surely do—he will demand of the Toressons that they accept offers of honourable atonement—"

"Think you," Olav broke in, " 'twill avail much if the lord Torfinn demand it? Before now the Bishop of Hamar has had to give away to the Steinfinnssons."

"Ay—in questions of property and the like. But for all that, they are not so ungodly as to deny that in this matter none has the right to judge but the fathers of the Church—whether marriage be marriage or not."

"I wonder. Oh no—then I have more mind to take Ingunn with me and fare south to my own country."

"Ah, not so long as I can wield a sword. In the devil's name, Olav, do you expect, because I have—lacked counsel so long—that I should sit here and shut my eyes while you steal my kinswoman out of my ward?" He saw that Olav was on the point of flaring up. "Be calm," he said curtly; "I know you are not afraid of me. And I am not afraid of you either. But I reckoned we were friends. If you feel yourself that your conduct to me has been something short of a trusty friend's, then do as I say, seek to make an end of this matter in seemliness and honour.

"I shall go with you to the Bishop," he added, seeing that the other still hesitated.

"Against my will I do this thing," said Olav with a sigh.

"Is it more to your liking as things are now," Arnvid rejoined hotly, "to let the talk go on, here on the manor and among the neighbours—of you and me and Ingunn? Can you not see that the womenfolk smirk and whisper behind her back wherever she goes—stare at her slyly? They look to see if she treads as lightly as ever—"

"There is no danger on that score," muttered Olav angrily; "so she says." His face was crimson again. "Ingunn must stay with us, then," he said reflectively. "Else it might be difficult even for Bishop Torfinn to get her out of Kolbein's clutches."

"Ay, I shall take Tora and Ingunn with me. Think you I would let her fall into Kolbein's hands after this?"

"So be it, then," answered Olav; he stared gloomily before him.

Two days later they rode down and reached the town late in the evening. The maids were long abed next morning, and Olav said he would go seek the smith and fetch his axe, while the others made ready to hear the last mass that was sung in Christ Church.

They had already set out when he came back to the inn. He hurried after them along the street, and the snow crunched under him—it was fine, frosty weather. The bells rang out so sweetly in the clear air, and the southern sky was so finely tinged with gold above white ridges and dark-blue water. He saw the others by the churchyard gate and ran up to them.

Ingunn turned toward him, flushing red as a rose—Olav saw that under her hood she wore a white coif about her face like a young wife. He turned red too, and his heart began to hammer—this was dead earnest; 'twas as though he had not known it till now. Young as he was and lacking friends and kinsmen, he had taken this upon himself—to face it out that she was his wife. And it made him terribly bashful to walk beside her thus. Straight as two candles, gazing fixedly before them, they strode side by side across the churchyard.

After the morning meal Olav accompanied Arnvid to the Bishop's palace. He was ill at ease during the walk, and it was no better when he had to sit waiting by himself in the Bishop's

stone hall, after a clerk had taken Arnvid up to Lord Torfinn in
the Bishop's bedchamber.

The time dragged on and on. Olav had never been in a stone
hall before and there was much to look at. The roof was also of
stone and vaulted, so that no light came in except from a little
glazed window in the back wall; but in spite of that it was not
so very dark, as the room was whitewashed within, and the walls
were painted with bright flowers and birds in place of tapestries
and to the same height. The room was without any sort of fireplace, but as soon as he had entered, two men came in bearing
a great brazier, which they placed in the middle of the floor.
Olav went up and warmed his hands over it, when he grew tired
of sitting and freezing on the bench. He was left to sit alone
most of the time, and he was ill at ease in this hall; there was
something churchlike about it which unsettled him.

After a while three men came in, clad in furs; they placed
themselves around the charcoal brazier and took no notice of the
boy on the bench. They had come about a case they had—of fish-
ing-rights. The two old ones were farmers from somewhere about
Fagaberg, and the younger one was a priest and stepson of one
of the farmers. Olav was made to feel very young and inexperi-
enced—it would surely not be easy for him to assert himself here.
Soon one of the Bishop's men came and fetched them away. Olav
himself would have been glad to go out into the palace yard too—
there were many things to look at. But he judged that this would
be unbecoming; he would have to stay where he was.

At last Arnvid came in great haste, snatched his sword, and
buckled it on, saying that the Bishop was to ride out to a house
in Vang and had bidden him go with him. No, he had not been
able to say much about Olav's case—folk had been coming and
going in the Bishop's chamber the whole morning. No, the Bishop
had not said much, but he had invited both Arnvid and Olav to
lodge in the palace, so now Olav must go back to the inn and
bring his horse and their things.

"What of the maids—they cannot be left behind in the inn?"

"No," said Arnvid. They were to lodge in a house in the town,
with two pious old women who had boarders. In a day or two
they would be joined by Magnhild, Steinfinn's sister from Berg;
the Bishop would send a letter tomorrow, bidding her come:
"He says you and Ingunn ought not to meet until a reconcilia-

tion be made in this affair—except, as you know, you may see
each other in church and speak together there." Arnvid dashed
out.

Olav hurried to the inn, but one of these women from the
guest-house was there before him, and Ingunn and Tora were
ready to go with her. So he was not able to speak to her. She
looked sorrowful as he gave her his hand in farewell. But Olav
said to Tora, so that her sister might hear, that the Bishop had
received them well; it was a great mark of favour that all four
were to be his guests.

But when he came back to the Bishop's palace, he was met by
a young priest, who said they were to be *contubernales*. Olav
guessed that this meant he was to sleep in this priest's room. He
was a tall, lean man with a big, bony, horse's head, and they
called him Asbjörn All-fat. He got a man to take charge of
Olav's horse, and himself showed the young man to the loft where
he was to sleep. Then he said he must go down to the boat-hithe;
a vessel had come that morning with goods from Gudbrandsdal—
maybe 'twould amuse Olav to go with him and look on? Olav
was glad to accept.

There was much shipping at Hestviken, Olav knew; and yet
no man could know less of ships and boats than he, so strangely
had his life been ordered. He used both eyes and ears when aboard
the trading vessel, made bold even to ask about one thing and
another. He took a hand with the men and helped to discharge
the freight—'twas a better pastime than standing by with idle
hands. Most of it was barrels of salt herrings and sea-trout, but
there were also bales of hides and a quantity of furs, butter, and
tallow. While the priest kept the tally, Olav helped him, notching
the stick; in this he had had practice at Frettastein, as he had
often done it for Grim; the old man was not very good at reckoning now.

He kept with Asbjörn Priest the whole day—followed him to
prayers in the choir of the church and to supper, which Olav
was to take at the same table as the Bishop's household. And
when at night he went to the loft with Asbjörn and another
young priest, he was in a much better frame of mind. He no
longer felt such a stranger in the palace, and there were many
new things to see.—Arnvid was not yet come home.

But in the course of the night Olav awoke and lay thinking of all that had been told him of Bishop Torfinn. He was afraid of the Bishop after all.

Rather let ten men lose their lives than one maiden be ravished, he was reported to have said. There was a case that had been much talked about in the country round, a year before. A rich man's son in Alvheim had set his mind on a poor peasant's daughter; as he could not tempt the woman with promises and gifts, he came one evening in springtime, when the girl was ploughing, and tried to use force. Her father was below in the wood, busy with the mending of a fence; he was old and ailing, but on hearing his daughter's cries he took his woodcutter's axe and ran up; he cleft the other's skull. The ravisher was left unatoned; his kinsmen had to be content with that. But, as was natural, they tried to get the slayer to leave the country. First they offered to buy him out, but when he would not have it, they fell upon him with threats and overbearing treatment. Then Bishop Torfinn had taken the poor peasant and his children under his protection.

Then there was that case of the man at Tonstad who had been found slain in his coppice. His wife and children charged the other tenant of the farm with the murder; the man had to flee to save his life, and his wife and young children suffered affliction and cruelty without end at the hands of the murdered man's relatives. Then it came about that the dead man's own cousin confessed that he was the one who had killed his kinsman—they had quarrelled about an inheritance. But it was said that Biship Torfinn had forced the murderer to avow before the people what he had confessed to the Bishop—saying that no priest had power to absolve him of the sin before he had shown sincere repentance and rescued the innocent who might be suffering from his misdeed.

Arnvid said that to the poor and sorrowing this Bishop would stoop with the gentlest kindness, praying them to turn to him as to a loving father. But he never bowed his neck the least jot when faced with self-willing or hard-hearted men, whether they were great folk or small, clergy or laity. Never would he excuse sin in any man—but if any sinner showed repentance and will to make amends, he received him with both hands, guided, consoled, and protected him.

This was nobly done, Olav had thought—and much of what he had heard of the lord Torfinn he had liked very well—a fearless man this monk from Trondheim must be, and one who knew his own will. But then he had never thought that he himself would have a case to submit to the Bishop's judgment. And what Arnvid said about the Bishop's being no respecter of persons seemed to Olav to be stretching his goodness somewhat far—he could see naught else but that it did make some difference whether it were a lowly peasant who killed his neighbour for a small matter, or Steinfinn revenging himself upon Mattias. In any case, he would not like anyone to think he had turned to the Bishop and sought his protection against the Steinfinnssons because—ay, because he felt himself in a way their inferior. Then there was this other thing, that Bishop Torfinn was so strict on the point of chastity. With all other men he might hold to his assertion that this life he and Ingunn had led since the summer was wedlock in a way. But he did not feel it so himself.

Next morning he sat waiting again in the little hall. It was so called because there was a larger hall or court-house beside it. There was no door between; none of the rooms in the stone building had more than one door, and that led into the courtyard. Olav had sat there awhile when a little young man came in, clad in a greyish-white monk's frock which was a little different from that of the preaching friars. The monk closed the door behind him and advanced rapidly to Olav—and the young man got up in great haste and knelt upon one knee; he knew at once that this must be the lord Torfinn. When the Bishop held out his hand, Olav meekly kissed the great stone in his ring.

"Welcome to Hamar, Olav Audunsson! 'Twas not well that I should be absent yesterday when you came—but I hope my house-folk have had good care of our guests?"

He was not so young after all, Olav saw—his thin wreath of hair shone like silver, and his face was shrunken, wrinkled, and grey as his frock almost. But he was slim and wonderfully lithe in all his movements—scarce so tall as Olav. It was impossible to guess his age—his smile took away the look of age; a brightness came into his great yellow-grey eyes, but upon his pale and narrow lips the smile became the faintest shadow.

Olav mumbled his thanks and stood in embarrassment—the zealous Bishop looked so utterly different from what he had expected. He remembered dimly that he had seen the former Bishop

—a man who filled a room with his voice and his presence. Olav felt that this one could also fill the room, slight and silver-grey as he was—in another way. When Lord Torfinn sat down and bade him be seated beside him, he modestly withdrew to the bench at a little distance.

"There is great likelihood that you must be content to bide here a part of the winter," said Bishop Torfinn. "You are a man of the Vik,[2] I hear, and all your kinsmen dwell far away, save only the Tveits folk out in Soleyar. It will take time ere we can receive their answer as to what their testimony may be in this matter. Know you if they have resigned their guardianship of you in lawful wise?"

"My father did so, lord—was it not he who had the right to that?"

"Yes, yes. But he must have spoken of it to his kinsmen and had their consent that Steinfinn should enjoy the payment for your wardship in place of them?"

Olav wås silent. This case of his did not seem so simple a matter —ay, he had guessed as much of late. No wardship payment from his estate had ever been made to Steinfinn—so far as he knew.

"I know nothing of this—I know little of the law; none has ever taught me such things," he said dejectedly.

"Nay, I supposed that. But we must be clear about this question of guardianship, Olav—first on account of your share in the deed of arson—whether you accompanied Steinfinn as his son-in-law or as a man in his pay. Kolbein and those have got their freedom now, but you were not included in it.[3] I shall speak with the Sheriff about this matter, so that you may be safe here in the town. But then there is that saying of Steinfinn before he died— that he desired the marriage between you and his daughter, as Arnvid tells me. Whether *he* were your guardian at that time, or these kinsmen of yours, who are so now."

"I thought," said Olav, turning red, "that I was come to man's estate. Since she was betrothed to me in lawful wise, and I have taken her to me as my wife."

The Bishop shook his head. "Can you suppose that you two

---

[2] *Vik:* the great bay in the south of Norway, of which the Oslo Fiord is the northern extremity.

[3] That is, Kolbein and the rest had been declared free to remain in the country, safe from outlawry.

children have acquired any right in law because you have gone to bed together, as seemed good to yourselves, without the presence of your kinsfolk and without banns in church? A duty you have taken upon yourselves, since you acted in the belief that it was binding wedlock—you are now bound under pain of mortal sin to live together till death shall part you, or to remain single if we cannot bring about a reconciliation between her sponsors and yours. But you have not come to man's estate through a marriage of this sort, and your spokesmen can demand no dowry on your behalf until you have fallen at the feet of the Toressons and made amends to them—and 'twould be unlike them if they should be willing to grant you such dowry with Ingunn Steinfinnsdatter as a man of your condition might otherwise look to get with his wife. This game may cost you dear, Olav. To the Church you must do penance, for making your marriage in secret, as she has forbidden all her children to do, since matters of matrimony are to be conducted in the light, in prudent and seemly fashion. Were it not so, too many young folk might deal as you have dealt; you and this woman are bound by the promises you have made to God, but no man is bound to grant you rights or afford you support, since no men were present, to make promises to you and for you, when you bound yourself."

"My lord!" said Olav; "I had thought that you would defend our rights—since you yourself deem that we are bound to keep the faith we gave to each other—"

"Had you submitted the case to the judgment of the Church as soon as you saw that the maid's uncles were minded to oppose the validity of the betrothal—that would have been the right way. You could have claimed of my official, Sir Arinbjörn Skolp, that he should forbid Kolbein under threat of ban to betroth Ingunn to another man, before it had been made clear whether you had already a right to this marriage."

"How much, trow, would Kolbein have cared for that?"

"Hm. *So* much you know, for all that. You have not learned law, but you have seen unlawfulness—" The Bishop moved his hands in his lap under the scapular. "You must bear in mind, Kolbein and Ivar have already so much on their hands that perchance they will not be so eager to have a matter of excommunication added."

"I thought 'twas held good enough," Olav began again obstinately, "that her father had handselled the maid to my father for my wife."

"No." The Bishop shook his head. "As I told you, guilt and duties you have gained, but no rights. Had you come to Sir Arinbjörn with the matter while the girl was yet a maid, you had gained more than the best you can win now. Either they would have been forced to give you both the woman and her goods, or she and you could have parted and been free to make another marriage. As the matter now stands, my son, you must pray God to help you, that you may not repent by daylight and in your manhood that you bound yourself hand and foot blindly and in darkness, before you were yet wholly out of your childhood."

"That day will never come," said Olav hotly, "when I repent me that I did not let Kolbein Borghildsson cheat me of what was mine by right—"

The Bishop looked at him searchingly, as Olav went on: "Oh no, my lord—Kolbein was resolved to upset this bargain, and small scruple will he have of the means he uses—that I know!" He told the Bishop of the betrothal ring.

"Are you sure," asked Lord Torfinn, "that Steinfinn had not replaced the ring in your coffer before he died? He may have thought it safer, so that you should surely receive again all that was yours and that he had in charge for you."

"No, for it was on the morning of his death-day that I saw Ingunn's betrothal ring; then it lay in the casket in which Steinfinn kept his own and his children's most costly jewels."

"Was it Steinfinn himself who brought out the casket—did he show you this?"

"No, 'twas Arnvid did it."

"Hm. Ay, then it looks as though Kolbein—" The Bishop paused for a moment, then turned to Olav. "As you two young people are placed, the best way will be—I do not say it is a perfect way, but the best—that your kinsmen and hers assent to a marriage according to the law of the land, and that you be allowed to enjoy one another and all that you possess and are to bring to one another. Otherwise life will be very difficult for you, and your feet will be beset with temptation to worse sins than this first sin, if you be parted. But you understand, I ween, that, even if we can bring witnesses to the validity of the betrothal, the Toressons may make such conditions for reconciliation that you will be poorer by your marriage than you were before?"

"Ay, that is all one to me," said Olav defiantly. "The word that was given to my father shall not be broken because he is dead. I will have Ingunn home with me, if I have to take her in her bare shift—"

"And what of this young Ingunn," said the Bishop quietly; "are you sure that she is of the same mind as you—that she would rather hold fast to the old bargain than be given to another man?"

"Ingunn was minded as I—we should not set ourselves up against our fathers' will because they were dead and strangers would minish their right to dispose of their own children."

Bishop Torfinn did his best not to smile. "So you two children stole into the bridal bed simply to be obedient to your fathers?"

"My lord!" said Olav in a low voice, turning red again, "Ingunn and I are of even age, and we were brought up as brother and sister from the time we were small. From my seventh year I have lived far from all my kinsfolk. And when she lost both mother and father, she betook herself to me. Then we agreed that we would not let them part us."

The Bishop nodded slowly; Olav said passionately: "My lord—meseems 'twould be a great dishonour both to me and to my father were I to ride brideless from Frettastein, where all have held us to be betrothed for ten years. But I also had the thought that, when I come home to my native place, where no man knows me, I could have no better wife than the one with whom I have been friends from childhood."

"How old were you when you lost your parents, Olav?" asked the Bishop.

"Seven years old I was when my father died. And I was motherless in my hour of birth."

"—And my mother is still living." Lord Torfinn sat silent awhile. "I see, 'tis natural you should not wish to lose your playmate." He rose and Olav sprang up at once. The Bishop said: "You know well, Olav, that motherless and friendless you are not—no Christian man is that. You, as we all, have the mightiest brother in Christ, our Lord, and His Mother is your mother—and with her, I trust, is she, your mother who bore you. I have always thought that the Lady Sancta Maria prays yet more to her Son for those children who must grow up motherless here below

than for us others.—True it is that none should forget who are our
nearest and mightiest kin. But it ought to be easier for you to
bear this in mind. You will not so lightly be tempted to forget
what power of kindred you have in the God of peace—since you
have no brothers or kinsmen in the flesh who might draw you
with them to deeds of violence and arrogance or egg you on to
revenge and strife. You are young, Olav, and already others have
drawn you into blood-guiltiness—you have thrust yourself into
strife and litigation. God be with you, that you may become a
man of peace, when you are answerable for yourself."

Olav knelt and kissed Bishop Torfinn's hand in farewell. The
Bishop looked down at his face and smiled faintly.

"You have a headstrong look—ay, so it is. God and His gentle
Mother preserve you, that you grow not hard-hearted."

He raised his hand and gave the young man his blessing. On
reaching the door Lord Torfinn turned with a little laugh: "One
thing I had forgot—to thank you for your help. My Asbjörn,
All-fat they call him, spoke of how you had already lent him a
hand since you came here. I thank you for it."

Not till the evening, when he was in bed and about to fall
asleep, did the thought cross Olav's mind like a chill breath:
what he had said to Bishop Torfinn about himself and Ingunn—it
was not altogether truthful. But he banished the thought at once—
now of all times he had no desire to think upon last summer and
autumn, the nights in the bower and all that.

He felt at home in the Bishop's palace, and every day the life
seemed better to him, with only men around him, all older than
himself and all with their regular tasks to perform, hour by hour.

Olav followed on the heels of Asbjörn All-fat wherever the
priest went. They were four men in the loft-room where Olav
and Arnvid slept; there was a young priest who had been at the
school with Arnvid, besides Asbjörn, who was a good deal older
than the others—close on thirty. Arnvid went to church and
sang the daily office with the clergy, and he had borrowed the
book from which he had learned when he was a pupil in the
school, and sat amusing himself with it in the leisure hour after
breakfast. He sat on the edge of the bed reading aloud the first
pieces that were written in it: *De arte grammatica* and *Nominale*.

Olav lay listening to him: 'twas strange how many names these
men of Rome had had for a single word; *sea*, for instance. At the
end of the book were some leaves on which to practise the art
of writing. Arnvid diverted himself by engrossing letters and sentences after the old copies. But it was chilly work in the cold loft—
and his fingers had lost their cunning for such things. One day he
wrote at the end of his copy:

> *"Est mala scriptura quia penna non fuit dura."* [4]

But when he had put away the book and gone out, Asbjörn Priest
took it and wrote in the margin:

> *"Penna non valet dixit ille qui scribere nescit."* [5]

Olav smiled quietly when he was told what it meant.

Asbjörn All-fat said his mass early in the morning, and Olav
usually went with him to the church; often he did not go there
again on week-days. At most times Asbjörn Priest was exempted
from service in the choir and read his hours from a book, where-
ever his duties might call him. He had much to do with the incomings and outgoings of the see, received rents and tithes in
kind, and spoke with people. The priest taught Olav to inspect
goods and judge their quality and how each kind should best be
stored; he explained to him the laws of buying and selling and of
tithes and showed him how to use the abacus. Mjösen was not yet
frozen over off the town, and folk came rowing and sailing
thither. Asbjörn Priest took Olav with him several times on short
journeys. He also bought two brooches of Olav, so now the boy
had ready money in his belt for the first time in his life.

In this way it was not much that he saw of Ingunn. He kept
his word to the Bishop and sought no meeting with her except at
church, but she seldom came there before one of the later masses,
and Olav was usually at the first. Arnvid often visited the house
where Steinfinn's daughters were lodged. From him Olav heard
that the lady Magnhild had been far from gentle with her niece—
in her words Ingunn had let herself be seduced; and Ingunn had
replied to her aunt in great wrath. The lord Torfinn had been
very friendly when he spoke with Ingunn and Tora—he had

---

[4] " 'Twas badly written, for the pen was lame."
[5] "Who knows not how to write his pen will blame."

sent for them to see him one day. But Olav was not at home when
the maids came to the Bishop's palace—he had accompanied Asbjörn All-fat on an errand to Holy Isle that day.

Nor could they have much speech together those times when
they met in church and he afterwards walked with her the little
way down to the house by Holy Cross Church. But he himself
deemed it best so. At times, indeed, he would remember how it
felt to hold her in his arms—so soft and slight, so warm and loving.
But he thrust the thought from him—now was not the time for
such things. They had all the years before them to live together
as good and loving friends. He was so sure that Bishop Torfinn
would help him to get his rights.

And besides this he felt as it were a dislike to thinking of the
life of the last months. Now that it was over, it seemed so unreal,
wellnigh unnatural, in his memory. Those nights in the bower
with Ingunn in black darkness—he lived and felt with all his senses
wide awake, except his sight; ay, 'twas so dark he might as well
have been blind. All day long he went about half-asleep and caring for nothing—feeling only the strain and uncertainty of all that
threatened him from without, like a booming inside his dazed and
empty head. Somewhere deep down within him he was always
uneasy—even when at the moment he could not tell what was the
newest thing that afflicted his conscience, he knew that there was
something wrong and that soon he would feel its urge. Even when
he was alone with Ingunn, he could not forget it quite—that something was out of gear. And then she irked him a little, because
she never seemed to be tormented by either fear or doubt, and he
grew tired of her, because she would always have him gay and
wanton and ready to caress her.

It distressed him not the least that he was now forced for a
while to lead a life in which there was no place for women and
secret love.

The Bishop himself was seldom seen by Olav. So far as his office
permitted, the lord Torfinn lived according to the rule of the
order he had entered in his youth. His bedchamber was over the
council hall, and there he worked, said his hours, and took most
of his meals. From this room a stair led down to the chapel in
which the Bishop said his mass in the morning, and from the balcony, which ran outside the rooms of the upper story, a covered

bridge led across to one of the chapels of Christ Church. Many of those who dwelt in the Bishop's palace were little pleased that they had gotten a starveling monk for their lord: the late Bishop, Gilbert, had kept house like a great noble, and yet he had been a devout priest and an able and zealous father of the Church. Asbjörn Priest said that he liked this Bishop well, but he had liked the old one better: Bishop Gilbert had been a man of cheer, a great saga-man and the boldest of horsemen and hunters.

Olav thought he had never seen a man who sat his horse more freely and handsomely than the lord Torfinn. And in every way a lordly house was kept, though the Bishop himself lived so strictly—every guest who came to the palace was sumptuously entertained; every serving-man was given strong ale every day and mead on holy-days. At the table in the Bishop's guest-hall wine was served, and when the lord Torfinn himself ate with the guests he specially wished to honour, he had a great silver tankard set on the board before him. During the whole meal his cup-bearer stood by his high seat and filled the tankard as often as the Bishop gave him a sign. It was a fine sight, thought Olav, to see Lord Torfinn take the cup, sip it, bowing with graceful courtesy toward him with whom he drank, and give it to be borne to him whom he honoured thus.

On the evening that Tore Bring of Vik was there, it fell to Olav's lot that the lord Torfinn drank with him. After supper the Bishop had him summoned from his seat far down the table; he had to come forward and stand before the Bishop's chair. Lord Torfinn raised the tankard to his lips and handed it to Olav: it felt icy cold in his hand, and the wine had a pale greenish look in the bright silver vessel. It was sharp and sour and pricked the boy's palate, but he liked the taste for all that, 'twas fresh, a drink for men, and afterwards it warmed his whole body with a rare, festal glow. He shook his head when Bishop Torfinn smiled and asked: "Maybe you like mead better, Olav?" Then he asked what Olav had thought of the service that day—there had been a festival mass and procession in the morning; and then he bade Olav drink again: "You are happy now, I dare say? I think we may be well content with what Tore has spoken."

The Bishop had not been able to get any satisfaction from the lady Magnhild—she would give no opinion as to what had happened at the Thing that time. She was inclined, indeed, to believe that her brother had thought of a marriage between Olav Audunsson and one of his daughters—at one time, in any case—but never that the match was made and settled. But Tore Vik declared that he was sure of it—Steinfinn and Audun concluded a bargain about their children that evening. They had given each other their hands on it, and Tore himself was the one who had struck the bargain; he named three or four men who had witnessed the taking of hands and who were still living, so far as he knew. What agreement was made as to settlements he knew not, but he had heard the men discuss it on a later day; he even remembered that Audun Ingolfsson would not hear of an equal division of property, unless Steinfinn increased his daughter's dowry a good deal; "My son will be much richer than that, Steinfinn," Audun had said.

During Advent, Arnvid went home to his farm in Elfardal for a space, and Olav went with him. Olav had not been there since he was a little boy. Now he came as the master's friend and equal, looked about him with discerning eyes, and put in his word as a man who himself had one thing and another on his hands. Here Arnvid's mother ruled supreme, and she received Olav with both hands, since he had upset Kolbein's plans for Ingunn; for she sincerely hated Kolbein and all the children her brother-in-law had had with his leman. Mistress Hillebjörg was a proud and handsome woman, old as she was; but there seemed to be a coolness between her and her son. Arnvid's children were three pretty, fair-haired boys. "They take after their mother," said Arnvid. Olav was well pleased with the thought that he would be a master himself when he came home to Hestviken.

Just before Yule the friends returned to the town; Arnvid wished to keep the feast there.

9

THE EVENING before Christmas Eve Olav was sent for to the Bishop.

A candle was burning on the reading-desk in the deep window, the little stone-walled chamber looked cosy and comfortable in its faint light. There was no other furniture but a chest for books and a bench against the walls. The Bishop slept and ate there; he used neither bed nor table. But there was a low stool on which his secretary could sit with his writing-board in his lap, when the Bishop dictated letters to him. At other times when Olav had been up, the lord Torfinn had bidden him sit on the stool, and Olav had liked to crouch at the Bishop's knee; it made it easy to speak to him, as to a father.

But this evening Lord Torfinn came straight up to him and stood with his hands under his scapular. "The Toressons will be here on Twelfth Night, Olav; I have summoned them hither and they have promised to appear. Now we shall have an end of this matter—with God's help."

Olav bowed in silence and looked anxiously at the Bishop. Lord Torfinn pursed his lips and nodded once or twice.

"To tell the truth, my son, they show no great mind to be reconciled. They spoke to my men about my having accepted penance of you for your share in the slaughter and suffered you to go to mass. They would have had me free them also from the ban before Yule; but that is another matter of which we must speak at our meeting. But you can guess, they are wroth that I did not receive you as though you had been a robber and a ravisher—" he gave a short and angry laugh.

Olav looked at the Bishop and waited.

"*You* have done wrong, never must you think aught else—but you are young and far from your kinsfolk and guardians—and these incendiaries seek to abate the rights of two fatherless children.—You will not be down-hearted, I trust," he said, giving Olav a little slap on the shoulder, "if you are forced to bow somewhat low to Ingunn's uncles? You know, boy, you have injured them. You shall not have to suffer wrong at their hands, if I am able to hinder it."

"I shall do as you say, my lord and father," said Olav, a little downcast.

The Bishop looked at him with a fleeting smile.

"You will not like it—having to bow your neck a trifle—no, no.—If you are going to church now, you may go by the balcony."

Bishop Torfinn nodded and held out his hand to be kissed, in token that the audience was at an end.

The Brothers of the Cross were in the middle of singing vespers. Olav knelt down in a corner with his fur cloak well spread under his knees and held his cap before his eyes, that he might the better collect his thoughts.

He was on the strain—but it was a good thing nevertheless that the decision was now at hand. He longed to escape from uncertainty. It had been like walking in the dark on a road where at any moment he might stumble and plunge both feet into the mire. *That* he had feared—of Kolbein and the rest he was not afraid. An end was to be made of all doubtful and—and half-concealed conduct; his case was to be brought to a conclusion. He would soon be seventeen years old—he liked to feel that he was the chief person in a suit. And he felt as though his bones had hardened within him in these weeks he had lived in the Bishop's palace—after all the slothful years at Frettastein among lazy house-carls and cackling women, joining in children's games. His pride in himself had grown with every day he spent here, where there were neither women nor frivolity, but only grown men who had taught him much and to whom he had taken a liking with all his youthful desire of meeting equals and superiors. It warmed his soul through and through to think that Asbjörn Priest had the greatest use for his help and that Bishop Torfinn bent over him with fatherly kindness.

When he had finished his prayers, he seated himself in a corner to hear the singing to the end. He thought of what Asbjörn Allfat had told him one day of the art of reckoning—how the nature of God was revealed in figures, through the law and order that reigned in them. *Arithmetica*, he thought it had such a fine sound; and all that the priest had expounded about the harmony of figures—how they swelled and cleft one another according to mystic and immovable laws; it was like being given an insight into one of the heavenly kingdoms; on golden chains of numbers the whole of creation was suspended, and angels and spirits ascended and descended along the links. And his heart was exalted in longing that his life also might rest in God's hand like one of these golden links—a reckoning in which there was no fault. When that which now weighed upon him should be effaced like false notches upon a tally-stick.

The midnight mass—the mass of the angels—was more beautiful than anything Olav had imagined. The whole great body of the church lay in pitch-darkness, but in the choir around the high altar so many candles, high and low, were burning that they seemed like a wall of living flame. There was a soft sheen of gold-embroidered silk and a brightness of white linen: tonight all the priests wore cantor's vestments of cloth of gold and silk, and the other singers were clad in linen surplices and held candles in their hands as they stood and sang from the great books. Arnvid Finnsson was among them, and other men of repute from the country round who had been at the school in their youth. The whole church was heavy with the scent of incense from the evening procession, and the grey clouds of perfume still ascended from the altar. When the whole choir of men and boys joined in the great Gloria, it was as though angels took up the song and swelled the music from the gloom of the roof.

Bishop Torfinn's face shone like alabaster as he sat on his throne with mitre and staff, in golden vestments. Now all the mass bells pealed out, and now all who had been standing or sitting knelt down, waiting in breathless silence for the transubstantiation, which tonight became one with God's birth in the world of men. Olav waited in eager longing; his prayers became one with his yearning for righteousness and a good conscience.

He had had a glimpse of Ingunn over on the women's side, but he did not go out after mass, when he saw her go. While they were singing the *Laudi* in the choir, he found a place to sit on the base of one of the pillars, and there, wrapped in his cloak, he shivered and nodded by turns till the priests left the choir.

On the ground outside the graveyard, there was still a glow of burned-out bonfires where the church folk had thrown down their torches in a heap as they came in. Olav went up to warm himself—he was chilled and numb from the many hours in church. The snow was melted far around, down to the bare earth, and the red and black embers still gave out a good strong heat. Many people were standing about. Olav caught sight of Ingunn—she was standing with her back to him; she was alone. He went up and greeted her.

She turned half round, and a reflection of the fire shown red upon the white linen wimple that showed under the hood of her cloak. She still seemed a little strange to him in this woman's dress—he could not grasp the thought that she should go about looking old and dignified because he for his part was determined to win his rights and to be respected as a grown man.

They took hands and wished each other a blessing on the feast. Then they talked a little about the weather; the cold was not too bad and the sky was half clear, with a few stars, but not many, for there was some mist, since the lake was not yet frozen over here.

Tora came up to them, and Olav greeted her with a kiss. He could never bring himself to kiss Ingunn now when they met—she was both too near and too far for him to embrace her as a foster-brother.

Tora went again at once, over to some friends she saw. Ingunn had scarcely spoken and had looked away the whole time. Olav thought perhaps he would have to go—it could not look well, their standing here together. Then she put out her hand and timidly took hold of his cloak.

"Can you not go with me, so that we may talk?"

"I can surely. Do you take the south road?"

The dark street was alive with heavy, fur-clad figures, swaying black against the snow—folk were going to rest awhile in their houses before the mid-morning mass. The drifts were banked high against houses and fences and trees—walls and branches were but little restless spots of black in the snow. Christmas Night lay close and dark upon the little town, and folk moved about silently as scared shadows, hurrying in where a door was opened and a faint light fell upon the snowdrifts in yard and street. But smoke issued from the louvers and there was a smell of smoke everywhere—the women were putting on the pots for the Christmas meal. Outside Holy Cross Church a gleam of light fell on the snow from the wide-open doors, and some old inmates of the spital dragged themselves in; there was to be mass now.

They tramped along the narrow alley behind the church. Here they did not meet a soul; it was very dark under the trees and heavy going, as the snow had been little trodden.

"We had no thought, when we came here that day last summer, that it would be so difficult for us," said Ingunn with a sigh.

"Nay, we could not know that."

"Can you not come in with me?" she asked as they stood in the yard. "The others were going to Holy Cross—"

"I can surely."

They entered a pitch-dark room, but Ingunn stirred the fire on the hearth and put fresh wood on it. She had taken off her cloak, and as she knelt forward to blow the fire, the long white wimple lay over her shoulders and down to her hips.

"Tora and I sleep here," she said, with her back to him. "I promised to do this for them—" she hung the pot on its hook. Olav guessed that this was the kitchen of the house; round about were things used in cookery. Ingunn busied herself to and fro in the glare of the fire, tall and slight and young in her dark dress and white coif. It was like a game, something unreal. Olav sat on the edge of the bed and looked on; he did not know what to say— and then he had grown so sleepy.

"Can you not help me?" asked Ingunn; she was cutting up meat and bacon on a platter by the hearthstone. There was a piece of back that she could not sever with the knife. Olav found a hatchet, chopped it, and broke it apart.

While they were busy with this, she whispered to him, as they knelt among the pots: "You are so glum, Olav! Are you unhappy?" As he only shook his head, she whispered yet lower: "It is so long since we were alone together. I thought you would be glad—?"

"You know that surely.—Have you heard that your uncles are coming on Twelfth Night?" he asked. Then it struck him that she might take that for an answer to her question, whether he were unhappy. "You need not be afraid," he said firmly. "We shall have no fear of *them*."

Ingunn had risen to her feet and she was staring at him, as she opened her mouth in a little gasp. Then she made as though she would throw herself into his arms. Olav showed his hands—they were smeared with fat and brine.

"Come here—you can wipe them on the bedspread." She moved one of the pots. "We can lie down a little, while we wait for it to boil."

Olav drew off his boots and unfastened his cloak. When he had lain down by her side, he spread it over them both. The next instant she had him in a close embrace, with her face pressed hotly against his cheek, so that her breath tickled his neck.

"Olav—you will not suffer them to take me away with them and part me from you?"

"No. But they will have no power to do that either. But you know that it is no trifling matters Kolbein will claim before he will be reconciled with me."

"Is it for that?" she whispered, clinging to him yet tighter. "Is it for that you are less fond of me now?"

"I am just as fond of you as I have ever been," he muttered thickly, groping to get an arm under her neck, but it was so tangled in the wimple.

"Shall I take it off?" she whispered eagerly.

"Oh no, 'twill give you trouble to put it on again."

"It will soon be a month since—we have scarce seen each other all this time," she complained.

"Ingunn—you know I only wish for your good," he pleaded—and recalled at once that he had said this before; when, he could not remember. "To think she has so little wit," he reflected sadly, "that she cannot see she is tempting me this moment—"

"Ay, but—I long so for you. They are kind, these women here, but, for all that, I long to be with you—"

"Ay. But—'tis so holy a night, this—we must go to mass again in a little while—" He turned red with shame in the dark at his own words. Such things should not even be *spoken*.—Quickly he rose in the dark, kissed her eyelids, and felt the eyeballs move and quiver under his mouth, while the tears trickled down and wet his lips.

"Be not angry," he whispered imploringly. Then he moved to the foot of the bed and lay with his face to the room, looking at the fire. Tormented by the tumult in his heart and in his blood, he listened for any sign of movement or weeping in her. But she kept as still as a mouse. At last he heard that she had fallen asleep. Then he stood up, put on his boots, and took his cloak, wrapping her in the bedcover instead. He was freezing, and felt sleepy and giddy and empty from his long fast. The cauldron of meat was boiling and smelt so good that it gave him a pain in his chest.

Outside, it had turned colder; the snow cried under his feet and there was more frost in the air, he could see that in spite of the darkness. Folk were beginning slowly to go up to the church again; Olav shivered a little under his fur cloak. He was so tired that he had no great mind to go to mass now—would rather have gone home and slept. And he had looked forward so much to this Christmas Night with its three services, each more beautiful than the last, they said.

• • •

In the days that intervened before that of the meeting Olav stayed for the most part within the palace and scarcely went beyond the church. Day after day there were splendid services, and the palace was full of guests for the feast; both priests and laymen had their hands so full with all kinds of duties that Olav was left mostly to himself. With the Bishop he had only once had speech—when he thanked him for his new-year's gift. Lord Torfinn had given him a brown cloth kirtle, reaching to the feet and bordered with fine black otter-skin. It was the first garment Olav had possessed which was altogether handsome and fit for one who would pass for a grown young man, and it added not a little to his self-respect that he could now feel perfectly well dressed—for Arnvid had lent him money to buy a handsome winter cloak, lined with marten, with hose, boots, and other things to go with it.

From Asbjörn All-fat Olav heard that the Bishop had now received an answer from the men he had charged to inquire of Olav's own kinsmen what they thought of the case. The Bishop was by no means pleased with their answers. So much was certain, that Steinfinn had never taken over the guardianship of Olav in a proper, binding way—and yet none of the men of the family had asked after the child or claimed his return from Frettastein.

"'Tis no little trouble and expense our reverend father is put to for your sake, Olav," said Asbjörn Priest with a little laugh. "Now he has summoned hither these kinsmen of yours from Tveit—it seems he of Hestviken is palsied and in poor case. But the men of Tveit must give consent to your marriage, I trow, before it can be lawful. And they let fall to the parish priest, who spoke with them on Lord Torfinn's behalf, that if the Toressons would have this marriage, then they must offer you the seduced maid—ay, 'twas their word, not mine—with such dowry as you may be pleased to accept. But they would never consent to your making more amends to her kinsmen than the law allows for fornication. And you know that Kolbein and Ivar cannot accept an atonement on such terms; 'twould be to their shame as long as they live."

"Methinks 'twould be to my shame and—and to hers," said Olav angrily. "'Twould be the same as were she a—leman—"

"Yes. Therefore the Bishop hinted of another way, which might be the last resort—that you leave the country and stay abroad four winters, till you be of full age and can parley on your own behalf. Lord Torfinn thought you could betake you to Denmark and seek refuge with your mother's kin—you know that in that land your mother's kinsmen are among the mightiest? Your uncle, Sir Barnim Eriksson of Hövdinggaard, is said to be the richest knight in Sealand."

Olav shook his head. "My mother's father was called Björn Andersson of Hvitaberg, and her only brother was Stig.—'Twas in Jutland, I have been told—"

"The lady Margrete was twice married; Björn was her second husband, and first she had a son named Erik Eriksson; he owned Hövdinggaard in Sealand. Think you, Olav, 'twould be the worst mischance if you had to live some years in foreign lands and could see something of other folks' manners and customs—and could associate with right wealthy and powerful kinsfolk to boot?"

The priest's words turned Olav's thoughts in a new direction. Since he came to the Bishop's see, he had indeed found out that it was a very small and narrow piece of the world he knew. These churchmen, they sent letters and messengers north, south, east, and west; in less than six weeks they managed to get word from folk whom it would have been impossible for Olav to reach—they might as well have lived in Iceland or in Rome. And now the Bishop knew more of Olav's own mother's kindred than he himself had ever done. In the church were books and candlesticks from France, silk curtains from Sicily sent hither by a pope, woven tapestries from Arras, relics of martyrs and confessors who had lived in Engelland and Asia. Asbjörn All-fat told him of the great schools in Paris and Bologna, where a man might learn all the arts and wisdom in the world—in Salerno one could learn the Greek tongue and how to become proof against steel or poison. Asbjörn was a farmer's son from the Upplands, and the longest journey he had ever made was north to Eyjabu church, but he talked very often of travelling in foreign lands—and he would surely be sent abroad in time, for he was an able man and useful in many ways.

On most days Olav spoke to Arnvid Finnsson only when they went to bed at night and when they got up. The friends had become strangers to each other since they came to the Bishop's palace. Arnvid was occupied with so much that Olav did not understand. And then Arnvid's presence reminded the young man of so many things that were difficult and humiliating. Olav felt a kind of remorse or shame when he remembered all the things of which Arnvid had been a half-willing, half-reluctant witness— though Olav himself could not understand how he had been able to compel a man who was so much older than he, a rich and powerful landowner, when one came to think of it. But it was as though he had used force upon his friend in one way or another, both in that matter of the ring—and afterwards when Arnvid held his peace about what he knew of Olav's nightly visits to his young kinswoman. This last would be judged harshly not only by the Toressons but by all others; Arnvid had gotten an ugly stain on his honour there—and for that he was too good. And Olav knew that Arnvid took things greatly to heart. Therefore he was not quite at his ease with Arnvid now.

With Asbjörn Priest he felt safe and easy. He was always the same, a steady, strenuous worker, whether he were saying his hours or passing salted hides. His long, thin, horse's face was just as unmoved and his voice just as dry and precise when he was saying his mass or when he stood by while goods were being weighed, or tested whether it were true that the supports of a cow-house were rotten on one of the farms of the Bishop's estate. Olav went with him, thinking of his own future; when he came to Hestviken and would go about in his own boats, among his own quays and byres and storehouses—unconsciously it was this friend he dreamed of imitating.

The memory of those hours alone with Ingunn on Christmas Night had reawakened his longing for her. He thought of the slender, girlish young wife in her woman's dress, on her knees blowing at the embers, moving in and out of the flickering light, and busying herself between the benches and the hearth. Thus he would lie at home in his own bed at Hestviken on dark winter mornings and look on while Ingunn made a fire on his hearth. He recalled her warm and affectionate embraces when they lay resting in the dark—when they came to Hestviken, they would sleep together in the great bed, as master and mistress of the house. Then he would be able to take her in his arms as often as he would, and every evening he could lie and talk to her of all that had happened to him that day, take counsel with her as to what he should do next. And he would no longer be forced to fear what he had hitherto dreaded as a misfortune—it would only increase their joy and their repute to have children. Then he would no longer be the last slender twig of a dying race; he would himself become the stem of the new tree.

Then it was that Asbjörn's words suddenly threw this new, unimagined thought into his mind. He had never thought it might fall to his lot to roam abroad and see the world. Far, far away—Valland,[6] Engelland, Denmark—they were all one to the boy, who, as long as he could remember clearly, had travelled no longer road than that between Frettastein and Hamar, had never dreamed of farther voyaging than out from Hestviken and back again with his trading craft. He had been willing to accept the fate prepared for him and had been content therewith—but that was before he had had any thought that it might be different. Now— It was as though he had been offered a gift—four years to look about him in the world and try his fortunes, see peoples and countries, and this just as he had found out what a small and out-of-the way corner of the world they were, these places which he had believed were all he was destined to see. And then there was this other thing, that he was said to come of such great folk on his mother's side—and they told him that now, just as the Steinfinnssons sought to make him a lesser man than they, and when it appeared that his kinsmen on his father's side either did not care or were not strong enough to defend his rights. But in Denmark he need only ride straight to the richest and mightiest knight's castle there was in the land and say to its master: "I am your sister Cecilia's son."—One evening Olav took out his mother's signet-ring and put it on his finger; he might as well wear it himself, till he was reconciled with Ingunn's kinsmen. And the little gold cross with the gilt chain he hung around his neck and hid on his breast under the shirt; he had heard his mother brought it with her from her home. Just as well to take good care of those things he had which might serve as tokens in case of need. Come what might, he would not be at a loss, even if his enemies set hidden snares for his feet, and his kinsmen in Norway availed him little.

The Steinfinnssons came to Hamar a few days later than they had been summoned. There were Kolbein with both his sons, Ivar Toresson, and a young nephew of the Toressons, Hallvard

[6] Northern France.

Erlingsson. Hallvard's mother, Ragna, was full sister to Kolbein; she too was one of old Tore's children by his leman; and Hallvard had been but seldom at Frettastein, so Olav scarcely knew him. But he had heard it said that Hallvard was very stupid.

Olav was not allowed to be present at their audience with the Bishop; Arnvid said it was because his spokesmen had not come, and therefore Olav could not appear himself. It was not on *his* behalf that the Bishop was acting, but on that of the Church, which alone had the right to decide whether a marriage was valid or not. Olav did not like this, nor did he see the difference clearly. But both Arnvid and Asbjörn Priest had been present at the interview. They said that at first Kolbein and Ivar had been very headstrong. What angered them most was that the lord Torfinn had sent Ingunn out of the town, to a farm near Ottastad church. Kolbein said that here in the Upplands it had never been the custom to let the Bishop of Hamar rule like a petty king—'twas easy to see that the man came from Nidaros,[7] for there the priests did as they pleased in everything. Nevertheless it was surely an unheard-of thing that the Bishop should harbour a seduced maid who had run from her kinsmen to hide her shame and escape chastisement, or should throw his shield over the ravisher.

Bishop Torfinn answered that so far as he knew, Ingunn Steinfinnsdatter had neither run away nor been ravished by Olav Audunsson; but Arnvid Finnsson had brought the two young people hither and requested the Bishop to search out a matter that came under the jurisdiction of the Church and to retain Olav and the girl in the meantime. It was the brothers themselves who had asked Arnvid to stay at Frettastein and take charge of the estate and the children; when therefore he found out that Olav had outraged the elder daughter, he had called the man to account for his conduct. Then it came out that these two childish people had fancied that because their fathers had made a bargain about them when they were small, and both Steinfinn and Audun were now dead and gone, they themselves and none else were now to see that the agreement was kept and the bargain accomplished: wherefore they had cohabited as a married couple ever since Steinfinn's death, believing that they did no wrong in this. Arnvid had then taken the course of bringing these two to Hamar, in order that learned men might inquire how the case stood.

[7] The old name for the town of Trondhiem.

One thing was certain: since Olav and Ingunn had given themselves to each other in the belief that they were fulfilling a marriage agreement, neither of them was now free to marry. anyone else. Equally certain was it that such a wedding was against the law of the land and the commandments of the Church, and the woman had forfeited her right to dowry, inheritance, and support of kinsfolk for herself and her child or children, if it should prove that she had conceived. But from the man her sponsors could claim fines for his infringement of their rights—and both were under an obligation to do penance to the Church for not having kept her commandments as to the proclamation of banns and the due celebration of matrimony.

But now the Bishop bade the woman's uncles remember that Olav and Ingunn were very childish, ignorant, and unlearned in the law, and that they had grown up in the belief that they were destined to be married. Tore Bring of Vik and two good franklins besides had deposed before him, the Bishop, that Steinfinn Toresson had handselled his child Ingunn to Audun Ingolfsson as a wife for Audun's son—they would make oath of this on the book. And Arnvid testified that just before his death Steinfinn had spoken of the agreement to Olav and said it was his wish that it should hold good. Therefore he asked Ingunn's kinsmen to accept atonement on such terms as might be agreeable to all: that Olav and Ingunn should fall at the feet of the Toressons and beg their forgiveness, and that Olav should make amends for his self-willed conduct according to the judgment of impartial men. But, this being done, Bishop Torfinn deemed that it would best become the Toressons if they were reconciled to Olav as good Christians and great-minded men—let him possess the woman with such dowry that the affinity would bring no shame to themselves, and Olav would suffer no disgrace in his native place for having made a marriage that did not add to his power and fortune. Finally the Bishop bade the brothers bear in mind that it is a good deed and specially pleasing in the eyes of God to care for fatherless children, but that to deprive such of their rights is one of the worst of sins, a sin that cries aloud for vengeance even here on earth—and it was the dead man's wish that their children should be given to each other in marriage.

But if it were as they sought to prove, that Olav and Ingunn had never been affianced in legal wise, and they could not agree with Olav's guardians on the course to adopt, then it was clear that they must bring a suit for fornication against the lad. And in that case the Bishop would hand Ingunn over to them, that they might punish her as they thought she deserved and divide her part of the inheritance among her brothers and sister, and afterwards her kinsmen would have to support her as seemed fit to them. But he himself would cause it to be published in all the bishoprics of Norway that these two were not free to marry any others, so long as both were alive—lest any third party, man or woman, might fall into the sin of adultery by taking a husband or a wife who was already bound in wedlock according to God's ordinances.

This last hit the mark, both Arnvid and Asbjörn thought. Neither of the uncles had a mind to receive Ingunn if they were to feed her and could never get her married off. Kolbein spoke at length to the effect that Olav Audunsson had well known how he and his brother regarded the betrothal and that they intended to dispose of Ingunn in another way; but he promised at the last that for the Bishop's sake he would make atonement with Olav. As to the conditions, however, he would say nothing until all was made plain about the old agreement and he had made tryst with Ingolf Helgesson of Tveit or whichever of Olav's kinsmen it might be who had authority to act on the boy's behalf. The Bishop hinted that so much at least was certain, that *sponsalia de futuro* had been made at that time at the Thing, so if only the Toressons gave their consent to what was already accomplished, Olav could act for himself; and then they would surely find him very compliant. But to this Kolbein gave a flat no: they would not take advantage of the boy's ignorance, but they claimed to deal with Olav's kinsmen, that the case might end in honourable and seemly fashion for them and their kinswoman.

10

THE NEXT evening Arnvid and Olav agreed to go down to the convent. Arnvid had promised the brothers a gift of wool, and Olav wished to speak to Brother Vegard about making confession to him one day. It was very dark outside, so they each took

a weapon. Olav had his axe, Kinfetch, which he carried whenever
he had an opportunity.

When they came into the courtyard, they found it was later
than they had thought; one of the monks, who had come out to
look at the weather, said that the lay brother had already gone to
ring the bell for complin. But Arnvid would fain have a word or
two with Brother Helge. Ay, he would find him in the guest-
room, said the monk. So they went thither.

The first they saw on entering were the sons of Kolbein and
their cousin, Hallvard, with three other men; they sat on the inner bench, eating and drinking. Brother Helge and another monk
stood on the outside, talking and laughing with them—the strangers were already very merry.

Olav stayed by the door while Arnvid went forward to Brother
Helge. At that moment the convent bell began to ring.

"Sit down," said Brother Helge, "and taste our ale; 'tis uncommon good this time—then I will ask leave of the Prior to go and
visit you after service. Sit down meanwhile, Arnvid!"

"Olav is with me," whispered Arnvid; he had to repeat it
louder a couple of times, for Brother Helge was hard of hearing.
When at last he understood, he went up to Olav and greeted
him, bidding him sit down too and drink; and now the sons of
Kolbein saw who was with Arnvid.

Olav answered the monk that he would rather go with him to
the church and hear the singing, but Haftor Kolbeinsson called
to him: "No, come here, Olav, and keep us company! We have
not seen you since you were our brother-in-law. Come, Arnvid,
sit down and drink!"

As Arnvid seated himself on the outer bench, Olav put away
his axe and threw back his hood. As he came forward to take his
seat. Einar clapped his hands together with a smile such as one
gives to little children:

"Nay, how big you are grown, boy! Truly you begin to look
like a married man already!"

"Oh, we were all as much married as Olav, I trow, when we
were his age," sneered Hallvard.

Olav had turned red as fire, but he smiled scornfully.

Brother Helge shook his head, but he gave a little laugh. Then
he bade them keep the peace. Haftor answered that they would
do that sure enough, and the monks went out. Olav followed them

with his eyes, murmuring that after all he was more minded to go to church.

"Oh no, Olav," said Einar. "That is discourteous—you must not show so little zeal to make acquaintance with your wife's kinfolk. Now let us drink," he said; he took the bowl that the lay brother had placed on the table and drank to Olav.

"That was a heavy, thirst you had on you," said Olav under his breath. Einar was already half-drunken. Aloud he said: "Oh, acquainted we are already. And as to drinking to our closer kinship—methinks we could as well wait for that till I am agreed with your father."

"It must be good enough when Father has agreed with the Bishop," said Einar, bland as butter, "—since he has adopted you. But 'tis a fine thing to see young people so quick to learn: do you see now, sometimes it is proper to wait? They say Lord Torfinn was so eloquent on patience in his Advent preaching—is that where you learned your lesson?"

"Yes," replied Olav. "But you know 'tis a new word to me, therefore I am so afraid I might forget it."

"Be sure I shall remind you," laughed Einar as before.

Again Olav made as though he would rise, but Arnvid pulled him back onto the seat.

"Is that how you keep your promise to the good brothers?" he said to Einar. "In this house we must keep the peace!"

"Nay, am I not peaceful? There is no harm in a little jesting among kinsfolk, kinsman!"

"I knew not that *I* was among kinsfolk," muttered Arnvid with vexation.

"What say you?"

Arnvid did not own kinship with Tore of Hof's offspring by Borghild, his leman. But he checked himself—turned his eyes upon the serving-men of the sons of Kolbein and upon the lay brother, who was listening inquisitively as he moved about.

"There are many here who are not kinsmen—"

Haftor Kolbeinsson told his brother to keep his mouth shut: "—though I think we all know Einar, all of us here, and are used to his teasing ways when he is in drink. But now, Olav, 'tis time you showed yourself a grown man—if you mean to set yourself up and play the master, it will not do to let yourself be provoked by Einar as when you were a little lad—crying with temper—"

"Crying—" Olav puffed with wrath; "I never did so! And playing the master—I trow there will be no play in it, when I go home and take over my property—"

"Nay, that's sure," said Haftor quietly.

Olav had a feeling that he had said something foolish; he turned scarlet again.

" 'Tis the chief manor in that country, Hestviken. 'Tis the biggest farm in all the parish."

"Nay, is it so?" said Haftor, imperturbably serious. "You will have much to answer for, young Olav—but you will be the man for it, sure enough. You know, brother-in-law, 'twill be worse with Ingunn, methinks. Can she cope with a mistress's duties on a great farm like that, think you?"

"We shall find a way. My wife herself will have no need to drudge," said Olav proudly.

"Nay, that's sure," said Haftor as before. "She is coming into great abundance, Ingunn, I see that."

"Oh, that may be saying too much—though Hestviken is no such small place. The shipping and fishery are the main things."

"Nay, is it so?" said Haftor. "Then you own much shipping too, down there in the Vik?"

Olav said: "I know not how it is with that—'tis so many years since I was at Hestviken. But in old days it was so. And now I mean to take it up again—I have followed Asbjörn Priest here and learned not a little of ships and trading."

"Meseems you could not possibly want *that*," said Einar with a smile. "With such great shipping as we saw you deal with—in Ingebjörg's goose-pond."

Olav rose and left the bench. They had only been making fun of him—Haftor too—he saw that.—That about shipping in the goose-pond was a game he had got up for Hallvard and Jon last summer, when the children of Frettastein were left so much to themselves.

"I cannot see that I demeaned myself in that," he said hotly, "if I carved some little boats for the children; none could think I was playing myself—" then he heard how silly and childish this sounded, and stopped suddenly.

"Nay, 'tis true," replied Einar; "that would be a very childish game for a boy who was already grown enough and bold enough to seduce their sister—'twas more manly work when you played with Ingunn in the outhouse and got her with child in the barn—"

" 'Tis a lie!" said Olav furiously. "The thrall's blood shows in you, when you use such foul talk of your own kinswoman. I know naught of a child either—but if 'tis as you say, you need not be afraid we shall ask your father to bring it up. We know that it is not to his liking—"

"Be silent now," said Arnvid; he had jumped up and gone to Olav's side. "And do you shut your mouths too"—he turned to the others. "Man's work, you said—do you call it man's work, after Kolbein has accepted atonement, that you sit here snarling like dogs? But you, Olav, should have more respect for yourself than to let them egg you on to barking with them."

But now the sons of Kolbein and Hallvard were on their feet—beside themselves with wrath at the last words Olav had spoken. Kolbein in his young days had freed himself by oath from the fathering of a child, but ill things had been said about the matter at the time, and as the boy grew up to manhood, 'twas thought he bore an ugly likeness to Kolbein.

"Hold your jaw yourself, Arnvid," said Haftor—he was fairly sober. " 'Tis true your share in this business is such that you had rather it were not talked about. But Olav must brook it, though I do not begrudge him atonement instead of the reward he deserves—he cannot expect us to embrace him as if he were *welcome* in our kin."

"Nay, *welcome* to our kin you will never be, my Olav," sneered Hallvard.

"Answer for yourselves, not for the kin," said Arnvid. "If that were so, think you Kolbein would have offered Olav your sister Borghild to wife instead of Ingunn, Hallvard?"

" 'Tis a lie!" shouted Hallvard.

"That may be," answered Arnvid. "But he told me that he meant to do so."

"Hold your jaw, Arnvid," Einar began again; "we all know of your friendship for Olav—'twill do you no good if we inquire into *that*. You keep nothing from this minion of yours—not even your own childish kinswoman for his leman—"

Arnvid leaned threateningly toward the other. "Have a care of your mouth now, Einar!"

"Nay, devil take me if I care for a rotten clerk. 'Tis a fine story,

methinks, this friendship of yours for the lily-white boy. We have
heard a tale or two, we have, of the kind of friendship you learn
in the schools—"

Arnvid took Einar by both wrists and twisted them till the
other fell on his knees with an oath and a groan of pain and rage.
Then Haftor came between them.

The Kolbeinssons' house-carls sat as before, seeming little
minded to meddle in the quarrel between the masters. Einar Kolbeinsson got on his feet again and stood rubbing his hands and
arms, swearing heartily below his breath.

Olav stood looking from one to the other. He did not understand it quite, but felt as though a hand squeezed at his heart: he
had brought Arnvid into a worse slough than he had guessed;
they fell upon his friend with grievous insults, flayed him merci-
lessly. It hurt him to look into Arnvid's face, chiefly because he
could not interpret what he saw in it. Then his anger flared up
hotly, and all other feelings were burned up in its flame.

Einar found his voice again, now that he had his brother and
cousin at his back. He said something—Olav did not hear the
words. Arnvid's face seemed to knit together—then he drove his
fist at Einar and caught him below the chin, so that the man fell
backward at full length and crashed against the bench.

The lay brother had rushed in among the men; he helped Einar
Kolbeinsson to his feet and wiped the blood from him, as he
shouted to the others: " 'Tis a banning matter, you know that,
to break the peace in our house—is this fitting conduct for nobles?"

Arnvid recovered himself and said to Haftor: "Brother Sigvald
is right. Now we will go, Olav and I—that is safest."

"Shall *we* go?" asked Olav sharply. " 'Twas not we who started
the quarrel here—"

"Let them end it who have kept their wits," said Arnvid curtly.
"I shall give Einar his answer in a fitter place. To you, Haftor,
I say that I can answer fully for my conduct in this matter—I *have*
answered both the Bishop and Kolbein, and *you* are not concerned
in it."

"You said you saw nothing of it," said Einar with a grimace;
"and that may well be true, if 'tis as folk say—that you were a married man yourself for a full year before you guessed what your
mother had given you a wife for—"

Olav saw Arnvid's face quiver—as when a man has a sudden knock on an open wound; he ran back and snatched his spear, which he had left standing by the door. Seized with insensate wrath on the other's behalf, Olav sprang between them—saw Einar swing an axe in the air and himself raised Kinfetch in both hands. He struck Einar's axe aside so that it rang and flew out of his hands, grazed Hallvard, who stood behind him, and fell to the floor. Olav raised Kinfetch once more and struck at Einar Kolbeinsson. Einar ducked to avoid the blow—it caught him on the back below the shoulder-blade, and the axe sank in deeply. Einar dropped and lay doubled up.

Now Kolbein's men had come to life—all three staggered out from the bench and thrust at the air with their weapons, but they were very drunken and seemed to have no great heart for a fight, though they yelled bravely. Hallvard sat on the bench holding his wounded leg, rocking to and fro and groaning.

Haftor had drawn his sword and made for the two; it was a rather short weapon and the others had axe and spear, so at first they only tried to keep Haftor from coming to close quarters. But soon they found this as much as they could do—the man was now quite sober and plied his sword with great skill; with a sullen determination to avenge his brother he took his aim, supple, swift, and sure in every muscle, with senses wide awake.

Olav defended himself, unaccustomed though he was to the use of arms in earnest—but there was a strange voluptuous excitement in this game, and in a vague way he felt acutely impatient every time Arnvid's spear was thrust forward to protect him.

Though aware in a way that the door had been opened to the night, he was yet overwhelmed with surprise when the Prior and several of the monks rushed in. The whole scene had not lasted many minutes, but Olav had a feeling of being roused from a long dream when the fight came to an end without his clearly knowing how.

It was fairly dark in the parlour now, as the fire on the hearth had burned low. Olav looked about him at the band of black and white monks—he passed his hand across his face once, let it drop, and stood leaning on his axe. He was now filled with astonishment that this thing had actually occurred.

Someone lighted a candle at the fire and carried it to the bench, where Brother Vegard and another of the friars were busy with

Einar. There was still life in him, and a sound came from him like
the retching of a drunken man—Olav heard them say that the
bleeding must be mostly *within*. Brother Vegard gave him such
a queer look once—

He heard that the Prior was speaking to him, asking if it were
he who first broke the peace.

"Yes, I struck first and cut down Einar Kolbeinsson. But the
peace was but frail in here the whole evening—long before I broke
it. At the last Einar used such shameful speech to us that we took
to our weapons—"

" 'Tis true," said the lay brother. He was an old countryman
who had entered the convent only lately. "Einar spoke such words
that in old days any man would have judged he died an outlaw's
death by Olav's hand."

Haftor was standing by his brother; he turned and said with a
cold smile: "Ay, so they will judge the murder in this house—and
in the Bishop's. Since these two are the Bishop's men, body and
soul. But mayhap the nobles of this land will soon be tired of such
dishonour—that every priest who thinks he has authority uses it
to shelter the worst brawlers and law-breakers—"

"That is untrue, Haftor," said the Prior; "we servants of God
will not protect any evil-doer farther than he has protection in
the law. But we are bound to do our best that law-breaking be
punished according to law, and not avenged by fresh unlawfulness, which begets fresh vengeance without end."

Haftor said scornfully: "I call them dirty laws, these new laws.
The old were better suited to men of honour—but 'tis true the
new are better for such fellows as Olav there, who outrage the
daughters of our best houses and strike down their kinsmen when
they call them to account for their misdeeds."

The Prior shrugged his shoulders. "But now the law is such
that the Sheriff must take Olav and hold him prisoner until the
matter be brought to judgment. And here we have these men
whom I sent for," he said, turning to some men-at-arms who, Olav
knew, lived in the houses next the church. "Bjarne and Kaare, you
must bind this young lad and carry him to Sir Audun. He has
struck a man a blow that may give him his death."

Olav handed Kinfetch to one of the monks.

"You need not bind me," he said sharply to the strange men;
"nay, lay no hands on me—I will go with you unforced."

"Ay, now you must go out in any case," said the Prior. "You can see that we cannot let *you* stay here—they are coming with Corpus Domini for Einar."

Outside, it had begun to snow again and there was much wind. The town had gone to rest more than an hour ago. The little band tramped heavily in the dark through drifts and loose snow between the churchyard wall and the low, black, timber houses of the canons; everything looked dreary and lifeless, and the wind howled mournfully about the walls and whistled shrilly in the great ash trees.

One of the watch went in front, and then came an old monk who was a stranger to Olav, but he knew him to be the subprior. Then walked Olav, with a man on each side of him and one behind, so close that he almost trod on his heels. Olav's mind was full of the thought that now he was a *prisoner*—but he was sleepy and strangely blunted and inert.

The Sheriff's house lay east of the cathedral. For a long time they had to stand in the drifts hammering on the locked door, while the snow worked through their clothes and turned the whole band white. But at last the door was opened and a sleepy man with a lantern in his hand came forward and asked what was the matter. Then they were admitted.

Olav had never been inside this gate. He could distinguish nothing in the darkness but driven snow between black walls. The Sheriff was away—had ridden out of town about midday in company with the Bishop, Olav heard in a half-dazed way—he was almost asleep as he stood. Reeling with tiredness, he let himself be led into a little house that stood in the yard.

It was bitterly cold inside and pitch-dark, with no fire on the hearth. In a few minutes some men came with a candle and bedclothes, which they threw down upon the bedstead within. They bade him good-night, and Olav replied half-asleep. Then they went out and barred the door, and Olav was alone—suddenly wide awake. He stood staring at the little flame of the candle.

The first thing he felt was a kind of chill. Then his rage boiled up, with a defiant, voluptuous joy—so he had paid out that unbearable Einar Kolbeinsson—and God strike him if he rued it. He cared not, whatever his hastiness might cost him! Kolbein and

those—how cordially he hated them! Now for the first time he
saw how he had fallen off in these last months: his dread, his
gnawing pains of conscience, all the humiliations he had been
exposed to, while he was trying to find a way out of the slough in
which he was sunk—it was Kolbein who had barred the way for
him wherever he tried to get a firm foothold again. Had not that
Kolbein crew stood in his path, he might long ago have been out
of all this evil, free and safe, able to forget the painful feeling
that he had been a false deceiver. But Kolbein had kept him under
his thumb.—And now it was avenged—and he *thanked* God for
it with all his heart. It mattered not that Bishop Torfinn and all
these new friends of his said it was sinful to have such thoughts.
A man's flesh and blood were not to be denied.

Olav's mind rose in revolt against all these new doctrines and
thoughts he had come under in this place—ay, they were fine in
a way, he saw that even now, but—no, no, they were unnatural,
impossible dreams. *All* men could never be such saints as to consent to submit all their concerns, great and small, to the judgment
of their even Christians, always being satisfied with the law and
with *receiving* their rights—never *taking* them for themselves. He
remembered that Haftor had said something of the same sort this
evening—that these new laws were only good for the common
people. And he felt at once that he was one with such as Kolbein
and his sons, if only in this—he would rather take his case against
them into his own hands, set wrong against wrong, if need were.
His place was among such as Kolbein and Steinfinn and Ingebjörg
—and Ingunn, who had thrown herself into his arms without a
thought of the law, in the warmth of her self-willed love—not
among these priests and monks, whose life was passed in clear and
cool regularity, who every day did the same things at the same
times: prayed, worked, ate, sang, lay down to sleep, and got up
again to begin their prayers. And they inquired into the laws,
copied them out and discussed their wording, and disagreed
among themselves and came into conflict with laymen about the
laws—all because they loved this law and dreamed that by its
means all folk might be tamed, till no man more would bear arms
against his neighbour or take his rights by force, but all would
be quiet and willing to listen to our Lord's new and gentle tidings
of brotherhood among all God's children.—He felt a kind of distant, melancholy affection for all this even now, a respect for the

men who thought thus—but *he* was not able always to bow beneath the law, and the very thought that they would slip these bonds about *himself* filled him with violent loathing.

It added to his rebellious feeling that he was dimly sure they now must look upon *him* as an outlaw. Bishop Torfinn could not possibly have any more love for him after the way he had repaid his fatherly kindness. And all the preaching friars had looked on him with such eyes—they must be full of resentment at his defiling their parlour with a man's blood. The old subprior had said something about repentance and penance before he went out just now. But Olav was not in any mood for repentance.

It must cost what it might. He ought never to have listened to Arnvid, never come hither, never let himself be parted from Ingunn.

Ingunn, he thought, and his longing for her came up in him as an incurable torment—she was the only one on earth whom he really knew and was allied to. Ingunn, such as she was and not otherwise, weak and obstinate, short of wit, alluring and tender and warm—she was the only one in the knowledge of whom he was quite secure; the only one of all his possessions that he could take and feel and see and own as something apart from unreal dreams and words and uncertain memories. But *she* was actually as his own body and his own soul, and now he cried out with her, silently, as he bent double, gnashed his teeth, and clenched his hands till the nails ran into the flesh. At the thought of how far he was from her now, and what chance he now had of getting her, all his desire blazed up, so that he moaned aloud and bit his own clenched fists. He would go to her, he would have her now at once, he was ready to tear her to pieces and eat her up in terror lest anyone should drag them apart.—"Ingunn, Ingunn," he groaned.

He *must* find her. For he must tell her what had happened—find out how she would take it, that he had killed her cousin. Ay, for Einar would die, of that he was sure, there was blood between them now, but, Holy Mary! what could that do, when they two were already one flesh? She was not fond of these sons of Kolbein, but kin is kin, and so she would weep and mourn, his poor darling—and yet he could not wish it were undone. And then he must find out whether it were with her as Einar had said—ah, then she would suffer cruelly indeed.—Olav was shaken by a short,

dry sob. Kolbein, who had demanded that she be handed over to
him for punishment—but if she fell into his hands, and if she
proved with child by his son's slayer—then they would surely torture her to death.

He must speak with Arnvid about this—Arnvid would surely
seek him out in the morning. Arnvid must get her away to some
place where Kolbein could not reach her.

The candle was but a thin wick wound about an iron spike.
Olav was not afraid of the dark at most times, but now he dreaded
the light's going out and leaving him in the dark with his thoughts.
With a cautious hand he trimmed the wick.

In a moment he threw off his cloak, his boots, and the fine kirtle
and leaped into the bed. He buried himself in the icy-cold bedclothes and dug his face into the pillow, moaning for Ingunn. He
remembered Christmas Night and felt a sort of resentment against
providence: was this his reward for having done what was right
that evening!

He drew the skins right over his head—so he would be spared
seeing when the light burned out. But soon he threw them off
again, rested his face in his hand, and lay staring at the little flame.

Ay, Arnvid was the only one he could ask to protect Ingunn,
when he could not do so himself.—And all at once he had such a
strange dislike of the thought of Arnvid.

He had not understood what Einar meant by the insults he flung
at Arnvid, but so much he saw, that Arnvid felt them like a kick
on an open wound; and whenever he thought of it, it turned him
sick at first, then beside himself with rage; it was as though he
had been witness to a nameless piece of brutality.

He had gradually become aware that he was very far from
knowing Arnvid thoroughly. He relied on him, more than on any
other person he had met—on his generosity, his loyalty; he knew
that Arnvid would fear nothing when it was a question of helping
a friend or kinsman. But there was something about Arnvid Finnsson which made him think of a tarn with unfathomable deeps.—
Or—Asbjörn All-fat had told a story one evening, of a learned
doctor in the southern lands who wooed a lady, the fairest in that
country. At last she made as though he should have his will; she
led him secretly into her bower, loosened her clothing, and let
him see her breasts. One of them was white and fair, but of the
other naught was left but a putrid sore. The other hearers praised

this tale greatly and called it good and instructive—for Raimond, the learned man, turned his heart altogether from the world after this sight and betook him to a cloister. But Olav thought it the most loathsome story he had ever heard, and he lay awake till far into the night and could not get it out of his head. But there was something about Arnvid which made him afraid—that one day he would see something like this in his friend, some hidden sore. But in secret he had always shrunk most painfully at the sight of sickness and suffering—could scarce bring himself to do anyone a hurt. And Olav had a vague suspicion that it might be the fear of being touched on a sore point that had paralysed Arnvid so strangely in the autumn. Now he came near to wishing that Arnvid had not been so meek, but called him to account earlier. He did not like the thought that he had taken advantage of a man's defencelessness. And here he lay, with the knowledge that he would be forced to ask Arnvid to have a care of Ingunn and protect her, whatever consequences his rash deed might involve; since God alone knew when he would be in a position to do so himself.

In a way Olav saw something of what ailed Arnvid. Arnvid had never made it a secret that his most heart-felt wish had always been to devote himself to the service of God in holy orders. And after this time he had spent in Hamar Olav guessed better than before that a man could wish that. But he suspected that there were more windings in Arnvid's brain than—well, than in Asbjörn All-fat's or Brother Vegard's, for instance. Arnvid longed to submit himself, to obey and to serve—but at the same time he had a sort of fellow-feeling with the men who demanded that the other law should hold: the law for men with fleshly hearts, hot blood, and vengeful minds. It was as though at some time Arnvid had been badly crushed between the two laws.

It had impressed Olav that Arnvid never spoke of the years he had been married. From other quarters he had heard this and that about Arnvid's marriage: Tordis, his wife, had first been promised to the eldest of the Finnssons, Magnus—a scapegrace, but of merry disposition, well liked and a remarkably handsome man. She had certainly been bitterly disappointed with the one she got instead—but there was no doubt Arnvid had had no great love for his wife either. Tordis was proud and quarrelsome; she made no secret of despising her husband because he was so young, quiet-mannered,

and rather shy among folk. With the mother-in-law she lived in
open conflict. Arnvid must have had a joyless youth between
these two imperious, quarrelling women. Doubtless it was for
that he now seemed to avoid all women—except Ingunn. Of her
he was intensely fond, Olav saw, and this must have been because
Ingunn was so weak, had need of men to defend and support her,
and had never a thought of ruling over them and giving them
orders. Often Arnvid would sit lost in thought, looking at her
with such strange sadness, as though pitying her.—But that was
a weakness of Arnvid, that he seemed too much given to pitying—
animals, for instance. Olav was kind to animals himself—but the
way Arnvid could nurse and tend a sick creature— 'Twas strange,
too, how often it mended and thrived when Arnvid took in hand
a sick animal. Even his dead wife—the two or three times Olav
had heard Arnvid speak of her, it struck him that the man felt
pity for her.

But lately Olav had felt a growing ill will toward Arnvid for being so ready to show compassion. Olav knew he was not free from
this weakness himself, but now he saw it to be a fault: it might so
easily make a man soft and cause him to give way before those
who were harder of heart.

Olav sighed, weary and at a loss. It made him so sad to think of
all those he had loved—Bishop Torfinn, Arnvid, Ingunn. But when
he called to mind Einar Kolbeinsson and his enemies, he was *glad*
he had done it, in spite of it all—nay, repent he *could* not. But he
could not bear being parted from Ingunn now.—He had reached
an utter deadlock.

The candle was almost burned out; Olav crept up and carefully
wound the last of the wick. He went to the door and scanned it
closely—not that he had any hope of being able to escape, but he
felt he must.

It was a heavy, solid door, but it did not shut tight—a deal of
snow had drifted in. He brought the light: there seemed to be a
big lock on the outside and a wooden bar, but there was no part
of the lock on the inside, only a withy handle nailed on. Olav
drew his dagger and tried it in the crack of the door. Then he noticed that the key had not been turned in the lock; the door was
only bolted with the wooden bar, and he could move that a little

with his dagger—only a little, for the bar was big and heavy and the blade of his dagger was thin.

But he was all on fire—his hands were trembling as he put on his boots and outer garments. He could not give up, when once he had found he was not locked in. He took his dagger in both hands and tried to force the bolt upward. At the first attempt the blade broke off in the middle. Olav clenched his teeth and thrust the rest of the blade into the crack right up to the handle. Then there was not room to work the dagger in the narrow crack. Sweating with excitement he coaxed it till he found how far in he could get the dagger—and then to bend it up and lift the bar. Several times he knew he had got it out of the catch, but it fell in again when he let go with one hand to pull the door-handle. But at last he did it.—The snow burst in upon him; he stepped quietly across the threshold and looked out into the night.

No sign of dogs—they must have shut them indoors for the weather. Not a sound but the infinitely fine whistling of dry, powdery snow blown by the wind. Slowly and cautiously Olav worked his way in the dark across the unknown courtyard. In a heap of snow by one of the houses stood a number of skis. Olav chose a pair and went on.

The gate to the street was shut, but close beside it a load of timber had been left. From that he could slip over the paling. He began to believe a miracle was taking place. He climbed the pile and dropped the skis over the fence—heard the soft sound as they fell into the snowdrift outside. "Mother!" he thought—"perhaps it is my mother who is praying for me, that I may get away."

It was awkward with his loose cloak and long kirtle, but he succeeded in getting over and dropped into the snow out in the street. He kilted up his kirtle as high as he could with the belt and bound the skis fast to his feet; then he threw his body forward and set out against the driving snow, which flecked the darkness with streaks of white.

As soon as he reached the end of the town, the road was lost in drifts. Only here and there he made out the tops of the fences, now that his eyes were used to the dark. But he kept on, with the snow in his face almost all the time. It was perfectly impossible to distinguish any road-marks on a night like this, though he knew the farm where she was; he had ridden past it many times on the highway in company with Asbjörn, but that would not help him in this weather. He was as good a ski-runner as the best, but the going was very heavy. Nevertheless he was undaunted and toiled on blindly—he was so certain of being helped tonight. It scarcely crossed his mind that he was quite unarmed—the dagger was useless now—and that he had no more than five or six ducats in money. But he was altogether dauntless.

He did not know what time of night it might be when at last he dragged himself into the yard of the farm where Ingunn lay. Here indeed the dogs were awake—a whole pack of them rushed out at him, barking ferociously. He kept them off with a pole he had picked up on the way, and shouted the while. At last someone appeared in a doorway.

"Is Ingunn Steinfinnsdatter within? I must speak with her instantly—I am Olav Audunsson, her husband."

The short winter day was already sinking and the grey dusk gathering over the snow-covered land as two sledges with worn-out horses drove into the little farm near Ottastad church. The three fur-clad strangers stood awhile talking to the master of the house.

"Ay, she sits within in the room," he said. "Her man is yet in bed, I wis—he came hither at early morn, and then they lay and talked in whispers—our Lord and Saint Olav know what there may be between them, the way they bore themselves—I fell asleep and left them to it—" he scratched his head and looked at the three with shrewd inquiry. Asbjörn Priest he knew well, and the others were Arnvid Finnsson from Miklebö, the woman's kinsman, who had been here more than once and spoken with her, and his old henchman.

The three strode into the room. Ingunn was sitting on the step below the farther bed; she held some sewing work in her lap, but it was too dark for her to sew in that corner. She rose at once on seeing who had come, and went toward them, tall and slender in her black garb, pale and dark-eyed under her woman's coif.

"Hush," she bade them in a low voice, "go quietly—Olav is asleep!"

"Ay, then 'tis time you wake him, little woman," said Asbjörn Priest. "Too much wit I never thought the boy was burdened with, but this is worse than the worst. Can he not guess they will search for him here first of all?—and here he lies asleep!" The priest neighed in his anger.

Ingunn posted herself in the men's way. "What would you with Olav?"

"We wish him no ill," said Arnvid; "but the way he has marred all— You must come with me now, Ingunn, and stay with me at Miklebö, for you can guess that now the lord Torfinn can hardly refuse to give you back to your kinsfolk."

"And what of Olav?" she asked as before.

The priest gave a despairing groan: "She there—is't not the very mischief that he should fly straight hither? She there will never keep a close mouth with what she hears."

"Oh yes, she will. When she sees it is for Olav's good. Ingunn, you must know that this priest here, and I too, we run no small risk in concealing a homicide and helping him to get away."

"I shall know how to hold my peace," said Ingunn seriously. She stepped aside and went up to the bed, where she stood for a moment looking at the sleeper like a mother who has not the heart to wake her child.

The priest thought: "Ah yes, she is fair after all." It seemed to him that these women for whom young boys committed folly and sin were seldom such that a sober and sapient man could see anything goodly in them. And for her here he had had uncommonly little liking: this Ingunn Steinfinnsdatter had the look of a slothful, loose-minded woman, feeble and cosseted, useful for nothing but to make trouble and strife among men. But now, he thought, perchance she was better after all than he had deemed her, she might even make a good wife, when she grew older and steadier of mind. In any case she had conducted herself like a person of sense, and she looked on her friend as though she loved him faithfully. And fair she was, he had to admit they were right who said so.

Olav looked very young and innocent as he lay asleep with his white, muscular arms under his neck and his fair hair spread over the brown woollen pillow. He slept as soundly as a child. But the moment Ingunn took hold of his shoulder and woke him, he started up wide awake, drew up his feet, and sat up in the bed with his arms clasping his knees as he looked calmly at the two men.

"Have you come hither to fetch me?"

"Arnvid has come to take your wife home with him. I—" The priest looked round at the others. "I think you must let me speak with Olav alone first."

Arnvid took Ingunn by the hand and led her to a seat at the farther end of the room. Asbjörn All-fat sat down on the bed beside Olav. Olav asked earnestly: "What says Lord Torfinn to this? An ill chance it is that I should repay his hospitality so badly."

"Ah, there you spoke a truer word than you know yourself. And therefore you must now see that you betake yourself yet farther, out of the land."

"Shall I fly out of the land?" asked Olav slowly. "Uncondemned—? Does Lord Torfinn say I must do this?"

"Nay, I say it. The Bishop and the Sheriff can scarce have heard of the slaying yet—ay, Einar is dead—we look not to see them home before tomorrow. And I made Audun's folk understand that, since they could not hold you better, they ought to keep Kolbein ignorant of your flight till the Sheriff himself could tell him. They are out searching for you now, but with this heavy going they cannot have come so far out as this, and now it will soon be night. Whatever betide, we must venture it, in God's name—we stay here till the moon is up, a little after midnight—'tis clearing up outside and freezing. Old Guttorm will go with you and show the way. Swift ski-runners such as you are should reach Solberga by the evening of the third day. There you must stay with my sister no longer than is necessary and keep in hiding till Sven Birgersson finds you a lodging somewhere in the neighbourhood."

"But can this be wise, to fly the country before I have been condemned to it?" asked Olav.

"Since you have taken wings, you must fly on," said the priest. "Will you have folk say of you that you broke out of prison merely to come hither and fondle your wife? Nay, you need not look at me so madly because I say this to you.—Young you are and bull-headed, and little thought have you beyond your own affairs; such is the nature of your age. And maybe you have not thought that a man like Lord Torfinn may have many matters on hand of greater moment than that you should enjoy your Ingunn and her goods in peace. And you came with this suit of yours at an inconvenient time—hardly could you have found a worse time to trouble the Bishop with your concerns—"

"Ay, 'twas Arnvid's counsel, not mine," Olav interrupted.

"Oh, Arnvid! He is as ill-timed as you, when it is a question of this frail wisp of a woman. But as I told you, Olav, we must now order it so that the Bishop shall not have to deal with this case of manslaughter too; here your kinsmen must come forward, and it will be their affair to obtain leave for your return, so that you may buy your peace in the lands of Norway's King."

"I wonder," said Olav pondering. "I scarce think Bishop Torfinn will like it that I go off in this way."

"No, he will not," said the priest curtly. "And it is for that I will have you do it. These new men, who rule the realm for our little King, are making ready for open war against Holy Church— and the lord Torfinn must have his hands free of such suits as yours. Had you been shut up in Mjös Castle, he would have leaped into the saddle for your sake—because you have sought his help and because you have few friends, and the lord Torfinn is so saintly and a true holy father to all the fatherless—and withal he is obstinate and headstrong as a he-goat; that is his chief fault. But I expect you to understand this: you have sought his protection *once*, and you were given it, and after that you disgraced yourself as you have done. 'Twould not be very manly of you to ask more of him now, knowing that you add to his difficulties thereby."

Olav nodded in silence. He stood up and began to dress.

"It will be more difficult for us now," he said quietly, "for Ingunn and me—to be brought together."

"At the last I trow her kinsmen will tire of having to keep her— when she is neither rightly married nor unmarried," said the priest. "But you two can surely wait a few years now."

Olav contracted his brows, looking straight before him. "That we have promised each other last night—we shall keep the troth we plighted to each other, and I shall come back to her, alive or dead."

"That was an ungodly promise," said Asbjörn dryly. "But 'tis as I thought.—It is an easy matter, Olav, to be a good Christian so long as God asks no more of you than to hear sweet singing in church, and to yield Him obedience while He caresses you with

the hand of a father. But a man's faith is put to the test on the day
God's will is not his. But now I will tell you what Bishop Torfinn
said to me one day—it was of you and your suit we were speaking.
'God grant,' he said, 'that he may learn to understand in time that
whoso is minded to do as he himself wills will soon enough see
the day when he will find he has done that which he had never
willed.' "

Olav looked earnestly before him. Then he nodded: "Ay. That
is true. I know it."

They took some food, and awhile after, they lay down in their
clothes, all but Arnvid; he offered to watch. He sat beside the
hearth, reading softly from a book he had brought in his travel-
ling-wallet. Now and again he went out of doors to see the time.
It had cleared now and the stars sparkled densely over the whole
vault of heaven—it was freezing hard. Once he knelt down and
prayed with his arms stretched out in the form of a cross.

At last he saw that the light of the rising moon was growing
over the top of the ridge. He turned and went in, to the bed where
Olav and Ingunn slept together, cheek to cheek. He roused the
man: "Now it is near time you were gone."

Olav opened his eyes, gently freed himself from the woman's
arms, and at once got out of bed. He was fully clad, all but his
boots and outer garment. He now drew on his footgear and a
coat of reindeer-skin; Arnvid had provided clothing more suited
to a long journey on skis than the kirtle and the red cordwain
boots, which had suffered badly on the night before.

"This Guttorm of mine knows his way everywhere about here
on both sides of the border," said Arnvid. This was Arnvid's old
henchman, his foster-father he might be called, who was to act as
guide for Olav. Arnvid handed Olav his own sword, a spear, and
a purse of money. "We will say that you have sold me your horse
Elk—you know I have always wished he was mine."

"So be it."

"That foul talk Einar came out with—" muttered Arnvid hesitatingly as he looked down into the fire. "He was always ill-natured and a liar— And a lecherous goat himself, and never guessed
that other men may—may turn sick at what he—"

Olav cast down his eyes, mortally embarrassed. He understood
not a word.

"I was fain you should have Ingunn, for I believed you would be good to her.—Will you swear, Olav, never to desert my kinswoman?"

"Yes. And I may rely that you will hold your hand over her? Did I not know that I can feel safe leaving her in your care, I would never in this world do as Asbjörn says and fly to Sweden. But I know you are fond of her—"

"I am." Arnvid burst out laughing. He struggled against it, but could not stop; he trembled with suppressed giggling till the tears ran down his cheeks. At last he sat doubled up and laughed till he shook, with his arms on his knees and his head buried in them. Olav stood by, profoundly uncomfortable.

"Nay—now you and Guttorm must be gone." Arnvid pulled himself together, wiped the tears of laughter from his face, and stood up. He went and called the three others.

Olav and old Guttorm stood out in the yard, with their skis bound fast to their feet, well armed, and furnished with all they required. The three others stood before the door of the house as Ingunn went up to Olav and gave him her hand. He shook it hard, and they spoke together, a few words, in low tones. She was calm and altogether self-possessed.

The waning moon had soared up into the sky high enough to cast long, uncertain shadows across the heaped-up drifts of the snow-field.

"In the forest the going will be fine, I trow," the priest encouraged them.

Olav turned and glided back to his two friends who stood at the door. He shook hands with them too and thanked them handsomely for their help. Then he faced about. Arnvid Finnsson and Asbjörn stood watching the two, Olav Audunsson and his guide, as they glided over the long stretch of fields toward the forest with powerful, dogged strokes. Then they passed into the shadow at the edge of the woods.

"Ay, *laus Deo*," said the priest. "So ill is it that this is the best. I was afraid Ingunn would break out into a fit, shriek and howl at the last minute."

"Oh no," said Arnvid. He looked up at the moon with a strangely frolicsome smile. " 'Tis only in trifles that she takes on like that. When serious matters are at stake, she is as good as gold."

"Say you so?—ay, you should know her better than I," said Asbjörn Priest unconcernedly. "Now it is we two, Arnvid. This may prove a dear jest for us, that we have helped Olav Audunsson to get away."

"Ay, but there was no other way."

"No." The priest shook his head. "But I wonder whether Olav has any notion that you and I have risked *much* by helping him in this?"

"Nay, have you lost your wits?" said Arnvid, and the waves of laughter heaved up in him again. "You surely know he has no notion of what *anything* costs, at his age."

Asbjörn All-fat gave a little laugh; then he yawned. And the three, the priest, the other man, and the woman, went in and lay down again.

THE AXE

PART TWO

INGUNN STEINFINNSDATTER

INGUNN
STEINFINNSDATTER

I

FTER Olav Audunsson's flight Bishop Torfinn said he no
longer had the right to keep back Ingunn Steinfinnsdatter
from her uncles. But Arnvid Finnsson answered that the
woman was sick and he could not send her away. Lord Torfinn
was very angry when he learned that Arnvid too refused to bow
to the law further than it suited himself. And now the Bishop
sought to order matters so that Ingunn should go to her father's
sister at Berg; but Arnvid said that she was utterly unfit for any
journey.

On their side Kolbein Toresson and Haftor were beside themselves with wrath that Olav had escaped, and they said the Bishop
certainly had had a finger in it—though the lord Torfinn had been
away from the town when the slaying was done and did not return home till after the slayer had fled—and though Arnvid Finnsson made known that it was he who had helped Olav over to
Sweden. When it came out that Asbjörn All-fat had been privy
to the matter and that the fugitive had been received by the
priest's sister, who was married in Sweden, Lord Torfinn was so
indignant that he sent Asbjörn away from him for a time, after
the priest had bought his peace for his part in the affair. But although no man seriously believed that the Bishop had been a party
to Olav's flight, there were many who counted him to blame in
that one of his priests had broken the law, connived with an outlaw, and helped him to safety.

The Sheriff proclaimed Olav's outlawry, and then at last Helge
of Tveit and his sons came forward and offered on Olav's behalf to make amends for the slaying according to the judgment
of good men and true at the Thing. However, these men were not
Olav's nearest kinsmen; they were descended from a brother of
his great-grandfather, and the two branches, that of Tveit and

that of Hestviken, had held little intercourse through the years. The old man at Hestviken was Olav's true guardian. It was therefore a long and difficult matter for Olav's spokesmen to accomplish anything in his case, and as Bishop Torfinn had to journey to Björgvin on another errand in the course of the spring, he let Jon Helgesson of Tveit go thither in his company, in order that he might beg permission of the King for Olav to return to the country.[1]

Kolbein demanded that Olav should be declared a felon. What could it be but a felony? he maintained—Olav had debauched Kolbein's niece in her father's house and afterwards struck down the girl's cousin when he called Olav to account for his misdeed. As his spokesmen at Björgvin, Kolbein chose the knight Gaut Torvardsson and his son Haakon. Sir Gaut was a kinsman of Baron Andres Plytt; Lord Andres sat in the council that was to govern Norway while the King was under age, and he was one of the leaders of those nobles who were now determined to join issue with the prelates over the rights and liberties of the Church. It appeared that these were the men on whose support the Toressons had relied, and Haakon Gautsson was to have had Ingunn to wife.

Then once more the Bishop of Hamar took upon himself to plead Olav's cause. He insisted that it was impossible to charge Olav with rape if he had taken Ingunn to himself in good faith in an old betrothal, and Ivar and Kolbein had already promised to grant Olav atonement on this score when the man had the misfortune to kill Einar in a brawl, as they sat drinking with several other men in the preaching friars' guest-house at Hamar. He said it would be the direst injustice if Olav were not accorded the same mercy as any other man who became a homicide—be given grace to remain at home and security for his possessions, if he was willing to pay weregild to the King and blood-fine to Einar Kolbeinsson's heirs. Although, for that matter, in every parish of Norway might be found men who had manslaughters or other outlawry charges hanging over them sitting safely on their estates with royal letters of grace—nay, those who thought them-

[1] "When a man had committed any offence punishable with outlawry (such as manslaughter or the abduction of a woman), he might, on making a payment to the Crown, be given leave to remain at his home under the protection of the law till his case was judged."—(Note to *The Mistress of Husaby.*)

selves powerful enough stayed calmly on without such letters.
But then it must be plain to every man that it was beyond measure unjust if harsher treatment were meted out to Olav, who was
so young that, had it not been for the last amendment of the law
under their late lord, King Magnus, none could have done him
any worse thing than order him to leave the country and stay
abroad until he was of age. And Olav had at once sent word to
Kolbein through Arnvid Finnsson and Asbjörn All-fat that he was
quite willing to pay the fine for the slaughter.

Olav had entered Norway again at Whitsuntide down in Elvesyssel, near Mariaskog convent. He owned a small farm there
which he held on udal tenure, and some shares in other farms;
this estate had come to the men of Hestviken with the wife of
Olav's grandfather, Ingolf Olavsson. Here no one attempted to
seize him, but the King's officers let him stay in peace till far on
in the autumn—it was a long way from the parts frequented by
Olav's enemies. But when proclamation was made in the autumn
that Olav Audunsson's goods in the north had been attached—the
movables he had left behind him in the Upplands and his estate
in the Vik, save only his udal lands—Olav left the country for the
second time, and now he sailed southward to Denmark.

At Miklebö, Mistress Hillebjörg had given Ingunn Steinfinnsdatter a good reception. She had liked Olav, the little she had
seen of him, and she liked him no less for having made an inroad
on the brood of Tore's leman. She treated her son with more
kindness than she was wont, and when a suit of outlawry was
brought against Arnvid for having helped Olav, she laughed and
patted him on the shoulder. " 'Twas none too soon either, my
son, that you too had a taste of the law; I never liked your meek
ways."

She was gentler with the sick young woman than Arnvid had
ever seen her with anyone. Ingunn was no more than moderately
well; she was so troubled with giddiness that when she got out of
bed in the morning, she had to stand a long while holding on to
something, for the room turned round with her, and dark mists
came before her eyes, so that she could not see. If she had to
stoop and pick up anything from the floor, this mist came on and
blinded her for a long time. She could not take food, and she fell
away and grew thin, till she was pale to the very corners of her

eyes. Hillebjörg brewed drinks for her, which were to remedy her affliction—but Ingunn could not keep these either. The old woman laughed and consoled her—'twas known such sickliness endured but for its time, and soon she would feel better. Ingunn made no reply when the mistress jested in this way, but bent her head and tried to hide the tears that filled her eyes. Otherwise she never wept, but was very quiet and patient.

She was not fit to perform the smallest piece of work, but sat with a ribbon in her hand, sewing a border of fine flowers and animals. Or else she was making the linen shirt she had cut out while she was at Hamar. She had always been skilful at fine needlework, and she put all her art and industry into this shirt, which Olav was to have when he came home; but the work went but slowly. Or she made playthings for Arnvid's sons, wove them breastplates of straw, feathered their arrows, and made bats and balls that were better than any they had had before. It was because she had always played with boys that she could do this so well, she told Arnvid. Olav had taught her this. She sang to the children and told them stories and rhymes, and she seemed to be of better cheer when caring for these three little lads—she would gladly have had one of the children on her knees always. Magnus was five years old now, and the twins, Finn and Steinar, nearly four. Magnus and Finn were strong, romping little fellows and did not care so much to be fondled by women, but Steinar was weaker and took a fancy to Ingunn. So she led the boy with her wherever she went, carried him in her arms, and took him to her bed at night. Steinar was also his father's favourite, and Arnvid often sat with Ingunn in the evening, while the child played on her lap, and he sang to them till the little one fell asleep with his head resting on Ingunn's bosom. Then she whispered to him to be quiet, and sat in silence, gazing before her and down at the sleeping child, kissed the boy's hair softly, and gazed into vacancy again.

But as it drew on toward summer, it became clear that there was no natural cause for Ingunn's disorder, and no one could guess what ailed her.

Arnvid wondered whether it could be sorrow alone that had broken her down so completely—for she grew no better, but rather worse: the fainting-fits gained upon her, and often she fell into a swoon, all the food she tried to eat came up again, and she complained of constant pains in the back across her hips, as though she had had a heavy blow with a stick—and there was such a queer feeling in her legs, as though they were withered; she was scarcely able to walk any more.

She longed for Olav day and night, Arnvid could see that, and then there was her sorrow over her parents, which had now come upon her again; for a while she had half forgotten it on Olav's account. But now she accused herself bitterly for this, saying she had thrown away by her fault a happiness that bade fair to be hers: "The night that mother died I became Olav's wife!"

A strange look came over Arnvid's face as she said this, but he held his peace.

She grieved also at being parted from her brothers and sister. Tora was at Berg with her aunt, and though there had never been any very warm affection between Ingunn and Tora, she now longed for her sister. But it was far sadder to think of her two young brothers; with them she had always been good friends, but now they were at Frettastein with Haftor and his young wife—and now of course Hallvard and Jon would be brought up in hatred of Olav Audunsson and anger with her.

She spoke of all this to Arnvid, without many tears—but it was almost as though she were too hopeless and heavy of heart to be able to weep. Arnvid wondered whether she would die of grief.

But Mistress Ingebjörg hinted that this sickness that had fallen upon Ingunn was so strange as almost to persuade her it was the work of some *guile*.

One evening at the beginning of summer Arnvid was able to coax Ingunn to walk down with him to look at the corn that was coming up so finely in the fair weather. He had to support her as she walked, and he saw that she moved her feet as though they were hindered by invisible fetters. He had got her as far as the edge of the wood when she suddenly sank to the ground and lay in a swoon. At long last he succeeded in bringing her back to life; so long he thought her fits had never lasted before. She could not stand on her feet, so he had to carry her in as one carries a child. She was so thin and weighed so little that he was quite scared.

Next morning it proved that she could not move her legs—the lower part of her body was quite paralysed. At first she lay moaning softly—the pains in her back were so grievous. But as the days went by they passed off, and now her body seemed to be entirely without feeling, from the waist downward. In this state she remained. She never complained, spoke but little, and often seemed absent from all around her. The only thing she asked for was to have Steinar with her, and when he crept up into the bed and played and frolicked over her half-dead body, which was now wasted to a skeleton, she appeared to be content.

During this time none knew where Olav was. Arnvid thought that Ingunn must surely die, and he could send no word to Olav of how matters were with her.

But Mistress Hillebjörg now said aloud to everyone she spoke with that it was certain someone had put the sickness upon Ingunn by witchcraft. She had stuck pins into the woman's thighs and calves and burned her with red-hot irons, but Ingunn felt nothing; she could bring witnesses to this, men and women of good repute and her parish priest and her son. But there was none beside Kolbein and Haftor who could be suspected of this misdeed. And here lay the unhappy child, wasting away and slowly dying. Now therefore she charged her son that he should call upon the Bishop to take up the matter and inquire into it.

Arnvid came near believing his mother had guessed rightly, and he promised to go to the lord Torfinn, as soon as the Bishop came home from his visitation. Meanwhile he made Ingunn speak to the priest and make her confession, and he had masses said for her. Thus the time passed till the birthday of our Lady.[2]

That day Arnvid had confessed and taken *corpus Domini,* and during mass he had prayed for his sick kinswoman so long and so earnestly that he was all in a sweat. It was past noonday before the church folk from Miklebö came home. Arnvid stood talking to Guttorm about his horse Elk, which had fallen lame as he rode homeward, when he heard loud cries for help from the room in which Ingunn lay.

He and Guttorm dashed headlong to the room. There they saw Ingunn, running barefoot and in her shift and tramping on the floor—the room was full of smoke and the straw was alight among the rugs she had thrown upon it. She held Steinar in her arms; he was wrapped in the bedspread, shrieking and wailing.

When the others came in, she sank down on the bench, kissing

[2] September 8.

and fondling the boy and trying to lull him: "Steinar, Steinar, my darling, now you will soon be better, now I will make you so well, my little one!" She called to the others that Steinar had burned himself and they must bring her cloths and ointment at once.

She had been lying alone, and Steinar was in the room with her; he had been sitting by the hearth, where a tiny fire was burning, and although the woman in the bed told him he must not, he had played with it, sticking dry twigs into the fire and letting them burn. The day was warm, and the boy had nothing on but a shirt—all at once the fire caught it. Then Ingunn knew no more till she was standing by the hearth with the child in her arms; she had put out the fire in his shirt by throwing the coverlet about him; but now she saw that the rushes with which the floor was strewed were burning, and so she threw down the cushions from the benches and trampled the fire as she cried for help.

The boy had been burned about the body, but Ingunn too had ugly burns on her legs and on the under side of both arms. But she heeded nothing but Steinar; they were not allowed to bind her wounds until the child had been tended, and then she laid him in her bed and lay watching over him, fondling and wheedling the poor little thing. And as long as the boy had fever and pain from his burns, she gave no thought to other things.

The palsy had slipped from her—she herself seemed scarce aware of it. She ate and drank what they brought her, greedily and unthinking, and the terrible vomiting and dizziness had altogether ceased. Arnvid sat by Steinar day and night, and, cruelly as it hurt him to see the boy suffer so, he nevertheless thanked God for the miracle that had happened to Ingunn.

From now on she quickly grew better, and when Steinar was well enough to be carried out into the sun to look at the snow that had fallen in the night, Ingunn had got back a little of her delicate roundness of face and form, and her cheeks flushed pink in the frosty air. She stood with Steinar on her arm waiting for Arnvid, who was away among the rocks collecting frozen haws in his hat—Steinar had said his father *must* find some berries for him.

The prospects of a reconciliation between Arnvid and the rest of Ingunn's kinsfolk had not been improved by these rumours Mistress Hillebjörg had spread abroad about Kolbein—that he had had spells cast upon his niece to bring her to her death. And when the betrothal ale was drunk at Frettastein, for Haakon Gautsson and Tora Steinfinnsdatter, a short time before Advent, no one from Miklebö was present at the ceremony. The wedding was held at the New Year in 1282, and afterwards the newly married pair went round visiting the young wife's kinsfolk, for Haakon was the youngest of many brothers and had no house of his own in the westland. It was intended that he should settle in the Upplands.

But now there came word from the lady Magnhild of Berg that she wished to take Ingunn. Ivar and Kolbein had promised that they would leave the girl in peace if she would stay there quietly and live in chastity. Arnvid swore horribly when Brother Vegard told him this, but he could not deny that he had no legal right to dispose of Ingunn. And Mistress Hillebjörg was beginning to be tired of her guest: now that Ingunn was well she had no patience with the young woman, who was only for show and no use at all. And the message Lady Magnhild had sent was no more than was reasonable: she had her old mother with her, Aasa Magnusdatter, the widow of Tore of Hov; the old lady was infirm and had need of her granddaughter for help and pastime.

Just before Easter, then, Arnvid went to Berg with Ingunn.

Lady Magnhild was the eldest of all Tore's true-born children; she was now a woman of two score years and ten—the same age as her half-brother Kolbein Toresson. She was the widow of the knight Viking Erlingsson. Children she had never had; in order to do good, therefore, she took to herself young maids, the daughters of kinsmen or friends, and taught them courtesy and such attainments as were suited to women of good birth; for Lady Magnhild had seen much of the King's court while her husband was alive. She had also offered to receive her nieces from Frettastein, but Steinfinn—or Ingebjörg—had been unwilling to send the little maids to her, and Lady Magnhild had been exceeding angry thereat. So when it came out that Ingunn had let herself be ensnared by her foster-brother, she said it had turned out as she expected: the children had been ill brought up, and their mother had been disobedient to her father and false to her betrothed, so it seemed most likely that Steinfinn's daughters would bring shame on their race.

Ingunn was tired and low-spirited as she sat in the sledge on the last stage of the journey through the forest. They had been several days on the road, for the weather had set in mild, with snow, as soon as they left Miklebö. Now toward evening it froze hard, and Arnvid walked beside the sledge and drove, as the road was bad—in places over bare rock, slippery with ice, in others through deep snowdrifts, for no one had passed this way since the last snowfall.

When they came out of the woods, the sun was low above the ridge facing them; it was an orange ball behind the mist, and the dark, rugged ice of the bay had a dull and coppery gleam. The mist had frosted the snow-covered woods and fens, so that all was grey and ugly as evening drew on. Down in the fields Arnvid's men struggled on; they and the sledge with the baggage went straight ahead through the snow. The manor lay down by the water, at some distance from the other houses of the parish—the woods formed a barrier, so that from Berg one could not see any of the other great farms about.

Ingunn had not seen her aunt since she came to Hamar, well-nigh a year and a half ago, and then the lady of Berg had been harsh toward her. She did not expect much good of the lady Magnhild this time either.

Arnvid hoisted himself onto the edge of the sledge, as it dipped into the first hollow.

"Look not so sorrowful, Ingunn," he begged her. " 'Twill be hard parting from you, if you are so faint-hearted."

Ingunn said: "Faint-hearted I am not; you know that I have not complained. But I shall not be in the hands of friends here. Pray to God for me, kinsman, that I may keep a firm mind, for I look to be sorely tried, so long as I must bide here at Berg."

But as they drove into the courtyard the lady Magnhild herself came out and received Ingunn in friendly fashion. She led her niece into the women's room and bade the maids bring warm drinks and dry footgear. She herself helped the young woman to take off her fur-lined boots and coat of skins. But then she said, taking hold of a corner of Ingunn's coif: "This you must now put off."

Ingunn turned red. "I have worn the coif ever since I was at Hamar. The Bishop bade me cover my hair—he said no virtuous woman goes bareheaded when she is no longer a maid."

"*He!*" sneered Lady Magnhild. "He has so many fancies— But now so much time has passed that the gossip has died down hereabouts. I will not have you blow fresh life into the rumours of your own shame by going here like a fool in married woman's attire. Take off the kerchief and turn your belt again. 'Twas a mercy at least that you were never *forced* to buckle it at the side."

Ingunn wore a leather belt around her waist, set with little silver studs and handsomely mounted at the end that hung down. Lady Magnhild took hold of it and pulled it straight, so that the buckle came in front. Again she ordered Ingunn to take off her headcovering.

"All *know* this about me," said Ingunn hotly. "If I do this, folk must think worse of me and deem me an immodest woman—if I am to go bareheaded when I have no right to that—as the wantons do."

Lady Magnhild said: "There is your grandmother too, Ingunn; she is old now. She remembers well enough all things that happened in her youth, but new tidings she forgets as soon as she hears them. Every day we should have to tell her afresh why you were to go in matron's dress."

"'Twould be easy to answer her that my husband is gone away."

"And soon it will come to Kolbein's ears that you stand by the old claims, and his hatred of Olav will never cool down. Be reasonable now, Ingunn, and cease these follies."

Ingunn unbound her coif and began to fold it together. It was the finest she had—four ells long and sewed with silk. Hillebjörg had given it her the year before, saying she could use it for a church-going coif and wear it the first time she went to mass with Olav, when he came home.

She drew the pins out of her hair and let the heavy yellow locks fall about her shoulders.

"And such goodly hair you have," said Lady Magnhild. "Most women would be glad to make boast of it awhile longer, Ingunn— if they could have no joy of their man, and the coif brought them no power or authority. Let it hang loose this evening, I pray you."

"Oh no, aunt," begged Ingunn, almost in tears. "*That* you must never ask me!" She divided her mass of hair and bound it in two plaits, stiff and unadorned.

Arnvid was already sitting at the table when Lady Magnhild and Ingunn came into the room. He looked up, and his eyes clouded over.

"Is it thus they will have it here?" he asked later, when they said good-night to each other. "You are not to be allowed the honour of a married woman?"

"Nay, you may see that," was all Ingunn said.

Aasa Magnusdatter had a house to herself at Berg with a loft-room and two maidservants to do the housework and cooking, and to spin and weave all the flax and wool that fell to her share. Grim and Dalla, the old bailiff and his sister from Frettastein, looked after her beasts, which stood in Lady Magnhild's byre; these two had been given a little cot to dwell in, close by the cow-house, but they were counted as part of Aasa's household.

Ingunn then had nothing to do at Berg but to be, as it were, at the head of her grandmother's little household and to be a solace to the old woman. She mostly sat with her grandmother when the maids were at their work.

As Lady Magnhild had said, Aasa was now grown somewhat childish, she remembered little of what was said to her, but asked again and again about the same things day after day. Sometimes she asked after her youngest son, Steinfinn, whether he had been there lately or whether they expected him soon. Often, however, she remembered that he was dead. Then she would ask: was it not four children he had alive? "And you are the oldest? Ah yes, I know that very well; your name is Ingunn—after my mother, for Ingebjörg's mother was still living when you came, and she had cursed her daughter for running away with Steinfinn. Ay, he was simple-minded and glad of heart, my Steinfinn, and it came to cost him dear that he was so nice in his choice of a leman that he carried off a knight's daughter by force. . . ." Aasa had never liked Ingebjörg, and she used often to talk of Steinfinn and his wife, without remembering that it was their daughter she spoke to. "But how was it now—did not a great misfortune befall one of these little maids of Steinfinn's? Nay, that cannot be so—they cannot be so old yet?"

"Dear Grandmother," Ingunn begged in her embarrassment, "you should try to get a little sleep now."

"Oh ay, Gyrid, perchance that were best for me—" Aasa often called her granddaughter Gyrid, taking her for a Gyrid Alfsdatter, a kinswoman who had been at Berg some fifteen winters before.

But all that had happened in her young days Mistress Aasa remembered clearly. She spoke of her parents and of her brother Finn, Arnvid's father, and of her sister-in-law, Hillebjörg, whom she both loved and feared—although Hillebjörg was much younger than Aasa.

When fourteen winters old she had been given to Tore of Hov. Before that he had lived with that Borghild for over ten years, and very loath he was to send away his leman—she did not depart from Hov until the morning of the very day when Aasa was brought there as a bride. Borghild continued to have great power over Tore as long as she lived—and that was for twenty years after the man's marriage. He consulted her about all matters of importance, and he often took his true-born children to her, that she might foretell their future and judge whether they seemed promising. But Tore bestowed his greatest efforts and his love chiefly on the four children he had had by his leman. Borghild was the daughter of a woman thrall and a nobleman—some said, one of those kings that Norway was full of at that time. She was fair and wise, and a bold schemer, but haughty, rapacious, and cruel to folk of low degree.

Meanwhile Aasa Magnusdatter was mistress of Hov. She bore her husband fourteen children, but five died in the cradle, and only four lived to grow up.

Aasa remembered all her dead children and used to speak of them. She mourned most for a daughter, Herdis, who became palsied from having slept out on the dewy ground. She died four years afterwards, when she was eleven winters old. A half-grown son had been kicked to death by his horse, and Magnus had lost his life in a brawl on board the ship, when coming home across the lake from a banquet in Toten together with other drunken young men. Magnus had just been married, but there was no child after him, and the widow married again in another part of the country. Aasa had liked her best of her daughters-in-law.

"But tell me, Grandmother," asked Ingunn, "have you had naught but sorrow in your life? Have you no good days to think upon now?"

Her grandmother looked at her and seemed not to understand. Now, as she lay waiting for death, she seemed to take as much pleasure in recalling her sorrows as her joys.

Ingunn did not thrive ill in this life with the old woman. Weak she was, even now when she had her health, and she had never liked to have to do anything that demanded hard work or continued thought. She would sit with some fine needlework that there was no need to finish in a hurry, lost in her own thoughts, while she listened with half an ear to her grandmother's talk.

In her growing years she had been restless and had found it hard to sit still for long at a time. But now it was different. The strange sickness that had fallen upon her after the separation from Olav seemed to have left behind a shadow that would not give way; it was as though she were always in a half-dreaming state.— At Frettastein she had had all the boys, and Olav first and last, and they had brought games and excitement and life to her, who herself lacked enterprise to undertake anything. Here at Berg there were only women, two old ladies and their servants, and a few elderly house-carls and workmen; they could not rouse her from the torpor into which she had sunk while she lay paralysed in bed, expecting to wither away altogether from among the living.

When Olav was whisked away, she seemed to have no strength to believe he would ever come back. All too many great events had overwhelmed her in the short time between her father's departure to seek out Mattias Haraldsson and Arnvid's taking her to Hamar. She felt she had been carried away by a flood, and the time at Hamar was like an eddy, in which she and Olav had been churned round in a ring, slowly but surely passing farther and farther from each other. There all had been new and strange, and Olav had changed till even he seemed to have become a stranger. She could understand indeed that it was right of him never to seek an opportunity for meeting her in secret while they were there. But that he should have taken it as he did when she brought about that meeting with him on Christmas Night—that had frightened her into a corner; she had felt so shamed and

abandoned afterwards that she dared not even *think* of him as
she had done before, lingeringly, with a sweet, hot desire for his
love. She was like a child that has been corrected and punished
by a grown-up—she herself had never guessed there could be anything wrong in it.

Then he had come to her that last night, out of the darkness
and the driving snow, worn out and agitated, shaking between
tiredness and suppressed ferocity—an outlawed man with her
cousin's blood yet warm on his hands. She had been self-possessed
in a way. But when he left her, it was as though all the waters
closed over her.

At first, when she was so sick, she too had thought that it was
with her as Mistress Hillebjörg said. But as time went on and it
became clear that she was not to have a child, she scarce had the
strength to feel disappointed. She was so worn out that it would
have seemed too much if she had had more to look for, of either
good or ill. She bore it with patience that she was so sick and
that none could tell what ailed her and that there seemed to be
no cure for her. If she tried to look forward into the future, she
saw naught but black, waving mists like the darkness that whirled
before her eyes when she had her swooning-fits.

Then she plunged deep into the memories of all that had been
between Olav and her that last summer and autumn. She closed
both eyes and kissed her own plait of hair and hands and arms
and made believe it was Olav. But the more she abandoned herself to dreams and desires, the more unreal it seemed to her that
these things had happened in truth. That the end of the matter
would be that they were united at last, in peace and with full
right, she had indeed believed, but never been able to imagine—
just as she believed, but was little able to imagine all that she had
heard of the priests about a blissful state in the other world.

So she lay powerless, not expecting ever to regain the use of her
limbs. With it the last rope was broken that still held her to the
everyday life and occupations of other men and women. She no
longer hoped that she would ever be lawfully married to Olav
Audunsson, would be mistress of his house and mother of his
children. Instead she allowed herself to drift as the sport of dreams
which she never looked to see fulfilled.

Every evening, when the candle was extinguished and the fire
raked out, she played that Olav came and lay down with her.

Every morning, when she awoke, she played that her husband
had risen and gone out. She lay listening to the sounds of the
great farm, playing that she was at Hestviken; and she played that
it was Olav who had the hay carted in, that they were his horses
and sledges, and that it was he who set his folk to their work.
When Steinar lay still for a moment in her bed, she laid her thin
arm about the boy, pressed his fair head against her breast, and
to herself she called the boy Audun, and he was her son and
Olav's. Then he wanted to get up and out, struggled to free himself from her embrace. Ingunn coaxed him to stay by giving him
dainty morsels of food she had hidden in her bed, telling him
stories, and playing at being a mother who was talking to her
child.

The first thing that waked her out of her dreams and play when
she came to Berg was Lady Magnhild's taking the coif from her.
Never before had she looked upon it as a shame that she had become Olav's own. At Frettastein she had thought so little, only
loved. Only when both Olav and Arnvid were suddenly so ur-
gent to go to Hamar and have Olav's right to her acknowledged
had anything like confusion been aroused in her. But when the
good Bishop sent her the modest white linen and bade her bind
up her hair, she grew calm again. Even if she had wronged her
uncles, who should have been her sponsors after her father's death,
the lord Torfinn would surely make all well again, and then she
would be as good a wife as all other married women.

She was chilled with humiliation in the unwonted feeling of
being bareheaded, after wearing the married woman's garb for a
year and a half. It was as though she had been immodestly bared
by violent hands—as they did with women thralls in the slave
market in former times. She excused herself from going across
to Magnhild's house when strangers were there. She did not willingly show herself abroad among folk except in church—there *all*
women had to cover their heads. Ingunn drew the hood of her
cloak over her face so that not a hair was seen. To make some
small amends for having to clothe herself as was unfitting for her,
she put away all jewels, wore none but dark, plain kirtles, and
did her hair in two hard, stiff plaits without ribbons or other
adornment.

Then came the spring. One day the ice sank in the bay, the
water lay open and clear and reflected the green hills on both
shores. Now Berg was at its fairest. Ingunn led her grandmother
out on the sunny side and sat with her, sewing the shirt for Olav
Audunsson. Olav had told her that Hestviken lay on the fiord.

She found some trifles to busy herself with in the loft-room that
belonged to Aasa. Morning after morning she spent up there, rum-
maging and tidying. Ingunn took the shutter from the little window and leaned out.

A boat was rowing under the opposite shore—the dark reflection of the wooded hill was broken by long streaks. Ingunn played
at its being Olav and the boy who were in the boat. They were
rowing this way—Ingunn could *see* it. They put in at the hard
and Audun helped his father to make the boat fast. The father
stood up on the wooden pier and the boy was busy in the stern
of the boat, collecting their things. At last he took his little axe,
Olav held out his hand and helped him up—ay, the boy was now
as big as Jon, her youngest brother. The two came up the path
toward the house, the father first and the son following.

She also had a little daughter, whose name was Ingebjörg. She
was out in the yard—she was just coming from the storehouse,
carrying a great wooden tray full of bannocks. She broke one of
them up and scattered the crumbs to the hens—no, the geese.
Ingunn remembered that they had had geese at Frettastein when
she was a little child, and there was something grave and imposing
about the heavy white and grey-flecked birds. They would have
geese at Hestviken.

Softly, as though she were doing something wrong, she stole to
the door and shot the bolt. Then she took a coif from her chest
and wound it about her head. Ingunn turned her belt, so that the
buckle was at the side; she hung on it all the heavy things she
could find—a pair of scissors and some keys. Thus adorned she
sat on the edge of the empty bedstead that was in the loft; with
her hands in her lap she turned over in her mind all the things
that had to be done before her husband and children came in.

At Berg it was only now and then that they heard anything of
the remarkable events which took place in Norway that year.
Almost no news reached Ingunn, shut up as she was in her grandmother's house. So it was like a bolt from the blue when she heard

one day that Bishop Torfinn had been declared an outlaw and was said to have left the country.

It was their parish priest who brought this news to the house, one day at the beginning of winter. For some months the lord Torfinn had been on a visitation in Norddalen, and from thence it seemed he had intended to meet the Archbishop somewhere in the outer islands. But before he could do so, these barons, who now possessed all the power in the realm, had outlawed the Archbishop and several of the other bishops and persecuted them till they fled the country in all directions. Bishop Torfinn was said to have gone on board a ship, but none knew what had become of him since, or when he might return to his see. The parish priest did not grieve for this—the Bishop had reproved him for indolence and for neglecting to punish the sins of great folks as they deserved; but the priest thought himself a good shepherd enough, and there was no need to treat *his* flock in the Bishop's way; he had been very angry with that stiff-necked monk, as he called him.

It was clear that the conflict between the bishops and the young King's advisers was concerned with great matters of state, and this marriage suit of Olav Audunsson was a trifle of no account—although it was brought forward as an instance of the Bishop of Hamar's intolerable obstinacy and desire to upset the ancient laws of the land. But the parish priest wished to remain good friends with the rich lady of Berg—and perhaps he had no idea how little this affair of the marriage of two children meant outside the parishes where the families of the young people were known. From the way he talked, it might be thought Bishop Torfinn had been outlawed mainly because he had held his hand over the Steinfinnssons' worst enemy.

Ingunn was seized by a terrible dread. Scared into wakefulness, she saw again her position as it was in reality, and all her dreams collapsed suddenly, as a flowery meadow is blighted by a frosty night. She realized with a shiver that she was but a defenceless and deserted orphan, neither maid nor wife; she had not a friend to maintain her rights—Olav was away, none knew where, the Bishop was gone, Arnvid was far off and she could not send him a message. She had no one on whom to lean, except her old grandmother, who was in second childhood, if her ungentle kinsmen were minded to take revenge on her.—She clung, a little trem-

bling, quivering creature, to the only firmness in her weak, in-
stinct-governed soul—she would hold fast to Olav and be true to
him, even if they were to torture her to death for his sake.

At about this time—during Advent—Tora Steinfinnsdatter and
her husband, Haakon Gautsson, came to Berg. Haakon had not
yet found a place where he cared to settle for good, and now Tora
was expecting a child before Yule. So it was the intention of the
young people to stay at Berg that winter. Ingunn had not seen
her sister for two years, and her brother-in-law she had never
met till now. He did not look amiss—he was a powerfully built
young man, with handsome features and curly chestnut hair, but
he had little brown eyes placed close together at the high root of
his hooked nose, and he squinted not a little.

From the first day he met his wife's sister with ill will. In words
and bearing he plainly showed that he counted Ingunn naught
else than a seduced woman who had disgraced herself and her
whole family. He was intensely pleased with his marriage, proud
of Tora's beauty and of her good understanding, proud that she
was soon to bear him an heir to all the riches he boasted of possessing; he allowed himself to be guided by his wife in all things—
which was well for Haakon. But though this was so, and though
poor Ingunn had been ignorant of the honour and good fortune
she missed in giving herself to Olav Audunsson—when she might
have been married to Haakon Gautsson—Haakon had conceived
a hatred for her, since she had preferred a young lad, her father's
serving-man and one of whose family and fortune none here in
the Mjösen country knew anything certain, to him, the knight's
son from Harland.

And the younger sister went about in her fruitfulness, gleaming
pink and white, proud of her matronly dignity, though she owned
neither house nor farm to rule over. The white wimple, which
she wore with honour and by right, reached nearly to her feet;
a heavy bunch of keys jingled at her belt—though God alone knew
what the houseless man's wife was to lock or unlock with them.
But Tora bore herself so that every mother's child at Berg, and
even the lady Magnhild, would do anything to honour her and
her husband, and the women made all preparations to receive the
child they expected with such pomp as became the son of so great
a man.

Through all the time of their growing up Ingunn had known well enough that Tora was seldom pleased with her conduct—thought her elder sister wanting in affection to their parents, thoughtless and lazy, and that she should have sat quietly with their mother and the maids in the women's room instead of always running out to play with Olav and his friends. But Tora never said anything—she was two years younger, and that is a great deal in childhood; Ingunn cared very little what Tora might *think*. And the last autumn at Frettastein Tora had kept silence about what Ingunn knew she must have guessed and been dismayed at. But only when they were in the guest-house at Hamar had her sister spoken of the matter, and then Tora had judged her and Olav's conduct with unexpected leniency and had been kind to Ingunn while they stayed there. One thing was that Tora had always been fond of her foster-brother with true sisterly affection—she liked Olav better than her own brothers and sister, because he was quieter and more natural—and then the Bishop had given some countenance to Olav and Ingunn, and all the people the sisters met in the town followed the lord Torfinn in their judgment; even if Olav had returned wrong for wrong, they had nevertheless done a greater wrong who had sought to break a handselled betrothal because the bridegroom was young and lacked powerful spokesmen. No one doubted that the Bishop in the end would force such a settlement of the suit as would be honourable to Olav. So at that time Tora had not thought that Ingunn's rashness might prove a disgrace to them all.

Now it was otherwise. She could not forgive Olav for having slain her near kinsman, and she spoke harsh words of the way he had rewarded them all for having taken him up, a friendless child, and fostered him in the Steinfinn kindred. Toward Ingunn she was not unfriendly—but, for all that, Ingunn guessed what Tora thought of her: that from a child she had been such that her younger sister was not surprised at her ending in misfortune—but Tora wished to be kind and not to make it harder for the poor thing to bear the fate she had brought upon herself.

Ingunn bowed in silence beneath Tora's gentle little words of pity, but when the talk turned to Olav's misdeeds, she tried to raise her voice in opposition. It availed but little; the other held such an advantage; that she was the elder was of no weight now, since Tora was the married woman. Tora had experience and the

right of judging between other grown people. Ingunn was left
with her experiences to which she had no right: of a love for
which all seemed minded to punish her, of household management and bringing up of children, at which she had played in her
dreams, but never set her hand to in reality. She felt poor and
down-hearted as she sat in her corner and saw how Tora and
Haakon filled the whole house with their life. In her dark, penitential garments, with the two smooth, heavy plaits hanging over
her shoulders, as though it were their weight that bowed her
head and bent her back, she looked like a poor maidservant beside
the young, richly clad wife.

Tora had a son, as no doubt had been the hope of her and
Haakon—a big, promising child, as all said who saw the boy. Ingunn was set to stay by her sister, while Tora was lying in, and
thus she was occupied in tending her nephew. She had always
been very fond of little children, and now she conceived a great
affection for this young Steinfinn Haakonsson. When she had to
take him into her bed at night to give the mother better rest, she
could not help it—she *had* to play at the boy's being her own. She
had to warm herself awhile at her old fancies that she was at
Hestviken, in her own house, and that she was living there with
Olav and their children, Audun, Ingebjörg, and the new little one.
But now she felt with bitter truth that it was but a poor web of
dreams that she had to wrap herself in, while she saw her sister
well and warmly enfolded in her tangible wealth, with husband
and infant son and all the crowd of their servants, who took up
so much room in the place, and the chests and sacks of their goods
that were stacked up in the lofts and storehouses.

Haakon wished to hold a great christening ale, and Lady Magnhild offered to bear half of the cost. Not only Haftor Kolbeinsson, who had become a great friend of Haakon, but the uncles,
Kolbein and Ivar, came to the feast, and these stayed for some
days after the other guests had left.

One evening the kinsfolk were sitting over the supper-table in
Lady Magnhild's room; Aasa Magnusdatter was there too and
sat in the high seat, with Ingunn by her side to help her with her
food and drink, for the old lady's hands were very shaky. Otherwise she had been in much better health this winter; it had rejoiced her greatly to be a great-grandmother; this last piece of

news she never forgot, but often asked after the child and wished to see it.

This evening the men's talk turned upon the conflict between the barons and the bishops, and the Toressons pretended it was certain which side would win. It was the bishops who would have to give in, content themselves with the power that was theirs by right as the spiritual fathers of the people, but let the old laws regarding laymen's dealings with one another stand unshaken. As to Bishop Torfinn, many of the priests here in his own diocese now thought he had gone too far: "I have spoken with three parish priests, good and learned men of God," said Kolbein, "and all three answered me that they were willing to say the bridal mass on the day we give away Ingunn here."

Lady Magnhild answered: "It is clear that the Bishop's interpretation cannot possibly be right. It cannot be God's commandment that His priests should hold with loose-minded and self-willed young people, or that Holy Church should help wicked children to force through their will against their parents—"

"Nay, indeed," said the others.

Ingunn had turned scarlet in the face, but now she straightened herself and defiance struggled with fear in her look—her eyes seemed unnaturally large and dark as she turned them upon her uncles.

"Ay, 'tis of you we are speaking," Kolbein answered back. "You have been a burden to your kinsfolk long enough now, Ingunn. It is time you had a man who can bridle you."

"Can you find a man who will take me?" asked Ingunn scornfully. "So wretched a wife as you would make me to be?"

"We shall not speak of *that*," said Kolbein furiously. "I thought you had had time to find your wits again. So shameless you cannot be, I ween, that you lust after living with a man who has stained his hands with the blood of your cousin—even if you could get him?"

" 'Tis not the first time a man has come to grief through his wife's kinsfolk," said Ingunn in a low and faltering voice.

"Say no more of that," replied Kolbein angrily. "Never will we give you to Einar's slayer."

"Ay, that you have power to refuse—maybe," said Ingunn. She felt that all around the table were staring at her. And she was strangely fired by the thought that she had thus stepped out of

the shadow of subjection. "But if you would give me to any other
—you will find *that* is not in your power!"

"In whose power think you that you are?" asked Kolbein scornfully.

Ingunn's hands grasped the bench she was sitting on. She felt
her cheeks go white. But this was herself—she was not dreaming.
It was herself who spoke, all were staring at her. Before she could
get out her answer, Ivar put in a conciliatory word: "In God's
name, Ingunn—this Olav—no man knows where he may be. You
yourself know not whether he is alive or dead. Will you pass all
your days as a widow, waiting for a dead man?"

"I *know* that he is alive." She thrust her hand into her bosom
and drew out a little silver-mounted sheath-knife which hung
by a string around her neck. She drew the knife and laid it before
her on the table. "Olav gave me this for a talisman, before we
parted—he bade me wait so long as the blade was bright, he said—
did it rust, then he was dead—"

She breathed hard once or twice. Then she became aware of a
young man sitting lower down the table, who stared at her excitedly. Ingunn knew that his name was Gudmund Jonsson and
that he was the only son of a great house in the neighbouring
parish; she had seen him once or twice here at Berg, but never
spoken to him. Now she guessed at once—this was the bridegroom
her uncles intended for her; she was quite certain of this. She
looked the young man straight in the eye; her own glance was
firm as steel, she felt.

Then said the conciliatory Ivar Toresson, scratching his hair:
"Such talismans—oh ay, I know not how much one may believe
in such things—"

"I trow, my Ingunn, you will soon see who is to decide your
marriage," Kolbein broke in. "So you will oppose us if we give
you to a man whom we reckon to be an equal match for you?
Whom will you turn to then—since your friend the Bishop has
taken to his heels, out of the country, so that you cannot crawl
under his cloak?"

"I will turn to God my Creator Himself," said Ingunn; her face
was white as a sheet and she half rose from the bench. "Relying
on His mercy, if you drive me to commit *one* sin to avoid a
greater. Ere I let you force me to be an adulteress and enter the

bridal bed with another man while my true husband lives, I will throw myself into the fiord out there!"

Both Kolbein and Ivar were about to answer her, when old Aasa Magnusdatter put her hands on the table, raised herself with difficulty, and stood up, tall and thin and stooping; she blinked at the men about her with her old red and running eyes.

"What is it you would do to this child?" she asked threateningly, laying her bony claw of a hand on Ingunn's neck. "You wish her ill, I know. Ivar, my son, will you do the work of this bastard brood of Borghild? They would harm Steinfinn's children, I see that—are you to lend them a hand in it, Magnhild and Ivar? Then I fear I have too many left to me in you two!"

"But, Mother!" entreated Ivar Toresson.

"Grandmother!" Ingunn nestled close to the old lady, creeping in under her fur cloak. "Ay, Grandmother, you must help me!"

The old lady put her arm around her.

"Now we will go," she whispered. "Come, my child, we will go."

Ingunn rose and helped her grandmother to reach the floor. Groping before her with her stick, and with the other arm round her granddaughter's shoulder, Aasa Magnusdatter staggered toward the door, muttering the while: "Lending a hand to Borghild's brood—my children—I have lived too long, I have—I mark that!"

"Nay, nay, Mother—" Ivar came after them, took the stick from his mother, and offered his shoulder to support her. "Now I have said the whole time that it were better they accepted an atonement from Olav, but— And now that he is clean gone—"

They had reached the door of Aasa's house. Ivar said to his niece: "I wish you no ill, you must know. But meseems it must be better for yourself—that you were married and mistress in your own house. Better than tarrying here to fade away—"

Ingunn gently pushed him aside as she almost lifted her grandmother over the threshold and barred the door after her, shutting Ivar out.

She undressed the old woman and laid her down, said the evening prayer with her, kneeling by her grandmother's bed. Mistress Aasa was now quite exhausted after her unwonted exertion. Ingunn busied herself for a while longer in the room before she began to prepare for bed.

She stood in her shift and was just about to jump into bed when there was a soft knock at the door. Ingunn went and drew the bolt—and saw a man standing outside in the snow, a dark bulk against the starry sky. Before he opened his mouth, she knew it was her wooer, and she felt a strange festal thrill, while at the same time she was a little afraid. After all—something was happening.

It was, as she thought, Gudmund Jonsson. He asked: "Had you lain down already? I wonder if I could say a word to you tonight. There is some haste in it, you can guess."

"Ay, you may come in. We cannot stand here in the cold—"

"But lay you down," he said as he came in and saw how thinly clad she was. "Maybe you will let me lie here by the bedpost, so that we may talk better?"

At first they talked a little of the weather and of Haakon Gautsson, who now seemed minded to settle at Frettastein, and so Haftor would go home to his father's. Ingunn liked Gudmund's voice and his quiet, pleasant manner. And besides, she could not help liking to lie here in the dark, chatting with a wooer, in cosy comfort. It was so long since anyone had sought her out or cared to talk to her for her own sake. In spite of her having to tell him that his wooing was useless, it was some reparation that a man of Gudmund's condition should have cast his eyes upon her, although her own kinsmen had declared her a worthless woman.

"Ay, there was a thing I wished to ask you," said her guest at last. "Were you in earnest in that you said this evening?"

"I was in earnest."

"Ay, then it is best I tell you," said Gudmund, "my father and mother would fain have me married this year, and we have agreed to ask Ivar Toresson for you."

Ingunn was silent. Gudmund began again: "But if I ask my father to seek elsewhere, he will do so. If it is so that you mean all that you said this evening?"

As he still got no answer, he said: "For you must know, if we once ask Ivar or Kolbein, we shall not get nay. But if you like it not, I will make it so that you shall not be troubled with the matter any more."

Ingunn said: "I cannot understand, Gudmund, how you and

your kinsfolk should think of such a one as I—seeing what a good
match you have the right to expect. You must know all that is
said of me."

"Yes. But we must not be too strict or too hard. Your kinsmen
would admit you to full inheritance with your brothers and sister
if this match could be made between us two—and for myself I
think you look well—and are right comely—"

Ingunn made no haste to reply. It was so good to be able to
lie thus talking with such a pleasing young man, to feel the
warmth of his presence and his living breath against her cheek
in the dark. There had so long been a cold, empty space about
her. Then she said very gently: "Now you know my mind—I
cannot let myself be married to *any* man but to him who owns me.
But for that, you must know, I would prize aright the good fortune which you would offer me."

"Ah," said Gudmund. "Think you not, Ingunn, that we two
might have agreed well together?"

"Indeed I think so. The woman would needs be a troll who
could not live happily with you. But now you must see that I am
not free—"

"Nay, nay," said Gudmund with a sigh. "Then I will take care
that you have no more torment for our sake. I would fain have
had you. But now I wis I shall have another."

They lay chatting awhile yet, but at last Gudmund thought it
time he was away, and Ingunn said it might be so. She followed
him to the door to bar it after him, and they parted with a clasp
of the hand. Ingunn felt strangely warmed and exhilarated as she
came back and went to bed for good. Tonight she would be able
to sleep so well—

In Lent Ingunn was allowed to ride into the town, that she
might make her confession to Brother Vegard—he had been her
father confessor since the day she was confirmed, at the age of
eight, until Arnvid took her with him to Miklebö.

It was no easy matter for her to tell the monk all about her difficulties. Until now she had always been able in confessing to give
each sin its name: she had prayed without reflecting, had answered
her parents discourteously, been angry with Tora or the maids,
taken things without leave, spoken untruthfully—and then this
last sin with Olav. Now she felt that it was mostly thoughts she

had to speak about—and she herself found it hard to grasp them and put them into words. There was especially this thought, that she was afraid she might let herself be scared or threatened into breaking the troth she had given Olav Audunsson under God's eyes.

Brother Vegard said she had done right in refusing to let herself be given to any other man, so long as she had not received true tidings of Olav's death. The monk had judged her and Olav's self-will far more strictly than the Bishop; but he too said they were bound to each other, so long as both were alive. But she must pray to God to save her from such thoughts as that she would take her own life; that was a deadly sin, no less than if she let herself be forced into a marriage without being a widow. And he cautioned her, in serious terms, against thinking too much, as she had said, of life with Olav and of the children she was to have by him. Such thoughts could only serve to weaken her will, to provoke lasciviousness and defiance of her kinsmen—and she must have learned by now that she and Olav had themselves brought about their misfortunes by their fond self-indulence and by their disobedience toward those whom God had set over them in their youth. It would be far better now that she should aim at the virtue of patience, bear her fate as the chastisement of a loving father, apply herself to a life of prayer, almsgiving, and ministering affection toward her kinsfolk, so long as they did not ask her to obey them in what was sinful. Finally Brother Vegard said that he believed it would be better for her if she could be admitted to a convent of nuns and dwell there as a pious widow while waiting to hear whether Olav could come home to his native land and take her to himself, if it were God's will that such happiness should be theirs. If she received certain tidings of his death, then she could choose whether she would return to the world or whether she would take the veil, devote herself to prayer for the souls of Olav and her parents and for all souls that had been led astray by self-will and by over-great love of the pomps and joys of this world. The monk offered himself to speak with her kinsfolk of this, and himself to conduct her to a convent, if she had a mind to it.

But Ingunn was frightened; she feared that if once she were inside a convent, it would not be easy for her to slip out—although Brother Vegard said that, so long as Olav lived, she could not take

the veil without his consent. So Ingunn replied that her grandmother was old and weak and needed her, and Brother Vegard
then agreed with her that so long as Aasa Magnusdatter had need
of her, she must stay with her grandmother.

When she came back to Berg after Easter, Haakon and Tora
had left with all their train; it had been settled that they were to
live at Frettastein. The place was very quiet after them. With the
old women one day was so much like another that for that matter
Ingunn might as well have been living in a convent.

And then she could not resist it—after a while she took up again
her imaginary life with husband and children in a dream-manor
that she called Hestviken. But now and again they came up in
her, those feelings which Gudmund Jonsson's wooing had called
to life—fear, but with it a sort of satisfaction. So after all she had
not misbehaved herself so badly but that a rich and well-born
young man could think of wooing her. And she dreamed of handsome and mighty suitors whom her uncles would seek to force
on her—and she showed her courage and her firm will, and no torments and humiliations they could think of would prevail against
her fidelity to Olav Audunsson.

2

At Berg one day passed like another. Time flew so fast that Ingunn could not guess what became of it. But when she saw how
much had happened in the others' lives, how everything about
them grew and spread, she felt a sting of anxiety—was it so long
ago already!

Tora came down from Frettastein and brought both the children with her. Steinfinn romped high and low like a whirlwind—
he was big and forward for his age, two years and a half. His little
sister could already push herself along the floor till she reached a
bench, when she would catch hold of it and stand on her feet.
Tora insisted that Ingunn must come with her to Frettastein. Ingunn had such a way with children—and as Tora expected her
third before Olav's Mass,[3] she thought it no more than reasonable

July 29.

that her sister should come to live with her and help to bring up all these children. But Ingunn said her grandmother could not manage without her. In her heart she thought she had no wish to see Frettastein again—unless she came there together with Olav.

She did not know where he was now. The only time she had heard news of him was last summer, when Arnvid was a guest at Berg. Asbjörn All-fat, the priest, had returned to Norway the same spring—he had followed Bishop Torfinn in his exile, accompanied him to Rome, and been with him when he died, in Flanders. On his way home Asbjörn had sought out Olav in Denmark; he was then with his mother's brother and was well. Asbjörn had afterwards become a parish priest somewhere in the Trondheim district. On his journey up through Österdal he had looked in on Arnvid at Miklebö and brought him greetings from his friend.

Arnvid had Steinar with him to give pleasure to Ingunn. But the boy had grown so big that she could not play with him as of old. His father said to Steinar that Ingunn had once rescued him from being burned up. But this did not seem to make much impression on the child.

Ingunn took him out in a boat on the lake—they were to fish. She paddled about near the shore, without the strength to row the heavy boat any distance, and Steinar had never been in a boat before. But they had a great deal of fun in this way, though their fishing did not come to much.

Gudmund Jonsson was married long ago and had a son by his wife. He came to Berg now and then and borrowed a boat there, when he had to go to his grandfather's on the other side of the bay.

There was only herself about the place, day in, day out, with the two old women, and now she was already twenty winters old. Fade away, Uncle Ivar had said that time—vaguely she knew that she was fairer than she had ever been. The shut-in life with her grandmother had paled her cheeks, but her skin was as clear as a flower. And she was no longer so thin; her flesh had grown firmer —and she did not hold herself so loosely and stoopingly. She had learned to walk gracefully, and she carried her tall, slender figure with a soft and supple charm of her own. On the rare occasions when she mixed among people, she felt that many men had their eyes on her; she noticed this, though she never returned their gaze, but always moved quietly, with eyes modestly lowered and a gentle melancholy in her look.

One evening, when some strangers had been at Berg on some business with Lady Magnhild, one of the men forced his way into the room after she had gone to bed. He was far gone in drink. Ingunn got him out again; old Aasa had not so much as noticed that anyone had come in. The man turned almost sober as he slunk out—like a whipped dog under the lash of her icy, low-voiced anger.

But when she had got the fellow out of doors, she collapsed altogether—she trembled and her teeth chattered with fright. And what frightened her most was—she herself had felt so strangely— though he could not have noticed anything, of that she were sure. While she was defending herself against him, cool and collected, far too angry and outraged to be afraid, she had felt deep down within herself, as it were, a temptation to let go, to give up.—She was so tired, so tired—it seemed to her all at once that she had been defending herself for years. She was tired of waiting.—Olav should have been here—he should have been here *now!* She did not get a wink of sleep that night; shaken and miserable she lay sobbing and weeping, buried beneath the bedclothes; it seemed to her she could no longer bear this life.—But next day, when this man came to make his excuses, she received his stuttering speech with a few words of gentle dignity, looking him straight in the face; the glance of her great dark eyes was so full of sorrowful scorn that the man crept rather than walked away from her.

Olav—she now knew nothing more of him. And oftener and oftener she lay weeping till far into the night, tortured by disquietude and longing and a dull dread: how long would it be—! She pressed his sheath-knife with both hands against her bosom. The blade was still as bright as ever. And that was all she had to cling to.

Then came a Sunday, toward the end of summer. Only Ingunn had gone to mass from Berg, together with some of the servants. She was on horseback; old Grim walked by her side, leading the dun. They came into the courtyard, the old man was just about to

help her off her horse—when she saw a young, fair-haired man
stooping his head as he came out of the low door of Magnhild's
house. It seemed a strangely long and stubborn moment before
she recognized the man—it was Olav.

He came to meet her, and in the first flash Ingunn thought
everything turned queerly grey and lustreless—as when one has
been lying on the ground face-downward on a scorching summer
day, and then opens one's eyes and looks around: the sunshine
and the whole world seem to have faded and all the colours are
much paler than one expected.

She had always remembered Olav as much taller, bigger in
every way. And handsomer—she remembered his fair colour as
something radiant.

He came up, lifted her out of the saddle, and set her on the
ground. Then they took hands in greeting, walked side by side
toward the house; neither said anything.

Ivar Toresson appeared in the doorway; he greeted Ingunn
with a great smile: "Are you pleased now, Ingunn—with the guest
I have brought to the house this time?"

Ingunn's whole face awoke—she turned pink right down to her
neck, a radiant smile broke out in her eyes and on her lips. "Have
you two come *together*?" She looked from her uncle to Olav.
Then he too smiled—the quiet brightening that she knew so intimately: the pale, handsome mouth moved gently, the lips were
not even parted; he dropped his eyelids slightly, and under the
long, silky white lashes his glance was blue and happy.

"So at last you have come home too?" she asked smiling.

"Yes, I thought I must look in at home some time," he said in
the same tone.

She sat on the threshold with her hands in her lap, looking up
at Olav, who stood talking to Ivar. With a strange suddenness all
became calm within her. Happiness, that was the same as allow-
ing rest to descend upon her—perfect rest.

Ivar had something to show to Olav—the men walked away.
Ingunn watched him and recognized his walk: she had never seen
a man who walked so well, carried himself with such easy grace.
He was not very tall, she well remembered that now; she was
herself perhaps a trifle taller than he—but he was so wonderfully
well built, with just the right breadth of shoulder, narrow in the

waist, well knit, and firm of muscle, though he was so slender, erect, and delicately limbed.

He had grown thinner in the face, his complexion was dry and hard. And his hair had darkened a little—it was not so bright a yellow—more the colour of ashes. But the longer she looked at him, the better she knew him again. There was only this, that when they parted, there was still a touch of childish softness in his good looks. Now he was a grown man—but a remarkably handsome young man withal.

Lingering over her deep happiness Ingunn sat at the supper-table and saw with glad surprise that both Ivar and Magnhild were so friendly toward Olav. Olav had come back to Norway a week ago—to Oslo.

"Methinks you ought to have seen to your own home first," said Ivar. "There could scarcely have been any danger in that—now that you are the Earl's man."

"Oh no, I might well have ventured *that*. But I had said to myself that I would not come home to Hestviken before I got back the control of my own estate. Time enough, I thought," he smiled, "when I can make all things ready there in the south to bring Ingunn home with me."

Ingunn guessed from their talk that Olav had not yet been given safe-conduct and leave to remain in Norway. But neither Ivar nor Olav himself seemed to count that any great matter. The Earl, Alf Erlingsson of Tornberg, was now the mightiest man in the land, and Olav had met him in Denmark and become his liegeman. The Earl had promised to obtain for him a bought peace and it was with leave from the Earl that he had journeyed up-country to find a man who could negotiate on his behalf concerning the atonement with Einar's kinsmen. Then he had thought that boldness pays best—he had ridden straight to Ivar Toresson at Galtestad. And they were soon agreed.

"Ay, you know I remember you since you were as high as that," said Ivar; "and I have always liked you. You know I was angry that time, when we heard you had helped yourself to your bride, as was natural enough—"

"Surely it was natural." And Olav laughed with him.

Ingunn asked timidly: "Then you have not yet come home to *stay*, Olav?"

"In Norway I shall stay—maybe. But here in the north I cannot stay many days. By Bartholomew's Day [4] I must be with the Earl at Valdinsholm."

Ingunn did not know where in the world Valdinsholm might be, but it sounded far away.

It was easy to see that Olav had learned to conduct himself among folk. The glum and silent country lad had become a mannerly young courtier, who knew how to choose his words: Olav could be lively and hold his own when he opened his mouth, but he listened readily to his elders, and most of what he said was in answer to Ivar's and Magnhild's questions. He rarely addressed his words to Ingunn, and never tried to have speech with her alone.

He said the times were very troubled in Denmark—the great nobles were discontented with their King in every way, although they had much greater liberties and rights in that land than here at home—but perhaps that was what made them open their mouths wide for more. His own uncle, Barnim Eriksson, did as he pleased in everything, Olav thought, and he had never seen that the knight paid any attention to the laws, which must hold good in that country too.

"You have not been able to lay your hands on any of the inheritance of your mother's kinsmen?" asked Ivar. "Surely you could claim that now?"

"Uncle says no," said Olav with a little mocking smile. "And that may well be true.—It was the first thing he made plain to me when I came to Hövdinggaard, that my grandmother had divided Sir Erik's estate with her children, before she married Björn Andersson. And my mother had lost all right of inheritance from her kinsfolk in Denmark when she left the country and married in Norway without asking their advice—that was the second thing. And the third was that the King has declared my mother's own brother, Stig Björnsson, an outlaw, and he is dead and his sons dwell in a foreign land; and the King has laid hands on the manor of Hvidbjerg. Now Duke Valdemar has taken up the cause of Stig's sons, and if he can get the estate back for them, Uncle Barnim thought that I ought to come forward: there might be a slice of the cake for me too." He laughed. "Ay, 'twas after uncle and I were better acquainted, that—we have been good

[4] August 24.

friends always, and he has kept me in seemly fashion and has been right generous with me. Only he will not have it that I should claim anything as my right."

Olav spoke with a smile. But Ingunn saw that a new look had come over his countenance; a touch of loneliness, which had been there always, but now appeared much more strongly, and something hard, which was new. She suspected that he had not fallen into unmixed joy and splendour when he sought shelter, a poor outlaw, among his mighty Danish kinsmen.

"But in all else I must say that Barnim Eriksson has treated me well.—For all that, I was a happy man the day I met with Earl Alf —when I took the oath to him on the hilt, I almost thought I had come home."

"You like him?" asked Ivar.

"Like—!" Olav beamed. "Had you met the Earl you would not say such a word. We would follow him—if he bade us sail across the smoking lake of hell—every man he looks at when he laughs. Those yellow eyes of his shine like gems. Small he is, and low— I am a head taller, I wis—and broad as the door of a house, shaggy and brown and curly-haired; ay, the Tornberg race comes of a king's daughter and a bear, they say. And Earl Alf has the strength of ten men and the wits of twelve. And there are not many men, I ween, who are not glad and thankful to obey him—nor many women either—" said Olav with a laugh.

"Is it true, think you, what they say of our Queen—that she would marry him?" asked Ivar inquisitively.

"How should I know that?" laughed Olav. "But if they say truly that she is so wise a woman—though there will be an end of the lady's rule in the land if she comes under the bear's paws—"

But Ivar thought it was in Queen Ingebjörg's service that Earl Alf lay in the Danish waters, harrying the coasts there and taking up the German merchant ships that tried to slip northward through the sounds.

Olav said it was true enough—the Earl sought to win for Queen Ingebjörg her fathers' inheritance in Denmark, while at the same time he chastised the German merchants for their late encroachments in Björgvin and Tunsberg. But no doubt he did it of his own will and not because the Queen had bidden him. Now there was certainly an agreement between the Earl and the Danish nobles—he was to support them in their feud with the Danish

King, and in return Count Jacob and the other lords were to rap
the King so hard over the knuckles that he would take his hands
off the Lady Ingebjörg's estates in Denmark.

They had sat drinking after supper, and Ivar already talked of
going to rest, when Olav stood up and drew the great gold ring
with the green stone from his finger. He showed it to Ivar and
Lady Magnhild. "I wonder if you know this again? With this
ring my father let me betroth her. Think you not it were fitting
Ingunn had it now and wore it herself?"

Ingunn's uncle said yes to this, and Olav set the ring on her
finger. Next he took from his saddle-bag a gilt chain with a cross
hanging to it and silver plates for a belt and gave these also to
Ingunn. Then he produced good gifts for Ivar and Magnhild, and
three gold rings, which he asked Ivar to give to Tora, Hallvard,
and Jon. Both the lady and Ivar were well pleased with this,
praised the gifts, and were now very bland with Olav; Lady
Magnhild had wine brought and all four drank together from the
Yule horn.

When Lady Magnhild said that now Ingunn must go across to
her grandmother and go to bed, Olav stood up—he said he was
going over to Grim's and Dalla's house to talk with them awhile.
Magnhild made no objection.

The sky was overcast, but between rifts in the clouds the sunset glow shone through, cold and brassy. The evenings were already beginning to be chilly and autumnal.

Olav and Ingunn strolled down between the outhouses. They
came to the fence of a cornfield; the man rested his arms on
the rail and stood looking out. The corn was thin, it shone
white under the heavy grey sky; down below, the bay lay in
a dead calm, reflecting the gathering darkness; under the opposite bank the image of the blue-black woods merged with the
land.

" 'Tis as I remember it," said Olav softly. "As it used to be in
autumn. In Denmark it blows almost always."

He turned half round to the girl, laid an arm about her shoulder, and drew her toward him. With a long breath of happiness
she leaned heavily against him. At long last she felt she had come
home; now she was in his arm.

Olav took her face in both his hands, pushed up her hair, and kissed her on the temples. "It used to curl here, where the hair begins," he whispered.

"It is because I comb it down so hard," she said softly. "I have combed away the curls. When they took the coif from me, I plaited it as flat as I could."

"Ah, now I remember it—you went in a coif that winter at Hamar!"

"Are you angry with me for letting them force me—to put it off?"

Olav shook his head with a little laugh. "I had almost forgotten it—when I thought of you, 'twas always as you were before that."

"Do you think I am like myself as I was then?" whispered Ingunn anxiously; "or have I fallen off?"

"No!" He squeezed her tightly in his arms. For a while they stood in close embrace. Then he let go. "Nay—we must go in. 'Twill soon be dark—" but he drew her plaits through his hands, twined them about his wrists, and shook her gently to and fro, standing at arm's length.

"How fair you are, Ingunn!" he said warmly. Again he let go, with a queer, short laugh. Then he asked abruptly: "Then it is more than a year since you saw Arnvid last?"

Ingunn replied that it was so.

"I would fain have met him this time. He is the only friend I had in my youth—he and you. The folk one meets later, when one is getting on in years, are not the same."

He was one-and-twenty and she twenty, but neither of them thought they were too young to talk thus. Far too much had happened to them both before they were quite out of their childhood.

When he had said this, Olav turned and began to walk back; Ingunn followed behind him up the narrow alley between the cattle-sheds. Grim and Dalla were sitting on the stone before the door of the byre. The two old people were delighted when Olav stopped to speak to them. Presently he took some money out of his belt and gave it to them—then there was no end to their joy.

Ingunn stood waiting by the wall of the byre, but no one spoke to her; and when she saw that Olav wished to stay here awhile with the old bailiff and his sister, she bade them good-night and went back to her grandmother's house.

Olav stayed five days at Berg, and on the morning of the sixth he said he must ride to Hamar that evening, for he had been promised a boat to take him to Eidsvold, if he could be ready early next morning.

He was now very good friends with Ivar and Magnhild, and all about the place thought that Olav had become much more of a man in these years he had spent abroad. But Ingunn and he had not had much talk together.

The day he was to ride away she asked him to go with her up into the loft where Aasa's and her own things were. She unlocked her chest, took out a folded linen garment, and handed it to him, turning her face away as she did so.

"This is your wedding-shirt, Olav. I wished to give it you *now*."

When at last she looked at him, he was standing with the shirt in his hands; he had turned red and his features were strangely discomposed. "Christ bless you, my Ingunn—Christ bless your hands for every stitch you have sewed here—"

"Olav—do not go!"

"You know I must go," he said quietly.

"Oh no, Olav! I never thought, when once you came home, that you would straightway go from me again. Stay here, Olav— only three days—only *one* day more!"

"Nay." Olav sighed. "Cannot you see, Ingunn—I am still an outlaw; 'twas rash of me to *come*, but I thought I must *see* you and talk with your kinsfolk. I own nothing in Norway today that I may rightly call mine. It is my lord the Earl who has promised me— And if it were not so—when *he* summons me to be with him on a certain day, I cannot stay away. I must make haste, as it is, to reach him at the right time—"

"Can you not take me with you?" she whispered almost inaudibly.

"You must surely see that I cannot. Whither should I carry you? To Valdinsholm, among the Earl's men—!" He laughed.

"I have had such evil days here at Berg," she whispered as before.

"I cannot see that. For they are kind, Lady Magnhild and Lady Aasa— While I was out there in the south—many a time I thought: what if Kolbein carried it so that *he* had you in his charge? And I feared for you, my dear. But here you have been as well off as you could be."

"I cannot bear to be here any more. Can you not take me with you—find me a lodging otherwheres?"

"I can find you no lodging so long as I have not been given control of my own estate," said Olav impatiently. "And how think you Ivar and Magnhild would like it if I took you away—Ivar, who is to be my spokesman with Kolbein? Be not so unreasoning, Ingunn. And Mistress Aasa cannot make shift without you."

They were both silent a good while. Ingunn went to the little window. "I have always thought, as I stood here looking out, that this must be like Hestviken."

Olav came up to her and laid a hand caressingly on her neck. "Oh no," he said absently; "the fiord is much broader at Hestviken, you must know. It is the salt sea there. And the manor stands higher, as far as I remember."

He went back, picked up the shirt, and folded it. "This must have been a great task, Ingunn—with all the stitches you have put into it."

"Oh—I have had four years to work at it," she said in a hard voice.

"Come, we will go out," said Olav hotly. "We will go out and talk!"

They walked together over the fields till they came to a meadow that sloped to the water. Junipers and other bushes grew on the dry, rocky ground, and here and there were patches of short, sun-scorched grass.

"Come, sit down here!"—He lay on his stomach facing her and gazed fixedly as though far away in his own thoughts.

In a way she thought they were brought nearer to each other merely by his losing himself in thought and remaining silent as soon as he had got her alone; she was so used to this from their childhood. She sat looking affectionately at the little scattered freckles over the root of his nose—they too were intimate, it seemed to her.

Great clouds drifted across the sky, throwing shadows that turned the forests dark blue—the patches of green meadow and white cornfield showed up so strongly between. And the fiord was grey with smooth dark currents farther out, which reflected scraps of the autumnal land. Now and again the sun came out, and its sharp, golden light baked them—but the next moment a cloud came by and the warmth was gone—and the ground was bleak.

At long last the girl asked: "What are you thinking of so, Olav?"

He sighed, as though awaking; then he took her hand and laid his face against the palm. "If you could be less unreasonable—" he answered, taking up again their talk in the loft. He paused a moment. "I ran off from Hövdinggaard without saying a word of thanks—"

Ingunn gave a little terrified cry.

"Ay," Olav went on. "'Tis ill done—'twas not seemly, for uncle had been a good man to me in many ways—"

"Did you quarrel?"

"Not that either. It came about that he did a thing I liked not. He had one of his house-carls punished—I cannot say it was more than the man deserved. But uncle was often cruel, when he was beside himself with rage—and you know I have never liked to see man or beast tortured needlessly—"

"And so you quarrelled?"

"Not that either. This fellow had turned traitor— They had been sitting drinking in the hall, uncle and some kinsmen and friends—ay, they were *my* kinsmen too—they had come to us to keep Easter—it was the evening of Easter Day. They spoke of the King, and there was none there who wished him well—and so they let out something of their plans against King Eirik. They weave many strange plots there now, you see—and we were all drunken and careless of our mouths. This Aake had been waiting at table, and he ran off to the King's captain at Holbekgaard and sold him the tidings he had heard; and this came to uncle's ears. So uncle had the man led out into the pleasance and bound to the biggest oak, and then he stretched up the traitor's right hand, the hand that had sworn fealty to Barnim, and nailed it to the trunk with a knife.

"Ay, 'tis not that 'twas undeserved, I say naught of that. But as the night wore on. I thought that Aake might have stood there long enough. So I went out and freed him and lent him a horse— I bade him send it back to a house in Kallundborg, where I was known, when he had found a chance to escape from Sealand.— But I thought that uncle would be mighty wroth with me for playing him this trick, and that 'twould boot me little to speak with him. I had heard that the Earl lay to the northward off the point—so I gathered together what I could of my goods and rode northward the same night. And so it came about that I was in England with the Earl this year.

"Ay, 'twas no fitting thanks I gave uncle—and I pray to God every day that he may not have more trouble through my setting Aake free. You know, I made him swear, but an oath and a belch are all one to such a fellow— Had uncle had him hanged, I should have said 'twas well done. But as he stood there by the oak, with his hand nailed fast— 'Twas just after Easter, you know; we had been to church every day, and I had crept to the cross and kissed it on Good Friday.—So it came over me that the man standing there was like one crucified—"

Ingunn nodded quietly. " 'Twas surely a good deed."

"God knows. Would I could believe it. And you know that if I go back to Denmark in the Earl's company, I can send uncle a message—maybe find occasion to visit him and beg his forgiveness. For I showed him gross ingratitude."

He gazed longingly over the dark-blue forests. "You say you are not in good case here, Ingunn. It has not been like keeping Yule every day with me either. I make no complaint of my rich kinsmen—but they are rich and proud men, and I came to them poor and a stranger, an outlawed man—a boy they counted me and no true-born scion of their race, since 'twas not they who had given mother in marriage. I will not say they might have received me better than they did—things being as they were."

"You must not be deaf to reason," he bade her again. He pushed himself forward and let his head fall heavily in her lap. "Gladly would I stay here now, or take you with me—were there any means to do it. Would you rather I had not come, since I could not come to stay?"

Ingunn shook her head, drew her hands through his hair, and ruffled it caressingly.

"But 'tis strange," she said in a low voice, "that your uncle would not do more for you—when he has no children living, other than that nun?"

"Had I been willing to stay in Denmark. But I always said I would not. And he must have seen that I yearned to be home again."

After a while Ingunn asked: "These friends of yours—in that town you spoke of—what kind of folk are they?"

"Oh, nothing," replied Olav a little crossly. "A tavern. I was

often in that town for uncle—selling bullocks and such errands—"
Ingunn stroked his hair again and again.

"A kiss you may give me for all that!" He rose on his knees, clasped her tightly in his arms, and kissed her on the mouth.

"You may have as many as you will," she whispered close to him. The tears came trickling from her eyelids as she felt his strong, hot kisses all over her face and down her neck. "As many as you will— You might have had kisses every day!"

"Then I fear I should have been far too greedy!" He laughed low in his throat. "My Ingunn!" He bent her head back till her neck nearly touched the ground. "But now 'twill not be long—" he muttered.

"We must go up," he said, letting her go. " 'Tis long past dinner-time. I wonder how Lady Magnhild will like it that we left the house in this fashion!"

"I care not," muttered Ingunn defiantly.

"Nay, nor I either!" Olav laughed as he took her hand and raised her. He dusted her and himself with his cap. "But now we must go home, for all that."

He walked on with her hand in his, until they came to the path where they could be seen from the house.

3

INGUNN went about her daily life, after Olav had gone, unable to conquer a trace of disappointment. It was as though his visit had been to *her* least of all.

She knew it was wrong to take it thus. Olav had behaved prudently in letting it seem that he had given up his old claim on her: that she was his to possess and enjoy. In any case they could never have carried that through here at Berg. And he had gained the assent of both Ivar and Magnhild to her staying here as his lawful betrothed.

Lady Magnhild gave her gifts for her bridal chest—it had been sadly empty till now. A cloak of green velvet, lined with beaver-skin, as good as new; a tablecloth and a towel with a blue pattern;

two shifts of linen and one of silk; the full furnishing of a cradle; three bench covers in picture weaving; a brass pot, a drinking-horn with silver mounts, and a great silver tankard—all this she received in the course of the next two months. And she got Aasa Magnusdatter to give her granddaughter the good bedding she had in store, with curtains and rugs, bolster, skin coverlets, and sheets of stuff. "Is Ingunn to be married?" the grandmother asked in surprise, each time her daughter begged some of her possessions. She forgot it from day to day.

Ivar promised to give her a horse and saddle, and money to buy six good cows—it would be too heavy a task to drive cattle from the Upplands to the Vik. And he bade her come south to Galtestad, so that she might choose from among the wearing-apparel left by his dead wife: "I would rather you had it than Tora—she is grown so high and mighty since she got this Haakon Thunderguts and became the royal mother of his sons."

He went so far as to find out what had become of Olav's clothes-chest, which was sold at Hamar when the boy was proclaimed outlaw. The chest was of white limewood, an unusually handsome piece of work, with the finest carving on the fore side. Ivar bought it back and sent it to Ingunn at Berg.

The axe Kinfetch had been with the Dominicans at Hamar the whole time. Brother Vegard hid it away when the Sheriff took possession of Olav's personal property. The monk said it was no great sin; for this axe, which had descended in the same family for more than a hundred years, ought not to come into the hands of strangers so long as Olav was alive. When Olav now came back to Hamar, Brother Vegard was in Rendalen preaching to the peasants there on the Paternoster and the Angel's Greeting—he had made up four excellent sermons on these subjects, and with these he travelled about the diocese in the summer. But Olav had sought out the Prior and had done public penance in church for the manslaughter in the convent. After that the Prior had given him back the axe. But when he set out again for the south, he left it behind in charge of the monks.

Kolbein was beyond measure furious when Ivar applied to him to treat of an atonement on Olav's behalf. Never would he accept fines for Einar's slaying—Olav Audunsson should be an unatoned felon, and Ingunn could stay where she was, without honour and without inheritance, unless she would accept such a match as her

kinsmen could provide for a debauched woman—a serving-man or
a small farmer.

Ivar merely laughed at his half-brother. Kolbein must be mad
if he knew so little of the times he lived in: if the King granted
Olav leave to dwell in the land, then Kolbein might, if he pleased,
refuse to accept the fines—let the silver lie by the church door for
crows and vagabonds to pick up; Olav would sit just as safely at
Hestviken for all that. And as to his betrothal with Ingunn, 'twas
nothing but folly to seek to deny that the bargain had been made
of old. That Olav had forestalled them, at the time they thought
of giving the bride to Haakon Gautsson, Ivar now thought a good
thing: he was well pleased that this nephew by marriage had
shown while still so young that he was a man who would not be
cheated of his lawful rights.

Haakon Gautsson was now engaged in litigation with his wife's
kinsmen about an inheritance that he claimed on Tora's behalf;
but Ivar had little thought of praising *this* nephew on this account;
it was for this he had given Haakon his pretty nickname. Thus
Haakon and Tora kept away this autumn, while Ivar and Magnhild were working to arrange Ingunn's marriage.

Haftor Kolbeinsson had a meeting with Ivar at Berg to treat of
the matter. Haftor was a hard, cold man, but upright in a way,
and much shrewder than his father. He saw full well that if Olav
Audunsson had made powerful friends who would advance his
cause, it was useless for his father to raise difficulties about the
atonement. The only way in which they could gain was by demanding that the fines be fixed as high as possible.

All this kept up Ingunn's spirits. She accepted every gift as a
pledge that now she would soon have Olav back, and then he
would take her home with him. She yearned so for him—and
when he was here last, he had spoken so little to her. It was natural, she saw, that he must now think above all of winning over
her kinsmen and securing their joint estate. And when she was
once his, she believed full surely that he would love her as in old
days. Although he was no longer so blind and hasty as he had
been then. The change in him was that he was now grown up—
it was in him that she first became fully aware how many years
had gone by since they were children together at Frettastein.

It was Haftor Kolbeinsson who brought news to Berg, when he came thither after Whitsuntide next spring to receive the second part of the blood-money for Einar.

Olav had made payment of one half at mid-Lent in Hamar—a German merchant from Oslo had brought the silver, and Ivar had appeared with him; Haftor received the money for his father. A part of the sum should now have been paid after Whitsuntide, and the remainder Olav himself was to hand over to the dead man's representatives at the summer Thing, which was held every year at Hamar after the conclusion of the Eidsiva Thing. After that he was to have received Ingunn at the hands of her kinsmen.

But this time no man had come from Olav; on the other hand, Haftor had strange tidings to tell of the Earl, Olav's lord. Queen Ingebjörg Eiriksdatter had died at Björgvin early in the spring, and Earl Alf must then have feared that the days of his mastery in Norway were over. The young Duke Haakon had hated his mother's counsellors heartily ever since he was a little boy. Now he sent word to the Earl bidding him send to Oslo the mercenaries he had hired in England the summer before—it had been done in the name of the Norwegian King, but Earl Alf had kept them with him at Borg, to the great annoyance and mischief of the folk of the country round. The Earl obeyed the command in this manner, that he came sailing in to Oslo with a whole fleet and went up into the town with more than two hundred men; he himself lodged with his following in the King's palace with Sir Hallkel Krökedans, the Duke's captain. One evening some of these Fi'port wights,[5] as the English hirelings were called, broke into a homestead near the town, plundered it, and maimed the master of the house. Sir Hallkel demanded the surrender of the malefactors, and when the Englishmen refused to give up the culprits, he had a number of them made prisoners, took out five men at random, and hanged them. Thereupon the Englishmen made an attack on the King's palace and it came to an open fight between the Earl's men and the townsmen, the town was plundered, and the whole of that part which lies from St. Clement's Church and the river down to the King's Palace and the quays was burned. The end of it was that the Earl sailed out of Folden [6] with his whole host,

[5] The Earl's mercenaries were drawn from the Cinque Ports.
[6] The Oslo Fiord.

and he carried Sir Hallkel with him as a prisoner—he sought to
throw the whole blame of the disaster upon him. But these tidings
were brought to the Duke while he lay under the coast in the
south, on his way home from his mother's funeral, and now he
collected a force in haste and got his brother, the King, with him.
They sailed across to Borgesyssel; Sarpsborg and Isegran were
taken by storm, and about three hundred of the Earl's men were
said to have fallen or were slain afterwards by the peasants of the
district; Alf's seneschal at Isegran and several men of his body-
guard were executed by the Duke—folk said in revenge for Hallkel Krökedans, who had been put to death in the castle there by
order of the Earl. Alf himself and the remnant of his host were
said to have saved themselves by flight to Sweden, and King Eirik
had made him an outlaw in Norway with all the men who were
in his following.

They were very silent, the Berg folks, when Haftor had told
this story, dryly and calmly. Olav's name he never mentioned,
but after a long pause Ivar asked in sheer despondency if Haftor
had heard any news of him—if he were among the fallen.

Haftor hesitated a moment and answered no. It chanced that
the men from whom he had first heard this—two white friars from
Tunsberg—could give him special news of Olav Audunsson, because he had been at the sister convent, Mariaskog, when the fire
of Oslo took place; Olav had been given leave by the Earl before
the move upon Oslo, and he had fared south to Elvesyssel to sell
some of the land he owned there to the monks of Dragsmark.
They said further that, when tidings came to him there of how
the Earl's greatness had been brought to an end, Olav had declared
that he owed Lord Alf all that he now possessed and had won
back, and he would not part without leave from the first lord to
whom he had sworn fealty. Thereupon he had set out into
Sweden to seek the Earl.

" 'Tis odd how unlucky he is, Olav, in the men he chooses to
back him," said Haftor dryly. "They end as outlaws, first the
Bishop and now the Earl.—But I trow 'tis in his blood; 'twas a
Baglers' nest, Hestviken, in his forefathers' time, I have heard."

"Ay, Baglers' nest and Ribbungs' den [7] were the names folk

[7] The Baglers (or "crozier men") were the party of the Church and
the old nobility, opposed to Sverre and his followers, the Birchlegs (see

gave in old days to Hov and Galtestad and many another manor of our kin, Haftor," Ivar protested, but his voice was very tame.

Haftor shrugged his shoulders. "Ay—Olav may be a good enough man, for all it seems his fate ever to be on the side of the loser. *My* friend he can never be, but, I will say, 'tis plain enough that his friends like the man. But if Ingunn is to wait for him, she will have to practise patience."

Ivar objected that this time it might well be that his affairs could quickly be set in order. Haftor merely shrugged again.

It was Ivar who told Ingunn there was but little hope that Olav could take her home this summer. It did not enter his mind to speak at length of Earl Alf's revolt to a young woman whom he counted somewhat simple and light-minded—so that at first Ingunn did not know that Olav was in as evil a plight as before he had found a helper in Alf Erlingsson.

All she knew was that nothing more was said about her marriage.

Ivar and Lady Magnhild felt somewhat at a loss. They had taken up this affair with both hands and had received Olav with such favour that they could hardly turn against him, now that he had been plunged so unexpectedly into a new strait. So they chose to be perfectly silent about the whole matter.

Kolbein Toresson was at his own home and lay abed for the most part—he had had a stroke. So Ingunn did not hear much of what he said. And Haftor held his peace. He had received one half of the blood-money in excellent English coin and judged it unprofitable to try whether the atonement could be upset after that. Moreover he had some pity for Ingunn, and he thought it might be just as well in the end if Olav got her and carried her off to another part of the country—her kinsfolk had neither honour nor profit of her. When old Lady Aasa was gone, she would only be a burden to her sister and brothers. And he was now foster-father to Hallvard and Jon, Steinfinn's sons, and good friends with the boys—Haakon Gautsson had also quarrelled with his young brothers-in-law.   . . .

---

note, p. 4). The Ribbungs (named after their leader) were a remnant of the Bagler party, the champions of a lost cause, and thus went down to history with the stigma of the under dog.

So Ingunn was left once more to herself, to sit brooding in her
corner with her grandmother.

The first autumn she still went on as she was wont—she span,
weaved, and sewed her bridal garments. But by degrees she lost
heart for the work. No one ever said a word of her future. She
left off hoping that Olav would come *soon*—and immediately it
was as though she had never believed it in earnest. Their meetings
during the days he had last been here had left behind a vague disappointment in her heart—Olav had been half a stranger to her.

She did not seem able to make his image fit into her old dreams
of living with him in his house, where they were master and mistress and had a flock of little children about them—and yet they
were the same two who had loved each other at Frettastein.

So she seized upon the memory of the only hour they two had
been alone together, face to face and lips to lips—that last day,
when they sat together in the meadow. She let her thoughts weave
fresh pictures from their talk and from his one ardent, passionate
caress—when he burned a kiss upon her and bent her neck backward to the ground. She dreamed that he had yielded to his own
desire and her prayers—and had taken her with him. She called
to mind what her mother had told her the night before her death
—of her bridal ride over hill and dale—the daughter now had this
to feed her fancies.—Next summer, the second since Olav's visit,
she chanced to go with Lady Magnhild far up into the Gudbrandsdal, to a wedding at Ringabu. They stayed some weeks
there with their kinsfolk at Eldridstad, and these took them up to
their mountain sæter, that Lady Magnhild might see their wealth
of cattle. For the first time in her life Ingunn went up a mountain,
so high that she was above the forests: she looked out over bare
wastes with osier scrub and stunted birches and greyish-yellow
bogs, and in the distance rose hill after hill, as far as the northern
horizon, where snow mountains closed the view, with clouds
about their sides.

At this great wedding she had been made to wear bright-
coloured clothes, a silver belt, and floating hair. At the time she
had been only shy and confused. But it left its mark in her. When
she was back in her grandmother's room at Berg, new images
floated before her mind—she saw herself walking with Olav,
jewelled and glorious—it might be in the palace of some foreign
king; this seemed to compensate her for all these years she had sat

in the corner. And in her dreams she wandered over the fells with
her outlawed man—they rode through mountain streams, which
foamed swifter and clearer than the rivers in the lowlands—there
was more music in their sound, less roar—and their beds shone
with white pebbles. Every sound under heaven, the light, the air,
were different on the mountains from what they were in the fields
below. She was journeying with Olav toward the distant blue
fells, through deep valleys and over wide moorlands again; they
rested in stone huts like the Eldridstad sæter.—At the thought of
these fells a wildness was born within her. She who had longed in
such meek abandonment to fate, who had only wept quietly under
the bedclothes now and then, when she seemed too bitterly oppressed—she felt an unruly spirit quicken within her. And her
dreams became chequered and fantastic—she wove into them such
incidents as she had heard of in ballads and stories, she imagined all
those things which she had never seen; stone castles roofed with
lead, and warriors in blue coats of mail, and ships with silken sails
and golden pennants. This was all more gorgeous and splendid
than the old pictures of the farmstead with Olav and their children—but it was far more airy and confused and dreamlike.

Arnvid Finnsson had been at Berg once or twice in the last
years, and they had spoken of Olav, but he knew no more of his
friend than that Olav was said to be alive and in Sweden. But the
winter after her journey to the fells—it was New Year, and men
wrote 1289 after God's birth—Arnvid came to Berg, very cheerful. Arnvid was wont to go almost every year to a fair at Serna,
and there he had met Olav that autumn; they had been together
for four days. Olav said that the Earl had himself released him
from his oath; he would have Olav think now of his own welfare
—and he had given him tokens to Sir Tore Haakonsson of Tunsberg, who was married to Lord Alf's sister. Olav had now entered
the service of a Swedish lord in order to provide himself with
means against his home-coming, but he intended to go home to
Norway at the New Year—perhaps he was already at Hestviken.

Ingunn was made happy; at least so long as Arnvid stayed at
Berg, she felt her courage awaken once more. But afterwards her
hope seemed to pale again and fade away; she dared not abandon
herself to the expectation that something was really going to
happen. Nevertheless there was a brighter background to her

thoughts and dreams that winter, while she watched the approach of spring—and perhaps Olav would come, as Arnvid had said.

In summer the women of Berg, when they had to smoke meat or fish, used to take it out of doors. In the birch grove north of the homestead there were some great bare rocks; they lighted a fire in a crevice of the rock and covered it with a chest without a bottom, within which they hung what was to be smoked; and then a woman had to sit and tend the fire.

One day before Hallvard's Eve,[8] Aasa Magnusdatter wished to have some fish smoked, and Dalla and Ingunn went out with it. The old woman lighted a fire and got it to burn and smoke as it should; but then she had to go home to tend a cow, and Ingunn was left alone.

The soil was almost bare here in the grove, brown and bleak, but the sun on the rocks was warm—fair-weather clouds drifted high up in the silky blue sky. But the bay, of which she could see a glimpse between the naked white birch-trunks, was still covered with rotten, thawing ice, and on the far shore the snow still glared white among the woods, right down to the beach. Here on the sunny side there was a trickling and gurgling of water everywhere, but the thaw had not yet given its full roar to the voice of spring.

Ingunn was happy and contented as she sat in the sunshine watching the smoke. She had already been there some hours and was just wondering whether she would have to go and look for more juniper when she heard someone come riding along the path above where she had been sitting. She looked up—it was only a man on a little shaggy, ill-kept dun pony.—In doing so she pushed against her water-bucket; it stood unsteadily on the rocks and upset.

She saw with annoyance that she would have to go and fetch water—and Dalla had taken the wooden bucket; the one she had was of stone, with two ears and a stick thrust through them to lift it by. She picked it up; then the man called from the path above—he had jumped off his pony and came running down through the withered heather: "Nay, nay, fair maid—I will do that for you!"

[8] St. Hallvard's Day is May 15.

He threw his arms around her waist to check himself, pressing her to him in his haste, took the bucket from her, and set off again briskly down to the burn. Ingunn laughed with him in spite of herself as she stood watching him—he had shown such a mass of white teeth when he laughed.

He was dark-complexioned and curly-haired—the hood of his cloak was thrown back and he was bareheaded. He was very tall and slight and active, but rather loose-jointed in all his movements, and his voice had been so merry—

He came back with the water, and she saw he was very young. His swarthy face was narrow and bony, but not ugly—the eyes were large, yellow or light brown, merry, and clear. His mouth was big, with its arched row of teeth, but the curve of his nose was fine and bold. The man was dressed in a proper moss-green kirtle and an ample brown cloak; he wore a short sword in his belt.

"There!" he said laughing. "If you would have more help, you need but to ask me!"

Ingunn laughed too; she said she had no need of more, and it was much that he had already done for her—the bucket was heavy.

"Far too heavy for so fine and young a maid. Are you from Berg?"

Ingunn answered yes.

" 'Tis thither I am bound—I have a message and a letter from my lord to your lady. But now I shall stay here and help you—then I shall be so late that Lady Magnhild must house me for the night. And then you will let me sleep with you?"

"No doubt I shall." Ingunn had no other thought but that the boy was jesting—he was no more than a boy, she saw, and she laughed with him.

"But now I will stay here and talk with you awhile," he said. " 'Tis a tiresome task you have, and lonely it must be for you to sit here alone in the wood, young and fair as you are."

"It were worse to sit here, I trow, if I were old and ugly. And 'tis not lonely in this wood. I have sat here but four hours, and already you have come this way."

"Ay, then I doubt not I was sent to pass the time for you—stay, I will help you; I am better at this work than you!" Ingunn went about it rather awkwardly, for she did not like to get the smoke in her eyes and throat. The boy dipped the juniper sprays in the water and laid them on the embers, jumping aside when the smoke blew out toward him. "What is your name, fair lass?"

"Why would you know that?"

"Why, for then I will tell you mine. It might be useful for you to know it—since I am to sleep with you tonight?"

Ingunn only shook her head and laughed. "But you are not from these parts?" she asked; there was such a strange tone in his speech, she heard.

"Nay, I am an Icelander. And my name is Teit. Now you must tell me yours."

"Oh, I have no such queer name as yours. I am called naught but Ingunn."

"That may be good enough for you—for the present; 'tis as fine a name as the finest I wot of. If I find a better, I will write it in golden letters and give it to you, Ingunn rosy-cheeks."

He helped her to take out the smoked fish and put in fresh. Lying on the ground, he picked out a trout, split it, and began to eat.

"You take the fattest and best," said Ingunn with a laugh.

"Is she so grudging of her food, Lady Magnhild, your mistress, that she would refuse us poor folks a fish-bone?" Teit laughed back at her.

Ingunn guessed he took her for a serving-maid. She was clad in a brown homespun dress with a plain leather belt at her waist, and she wore her hair as usual, in two plaits without ornament, simply bound with blue woollen knots.

Teit seemed disposed to stay with her for good. He tended the smoke for her, dipped juniper, and laid it on; between whiles he stretched himself on the ground by her side and talked. She learned that he was now clerk to the Sheriff's officer in these parts. He was the son of a priest whose name was Sira Hall Sigurdsson, and he had been at the school in Holar; but Teit had no mind to be a priest, he chose rather to go out into the world and seek his fortune.

"Have you found it, then?" asked Ingunn.

"I will give you an answer to that tomorrow"—he smiled darkly.

She could not help liking this merry boy. And then he asked if he might take a kiss. It came over her—there could be no harm. So she said neither yes nor no—simply sat still and laughed. And

Teit took her round the waist and kissed her full on the mouth. But after that he would not let her go—and he slipped his hands in under her clothes, grew somewhat indelicate in his advances. Ingunn tried to defend herself, she was near being afraid—and she bade him cease.

" 'Tis unmanly of you, Teit," she begged—"I sit here and must tend my work—I cannot run, you know that well!"

"I had not thought of that!" He let her go at once, rather shame-facedly. "I must go and see what has become of my jade," he said a moment later. —"We shall meet at Berg?" he called to her from the bridle-path above.

When Ingunn and Dalla came down to the house in the evening, there was no one in the courtyard, but when the door of Lady Magnhild's living-room was opened, they heard laughter and loud voices within. Lady Magnhild had guests, two young maids, Dagny and Margret, the twin daughters of one of her foster-daughters, and this evening a number of young people had come to Berg, the girls' kinsfolk and their friends.

Ingunn went into her grandmother's house. Taking the bowl on her knees, she sat by the bedside and gave the old lady porridge and milk, taking a spoonful herself now and then, after that she took a knife and a basket and went out. The evenings were already fine and bright, and cummin and other wild herbs had come up on the sunny slope facing the bay, below the Bride's Acre, as they called the best and largest cornfield on the place. She wished to dig up a basketful and make broth for her grandmother—the old lady must need to cleanse her body of rheum and unwholesome humours after the winter.

The plants were so small and young, before she had filled her basket the grey-blue dusk of the spring evening had fallen upon the land. As she came up toward the house she was met by a tall, slight man coming down in the twilight—Teit, the Icelander.

"Is it so—must you go out and toil and swink so late?" he asked kindly. He put his hand into her basket, took up a handful of the green herbs, and smelled them. Then he took hold of her wrist and stroked it gently up and down.

"There is frolic and dance in the hall. Will you not join in it, Ingunn? Come—and I will sing the best I can."

Ingunn shook her head.

"Surely she cannot be so hard on you, your mistress? All the others are within, the whole household—"

" 'Twould surprise them if I came," said Ingunn quietly. " 'Tis long since I was seen in the young folks' dance. Dagny and Margret would wonder, if I went in to them and their friends."

" 'Tis only that they are jealous of your beauty. They like it not that the maid is fairer than—" He clasped her, crushing the basket she held before her. "I shall come to you by and by," he whispered.

Ingunn stood for a while before the door, looking out into the grey spring night and listening to the sound of song and harping which came faintly from Magnhild's hall. She would not go in there—they were young and wanton. But there could not be any harm in it if she let Teit in tonight. She too had a mind to talk with a stranger once again. She left the door ajar and lay down fully clad.

The time dragged on, and she tried to deny to herself that she was disappointed at his not coming after all. At last she must have fallen asleep—she was awakened with a start by the man's jumping into her bed and lying down beside her, in no very seemly fashion. But when she thrust him roughly from her, he was tame at once.

He excused himself, saying there had been so much noise and revelry in the hall. But when Ingunn lay so still and answered so coldly to all he told her of their merry-making, Teit grew more and more subdued. At last he said meekly: "You must know, what rejoiced me most was that I was to speak with you—and now you are angry with me, I wis? My sweet, what would you that I should say to you that will give you pleasure in the hearing?"

"Nay, that you must find for yourself," said Ingunn; she fell to laughing again. "If you have come a-courting, you must not ask me how to set about it!"

"How so? Could I then win your heart—would you not gladly leave Berg, Ingunn?"

"Oh—oh—that may well be—"

"Would you have a mind to flit over to Iceland and dwell there?"

"Is it very far to Iceland?" asked Ingunn.

Teit said yes. But it was a good land to live in, better than Norway—in any case better than the Upplands, for here the winter was so horridly cold. At home where he came from there was many a winter with no snow on the ground—the sheep were out all year round and the ponies.—This sounded tempting to Ingunn, for she too thought the winter was horrid—when the beast starved in the byre, and the bedcover was frozen fast to the wall in the morning, and one's feet were always cold, and one had to break a hole in the ice for every drop of water wanted in the house.

Teit waxed eloquent as he spoke of his native land. Ingunn thought it must be beautiful—those heaths, where they herded sheep and goats in the autumn, must be like the mountain she had climbed, when they were north in the dale. The world was wide and great—for the men, who could roam afar in it. She fell to thinking of Olav, how he had roamed abroad—to England and Denmark and Sweden—Teit had seen no other lands but Iceland and Norway. She wished Olav had been one who would tell her something of all he had seen—but Olav was always so silent about the things that had happened to him. But it might be because Teit had great learning—she had never thought that a learned man could be so young and frank and full of life. But then she had never before met a layman who was a clerk—save Arnvid, and he was so much older and so serious-minded.

At last they grew sleepy, both of them—several times their talk came to a standstill. Then the boy crept closer to her and began to fondle and caress her. Ingunn repelled him, at first rather sleepily and half-heartedly—but then she took fright, Teit was so wild. She bade him remember that Lady Aasa slept in the other bed; were she to wake and find that Ingunn had a bedfellow, it would go ill with her.

Teit made some show of wailing and lamenting, as if in jest— but then he mended his manners, wished her good-night, and thanked her. Ingunn followed him to the door and barred it—then she saw that it was already past midnight.

She was up late next morning and it was the middle of the day before she was out in the courtyard. She caught sight of the Icelander, who was hovering by the stable door, looking as if he had sold butter and not been paid for it. Ingunn went up to him, wished him good-morning, and thanked him for their last meeting.

Teit feigned not to see her outstretched hand; he gazed gloomily before him.

" 'Twas a good jest you thought to play on me, that—I was such a dullard that you could cozen me to your heart's content?"

"I know not what you mean!"

"Was it not a fine conceit to lead on a poor young lad to woo you—the daughter of Berg?"

"I am not the daughter of Berg, Teit—the niece am I. That makes a great difference."

Teit looked at her suspiciously.

"I thought it was *you* who jested—when you spoke of wooing, and when you would fondle—I took it not for earnest. But I did not believe you would mock me—for my simplicity, I mean. And you must know that I, who have never been beyond these parts, where I was born, have little wit or knowledge; I thought it solace to speak with you, so wise and learned and far-faring a man as you are."

She smiled at him with gentle entreaty. Teit looked down. "That you surely do not mean."

"Yes, I mean it. I had thought perhaps you would stay here some days—and that I should be cheered by hearing and learning more of you."

"Nay, I must go home now. But I expect that Gunnar Bergsson will send me hither again after the holy-days," he said, a little annoyed.

"Then you will be welcome!" Ingunn gave him her hand in farewell and went back to her house.

4

ARNVID FINNSSON came down at John's Mass to see to his aunt— it was up and down with Mistress Aasa now; she might go out at any moment, but she might also live a good while yet, if it was God's will. Arnvid had heard no more news of Olav since his last visit.

The day after he came, he and Ingunn were walking together in the courtyard. Then Teit Hallsson came in, ran past them, and went into Magnhild's house. Arnvid stopped and followed the young man with his eyes: "He has errands here day after day, that clerk?"

Ingunn said yes.

"I know not whether you ought to talk so much with him, Ingunn—"

"Why so?—know you aught of him?" she asked after a moment.

"I heard of him at Hamar," said Arnvid curtly.

"What was it?" asked Ingunn rather uneasily. "Do they charge him with—any *vice*?"

"A double one," said Arnvid quietly, as though with reluctance. It was Master Torgard, the cantor, who had first had the knave in his service, and he praised him too. The Icelander wrote the fairest hand, and he wrote quickly and correctly; he also knew how to illuminate, so Master Torgard had entrusted him with drawing and colouring the initials in an antiphonal and in a copy of the law of the land, and the work was fairly done. And when the book-binder's wife, who usually helped her husband, fell sick, Teit had assisted the man in her place, and he proved to be as skilful a book-binder as the Bishop's own man. So Master Torgard had been loath to send the lad away. But his weakness was that he went clean out of his wits when he touched dice or tables. And there was a good deal of such play in the town. He was a man who could play away hose and shoes, this Teit, and then he would come home to his master in borrowed clothes. In short, he had no sense to take care of his own welfare—he was in debt to ale-wives and chapmen. Unwilling as he was to be rid of so skilful a writer, Master Torgard thought that for the boy's own sake he must get him disposed where so many temptations would not beset his feet. He was in other ways a likable fellow, the cantor had said. But when the Sheriff at Reyne required a clerk who was good at reading and writing, Master Torgard had got the Icelander the place.

That he had also been involved in some irregularities with women Arnvid thought there was no need to mention to Ingunn; he was loath enough to spread rumours about the boy in any case. But he thought he must tell her this other thing about Teit—the Icelander had borrowed money from Master Torgard's old sisters and the like.

The day before John's Mass the people of Berg had been to morning mass—it was Sir Viking's anniversary—and as they were on their way home from church, a terrible thunderstorm broke.

It rained so that one would have thought the world had not seen the like since the days of Noah. The church folk sought shelter under some great overhanging rocks; for all that, they were drenched to the skin when they reached home late in the day.

Tora Steinfinnsdatter was visiting her aunt for the holy-day and had brought her two eldest children with her. She had been very friendly with her sister this time, and in the course of the afternoon she came into Aasa's house to get Ingunn to come over to them—they had several guests today.

Ingunn sat crouching by the fire on the hearth; she had let down her hair to get it to dry quicker. She objected at first that she could not leave her grandmother. Tora thought Dalla might well sit with the old lady. Then Ingunn said she had no fitting gown to wear—her only Sunday kirtle had been soaked that day on the church road.

Tora walked about the room, humming to herself. She was still a very handsome young wife, though she had grown very stout with years. But she was bravely clad, in a blue velvet kirtle and a silken coif—and her brooches and gilt belt made a goodly show on her broad figure. She had opened Ingunn's clothes-chest.

"Can you not put on this?" Tora came forward into the light of the fire carrying the green silk gown that her mother had given Ingunn for the feast after Mattias Haraldsson's slaying.

Ingunn bent her head shyly. Tora went on: "You have not worn it many times, sister. I mind me I grudged it you a little when Mother gave it you. *Have* you worn it more than that one evening?"

"I wore it to the wedding at Eldridstad."

"Ay, I heard say you looked so bravely there." Tora sighed. "And I lay abed and was vexed I could not be there too—the greatest wedding there has been in the dale these twenty years. Come now, sister," she begged. "Oh, I have such a mind to dance and play tonight—'tis the first summer I have been free to do the like since I was wed. Come now, my Ingunn—we have Arnvid to sing for us, and that Icelander, your friend—I know not which has the finer voice!"

Ingunn got up hesitatingly. With a laugh Tora took the gown, cast it over her head, and helped her to arrange the folds under the silver belt.

"My hair is still half wet," murmured Ingunn in embarrassment, as she gathered it in her hands.

"Then let it hang loose," laughed Tora. She took her sister's hand and led her out.

"Nay, look at Aunt Ingunn, look at Aunt Ingunn!" screamed Tora's little daughter as she came into the light. Ingunn picked up the child in her arms. The little maid threw her arms about her neck and sniffed at her half-dried hair, which enshrouded the woman like a mantle of some dark golden texture and reached below her knees. "Mother," she cried, "I will have hair like that when I am a grown maid!"

"Ay, you may well wish that."

Ingunn put the little one down. She was conscious of her own beauty tonight, it even dazzled herself. Olav, she thought, and her heart beat with a heavy thump—he *must* be here tonight. She passed her hand over her face, pushing the hair from it, and looked about her; she met Arnvid's strange, dark glance; and Teit's yellow-brown eyes blazed at her like torches. But the one she sought was not there. She clasped her hands crosswise over her bosom—*he* was not here who ought to have seen that tonight she was the fairest woman present. For an instant she felt she would rather run back to her grandmother, pluck off her finery, and give way to her tears.

As the evening wore on, there was talk of dancing—they called for the *Kraaka-maal*, the stately old sword-dance. Arnvid admitted that he had known it, and Tora said both she and her sister had learned the steps. Teit cut in, flushed and keen—he knew the *whole* lay, would gladly sing for them. Lady Magnhild laughed and said that if it would amuse the young people to see the old dance once more, she could bear a part—"And you, Bjarne?" She turned to an old knight, the friend of her youth. Then two or three of the older house-folk came forward, somewhat bashfully. It was easy to see that they were eager to essay their youthful exercise once more.

Arnvid said that Teit must lead the dance—he doubtless knew it best—and then Lady Magnhild and Sir Bjarne ought to stand next. But the old people would not have this. The end of it was that

Teit came first in the chain, then Ingunn, and Arnvid with Tora.
There were in all seven men with drawn swords and six women.

The dance went right well—Teit was an excellent leader. His
bright, full voice was a little sharp, but it could be heard that he
was a trained singer. Arnvid's fine, rich voice supported him well
in the lower part, and Sir Bjarne and two of the old house-carls
still had very good voices—and they all warmed to it, so well did
Teit carry on the lay and the dance. None of the women joined
in the song—but thereby the old sword-dance seemed to gain in
seriousness and force: it was the weapons that were to the fore,
the men's rhythmical tramp and the rising fire of their singing;
the women only glided silently in and out beneath the clashing
play of the swords. Ingunn danced as though in a dream—she was
tall and limber, had to stoop lower than the other women; and she
turned pale and breathed heavily, keeping her eyes half-closed.
As she sprang forward under the blades, her loose mantle of hair
fluttered out, as though she were rising on heavy wings. One of its
strands swept across Teit's chest and caught in a buckle; it gave
her a wrench each time she crossed over, but she did not think of
stopping the dance to free herself.

They had danced fifteen or sixteen of the verses when Lady
Magnhild gave a loud cry that brought the whole chain to a standstill. The sweat was pouring down her red face—she clutched herself with both hands below the breast—now she could do no more,
she cried with a laugh.

Arnvid signed to Teit with a fling of his compact little head;
his eyes glistened wildly and he called out something, as he took
up the strain, and all the men with him:

> *"Swiftly went the sword-play—*
> *Aslaug's sons would quickly*
> *Rouse up Hild with weapons*
> *Keen, if they could see me—"*

the men *would* have the last stanzas, even if they had to skip over
ten or twelve verses between—

> *"Strong meat gave I my sons,*
> *Strengthening their manhood!"*

The men dancers were so wrought up by the game that they
glowed with excitement and their voices boomed in chorus:

"Swiftly went the sword-play!—
Fain am I now for the end!
Home the bright ones call me,
Whom from Herjan's halls
Odin has sent out.
Gladly shall I in the high seat
Drink ale with the Æsir;
Gone are the hopes of life:
Laughing I go to my death!"

Then they broke the chain and reeled back to the benches, while the men laid aside their swords and wiped the sweat from their faces, laughing with delight. And the young people who had looked on cried out—so fine it had been! Lady Magnhild held her sides, panting with exhaustion: "Ay, 'tis another sort of dance than the way you hop and jump nowadays—'tis your turn now, Margret; dance one of these sweet love-ballads you young ones like so well:

'It was the King Lord Eirik
Rode north upon the hill—'

for they are dainty and sweet as honey, and I trow the old lays must be too rough for such silken dolls as you are!"

The young ones did not wait to be asked twice—most of them had thought rather that the old people kept the floor too long, though 'twas a rare sight to have the old sword-dance for once.

Teit came over to where Ingunn was sitting, crouched against the wall, wrapped in her own lovely hair. The dance had not flushed her, but her face was bedewed with a waxy pallor.

"Nay, I have no more strength to dance. I will sit here and look at you."

Teit rushed back to the others. He was unwearying and seemed to know everything, both the old lays and these new ballads by the score.

Ingunn paused in the courtyard—she had left the dancing to cross to her grandmother's house and go to rest.

It must be nearly midnight, she thought; the sky was pale and clear all round the horizon with a white sheen that deepened to yellow in the north. Only upon the ridge on the far side of the bay was there a grey-blue veil of thin clouds, and among them the moon was setting in a trail of moist vapour.

Although the night was so clear, it was darker over the land than was usual at this time of year—meadows and cornfields and groves were still soaked from the storm earlier in the day; a cold, damp mist was rising everywhere. Over the water floated thin wisps of brownish smoke, but all the bonfires had now died down, save one which blazed fiercely on a headland far away and threw its reflection like a narrow, glowing blade upon the steel-blue water.

Teit came out to look for her—she had known he would do so. Without looking back she walked out toward the cornfield that stretched down to the fiord. When she reached the gate and stood pulling up the stakes, he came up with her.

They did not speak as they walked on, she in front and he following, along the narrow path through the tender young corn. At the end of the cornfield ran a burn, and the path followed it through a thicket of alders and osiers down to the manor hard.

Ingunn stopped as soon as she entered the shadow of the foliage. It was so dark in there—she was afraid to go on.

"Ugh—'tis so cold tonight," she whispered almost inaudibly, shivering a little. She could barely make out the man's figure in the darkness, but she felt the warm breath of his body as something mild and sweet amid the cold and acrid scent of wet leaves and raw mould. He said not a word, and his silence seemed all at once to loom threateningly and terrifyingly—with a sudden uncontrollable dread she thought she must get him to say something; then the danger would pass.

"That verse you sang in the hall," she whispered; "of the willow —say it again!"

In a low, clear voice Teit repeated in the darkness:

> *"Blest art thou, willow,*
> *Standing out on the shore;*
> *Fair is thy garment of leaves.*
> *Men shake from thee*
> *Dews of the morning.*
> *And my longing is to Thegn*
> *By night and by day!"* [9]

Ingunn reached up and drew down an armful of the bitter-scented foliage—rain and dew showered over her in the darkness.

[9] *Aan Bogsveig's Saga.*

"You will spoil your fine clothes," said Teit. "Are you wet?—let me feel—"

But as his hands lightly brushed her bosom in the dark, she darted quick as lightning under his outstretched arms; with a low scream of fright she rushed along the path—catching up her gown in both hands, she ran as though for her life through the cornfield.

Teit was so surprised at the turn things had taken that it took him a moment to collect himself and follow her. And then she had such a start that he did not catch her up till they were at the gate. From there they could be seen and heard from the yard, where the guests were now passing to seek their quarters. So he stopped and let her go.

He showed a black and offended look when they met next day. Ingunn greeted him almost humbly; she murmured shyly: "I trow we had both lost our wits last night—to think of going down to the lake at midnight."

"Oh, was it that you thought of?" asked the Icelander.

"And yet there were no more bonfires than we could see from the house. So it had been waste of time to go down to the hard."

"Nay, I doubt not we could have had more pleasure of each other if we had stayed together within doors," said Teit bitterly. He bowed and went his way.

5

THEN there came an afternoon in the autumn—three months after Midsummer Night. Ingunn went through the gate, from which the stakes were now removed, as the cattle had been brought in from the sæter and were grazing freely over all the home fields.

Today the cows were in the meadow below the cornfield—no fairer sight could be seen than these fat sæter-fed beasts glistening in the sun; they were of every hue that cattle can be—and the after-grass was so green and thick that it seemed in a ferment of plenty, with masses of shimmering dog-fennel among the grass. The sky was blue, and blithe little fine-weather clouds drifted high up; the fiord was blue and reflected the autumnal brightness of the land, the red and yellow woods surrounding the home fields. Farther off stood the dark, blue forests, where each single fir tree stood out by itself, as they stood drinking in light in the strong, cool air.

The glad radiance of the day forced her to shrink beneath her own desperate dread and misery. She dared not fail, when he had trysted her. She was in mortal fear of being alone with him; but she dared do naught else. For if she did not come, he might seek her out up at the homestead and others would hear.

The stubble shone like pale gold on either side of the path—now there was a wide view over the open, reaped fields. His little dun jade was grazing in the coppice by the burn.

Ingunn prayed in her heart, a wordless prayer that was but a groan of her deep distress. As she had prayed that night when he stood outside her door, knocked softly, and called her by name. In the darkness she had knelt at the head of the bed, clasping the carved horse's head of the bedpost, and called for help, soundlessly within herself, shaking with terror. For if the disaster *had* happened, if she had sunk into the worst that could befall—she would no more, she would not sink yet deeper. But it came over her that he could force her against her will, so that she *must* cross the floor and let him in.

When she guessed that he had gone from her door, she had sobbed from very gratitude. For it seemed that not her own tiny spark of will had held her back, but an invisible power, strong and stern, had filled the darkness between her and the terror at the door. As she huddled exhausted beneath the bedclothes, humbly thankful for her deliverance, she had thought that no punishment for her sin could be so hard that she would not accept it with gratitude, if only she might never more fall into Teit's power.

And when they met next day and he jested at her sleeping so heavily that he had to go unsolaced from her door, she had answered: "I was awake, I heard you." She was quite calm, for she was sure that the good powers that had kept her back last night would not suffer him to compel her any more.

When he asked why she had not opened, whether she had not dared, or someone had been within, she made bold to answer: "No; but I would not. And you must not come here any more, Teit. Be good, do not come after me any more!"

"Now, I have never heard the like—be good, you say! The other night—"

"Ay, ay," she had interrupted him, with a groan of suffering. " 'Tis ill enough, sin enough—"

"*Sin?*" he exclaimed, overwhelmed with astonishment. "Is it *that* you think of!"

She had remembered it then, and she remembered it now as she walked here, and she felt a sort of pity for the lad. *He* could not know how great a sin had been committed when she let herself be his: that she had broken a troth of which she could not even bear to think in this outpost of hell where now she had her dwelling.

Six weeks—six weeks it was already since that day and that night which she had begun to hope, deep down below her conscious thoughts, might be forgotten—some day; she could do penance and be shriven, and then she could let herself forget this matter of Teit. For she had neither seen nor heard anything of him since. Until today he came to Berg—had found himself an errand to Lady Magnhild. And he had made this tryst with her—and she dared do naught but go.

Now she could see the man; he was sitting on a rock within the thicket. And silently she cried within her: "Help me, let him not affright me, so that I do his will again!"

Where he sat was almost the same spot on which they had stood together in the dark on Midsummer Night, when he had repeated the verse about the willow for her. But she did not think of that—it was now a light and airy bower under the fading trees. Sunshine and blue sky reached them through the half-stripped branches; a glitter of light danced on the burn behind the bushes, dewdrops glistened on pale blades of grass and on the coarse weeds that were already touched and browned by the frost. The patch was bright with fallen leaves.

Even the moss-grown rock on which he had been sitting was so fair to see, with the wealth of green cushions clinging to it, that she was in sheer despair at being so alone with her terror and hopelessness in this fair and glorious world.

"Christ save me! What has come to you?" He had leaped up and stood looking at her. Then he made as though he would clasp her to him—she raised her hands with a little blunted gesture, weakly warding him off, as she shrank away. Quickly he set her on the rock and stood looking at her. "You seem not to have been right merry all these weeks that I have not seen you!—Has anyone got wind of it?" he asked quickly.

Ingunn shook her head. She trembled as she sat.

" 'Tis best I tell you my good news at once," he said, smiling a little at her. "I have been at Hamar, Ingunn, and spoken with Master Torgard about the matter. He has promised that he himself will speak for me with your kinsmen—he and Gunnar Bergsson. So I am not so badly off for spokesmen to my suit, how think you?"

She felt as if she had once been carried away by a landslide—and had crawled out, bruised and bleeding. And now this fresh fall came and buried her.

"What say you to that?"

"I have never thought any such thing," she whispered, wringing her hands. "That you could—ask for me—"

"I have thought of it before, I have—last summer, sometimes. I liked you from the first time I saw you—and as you made no secret of your liking for me— But 'tis not certain"—he looked down at her with a crafty laugh—"that I should have bestirred myself so speedily had you not barred your door to me even the second night. Nay, I saw myself afterwards that 'twould have been too perilous had we carried on with that game at Berg. And to lose you I am loath.—So now you may cease to mourn for your *sin*, if 'tis that has troubled you!" He smiled and stroked her cheek —Ingunn cowered away, like a dog that expects to be whipped. "I had scarce thought you would take *that* so sadly— But haply you can take comfort now, my poor one?"

"Teit—'tis impossible we two can come together—"

"Neither Gunnar nor Master Torgard seemed to think so."

"What is it you have told them?" she whispered almost inaudibly.

"I have told them all there has been between us—save the thing you wot of," he laughed. "But I have told them that we two have gotten such a heart-felt kindness for each other. And now at last you had let me know for certain that you would fain we should be wed.—But you must know I have said naught that may let them guess I have had more of you than your *word*." He gave a wanton laugh, took her by the chin, and tried to make her look up. "My Ingunn?"

"I have never meant that."

"How so?" Teit's face darkened. "Do you mean perchance I am too poor a match for you? Gunnar and Master Torgard did not think that, I ween. You must know I have no thought of staying in Gunnar's service after I am married—we are agreed that I shall leave him even now, after Yule. 'Tis not my purpose to stay longer in this part of the country either—unless you wish it and your kinsfolk will give us land to live on, but haply they will not do that. Nay, but Master Torgard will give me letters to the Archbishop himself, Ingunn, and to certain friends of his in the chapter there—and he will write in them that I am a most skilful clerk and painter of images on vellum. I can support you much better by my handicraft, when I come to such a place as Nidaros, than any of you country folk think. There I might find many roads to wealth, Ingunn—when I get woods that I can trade in.—And then we can sail home to Iceland. You spoke of that many a time in the summer, and said you were so fain to come to Iceland. I think I can promise you that I shall be able to take you thither, and that right handsomely."

He looked down at her white, terror-stricken face and it made him angry. "You ought to think of it, Ingunn—you are not so young either: you have entered on the second score of years. And your suitors have not worn down the grass of your kinsmen's courts lately, I have heard—" he looked away, a little ashamed of his own words.

"Teit—I *cannot!*" She twisted her hands violently in her lap. "There is another—another to whom I have given my troth—long years ago—"

"I marvel whether he would deem you have kept it well, if he knew all," said Teit dryly. " 'Tis not I would be content with such a troth if 'twere *my* betrothed that gambolled with a strange man and jested with him so freely—as you have shown me that you liked the game we two have played last summer. Nay, the troll trounce me if I would—not even if you had kept back that which you parted with the first day we chanced to be alone in the house!"

Ingunn put her hand to her face as though he had struck her. "Teit—'twas against my will!"

"Nay—I know that!" He gave a sneering laugh.

"I did not believe—I could not think you would do such a thing."

"Nay, how could you?"

"You were so young—you are younger than I am; I thought it was but wanton frolic, for you were so young a boy—"

"Ay, that was it."

"I resisted—and tried to defend myself—"

Teit gave a little laugh. "Ay, 'tis the way with most of you—but I am not so young but that I have learned this—that nothing makes you women so angry and so scornful of a young and innocent lad as when he lets himself be checked by such—resistance!"

Ingunn stared at him, stiff with horror.

"Ay, had you been a pure young maid—never have I shamed a young maid, I am not like that. But you cannot ask me to believe you did not know full well how the dance would end that you led me the whole summer long?"

Ingunn continued to stare—slowly a blush crept over her grey face.

"I may tell you," said Teit coolly, "so much have I heard of you that I know of that man who served in your father's home—with whom you had a bastard when you were but fourteen—"

"He was no serving-man. And never have I had a child." Then she bowed low; with her arms clasping her knees and her head hidden in them she began to weep very softly.

Teit smiled doubtfully as he stood looking down at the weeping girl.

"I know not if 'tis he you wait for—to come back and marry you? Or if you have had others since— However that may be, he seems not to kill himself with haste, this friend of yours—I greatly fear, Ingunn, 'tis of no use you stay for him. For if you did that, there might easily come too many between you."

She sat as before, weeping silently and in bitter pain. Teit said, more gently: "Better take me, Ingunn, whom you have in your hand. I shall be—I shall be a *good* husband to you, if only you will put off this—flightiness of yours—and be steady and sane from this day. I—I am fond of you," he stammered awkwardly, stroking her bowed head lightly. "In spite of all—"

Ingunn shook his hand from her head.

"Weep not so, Ingunn. I have no thought of deceiving you!"

She raised her head and gazed fixedly before her. It would be idle, she guessed, to try to tell him the truth of what he had heard. Such must indeed be the talk hereabouts, where none knew Olav, and few had known her as other than a worthless woman, the shame of her race, whom her kinsfolk had thrust aside in disgrace.

She had not strength to speak of it either.—But this new thing that had befallen her with Teit—she thought she must tell him how it had been brought about. So she broke silence: "I know well that this is a punishment for my sin—I knew I sinned grievously when I would not forgive Kolbein, my father's brother—I rejoiced when he was dead, and I thought of him with hatred and lust of vengeance; I refused to go with the others to his funeral feast. He it was who was the chief cause that I was parted from one to whom I was promised in childhood and would have taken before all. Not one prayer would I say for Kolbein's soul, though I guessed he might need all the prayers that— When they said the *De profundis* at even, I went out of the room. And I refused to go north with the others to his burial.

"God have mercy on me. I knew well that it is sinful to hate an enemy after he has been called to judgment. Then you came— and I was fain to think of other things—I was happy. And when you would bear me company up in the weaving-loft—I had no other thought but that you were a boy—and as it was with me then, I had most mind to play and romp with you, for I would think no more of the dead man; and when we took to throwing the wool from the sacks at each other— But I never thought, nay, I never thought, that if you were uncourtly and said lewd words —I thought 'twas only that you were so young and wanton—"

Teit stood looking down at her with the same doubtful little smile.

"Well—let that be so. I got you first against your will. But afterwards—at night?"

Ingunn dropped her head, hopelessly. Of *that* she could say nothing—she was scarce able to unravel it to herself.

She had lain awake hour after hour, crushed by dismay and shame. And nevertheless it was as though she could not bring herself to see that it was true—that now she was lost and branded with shame. For already it seemed but as the memory of a dream or an intoxication, her own wild merriment of the afternoon in the wool-loft. And that Teit had caught her—but all the time his image appeared to her as she had brought herself to see it after

Midsummer Night, when next day she had been angry with herself for her foolish fear of him: for he was but a boy, a likable,
clever, lively boy, who had brought her nothing but pleasure; a
little wanton of speech, but then he was so young— And yet she
knew, as she lay there, that now she had brought disaster upon
herself even to death and perdition, and now she was an adulteress.

At last she had fallen asleep. And she was awakened by Teit
taking her in his arms. She had not thought to bar the door—they
never did so when they slept in the loft in summer. She no longer
remembered clearly why she had not tried to be rid of him. Perhaps she had thought it would make her shame yet deeper if she
now said she would have no more to do with him who had already
possessed her—that she was loath to see him again and hated him.
And when he himself came and she heard his bright young voice,
she may have thought that after all she did not hate him so terribly
—he was so simple-hearted and had no inkling of *what* he had
brought upon her. For he knew nothing of her being bound to
another, married in the sight of God.

Only next morning, when she looked at her misfortune in the
clear light of day, was it borne in upon her that she must escape
from this at once—must not let herself be dragged yet deeper.
She felt that she herself had no power to do anything, of her own
strength she could not break with him. But she had cried for help
in her bitter woe— "Whatever may become of me, I shall not
complain, if only I be saved from further sin—"

Teit stood looking at her. And as she still kept silence, he held
out his hand to her. "Better not to quarrel, Ingunn. Let us try to
agree and be friends."

"Yes. But I will not marry you. Teit—you must tell these friends
of yours they are not to bring forward your suit—"

"That I will not do. And if your kinsmen say yes?"

"Still I must say no."

Teit paused for a moment. She saw his rage seething in the
young man. "And what if I do as you wish—cease my wooing and
come here no more? And if your kinsfolk should see for themselves, in a little while, that you have strayed again into your old
bad ways?"

"Still I would not marry you."

"You must not be too sure of finding me and catching me again, if you should need me this winter. I *have* offered once to do rightly by you, and you met me with scorn and cruel words."

"I shall not need you."

"Are you so sure of that?"

"Yes. Before I would send for you—I would cast myself into the fiord."

"Ay, ay. That will be your doing and not mine—your sin and not mine. Since you seem to think we have no more to say—?"

Ingunn nodded in silence. Teit paused a moment—then turned on his heel, leaped across the burn, and ran after his pony.

She was standing in the same place as he came riding up the path. He pulled up beside her.

"Ingunn—" he pleaded.

She looked him straight in the face—and, beside himself with rage and agitation, he leaned forward and struck her with all his force below the ear, making her reel. "A wicked wretch you are, a cursed, fickle bitch!" His voice was broken by sobs. "And may you have such reward as you deserve for the false game you played with me!"

He struck his heels into the pony's sides, and the little jade broke into a trot—for a few paces. But where the hill began, it fell into its usual amble.

Ingunn stood watching the rider—she held her hand to her flaming cheek—but she was no longer angry with Teit for this. With a strange and painful clearness she saw that Teit could but think her what he had called her. And it added to her sorrow—even now she could remember that she had liked him. And she pitied him, for he was so young.

She would have to go home now, she thought. But she felt she must break down at the thought of the house above—nowhere could she turn without being reminded of this boy.

And yet she could not resist the rising thought at the back of her mind—in a few months it would all be easier for her. When she was no longer forced to think of—and a sudden pang of fear came over her like a hot wave. Though there was little likelihood of that— But would to God Teit had said nothing of it—she had dreaded it enough already. Sick as she now was, with grief and anxiety, she nevertheless knew that, when so much time had gone by that she might be quite sure she was safe from *that*, then she would not suffer so terribly. Then she would not feel, as now, that her *whole life* had been ruined by this disaster and this sin.

Old Mistress Aasa failed greatly during the autumn, and Ingunn tended her lovingly and untiringly. Lady Magnhild marvelled at the girl: for all these years she had seen her niece dragging herself about like a sleepwalker, doing only what she could not avoid, and that little as slowly as might be. Now it seemed that Ingunn had waked up; her aunt saw that she could work when she chose —she was by no means so incapable when she took herself in hand. Now and again the thought occurred to Lady Magnhild: perhaps the poor thing was afraid of what might become of her when the old lady was gone; her unwonted diligence was a prayer to them not to look on her too ungraciously when the grandmother no longer needed her care. Perhaps they had not been friendly enough to the poor, frail child.

Ingunn snatched at everything she could find to occupy her. When her hands were not full with the sick old woman, she applied herself to any work she could find—anything that might help her to keep her thoughts from the one thing to which they constantly flew back in spite of herself; she waited in breathless tension for her fear to be proved groundless.

All the thoughts with which she had played for years—of life with Olav at Hestviken, of Olav coming to take her away, of their children—it was like the touch of the angel's flaming sword merely to approach the memory of these dreams. She could scarce keep herself from wailing aloud.

She threw herself upon all such tasks as demanded thought—and told upon the body. She *would* not give in, if she felt sick this autumn—for she was not near so ailing as she had been the first days at Miklebö.

It had always been the way with her, that when she had been badly frightened, she felt giddy and had violent qualms afterwards. She had only to think of the day they drove over the rocks in the sledge, she and Olav. It was Yuletide, not long before they were grown up; they had taken it into their heads that they would go to mass in the parish church, and so they drove off in the dark winter morning, though none of the others at Frettastein would go to church that day—a strong south wind was blowing, with rain and mild weather. She remembered so clearly the long-drawn, dizzying fear that seemed to descend on her whole body and dissolve it as she felt the sledge swerve and slide backwards over the smooth ice-bound rocks—it came across the horse's quarters, as he struggled to keep his feet, striking sparks and splintering the ice, but was carried away and thrown down—Olav, who had jumped off to support the sledge, was flung headlong and fell on the frozen ground; and then she knew no more. But when she came to herself again, she was on her knees in the soft snowdrift, hanging over Olav's arm and retching till she thought her whole inside would be turned out, and Olav with his free hand was pressing lumps of snow and ice to the back of her head, which she had struck against the rock. This time too it was only fear that ailed her.

On the eighth day of Yule she sat alone with her grandmother —the others had gone to a feast. She had laid plenty of fuel on the hearth, for her feet were so cold. The flickering gleam of the fire lent a semblance of life to the sleeping face of the old woman in the bed—dead-white and wrinkled as it was. By the pale light of winter days Ingunn had often thought it already as peaceful as the face of a corpse.

"Grandmother, do not die!" she wailed below her breath. Her grandmother and she had been companions so long that they had drifted into a backwater of their own, while the life of other folk ran past outside. And she had come to love her grandmother in the end, unspeakably, she thought—it was as though she herself had found support, her only support, in the old woman, as she led her faltering steps, dressed her, and fed her. And now it would soon be all over—if only she could have laid herself down beside the aged woman. Sometimes she had dared to hope that this would be the end—she would be permitted to die here in her dim corner screened by her grandmother's protection—before anyone had guessed.

But now she would soon be dead. And then she would have to go out among the others. And she would be haunted by the terror that one day someone would see it in her.

But it was not certain, it was *not* certain even yet. It was only the fear of it that drove and forced the blood in her body: she had felt such violent shocks in her heart as almost to make her swoon. At times there was a sudden throbbing in the veins of her throat, and her pulses seemed to race through her head behind the ears. And that feeling she had had yestereven—and in the night— and today again, time after time, deep in her right side—like a sudden blow or thrust—haply it was but the blood hammering in a vein.

For even if there had been anything, 'twas not possible it had quickened, the way she had starved and laced herself tight.

The week went by, and more than once Lady Magnhild said to Ingunn that she must spare herself somewhat—the unwonted hard work must be too much for her in the end. Ingunn made but little reply and continued to tend her grandmother; but the active fit seemed to have left her again. She had slipped back into herself, as it were.

She felt as though the soul within her had sunk to the bottom of a thick darkness, in which it fought a blind struggle with the sinister foreign being that she housed. Day and night it lay tossing and would have room for itself and burst her aching body. At times she felt she could bear no more—she was in such pain all over that she could scarcely see—for not even at night did she dare to relax the bandages that caused her such intolerable torment. But she could not give up—she must get it to stop, to move no more.

There was one memory that constantly floated before her at this time; once, when she and her sister were children, Tora's cat had caught a bird which Olav had brought her that she might tame it. The cat had just kittened, and so she stole two of its young, ran down to the pond, and held them under water. She had expected them to die as soon as they went under. But it was incredible how long the little beasts kept on wriggling in her hands and struggling for their lives, while little air-bubbles came up all the time. At last she thought they were dead—but no, there was another jerk. Then she took them out, ran back with them, and laid them down by their mother. But by that time they were indeed lifeless.

She never thought of it as her child, this alien life which she felt growing in her and stirring ever stronger, in spite of all her efforts to strangle it. It was as though some deformed thing, wild and evil, had penetrated within her and sucked its fill of her blood and her marrow—a horror she must hide. What it would look like

when once it came out into the light, and what would happen to
herself if anyone found out she had borne such a thing—of this she
dared not even think.

At last, six weeks after Yule, Aasa Magnusdatter died, and her
children, Ivar and Magnhild, made a great funeral feast for her.

The last seven days and nights of her grandmother's life Ingunn
had only slept in snatches, lying down in her clothes. And when
the corpse was borne out, all she asked was to be allowed to rest.
She crept into her bed; now she slept and now she lay staring before her, with no power to think of the future by which she was
faced.

But when the feast came, she had to get up and busy herself
among the guests. No one wondered at her looking like a ghost of
herself in her dark-blue mourning gown, wrapped in her long,
black veil. Her face was grey and yellow, her skin lay stretched
and shiny over the bones, her eyes were wide and dark and tired
—and the men and women, her kinsfolk, came up and said kind
words of praise to her, almost all of them. Lady Magnhild had
spoken of her faithfulness to the dead woman during all these
years.

Both Master Torgard, the cantor, and the Sheriff of Reyne were
among the funeral guests. And at once it flashed upon Ingunn—
Teit! She had almost forgotten him. It was as though she could
not make out the connection between him and her misfortune—
even now, when she called him to mind, it was only as an acquaintance she had liked at one time, but then some ugly thing had befallen them, so that she scarce cared to think of him again.

But now the thought came to her: what had he said to his
spokesmen when he withdrew his suit? If he had exposed her to
them—ah, then she would indeed be lost. She must try to find out
whether they knew aught. She felt like a worn-out, poor man's
jade that had toiled in harness under a grievous load till she was
almost broken-winded, and now was to bear yet more.

"You have not brought your clerk with you?" she asked Gunnar of Reyne, as indifferently as she could.

"Is it that Teit you mean? Nay, he has run from me. So now,
you ask for him? They tell me he had errands hither to Berg early
and late—is it true that 'twas you he was after?"

Ingunn tried to laugh. "Not that I know. He said—he said he

would send suitors to ask for me—and that you were to be one of
them. I counselled him against it, but— Can it be true?"

The Sheriff's eyes twinkled. "Ay, he said something of the
same to me. And he had the same counsel from me as from you!"
Gunnar laughed till his stomach shook.

"What became of him, when he ran away from Reyne?" asked
Ingunn, and she too laughed a little. "Do you know that,
Gunnar?"

"We will ask the cantor—'twas to him he would go. Hey,
Master Torgard, will you deign to come hither? Tell me, good
sir—know you what became of him, that Icelander, my writer?
Mistress Ingunn here asks after him—you must know he intended
her such honour that he would sue for the hand of Ingunn Steinfinnsdatter."

"Nay, say you so?" said the priest. "Ay, he had many strange
devices, my good Teit. So then, you are left to mourn his absence,
my child?"

"I can do naught else. For he was such a marvellous cunning
man, I have heard, that you, master, would send him to the Archbishop himself, since there was none other in this land who could
make use of such skill. This must be true, I ween, for he said it
himself."

"He-he, he-he. Ay, he could make up a tale. Half crazed he was,
forsooth, though the boy could write better than most. Nay, he
came in to see me awhile ago—but by my troth, I'll not have him
in my household again—though he is a good clerk, but a madcap.
So 'twill profit you nothing to weep for him, my little Ingunn.—
Nay, but is it true—was the boy so bold that he dared speak of
seeking a wife at Berg? Nay, nay, nay—" the priest shook his little
birdlike old head.

So she guessed it could not be altogether true, what he had said
to her that last day they spoke together. But now she had added
this to her other anxieties—had she done a madly foolish thing in
letting these men see that she thought enough of Teit to care to
ask after him?

When the guests departed after the funeral, Tora stayed behind
with her two eldest children and old Ivar Toresson of Galtestad.
One evening when they were sitting together—they had brought
out the treasures they had inherited from Lady Aasa and were

looking at them—Tora said once more that her sister ought now
to take up her abode with her.

Lady Magnhild said that Ingunn must do as she would: "If you
would rather go to Frettastein, Ivar and I will not hinder you."

"Rather will I stay here at Berg," replied Ingunn in a low voice.
"If you will still grant me lodging here, now that grandmother is
gone?"

Tora renewed her demand: she herself had now five children
and she had charged herself with the fostering of the motherless
twins left by Haakon's sister, so she needed Ingunn's help.

Lady Magnhild saw a look of perfect misery in Ingunn's thin
and wasted face, and she held out her hand to her. "Come hither
to me, Ingunn! Shelter and food and clothing you shall have with
me, as long as I live—or till Olav comes and takes you home; for
I believe full surely that he will come one day, if God be willing
and he is alive.—Think you," she said scornfully to Tora, "that
Haakon will show his sister-in-law such honour at Frettastein as
Steinfinn's daughter has the right to look for? Haply she is to
dwell in her father's home and be nurse to his and Helga Gauts-
datter's offspring! That Ivar and I will not consent to.—I
had thought I would give you this"—she took up the great gold
ring that she had inherited from her mother—"as a memorial
of the faithful care with which you tended our mother all these
years."

She took hold of Ingunn's hand and was about to put the ring
on it. "But what have you done with your betrothal ring—have
you taken it off? Poor thing, I believe you have worked so hard
that your hands are quite swollen," she said.

Ingunn felt that Tora gave a little start. She dared not look at
her sister—yet did so for an instant. Tora's face was unmoved, but
there was an uneasy flicker in her eyes. Ingunn herself could not
feel the floor under her feet—she clung fast to one thought: "If I
fall into a swoon now, they will know all." But she seemed to be
listening to another's words as she thanked her aunt for the costly
gift, and when she was back in her usual place, she did not know
how she had come there.

Late in the evening she stood by the courtyard gate, calling and
whistling for one of the dogs. Then Tora came across to her.

There was no moon, and the black sky sparkled with stars. The two women drew their hooded cloaks tightly about them as they tramped in the loose snow and talked of the wolves, whose inroads had been very bold in the last few weeks—now and again Ingunn whistled and called in an anxious voice: "Tota—Tota—Tota!" It was so dark that they could not see each other's faces; Tora asked in a low and strangely dejected tone: "Ingunn—you are not sick, are you—?"

"I cannot say I am well," answered Ingunn, quite calmly and easily. "Thin and light as Aasa had grown at last, I can tell you it was a trying task to lift her and move her, day in, day out, for months. And there was little rest at night. But now it will soon be better with me—"

"You do not think it is anything else that ails you, sister?" asked Tora as before.

"Nay, I cannot think that."

"Last summer you were so red and white—and as slender as when we were both young," whispered Tora.

Ingunn managed to answer with a melancholy little laugh: "Some time I must begin to show, I wis, that I am on the way to thirty. Look at the great children you have, my Tora—do you remember that I am a year and a half older than you?"

In the darkness between the fences a black ball came rushing along—the dog jumped up at Ingunn, nearly sending her headlong into the snowdrifts, and licked her face. She caught it by the muzzle and forepaws, keeping it off as she laughed, and spoke to it fondly: "—And well was it the wolf did not get you tonight either, Tota, my Tota!"

The sisters wished each other good-night and separated.

But Ingunn lay sleepless in the dark, trying to bear this new anxiety—that Tora must have a suspicion. And the temptation came to her—what if she told Tora of her distress, begged her help? Or Aunt Magnhild—she thought of the lady's marked kindness that evening and felt tempted to be weak and give herself up. Dalla—it had also flashed across her mind, when she thought she could no longer bear this secret torment alone—perhaps if she turned to Dalla—

In breathless suspense she kept her eyes on her sister during the days Tora stayed on at Berg. But she could notice nothing—neither by look nor by word did Tora betray any sign that she guessed how it was-with her elder sister. Then she went away, and Ingunn was left alone with her aunt and the old house-folk.

She counted the weeks—thirty were gone already; there were but ten left. She *must* hold out so long. Nine weeks—eight weeks— But as yet she had never clearly acknowledged to herself what the purpose was to which she clung, as she struggled on and suffered, as though stifled in a darkness full of formless terrors, with a dull pain over her whole body and a single thought in her head: that none must have any inkling of the misfortune that had befallen her.

The end that she saw before her—when she thought of it, she was filled with a horror that was like the stiffness of death; but it appeared to her that it was the end of the road, and she *must* reach it, though she would try to walk the last piece with closed eyes. Even when she sought a kind of easement by playing with the thought of crying for help, speaking to someone before it was too late—she never thought in earnest that she would do so. She must go on, to what she saw before her.

So far on in the spring the ground was almost always free of snow hereabouts. They would not find her footprints.—The great birch wood north of the manor stretched from the rocks where they smoked fish almost down to the lake. At its lower end it narrowed to a strip between crags—where folk hardly ever came, and where they could not be seen or heard from the house. The ice did not leave the bay so early. But on the southern shore and on the screes below the birch wood lay great heaps of stones that had been cleared off the fields in former times; there the people of Berg were used to throw down carcasses of horses and other beasts that died a natural death.

6

She had gone up into the bower where she had kept her things since Lady Aasa's time, one morning of early spring—it was a few days before Lady Day. She sat and shivered with fur boots on her feet and a big sheepskin cloak over her clothes; it was now colder indoors than out. Long, glistening drops kept falling from the roof

past the opening, and the air quivered and steamed over the
glimpse she saw of white roofs against the bright blue sky. She
had taken the shutter from the little window to have more air—
she could hardly get her breath, and she felt as though a heavy
leaden hood lay upon her brain inside her skull; it pressed upon
her so that the blood hammered in her neck behind the ears, and
patches of red and black flickered before her eyes. She had taken
refuge up here for fear anyone should speak to her—she had no
strength to talk. But it was some small relief to be able to sit here
in her prostration.

Ever afterwards she believed for certain that she had known
what was coming when she heard the horsemen at the courtyard
gate. She got up and looked out. That was Arnvid, the one who
rode first through the gate; he had his black horse and the ring-
bridle that he used when he went on a visit. The second horse she
also knew to be his, a big-boned grey, which his groom rode. And
the third horseman, he who was riding a high dappled roan, was
Olav Audunsson—she knew that before he had come near enough
for her to recognize him.

He looked up as he held in his horse, saw her at the window,
and waved his hand in greeting. He was wearing a great black
travelling-mantle, which lay in ample folds over the horse's
quarters and covered his legs down to the feet in the stirrups. He
had thrown back the hood, and on his head he wore a black, foreign hat with a high crown and a narrow brim—his fair hair fring-
ing it all round and falling to his eyebrows in front. He had smiled
at her when he threw up his hand.

Ever afterwards it seemed to her she had been awakened from
a nightmare at the instant she saw him—Olav had come home. To
her misfortune, it was true—he would crush her in one way or
another—she faced that at once. But it was as though the blinding
gloom fell away from her on every side, and the devils who had
swarmed about her like the stirring of the darkness itself, so
thickly that they jostled each other with elbows and knees, while
they surrounded her and led her blindly with them—they fell
away from her too. She seemed to know, even as she came down
the stairs of the loft, that, now Olav was come, she could do
naught else than tell him all and accept her doom from him.

Olav stood there with the house-carls who had come to take
the strangers' horses—he turned toward her. With a pang of

wounded pride she saw how handsome he was, and she had fallen away from him—those black clothes suited the bright fairness of the man so well. He gave her his hand. "Well met, Ingunn—" Then he had a sight of her wasted face. And, unheedful of good manners and of all the strangers who stood by, he threw his arms about her, drew her to him, and gave her a kiss full on the mouth. "'Twas a long time you had to wait for me, Ingunn my dear. But now it is over, now I am come to take you home!"

He released her, and she and Arnvid greeted each other with a kiss on the cheek, as became kinsfolk.

She stood by while the young men cried: "All hail!" to Lady Magnhild. They told her laughing that Ivar was with them, but they had ridden from him up by the church—for neither the Galtestad sorrel nor his master was in good trim for speedy travelling.

"Nay, you know how angry he was with the haste you made in your young days," laughed Lady Magnhild. "But since you have put off that bad habit, Olav, I believe my brother has grown more and more fond of you!"

"Have I ever seen such a fair day?" thought Ingunn. The hard snow shone like silver in the spring sun, over the fields and out on the bay. After the mild weather earlier in the week, all the snow had vanished from the woods, and the bare ground shone with young grass, as though newly washed. Across the fields the aspen trees stood with pale green stems within the brown, leafless groves.

And she felt joy bubbling up in her heart—that the world was so full of sunshine and beauty and gladness. And she had put herself outside it, banished herself to her corner. For all that, it was a good thing that it was so good to live—for the others, for all who had not undone themselves. And when at that moment she felt a violent quickening of the child within her, her own heart seemed to stir and answer it—"No, no, I no longer wish you ill. . . ."

They sat at table, and Ingunn listened in silence to the men's talk. She learned that it was intended Arnvid and Ivar should go on the very next day, northward to Haftor Kolbeinsson, and place in his hands the third quarter of the blood-money for Einar. Olav held that it was more seemly he himself should not meet Haftor until he came to pay the rest of the sum, when at the same time he would receive Ingunn and her dowry at the hands of her kinsmen.

"You have no mind to go farther with us, I guess," chuckled Ivar Toresson. "I believe 'tis not your purpose to stir from Berg till you be driven out of the house!"

"Ay, so long as Lady Magnhild will grant me shelter, and fodder for my horse." He laughed with the others, at the same time giving Ingunn a rapid glance out of the corner of his eye. "Sooth to say, I have most liking to stay here, make an end of this matter between Haftor and me—and take Ingunn with me, so soon as I go southward to Hestviken."

"I doubt not that could be done," said Arnvid.

"Ay, I guess what you mean, and I thank you for it—but nevertheless I will not ask more help of you, Arnvid, since I can make shift without it. And I must do as I told you at Galtestad—go south and see how things look at Hestviken, before I bring my wife thither; and fetch the money I am to get in Oslo. And 'twill be far easier to collect the men who ought to be witnesses to our atonement if the feast be held at the time folk are on their way homeward from the Things—whether you wish that I shall receive Ingunn here or at Galtestad. Ivar is right in saying that, since this suit has been so long drawn out and tortuous, it should be brought to an end as openly as may be."

When folk went home from the Things—that was the middle of summer. The thought crossed Ingunn's mind like a whisper from the devils that had had her in their power the whole winter. But now she did not even feel tempted. It was impossible that she could go the rest of that road, now she had seen Olav again. All that she had fancied of her life at Hestviken with him and their children hovered before her mind. To that she could never return—if she tried to free herself of her secret in the gloom of night and hide it among the rocks, it would avail her nothing. Never more could she come to Olav.

Ivar only held up his hands in humorous amazement as he told the others that Olav had not yet set foot in Hestviken. Had anyone ever heard of such a man!

Olav laughingly excused himself—he turned red at the old man's teasing and it made him look very young. He looked younger, more like his former self, than when he was here last—though he now had some lines across his straight, round neck, and when he stretched, a red scar could be seen under his wristband. And his face was thinner and more weatherbeaten. For all that, he looked very young—and Ingunn guessed this was because he was so happy. Her heart sank sickeningly—would it be a *great* grief she was bringing upon him, when he heard that she had thrown herself away?

But he had been given grace, he had got his estate back, she understood that he was a man of some wealth. He had now sold Kaaretorp, the farm he had owned in Elvesyssel, where he had dwelt when at length he had been allowed to return to the country, last autumn. It would not be difficult for Olav to find a better match than she would have been—according to the agreement with her family he would have received no great portion with her, she understood.

Olav went out with her when she was crossing the yard to go to bed. "Do you sleep alone in Aasa's house? Ay, then 'twould scarce be fitting if I came in when you are in bed," he sighed, and gave a little laugh.

"Nay, we can scarce do that."

"But tomorrow night? Can you not get one of the maids to sleep in the house with you—so that we may speak privily in the evenings?"

He clasped her to him, with awkward haste, so hard that she uttered a groan, and kissed her before he let her go.

Ingunn lay awake, trying to think of the future. But it was like trying to clear a path for herself amid a fall of rocks too heavy for her to move. She had no power to think what would become of her now. Nevertheless, she had staggered as far as this in a blinding darkness that lived and moved with unseen terrors, and now she saw the day before her—even if it was as grey and hopeless and impassable as a rainy day in midwinter. Forward she must go: from what she had brought upon herself there was no escape, unless she sought refuge in hell.

She knew that she had lost her rights. She had lost them already in giving herself to Olav without the knowledge and consent of her lawful guardians—they had let her know that plainly enough. If her kinsfolk had afterwards been willing to grant her the right of inheritance, this was for Olav's sake—since they had changed their view of him and found out that it was more profitable to accept his offer of atonement and let him take her to wife in lawful fashion. What they would do when they heard that she had made it impossible for Olav to take her—of that she dared to think only vaguely. When it came to their ears that she was with child—and the father was a man whom it were bootless for her kinsmen to pursue. They would have to let Teit go—they could have no profit of him, and if they would seek him out and punish him, the shame would only be made worse—when it was heard that she had let herself be seduced by such a man.

No, she could not guess what they would do with her—and it. But tomorrow—or in two or three days at the latest—she would have to make trial of it. And, impossible as it was for her to imagine it—it was nevertheless as sure as death that when the birch was green, she would be sitting here with her bastard in her lap, and then she would have to accept all that her kinsfolk might visit upon her in their wrath at her bringing such shame on them all, and at being forced to support her and the child.

She had bowed so completely beneath her fate that her thoughts of yesterday seemed scarcely real, when she believed she could cast off her burden. Her only thought now was that she must drag this child with her all the rest of her life. Nor did she yet feel anything like kindness or affection for it; but it was there, and she must go through with it.

Only for a moment—at the thought that Tora might again claim her for Frettastein, and she saw herself with *her* child, two outcasts, living in Haakon's house among his rich children—only then did something wholly new awaken within her, the first tiny stirring of an instinct to protect her own offspring.

It was her brothers and sister who before all others had the duty of providing for their sustenance. That meant Haakon on Tora's behalf and her two young brothers, whom she had scarcely seen during these years while they were growing into men. Oh, but now she might perhaps dare to hope that Lady Magnhild would be charitable enough to let her remain at Berg, until she had given birth to the child.

Arnvid—she thought of him. If he would offer to receive them; he would be kind to them both. In spite of his being Olav's best friend—he was the friend of *all* who needed help. What if she told her story to Arnvid—to Arnvid and not to Olav? He could speak to Olav and to Lady Magnhild—and she would be spared what was as bad as walking into a living flame.

But she knew that she dared not do this. How she should find courage to speak to Olav she could not tell—but worst of all she feared to hide the truth from Olav. He it was who was her master, he it was whom she had failed, and all at once she felt that, when she had gone through this meeting with Olav, it would come about of itself that she must fall on her knees to God repenting her sin and all the sins she had committed in her whole life—*quia peccavi nimis cogitatione, locutione, opere, et omissione, mea culpa*—the words arose in her of themselves. For each time she had said them, kneeling by Brother Vegard's knee, they were now illumined and brought to life; as when the dark glass of the church window was suddenly illuminated by the sunshine—"because I have sinned most grievously, in thought, word, deed, and omission, *through mine own fault.*"

She arose to her knees in the bed and said her evening prayers —it was long since she had dared. *Mea culpa*—she had been afraid of being saved from doing what she wished and accepting what she had brought upon herself. Now it dawned on her that, when she received God's forgiveness for the evil she had done to herself and to Olav, she would no longer desire to escape her punishment. The mere sight of Olav had been enough to make her see the nature of Love. She had done him the most grievous wrong. And when he suffered, she could not wish herself a better lot. And behind it she caught a glimpse, as in an image, of the origin of Love. In the cup which our Lord was compelled to receive that evening in the Garden of Gethsemane He had seen all the sin that had been committed and was to be committed on earth from the creation of mankind to the last judgment and all the distress and misery that men had caused to themselves and others thereby. And since God had suffered, because of the suffering her own fault would bring her, she too would desire to be punished and made to suffer every time she thought of it. She saw that this was a different suffering from any she had suffered hitherto; that had been like falling from rock to rock down a precipice, to end in a bottomless morass—this was like climbing upward, with a helping hand to hold, slowly and painfully; but even in the pain there was happiness, for it led to something. She understood now what the priests meant when they said there was healing in penance.

Olav and Ingunn were together in the courtyard at noon next day when Ivar and Arnvid were setting out. It was the same fine weather as the day before, thawing and dripping everywhere. The snow settled with a crisp little sound in the shrinking drifts, and the yard was full of tiny streams that washed smooth channels of rock in the winter's carpet of horse-dung and chippings of wood. Ivar was fuming because Arnvid wished to ride over the ice—it was certainly unsafe in many places off the Ringsaker shore; Ivar had once driven into a gap of open water many years before, and ever since he had been a great coward on the ice. But Arnvid laughed him to scorn—what, in broad daylight? Nay, kinsman! They would reach Haftor's before it was quite dark. Toiling uphill and down across country in this going—Arnvid swore he would have none of it— "If you can get your men to follow you, ride where you will, for me, but Eyvind and I will go our own way—"

But the three grooms were already far down the fields. The winter road from several farms higher up led through Berg and down to the bay; from there folk made their way south to the town, or north and west across the high ground on the other side and down to the ice of Mjösen.

Olav and Ingunn walked down with them—Arnvid and Ivar rode at a foot's pace. The snow was thawed away on the upper side of the track here on the sunny slope, and the water ran down. Arnvid warned Olav that he was being well splashed—Olav walked bareheaded, without a cloak, in a sky-blue kirtle reaching to the knees, light leather hose, and low shoes with long, pointed toes. His fine footgear was soaked and dark. "Ingunn is better clad to walk abroad—"

"I know not how she can bear it in this heat—"

She wore the same short, sleeveless sheepskin coat as the day before and tramped along in her fur boots—had done no more to deck herself than tying some red silk ribbons in her hair.

The air breathed warmly about them on the slope and there was a shimmer afar off wherever they looked.

" 'Twas over there we sat that time—do you remember?" whispered Olav to Ingunn. Today there were great bare patches of grass—even yesterday the whole had been silvery white, with only here and there a rock or a juniper bush showing. "We may look for a late sowing this year, since so much is thawed before Lady Day."

They stopped in the dingle and watched the riders. Arnvid turned once in the saddle and waved—Olav threw up his hand in answer. He broke off a branch of bramble and offered it to Ingunn, but when she shook her head, he plucked some of the berries himself, sucked them, and spat out the skins into the snow. "Ay, 'tis time to go back again."

"Nay. Stay a little. There is a matter I must tell you of."

"What is it?—You look so cheerless, Ingunn."

"Indeed, I am not cheerful," she managed to say.

Olav looked at her, at first in surprise—then his face too became serious and he looked half away again. "Is it that you think I stayed from you too long?" he asked in a low voice.

Too long. She would have said it, but could not.

"I thought of that," he said, gently as before. "I thought of you when I followed the Earl—I must tell you, I knew it was to share his outlawry. But he was my lord, Ingunn, the first lord to whom I had sworn fealty. 'Twas not easy for me to know what I ought to do. But I lost desire of food, Ingunn, when I thought of sitting down at Hestviken, eating bread and drinking ale, while he, who had helped me to get back all I possessed, was doomed to wander an outlaw in another land and had lost all he had at home.—But, you know, I did not believe it would be so many years— Think you that I failed you, when I followed the Earl?"

Ingunn shook her head: "In such matters you know well I cannot judge, Olav."

"I thought—" Olav drew a deep breath; "since I was such good friends with Ivar—and the fines for Kolbein were half cleared off —in good English coin—and you were affianced with my ring and gifts—I thought your lot would be a better one where you were. *Has* not your lot been a good one among your kindred, Ingunn?"

"Oh yes. 'Tis not of *that* I can complain—"

"Complain—?"

She heard the first faint catch of fear in his voice, summoned all her courage, and looked at him. He stood with the bramble in his hand, looking at her as though he did not understand, but dreaded what might be coming.

"Have you anything to complain of, then, Ingunn?"

"It was so ordered—that I—I had not strength to—I am no longer fit for you, Olav."

"No longer—fit for me—" his voice was utterly devoid of expression.

Again she had to rouse herself with all her force before she dared look at him. Then they stood staring each other in the eyes. She saw that Olav's face seemed to fade, congeal, and turn grey— he moved his lips once or twice, but it was long before he got the words out: "What do you mean by that—?"

Again they stood staring each other in the eyes. Till Ingunn could bear it no longer. She raised one arm and held it before her face. "Do not look at me like that," she begged, trembling. "I am with child."

After an eternity she felt she could hold out no longer; she let her arm drop and looked at Olav. His face seemed unknown to her—the lower jaw had dropped like that of a corpse, and he stared at her, still as a rock, and this went on and on.

"Olav!" she burst out at last, with a low moan— "speak to me!"

"What do you wish me to say?" he said tonelessly. "If another had told me this—of you—I had killed him!"

Ingunn gave a faint, shrill whine, like a dog that is kicked.

Olav shouted at her: "Hold your peace! You deserve no better —you vile bitch—than to die!" He thrust his shoulders forward as he spoke—again she whimpered like a beaten dog, stepped hastily away from him, and supported herself against the trunk of an aspen. The dazzling light from the snow-crust all around struck her with a sudden blow, unbearable; it made her close her eyes tightly, and she felt the pain shrivelling her body, as meat shrivels when it is thrown upon the fire.

Then she opened her eyes again, looked at Olav—no, she dared not look at him; she looked down at the brier with the red haws which he had thrown down on the snow. And she fell to wailing softly: "It were far better—it were far better—you did it—"

Olav's face contracted violently, became inhuman. His hands grasped the hilt and sheath of his dagger—then he tore it from him, belt and all, and flung it far away. It buried itself somewhere in the thawing drifts.

"Oh, would I were dead, would I were dead!" she moaned again and again.

She felt his wild, red, animal's eyes upon her—and, terrified as she was, her greatest wish was that he would murder her. She put her hands to her throat for an instant—whimpered softly—

The man stood staring at her—at the tense white arch of her throat, as she stood leaning against the tree. Once he had done it— the sword had been struck out of his hand, he was unarmed, and he had taken the other man by the waist and throat and broken him backward—had felt that never before had he put forth his strength to the uttermost.— And as she stood now he could see it— the shameless change that had come over her face, over her form —the mark of the other man.

With a loud groan, like the cry of an animal, he turned his head from the sight and fled up the path.

He heard her calling after him, calling his name. He knew not whether he had cried it aloud or only within himself— "No, no, I dare not come near you—"

She lay in a heap on the little spot of bare earth by the roots of the aspen, rocking herself and wailing. A good while must have gone by. Then Olav was there again. Now he stood bending over her, breathing down on her: "Who is father—to the child you bear?"

She looked up, shook her head. "Oh—'tis no— He was clerk to the Sheriff of Reyne. Teit was his name, an Icelander—"

" 'Twere a sin to say you were hard to please," said Olav with a sort of laugh. He took her roughly by the arm, gripped it till she wailed aloud. "And Magnhild—what says she to this? She laughed so merrily with the others yestereven—" he ground his teeth— "at me, I wis, silly gull that I was to be so glad and easy, never dreaming of such increase in my fortune. Oh—God's curse upon you all!"

"Magnhild knows nothing. I have kept it hid from every soul, until I told it to you but now."

"That was gracious of you indeed! I was to be the first to know! Now, I had always thought I could get my children myself, but—"

"Olav!" she cried piteously. "Had you not come so soon"—her voice broke—"none would ever have known of it—"

Again they looked each other in the eyes for an instant. Ingunn's head dropped forward.

"Jesus Christ! You are not human, I trow!" whispered Olav in horror.

He straightened himself and stretched once or twice, and each time she had a glimpse of a red scar on his chest near the throat. He said, more to himself than her: "If they had brought me tidings that you were a leper—I believe I should still have longed for the day I could take you home.—'Wilt thou keep this woman in sickness as in health?' asks the priest at the church door.—But this —nay, this—! God forgive me, I cannot do it!"

He took her roughly by the shoulder. "Do you hear, Ingunn? —I cannot do it! Magnhild must—you must tell Magnhild I cannot. And since she has had no better care of you—this has befallen while you were in her charge, so she must herself— I cannot bear to see you again, before you are rid of it—

"Do you hear?" he repeated. "You must tell Magnhild yourself!"

Ingunn nodded.

Then he went up the road.

The ground was soaking wet where she sat, and she felt the cold stiffening and crippling her; it was an alleviation. She put her arm about the trunk of the aspen and leaned her cheek against it. Now it was time to search within herself for the consolation that was to come after she had told him. But she could not find it—only a bitter remorse, but not the contrition that brought hope. Her only wish was to be allowed to die at once—she had no strength to think of arising and going on to face all she must go through.

She called to mind all the words of comfort she had meant to say to Olav—that he should think no more of her; when he went out into the world, he must enjoy his happiness without thinking of her; she was not worth it. She saw now that it was true, and it was no consolation—that was the worst of all, that she was not worth his thoughts.

She did not know how long she had lain there when she heard the sound of sledges on the road. She struggled painfully to her feet—she was stiff with cold and her body ached all over when she moved—her feet were asleep and she could hardly stand or walk. But she made her way into the bushes and pretended she was eating haws as the two loaded sledges drove past. The workmen greeted her quietly and she answered them. They were folk from the farms above.

The sun had sunk a long way toward the west—the light on the snow was now orange, and the rising vapour began to be visible as a low-lying mist. She tramped hither and thither on the road for a while, not knowing where to go. Then she caught sight of some horsemen out on the ice—it looked as if they were coming this way—she took fright and turned toward the house.

She was about to steal into her own bower when Lady Magnhild came up to her from the other house. To Ingunn's scared senses her aunt appeared terrible, with her fleshy, florid face surrounded by its wimple, and her stomach thrust forward under the silver belt, with all the clatter of heavy keys, dagger, and scissors dangling at her side—like the time the mad bull came charging straight toward her. She put out her hand to the doorpost for support. But at that moment it seemed her powers of being frightened had been stretched too far.

"Holy Mary, where have you come from—have you been out loitering all day?—rolling in the road, one would think—you are smothered in wet and horse-dung up to your neck! What has come to you—and Olav, what is it with him?"

Ingunn did not answer.

"Do *you* know what took him to Hamar so suddenly? He came here and got out his horse, Hallbjörn could make nothing of him —he must go to Hamar, he said; but he left his bag behind, and he rode as though the devil sat behind him—'twas an ugly sight, the way he used his spurs, said Hallbjörn—"

Ingunn said nothing.

"What is this?" asked Lady Magnhild, flashing with wrath. "Do *you* know what is afoot with Olav?"

"He is gone," said Ingunn. "He would stay here no longer, when he had heard—when I had told him how it is with me—"

"—*is* with you?" Lady Magnhild stared at the girl—in her drenched clothes, her tousled hair out of its plaits and full of bark and refuse, her face a dirty grey and thin as a scraped bone—she was ugly, nothing else—and the way she held herself in the filthy wet sheepskin—

"Is with you!" she shrieked; she caught Ingunn by the upper arm and pushed her through the door, making her stumble over the threshold. Then she flung the girl across the room, so that she fell and lay in a heap by the draught-stone. Her aunt barred the door behind them.

"Nay—! Nay—! Nay—! 'Tis not I can guess what you have been doing!"

She took hold of Ingunn and pulled her up. "Take off your clothes—you are as wet as a drowned corpse. Ay, 'tis what I have always thought of you—half-witted you are; 'tis not possible you have your right senses!"

Ingunn lay in bed, half-numbed, and listened to her aunt's talk as she hung her wet things on the clothes-horse over the hearth. It was the first time in all these months she had lain down wholly undressed, and it was such a relief to be free of all these cruel bonds she had put upon herself—to get rest. It scarcely occurred to her that Lady Magnhild might justly have been far, far harsher with her—she had neither cursed nor struck her, nor dragged her by the hair—she did not even say much of what was in her mind.

Lady Magnhild took it in this way, that she demanded a full confession of how it had come about—then it was for her to see if some means could be found of keeping it hid.

She asked who was the father, but when Ingunn told her, Lady Magnhild sat for a long while perfectly speechless. This was so utterly beyond all she had ever believed possible that she could only think it must be so—the poor thing was something wanting. Ingunn had to give an account of all there had been between her and Teit—she gave short and broken answers to Lady Magnhild's rigorous questions. It was six months since she had seen him—no, he knew nothing of how it was with her—she expected the child in six weeks—

It was wiser to let the bird fly, thought Lady Magnhild. And there must surely be some means of keeping the girl hidden here in Aasa's house for the rest of her time; it could be said that she was sick—there were not many who asked after Ingunn; it was a lucky chance that she had lived so much in the shade all these years. Her aunt strictly forbade her to move beyond the door during the hours when the folk of the house were out of bed. Dalla would have to live with her for the present, and when her time came, they would send for Tora.

Ingunn lay still and let her weariness overcome her. It was almost good to be alive—her feet had grown warm between the bedclothes, and sleep poured over her like sweet tepid water. Half-dazed she heard Lady Magnhild discussing with herself how they might best smuggle out the child as soon as it was born.

When she awoke, she guessed it must be late in the evening; the fire on the hearth was almost burned out, but not yet raked over. Dalla sat on a stool beside it, nodding and spinning. Outside, a storm was rising—Ingunn heard the wind on the corners of the house, and just then something wooden clattered against the wall outside. She was still sunk in placid ease.

"Dalla," she said after a while. The old woman did not hear.

"Dalla," she repeated a little later. "Cannot you go out and see what it is that knocks so against the wall—see if you can move it—"

Dalla rose and came up to the bed. "So you are yet proud and grand enough to send folks on errands for you, lazy-bones! I am here to herd you, but not to run and do your bidding—shame on you, paltry jade!"

Lady Magnhild looked in on her niece for a moment once or twice each day; she gave Ingunn no more angry words—said very little to her at all. One day, however, she told Ingunn that she had found a foster-mother for the child—the wife of a cottar who lived in a clearing in the woods far to the north. It was settled that Lady Magnhild should send for her at once when Ingunn's birth-pangs came on; then they could get it out of the way as soon as it was born. Ingunn said nothing to this, and Lady Magnhild guessed it must be as she thought—the girl was only half-witted.

Then she was left alone with Dalla, day and night. She crouched, still as a mouse; if she did but move or breathe heavily, she feared Dalla would fall upon her with scorn and abuse, all the foulest and most cruel words she could think of.

Dalla and Grim had never been thralls in the way that folk in old time were as their masters' cattle. But in many places it had made very little difference between free-born and serf-born that the latter now had rights under the law. And least of all where it was a question of the descendants of the ancient noble families and their married servants who were the offspring of the old thrall stock of the house. It could never occur to such a master or mistress to part with such a couple, were they never so troublesome or incapable or sick or infirm; nor had it ever been the custom in these families to sell their thralls: an unusually good-looking

or promising thrall child might be given away to a young relative
or a godchild, and a thrall who gave far more trouble than service, or who was guilty of a misdeed, disappeared.—And even now
the serf-born serving-folk hardly ever thought of anything but
staying and earning their livelihood where they were born—in the
inland districts. The honour of their master's house was their honour, its happiness and prosperity were theirs; they followed it in
good and evil fortune, and the subject they threshed out again and
again among themselves was the life of their masters in hall and
chamber and bower, every scrap of it they could seize upon.

Aasa Magnusdatter had had Grim and Dalla with her since all
three were children, and when she sent them to Steinfinn, it was
as a gift from mother to son. Steinfinn's lot had been theirs, and
since Aasa thought that his misfortunes were due to his marriage,
they conceived a hatred for his wife, though they dared not show
it. Although Ingunn by no means took after her mother, she had
come in for a share of their ill will—without very much reason.
But Olav and Tora had been their favourites among the children;
these two were calm and considerate in their behaviour to the old
bailiff and his sister—Ingunn was thoughtless and flighty, and they
decried her yet more in order to exalt the others. And besides this,
Dalla had been violently jealous all these years, that Ingunn and
not she should have the care of Lady Aasa, and she saw the grandmother's fondness for the girl. And now that Ingunn had brought
this unheard-of shame upon the Steinfinnssons and proved false
to Olav, and had been handed over to Dalla, perfectly helpless and
without the power of defending herself, the thrall woman took
her revenge, according to her lights.

In the crudest and cruellest language she spoke at length of all
the things of which Ingunn was only dimly aware—of Teit and of
Olav—till the young woman was scalded with shame and wished
the floor would open and hide her in the earth. Whether Ingunn
sat or stood or walked, Dalla fell upon her with mockery for being so ugly. And then the old woman tried as well as she could to
scare Ingunn out of her wits with talk of what awaited her when
she should be laid on the floor; she predicted her the hardest of
childbirths and said she could see it in her that she was to die.

Ingunn had always known that Dalla disliked her and counted
her a fool, but she had never paid much attention to that. And it
came as an altogether unlooked-for blow that the old thrall

woman should apply herself to torturing her with such untiring malignity. Ingunn could guess no other reason for it but that she herself must be so disgraced and besmirched and abominable that those who had to be with her were minded to trample on her, as one tramples on a loathsome reptile.

So she gave up all thought of peace or preservation. That she might die was the best she dared hope. If only she might be free of this strange creature—for which she could still feel nothing but terror and hatred—she had no wish in the world but to be allowed to die.

Ten days passed in this way. Late in the evening they were sitting, each in her corner, Ingunn and Dalla, when someone came to the door. Dalla started up. "None comes in here!"

"Oh yes, I come in," said the man who stepped across the threshold; it was Arnvid.

Ingunn got up and went to meet him; she laid her arm about his neck and leaned forward to him—he was the only one she knew of on earth who would be good to her, even now. Then she felt him draw back a little and loosen the hold of her hands on his neck— and this sank into her, deeper than Dalla's abuse. Even Arnvid abhorred her—was she as befouled as that? The next moment Arnvid stroked her cheek, took her hand, and made her sit by him on the little settle by the fire.

"Go out with you, Dalla," he said to the old woman. "The Fiend himself must have put it into Magnhild's head to send that half-crazy witch to help you.—Or do you like to have her here perhaps?"

"Oh, no," she said weakly. And little by little Arnvid got from her something of Dalla's conduct—though it was not much that Ingunn could bring herself to mention. He took her hand and laid it on his knee. "Never fear—I trow you will be plagued with her no more!"

But there was so little that he could bring himself to say. He wished that she herself would tell him how Olav had taken this, and whether she knew what the man would do, or where he was now, or what was to become of herself; but it was impossible for him to speak of it first.

So Olav's name was never spoken between them, though Arnvid sat there a pretty long time. As he was going, he said: "'Tis an ill thing, Ingunn—I cannot help you. But you must try to send me word as soon as there comes a time when a man can be of use to you. I would fain have a word to say when they take counsel how you and the child shall be bestowed."

"There is no man can help me."

"Nay, that is true enough. You must put yourself in God's hands, Ingunn—then you know all will be well in the end."

"Ay, I know that. And you can say it. But 'tis not you that are in this case." She squeezed his hand in her distress. "I cannot sleep at night—and I have such dreadful thirst. And I dare not get up and drink for fear of Dalla—"

"Nay, nay," said Arnvid softly. "There is none of us that has known what it feels like to hang upon a cross. But that robber, he knew—and he hung there rightfully. And you know yourself what he did—"

Awhile after Arnvid had gone out, Lady Magnhild came and rebuked Dalla sharply. She bade her remember that Ingunn was Steinfinn's daughter, whether she had done wrong or not, and she was not to be troubled with unseemly prating from a serving-woman. And when Ingunn was in bed, Dalla came in with a great bowl full of whey and water and set it down on the footstool beside the bed with a smack, so that the drink splashed over. But in the course of the night, when Ingunn wanted to drink, she got a mouthful of refuse—it tasted like straw and sweepings from the floor.

Arnvid came in to see her next day, before he left, but they had not much to say to each other.

Ivar had come to Berg in Arnvid's company, but he did not go to see his niece. Ingunn did not know whether he was so angry with her that he would not look at her, or whether any had asked him to stay away so as to spare her.

Arnvid reached the convent of the preaching friars in the middle of the day and learned at once from the porter that Olav was there —he had come more than a week ago. He did not lie in the guest-house, but in a little house that the new Prior had had built in the kale-yard—he had bethought him that men and women ought not to be lodged together in the hostel, but that the women must stay outside the convent walls. But the women would not lie there, separated from their company and close to the graveyard. More-over the house was badly built, and draughty in winter, and instead of a hearth Sir Bjarne had had a stove built in the corner by the door, but it gave no heat, and the smoke from it would not draw out through the louver.

It was cold under the shadow of the church and chapter-house, and the thin coat of ice crunched with the jingling of his spurs as Arnvid walked through the garden. Here the snow had now thawed enough to leave the rows of peas and beans standing out as black banks with pale rotting stalks above. The women's house abutted on the churchyard fence; it was darkened by some big old trees even now, when they were bare.

The house had no anteroom; Arnvid walked straight in. Olav was sitting on his bed with his legs hanging over the side and his neck resting against the wall. Arnvid saw with a shock how changed his friend was. His ashen hair seemed faded, because his whole complexion was now the same, a greyish yellow, and it was so long since he had shaved that the lower part of his face seemed flooded—Olav was blighted and haggard all over. The fresh timber walls were still yellow, and there was some smoke in the room, but only a few embers glowed in the stove—and Arnvid felt that he had come into a place where all was wan and frozen.

Neither man noticed that they forgot their greetings.

"Have you come?" asked Olav.

"Yes—" said Arnvid stupidly. Then he remembered to say—as Olav knew it had been his intention the whole time—he had come to see Finn, his son, who was a pupil in the school. After that it occurred to him that he must tell Olav how they had fared with Haftor Kolbeinsson.

"How fared you, then?" asked Olav.

Oh, Haftor had been well pleased with the money—

"How long were you at Berg?" Olav gave a little frozen laugh. "I can see you have been there."

"I lay there last night."

"And how goes it there?"

"As you may well conceive," said Arnvid curtly.

Olav said no more. Arnvid sat down, and they were both silent. After a while a lay brother came in with bread and ale for the new-comer. Arnvid drank, but could not eat. The monk stayed for a few moments, chatting with Arnvid—Olav only sat and glared. And when the brother was gone, the silence fell between them again.

At last Arnvid pulled himself together. "What will you do about the atonement now, Olav? Will you give me and Ivar authority to act for you, when the matter is to be concluded? For you will have no mind to come north yourself and meet Haftor this summer?"

"I cannot see how I am to escape it," replied Olav. "She cannot journey alone over the half of Norway and home to me. There might be a danger that the next bantling was on the way before she reached her journey's end—" he smiled maliciously. "Oh nay, it were safer that I take her in hand myself; so soon as may be."

After a pause Arnvid asked, in a low and tremulous voice: "What do you mean by that?"

Olav laughed.

"Do you think of taking her to you after this?" asked Arnvid softly.

"You must know that, I suppose, you who are half-trained for a priest," said Olav bitterly. "That I cannot part from her."

"No," replied Arnvid quietly. "But I was not sure whether you saw that yourself. But, you know, none can force you take her into your house and live with her after this."

"I must have someone to live with, I trow, like the rest," said Olav in the same bitter tone. "I have lived among strangers from my seventh year. 'Tis not too soon to have a house and home of my own. But, you know, 'tis more than I had reckoned for, that she should bring into the household a brat ready-made—"

"Magnhild has provided already for the fostering of the child," said Arnvid softly. "It will be set out to nurse the same day it sees the light."

"Nay. I will not be shackled with any dealings in these parts. I will have nothing to do with anyone from here. Neither she nor I shall set our foot here in the north when once we have come away from it. In the devil's name, has my wife turned whore, I must be able to take her bastard into the bargain—" He ground his teeth.

"She is in such shame and distress now, Olav," pleaded Arnvid.

"Ay—we must smart, I wis, both one and the other, for the favours she allowed that vagabond Icelander of hers—"

"Never have I seen a child so wretched and cast down. Remember, Olav, when you had to leave her and fly the country—she was in an ill way even then, Ingunn. Weak she has always been, had little strength or wit to choose wisely for herself—"

"I know that well enough. It is not that I have ever thought her shrewd or firm of mind. But still this is a hard thing for a man to have to stomach.—Have they—" his voice suddenly failed him—"have they been *very* harsh with her? Know you that?"

"Nay, they have not. But it needs not much to break *her*. You know that yourself."

Olav made no reply. He leaned forward, with his hands hanging over his knees, and stared at the floor. After a while Arnvid said: "At Berg, I ween, there is none but thought you would put her away."

Olav sat as before. Arnvid dared not bring out what he had at heart. Then suddenly Olav himself spoke: "I said to her that I should come back—to Ingunn. Half a heathen she has been all her days, but I thought she had guessed so much—that we are bound together, while we are in life—"

Arnvid said: "When they wished to give her to Gudmund Jonsson, you know that would have been a right good match for her—but then she spoke as though she understood full well."

"Ha! But now, when she herself has broken her troth, she expects that I too shall go back on all I have spoken before God and men—?"

"She expects she is to die, I believe."

"Ay, that were the easiest way out, for both her and me."

Arnvid did not answer.

Then Olav asked: "I promised *you* once—that I would never fail your kinswoman. Do you remember?"

"Yes."

At last Arnvid broke the silence: "Ought they not to know it, Ivar and Magnhild—that you will take her in spite of all?"

He received no answer; and spoke again: "Will you consent that I tell them what you will do?"

"I can tell them myself what I will do," answered Olav shortly. "I forgot some of my things there too," he added, as though to soften it.

Arnvid said nothing. He thought that, in the mood Olav was in now, it was uncertain that they would have much comfort of him when he came to Berg. But he deemed he had no right to meddle with the affair further than he had done.

In the course of the afternoon, when Olav was ready for the road, he asked Arnvid: "When had you thought of going home again?"

Arnvid said he had not thought of that yet.

Olav did not look at the other, and he spoke as though he were ashamed and had difficulty in getting the words out: "I would rather we did not see each other again—before the atonement feast. When I come back from Berg, I would rather not—" he clenched his fists and ground his teeth sharply—"I cannot bear the sight of anyone who knows of this!"

Arnvid turned crimson in the face, but he swallowed the insult and answered coolly: "As you will.—Should you change your mind, you know the way to Miklebö."

Olav gave Arnvid his hand, but would not meet the other's eyes. "Ay—thanks for that—'tis not that I am ungrateful—"

"Nay, nay— You go south now, to Hestviken?" he asked nevertheless.

"No, I have thought to stay here—for a time. Haply I ought to find out if I am to prepare a home-coming feast or not—" he tried to laugh. "If she is not to live, there is no need—"

Ingunn sat crouching in the corner by the bed, and it was so dark both indoors and out that she could not distinguish who it was that came in, but she thought it was Dalla, who had finished in the byre. But the figure did not move, after closing the door behind it—and a terrible fear seized her, though she could not guess what it was that had come in; her heart flew up into her throat and throbbed like a sledge-hammer if anyone spoke to her. She struggled to quell her loud breathing and drew back into her corner, still as a mouse.

"Are you here, Ingunn?"

When she heard Olav's voice, it was as though her heart beat itself to pieces—it faltered and stopped, and through her whole body went a feeling that she was stifling to death.

"Ingunn—are you here?" he asked again. He advanced into the room—she could make out his form, square-shouldered and broad in his cloak against the feeble glow from the hearth. He had heard her groaning breath and felt about, trying to find where she sat in the dark.

And now terror gave back her speech: "Come not near me! Olav—come not near me!"

"I shall not touch you. Be not afraid—I will do you no harm."

She cringed away, speechless, fighting to overcome the terrible breathlessness that her fear had brought on her.

Olav's voice was heard, calm and level: "It came into my mind —'twere best after all that I myself speak with Ivar and Magnhild. Have you told them who is the father?"

"Yes," she whispered painfully.

Olav said, hesitating a little: "That was bad. I should have thought of it before—but I was so—surprised—I knew not what I said. But now I have bethought me, 'tis best I take upon myself the fatherhood. It will surely come out—such things are always noised abroad—and then we must say the child is mine. We must spread the report that I came secretly here to Berg last year at that time—"

"But it is not true," she whispered feebly.

"No. I know *that*." He said it so that it struck her like a whip. "And folk will surely doubt it—but that is all one, if they only see they must not speak their doubts too loudly. You must all say as I have said. I will not have it that you should keep such a child here in the Upplands; we should never feel safe that the story would not be ripped up again. You must take it south with you—

"Do you understand what I say?" he asked hastily, as she gave no sound beyond her heavy breathing in the darkness.

"No," came her answer all at once, clear and firm. It had happened to her before, very rarely—when tormented and frightened to the uttermost it was as though something broke within her mind, and then she was able to face anything, calm and composed. "You must not think of that, Olav. You must have no thought of taking me to you after this."

"Talk not so foolishly," replied Olav impatiently. "You ought to know as well as I that we two are bound to each other hand and foot."

"They told me—Kolbein and those—that there were many good and learned priests who judged your case otherwise than Lord Torfinn—"

"Ay, there is no case that all men are agreed on. But I hold to Bishop Torfinn's judgment. I gave him an ill reward for his kindness that time—but I laid this case in his hands and bowed to his judgment, when it fell out as I desired. And I must bow to it now likewise."

"Olav—do you remember that last night, when you came out to me at Ottastad?" Her voice was mournful, but calm and collected. "Do you remember saying you would kill me?—you said the one who broke troth with the other should die. You drew your knife and set it against my breast.—I have that knife—"

"Ay, keep it and welcome.—That night—oh, you must not speak of it—we swore so many oaths! I have since thought it was a greater sin, all we said then, than Einar's slaying. But I never thought it would be you who—"

"Olav," she said as before, "it is impossible. You could never have any joy of me if I came with you to Hestviken. I was sure of that as soon as I saw you. When you said you would come and fetch me in the summer—I saw that I had time enough to keep this concealed—"

"Ah—so you thought of that!" The words struck her like a blow, so that she threw herself upon the bed and clasped the bedpost as she broke into sobs, wailing in her abyss of shame and humiliation.

"Go from me, go from me," she whimpered. She remembered that Dalla might come in at any moment, bringing light into the room. At the thought that Olav might *see* her she was wild with despair and shame. "Go," she begged; "Olav, have pity on me and go!"

"Ay, now I will go. But you must know, 'twill be as I have said.—Nay, weep not so, Ingunn," he pleaded. "I wish you no harm—

"Much joy of each other we may not have," his bitterness got the better of him and he could not keep back the words. "God knows, in all these years—I often thought how I would make you a good husband—how I would do you all the good I might.—Now I dare give no such promise—it may well be difficult many a time to keep me from being hard on you. But, God helping me, our life will be no worse than we can both endure."

"Ay, would you had killed me that day," she wailed, as though she had scarce heard what he said.

"Be silent," he whispered, revolted. "You speak of killing—your own babe—and of my killing you—you are more beast than human, methinks; lose your wits when you see no escape. Men and women must bear resolutely what they have brought upon themselves—"

"Go!" she beseeched him; "go, go—"

"Ay, I will go now. But I shall come back—I shall come back when you have had this child of yours, Ingunn—then maybe you will find your wits again, so far that one may talk with you—"

She felt that he came a few steps nearer—and cringed as though she awaited ill treatment. Olav's hand felt for her shoulder in the dark; he bent over her and kissed her on the crown of her head, so hard that she felt his teeth.

"Be not so distressed," he whispered, standing over her. "I wish you no worse than— You must believe I do but seek a way out."

He took his hand from her and went out quickly.

Next morning Lady Magnhild came into her. Ingunn lay in bed gazing vacantly before her. Lady Magnhild's wrath was roused when she saw that the girl looked just as despairing today as ever.

"Have you not brought this misfortune on yourself?—and now you are to be rid of it far more lightly than you had a right to expect. We must all thank God and Mary Virgin on our knees that Olav is the man he is. But I say—God requite Kolbein as he deserves, for that he set himself against Olav's taking you long ago, and cozened that silly gull Ivar to be on his side! If they had only let Olav have you then, nine years ago!"

Ingunn lay motionless and said nothing.

Lady Magnhild went on talking: "Be it as it may, I'll not send for Hallveig at present. Since you are in such a wretched state, we may well doubt if it will live," she said consolingly. "And should it live, 'twill be time enough to speak of what will be best."

On the fourth day of Easter came Tora Steinfinnsdatter. Ingunn rose to meet her sister as she came in, but she had to take hold of the bedstead to keep on her feet, such was her dread of hearing what Tora would say.

But Tora took her in her arms and patted her. "My poor, poor Ingunn!"

And then she began to speak of Olav's generosity and of how black it would have looked if he had acted as most men in his position—sought to be rid of a wife who had never been given to him in lawful wedlock. "Sooth to say, I knew not Olav was so pious a man. He had much to do with the priests and the Church —I thought 'twas mainly for his own profit. I did not believe it was because he was so God-fearing and steadfast in the faith—

"And he will not claim that you part with your child," said Tora, beaming. "That must be such a comfort to you—are you not overjoyed that you need not send away your child?"

"Oh yes. But speak no more of that," begged Ingunn at last, for Tora never ceased her praises of this good luck in the midst of misfortune.

Tora said nothing of what she might have guessed or feared in the winter, nor did she censure her sister with many words, but tried rather to put a little heart into Ingunn: when relief came in a little while, she would find that the whole world would appear to her in brighter colours, and then there would come good days for her too; but she must not abandon herself as she did—she sat there in her corner all day long, never moved nor spoke a word unasked—only gazing before her in black despondency.

Dalla had taken Lady Magnhild's correction in such wise that never since had she opened her mouth to Ingunn. But she found ways enough, for all that, to torment the sick woman. Ingunn never dared lie down at night till she had felt under the bed-clothes whether anything hard and sharp had been put there. And all at once she found a mass of vermin in her bed and in her day-clothes—they had been perfectly clean before. There were constantly cinders and chips and mouse-dirt in the food and drink that Dalla brought her. Every morning she tied Ingunn's shoes so tightly that they hurt her, and while Ingunn struggled painfully to loosen them, Dalla stood by with a sneering smile. Ingunn never said a word about this.

But Tora guessed at once a good deal of what had been going on—she took Dalla to task right heartily, and the old thrall woman cringed before her young mistress like a beaten dog. And when Tora saw that Ingunn could not overcome her terror if Dalla did but approach her, she drove the old woman out of Aasa's house for good. She helped her sister to be rid of the worst of the vermin, got her clean clothes and good food; and she checked her aunt when Lady Magnhild grumbled at Ingunn's ingratitude— saying that she herself had had a part in the disaster, and they had assuredly treated her more gently than she had a right tó expect; she would put up with no more of this sullen crossness toward Ingunn. But Tora implored the lady—let them do all they could to make these last days easy for her; when she was on her feet again after her lying-in—it would be another matter. Then she would be strong enough to hear some grave words from them both.

7

SINCE Olav Audunsson had done penance for the slaying in the preaching friars' guest-house, he had formed fairly close ties with this monastic community; Brother Vegard, too, had been his confessor ever since he was a child, and he was a good friend of Arnvid Finnsson, who was one of the benefactors of the house. And before this last turn of events with Ingunn, Olav had had thoughts of joining the Dominicans as a brother *ab extra*. When the friars now saw that something weighed upon his mind, they left him in peace and avoided as far as possible lodging other guests in the women's house, where he lay. There was no little coming and going in the convent during Lent, for many folk from the country round were wont to make their Lenten confession here and celebrate Easter in the convent church.

Olav put off his confession again and again. He could not see how he was to make it in the right way—Ingunn could not have confessed yet, for Olav knew that Brother Vegard was still her confessor, and the monk had not been absent from the convent for six weeks. So Olav sat in the women's house and went nowhere—except to church.

But on Wednesday in Holy Week he thought he could not put it off any longer, and Brother Vegard promised to be in the church at a certain hour.

It felt cold and dark as he entered through the little side door from the cloister garth—it was the same spring weather out of doors. Brother Vegard already sat in his place in the choir, reading a book that he held on his knee, with the purple stole over his white frock. From an opening high up a sunbeam fell straight upon the pictures that were painted above the monks' choir stalls —lighting up the likeness of our Lord at the age of twelve among the Jewish doctors. "God, my Lord," prayed Olav in his heart, "give me discretion to say what I have to say and no more and no less." Then he knelt before the priest and said *Confiteor*.

With scrupulous care he rehearsed his sins against all the ten commandments, those he had broken and those he had kept, so far as he knew—he had had good time to think over his confession. At last he came to the hard part: "Then I confess that there is one to whom I bear the most bitter grudge, so that it seems to me most difficult to forgive this person. It is one whom I have loved with all my heart, and so soon as I heard what this friend had done to me, I felt I had been so deceived that thoughts of slaughter and wicked and cruel desires arose within me. God preserved me so that I curbed myself at that time. But so hard is it for me to bear with this person that I fear I can never forgive my friend—unless God give me special grace thereto. But I am afraid, father, that I must say no more of this matter."

"Is it because you are afraid you might otherwise disclose another's sin?" asked Brother Vegard.

"Yes, father," Olav drew a deep breath. "And it is for that reason that it seems so difficult to forgive. If I could tell the whole matter here in this place, I think it would be easier."

"Consider well, my Olav, whether it does not seem so to you because you think that, could you speak freely of the wrong your even Christian has done you, you own evil thoughts, your hatred and desire of blood, would then be justified according to what we sinful men call justice?"

"It is so, father."

The monk asked: "Do you hate this your enemy in such wise that you could wish him evil fortune every day upon earth and eternal perdition in the other world?"

"No."

"But you could wish that he might smart for what he has done to you, often and sorely?"

"Yes. For I can see naught else but that I myself must smart for it as long as I live. And I fear that, unless God work a miracle with me, I shall never more have peace in my soul, but wrath and ill will will arise in me time after time—for after this my affairs—my welfare and my repute—will grow worse, so long as I live upon earth."

"My son, you know that if you pray with your whole heart,

God will give you strength to forgive him that trespassed against you, for it has never yet been known that God was deaf to such a prayer. But you must pray without reservation—not as that man of whom Saint Augustine tells us: he prayed that God would give him grace to lead a chaste life, but not at once; it is in such wise men are wont to pray for grace to forgive their enemies. And you must not be downcast, even if God lets you pray long and persistently before He grants you this gift."

"Ay, father. But I fear I shall not always be able to curb myself while I wait for my prayers to be heard."

As the monk did not reply at once, Olav said hastily: "For it is so, father, that this thing which—which my friend—has done to me—has disórdered my whole life. I dare not say more of it, but there are such difficulties— Could I say more, you would see that—this person—has set so heavy a load upon my neck—"

"I can guess that it is heavy, my son. But you must be steadfast and pray. And when on Good Friday you come forward to kiss the cross, look on it closely and reflect in your heart whether your sins did not weigh something in the load which our Lord bore, when He shouldered the sins of us all. Think you then that the load which your friend has laid upon you is so heavy that you are not able to bear it—a Christian man and His man?"

Olav bent so low that he touched the monk's knee with his forehead. "Nay. Nay, I think not that—" he whispered falteringly.

The night between Good Friday and Easter Eve Olav awoke drenched with sweat—he had been dreaming. As he lay in pitch-darkness trying to be rid of the horror this dream had left in his mind, their childhood came back to him in the very life: in his dream they had been boy and girl. But when he thought how all had promised then and how their future looked now, all that he believed himself to have secured through his constant prayers of the last few days seemed to fade away like smoke between his fingers. He drew the bedclothes over his head, and, lest he should burst into tears, he lay as a man lies on the rack, straining his whole will to a single end—the torturers shall not force one moan out of him.

That summer—that summer and that autumn, when she awaited his coming every night in her bower. Uneasy he had been; the guileless young heart in his breast had quivered with excitement and disquietude from the moment he awoke and saw that he was naked. But of *her* he had always felt easy. That she could fall out of his hands and into another man's—no, that he had never imagined. That last night, when he had come to her a homicide and an outlaw, when he had put the cold blade against her warm breast and bade her keep the knife for a token—it was not that he thought she might prove faithless. His thoughts were of himself, who was about to face an uncertain fate, young and untried and doubtful as he was.

When he crept close to her and hid his face in her wheat-coloured hair, it smelt like new-mown hay. And her flesh was so soft and limp, it always made him think of corn that had not fully ripened—was still milky. Never had he taken her in his arms without the thought: "I must not be hard-handed with her, she is so slight and weak; she needs my protection against every shock and scratch, for this flesh of hers cannot be such as heals quickly." And he had spared her all talk of that which weighed upon him, for he thought it would be a shame to shift any of his burden onto her feeble shoulders. Uneasy conscience, anxiety for the future—what should she understand of such things, with her childlike nature? The very insatiability with which she demanded his caresses, set herself to provoke them if he became absent for a moment or chanced to speak of any but their own concerns—this he took to be a kind of childishness. She had little more understanding than a child or an animal, poor thing—nay, he had often thought her like a gentle, timid beast—a tame doe or a young heifer, so fond of endearments and so easily scared.

Now he remembered that he had divined this at the same moment as he divined what it meant that she was a woman whom he would possess and enjoy—it had been clear to him that she was a weak and tender creature and that he must shield and defend her.

And now it appeared to him that this dream might have been sent him as a gift, though it had at first called up such grim torment in his mind. He had believed himself capable of wishing she might suffer abundantly for her weakness. Far from it.—He would do all in his power to help her to be let off lightly.

"My little doe—you have let yourself be chased straight into the pit—and now you lie there, battered and besmirched, a poor little beast. But I shall come and take you up and bear you away to a place where you will not be trampled upon and crushed."

—Now it was revealed to him that what had happened when he had taken her in his arms, plucked her flower, and breathed its sweetness and its scent, was only something that had chanced by the way. But what really mattered, when it came to the point, was that she had been placed in his arms in order that he might carry her through everything, take the burden from her and defend her. That was to be his happiness, the other was no more than passing joys.

Throughout the holy-days of Easter he was as one who had just risen from a grievous sickness—not that he had ever been sick in his life; but so he felt it. "My soul is now healed— Ingunn, you must know that I wish you naught but well."

He wondered whether he ought to tell his dream to Brother Vegard. But in these wellnigh twenty years during which the monk had been his confessor, he had never spoken a word to him in confidence outside the confessional. Brother Vegard Ragnvaldsson was a good man and a man of intelligence, but dry and chilly by nature—and then he had a sly and witty way of talking of folk, in which Olav delighted, so long as he was not himself the victim. Nor had he ever before felt any impulse to cross the fence that separated him and his confessor; rather had it seemed an advantage that the man outside the church was almost another person than the priest who heard his self-reproaches and guided him in spiritual things.

Before now he had thought of confiding this matter of Ingunn to the monk outside the confessional. But this would be like justifying himself and accusing her; so he would not. Doubtless Brother Vegard would soon be sent for to Berg; the poor soul must soon prepare herself to face the peril of death.

Then came the Wednesday after *Dominica in albis*.[1] As Olav was passing through the church door after the day's mass, someone touched his arm from behind.

"Hail, master. Is it you they call Olav Audunsson?"

Olav turned and saw a tall and slight, dark-complexioned young man behind him. "That should be my name—but what would you with me?"

[1] The first Sunday after Easter.

"I would fain speak with you, a word or two." Olav could hear by his speech that he was not from these parts.

Olav stepped aside to let the people come out of church and went a few paces along the covered way. Through the arches of the corridor he saw the morning sun just bursting over the blue-black ridges in the south-west, glancing on the dark open water between the island and Stangeland and lighting up the brown slopes, now bare of snow.

"What would you, then?—I cannot call to mind that I have seen you before."

"Nay, we can scarcely have met before. But you will surely know me by name—Teit Hallsson I am called; I am from Varmaa-dal in Sida, in Iceland."

Olav was struck speechless—Teit. The boy was shabbily dressed, but he had a handsome, dark, and slender face under his worn fur cap, clear tawny eyes, and an arched jaw with a mass of shining white teeth.

"So now maybe you guess why I have sought you out."

"Nay, I cannot say that I guess that."

"If you knew of a place where we could talk privily," said Teit, "it might be better."

Olav made no reply, but turned and went in front under the covered way round the north side of the church. Teit followed. Olav was aware as he walked along that no one could see them. The roof of the corridor came down so far that people outside could not distinguish who was moving in the shadow behind the narrow arches.

Where the corridor followed the curve of the apse, there was a way into a corner of the graveyard. Olav led the other by this path and leaped the fence into the kale-garden. This was his usual way to and from church; it was shorter for him.

When they reached the women's house, Olav barred the door behind them. Teit seated himself on the bench unbidden, but Olav remained standing and waited for him to speak.

"Ay, you can guess 'tis of her, Ingunn Steinfinnsdatter, I would speak with you," said Teit with an uneasy little smile. "We were friends last summer, but now I have neither seen nor heard aught of her since early autumn. But now the talk is that she is with child and near her time—and so it must be mine. Now, I know

that she was yours before she was mine, and therefore I thought
I would speak with you of what we should do—"

"You are not craven-hearted, methinks," said Olav.

"No man can be possessed of *every* vice, and I am free of this
one—" the boy smiled lightly.

Olav still held his peace, waiting. Instinctively he gave a rapid
glance at his bed: his arms hung in their place.

"So long ago as the autumn," Teit began again, "I let her know
that if it could be so ordered, I was willing to marry her—"

"*Marry* her!" He laughed, two short blasts through the nose,
with mouth hard set.

"Ay, ay," said Teit calmly. "Meseems 'twas no such unequal
match either—Ingunn is no nurseling, and her name has been in
folk's mouths once before. None had heard from you for ten
years, and it seemed little likely that you would ever come back.
Ay, *she* talked as if she believed it, and so she sent me packing;
and I was angry, as well I might be, at such fickleness and said I
would go my way, if she would have it so, but then it would be
bootless to send for me later. She has not done so either—not a
word have I heard from her, that she is in distress—and I know
not if I would have gone to her now—I parted from her in no
friendly fashion—

"But when I heard that you had come back and had been at
Berg—and that you would have no more of her and went your
ways when you saw how things were—then I took pity on her
after all. And now they say she lies shut up in one of the outhouses and is given nothing to live on but dirty water and ashes
in her porridge, and they have beaten her and kicked her and
dragged her by the hair, till it is a marvel she is still alive—"

Olav had listened to him with frowning brows. He was about
to answer gruffly that these were lies; but he checked himself. It
was impossible for *him* to discuss this matter with Teit. And then
he reflected how it would add to all their difficulties if these
rumours got abroad.—And to how many people had this young
coxcomb boasted of his paternity?

Teit asked: "Is it not so that you are a good friend of this rich
Arnvid of Miklebö in Elfardal, her kinsman?"

"Why so?" asked Olav sharply.

"They all say he is helpful and good—the friend of every man

who needs help. So I thought haply it were better if I betook me
to him first, not to the Steinfinnssons or the old man at Galtestad.
What think you of that? And if you would give me a token to
your friend, or let one write a letter to him and set your seal on
it—"

Olav sank straight down upon the bench. "Now methinks—! Is
that your suit to me—I am to back your wooing?"

"Yes," said Teit calmly. "Does it seem so strange to you?"

"It seems strange to me indeed." He burst into a short, harsh
laugh. "Never did I hear the like!"

"But 'tis seen every day," said Teit, "that a man of your condition marries off his leman when he wants her no longer."

"Have a care of your mouth, Teit," said Olav threateningly.
"Beware what words you use of her!"

As though absently, Teit took the little sword that hung at his
belt and laid it across his knees, with one hand on the sheath and
the other on the hilt. He looked at Olav with a little smile. "Nay,
I had forgot—'tis here in this room you use to strike down your
enemies?"

"Nay, 'twas in the other guest-house—and as for striking down,
we came to blows—" he checked himself, annoyed at having been
drawn into saying so much to the man.

"Be that as it may," said Teit with the same little smile, "since
it seems now that I have more part in her than you—"

"There you are mistaken, Teit. Never can you have part in her
—Ingunn belongs to *us*, and whatever she may have done, we will
never give her away outside our own rank."

"Nevertheless it is mine, the child she bears—"

"Know you not, with your learning, Icelander, that an unmarried woman's child follows the mother and has her rights, even
if it be a freewoman who had been seduced by her thrall?"

"I am no thrall," said the Icelander hotly. "Both my father and
my mother came of the best stock in Iceland, though they were
poor folk. And you need not fear that I shall not be able to support her, if you do but give her a fair dowry—" and he enlarged
on his future prospects—he would become a man of substance if
only he came to a place where he had opportunity to exercise all
his art and knowledge—and he could train Ingunn to help him.

Olav called to mind the bookbinder who had been here in his
youth—a master craftsman whom the Bishop of Oslo had sent up

to Lord Torfinn, that he might finish the books that had been written in the course of the year. Olav had accompanied Asbjörn All-fat to the room where they work—the wife was there helping, boring holes in the parchment, many sheets at a time, and between whiles she pushed with her elbow the great kneading-trough which she had hung by her side; within it lay her child, shrieking and grimacing and dropping the morsel it had been given to suck —till Asbjörn bade her give herself a little rest and comfort the child. He felt sorry for her, said Asbjörn. When their work was done, the Bishop sent her a winter kirtle besides the man's wages, calling her an able woman. Olav had seen them the day they departed: the master rode a right good horse, but his wife was mounted on a little stumpy, big-bellied jade, with the infant in her arms and all their baggage stowed about her.

Ingunn thrust into such a life—holy Mother of God, no! That was not even to be thought of. Ingunn outside the rank in which she had been born and brought up; it was so crazy a thought—he simply could not understand how it had come about that a fellow who stood so utterly outside had fallen in with her.

He sat watching Teit with a cold, searching glance as the other was speaking. Amid all the rest he saw that the boy was likable in a way. Unafraid, accustomed to make his own way in the world, Olav could guess; it would need no small thing to wear him down or quell his cheerful spirit—he was so quick to smile, and it became him well. He must have grown a tough hide in his roaming life among strangers, knaves, and loose women; but— He himself had now roamed about the world for nine years; he himself had had a hand in doings that he did not care to think of when he came home to settle. But that anyone from *that* world should have stepped between him and Ingunn, should have touched her—

Touched her, so that she lay there at Berg awaiting the hour when she must go on her knees upon the floor and give herself over to the pains and humiliation of childbirth—Ingunn's child. No one, she had said, when he asked her who the man was. He remembered that he himself had said: "No one" when she wished to know who had helped him to escape to the Earl, when he ran away from Hövdinggaard. And in those years when he had followed the Earl he had met so many, both men and women, who, he knew, would be "No one" to him when once he was settled at home in Hestviken—he had known many lads like this Teit, had

caroused with them in comradeship and liked them. But then he
was a *man*, nothing else. When any from that world outside
crossed the bond that held a man to his wife—then the life of both
was stained for all time. A woman's honour—that was the honour
of all the men who had the duty and right of watching over her.

"Now, what say you?" asked Teit, rather impatiently.

Olav woke up—he had not heard a word of what Teit had just
been saying.

"I say, you must put this—folly—out of your mind. But see that
you get you out of the Upplands as quickly as you can—take the
road for Nidaros today rather than tomorrow. Know you not she
has grown-up brothers?—the day they hear of their sister's misfortune, you are a dead man."

"Oh, that is not so sure. If I say it myself, I am none of the
worst at using arms. And I hold, Olav—since she was once *yours*—
that you might well do something to help her to marry and retrieve her honour."

"So you think I would count her case bettered if she married
you?" said Olav hotly. "Hold your peace, I say—I will hear no
more of this fool's talk."

Teit said: "Ay, then I must go to Miklebö alone. I will try it—
will speak with this Arnvid. *I* hold that her case will be better as
my wedded wife than if she is to be left with these rich kinsfolk
of hers till they have tortured both her and our child to death—"

"But I once said that myself," thought Olav, wearied out— "torture her and the child to death.—But then we were not to have a
child—"

"For I have seen myself the plight she was in with the folk of
Berg, ere ever this came about. And I cannot be sure that *she* will
not count it a gain if she gets a man who can take her far away
from this part of the country and from all of you. 'Tis true, when
first she had let me have my will with her, she turned clean round,
raved at me like a troll. But maybe she was affrighted—haply 'twas
not so senseless as I thought at first. And until this time we had
always been friends and agreed well together, and she never made
it a secret that she liked me as well as I liked her—"

Liked him—so there it was. Until this moment Olav had felt no
jealousy, in such a way that he could fix it on this Teit—it was
she and her disaster that had troubled him to the depths of his
being. The cause—had been "No one" to him too. But so it was,

she had liked this rascal and been good friends with him the whole summer. Ay ay, in Satan's name, the boy was comely, brisk, and full of life. She had liked him so well that she let him have his will —afterwards she had taken fright.—But she had given herself to this swarthy, curly-haired Icelander, in the kindness of her heart.

"So you will not give me any token or message to Miklebö that may serve me in good stead?" asked Teit.

" 'Tis strange you do not bid me go with you and plead your cause," said Olav scornfully.

"Oh nay—I thought that were too much to ask," replied the other innocently. "But I had it in my mind, if perchance you were bound thither in any case, that we might travel in company."

Olav burst into a laugh—a short bark. Teit rose, took his leave, and went out.

As soon as he was gone, Olav started up as though from sleep. He went to the door, and saw as he did so that he had picked up his little axe—a working-axe that had lain on the bench beside his hand among knives and gouges and the like. Olav was engaged in making some footstools for use in the church—the Prior had said they wanted some, and Olav had offered to make them.

He went into the convent yard and through the gate. The lay brother who acted as porter was standing there idly. Olav went up to him.

"Know you aught of that fellow yonder?" he asked. Teit was striding up the hill toward the cathedral; no others were in sight just then.

"Is it not that Icelander," said the porter, "who was clerk to Torgard the cantor last year? Ay, 'tis surely he."

"Know you aught of the fellow?" asked Olav again.

Brother Andreas was known for the strictness of his life, but his chastity was of the kind that has been likened to a lamp without oil: he had not much charity toward other poor sinners. He then and there bestowed upon Olav all those chapters of Teit Hallsson's saga which were known to Bishop's Hamar.

Olav raised his eyes to the churchyard wall, behind which the young man had just disappeared.

No greater harm could possibly befall than that the man came off scot-free.

Next day the sky was again blue and the air quivered with warmth and moisture about the bare and brown tree-tops. As Olav entered the courtyard of the convent late in the afternoon, the cook, fat Brother Helge, stood watching the pigs, which were fighting over the fish offal he had just thrown out.

"What has come to you?" he asked. "You were not at mass today, Olav."

Olav replied that he had not slept till near morning, and so he had overslept himself. "But I wonder if you could get me the loan of a pair of skis about the house, Brother Helge." Arnvid had asked him to come north to Miklebö after Easter; he thought of going today.

But would he not rather ride, suggested the lay brother. Olav said that with this going he would get on faster by following the ski-tracks through the forest.

He had just shaved himself when Brother Helge came to the door of the women's house with his arms full of all the convent's skis and a wallet of provisions over his shoulder. Olav had cut himself over the cheek-bone and was bleeding freely—the blood had run down his cheek and stained his shirt; his hand was covered with it. Brother Helge could not stop the bleeding either, and he wondered that such a little scratch could bleed so much. At last he ran off and came back with a cupful of oatmeal, which he clapped against the wound.

The sweet smell of the meal and the coolness of it against his skin sent a sharp thrill of desire and longing through the man— for a woman's caresses, tender and sweet, without sin or pain. It was of that he had been robbed.

The monk saw that a veil came over Olav's eyes; he said anxiously: "Methinks, Olav, you should give up this journey of yours —inquire first, in any case, if there be no other man in town who goes that way. 'Twas not natural that a paltry cut should bleed so freely—look at your hands, they are all bloody."

Olav only laughed. He went outside, washed himself in the puddles under the drip of the roof, and chose a pair of skis.

He was standing in the room, fully dressed, telling the lay brother about his horse and the things he was leaving be-hind—when there was a sharp ring of steel somewhere. Both men turned instinctively toward the bed. Kinfetch hung on the wall

above it, and it seemed to them both that it shifted slightly on
its peg.

" 'Twas your axe that sang," said the monk in a hushed voice.
"Olav—do not go!"

Olav laughed. "That was the second warning, think you?—
Maybe I shall bow to the third, Helge."

Hardly had he uttered the words when a bird flew in at the
door, fluttered hither and thither about the room, and flapped
against the wall—it was incredible how much noise the little wings
made.

The cook's round red face whitened as he looked at the other—
Olav's pale lips seemed livid.—But then he shook his head and
laughed. He caught the bird in his cap, carried it out of the door,
and let it go.

"These tomtits are ever perching on the log walls, scratching
and pecking at flies at this time of year; the noise they make every
morning— You are easily served with portents, brother, if you
reckon it one when the tomtits fly indoors!"

He took up the little working-axe and hung it to his belt.

"Shall you not take Kinfetch?" asked Brother Helge.

"Nay, she would be unhandy to drag on this journey." He
bade the lay brother put away the battle-axe together with his
sword, took a ski-staff that was tipped with a little spear-point,
and then with a farewell to Brother Helge he set out.

It was full moon as Olav mounted the slopes under Furuberg.
The sunshine had paled, the sky had become dull and chilly—grey
and thick in the north. It looked as though there might be snow.
Olav halted with the skis on his shoulder and looked back.

In the fading sunshine the lowlands looked bare and dark and
withered—patches of snow were few and small. In the town the
dark roofs of turf or shingles and the bare branches of the trees
clustered about the bright stone walls of Christ Church, with its
heavy, lead-roofed tower standing out against the pale and ruffled
waters of the lake. Olav cursed within himself at the feeling of de-
pression that came upon him—well, it would be bad luck if snow
came just when he had to find his way through the woods. He
had passed that way only once before, and that was in Arnvid's
company, so that they dashed along and took short cuts over

the roughest ground—on skis Arnvid could outrun any man he knew.

It chanced that he knew which of these little huts on the out-skirts of the forest the Icelander had taken for himself; a foul murder had been done there in Bishop Torfinn's time: a father and his two children, a son and a daughter under age, had killed and robbed a prosperous old beggar. Since then folk had not cared to live there. But this Teit was altogether penniless.

Olav pretended to himself that he had no plan—it must fall out as fate would have it. Teit might have set out for the north the day before, or he might have thought better of it, given up that idea. But if that were so, Olav saw at once he would have to keep him to it again; he could not have this man going at large in these parts. He would have to get him to Nidaros, or to Iceland—any-where out of the way.

He pushed the door; it was not bolted. The cover was over the smoke-vent, so it was very dark; the little room was cold and dismal, with a raw smell of earth and mouldiness and dirt. But Teit sprang out of bed fully clad and looked as fresh as ever—a fleeting smile came over his face as he saw who his visitor was.

"You will have to sit on the bench—I cannot set out a seat for you, for there is not a stool in the place, as you see."

Olav seated himself on the fixed bench. So far as he could see, there was not a loose piece of furniture in the hut—only some fire-wood lying about the floor. Teit threw some on the hearth, blew it into a flame, and opened the vent.

"And I cannot offer you a cup of welcome—for a very good reason. But you gave me none yesterday either, so—"

"Did you expect it?" Olav laughed grimly.

The other laughed too. And again Olav felt that there was a sort of charm about the lad—barefaced perhaps, but spirited, un-daunted by poverty and desolation.

"I have changed my mind, Teit," said Olav. "I am on my way to Miklebö now. And if you think it may serve your turn to speak with Arnvid Finnsson—you are welcome to join me."

"Ah—but, sooth to say, I have not my horse with me now. But maybe you can get me the loan of one?" He laughed as if he had made a good joke.

"I go through the forest, on skis," said Olav curtly.

"Ah. Such conveyance I can well find. I have seen a pair out in the shed—" he darted out and came back with them. The ski was split for a good part of its length and the hide of the *aander* was almost worn away.[2]

Teit fastened on his belt and sword and threw his cloak about him. "Ay, now I am ready when you will!"

"Food you must take, I ween?"

"Nay, such heavy gear I thought to spare myself—for a good reason."

Olav felt very ill at ease. Was he to share his food with a man whom perhaps he would afterwards—break peace with? And something prompted him to offer the lad the whole; Teit must have gone very short of food lately.—But in any case that would have to wait till they came up into the hills.

"Think it well over, though, Icelander," he said, almost threateningly. "Might it not be foolhardy for you to join company with me through the forest, think you?" He felt he was giving his conscience a little more than its due in saying this—it might sound like a sort of challenge. What would happen was uncertain, but in any event—

But Teit only smiled coldly and slapped his sword. "Methinks I am better armed than you—I believe I will venture it, Olav. And for that matter—a great man like you does not cast his hawk at every fly."

As they were going out, Olav looked back at the hearth; the fire was now burning briskly.

"But—will you not put it out?"

"Nay, I care not. 'Twill be no great harm anyhow if this hut be burned up."

As soon as they stepped outside, Olav noticed that the mist in the air had now grown so dense that he could look at the sun— there was a grey veil before it.

The surface was good when they reached the high ground. Olav kept to the northern slopes of the ridge that lies between Ridabu and Fauskar. As far as he remembered, he ought to go due

---

[2] In some districts of Norway a pair of skis consisted of one *ski* (left foot) of naked wood and one *aander* (right foot), which was a shorter ski, covered on the under side with hide, preferably sealskin, with the hair on. This made the *aander* run very smoothly downhill and prevented balling on wet snow; uphill the hide acted as a brake against backsliding.

north and then slightly to the north-east; then in the course of the
afternoon he would come into a tract that contained not a few
sæters belonging to farms in the Glaama Dale, and they would
be sure of finding shelter for the night. The evenings were already
long.

The snow lay six or eight feet deep on these slopes, and after
the thaw of the last weeks' mild weather and the sudden frost, it
gave excellent going. But ever and anon Olav had to wait for
Teit, who lay floundering, sunk in masses of snow. He was just
as likely to fall at the top of a slope as at the bottom.

"I think we shall have to change skis," said Olav after a while.
The hide of Teit's *aander* was so ragged that Olav simply ripped
it off.

The change did not help Teit much; it was marvellous how
many tumbles the boy got. He lost his ski and went through the
frozen crust up to his waist, laughing at his own clumsiness as he
scrambled out.

"You are not much used to running on skis, Teit?" asked Olav;
he had been far down a bush-grown scree after the other's ski.

"Not much." Teit's face was red as fire from his struggles and
he had scratched both face and hands on the frozen snow, but he
laughed heartily. "At home in Iceland I never set foot on a ski.
And here in Norway I have not tried the art more than two or
three times before today."

" 'Twill be hard work for you to cover the long road to
Miklebö, then," said Olav.

"Oh, I shall come through well enough—have no fear of that."

"God knows if he even sees how it plagues me to run back and
forth in my own tracks like a dog to pull up him and his skis,"
thought Olav. Aloud he suggested that they might rest awhile and
take a bite of food. Teit was quite willing, and Olav broke off
branches and laid them on the snow.

He looked the other way while the lad was eating. "Ay, he
suffers no want who is victualled by convent folk!"

The sky was now grey all over. From where they sat, high on
the shaded slope, they saw nothing but forest, ridge behind ridge,
blue-black beneath the heavy sky; in the valley that lay just below
them the forest looked black as coal around a little white patch—
a lake or a marsh.

But round about the birds began to pipe and chirp in tones of spring—a little uncertain and hesitating in the face of the weather that was coming. Now and again a sough went through the forest, advancing from ridge to ridge. The land to the northward was wrapped in a snow-squall, which hid the dark-grey cliff and the wooded slope below it—it was coming this way.

"Nay, Teit—we must go on."

Olav helped the Icelander to bind his skis securely. And then this sword—for a man who fell at every turn. He could not help saying it—sword and skis do not go together.

"'Tis the only weapon I have." He drew it and handed it to Olav, with some pride. It was a good weapon—a plain hilt and a fine blade. "That is my whole patrimony—all my father left me. And I will never part with it!"

"Is your father dead?"

"Ay—three years ago. 'Twas then it came into my head to try my luck in Norway. Well—I made for Fljotshverv first, to Mother. She ran off from Father and me when I was seven winters old and I had not seen her for ten years—she had found one she wished to marry, and then her conscience smote her for having been a priest's paramour so long. But she would fainer see my heel than my toe—ay, there had been lean years in our part of the country, and the children swarmed on their farm; I could never find out how many were mother's and which belonged to the other women—"

"Nay, Teit—" Olav leaned forward on his skis and set out again.

Tacking this way and that, he plunged down; the ground was broken here—he had to crouch under the trees. The sun had beaten down on the snow and left the ski-track standing out like a ridge. But yon fellow must get on as best he could.

Down by the tarn he stopped, waiting and listening. A gust of wind swept the ridge, there was a creaking and grating and soughing through the forest. Ah, at last, there came the sound of skis on the frozen slope.

Teit accomplished the last lap in fine style and came down to the tarn. He was white all over from his falls, but he grinned with all his gleaming teeth and his grazed and ruddy cheeks.

"Soon I shall be as good a ski-runner as a Norseman!" He showed what he had done with his awkward cloak—by degrees it had become so ragged that he had thought it as well to thrust his arms through two of the holes and fasten his belt outside. Thus he was rid of *that* hindrance.

"Are you very tired?" asked Olav.

"Oh no." He put his hand to the back of his neck and rocked his head a little: just there in the bend of the neck he was stiff and sore—it felt as if the devil himself had caught him there.

Olav himself felt a slight stiffness in the same place—it was the first time he had been on skis this year. So he could imagine what the other felt. And all at once there came into his mind—his rowing to Hamar with Ingunn on the lake; he was only a boy at the time, and he had toiled and pulled at the oars, but his neck ached worse and worse and he clenched his teeth, spurted, and would not give in and show that he was tired; he felt perfectly hopeless—"Shall we never get there?"

He looked at Teit—and clenched his teeth. He must stifle this feeling that tried to get the better of him. He would think of her —how *she* was suffering now; of the hatred and loathing that had filled him when he heard of her ruin; of all the hopes that had been destroyed. "And we shall live in the shadow of this sorrow and shame all our days." But here was this malapert youth, who was the cause of their misfortunes—and had no idea of it all. They went on side by side across the flat, and Teit chattered incessantly, puffing and blowing and groaning—asked Olav questions about the animal tracks they saw—old trails that glistened on the frozen crust, fresh ones of elk that had gone through—boasted of his newly acquired skill as a ski-runner. He confided in him, almost as a boy confides to his father.—And more than anything else Olav felt a kind of pity for this fatuous simplicity. No! This was so utterly preposterous—

The first hard grains of snow began to drizzle down as they entered the forest on the other side of the tarn. And the daylight was already on the wane. They had not gone far up the slope when they found themselves in a flurry of snow. Olav pushed on, stopped and waited for the other, who was hanging back—pushed on again. Now he was restlessly longing to make an end of this journey, to come under a roof—and at the same time he shrank from thinking of what then. From the height where they had rested, he had seen that beyond the ridge they were now on was a higher one, and at the top of it were some white patches on which there seemed to be

houses. They might be crofters' homes, they might meet folk
tonight—or they might be sæters, which was more likely. It must
fall out as it was fated.

Higher up there was a strong breeze against them. For a time
the snow had fallen thickly in great soft flakes, but now the wind
lashed their faces with hard, dry grains; the whistling sound of
the snow seemed to fill the whole forest with a sharp note that
penetrated the droning and howling of the wind in the fir-tops.
And the weather was felt the more since the dusk was now growing rapidly denser.

The ski-tracks had vanished long ago, a good deal of fresh
snow had fallen already, and where it had been blown into drifts,
their skis sank in deep.

Again he had to stop and wait for Teit. The Icelander drew up
beside him, groaning as if his chest would burst; breathless, but
as cheerful as ever, he said: "Bide awhile, friend—let me go ahead
and break the trail."

Olav felt his will sink impotently—before this feeling that arose
within him, which he must grapple with and trample underfoot
ere he could do aught to this boy. He flung himself forward and
ran on with all his strength. Now and again he had to halt and
listen whether the other was after him, but he never waited till
Teit had quite overtaken him.

It was almost dark when they reached the clearing. It looked
like a little cluster of sæters. Through the snow and the darkness
he had a glimpse of scattered black objects—some might be large
rocks, but some were huts.

Olav threw down the wallet as soon as they were inside the
dark hole, took out his tinder-pouch, and set about striking fire.
He knelt over the hearth, breathing upon the little flames that
struggled to catch the half-damp twigs—heard Teit's cries of satisfaction as he looked about him in the little cabin. There was hay
on the pallet, a skin coverlet, and some sacks for pillows—and the
boy strode into the black hole beyond, a sort of shed of stones
and turf. There were bannocks, Teit announced, and a tub of
whey and water; he came into the opening with a baler in his
hand and offered Olav some of the half-frozen drink.

"To be sure, Teit, we are in a Christian land; folk do not go
from their sæters without leaving behind the wherewithal to keep

body and soul together, should any need it when faring through the forest."

Teit stretched himself on the pallet while they took their meal, lying with his knees drawn up and his head low on account of the smoke; they could not make a draught, for the little room was so narrow that the flames might catch the bedstead or the pile of fuel on the floor. Olav sat on the bench opposite, in spite of the smoke, which tore at his chest and made his eyes smart. The man sat with his arms crossed, staring under drooping eyelids into the fire and listening to the boy's chatter, silent as a stone. 'Twas all folly; neither the weather nor the road was anything to talk about —had he not been burdened with this companion, who was like a new-born calf on skis, he would have run hither in half the time. But the fool talked as though they had been comrades in the mightiest adventures and dangers.

"Are you tired?" asked Teit, suddenly aware that the other had not replied a word to his flood of talk. He made room on the pallet—"Or maybe you will lie inside?"

Never, thought Olav. Share a couch with this guest for a night —no. There was reason in all things.

"Nay, I am not tired."

He tried to collect his thoughts. For they seemed to be slipping away from him all the time—Ingunn and he were *married;* he must keep that clearly before him; and therefore Teit *must* be put out of the way; he had ruined her from pure frivolity, but this nonsense the boy talked about repairing her misfortune—the young goat could do nothing there; he must do it himself, the little that could be done. Hide the shame. Believe—let folk believe what they pleased, so long as they saw where he stood and where her kinsmen must stand with him—he acknowledged the child for his and intended to defend his word against any who dared to utter doubts aloud.

"When did you hear these rumours?" he asked abruptly. "That she is—in trouble? This must have got abroad quite lately?"

Teit said ay, 'twas not so long since he had heard it. Some people he knew in the town had a daughter who was married to one of the crofters under Berg. And both they and their daughter had seen her walking hither and thither on the slopes below the manor in the evenings—but now of course it was light till late at night.—Teit dwelt upon their gossip.

Olav sat listening with lowered brows. The blood began to surge in his ears. But this was better. Let the boy keep on; now he would soon get over this unmanly—kindliness, which had been in a fair way to corrupt him.

"And what of you?" asked Olav; his mouth was twisted into a sort of smile. "Could you forbear to let them know that this was your doing?"

"I dare say I said some such thing."

"Have you spoken of it to others?"

If it could be made to seem like crofters' tattle and naught else, that would be bearable. Carry one's head high among one's equals, look them straight and hard in the face, and pretend to have no inkling of what was murmured behind one's back—malicious gossip that the maids had carried to their mistresses—

Teit said, with some embarrassment: "I had been so furious with her that it made me glad when first I heard she was so heavy on her feet.—The devil knows she was light and quick enough last summer—like a cat that strokes herself against one's leg and slips away when one tries to take her up. Then at last, when I had got her in my clutches—"

Olav hardly heard what the other was saying—the blood hummed and hammered so in his head. But this was enough, it had given him back the will to revenge—and a dear vengeance it must be, for it would be long ere he forgot this that he had just heard.

"—But the next night she had changed her mind again, barred her door against me. And when I came to her and spoke of marrying, she drove me from her as though I had been a dog—"

"Then I almost think you must put this marriage out of your head, Teit."

Warned by the ring of the man's voice, Teit looked up—Olav had risen to his feet and held the little woodcutter's axe in his hand. Quick as lightning the boy seized his sword and drew it, as he leaped to his feet. Olav was seized with a wild joy on seeing that Teit now grasped it all—the boy's face seemed to blacken with rage; he saw he had been fooled and he met the other's wordless challenge with an eager cry of youthful valour.

He did not wait for Olav to attack, but dashed in at once. Olav stood still—three times he warded off the boy's strokes with the head of his axe. The lad was deft and agile, Olav saw; but not strong in the arm. When Teit cut at him the fourth time, Olav

swerved unexpectdly to the right, so that the sword caught him
on the left arm, but the young fellow lost his head for an instant. Olav's axe struck him on the shoulder, and the sword fell
out of his hand. He bent down to pick it up with his left, and
then Olav planted the axe in the skull of him; the boy fell on his
face.

Olav waited till the last spasms had left the body, and a little
longer. Then he turned him over on his back. A little blood had
run down through the hair, making a streak across the forehead.
Olav took the corpse by the arm-pits and dragged it out into the
dairy-shed.

He went to the door of the sæter—night and wind-driven snow,
the roar and soughing of the wind in the forests. He would have
to wait here till daylight.—Olav lay down on the pallet.

So many a man had fallen by his hand, of greater worth than
this one.

Olav threw more wood on the fire. He must shake off this unwholesome—remorse, or whatever it was. Teit had brought it on
himself. Bishop Torfinn himself had said a ravisher who was slain
by the maid's kinsmen must be reckoned almost as a self-slayer;
he had begged his own death. Teit—had begged his own death. It
were absurd that he should feel it as anything worse than—than
felling a man in battle. Teit had fallen weapon in hand—there lay
his sword on the floor.

Never could he settle Ingunn securely so long as this wretched
jackanapes could run hither and thither blabbing of his misdeed,
the nature of which he had not the sense to see.

Olav was so cold that his teeth chattered, though one side of
him was being baked as he lay. But his elkskin coat stuck to his
back, wet and stiff and icy cold, and his footgear was wet through.
And he felt the wound he had got on his left arm—he had forgotten it, but now it ached and smarted.

He heaped fresh fuel on the hearth. If the hut burned, let it
burn.

Nay, but he must preserve his life for Ingunn's sake. Long
enough she had had to wait for her husband—he must not be missing when she needed him most.

"Nay, my good Teit, 'tis *you* must give way, for *I* will not."
He struggled to hiss out the words; the other was pressing on his
chest with all his weight, and Olav could not get a hold, his

strength seemed to be taken from him. Teit showed his whole white row of teeth, smiling as frankly as ever, though the back of his head was split open. "Cannot you see it, you wretched half-wit?—the woman is mine, so you must give way—take yourself off—"

He was awakened by his own hoarse cry as the nightmare left him. It was almost entirely dark in the room, with only a little glow from the embers. Wind and snow came in through the walls —and the elkskin qerkin was like an icy coat of mail.

Olav got up and went into the dairy, fumbling in the dark. The dead man lay there stiff and still, cold as ice. He had only been dreaming—he must have slept for several hours. He fed the fire again, nor could he endure to sit and stare at it—so he had to take to the pallet again. He got the sacks of hay under his back and the skin coverlet over him as well as he could.

Now and again sleep wrapped him as in a mist, and each time it veiled his thoughts he was awakened by the same dull throbbing pain within him—the smarting of his wound was only an echo of some deeper hurt. Then he was wide awake and lay thinking round in the same ring.

That fellow had got his deserts. He had had to kill so many a better man in battle, and never taken it to heart. There might be sense in pitying Ingunn, but not this one—no. If there were none to mourn the lad, either here or in his own land, that were well; then no innocent would suffer because the guilty had found his punishment. These years, first with his uncle and then with the Earl, ought to have been enough to harden him. This was uncalled for—he had got his deserts. And so on, round in a ring.

He started up—no, it was only a dream that Teit stood there in the doorway with the baler, offering him a drink. He lay safe enough where he should lie. "Oh nay, Teit, I am not afraid of you. And if I am afraid, you never had the wit to know what it is I am afraid of. My poor little Ingunn, you must not be afraid of me."—He was wide awake again.

Then there was this new burden that he had to face—what should he do? Give notice of the slaying at the first house he passed, when he came down from the wilds? And take upon himself this new case of manslaughter before he was wholly quit of the old one, with weregild and fines?—And feel the common talk barking in his tracks—what quarrel could such a man as he have

had with that vagabond Icelander?—ay, to be sure, 'twas Ingunn
Steinfinnsdatter— No, not that either.

But then—how was he to be rid of the corpse?

So many a better man had he seen fall from the ship's side and
be lost in the sea. So many a good thane's son of Denmark must
have been left to the wolf and the eagle after the Earl's attack. But
that was the Earl's doing, not his; it had never been his fault if a
dead man was left without Christian burial. And since he was so
soft that the mere slaying of such a one as this Teit, his wife's
paramour, weighed upon him, he would be ill fitted to go through
with the other thing, which *was* sin. *That* would be a sin that he
could not throw off.

But if he declared Teit's slaying at his hands, then they could
not even *pretend* that Ingunn's honour was saved.

At last he must have fallen asleep and slept long and dreamlessly. The sun shone in through the cracks between the logs when
he opened his eyes. The hearth was black. He heard nothing of
the wind—not a sound but the black cock's note from far and
near, and now and again a belated chirping.

He stood up, stretched and rubbed himself. His arm was stiff
and rather sore—not much. He went to the door and looked out.
The world was white and the sun was high in a blue and cloudless sky. The mist had sunk and lay like a white sea, made golden
by the sun, with points of rock and wooded ridge jutting out, and
they were golden with fresh snow on which the sun was shining.
The white carpet of the hillside sparkled red and blue; hare and
bird had already printed their tracks in the fresh snow, and the
call of the black cock resounded everywhere in the woods.

In this infinitely white world of wild, snow-covered forest he
stood, the only human being in the wastes, and knew not where
to hide that other little carcass, the dead man. Break through the
carpet of snow and bury him—no. It must be done in such a way
that beasts could not come at it—that he would not have. Let it
lie and be found when folk moved up to the sæter—that was impossible; then it might come out who the dead man was—and
after that all the rest.

The two pairs of skis stood in the drift beside the wall, snowed
under. Olav took the good pair, which he had borrowed from the
convent, cleared them of snow, and laid them down. He clenched
his teeth firmly; his face grew stiff and blank.

He went in and smoothed out the couch. Then he fetched the corpse and laid it there—tried to straighten it out. There was clotted blood and brains in the hair, but not much on the frozen grey face. He gaped hideously, Teit. Olav could not get the mouth and eyes closed. So he covered the dead man's face with the worn and blood-stained fur cap.

Underneath the ashes he found some sparks, and when he laid on bark and twigs and a mass of wood, the fire soon burned up. There was a load of hay in the dairy; Olav brought it in and threw it down between the hearth and the bed. His foot stumbled against Teit's sword—he picked it up and laid it on the boy's breast. Then he scraped up an armful of bark and twigs and threw it on the heap of hay.

Now the fire was burning briskly on the hearth. Olav took a long stick and raked the brands into the hay—with a flicker and a hiss as they caught the bark the flames shot up. Olav sprang out, carrying the skis under his arm, and waded up the slope through the fresh snow.

Up at the top, where the wind had bared the old crust, he halted, knelt, and bound the skis fast to his feet. Then he took the staff in his hand. But he stood there till he saw the grey smoke curling out of every crack in the walls. He repeated the burial prayers in a low voice—almost overcome by terror: was this blasphemy? But it seemed he had no choice—a dead man lay within; he *must* do it.

He had left his axe in the hut, he remembered, and the wallet, but it was empty. Now both the whey-vat and the store of bread would be burned; it was a small matter among all the rest, but— Never had he disdained God's gifts; the smallest piece of bread that he dropped on the floor he would take up and kiss before he ate it. This was almost the only thing he remembered of what his great-grandfather had taught him.

To hell with it. In the wars he had seen whole storehouses of food and franklins' homes given over to the flames. And better men than this one had been caught in the fire, both living and dead. Why should he count this as so much worse—?

In old days they burned their fallen chieftains thus. "I have given you a funeral pyre fit for a sea-king, my Teit—with your sword clasped in your hands, food and drink beside you."

The smoke kept creeping out—now it enshrouded the whole

sæter. The fire shone through it—the first flames found their way
out under the eaves. Olav set out swiftly, with no trail to follow.

When the sæter-folk came up in the summer, they would find
the bones among the ashes—he tried to console himself. He would
be laid in Christian ground in the end.

He swept down to a watercourse, while his ears sang and the
snow spurted from his skis; flew across the bottom of the slope,
halted on the other side, and looked back. The fine, long hump
of the ridge he had left stood out golden in the sunshine against
the blue sky. In one place a little cloud of dark smoke was
spreading.

An hour later he crossed the top of a fence, buried in the snow,
into white meadows. There were houses here; the snowdrifts
made them level with their surroundings in many places but smoke
was rising from a louver. There were tracks between dwelling and
byre, and fresh refuse on the midden.

Olav looked out over the landscape as he brought himself to a
standstill. The country was white, tinged with yellow, and blue in
all the shadows. Far to the northward he had a view of a broad
valley in which were great farms.

Say that he had quarrelled with his companion last night and
it ended in their seizing their weapons. And then brands from the
fire had been flung into the straw.

He pulled himself together and set out again over the fields.

Late in the afternoon he came to Miklebö. Arnvid was out—
had started for the woods two days before with both his sons to
look for capercailye. But his house-folk gave their master's best
friend a good reception.

Olav was out in the courtyard next day at sunset when Arnvid
and his sons came home. Magnus was leading the horse—both
it and the men wore snowshoes—and it was packed with knapsacks
and the like and a fine bag of game. Arnvid and Steinar were
loaded with skies and bows and great empty quivers.

Arnvid greeted his guest with quiet heartiness, the sons received
him frankly and becomingly. They were half-grown now, two.
fine, fair-haired, promising youths.

"As you see, I changed my mind—"

"That was well." Arnvid smiled a moment.

"But—have you fared through the forest with no weapons but that little spear?" asked Arnvid as they sat talking while the food was being brought in.

Olav said no, he had had an axe with him too, but he lost it yestereve; he was cutting some branches to make a bed—ay, he had found a shealing and slept in it. Graadals booth?—it might be that. Nay, in the snow and the darkness he had not been able to find his axe again. For that matter, he had given himself a scratch on the upper arm as it flew out of his hands.

Arnvid wished to see the wound before they went to rest. It was a clean, straight slash—looked as if it would heal quickly. But how Olav could contrive to wound himself just there, Arnvid could not make out—well, these old axes with a long pointed barb at each end might play one many tricks—and surely they were unhandy for lopping branches.

8

INGUNN had the child on the third day after Hallvard's Mass.[3] When Tora lifted the new-born babe from the floor, the mother clasped her head in her arms and shrieked, as though afraid to see or hear.

When Ingunn was put to bed, Tora brought her the child, ready wrapped.

"You must *look* at your son, sister;" Tora implored. "He is so pretty—he has long, black hair—"

But Ingunn shrieked and drew the coverlet over her face.

Tora had sent for the priest the evening before, when the case looked ill; and as she thought there was little life in the boy, she asked him to baptize him before he left. They asked the mother what name he was to have, but she only groaned and hid under the bedclothes. Neither Magnhild nor Tora cared to recall any of the men of their kindred in this child, and so they asked the priest to give him a name. He replied that today the Church commemorated Saint Eirik, king and martyr, and therefore he would call Ingunn's child after him.

[3] May 15.

Tora Steinfinnsdatter was both angry and sorrowful as she sat with this ill-omened little one, her own nephew, on her lap, and the mother would take no notice of him.

On the third day after the birth Ingunn was very ill. Tora guessed she was suffering from the milk, which was now bursting her breasts. She was unable to move, or to bear any one's touching her, and she could not swallow a scrap of food, but complained of intolerable thirst. Tora said it would be much worse if she drank—the milk would then rise to her head: "Not a drop dare I give you, unless you will let me give you Eirik—" But still Ingunn would not take her child.

In the evening, when Tora was preparing the boy for the night, she chanced to upset the basin of water, and she had no more warm water in the room. For a moment she was uncertain what to do. Then she wrapped a cloth about the naked child and bore him to the bed. Ingunn lay in a feverish doze, and before she could prevent her, Tora had laid Eirik on his mother's arm and gone out.

She made no haste in the cook-house—but all at once she was struck with fear and ran back. In the doorway she heard Ingunn's loud and piercing sobs. Tora rushed forward and pulled back the coverlet. "In God's name—you have not done anything to him!"

Ingunn did not answer. Eirik lay there, with his knees drawn up to his stomach, and his hands to his nose; small and thin and brownish red; the warmth of his mother seemed to do him good. His wide, dark eyes looked as though he were thinking.

Tora drew a breath of relief. She took the basin that Dalla brought her, lifted the boy, and finished washing him. Then she wrapped him in swaddling-clothes and carried him back to the bed.

"Shall I lay him beside you?" she asked, as indifferently as she could.

With a long-drawn plaint Ingunn raised her arms, and Tora laid the child in them. Her hands trembled a little, but she made an effort to talk in a calm and level voice as she propped her sister up, laid Eirik to her breast, and strove to get him to suck.

After this Ingunn obediently took the boy when Tora brought him and laid him to her breast. But she remained as sorrowful as before and seemed to have lost heart entirely.

She was still in bed when Arnvid came riding one evening to Berg. Lady Magnhild had sent word to Miklebö as soon as Ingunn was delivered.

Arnvid came into the room, greeting Lady Magnhild and Tora as calmly and courteously as though nothing unusual were afoot. But when he came up to the bed and met Ingunn's look of mortal dread, his own face became stiff and strange. A burning flush spread over her face and throat as she fumbled shyly with her thin fingers at her breast—drew her shift together and turned the child's face, which was instantly convulsed in a scream, toward the man.

"Ay, is he not what women call pretty?" said Arnvid with a smile touching the child's cheek with one finger. " 'Twas a shame you made such haste to have him christened. You should have been my godson, kinsman."

He seated himself on the step beside her bed and slipped his hand under the bedcover so that he touched the child's head and the mother's arm. It was uncanny, the way she trembled—and then came what he was waiting for, Lady Magnhild asked after Olav.

"I was to give you all greetings from him. He parted from me at Hamar, would hasten home now; he thought he could be back here about the Selje-men's Mass; [4] by that time Ingunn should be strong enough to go south with him." He pressed her arm tightly to make her keep calm.

He replied to Magnhild's and Tora's questions, told what he knew of Olav's plans. All three made as though all was well— though each one knew that they all thought the same: how would life shape itself for these two? Here lay the bride with another man's child at her breast, and the bridegroom knew it, as he rode south to make his house ready to receive its mistress.

But at last Arnvid said he would fain speak a few words with Ingunn alone. The two ladies stood up; Tora took the child from its mother to carry it to the cradle.

"And this one?" she asked. "It is Olav's wish that he shall go southward with his mother?"

"Ay, so far as I understood, that was his wish."

Then he was left alone with her. Ingunn lay with closed eyes. Arnvid stroked her under the roots of the hair, wiped away the

[4] July 8.

perspiration. "Olav bade me stay here till he himself can come and fetch you."

"Why so?" she asked in fear.

"Oh, you know—" he hesitated. "Folk are a little more wary of what they say when there is a danger their talk may reach a man—"

Beads of perspiration came out on Ingunn's forehead. She whispered almost inaudibly: "Arnvid—is there no way out—for Olav —so that he may be free—?"

"Nay.—Nor has he given any sign," Arnvid added, "that he wished it."

"If we besought—the Archbishop—on our knees—promised to do penance—?"

"His Bishop could give him leave to live apart from you—if Olav would ask it of him. That he will fetch you home and live with you—this he does of his own free will. But no man can sunder the bond there is between you, so that Olav could freely take another wife—not even the Pope in Romaborg, as I believe."

"Not even if I went into a nunnery?" she asked, trembling.

"So far as I know, you must have Olav's consent to that. And he would not be free to marry again. But to be a pious nun I trow you are the least fitted of women, my poor Ingunn.

"Then you must remember what Olav himself said to me. It was he who once staked all upon the judgment of Holy Church in the question whether you two were husband and wife or not. He himself called for Bishop Torfinn's decree, whether your living together were binding wedlock according to God's law and not fornication—and Lord Torfinn said yes to that. Strict as this Bishop was wont to be toward ravishers and all who violated the honour of women, he claimed on Olav's behalf that this man should be suffered to do penance and make atonement with Einar's kinsmen.—Do you understand—Olav *cannot* depart from his own word, nor will he either, he says.

"Nay, here I talk on, forgetting that you are still weak. Be easy now, Ingunn—remember what manner of man Olav is. Stubborn and headstrong; when he wills a thing he must have it. But you must have heard the saying, trusty as a troll—"

But it could not be seen in Ingunn that she had plucked up heart. The other women were mightily consoled when they knew for certain that Olav Audunsson would make no ado, but would take to himself the wife he had once claimed in so boastful and headstrong a fashion—and bear with her ill conduct in the meantime. Ingunn's kinsmen, Ivar, her brothers, and Haakon, when they heard of the whole matter, said that Olav had injured them all so deeply, by first taking the bride to himself, then summoning her guardians before the Bishop's court, and finally by killing Einar when he called him to account—that it was no more than justice if he held his peace, cloaked Ingunn's shame, and did what he could to put a good end to a bad business. Moreover, Hestviken was far away. And even if folk in the south got to know that his wife had had a child by another man before Olav Audunsson married her, he would not be worse wed than many another good and worthy man. No man in his native district need know more than that, unless they themselves were foolish enough to let it come out that she had already been bound to Olav before she had the child, in such a way that some priests in any case would say the boy was begotten in adultery.

This was pointed out to Ingunn by Ivar and Magnhild. She listened to them, palefaced, and dark about the eyes; Arnvid saw that she was greatly disturbed by what they said.

"What say you to this, Arnvid?" she asked one day when Ivar and Haakon had been sitting with her, discussing their view of the case. She now left her bed in the daytime.

"I say," replied Arnvid quietly, "God knows 'tis an ill thing it should be so—but you must see yourself, there is some truth in it—"

"You say that—you who call yourself Olav's friend!" she burst out angrily.

"That I am—and I thought I had shown it more than once," replied Arnvid. "And I will not deny that I have my part of the blame for the bad turn all this has taken. I counselled Olav unwisely, perhaps—I was too young and lacking in wisdom—and I should not have stayed in the guest-house that evening, when Einar picked a quarrel with us. But I shall do my friend no good, nor will you either, if we hide our heads under our wings and refuse to see that the Steinfinnssons too have *some* right on their side!"

But Ingunn burst into tears. "Not even you wish Olav better than this! None of you count his honour of any worth, none but I—"

"Nay," said Arnvid —"and now he must lie in the bed you have made for him."

Ingunn's weeping stopped suddenly—she raised her head and looked at the man.

"Ah well, Ingunn—I should not have said it. But I have been stretched upon the rack of this case of yours so long now—" he said wearily.

"But what you said was true."

The child lay in the bed screaming; Ingunn went and took it up. Arnvid noticed again what he had seen before—though she handled the little one tenderly and seemed to be fond of him, she always seemed to touch her child rather reluctantly, and she was very clumsy when she had to tend the boy herself. Eirik indeed always screamed and was restless and fretful in his mother's arms; she could only quiet him with the breast for a very little while. Tora said this was because Ingunn was depressed and uneasy, so that she had little milk for him; Eirik was always hungry.

This time too he had soon finished sucking, and then he lay grimacing as he pulled at the empty breast. Ingunn gave a little sigh; then she fastened her clothes, stood up, and began to walk up and down the room, carrying the child. Arnvid sat looking at them.

"Will you accept it, Ingunn," he asked, "if I offer to foster the child? I will bring up your son in my house and be to him as I have been to my own sons."

Ingunn did not reply at once; then she said: "You would be a faithful kinsman to the boy, I know that. You had the right to expect that I should thank you for the friendship you have shown me all these years, better than I do.—But should I die, you must—you must take care of Eirik—then 'twill be easier for me in my last hour."

"You must not speak of such things *now*," said Arnvid, trying to smile. "You who are just up and out of danger."

When Eirik was six weeks old, the woman came with whom Lady Magnhild had bargained early in the spring—that she should receive and foster a child that would be born in secret at Berg. Now the rumours about Ingunn had got abroad nevertheless. So many different things were said as to who might be the father—but most people thought it was that Icelander who had been so often at Berg last summer—now he was gone, doubtless run away for fear of the woman's rich kinsmen. Now the foster-mother, Hallveig was her name, came one evening to Berg to ask what had become of the child—she had heard no more of the matter.

Before Lady Magnhild had thought of what she should say, Ingunn came forward and said she was the mother of the child, and Hallveig should take it with her when she went home the next day. Hallveig looked at Eirik and said he was a fine child; while waiting for her food, she took him up and laid him to her breast.

The mother stood over them and looked on while Eirik took a full draught—it must have been the first time in his young life that he had drunk his fill. Then Ingunn took the child and carried it away to her bed; but the woman was shown into another house, where she was to sleep. It was intended that she should ride home betimes next morning, before folk were about upon the farms.

The sisters were left alone in Aasa's house, and Tora lighted the holy candle, which they still burned every night. Ingunn sat on the edge of the bed with her back turned to the child; Eirik lay against the wall, cooing cheerfully.

"Ingunn—do not this thing," said Tora seriously. "Do not send your child away like this. It is a *sin* to do such a deed, unless you are forced to it."

Ingunn said nothing.

"He is smiling—" said Tora with emotion, beaming at the boy. "Look at your son, Ingunn—he can smile now—he is so sweet, so sweet—"

"Ay, I have seen," said Ingunn. "Many times he has smiled of late."

"I cannot understand that you *will*—that you *can* do this."

"Cannot you see that I will not bring this child of mine under Olav's roof—ask him to foster this brat that a vagabond clerk has left behind—"

"Shame on you for speaking thus of your own child!" exclaimed Tora, revolted.

"I am ashamed."

"Ingunn—be sure you will regret it as long as you live if you do this thing, sell your child into the hands of strangers—"

"I have now brought myself into such a plight that I can never cease to regret."

Tora answered hotly: "You speak truly, and on that score there is none on earth can help you. With Olav you have played right falsely, there is none of us but thinks that—and your shame falls heavier on him than on the rest of us. But if you will be false to your child too—the guiltless young being that you have housed forty long weeks under your own heart—I tell you, sister, I cannot believe that even Mary, Mother of God, will pray for mercy on the mother who betrays her own son—"

"Beware, sister," said Tora once more. "You have wronged us all, and Olav worst. There is only left this boy, him you have not yet failed!"

No more was said between the sisters. They went to bed. Ingunn took the boy with her. She lay with her lips pressed against the silky, moist skin of the child's forehead and heard her sister's words ring and ring again within her. Even as Eirik's little head lay now against her throat, lay Jesus Christ against His mother's bosom in the image in church. What did He think of the mothers who flung a little boy from them? "And He called a little child unto Him and set him in the midst of them—" On the wall of the church in Hamar there was a painting where He hung nailed to the cross between two thieves, but beside Him stood His mother: fainting with sorrow and weariness she watched by her Son in His last agony, as she watched over His first sleep in the world of men. Nay, she saw it now—she dared not pray to Mary's Son for forgiveness of her sins unless she stopped here. She dared not pray Christ's mother to intercede for her with her Son if she held fast to her purpose and betrayed her boy.

"Ingunn," whispered Tora, weeping. "I spoke not so harshly to you because I wished you ill. But it will be worse than all the rest if you forsake your child."

Ingunn's voice was as hoarse as her sister's as she answered: "I know it. I have seen that you are fond of Eirik. You must try—when I am gone, you must—you must look after Eirik as well as you can."

"I will—as much as I dare—for Haakon," said Tora.

None of the three slept much that night, and just as they had fallen into a doze toward morning, Lady Magnhild came and woke them. The woman was ready to start.

Tora watched her sister as she wrapped the child—"I do not

believe she will dare to do it," was her hope. Then Lady Magnhild began again with her talk that Olav had transgressed so deeply against them all that it could not be called sheer injustice if he had to suffer Ingunn to take her child south with her. They need not have it at Hestviken; Olav could very well have it fostered outside.

Then Ingunn seemed hard and resolved as she carried the child out and gave it to Hallveig and watched her and the little boy who accompanied her ride away with it.

At breakfast-time it appeared that Ingunn had left the house. Arnvid and Tora ran out to search for her—she was walking hither and thither in the field behind the barn, and, beg as they might, they could not get her to go in with them. Tora and Magnhild were quite bewildered—it was dangerous for a married woman to go out in this way, before she had been churched—and what were they to say of a mother in Ingunn's case? Arnvid thought they must send for Brother Vegard, for Ingunn ought to obtain absolution and make her peace with God and the Church before Olav came back, so that they might go together to mass, when he had received her with her kinsmen's consent. He himself promised to stay with Ingunn and keep watch over her until he could get her to come in.

Once they came right up to the birch grove north of the manor. Arnvid followed close on the woman's heels—not a word could he find to comfort her. He was as tired as a drudge and hungry; the afternoon was far spent, but when he begged her to use her wits and come in with him, he did not get so much as a word in answer; he might just as well have spoken to a stone.

Then she went up to a birch tree, laid her arm against its trunk, and ground her forehead on the bark, uttering groans like those of an animal. Arnvid prayed aloud for God to help him. He guessed she must be half mad.

At last they reached a little knoll, where they sat side by side in silence. All at once she tore open her dress and squeezed her breast so that the milk spouted in a thin jet onto the warm rock, where it dried into little shiny spots.

Arnvid jumped up, caught her round the waist, and set her on her feet, shook her this way and that. "Now you must behave yourself, Ingunn—"

As soon as he took his hand from her, she let herself fall at full length; he raised her again. "Now you must come in with me—or else I'll take and *beat* you!"

Then her tears came—she hung in the man's arms and wept impassively. Arnvid kept her head buried against his shoulder and rocked her this way and that. She sobbed till she could sob no more. Then she wept silently, with streaming tears, and now Arnvid could fasten her clothing over the bosom; after that she allowed herself to be half led, half dragged home, till he could hand her over to the women.

Late in the evening Arnvid sat out in the courtyard talking to Grim and Dalla—when Ingunn came out of her door. As soon as she saw the old people, she halted in fear. Arnvid rose and went up to her. Dalla went in, but Grim stood where he was, and as Ingunn came past him by Arnvid's side, he raised his hairy old face and spat at her, so that the spittle trickled down on his bushy beard. When Arnvid took hold of him and pushed him away, he made some nasty gestures and muttered all the coarsest names the thralls of old had for loose women as he turned after his sister and left the yard.

Arnvid took Ingunn by the arm and drew her indoors. "You cannot look for aught else," he said, half in anger and half consoling her, "than to suffer such things while you are here. It will be easier for you when you come away, where folk know not so much of you. But go in now—you have tempted fate more than enough in running out today, and now the sun is going down."

"Stay a little while," begged Ingunn. "My head is burning so— it is so good and cool here."

It was rather dark for the time of year; clouds were spreading over the whole sky, and in the north the sunset turned them to gold. A rosy light came over the valleys, and the bay reflected the glory of the clouds.

Ingunn whispered: "Speak to me, Arnvid.—Can you not tell me something of Olav?"

Arnvid shrugged, as though impatiently.

"I would but hear you speak his name," she said plaintively.

"Methinks you must have heard it often enough these last weeks," replied Arnvid with annoyance. "*I* am sick of all this long ago—"

"I meant it not so," she begged quietly. "Not of how useful a man he might be to us and such things. Arnvid—can you not speak to me of Olav—you who love him? For you are his friend—?"

But Arnvid would not say a word. It occurred to him that now he had allowed himself to be tormented year in, year out by these two; he had done so many things that were like cutting into his own flesh and turning the knife in the wound. He would do no more.—"Come in now—"

Tora met them and thought that she and her sister might well sleep in Magnhild's house tonight. It was so cheerless in the other house, now the child was gone.

When they were about to go to rest, Ingunn asked her sister to sleep with Lady Magnhild in the chamber: "I am afraid I shall get but little sleep tonight, and sleeplessness is catching, you know."

There were two bedsteads in the room. Arnvid slept in one, and Ingunn lay down in the other.

For a long time she lay waiting for Arnvid to fall asleep. The hours passed; she felt that he was still awake, but they did not speak.

Now and again she tried to say a Paternoster or an Ave, but her thoughts roved hither and thither and she could seldom repeat a prayer to the end. She said them for Olav and for Eirik; she herself must be beyond prayers, since she had determined to cast herself into perdition with her full knowledge and will. But since she *had* to do it, perhaps she would not be given the very hardest punishment in hell—even there she thought it must be an alleviation to know that when she cut the bond between them and plunged into the depth, she left Olav a free man.

She could not feel that she was even afraid. She seemed worn out at last—hardened. She did not even desire to see Olav again or her child. Tomorrow Brother Vegard would come, they had told her; but she would not see him. She would not look *upward*, and she would not look *forward*, and she recognized the justice of her perdition, since she refused to receive anything that was necessary to her soul's salvation. Repentance, prayer, work, and the further pilgrimage of life, seeing and speaking to those with whom she must dwell, if she should try to live on—the thought of all this was repulsive to her. Even the thought of God was repulsive to her now. To look *downward*, to be alone and surrounded by darkness —that was her choice. And she saw her own soul, bare and dark as a rock scorched by the fire, and she herself had set fire to and burned up all that was in her of living fuel. It was all over with her.

Nevertheless she said another Paternoster for Olav—"Make it so that he may forget me." And an Ave Maria for Eirik—"Now he has a mother in me no longer."

At last Arnvid began to snore. Ingunn waited awhile, till she thought he was sound asleep. Then she crept up and into her clothes and stole out.

It was the darkest hour. Behind the manor a wing of cloud rested upon the ridge and seemed to cast its shadow over the country. The woods surrounding the farm were steeped in gloom —a thin grey vapour floated over the corn and gathered about the clumps of trees, effacing their outlines. But higher up, the sky was clear and white and was palely reflected in the bay; on the heights beyond the lake there was already a gleam of the coming dawn above the woods.

At the gate of the paddock Ingunn stopped and set the stakes in after her. There was not a sound in the summer night but the grating of the corncrake. Dew dripped from the alders on the path by the burn and there was a bitter scent of leaves and grass in the darkness of the thicket.

The grove went right down to the manor hard. And now Ingunn saw that the lake had risen greatly while she had been lying in. The water came over the turf and covered the shore end of the pier.

She stopped, uncertain—in an instant terror quickened within her and shattered her hardened resolve. Nay, for this she had no heart—wade through the water out to the pier. She wailed helplessly in her fear. Then she lifted up her dress and put one foot into the water.

Her heart seemed to thrust itself into her throat as she felt the chill water running into her shoe; she gasped and swallowed. But then she ran on, wading through her own fear, tottering unsteadily over the sharp stones of the beach. The water splashed and gurgled about her with a deafening noise as she went forward. Her foot reached the pier.

It was flooded for a good way out; the plank bent between the piles, it gave under her feet, and the water came far up her legs. Farther out the planks were just above the surface, but sank under

as soon as she stepped on them. Each time she held her breath in
fear of losing her foothold and falling into the lake. At last she
reached the extreme end of the pier; it was clear of the surface.

There was nothing left of her callousness now—she was beside
herself with fright. But her trembling hands busied themselves
blindly with what she had thought out beforehand. She took off
the long woven girdle that was wound thrice about her waist,
drew her knife, and cut it in two. With one piece she bound her
clothes together around her legs below the knees—that she might
appear seemly if she should drift ashore. The other piece she tied
crosswise over her bosom and slipped her hands underneath—she
had thought that it might be over sooner if she did not struggle as
she sank. Then she drew a last, long breath and threw herself in.

Arnvid half woke, lay in a doze, and was on the point of dropping off to sleep again when, with a dull thump of the heart, he
started up, wide awake—and knew that what had half awakened
him was that he had heard someone go out.

He was on the floor in an instant and over by her bed, fumbling
in the dark. The couch was still warm, but empty. As though still
distrusting his own senses he searched on, along the logs of the
wall, the head of the bed, the foot—

Then he thrust his naked feet into his shoes, slipped his kirtle
over his head, groaning the while—he did not even know how long
it was since she had gone out. He set out at a run straight through
the corn and came down into the meadow that led to the lake—
there was someone on the pier, he made out. He ran across the
meadow and heard his own footfalls thudding on the dry turf. On
reaching the water's edge he ran on, wading until he could strike
out and swim.

Ingunn awoke in her old bed in Aasa's house. At first she was
aware of nothing but that her head ached as though it would burst
and the skin of her whole body was as sore as if she had been
scalded.

The sunshine poured in; the louver was open and she had a
glimpse of the clear sky. The smoke, which showed blue under the
ridge of the roof, turned brown in the bright air outside—it was
caught at once by the breeze and whirled among the grass on the
roof.

Then she remembered—and fell almost into a faint. The feeling of relief, of being saved, was so overpowering—

Arnvid came up at once from somewhere in the room. He supported her with one arm and put a wooden cup to her lips. There was tepid water-gruel in it, with a flavour of herbs and honey.

Ingunn drank every drop, keeping her eyes on him over the rim of the cup. He took it from her and put it on the floor, then seated himself on the step beside the bed with his hands hanging between his knees and his head bowed. It was as though both were overcome by a sore sense of shame.

At last Ingunn asked in a hushed voice: "I cannot think—how was it I was saved?"

"I came at the last moment," said Arnvid shortly.

"I cannot tell," she began again. "I am so stiff in all my limbs—"

"Today is the third day. You have lain in a swoon—'twas the milk went to your head, I wis—and you had grown so cold in the water, we had to pour hot ale and wine into you. You have been awake before this, but haply you do not remember—"

The bad taste in her mouth seemed worse than before and she asked for water. Arnvid went out for it.

As she drank, he stood and watched her. He had so much at heart that he knew not what to take first. So he said it without more ado: "Olav is here—he came yesterday in the afternoon—"

Ingunn gave way, sick and dazed. She felt herself sinking down and down—but deep within her there was a little spark that was alive and tried to catch and break into flames—joy, hope, the will to live, meaningless as it was.

"He was in here for a while last night. And he bade us tell him as soon as you were awake. Shall I go and fetch him now?—the others are in the hall—'tis breakfast-time—"

After a moment Ingunn asked, trembling: "Said Olav aught—have you told him—of this last?"

Arnvid's face contracted suddenly—he set his teeth in his lower lip. Then it burst out of him: "Had you no thought—have you no thought, Ingunn, of where you would be dwelling today if you had carried out your purpose?"

"Ay," she whispered. She turned her face to the wall and asked in a low voice: "Did Olav say *that*? What said he, Arnvid?"

"He has said naught of that."

After a while Arnvid asked: "Shall I bring Olav in now?"

"Oh nay, nay—wait a little. I will not lie here—I will sit up—"

"Then I must send in one of the women—you have scarce the strength to dress yourself?" asked Arnvid doubtfully.

"Not Tora or Magnhild," Ingunn begged.

Then she sat on the bench by the end wall and waited. She had put on her black cloak, without really knowing why she did so; and she held it tightly about her and drew the hood over her head. She was white and cold in the face with fear. When the door opened—she had a glimpse of the man stooping as he came in—she shut her eyes again and her head sank on her breast. She planted her feet hard against the floor and held on to the edge of the bench with both hands to master her trembling.

He stopped when he had passed the hearth. Ingunn dared not raise her eyes; she saw only the man's legs. He wore no shoes, but tight-fitting buff leather hose, split and laced over the instep—she fixed her eyes upon this lacing, as though it would save her from her crowding thoughts. Such a fashion of men's hose she had never seen before, but it was cunning—they could thus be made to fit the ankle like a mould.

"Good day, Ingunn."

His voice went through her like a thrust, she sank yet farther forward. Olav came on, now he was standing just before her. She saw the hem of his coat; it was light blue, came down to the knees, and had many folds—her eyes stole upward as high as to his belt. It was mounted with the same silver roses and the buckle with Saint Olav's image; he had a dagger with an elk-horn sheath and silver mountings.

Then she saw that he was standing with outstretched hand. She laid her thin, clammy hand in it, and his closed about it—his hand was rough and dry and warm. Quickly she drews hers back.

"Will you not look up, Ingunn?"

She felt that she ought to rise up and greet him.

"Nay, sit still," he said quickly.

Then she looked up; their eyes met, and they continued gazing into each other's face.

Olav felt all his blood being sucked back to his heart—his face was frozen and stiff. He had to set his teeth; his eyelids drooped half over his eyes and he could not raise them again. Never had he known that a man could be struck so powerless.

The boundless pain and distress in her poor eyes—it was that which drew his soul naked up into the light. Away went all that he had thought and determined—he knew right well that they were great and important things that now dropped from his mind, but he had not the power to hold them fast. He was left with the last, the inmost cruel certainty—that she was flesh of his flesh and life of his life, and this could never be otherwise, were she never so shamefully maltreated and broken. The roots of their lives had been intertwined as long as he could remember—and when he saw that death had had hold of her with both hands, he felt as though he himself had barely escaped from being torn to pieces. And a longing came over him, so intense that it shook him through and through—to take her in his arms and crush her to him, to hide himself with her.

"Perhaps you will grant me leave to sit down too?"—he felt so strangely weak in the knees. Then he seated himself on the bench, at a little distance from her.

Ingunn's trembling increased. His face had been hard as stone—grey around the bloodless lips, and his strangely bright blue-green eyes had stared sightlessly under the drooping lids. "O God, God, have mercy upon me—!" As yet, she thought, she had not fully guessed the extent of the misfortune she had caused—but now she was to know it; she read that in Olav's face of stone. Now, when she could bear no more, came the worst.

Olav glanced at her under his half-closed lids. "You need not be afraid of me, Ingunn." He spoke calmly and evenly, but there was a slight hoarseness in his voice, as though his throat was not quite clear. "You must not think any more of what I said when I was here last—that I might prove a hard man to you. When I said it, I was still—wild—about this. But now I have bethought myself, and you must not be afraid. You shall live at ease in Hestviken, so far as depends on me."

Ingunn said, in a low, despairing voice: "Olav, you cannot— We cannot dwell together in Hestviken after this? How will you live there with me, remembering every day—"

"If I must, I can," he said shortly. "There is no help for it, Ingunn. And never shall you be reminded of it by me. That you may depend upon—safely."

Ingunn said: "But you are not one who forgets easily, Olav.

Oh—! Do you think you could do aught else but remember, every night when you lay down by my side, that another—"

"Ay—" he broke in. "Then you must remember," he went on, calmly as before, "Hestviken is a long way off—farther than you think. You will see, Ingunn, that it may be easier for us than we believe, when we live so far away from the places where all this has befallen us.—You will never see any sign in me that I remember it," he added hotly.

Ingunn said: "Olav, I am crushed and broken.—And if it be true that there is no way at all of setting you free, now that I have disgraced myself— But I do not see that it can be so, since they said once that they could part us, though we had been betrothed since we were children and we had slept in each other's arms—"

"I have never asked if I could wriggle out of my marriage. In all these years I have counted myself bound and been content that it was so, and I am still content. Such was my father's will. I am not one who forgets easily, you say—no, but I cannot forget this either, that we were betrothed to each other by our fathers when we were so young—and as we grew up together we slept in one bed and ate of one dish, and most of what we owned was in common. And when we were grown up, it was with us as you said.— There may be many things for which I must answer before God's judgment-seat," he said in a very low tone; "so I may well forgive you!"

"That is handsome of you, Olav, and it is good to know it. But now I will ask you to wait a year and meanwhile to let this matter rest. I am weary and sick, maybe I shall not live so long. Then you will be glad that you can take a wife to whom no blemish clings—that no woman without honour has ever been mistress of your house, or brought shame on your bed and board."

"Be quiet," whispered Olav huskily. "Speak not of that. When they told me what you had tried to do—" he stopped, overcome.

"I shall scarce have the strength to go to such a deed another time," she said; a quiver, a sort of smile, passed over her face. "I shall be a pious woman now, Olav, and repent my sins for such time as God wills I shall live. But I believe it will not be long—I believe I bear death within me already."

"You believe that because you are not yet over your sickness," said Olav sharply.

"Tainted I am," she wailed—"faded. I have lost all my fairness, so say they all. Little skill have I had all my days, and now I have lost heart and strength—what profit or joy can you have of such a wife as I? You have sat here and never looked at me once," she whispered shyly. "I am not much to look at, I know that. And 'tis no wonder you are unwilling to come near me. Think of it, Olav —you would soon feel it unbearable if you had such a wretched wife by your side day and night, always—"

Olav's features grew yet stiffer; he shook his head.

"I marked it already when you came in," she whispered almost inaudibly, "and you did not greet me with a kiss—"

At last Olav turned his head slightly and looked at her with a melancholy smile. "I kissed you last night—more than once—but I trow you did not feel it."

He passed both hands over his face, then bent forward, with both elbows on his thighs, and rested his chin in his hands.

"I dreamed a dream last spring—'twas Good Friday night to boot—I have thought of it often since. I remembered it so clearly when I awoke, and afterwards I have not been able to forget it. Now I will tell you what manner of dream this was.

"I dreamed I was on a hill in the forest, where all the trees were cut down, so that there was no shade—ay, the ground was hot there, and you lay in the full blaze of the sun, on the heather— there was heather and cranberries all around the stumps. You lay still—I know not whether I thought you slept—

" 'Tis strange—in all these years I have roamed about the world I often wished you would show yourself to me in dreams. You know that there are means one can use if one would dream of one's dearest friend—many a time I tried them, though you know I have never had a very firm belief in such devices. But I used them many times while I was still in Denmark, and also since. But I never saw you—

"But I dreamed this dream on Good Friday night, and I saw you as clearly as you are sitting there. You still seemed a child; we were both children, methought, as when we were together at Frettastein. Your hair had come unplaited, and you had on your old red gown of wadmal, but it had rucked up and I saw your legs bare to the knee—you were barefooted—

"Then a viper darted out of the heather—"

Olav drew a few heavy breaths; then he went on: "I was so

affrighted that I could not move. And this seemed strange, for I am bold to say that if only I can *see* the danger, I am not easily frightened—but in this dream I felt a terror beyond bearing—when I think of it, it seems I have never known what terror was, before or since. The snake moved through the heather, and I guessed it would strike you.

"But it did not move all the time after the manner of vipers; sometimes it thrust its way along as caterpillars do, and then it was no serpent, but a fat, hairy caterpillar—but then it was a viper again, coiling in the grass. It seemed to me I had a knife in my hand, and I thought I would strike the snake over the neck with a stick and kill it—'twould be easily done. But I dared not, for it turned into a caterpillar again.—Do you remember how I was a boy—how unspeakably I loathed the sight of worms and caterpillars, and maggots worst of all? I strove to hide it, but I know that you saw it."

Again he passed his hands over his face and breathed deeply.

"Ay, I stood there as though stunned. And then the snake lay about your foot, and now it was a viper, and it coiled about your calf, but you slept on as soundly as before. And then the snake raised its head and darted hither and thither in the air and flickered with its tongue. Now I know not what I shall say—there was a horror in it, yet I was drawn to look upon it; nay, it was as though I waited with delight for it to strike.—I saw that now I could easily take it by the neck, but I dared not. And—and—I saw that it was seeking out the place, on your instep, where it could set its teeth in deep.—But I felt—pleasure—in looking on at this. And then it struck—"

He stopped abruptly, with closed eyes, and bit his lip.

"Then I awoke." Olav strove to speak calmly, but his voice was thick. "And I lay and was angry with myself, as you know one often is when one has behaved in a dream as one would never do awake. For, you know, then I should have killed the snake. And I ween I would never have stood idly and watched my worst enemy asleep if a viper crept upon him, nor would I have thought it any delight to see it strike.— But there were not many things in the world, I wis, that I would not have done for you, when we were children.

"And I have thought and thought upon this dream—"

Again he broke off abruptly—sprang up and staggered a few

steps away from her. Then he turned to the wall and threw himself against it, with his arms raised in a cross and his head buried between them.

Ingunn rose and stood as though thunderstruck. Something was happening that she had never dreamed possible. Olav was weeping —it was as though she had never thought he could.

The man sobbed aloud—strange rough and raw noises were torn from his chest. He made a great effort and forced himself to silence; but his back quivered, his whole frame was shaken. Then his tears broke out again—at first in little gasping spasms, then another storm of harrowing sobs. He stood with one knee on the bench, his forehead against the wall, and wept as if he could never cease.

Ingunn stole up, beside herself with terror, and stood behind him. At last she touched his shoulder.—Then he turned round to her, threw his arms about her, and crushed her to him. They sank into each other's arms as though both seeking support, and their lips, open and distorted with weeping, met in a kiss.

THE SNAKE PIT

THE SNAKE PIT

I

ESTVIKEN had been a seat of chieftains in old time. Traces of many great boat-sheds could still be seen by the water-side, and rotting logs strewed the slope over which the Hestvik men had drawn their longships in spring and autumn. They showed like the remains of an old roller-way, reaching from high-water mark up to the little plain between the crags.

Then Christian faith and morals came to Norway; Saint Olav forbade his subjects to go a-viking. Men were to believe, whether they liked it or no, that God will not suffer a man to rob his even Christian, even though he be of strange race. The Hestvik men sailed on merchant voyages, and from of old shipbuilding had been carried on at Hestviken. Even Olav Ribbung, while he was in his best years, kept a shipwright at his manor, and when, after the Birchlegs [1] had burned Hestviken, he rebuilt both the manor farm on the high ground and the houses by the shore, he set up the boat-house and the two sheds and the workshop as they stood to this day down by the hithe.

A couple of hours' rowing southward from the Thingstead, Haugsvik, brings one to a lofty crag; this great dull-red rock, which falls abruptly to the fiord and is bare of trees to near its summit, is called the Bull. Behind the point Hestviken runs up into the land; it is a small and rather narrow creek. On its northern side the Bull Crag falls sheer into the sea, and below it is deep, dark water. Upon the neck of the Bull grow sparse and wind-bent firs, but they thicken farther up the height—the promontory is like a foot thrust out into the sea from the low ridge, which extends on the whole northern side of the inlet and of Hestviksdal or Kverndal, as it is also called,[2] eastward into the heart of the dis-

---

[1] The Birchlegs (see note to *The Axe*, p. 4) were the adherents of the pretender Sverre, who became King of Norway in 1184. The Ribbungs were a remnant of the Church party, opposed to Sverre and the Birchlegs.

[2] Kverndal: Mill-dale.

trict. Inland along the valley the ridge falls steeply to the water-course—a little stream runs through Kverndal and comes out into the sea at the head of the creek. Here trees and grass and flowers grow luxuriantly among cliffs and screes, and the ridge itself is thickly wooded with spruce; but as it descends to the level ground this passes into foliage, with many oaks even, belonging to Hest-viken.

On the south side of the creek the rocks are rounded off into the fiord, much lower and less steep; juniper bushes combed flat by the wind and thickets of brier grow in the crevices of the rock, and here and there are short stretches of dry turf. But then the hill rises in a sheer cliff, dark grey and almost bare, facing north; and underneath this crag, which is called the Horse,[3] lies the manor, fairly high up and turned toward the north. The path from the hithe up to the houses runs along the edge of the manor fields on the fiord side and is fairly steep. Farther inland there is deep and good soil on the slopes, and fields and meadows suffer less from drought than in most other places on the Oslo Fiord, as many runnels trickle down from the Horse Crag, and higher up, the valley is somewhat moist. But almost all the plough-land of Hestviken lies on the south side of the valley and faces north.

The manor farm of Hestviken was built so that the houses stood in two rows enclosing a long and narrow courtyard, in which the bare rock cropped out everywhere like a ridge through the midst of it. Between this rock and the Horse Crag there was a hollow, marshy from the water trickling down the cliff, and the buildings on that side of the courtyard had therefore sunk and become damp; the logs of the lowest courses on the side facing the rock had rotted, so that the houses were draughty and the damp came in both above and below, but in summer nettles and weeds grew in the hollow, almost to the height of the turf roof. It was the stables, byres, and a few sheds that stood here.

Toward the sea, on the north side of the courtyard, lay the dwelling-houses, the cook-house, and the storehouses. Looking up the fiord the view was shut in by the Bull; but from the western end of the courtyard one could look across the creek to Hudr-heimsland and southward a great way down Folden.[4] And in

---

[3] *Hesten. Hestviken* may be translated "Horse-wick."
[4] The Oslo Fiord.

former days the lords of Hestviken, when there was war in the land, had been wont to keep a watch on the hill above the Bull; the turf hut was still there in which the watchmen had lived when they relieved one another on the lookout.

At the end of the courtyard, toward the meadows and Kverndal and a good way from the other houses, stood the barn, all that was left of the old manor. It was immense and strongly built, of heavy timber. The other houses were small and without embellishment, of somewhat light logs bonded together. It had been no easy matter for Olav Ribbung to rebuild his manor after the fire—his losses had been great, as his warehouses were crammed full of goods at the time of the burning, and in those days it was often difficult for landlords to get in what their tenants owed them. But it was the tradition of the neighbourhood that the old houses at Hestviken had been large and splendid. There had been a hall, built of upright staves with a shingle roof like a church; two rows of carven pillars supported the roof internally, and the hall was richly decorated besides with wood-carving and painting. And for high festivals they had blue hangings and a tapestry that was spread under the roof; it was of red woollen stuff embroidered with fair images. Of this tapestry two pieces still remained—one that had been given to the church and one that was in the manor; this latter piece was so long that it stretched over both sides and the end wall of the new living-room, and yet a part of the tapestry was said to be lost—so one could imagine the difference in size between the old hall and Olav Ribbung's house. Apart from this no more was left of the old glories than a carven plank, which people said one of Olav's house-carls had torn out to defend himself with as he ran from the burning hall. In the new house this plank was one of the doorposts of the bedchamber.

Olav Audunsson knew it again the moment he stepped into his own house, which he had not seen since he was a child of seven years. Never had he thought of this carving or known that he remembered it—but the moment his eye fell upon it, recognition came like a gust of wind that passes over the surface of a lake and darkens it: 'twas the doorpost of his childhood. The image of a man was carven upon it surrounded by snakes; they filled the whole surface with their windings and twistings, coiling about the man's limbs and body, while one bit him to the heart. A harp lay trampled under his feet—it was surely Gunnar Gjukesson in the snake pit.[5]

This doorpost was the only ornament of the hall, which was otherwise no different from the hearth-room of an ordinary farmstead; an oblong rectangular house, divided off by a wooden partition near the east end, so as to make two little rooms beyond the hall: the bed-closet at the far end and an antechamber by the door leading to the courtyard; for safety's sake the entrance was placed as far as possible from the sea. At the other end, farthest from the door, were two box-beds with a raised floor between them, and along both side-walls ran benches packed with earth. Of movable furniture there was none but a few three-legged stools—not so much as a side-table by the antechamber door or a backed chair or settle. The top of a long table hung on the north wall, but it could not have been taken down and used may times since Olav Ribbung's death.

The bed within the closet was intended for the master and mistress. But Olav Audunsson bade his old kinsman Olav Ingolfsson use this resting-place in which he had slept hitherto; he himself would take the bed on the south of the hall, where he had slept as a child.

He had no desire to move into the bed-closet. At the sight of the doorway leading to the pitch-dark room, ghosts of his childish loathing of this black hole arose within him. There his great-grandfather had slept, with his mad son, and when the fit came upon Foulbeard, they bound him and he lay roaring and howling and tossing in his bonds on the floor in the darkness. The child had been—not so badly frightened; in any case it was a kind of calm and composed horror, for he had been a witness of Foulbeard's attacks as far back as he could remember, and the madman had never harmed anyone; that he might do some hurt upon himself was all they had to fear. But of his own free will the boy never went near the closet—and indeed there was always a terrible stench within; a breath of pestilential air met him whenever he approached the doorway. His father and Aasa, the old serving-woman, did their best to clean up the madman's lodging, but it

---

[5] This is Gunnar of the *Völsunga Saga*, the husband of Brynhild. Gunnar was thrown into the snake pit by Atle (Attila); his sister Gudrun, Sigurd's widow and Atle's wife, secretly sent him a harp, and by his playing he charmed all the snakes save one, which bit him to the heart.

was difficult, so dark was it within. They changed the straw of the bed when they could come at it and strewed fresh mould on the floor so often that from time to time old Olav had to have it dug and carried out again, as the floor of the closet grew into hills and mountains. But all this availed but little.

And now Olav Audunsson remembered them so vividly—the two old men who used to appear at the door of the closet. When the madman had had a fit and struggled till he was faint and calm again, his father led him outside to sun him if the weather suited.

First the great-grandfather entered—a giant in stature, with long thick hair and a beard that fell over his chest; there was still as much black as white in it. He helped his son out, putting an arm about his neck and bending him, lest he should strike his face against the frame of the door. The madman had not the wit to turn aside from anything, but went straight on.

Torgils Foulbeard seemed a small man, for he was shrunken and bent. His whole head was overgrown with hair; the beard reached up to the eyes. All this tangle of his was matted with filth, grey and yellow of every dirty shade; from the midst of it shone the great eyes, pale greyish-green like sea-water, bloodshot in the whites, with an uncanny stare, and the nose small, straight and finely shaped, but red; it had been frostbitten one winter night when he had slipped out unknown to his father. But when old Olav had taken his son to the bath-house, cleansed him with lye and sand, and combed his hair, the whole shaggy head of Torgils shone silvery white and soft as a great tuft of bog-cotton. Torgils looked much older than his father.

Old Olav fed him as though he had been a child. Sometimes he had to shake and beat Torgils to make him open his mouth; at other times the trouble was that he would not shut it again, but let the food run out upon his beard. His father could get him to take meat and solid food by stuffing mouthfuls between Torgils's teeth and then thrusting his face close to his son's and chewing with empty jaws, up and down with all his force—then it might be that the madman mimicked him and chewed too.

Aasa sighed when she saw it. It was her charge to be like a foster-mother to young Olav, and he slept in her bed. But Aasa was more minded to herd Foulbeard and tend him, she as well as the great-grandfather. Koll, the old house-carl, was the only one who had care of the boy Olav.—Other than these four had not been dwelling at the manor, that Olav could remember. There were some who came and worked on the farm and down by the waterside.—Like enough the decline of Hestviken had already begun in those years. And after Olav Ingolfsson took over the conduct of the place, it had gone steadily downhill.

Now, farming had never been the main thing at Hestviken; but neither Olav Ribbung in the last years of his life, nor Olav Ingolfsson had made such use of the sea as had been the custom here from old time. Then it came about that the rightful owner was outlawed, and the larger craft that still belonged to the place were seized by the King's officers. Olav Ingolfsson had never succeeded in providing new boats, nor yet in restoring the herds of cattle and making good the number of horses.

Olav guessed that the heritage that had fallen to him on the death of his father, Audun Ingolfsson, was so great that he would have been a very rich man at that time; but he himself had not known this and Steinfinn had never made any inquiries on his behalf. And even before his outlawry the estate had greatly shrunk. Now he owned no more than his ancestral manor and some farm-lands in the surrounding district, with others over in Hudrheim, across the fiord. He had sold the udal estate in Elvesyssel that had come to him from his grandmother, when he had to make atonement and pay weregild for the slaying of Einar Kolbeinsson; but there was still so much money owing to him by the monks of Dragsmark, who had bought most of the land, that he could again fit out ships and resume the trading by water.

And at that time there were not so many franklins in the country round the Oslo Fiord who possessed their udal estates whole and undivided. A great part of their property had come into the hands of the great landlords, or into those of the King or the Church. So Olav Audunsson of Hestviken might nevertheless be reckoned a man of substance and leading in his native district—and as such he was honoured as was meet, when at last he returned to his ancestral home.

Folk judged that he had shown himself generous when he took over his property from the aged man who had been his guardian and had acquitted himself so ill of his trust. But none had heard Olav complain of this, and he showed his namesake filial respect. And when certain men tried to find out what Olav himself thought, and asked how he had found his affairs situated, Olav replied very soberly: "Not well." But it could not have turned out otherwise—with the doom that had fallen on himself—and even before that the work of this place must have been more than Olav Ingolfsson could accomplish, crippled as he was. One of Olav Half-priest's legs had been broken, so that it was quite stiff and the foot was turned outward; he was very lame and could not move without a staff, and his stiff and straddling leg made it difficult for him to sit a horse or travel in a boat.

Olav Ingolfsson was a good deal more than threescore winters and he looked older yet—he seemed old as the hills. He was tall and thin and bent; his face was narrow and well-featured, with a fine curved nose—the younger Olav had a feeling that his namesake was not unlike his own father, so far as he remembered him. But Olav Ingolfsson was bald as a stone, with red and bleary eyes; the skin hung in shrivelled puckers under his eyes, on his shrunken cheeks, and below his chin. To cure the pain in his lame leg he used dogskin and catskin and many kinds of unguents. Whether from this or other causes, there was always a peculiar smell about the old man—as of mice—and the closet where he slept smelt of mice.

He was a son of Olav Ribbung's twin brother, Ingolf Alavsson, priest of St. Halvard's Church at Oslo. When the order came that the priests of Norway were to live in celibacy, Ingolf Priest sent his wife home to Tveit, the estate in Soleyar which she had brought him as her dowry; and all the children followed their mother, save the youngest son, Olav; he was himself set apart for the priesthood and newly ordained deacon when the accident befell him that made him a cripple. But he had lived in chastity all his days, and folk thought he had such great insight into many things that some held him to be more learned and pious than their parish priest. It was above all when folk were troubled by the walking dead and by goblins on sea and land, or when they had some sickness that was thought to be the work of witchcraft or evil spirits, that they sought counsel of Olav Half-priest, for he had more understanding of such things than all men else.

Olav Audunsson took to his namesake at once—in the first place because he was his nearest kinsman and the first man of his father's race whom he had met. It was strange to be here and to know that this was his ancestral manor and these surroundings his native soil; here he was destined to live the rest of his life—and he would have grown up here, but that his lot had been so markedly unlike that of other young men. But fate had cast him far from his home while he was yet a child, and since then he had been homeless and rootless as a log adrift in the sea.

Now he had come back to the place from which he had sprung. In a way he felt at home with many things, both indoors and out; but for all that it was very different from what he seemed to remember. The mill in Hestvikdal was familiar, but all that lay on the other side of the creek—the Bull, the wooded ridge—was as though he had never seen it, nor could he remember the marshy valley along the stream, a waste full of foliage trees. He could never have known what the country was like to the north of the creek—perhaps he had believed it settled and tilled like the shores of Lake Mjösen. But from Hestviken not a single human dwelling was to be seen.

The houses of the manor he remembered much bigger than they were. And the little strip of beach hemmed in by rocks, which had seemed to him a whole stretch of country with many distinctive marks—a great bluish rock on which he used to lie, some bushes in which he could hide—now he saw that the little strip of sand was scarcely fifty of a grown man's paces in length. He looked in vain for a hollow in the meadow above the manor, where he had been wont to sit and sun himself—it might have been a little pit east of the barn, which was now overgrown with osiers and alders. In a crack of the rock in the courtyard he had once found a curious snow-white ring—it must have been a vertebra of some bird or fish, from which the points were broken off, he now thought. But at that time he had taken it for a rare treasure, had preserved it carefully and often searched in the crevices of the rock to see if he could find others like it. It was almost like remembering old dreams—the scenes of the past floated before him in fragments—and at times he recalled a forgotten feeling of eeriness, as though after bad dreams he remembered no more than the dread.

So he snatched at everything that might help him to overcome this sense of insecurity, of dreams and shadows, and make him feel that Hestviken was his, and that when he walked over the fields here he had his own ancestral soil under his feet—the Bull, the woods and hills on both sides of the valley, all was *his* land.

And he was glad to think that now he was dwelling under the same roof as a kinsman, his own grandfather's cousin, who had known all the men and women of his race since the days of his great-grandfather's, Olav Ribbung's manhood. When he sat in the evening drinking with his namesake and the old man told him of their bygone kinsmen, Olav had a sense of fellowship with his father's stock which he had never known when he was in Denmark among his mother's kindred.

And he was drawn to the old man by the belief that Olav Priest's son was so pious and learned. During these weeks, while he was awaiting the time when he could go northward and fetch Ingunn, he felt in a way as though he were settling his account with God.

He himself was fully aware that it would not be easy for him to show perfect serenity and a glad countenance when he came to Berg to conclude the atonement with Haftor and receive Ingunn as his wife at the hands of the Steinfinnssons. But it could not be otherwise—and to get her was what he himself wished, in spite of all—and so he would surely be man enough to put a good face on it. But he could not defend himself against the insistence of childish memories—the certain knowledge that they belonged to each other and should always be together. That anything could come between them had been so far from their thoughts that it had never moved their hearts to either joy or wonder—they had taken it for granted that it should be as it had been determined for them. Until that summer when, locked in an embrace, they had fallen out of childhood and innocence, frightened, but at the same time giddy with rapture at the new sweetness they had found in each other—whether it were right or wrong that they abandoned themselves to it. Even when he awoke to a fear and defiance of all who would meddle with their destiny, he had been full sure that at last they two would win their cause. These memories would come suddenly upon Olav, and the pain of them was like the stab of a knife. That dream was now to take its course—but not the course he had imagined. And remembering himself as he was then was like remembering some other man he had known—a boy of such infinite simplicity that he both pitied and despised him, and envied him excruciatingly—a child he had been, with no suspicion of deceit, either in himself or in others. But he knew that for this anguish of the soul there was but one remedy—

he would have to hide his wound so that no one, she least of all, might see that he bore a secret hurt.

These thoughts might assail him while he sat conversing with the other Olav, and he would break off in the midst of his talk. The old man scarcely noticed it, but talked on and on, and the young man stared before him with a face hard and close—till old Olav asked him some question, and young Olav became aware that he had not heard a word of what the other had been saying.

But he made ready to shoulder the burden he had to bear—without wincing, should it be God's will to chasten him sorely in the coming years. For in a way the memory of that ski journey he had made with another and of the night at the sæter was ever present to him—except that he did not seem to see *himself* as the murderer. Rather was it as though he had witnessed a settling of scores between two strangers. But it *was* he, he knew that in a strange, indifferent way, and the sin was *his* sin. The slaying in itself could hardly be any mortal sin: he had not enticed the other into an ambush, the lad himself had planned this journey, and he had fallen sword in hand—and even a thrall had had the right to avenge his wife's honour in old days, he had heard; 'twas a man's right and duty by the law of God and men.

It was what came after—

And he had a feeling that he was offering God a makeshift in squaring his shoulders and making ready to bear the burden of Ingunn's misfortune. Never would he let anyone see it if it became too heavy. And he would live piously and in the fear of God from now on—so far as that was in the power of a man who had an unshriven sin on his conscience. He would act justly by his neighbour, be charitable to the poor, protect the forlorn and defenceless, honour the house of God and his parish priest and render such payments as were due, say his daily prayers devoutly and with reflection and repeat the Miserere often, pondering the words well. He knew that he had received far too little instruction in the Christian faith during his youth; Brother Vegard had done his best, but he came to Frettastein only once or twice a year and stayed there but a week, and there was none else who so much as made inquiry whether the children said their prayers every day. And the good instruction he had received while with Bishop Torfinn had fared as in the parable—so many tares had been sown among the wheat during the years he spent abroad that the wheat, just as it was beginning to sprout, was choked by the weeds. For the first time something like remorse for the slaying of Einar Kolbeinsson dawned upon Olav Audunsson: he had regretted it because it was an ill reward to Bishop Torfinn for his kindness and because, as his affairs were then situated, it was the most unlucky chance that could befall him—ay, and then he knew that he *ought* to repent it, because it *was* sin, even if he could not see why it was so sinful. Now he began to divine that a deeper meaning and a deeper wisdom underlay our Lord's commandment "Thou shalt not kill" than merely that which he had been told—God desires not the death of any sinner. Behind the commandment lay also a care for the slayer—the slayer also exposed his soul to many kinds of evil powers, which now found occasion for sudden assaults.

Therefore it might well be of service to him to dwell with so pious a man as Olav Half-priest; his kinsman could surely afford him useful guidance in many things. Such as the penitential psalms —he had learned a number of them of Asbjörn All-fat and Arnvid in his days at Hamar, but now he had forgotten the most part.

Olav invited his neighbours to a home-coming feast and told them that the wife he was to bring home was the daughter of Steinfinn Toresson, his foster-sister, to whom he had been betrothed when both were of tender age. So soon as he had looked about him at home and seen how his affairs stood he would ride back to the Upplands and fetch his wife. But as to the wedding he said not a word, whether it had already been drunk or was still to come; nor did he ask any of his neighbours to accompany him, though it was impossible for his kinsman to make the journey. Folk were quick to remark that the young Master of Hestviken was one who kept his own counsel and knew full well how far he would give an account of himself—not much was to be got out of him by asking questions.

Olav had thought long and deeply whether he should mention that there was a child. Perhaps it might make the matter easier if he spoke of this beforehand. But he could not bring himself to it. And then he thought that after all it might be dead. It had been born quick—but death came easily to young children, he had heard it said. Or they might hit upon some means—put it out to foster-parents on the way, perhaps. That Ingunn should give him out as the child's father, as he had told her in his first bewilderment and desperation, he now saw to be madness. He could not understand how he had come to conceive such a thought—bringing a bastard into the race. Had it but been a daughter, they could have put her in a convent, and no man would have suffered any great wrong by his letting her pass as his; but Ingunn had had a man-child— Oh, he had been witless at the time, from grief and anger. But he felt bound to accept the child, if the mother wished to have it with her. It must now fall out as fate would have it; useless to take up an evil before it was there.

Nevertheless he crept one day up to the little room that was above the closet and the anteroom. The thought occurred to him that the child and its foster-mother might live there, if Ingunn wished to have her son in the house. Olav Ribbung's daughters had slept in this loft with their serving-maids; but it was an age since the young women had lodged there. The dust and cobwebs of at least twenty years had collected there undisturbed, and the mice scrambled out of the bedstead when he went to see what might be stowed away there. Some old looms stood against the wall, and trestles for a table, and then there was a chest, carven with armorial bearings, which showed him that it had been his mother's. He unlocked it: within lay spindles, spools, and combs and a little casket. In the casket was a book and a child's swathe of white linen—a christening-robe, Olav guessed, no doubt the same that had been wrapped round him when he was lifted out of the baptismal font. He lingered, sitting on his haunches and twisting its embroidered border between two fingers.

He took the book down with him and showed it to Olav Half-priest. But although the old man had always let it be thought that he could read and write as well as any priest—and much better than Sira Benedikt, their parish priest—there was in any case not much that he could make out of Cecilia Björnsdatter's psalter. In the evening Olav sat and looked at it: little images were drawn within the capital letters, and the margins were adorned with twining foliage in red and green. When he went to bed he buried the book under the pillow, and there he let it lie.

A few days before he was to set out for the north there came a poor woman to Hestviken who wished to speak with the master. Olav went out to her. She bore an empty wallet on her shoulder, so he guessed her errand. But first she greeted Olav with tears in her voice—tears of joy, she said; 'twas such a glad thing to see the rightful master stand at his own door at last, "and a fair and lordly man have you grown, Olav Audunsson—ay, Cecilia ought to have seen her son now—and they speak well of you among the neighbours, Olav. So methought I must come hither and see you—and I was among the first who saw you in this world, for I served at Skildbreid at that time and I was with Margret, my mistress, when she came to help your mother—I gave her a hand when she swathed you—"

"Then you knew my mother?" asked Olav when the woman had to pause for want of breath.

"You know, we saw her at church sometimes, when first Audun had brought her hither. But that winter she grew so sickly that she never went abroad—'twas too cold, the house she lived in, her handmaid said, and at last she had to move into the great room, where the old men were, for the sake of the warmth. It was right ill with Torgils that winter and spring. I mind me he raved most foully the night you were born, and the fit was upon him a whole week—Cecilia was in such fear of him, she lay trembling in her bed, and Audun himself could not comfort her. 'Twas that, I ween, that broke her, that and the cold. Audun carried her up to the loft-room when the weather was warmer; he saw she was not fit to dwell in the house with the madman—but she died straight. You must have been a month old then—"

The woman's name was Gudrid, she told him, and she lived in the cot that maybe Olav had seen when he rode east to the church town—to the north of the bogs, just before the road turns off toward Rynjul. In her first marriage she had had a little farm in the Saana district—with a good and worthy husband, but she had had no child by him. Then he died, and his brother moved to the farm with his wife; and as she could not be agreed with them, she married this Björn, with whom she was now. This was the most foolish counsel she could have taken. Nay, he was no poor man at that time; when they put together their goods, they might have had an easy lot. He was a widower and had only one daughter, and so they deemed that all might turn out well: she was minded to take a husband again, and she greatly desired to have children. And that wish alone was granted, of all she had looked for—eight children, and five of them lived. But the very first winter they were married Björn chanced to slay a man and had to pay fines, and there was soon an end of their prosperity. Now Björn was mostly out in the fiord, hunting seal and porpoise and sea-fowl, or fishing for Tore of Hvitastein—and she herself sat in the cot with all her little children and the stepdaughter, who was shrewish and ungodly—

Olav listened patiently to the woman's torrent of words, and at last he bade her follow him to the storehouse. He had laid in all that was needed for his home-coming feast, and he filled Gudrid's sack abundantly—"and if you are in straits this winter, you must come hither and tell us, foster-mother!"

"God bless you, Olav Audunsson—but you are like your mother when you smile! She had so gentle a smile, Cecilia, and she was always good to poor folk—"

At long last the old wife departed.

There was no one in the hall when Olav entered. And he stood awhile musing. With one foot on the edge of the hearth, and his hands clasped about his knee, he stared into the little heap of burned wood in which there was still a gleam—it hissed and crackled with crisp little sounds, and a faint breath came from the dying embers.

"Mother," he thought, and recalled the little he had heard of her. She had been young—and fair, they said; she had been reared as became one of noble birth in the rich nunnery, where she was the playmate of a King's daughter. And from the Queen's court she had been removed to this lonely manor, far from all she knew. In these poor and rustic rooms she had borne him under her heart, starved with the cold and left alone with two aged men—the madman, of whom she was afraid, and the master himself, who misliked his grandson's marriage.—It was hateful.

He smote his thigh hard with the palm of his hand. Intolerable it must be to be born a woman, to have so little say in one's own destiny. He seemed to pity *all* women—his own mother in silk and fine linen, this beggar woman Gudrid, Ingunn—it availed one as little as the other to meet force by force. Ingunn—a wave of desire and longing rose within him—he thought of her slender white neck: poor thing, she had learned perforce to bend her proud young head. First for his sake; and now she had been brought full low. But he would take her head upon his breast, softly and tenderly he would caress that poor, weak neck. *Never* should she hear a word from him of her misfortune; never should she see a sign, in word or in deed, that he bore her resentment.—At that moment he did not feel that there was any resentment in his soul toward the defenceless creature who would soon be in his power —his only wish was to protect her and do well by her.

Later in the day Olav saddled his horse and rode eastward to the church town. He was not sure what he wanted there, but his mind was in a turmoil that day. And when he came there, he tied his horse to the fence and walked across the graveyard up to the church.

He laid his sword and hat on the bench that ran along the wall, but chanced to sweep them to the floor with the skirt of his mantle. The echo within the stone walls made him ill at ease. And the light was unpleasantly pale and strange, for the walls had just been whitewashed—pictures were to be painted on them this summer.

Audun and Cecilia lay at the top of the nave on the left, between the Lady chapel and the apse. As Olav knelt by their tomb and said his prayers as softly as he could, his eye was caught by an image that the master painter had newly finished on the pier of the chancel arch. It was of a tall, slender, and graceful woman with bandaged eyes and a broken reed in her hand—her mien and bearing, nay, the very colour of her dark garment, were also unspeakably mournful. Olav had often seen this image in the churches, but had never remembered to ask what was its significance. But never had the woman looked so melancholy or so beautiful as here.

Bishop Torfinn's words about the motherless children suddenly occurred to his mind. For the first time he thought he was almost glad he had not required of Ingunn that she should part with her child. At that moment he felt able to think of this infant with a kind of compassion. Since she had borne it, he must find means to rear it.

When he came out of the church, he saw that the priest, Sira Benedikt Bessesson, was standing by his horse. Olav greeted him courteously, and the priest returned his greeting blithely. From the little he had seen of his parish priest Olav liked him uncommonly well. The priest had a fine and dignified presence—thickset, broad-shouldered, and well-knit. His face was wreathed about with reddish-brown hair and beard, and it was a broad face, but shapeful, with bold features, much freckled; he had large, clear eyes, sparkling with life. Olav judged him to be a pious, discerning man of cheerful disposition—and he liked the priest for having a strong, fine, and flexible voice, whether in speech or song.

At first they talked of the gelding. Olav had got him in Skaane —he was seven years old, big and strong-legged and handsome, white and dapple-grey over the quarters. He always groomed and curry-combed the horse himself, making him smooth and glossy, for he was very fond of the animal and he liked to hear that the priest could see what he was worth. Then Sira Benedikt closely examined the bridle, which was of red leather. Olav concealed a smile—the priest practised much tanning and dyeing of leather, and such work was his joy and delight. This was one of the faults Olav Half-priest had to find with Sira Benedikt—he thought this work altogether unseemly for a priest, since it made him soil his consecrated hands with the worst impurities. To this Sira Benedikt replied that he did not believe such impurities to be unseemly in God's eyes, since the priest's hands were as clean as before, when he had washed them. Our Lord Himself had done in like manner and honoured the work thereby, when He took axe and chisel in the same blessed hands that created and redeemed mankind, and wrought the logs in the workshop of his holy foster-father—He surely would not deem His poor servant disgraced by following a noble and ingenious craft.

The priest invited Olav to accompany him home, and Olav accepted with thanks. Another thing at which Olav Ingolfsson turned up his nose was the smell in the priest's yard, like that of the dyers' booths in the town. But the house was clean and fair within; his living-room was far finer than that of Hestviken. Three well-favoured young maidens brought in butter, white bread, and ale, greeted the guest with comely grace and went straight out again. They were daughters of the priest's nephew; the eldest undertook the duties of his household, and at this time she had her sisters on a visit.

The ale was excellent, and the men sat a good while talking of this and that. Olav like Sira Benedikt better and better. Then their talk fell upon Olav Ingolfsson, and the priest praised the young man for having shown such loving-kindness toward one

who had misgoverned his affairs so ill. Olav answered that it was
his own outlawry that was chiefly to blame for the neglected
state of Hestviken; the old man had doubtless done his best, seeing
that he was a cripple and ailing. But indeed he held old Olav to be
a remarkably wise and holy man.

"That addle-pate?" said the priest.

Olav said nothing.

The priest went on: "Holiness, I trow, he had good cause to
seek—to judge by the fellows he resorted to in his youth, his holiness cannot have been much to boast of. And were he wise, he
would think and speak more of Christ and Mary Virgin, and less
of witchcraft and spectres and mermen and water-wraiths—would
pray, rather than practise these sorceries and incantations of his—I
marvel whether much of what he deals with be not downright
heresy. But he came out of school a half-taught priestling—and
the half he had learned was learned wrong. It may be diverting to
listen to his tales some evening or other—but you seem to be a
man of sense, Olav Audunsson, you surely do not believe all his
preaching—?"

Ah, thought Olav, now he knew it. And in fact he thought he
had already suspected how it was. Aloud he said with something
like a smile:

"There would seem to be no very warm friendship between
you and my kinsman?"

The priest replied: "I have never liked him—but that is not
merely because he was foster-brother of him who wronged me
and mine most grievously. And none of us bore hatred to the
other men of Hestviken—they were brave and honourable, all but
he. You may see that yourself, Olav—I have liked you since I saw
you for the first time, and I was minded that you should see I wish
you well, and I think myself that the old enmity between us of
Eiken and you of Hestviken should now be buried and forgotten.
Not that we ever counted Olav Ribbung and his other sons our
enemies—but we kept out of each other's way as much as we
could, as you may well suppose."

Olav busied himself with wiping off some ale he had spilt on
his jerkin; he did not look up as he asked:

"I know not what you mean, Sira Benedikt. I am but newly
come home and am strange to these parts—I have never heard
aught of this enmity between your kindred and mine."

Sira Benedikt seemed greatly surprised, and a little embarrassed as well. "I thought surely Olav Half-priest had spoken to you of this?"

Olav shook his head.

"Then 'tis better I tell you myself." The priest sat in thought awhile, jogging the little dipper that floated in the ale-bowl and making it sail round.

"Did you look at those fair children of mine, the little maids that came in here, Olav?"

"Indeed they were fair. And were it not that I have a young bride waiting for me in the Upplands, I had used my eyes better while your kinswomen were here, Sira!" said Olav with a little smile.

"If I guess your meaning aright," replied the priest, and he too smiled, but with a troubled look, "you cannot be aware that they are your own kinswomen, and near of kin too?"

Olav turned his eyes upon the priest and waited.

"You are second cousins. Torgils Foulbeard was the father of their father. He ruined my sister—"

Involuntarily Olav's face was convulsed with horror. Sira Benedikt saw it, guessed the young man's thought, and said:

"Nay, 'twas before God took his wits from Torgils, or the Evil One, whom he had followed so faithfully, while sin and lust tempted him. Ay, God knows I am not an impartial man when I speak of Olav Half-priest; he and Torgils were foster-brothers, and Olav backed the other through thick and thin. Olav Ribbung would compel Torgils to marry Astrid; he was an honourable, resolute, and loyal man—and when Torgils left her to her shame with his bastard son, while he himself kept to his leman in Oslo and would marry her, Olav Ribbung commanded his son to come hither. Ingolf, your grandfather, and Olav's daughters, and Ivar Staal, his son-in-law, all said they would not sit at meat with Torgils nor speak to him while he held fast to his purpose. But Torgils was living with the priest, the father of Olav Ingolfsson— the more shame to them that they received him; one was a priest and the other was to be one.

"Ay, and the end was that my father and brothers accepted fines and made atonement with the Hestvik men when we saw that neither Olav Ribbung nor Ingolf could do aught to shake Torgils or force him to make amends for Astrid's misfortune.

'Twas the better and more Christian way—that is true. But had I
been of an age to bear arms, I know full sure I would not have
rested till I had laid Torgils low—I had done it even if I had been
a priest, ordained to the service of God. I have hated that man so
that—God sees my heart, and He knows it. But He knows too, I
ween, that the hardest thing He can require of a man is that he
shall not avenge his kinswoman's honour with the sword.—I was
ten years old when it happened. Astrid had been to me as a
mother; she was the eldest of our family, and I was the youngest.
I shared a bed with her that summer: she wept and wept; I know
not how it was she did not weep herself to death. I tell you, Olav,
the man who can forgive such a thing from his heart, him I would
call a holy man."

The priest sat in silence. Olav, still as a rock, waited for him to
say more. But at last he thought he must say something.

"What became of her, your sister?" he asked in a low voice.
"Did she die?"

" 'Tis eight winters since she died," said the priest. "She lived
to be an old woman. She was married some years after, to Kaare
Jonsson of Roaldstad, north in Skeidis parish, and she had a good
life with him. Father was too hard on her and could not bear the
sight of her child; had it been another man's—but that a daughter
of his should swell the flock of Torgils's concubines— But Kaare
was good to them both; it was he too who brought about the good
marriage for his stepson, with the daughter and heir of Hestbæk.
And when disaster fell upon Olav of Hestviken and he began to
feel the lack of kinsmen, he sent word to Astrid—if she would let
him have the child, Arne, he would make the boy heir to his
father's name and goods. Kaare answered that the lad no longer
needed the support of his father's kindred, and both he and Astrid
loved Arne Torgilsson far too dearly to send him out to Hestviken
to inherit the fortunes of the Hestvik men. So Olav fetched home
Aasa, who had served there at one time, and the son that she had
had by Torgils; but he was not long in life—

"But these are all old matters, and I deem that we should now
forget our enmity and you young ones should claim kinship and
meet in charity. I believe that Arne of Hestbæk and you would
like each other. You must go thither with me one day, Olav, and
greet the kinsfolk you have in this part of the land."

Olav said he would do so more than gladly. But then he asked:

"That word you spoke of the Hestvik men's fortunes—what meant you by that?"

The priest looked as though the question troubled him.

"You know that your great-grandfather was not blest in his kindred. That was the time when he sat there in Hestviken with the madman—his other children he had lost, all but Borgny, who was in a convent, and he had no true-born heir to follow him other than the little lad Audun, your father—and him Ingolf's widow had taken with her, when she went home to the place she had come from, south in Elvesyssel. So it may well have seemed to Kaare and Astrid that the race would not prosper after him."

Olav said pensively: " 'Tis true for all that, Sira Benedikt, favoured of fortune they were not, from all that my kinsman has told me of them."

"They were brave men and loyal, Olav, and that is worth more than good fortune."

"Not Torgils," said Olav. "I knew not this thing of him. I knew naught else but that he had been witless all his days—old Olav has never spoken his name."

"Bitterly as I have hated him," said Sira Benedikt, "I will yet tell you the truth of him—he was a brave man—and with men he kept faith. And all say that no goodlier youth has been seen within the memory of man in the country about Folden. Ay, 'tis strange I should have liked you so well, when first I saw you, for you bear great resemblance to Torgils. But then Arne too is like his father, and his daughters—methought perchance you had seen it, when all three came in—they might well be your sisters. You all have the same abrupt little noses and the white skin—and the same fair hair, pale as thistledown; nay, so handsome as he was you are not—though I hated him, I must say with the rest, a fairer man have I never seen. So there may well be truth in what they report of him, that he had no need to run after women or to allure them with wooing arts and false words. They followed him of themselves—as though bewitched if he did but fix those strange blue-green eyes of his upon them. Ay, you have the same light eyes, you too, Olav—"

Olav had to laugh at this—and he laughed on, trying to laugh off his sense of oppressive discomfort.

"Nay, Sira Benedikt—I cannot be very like my kinsman Torgils

—in the eyes at least. For *I* have never marked that I could charm women—"

"You are like him, Olav, though you be not so handsome—and you have the same light eyes, both you and these little maids of mine. But the evil power of bewitching folk dwells not in the eyes of any of you, God be praised. And this prating of misfortune that is thought to pursue certain houses and kindreds—it may have been so in heathen times, I am ready to believe that. But you are surely wise enough now to lay your life and destiny in the hands of God Almighty and not to believe such things.—God be gracious to you, my Olav—I wish you happiness and blessing in your marriage, and that your race may be called fortune's favourites from now on!"

The priest drank to him. Olav drank, but could not bring himself to say anything. But now Sira Benedikt fetched in the three daughters of Arne—Signe, Una, and Torgunn—and Olav greeted his kinswomen with kisses. They were so fair and debonair that Olav warmed little by little and stayed a good while in cheerful converse with them. To his home-coming feast at Hestviken they thought they could not come, for it would be just at the time when they were to go to a great wedding near their own home. But late in the autumn they would return to the priest's house and stay with him awhile, and then they promised to visit him and pay their respects to his wife.

Olav was profoundly troubled in his mind as he rode homeward. That he should have been impelled to visit the church today—and that he should have met Sira Benedikt and learned this of his grandfather's brother and the priest's sister, this seemed so singular to Olav that he could scarce believe it to be pure chance.

For though it was true that only the Bishop could give him absolution for the slaying of Teit, yet he could confess it to Sira Benedikt first. And with a sort of terror Olav felt how unspeakably he longed to do so.

He knew that if he knelt at Sira Benedikt's knee and laid it bare to him that he was a murderer, and how it had come about that he was one—then he would find himself in the presence of a servant of God who was not merely a spiritual father. Sira Benedikt would understand him as a father understands the son of his body.

He had loved Bishop Torfinn because that monk from Tautra had suffered him to approach a world of riches and beauty and wisdom, which before he had only known as something distant and strange. The Christian faith had been to him a power like the King and the law of the land—he knew that it was to govern his life, and he bowed to it, without reluctance, with reverence and with the recognition that a man must be loyal to all these things if he was to be able to meet his equals and look them freely in the face without shame. In Bishop Torfinn he had seen the man who could take him by the hand and lead him on to all that gave happiness and self-knowledge to serve and to love. What manner of man he would have been had it been his lot to follow the lord Torfinn for a longer space, he could not tell. To Olav the Bishop remained an advocate from the eternal heights—and he himself was as a child, who had only understood a little of that to which the other opened his eyes, before his own conduct forced him to fly from his good instructor.

Of Arnvid he was fond, but their tempers were so unlike that he had felt Arnvid's piety as merely a part of what he did not understand in his friend. Arnvid was reserved, Olav felt, though he was far from being a taciturn man—but Arnvid's loquacity seemed a part of his readiness to help. Time and again Olav remembered that it was always himself who had received and Arnvid who had given—but such a man was Arnvid Finnsson that Olav could not feel humiliated by it; he might have accepted even more of the other, and still they would have been close friends. Arnvid knew him through and through, thought Olav, and yet was fond of him —*he* did not know Arnvid, but yet was fond of him.

It had diverted him greatly to listen to Olav Half-priest's talk of spiritual things. But all that the old man talked of, angels and devils, pixies and sprites and fairies and holy men and women, seemed as it were to belong to another side of life than that in which he himself contended with his difficulties. The Lady Sancta Maria herself became almost as a king's daughter in a fairy tale, the fairest rose of paradise—but it seemed very far from his part of the world, this paradise, when old Olav talked of it.

Sira Benedikt was the first man he had met in whom he had recognized something of himself—a man who had fought the fight in which he himself was engaged. And Sira Benedikt had won, had become a God-fearing man, strong and steadfast in the faith.

And Olav felt longing and hope pulsing in his veins. All he needed
was to take heart. Pray for strength, as Brother Vegard had said,
without the reservation: O God, grant not my prayer too quickly.

He lay awake most of that night. It came over him that now he
understood one thing: a conflict had been waged in the whole of
creation since the dawn of the ages between God and His enemy,
and all that had life, soul, or spirit took part in the fight in one host
or the other, whether they knew it or not—angels and spirits, men
here on earth and on the farther side of death. And it was most
commonly by a man's own cowardice that the Devil could entice
him into his service—because the man was afraid God might demand too much of him—command him to utter a truth that was
hard to force through his lips, or to abandon a cherished delight
without which he believed himself not strong enough to live:
gain or welfare, wantonness or the respect of others. Then came
the old Father of lies and caught that man's soul with his old
master lie—that he demanded less of his servants and rewarded
them better—so long as it lasted. But now Olav himself had to
choose whether he would serve in one army or in the other.

It was thick weather, mild and grey, when he came out next
morning. The mist shed tiny drops of water over him, which fell
gratefully on his face and refreshed his lips after the sleepless
night.

He went out on the high ground west of the manor, where the
hill sloped in a rounded curve toward the open fiord, with
stretches of bare rock and flowery crevices. It was already his
habit to turn his steps thither every morning and to stand and
watch the weather. He was beginning to be familiar with the
voice of the fiord. Today the sea was calm. A light swell lapped
the smooth sides of the Bull, breaking through the mist with little
gleams of white, where the spray was thrown high into the air
when the slightest breeze blew on the shore. There was a trickling
of water among the rocks down on the beach, a lapping of the
wreath of seaweed just beneath him, where the smooth rock slid
down into the sea; a breath of good salt water came up to him.

Olav stood motionless, gazing out and listening to the faint
sound of the fiord. Now and again the fog thickened so that he
could scarcely see it.

He had seen long ago that he had committed a sinister folly in not proclaiming the slaying straightway at the first house he came to. Had he done *that*, 'twas not even certain that he would have been condemned to make amends—Teit's life might have been found forfeit, if Ingunn's kinsmen had been willing to witness that he, Olav, had an older right to the woman. He had now thought so long this way and that, that he scarce remembered what had been in his mind, when he chose to remain silent and wipe out all traces of the deed—but he must have fooled himself into the belief that so the shame might be kept hid. No man must learn that he had rid himself of Teit Hallsson, since thus he thought no man would learn that Ingunn had been disgraced by Teit. Now it seemed to him incomprehensible that he could have thought anything so totally fatuous.

But now he was caught in his own snares. Never would the Bishop give him absolution for a manslaughter on other terms than that he should publicly acknowledge the deed, that justice might be done. But now it had become a secret murder and dastard's work, and never could it be anything else.

Behind him he had his manor, his lands along Kverndal, the forest on the ridges north and south of Hestviken—his property extended far inland into the mist. The sheds, the quay, his boats he could glimpse down in the creek; the smell came up to him of nets and tar and fish offal and salt water and wood soaked by the sea. And far away in the north Ingunn waited; God knew how she fared now. To take her out of her misfortune, bring her hither to a place of refuge, that was the first duty that lay upon him.

No. The burden he had been mad enough to fasten upon himself he would have to bear henceforward. He could not lay it down now. Perchance he would have to drag it on till he saw the gates of death open before him. And he might die—a sudden death— But that too he must venture. His case was not such that he could turn about and retrace his steps to the point where he had gone astray. He could only go on.

It was with such thoughts that he journeyed northward. Arrived at Berg, he learned from the mouth of Arnvid that Ingunn had tried to slay herself. Six weeks later he came home to Hestviken for the second time, bringing his wife with him.

The sea lay glittering white in the sunshine beneath the burning hot cliff of the Bull when at noonday Olav led Ingunn ashore at the Hestvik hithe. It was the day after Lavransmass.[6]

The water gurgled under the boat's side and smacked against the piles of the quay; the air was heavy with smells—salt water, sweating tar, rotten bait, and fish offal, but now and again there was a breath of flowery scent, sweet and warm and fleeting—Olav caught it and wondered, for it was so familiar. Memories were called forth by it, but he knew not what it was that had this scent.—All at once Vikings' Bay and Hövdinggaard came vividly before him—that world which had wholly vanished from his memory since he fled from it to serve the Earl. At once he knew the smell—'twas lime trees. That fine moist breath as of honey and pollen and mead—there must be flowering lime trees somewhere in the neighbourhood.

The scent grew stronger as they walked up the slope. Olav could not understand it; he had never seen limes at Hestviken. But when he came up to the courtyard, he saw them growing on the steep cliff behind the cattle-sheds. They were firmly rooted in the crevices, clung flat against the face of the rock and let their branches sweep downward. The dark-green heart-shaped leaves lay one over another like the shingles on a church roof, covering the golden bunches of blossom—Olav could glimpse them underneath. They were fading and turning brown, and their scent was somewhat sickly and past, but there was a faint, soft buzz of bees and a swarm of flies about them.

"Nay, Olav, what is it that smells so sweet?" Ingunn asked in wonder.

"It is lime. You have never seen limes before, I ween—they grow not in the Upplands."

"Ay, but they do. I mind me now—there is a lime tree in the garden of the preaching friars at Hamar. But I cannot see the trees."

Olav pointed up at the cliff. "They are not like the trees that are planted on level ground, the limes that grow here."

He recalled the mighty lime that stood in the castle court at Hövdinggaard—its waxen, honey-dewed flowers hung in the midst of the foliage as though under a tent of leaves. When the lime flowered at Hövdinggaard he had always had a longing— and it

[6] St. Laurence's Day, August 10.

was not Frettastein or Heidmark or any of the places where his
destiny had been set moving, but the half-forgotten home of his
childhood that came to his mind. It must have been the scent of
the lime blossom that he recognized—though he did not seem to
have known that there were limes at Hestviken.

Toward sundown he wandered up Kverndal, to look at the
cornfields on that side. The smell of lime blossom was so heavy
and strong—Olav moved his feet languidly; the sweet fragrance
seemed to weigh upon him. He felt quite weak with happiness.
And now he saw that limes grew all over the ridge on the north
side as well.

The sun had left the valley; the dew was falling as he turned
homeward. He passed through an enclosure of alders and thought
he remembered that there had been a meadow here, where they
cut grass; but now it was overgrown with alders. There was a
rustling and crashing of leaves and bushes as the cows burst their
way through the thicket. They were strange beasts, the Hestvik
cattle—long-haired, deep-bellied, with misshapen legs and curiously twisted horns, big heads and mournful eyes. Most of them
had but three teats, or some other malformation of the udder. Olav
patted their cheeks and spoke kindly to them as he passed through
his herd of melancholy beasts.

Ingunn came out on the path behind the barn, tall and slender
as a wand in her blue habit, with the linen coif waving about her.
Quietly, as though hesitating, she advanced along the path by the
edge of the field. Meadowsweet and setwall, which had almost
shed its blossoms, reached to her waist and almost met around her.
She had gone out to meet him.

When he came up to her he took her hand and led her as they
walked homeward. Their guests were to come next day, but this
night they two and the old man in the closet were the only ones
in the house.

2

THE fine weather lasted over the late summer. In the middle of the
day the bare rocks glowed with heat; the vapour rose from them,
and the sea glittered and the spray dashed white beneath the crags,
in the places where it was never at rest.

Olav was up early in the mornings, but he did not go out on the rocks now. He would stand leaning over the fence round the northernmost cornfield, where the path from the waterside came up. From there he could see down to the creek and up the valley, almost the whole of his home fields. But toward Folden and southward the view was shut in by a crag that jutted out and gave shelter to the last strip of arable land in Hestviken—of the fiord he had only a glimpse northward past the smooth skull of the Bull and its shaggy wooded neck. Over on the other side lay Hudrheim in the morning sun—a low ridge of waste, with sparse fir trees; the higher ground was tilled, with great farms; he had been over there one day, but from here nothing could be seen of any dwellings.

In the cornfield the rock cropped out in so many places that the pale carpet of stubble seemed riddled with it—here and there a ribbon of soil between two brown rocks. But they often had good corn here—it was manured with fish offal from the quayside—and it ripened early. In the crevices of the rock grew a flowering grass that Olav had never seen before; when he came hither in the early summer it blossomed with fair purple stars, but now the grass itself was blood-red and rust-red in all its fringed blades and bristled with seed-bolls that looked like herons' heads with long beaks.

The work of the farm was what Olav understood best. He saw that there were tasks enough before him—the old meadows to be cleared of scrub, the herds to be brought up to their number, the houses to be repaired. He had hired Björn, Gudrid's husband, to fish and hunt seals for him in the fiord during the coming half-year. Of such things he had no expérience, but he intended to go out with Björn this winter, to gain a knowledge of the pursuits on which the ancient prosperity of Hestviken had most depended. Björn also advised him to take up again, next summer, the salt-pans on the creek south of the Horse Crag.

But behind his thoughts, which were busy with the work of the day and the work of the future, a deep, happy calm dwelt in Olav's mind. His day flowed over him now like a stream of nothing but good hours. And since he knew that the dangerous memories lay sunk beneath this stream, and that it was only by virtue of a kind of strength that he was able to let them lie there in peace and not think about them, he felt at the same time proud that he was now happy and safe.

He knew, in a clear and cool fashion, that the old disasters might return and afflict them. But he took the good days while they were there.

So he stood, morning after morning, gazing and thinking of this and that, while this dreamlike feeling of happiness surged beneath his thoughts. His fair face looked hard and angry at times, and the black pupils of his eyes grew small as pin-points. When he might expect Ingunn to be up, he went back to the house. He greeted his wife with a nod and the shadow of a smile when they met, and watched the little blush of joy that appeared on her healthy face and the calm, meek happiness that beamed in her looks and bearing.

Ingunn was so fair now, never had she been fairer. She was a little fuller than of old, and her skin was shining white; her eyes seemed larger and a deeper blue under the white coif of the wedded woman.

She moved in a gentle, subdued way—her manner had become quiet and simple; she was meek with all, but almost humble toward her husband. But all could see that she was happy, and all who had met Olav's wife liked her.

Olav still slept but little at night. Hour after hour he lay awake without stirring, unless he moved the arm on which she lay, when it was numb. She reposed so confidingly against him in her sleep, and he breathed in the sweet hay-scent of her hair. Her whole being exhaled health, warmth, and youth—and in the pitch-darkness it seemed to Olav that the smell of old folk dwelt in the corners, overcome and driven out. He lay thus and felt the time go by, not longing for sleep to come—it was so good to lie like this and simply be aware of her presence; now at last they were safely together. He passed his hand over her shoulder and arm—it was cool and soft as silk; the coverlet had slipped down. He drew it up, bending over her with caresses, and she replied from her drowsiness with little sleepy words of endearment, like a bird twittering on its nightly perch.

But his heart was wakeful and easily scared—it started like a bird that flies up. He noticed this himself, and was on his guard lest others should see it.

One morning he stood by the fence, looking at his cows, which had been let into the stubble-field; the big bull was there. It was the only really handsome animal in his herd, massive and sturdy, black as coal, but with a pale buff stripe down its back. As he stood and watched the bull striding along, slow and heavy, he thought all at once that the pale stripe on the dark back wriggled like a snake, and for a moment it made his flesh creep. It was only for a brief instant, then he collected himself. But after that he was never quite so fond of the bull as he had been, and this feeling clung to him so long as the bull was in his possession.

While the summer weather lasted, Olav was in the habit of going down to the beach daily during the midday rest. He swam out till he could see the houses of the manor above the rocks—lay floating on his back and then swam again. Usually Björn bathed with him.

One day, when they had come out of the water and were letting the wind dry them, Olav chanced to look at Björn's feet. They were large, but high in the instep, with strongly curved soles—the sure sign of gentle birth. He had heard it said that it could be seen at once by a man's feet if a drop of blood from the old thralls' stock were mingled with his. Björn's face and limbs were tanned brown as the bark of a tree, but his body was white as milk and his hair was very fair, but much grizzled.

The question slipped out of Olav's mouth: "Are you akin to us Hestvik men, Björn?"

"No," said Björn curtly. "The devil! Know you not who are your own kindred, man?"

Olav was rather embarrassed and said: "I grew up far from my own people. There may be branches of which one has scarce heard."

"You thought maybe I was one of these wild shoots that have grown up after that Foulbeard," said Björn gruffly. "Nay, I am true-begotten, and so were my forefathers for seven generations. I have never heard that there were bastards in our stock!"

Olav bit his lip. He was angry—but then he had himself provoked the man. So he said nothing.

"But there is one fault in us," Björn went on; " 'tis as though the axe leaps up of itself in our hands when we are goaded—if you will call that a fault. And short is the joy that comes of a stroke—unless the hand that strikes have gold within its reach."

Olav was silent.

Björn laughed and said: "I slew my neighbour, when we fell out over some thongs. What think you of that, Master Olav?"

"Methinks they must have been costly thongs. Were they so wonderful?"

"I had borrowed them of Gunnar to carry in my hay. What think you of that?"

"I think you to be such that I cannot believe it your custom to reward folk thus for a service," said Olav; "so I think there must have been something rare and strange about those thongs nevertheless."

"Gunnar must have thought I thought so," replied Björn, "for he charged me with cutting off a piece of them."

Olav nodded.

Björn asked, bending down to tie his shoe: "What would you have done in my place, Olav Audunsson?"

" 'Tis not easy for me to say—" said Olav. He was struggling to get the pin of his brooch through his shirt.

"Nay, for none would think of charging a man of your condition with stealing a wretched piece of thong," said Björn. "But you held not your hand either, Olav, when your honour was at stake."

Olav was about to put on his kirtle, but he let his arm drop with it.

"What mean you—?"

"I mean—when word came hither, how you had served your brother-in-law for seeking to deny you the maid you were promised and giving you foul words withal—methought I could have a mind to do you a friendly office when you came home some day. But for that I had not taken service so near the haunts where once I owned a farm myself—though 'twas not a great one—"

Olav was putting on his belt. He unfastened the dagger that hung to it: a good weapon with a blade forged by a foreign armourer and a plate of silver with a hook to hold it to the belt. He handed it to Björn:

"Will you accept this as a token of friendship, Björn?"

"No. Have you never heard, Olav, that a knife is not a gift between friends?—it cuts friendship asunder. But you must do me this friendly office—you will cease giving to the wife who is here ever and anon."

Olav blushed—he looked very young for the moment. To hide

his embarrassment he said lightly, as he leaped onto the rock and began to walk up:

"I wist not that they knew so much hereabout of what has been between the Kolbeinssons and me."

Björn had given him a start with what he said about being quick of hand when honour was at stake. The slaying of Einar Kolbeinsson had been far from his mind, it weighed so little on his spirit, except as the cause of the difficulties from which he was now free. So it had not occurred to him that Björn was alluding to *that*—

Olav had taken to Björn when he came and offered him his service, and he continued to like him. But he saw that the man had an ill report in the neighbourhood. His wife, Gudrid, came down to Hestviken at all times; Björn showed little joy at meeting her, and he seldom went home. Olav soon found out that she was the most arrant gossip, who preferred to roam from house to house mumping with her wallet rather than look to her home. Nor were they so poverty-stricken over at Rundmyr as she pretended; Björn took better care of his own than Gudrid gave him word for, he sent home both meat and fish and a little meal, and they had cow and goat. But now Olav had once called the woman foster-mother, so she never went from him without a gift. Now he was sorry he had put himself in this difficulty—he guessed it must be intolerable for Björn, when the man was to be chief of the serving-men at the manor, and his wife came and accepted alms in this way.

A desire had come upon Olav to associate with older men. Without his knowing it he had felt the want of someone who might have cared to teach him and be a guide as he grew up. He was now very courteous and respectful toward all old men among his equals, and helpful to the aged poor, received old men's advice patiently, and followed it too, when he saw that it was beneficial. Moreover Olav was himself a man of few words when he came among strangers—but old folk could usually succeed in keeping the talk going, without his having to say much for his part or to listen the whole time. So they thought very well of the young Master of Hestviken.

Nor was he ill liked among those of his own age, though they thought it could scarce be said that Olav Audunsson brought mirth and gladness with him, and some mistook his quiet and silent manner for pride. But others deemed that the man was only somewhat heavy of disposition and not too keen-witted. That Olav and his wife were uncommonly fair to look upon and knew well how to demean themselves among folk, all were agreed.

One Saturday afternoon, about the time when the work ceased, Olav and Björn with both the house-carls were coming up from the waterside when they saw a company ride out of the little wood in Kverndal and go up the slope toward the manor. There were two men and three young maids whose flaxen hair floated freely down to their saddles; their gowns were red and blue. It was a fair sight on the meadow, which was still fresh and green with the after-grass—and Olav was glad when he recognized the daughters of Arne.

He took them in his arms and kissed them with a merry greeting as he helped them from their horses, and then he led them forward to his wife, who stood at the door and received her guests in her quiet and gentle way.

They had not been to the home-coming feast, and during the holy-days the two younger were to go home to their father; so the priest had sent them hither that they might bring greetings and gifts to the wife of their kinsman. The priest's house-carl accompanied the maids, and as they rode past Skikkjustad, the son of that house came and offered to join them; he had spoken with Olav the week before about a bargain.

Olav went over to the loft-room, changed his sea-clothes, tidied himself, and put on his Sunday garments. He was glad to have these young kinswomen in the neighbourhood, so Ingunn would be less lonely. He had heard a rumour that Sira Benedikt and Paal of Skikkjustad were thinking of a marriage between Signe and Baard Paalsson, and it looked as though the two young people were not disposed to gainsay the matter either; indeed, it might be a comfort to them at Hestviken too if this bargain were made.

Outside, the weather was still and cold; the pale, clear air was a sure presage of frost at night. It was cold indoors too—much wood was thrown on the hearth, and after the household had been fed, the young people were minded to play in the courtyard awhile, till darkness came on, to warm themselves. But Ingunn would not take part in the game. She sat with her cloak wrapped about her and looked as though she felt the cold; she was so quiet that something seemed to have depressed her spirits. Seeing it, Olav left the dance and seated himself by his wife—and soon after, it grew so dark that they all came into the house. It then appeared that the three sisters knew many games, riddles, and jests that were fitted for indoors, and they had sweet voices when they sang—in everything they were courtly and well-bred maidens. But Ingunn remained in ill humour, and Olav was not able to enjoy himself fully, for he could not guess what ailed his wife.

Olav put his arm about Torunn and led her to Ingunn. Torunn was not yet thirteen, a fair and merry child. But not even she could thaw the mistress of the house.

In the evening Olav accompanied his guests on the way. It was fine weather; the full moon shone brightly in the clear sky, but the frost fog was beginning to creep in from the fiord, blotting out the shadows. Olav walked, leading Torunn's horse.

"Your wife likes us not, Olav," said the little maid.

"Can you think that?" said Olav with a laugh. "Not like you! I know not what it is that has gone against Ingunn tonight."

Ingunn was in bed when Olav came home, and when he lay down beside her, he found that she was weeping. He stroked her and bade her say why she was so sorrowful. At long last he got her to come out with it—she felt so mortally unwell; it must come from her having eaten some shellfish when she was down by the waterside that morning. Olav told her not to do such things—she could speak to him or to Björn if she had a mind to such food, and they would find her some shellfish that was good to eat. Then he asked if she did not think his kinswomen were pleasant and comely maids.

Ingunn answered yes, "and merry indeed were these daughters of Arne," she said in a tone of disapproval. "And you sported right wantonly with them, Olav—utterly unlike you. I can guess that *you* like them."

"Yes," said Olav, and his voice was filled with gladness at the thought of the mirthful evening. 'Twould be a great comfort to them both that he had these blithe and courtly young kinswomen so near at hand, he said again.

Olav could hear that she was breathing heavily. After a while she whispered:

"Were we not as sisters to you, Tora and I, in your boyhood?—
but never do I mind me that you romped and jested so wantonly
with us."

"Oh, maybe 'twas not unknown," replied Olav. "But I was under another man's roof," he added quietly. "Had I grown up
among my own kindred and in my own home, I trow I had been
less grave and silent as a boy."

Soon after, he heard that she was weeping again. And now her
sobs took such hold that he had to get water for her. On lighting
a splinter of wood he saw her face so red and swollen that he
feared she had eaten something downright poisonous. He threw
on some clothes, dashed out, and fetched fresh milk, which he
forced her to drink, and then at last she began to mend and fell
asleep.

One day just before Hallowmas Olav was at the manse together with certain other franklins; they had come to have letters drawn up by the priest. Olav had—not exactly fallen out—
with another man, named Stein; but yet the two had exchanged
words somewhat sharply once or twice.

As they were about to ride home again, some of the men went
out to look at Apalhvit, the horse Olav Audunsson was riding.
They praised the horse highly and remarked how well groomed
he was. And they teased Stein, who also had a white horse, but his
was ill kept and rusty yellow, and it was easy to see that he had
been roughly handled by his rider.

Stein said: "It has been Olav's calling to break and tend horses—
'tis but meet that a knight's horse should be well groomed. But
wait till you have known a few years of husbandry; then you will
have forgotten all your courtly ways. And then you will own the
truth of the old saying that white horses and too fair wives are
not for country folk, for they have no time to watch them."

" 'Twill surely never go so hard with me that I have not the
means to keep two white horses," said Olav proudly. "Will you
sell me the horse, Stein?"

Stein named a price, and at once Olav held out his hand and
bade the others witness the bargain. It was settled on the spot how
and when Olav should pay over the purchase money. Stein took
the saddle off his horse and went into the house to borrow a halter
of Sira Benedikt. The other men shook their heads, saying that
this time Olav had made a bad bargain.

"Oh well—" Olav shrugged his shoulders and gave a little laugh. "But I care not always to be so thrifty as to split a louse into four."

He put his saddle on the horse he had bought and let Apalhvit trot behind. The other men stood and watched him; one or two of them gave a little sneering laugh. The first trial of strength between horse and rider came at the bend of the road. It looked as though Olav would be well warmed ere he reached home.

Ingunn sat sewing alone in the hearth-room when she heard the beat of hoofs on the rocky floor of the courtyard. She went to the outer door and looked at her husband in surprise: in the rarefied autumn sunlight he was holding in a strange and restive horse; his face was fiery red and both he and the horse were bespattered with the foam that covered the bridle, while the horse champed and pranced till the stony ground rang again, and would not stand still. Olav greeted her and the house-carl, who came up, with a laugh.

"I will tell you all when I come in," said Olav; he leaped from the saddle and stayed by the house-carl who was to lead the new horse to the stable.

"What is it?" she asked in wonder when he came in. He stopped just inside the door—looking like a drunken man.

"Is the old man at home?" asked Olav.

"No, he went down to the sea—shall I send Tore for him?"

Olav laughed and closed the door behind him. Then he came forward, lifted his wife as one takes a child in one's arms, and squeezed her till she gasped.

"Olav—" she cried in terror. "What has come over you?"

"Oh, naught else but that you are too fair a wife," he muttered with the same drunken laugh, and pressed his heated face against hers till she thought he would break her neck.

Late in the afternoon Olav betook himself to the mill, and Ingunn went into the cook-house; she had a pan of cheese standing by the fire, below the bake-stone.

The lid could not have been fitted on tightly, so much ash had got in. And it smelt ill—had doubtless stood too long, but it would not curdle sooner. Ingunn could never get her cheeses to work in the right way: the cheeses she had made the week before had gone soft again and run over onto the shelf where she had put them to dry.

Her mouth twitched as she stood kneading the sticky, evil-smelling cheese in the pan, with slow and clumsy hands. She was no skilful housewife—all work was to her heavy and difficult, and accidents were always happening. Each new misfortune made her so utterly despondent—when would it strike Olav that his wife was incapable besides her other faults? At the end of a day like this, when everything she put her hand to had gone wrong, she felt bruised all over, as though from a number of falls.

He had not been drunken after all, Olav. At first she had sought comfort in the thought that he must have partaken more freely than was his wont of that ale of which their priest made such boast. But he had been quite sober. And her heart fluttered fitfully as she pondered—what could have come over Olav to make him so utterly unlike himself? Never had he been aught but kind and affectionate and tender in his love. At times she would fain have had him—not quite so calm and sober-minded.

The thought weighed heavily upon her: true enough, he was calm in his bearing, master of himself—as long as might be. But she had seen occasions when he lost his self-control. But even in that night of madness when the boy came to her and said he had slain Einar, she had felt his love for her as a safeguard. His rage she had seen *once*—when it was turned against herself; once she herself had lain cowering, mortally afraid, face to face with his white-hot anger. It was a thing she could not bear to think of— and she had not thought of it, till now. But now she recalled it, with such stifling vividness— But *now* she could not have done anything to make him angry?

She had felt so easy in these four months they had been married. Unconsciously she reckoned her marriage from the hour when her kinsmen in the presence of witnesses had given her into the hands of Olav Audunsson. He had been so good to her that the memory of all the terrible things that had befallen her on the eve of that event was now but as the shadow of a horrible dream. And she had been obliged to acknowledge the truth of what he said— Hestviken was far away; it had been easier than she could ever have imagined to forget what had happened there in the north. But at the same time she had striven to show him that she was grateful and loved him—unspeakably.—Surely, then, *she* could not have done anything to cause him to be so—strange—just now, when he came home. But then she was seized with terror at the thought of *what* might have caused it—

And yet that was foolish—for he had shown no sign of wrath; it had all been caresses, in a way, the whole of it. Only wild ones— and then he had played with her, roughly, mad with an ungovernable merriment that had scared her, for she was not used to seeing Olav thus. But perhaps that was no proof that anything out of the common had befallen him—perhaps it was the way with all men, that such a fit came over them now and again. It had been Teit's way—

Teit—she felt a kind of sagging at the heart—it had been just like Teit. Her memory of him had grown distant and unreal like all the rest that sank below the horizon as she moved farther and farther away from it with Olav. Now it had again come nigh her, alive and threatening, the memory that she had been Teit's—

She uttered a scream and started, trembling all over, as Olav suddenly appeared just behind her—she had not noticed his coming.

He had stood in the doorway for a while watching her, the tall and slender young wife bending over the board, narrow-shouldered and lithe, working slowly and awkwardly with her long, thin-fingered hands in the mess of cheese. He could not see her face beneath the coif, but he had a feeling that she was in low spirits.

He was ashamed of himself for the way he had behaved to her when he came home before. 'Twas far from seemly for a man to show his wife such conduct. He was afraid she might feel insulted.

"Have I frightened you?" Olav spoke in his usual voice, calmly, with a shade of tender solicitude. He placed himself beside her, a little awkwardly—took a pinch of the curds she was now kneading into balls, and ate it.

"I never did this work until I came hither," she said in excuse. "Dalla would never let me. Maybe I have not pressed out the whey enough."

"You will learn it, I doubt not," her husband comforted her. "We have time enough, Ingunn.—I was so vexed over that matter of the horse—but the man Stein provoked me to it." He looked down with embarrassment, turned red and laughed with annoyance. "You know 'tis not like me—to make a fool's bargain. I was so glad when you came out to meet me—" he looked at her as though begging forgiveness.

She bent yet deeper over her work, and her cheeks flushed darkly.

"She is not yet fit for much," thought her husband. "The unwonted labour tires her."—If only the old man in the closet would keep quiet tonight. His poor frame was rent by rheumatic pains, so that he often wailed aloud for hours at night, and the young people got little rest.

Olav Ingolfsson had broken down completely as soon as his young kinsman had relieved him of the duties of master. He had worn himself out at Hestviken, though there was but little to show for it. Now he abandoned himself wholly to the afflictions of old age. The two young people were kind to him. Olav felt it as a support—without being clear in what way he needed support—that after years of waiting he was living under the same roof as a man of his father's kindred. And he was glad that Ingunn was so kind and thoughtful in her manner toward the feeble old man. He had been a little disappointed that she seemed to like neither the daughters of Arne nor their father, whom they had since met. Olav himself had a great liking for this cousin of his father's. Arne of Hestbæk was a man of some fifty years, white-haired, but handsome and of good presence; the family likeness between him and Olav Audunsson was striking. Arne Torgilsson received Olav very open-heartedly and bade him be his guest at Yule. And for this Olav had a right good mind; but Ingunn did not seem so set on going.

But he was glad that in any case she seemed to take to Olav Ingolfsson, though the old man gave no little trouble. He was often restless at night—and then he befouled the place with all the simples and unguents he prepared for himself—and the old dog, who lay in his bed at night and was to draw out the pain from his sick leg, was uncleanly, thievish, and cross-tempered. But Ingunn patiently assisted the old man, spoke to him gently as a daughter, and was kind to his dog.

Both the young people found it diverting to listen to old Olav's talk in the evenings. There was no end to what he knew of men and families and their seats in all the country around Folden. Of the warfare that followed Sverre Priest's coming to Norway he could tell them many tales learned from his father; but in King Skule's cause Olav Half-priest had fought himself. Olav Audunsson's great-grandfather, Olav Olavsson of Hestviken, had followed Sigurd Ribbung to the last, and then he had fought *against* Skule. But when the Duke was proclaimed King at the Öre Thing, Olav Ribbung mustered men about him and marched northward with his three sons to offer him his support; and his brother, Ingolf the priest, gave his son leave to accompany his cousins: "We were then in our fifteenth year, Torgils and I—but we gave a good account of ourselves. The scar I bear on my back was gotten at Laaka. They made such sport of me, the Vaarbelgs,[7] for getting hurt *there*—but we had come into a deep cleft with a stream between landslides and had the Birchlegs above us both behind and before—there were Torgils and I and three other lads—there were so many young lads among our party. One of them we called Surt, for he had the reddest hair I have seen on any man.[8] It chanced, as we followed Gudine Geig into the Eastern Dales, that we lay one night at a little farm and woke to find the house afire. 'You have lain with your shockhead against the bare wall, you devil,' said Gudine. 'Yes, and then you blew on it,' said Surt—he-he-he, his words were less decent than I will repeat for Ingunn's sake; we lay all over the floor, Surt just behind Gudine. The penthouse was all ablaze, but out we came and hacked our way through. They had an ill habit of setting fire to houses, the Birchlegs—'twas a jest with us that there were so many sons of bathhouse carls and bake-house wives among them. But now you are to hear how we fared, Torgils and I, at Laaka—nay, first let me tell you a little of this Gudine Geig—"

Olav noticed that it vexed Ingunn when the old man questioned her impatiently whether she would not soon have news for them. Now she and Olav had been married five months—

[7] *Vaarbelger* was the name given to the followers of Skule by their enemies, the Birchlegs. Various explanations of the name have been suggested, the most probable being "hides taken in springtime" (*vaar*, spring, and *belg*, hide), the hides being almost valueless during the spring months. Duke Skule was proclaimed King in 1239. In the following year he was victorious over the Birchlegs at Laaka, but the Vaarbelgs were afterwards defeated by King Haakon at Oslo. Skule fell at Trondhiem in May 1240.

[8] *Surt* is the Norwegian name for a ferruginous earth used as a dye.

"We do what we can, kinsman," said Olav with a little laugh.

But the old man was angry and told him not to jest lightly with the matter, but rather to make vows and pray God to grant them an heir betimes. Olav laughed and thought there was no such haste. In his own mind he deemed it hard enough for Ingunn, even now when she was in full health, to cope with the affairs of the household and keep her three serving-women to their work.

But Olav Ingolfsson complained: he believed he had not long to live. Now he had known four generations of the family, great-grandfather, grandfather, father, and son—"I would fain greet a son of yours, Olav, before I quit this world."

"Oh, you will live sure enough to greet both my son and my grandson," Olav consoled him. But the old man was despondent:

"Olav Torgilsson, who was the first man of our race here in Hestviken, was married to Tora Ingolfsdatter ten years before they had children—and he fell before his sons saw the light. That was his punishment, to my mind, for having married her against his father's will. Ingolf of Hestviken and Torgils of Dyfrin had been enemies, but Olav Torgilsson said he would not forgo this good marriage because the two old men had quarrelled once in a drinking-bout. Tora was the heiress here, for Ingolf was the last man of the old Hestvik line, who are said to have dwelt in this spot since there were men in Norway. And Torgils Fivil was the last of the barons' line at Dyfrin. Sverre gave the manor and Torgils's young widow to one of his own men—he had been thrice married, Torgils Fivil. He had been given the name in his youth from his flaxen hair and the fine, white skin that has ever been an inheritance in our kin.[9]

"So you may see, our ancestor had cause enough for vengeance upon Sverre—his manor, his father, and three brothers. And the winter that his wife perceived there was a hope that the race would survive them was the same winter when the country folk here around Folden rose to take vengeance for Magnus, their crowned King, and strike down that Sverre, who had no right to the kingdom and sought to upset all our ancient rights and bring in new customs, which we liked not. Men of the Vik and of the Upplands, of Ranrike and Elvesyssel, wellnigh the whole people of Norway were with us. Olav Torgilsson was among the

[9] *Fivil*: bog-cotton.

nobles who were foremost in counsel and boldest in fight from the very first.

"You know how we fared at Oslo that time. The Devil helps his own, and he bore up Sverre Priest till he had him well housed within the gates of hell, 'tis my belief. Olav Torgilsson fell there on the ice; but some men from these parts rescued the body and carried him home. So many men had fallen above Olav there around the standard that the Birchlegs had not despoiled him, and home he came, axe in hand; they could not loosen the dead man's grip of the weapon. But when the widow came up and took hold of it, he let go—the arm dropped, and Tora was left with the axe, and at the same moment the child quickened within her—'twas as though the unborn babe had struck out with his clenched fist, she told the sons she bore that spring. From the time they were big enough to understand, she spoke of this early and late, that they had vowed to avenge their father while they were yet in the womb. That axe was the one you have now, 'Kin-fetch.' Tora gave it that name; of old it was called 'Wrathful Iron.' It came to Olav, since he was the elder of the twins, when she sent the boys to a man named Benedikt, who was said to be a son of King Magnus Erlingsson. His was the first company in which these brothers took part.

"I can well call to mind my grandmother, Tora Ingolfsdatter. She was a large-hearted woman, of great judgment, feared God, and was charitable toward the poor. While she was mistress here—and she had a long life; your great-grandfather and my father obeyed her to her dying day—there was great fishery here in Hestviken. Grandmother sent her ships along the whole coast, as far as the border by the Gauta River and down to Denmark—you can guess, she spied out news of what was brewing against the race of Sverre. Tora always had scent of all such plans that were afoot, and all who were minded to oppose the Birchlegs found good backing with the widow of Olav Torgilsson. Tora had loved her husband with marvellous devotion. Olav Torgillson was a little fair-skinned man, but full of strength, and handsome—somewhat lacking in chastity, but so they were, the men of King Magnus's time.

"Grandmother herself can never have been fair of face. At the time I remember her she was so tall and so portly that she had to go sideways and bend double to get through the door here in the new house. She was half a head taller than her sons, and they were big men. But fair she was not: she had a nose so big and so crooked that I know not to what I can liken it, and eyes like gulls' eggs, and her chins hung down upon her chest and her breasts upon her stomach.

"First she sent her sons to Filippus, the Bagler King,[1] but soon she grew very dissatisfied with him, deeming him lacking in energy, lazy, and a lover of peace. When therefore this Benedikt came forward in the Marches, she bade the lads go to him. His company was for the most part a rabble of vagabonds of every kind—my father always said that this Benedikt was of little worth as a leader. He was rash and heedless and somewhat foolish—sometimes a coward and sometimes overbold. But Olav held staunchly to him, always, for he firmly believed that Benedikt was King Magnus's son, though he did not come up to his father. Now, it befell Bene that at the first he had but this herd of rogues that they called the ragged host, but soon more and more good franklins took up his cause, since no more likely leader could be found at the time. But then they were minded to rule Bene and not let themselves be ruled by their claimant to the crown. And when, after a time, Sigurd Ribbung came forward and gained the support of the nobles, the old Bagler leaders, the chiefs of the ragged host took Bene with them and went over to Sigurd, and Benedikt had to content himself with being one of Sigurd Ribbung's petty chieftains. But Olav Olavsson always bore in mind that Benedikt was the lord to whom he had first sworn fealty, and served and honoured him accordingly. Olav was a loyal man.

"Tora made good marriages for her sons—for Olav, Astrid Helgesdatter of Mork; they were very young, some sixteen years both of them, and they had a goodly life together and loved each other with true affection. Their sons were Ingolf, your grandfather, he was the eldest; then there was the Helge who fell at Nidaros with King Skule, and Torgils, he was the youngest of the sons; he and I were of equal age. The daughters of Olav and Astrid were Halldis, who was married to Ivar Staal of Aas in Hudrheim, and Borgny, the nun—a lovable, holy woman. She died the year after you were born.

[1] The Baglers (or "crozier men") were the party of the Church and the old nobility, opposed to Sverre and his followers, the Birchlegs.

"Father was older when he married, for he wished to be a priest. It was the Bishop himself, Nikulaus Arnesson, who ordained him, and he loved my father very dearly, for Father was exceeding pious and learned and wrote books more fairly than any priest in the diocese. My mother, Bergljot of Tveit, was merry, fond of feasting and show, so she and Father were ill matched and did not agree well together, though they had many children—five of us lived to grow up. She was somewhat greedy of money, my mother —Father was so generous that he robbed his own larder behind Mother's back to give alms. But it chanced unluckily that the townsmen got word of this and laughed at it—you know, it looks ill if a priest be not master in his own house. I remember one day Mother was angry over something—she took two sheets of a book Father had just finished writing and threw them on the fire, but then he beat her. Father was a big, strong, valiant man and he had fought bravely against the Birchlegs, but toward his even Christians he was the most gentle and peaceful of men—but with Mother there was ever some dissension. Between our house at Oslo and the sea there was a piece—one could not call it ground; 'twas but beach and weeds and bare rock. The townspeople had been wont to use a path across it to shorten the way. Mother wished to close this path—Father deemed it unseemly for a priest to wrangle over such a small matter. But there were quarrels without end on account of this right of way—between Father and Mother and between us and our neighbours.

"When the order came that the priests of Norway were to live in celibacy like those of other Christian lands, Father bade my mother go home to Tveit, to enjoy the manor and a great part of his estate. But she and her kinsmen and my brothers and sisters were very wroth, for they thought in their hearts that Father was more glad than sorry to be forced to break up their married life. I know full well that my father had always held the marriage of priests to be an evil custom, and that was also the opinion of Bishop Nikulaus—but 'twas the usage when my father was a young man, and then he had to do as his mother willed. My brothers and sisters and my mother then went upcountry, and I have not seen much of them since: Kaare, my brother, got Tveit, and Erlend got Aasheim; now both the manors are divided among many children. I stayed with Father; I had always been intended for the priesthood—and Father and I lived happily together and looked on Halvard's Church as our true home. I was ordained subdeacon three years after King Skule's fall. Grandmother Tora died soon after.

"But it was of your great-grandfather Olav Ribbung and his kin that I was to tell you. Ingolf, you know, was married to Ragna Hallkelsdatter from Kaaretorp—'twas Tora who had busied herself to secure this good marriage for her grandson, as soon as he was grown; Audun, your father, was already some two years old when we kinsmen set out to follow King Skule and the Vaarbelgs. When Torgils turned mad, Ingolf and Ragna had an uneasy life at Hestviken, and afterwards they lived mostly at Kaaretorp. But one Yule, when they were here, Ingolf wished to accompany Halldis, his sister, and her husband across the fiord to Aas and to stay with them awhile. They ran upon a rock, and all who were in the boat were drowned.

"Olav Ribbung bore this disaster so well that my father used to say he had never seen a man bear adversity so nobly—he always named his brother as a pattern of firmness and strength—those twin brothers loved each other so dearly.—Ay, 'twas his son and daughter and son-in-law who were lost. Olav merely said that he thanked God his mother and Astrid, his wife, had died before these disasters had fallen upon his children. He dwelt on there with the madman, and there were no others of his offspring left but Borgny, the nun, and Audun, a little lad. Ingolf's widow married again in Elvesyssel, and Olav gave his consent that Audun should be brought up by his mother and stepfather. Olav Ribbung then adopted the son that Torgils had gotten by a serving wench here at Hestviken, but the boy lived no long time.

" 'Twas the third year I was lame from my broken leg, when Ingolf and the others were lost. And I bore it ill—I thought it unbearably hard to be a cripple, young as I was, and that I could never be a priest. Then father always held up Olav Ribbung to me as an example.—But I know that Olav took it sorely to heart that Audun would not marry again after your mother's death and would not bide at home in Hestviken—and the race bade fair to die out.

"But now there is good hope, I ween, that it will thrive again, with such young and sound and goodly folk as you and your wife. And you may be well assured that I yearn to take a son of yours in my arms. Four generations have I known—five, if I may

reckon our ancestress among them—gladly would I see the first
man of the sixth ere I die. 'Tis not given to many men to know
their own kindred through six generations. And I would deem it
a reasonable thing, my Ingunn, if your husband too should conceive a great longing for the same—his departed kinsmen have
possessed this manor of Hestviken since there were men in Norway. Do you hear that, young woman?" he said, laughing to himself.

Olav saw how red she turned.—But it was not the modest blush
of happy longing; it was the hot glow of shame that mantled her
face. Her eyes grew dark and troubled. In charity he took his
glance from her.

3

Ingunn came out into the balcony and stood gazing at the falling
snow. High up against the pale clouds the great wet flakes looked
grey as they whirled in the air, but when they settled they seemed
pure white, a gleaming white mass against the obliterated white
heights toward Kverndalen.

When she looked up for a while into the driving flurry, she felt
as though she herself were being sucked up, to hover in the air for
an instant; then she sank down and all grew dark. She tried this
again and again. The unbearable giddiness that came over her all
at once was somehow turned to gentle rapture as she felt herself
borne upward; but when the drop came she could not see that she
was falling—nothing but grey and black streaks that whirled
around.

There was such a strange hush that the very sea-mews were silent—she had seen how they settled in such weather, in cracks of
the rock and on the great stones of the beach. Now and again they
moved a little, but without uttering a note. When first she came
here she had thought these great white birds with their wide
stretch of wing were fairer than anything she had seen—even their
curious screams made her strangely happy at heart. She had been
brought to a new land, far from the region where she had suffered
intolerably. In summer, when she came out in the morning and
heard the regular pounding of the sea at the foot of the rock on
which she stood, saw the wide and bright expanse of the fiord and

the bare shore on the other side, and the circling white sea-mews screamed hoarsely, unreal as wraiths—it had made her so light at heart: the world was so great and so wide; what had befallen her somewhere in a spot far, far away could not possibly be so great a matter—it must surely be forgotten in time.

But as autumn drew on out here by the fiord she was alarmed by its being never still. The unceasing murmur and booming of the waves, the cries of the sea-birds, the sweep of the storm over the wooded ridge—all this made her dizzy. If she had but to cross the yard, the wind seemed to rush in at her ears and fill her whole head with noise. And rain and fog drifted in from the sea and took away her courage. She thought of the autumn at home—the ground hard with black frost, the air bright and clear, so that the blows of an axe or the baying of a dog could be heard from farm to farm; there the sun made its way through the morning mist and thawed the rime to dew in the course of the day. And she longed to listen to a stillness around her.

It was as though she had sunk lower and lower as the days and the year grew shorter and darker. Now she was at the bottom—midwinter was past, the year was climbing again. And she felt utterly powerless at the thought that now she was to take the uphill road. Soon the sun would rise higher and higher—the time was near at hand when day by day it would be manifest that brighter and longer days were drawing on—the springtime. But to her it was as though she faced a lofty mountain up which she was to climb—with the burden she now knew full surely that she bore—and it made her sick and giddy to think of it.

Still, still was the air, though the snow whirled so madly—the flakes drifted hither and thither, but at last they fell straight down. The sea was dark as iron, when she had a glimpse of it, and the surf-beat on the beach sounded faint and monotonous in the mild, snowy air.

All was covered now—the road down to the wharf was blotted out. The footprints of the maids who had gone to the byre, her own tracks across the yard, were snowed under. And all the white was turning grey and slowly fading as the first shades of dusk came on.

The door of the bath-house burst open, and in the cloud of white steam that poured out she caught a glimpse of the men's bodies, dark against the snow. They ran up toward the barn, where they had left their clothes, rolling in the drifts as they went, with shouts and laughter. She recognized Olav and Björn, who came first; they closed and wrestled, ducking each other in the snow.

She lifted up the platter of pickled fish and threw her cloak over it. It was so heavy that she had to carry it in both arms; she could not steady herself or see beyond her feet and was afraid of slipping on the snow-covered rocks. The dusk had deepened and the flickering snow made her yet more giddy.

Olav came into the house and took his place in the high seat at the end of the room. He was hungry and tired—settled down in ease at the thought that it was Saturday and the eve of a holy-day, and that three women were busied about him, bringing in food.

The fire on the hearth glowed red, with little low flames playing over the burned-out logs, but through the dim light of the room the man in the master's seat was conscious of the new comfort that had been brought in. The table was always set up now on the raised floor along the end wall; there were cushions in the high seat, and a piece of tapestry had been hung over the logs of the wall behind it. By the side of this the axe Kin-fetch hung in its old place, together with Olav's two-handed sword and his shield with the wolf's head and the three blue lilies. A blue woven curtain had been hung about the southern bed, where the master and mistress slept.

A faint light showed within the closet—the old man was reciting his evening prayers in a half-singing voice. Sira Benedikt might say what he would, thought Olav—his kinsman was a man of no little learning: he said his hours as well as any priest. When the old man had finished, Olav Audunsson called to him: would he not come in and sup?

The old man answered that he would rather have a little ale and groats brought to him in bed. Ingunn hastily filled a bowl with the food and carried it in to him. At the same moment the house-carls appeared at the door—Björn with a bundle of wood, which he flung on the floor. He made up the fire, threw open the outer door and raised the smoke-vent, so that snowflakes drifted down to the hearth with a hiss. Ingunn stayed with the old man till the wood had caught and the worst of the smoke had cleared away. Then Björn closed the door and the smoke-vent.

Ingunn came in and stood at her table. She made a cross with her knife on the loaf before cutting it up. The five men on the bench ate in silence, long and heartily. Ingunn sat on the edge of the bed and picked at a little fish and bread, enjoying it, for the salmon was good and well pickled. The ale was of the Yule brewing and might have been better, but she had had such dirty grain for the malt, mixed with all manner of weeds.

She glanced over at her husband. His hair was dark with wet; the eyebrows and stubbly beard stood out with a golden gleam against his face, which was red and weatherbeaten this evening. He seemed to have a good appetite.

The three serving-maids sat on the bench below the bed, facing the hearth, and ate their supper. Herdis, the youngest of them, whispered and giggled as she ate; that child was always full of laughter and games. She was showing the other maids a new horn spoon that she had been given; the laughter spurted out of her as she did so—then she gave a terrified look at the mistress and struggled to keep quiet, but the girl was all squeaks and gurgles.

The house-folk went out soon after the meal was ended. The men had been on the water from early morning, and the road from Hestviken to the church was so long that they could not lie late abed on the morrow, when the going was as heavy as it was now.

Olav went in to his kinsman—the old man always needed a hand with one thing or another before he lay down to rest. Olav Ingolfsson was specially inclined to talk toward bedtime and wished to hear all about the fishing and the day's work on the farm. And every answer he received of the younger Olav put him in mind of something that had to be told.

Igunn was sitting on a low stool before the hearth, combing her hair, when Olav came back into the room. She was half undressed—sitting in a white, short-sleeved linen shift and a narrow, sleeveless under-kirtle of russet homespun. Her thick dark-yellow hair hung like a mantle about her slender, slightly stooping form, and through it gleamed her delicate white arms.

Olav came up behind her, filled his hands with her loosened hair, and buried his face in it—it smelt so good.

"You have the fairest hair of all women, Ingunn!" He forced her head back and looked down into her upturned face. "But you have fallen away since Yule, my sweet one! You must not work beyond your powers, I will not have it! And then you must eat more, else you will grow so thin, ere Lent comes and we must fast, that there will be nothing left of you!"

He struggled out of his jerkin and shirt and sat down on the edge of the hearth to warm his back. The sight of the man's naked chest, the play of the muscles under the milk-white skin, as he bent down to pull off his boots, affected the young wife painfully. His sound health made her feel her own weakness all the more.

Olav scratched himself on the shoulder-blades—a few little drops of blood trickled, red as wine, down his smooth skin. "He is such a rough fellow, Björn, when he bathes one," laughed Olav.

Then he bent over the bitch that lay with her litter on a sack by the hearth, and picked up one of the puppies. It squealed as he held it to the light—its eyes were only just opened. The mother gave a low growl. Olav had bought the dog but a little while before and had paid so much that his neighbours had again shaken their heads at his grand ways. But it was a special breed of dog, with hanging ears, soft as silk, and a short coat—keen-scented, excellent sporting dogs. Olav handled the puppies with satisfaction: it looked as if they would take after their mother, all five of them. He laughingly laid one in his wife's lap, amused at the dog, which now growled more threateningly, but dared not fly at him.

The tiny, round-bellied creature, still soft of bone, crawled and scrambled, trying to lick Ingunn's hands. It was so weak and jointless—all at once she felt unwell, a lump came into her throat.

"Let its mother have it back," she begged feebly.

Olav looked at her, stopped laughing, and laid the puppy back beside the bitch.

Torre was past and the month of Gjö came and froze the fiord—the ice stretched far to the south of Jölund.[2] The days began to lengthen and grow lighter. The frost fog crept up the fiord from farther out where there was open sea, and when clear days succeeded, with blue sky and sunshine, the whole world glistened with rime. Olav and Björn went out hunting together.

Ingunn's only thought was how long yet would she be able to conceal it. Her tears burst forth—an impotent despair she knew

.[2] Torre and Gjö were the names of two of the old Scandinavian months, the former beginning with the next new moon after the "Yule moon." Gjö would usually include the latter part of February and most of March.

that now indeed she had no need of concealment: was she not Olav's wife in Hestviken, where she was to bear him a child in the old manor that had been the seat of his kin from time out of mind? And yet she would fain have crept underground and hidden herself.

She saw that Olav had guessed how it was with her. Still she kept going and could not bring herself to utter a word of it. She kept the fast like the others, though her chest was drawn with hunger so that it gave her pain. She noticed that Olav stole a glance at her more and more often, with something of wonder and covert anxiety in his looks. Afterwards he would remain silent a long while. Her heart was filled with dread when she saw him thus, brooding and wondering about her. But she did not get herself to say anything.

Then there came a Sunday; they had just come home from church and were alone in the room for a moment. Olav seated himself on the bench; as she was hurrying past he caught her by the wrist and held her.

"Ingunn mine—you must do a kindness to Olav Ingolfsson and tell him of it. I believe he will scarce live through the spring. You know how eagerly he awaits it!"

Igunn bowed her head; her face was red as fire.

"Yes," she whispered obediently.

Then her husband drew her to him and would set her on his knee.

"How is it with you?" he asked in a low voice. "You are so unhappy, Ingunn? Does he plague you so ill, this little guest of yours? Or are you afraid?"

"Afraid!" For an instant the young wife seemed to flare up, like her old headstrong self of former days. "You must surely know how it is— Never have you been anything but good to me—and now I must think day after day that I am not *worth* it!"

"Be silent!" He squeezed her hand hard. Ingunn saw Olav's face shut up. When he spoke again, his voice was forced, though he made an effort to speak calmly and gently:

"Think not of that, Ingunn, which we do much better to forget. 'Twere foolish indeed of us to awaken memories that—that— And you know full well that I love you so dearly that I could never have the heart to be aught but good to you."

"Oh, I should be worth still less, if I could forget—!"

She sank on her knees before him, hid her head in her husband's arms, and kissed his hand. Olav quickly withdrew it, leaped up, and raised his wife to her feet. Ingunn bent backward in his arms, looked into his eyes, and said in a kind of defiance:

"You are fond of me—ay, God knows I see it—but I believe, Olav, that had I offered to treat you as of old—with an overweening, fanciful humour, claiming to have my own way in all things —I scarce believe you would have suffered it in me, or loved me so much, after what I have done to you—"

"Oh, be quiet now!" He let her go.

"I often wish you had treated me harshly, as you threatened that time—"

"That you do not wish," he said with the cold little smile she knew so well from old days.

But then he drew her passionately to him, hid her head on his breast.

"Do not weep," he begged.

"I am not weeping." Olav raised her face and looked into it— he felt strangely ill at ease. He would much rather she had wept.

In the time that followed, a kind of paralysing dread crept over Olav again and again. He had a feeling that all had been in vain. In vain the payments he had made to buy peace for himself and her, in vain that he had sunk his own bitterness to the bottom of his soul and quenched it with all the old streams of his love: his life with her was a dear old habit of his childhood; when he took her in his arms, he recalled the first rapture of his life. Never had he let her see that he remembered her—weakness, he called it now. And now he was at his wit's end, recognizing that against the sense of shame that gnawed at her heart he could do nothing.

And when he saw her in this state, he himself could not avoid the thought—it was not her *first* child.

During their first months together at Hestviken he had been so pleased with her quiet bearing, knowing it was happiness that made her so meek and gentle a wife. But now it hurt him. For she had spoken the truth—had she been as in old days, when she would have her own way and always expected him to give in to her—he would not have brooked that of her *now*.

Then he straightened himself, as though shouldering his burden anew. At home he always appeared calm and contented, he had a cheerful answer when anyone spoke to him, and put a good face on the prospect of the old stock sending out fresh shoots. He was affectionate toward his wife and tried to console himself: Ingunn had never been strong, and this sickliness must prey heavily on her meagre powers. No doubt her melancholy would pass off when she grew well again.

Old Olav Ingolfsson had failed greatly during the spring, and Olav Audunsson tended him as well as he could. He often lay at night in the closet with his kinsman; at any moment the old man might require help of one kind or another. A little oil-lamp burned all night long, and the younger Olav lay on the floor in a leather bag. When old Olav could not sleep he would babble by the hour together, and now it was always of their kin: how possessions and prosperity had come into the hands of the Hestvik men, and how they had been lost again.

One night, as they lay talking of such things, young Olav asked his namesake about Foulbeard. All he knew of this man was but scraps—and these scraps were scarcely more agreeable, he thought, than what he himself remembered of the madman.

Old Olav said: "I have not told you much of him before—but maybe you ought to have knowledge of this too, since you are now to be the head of our line. Is your wife asleep?" he asked. " 'Twere better she did not hear this.

"It was truly spoken of him that he acted cruelly and faithlessly toward—many women. And many spoke ill of me, because I was always in company with Torgils, I who was intended for the priesthood. But Torgils I have loved more dearly than any man on earth—and never have I been able to understand his evil life, for I never saw that he sought the company of women or paid court to young maids, when we were at feasts and merrymakings. And when the talk fell upon women and loose living, as you know will often happen among idle young men in hall, Torgils would sit in silence with a little scornful smile—and never have I heard him use immodest or lecherous speech. He was rather sparing of words and grave in all his dealings, a bold, manly, and valorous man. I never knew him have any friends, save me—but we had been as foster-brothers from childhood. I grieved at his evil living—but I could never bring myself to say a word about it to my cousin. Father reproved him often with hard words—he was so fond of Torgils, he too: he would remind him of the day that awaits us all, when we must answer to our Lord for all our deeds —'It had been better for you, Torgils,' my father often said, 'if you had been sunk in the fiord with a millstone about your neck, as the inhuman wretches did to God's beloved Saint Halvard when he sought to protect a poor, simple woman—but you do outrage to such poor and simple ones.' Torgils never said a word in return. There was something secret about Torgils: I never saw him go up to a woman, sit down by her, and talk to her but I noticed that she was uneasy so soon as he looked at her—he must have had an evil power in his eyes. He had a kind of power over men too. For when King Skule's cause was lost, Torgils lent assistance to the Bishop—and afterwards he was made captain of the Bishop's men. But more than once the Bishop was minded to turn him away on account of the ugly rumours. When the matter of Astrid Bessesdatter and Herdis of Stein came out, the Bishop threatened him with excommunication and outlawry and with expulsion from the town—but nothing came of it.

"It was at Yule, seven years after King Skule's fall, that Torgils had been at home in Hestviken, and in Lent Besse and his sons and Olav, my uncle, came to Oslo, and it was agreed that Torgils should marry Astrid as soon as might be after the fast. That was the only time Torgils spoke to me of such matters—he said he would stay here and not go home to his wife; but Besse and his children were such good folk that there was no way out, he must take Astrid. But I guessed that he had taken a dislike to her. Never have I been able to understand how a man can have the heart to bring ruin upon such a young child, when he did not even like her better than that. But Torgils replied that he could not help turning against them always—God be merciful to his soul.

"He met Herdis Karlsdatter just after, and then he did not go home to his own betrothal feast. Olav was beside himself with shame and anger over his son's behaviour, but Torgils said he would rather fly the country than let himself be pressed into taking a wife whom he could not bear to set eyes on. When the rumours got abroad about Torgils and Herdis, it was yet worse; they both begged and threatened him, Uncle Olav and Father and the Bishop, but Torgils heeded them not at all. Astrid Bessesdatter was not surpassingly fair, but she was young, red and white —Herdis Karlsdatter was fat and yellow of skin, thirteen years older than Torgils, and eight children had she borne, so no one could understand it, but folk thought that Torgils had been bewitched. I myself thought it must be the Devil—that he had now got Torgils wholly into his power, after he had treated the young maid, Astrid, so heartlessly. I told him this, but then his face turned so white and strange that I was sheer afraid, and he answered me: 'I think you are right, kinsman. But now it is too late.' And all my prayers and persuasion were as though I had preached to stocks and stones. Some days after came the news that Jon of Stein, Herdis's husband, was dead."

Olav Audunsson started up in his sleeping-bag—stared at the old man in horror, but said nothing. Olav Ingolfsson was silent for a moment, then he said in a low voice, as though it irked him:

"He was on his way home from a gathering, had been absent for the night, and two of his own faithful men were with him—he fell right down by the roadside and died at once. Jon was old and weak—God knows I surely think neither Herdis nor Torgils had a hand in this. But you may well suppose that much was said when it was rumoured that Torgils would marry the widow. Olav Ribbung said he wished the sons of Besse had cut down Torgils before this happened, and he declared that so long as Astrid was left unmarried with Torgils's son, he would not suffer Torgils to offend her kinsmen yet worse by marrying any other. But if it were true that his son had ended by loving a married woman, he would himself pray God to smite Torgils with the hardest of punishments if he did not turn from his sinful life, do penance, and put away his leman. And ere he would let Torgils marry her, his father would bind him as a madman.

"Not long after, Herdis died suddenly. I was with Torgils when the news came. But I cannot tell you how Torgils looked—first his eyes grew so big that I have never seen the like, then they shrank in again and the whole man shrivelled and faded. But he said nothing, and in the days that followed he went about and performed his duty as though nothing had happened—but I felt that something was brewing, and when I was not at church I did not move from his side, day or night. I noticed too that he wished me to be with him—but when he slept I know not; he lay down in his clothes and neither washed nor shaved himself, and he began to be strange in his manner and unlike himself to look at.

"Herdis was buried in the church at Aker. That day week the

Bishop sent Torgils up to Aker, and I went with him. It was the
eve of a holy-day and the tenant of the nuns' farm offered us
baths; then I got him to shave off his foul yellow stubble, and I
cut his hair. 'Ay, now I am ready,' said Torgils—and an uncanny
feeling came over me, for he smiled so queerly—and I saw that
his face was ravaged and wasted, and skin and hair were yet paler
than before, but his eyes had grown so big, and they too had paled
till they were of the colour of milk and water. He was handsome,
for all that—but he little resembled a living man as he sat motionless on the bench, with a fixed stare.

"At last I lay down on the bed awhile, and then I fell asleep.
But I was awakened by a knocking at the door, three blows, and
I started up.

"Torgils had risen and moved as a man walks in his sleep. 'I am
sent for—'

"I rushed up and took hold of him—God knows what I thought
at that moment—but he pushed me aside, and again there was a
knocking at the door.

" 'Let me go,' said Torgils. 'I must go out.'

"I was a tall man, much taller than Torgils, and very strong I
was in my youth, though never so strong as Torgils—he was thickset and small of limb like you and had immense bodily strength.
I threw my arms around him and tried to hold him, but he gave
me a look, and I knew that he was beyond human aid.

" 'It is Herdis,' he said, and again there were three blows on
the door. 'Let me go, Olav. Never did I promise the others aught,
but her I have promised to follow, living or dead.'

"Then he flung me from him, so that I fell on the floor, and he
went out; but I got on my feet, grasped my axe, and ran after
him. God forgive me, had I taken my book or the crucifix in my
hand, it had gone better, but I took no time to think. I was young
—more of a warrior yet than a priest at heart, maybe; I put more
trust in the sharp steel when it came to the push.

"When I came out into the yard I saw them by the castle gate.
'Twas moonlight, but open weather with driving clouds and the
ground was dark, for we had no snow lying in the lowlands that
year. But it was just light enough for me to see them before me
out in the field as I came through the gate—the dead woman went
first, and she was like a shred of mist, scarce touching the ground,
and after her ran Torgils, and I followed. At that moment the

moon peeped out and I saw that Herdis stopped, and I guessed her purpose—so I called to her: 'If he promised to follow you, he must—but he has not promised to *go before* you.'

"But to bid her begone in the Lord's name and let go her prey—that did not cross my mind. And as we were near the church a gleam of moonlight shone on the stone wall. The dead woman glided in by the churchyard gate and Torgils ran after her, and I leaped—I was through the gate in time to see Herdis standing by the wall of the church and reaching out an arm for Torgils. I swung my axe with all my force and threw it, so that it flew over the head of Torgils and rang on the stone wall. Torgils fell flat down, but in an instant they were upon me from behind and flung me to the ground so hard that my right leg was broken in three places—the thigh, the kneecap, and the ankle.

"After that I knew no more till folk came to mass in the morning and found us. Torgils was then as you remember him—his wits were gone, and he was more helpless than a suckling, only that he could go about. If he came near edged tools he roared like a beast and fell down, foaming at the mouth—and he had been the boldest wielder of his weapons that I have known. I have been told that his hair turned white in the very first winter.

"I lay in bed year after year with my broken leg, and in the first years the splinters of bone worked out of the wounds, and the matter ran out and stank so that I could not bear myself—and many a time I besought God, with floods of tears, to be allowed to die, for my torments seemed intolerable. But Father was with me and helped me and bade me bear it as befitted a man and a Christian. And at last my leg was healed—but Torgils knew me not when I came hither—'twas five winters after. And Olav Ribbung bade me keep away, for he could not brook seeing his nephew dragging himself about as a wreck—I went on crutches at that time—when his own son had been the cause of it."

Olav lay awake long after the old man had fallen asleep. Favourites of fortune they had not been, the men of his race. But they had endured one thing and another—

The broken man there, asleep in his bed. His other namesake, the great-grandfather, whom he remembered living here with his grisly mad son—Olav felt warmed by a fellow-feeling with them. The aged woman, Tora, Ingolf the priest: loyal they had been, to

a lost cause, to dead and doomed ones who were their own flesh
and blood.

He thought of the Steinfinnssons—such, no doubt, were the
favourites of fortune. Carefree, reckless folk—to them misfortune
was as a poison they had swallowed. They held out till they had
thrown it up again—but then they died. And tonight he saw it,
fully and clearly—Ingunn too was of that sort—she too had been
stricken by misfortune as by a mortal sickness; she would never
hold up her head again. But it was his fortune to be so moulded
that he could endure, even without happiness. His forefathers had
not abandoned a lost cause—they had raised the old standard so
long as there was a shred left of it. In his heart he never knew
whether he regretted or not that he had accepted Earl Alf's offer
and taken his discharge from the service of his lord—but he had
accepted it for the sake of the woman who had been given into
his hands while both were yet little children. And he would protect her and love her, as he had protected her when a boy and
loved her since first he knew he was a man—and if he got no happiness with her, since she could never be aught but a sick and useless wife, that made no difference, he now realized—he would
love her and protect her to her last hour.

But in broad daylight he knit his brows when he recalled his
thoughts of the night. One has so many queer fancies when one
cannot sleep. And she had been happy and well in the summer—
fair as never before. She was utterly disheartened now—but then
she had never been any great one at bearing trouble, poor girl.
After the child was born she would surely be both happy and
well.

For an instant it crossed his mind: "Can it be that she is thinking of the child she bore last year?" She had never mentioned it,
and so he had not been willing to do so either. He knew no more
than that it had been alive when they left the Upplands the summer before.

4

INGUNN was thinking of Eirik now—night and day. This too had
grown pale and unreal to her in the first happy days—that she had
had a little son who slept in her arm, sucked her breast, and lay

against her, small and soft and warm, and she breathed the sourish
milky scent of him as she flooded him with her tears in the blind,
dark nights. And she had parted from him, as though tearing herself in two, before she faced the final horror and the outer
darkness.

But all these horrors lay sunk beneath the horizon of her fevered
nights of darkness and tumult, when she was tossed high and
drawn down into the abyss by waves of dizzy swooning. When
she came back into the light of day, Olav was there and took her
to him. When she was made happy, it was as though the hapless
being of her memory were not herself. Weeks passed without
her thinking once of the child; as though she wondered, vaguely
and almost indifferently: "Is he still alive?" And she would not
have been greatly moved, she thought, if she had heard that he
was dead. But then it might chance that an uneasy thought stirred
within her: "How *is* he, is Eirik *well*—or is he ill-treated among
strangers?" And from among the pale and distant memories of
last year's misery, one shot out and came to life—the little, per-
sistent scream that nothing could quiet but her breast. The truth
smote her with a cruel stab: she was mother to a whimpering babe
that had been flung out among strangers far away and perhaps at
that moment was screaming himself hoarse and tired for his
mother— But she thrust these thoughts from her with all her
might. The foster-mother had a kind look, so perhaps she was
more charitable than the mother who had brought the child into
the world. No—she thrust the thought aside, away with it! And
the memory of Eirik faded out again. And here she was at Hestviken, as Olav's wife, in all good fortune—and she felt her youth
and beauty flourish anew. She bent her head, radiant with bashful joy, if her husband did but look at her.

But as the new child grew within her—from being a secret,
wasting exhaustion which turned her giddy and sick with fear of
the shadows it might conjure up to stand between Olav and her,
it had become a burden that weighed on her and obstructed her
whenever she would move. And meanwhile the most important
thing about her now in the eyes of all was that she should bring
new life into the old stock. Olav Ingolfsson talked of nothing else.
Had she been queen of Norway and had the people's hopes of
peace and prosperity for generations been centred on the expected
child, the old man could not have regarded the coming event as

more momentous. But the neighbours too, when they met the young mistress, let her know that they counted this glad tidings. Olav Audunsson, since he was seven years old, had been the only one on whom rested the hope of carrying on the Hestvik race, and ever since that time he had wandered far from the spot where his home was. After twenty years of roaming he had come back to the lands of his ancestors. When children began to grow up about him and his wife, something that had long been out of joint would be put right again.

Her own household also took their share in what awaited their mistress. They had liked Ingunn from the first, because she was so charming to look at, kind and well-intentioned, and they had pitied her a little for being so utterly unfitted for all the work of her house. And now they pitied her, seeing her sorry state. She turned pale as a corpse if she did but enter the cook-house when they were cooking seal-meat or sea-birds—she was not used to this oily smell in the food where she came from, she murmured. The maids laughed and pushed her out—"We will get through it without you, mistress!" She could not stand up to serve out the meat without the sweat bursting out on her face—the old dairy-woman gently pressed her into a seat on the bench and stuffed cushions behind her back—"Let me be carver today, Ingunn—you can scarce stand on your feet, poor child!" She laughed, seeing that the mistress was shaking with weariness. And they were fearful how it would go with her. She did not look as if she could bear much more. And it was over three months to her time, from what she herself said.

Olav was the only one who never showed sign of joy at the expected child; he never uttered a word about it—and his household marked that well. But Ingunn thought in her heart that, when once the boy came into the world, he would be no less wonderful in his father's eyes than in those of all the others. And the bitterness, at which she herself was terrified, welled up anew.

Not a spark of affection did she feel for the child she bore, but a yearning for Eirik and a grudge against this new babe, whom every good thing awaited and all were ready to caress when he came. And it seemed to her as though it were the fault of this child that Eirik was cast out into the darkness. When she felt that folk looked kindly upon her, took pains to clear her path and make things easy for her, the thought struck her: "When Eirik

was to be born I had to hide myself in corners; the eyes of all
stoned me with scorn and anger and sorrow and shame; Eirik
was hated by all before he was born—I hated him myself." As she
sat at her sewing she recalled how she had staggered from wall
to wall when the first pangs came upon her: Tora made up a
bundle of swaddling-cloths, the worst and oldest she had left over
from her own babes. And she, the mother, had thought they were
good enough and more, for this one. The maid sitting with her
looked in astonishment at her mistress—Ingunn tore impatiently
at the fine woollen swathing she was sewing, and threw it from
her.

Now he was a year old, a little more. Ingunn sat out of doors
the first summer evenings, watching the little child, Björn's and
Gudrid's youngest, as he stumped about, fell and picked himself
up, stumped on and tumbled again in the soft green grass of the
yard. She did not hear a word of all Gudrid's chatter. My Eirik—
barefoot, poorly clad like this one here, with his poor foster-
parents.

Old Olav died a week before the Selje-men's Mass,[3] and Olav
Audunsson made a goodly funeral feast for him. Among the
ladies who came out to Hestviken to help Ingunn with the preparations was Signe Arnesdatter, who was newly married and
mistress of Skikkjustad. Her younger sister Una was with her,
and when the guests were leaving, Olav persuaded Arne and the
priest to let Una stay behind, so that Ingunn might be spared all
toil and trouble at the end of her time.

Olav was somewhat vexed, for he could not help seeing that
Ingunn did not like the girl. And yet Una was deft and willing
to help, cheerful, and good to look at—small and delicately built,
nimble and quick as a wagtail, fair-haired and bright-eyed. Olav
himself had grown fond of his second cousins. He was slow to
make acquaintances, with his reserved and taciturn nature, but
there were not many folk he disliked. He took them as they were,
with their faults and their virtues, was glad to meet them as
acquaintances, but not unwilling to make friends with those he
liked, if only he were given time to thaw.

· · ·

[3] July 8.

Olav Ingolfsson had got together a quantity of good timber, and in the previous autumn Olav Audunsson had already done a good deal to repair the most pressing damage in the houses of the manor. This summer he pulled down the byre and rebuilt it, for the old one was in such a state that the cows stood in a slough of mire in autumn, and in winter the snow drifted in so that the beasts could hardly have suffered more from cold if they had been out in the open.

One Saturday evening the household was assembled in the courtyard. It was fine, warm summer weather and the air was sweet with the scent of the first haycocks. And the fragrance of lime blossom was wafted down from the cliff behind the outhouses. The byre was set up again and the first beams of the roof were in place; the heavy roof-tree lay with one end on the ground and the other leaning against the gable as the men had left it when work ceased for the week.

Now the two young house-carls took a start and ran up the sloping beam, to see how high up they could go. Presently the other men joined in, even the master himself. The game went merrily, with laughter and shouts whenever one of the men had to jump off. Ingunn and Una were sitting against the wall of the house, when Olav called to the young maid:

"Come hither, Una—we will see how sure of foot you are!"

The girl excused herself with a laugh, but all the men crowded round her—she had laughed at them when they had to jump off halfway up the beam—no doubt she would be able to run right to the top, she would. At last they came and dragged her forcibly from the bench.

Laughing, she pushed the men aside, took a run and sprang a little way up, but then she had to jump down. Again she took a run and reached much higher this time—stood swaying for an instant, lithe and slender, waving her outstretched arms, while her little feet in the thin summer shoes, without soles or heels, clutched the beam like the claws of a little bird. But then she had to jump to one side, like a tomtit that cannot get a hold on a log wall. Olav stood below and caught her. Now the young maid had entered into the sport and ran up time after time, while Olav ran backwards below and received her laughing in his arms every time she had to jump down. Neither of them had an idea of anything, till Ingunn stood beside them, panting and white as snow beneath her freckles.

"Stop it now!" she whispered, catching at her breath.

"There is no danger, I tell you." Olav comforted her with a laugh. "Do you not see that I catch her—"

"I do see it." Olav looked at his wife in astonishment; she was on the point of tears, he could hear. Then she burst out, in mingled sobs and scornful laughter, with a toss of the head toward the girl: "Look at her—she is not so foolish but she has the wit to be ashamed."

Olav turned round to Una—she was red in the face and looked troubled. And slowly a flush rose in the man's cheeks. "Now I never heard—are you out of your senses, Ingunn?"

"I tell you," cried his wife, with bitterness in her voice, "she there, 'tis not for nothing she comes of Foulbeard's brood—and I trow there is more likeness between him and you than—"

"Hold your mouth," said Olav, revolted. "'Tis *you* should have the wit to be ashamed—are *you* to say such things to me!"

He checked himself, seeing her wince as though he had struck her in the face. She seemed to collapse with wretchedness, and her husband took her by the arm.

"Come in with me now," he said, not unfriendly, and led her across the yard. She leaned against him with her eyes closed, so heavy that she could scarcely move her feet; he had almost to carry her. And within himself he was furious—"She makes herself out far more wretched than she is."

But when he had brought her to a seat on the bench and saw how miserable and unhappy she looked, he came up and stroked her check.

"Ingunn—have you clean lost your wits—can it displease you that I jest with my own kinswoman?"

She said nothing, and he went on:

"It looks ill and worse than ill—you must be able to see that yourself. Una has been here with us four weeks, has taken all the work she could from your shoulders—and you reward her thus! What do you suppose she thinks of this?"

"I care not," said Ingunn.

"But I care," answered Olav sharply. "'Tis unwise of us too," he went on more gently, "to behave so that we challenge folk to speak ill of us. Surely you must see that yourself."

Olav went out and found Una in the cook-house; she was cleaning fish for supper. He went up and stood beside her—the man was so unhappy he did not know what he was to say.

Then she smiled and said: "Think no more of this, kinsman—she cannot help being unreasonable and ill-tempered now, poor woman. The worst is," she added, making the cat jump for a little fish, "that I cannot be of much use here, Olav, for I saw from the first day that she likes not my being here. So I· believe it will be wiser if I go to Signe tomorrow."

Olav answered warmly: "To me it seems a great shame that she —that you should leave us in this wise. And what will you say to Signe and to Sira Benedikt about your not staying here?"

"You may be sure they have more wit than to make any matter of this."

" 'Twill grieve Ingunn most of all," the man exclaimed dolefully, "when she comes to herself again—that she has offended our guest and kinswoman so abominably."

"Oh no, for then she will scarce remember it. Let not this vex you, Olav—" she dried her hands, laid them on his arms, and looked up at him with her bright, pale-grey eyes, which were so like his own.

"You are kind, Una," he said in a faltering voice, and he bent over her and kissed her on the lips.

He had always greeted the sisters with a kiss when they met or parted. But he realized with a faint, sweet tremor that this was not the kiss that belongs to courtesy between near kinsfolk who count themselves something more than cottagers. He let his lips dwell upon the fresh, cool, maidenly mouth, unwilling to let go, and he held her slender form to him and felt a subtle, fleeting pleasure in it.

"You are kind," he whispered again, and kissed her once more before reluctantly releasing her and going out.

"There can be no sin in it," he thought with a mocking smile. But he could not forget Una's fresh kiss. It had been—ay, it had been as it should be. But that was a small thing to trouble about. He had been *angry* with Ingunn—had never believed she could behave so odiously and ridiculously. But no doubt Una was right, there was little count to be taken of what she said or did at this time, poor creature.

But when he had accompanied Una to Skikkjustad next day

after mass—it was the feast of the Translation of Saint Olav [4]—and was riding homeward alone, his anger boiled up anew. Had she come to such a pass that she now suspected him of the worst, simply because she herself had sinned? No, now he remembered that she had shown his kinswomen ill will before, in the autumn, when there was naught amiss with her. She *was* jealous—even at Frettastein she had been quick to find faults and blemishes in other women—the few they met. And that was unseemly.

Olav was indignant with his wife. And then the fact that she should mention Torgils Foulbeard. All his childhood's vague aversion to the madman had turned to open hate and horror since he had heard the whole story of Torgils Olavsson. He had been a ravisher whom God struck down at the last, a disgrace to his kin. And *he* lived in folk's minds, while none remembered the other Olavssons who had lived and died in honour. Surely he might just as well be said to take after them—Olav was always ill at ease when he heard it hinted that he was so like Foulbeard. But he was annoyed with himself for feeling as it were a cold blast of ghostly terror at the back of his neck when such things were said.

His worst enemy could not accuse him of being mad after women. In all the years he had lived in outlawry he could scarcely recall having looked at a woman. When his uncle Barnim suggested that he ought to take the pretty miller's daughter and keep her as his leman, while he was at Hövdinggaard, he had sharply refused. Fair she was, and willing too, as he could see—but he had held himself to be a married man in a way, and he would keep his troth, even if his uncle teased him for it and laughingly reminded him of Ketillög.—This was a poor vendible girl he had fallen in with one night when he was in the town in company with other young men from the manor and they were all dead-drunk. In the morning, when he was sober again, he fell to talking with the girl, and after that he had conceived a sort of kindness for her—she was unlike others of her kind, sensible and quiet in her ways, preferring a man who did not care to play the fool and raise a riot in the inn. And then he had continued to look in on her when he was in the town on his uncle's business. Often he simply came in and sat with her, ate the food he had brought, and sent her for ale: he took pleasure in her quiet way of waiting upon him. But his

[4] August 3.

friendship for her had been no heavy sin—and no one in his right mind would assert that he had been unfaithful to Ingunn with *her*. He had often thought of her, however, in the first years that succeeded—hoped she had got into no trouble for helping him to get away to the Earl that time. He wished he could have known for certain that she had been able to hide from the others in the inn the money he gave her at parting, and whether she had carried out the plan she often spoke of: that she would turn her back on that inn and seek service with the nuns of St. Clara's convent. In truth she was far too good to be where she was.

It was the sense of this secret guilt that made him insecure—he felt defenceless against the Evil One, like a man who must go on fighting though crippled by a secret wound. His wife's prolonged ill health and her unreasonableness—and her being herself the cause that he was never allowed entirely to forget what *must* be forgotten—all this made him uneasy, wavering in his mind. And he felt a little thrill of pleasure as he remembered how good it had been to hold Una in his arms.

It angered him as he thought of Ingunn—it was her senseless behaviour to the kind, fair child that had been the cause of this.

But he would have to take it patiently—she had so little to comfort her now, Ingunn.

But the same evening Ingunn fell sick; it came so suddenly that before the ladies who were to help her could reach the place, it was over. None but Ingunn's own serving-women were with her when the child came—and they were all terrified and bewildered, they told Olav afterwards, with tears in their eyes. They thought the boy was alive when they lifted him up from the floor, but a moment later he was dead.

Never, thought Olav, had he seen a creature look so like a piece of broken, washed-out wreckage cast up on the beach as did Ingunn, lying there crouched against the wall. Her thick, dark-yellow hair lay tousled over the bed, and her dark-blue eyes, full of unfathomable distress, stared from her swollen, tear-stained face. Olav seated himself on the edge of the bed, took one of her clammy hands, and laid it on his knee, covering it with his own.

One of the weeping maids came in bearing a bundle, unwrapped it, and showed Olav the corpse of his son. Olav looked for a few moments at the little bluish body, and the mother burst into another harrowing fit of weeping. Quickly the man bent over her.

"Ingunn, Ingunn, do not grieve so!"

He himself was unable to feel any real grief over his son. In a way he was fully aware how great was the loss—and his heart was wrung when he reflected that the boy had died unbaptized. But he had never had peace for rejoicing in the past months—had felt nothing but a vague and faltering jealousy of what had gone before, anxiety for Ingunn, and a longing for the end of this cheerless time. But he had never realized that the end would be the birth of a son in his house—a little boy whom he would bring up to manhood.

The mother was not very sick, said the neighbours' wives when they came and nursed her. But when the time came for her to be helped to sit up in bed in the daytime, she had no strength. She was drenched with sweat if she did but try to bind her hair and put on her coif. And Sunday after Sunday went by without her being strong enough to think of churching.

Ingunn lay on her bed, fully dressed, with her face turned to the wall the whole day long. She was thinking that she herself had been the cause of this child's death. She had received it with loveless thoughts as it lay within her, groping for its mother's heart-strings. And now it was dead. Had skilful women been with her at its birth, it would surely have lived, the neighbours told her. But she had always insisted, when they came to see her this summer, that she did not expect it before St. Bartholomew's Day.[5] For she had been afraid of these wise neighbours of hers—lest they might find out and spread it abroad that Olav Audunsson's wife had had a child before. And the morning she woke up and felt it was coming, she had risen and kept on her feet as long as she was able.— But Olav must never know this.

But at last it could be put off no longer—it was on the Sunday after Michaelmas that Ingunn Steinfinnsdatter had to submit to be led into church. Olav had learned that there were four other women newly delivered who were to go in; one of them was the daughter-in-law of one of the richest manors of the neighbour-

[5] August 24.

hood, and she had just brought an heir into the world; the church would surely be half full of her kinsfolk and friends alone, who would come to make offerings with her. Olav could scarce bring himself to think of Ingunn, kneeling before the church door, poor and empty-handed, while the others bowed to receive the lighted candles—as the psalm of David was sung over the women: "Who shall ascend into the hill of the Lord? or who shall stand in His holy place? He that hath clean hands and a pure heart . . . he shall receive the blessing from the Lord, and righteousness from the God of his salvation."—To Ingunn and him this would sound like a judgment.

Olav had been shy of going near Sira Benedikt since the day Ingunn drove Una Arnesdatter out of their house in such a shameful manner. But now he rode one day up to the priest's and begged him to be kind and bring consolation to Ingunn.

Sira Benedikt had ordered that all corpses of unbaptized infants should be buried on the outer side of the churchyard fence; they were not to be hidden under a heap of stones, like cattle that had died a natural death, or buried in waste places like evil-doers. He reproved people severely for believing in the ghosts of such children: dead infants could not appear, he said, for they were in a place which is called Limbus Puerorum, and they can never come out from thence, but they are well there; Saint Augustine, who is the most excellent of all Christian sages, writes that he would rather be one of these children than never have been born. But if folk have been scared out of their wits and senses in those places where the corpses of infants have been hidden away, it is because they themselves have such sins on their consciences that the Devil has power over them to lead them astray. For it is clear that the place where a mother has made away with her babe is wellnigh an altar or a church to the Devil and all his imps—they are fain to haunt it ever after.

The priest consented at once to accompany Olav home. Olav Ingolfsson had firmly believed in infant apparitions and thought indeed that he himself had once laid such a ghost. So Sira Benedikt was zealous to dissuade Ingunn from this heresy and give her consolation.

The woman sat, white and thin, with her hands folded in her lap, and listened to their parish priest discoursing of the Limbus Puerorum. It was written of this in a book—a monk in Ireland

had been rapt in an ecstasy seven days and seven nights, and he
had had a vision of hell and purgatory and heaven; he had also
been in the place where are the unbaptized infants. It appears as a
green valley, and the sky is always clouded as a sign that they can
never attain the bliss of beholding God's countenance; but light
is shed down between the clouds, in token that God's goodness
dwells upon the children. And the children appeared to be happy
and in good case. They do not feel the lack of heaven, for they
know not that there is such a place, nor can they rejoice at being
saved from the pains of hell, for they have never heard of it. They
play there in the valley and splash water upon one another, for the
place is passing rich in brooks and meres.

Olav interrupted: "Then meseems, Sira Benedikt, that many a
man might be tempted to desire he had died an infant and unbaptized."

The priest replied: "It is so ordained, Olav, that in our baptism
we are called to a great inheritance. And we must pay the price of
being men."

"Are the parents suffered to come thither sometimes?" asked
Ingunn in a low voice—"to have sight of their children and watch
them at play?"

The priest shook his head:

"*They* must go their own way, up or down—but it will never
take them over that valley."

"Then meseems God is cruel!" exclaimed the woman hotly.

"That is what we human creatures are so prone to say," replied
the priest, "when He grants not our desires. Now, it was of great
moment to you and your husband that this child should have
grown to man's estate—he was born to take up a great inheritance
and carry on the race. But if a woman bear a child whose only
destiny is to be a testimony of her shame and whose only inheritance is his mother's milk—then her mother's heart is oftentimes
not to be depended upon. It may be that she will hide herself and
give birth to it in secret, destroy her child body and soul or put
it out with strangers, well pleased if she neither hear nor see it
more—"

Olav sprang up and caught his wife as she fell forward in a
swoon. Kneeling on one knee, he supported her in his arms; the
priest bent down and quickly loosened the linen coif that was
tightly wound about her neck. With her white face hanging back-

ward over her husband's arm, and the bare arch of her throat, she looked as one dead.

"Lay her down," said the priest. "Nay, nay, not upon the bed —on the bench, so that she may lie flat." He busied himself with the sick woman.

"She is not strong, your wife?" asked the priest as he was about to ride away. Olav stood holding his horse.

"No," he said. "She has ever been weak and frail—ay, for you know we are foster-brother and sister; I have known her from childhood."

5

EARLY in the following spring Duke Haakon made ready for an inroad upon Denmark; the Danish King was to be forced to make a reconciliation with his outlawed nobles upon such terms as they and the Norwegians should impose on him.

Olav Audunsson set out for Tunsberg; he was one of the subordinate leaders under Baron Tore Haakonsson. He was not altogether glad to be away from home this summer. He was now striking root at Hestviken: it was his ancestral seat and his native place —he had so long been homeless and an outlaw. As he proceeded with repairing the decay of his property, so that the source that had long been dried up began to flow again with riches, and as he himself acquired a grasp and a knowledge of the work ashore and afloat, he came to take pleasure in these labours on his own behalf. He would have liked Björn to stay behind as his steward, but Björn had no mind to it. In the end Björn accompanied Olav as his squire, and an older man named Leif was to take charge of Hestviken together with the mistress of the house.

He also felt some anxiety for Ingunn—about midsummer she would be brought to bed again. True, she had been in much better health than last time; she had managed her housekeeping and her share of the farm work the whole time—and now she had learned and was not nearly so helpless as she had been when they were newly married. But Olav was uneasy, just because he guessed that she awaited this child with impatient longing. If a disaster should befall it, she would be utterly struck down with sorrow. And he seemed to have a presentiment—that he should find a child in the house when he came home in the autumn, seemed to him well-nigh unimaginable.

As soon as he reached Tunsberg, Olav Audunsson found old acquaintances of his years of outlawry wherever he turned. Earl Alf's men had flocked to the son-in-law of their slain chief, begging Lord Tore to take them into his service. Also among the Danish outlaws and their men, of whom the town was full, he met many that he had known while he was with the Earl. And one day a vessel ran into the harbour with letters from the Danish lords at Konungahella; her captain, Asger Magnusson, was from Vikings' Bay and he and Olav had been friends when Olav was at Hövdinggaard; they were also kinsfolk, but very distant. In the evening he went up into the town with his Danish kinsman and took a good rouse—he was much better for it afterwards.

Lord Tore made Olav captain of a little sixteen-oared galley, and his ship, with three small war-vessels from the shipowners of the south-east of the Vik, was to sail under the orders of Asger Magnusson in the *Wivern*, which the Norwegians called *Yrmlingen*.[6] Feeling between the Danes and their allies was often barely friendly, for this time the greater part of the force was Norwegian. And now the Norwegians made no secret of what they intended by the expedition: King Eirik and Duke Haakon would claim the whole kingdom of Denmark in succession to their grandfather, the holy King Eirik Valdemarsson, and make the country tributary to the crown of Norway. But the Danes did not like to hear this; they jeered at it, saying that their lords, the Constable, Stig Andersson, and Count Jacob, had never bound themselves by promises to any king, and that the Norwegians would have reward enough for their aid when they helped themselves with both hands among the towns and castles of the Danish King. The Norwegians answered that when it came to dividing the spoil, the Danes were great tricksters who always knew how to get the best share for themselves. The Norwegians were the more numerous, but they were mostly peasants and seamen, less inured to war than the Danes. For nearly all of these had served for years under their outlawed chiefs, had grown hardy and resolute, and let the Devil take every law but those of the fighting trade. But in this matter Earl Alf's old band were a match for

[6] *Little Snake.*

the Danes and more than that. Olav and Asger had their hands full keeping the peace among their men.

The war fleet lay off Hunehals, and the squadron to which Asger's and Olav's small vessels belonged harried the northern coasts of the Danish islands. To Vikings' Bay they did not come. Olav had heard from Asger that the Danish King's men had stormed Hövdinggaard, burned the manor, and pulled down the stone hall; Sir Barnim Eriksson had fallen, sword in hand. So it booted not to think of him any more, else Olav would have had a mind to see his uncle again. Now he could only let say a mass for the man and let it go. For that matter he felt even less bound than before to his mother's land and kindred.

There was something light-minded and foolhardy about these low, defenceless coasts that lay awash in the midst of the glittering sea. Above the broad white beach the yellow sand-dunes sloped up, and forest trees grew right out to the point: the trunks of full-grown beeches and gnarled oaks stood just above the stormy waves; turf and roots overhung the edge of the bluff like the threads of a torn tissue. It looked as if the sea had seized and bitten out great pieces of the naked bosom of the land. Olav thought it ugly. Inland there were indeed fair tracts—great and lordly manors, rich soil, swine in the woodland, fat cattle in the meadows, fine horses in the parks—nevertheless, he had never felt at home here. His homeland, the coast of Norway, ring within ring of rocky defences—shelves, skerries and holms, the inner channel, and at last the bright rocks of the mainland, before the first streaks of green soil stole down to the head of an inlet, as though spying out. The great manors lay inland, built mostly on ground from which one could see far afield and know what was coming.

He thought of his own home—the bay within the bare rocks, the manor on the slope of the hill with the Horse Crag at its back. Ingunn would be up again by now—maybe she was standing out in the yard, fair and young and slender again, sunning the child. For the first time he felt an intense desire for children in his home. But the bright vision was far off and incredible.

He was back in the same life he had led when he was outlawed from Norway. The very feeling of wearing a coat of mail again was strangely good; under the weight of it his bodily forces seemed gathered together—it was good to feel the coolness of it when he was at rest, and how it shut in and saved up the heat of the body when fighting; it was like a warning to husband his strength, not to waste himself without plan or object. The trials of strength, afloat in rough weather, or in a descent ashore—both one and the other demanded of a man that he should be prompt and vigilant, but at the same time reckless in his inmost will, not caring if he were conquered by the danger he was using all his powers to conquer. It was something of this sort that loomed within Olav, more as feelings than thoughts—and at times he felt a kind of repugnance as he recalled the two years he had lived upon the land as a married man. A vague pang at the heart, like a faint throbbing beneath a healed wound—was he wasting his manly strength as he toiled in his loose woollen working-clothes, power-less to determine what he would gain in the end by his trouble? And a kind of revulsion against the memories of his intimate life with the sickly woman—it was as though he surrendered his pow-erful youth and unbroken health in order that she might absorb vigour from his store, and in his heart he did not believe it would be of any use. Like swimming with a drowning companion hang-ing about one's neck—no choice but to save the other or go down with him, if one would deserve the name of man. But one might be pardoned a failing at the heart, at the thought that the end was certain—to be drawn under—though one would struggle to the last, because a man can do no less.

Had she been in good health, and had it seemed natural to him that they would have children to reap where he sowed and in-herit all his gains, then he would have looked upon his lot with different feelings. And now and then, when he tried to persuade himself into the belief that Ingunn might be well again, and that, for all he knew, he had a healthy, squalling infant son or daughter in the cradle at home—he would long for his own house. But usually this longing was absent—he had a profound sense of well-being at having no one but himself, no other care but his duties as one among many subordinate captains in the army.

He liked this life among none but men. The women he saw ashore, old or aging women who were charged with the food, venal hussies who were to be found wherever men were, he did not count these. There were wet days and nights afloat, fighting when they forced a landing—this had not fallen to Olav's lot very often, nor was he altogether sorry for it: in all the years he had followed Earl Alf he had never been able to overcome his dislike

of useless cruelty—and the Danes were cruel when they harried
their own country. Indeed, they would scarce have been anything
else if they had harried another country. But down here they
were used to the game; these coasts had seen plunder and rape and
burning since there were men in Denmark. Olav felt himself a
stranger among his mother's people. It was true his heart had
been set upon warfare and fighting in his young days, but then
the struggle was to end in a decision: death or victory. At times
an image would rise before him—a hostile attack upon Hestviken;
he defended himself in this home on the rock, with its back to
the cliff, drove the enemy downhill into the sea, or fell on his own
lands.

The Danes were different, softer and tougher. They let themselves be chased away—peasants into the depths of the forests,
lords overseas—but they came back, even as the waves of the sea
retire and come again. They lost and they won, and neither one
nor the other made much difference to their appetite or en-
joyment of life. And with a strangely buoyant patience they
bore the thought that things would never be otherwise—they expected to have to fight to all eternity, winning or losing along
the low, wet shores, without calling any victory or defeat the
last one.

Then they were quartered ashore for a time. The men were
closely packed in the houses of the town; the air was dense and
hot with rank smells, foul talk, ale and wine, belching, wrangling
and quarrelling. There was fighting every night in the streets and
yards—the captains had hard work to keep anything resembling
peace and discipline among their bands.

Rumours were ever in the air—of ships' crews that were reported to have made descents and carried off great booty. At
Maastrand a body of Earl Alf's old men-at-arms had fought with
some German merchants and killed all their prisoners—in payment
of an old score of their dead lord's, it was said. The Danish King's
fleet had taken the Constable's fortress on Samsö, and Sir Stig
Andersson himself had fallen, folk said. Among the Norwegians
it was believed that Duke Haakon aimed at winning Denmark
for himself, and that it was over this he had quarrelled with his
brother the King; it was for this reason that King Eirik had sailed
home to Björgvin already in the early summer, and that the captains of the King's fleet, lords from the west country and some

few from Iceland, had wrought such destruction. But the Duke
caused strict discipline to be kept in his army: he did not wish to
see the total ruin of the land he intended for himself.

Olav thought that even if the great lords knew the truth or
falsity of all these rumours, the rank and file of the army had
little grasp of what was going on. And the lesser captains, like
himself, were reckoned with the rank and file, not with the lords
—whom the fighting men usually knew only by name; but the
less they knew of them, the more inclined they were to talk about
them. That he himself was related to many of the outlawed
Danish nobles, he was too proud to mention, if they did not remember him. His own chief, Baron Tore, counted him as no
more than a subordinate captain on the same footing as the masters of the ships of the country levies; he deemed Olav of Hestviken to be a brave man and a useful leader—but he had not distinguished himself in any way above the rest; he had had no
opportunity of performing deeds that attracted attention.

One thing resulted from this life: when Olav recalled his secret dread that there was some connection between the load on
his conscience and the fact that there had been so little joy in his
life with Ingunn, this now seemed to him a very preposterous
thought. Imperceptibly an idea of this sort had grown up in him
during these two years. But these men among whom he was had
robbed the peasants of their cattle, burned houses and castles, had
not only reddened their weapons in fight, but often slain and
maimed defenceless folk without just cause. Some had on them
treasures that they were mightily afraid of showing—likely enough
these things were stolen from churches. And though it was Duke
Haakon's order that rape should be punished with death, it could
hardly be thought that all the women and girls who drifted
among the fighting men while the army was ashore had taken to
this life entirely of their own free will.

His own settlement with that Icelander seemed an utterly un-
important affair. Surely no one believed that all these fellows here
confessed every scrap to such priests as were to be found—it was
impossible that the men could remember all or the priests find
time to hear such scrupulous confessions. Many a man who cheerfully took *corpus Domini* before setting out certainly had heavy
sins on his conscience which he had forgotten to confess. The
wretched Teit had his deserts—Olav now thought himself

strangely foolish to have seen signs in this and that: in the chance words of strangers, in dreams that had come to him, in the colour and markings of his beasts. He had believed at last he felt God's hand over him, seeking to make him turn aside from the path he followed. Here, among all these men, where he himself was of so little account, his own affairs were also lessened in his eyes: so many a brave man's death had he seen and heard of that it was unreasonable to think that the Lord God was so scrupulous over the slaying of Teit, or that He singled out him, Olav Audunsson, for chastisement, penance, and salvation, when there were great men enough who needed it much more—such as the Danish lords, for the way they treated their own countrymen. Even Ingunn's transgressions seemed to grow less—he heard and saw so much out here.

One day in late autumn he steered into the fiord. The sun was hot, between the rain-squalls that swept over the sea. There was a fresh breeze; the white spray shooting high under the Bull gave him a greeting from afar. Up at the manor they had recognized his little craft—Ingunn stood on the quay as he came alongside, her coif and cloak fluttering about her thin, stooping figure. And as soon as he saw her, the husband knew that all was as it had been:

The child had been stillborn, a boy again.

Two months after the new year Ingunn fell sick again—she had miscarried, and this time her life was in danger. Olav had to fetch the priest to her.

Sira Benedikt counselled husband and wife to live apart for a year and employ the time in penitence and good works; weak as Ingunn Steinfinnsdatter now was, the priest deemed it impossible that she could bear a living child.

Olav was willing enough to try this expedient. But Ingunn was clean beside herself with despair when he spoke of it to her.

"When I am dead," she said, "you must marry a young and healthy wife and have sons by her. I told you that I was broken down—but you would not let me go then. I have not long to live, Olav—give me leave to be with you the little time I have left!"

Olav stroked her face and smiled wearily. She often talked of his marrying again—but she could not bear him to look at another woman or to say two words to their neighbours' wives when he met them before the church door.

Sleeplessness troubled him this spring even worse than the other years. With a heart heavy with compassion he lay with his arm about the poor, ailing woman—but he felt her clinging love as an encumbrance. Even in her sleep she lay with her thin arms clasped about his neck and her head resting on his shoulder.

He was glad to get away from home when he set out for Tunsberg in the spring. The summer passed like the previous one. But whenever he thought of his home, Olav was sick at heart. It mattered not, he felt, that he had had so little joy in his life with her—the loss of Ingunn would mean the loss of half his life.

But she was well and cheerful when he came home late in the autumn, this time she was so certain that all would go well. But six weeks before Yule the boy was born, more than two months before his time.

Awhile before this happened it became known in the countryside that Lord Tore Haakonsson had had Björn Egilsson beheaded at Tunsberg. After the first campaign in Denmark he had entered the Baron's service—he would not go back to Hestviken any more. When the war fleet returned to Norway this autumn, Björn had been on board the ship that brought Lord Tore himself home, and while on shipboard he had fallen out with another man and cut him down. When the Baron ordered him to be seized and bound, he had defended himself, wounded two men to the death, and given several others lesser hurts.

Gudrid, Björn's wife, had died during the summer, and now Olav Audunsson thought he ought to help the orphans of the man he had liked so well. Torhild Björnsdatter had held aloof from all —she was cross and taciturn; Olav had rarely seen her and scarcely exchanged two words with the girl, so he did not rightly know how he was to put his offer to her.

But when Ingunn lay sick so near to Yule and there was no mistress at Hestviken to cope with all the work that was at hand —their numbers were increased during the fishing season, with the hunting of seals and auks—Olav considered whether he should speak to Torhild Björnsdatter and ask if she would move to Hestviken and keep house for him. She was said to be a capable and industrious woman—and the mismanagement had now reached such a pitch that any housekeeper at all must be able to do the work better than the mistress; Ingunn was of little use when she was well, and she had had scarcely a day's health in three years. The food was so wretched that Olav had had difficulty in getting house-carls this winter, and when strangers visited the house, he dreaded and was ashamed of what might be sent to table. Except the fresh fish and frozen meat in winter, there was hardly anything that did not smell and taste abominably. The stores in the larder lasted an unaccountably short time—until Olav discovered that many of the servants stole like magpies. Bought ale from town he always had to keep in the house, dear though it was, for Ingunn's brew had a bad name all along the fiord. Even the drink in the curd-tub was not merely sour, but rotten. He himself had hardly had a new garment made at home since he was married, and his everyday clothes looked like a beggar's rags—they were neither kept clean nor properly mended.

He had proposed to Ingunn more than once that they should take a housekeeper, but each time she had been in utter despair, weeping and begging him not to bring such a shame upon her. It was in vain he replied that sickness is every man's master; it could be no shame to her. He saw that if he was to speak to Torhild, he would have to do it without consulting his wife. The worst thing was about her children—she would have to bring the younger ones with her, and that was likely to lead to noise and disturbance, which Ingunn could not bear.

The six surviving offspring of Björn and Gudrid were known to all as "Torhild's children." Gudrid had been an unnatural mother—she shook off one child after another; her stepdaughter took it up, laid it in her lap, and fed it from a cow's horn. Gudrid cared for nothing but gadding about the neighbourhood. Torhild had been betrothed in early youth to a lad of substance and honour, but he was near akin to that Gunnar whom Björn had had the misfortune to slay, and so the marriage came to naught. Since then she had been drudging in their poor home, doing the work of a man and a woman together. Folk knew little about her, but the maiden was of the best repute. Nor was she ugly, but no one seemed able to conceive that Torhild Björnsdatter might change her condition. She was now no longer young—eight or nine and

twenty winters old; the two eldest of her half-brothers were of
an age to take service, but when this was spoken of, Torhild answered that she needed them at home.

One Sunday, not long after Ingunn fell sick, Olav saw Torhild
Björnsdatter in church. She stood farthest back on the women's
side and was completely shrouded in a long and ample black
cloak, which she held closely about her. She had drawn the hood
forward, and from time to time the man saw her face in profile,
pale against the black woollen stuff. She was like her father: the
forehead high and abrupt, the nose long, but finely curved, the
mouth broad and colourless, but with lips tightly closed as though
in mute patience; the chin was powerful and shapely. But her
fair hair was faded and hung straggling about her forehead; her
complexion seemed grey and turbid from smoke and soot that
had eaten into the skin. She had large grey eyes, but they were
red-rimmed and bloodshot, as though she had stood too long over
the fire in the narrow, smoky cot. Her hands, which held the
cloak together, even when she clasped them in prayer, were not
large, and the fingers were long—but they were red and blue,
covered with broken chilblains, ingrained with black, and the
nails were worn. And though she was so well shrouded, it could
be seen that the girl held herself very erect.

After mass Olav stayed outside the church talking with some
other franklins, and it came about that he rode home alone—his
people had gone on ahead.

He had reached the place where the forest gives way to open
ground, with some great meres and a little croft on the edge of
the largest of them. The bridle-path divides here just behind the
outhouses, one path going to Rynjul and southward, and another
down to Hestviken. As Olav was turning into the road for home,
he saw Torhild Björnsdatter standing outside the hut; she had
taken off the cloak and gave it back to the woman from whom
she had borrowed it. As she caught sight of the horseman, she
turned abruptly and crossed the frozen mere, as quickly as if she
were flying from him. But Olav had seen why she kept the cloak
so closely about her—without it she was in her bare shift, of
coarse, undyed homespun. It was cut low at the neck, the sleeves
reached to the elbows, and her arms were blue with cold, as were
her naked ankles, which showed between the edge of the shift

and the big, worn-out man's shoes she wore on her feet. She had bound a strip of homespun about her waist for a belt—again Olav could not help being surprised at her erect bearing.

She was dressed like working-women when they cut the corn on a summer's day. A memory flashed across Olav's mind—of blue sky, sunshine, and warmth over the fields, where the women bent to grasp the sheaves of ripe, sweet-smelling corn. He watched the summer-clad maid flying across the frozen mere toward the edge of the wood, where the spruces were grey with rime. How she must feel the cold!—she was bareheaded, her plait of hair hung thick and straight down her resolute, unbending back. All at once Olav felt an intense liking for her. He halted awhile on the path, watching the girl. Then he rode on a little way—turned his horse and set out across the mere.

The croft that Björn Egilsson had owned lay up the slope on the other side—an alder thicket almost hid it from travellers on the road. Olav saw that a good deal of clearing had been done since he had last had occasion to come here, two years ago. Some small patches must have been dug last autumn: some stones and roots were not yet cleared away. Farther up, the strips of stubble showed lighter than the rest of the rime-covered, swampy ground. The little byre that Björn had put up a few years before shone yellow with its fresh logs, but he had never got the dwelling-house built: they were still living in the round turf hut.

Torhild Björnsdatter came out on hearing the horseman. The children peeped behind her in the doorway. She stepped outside and stood erect, blushing slightly and glancing ungraciously at the man as he dismounted, and she guessed he had some business with her. Olav tied Apalhvit to a tree and covered him with his grey fur cloak. "You must let me come in, Torhild; there is a matter about which I would fain speak with you." He did not wish her to stand there in the cold; she was now barefooted.

Torhild turned and went in. She laid a worn sheepskin on the earthen bench, bade her guest be seated, and offered him a ladle of goat's milk from a bowl that stood behind him on the seat. The milk tasted and smelt strongly of smoke, but Olav was fasting and thought it good. The room was like a cave, with a narrow passage between the two benches of earth that filled it entirely. Torhild sat down opposite her guest; she had a two-year-old child on her lap; another girl, a little older, stood behind her with her arms about her neck. The two eldest boys lay by the fire near the door, listening to the talk between their sister and the stranger.

After they had spoken of other things for so long as was proper, Olav mentioned his business. She must have heard what a pass he had come to at home—how little likely it was that his wife would be fit for any work that winter. If Torhild would grant them a boon and help Ingunn and him in their difficulty, they would never be able to thank her enough. Olav spoke as one asking a favour, he liked her so cordially. Strong she looked, with her broad, straight shoulders, high, firm bosom, and powerful hips. *She* had never let herself be bent double by all her drudgery here between the cot and the little byre.

Torhild raised some objections, but Olav replied that it was clear she should have leave to bring all six children with her to Hestviken. He had not thought of offering to receive more than the two eldest—they could no doubt be of some service—and the two youngest, who could not be parted from their foster-mother. The middle ones they could surely find a home for in the neighbourhood. Her beasts—the cow, four goats, and three sheep—he would also receive; when the roads were fit for sledges they would send for the fodder she had stacked. And he would see to it that the fields here at Rundmyr were manured and sown in the spring.

The end of it was that Torhild took service with Olav and was to move to Hestviken as soon as she had made ready a few clothes for herself and the children. Olav promised to provide the stuff. He himself rode up with it next day; there was no need for her fellow servants to know how poor she had been.

He had thought of telling Ingunn of his agreement with Torhild the same evening. But when he came in to the sick woman, she lay in a doze, so faint and bloodless that she looked as though she could neither hear nor answer him. So he merely sat on the bedstead beside her. Her face was fearfully wasted; the eyelids lay like thin brown membranes over the sunken eyes, her skin was grey and flecked with brown over the cheek-bones—the dark streaks that had come with her second child had never gone away. Her white linen shift was fastened with a good brooch—her throat was wizened like a plucked fowl's. He remembered that Torhild's grey woollen shift had been held together with a pin of sharpened bone—but her throat was round as the stem of a tree, and her bosom was full and high. She was sound and strong, although her lot in life had been so heavy and toilsome. His own poor creature was well provided with all that was needed to make pleasant the lot of a young wife—and here she lay, for the fourth time in three years, childless and broken in health.—Olav stroked her cheek.

"Did I but know some means of helping you, Ingunn mine!"

He did not bring himself to tell his wife that he had hired a housekeeper until Torhild moved in with all her following of children and animals. Ingunn looked displeased, but all she said was:

"Ay, so it is, I ween; you must have one that can take charge of the house. I was never good for aught—and now it seems I can neither live nor die."

Ingunn lay sick a great part of the winter, and it looked as though she had spoken truly—she could neither live nor die. But then she began to mend, and by the first days of Lent she could sit up. Spring came early on the fiord that year.

It was expected that the levies would be called up again for the summer. The franklins were now heartily sick of the war with Denmark. No man believed that either the King or the Duke would reap anything by it in the end but the loss of their mother's inheritance, which indeed they *had* wrested from their cousin, the late King of Denmark,[7] before he was murdered.

That spring Sira Benedikt announced that he intended to repair to Nidaros for the Vigil of St. Olav. Many of the folk of his parish joined him for the sake of having good company on this pilgrimage, which every man and woman in Norway desired to make at least once in his life.—Olav leaped at the thought, seeing in it a hope and a remedy—Ingunn should take part in the journey. It seemed a very prodigy that she had been so well of late and ailed not at all—she must needs make use of this rare occasion.

At first Ingunn was by no means willing to go—if Olav could not go with her. But then the thought came to her that she would go home and see her sister and brothers—accompany the pilgrims only as far as Hammar. Olav was displeased with this; he wished her to make the pilgrimage, then perhaps she would be restored

[7] Erik Glipping.

to health at Saint Olav's shrine. If she was equal to travelling so far into Heidmark, then she could surely make the whole journey: they were to move slowly, for there were many sick people in the company. But when he saw how she longed to see her own family again, he gave his consent.

He accompanied her as far as Oslo and stayed in the town a few days, buying and selling. One morning Ingunn was sitting in the inn when Olav entered hastily. He searched in their leather bags, did not find what he wanted, and opened another bag. There he came upon some little garments—they might have fitted a child of four years. Unconsciously his eyes fell upon his wife—Ingunn's head was bent and her face was red as fire. Olav said nothing, packed the bag again, and went out.

6

HAAKON GAUTSSON had bought Berg after the death of Lady Magnhild Toresdatter. Now Tora Steinfinnsdatter had dwelt there as his widow for over a year. Ingunn guessed from her talk that she had had a good life with Haakon, but she lived well without him too. She was a very capable woman. Ingunn never ceased to marvel at her sister, who busied herself deftly, promptly, and shrewdly both indoors and out, although her bulk was prodigious. She still preserved her fair red and white complexion and her regularity of feature, but her cheeks and chin were grown to an immense size and her body was so unwieldy that she could scarcely sit on horseback; even her hands were so fat that the joints only showed as deep hollows—but Tora could make full use of them. Wealth and prosperity surrounded her, and her children were handsome and promising. She had had six, and all were alive and thriving.

On the third evening the sisters were sitting together in the balcony before going to rest. Ingunn sat in the doorway listening to the stillness—far away in the woods the cuckoo still called now and again, and the corncrake chirped in the fields. But she had now lived so long in a place where the very air seemed always to be full of voices, the soughing of the wind, the roar of the sea

dashing against the rocks below: under this clear and silent vault
the little sounds of birds seemed only to make the stillness more au-
dible—to Ingunn it was as though she drank deep draughts of refreshment. The bay was so small and so dear; bright and smooth
it lay, with dark reflections of the wooded headlands. The last
banks of cloud had settled upon the distant hills—the day had been
showery with gleams of sunshine, and a sweet scent came up to
them from the hay spread out below.

Her longing would not be kept back—all at once, without
thinking, Ingunn declared the purpose for which she had come.
She had fought with herself these two days, now to speak out,
now to hold back the question:

"Do you ever see aught of my Eirik?"

"He is well," said Tora, with some hesitation. "Hallveig says
he is thriving and promises well. She comes hither every autumn,
you know."

"Is it long since you saw him?" asked her sister.

"Haakon was so much against my going there," said Tora as
before. "And since then I have put on so much flesh that I am
little suited for such a journey. But you know that he is with
honest folk, and Hallveig has naught but good news to tell of
him. I have much upon my hands here at home—and little time
to wander so far afield," she concluded, with some heat.

"When saw you him last?" Ingunn asked again.

"I was there in the spring after you left home; but then
Haakon would not have me go thither any more; 'twas only keeping the gossip alive, he said," Tora replied impatiently. "He was
a fine child," she added, more gently.

"Then that is three years ago?"

"Ay, ay."

The sisters were silent awhile.

Then Tora said: "Arnvid went to see him—many times—in the
first years."

"Has he too given up, Arnvid? Has he too forgotten Eirik
now?"

Tora said reluctantly: "You know—folk could never find out
who was the father of your child."

Ingunn was silent, overcome. At last she whispered: "Did they
believe then that Arnvid—!"

"Ay, 'twas foolish to make such a secret of the father, since the child could not be hid," said Tora curtly. "So they could but guess the worst—a near kinsman or a monk."

There was a little pause. Then Ingunn said impulsively:

"I had thought of riding up their tomorrow—if the weather suits."

"I think it unwise," said Tora sharply. "Ingunn, remember we have all had much to suffer for your misdeeds—"

"*You*—who have six. How think you it feels to have but a single one, and to be parted from him? I have longed and longed for Eirik all these years."

"It is too late now, sister," said Tora. "Now you must remember Olav—"

"I *do* remember Olav too. He has had four dead sons by me. He claimed his own, the child I deserted and betrayed—he claimed his mother; he has sucked at me without ceasing, he almost sucked the soul out of my body, and he sucked the life out of my children while they were yet unborn, the outcast brother. There was yet a little life in the first son I bore to Olav, they say, when he came into the world—he died before I could see him, unbaptized, nameless. You have seen all your children come living into the light of day, and grow and prosper. Three times have I felt the child quicken within me and grow still and die again. And I knew I had nothing to hope for, when the pains came upon me, but to be quit of the corpse that burdened me—"

After a long silence Tora said:

"You must do as seems good to you. If you think the sight of him will make it easier for you, then—"

She patted her sister's cheek as they went in to bed.

It was drawing near to midday when Ingunn halted her horse at a gate in the forest. She had refused to listen to all Tora's prayers, but had ridden off alone. No worse thing had befallen her but to mistake the road; first she had come to a little farm that lay high up the slope on the other side of a little river. The people who lived there were the nearest neighbours to Siljuaas, and two children from this croft had gone with her down the hillside to a place where she could cross the river.

She stayed awhile sitting in the saddle and looking out over the country. The forests rolled endlessly, wooded ridge behind ridge into the distant blue—toward the north-west there was a gleam of snow under the shining fine-weather clouds. Deep down and far away she saw a small stretch of the surface of Lake Mjösen glittering beneath the foot of wooded hills, and the land on the other side lay blue in the noontide heat, with its green patches of farms and crofts.—From Hestviken one could not see a scrap of cultivation beyond the fields of the manor itself.

Homesickness and yearning for her child united in a feeling of crying hunger within her. And she knew she had but this one little hour in which to assuage it, for once only. Then she must turn back again, bow her neck, and take up her burden of unhappiness.

It seemed to her that in the south, by the fiord, the sunshine was never so clear and deep as here under the blue sky. It was glorious to be up on a high ridge once more. Below and to the right of her she had the dark, steep wooded slope, up which she had toiled on foot, leading her horse. The roar of the stream at the bottom of the ravine came up to her, now louder, now softer. Right opposite, on the other side of the secluded little valley, lay the croft that she had come to first, high up under the brow of the hill, and between her and it the air quivered in a blue haze over the hillside.

Before her was the clearing. The houses stood on a little knoll of rock-strewn, tussocky turf—they were grey and low, not more than a couple of logs high. The little patches of corn lay for the most part at the foot of the knoll, toward the fence.

Ingunn dismounted, pulled up the stakes of the gate—and a group of grey-clad little children came in view on the knoll. Ingunn was unable to move—she was trembling all over. The children kept as still as stones for a few moments, watching her; then they whisked round and were gone—not a sound had she heard from them.

As she walked up the knoll, a woman appeared at the door of one of the little houses. She seemed rather scared at sight of the stranger—perhaps she took her for something other than human, this tall woman with the snow-white coif about her heated face, and the sky-blue, hooded mantle and silver brooch, leading a great sorrel horse by the bridle. Ingunn hastened to call out, greeting the woman by name.

They sat indoors for a while, talking, and then Hallveig went out to fetch Eirik. The children could not be far away, she thought—they were scared of the lynx; it was abroad and had been sitting on the fence that morning. But they were shy of the visitor, for lynxes were more common than strangers here.

Ingunn sat and looked about her in the tiny room. It was low under the gabled roof and darkened by smoke; tools and earthen pots lay all about, so that there was scarce room to turn. A baby was asleep in a hanging cradle, snoring soundly and regularly. And then she heard a fly buzzing somewhere with a high, sharp, piercing note, incessantly, as though caught in a cobweb.

Hallveig came back, dragging with her a very small boy who had nothing on but a grey woollen shirt. Behind them swarmed the whole flock of the woman's own children, peeping in at the door.

Eirik struggled to be free, but Hallveig pushed him forward and held him in front of the strange woman. Then he raised his head for an instant, glanced in wonder at this splendidly clad person—crept back behind his foster-mother and tried to hide.

His eyes were a yellowish brown, the colour of bog-water when the sun shines into it, and the long, black eyelashes were curled up at the end. But his hair was fair and curled about his face and neck in great glistening ringlets.

His mother stretched out her arms and drew him onto her lap. With a voluptuous thrill she felt the hard little head on her arm, the silky hair between her fingers. Ingunn pressed his face to hers —the child's cheek was round and soft and cool; she felt the little half-open lips against her skin. Eirik resisted with all his force, struggling to escape from his mother's impetuous embrace, but he did not utter a sound.

"It is I who am your mother, Eirik—do you hear, Eirik?—it is I who am your real mother." She laughed and wept at once.

Eirik looked up as if he did not understand a word of it. His foster-mother corrected him sharply, bidding him be good and sit still on his mother's knee. Then he stayed quietly in Ingunn's lap, but neither of the women could get him to open his mouth.

She kept her arm about him and his head against her shoulder, feeling the whole length of his body. She passed her other hand over his round, brown knees, stroked his firm calves and his dirty little feet. Once he plucked a little at his mother's hand with his grimy little fingers, playing with her rings.

Ingunn opened her bag and took out the gifts. The clothes were

far too big for Eirik—he was very small for his age, said his foster-
mother. That these fine shirts and little leather hose were for him
seemed quite beyond Eirik's comprehension. Not even when his
mother tried on him the red cap with the silver clasp did he show
any sign of joy—he only wondered, in silence. Then Ingunn took
out the loaves and gave Eirik one that he was to have for himself—a big round wheaten cake. Eirik seized it greedily, clutched
it to his chest with both arms, and then ran out—to all his foster-
brothers and sisters.

Ingunn went to the door—the boy was outside with the cake
held tightly in his arms; he thrust out his stomach to support it
and straddled with his bare brown legs. The other children stood
round in a ring staring at him.

Hallveig produced food for her guest—cured fish, oaten bannocks, and a little cup of cream. The children outside were given
the pan of milk from which the cream had been skimmed. When
Ingunn looked out again, they were sitting round their food;
Eirik was on his knees, breaking off big pieces of the cake and
passing them round.

" 'Tis his free-handed way," said the foster-mother. "Tora gives
me a cake for him every year when I go down to Berg, and Eirik
always shares it and nigh forgets to eat any himself. 'Tis such
things, and others too, that show the boy comes of gentle kindred."

Now that all the children were sitting in a ring in the sunshine,
Ingunn saw that Eirik's fair hair was quite different from the
coarse flaxen shocks of the others; Eirik's was curly and shining,
all unkempt as it was, and it was not yellow, but more like the
palest brown of a newly ripened hazelnut.

Ingunn had to set out for home about the hour of nones, to be
sure of reaching Berg before evening. She had not been able to
conquer Eirik's shyness of the strange woman, and she had scarce
heard his voice, except when he spoke to the other children out
of doors. It was so sweet, so sweet.

Now Eirik was to have a ride on her horse as far as the forest.
Ingunn walked, leading the horse and supporting the child with
one arm, while she smiled and smiled at him, trying to coax forth
a smile on his pretty little round and sunburned face.

They had passed through the gate: here no one could see them.

She lifted the boy down, hugged him in her arms, kissed and kissed again his face and neck and shoulder, while he struggled, making himself long and heavy in her embrace. When he began to kick her as hard as he could, his mother took a firm hold of his smooth bare calves—feeling with painful joy how firm and strong his little body was. At last she sank into a crouching attitude, and as she wept and muttered wild endearments over the child, she strove to coax and force him to sit in her lap.

When she was obliged for a moment to loosen her grip of him, the boy managed to wriggle away from her. He darted like a hare across the little clearing, was lost among the bushes—then she heard the gate close.

Ingunn stood up—she wailed aloud with pain. Then she staggered forward, bent double by sobs, with drooping arms. She came to a hedge, saw Eirik running over the turf so fast that his heels nearly reached his neck.

The mother stood there, weeping and weeping, as she bent over the hedge. The withered, rust-red branches of spruce had been felled to fence in a little field, where the corn had just begun to shoot—still soft and pinched like some kind of new-born life, it appeared ever after to her inner vision, when she thought of her sorrow, though now she had no idea of what her tear-blinded eyes looked upon.

But at last she had to go back to her horse.

7.

IN the course of the autumn Sira Benedikt Bessesson fell sick. And one day a message came for Olav of Hestviken—the priest would bid him farewell.

Sira Benedikt did not look like a dying man as he lay propped up by pillows. But the wrinkles, which had seemed few and shallow in his fleshy, weatherbeaten face, were deeper and there were more of them. Nevertheless he predicted his approaching departure with certainty. When Olav had seated himself on the edge of the bed, as the other bade him, the priest, as though absently, took the riding-gloves out of the franklin's hand, felt the leather,

and held them critically to his nose and eyes—Olav could not help
a little smile.

They talked for a while of one thing and another—of Arne Torgilsson and his daughters. Two of them were now married in the
neighbourhood, but Olav had seldom met them or their husbands
of late.

"Folk see less and less of you, Olav," said the priest; "and many
wonder at it, that you always keep to yourself as you do."

Olav reminded him that he had been at sea the last few summers, and every winter his wife had been sick.

Again the priest spoke of his imminent dissolution, asking Olav
to be diligent in prayers for his soul. Olav gave him his promise.
"But you have surely little need to fear what may await you, Sira
Benedikt," said he.

"I think there is none of us but needs must fear it," replied the
priest. "And I have always lived negligently, in that I took little
thought of the small daily sins—I spoke and acted as my humour
prompted me and consoled myself with the thought that it was
no great and deadly sin—thinking it could be no such great matter
what I did from frailty and natural imperfection, though I well
knew that in God's eyes all sin is more loathsome than sores. And
you and I would not like to live with a man and take him in our
arms if he were full of sores and scabs all over. Now I have every
day partaken of the remedy that surely heals the leprosy of sin.
But you know that even the surest remedy and the most precious
ointment is slow to heal the sickness if every day a man shall
scratch himself again and tear his skin anew. And so it is with us,
when our Lord has washed away our sins with His blood and
anointed us with His mercy, but we are careless to do the deeds
to which we were anointed—thus we scratch ourselves as soon as
He has healed us, and we must bide in purgatory, bound hand
and foot, until we are cleansed from our scabs and taints."

Olav sat in silence, twisting his gloves.

"Too great love have I borne to mine own, I fear. I thank God
I have never been the cause of sin in them or backed them in an
unrighteous cause—to that I was never tempted, for they were
honest folk. But I ween I have been over-zealous sometimes for
their advancement and wealth—it is written in my testament that
it is to be given back.—And I have been headstrong with my en-

emies and my kinsmen's enemies—hasty and ready to believe evil
of every man I liked not."

"Nevertheless we others must have worse than ill to fear," said
Olav, trying to smile, "if you think your case stands thus."

The priest turned his head upon the pillow and looked the
young man in the eyes. Olav felt that he went pale under the
other's glance; a strangely impotent feeling came over him. He
tried to say something, but could not find words.

"How you look at me—" he whispered at last. "How you look
at me!" he said again a few moments later, and he seemed to be
pleading for himself.

The priest turned his head again, and now he looked straight
before him.

"Do you remember I always scoffed at Olav Half-priest for
his talk of having seen so much of those things of which I had
little knowledge? I think now that it may enter into God's counsels to open the eyes of one man to that which He conceals
from another. I was never permitted to *see* aught of those things
with which we are surrounded in this life. But now and again I
have had an inkling of them, I too."

Olav looked at the priest attentively.

"Of *one* thing I have always had foreknowledge," said Sira
Benedikt. "I have always known—almost always, perhaps it were
well to say—when folk were on the way to fetch me to the dying.
Above all, to such as had greatest need of help—such as were burdened by an unshriven sin—"

Olav Audunsson gave a start. Unconsciously he raised one hand
slightly.

"Such things set their mark upon a man. Few are they who become so hardened as to show no trace that an old priest can note.
This befell me one evening in this room, as I was putting off my
clothes. I was about to climb into bed when it was borne in upon
me that one was on the way hither and encountered great difficulties, and that he had sore need of intercession. I knelt down
and prayed that he who was faring hither might find safe guidance—and then I thought to lie down and take a little rest before
I had to go out. But when I had laid me down, I felt ever more
strongly that someone was in great danger. At last it was clear to
me that there was one present in the room with me, who aroused
terror in my heart, but I knew it to be holy awe—'Speak, Lord,

Thy servant heareth,' I prayed aloud. And immediately it was as though a voice had called within me: I arose, clothed myself and waked one of thy servants, an old and trustworthy man. I bade him go with me up to the church, enter the belfry, and ring the midmost bell. I myself went into the church and knelt on the steps of the altar—but first I took a taper from the altar of Mary, lighted it and carried it to the church door, which I set open wide. The taper burnt with a calm, clear flame, though the night was wet and raw, misty and somewhat tempestuous.

" 'Twas not long before a man came and begged me to bring extreme unction and the viaticum to a sick man. The messenger had been so long on the road that he never thought he would arrive in time, for he had followed his own tracks in a ring and gone astray in bogs and rough ground. But we were able to bring succour in due time to one who needed it more sorely than most.

"Now I have been fain to think that even he who brought the message was one whose life had been such that evil spirits were more likely to guide his footsteps than his guardian angel, to whose voice he had ceased to listen. And it may well be that 'twas this angel, or the guardian spirit of the dying man, who turned to me and sent me to the church to ring the bell.

"But when I came home toward morning and went past the church, I saw that I had forgotten to close the door; the candle still stood there burning in its candlestick, and it was not consumed, nor had the wind and rain that drove in at the open door quenched it. I was afraid when I saw this sign, but I took courage and went in to bring the Virgin Mary back her candlestick and to close the door. Then I was ware that one bent over the candle and guarded the flame, for about it I saw as it were a reflection of the light falling upon something white—whether it was an arm or the lappet of a garment or a wing, I know not. I crept up the steps on my knees, and as I reached out my hand to take the candlestick, the light went out, and I fell upon my face, for I felt that one swept past me, whether it was an angel or a blessed soul—but I knew that this one had seen his and my Lord face to face."

Olav sat motionless, with downcast eyes. But at last he looked up, he could do naught else. And again he met Sira Benedikt's glance.

He knew not for how long they stayed thus, staring into each other's eyes. But he felt time passing over them like a roaring stream, and he and the other stood at the bottom beneath the stream, where was eternity, unchanging and motionless. He knew that the other could see the secret sore that preyed upon his soul and was eating its way out—but he was too cowardly to allow the healing hand to touch the festering cancer. In extreme terror lest the diseased spot might be disturbed, he summoned all his will and all his strength—he closed his eyes. He sank into darkness and stillness—time ceased to roar and sing, but he felt the room turning round with him. When again he opened his eyes, the room was as usual, and Sira Benedikt lay with averted head on the green-spotted pillow. He looked weary and sorrowful and old.

Olav stood up and took his leave—knelt down and kissed Sira Benedikt's hand in farewell. The old man took his firmly and pressed it as he murmured some Latin words that were unknown to Olav.

Then he went out, and the priest did not attempt to hold him back.

A week after came the news of Sira Benedikt's death. The folk of the parish counted it a loss—they had esteemed him as an able priest and a bold and upright man. But the franklins had never reckoned him to be endowed with any conspicuous mental gifts—he was like one of themselves in manners and disposition and had had no learning beyond what was necessary.

Olav Audunsson alone was strangely stricken in spirit when he heard the news. It had seemed as though a door stood open—and vaguely he had reckoned that one day he would be given courage to enter it. But as yet he had not had the courage. And now the door was closed for all time.

He had not had much talk with Ingunn about her visit to the Upplands, and the child had not been mentioned between them.

But toward Yule, Olav again had fears that the worst had happened—so he called it in his own mind when Ingunn was clearly with child.

Ever since Torhild Björnsdatter had been with them, Ingunn had shown a more active spirit than ever before in all the years they had been married. There was now no need for the mistress to do anything herself; Torhild was so capable that she accomplished all the household duties alone, and she had learned how everything was done at Hestviken. But it seemed that the other's presence had aroused a kind of ambition in Ingunn—Olav guessed that his wife had felt injured at his taking a housekeeper, and that without first consulting herself. And though Torhild was very accommodating, inquiring her mistress's desires in everything, keeping out of the way as far as possible and living with her children in the little old house on the east of the courtyard, where Olav's mother had once dwelt, the husband noticed that Ingunn did not like Torhild.

Fine needlework was the only thing in which Ingunn had excelled in her youth, and now she took it up again. She made a long kirtle for Olav—it was of foreign cloth, woven in black and green flowers, and she adorned it with broad borders. Her husband had little use for such a garment now—but she left the making of his working-clothes to Torhild. For the daily work about the manor she remained as useless as ever, but she insisted on taking part in it all, and for Yule she toiled at preparing the meat, brewing, and cleaning houses and clothes, running between the storehouses and the quay in driving snow-squalls that came in from the fiord and turned the whole courtyard and the road down to the sea into a mass of slippery green slush.

But the evening before Christmas Eve, when Olav came in, he found her standing by herself up on the bench, struggling with the old tapestry, which was to be hung on wooden hooks along the uppermost of the wall-logs. It was all in one piece and very heavy; Olav came up to help her, holding up a length at a time.

"I doubt if it be prudent for you to work so hard," he said. "If you think it will be well this time, all the more reason to be careful of yourself—so that it may turn out as we both desire."

Ingunn said: " 'Twill fall out, sure enough, as 'tis fated—and rather will I face now the suffering I cannot escape than go through months of torment in the prospect of it. Think you not that I know I shall never see the day when any child calls me mother?"

Olav looked at her a moment—they were standing side by side on the bench. He jumped down, lifted her after him, and stood for a while with his hands on her hips.

"You must not talk in that way," he said feebly. "You cannot be sure of it, Ingunn mine!"

He turned from her and began to clear away the hooks and pegs that were lying on the bench.

"I thought," he asked in a low voice, "that you had a mind to go and see that boy—when you were at Berg in the summer?"

Ingunn made no reply.

"I have sometimes wondered whether perchance you longed for him," he said very softly. "Do you ever long for him?"

Ingunn was still silent.

"Is he dead mayhap, the child?" he asked gently.

"No. I saw him once. He was so afraid of me—clawed and kicked—he behaved like a young lynx when I tried to hold him."

Olav felt old far beyond his years, weary and worn at heart. This was the fifth winter he and Ingunn had lived together—it might have been a hundred years. But the time must have seemed yet longer to her, poor woman, he reminded himself.

Meanwhile he tried to rouse himself—to hope. If this time it went well, that would indeed be the only thing that could make her happy again. And now she had been in good health longer than any time before—so maybe she was equal to going through with it.

As for himself, all desire of having children had been tortured out of him long ago. He thought indeed of his manor and his race —but now these affected him so little. And then there loomed before him a shadowy vision of something immensely far off in the future: when he had grown old, and his pain and anxiety and this strange morbid and uneasy love of his was no more— For she could not live to be old. And then his life might be like that of other men. Then he would be able to seek atonement and peace for his tortured conscience. And then there might yet be time to think of his manor and his race—

But when he had reached this point in his vague conjectures, a sharp pang went through his heart, as when a wound opens wide. Dimly he divined that, in spite of his having no peace, no joy, in spite of his soul being hurt to the death—he yet possessed happiness, his own happiness, even if it were unlike the happiness of other men. Sick and almost bled to death, his happiness yet lived within him, and his aim must be to find courage and means to save it, before it was too late.

Ingunn seemed to keep in good health, even into the new year. But by degrees it made Olav uneasy to see her so utterly unlike herself—in a continual state of futile bustling. That Torhild could have patience with such a mistress was beyond his comprehension; but the girl followed her mistress with calm endurance and made work for herself out of all Ingunn's restless confusion.

Matters stood thus when at the beginning of Lent word came to Hestviken that Jon Steinfinnsson, Ingunn's younger brother, had died unmarried at Yuletide. There was indeed no necessity for Olav to journey northward at this winter season in order to take up his wife's share of the inheritance. But to Olav Audunsson this thing came as a token.

For four nights he lay with lighted candles, scarcely closing his eyes in sleep. He was bargaining with his God and judge. Some means he *must* find now of saving himself and this unhappy wreck of whom he was so fond that he knew of no beginning or end between them. The whole of Hestviken as his patrimony and the name of his own son—that must surely be amends in full for the brat of the vagabond Icelander.

Olav had been twelve days at Berg when he spoke of this one evening as he sat in the hall drinking with Hallvard Steinfinnsson, while Tora was present: now there only remained his most important business, to fetch home his son.

Hallvard Steinfinnsson stared at him agape—speechless. Then he flared up:

"Your—! Do you tell me that you *yourself* were father to the brat Ingunn had to creep into the corner and give birth to like a bitch?" He smote the table, crimson with rage.

"You well know, Hallvard, how my fortunes stood at that time," replied Olav with composure. "Had my enemies had this against me, that I was here in secret while still under sentence of banishment, they would scarce have been easy to deal with. And it might have cost their aunt and Lady Magnhild dearly if it had come out that they had housed me, an outlaw."

But Hallvard swore till the sparks flew. "Think you not, Olav Audunsson, my aunt and Magnhild would rather have paid all they had in fines for your thrusting yourself upon them, an outlawed man, than that it should have been said that one of our women had disgraced herself so foully that she dared not name the father of her child?" He mimicked all the guesses folk had brought forward, each one uglier than the last.

Olav shrugged his shoulders. "I know not how you care to

speak of these rumours now. For now the truth will come to light —and had you let me know a little sooner that such things were said, I should not have waited so long. We deemed we ought to keep silence about it awhile for Magnhild's sake—but you may be well assured I have never had any other thought than to acknowledge my son."

"You had—God knows what you had!" the other mocked. All at once he sat straight up, with a stiff stare: "You had so! I wonder whether Ingunn believed it so surely—or that you would hold to your boast that 'twas a lawful marriage you made when you went to bed with her before you had hair on your chin? Why then did she throw herself into the lake?"

"Ask Tora," said Olav curtly. "She thinks it was the milk that had gone to her head."

"Nor do I believe," said Hallvard slyly, "that Haftor would have sued Magnhild for this—for you and he were reconciled—"

"Believe what you will," said Olav. "To be sure Haftor and I were reconciled—'twas on account of the Earl I was then an outlaw. A numskull you have been all your days, Hallvard, but you can scarce be so foolish as not to see that for you and your kinsfolk the more profitable way is to believe what I have now told you. Even if you should miss the inheritance you would have gotten had your sister died childless."

Hallvard started up and made for the door.

But when Olav was left alone with Tora, he felt all at once that this thing he had taken upon himself was intolerably difficult. As she remained silent, he began with a kind of sneer:

"And you, Tora; do you believe me?"

Tora looked him straight in the face with eyes that betrayed nothing:

"I am bound to believe you, when you say it yourself."

And Olav felt it as a physical pressure upon his neck. Weary as he was, he had now taken upon himself a new burden, in addition to the old. Nothing of it could be cast off, and nowhere could he turn for help. He must go through with it—alone.

On the evening of the next day Olav came down to Berg with the child. Tora did her best to receive her sister's son kindly. But, for all that, the boy seemed to feel he was not very welcome in this house; he kept close to his new-found father, trotted at his

heels everywhere and stood by Olav's knee when the man sat
down. Then if it chanced that he was allowed to hold his father's
hand, or that Olav took him up and set him on his knees, Eirik's
pretty little face beamed with joy—all at once he had to turn and
look up at his father in glad wonder.

After this Olav stayed no longer at Berg than he was obliged.
Already on the morning of the third day he was ready for the
journey.

Eirik sat well wrapped in the sledge, turning this way and that,
looking about and laughing with joy. Now he was to drive in a
sledge again—he had had one drive when his father fetched him
from Siljuaas; the sledge had been waiting for them at the last
farm in the parish. Anki laughed and chatted as he made fast the
baggage—the kind man who had carried him down on his back
when his father fetched him. His father looked shapelessly huge
in his fur mantle—and the rime on the fur of his own cape showed
as white as it did on the hairs around the men's hoods.

Tora stood looking at the boy's red and happy face—his brown
eyes were bright and quick as those of a little bird. There sprang
up in the woman's heart a few drops of the tenderness she had felt
for Eirik when he was a baby. She kissed him farewell on both
cheeks and bade him bring greetings to his mother.

Olav came home to Hestviken early one day, as the pale sun
shone red through the frost fog; he had driven from Oslo in the
pitch-dark early morning. When they came into the valley he gave
the reins to Anki, lifted the sleeping boy out of the sledge, and
carried him up the slope to the house.

Ingunn sat by the fire combing her hair when Olav came in.
He set down the child on the floor and pushed him forward:

"Go on, Eirik, and bid your mother good-morrow as you
ought"—whereupon he turned back into the anteroom. From the
door he saw with the corner of his eye that Ingunn crept toward
the boy on her knees, stretching out her thin, bare arms; her hair
swept the floor behind her.

He was out in the yard by the sledges when she called to him
from the doorway. In the dark anteroom she threw her arms
about his neck, weeping so that it shook her as she clung closely
to him. He laid his hand upon her back—underneath the hair and
the shift he felt her shoulder-blades standing out like boards. With

that wealth of unbound hair streaming over the weak, drooping shoulders she reminded her husband in a strange way of what she had been like when she was young. Heavy and awkward she was now in her movements—it was not easy to see traces of her freshness and beauty in the tear-swollen, wasted face. And yet it was not so many years since she had been the fairest of all.—For the first time he felt the full wretchedness of her useless fecundity. He put his arm around her again.

"I thought 'twould make you happy," he said, for she wept and wept.

"Happy—" she trembled, and now he found that she was laughing through her sobs. "I am surely happier than the angels—though you know full well, Olav, I love you more than ten children—"

"Go in and dress yourself," he begged her; "you will take cold here."

When he came in she put on her clothes and her wimple and was carrying in food from the closet where they kept it in winter. Eirik still stood where Olav had put him down, but his mother had taken off his leathern jacket. When he saw his father coming, he turned to him quickly and tried to take his hand, smiling a little anxiously.

"Nay, go to your mother now, Eirik," said Olav. "Do as I tell you," he repeated, rather sharply, as the boy shyly drew nearer to him.

8

EIRIK was nearly five years old, and he was beginning to find out that it was counted a great blemish in him that he had no father. A year before, when they had been down to the village for Lady Day in the spring, he had heard certain folk saying that he was base-born; the same word had been used by the men who called at Siljuaas on their fowling—and it was surely said of him. But when he asked his foster-mother what it meant, she boxed his ears. Afterwards she had muttered angrily that they had better deserved the blows who said such things to the poor little creature—ay, and his mother too—'twas not the boy's fault that he was a bastard and a straw-brat. But Eirik guessed it was better not to ask more questions about these queer words. They meant something it was wrong to be, and that was why Torgal did not like him—he could not tell how he knew it, but it had come to him in some way that Torgal, the father of the house, was not *his* father.

Torgal, the crofter of Siljuaas, was a kindly, home-loving man. He trained up his sons: the eldest of them already went hunting with him in the forest, the younger ones had to work on the clearing at home, and their father showed them what to do and chastised them when they needed it. But Eirik he heeded not at all, whether for good or for evil. He showed his wife the honour of never meddling with her affairs, and he reckoned this adoption of the bastard of a great man's daughter to be a venture of hers with which he had nothing to do—he left her a free hand both with the child and with the payment for his fostering.

Eirik knew well enough that Hallveig was not his mother, but he thought nothing of it, for Hallveig never made any difference between him and her own children. She was just as ready with blows and angry words whichever of them might get in her way while at work. And on the eve of holy-days she bathed them all in order of age in the big tub, and he was clad in a sheepskin coat the day before winter night,[8] and as soon as the cuckoo was heard he had to be content with a homespun shirt and nothing else, like the other children, whatever the weather. On those days in the year when the people of Siljuaas went down to the village to mass, and Hallveig had the use of the horse, Eirik was allowed to ride behind her just as far as each of the other children, and she kissed them all with equal affection when she had received *corpus Domini.*

They never went short of food—cured fish or game; with it a piece of bread or a ladleful of porridge, small beer now and again, and water when milk ran short in winter. Eirik had been very well off and quite content with his lot in the lonely clearing far away in the forest.

Every hour of the day something happened, so many people and animals were there in the little homestead. And round about its fences the forest was thick on every side: within it, behind the wall of murmuring fir trees and glistening bushes, was a teeming, hidden life. Creatures lived and moved in there, keeping an eye on them from the edge of the wood, luring the boy and drawing him right down to the fence: at the slightest movement or sound

[8] October 14.

within the forest the whole flock of youngsters would spin round
and take to their heels across the turf, back to the shelter of the
houses. Not much had the children seen of the folk from beyond,
but they heard the grown-ups tell tales of strange happenings,
so they knew of the troll of Uvaas and the pixy who mostly
haunted the mossy rocks by the Logging Stone, and of the bear—
one year he had appeared at the byre and tried to break through
the roof on a frosty night—but that was before Eirik could remember. Under a fixed rock in the meadow there dwelt little men
and women in blue, but with them they were good friends—Hallveig carried out food to them now and then, and they did her
many a good turn in gratitude. Eirik had often seen their footprints in the snow. Those who dwelt outside the fences were of
course more evilly disposed. There was no great difference, to
the boy, between the beasts of the forest and these others who
haunted it.

The sound of something moving within the thicket on a summer's day, the calls of beasts and other noises from the forest at
nighttime, tracks in the snow on winter mornings. Beisk, the dog,
who would start up and bark furiously on dark evenings, without
Eirik ever finding out what made him do it—all such things made
up the wonderful world outside the homestead which greeted the
child. It was misty and dreamlike, but it was real enough, only
he was so small that he had to stay inside the fence. But Master
Torgal and the big boys went in and out of it and told of the
strange things that happened there.

Eirik never came into the forest except on those days in the year
when Hallveig took him with her to church. Then they passed
through it, a long, long way down. At last they came to a new
world that was even farther away and more dreamlike. The bells
that pealed and rang again across the great open fields with big
houses on them; the church hill where stood horses and horses and
yet more horses—little shaggy ones like their own on the lower
side, but up by the churchyard fence there was a neighing of big,
shiny colts with hog manes and red, green, and violet harness
glittering with gold and silver. Within the church stood the priests
with gilt cloaks on their backs, singing before the lighted candles
on the altar, and some young ones in long white shirts swung the
golden censers so that the church was filled with the sweetest fragrance. His foster-mother pushed her flock down on their knees

and hoisted them up, according to the movements of those in the brilliant light of the choir. At last came God, as Eirik knew, when the priest lifted up the little round loaf and the bell in the tower above began to ring, chiming with a sharp note of joy.

At the upper end of the church stood a whole crowd of men and women in bright-coloured clothes, shining belts, and big brooches, and Eirik knew that it was they who owned all the horses with the fine saddles and the gleaming arms that were left in the room under the tower. Eirik believed they were a kind of fairies—only that they lived and moved even farther away from his life than those others in the woods at home. One day Hallveig pointed to one of them, the bulkiest of all the women, clad in flaming red, with a triple silver belt about her big stomach and a brooch like an ale-bowl in the middle of her mighty bosom: that was his aunt, said Hallveig. Eirik was none the wiser, for he did not know what an aunt was. Fetches he had heard of and angels; nay, sometimes a woman came to Siljuaas whom the children called Aunt—her name was Ingrid and she had a great hump on her back—but this one did not look like anything of that sort.—

He had been properly scared when that lady in blue came. And it was for him she had come—she was his mother, they said. It made him extremely uncomfortable, for it seemed to be not only a great danger but a disgrace. She was certainly one of the women who stood in front at church—fairies of the farthest-off kind. And now he had got his eldest sister to tell him what a straw-brat was: when women lie with men out in the woods, they get a straw-brat. The blue woman had had him, just as Mother had had little Inga in the spring; all the other children in the house Mother had had, but not him. The child had a horrified suspicion that he had been born out of doors and carried in from the woods. But now he was mortally afraid he would be taken out there again, and he did not want that at all. For a long time he was haunted by a terrible dread lest the blue woman should come back and fetch him out to where she lay—with a man whom he imagined to be like a tree blown down by the storm, with tangled roots in the air. They passed a tree like this on the way to church; it lay on a flat piece of dry ground under a knoll, and Eirik had always been afraid of this dead, fallen fir tree, for it had something like an ugly man's face amid the tangle of its roots. The boy imagined that the blue woman lived in a little glade like this among the woods, and there he would be alone with her and her tree-man and the big sorrel horse with bright things on its bridle; never would anybody else come there, neither people nor animals. But he would not have that—he wanted to stay at home in the safe, open clearing and sleep indoors, and he would never be parted from Mother and Gudda, his foster-sister, and Kaare and the other children and Beisk and the horse and the cows and the goats and Torgal—and he would not be squeezed and kissed as he had been by the strange woman. For a long time he scarcely dared to go three steps from the house door, so frightened was he that she would come again, this mother of his. But if he had had a father, she could not have done anything to him—for sister had said that only those children who had no father could be straw-brats.

All the same, as time went on, Eirik thought less of that visit. But one day in the winter some men who were following a ski-track through the forest to Österdalen called at Siljuaas. Again he heard that they were talking about him, but this time they mentioned his mother by name: "Leman" they said she was called. Eirik had never heard that word before, but it sounded strange and unsafe—as if she were not human, but rather some kind of great bird. He imagined vaguely that Leman might come flapping her great blue cloak like a pair of broad wings and pounce down on him. It grew more and more clear to him how evil was his plight, since he had no father to own him, so that nobody would dare take him away.

Then one day there came a father to him. Eirik was not very surprised at this. When he was led up to the man, he took a good look at him. It must have been the fact that Olav's complexion was so fair that made the boy feel confidence in him from the first. This father with the broad, straight shoulders and the upright bearing—Eirik felt at once that he knew this was another of those who stood in front at church—but he was not afraid of him. Gay clothes he wore—a leaf-green kirtle, a silver clasp in the breast of his jerkin, bright metal on his belt and on the long sheath of his dirk. And then Eirik took such a fancy to the queer big axe his father held between his knees as he sat; the hand that rested on the head of the axe was covered with rings. The more he looked at him, the more pleased he was with his father. He stood calmly meeting the other's searching glance—at the first sign of something like a smile on the man's face Eirik beamed and went up close to Olav's knee.

"He is small, this son of mine?" said the father to Hallveig, holding the boy's chin a moment. Beyond that he said nothing to Eirik while he was at Siljuaas, but that was enough for the boy. Hallveig wept a little, Torgal lifted him up when he said farewell, the brothers and sisters stood staring at him who was to go away with the two strange men. Eirik felt a little clutch at the heart when he saw his mother cry; he put his arms about her neck, and his lips began to quiver—then his father called, and at once he turned and trudged to the door, clumsy in his new fur coat that came down to his feet.

Eirik and Olav became good friends on the journey. It was not much that his father said to him; he let Arnketil, his man, look after the boy. But all the strange new things he met with, the sledge and horses, a fresh house to sleep in every night, all the good food, and then the many people everywhere, who talked to him, many of them—Eirik knew that all this was his father's doing. And his father wore a shirt and breeches of linen next his skin, and he did not take them off at night.

The new mother that he found when he came to the end of the journey made much less impression on Eirik. He did not know her again; when she asked if he remembered that she had been at Siljuaas, he answered yes, for he guessed that was what he ought to say. But he had no feeling that she was the same. This mother here had brown clothes, she was thick about the waist and trod heavily and slowly as she went ceaselessly in and out, busying herself between the houses. The tall, blue mother, Leman, with the quick, birdlike movements, he imagined standing in the little clearing in the forest, where she dwelt with her tree-man and the big sorrel horse. Only when the new brown mother crushed him to her and smothered him with kisses and wild words of endearment did he know in a way that she and Leman were one and the same—although they called this one Ingunn.—Eirik did not like being kissed and squeezed in this way—he had never in his life been

given other kisses than those which went with a mass Sunday and
fresh meat and a drink from the ale-bowl when they came home—
rare and festive occasions.

But here the way of it was that he got ale every day, and these
folk ate cooked fresh food, fish and meat, day after day for many
days, so maybe the women had the habit of kissing every day too.

When Eirik came up to Olav, laid his hands in his lap, and asked
him all kinds of questions—whether the seal lived in the forest
that he could see straight across the fiord, and why his two horses
were white, and why he was not the father of Torhild's children,
and what they were to do with the train-oil they were boiling, and
where the moon was going when it flew so swiftly across the sky
—Ingunn watched the two with a strange tension. For one thing,
she was afraid Olav might be impatient with the boy. She was so
unspeakably humble in her gratitude for this thing her husband
had done for her in bringing home the child for whom she had
longed to the very death; and now she was only afraid the boy
might worry Olav, or that he might be angry at the sight of her
child if he saw too much of him. She could not discover that Olav
entertained any dislike for Eirik. He took little notice of him, unless the boy sought him out, but then he was always friendly and
replied as well as he could to Eirik's endless questions. But it was
not easy to make Eirik understand the nature of anything. The
boy seemed to have no grasp at all—he made no difference between living and dead things, asked whether the big rock on the
beach was fond of the gulls and why the snow wanted to lie on
the ground. He could not make out that the sun that glimmered
through the fog was the same as shone in the sky on a clear day,
and once he had seen a moon that was quite unlike all other moons.
—The priest came to see them one day, but Eirik never guessed
that he was the same person he had seen up at the church—that
his vestments could be taken off and that he could ride about like
other men. Sometimes Eirik would take it upon himself to hold
forth to them, but all his stories were strange and absurd—impossible to find any sense in them. Ingunn feared the boy was very
stupid and backward for his age—and she was afraid Olav would
dislike him still more for having so little sense. He was so pretty
and so sweet that she thought she could never feast her eyes
enough on him—but clever he was not.

The secret pang of disappointment and pain that she felt because the boy showed so openly that he liked his father better than her was another reason for her seeking to keep her husband and her son away from each other as much as she could.

At the outset Olav entertained no ill will toward Eirik. The violent mental tumult that had shaken him when he heard of Ingunn's infidelity, and afterwards time after time when he recalled that another man had possessed her—this had become a thing of the distant past during these years of their joyless life together. His love of her was a fixed thing and a habit; it was intertwined with his whole being as the mould of a meadow is intertwined with a mass of roots. But now he did not feel this love otherwise than as an infinite compassion with this poor sick creature, whose life was his own life. What was now the living warmth in his feelings for Ingunn—what throbbed, flared up, and sank again— was tenderness and anxiety for her; desire only stirred sluggishly and lukewarm, as in a doze. But thus it was that his jealousy had also grown weak and numb—it was but rarely that he thought of what she had gone through in the past, and then it seemed very far away. And Olav could not realize any connection between the shame and agony of that time and this little boy whom they had brought into their home. Eirik was there, that was to be—God had made known to him that he was to take Eirik to himself, and that was an end of the matter. And Olav was more inclined than not to like the boy in himself—he was a pretty boy, and he wooed his father's affection so openly. Olav, himself slow in taking to others, was always surprised and glad when any sought his friendship.

Olav often guessed the train of thought behind the boy's strange jumble of talk much better than his mother did. And when she interrupted Eirik's faltering explanations with inappreciative words and would not leave the boy alone so that he and Olav might reach an understanding, her husband more than once felt a kind of fretful impatience. *He* remembered—not in such a way that he could form clear images of it, much less put it into words, but in brief and fleeting visions he remembered a great deal of how the world had appeared to himself when he was a child.

9

THE ICE broke up and the spring came. The dull-red rocks down by the fiord were baked in the sunshine, and the spray gleamed white under the Bull Crag, as though new-born. The soil turned green and breathed its sweet smell of grass and mould, and then came the time of bursting buds, filling the evening air with a cool and bitter scent of young leaves along the valley.

One morning in May, Olav came across a nest of vipers on a slope; he killed three of them. He brought them home in a closed wooden cup and during the midday rest he stole to the cook-house with them. Snakes' fat and snakes' ashes are good for many things, but they have much more power if one goes secretly about the preparation of them.

He was about to slip into the cook-house when he heard voices. Ingunn was there, and the boy. The child's voice said:

"—because father gave me the breast, you see."

"He gave you the breast?" his mother wondered. "What nonsense are you talking now?"

"Oh yes, he did. And then Father said I might eat up the wings too, if I had not had enough, but there was nothing left of the cock but the wings—"

Olav laughed quietly to himself. Now he remembered: in the inn at Oslo the woman had set before him a roast cock, and the boy had liked the meat hugely.

Then he heard Ingunn say: "A whole cock I will roast for you, Eirik—will that make you think I am as kind as your father? You shall have it next time he goes away from home—"

Olav stole back across the yard and went east to the smithy. He felt a strange sense of shame on her behalf. What was the use of such talk? Surely she could roast one of her own cocks for the child, whether he were at home or not.

Whether it was that the unaccustomed food was too rich for Eirik's stomach or from some other cause, as spring went on the child took to waking up and screaming nearly every night. Olav heard Eirik start up with a shriek, crawl around and grope this way and that in the big north bed, where he slept alone—then he shrieked again, even louder, as though in utmost terror.

Ingunn tumbled out of bed and went to him. "Eirik, Eirik, Eirik mine, hush, hush, hush, you will wake your father—oh be quiet now—there is nothing here that you need be afraid of, my little son!"

"You had better bring him over to us," came Olav's voice, wide awake, from the darkness.

"Oh, has he waked you again!" complained Ingunn as she came back with the boy and lay down—the two tossed and wriggled till they were comfortable.

"I was not yet asleep. What have you dreamed of this time, Eirik?"

But at night it was only his mother who would serve Eirik's turn. He simply nestled closer to her and did not answer his father. They never got to hear anything of his dreams. He made a gesture of wiping something from his hands and throwing it from him two or three times. Then he gave a sigh of relief and lay down to rest. Very soon they were both asleep.

Olav was always more sleepless in spring than at other seasons; he seldom fell asleep before midnight and woke very early. On these early summer mornings the fiord often lay smooth as a mirror, pale blue and glistening in the sunlight, and the desolate shore opposite seemed bright and tranquil as a mirage. Olav was absurdly happy and light-hearted when he went out on such a morning. Torhild Björnsdatter was singing somewhere in the outhouses; she had already been long at work. Olav and the girl met in the yard; they stood and talked together in the morning sunshine.

When he came in again some hours later he sometimes stood for a moment looking at the two, mother and child, who were still asleep. Eirik lay with his face against his mother's neck, breathing with half-open mouth. Ingunn held her narrow hand, heavy with rings, about his shoulder.

A fortnight before St. John's Day, Ingunn gave birth to a man-child. Olav had him christened at once, Audun.

It was a tiny boy, purple and skinny. Olav put two fingers around his son's hand one day, when he lay in Signe Arnesdatter's lap and was being washed—it was so thin, that little hand, almost like a chicken's leg, and just as cold.

Olav felt no very deep affection for his son or joy that at last he had one. The waiting had been so long that the bare suspicion that Ingunn might be with child again had struck him with black despondency. He had grown so unused to the hope that all this misery might end at last in rejoicing that he had to have time to take it in.

But he saw that it was not so with the mother. In spite of her having expected nothing but bitter pain, against her own will her heart had trembled each time with hopeless and despairing love for the little unborn creatures. Now Audun inherited this love from all his brothers, who had left behind them not even a name or a memory.

Eirik was boisterously happy at having a brother. He knew from Siljuaas that the birth of a child was the greatest of great events. Then there were two or three strange women in the house, and they brought with them good food, and candles were burning in the room all night long. The child in the cradle was tended as a most precious thing—those outside the fence were lying in wait to steal it—and its health and well-being were constantly inquired after. That it was the worst off of all in the home when the next child came and took its place in the cradle—the child of yesteryear was abandoned to the care of its little sisters, always in the way and always in danger—of this Eirik took no account. Here in this house the time was one of immense festivity, so many wives, each with her maid, and masses of food—but the candles at night he and his father were cheated of; his mother and the new brother lay in another house.

"It's my silken brother, but it's only your woollen brother," he said to Torhild's two youngest children as they stood together watching Audun being dressed.

Olav was sitting with his wife at the moment; he heard it. He glanced at Ingunn. She lay looking at her two sons, radiant with joy.

His son—that little creature there, that the maid was pulling about. The other bent his healthy, beaming face over him and prattled to the little brother, whom all unwittingly he had deprived of his birthright.

It had caused a certain mild stir in the neighbourhood when the people of Hestviken so unexpectedly produced a big son of five who had been hidden away all this time.

Olav was not very well liked in the neighbourhood. He had been received with evident and cordial goodwill when he came home to his own—but little by little a feeling grew up among the people of the countryside that he had repelled their offers of friendship and good-neighbourship. Olav kept to himself more than they liked, and in company he was little inclined to be sociable; never discourteous—and this did not make him more popular, for it was taken as a sign that he thought himself something above the other franklins—but taciturn, quiet, and unapproachable. It was hinted in private, with a slight sneer, that Olav must think himself something like a courtier, since he had been Earl Alf's man and was kinsman on his mother's side to these great Danish lords who lay here in Norway half a year at a time and fed at the Duke's table. Ay, ay. He owned his fathers' manor yet, whole and undivided—but let him wait and see how long that would last, in days such as these. Although he never shirked doing anything that was his due, and was not ill-natured when it was a question of helping anyone, nobody *cared* to ask Olav Audunsson to do him a favour. For if folk who were in difficulties went to the rich Master of Hestviken, it was as though he scarce troubled himself to listen to them. When they had explained to him their situation at length, he would ask at the end of it all, as though he had been thinking of other things: ay, what was it they wanted—? No one could deny that Olav was generous in both giving and lending, but if anyone would ease his heart and discuss his affairs with him, there was no comfort to be had of it in that house—he gave such answers that one knew not whether the man was foolish or indifferent. So that unless folk had the most crying need of a helping hand, they preferred to go to another, who would listen to what they said, express an opinion, and give them counsel and consolation, even if this man might not grant them help without some hanging back, saying he was badly off himself— but in God's name—

Another matter which had been remarked by the neighbours was that no man had seen Olav get honestly drunk or free-spoken in a carouse. He drank no less than other good men at a banquet. But it seemed that God's gifts did not bite on him.

And by degrees there grew up a feeling in the countryside—vague and formless, for no one really knew on what they based it, but with all its obscurity it was strong as a certainty—that this man had something on his mind, a secret misfortune or a sin. The handsome, erect young master, with the broad, fair face beneath his curly flaxen hair, was a marked man.

It was a strange thing too about his wife, that she could not give birth to living children. Little it was that one saw of Ingunn Steinfinnsdatter, and the poor thing was not much to look at either. But folk still remembered how fair she had been—and that not so many years ago.

And now it came out that they *had* a child. For all these years they had had a son hidden away, the Fiend knew where, far in the north in her home country.

Begotten while the father was an outlaw, ay, that was it. Olav had made that known, briefly and clearly. Folk knew that his quarrel with his wife's kinsmen had arisen from this, that Steinfinn on his deathbed had given into Olav's charge the daughter to whom the lad had been betrothed since their childhood. Olav had accepted her as his wife, and it was impossible to interpret Steinfinn's words otherwise than that this accorded with his wishes. But the new sponsors had thought they might dispose of the fair and wealthy maid in another manner. Now Olav declared that the summer before he made final reconciliation with his wife's kinsmen, he had secretly visited the house where she dwelt. But in the meantime this had had to be kept secret.

So said Olav Audunsson. But folk began to wonder. Perhaps it was not so sure that Olav had accepted purely of his own free will the wife he was made to marry by Steinfinn's order, while he was a mere boy and subject to Steinfinn's authority. Had he not rather tried to shuffle out of a marriage into which he had been forced in childhood? Folk who had seen a little of their life together—their serving-folk and the neighbours' wives who had been with Ingunn when she lay sick—spoke of what they knew. True enough, Olav was good to his wife in a way, but he was sulky and silent at home as he was abroad; days might pass when he spoke not a word to his wife even. Ingunn never looked happy, and that was not so strange either—a woman who was tied to this

cross-stick of a husband, always in bad health and giving birth to
one dead child after another.

One day the new priest, Sira Hallbjörn, came to Hestviken.
He was a fairly young man, tall and slight, with a handsome
face, but his hair was fiery red and folk thought he had a haughty
look. He had made himself somewhat disliked in a short time.
Scarcely had he come to the parish when he raised dissension on
every side, over the property of the Church and the incomings
of the glebe, over old agreements which Sira Benedikt had made
with the owners of the land, but which this new man found to be
unlawful. Both the monastery on Hovedö and the nuns' convent
of Nonneseter owned farms and shares of farms in the parish, as
did several of the churches and pious foundations in Oslo. The
deputies of these institutions were for the most part wise and
kindly men who were on good terms with the country folk, many
of whom had bought themselves a resting-place within the walls
of the convents; and when it happened that any of the Hovedö
monks themselves came to visit their farms, the franklins flocked
from far around to hear mass in their chapels. And then it was
not long before Sira Hallbjörn fell out with the convent folk. On
the other hand the priest had set his whole heart upon some monks
of a new order that had just come into the country: they went
barefoot, in habits that were like sackcloth and ashes, and the
virtues they chiefly practised were said to be humility, meekness,
and frugality—ay, 'twas said these friars begged their daily bread
as they went about teaching rich and poor the true fear of God,
and had they aught left in their bag after vespers, they were to
share it among the poor and themselves go out each morning with
empty hands. Now it was sure that Sira Hallbjörn was neither
humble nor meek, but proud of his birth—he came of noble stock
far away in Valdres—and he was little fitted to teach the fear of
God, for he was so learned and his speech was so hard to understand that folk had no great benefit from listening to him. But
he could never praise these beggar friars enough—Minorites
they called themselves—and made himself as it were their protector, gave great gifts to the house they had set about building
in the town, and tried to persuade his parishioners to do the same.
But folk found out that this must be because the Duke favoured

these new monks greatly, while the Bishop and most of the priests and learned men in the town liked them ill and thought that the rule of this order was dangerous and unsound. And folk knew that Sira Hallbjörn had been sent out to this parish because he, a man who by his birth and rare learning seemed destined for the highest offices of the Church, had fallen out with the Bishop and the whole chapter of Oslo, through being so proud and quarrelsome and thinking he knew and understood and could teach everything better than all the others. But they were not able to do any worse thing to him than banish him to this good call—his conduct was blameless in all else, he had studied in foreign lands for many years, and he knew all that was to be known of the law and justice of the land, from the oldest times down to his own day.

It was in order to hear what Olav knew about a right to salmon-fishing in a little river over on the Hudrheim side that he had come today. Olav could not tell him much—the farm with which the right went had been sold by his grandfather to his son-in-law and since then it had been divided and had passed into many hands. He could see that Sira Hallbjörn was vexed because he could tell him so little of the matter; nevertheless Olav asked, while the priest sat at meat, if he could throw light on a question that weighed on his mind. "It concerns my sons—"

It was thus: he had heard that a child begotten while the father is under ban of outlawry is outside the law and has no rights, even if the mother be the outlaw's duly married wife.

"Nay, nay," said Sira Hallbjörn, with a sweep of the hand. "You have heard of the wolf's cub—such was the name they gave to an outlawed man's child in old days. Then it was so that the outlaw was treated as a dead man: his estate was divided and his wife held to be a widow; and if he were granted grace, he had to ask her again of her kinsfolk and wed her anew. But you know full well that such a law cannot hold among Christian men—among us no sin and no sentence can sever the bond of wedlock between man and wife."

"Her kinsmen would not have it that 'twas lawful wedlock, that which had been made between us when we were young," said Olav. "'Twas only after Eirik was born that I got her with her kinsfolk's consent."

"You need have no fear on that score now. Whether the boy were true-born or not, he enjoys the same rights now that you are married with her kinsfolks' consent, so none can dispute with you whether 'tis lawful marriage."

"Then is it certain," asked Olav, "that Audun can never come forward and oust Eirik from his right as our first-born?"

"Certainly he cannot," said the priest decisively.

"Nay, nay. I wished but to be sure how this matter stood."

"Ay, 'twas natural enough," replied Sira Hallbjörn.

Olav thanked him for his information.

While his mother was lying in, Eirik took to talking of one he called Tötrabassa. At first the grown people thought this was a beggar woman—one of those who came in greater numbers now that the house was overflowing with food and drink.

Ay, Tötrabassa was a woman with a bag, said Eirik. But another day he said that Tötrabassa had been there and had played with him in the field behind the barn. There was a little hollow in the meadow where he was fond of going with his things. Tötrabassa was a little maid. No one paid much attention to this— they were all used to the queer nonsense Eirik so often talked.

But after a while he began to tell of more playfellows, and they all had strange names like Tauragaura, Silvarp, Skolorm, Dölvandogg, and Kolmurna the Blue—whether they were men or women, grown-up or children, it was not easy to make out.

The house-folk grew alarmed. It still happened sometimes that a whole household left croft or cabin, great and small, and took to the wood, either because they were pursued by the law or from sheer poverty, and chose a vagabond life, in summer at any rate, rather than be brought to justice. Just at this time a fat sheep was lost that had been kept in the home pasture, and now the housecarls thought that these friends of Eirik's must be vagabonds of this sort, who lived chiefly by pilfering and stealing. Folk kept an eye on Eirik, when he was playing in the hollow, whether any unknown children or grown people might come to him. But nothing was seen. And one day the sheep's carcass was washed up in the bay—it had fallen from the cliff.

And now the people of Hestviken were afraid in earnest. This must be some of the underground folk. They asked Eirik if he knew where they came from. Oh, from away under the crag. But when he saw how frightened the others were at this, he was a little scared himself. Nay, they came from the town, he said—in a sledge they came. Or maybe they sailed, he corrected himself, when Olav said no one could drive a sledge from Oslo in summertime, he must not talk such nonsense. Anyhow, they came from the woods—ay, they dwelt in the woods, Tauragaura had said. Tauragaura was the one he talked most about.

Ingunn was quite beside herself with despair. These must be the evil spirits who had turned all luck from this house, generation after generation; now they were surely after her children. Eirik was shut up in the women's house and watched—and then he talked and talked of these friends of his, till it looked as if his mother would lose her wits with despair. She would have Olav fetch the priest.

"Now, you are not lying, Eirik, by chance?" asked Olav severely one day when he had been listening while Eirik replied to his mother's anxious questions.

Eirik stared in terror at his father with his great brown eyes and shook his head vehemently.

"For if I find out one day, boy, that you bear untruthful tales, it will go ill with you."

Eirik looked at his father in wonder, seeming not to understand.

But Olav had conceived a suspicion that the whole story was a thing the boy had invented—unreasonable as such an idea appeared to himself, for he could not make out what object the child could have in spreading such vain and purposeless lies. And the next day, when Olav and a man were to mow the meadow that lay below the hollow, he let Eirik come with them, promising Ingunn that they would keep a sharp watch on the child all the time.

Olav did so, looking out for the boy now and then. Eirik pottered about, good and quiet, up in the hollow, playing with some snail-shells and pebbles that the boatmen had given him. He was quite alone the whole time.

When the other man and the girls went up to the morning meal, Olav came up to Eirik. "So they did not come to see you today, Tötrabassa and Skolorm and the rest?"

"Oh yes," said Eirik radiantly, and he began telling of all the games he had played with them today.

"Now you are lying, boy," said Olav harshly. "I have watched you the whole time—none has been here."

"They took to their heels when you came—they were afraid of your scythe."

"Then what became of them—where did they run to?"

"Home, to be sure."

"Home—and where may that be?"

Eirik looked up at his father, puzzled and a little diffident. Then his face brightened eagerly: "Shall we go thither, Father?" and he held out his hand.

Olav hung his scythe on a tree. "Let us do so."

Eirik led him up to the manor, out of the yard and on to the rocks to the west of the houses, where they could see over the fiord.

"They must be down there," he said, pointing to the little strip of beach that lay far below them.

"I see nobody," said Olav shortly.

"Nay, they are not *there*—now I know where they are—" Eirik first turned back toward the manor, but then he took a path that led down to the waterside. "Now I know, now I know," he called eagerly, hopping and skipping as he waited for his father; then he ran on ahead again, stopped and waited and took his father by the hand, dragging him down along the path.

He showed the way to the farthest of the sheds by the quay. Olav hardly ever used this one—there was not so much trade at Hestviken now. Only in spring, when Olav was preparing to visit the Holy Cross fair at Oslo, did he store some of his winter goods here. Now the shed was empty and unlocked. Eirik drew his father into it.

The sea splashed and gurgled about the piles under the floor of the shed. This was leaky and the walls were gaping, so that reflections of the sunlight from the water rose and fell in bright streaks on walls and roof. Eirik sniffed in the salt smell of the shed, and his face sparkled with excitement. He looked up into his father's eyes with a smile of expectation and, stealing on tiptoe, led him to an old barrel standing bottom-upwards, which Olav used to pack skins in.

"Here," he whispered, squatting down. "In *here* they dwell. Can you see them—now the cracks have grown so big again, else we could see better, but they are sitting there eating—can you see them?"

Olav turned the barrel on its side and gave it a kick so that it rolled away. There was nothing underneath but some litter.

Eirik looked up smiling and was about to say something—when he noticed the expression of his father's face and stopped in terror, open-mouthed. With a scream he put up his arms to ward off the blow, bursting into a heart-rending fit of weeping.

Olav let his hand drop—felt it was unworthy of him to strike the boy. So puny and miserable Eirik looked as he stood there in tears that his father was almost ashamed of himself. He just took the child's arms, drew him away, and sat down on a pile of wreckage, holding Eirik before him.

"So you have lied, I see—'twas a lie every word you said of these friends of yours—answer me now."

But Eirik answered nothing; he stood staring up at the man's face, clean dazed—it seemed he could not make it out at all.

The end of it was that Olav had to take Eirik on his knee to stop his bitter weeping. He said again and again that Eirik must never say what was untrue or he would get a beating—but he spoke much more gently now, and between whiles he stroked the boy's head. Eirik nestled close to his father's chest and put his arms tightly about his neck.

But he did not understand—Olav was sure of that, and it affected him almost uncannily. This boy that he held in his arms seemed to him so strange and odd—what in God's name had come over him that he could invent all these lies? To Olav it was so utterly aimless that he began to wonder: was Eirik altogether in his right senses?

Ingunn stayed indoors for nearly nine weeks after her lying-in. She was not notably sick or weak; it was rather that she had grown too fond of her life in the narrow chamber, where all was done for the comfort of herself and the infant, and all was shut out that might disturb her. She let herself sink deep into this new happiness—the infant she had at the breast, and Eirik, who ran in and out of her room all day long. Toward the end Olav began to grow impatient—they had passed so many bad years together, and in all that time she had clung to him. Now she was happy and well, ay, she had recovered some of her youthful beauty, and she barred herself in from him with the children. But Olav allowed nothing of this to appear.

At last, on the Sunday after St. Laurence's Mass, she kept her churching. Eirik was asleep when the company left home in the early morning, but he was out in the yard when the church folk came back.

A new custom had grown up—although many liked it not, nay, said it was tempting God with overweening pride: young wives at their first churching, especially if the child was a son, wore again on that day their golden circlet, the bridal crown of noble maids, outside their wedded women's coif.

Ingunn had fastened her white silken kerchief with the golden garland; she wore a red kirtle and her blue mantle with the great gold brooch in it.

Olav lifted his wife from her horse; Eirik stood rapt, gazing at his mother's loveliness. She seemed much taller in this splendid dress, with the silver belt around her slender waist; her movements were lithe and supple, light as a bird's.

"Mother!" Eirik exclaimed, beaming; "you *are* Leman after all!"

In an instant his father seized him by the shoulder; the blow of a clenched fist fell on his cheek-bone, making his head swim. Blow followed blow, leaving the child no breath to cry out—only a hoarse whistling came from his throat—till Una Arnesdatter came running up and caught the man by the arm.

"Olav, Olav, curb yourself—'tis a little boy—are you out of your senses, to strike so hard?"

Olav let go. Eirik let himself fall backward flat on the ground; there he lay, panting and whining, black and blue in the face. It was no swoon—half on purpose, the boy behaved as if he were dying. Una stooped down to him and lifted him to her lap; then his tears began to flow.

Olav turned toward his wife—he was still trembling. Ingunn stood bending forward; eyes, nostrils, the open mouth were like the holes in a death's-head. Olav laughed, a harsh and angry laugh —then he took her by the upper arm and drew her into the hall, where the maids were now bringing in the banquet.

None of the company had heard what the child said. But all thought the same—no matter what he had done, it had been an ugly sight to see the father correct the little boy so roughly. They sat about on the benches, waiting to be bidden to table, and all were ill at ease.

At last Una Arnesdatter came in, carrying Eirik in her arms.

She set him down beside his father's knee. "Eirik will not disobey you again, Olav—you must tell your son you are angry no longer."

"Has he told you why I chastised him?" asked Olav without looking up.

Una shook her head. "Poor little fellow—he has cried so he had no power to speak."

"Never more shall you dare to say that word, Eirik," said Olav hotly in an undertone. "*Never* more—you understand?"

Eirik was still hiccuping spasmodically. He said nothing, but stared at his father, frightened and bewildered.

"Never again are you to speak that word," his father repeated. laying a heavy hand on the boy's shoulder. Till the child nodded. But then Eirik's eyes wandered longingly to the dinner-table, which was groaning with good things.

And so the company seated themselves.

Eirik was to sleep in Torhild's house that night, for there were so many guests at the manor. In the evening, when he was going across, his father came after him into the yard. Eirik stopped short, trembling violently—he looked up at the other in such mortal fear.

"Who taught you to say that ugly word—of your mother?"

Eirik looked up, frightened; the tears began to rise. Olav could get no answer to his question.

"*Never* say it again—do you hear, *never* again!" Olav stroked the boy's head—saw with something like a sense of shame that one side of Eirik's face was all red and swollen.

The boy was on the point of falling asleep when he felt that someone was bending over him—his mother; her face was burning hot and wet.

"Eirik mine—who has told you this—that your mother was a leman?"

The boy was wide awake in a moment:

"But *are* you not Leman?"

"Yes," whispered his mother.

Eirik threw his arms about her neck, nestled up to her, and kissed her.

I O

AUTUMN came early that year. Bad weather set in about Michaelmas, and then it rained and blew, day in, day out, except when the gale was so high that the clouds could not let go their rain. This weather lasted for seven weeks.

At Hestviken the water rose above the quays. One night the sea carried away the piles under the farthest shed: when the men came down in the grey dawn, they saw the old house lying with its back wall, which faced the rock, leaning forward, and the front wall, toward the fiord, sunk half under water. It rocked in the heavy seas like a moored boat, and every time the wreck was lifted by a wave and sank again, the water poured out between the timbers, but most of all through a hatch under the gable. It looked like a drunken man hanging round-shouldered over the side of a boat and spewing, thought Anki.

With axes, boathooks, and ropes the men now had to try to cut the wrecked shed adrift and warp it out of the way; otherwise it was likely to be flung in against the quay and the shed in which Olav stored all the salt he had dried during the summer, and his fish—of this there was not much, for the autumn fishing had failed. In the course of this work Olav bruised his right arm badly.

He paid little heed to it while he was toiling in the spray and the storm, which was so violent that at times the men had to lie flat and crawl along the rocks. But at dusk, as they walked up to the manor, he felt his arm aching and it hurt when he touched it. As he was shutting the house door a gust of wind blew it in, carrying Olav off his feet; his bad arm was given a violent wrench as the man stumbled over the threshold and fell at full length on the floor of the anteroom. He had to call for help to be rid of his soaking sea-clothes, and Torhild bound up his arm in a sling.

It was unbearable in the hall that evening; the room was chock-full of smoke, for it was impossible to open door or louver in this wind. Eyes smarted and chests were racked; and when the men's wet clothes began to steam on the crossbeams, the air was soon so thick that it could be cut with a knife.

Ingunn lay in the little closet with both the children—there was less smoke, but it was so cold that they had to creep under the bedclothes. The men went out as soon as they had supped. Olav threw some skins and cushions on the floor by the hearth and lay down there, to be below the smoke.

His arm was now swollen. His face was burning from the weather and his head and body were hot and cold by turns. Feverish and light-headed, he heard the storm as a multiplicity of voices—it howled about the corners of the house, slamming a loose shutter somewhere—now and then he could distinguish its roaring in the trees on the crag above the manor. The deepest note was that of the raging fiord; where he lay he thought he could hear the thunder of the waves breaking on the rock on which the houses stood as though the booming came from beneath him, up through the rock.

In a doze he saw the huge white-crested seas coming, their water brown with mud; and he crawled again up the wet rock on hands and knees, with the boathook gripped under him, and the rope he had to fasten in a cleft of the rock. The spray, thick as rain, lashed him even up here. The black welter of clouds was split at that moment with a brassy yellow rift, and far beneath him, where the black and foaming fiord seemed hollow as a cup, a single shaft of sunlight fell glittering upon the racing waves.

Then another vision appeared under his closed eyelids—a great bog, pale with rime, grass and heather frosted and white. But a kind of light glimmered within the morning mist, and he could tell that as the day wore on, the sun would break through. Never is there such a day for riding out with hawk and hound: bog-holes and tarns scattered over the moor are held fast in dark, smooth ice with little white air-bubbles that crack. The wooded hillsides are clear and carry sound, for trees and bushes are bare, and the fallen leaves are bright over the ground, but the fir forest stands dark and fresh after the rime has thawed—and then there is the suspense, whether the bird will make for impassable ground or will take to the bogs and the frozen water.

The only hawk he owned now was in the loft of the men-servants' house, sick and reddish about the feet, nor did it breathe as it should either. It would be as well to make an end of it now—it would never be fit for hunting again. And he had lost his falcon last autumn.

Now Audun was fretting again. Ingunn hushed him and lulled him to sleep in there.

Torhild Björnsdatter came up and spread some blankets over her master. Olav opened his eyes—from where he lay he could see the girl's strong figure moving in the red glare from the embers on the hearth. Torhild was putting things straight—moving the clothes on the crossbeams.

"Are you not asleep, Olav—are you thirsty?"

"Oh, ay. Nay, I will rather have water—"

Olav raised himself on his elbow. His bandaged arm hurt him when he tried to stretch it out and take the cup of water. Torhild sat on her haunches and held it to his mouth. When he lay down again, she drew the coverlet over his shoulder. Then he heard her asking in the closet whether the mistress wanted anything.

"Hush, hush," Ingunn whispered impatiently in reply; "you will wake Audun for me—he was almost asleep."

Torhild covered the embers and went out. Olav lay on the floor all night.

The severe autumn weather was not good for Audun. He got sore eyes from being always in the pungent smoke, and he coughed a great deal.

On the approach of Yule the weather fell calm; the sun glowed red behind the frost fog every morning. Early in the new year the fiord froze over, but the cold increased. In the farms round about, folk had to move all into one house and keep the fire burning on the hearth night and day.

It had been a good spring the year before, so the farmers had as much live stock as they could in any way find room for. But in spite of their byres and stables being overfilled, the beasts suffered so much from the cold that folk had to wrap in sacks and cloths those it was most important to save, and they had to spread the floor with spruce boughs, lest the animals should freeze fast in the clay. The dung was frozen stiff every morning, so it was almost impossible to clear it away.

About the time of St. Agatha's Mass [9] it was said in the countryside that now men could drive on the ice right down to Denmark. But now no man had business in that land; peace had been concluded between the Kings the year before.

About this time Olav was called upon to show cause why he had stayed at home in the summer, when the Duke proceeded to

[9] February 5.

Denmark to negotiate the peace of Hegnsgavl. The matter was thus: that Olav, who had been out for three summers in succession with the war fleet as one of the lesser captains, had been given a half-promise of furlough by Baron Tore Haakonsson for the fourth summer; but Tore ordered him to provide two fully armed men and their victuals for the Baron's service instead. Olav had not been able to do this, but in spite of that he had not presented himself at the muster of the army in the spring—the levy this year was much smaller, since the Duke only went south to negotiate. Now Olav found himself in trouble over this, and in the bitter cold about mid-Lent he had to ride once to Tunsberg and then several times to Oslo, first to account for his absence and then to raise ready money. He lost much cattle that winter, and the white horse died that he had bought of Stein.

The two little children filled the crowded house with commotion.

Eirik had a bad fault: Olav found out by degrees that this boy was greatly given to lying. If his father asked whether he had seen this or that member of the household, Eirik was always quick to answer yes, he had just spoken with the other in the house or out in the yard, and gave an account of what had been said or done. Usually there was not a word of truth in it. Some of the servingfolk, and his mother too, hinted that perhaps the child had second sight—Eirik was not like other boys. Olav had not much to say to this, but he kept an eye on him—he could see no sign that it was anything but mendacity.

Another bad habit of Eirik's was that he would sit humming or singing some rigmarole that he made up himself, interminably, till Olav's head ached and he felt inclined to beat the boy. But he had grown wary of laying a hand on the child since he had thrashed him so pitilessly the day Ingunn came home from her churching.

Eirik knelt before the bench in the evening, arranging these snail-shells and animals' teeth of his in rows and chanting:

> *"Four and five of the fifth dozen,*
> *Four and five of the fifth dozen,*
> *Fifteen mares and four foals*
> *I got in the daytime and got in the nighttime.*

*Four and five of the fifth dozen
Were the horses I owned upon the morrow.*"

He repeated this about cows and calves, sheep and lambs, sows and pigs.

"Be still," his father checked him sharply; "have I not told you I will have no more of these gowling cantraps of yours?"

"I had forgotten, Father mine," said Eirik in alarm.

Olav asked him: "How many horses would you choose to have, Eirik—four and five of the fifth dozen or a hundred horses?"

"Oh, I would have many more," replied Eirik. "I would have— seven and twenty!"

So little did he understand of his own crooning.

Audun was fretful and ailing. Ingunn boasted of her son and said there was no fairer child, and indeed he had been better of late; but Olav saw the smouldering anxiety in her eyes when she spoke thus. Eirik repeated what he heard his mother say, hung over the cradle, rocking and wheedling his silken brother, as he always called Audun.

Olav felt a strange distress when he saw it. Audun seemed to him a most miserable little creature—always scurfy about the scalp, sore about the mouth, lean and raw about the body, which was backward in its growth. Never had this son made him feel anythink like paternal joy; but that he was father to this poor sick, fretting child gave him a feeling of bitter pain when Eirik was bending over the cradle: the other was so fair and full of life, with his glistening nut-brown locks falling about Audun's wrinkled face.

One day Olav asked Torhild what she thought of Audun.

"He will surely mend, when the spring comes," said Torhild; but Olav felt in himself that the girl did not believe her own words.

They had turned loose the cattle at Hestviken and drove them up to the old moss-grown pastures in Kverndal in the daytime, when Audun fell very sick. He had coughed the whole winter and had had many fits of colic, but this time it was worse than ever before.

Olav saw that Ingunn was ready to drop with fatigue and anxiety, but she kept wonderfully calm and collected. Untiringly she watched over the child night and day, while every remedy was tried to help Audun—first those familiar to the people of the house, and then all those known to the neighbours' wives for whom Ingunn sent.

At last, on the sixth day, the boy seemed to be much better. By supper-time he was sleeping soundly, and he did not feel so cold to the touch. Torhild put warm stones underneath his cradle clothes; then she went out, taking Eirik with her. She had watched nearly as much as the mother and had had all the housework in the daytime; now she could do no more.

Ingunn was so tired that she neither heard nor saw—at last Olav led her away by force, took off her outer garments, and made her lie down in the bed. He promised that he himself would sit up with the maid and would wake her if the boy was restless.

Olav fetched three tallow candles, set one on the candlestick, and lighted it. But, though he was usually such a bad sleeper, he felt heavy and drowsy tonight. If he stared at the flame of the candle, his eyes began to smart and run, and if he looked at the maid, who had taken her distaff and was spinning, he grew sleepy from seeing and hearing the spinning-wheel. From time to time he made up the fire, snuffed the candle, gave a look to the sleeping child and to his wife, drank cold water, or went outside for a moment, to look at the weather and refresh himself with a breath of the calm, cold spring night—bringing in a piece of wood, which he whittled as he sat. Thus he kept himself awake till he had set the third candle on the stick.

He started up on hearing the cradle rockers bumping queerly against the clay floor; such a strange sound was coming from the child. It was almost dark in the room; the candle-end had fallen off the spike, almost burned out—the wick flickered and smoked in the molten tallow on the iron plate. On the hearth there was still a faint crackling amid the smoke of the wood ashes. Olav was beside the cradle in two noiseless steps; he lifted up the child, wrapping him in the clothes he lay in.

The little body struggled, as though Audun would free himself from his swaddling-clothes—in the dim light Olav thought the boy gave him a strangely accusing look. Then he stretched himself, collapsed limply, and died there in his father's arms.

Olav was benumbed, body and soul, as he laid the corpse down again and covered it over. It was vain to think when Ingunn would wake.

The maid had fallen asleep with her head in her arms over the table. Olav waked her, hastily hushing her as she was about to utter a cry. He bade her go out and tell the house-folk, begging them not to come near the house—Ingunn must be allowed to enjoy her sleep while she could.

He opened the smoke-vent—it was daylight outside. But Ingunn slept and slept, and Olav stayed sitting with her and their dead son. But once when he got up to look at her, he chanced to jerk her belt onto the floor. It made a clanging noise, and the woman started up and looked into her husband's face.

She sprang up and pushed him aside when he tried to hold her back, threw herself upon the cradle so violently that it looked as if the dead child was upset into her arms.

As she sat on her haunches, rocking the corpse in a close embrace and weeping with a strange, spluttering sound, she checked herself all of a sudden and looked up at her husband:

"Were you two asleep when he died—were you both asleep when Audun drew his last breath?"

"No, no, he died in my arms—"

"You—and you did not wake me—Lord Christ, how had you the heart not to wake me—in *my* arms he should have died, 'twas me he knew, not you—you never cared for your child. Is it thus you keep your word!"

"Ingunn—"

But she leaped up, holding the child's corpse high above her head with both hands and screaming. Then she tore open the dress over her bosom, pressed the little dead son to her bare body, and threw herself on the bed, lying over him.

When Olav came up after a while and tried to talk to her, she put her hand against his face and thrust him away.

"Nevermore will I be parted from my Audun—"

Olav knew not what to do. He sat over on the bench with his head between his hands, waiting if perchance she should recover her senses—when Eirik burst open the door and ran to his mother, in a flood of tears. He had been told it when he awoke.

Ingunn sat upright—the child's corpse was left lying on the pillow. She drew her son to her in a close embrace, let him go and took his little tear-stained face in both hands, laid her own against it and wept, but much more quietly.

The day Audun was borne to the grave was gloriously fine.

During the afternoon Olav stole away from the funeral guests, down to the fence around the farthest cornfield. The sea gleamed and glistened so that the air seemed all a-quiver with it; the quiet surf at the foot of the Bull shone fresh and white. The smell that came up from the quay was so good and full-laden today, and it was met by the scent of warm rocks and mould and young growth. The little waves breaking on the beach trickled quietly back among the pebbles, rills were gushing everywhere, and from Kverndal came the murmur of the little stream. The alder wood up there was brown with bloom, and the hazel thickets dripped with yellow catkins. Summer was not far off.

He heard it was Ingunn who came up behind him. Side by side they stood leaning over the fence, gazing at the reddish rocks on which the sun was blazing and at the gleam of blue water.

All at once Olav felt strangely ill at ease, oppressed with longing. To be on board ship, at sea, with a clear horizon on every side. Or at home upcountry, where the scent of mould and grass and trees welled out of broad hills and ridges as far as one could see. Here all was cramped and small, this narrow fiord with its strips of land bordering the lonely creek.

He said gently: "Do not grieve so much over Audun, Ingunn. It was best that God took home His poor innocent lamb, whose only heritage was to bear the burden of all our misdeeds."

Ingunn made no answer. She turned from him and went back toward the houses, quietly, with bowed head. Up by the houses Eirik came rushing to meet her—Olav saw that his mother hushed him as she took his hand and led him with her.

I I

In the summer the year after they had lost Audun, Olav and Ingunn were at a working meeting on a farm in the neighbourhood; they had Eirik with them. The boy was now seven winters old, and he was apt to be unmanageable when amusing himself.

When work was over in the evening the people sat in a meadow near the house they had been roofing. Some of the younger ones then began to dance. Eirik and some other little boys ran about and made a noise; the ale had gone to their heads—they ran straight at the chain of dancers and tried to break it, shouting and laughing as they did so. They mixed among the older folk, jostling one after another, and interrupted the men's talk. Olav had spoken to Eirik time after time, rather sharply at last—but it only kept the boy quiet for a little while.

Ingunn had not noticed it—she was sitting a little way off by the wall in company with other women. All at once Olav appeared before her, dragging Eirik with him; he lifted him by the back of his shirt, so that the boy hung from Olav's hand as one takes a puppy by the nape of the neck. Olav was red in the face, somewhat drunken—his ale was apt to tell on him more than usual when these fits of sleeplessness had been very frequent.

"You must look after your boy and keep him in order, Ingunn," he said angrily, giving Eirik a shake. "He will not obey me, unless I thrash him—take him, he belongs to you—" and he flung the boy so that Eirik pitched into his mother's arms. With that he went away.

In the course of the evening, when folk sat drinking in the shed after supper, some of them began to tell stories. And Sira Hall-börn told the tale of Jökul:

"A rich merchant fared forth and was away from home three winters. So every man may judge whether he was more surprised or joyful when he came home and found his wife abed and with her a little boy of one month old. But the traveller's wife was a crafty and quick-witted woman; she said:

"'A great miracle has befallen me. Sorely have I longed for you, my husband, while you wandered so far abroad. But one day last winter I stood here at the door of the house and the icicles hung from the eaves; I broke one off and sucked, yearning for you the while with keen and ardent desire—and then I conceived this child; judge for yourself whether you and none other are not his father, Jökul [1] I have had him called!'

"The traveller had to rest content with that; he spoke her fair, this loving wife of his, and seemed to have great joy of the son,

[1] *Jökul:* icicle.

Jökul. He would have the boy ever near him when he was at home. And when Jökul was twelve years old, his father took him out on one of his voyages. But one day, when they were in the midst of the sea and Jökul stood at the ship's side, the merchant came behind him, while no man saw; he dropped the boy overboard.

"On returning to his wife he told his tale with sorrowful mien and mourning voice:

" 'A great misfortune has befallen us and a heavy loss have we suffered, my sweet one—Jökul is no more. Know that I lay becalmed in the midst of the sea, the day was hot and the sun poured straight down. Our Jökul stood upon the deck and he was bareheaded. We begged him hard that he would cover his head, but he would not—so he thawed in the heat of the sun, and there was nothing left of Jökul, our son, but a wet spot on the deck-planks!'

"With that the wife had to rest content."

Folk laughed greatly at this tale. None took note that Olav Audunsson kept his eyes on the floor, while blushes overspread his face. If his life had depended on it, he did not believe he would have dared to turn his eyes to the dais, where his wife sat among the other ladies. Then there was a disturbance up there—Olav leaped over the table and forced his way through the crowding woman. He lifted up his wife, who had slipped from the bench in a swoon, and carried her out into the fresh air.

The best thing Eirik knew was to be allowed to go out with his father—in a boat when Olav rowed out alone to fish with a handline, as he did now and then, mainly for pastime, or across the fields. Afterwards he always came to his mother and told her about it—with beaming eyes, so eagerly that he stumbled over the words—all that had happened to them and all that he had learned of his father: now he could both row and fish, make knots and splice ropes after the fashion of seafaring men; soon he would be able to go out and fish in earnest with his father and the men. He had become such a good hand at shooting and casting—his father said he had never seen his match.

Ingunn listened to the boy's chatter, perplexed and distressed. Her poor, simple-minded little boy loved Olav more than anyone else on earth. It was as though the man's unfriendliness did not bite upon Eirik: he was given curt answers to all his questions, and at last he was told to hold his tongue. Olav coldly chid him when the boy was wild and wanton, and harshly bade Eirik speak the truth, when his mother guessed that only the child's memory was at fault. But she dared not say that to her husband, dared not take Eirik's part and remind Olav that he was so young—or tell the man Eirik called father how dearly the child loved him. She had to bow the neck and keep silence; only when she was alone with her son did she dare to show her love for him.

Ingunn did not know that what Eirik said was true, and that it was for this that Olav's bad humour neither frightened the boy for long at a time nor lessened his love for his father. They agreed much better when they were alone together. Eirik was then more obedient and not so restless, and even if he was too fond of asking odd questions, there was often some sense in them. He swallowed every word from his father's lips with eyes and ears, and this made him forget to come out with his fables and rigmaroles. Without being himself aware of it, Olav was warmed by the affection the child showed him; he forgot his dislike of other days and let himself be warmed, just as he had felt warmed whenever anyone showed him the friendship he found it so hard to seek for himself. So he met Eirik halfway with calm goodwill; he instructed the boy in the use of weapons and implements, which were still more like playthings, smiled a little at Eirik's eager questions, and chatted with him as a good father talks to his little son.

They fished for wrasse under the cliff north of the Bull, and Olav showed the boy the cleft in the rock where an old she-otter had her lair. Every year Olav took the cubs—one year two litters—and the dog-otter. As soon as the dog was gone she got a new mate, said Olav, and he mimicked for the boy the otter's cry. Yes. Eirik should come with him after the otter one night, when he was a little older—ah, when it would be, his father could not say.

One day when they were up in his father's game-covert to see to some traps, Olav chanced to speak of his own childhood at Frettastein, while he and Eirik's mother were young. "Your grandfather," said Olav, telling some story of Steinfinn at which he himself smiled and Eirik roared with laughter. "One day I had coaxed Hallvard, your uncle, with me—he was very small at that time, you must know, but all the same I had taken the boy with me up to the tarn, where we had a dugout we used to row in—"

Till Eirik mentioned Tora of Berg; he remembered her. Olav broke off his story, answered absently when the boy went on asking questions—at last he bade him hold his tongue. It was as though the sky had suddenly clouded over.

But whenever Olav was with his own house-carls, either on the quay or up at the manor, and Eirik ran about among them, he was at once more impatient with the boy. It was the way with Eirik that the more people he saw about him, the more noisy and foolish and disobedient he became. The men were amused at the boy, but they noticed that the master disliked their laughing at the things he said, and they thought Olav was very short-tempered and strict with his only son.

But it was when the mother was there that Olav felt most provoked to an intolerable ill will toward the boy. Many a time he itched to give Eirik a thrashing, to break him roughly of all his bad habits.

One thing was that Ingunn provoked him to a dull exasperation when she fussed with the child—he was to be quiet and behave in a seemly way, she said severely. Olav knew only too well that the moment his back was turned on the two, she would be on her knees trying to please Eirik. He saw how deeply she distrusted his feeling for the boy; she spied on him secretly when he was occupied with Eirik. He knew in himself that he had never done the child any harm—he might surely be trusted to punish the boy when he needed it. It was Ingunn who egged him on to anger, but it was his lifelong habit, when she was concerned, to hold himself in—and of late years it had come to this, that she was a poor, sick creature, and he had to be doubly careful not to make things worse for her. So when Ingunn tried Olav's patience too far, it was usually Eirik who suffered.

The boy had come between man and wife, and he was the first who had sundered their hearts in earnest. In their youth Olav had had to leave his playmate and fly the country—and in a way he had felt that Ingunn had gone astray simply because he had been forced to abandon her. Far too great a burden of evil fortune had been thrown upon her when she had to have recourse to her angry kinsfolk, who refused to count her as anything but a disobedient and dishonoured woman. Young she was, weak-shouldered and pampered—but her nature was not such that she could have been unfaithful to a husband with whom she shared bed and board, he knew that. He had had a feeling that Teit was but an unhappy accident—and in making an end of this confiding fool he had acted more from a belief that it would be so hopelessly difficult to remedy the disaster so long as he was alive and could blurt out the truth than because he had felt himself wronged by Teit. But even when the slaying had been accomplished, this had not done much to allay his pain of mind. His thirst to avenge the destruction of his happiness—this the poor corpse in the sæter had not been able greatly to assuage.

Now Olav saw that Ingunn loved another, and he guessed how often she had wished him out of the way, so that she might freely shed her affection upon Eirik—as one smuggles food to an outlawed friend behind the back of the master of the house.

And together with this bitterness and unrest something like a ghost of his youthful desire awoke in Olav's heart and senses; he longed to possess Ingunn as he had possessed her in former days, when they were young and healthy and could find happiness in each other's arms in spite of all their cares. Olav had never quite forgotten that time; the memory of her sweet beauty had warmed his pity to a painful tenderness—this poor faded wreck to whom he was bound was the wreck of the lovely, useless Ingunn he had once loved, and his will to protect her became stubborn and intense, as had once been his will to defend his right to his wife.

Now there blazed up in him a desire to feel that she too remembered the madness of their youth. Year in, year out a latent repugnance had smouldered within him when she clung to him with her morbid and insensate demand for caresses which, he knew, ought to be withheld from his sick wife. Now, when she avoided him, hiding herself away with what was her own, what she thought he could have no share in, it was Olav who felt he would fain have crushed her to pieces in his arms in the effort to make her answer such questions as these: Have you forgotten that I was once your dearest friend in all the world?—Why are you afraid of me?—Have I ever willingly brought sorrow upon you in all these years? For it cannot be *my* fault that we have had so little happiness in our married life?

And then his fear awoke, when he touched upon the sick spot in his mind; the dull ache became a pain that shot through his whole being: whether it was so that he *might* all the time—have averted her misfortunes. If he had had the courage to hand himself over—to men's justice and God's compassion.

Olav noticed that his unwonted impetuosity now frightened Ingunn and made her shrink; so he withdrew into himself, while his secret wound throbbed and stung. "Why is she afraid of me? Does she know—?"

There were times when he almost believed it—believed that all knew it. For he had not a friend here in his native country. It could not be helped; but that was not all: Olav guessed that no one *liked* him. Coldness and distrust met him everywhere, and often he thought he could detect a hidden malicious satisfaction when things went ill with him. Yet in this part of the country he had always acted rightly and had never done any man an injustice. He could not even bring himself to be angry at this—he received his sentence without wincing. It must be that folk saw the secret mark upon his brow.

But when he thought of Ingunn, the fear quivered through him: did *she* see it too? Was it for that she turned cold in his arms, and was it for that she seemed to be afraid when he came near her son?

On the day of St. Olav's Mass,[2] Olav always held an ale-feast. He never prayed to his patron saint—the lawmaker King would certainly not aid him with his intercession except on one condition. But nevertheless he thought himself bound to show Holy Olav due honour.

The floor was strewed with green and the hall was decorated with hangings—the old tapestry that otherwise only appeared at Yule.

On St. Olav's Eve, Olav himself was busy hanging up the tapestry. He moved along the bench and fastened the long piece with wooden hooks, which he drove in between the topmost log of the wall and the roof. Eirik followed him on the floor, gazing at the worked pictures: there were knights and longships with men on board. He knew that soon the best picture of all was coming—a house with pillars and shingled roof like a church and a banquet going on inside with drinking-horns and tankards on the table. Eirik had to peep into the roll of stuff that still lay on the bench—and in so doing he chanced to pull down a long piece of that which his father had just made to hang right.

[2] July 29.

Olav jumped down, pulled the boy from under the folds of
tapestry, and flung him on the floor:

"Out with you—you are ever in my way, bastard, doing mischief—"

At that moment Ingunn appeared in the door of the anteroom
with the lap of her gown full of flowers. She let her burden fall
straight on the floor.—He saw that she had heard.

Olav did not get a word out. Shame, anger, and a confused feeling that soon he would not know which way to turn made a
tumult within him. He stepped up on the bench and began to
hang up the tapestry that had been torn down. Eirik had fled out
of the door. Ingunn picked up her flowers and strewed them over
the floor. Olav dared not turn round and look at her. He did not
feel equal to talking to her now.

One morning a few days later Ingunn was sitting with Eirik on
the top of the crag behind the houses of Hestviken. She had been
down to Saltviken—a path led over the height; it would serve at a
pinch for riding, but was little used: the common way between
Hestviken and Saltviken was by boat.

There was sparkling sunshine and a fresh breeze; from where
Ingunn sat she saw the fiord dark blue, dotted with white foam.
The breakers dashed up in spray, glittering white along the reddish rocks that planted their feet out into the water all along
the coast. The morning sun still lay over Hudrheimsland. From the
height where she sat she could see a little of the cultivation on the
hillside—it was for that she liked this spot. And up here it sounded
fainter and farther off, that intolerable roar of the sea which tormented her at home at the manor till she thought it must come
from within her own weary, bewildered head. But there was a
kind of taste of salt, and that flickering of light from the sea
in the uneasy air—she could never accustom herself to that. She
grew tired of it.

Eirik lay half in his mother's lap playing with a bunch of big
bluebells. One after another he tore off the flowers, turned them
inside out, and blew into them. Ingunn laid her thin hand on his
cheek and looked down into his sunburned face. How handsome,
how handsome he was, this son of hers—his eyes the shade of bog
water in sunshine, his hair as fine as silk! It had grown much
darker in the last year; it was brown now. Eirik scratched his head.

"Louse me now, Mother mine. Ugh, they bite so hard in this heat!"

Ingunn gave a little laugh. She took out her comb from the pouch at her belt and began to clean the boy's head with slow, caressing strokes. It made Eirik sleepy—and the scent of the fir woods in the sun's heat and the sourish fragrance of the hair-moss on which she was lying, the clanging of bells from the cattle moving on the slope farther up the valley, lulled Ingunn to sleep.

She started at the little sound of a dog that came swimming through the high bilberry bushes. It sniffed at the two, jumped without a sound over their knees, and set off again down the path.

Her heart still trembled from being waked so suddenly. Now she heard horse's hoofs on the rock far below. Her head fell back against the trunk of the fir tree by which she sat—oh, that he should be back already! She had felt so sure he would not come home before evening at the earliest, perhaps not before the morrow.

They came over her again, the same thronging fears and despair. This thing that she had gone in dread of the last month—she could not face it, she felt that; it would be her death this time. And she could almost have wished it—had it not been for Eirik's sake; then he would be left alone with Olav. And in the midst of her great dread this little anxiety started up—why had Olav come home so soon? Had he not been able to accomplish his errand in the neighbouring parish, or had he fallen out with those folk?—and maybe he came home in yet worse humour than when he set out.

Instinctively she had thrown her arm about her child, as though to protect and hide him. Eirik struggled and freed himself:

"Let me go now—father is coming." He got on his feet, and his mother saw that he turned red as he went along the path, seeming a little uncertain and hesitating. Ingunn followed.

She saw the white horse among the trees; Olav was walking by its side. When Ingunn came up he was showing Eirik something that lay at his foot—a great lynx.

"I found her over on the mountain here to the south—she was out in broad daylight. She has young in her lair—her teats are full of milk." He turned over the dead lynx with his spear, shooing off the dog, which lay on its front paws barking, and holding the uneasy horse. Eirik cried aloud with joy, squatting down over his father's quarry. Olav smiled at the boy. "We could not find the lair—though it cannot have been very far away. But there was a scree with fallen trees on it—she must have had her track among the trees."

"Will they starve to death now, the young ones?" asked Ingunn. Eirik fumbled in the light fur under the belly of the lynx, found the swollen teats, and squeezed them—the boy's hands were all bloody. Olav was telling him how it was easy enough to get the lynx when it strayed out in broad daylight.

"Starve to death?—ay, or else they will eat each other in the lair, the strongest will come through. Unless they were born very early in the summer—that is like enough, since the dam was not with them."

Ingunn looked at the dead beast of prey. A soft and warm place the young had had as they huddled together, nosing for the sources of milk in the light fur under her soft belly. The heavy thigh that she had protected them with was tense with muscle and sinew, the claws were like steel. When she licked her young, the cruel white fangs showed up. The tufts of hair in the ears had been given her to make her the more wary and sharp of hearing; the black streaks in her yellow eyes had been like keen slits. She had been well fitted to protect and defend and discipline her offspring.

Her own child, he had such a poor wretch of a mother, unable to defend her own. And she herself had brought it to such a pass that he had none to protect him, and most he needed protection against the man he called father.

"I cannot believe even Mary, God's Mother, will pray for a mother who betrays her own son," Tora had said. And she had already betrayed her child when she suffered him to be begotten; she saw that now.

Olav and Eirik were pulling up bunches of moss and wiping away the blood that had got on the saddle and had run down the side of the white horse. Olav helped the boy into the saddle and placed the reins in his hand.

"He is so quiet, Apalhvit; Eirik will be able to ride him home, though it is a little steep below here." He walked a few steps down, cheering the boy and the horse with kind words. Then he returned to the lynx, bound its limbs together with thongs; now

and again he looked up, watching the boy on the big white horse,
till they were lost among the trees.

"Nay, we came to no agreement—'twas vain to stay there dis-
puting with those Kaaressons," he said. "I think that Eirik ought
to have Apalhvit—is he not seven winters now, the boy? 'Twill
soon be time he had his own horse—and 'tis unsafe to let the boy
ride Sindre, he is too skittish.—What are you crying for?" he
asked rather sharply, as he rose to his feet.

"If you gave Eirik the fairest colt ever bred—with saddle of
silver and bridle of gold—what would that serve, Olav, if you
cannot alter your feelings—can never look at the boy without a
grudge?"

"That is not true," said Olav hotly. "You are heavy too, you
sow of Satan"—he had got the lynx on his spear and hoisted it over
his shoulder. "Do use your wits, Ingunn," he went on, rather
more gently. "Can I have any joy of the son who is to take this
manor after me, if he is always to hide behind your skirt, now that
he is of an age to need a father's teaching and discipline? You
must venture it now, to let *me* take Eirik in hand; else there will
never be a man of him."

The breeze up here on the height fluttered his long grey cloak;
the wide brim of his black cloth hat flapped. Olav had come to
look much older in the last few years; he was no stouter than before, yet his figure seemed much more burly, broader and rounder
behind the shoulders. And the pale eyes looked smaller and even
sharper than of old, as his face was now browned by the weather.
The whites were somewhat bloodshot, no doubt because the man
had too little sleep.

He felt her staring at him, till he was forced to turn his head.
He met her complaining glance with a hard eye.

"I know what you are thinking of, Ingunn, I spoke a word in
wrath—God knows I wish it unsaid."

Ingunn crouched as though expecting a blow.

Olav began again, forcing himself to be calm: "But you must
not act so, Ingunn, as to entice him away from me, as though you
were afraid I should— Never have I chastised Eirik excessively—"

"I do not remember that my father ever laid a hand upon you,
Olav."

"No, Steinfinn cared not to trouble himself so far on my account as to correct me. But I have never departed from my own

word—not from my word to you, Ingunn, in any case. And now I have let all men know that Eirik is *our* son—yours and mine."

He saw that she was ready to faint. But it seemed to him that this time he *could* not turn aside—saying some new thing to blot out the traces of what he had already said. He went on:

" 'Tis worst for us all if you steal away with your motherly love and dare not take Eirik on your lap when I am there to see. Deal with the boy in hole-and-corner fashion, as though you crept away by stealth to meet a leman."

He took her hand, pressed it hard and kept it. "Remember, my dear—by so doing you serve Eirik worst."

On the Eve of St. Matthew,[3] early in the day, Eirik came rushing in to his parents, who were in the hall. He was screaming at the top of his voice. Kaare and Rannveig, the two children Björn had left, who were still with Torhild, came after him, and Olav and Ingunn heard from them what had happened.

The stoat that lived in the turf roof of the sheepcot had had another litter of young, and Eirik had tried to dig out the nest—though Olav had said they were to be left in peace this summer. Eirik had been bitten in the hand.

Olav seized the boy, lifted him up, and carried him to his mother's arms. Hurriedly he took the child's hand and looked at it—the bite was in the little finger.

"Are you able to hold him—or shall I fetch in Torhild? Be quiet—say nothing to Eirik. He can be saved if we are quick enough about it."

The stoat's bite is the most poisonous of all animals'; the flesh of him who is bitten by an enraged stoat rots and falls from the bones till the man dies, or else he gets the falling sickness, for all stoats have falling sickness. Only if one be bitten in the tip of one finger there may be a chance of saving life and health, if the finger be cut off and the wound burned out.

Quick as lightning Olav made all ready. Among the smaller implements kept in a crack of the wall he found a suitable iron and put it in the fire, bidding Kaare Björnsson blow. Then he drew his dagger and set to sharpening it.

But the serving-maid who had been called in to hold the boy began to scream loudly. Eirik was scared already—now he guessed

[3] St. Matthew's Day is September 21.

what his father would do to him. With a howl of the utmost terror
he tore himself away from his mother and ran like a rat from wall
to wall howling worse and worse, and Olav after him.

A ladder stood leading to the loft above the closet. Eirik ran
up it, and Olav followed him. In the darkness among all the piled-
up chattels he got hold of the boy at last and came down the ladder
carrying him. Eirik kicked and sprawled and yelled inside the flap
of his father's kirtle, which Olav had had to wrap about his head
so as not to be bitten by the maddened child.

Ingunn did not look as though he could expect help of her.
Torhild had come in—Olav gave Eirik to her, and the two other
serving-women also took a hand. Eirik fought and screamed in
mortal fear as they struggled to wind a cloth about his head.

Then the father pulled the cloth from the boy's eyes.

"Your life is at stake, Eirik—look at me, boy—you will die, if
you will not let me save you—"

Olav was in a raging tumult. This was the last of her children
and she loved the child as she had never loved him—if she were
to lose Eirik, it would be the end of all. He must and would save
the boy; if it might cost his own life, he must! At the same time
he felt a cruel desire and longing to get home at last on this flesh
that had come between him and her, to maim and burn it—and in
spite of that, something arose from the innermost depths of his being and forbade him to harm the defenceless child.

"Do not scream like that," he yelled in fury. "You wretched
whelp—do not be so afraid—it is no worse than—look here!"

He set the point of his dagger to the lining of the sleeve at his
left wrist and slit and cut till his shirt and the sleeve of his kirtle
hung in tatters right up to the shoulder. He quickly wound the
rags about his arm, so that they should not be in the way, took the
red-hot iron by the tongs, and pressed it against his upper arm.

Eirik had stopped howling from fear and surprise at what his
father was doing; he lay limply in the women's arms and stared.
But now he set up a fresh shriek of terror. Olav had had a vague
idea of putting heart into the boy, but all he had done was to
scare away the rest of his wits: the smell of the scorched flesh, the
sight of the spasm that passed over Olav's face as he withdrew the
iron from the burn, made the boy clean mad. A straight stream of
blood ran down the man's white arm as he let it drop; his dagger
had entered the flesh as he started.

Then all at once Ingunn was there. She was white in the face,
but perfectly calm now as she took the child on her lap, held his
legs tight between her knees, threw the end of her coif across his
face, and caught it under one arm. With her other hand she took
him by the wrist and held the little fist against the table. The
serving-maids helped to hold the boy, smothering his hideous
screams of pain with more cloths, while Olav took off the damaged finger at the inner joint, burnt out the wound, and bound it
up—he did it so rapidly and so neatly as he had never guessed
himself able to accomplish leechcraft.

While the women attended to the wailing child, got him to bed,
and poured strengthening drinks into him, Olav sat on the bench.
Only now did he feel the pain of his burn, and he was ashamed
and furious with himself for being capable of such senseless conduct—maltreating himself to no purpose like a madman.

Torhild came up to him with white of egg in a cup and a box
of fuzz-ball fungus. She was going to tend his arm; but Ingunn
took the things from the serving-woman and pushed her aside:

"I shall tend my husband myself, Torhild—go you out, find a
tuft of grass, and wipe the blood from the table."

Olav stood up and shook himself, as though he would be rid of
both women. "Let be—I can bind this little thing myself," he said
morosely. "And find me some other clothes than these rags."

Eirik recovered rapidly; that day week he was already sitting
up, eating with a good appetite of the dainties his mother brought
him. It looked as though he would escape from the stoat's bite
with no worse harm than the loss of his right little finger.

At first Olav would not allow that the burn on his arm troubled
him; he tried to work and use the arm as if nothing had happened.
Then the wound began to gather and he had to bind up his arm.
After that he had fever, headache, and violent vomiting, and at
last he had to take to his bed and let a man practised in leechcraft
tend his arm. This lasted till near Advent, and Olav was in the
worst of humours. For the first time since they had lived together
he was unfriendly to Ingunn; he constantly used a harsh tone toward her and he would not have a word said as to how he had
met with his hurt.—The housefolk guessed too that he had very
little joy of his wife being with child again.

When Eirik was up and out of doors once more, he talked of

nothing but his misfortune. He was unspeakably proud of his maimed hand and showed it off outside the church to all who cared to see, the first Sunday the people of Hestviken were at mass. He boasted fearfully, both of what his father had done, which seemed to him a mighty exploit, and of his own hardiness —if Eirik was to be believed, he had not let a sound out of him under the ordeal.

" 'Tis my belief that boy is a limb of the Fiend himself, the way he lies," said Olav. "It will end ill with you, Eirik, if you do not give up this evil habit."

I 2

About St. Blaise's Mass [4] they had a guest at Hestviken whom they had never thought to see here: Arnvid Finnsson came to the manor one day. Olav was not at home, and the house-folk did not expect him till after the holy-day.

Olav had a happy look that evening when he came in with his friend—Arnvid had gone out to meet him on the hill. He received the ale-bowl that Ingunn brought, drank to the other, and bade him welcome. But then he saw that Ingunn had been weeping.

Arnvid told him he had brought her heavy tidings: Tora of Berg had died in the autumn. But when Olav heard that Arnvid had already been here for some days, he wondered a little—had she wept over her sister for all that time? They had not been so very closely attached. But, after all, she was her only sister—and maybe at this time her tears flowed more readily than usual.

Ingunn bade them good-night as soon as supper was over. She took Eirik with her and went out—she would lie in the women's little house tonight—"You two would rather sleep together, I ween; you must have many things to speak of."

Olav could not help wondering again: was there any special thing that she thought they wished to speak of so privily? For otherwise she might simply have lain in the closet.

After that their talk went but sluggishly as they sat at their drink. Arnvid spoke of Tora's children—'twas a pity they were all under age. Olav asked after Arnvid's own sons. Arnvid said he

[4] February 3.

had joy of them: Magnus had Miklebö now; he was married, and Steinar was betrothed. Finn had taken vows in the convent of the preaching friars; they said he had good parts, and next year they would surely send him to Paris, to the great school there.

"You never thought of marrying again?"

Arnvid shook his head. He fixed his strange dark eyes upon his friend, smiling feebly and bashfully like a young man who speaks of his sweetheart. "I too shall be found among the friars, once Steinar's wedding is over."

"You are not one to change your mind either," said Olav with a little smile.

"Either—?" said Arnvid involuntarily.

"So you will be father and son in the same convent."

"Yes." Arnvid gave a little laugh. "If God wills, it may be so turned up and down with us that I shall obey my boy and call him father."

They sat in silence for a while. Then Arnvid spoke again:

"It is on the convent's business we are now come south, Brother Vegard and I. We would rebuild our church of stone after the fire, but Bishop Torstein has other use for his craftsmen this year; so we were to see whether we can hire stonemasons in Oslo. But Brother Vegard said that you must do him a kindness and come into the town—and bring Ingunn with you if you could—so that he might see you."

"Ingunn is not fit for any journey—you may guess that.—But he must be as old as the hills now, Brother Vegard?"

"Oh, ay—three and a half score, I believe. He is sacristan now. —Ay, 'twas that I was to say, that you must not fail to come. There was something he must needs say to you"—Arnvid looked down and spoke with a slight effort—"about that axe of yours, the barbed axe. He has found out a deal about it—that it is the same that was once at Dyfrin in Raumarike, at the time your ancestors held the manor."

"I know it," replied Olav.

"Ay, Brother Vegard has heard a whole saga about that axe, he says. In former times it was the way with it, they say, that it sang for a slaying."

Olav nodded. "That I have once heard myself," he said quietly. "That day when I was in the guest house, ready to fare northward —you know, the last time I visited you at Miklebö—"

Arnvid was silent for a while. Then he said in a low voice: "You told me that you had lost your axe on that journey?"

"You think me not such a fool as to set out through the forest with that huge devil of an axe?" Olav laughed coldly. "'Twas a woodcutter's axe; it served me well enough, that one. But true it is, I heard Kinfetch ring—she would fain have gone with me."

Arnvid sat with his arms crossed before him, perfectly silent. Olav had got up and walked uneasily about the hall. Then he came to a sudden stop.

Aloud and as though defiantly he asked: "Was there none who wondered—was nothing rumoured, when that Teit Hallsson disappeared from Hamar so abruptly?"

"Oh—something was said about the matter, no doubt. But folk were satisfied that he must have been afraid of the Steinfinnssons."

"And you? Did you never wonder what had become of him?"

Arnvid said quietly: "It is not easy for me to answer that, Olav."

"I am not afraid to hear what you thought."

"Why do you wish me to say it?" whispered Arnvid reluctantly.

Olav was silent a good while. When he spoke, it was as though he weighed every word; he did not look at his friend meanwhile:

"I trow Ingunn has told you how it has gone with us. I thought it must be because He would that I should offer atonement to the boy for the man I put out of the world. That vagabond"—Olav gave a little laugh—"he was mad enough to imagine he would marry Ingunn—keep her and the child, he said. I *had* to put him out of the way, you can see that—"

"I can see that you thought you had to," replied Arnvid.

"Well, he struck first. It was not that I decoyed the fellow into an ambush. He came of himself, stuck to me like a burr—I was to help him, as a man buys a marriage for his leman when he would be rid of her."

Arnvid said nothing.

Olav went on, hotly: "So said this—a man of his sort—said it of Ingunn!"

Arnvid nodded. Nothing was said between them for a while. Then Arnvid spoke with hesitation:

"They found the bones of a man among the ashes, when they came up in the spring, my tenant of Sandvold; those sæters up there on Luraasen. That must have been he—"

"Oh, the devil! Was it *your* hut? That is well so far—now I can make amends to you for it."

"Oh, no, Olav, stop!" Arnvid rose abruptly and his face contracted. "What is the sense of that? So many long years ago—"

"That is so, Arnvid. And every day I have thought of it, and never have I spoken of it to any living soul until this evening.—Then he was given Christian burial?"

"Yes."

"Then I have not that to grieve over—to think of. I need not have vexed myself with that for all these years—that maybe he still lay there. I have not that sin upon me, that I left a Christian corpse unburied.—And no one asked or made search, who it might be that lay there?"

"No."

"That seems strange."

"Oh, not so strange either. The folk up there are wont to do as I say, when for once I let them know my will."

"But you should not have done that!" Olav wrung his hands hard. "It had been better for me if it had come to light then—if you had not helped me to carry out my purpose, hush the matter up. That *you* could lend your hand to such a thing—you, a God-fearing man!"

Arnvid burst out laughing all at once, laughed so that he had to sit down on the bench. Olav gave a start at the way the other took it; he said heatedly:

"That ugly habit of yours—bursting into a roar of laughter just as one is speaking of—other things—you will have to give that up. I should think, when you are a monk!"

"I suppose I must." Arnvid dried his eyes with his sleeve.

Olav spoke in violent agitation: "*You* have never known what it is to live at enmity with Christ, to stand before Him as a liar and betrayer, every time you enter His house. I have—every day for—ay, 'twill soon be eight years now. Hereabouts they believe me to be a pious man—for I give to the church and to the convent in Oslo and to the poor, as much as I am able, I go to mass as often as I have the means to come thither, and two or three times a day when I am in the town. Thou shall love the Lord thy God with all thy mind and all thy heart, we are told—methinks God must know I *do* so—I knew not that such love was within the power of man until I myself had abandoned His covenant and lost Him!"

"Why do you say this to *me*?" asked Arnvid in distress. "You ought rather to speak to your priest of such things!"

"I cannot do that. I have never made confession that I slew Teit."

As he received no reply, he said hotly: "Answer me! Can you not give me a counsel?"

"It is a great thing you lay upon me. I can give you no other counsel than that which your priest would give you.—I can give you no other counsel than that you know yourself— And that is not the counsel you wish for," he said a moment later, as the other stood silent.

"I cannot." Olav's face turned white, as though congealed. "I must think of Ingunn too—more than of myself. I cannot condemn her to be left alone, poor and joyless and broken in health, the widow of a secret murderer and caitiff."

Arnvid answered doubtfully: "But I trow it is not certain—quite certain it cannot be, that the Bishop could not find a way out—since this happened years ago—and no innocent man has suffered for the misdeed—and the dead man had done you grievous harm, and you fought together. Mayhap the Bishop will find a means of reconciling you with Christ—give you absolution, without demanding that you accuse yourself of the slaying also before human justice."

"That can scarce be very likely?"

"I know not," said Arnvid quietly.

"I cannot venture it. Too much is at stake for those whom it is my duty to protect. Then all that I have done to save her honour might as well have been undone. Think you I did not know that had I proclaimed the slaying there and then, it would have been naught but a small matter?—the man was of no account, alive or dead, and had you then backed me and witnessed she was mine, the woman he had seduced— But Ingunn would not have been equal to it—she could face so little always—and then is every mother's son in these parts to hear this of her now that she is worn out—?"

It was a little while before Arnvid could answer. "It is a question," he said in a low voice, "whether she could face the other thing better. Should it go with her this time as all the other times —that she lose her child again—"

A quiver passed over Olav's features.

"However that may be—she is not fit to go through it many times more."

"You must not speak so," whispered Olav. "Then there is Eirik," he began again, after a pause. "This promise I have made to God Himself, that Eirik should be treated as my own son."

"Think you," asked Arnvid, "that it avails you to offer God this and that—promise Him all that He has never asked of you—when you withhold from Him the only thing you yourself know that He would beg of you?"

"The only thing?—but that is *everything*, Arnvid—honour. Life, maybe. God knows I fear not so much to lose it in other ways—but to lose it as a caitiff—"

"Nevertheless, you have nothing that you have not received of Him. And He Himself submitted to the caitiff's death to atone for all our sins."

Olav closed his eyes. "Nevertheless I cannot—" he said almost inaudibly.

Arnvid rejoined: "You spoke of Eirik. Know you not, Olav, you have not the right to act in this way—to make a promise to set aside an heir—since by so doing you play your kinsmen false."

Olav frowned in anger. "Those men of Tveit—never have I seen them, and they did not deal by me as kinsmen when I was young and had sore need of their coming forward."

"They came forward after you had fled to Sweden."

"And they might just as well have stayed where they were, for all the good I had of them. Nay, then I should rather let her son take Hestviken."

"That will not make wrong right, Olav.—And neither you nor she can know whether it will tend to the boy's happiness that you two make him a gift that he has no right to receive."

"Oh, ay, I thought as much: she has been talking to you of what is in her head—that I hate her child and wish him ill. 'Tis not true," he said hotly. "I have never had aught else in mind for Eirik but his own good—'tis she who corrupts him; she trains him to be afraid of me, to lie and sneak out of my way—"

On seeing the expression in Arnvid's face he shook his head. "Nay, nay, I blame her not for that—Ingunn knows no better, poor woman. I have not changed my mind either, Arnvid. Do you remember, I promised you once that I would never fail your kinswoman? And I have never regretted it—in whatever shape my

last hour may come, I shall thank God that He held my hand
when I was tempted to do harm to *her*—showed me, ere it was too
late, that I must protect and support her as well as I was able.
Even if I had come back and found her stricken with leprosy, I
could have done no less than remember that she was my dearest
friend—the only friend I had in all the years I was a child and
brought up among strangers."

Arnvid said calmly: "If you think, Olav, that it would make
it easier for you to judge what you ought to do in order to make
your peace with God, should you be unable to care for those
belonging to you, I promise to be as a brother to Ingunn, to provide for her and the boy. I shall take them under my roof, if need
be—"

"But you have given up Miklebö to Magnus. And you yourself
will enter the convent—" Olav said it almost with a touch of scorn.

"Thereby I have not parted with my whole estate. And if I
have endured the world so long, I doubt not I can endure it to my
dying day, if it must be—while my near kinsfolk need me by
them."

"Nay, nay," said Olav as before. "I will not have you think of
the like for my sake or for the sake of any who are properly in
my care."

Arnvid sat gazing into the dying embers on the hearth, feeling
the presence of his friend in the gloom. "I wonder if he does not
see himself that it is no small burden he has thrown upon me tonight," he thought.

Olav pulled a stool toward him with his foot and sat down by
the hearth, facing his friend.

"Now I have told you much, but not that which I had it in my
mind to say: I have told you that I yearn, day and night, to be
reconciled with the Lord Christ—I have told you that never did
our Lord seem to me so lovable beyond all measure as when I
knew that He had marked me with the brand of Cain. But I marvel that I yearn so, for never have I seen Him so hard on other
men as on me. *I* have wrought this one misdeed; and then I was
so—incensed—that I do not now recall what were my thoughts at
the time; but I did it because I judged that 'twould be even worse
for Ingunn if I did it not—I would save a poor remnant of respect
for her, even if it cost me a murder. And then it all came about as
easily as if it had been laid out for me—*he* begged me to take him

on that journey; no man was aware that we set out together. But had God or my patron or Mary Virgin directed our way to some man's house that evening and not to those deserted sæters under Luraas—you know it would have fallen out otherwise."

"I scarce think you had prayed God and the saints to watch over your journey, ere you set out?"

"I am not so sure that I did not—nay, *prayed* I had not truly. But all that Easter I had done nothing but pray—and I was so loath to kill him, all the time. But it was as though all things favoured me, so that I was driven to do it—and tempted to conceal it afterwards. And God, who knows all, He knew how this must turn out, better than I—why could not He have checked me nevertheless, without my prayers—?"

"So say we all, Olav, when we have accomplished our purpose and then see that it would have been better if we had not. But beforehand I ween you think like the rest of us, that you are the best judge of your own good."

"Ay, ay. But in all else beyond what this deed has brought in its train I have dealt uprightly with every man, to the best of my power. I have no goods in my possession that were come by unjustly, so far as I know; I have not spread ill report of man or woman, but have let all such talk fall to the ground when it reached my door, even though I knew it to be true and no lie. I have been faithful to my wife, and 'tis *not* as she thinks, that I bear the boy ill will—I have been as good to Eirik as most men are to their own sons. Tell me, Arnvid, you who understand these thinks better than I—you have been a pious man all the days of your life and have shown compassion to all—am I not right when I say that God is harder on me than on other men? I have seen more of the world than you"—Arnvid was sitting so that Olav could not see him smile at these words—"in the years when I was an outlaw, with my uncle, and afterwards, when I was the Earl's liegeman. I have seen men who loaded themselves with all the seven deadly sins, who committed such cruel deeds as I would not set my hand to, even if I knew of a surety that God had already cast me off and doomed me to hell. They were not afraid of God, and I never marked that they thought of Him with love or longing to obtain His forgiveness—and yet they lived in joy and contentment, and they had a good death, many of them, as I myself have seen.

"Then why can we have no peace or joy, she and I? It is as though God pursued me, wherever I may go, vouchsafing me no peace or rest, but demanding of me such impossible things as I have never seen Him demand of other men."

"How should I be able to give you answers to such questions, I, a layman?—Olav, can you not go with me to the town and speak with Brother Vegard of this?"

"Maybe I will do so," said Olav in a low voice. "But you must tell me first—can you understand why it is to be made so much harder for me than for other men?"

"You do not know everything about the other men you speak of, either. But you must be able to see that, if you feel that God pursues you, it is because He would not lose you."

"But He has so ordered it for me that I cannot turn about."

"Surely it was not God who ordered it so for you?"

"Nay, but I have not brought it about myself either—I had to do what I did, it seems to me; Ingunn's life and welfare were laid in my hands. But that which was the cause of all this, Arnvid— that the Steinfinnssons would steal from me the marriage that had been promised to my father—should I have been content with that—bowed before such injustice? I have never heard aught else but that God commands every Christian man to fight against wrong and law-breaking. I was a child in years, unlearned in the law—I knew no other way to defend my right than to take my bride myself, ere they could give her to another."

Arnvid said reluctantly: "That was the answer you gave me when I—spoke to you of your dealings with my kinswoman. Do you remember yet, Olav, that—that you did not speak the truth that time?"

Olav raised his head with a jerk, taken by surprise. He paused a moment with his reply. "No.—And I believe," he said calmly, "most men would have done the same in my place."

"That is sure."

"Do you think," asked Olav scornfully, "that God's hand has pressed so hard upon me—and upon her—because I lied that time —to you?"

"I cannot tell."

Olav gave a fretful toss of his head. "I cannot believe that it was so grievous a sin. So many a man have I heard tell worse lies— needlessly—and never did I see that God raised a finger to chastise him. So I cannot understand His justice, which deals so hardly with me!"

Arnvid whispered: "You must have petty thoughts of God if you expect His justice to be the same as man's. Not two of us outlawed children of Eve did He create alike—should He then demand the same fruits of all His creatures, to whom He has given such diverse talents?—When first I knew you, in your youth, I judged you to be most truthful, upright, and generous; there was no cruelty or deceit in you, but God had given you a heritage of brave and faithful ancestors—"

Olav rose to his feet in violent agitation. "Methinks that if it were so—. If 'tis as you say—and truly I have often shrunk from doing what other men do every day, without a care, for smaller matters— Methinks that what you call God's gifts might just as well be called a burden not to be borne, which He laid upon my back when He created me!"

Arnvid leaped up in his turn. He moved forward to the other and stood before him, almost threateningly. "So many a man may say that of the nature he was given; unless he have a faith firm as a rock in his Redeemer, he must think himself born the most unfortunate of men." He put his foot on the edge of the hearth; with his hand resting on his knee he stood bending forward and looked down at the embers. "You often wondered that I longed to turn my back upon the world—I who had riches in abundance, and more power than I cared to use—and some respect withal. Pious you say I have been, and compassionate to all— God knows if you do not deem it must be because I *love* my even Christians!"

"I believed you helped every man who sought your aid because you were—meek of heart—and pitied everyone who was in any —difficulty—"

"Pitied—oh yes. Many a time I was tempted to reproach my Creator because He had made me so that I *could* do naught else— I had to pity all, though I could love none—"

"I believed," said Olav very low, "that you—supported me and Ingunn with deed and counsel because you were our friend. Was it only for *God's* sake you held your hand over us?"

Arnvid shook his head. "It was not. I was fond of you from our childhood, and Ingunn has been dear to me since she was a little maid. Nevertheless I was often so mortally weary of all this—it came over me that I desired more than all else to be rid once for all of this suit of yours."

"You might have let me know this," said Olav stiffly. "Then I should have troubled you far less."

Again Arnvid shook his head. " 'Tis you and Ingunn who were ever my best friends. But I *am* not pious and I am not good. And often I was weary of it all—wished I could transform myself and become a hard man, if I could not be meek and let God judge mankind, not me. There was once a holy man in France, an anchorite; he had taken upon himself a work of charity for the love of God, that he would harbour folk who fared through the forest where he dwelt. One night there came a beggar who sought shelter with the anchorite—Julian was his name, I think. The stranger was full of leprosy, grievously tainted with the sickness, gross and foul of mouth—returned ill thanks for all the kindness the anchorite showed him. Then Julian undressed the beggar, washed and tended his sores and kissed them, put him to bed— but the beggar made as though he was cold and bade Julian lie close and warm him. Julian did so. But then his foulness and ugliness and evil speech slipped from the stranger as it were a disguise —and Julian saw that he had embraced Christ Himself.

"It has been my lot that, when I thought I could not bear all these folk who came to me, lied and threw the burden of their affairs on me, begged advice and acted as seemed good to themselves, but blamed me when things went wrong, greedy and envious of everyone they thought had been better helped—it was borne in upon me that they must be disguised, and that under the disguise it would one day be granted to me to see my Saviour and my Friend Himself. And indeed it was so in a way—since He said that everything ye do unto one of My little ones— But never would He throw off the disguise and appear to me in the person of any of them."

Olav had seated himself on the stool again, hiding his face in his arms.

Arnvid said in a yet lower voice: "Do you remember, Olav, what Einar Kolbeinsson said that evening—the words that goaded me so that I drew my weapon upon him?"

Olav nodded.

"You were so young at that time—I knew not whether you had guessed their meaning."

"I guessed it later."

"And afterwards, those rumours of Ingunn and me—?"

"Hallvard said something of that—when I was north to fetch the boy."

Arnvid drew a couple of deep breaths. "I am not so holy but that I took it greatly to heart, both one thing and the other. And I often thought God might have granted me my only prayer—given me leave to serve Him in such guise that I dared work deeds of compassion, as far as I was able, without folk whispering behind my back and defaming me or calling me a sanctimonious fool. Or believe the worst of me, because I took to myself neither wife nor leman after Tordis's death." He struck out with his fist and brought it down on the other hand with a crack. "Often I had a good mind to take my axe and make an end of the whole pack!"

Thereafter, during the two days Arnvid yet stayed at Hest-viken, the friends were shy and taciturn with each other. It pained them both that they had said far too much that evening; now it seemed they could not talk freely of the simplest trifles.

Olav rode with Arnvid a part of the way up the fiord, but when they were halfway to the town he said he must turn back. He drew out something from the folds of his kirtle—a hard thing, wrapped in a linen cloth. Arnvid could feel that it must be the silver cup that Olav had shown him a day or two before. Olav said he was to give it to the convent at Hamar.

"But so great a gift you ought to place yourself in the hands of Brother Vegard," thought Arnvid.

Olav replied that he must be home that evening—"but it may be that I come in to Oslo one day to greet him."

Arnvid said: "You know full well, Olav, that it is vain to seek to buy your atonement with gifts, so long as you live as you do now."

"I know it—'tis not for that. But I had a mind to give to their church—many a happy hour have I had in the old Olav's Church."

So they bade each other farewell and rode their ways.

Olav did not come to Oslo. Arnvid spoke with Brother Vegard about it, saying that he was doubtless unwilling to come while Ingunn was unfit to accompany him. But she had grieved so much that she could not see the instructor of her youth while he dwelt so near, Arnvid proposed that the monk should borrow a sledge and drive south to Hestviken one day. Brother Vegard was well minded to make the journey, but he had been so unwell and full of rheum ever since he came to Oslo. By Peter's Mass [5] a hard frost set in. A few days after, the old man fell suddenly sick of a fever in the lungs and died the third night. Thereafter Arnvid had to deal single-handed with the hiring of the stonemasons, and it took up all his time, until he had to take the north road again.

Olav got Ingunn to keep her bed in the daytime when the weather turned so cold: she was scarcely able to move now, so far gone was she, and then her feet were frostbitten so that there were great open holes in the flesh. Olav tended them himself and smeared foxes' fat and swine's gall on the sores. Ever since Arnvid's departure he had been gentle and solicitous with his wife; he had quite put off the cross and unfriendly air that he had shown her during the autumn and winter.

Ingunn lay huddled under the skins, whispering a little word of humble thanks whenever Olav did anything for her. She had bowed beneath his displeasure and harsh words, silent and submissive; now she accepted his affectionate care with almost the same dumb meekness. Olav kept an eye on her privily as she lay motionless by the hour together, staring out into the room, almost without blinking. And the old, wild fear rose up in his heart, as hot as ever—it was no matter if he had neither use nor joy of her; he could not lose her.

Ingunn was glad to be allowed to creep thus into hiding. She had come to feel it as an unbearable disgrace every time she was to have a child. Even before she had her first two she had been distressed and shy, because it made her so ugly—Dalla's insults had bitten into her mind so that she never got over them. She winced when she had to appear before Olav—and when he was away from her, she felt as though she could not sustain herself without his sound health close at hand to draw strength from.

But as time went on and it proved that she could not bring into life a single one of these creatures who came and dwelt in her, one after the other, she was filled with a horror of her own body. She

[5] February 22.

must be marked in some mysterious way, with something as terrible as leprosy, so that she infected her unborn infants with death. Her blood and marrow were spent, her youth and charm wasted long ago by these uncanny guests who lived their hidden life beneath her heart for a while and then went out. Till she felt the first warning grip as of a claw in her back, and had to let herself be led by strange women to the little house on the east of the courtyard, give herself into their hands without daring to show a sign of the mortal dread that filled her heart. And when she had fought through it, she lay back, empty of blood and empty of everything—the child was as it were swallowed up by the night, taken back into a gloom where she had not even a name or a memory to look for. The last premature births the women had not even let her see.

And yet she sometimes thought that it was even worse with Audun. When she lost the year-old child, he had already shown in many ways that he knew her for his mother; he would not be with others than her, and he was so fond of her. But he must be so still. When they sang in the litany: *Omnes sancti Innocentes, orate pro nobis*, Audun was one of them. In purgatory she would know that Audun was one of the holy Innocents who prayed for her. And when her hour of grace arrived, perhaps our Lord Himself or His blessed Mother would say to Audun: "Run down now and meet your mother."

How it might go with her this time, she tried hard not to think.

But when the men came in at mealtimes, Olav and Eirik together, a deep, uneasy tension came to life in the sick woman's great lustreless eyes. Olav noticed how wide awake she was, watching every movement of his features, listening to every word he spoke, when he was with the boy. And he always kept a guard over himself, taking care not to show it, when he was impatient or annoyed with Eirik.

The boy was troublesome enough; Olav liked him but moderately, now that he was big enough to show his nature. Noisy, full of boasting and idle tales, he chattered more than becomes a youth; not even when the men sat over their food, tired and worn out, could Eirik keep his mouth shut. There was that Arnketil, or Anki, as they called him. Olav had had him in his service some six years, and the man was now well on in the twenties, but he had

poor parts, might indeed be called almost half-witted, though he
was useful for many kinds of work. He had always been Eirik's
best friend. They quarrelled—half in jest—raising their voices, till
Eirik flew at Anki as he sat on the bench, pushing and pulling him
till he got him to join in the game; they thrust each other hither
and thither about the room, laughing and screaming and shouting
without a thought of the other men who sat there and wanted
rest and quiet. Grossly disobedient he was too; whether his father
taught him something or forbade him to do this or that, he forgot
it at once.

And Olav was angry that Eirik did not show his mother more
affection. He was himself aware of the unreasonableness of this:
formerly he had felt a secret exasperation when he knew that
mother and son clung together behind his back. But now it made
him angry to see Eirik spend the whole day out of doors among
the men, never going in to sit by his sick mother. Olav himself had
taught the boy his prayers some years ago—when he saw that Ingunn did not seem to think it was yet time. Now he made Eirik
say a Paternoster and three Aves for his mother every evening,
when he had prayed for himself. The boy gabbled off his prayers
while his father stood over him—Eirik rose to his feet before he
had finished the last Ave; at *In nomine* he was up on the bed,
hastily crossed himself, and plunged headlong beneath the skins
in the northern bed, which he shared with his father. He was
asleep in an instant, and when Olav had finished smearing Ingunn's
feet, he found Eirik curled up in the middle of the bed, so that
he had to straighten him out and push him against the wall to
make room for himself.

At times Olav felt a stab of pain when Eirik sought him out
with his foolish talk, boasting of his little, unhandy attempts to
make himself useful among the men—"If only the boy had been
so that I could have liked him." In his innocent stupidity Eirik
seemed never to guess that his father was not so fond of his company as he was of his father's. But Olav had taken his resolution:
he had acknowledged this child and raised him up in order to set
him in the high seat here at Hestviken in succession to himself—
though God knew Eirik was unpromising material for a great
franklin and the head of a manor: the boy seemed to be a loose-
tongued chatterer, untruthful, boasting and cowardly, lacking in

hardiness, and born with little sense of seemliness and quiet good manners. But he would have to do what he could to teach Eirik good behaviour and drive the bad habits out of him—even if he had to let the discipline wait till Ingunn was stronger—so that the lad might learn to comport himself as became Eirik Olavsson of Hestviken.

Some years before, herds of deer had moved into the districts on the west side of Folden, and there were now not a few deer on Olav's land—they were to be found up in Kverndal, on the ridge of the Bull and in Olav's oak wood, which lay inland, toward the church town. The summer before, they had grown so much fodder in Hestviken that they had stacks of hay and dried leaves standing in the open. Now, in late winter, the deer came as far as the manor in the early morning to snatch what they could of the fodder. Hiding behind some timber that lay in the yard, Olav one morning shot a fine young stag of ten points. Eirik was then quite wild to go with him—he would bring down a stag too.

Olav laughed a little at the boy's chatter. The next few days the wind was off the fiord and he made Anki go out in the morning so that the deer might get scent of him and keep off the hay, and Eirik was allowed to go with them. The boy lay stiff with cold—with bow and spear by him— but when he came in he made out that he had both seen and heard the red deer.

Then one night Olav woke up and went to the outer door to see the time. It was two hours to daybreak, intensely cold and a dead calm—with the faintest breath from the east down Kverndal. In the early morning the deer would certainly come down and take tithe of the stacks. Olav dressed in the dark, but in order to choose his arrows he had to light a torch. That waked Eirik—and the end of it was that his father gave him leave to go with him, but he was not allowed a weapon.

As soon as they had crept into hiding behind the timber stacks, Olav had hard work to keep the boy quiet. Eirik forgot himself every minute and would whisper. Then he fell asleep. He had on a thick leathern jacket of his father's; Olav wrapped it well about the child, so that he should not get frostbites—it was bitterly cold just before dawn—and thought with satisfaction that now Eirik could do no harm.

Olav had a long time to wait. The eastern sky was already turning yellow above the forest when he espied the deer coming out of the thicket. Four dark spots moved against the dun-coloured ground; patches of it were clear of snow. Now and again they stopped, looked about and sniffed the air—now he could see that they were a stag, two does, and a calf.

Excitement and joy warmed his stiffened body as he rose on one knee, took his bow, and laid an arrow to the string. He held his breath. The stag came on, proud and stately—now he saw it against a snowdrift. It climbed onto an old balk of sods—stood there with feet close together: the neck and head with the antlers showed clearly against the yellow sky. Olav gave a noiseless gasp of joy—he had not met this old fellow before: a mighty beast, full-shouldered, with a great crown of antlers, fifteen or sixteen points, no less. It moved its head this way and that, spying out. It was a rather long shot, but the target was just right: Olav took his aim, and his heart laughed with joy—he felt too that Eirik was on the point of waking.

The boy started up with a shout—he too had seen those glorious horns against the sky. Olav sent his arrow after the flying deer, chanced to graze the shoulder, making the stag leap high into the air—it went on in flying leaps and the whole herd disappeared in the thicket.

Eirik received a couple of hearty cuffs on the side of the head—he took them with a little gasp, but did not cry out; he had wit enough to be ashamed of what he had done and did not cry out; besides, the thick leather cap he wore must have deadened the blows.

"Say nothing to your mother about this," said Olav, as they went back to the houses. "She need not know that you can behave yourself like an untaught puppy, old as you are."

Later in the day Olav followed the blood-tracks of the stag with his hound, found the deer, and killed it on the hillside at the top of Kverndal. And when the quarry was brought home at evening, Eirik went about boasting—it was he who had warned his father when the great stag came within range.

Olav did not care to say a word to the boy—he was afraid of losing his temper.

The seal now came in thickly on the approach of spring, and the farmers of the country round took their boats out to the edge of the ice and went seal-hunting in the south of the fiord. Olav let Eirik go with him, but the result was not very happy; the massacre of seals and the brisk life among the hunters made him wild with excitement. It was quite incredible that the boy should have so little idea of how to behave anywhere in seemly fashion. But on coming home again he had the most extraordinary tales to tell. It was not easy for Olav to listen to the boy's talk without losing patience.

St. Gregory's Day [6] brought a change of weather, southerly winds and rain—this was thought to presage a good year both on land and on sea.

On the morrow Ingunn was lying alone in the house early in the day. It was fairly dark indoors, for the smoke-vent was closed; it was raining outside.

Olav came in. He sat down on the bench, drew off his boots, struggled out of his jerkin and shirt, and opened his clothes-chest to find other garments.

"Are you asleep, Ingunn?" he asked with his back toward her. "How is it with you?" he said when she whispered in reply, no, she was not asleep.

"Oh, well. Will you ride out?"

Olav said yes, the Thing at Vidanes was summoned for today. He came up to the bed, naked to the waist, and put one foot on the step. "Must I change my hose, think you?"

Ingunn involuntarily drew her head away. "Indeed you must— they smell so ill."

"They will scarce smell sweeter, the other men who come there —we have been out seal-hunting day and night of late, all of us."

"But if you are to meet strangers from other parts—" suggested Ingunn.

"Ay, ay, as you will." He drew off his breeks and hose, stood quite naked, stretched himself and yawned.

The sight of his faultlessly shaped body hurt her, it made her own ravaged wretchedness so hopeless. That time was so impossibly long past when she had been young and lovely, when they were well matched—but Olav was yet a young man, sound and handsome. His muscles were more knotted than of old, chiefly about the shoulder-blades and upper arms; they moved freely and powerfully as he stretched himself, raising his arms and lowering them. His flesh was still white as milk.

[6] March 12.

He came back to his wife when he had put on his red woollen shirt, long hose of black leather, and linen breeks.

"Then I must wear the blue kirtle too, think you—since you will have me so tricked out?" he asked with a smile.

"Olav—?" As he bent over her, she suddenly threw her thin arms around his neck and drew him down to her, pressing her face against his cheek. Olav felt that she was trembling.

"What is it?" he whispered. She only clung to him and made no answer.

"Are you sick?" He loosed her arms from about his neck; it was so uncomfortable to stand bent double. "Would you have me stay at home today? I can ride to Rynjul and fetch Una to you— at the same time ask Torgrim to speak for me at Vidanes."

"No, no." She pressed his hand hard in hers. "No—there will be no change with me till mid-spring be past. But stay with me a little while"—it came as a faint moan. "Sit here a little while, if you have the time."

"That I may well do." He held her hand, stroking her arm. "What is it with you, Ingunn? Are you so afraid—?" he asked quietly.

"Nay. Yes. Nay, I know not that I am so afraid, but—" Olav pushed the step out of his way, sat on the edge of the bed, and patted her wasted cheek, time after time.

"I had a dream," said his wife softly. "Just before you came in."

"Was it an evil dream, then?"

The tears began to pour down her cheeks, but she wept without a sound; only her voice was more veiled and broken:

"It seemed not evil while I dreamed it—*then* it was not evil. I saw you, walking along a path in a forest; you looked happy and seemed younger than you are now; you sang as you walked. I saw you here at Hestviken too, out in the yard, and it was the same, you looked happy and well. I could see it all, but it was as though I myself was not—I was dead, I knew. Children I saw not here— not one."

"Ingunn, Ingunn, you must not lie here thinking such thoughts." He knelt down so that he could get his arm in under her shoulder. "There would be little joy for me here in our house were I to lose you, Ingunn mine."

"A joy for you I have never been—"

"You are the only friend I have." He kissed her, bending lower over his wife, so that her face was quite hidden against his breast.

"If now it is as Signe and Una say," he whispered, hesitating, "that you are to have a daughter this year— They were all sons till now. But a little maid—her maybe God would let us keep."

The sick woman sighed: "I am so weary—"

Olav whispered: "Have you never thought, Ingunn—that maybe I have paid Eirik no more than—the price of his father's slaying?"

As he received no answer, he asked her—and he could not make his voice sound quite firm: "Have you never wondered what became of—that Teit?" She clasped him closer. "I never believed that you did it."

The man felt strangely overpowered—as though he had suddenly come into a bright light and were trying to distinguish things in it. She had *known* it, all the time. But what did that mean —had she guessed what was on his mind, or had she been afraid of his blood-stained hands—?

Ingunn turned her face to his, clasped his neck, and drew his head down to her. She kissed him on the lips, with a wild gulp. "I knew it. I knew it. Yet I was afraid, sometimes—when things were at their worst with me and I almost lost heart. I could not help it— I thought, what if he were alive and came after me, avenged himself. But indeed I believed you had done it, and I could feel safe from him!"

Olav had a queer feeling—as though numb or frozen. Was *that* what she had thought?—ay, ay. Perhaps that was all she could take in, poor thing. He kissed her again, a gentle little kiss. Then he said with a laugh of embarrassment:

"You must let me go now, Ingunn—you will break my ribs against the bedpost soon."

He got up, patted her cheek once more, and crossed the room to his chest, searched among the clothes. Then he asked again:

"Are you sure, Ingunn—should you not rather I stayed at home today?"

"Nay, nay, Olav, I will not keep you."

Olav buckled on his spurs, took his sword, and threw his raincloak of thick, felted homespun over his shoulder. He was already at the door—when he turned and came back to her bed.

Ingunn could see that a change had come over him and he was

not as she had seen him for a long, long time—his face was still as a rock, his lips pale, his eyes veiled, unseeing. He spoke as though in his sleep:

"Will you promise me one thing? Should it go with you as— as you said—should it cost your life this time—will you give me your promise that you will *come back* to me?" He looked at her, bending slightly toward her. "You must promise me, Ingunn—if it is so that the dead may come back to the living—then you must come to me!"

"Yes."

The man bent down hastily, touching her breast with his forehead an instant.

"You are the only friend I have had," he whispered quickly and shyly.

Olav came riding home late in the evening, wet and cold, so that he could not feel his feet in the stirrups. His horse trotted wearily, splashing the snow-slush over him at every beat of the hoofs.

Clouds and fog rolled over the landscape, the earth breathed moisture—it was an evening of steaminess and mist, the whole world strangely dissolved, forest and field bare and dark in patches among the melting snow. The fiord spoke in dull surf-beats with long intervals, like a sluggish pulse, but the stream in Kverndal roared with a glut of water. A sigh went through the woods as the firs shed their snow, and water purled and gurgled everywhere in the dusk—the cold scent from the fields and the sea brought the first reminder of springtime and growth.

On the hillside by the barn a dark figure came toward him—a woman in a hooded cloak.

"Welcome home, Olav!" It was Signe Arnesdatter; she hurried to meet him as he drew nearer.

"Ay, now Ingunn is over it for this time—and she does better than we had looked for." Olav had reined in his horse, and Signe caressed its muzzle. "And the child is so big and fine—none of us has even seen so big and fair a new-born babe. So you must bear with it that 'tis not a son!"

Olav thanked her for the good news, feeling that, had he been as in his younger years, he would have leaped from his horse, embraced his kinswoman, and kissed her. He *was* relieved and he *was* glad, but as yet he did not *feel* it to the full. Then he thanked Signe again for the kindness she had shown once more to Ingunn.

It had come upon her so suddenly, said Signe, that they had not been able to take her out to the women's house. Olav would have to put up with sleeping in the closet while they had the cradle and kept watch in the great room.

But in a moment he saw Ingunn herself—her face shone snow-white, she lay on her side with one light-brown plait showing from under her cheek. Una knelt behind her in the bed, plaiting her other thick rope of hair. The other times Olav had seen her lying thus, she had been ugly, swollen and blotched in the face—but now she was unlike herself, marvellously fair, as if an unearthly light were shed upon her white and wasted countenance. Her great dark-blue eyes glittered like starlight mirrored in a well. And the thought sank into the man that a miracle had taken place.

Signe came with a little bundle—white swaddling-bands wound crosswise about the leaf-green woollen wrapper. She laid the child in Olav's arm. "Have you ever seen so fair a maid, kinsman?"

And again it was as though he had fallen among incredible things—a girl's face, impossibly small, but perfect, the fairest! A new-born life, and it could look like that. Her eyes were open; dark they were and bottomless—and she was red and white like a brier-rose and had nose and mouth like a human being, but so small that he could not understand it.

Signe drew the swaddling-cloth aside so that the father might see that she had fine hair too. Olav cupped his hand under the delicate, round head: it lay in his palm no larger than an apple and as sweet and soft to hold.

Olav still held his little daughter in his hands—a gift, a gift she was. It softened him—so grateful beyond measure he had never been before. He laid his face against the baby's breast—her face was so pure and fine that he durst not touch it.

Una leaped to the floor, arranged Ingunn on her back, with the plaits over her bosom. They took the child from him, and he sat down on the edge of the bed by his wife. He held her hand in his for a while and took up one of her plaits; neither of them said anything.

Then a maid came in with food and drink for him, and after-

wards they said that he must go into the closet and lie down—
Ingunn needed sleep. Then she called to him softly.

"Olav," she whispered, "there is one thing I would beg of you,
husband"—at other times she never called him that—"will you do
what I ask of you?"

"I will do all you ask of me." He smiled as in pain, so unmanned was he by his joy.

"Promise me that she shall not be called after my mother. Cecilia
I would have her named."

Olav nodded.

He lay awake in the darkness—against the wall Eirik was sleeping like a stone. Through the door opening he could see the reflection of the fire flickering on the logs of the wall; it rose and sank.
But the holy candle burning beside the mother and child shed a
mild and golden light.

The watching women whispered and went about their work,
clattering with the kettle and the pot-hook. Once the new-born
child began to cry—and her cries called to his heart; he listened
to her and was tender and happy. The women got on their feet;
the cradle was set rocking, and Signe sang softly.

Here he lay before her door; it seemed as natural as a dream
that he should lie and listen while they watched over her sleep.
Ingunn slept sweetly now; she had given birth to a child, and now
she was to take a long rest, which would make her young and
healthy and happy again. A child had been born here in his house,
the first one. All that had gone before had been as one endless,
unnatural sickness—an uncanny spell upon the unhappy woman.
The little lifeless deformities that the women had brought to him
that he might see them, though he was so loath to do so—the sight
of them had filled him with infinite disgust; and the poor little
abortion that had lived his brief, tormented life, until God had
pity on him and took him to Himself—in his heart he had never
been able to acknowledge that these were his children—the fruit
of his and Ingunn's bodies.

Never had he known how it felt to be a father—till now, when
he had a daughter, a treasure like this little, little—Cecilia.

I 3

CECILIA OLAVSDATTER grew and throve so that the neighbours' wives said they could see a difference in her from day to day. What fattened her none could guess, for the mother would nurse her at her own breast, and there she could hardly suck many drops of milk. But that she grew more in one month than other infants in three was the boast of Signe and Una. Now and then they poured cream into her, or let her chew at deer's marrow in a cloth.

Folk who came out to Hestviken asked to see this little maid whose fame was already abroad—she was so peerlessly fair. They let it be seen that they wished Olav and his wife well of their happiness. True, there was none who liked the Hestvik folk very well. Olav was strangely reserved, a man of few friends—folk thought it a trouble if they had to be in company with this cross-stick—but no doubt this was mostly his manner: one had to admit that in his actions he had always shown himself an upright and pious man, by no means unhelpful either. The wife was incapable and weak-minded, but indeed she wished nobody ill, poor thing. So it was a happy thing after all that at last they had gotten a child that looked as if it would grow up.

But Ingunn continued poorly for a long time—she must have suffered some hurt in her back, and she could not regain power over her legs, when at last she was up again.

One Sunday when Olav came home from church, it was such fine weather—that day summer had come. In the fair-weather breeze the leaves and green meadows gleamed with light, and every puff of air was like a warm and healthy breath from the growing grass and the new foliage and from the earth, which still had the moisture of spring within it. When he entered the house and saw Ingunn lying outstretched on the bench, he was a little uneasy; then he said that when they had broken their fast she must go out with him and look at the "good acre," the corn there was coming up so thick and fine this year again.

This was the field that lay farthest out toward the fiord under the crags; Olav had a peculiar affection for it and always chose the best and heaviest corn to sow there. He had fishes' heads and offal from the quay brought there, and it suffered less from drought than was to be expected—for the mould was not very deep—but it was ready for reaping before any of the other fields of Hestviken.

Olav had to carry Ingunn over the threshold, and when he had set her down outside the door, he saw that she walked as though she could not lift her feet—she slid them along the ground in short, uncertain jerks, and at the slightest obstacle she nearly fell forward. He took her by the waist and she leaned heavily against him, with one hand on his shoulder; at every third or fourth step she had to pause, and he noticed that she was sweating profusely and trembling with fatigue.

On arriving at the look-out rocks Olav spread his fur-lined winter cloak, which he had brought with him, in a hollow among the rocks. There she could lie in shelter and watch the breeze caressing the young blades of corn as though currying them, sending flames of light down the green slope.

Sea and land were all aglitter; the summer waves ran in toward the rocks, splashed, and trickled back with the pebbles of the beach—the sound of the surf was a gentle murmur; but farther off under the Bull the spray was thrown higher; the wind was going round to the south-west now. Olav sat following with his eyes a heavily laden trading vessel that was making her way up the fiord, rather fast. He was lost in thought; old memories floated before him of the time when he was an outlaw and free as a bird—knew nothing of bearing another's burdens. Alone he had been, one man among many others, who were never so near to him that he felt their pressure—it was strangely far away now, after all these years he had had the whole of Hestviken depending on him, and his sick wife as close to him as his own flesh. He had struggled on with her, who was always infirm and suffering; it was like fighting with one arm hanging broken and useless. Nevertheless he did not feel unhappy as he sat here in the midday sun—he did not think of the old days in such a way that he wished himself away from the present or fretted at his lot with Ingunn. He sat and took his rest—in a kind of melancholy, but even that which oppressed him was his infinite affection for her; it seemed too great for him to carry it alone.

He turned to Ingunn, was going to say something about the vessel; then he saw that she had fallen asleep. She looked like one dead.

He felt with wonder that he was even fonder of her now than
he had ever been before—just because he could see that every trace
of her beauty was so utterly destroyed. No one who had not seen
her in her youth could imagine that this middle-aged, faded wife
had once been fair. She had been lovely, as a pure and delicate
flower is lovely—now the yellow skin, flecked with brown patches,
was drawn tightly over her hollow-cheeked and long-chinned
face. Her tall and slender form had long lost its willowy suppleness: she was flat as a board over the narrow chest, heavy and
shapeless about the waist—looked like an aged and worn-out cottar's wife who has borne many children.

The husband sat and looked at her—not daring to touch her; she
must be in need of sleep. He merely took the ends of her linen coif
and tucked them in, lest the wind should blow them in her face,
and wrapped the cloak better about her—she looked so bloodless
that he must not let her take cold.

Both Olav and the house-folk saw that she was less able to walk
day by day, and about the time of St. John's Mass she could not
get up from her seat without help, nor push one foot before the
other without someone to support her. But still they dressed her
every morning; it was Torhild who had to do this now, for Liv,
Ingunn's own maid, was fit for nothing at this time.

Olav had never been able to understand Ingunn's obstinate dislike of Torhild Björnsdatter in all these years. Torhild was a
woman whose match was not often to be met—loyal, capable, and
strong—and however unreasonable Ingunn might be with the
housekeeper, Torhild remained as patient and attentive as ever
toward her sick mistress.

Equally incomprehensible did it appear to Olav that she should
have taken a fancy to this Liv, who had entered her service the
year before. For one thing, the girl was almost the ugliest being
Olav had ever seen: at the first glance one was tempted to doubt
whether she was human—undersized, hugely broad, and notably
squat and bandy-legged. Her red hair was thin and straggling, her
skin·was a reddish grey, with freckles over her arms and hands
and down to her chest, and her face was marvellously hideous,
with little blinking pig's eyes, a pointed nose, and no chin—the
lower part of her face slanted in and made one with the flabby
flesh of her throat. Nor was she of kindly disposition—lazy and

unwilling with Torhild and the dairymaid, and exceedingly stupid.
But Ingunn had set her affection on this girl. When it came out
that she had gone astray the autumn before, when she was given
leave to go home and visit her parents at Michaelmas, her mistress
besought Olav not to turn Liv out of the house. Olav had had no
such thought; he knew that there was great poverty and many
children in the croft from which she came, so it was better for her
to stay at Hestviken. But as she was under his roof and very young
—fifteen—he thought he would have to try to see justice done to
the girl and questioned her about the father. But all she knew was
that it was a man who had borne her company a part of the way
through the forest, when she was going home at Michaelmas.

"Ay—and did he maltreat you then?" asked Olav.

"Nay, nay"—Liv beamed all over her face. He had been so
merry and kind. Jon he said was his name.

"Ay, so every man is called who has no other name."

Now in any case she would soon be a fit foster-mother for
Cecilia. For it would go ill if the sick mother were to nurse this
big and greedy child—but hitherto Ingunn had refused to hear
of Cecilia being taken from her breast.

Olav had sent for all the men and women of the country round
who had a knowledge of sickness and leechcraft. None could say
what ailed the mistress of Hestviken—and most of them thought
it must be caused by treachery or envy. Olav knew that she had
been sick in the same way sixteen or seventeen years before, when
she was at Miklebö, and then Mistress Hillebjörg had said it was
certain that Kolbein had caused spells or other witchcraft to be
put upon her. He wondered whether this might not be true after
all, and that she had never been entirely set free from the power
of evil.

Then he became acquainted with a German merchant, Claus
Wiephart, in Oslo, who was said to be a very learned leech—he had
been a captive among the Saracens in his youth and had acquired
their knowledge. Olav fetched him, and this man saw at once
what ailed Ingunn.

What might have been the origin of it he was not able to say;
it might be one thing or another, but most probably it came from
the stars: for example, that her husband had first had knowledge
of her in an hour when the position of the heavenly bodies was

hostile to them, according to the stars under which they had been born. It might be a question of less than an hour—a little before or a little after, the auspices might have been particularly favourable to them. But this might have had such an effect upon her, who was the weaker, as to disturb the harmony in her body between the solid matter and the humours, so that the solid matter had shrunk and the humours had obtained the mastery—nay, she might even have had a disposition toward this disharmony in her hour of birth, but the disharmony was the especial cause of her weakness. The proof of this was that she had not been able to bear children of the male sex that were capable of surviving, beyond the first one; for man's body is by nature drier than woman's and demands from the very beginning more of the solid matter; but a daughter she had been able to bring forth alive. Even so, this child too had absorbed more solid matter than the mother's body could afford to give up; she was now, Clause Wiephart would say, in a state of decay, as it were; bones and flesh were saturated with humours—even as wood floating in the sea becomes soft and full of water.

In the first place they must see to getting her body drained of moisture, said the German. The child should by no means be taken from her breast; she must be given sudatory and diuretic medicines, she must drink very little, but take burnt and pounded bones and *terra sigillata*, and eat hard, dry food with hot spices in it.

The learned man's opinion filled Olav with fresh courage. It sounded so reasonable—and the Latin words used by the German came back to Olav from his young days. *Prima causa, harmonia, materia*, and *umidus, disparo, dispono*—these words he remembered to have heard from Asbjörn All-fat, Arnvid, and the friars at the convent, and, as far as he could judge, Claus knew them rightly. And then, even before they were grown up, he himself had noticed that Ingunn's body was strangely weak and without firmness—it made him think of green corn—surely she had always had too little of the solid matter. *Terra sigillata* must certainly be good for her—it was good for so many things, he knew.

And he had learned about the four elements of which the human body is composed, and had heard that the position of the heavenly bodies influences a man's destiny. Learned men at home did not know so much about this; Asbjörn All-fat said that Christian men have no need to inquire what is written in the stars. But the Saracens were said to have more knowledge of the stars than any other folk.

Olav was unspeakably relieved at heart. Perhaps he had been on an entirely false scent all these years—he had always believed it was he who had brought misfortune upon them both, because he dared not break out of the sin in which he lived. He *was* living in sin, there was no doubt of that, so long as he made no offer to atone for that unhappy deed, but God must know that he could not; he could not jeopardize the welfare and honour of his wife and child. In all else he had endeavoured to walk as a Christian man. And God must know even better than himself how unspeakably he longed to live at peace with Him, to be allowed to love Him with his whole heart, to bend the knee in prayer, without grieving at his own disobedience.

But what if he might now believe that all their misfortunes had a natural origin? Cecilia was the pledge that God had remitted his debt—or would give him respite till the hour of death. That the stars had been the cause of Ingunn's weakness in body and soul—

But *Prima Causa*—that was one of God's names. He knew that.

She said herself that she was better for these remedies of Claus Wiephart's. As yet she had not regained sufficient vigour to be able to move her legs, but she felt less of the pain in her back.

He came into the cook-house one evening just before Olav's Mass [7]—there was something he wished to say to Torhild Björnsdatter before he forgot it.

She was baking bread for the holy-day. The flour dust floating in the air was golden in the evening sun as he opened the door and the light filled the sooty little room. A sweet, yeasty scent came from the round loaves that lay baking on slanting stones around the glowing, heaped-up fire—Olav's mouth watered at the smell. The girl was not there.

Olav was turning to go out when Torhild appeared at the door, carrying a board so heavy that she supported it on her head with both arms. She was obliged to walk even more erect than usual, and in the warm summer evening her light clothing looked but well and suitably free; she was in her working-clothes, a short-

[7] July 29.

sleeved shift of homespun, and bare legs; she was so deft in her movements, firm and strong.

Olav took the board from her; it was of oak and very heavy. He carried it in and laid it on the trestles. Torhild followed, filled both her fists with chopped juniper from a basket, and spread it over the board. She gave off a fragrance in her rapid movements—of meal and fresh bread, of the healthy warmth of work. Olav threw his arms about the maid and pulled her roughly to him. His chin came near her shoulder—for an instant he pressed his cheek against her skin—her neck was dewy, at once cool and warm. Then he let her go and laughed to cover his confusion and shame at this foolish wantonness that had come over him so suddenly.

Torhild had turned red as blood—and the sight of her added to his embarrassment. But she said nothing and showed no sign of anger—went about quite calmly, moving the loaves that were done from the stones onto the board.

"You can lift as much as a man, Torhild," said her master. And as she did not answer, but went on with her work, he began again, more seriously: "You support our whole household—do more work than all the rest of us together."

"I do my best," muttered Torhild.

"Ay, I know not how you think—perhaps you think we might reward you better—if so, you must tell me; we shall soon be agreed—"

"Nay I am well content with what I have. I have now put out all mine own into the world, save the two youngest—and you have helped me well."

"Nay, say naught of that—" He gave her the message he had come for, and went out.

Ingunn continued to use the wise German's remedies, but after a while it was seen that the results were not entirely beneficial after all. She had violent pains in the stomach and burning of the throat from all the pepper and ginger. But she held out as long as she could, struggling to get down the dry and irritating diet, although she seemed to feel the pains even at the sight of the food. She was tortured by thirst day and night; but she bore it all with patience and made little complaint.

Then Olav had to be away from home for a few nights, and

Signe Arnesdatter came to sleep with the sick woman meanwhile. Afterwards Signe told Olav it was quite wrong that Ingunn should still have Cecilia with her at night; the mother no longer had a drop of milk in her breast, and it was hunger and temper that made the child shriek so wildly at night, keeping Ingunn and all awake. Olav had never known any other infant than Audun, and he shrieked almost continually, so the man thought it was the way of little ones. Now Liv had long nursed Cecilia in the daytime, and her own child was lately dead, and the girl was as full of milk as a fairy cow; the only natural thing was to let Liv be Cecilia's foster-mother and have the child both day and night.

But when they spoke of this to Ingunn, she was quite beside herself with grief. She begged and besought that they would not take Cecilia from her: "She is all that is left of me; I bought you this daughter at the price of lying here powerless and palsied to the waist. If you love her, Olav, have pity on me—take not Cecilia from me, the little while I have left to live. 'Twill not be long ere you be freed from this wretched life with me."

He tried to make her see reason, but she screamed, thrusting her elbows into the bolster under her, raising her shoulders and struggling, as though she would force her palsied body to rise. Olav seated himself on the edge of the bed, comforted her as well as he could, but it was in vain; and at last she had raged and wept till she was so weary that she sank into a doze, but even in her sleep she gasped and shook.

The end was that he promised she should have Cecilia in bed with her at night, but Liv was to lie on the bench near by, so that she might quiet the child when it shrieked.

When he came to say good-night to her before he went to bed, she put an arm about his neck and drew his head down.

"Be not angry, Olav. I cannot sleep but I have her with me. I have ever been afraid when I had to lie alone," she whispered; "ever since the first night you slept with me it has seemed as though I could not feel safe unless I had your arm about me. And now that will never be again."

Olav knelt down, took her under the neck, and let her head rest against his shoulder.

"Do you wish me to hold you thus until you fall asleep?" he asked.

She fell asleep almost at once. Then he arranged the pillows

under her shoulders, stole quietly across the floor and crept in to
Eirik in the north bed.

He kept a little charcoal lamp burning on the hearth at night—
he had to get up so often, to help Ingunn and turn her. And now
he had to get up and take Cecilia too, when she shrieked, and
carry her to the girl—Liv never woke.

At last he must have fallen asleep and slept heavily—the child
must have been shrieking a good while, so persistently as to succeed in waking Liv. In the feeble light of the little lamp he saw
the maid padding about by Ingunn's bed with Cecilia in her arms.
She looked so shapelessly broad and squat that he could not help
thinking of tales he had heard of ogres and gnomes. Though he
knew how foolish it was, it made him uncomfortable to see Cecilia
in the arms of this foster-mother.

Olav came in to Ingunn about midday on the morrow—he and
one of the house-carls had been bringing in the hay on pack-horses
from some outlying meadows on the high ground. The nap of
his short cloak was thickly beaded with drops of mist, and his
boots were heavy with wet earth and withered leaves. He gave
off a raw scent of autumn as he bent over Ingunn and asked her
how she did.

With a little embarrassed smile he showed her what he had
brought in his hand—some big watery strawberries threaded on
straws—as they had used to do when they were children. The
berries were soft, so that the palm of his hand was red with them.
"I found these up by the mill."

Ingunn took them, without remembering to thank him. It was
these little red spots within his coarse, worn hands—and she recalled their life together from childhood, all the way till now.
Twice he had reddened that hand with blood for her sake, and it
was the same hard, resin-smirched boy's fist that had helped her
over fences and opened to show her gifts.—Their life appeared as
a tapestry to her—as one long tissue: little images of brief, hot,
happy love, with long intervals between of waiting and longing
and barren dreams, the time of shame and mad despair like a big
dark spot, and then all these years at Hestviken—all appeared to
her in an instant as though embroidered on a ground—a single
fabric, a whole tapestry of the same stuff from their childhood's
days until now, until the end.

True, she had always acknowledged to herself that Olav was good to her. She had known in a way that few men would have had patience with her so long, would have been equal to the task of protecting her and sustaining her all these years. She had indeed thanked him in her heart—thanked him sometimes with burning intensity. But only now did she see, as a whole, how strong his love had been.

He was standing by the cradle now. The rockers bumped and bumped against the floor, and the child gurgled and cried with delight, drumming its heels with wild persistence against the skin rug under it—the mother could just see its little pink hands waving above the side of the cradle.

"Nay, Cecilia—you will soon strangle yourself in these snares!" Olav laughed and lifted up the child in his arms. She had wriggled so violently that her clothes were quite undone, and the swaddling-band had become so tangled about her arms and legs and neck and her little body that it was a wonder she had not strangled herself with it. "Can you get this straight?" He laid the child on the bed by its mother.

"Are you weeping?" he asked, saddened. Ingunn was blinded by tears, so that she could scarcely see as she tried to free Cecilia from her bands.

"She will be just as fair-haired as the rest of us Hestvik folk," said the father; "and now you have seven curls—" he passed his hand over the child's forehead, where the hair had grown long and curly in little, pale-yellow locks. "Are you in such pain today, my Ingunn?"

" 'Tis not that. I am thinking that, though you have been good to me and faithful so long as I have known you, I have never had it in my power to reward you for your affection."

"Say not so. You have been a—gentle—" he could not find another word in her praise on the spur of the moment, though he was trying to say something to please her. "You have been a gentle and—and quiet wife. And you know how fond I am of you," he said with feeling.

"And now it will soon be a year," she whispered, distressed and shy, "that you have been as a widower—with an infirm sister to take care of—"

"Ay, ay," said her husband softly. "But if I love you— Sister, you say. Do you remember, Ingunn, the first years we lived together; we slept in the same bed, drank from the same bowl, and were as brother and sister; we knew of naught else. But then too we were happiest when we were together."

"Yes. But we were children in those days. And then I was fair—" she whispered with more passion in her voice.

"You were. But I fear I was too childish to see it. I believe in those years I never had a thought whether you were fair or not."

"And I was not a burden on you. I was healthy and strong—"

"Oh nay, Ingunn—" Olav smiled weakly and stroked her arm. "Strong you have never been, my dearest friend!"

It was a long winter for them at Hestviken.

Olav was at home all the time; he thought he could not leave her for a single night. She now suffered greatly from lying in bed, since she was so emaciated, and then she had got some hurt in her back: when she had lain awhile in one position, it felt as if a pain crept over her ribs and filled her whole chest. The only thing they could do to relieve her was to move and turn her constantly. She could take no food at all; they kept life in her by giving her gruel, broth, and milk, a mouthful at a time.

She had tried to do a little needlework as she lay in bed, but her hands became numbed whenever she held them raised a little while, so that she could neither sew nor plait. And then she lay in a doze, altogether motionless. She never spoke a word of complaint, and she thanked them gently when anyone came and turned her or arranged her pillows. Sometimes she slept a good deal in the daytime, but at night she seldom had any sleep at all.

Olav had the fire burning on the hearth all night and he had shut off the closet with a door, to make the great room warmer. The winter was not a very cold one, but all this smoke day and night was troublesome.

He watched by the sick woman night after night. Eirik lay in the bed behind his back asleep, Liv slept on the bench, and Cecilia slept in her mother's bed. Olav lay in a sort of doze, but it was never too deep for him to hear an ember shooting out of the fire, or Ingunn's almost inaudible groans—he was up and beside her in a moment. All that winter he was never out of his clothes, except every washing-day, when he went to the bath-house.

He knelt beside her bed, laid the palms of his hands under her shoulders, then under her back, and then he held her heels in the

hollows of his hands for a while. In his heart he expected with a
kind of morbid horror that she would get bed-sores there. It was
like the last glowing ember of all he had once felt for her body—
he thought he could not bear to see the skin broken and the sores
eating into Ingunn's flesh while she yet lived. Never had it been
so hard for him to endure the sight and smell of wounds and impurities—though he was ashamed of this weakness. But he prayed
desperately to God that at least it might not come to this—he asked
it as much for his own sake as for hers.

He was away tending the fire.

"Are you thirsty, Ingunn?—Shall I take you in my arms, Ingunn?"

Olav wrapped the bedclothes about her and lifted her up in his
arms. He sat with her on the settle before the fire. Carefully he
bent the lifeless legs, laid down pillows under her feet on the
bench, supporting her hips and back on his thighs, as he laid her
head to rest on his shoulder.

"Is that better?"

Sometimes she fell asleep when she lay thus in his arms. And
Olav sat by the hour holding her, till he was chilled through about
the shoulders, stiff in all his limbs. She woke if he made the slightest movement. Then she extricated a hand from the bedclothes
and passed it over his face.

"Now I am much better. Carry me back to bed now, Olav, and
go and lie down—you must be tired."

"I am become a heavy burden for you, Olav," she said one
night. "But bear with me a little—'twill not last longer than this
winter."

He did not deny it. He had thought the same himself. When
spring came, it would take her with it. And now at last he was
ready to submit to it.

But as winter drew to a close, she seemed rather to be slightly
on the mend. In any case she revived sufficiently to ask how things
were going on the farm and in the fishery. She listened for the
cow-bells morning and evening, mentioned her cows by name,
and said one day that when spring was fully come they must
carry her out of doors, that she might see her cattle once more.

Cecilia was now a very pretty child, and big for her age; Ingunn had great comfort of her in the daytime, but then she had to

have Liv in with her. At night she slept with her foster-mother in another house—Ingunn could no longer bear the big, heavy child in bed with her: Cecilia rolled over on her mother in her sleep, and when she was awake she stumped about the bed and fell heavily over her palsied body.

Olav had so little liking for Liv that he avoided the room while the maid was there. He knew too that she stole in a small way, and he had more than a suspicion that she was too good friends with Anki and thus taught the man to pilfer and lie— Arnketil's word had always been untrustworthy, but till now it had mostly been because he had no better wit. What they stole was no great matter, but he did not like having dishonest folk in his house. And now there was such disorder in the household in many ways—he himself was so tired every day that he could not accomplish all he ought, and downhill is an easy road.

So now he did not see much of Cecilia in the daytime. But by degrees it had come to this, that his affection for his daughter was mingled with a profound soreness—it pained him sharply when he recalled that blue, damp night of spring when he came home and found her in the cradle. The first time they laid her in his arm he had believed so surely that she betokened a turn in their fortunes, that Cecilia came into the world bringing their happiness with her.

He loved this little daughter, but his affection was, at it were, spread within him, it lay at the bottom of his heart, shy and mute. In the first days of her life her father had often stopped before her cradle and touched her with a couple of fingers, playfully and caressingly—full of quiet joy and wonder when he got her to smile. And he had lifted her up and held her to him a moment, in his clumsy, unpractised way: Cecilia, Cecilia— Now he usually stopped at a little distance when he saw her being carried from house to house; he smiled at his daughter and beckoned; she never took the smallest notice. The very fact that she was so pretty, and that he recognized in her the fair complexion of his own race, seemed only to increase the father's melancholy.

Not much was seen of Eirik now. The nine-year-old boy instinctively kept away from the grown people, whom he saw to be always heavy at heart. He found enough to do about the manor and only came into the hall to eat and sleep.

. . .

Olav had to go in to Oslo for the Holy Cross fair [8] in the spring. There he received a message asking him to go to the convent of the preaching friars.

The Prior had news for him that his friend Arnvid Finnsson had died during the winter. In the middle of last summer he had adopted the professed habit among the friars at Hamar. But by the second week of Lent he died suddenly—none could say of what. As they went to morning mass, the monk who walked beside him saw that Brother Arnvid turned pale and faltered, but on his asking in a whisper if he were sick, Arnvid shook his head. But when they knelt at *Verbum caro factum est*, his neighbour saw that Brother Arnvid was not able to rise to his feet again, and when the mass was at an end he lay in a swoon. Then they carried him into the dormitory and laid him on his couch; he moaned a little now and again, but was unconscious. In the middle of the day, however, he came to and asked in a low voice for the last office. As soon as he had received the sacraments he fell asleep, and when the monks came from vespers he was dead, so calmly that the friar who sat with him could not say when he ceased to breathe.

The Prior told him also that before Arnvid entered the convent he had disposed of a great part of his treasure to kinsmen and friends, and he had bidden his sons send these two drink-horns to Olav Audunsson. But the Arnvidssons were so unlike other men that they would never leave their home parish, and only when they went down to Hamar for their father's burial had Magnus brought the horns to the convent; and Father Bjarne had been unwilling to send these rare treasures south until he could place them in the hands of one of his own order.

Olav knew the horns well from Miklebö. They were small, but very costly: two griffin's claws mounted in silver and gilt. Olav and his friend had used them on the evenings of high festivals, when they drank mead or wine—they only held drink for one man.

The news of Arnvid's death shook Olav to the heart. He could not bear to stay in town among the other men, but sailed out to Hestviken the same evening.

There had been times when he thought of his friend and recalled their last talk together, and it pained him that he had stripped himself so bare to the other. He regretted this weakness

[8] May 3.

so, that at times he had doubtless thought it would be easier for him if he heard that Arnvid was no more.—And then he felt all at once that this was the last stroke, and now he was no longer capable of fighting against his own heart—now that he knew that not a single one shared his secret: alone he would not be able to keep it any longer.

And for the first time he saw the true nature of this friendship. It was he who had taken advantage of the other—and Arnvid had allowed him to do so. He had lied to his friend, and his friend had seen through his untruthfulness; not only the first time, but always he had told Arnvid what suited himself—even to their last meeting; and Arnvid had accepted it and held his peace. It was always he who had sought support, and Arnvid had supported him—as Arnvid had given to all, whatever was asked of him. And the reward they had given him was to scourge him—he had found such reward as awaits the man who has courage to follow Christ's example. And nevertheless Arnvid had blamed himself and thought himself an unfaithful follower, whenever he was unable to see his path clearly and whenever his heart was full of bitterness and contempt for men's baseness—as must at times befall a sinful man, when he ventures to follow where God went before.

Olav stayed at home during the spring sowing, even more silent than usual.

But one morning, when he had set his folk to work, he walked back to the houses alone.

The sunshine flooded the room through the open smoke-vent, the light fell upon the fireless hearth, upon the clay floor, and touched Ingunn's bed. Both the children were with her: Eirik lay with his dark, curly head in his mother's arm and his long legs hanging over the edge of the bed. Cecilia crawled about, climbing up the bedpost and dropping down with a thump and a little scream of joy upon the lifeless form under the clothes. The little maid had nothing on but a flame-coloured woollen shift; her skin was pink and white and her hair had grown so that it fell in bright, flaxen ringlets about her face and neck. Her bright eyes were so blue in the whites that they seemed blue all over, and this gave the charming little face a strangely wide-awake look, like that of an animal.

"Your mother cannot bear you to weigh so heavily upon her,

Eirik." Olav took Cecilia and seated himself on the edge of the bed with the girl on his knee. Once he clasped his daughter impetuously, and the child struggled—she was not used to being with her father. Olav felt how good and firm the little body was between his hands, and the silken hair had a fresh, moist scent.

As she was not allowed to get at her mother, she wriggled in her father's arms and tried to reach her brother. Eirik took her, held her under the arms, and tried to make her walk. Cecilia thrust out her round stomach, straddling with her arms and one foot, as she threw her head back and laughed up in her brother's face. Then she humped herself along with wild little kicks—laughing and shrieking: "Goy, goy, goy"; she curled up all her toes under the sole of her foot, which was quite round—as yet it had scarcely trodden the ground.

Olav swept his hand over the bed—it was strewn with half-withered flowers, such as bloom between spring and summer: wild vetch, catchflies, buttercups, and great violets. Ingunn gathered them into a bunch:

"They have long come out, I see."

Olav sat looking at the children. They were of rare beauty, the two of hers that had lived. Eirik was a big boy now, tall and slight, with his knife-belt on his slender hips. Olav could see he was handsome: his face had lost its childish roundness, it was narrow and sharp, with a slightly curved nose and a high, arched jaw; he was brown-skinned and black-haired, had golden-yellow eyes. Could his mother help thinking of whom he resembled?

"Take your sister with you, Eirik, carry her out to Liv. There is a matter your mother and I would speak of."

Ingunn raised the bunch of flowers with both hands to her face and drank in with open nostrils the acrid scent of spring.

"Now, my Ingunn," said Olav in a clear, calm voice, "you shall soon be released from lying here in torment. I have bespoken a passage for us in a vessel to Nidaros this summer, to St. Olav, so that you may recover the use of your limbs at the shrine of him, the martyr of righteousness."

"Olav, Olav, do not think of such a thing. Never could I bear the voyage—I should not come to Nidaros alive."

"Oh, but you will." The man closed his eyes, smiling painfully —his face had gone pale as death. "For now, Ingunn, now I have the courage to do it. When I come thither, to the sanctuary—I will confess my sin. Of my own free will I shall put myself in God's hands, make amends for my offence toward Him and toward the law and justice of my countrymen."

She looked at her husband in dismay; he went on with the same haggard smile:

"The thing which befell you that time at Miklebö—when you rose from your bed and walked—that must have been a miracle! —Think you not that God can perform another miracle?"

"Nay, nay!" she cried. "Olav, what are you saying—what is this sin you speak of?"

"That I slew Teit, what else? Set fire to the hut where the body lay—and never made confession of it. I have been to confession all these years, have been shriven for all else, great and small—received *corpus Domini* like other Christian men, gone to mass and prayed and pretended, pretended—but now there is an end of it, Ingunn—I will have no more of it. Now I will put my case in the hands of my Creator, and whatsoever He will that I shall suffer, I will thank Him and bless His Name."

He saw the look of terror in her face and threw himself down by the bedside with his head in her lap.

"Ay, Ingunn. But now you shall suffer no more for my sins. If only you will *believe*, you know that you will be helped."

She put her hand under his chin and tried to raise his head. The sun was now shining full upon the bed, upon the crown of his bowed head—she saw that Olav's hair was quite grizzled. It did not show unless the sun shone straight upon it, as it was so fair in colour.

"Olav, look at me—in Jesus' name, have no such thoughts as these. Have I not sins enough myself to atone for? Do you remember"—she forced him to raise his face—" 'you are not *human*,' you said to me that time—you know what I would have done with Eirik, if you had not prevented me. Should *I* cast reproach upon God for deeming I was not fit to bear children?—all that winter long I thought of nothing but of stifling the innocent life I felt quickening within me."

Olav looked at her in surprise. He had, as it were, never thought she remembered this, much less recalled it as guilt.

"I may thank God's mercy and naught else that I have not child murder on my conscience. And no sooner was I saved from that

sin than I went about to do a worse one—God stretched out His
hand again, when I was already halfway through the gates of hell.
I perceived it long ago—I was not allowed to send myself straight
to hell; every day I have lived since has been a loan, a respite given
me to bethink myself and understand—

"I do not complain as I lie here—Olav, have you *once* heard me
complain? *I* know well that God has chastised me, not from un-
kindness—He who has twice plucked me out of the fire into which
I would have thrown myself—"

Olav stared at her—a light was kindled far in behind his pupils.
Unspeakably dear as she had been to him in all these years, he had
never expected much more thought in her than in an animal, a
tender young hind or a bird, that can love its mate and offspring,
and lament its dead young—easily scared out of its wits, helplessly
at the mercy of wounds and pain.—Never had he imagined he
could talk to his wife as to another Christian person of that which
had been growing in his soul for years.

"Oh nay, Olav!" She took his hand, drew him down and clasped
his head to her bosom. He heard her heart beating violently within
the narrow, wasted chest. "Say not such things, my friend! Your
sin—'tis white by the side of mine! You must know that they were
long for me, these years, and ofttimes heavy—but now it seems to
me they were good in spite of all, since I lived with you, and you
were always good!"

He raised his face. "It is true, Ingunn, that we two have had
some good here in Hestviken—in that we were always friends. In
sickness and in health I have had you with me always, and you
have been dearest to me of all human creatures, in that I grew up
away from all my kinsmen and friends, and you were the one with
whom I consorted most. But then God was so kind to me, in spite
of all, that He gave you to me—and I see now that it would have
been difficult for me to prosper here, had I dwelt here alone without a single person that I had known from my youth.—You see,
then, 'tis for that I can no longer bear to be God's enemy—of my
own will I will no more live apart from Him. Let it cost what it
may—

"I am no poor man either. There too God spared me—He gave
success to many of the enterprises I undertook to better our fortunes. I own more now than when we came together. And you
know that by our marriage bond half our estate is yours, what-

ever may befall. You and your children will not be unprovided
for."

"Speak not so, Olav. It *cannot* be so grievous a sin that you slew
Teit. I have never told you before, I have never made complaint
of it to any soul—but he took me by force! I could not bring myself to say it—'twas a thing I could not bear to speak of—" she
sobbed aloud—"nor was I myself innocent, I had borne myself so
that he must have thought I was not above such things—but I had
never thought it would end as it did—and then he forced me. 'Tis
true, Olav, I swear—"

"I know it." He put out his hand as though to stop her. "He
said it himself. And I know that this slaying was a small matter in
the beginning—had I declared it at once. But I took the wrong
road at the start—and now the guilt has grown, and I see that it
will go on and breed new guilt. And now I must turn about, Ingunn—else I shall become the worst of inhuman wretches. It has
come to this, that I scarce dare utter three words, for I know that
two of them will be untrue."

She laid her arm across her face, wailing low.

"You know," said Olav, trying to hush her, " 'tis not certain
either that the Archbishop will demand that I accuse myself before the King's judges. Haply he will deem it enough that I confess my sin before God. I have heard that men have been given
absolution for the gravest of sins without being forced to destroy
all their kinsfolk's honour and welfare—they were made to do
such penance as a pilgrimage to Jerusalem—"

"Nay, nay!" she cried out again. "You would be sent away
from us—to the world's end—"

"But 'tis not impossible"—he laid his hand on her bosom to
quiet her—"that I might come home to you again. And you know
you would dwell here and possess Hestviken—"

"But then it would come out that Eirik is not your son!"

Olav said quietly: "I have thought of that too, Ingunn—and it
held me back, so long as I had no child of my own by you.
Whether you might be driven out of Hestviken with your son—
by my remote heirs. But now there is Cecilia. You can adopt the
boy to full inheritance in your share of the estate—and he has a
rich sister beside him—"

"Olav, do you remember what you said yourself?—that you
had made Eirik no more than amends for his father's death—"

"I remember. But I see now, Ingunn, that I had no right to do it—give away my daughter's inheritance as amends to the child of a stranger—"

"Cecilia—Olav, Cecilia will be a rich maid for all that; she is rich and born in honour, of noble race—she will be fair besides. She will not be among the unfortunate—if she must be content with sister's share after you—"

Olav's face was stiff and closed. "A child of such birth as Eirik's has no *right* to amends for his father."

"Nay—you have always hated—my bastard." She burst into a wild fit of weeping. "I have heard you call him that."

"Oh ay—'tis a bad name that may escape the lips of an angry man, even when he speaks to one who is true-born." He made an effort to speak calmly, but could not help showing a touch of bitterness. "But I will not deny I have regretted it—'twere better I had called the boy by another name when he vexed me."

"You hate him," said the mother.

"That is not true. I have never been too hard with Eirik. God knows, he has had less of the rod than he needs—I *cannot* do it, when you look at me as though I stabbed you with a knife if I do but speak a little harshly to him—and you spoil him yourself—"

"I! who lie here and see naught of the boy from morning to night—" she had picked up the flowers and was pulling them to pieces. "Weeks pass, and he never comes to see his mother—has no time to speak to me—as today. You came at once and drove him out."

Olav said nothing.

"But if Eirik is to suffer for my misdeeds—then it had been better he had not come living into the world—though I myself should have suffered death and perdition for it—"

"Be reasonable, Ingunn," her husband begged her gently.

"Olav, listen to me—Olav, have pity! Too dearly will you have bought my life and my health, if on this account you should wander through the world, a poor and homeless pilgrim in the lands of the black men, among wicked infidels. Or if the worst should happen—that you should be forced to stand naked and dishonoured, in danger of your life maybe, be called caitiff and murderer—for the sake of that man—you, the best among franklins, upright and gentle and bold above all—"

"Ingunn, Ingunn—that is what I am no longer. A traitor I am to God and men—"

"You are *no* traitor—it *cannot* be a mortal sin that you made away with yon man.—And you know not how it feels to have to bend beneath shame and dishonour—*I* know it, *you* have never tried what it is to be disgraced. I cannot, nay, so help me Christ and Mary, I *cannot* have this brought upon me again—even if I were granted life and the use of my limbs—and I should feel that everyone who looked upon me knew of my shame: what manner of woman you had brought home to be mistress of Hestviken—and my Eirik a base-born boy without rights or family, whom a runaway, outlandish serving-man had begotten on me—tempting me among the wool-sacks in the loft, as though I had been a loose-minded, man-mad thrall woman—"

Olav stood and looked at her, white and stiff in the face.

"Nay, were I granted life to suffer in such wise—to stand up and walk with this to face—with your little Cecilia and my bastard holding my hands—and you away from us three, all of us equally defenceless—then I should surely regret the time I lay here waiting for my back to rot away—"

She stretched out her arms to him. Olav looked away—his face was immovably stiff—but he took her hand in his.

"Then it shall be as you wish."

14

NEXT year, at the beginning of Lent, Torhild Björnsdatter moved home to Rundmyr. And at once it was over the whole country-side that she had to leave Hestviken so suddenly because she was to have a child by Olav Audunsson.

If such a misfortune had befallen another man, who had been as a widower for years with a sick wife living, no one would have spoken aloud of the matter, but all the best men and women of the neighbourhood would have given thoughtless youths and those who knew nothing of good manners to understand that the less there was said about it, the better. Olav knew that. But he also knew that *he* was the man—and that he was regarded almost as a sort of outcast. Not that he had ever wronged any of his neighbours, so far as he knew. And at times folk had remembered this—when they thought it over, they knew of no particular stain on his name; no ugly or dishonourable action could be laid at his door. Olav Audunsson had simply acquired the reputation of being unpopular, a most uncongenial fellow.

In the brief days of sunshine after Cecilia had come into the world—before it became clear that her birth had cost the mother the last remnant of her health—the folk of the country round had met Olav with goodwill. Now that this strange curse had been lifted that denied them living children at Hestviken, his equals had rejoiced with him, and they had thought that now perhaps the man would be more sociable, not such a kill-joy as he had been—he extinguished life and merriment around him simply by the way he sat in silence, glaring with unseeing eyes in good company.—But Olav seemed so little able to meet them halfway—he remained the most arrant cross-stick, with whom nobody could get on.

Then there came to light this matter, which was as ugly as need be. While his wife lay palsied and full of torment, broken by one childbirth after another, each harder than the last, the man had been whoring with his housekeeper under his own roof. They had known it for years, folk called to mind now—this man and that knew that Olav had often brought his servant gifts from the town, far too costly for her position. He had helped her to provide for Björn's and Gudrid's children. And all the time he had worked the land for her up at Rundmyr, whither she had now betaken herself again. It was no long way between Rundmyr and Hestviken—so they showed no great shame: folk had seen Torhild swaying about in broad daylight, broad as she was now below the belt—she carried pails between her cot and the byre, far abroad she went along the edge of the wood, chipping bark and cutting twigs.—While they were about it, folk dug up again all the talk there had been at Björn Egilsson and Gudrid.

Olav's nearest kinsfolk in the neighbourhood, Signe of Skikkjustad and Una of Rynjul, had taken his part all through and done their best to excuse their cousin. But now even they were silent and looked ill at ease if anyone did but name Olav of Hestviken.

Olav knew most of what was said of him and Torhild. When he had made his confession, Sira Hallbjörn asked if that was *all*.

And then he discovered what kind of rumours were afloat about him—that this affair between him and Torhild had been going on for years, and that some folk hinted that maybe he was also father to the child Liv Torbjörnsdatter had had a year or two ago out at Hestviken.

One of the first Sundays when he was not permitted to ride to church with other people, the weather was mild. Olav was walking about the yard. A great washtub stood there; it had thawed so much that there was water on the top of the ice. Olav chanced to bend over it and saw his own reflection in the water. The face that looked up at him from the dark depth of the vessel, blurred and somewhat indistinct, was like the face of a leper—his pallor showed like patches of rime-frost against the weatherbeaten skin, and the whites of his eyes were red with blood.—Olav was frightened at the sight of himself.

He had almost expected it to come as a relief in a way when he was forbidden to enter the church this year. In the end he had felt he could no longer endure to go to mass with his unshriven sin. But, for all that, it was worse to be shut out. He had thought that the heavy penance for his adultery would at the same time heal some of his old wound. But it only caused him to reflect that this last sin was but a consummation of the old sin.

But this was the last thing in which he had ventured to put trust in himself—that nothing on earth would be able to break down his fidelity to Ingunn.

Not a word had been spoken between them of his faithlessness. But he knew that she knew of it.

The beginning of it all was that he felt all at once that he could no longer bear the burden of Ingunn. After that day in the previous spring when he had told her that he could live no longer with a deadly sin stirring in his mind, begetting fresh sins from day to day—and she had begged him to go on enduring it, for the boy's sake and hers. And in her sick and tortured state she had the advantage—no man worth calling a man could have opposed such a living bundle of pain.

He could not humiliate himself so far as to broach the subject again. He made as though nothing had been said, helped her through the long nights as before. But now, when at last his heart had run dry of love and patience, it was far more trying. Now

not a day passed but he felt how tired and worn he was from the
endless watching in the air of the sick-room. And the great bitterness in his heart received constant accessions of petty bitterness
every time he found himself growing sluggish and forgetful in
his work, heavy and inactive of body.

One night before midsummer he had gone out toward morning.
Ingunn had fallen asleep at last, and he wished for a breath of the
cool night air before lying down. Olav paused before the door of
the house—it was light, calm, and grey outside. The boat's crew
were not expected home for some hours yet; all on the manor
were asleep. Then he noticed a thin column of smoke above the
roof of the cook-house. At that moment Torhild Björnsdatter
appeared at its door and emptied a cooking-pot—her wet hair
hung about her, dark and straggling.

Olav had always been strangely touched to see how Torhild
strove to keep herself clean and tidy in spite of all she had to do.
She was always first up and last in bed, and thus she found time
to wash and plait her hair even in the middle of the week, and
mend her clothes. Ingunn had given up all such things before they
had been married four years.

Olav went across to Torhild and they spoke together for a
while—instinctively whispering, as it was so still—not a sound but
that of the birds beginning to wake. He had dozed a little at times,
he said in answer to her questions. But now he would go in and lie
down.

"Could you not come over to us and lie down in my bed?"
asked the girl. "Then you would have more peace." She herself
and the children lay in one of the lofts now that it was summer.

Torhild lived in the house that Olav's parents had had when
they were first married. It was a little old house which stood a
little way apart, in a line with the cattle-sheds, under the Horse
Crag, on the east of the yard toward the valley. Olav had had it
set in order, so that it was now good and weather-tight, but it
was very cramped inside.

Torhild accompanied him to the house and drew out the cudgel
with which she had bolted the door. The air from within smote
him like a sweet breath: the floor was strewn with juniper. The
room was so narrow that the bed at its end filled it from wall to
wall: in the dim light its sheepskin covers shone white as snow;
around it were hung wreaths of flowers to keep off flies and

vermin. Torhild had made it all trim before she moved out for the summer.

She bade him sit on the edge of the bed while she pulled off his shoes. Olav felt sleep well up from this clean, fresh couch, rising about him like sweet, tepid water. He was already half off as he rolled over into the bed—was just aware that Torhild lifted his feet in and spread the coverlet over him.

When he came to himself again, he saw the evening sun shining yellow on the meadow outside the open door. Torhild stood over him with a bowl in her hands—it was fresh, warm milk. He drank and drank.

"You got some sleep?" asked Torhild; she took the empty bowl and went out.

His shoes stood before the bed; they were soft, well smeared with tallow. And a clean everyday jerkin was laid out for him— still damp across the chest where she had washed away the stains, and the tear was mended that had been there when he wore it last.

During the summer it happened more and more often that he went and lay down in Torhild's house to get a night's sleep. But each time he rested thus made it harder to go back to the nights of watching; he was fairly hungry for sleep and again sleep—he could not have had his fill of sleep for many years, he thought.

Torhild brought him his morning bread when she came to wake him. If his clothes were wet the night before, he found dry ones ready when he woke, holes and tears were mended. Olav asked her not to do this—it was Liv's work, though she seldom did it. Torhild had enough to do as it was. The girl gave a little smile and shook her head.

And then there arose in him a desire for her—to know for once in his life what it was like to hold a sound and healthy woman in his arms, one he need not be afraid of touching. But, for all that, it was as though he had never *willed* it—even that morning when he reached out and took hold of her, he had expected her to thrust him back, perhaps in anger.—But she yielded to him, without a sigh.

All through that autumn and winter he seemed to be walking at the bottom of a thick sea of mist. He could not bear himself, and sometimes he could not bear her either; but he had no force to pull himself out of the mire. When she moved back into the house with the children, it must surely come to an end, he comforted himself; but it did not.

He stayed indoors with Ingunn from early in the morning till late in the evening. He had not been away from home a night except for a week in the seal-hunting. Now that he had betrayed his wife, he remembered his bitterness toward her as a temptation of the Devil to which he had yielded. "Ingunn, my Ingunn—how could I treat you thus, while you lie here, patient and kind, helpless as a maimed animal? Was that to be the end of our friendship, that I turned traitor to you?"

Night after night Olav carried her wrapped in skins and blankets, as one carries a child, so that she might have some relief from the stress of lying in bed. The more weary and cold and sleepless it made him, the greater was the relief he got from it.

He and Torhild had scarcely exchanged a word since that fatal morning. In all these years Torhild had been almost the only person with whom Olav had much talk—as with a grown-up equal. He remembered that—remembered what he owed this Torhild, whom he had rewarded thus. He could find nothing to excuse his misdeed. She had known no man before him—all she had known was hard work for other folk's welfare—and to make no complaint if life was too hard for her. And now he durst not speak to her, checked her when she would speak—in his heart he knew full well what she had long treasured up, and why this upright and scrupulous woman who was no longer young had allowed him to possess her without resistance. He was aware of it in her silent caresses. But if she *once* forgot herself and put it into words, his shame would stifle him.—

Of Björn, her father, he also thought. Ay, had he been alive now, he would have cut him down straight.

He guessed that it would not remain hidden either. It was in the darkest days before Yule that his fear changed to certainty. And in his despair temptation came to him. It was as though the Devil, who had led him for all these years into an ever increasing slough, going before him cloaked and half disguised—had now turned about, thrown off his hood of concealment, and shown him his true face:

He knew that Torhild would do whatever he asked of her. In former years it had often happened that they had been out together in a boat alone. She would go with him again—even if she guessed what was in his mind, she would follow him, he felt that. Then something might easily happen.

And Ingunn would be spared the knowledge of this. And he would be spared the shame of being exposed to every mother's son around the fiord as the worst of wretches. If he was already in the Devil's power neck and crop—he could no longer have a soul to lose.

But no, for all that. It was Satan who held out all this to him, but he himself said no. "This crime I will not be guilty of—no matter whether you have my chair ready for me in hell. I have nothing to lose, I can well believe that—honour and hope of salvation and my happiness with Ingunn, which I had saved so far—all this I have sold. But nevertheless you will not get me to do this. I will not do Torhild more harm than I have done already. Not even for Ingunn's sake—

"Lord, have mercy! Holy Mary, pray for us! Not for me, I beg nothing for myself—but, Lord, have mercy—upon the others."

"Ay, now it is too late," he said scornfully to the Devil. "They have guessed it, my whole household has guessed it; now you may cease to mutter about it. Be quiet! You will get me, when the time comes."

An ugly silence had fallen about him. The house-folk ceased speaking when the master came near. Scarcely a whispered word was spoken at mealtimes. Olav sat in the high seat; the housekeeper brought in the food and served it out. No one could mark the slightest change in her bearing; she was about from dawn to late in the evening, industrious as ever, her back was as straight and her foot as nimble, though it was plain to all that she no longer went alone.

Ingunn turned her face to the wall when Torhild came into the room.

So much had already gone by of the new year that Lent was at hand, and yet not a word had been said between Olav and Torhild of that which awaited them. But one day he saw her go up to the storehouse loft after the morning meal. He followed. She was taking pieces of bacon out of the salt-barrel and scraping off the worst of the scum that had formed on them.

"I have been thinking, Torhild"—Olav went straight to the point—"that it is not much I can do for you; I cannot help you much. But I will do what is in my power. And therefore I thought —that farm of Auken that I bought over on the Hudrheim side five years ago—that I give you a deed of it and make it over to you. Rundmyr I can continue to work for you and your brothers and sisters, as we have done in these last years."

Torhild reflected for a moment. "Nay, it may well be better that I do not stay up there at Rundmyr—"

"It will surely be better for you if you do not have to live hereabouts. After the trouble I have brought upon you," said the man in a low voice.

"Auken—" Torhild looked at him. "That is no small gift to make to a woman of my condition, Olav."

"It was reckoned to be a three-cows' croft, and there were some good cornfields on the south side of the knoll the houses stand on. But you know that no folk have lived there for a score of years, and they who rented the land of me have not kept it in good tilth."

Torhild turned round to him and held out her hand. "Then I say thanks, Olav. I see that you wish to make good provision for me."

Olav squeezed her fingers. "I have behaved worst to you of all people," he whispered. "You had the right to expect a different reward of me—"

Torhild looked him in the eyes. "The fault is mine as much as yours, I ween, master."

He shook his head. Then he said quietly: "Will it not be too hard for you now—all the work of the house here?"

"Oh no." She smiled feebly. "But perhaps it were best that I stay here at Hestviken no longer—?"

Olav nodded stiffly. "But the houses over at Auken are in a sorry state—sunken and roofless. I shall have them repaired and put new roofs—but you cannot move in before the summer."

"Then I must stay at Rundmyr meanwhile," Torhild suggested.

"Ay, I see no other way," said Olav.

.   .   .

A week after, Olav left home for a few days, and when he came back, Torhild had moved home to the croft at Rundmyr. And Olav discovered that he missed her—unspeakably.

It was not that his affection for Ingunn was less or other than it had been. This was something that had grown up entirely outside it. As in a sort of mirage he had had a vision of a life very different from his own; had seen how it might be for a man to have a sound and sensible wife by his side in all things, one who took her share of their common burden and bore it with as much discretion and strength as he bore his—or even more. And to see children, sons and daughters, succeeding one another, without its breaking and slowly killing the mother to bring them into the world. It was not that he would have changed his lot for this that the vision showed him—he thought that, had he known from his first meeting with the child Ingunn what she would bring him as a dowry, he would nevertheless have reached out both hands for her.

And yet he missed Torhild painfully. She had done him more good than any other creature. And he had repaid her in the worst way.

Eirik had seen how it was with Torhild, like everyone else in the house, and he had not given it much thought. But there was this silence that spread around Torhild—and it began to dawn upon Eirik that there was something sinister behind it. It could not be merely that she had gone the way of so many other serving-maids.

This silence which spread like the soundless rings in water when a stone is thrown into it. And by degrees, without a word having been said to him, Eirik became aware that this same sinister silence surged about his father too. A vague, evil dread stirred in the boy's soul—but he could not guess what his father had to do with Torhild's being with child. For his father was married to their mother—

Sira Hallbjörn sent word to Hestviken that this year Eirik Olavsson must go to confession in Lent and receive the Easter sacrament; the boy was now in his tenth winter, he ought to have come the year before. Eirik forgot all his gloomy anxieties on the morning his father sent him off—the priest wished to have the children with him for a week to teach them. It was the first time Eirik was to ride alone right up to the church town; his father had lent him a little light sword, and behind his saddle he had a bag of gifts for the priest and provisions for himself.

The day after his return he asked Olav:

"Father—who is my godmother?"

"Tora Steinfinnsdatter, your aunt, who is dead." Olav was not sure of this, but believed he had heard it once. Eirik asked no more.

Memories that he had not thought of for years began to swarm upon the boy. Half-forgotten feelings of insecurity and bewilderment were revived.—The other children had spoken of godmothers and godfathers—Sira Hallbjörn had wished to hear on the first day how much they knew of Christian religion from their homes. His father had taught Eirik his Credo, Paternoster, Ave Maria, and Gloria Patri, but that was long ago, and now he never saw that the boy said his prayers. So Eirik did not know them well, and he had almost forgotten what they meant in Norse. Nearly all the other children were better taught—and most of them had learned something from their godmother or godfather.

Eirik remembered that while he was at Siljuaas the mother he had there pointed out a stout, splendidly clad woman one day when they were at church, saying that she was his aunt. But she had not so much as looked at him as she walked past them. He was not even sure that she was the same aunt as the one in whose house they had lodged when his father fetched him from Siljuaas. At any rate, he had never heard that she was his godmother. For the first time it occurred to him to wonder why he had been there, at Siljuaas, when he was small.—He had often heard of other children being brought up away from their parents; but it was always with kinsfolk, solitary people or old. That little maid Ingegjerd who was so pretty and wore a silver belt about her waist like a grownup maid, only that the plates were quite small, and who knew all the penitential psalms almost right—she was with her godmother, and she ruled the whole house for the childless couple and was given everything she asked for. But at Siljuaas the cabin had been poor and narrow, and Hallveig and Torgal had had plenty of other children—and he had never heard his parents mention these folk since; so they could not be kinsfolk of theirs.

Bastard and straw-brat, he knew well enough now what those words meant, and leman too. The memory of his mother's visit, which had frightened him so much that time—now it came up again, a living riddle. Words that he had heard his mother murmur almost to herself, when she could not hide her tears—they came up; and he remembered that his mother had once borne the keys, but they had been moved to Torhild's belt even before her mistress became bedridden.—And now, since his mother had lain low, palsied and unfit for anything, his father had taken to himself Torhild in her stead, and she was already far gone with child, and Eirik guessed now that it was his father's. But if his father had been *married*, this was a sin so grievous that scarcely any man would dare commit it. But then it must be so, that his mother was only his father's leman.

But then, but then—! That a rich franklin sent away his leman and children, assigned them a little home to dwell in far from his own, while he himself took in another or married—that had happened many times in the country round, and Eirik had heard of it.

The boy's heart was gripped by the dread of it, so that he could not sit still or stay quietly in one place. His father might send them away, if he wished. And he no longer cared for any of them. It was over a year since his father had taken Eirik about with him; he no longer taught him anything, scarcely spoke to him. Nor did he take any notice of Cecilia. And his mother lay there, needing constant attention and unable to do the merest trifle of work. If his father ordered them all three to leave Hestviken, he would bring Torhild and her child hither in their stead.

He had always remarked his mother's dislike of Torhild and never thought about it. *Now* he saw— And hatred, of which hitherto he had known nothing, was born in the boy's heart. He hated Torhild Björnsdatter, his cheeks turned white and he clenched his fists if he did but think of her. He took it into his head that one night he would steal up to Rundmyr and kill her, who would force his poor sick mother and all of them out of their home—drive his knife straight into her wicked, false heart.

But his father, his father— Eirik stood as it were with two arrows in his hand, not knowing which to lay to his bow. Should he hate his father too—or love him even more than before, now that he was in danger of losing him? To Eirik, Olav had always appeared the most perfect being on earth—the man's impatience, taciturnity, and coolness had made no impression on the child; he shook them from him as the sea-bird shakes off the water, and thought only of the times when his father had treated him differently. Above all when they had been out together without other company, in the forest or on the fiord, and his father had been the all-knowing, helpful being who warmed the child and gave him a feeling of security by his quiet good humour; but even at other times Eirik had often been able to feel that his father wished him well. And then there was that time when his father had to cut off his poisoned finger, and thrust the red-hot iron into his own flesh to show his son there was nothing to be afraid of. To the boy this was such a shining deed that he did not remember it clearly—it dazzled him to think of it.

Lose his father—Eirik turned to fire and ice with pain at the thought. Then he had dreams of doing something or other—a manly deed that would bring him fame. He imagined many things, but did not quite know which to choose. But when his father's eyes were opened to the kind of son he had, when he saw that he was bringing up a lad of spirit—when Eirik had won his father's heart, then he would say to him that he claimed an honourable position for his sister and himself, and his father should not send away his mother, were she never so sick and useless and in the way. But Torhild he should drive so far abroad that he need never more fear her coming with her child to claim their place.

But even if his affection for his father was more lively than ever, his confidence and sense of security were gone; and now Eirik noticed this—that his father was not fond of him, although the man never corrected him now, scarcely paid heed to him.

Olav hardly gave Eirik a thought now, only noticed with a vague relief that the boy was quieter than before, less in the way.

Not to a living soul did Eirik so much as hint at the conflict of thoughts that possessed him.

At last, one day in the course of spring, Olav stayed behind when the household went out after the morning meal—and then he said it:

" 'Tis likely you have heard—Torhild has a son—" he spoke in a low voice, which sounded husky.

"I heard it—" With a painful effort she turned her head so far as to see a glimpse of her husband as he sat leaning back in the high seat. His face was white and patched with red, his eyes swollen and bloodshot. She guessed he had been weeping.

She had not seen him thus in all these years, not when Audun died, not when she herself received the last sacraments, that time

the women expected her to bleed to death. Only once before had
she seen Olav weep.

"What is it like?" whispered his wife—"Torhild's child?"

"Fair and shapely, they say."

"Have you not—*seen*—your son?"

Olav shook his head. "I have not seen Torhild—not since she
left us."

"But surely you will *see* it—?"

"I can do no more than I have done—for her. I cannot amend
the boy's lot. And so—"

Olav got up and crossed the room—was going out.

Ingunn called to him: "What name has she given him?"

"Björn." Ingunn saw that his tears were about to overcome
him again.

"That was the name of your mother's father."

"She can have had no thought of that. 'Twas her father's name,
you know."

Olav made as though he would bend over his wife, but then he
turned abruptly and went out.

She said no more to him till supper-time. From Liv she had
heard that he had gone straight off to the smithy in the morning,
and no one in the place had seen the master all day. He looked as
if he had wept most of the time.

Then came the night. Olav and Ingunn were left alone in the
house—with Eirik, who was asleep against the wall in his father's
bed. The man tended the sick woman as he did all the other nights.
Several times his wife saw that he was near bursting into tears
again. And not a word did she dare to say—to him, who had now
gotten a son, and who could never lead in his own son to sit beside him in the high seat in his ancestral manor. But what of Eirik
—when she herself was no more—?

Withal Ingunn had an obscure feeling that it was not only sorrow over his son that had so shattered Olav.

The man himself was not thinking so much of his child. He
wept chiefly over himself—it was as though he saw the last remnant
of his honour and his pride lying crushed before his feet.

Not till after Olav's Mass had Olav Audunsson finished repairing the houses at Auken so far that Torhild Björnsdatter could
move thither with her belongings. His house-carls were to carry

her and her goods across the fiord. Olav himself had gone off
south to Saltviken the day she was to move.

Ingunn lay listening—she had had both doors thrown open to
the yard. She heard the coming of the pack-horses, the hoof-beats
on the rock. Then the cow-bell, the tripping of little hoofs—the
children, Rannveig and Kaare, ran about, driving and keeping together their flock of sheep and goats.

Liv stood at the outer door, sniffing and making game of the
procession. "Torhild takes the lower path along the creek," announced the maid, buzzing with excitement. "To bring her whoreson among the houses here—that's more than even she has a mind
to."

"Hush, Liv!" whispered Ingunn, breathing rapidly. "Run down
to her—bid her—ask if she will—tell her I would so fain have a
sight of her child."

A moment later Eirik dashed in hurriedly. His narrow, swarthy
face was burning—his yellow eyes sparkled with indignation:

"Mother! Now she is coming hither! Shall I drive her off? We
must not let the filthy hell-sow drag her bastard in here!"

"Eirik, Eirik!" His mother called to him in a wail, stretching out
her thin, yellow hand. "For God's mercy's sake, say not such ugly
words. 'Tis a sin to scoff at a poor creature and call her bad
names."

He was so tall now, her boy, slender as a reed and slight of
build. Angrily he tossed his shapely head with its black curls.

"It is I who sent for her," whispered Ingunn.

The boy frowned and turned on his heel; then he went and
flung himself down on the edge of the north bed, sat there staring
with an angry, scornful smile as Torhild entered.

The girl came forward with bent head—she had bound up her
hair under a coarse, tight-drawn coif—but her back was as straight
as ever. She carried a bundle in her arms, wrapped in a kerchief
with a red and white border. It was strange to see that she bore
herself with all her old dignity and calm, even as she appeared before Olav's wife, humble and sorrowful.

The women greeted each other, and Ingunn remarked that
Torhild would have good weather for the passage across. Torhild agreed.

"I had so great a mind to see your boy," whispered Ingunn
shyly. "You must do me the kindness to let me see him. You must

lay him down here before me; you know I cannot raise myself," she said as Torhild held out the bundle. Then the girl laid the child down on the bed before the mistress.

With trembling hands Ingunn undid the kerchief that was wrapped about it. The boy was awake—he lay staring, at nothing in particular, with big blue eyes; a little smile, as it were a reflection of a light none but himself could see, hovered about the toothless, milky mouth. A fine, fair down curled from under the border of his cap.

"He is big?" asked Ingunn—"for his age—three months, is it not?"

"He will be three months by Laurence Mass." [9]

"And fair he is. He is like my Cecilia, methinks?"

Torhild stood silent, looking down at her child. There was no great change to be seen in the housekeeper—though in some way she had grown younger and fairer. It was not only that her figure seemed yet more shapely: she was broad-shouldered and had always been high-bosomed, with a chest as deep and broad as a man's. But now her full, firm breast looked as if it would burst her kirtle, and this made her seem slighter in the waist. But it was not that alone—her grey, bold-featured face had softened as it were and become younger.

"He has no look of knowing what hunger is, this fellow," said Ingunn.

"Nay—I thank God," replied Torhild quietly; "he knows not what it is—and with His help he shall never know it either, so long as I am alive."

"You may be sure Olav will see to it that the boy shall never lack aught, even if you be taken from him," said Ingunn in a low voice.

"That I know full surely."

Torhild threw the cloth over her child again and lifted him in her arms. Ingunn held out her hand in farewell—Torhild bent deeply over it and kissed it.

Then Ingunn burst out—she could not keep back the words:

"So in the end you got your old desire fulfilled, Torhild!"

Torhild replied calmly and with a mournful air: "I tell you, Ingunn—as truly as I hope in Christ and Mary Virgin for mercy for myself and this my child—I do not believe, mistress, that I ever

[9] August 10.

desired to deceive you—and he, your husband, never desired it, as you must know—but it came about nevertheless—"

Ingunn said bitterly: "Nevertheless I have seen it, years before I lost my health, what thoughts you had of Olav—you liked him better than all beside—and that has been so for more than three years or four—"

"Ay, from the time I knew him first I have liked him best of all." She bowed stiffly and went out.

Eirik started up, spat after the woman, and swore.

His mother called to him, in a hushed and frightened voice. "Eirik mine, be not so sinful—never say those ugly words of any mother's child," she begged him, bursting into tears and trying to draw the boy to her. But he wrested himself from her and dashed out of the door.

15

NEVERTHELESS it overtook Olav as something quite unexpected when the end came.

The winter following the misfortune with Torhild Björnsdatter passed like the two that preceded it. Everyone marvelled that life still clung to Ingunn Steinfinnsdatter—it was more than two years since she had been able to take dry food. She had bed-sores now, and in spite of all Olav's efforts they grew worse. She herself felt little of the sores, except those under her shoulders; they sometimes burned like fire. She always had to have linen cloths under her, and although Olav smeared the places where the skin was broken thickly with grease, the linen often clung fast to the sores, and then it was pitiful to see her torments. But she complained wonderfully little.

One morning Olav had carried her over to his own bed, and while Liv spread clean skins and linen on hers, he tended her back; he had laid her on her side. He was dizzy with fatigue and sickened by the bad smell there was now in the room. Suddenly he bent over his wife and cautiously touched with his lips the moist, open sores on her thin shoulder-blades; he had recalled something he had heard—of holy men who kissed the sores before they bound up the lepers whom they tended. But then this was the other way about: it was he who was the leper, though he seemed

clean and sound outside—and she must indeed be washed clean
now, who had borne the torments of all these years meekly and
without complaint.

He accused her of *nothing* now.

Ingunn guessed it must be hard for Olav to be shut out of the
church. And one night, when her husband had fasted on bread
and water during the day, so that he was quite worn out when he
had to watch by her, she whispered, as she drew him down to her:

"I *will* not complain, Olav—but why *could* I not be suffered to
die, when Cecilia was born? Then you would not have fallen into
this sin with Torhild—"

"Speak not so." But he could not tell her that was not what
had brought about the misfortune. It was that he had been em-
bittered against her, and then he had grown careless and weary of
himself, had longed for rest from all that weighed upon him. Now
he no longer gave her any blame for it—she had known no better.
He had known for close on thirty years that Ingunn had little wit,
and God had laid it upon him to judge and answer both for himself and for her. Simple she was—and unspeakably dear to him. He
put no blame on any but himself. *Mea culpa, mea culpa*—and the
fault of no one else.

All things went regularly at Hestviken now, both with the
farming and the fishery. If the master could not take part himself
—but he had to be with her. He always consoled himself with the
thought: "It cannot possibly go on much longer." But at the same
time he could not imagine it would be today, or tomorrow, or the
next day. The end must indeed come soon, but there was still a
little time.

Easter fell early that year, so that the Oslo fair was held in the
week before St. Blaise's Day. Olav had to go into town: he had
some goods lying in the hands of Claus Wiephart—had entered
into a kind of trading partnership with the German, but he did
not trust that fellow farther than he could see him, nor had he
cared to lodge with Claus on his recent visits; it came too dear.
Hitherto he had excused himself by saying that he would lie in
the guest-house of the preaching friars, since from his youth up
he had been a friend of that order. But this year he could not very
well be in the convent, since he was banned from taking part in
the mass. So this time he had put up at the Great Hostelry.

On the evening of the last day of the fair he sat in the great room of the hostelry munching the provisions he had brought and washing them down with their indifferent ale, when Anki came in and asked for Master Olav of Hestviken.

"Here am I. Is there any news from home, Arnketil, or what brings you hither?"

"God help you, master. Ingunn lies at the point of death—she was given extreme unction as I left home."

She had had a fit of colic, but no worse than often before, and she had coughed violently for some nights. But when she collapsed that morning they did not guess that she was dying—until old Tore came in to dinner. As soon as he saw the state the woman was in, he went out, saddled his horse, and rode for the priest. Sira Hallbjörn was again away from home—ay, now his parishioners would complain to the Bishop on his next visitation—but one of these barefoot friars of his occupied the parsonage and was called his vicar. Even before the monk began his ministrations to the dying woman, he told the house-folk that they must send for the master in all haste—it was uncertain at the best whether he could reach home in time to say farewell to his wife.

There had been no cold worth talking about that winter; beyond the islands the fiord had been open, so that Olav had come by boat. But then here had been a few nights' frost, followed by a strong southerly wind, and now it was freezing again—Anki had been able to row as far as Sigvaldasteinar, but there he had had to take to the land and borrow a horse. And now it was likely that the fiord was full of ice a long way out; it was hard to say how Olav would reach home quickest. No doubt he would have to ride round inland. Claus would be able to find him a horse.

People had collected about Olav Audunsson and his man; they stood listening and offering advice. Some young, well-dressed squires in long, coloured kirtles and cloaks also came up; they had been sitting farther up the hall, laughing rather noisily as they drank German mum and threw dice. Now one of them spoke to Olav—he was a tall, fair lad with silky, flaxen hair, which he wore long upon his shoulders according to the latest foreign fashion. Olav knew him by sight: he was one of the sons of the knight of Skog and was in company with his brother; the others were doubtless pages from the King's palace.

"It means much to you to reach home quickly, I can guess. You can borrow a horse of me—I have a well-paced horse out in the friars' paddocks—if you will go thither with me?"

Olav protested that this was too much—but the young man was off already, settled his gaming debts and drank up his ale while he took his sword and cloak. Then Olav gave Arnketil orders about his baggage and threw his cloak about him.

The snow crunched under their feet as they came outside. The sky was clear and the hills were still green; the first stars were coming out. " 'Twill be villainously cold tonight," said Olav's companion. They struck out eastward through the alleys toward Gjeitabru.

Olav asked the other about the road—he was totally unacquainted with the districts lying east of the town toward Skeidissokn, had never come to Oslo overland. The young man answered that he could ride across the whole of the Botnfiord, the ice was safe enough—well, it was unsafe too, in some places, "but I can ride over with you."

Olav said that was far too much and he would find his way sure enough; but his companion, Lavrans Björgulfsson was his name, made off at once: "I have my horse standing in Steinbjörn's yard; if you will wait for me in the church—I shall not be long—" He turned and went back to the town.

The Franciscans' church was not yet dedicated and the friars said mass in a house within the garth; but the church was roofed, Olav had heard, and they preached there in the evenings during Lent. Not before Easter would his first year of penance be ended, but he was free to enter this edifice, which had not yet become the house of God.

For all that, he had a queer feeling as he crossed the bridge and took the trampled path over a field, where the snow shone grey in the falling darkness, toward the church, whose black gable-end was outlined against the blue, star-set gloom.

It was colder inside than out. From habit he bent the knee as he came in, forgetting that the holy sacrament had not yet been brought into this house. From the farther end of the dark nave his eye was met by the blaze of a great number of little tapers—they were burning at the foot of a great crucifix that stood against the grey stone wall. Beside it the chancel arch yawned before a pitch-dark empty space.

A little farther down the nave a solitary candle was burning by a lectern; before the book a monk stood reading, clad in the order's brown garb of poverty. He was standing on an inverted tool-chest, and about him were assembled a score of men and women in thick winter clothes—some stood and some had drawn up beams and overturned vessels to sit upon. Their breath showed like white smoke in the light of the candle.

The very incompleteness and desolation of the place caught at him like a hand clutching at his anxious heart. The openings for windows in the wall were boarded up; the scaffolding still stood at the western end of the nave, and he made out boxes and mortar-vats and boards and ends of beams as his eyes grew accustomed to the darkness. But most desolate of all was the black chasm of the choir—and above this image of the world, without form and void, rose the great crucifix with the glittering assemblage of candles at its foot.

It was not like any crucifix he had seen before. At every step he took forward, an immense pain and dread rose within him at the sight of this image of Christ—it *was* no image, it seemed alive— God Himself in mortal agony, bleeding from His scourging as though every wound men have inflicted upon one another had stricken His flesh. The body was bent forward at the loins, as though contorted with pain; the head had fallen forward, with closed eyes over which streamed the blood from the crown of thorns, down into the half-open, sighing mouth.

Beneath the crucifix stood Mary and John the Evangelist. The Mother held her thin hands clasped, one above the other, against her bosom, as she looked up—mournfully as though she raised the sorrows of all races and all ages to her Son, praying for help. Saint John looked down; his face was contracted with brooding upon this mystery.

The monk read—Olav had known the words since he was a child: *O vos omnes, qui transitis per viam, attendite, et videte, si est dolor sicut dolor meus.*[1]

The monk closed the book and began to speak. Olav did not hear a word—he only saw the image on the cross before him: *et videte, si est dolor sicut dolor meus.*

Ingunn lay at home, in the agony of death, if she were not dead

[1] Lamentations, i, 12.

already. It did not seem real to him, but he knew now that this
sorrow of his was also as a bleeding wound upon that crucified
body. Every sin he had committed, every wound he had inflicted
on himself or others, was one of the stripes his hand had laid upon
his God. As he stood here, feeling that his own heart's blood must
run black and sluggish in his veins with sorrow, he knew that his
own life, full of sin and sorrow, had been one more drop in the
cup God drained in Gethsemane. And another sentence he had
learned in his childhood came back to him: he had believed it was
a command, but now it sounded like a prayer from the lips of a
sorrowing friend: *Vade, et amplius jam noli peccare—*[2]

Then it was as though his eyes lost their power of sight, and
his blood rushed back to his heart, so that he grew outwardly cold
as a dead man. All this was as it were within him: his own soul
was as this house, destined for a church, but empty, without God;
darkness and disorder reigned within, but the only sparks of light
that burned and sent out warmth were gathered about the image
of the rejected Lord, Christ crucified, bearing the burden and the
suffering of his sin and his despair.—*Vade, et amplius jam noli
peccare.*

My Lord and my God! Yea, Lord, I come—I come, for I love
Thee. I love Thee, and I acknowledge: *Tibi soli peccavi, et malum
coram te feci*—against Thee alone have I sinned, and done evil in
Thy sight.—He had said these words a thousand times, and only
now did he know that this was the truth that held all other truths
in itself as in a cup.

My God and my all!—

Then someone touched him on the shoulder—he gave a start: it
was Lavrans Björgulfsson; the horses were standing in the garth.
This was the shorter way—the young man went in front, up
through the church, into the choir. Now that Olav's eyes were
used to the darkness he could make out the altar—the naked stone,
as yet undedicated and unadorned, a cold, dead heart. There was
a little door on the south of the choir:

"Look how you go—the steps are not finished—" Lavrans
jumped down into the snow. Out in the yard stood two of the
friars. One held the horses, the other carried a lantern. Lavrans
must have told them how things stood, for one of them came up

[2] St. John, viii, 11.

to Olav—it was one of those who had been with Sira Hallbjörn, and he had come out to Hestviken once. Olav knew the monk's face, but did not remember his name.

"Patiently and meekly she bore it all, your wife. Ay, and now it is Brother Stefan who is with her—ay, we shall remember her in our prayers here too tonight."

The north wind was at their backs as they rode over the ice—long stretches of it were like steel, swept of the little snow that had fallen lately. The moon would not rise till toward morning; the night was black and strewn with stars.

"We shall have to ride up to Skog," said Olav's guide, "and get fur cloaks on."

It was a great manor, Olav saw—many great houses stretching away in the darkness. Young Lavrans sprang from the saddle, unhindered by the long folds of his mantle, stretched his tall, supple frame, and went across and opened the door of one of the houses. Then he stood by his horse, caressing and talking to it, till a man came out with a lantern—the light seemed to hover over the snow.

"You must dismount, Olav, and come in with me." He took the lantern from his man and showed the way across the courtyard. "We live where we have been since we were married—my stepmother and Aasmund, my brother, have the great house, as in father's time—" he seemed to take it for granted that everyone knew all about the great people of Skog.

"Is your father dead?" asked Olav for the sake of saying something.

"Ay, 'tis a year and half since—"

"You are young though—to be master of this great manor."

"I? not so young either—I am three and twenty winters old." He opened a door. They did not seem to bar their houses here at Skog. Through an anteroom they entered a little hall, warm and tidy. Lavrans lighted a thick tallow candle that stood near a curtained bed, threw the pine torch on the hearth, and spoke to someone within the bed. He handed in some woman's clothes behind the curtain.

A moment after, a young woman stepped out, lightly clad, with a red cloak over her long, blue shift—she was tucking locks of jet-black hair under the coif she had flung around her narrow, large-eyed face. While she busied herself, with easy, youthful briskness, her husband lay half-hidden within the bed. There were sounds of a little child behind the curtains, and the young father laughed aloud:

"Nay, Haavard—will you pull your father's nose off? Leave go now. Or maybe you want to feel if 'tis frozen off me—" The hidden youngster choked with laughter.

The mistress had brought in food from the closet and offered her guest a foaming bowl of ale. Olav thanked her, but shook his head—he could no more eat and drink now than if he had been dead. Lavrans shook off the child he was playing with, came up, and took some food standing.

"You must give me a drink of water then, Ragnfrid.—My wife and I have made a vow to drink naught but water in Lent, except we be in company with guests or on a journey"; he gave an affectionate look at the foaming bowl of ale. With a little crooked smile Olav accepted the draught of welcome, took a taste of it, and passed the bowl to the master of the house, who now did justice to his guest—the young man did not seem minded to say good-bye to the slight intoxication that had been on him when they left Oslo. It had been passing off as they rode along, but now he made up for it, generously.

The single draught he had taken worked upon Olav so that he felt awakened from his ecstasy. Gone was the strange sense that all he saw and felt was a shadow, but that he himself had been taken away this night by God from the paths of men, brought before His face alone in a desolate spot—for now He willed that this His creature should understand at last.—And he heard all sounds from the visible world outside as he heard the voice of the fiord under the crags at home in Hestviken, sensed them without hearing. Voices reached him as though they were speaking outside a closed hall, where he was alone with the Voice which adjured and complained, full of love and sorrow: *O vos omnes, qui transitis per viam, attendite, et videte, si est dolor sicut dolor meus!*

But now the door of the closed room was thrown open, the Voice was silent—and he sat in a strange house with total strangers, the night was far spent, and he was to find his way through country that was quite unknown to him ere he reached home. And there death awaited him, and the choice that, as he now saw, he had made more and more difficult for himself every day and every year he had put it off. But now he *must* choose—he knew that, as he sat here feeling dazed and frozen, roused out of his strange visionary state: after that vision or whatever it might have been, he could not go on drowsily hoping that one day God would choose for him—*force* him.

So many a time had he allowed himself to be driven out of his road, upon false tracks that he had no desire to follow. Long ago he had acknowledged the truth of Bishop Torfinn's words: the man who is bent upon doing his own will shall surely see the day when he finds he has done that which he never willed. But he perceived that this kind of will was but a random shot, an arrow sent at a venture.—He still had his own inmost will, however, and it was as a sword. When he was called to Christianity, he had been given this free will, as the chieftain gives his man a sword when he makes him a knight. If he had shot away all his other weapons, marred them by ill use—this right to choose whether he would follow God or forsake Him remained a trusty blade, and his Lord would never strike it out of his hand. Though his faith and honour as a Christian were now stained like the misused sword of a traitor knight, God had not taken it from him; he might bear it still in the company of our Lord's enemies, or restore it kneeling to that Lord, who yet was ready to raise him to His bosom, greet him with the kiss of peace, and give him back his sword, cleansed and blessed.

Olav felt a vehement desire to be left alone with these thoughts —though he did not forget that this young Lavrans had shown himself very kindly, and he knew it might be difficult for him to reach home that night without the other's help. But the young folk troubled and disturbed him by their constant services. The wife knelt before him and would help him change his boots—she had brought out foot-clouts of thick homespun and big fur boots stuffed with straw. The scent of her skin and hair was wafted to him, warm and healthy—it made him shrink within himself, as though to ward it off. The young mother breathed a fragrance of all the things in life from which he had been led away step by step, until tonight he saw that he was parted from them as completely as though he had already taken a monk's vows.

The husband came in with his arms full of fur clothing and set about finding something that would fit his guest. Olav was queerly abashed to see how much too large for him the other's clothes were—he was quite lost in them when he got them on. Olav's broad shoulders gave him a look of bulk, and the other seemed so slight; but he was doubtless more substantial than he looked, and he was tall besides. And in the pride of his grief Olav felt mortified that he should appear a lesser man than Lavrans Björgulfsson in everything, stature and worship and power—this tall, fair-skinned boy who breathed this air of home with wife and child, who was master of this rich knightly manor, helpful, kind, and well content. He had a long face with handsome, powerful features, but his cheeks were still smooth and of a childlike roundness; life had not marked his young and healthy skin with a single scratch—was never likely to do so either: he looked as though destined to take his course through the world without ever meeting sorrow.

Olav protested that he could well find his own way through the forest in Skeidissokn, and Lavrans must not think of riding from home so late at night for his sake in this cold. But his host was quick to reply that, as it had not snowed properly for so long, the forest was full of old trails; a man must be well acquainted with the paths by Gerdarud to find the shortest way. And as for a night out of doors—nay, he made nothing of that.

Outside in the courtyard a groom held two fresh horses, fine, active animals. An excellent horseman was this young squire, and he had the best of horses. Olav was secretly vexed that he had to be given a hand in mounting—it was these boots that were far too big.

The road lay through forest most of the time, and the thin coating of snow was frozen hard and broken in every direction by old, worn tracks of ski-runners, horsemen, and sledges—and the moon could not be expected for an hour yet. Olav guessed that he might have strayed far and wide ere he had found his way out of these woods alone.

At last they came through some small coppices and saw Skeidis church ahead of them on the level. The moon, rather less than full, had just risen and hung low above the hills in the north-east. In the slanting, uncertain moonbeams the plain was raked with shadows, for the snow had been blown into drifts with bare

patches of glimmering crust between; all at once Olav recalled
the night when he fled to Sweden—more than twenty years ago.
It must have been the waning moon that reminded him—then too
he had had to wait for moonrise and had started at about this
time of night, he remembered now.

He told his guide that from here he was well acquainted with
the roads southward, thanking Lavrans for his help and promising
to send the horse north again at the first opportunity.

"Ay, ay—God help you, Master Olav—may you find it better
at home than you look for.—Farewell!"

Olav remained halted until the sound of the other's horse had
died away in the night. Then he turned into the road that bore
south and west. It was fairly level here, and the road was well
worn and good for long stretches; he could ride fast. It was not
far now from farm to farm.

The moon rose higher, quenching the smaller stars, and its
greenish light began to flood the firmament and spread over the
white fields and the grey forest; the shadows shrank and grew
small.

Once the crowing of a cock rang out through the moonlight;
it was answered from farms far away, and Olav became aware
how still the night was. Not a dog barked in any of the farms, no
animal called, there was not a sound but that of his own horse's
hoofs, as he rode in solitude.

And again it was as though he were rapt away to another world.
All life and all warmth had sunk down, lay in the bonds of frost
and sleep like the swallows at the bottom of a lake in wintertime.
Alone he journeyed through a realm of death, over which the
cold and the moonlight threw a vast, echoing vault, but from the
depths the Voice resounded within him, incessantly:

*O vos omnes, qui transitis per viam, attendite, et videte, si est
dolor sicut dolor meus!*

Bow down, bow down, yield himself and lay his life in those
pierced hands as a vanquished man yields his sword into the hands
of the victorious knight. In this last year, since he had turned
adulterer, he had always refused to think of God's mercy—it
would be unmanly and dishonourable to look for it now. So long
had he feared and fled from the justice of men—should he pray
for mercy *now*, when his case had grown so old that perhaps he
would be spared paying the full price of it among men? Some-

thing told him that, having evaded men's justice, he must be honest enough not to try to elude the judgment of God.

But tonight, as he journeyed under the winter moon like one who has been snatched out of time and life, on the very shore of eternity, he saw the truth of what he had been told in childhood: that the sin above all sins is to despair of God's mercy. To deny that heart which the lance has pierced the chance of forgiving. In the cold, dazzling light he saw that this was the pang he had himself experienced, so far as a man's heart can mirror the heart of God—as a puddle in the mire of the road may hold the image of *one* star, broken and quivering, among the myriads clustered in the firmament.—That evening many, many years ago, in his youth, when he had arrived at Berg and heard from Arnvid's lips how she had tried to drown herself, fly from his forgiveness and his love and his burning desire to raise her up and bear her to a safe place.

He saw Arnvid's face tonight, as his friend admonished him: you accepted all I was able to give you, you did not break our friendship, therefore you were my best friend. He remembered Torhild—he had not seen her since the day he had had to drive her out of his house, because she bore a child under her heart, and it was his, the married man's. He had never seen his son—could not make good the disgrace, either to the boy or to his mother. But Torhild had gone without a bitter word, without a complaint of her lot. He guessed that Torhild was so fond of him that she saw it was the last kindness she could do him, to go away uncomplaining—and that it had been her chief consolation in misfortune that she could yet do him a good deed.

Even for poor sinners it was the worst of all when one's friend in distress refused to accept help. In spite of his being sunk in sin and sorrow, God had let him have his happiness in peace: he had been allowed to give to Ingunn, and never had it been said to him that now the measure was full. Again it was words from his childhood's teaching that arose, illumined so that he understood their meaning to the full: *Quia apud te propitiatio est: et propter legem tuam sustinui te, Domine.*[3]

The strange horse began to tire under him; he halted in a field and let it recover its wind. The steam rose from its sides like silvery smoke under the moon, which now shone from the height

[3] Psalm cxxx. *De profundis.*

of heaven. They were covered with rime, both he and his horse
—Olav woke up and looked about him. Behind him, under the
brow of the wood, lay a farm he did not recognize; before him
he saw a great white surface bordered by high rushes, glittering
with rime and rustling feebly in the breeze—a lake. No, he did
not know where he was. He must have gone much too far inland
to the eastward.

The moon had sunk low in the south-west and had lost its
power, the sky began to grow light, blue with a touch of orange
on the land side, when at last Olav came out of a wood and knew
where he was—he had reached some small farms in the south of
the parish. The shortest way home to Hestviken was over the
Horse Crag. Stiff, frozen, and deadly tired he stood stretching
himself and yawning—he had dismounted to lead the poor horse
over the height. Silently he caressed the strange animal, taking its
muzzle in his hand. Its coat was covered with rime and frozen
foam.—It was now full daylight.

Arrived at the top of the ridge, he stopped for a moment and
listened—an unwonted stillness penetrated him through all his
senses: the last frost had silenced the fiord. The ice lay as far as
he could see up and down, rough and greyish white. The southern
wind at the beginning of the week had broken up the first sheet
of ice and driven the floes inshore; the last night's cold had bound
them all together. A thin mist rose from the ground, covering
everything with a downy greyness, and the air was tinged pink
by the sun, which was rising behind the fog.

The monk came into the doorway to meet him, when his horse
was heard in the yard. "God be praised that you are here in time!"

Then he stood by her bed. She lay in a doze, with her narrow
yellow hands crossed upon her sunken bosom—looking like a
corpse but that her pupils just moved under the filmy eyelids.
With a sharp stab of pain the husband felt that soon she would lie
here no more. For more than three years he had gone in and out
while she lay stretched here in bed, racked with pain, unable to
move more than her head and hands.—Lord Jesus Christ, had it
been worth *so* much to him, merely to have her here alive!

The monk talked and talked—what a happy thing it was that
at last she was to be released from her sufferings, after the way

she had been lying of late, with the flesh of her back raw and
bloody; Patient and pious—ay, he, Brother Stevne, had prayed as
he was about to administer extreme unction: "God grant we may
all be as well prepared to meet death, when the hour comes, as
Mistress Ingunn."—As soon as she had received the sacrament she
had sunk into a doze—she had lain as she lay now for twenty
hours, and like enough she would not come to herself again; it
seemed she would be allowed to die without a struggle.

Then he began to question Olav about his journey home—his
mouth was never still—but now they must see that the master had
something to keep him alive!

The serving-maid brought in ale, bread, and a dish of steaming,
freshly boiled salt ling. Olav turned sick at the nauseous, washy
smell that rose from the fish and set himself against it, but the
monk affectionately laid a dirty, frost-bitten hand on his shoulder
and forced him. Olav felt repelled by this Brother Stefan—his
frock smelt so foully, and his face had the look of a water-rat
with its long, pointed nose that seemed to have no bone in it.

At the first mouthful of food he was almost sick—his throat
hurt him and his mouth filled with water. But when he had got
down a bite or two, he found he was famishing. While he was
eating he stared, without knowing it, at Eirik, who was busy with
something in his place on the bench. When the boy noticed his
father looking at him, he came up and showed what he was doing
—he was so eager about it that he forgot his shyness of Olav: he
had kept two pairs of shells from the walnuts his father had
brought home from the town the year before, and now he had
found good use for them. He was collecting the wax that dripped
from the candle by his mother's deathbed and filling the walnut-
shells with it; one was for Cecilia and one for himself. Brother
Stefan was at once interested in the boy's occupation; he pulled
off the lump of wax that had run down the candle and discussed
with Eirik how they should prevent the shells bursting apart
afterwards.

Olav was overpowered by fatigue when he had eaten his fill.
He sat with his neck leaning against the logs of the wall, the pulses
throbbed in his throat and about his ears, and his eyes would not
keep together when he tried to fix them upon anything—he saw
the flame of the holy candle double. Now and then his eyelids
closed altogether—images and thoughts whirled within him as a

mist rolls and drifts along—but when he took a hold of himself and opened his eyes again, they were all forgotten. He felt numbed and empty, and the memory of the last night and all he had gone through in it was as far off as the memory of an old dream.—This untiring Brother Stevne came and pestered him again, wanting him to lie down awhile in the north bed—he would be sure to wake him if there was any change in his wife. Olav shook his head crossly and stayed where he was. Thus the hours wore on till midday.

He had slept and dozed by turns when he saw that Brother Stefan was busy beside the dying woman. Kneeling, he held a crucifix before Ingunn's face in one hand, while with the other he beckoned eagerly to Olav.

Olav was there in an instant. Ingunn lay with eyes wide open; but he could not tell whether she *saw* anything—whether she recognized either the crucifix in the priest's hand or himself bending over her. For a moment something like an expression came into the great, dark-blue eyes; they seemed to be seeking. Olav bent lower over his wife, the monk held the crucifix close to her face— but the feeble, fluttering disquiet was still there.

Then the husband got up, took Eirik by the hand, and led him forward to his mother's bed. The monk had begun to say the litany for the dying.

"Are you looking for Eirik, Ingunn? Here he is!"

He had put his arm about the boy's shoulder and stood holding him close. Eirik came up to his shoulder now. Olav could not see whether Ingunn knew them.

Then he knelt down, still with his arm around the child. Eirik was sobbing, low and painfully, as he knelt side by side with his father and said the responses.

"*Kyrie, eleison.*"

"*Christie, eleison,*" whispered the man and the boy.

"*Kyrie, eleison.—Sancta Maria—*"

"*Ora pro ea—*" The two kept their eyes on the dying woman. The man was watching for a sign that she knew him. The boy looked at his mother, in dismay and wonder, as the tears streamed down his cheeks and he sniffled between the responses—"*ora pro ea, orate pro ea—*"

"*Omnes sancti Discipuli Domini—*"

"*Orate pro ea.*"

Ingunn sighed, moaning softly. Olav bent forward—no word came from her white lips. The three continued the prayer for the dying.

"*Per nativitatem tuam—*"

"*Libera ei, Domine.*"

"*Per crucem et passionem tuam—*"

"*Libera ei, Domine.*"

She closed her eyes again; her hands slipped from each other, down to her sides. The monk crossed them again over her bosom, as he prayed:

"*Per adventum Spiritus sancti Paracliti—*"

"*Libera ei, Domine.*"

—Ingunn, Ingunn, wake up again, only for a moment—so that I may see you know me—

"*Peccatores,*" recited the monk, and the father and son replied:

"*Te rogamus, audi nos.*"

She still breathed, and her eyelids quivered very slightly.

"*Kyrie, eleison.*"

Olav remained on his knees by the bedside, holding Eirik to him, even after they had reached the end of the prayer. Inwardly he was beseeching: "Let her wake up, only for a little instant—so that we may bid each other farewell." Although every night of these three years had been like entering the valley of death with her, he felt he could not part from her yet. Not till they had given each other one last greeting before she went out of the door.

Eirik had laid his face on the edge of the bed; he was weeping in an agony of grief.

Suddenly the dying woman opened her lips—Olav thought he heard her whisper his name. Quickly he bent over her. She muttered something he could not distinguish; then more clearly: "—not go forth—'tis uncertain—out yonder—Olav—do not—"

He could not guess her meaning—whether she spoke in a dream or what. Almost without knowing it, he put his arm around Eirik, stood up, and raised the boy to his feet.

"You must not weep so loudly," he whispered as he led his son to his seat on the bench.

Eirik looked up at him in despair—the child's face was all swollen with weeping.

"Father," he whispered, "Father—you will not send us away from Hestviken, will you—because our mother is dead?"

"Send away whom?" Olav asked absently.

"Us. Me and Cecilia—"

"No, surely—" Olav broke off, held his breath. The children
—they had never entered his mind when he was thinking of all the
rest last night. It took him by surprise—but he would not think of
this now, would thrust it from him. As though asleep he sat down
on the bench a little way from Eirik.

He was not fit to contend with it now. But the children—he had
not thought of that.

The day wore on to nones. And little by little the inmates of
the house tired of watching and waiting for the last sigh. Liv had
been in once or twice with Cecilia, but as the mother lay in a doze
and the child was noisy and restless, the maid had to take her out
again. The last time Eirik went with her—Olav heard their voices
outside.

He had seated himself on the step by the bed. Brother Stefan
was dozing at the table with his book of hours open before him.
The house-folk came in quietly, knelt down and softly said a
prayer, paused awhile, and quietly went out again. Olav dropped
off—he did not sleep, but it was as though his head were full of
grey wool instead of brains, so tired and spent was he with the
strain.

Once, when again he looked at Ingunn, he saw that her eyelids
had half-opened, and underneath he had a glimpse of her eyes,
sightless.

In the first weeks after Ingunn's death Olav could not have said
when he had slept. For slept he must have at times, since there was
still life in him. Toward morning he felt as if the grey fog rolled
within his head, leading his thoughts astray and deranging them.
Then the fog settled, grey and dense, but never so that he escaped
feeling the pressure of his burden even in his light morning doze,
while his thoughts were busied with the same things deep down
within him, and he was aware of every sound in the room and
out of doors. He longed to be given real sleep for once—to sink
into perfect darkness and forgetfulness. But as far as he was aware,
it never happened that he enjoyed a deep sleep.

It was the thought of the children that kept him awake.

He knew that that night as he rode home to Ingunn's deathbed, he had formed a resolution. He had answered yea to God. "I will come, because Thou art my God and my All; I will fall at Thy feet, because I know that Thou longest to raise me up to Thee—"

But the children—it seemed as though both God and himself had forgotten them. Until Eirik asked—he would not send them away from Hestviken, haply?

He could not guess how the boy had come to think of such a thing. It could not have come about in any natural way.

And then he recalled Ingunn's last words, pondered over them: "—Do it not, Olav. Not go forth—'tis uncertain out yonder—" Perhaps she had only spoken in a dream—dreaming that he was about to venture on to unsafe ice. But it might also be that, as she lay with her soul scarce in her body, she had learned what had befallen him that night. That both she and Eirik had had knowledge of it—and both had pleaded with him.

The children had none but himself to look to. Hallvard Steinfinnsson far away in the north at Frettastein was their nearest kinsman. And he could imagine how Hallvard would take it if he now came forward and accused himself of a secret murder twelve years old. His children would not be given a very cordial reception at their uncle's. And no doubt it would be revealed who Eirik was.

For that too he would be forced to confess, that he had tried to push forward a bastard heir, cheat his nearest kinsmen of the family manor in favour of a stranger.

If he carried out what he had resolved that night, he could see only one way of dealing with the children: Cecilia he would have to offer as an oblation to the sisterhood at Nonneseter, with her mother's inheritance, and Eirik to the Church or to the preaching friars.

The man shuddered to his very soul—was *that* the meaning? Was his race to die out with him because he had struck the crown from his own head by a dastard's deed? He *was* to be a childless man, because it is an ill thing that a dastard carry on the race? And those children he had begotten while he lived in rebellious outlawry might not carry on the line on which he had brought misfortune. A son he had, a single one, whom he could never adopt into his kin. And his only daughter was to be lost to the world behind the gates of a convent.

Eirik— At times he thought he was sorry for the boy. It would

be hard for him to send the young lad back to the state of life
from which he had once been willing to raise Ingunn's son, born
in secret. Now and then he had thought he was fond of the boy
too, in spite of all.

It was chiefly at night, when Eirik slept with him on the inside
of the bed, that he thought, no, he could scarcely have the heart
to thrust the child back into the lot to which he had been born.

At other times, when he heard the boy roistering among the
house-carls, laughing as if he had already forgotten his grief at
his mother's death, it seemed to Olav that Eirik was now the chief
of his burdens; it was the boy above all who stood in the way,
made it difficult for him to break through all that kept him from
winning peace and relief for the sickness of his soul.

He noticed that he was drifting farther and farther away from
the resolution he had made on the night before Ingunn's death.
But he did not know whether he was being drawn back into the
old slough against his will, or whether he had taken flight of himself, because after all he dared not come forward, when it came to
the point.

One night Olav got up and went across to the house where Liv,
the maid, lay with his daughter. With great trouble he succeeded
in shaking her awake.

The girl lay huddled under the bedclothes, blinking with her
little screwed-up pig's eyes, at once afraid and expectant, at the
master who stood by her bed with a candle in his hand. Under his
shaggy, unkempt, grizzling hair his face was furrowed and pale as
ashes, the firm edge of his chin lost in a fog of stubble; he had
nothing on but his linen beneath the long, black cloak, and his
feet were thrust bare into his shoes.

Olav looked down at her and guessed that the maid must think
he had come to let her share the fate of Torhild Björnsdatter
without more ado—she had already moved as though to make
room for him by her side. He gave a short, harsh laugh.

"Cecilia," he said—"I was dreaming so of her. There is nothing
wrong with Cecilia?"

The girl turned aside the coverlet so that he could see the child.
She lay asleep in the bend of her foster-mother's arm, with her
little pink face well buried, half concealed by her own shining,
silky curls.

Without more words Olav put down the candle, bent over, and lifted up his daughter. He wrapped her well in the folds of his cloak, blew out the light, and went out with his child.

Coming into the great room, he dropped his cloak on the floor, kicked off his shoes, and crept into bed with his daughter, who was still fast asleep against his chest.

At first all he felt was that sleep was just as far from him as before. But it was good to hold this tiny young creature in his arms. Her baby hair was soft as silk under his chin, with a sweet, fresh smell of sleep, and her little breath played over his chest and throat, warm and dewy. Silky of skin, her body was firm and plump and strong; the little knees that bored their way into her father's body were quite round. Olav allowed himself the luxury of loving his child as a miser indulges himself by taking out his hoard and handling it.

But by degrees the little maid acted like a hot stone. The warmth of the sleeping infant penetrated the father, soothed the throbbing, aching unrest in his heart; it flowed through his whole body and resolved its strain into a sweet, soft tiredness. He felt slumber settling down upon him, a blessing worth he knew not what. With his chin buried in Cecilia's soft, curly hair he sank into a deep sleep.

He was awakened by her howling wildly and furiously. The little maid was sitting up, half on his chest, roaring, as she rubbed her eyes with two small fists. On the inside of the bed Eirik sat up in surprise. Then he leaned over his father's chest, coaxing and trying to quiet his little sister.

Olav did not know what time of night it might be—the smoke-vent was closed; the little charcoal lamp standing on the edge of the hearth was still burning—it must be very early.

When her father took hold of the little one, she raged more violently than ever, hitting about with her little round fists and shrieking at the top of her voice. Then she swung round, threw herself upon her father, and tried to bite him, but could not get a proper hold of his thin cheek. Eirik was laughing boisterously.

Then she took to nipping Olav's worn eyelids between two of her nails—she pulled them out and pinched them, and this gave her so much amusement that she kept quiet—stopped screaming for a while as she punished her father all she could. After that she looked helplessly about her.

"Liv—where Liv?" she wailed loudly. "Bringlum!" she said in a tone of command.

That was her name for food, Eirik interpreted. Olav got out of bed, went into the closet, and returned with a thick slice of the best cheese, a bannock, and a cup of half-frozen milk.

While he revived the fire on the hearth, holding the cup of milk he was going to warm, Cecilia sat up, stared angrily at the strange man with her deep-blue kitten's eyes, and threw bits of bread at him. She gobbled up the slice of cheese till nothing was left but the crust. "Bringlum," she said as she threw the last of the cheese on the floor.

Olav went to fetch more food for his daughter. She ate all she was given, and when there was no more, she screamed again that she wanted to go to Liv.

When the milk was warm enough, Olav gave it to his daughter. She drank it to the last drop and then would not let go the cup, but hammered on the edge of the bed with it. It was a fine cup, made from a root, very delicately turned, so Olav took it from her. Cecilia caught hold of his hair with both hands and pulled it; then she got her claws into his face and scratched all down her father's cheeks with her sharp little nails. She clawed him to her heart's content—Eirik tumbled all over the bed in fits of laughter. He knew his sister better than her father did and could witness that Cecilia was the most spiteful little monster: "She has drawn blood from you, Father!"

·Olav fetched more food, all the dainties he could find, but Cecilia seemed satisfied now; she refused all he offered her. She scarcely seemed to have the makings of a nun, this daughter of his.

Finally he had to let Eirik take the ill-tempered brat and carry her back to her foster-mother.

Then one night Olav awoke in black darkness—the charcoal lamp had gone out. He had slept—for the first time since Ingunn died he had had a deep, sound sleep. His gratitude made him strangely gentle and meek, for he felt born anew and healed of a long sickness, so good was it to wake without feeling tired.

He closed his eyes again, for the darkness was so dense that it seemed to press against them.—Then it dawned upon him that he had dreamed too, while he slept. He tried to put together the fragments of his dream—he had dreamed of Ingunn the whole time, and of sunshine—the glow of it still lingered in him.

He had dreamed that he and she were standing together in the little glen where the beck ran, due north of the houses at Frettastein. The ground still looked pale and bare with the withered, flattened grass of the year before, but here and there along the bank of the stream some glossy leaves, reddish brown and dark green, shot up among the dead grass. They were just by the white rock that filled the whole bed of the stream, so that the water swept over it and round the sides in a little cataract, swirling and gurgling in the pool below. They stood watching the bits of bark that floated round in the whirlpool. She was dressed in her old red gown—they were not yet grown up, he thought.

Throughout the whole dream he seemed to have been walking with Ingunn by the side of their beck. Olav thought they stood together under a great fir in the middle of the steep scree; this was farther down, where the stream ran at the bottom of a narrow ravine; great fallen rocks choked up the little river-bed, and on the rough slopes on both sides grew monk's-hood, lilies of the valley, and wild raspberries so thick that one could not see where to plant one's foot among the stones which gave way and rattled down. She was afraid of something, put out both hands to him with a little moan—and he felt oppressed himself. Above their heads he saw the narrow strip of sky over the glen—the clouds were gathering and threatening thunder.

Once they had been right down on the beach, where the stream runs out into Lake Mjösen. He saw the curve of the bay, strewed with sharp, dark-grey rocks under the cliff. The lake was dark and flecked with foam farther out. Ingunn and he had come there to borrow a boat, it seemed.

It must have been that journey long ago to Hamar that came back to him, he thought—his memories were confused and transposed, as they always are in dreams. But his dream had held the sweetness of their fresh young days, so that the savour of it still lingered in his mind.

In another way it was as though he had gone through his whole life with Ingunn again in his dream.

However that might be, he must have slept a whole night to have dreamed all this. It must soon be morning.

He stole out of bed in the darkness, found some clothes and put them on. He would go out and see how far the night was spent.

As he stepped out on the stone before the door, he saw the back of the Horse with its mane of trees at the highest point—it stood out black against the starry sky. Between the houses the yard was dark, but there was a faint light on the edge of the crags that closed the view toward the fiord, like moonlight on ice. Olav wondered—could it be possible?—the moon set before midnight now. But over the forest along Kverndal there was a faint uncertain glimmer of low, slanting moonbeams.

He could hardly believe it—that he had been so mistaken in the time. Hesitating, he slowly made his way westward through the yard and to the lookout rock. It was glazed and slippery to climb.

The half-moon touched the tree-tops on the other side—yellow at its setting. Under the dim, oblique beams the whole surface of the frozen earth was made rugged by the faint light and the pale shadows that scored it. The glazed surface of the rock beneath him still gleamed dimly. He saw that he had not slept more than three hours.

Again that light of the moon lying low over the brow of a hill made Olav think of the far-off night when he fled the country, an outlawed man. The sudden memory plunged him into an endless, weary despondency.

He thought upon his dream—it was so infinitely long since they had walked together along the beck, by the hillside path, down to the village. She was dead, it was only three weeks since—but so long ago.

He felt a clutching at his throat; the tears collected under his smarting eyelids as he stood gazing into the distance, where the moon was now but as a spark behind the forest. He wished he could have wept his fill now—he had not wept when she died, nor since. But the two or three times he had wept since he grew up, he had not been able to stop—furiously as he had striven to master himself, the fits of weeping had come again and again without its being in his power to hinder them. But tonight, when he wished he could weep on out here alone, without a soul to see him, it came to nothing but this strangling pain in his throat and a few solitary tears that flowed at long intervals and turned cold as ice as they slowly ran down his face.

When spring came—he thought he would go away somewhere

when spring came, the idea had just struck him. He could not face the summer at Hestviken.

The moon was quite gone, the light faded away over the distant forest. Olav turned and went back to the house.

As he was about to lie down he felt in the darkness that Eirik had stretched himself across the bed, taking up all the room between the wall and the outer board. All at once a disinclination to take hold of the boy came over him—whether it was that he shrank from disturbing his rest or felt he could not have him as a bedfellow tonight.

The south bed stood empty, since the bedclothes had been carried out and the straw burned on which she had died.

Olav went to the door of the closet and pushed it open—he was met by an icy air and a peculiar stale and frozen smell of cheese and salt fish; they kept food in the closet in winter and shut it up to make the outer room warmer; but the bed was always made up, in case they might have guests to lodge for the night.

Olav stood for a moment with his hand on the old doorpost. His fingers felt the carving that covered its surface—the snakes wreathed about the figure of Gunnar.

Then he went in—butting against tubs and barrels, till he found the bed. He crept into it and lay down—closed his eyes upon the darkness and gave himself up to face the night and sleeplessness.

IN THE WILDERNESS

PART ONE

THE PARTING OF THE WAYS

THE PARTING OF
THE WAYS

I

ON a day in spring Olav was out with one of his house-carls spreading dung on the frozen soil of the "good acre."

The fields that faced north still gleamed and glittered with ice, but from above on the Horse Crag water trickled and ran. And on the sunny side, across the creek, the cliff was baking—the Bull rose out of the sea with a flickering reflection of the ripples on its rusty-grey rocks. Brown soil showed under the pines over there, and the thicket on the hillside toward Kverndal was hung with yellow catkins.

Out in the creek Eirik was rowing—the lad's red kirtle shone sharply against the blue water. Olav stood for a while leaning on his spade and looked down at the little boat. 'Twas ever the same with Eirik—he took such a time! He had only had a few sheep to ferry across; sheep and goats were now turned out in the wood on that side. Today there was good use for the boy at home.

There came a tripping of feet on the rocks behind Olav's back— the great bare rocks that rounded off the "good acre" toward the fiord. There stood Cecilia with the sun behind her so that its rays shone through her fair, curly hair, lighting it up. She sat on the rock and slid down, crying out to her father and holding up a bunch of coltsfoot.

Olav turned and waved her off.

"Come not too close, Cecilia—you will be all besmeared." He lifted her onto a stone. The little maid dabbed her posy into his face and looked to see how yellow she had made her father with the pollen. 'Twas not much, for Cecilia had already pulled the flowers to pieces, but she laughed none the less and tried again.

Olav caught the faint scent, fresh and acrid—the first of the

year's new growth. The winter that lay behind him had been as
long as the Fimbul winter.[1] But now he felt with a zest all through
him that his boots were wet and heavy with earth. Even here in
the shadow of the rock the ice shield covering the ground had
shrunk away and exposed a strip of raw mould along its edge.
The manure that lay spread over the field steamed with a rich
smell, and from the waterside came a powerful springtime breath
of sea and tar and fish and salt-drenched timber.

The little sailboat that he had sighted just now off the Bull was
making this way. The craft was unfamiliar—no doubt some folk
who were going upcountry.

He wiped the worst of the dirt from his fingers and led Cecilia
back over the rocks.

"Go away to Liv now. You must not let the child run so far
from you, Liv—she might fall over."

The serving-maid turned toward him—"such fine weather"—
with a great smile on her face. She sat sunning herself; the garment she should have been mending was flung aside into the
heather.

Olav turned from her with distaste and went back to his work.
The boat now lay alongside the quay; the strangers were walking
up in company with Eirik. Olav made as though he had not seen
them until they stopped by the fence and greeted him.

They were two men of middle age, tall, thin, with keen, hook-
nosed faces and merry, twinkling eyes. Olav knew them now, he
had often seen them in Oslo, but never spoken with them; they
were sons of that English armourer, Richard Platemaster, who
had married a yeoman's daughter from the country west of the
fiord and had settled in the town. What business these men might
have with him Olav could not guess. But he went with them up to
the houses.

When the Richardsons had been given a meal and they were
sitting over their ale, Torodd, the elder, set forth their errand: he
had heard it hinted that Olav was minded to make an end of his
trading partnership with Claus Wiephart. Olav answered that he
knew nothing of it. But, said Torodd, he had heard in the town
that this year Olav Audunsson had withheld his goods and not
allowed Claus Wiephart to sell for him.

[1] In Norse mythology the Fimbul (i.e., mighty) winter, lasting for three
years, precedes Ragnarok, the death battle of the ancient gods.

'Twas not so either, replied Olav. But he had made a funeral feast for his wife here during the winter, so that much had been consumed in the house, and with the death of his wife he had also been hindered in his work in many ways.—Olav thought he could now see whither they were tending. And perhaps it might be worth considering, to find another trader for his wares.

Then said the other brother, Galfrid: "The matter is thus, Olav, that my brother and I have business in England this summer. And we know you to be a skilful shipmaster, and you are acquainted with that country from your youth. We have never been there, though it is the home of our father's kinsfolk. Now we have been surely told that you purpose to make a voyage this summer—"

While he was speaking Eirik had come in at the door, with a chaplet of blue anemones in his hand. Olav knew that the hazel thicket on the other side of the creek was now blue with these flowers. With such childishness as plucking flowers this long lad idled away his time on a bright and busy day of spring.

Eirik stayed by the door, listening intently and only waiting for his father to send him out of the room.

"Who told you that, Galfrid?" asked Olav.

It was Brother Stefan—that barefoot friar who had been hereabouts so much during the winter. The Richardsons were free of the Franciscan convent, as one of their brothers was a monk there. And there they had heard that Olav of Hestviken had thoughts of faring to foreign lands this summer, though doubtless he had not yet made any bargain about a ship.

Olav kept silence. But how the friar had got hold of this he could not guess—he did not recall having spoken of it to a soul. Go away—ay, God knew he had wished he could—but still he had not thought of *doing* it. He owned neither ship nor freight, and to seek out an opportunity of sailing with other folk had seemed somehow too troublesome a matter. Moreover there was enough to be done at home now, seeing how everything had been neglected during the long years of his wife's sickness.

But when an opportunity was offered—! He felt his heart contract in his breast as a hand is clenched to strike the table, the moment he fully realized that he *could* get away from everything. Far away—for a long while—Yes, oh yes!

"I said no such thing to Brother Stefan—" Olav shook his head. "Maybe I let fall something—I do not remember—I may have said

I might have a mind to see the world again, now that I am a man without ties—"

Then he became aware of the boy standing there, all ears, and he bade Eirik go out. Eirik came forward quickly and flung his chaplet about the little crucifix that hung on the wall within the bed where his mother had lain. But having done so, he had to go out.

How Brother Stefan's long nose had sniffed out these thoughts that he harboured—that was nevertheless more than Olav could make out.

In the course of the afternoon the men had reached so far in their colloquy that Olav took the two strangers and showed them what wares he had for sale. It was not much—less than a score of goats' pelts, three otters' skins and a few other skins of game, some barrels of oak bark. He would have to take with him all his store of fish and herrings—his house-folk could be content with fresh fish this summer. He had also some oak logs and barrel-staves he had intended for his own use—but if he himself were absent, they would only lie unused.

Late in the evening Liv came in and asked her master to go with her to the byre; there was a cow that was to calve, but the dairy-woman had fallen so grievously sick, said Liv—and besides, it was not her work to see to the cattle.

The night was moonless, cold, and still as Olav came out of the byre again. Now he had to go and wake old Tore, ask him as a favour to watch in the byre tonight, for it was of no use to let Liv be there alone. Lazy she was and thoughtless. One would scarce have believed it, but not even while they were struggling to tend the poor beast that lay there lowing plaintively—not even in the dark and narrow byre could the girl leave him in peace. She was after him like a kitten seeking to be caressed—time after time he had almost to fling her from him so that he might use his hands freely. She had taken the idea, Olav guessed, that now she would be his leman and mistress of the house. And however he let her see that it was bootless to aspire to *that* dignity, it made little impression on Liv.

He was secretly ashamed before his own house-folk—they must be laughing behind his back and watching whether the girl would

coax him the way she wanted in the end. He thought he saw it—
Liv playing the lady here with the keys at her belt. Oh no.—He
did not care to go in even with Tore, when he had roused the old
man.

There was ice on the top of the water-butt as Olav plunged
his arms into it and rinsed his hands. He listened and gazed out
into the darkness as he bethought himself whether anything had
been forgotten.

It was still now—the merry purling of little brooks on the slope
was frozen into silence and there was only the faint splash and
ripple of the sea beneath the cliff—and over in Kverndal the murmur of the stream. The stars seemed so few and so far away tonight—there was a slight mist in the air.

The calf was full-cheeked and long-eared—looked promising;
that was so far well; he had lost three calves this spring. And not
one cow-calf had he had yet.

In the northern sky above the dark back of the Bull pale flickers
of northern lights came and went—like a dewy breath over the
vault of heaven. They were not often seen here in the south. At
home in the Upplands the lights flashed half across the sky; and
when as children they used to tease them, by whistling and waving
linen cloths at them, there was a crackling sound and long tongues
shot down toward the earth and back to the sky. Once when they
had stolen out behind the outhouses and stood there flapping one
of Ingebjörg's longest wimples, Arnvid had come upon them, and
then he had beaten them. It was a great sin to do so, for it meant
storm when the northern lights were disturbed.

Here in the south the lights were usually but pale and faint.—

Olav gave his shoulders a hitch in his reeking clothes—'twas
still four days to washday and Sunday.

Instinctively he went quietly as he crossed the yard: the little
ice pockets made such a crackling, and he was loath to break in on
the low murmuring sounds that came up from below, as from the
depths of the night.

Within the room a little lamp was burning at the edge of the
hearth.

Olav had given the two strangers beds in the closet, and seated
on the edge of Ingunn's bed he undressed—slowly, with a pause
after each garment. He rose to pinch out the wick.

A whisper came from the northern bed: "Father!"

After a moment Olav answered in a hushed voice: "Are you awake, Eirik?"

"Yes. When shall we sail, Father?"

Olav was silent. But Eirik was so used to his father's seeming not to hear, or answering like the echo when one shouted toward the Bull—after a pause and as though across a distance.

"Father—take me with you! I shall stand you in good stead"—Eirik spoke in a loud and eager whisper—"I shall serve you as well as a full-grown man. I can do the work of an able-bodied man, ay, and more!"

"You can indeed." Eirik could hear that his father was smiling, but then there was neither anger nor refusal in his voice.

"May I go with you, Father—to England this summer?"

"None has yet said that I go myself," said Olav soberly.

He blew out the little flame, pinched off the burned wick, and dropped it into the oil. Then he got into bed. Something fell down and touched his neck in the darkness. It was soft and cool, reminding him of young, living skin, among the coarse, rough wool and sheepskins of his bedclothes. It was Eirik's chaplet. Olav groped for it and hung it in its place again. It had reminded him of her body—her shoulder so slight and soft and cold, when the coverlet had slipped off while she slept and he drew it up and spread it over her again.

Of course he would go—he was firmly resolved on that in his inmost heart, and he would suffer nothing to come in the way and hinder him. Only for appearance' sake he still let it seem uncertain whether he would accept; it would not do to acknowledge that he had let himself be persuaded so easily by two perfect strangers—nay, that he had seized their offer with both hands.

But he would not stay here at Hestviken the whole summer, now that he espied a means of escape. No matter that this little old hoy that the Richardsons' grandfather owned was a wretched craft—and that he himself was no more of a seaman than that they might easily have found many a better one. *Once* before he had been in England, some fifteen years ago with the Earl—so it was but little he knew of that country; a great lord's subalterns cannot stir far abroad. But as the Richardsons had not questioned him of it— He knew nothing of these two, but he could see that they were untried men and not over-wise. And by degrees he had been forced to admit that he himself would never be a good tradesman. It made him angry when he saw he had been cheated. But he had accustomed himself to say nothing and put a good face on it; 'twas bootless for him to wrangle with folk who were sharper than himself in such matters. He had not even thought of dissolving his partnership with Claus Wiephart—he might fall into the hands of others who would shear him yet closer.

These Richardsons looked as if they themselves might stand to be shorn. In that case there would be even less profit in throwing in his lot with them. Howbeit—

He missed her who was gone so sorely that he could not guess what it would be like to live here without her in all the years that were to come. He went about as one benumbed with wondering.

He could remember the thoughts he had sometimes had in her last years: that it would be a sin to wish her to lie on here and suffer torment to no purpose. But now that she was gone—ay, now he remembered that shred of saga that Brother Vegard had once repeated to them while they were children, of King Harald Luva, who sat brooding three years over the corpse of his Lapp wife. He was bewitched, the monk had said. Maybe—ah yes, but maybe 'twas not all madness either.

As far back as he could remember, he had been used to think of her as much as of himself, whatever he were doing or thinking. When two trees have sprung up together from their roots, their leaves will make *one* crown. And if one falls, the other, left standing alone, will seem overgrown. Olav felt thus, exposed and grown aslant, now that she was gone.

He knew full well they had been joyless years, most of them, but his memories of the happiness they had shared were far clearer and more enduring. It was as with the lime trees here on the hills about the inlet: they made no great show to the eye, but in summer when they blossomed, the whole of Hestviken seemed laden with the scent of them, so that one almost felt its sweetness clinging to the skin like honey-dew. In all the years he had been away from here, as boy and as man, fostered among strangers or an outlaw in other realms, this scent of lime blossoms had been the only thing to remind him that he owned lands that were his—all else about them he had forgotten.

And even in the saddest days of their life together she had been his—the same as that little Ingunn who had been so sweet and fair

when she was young, so slight and supple to take in his arms, with
the scent of hay breathing from her golden-brown hair when he
spread it over him in the darkness. He had often loved her with
the same gentle goodness as one loves a favourite faithful, innocent animal—a handsome heifer or a dog. And at other times he
had loved her so that his body trembled and quailed in anguish
when he recalled it now and remembered that it was done, had
been done for many a day before she died. And nevertheless she
was the only woman of whom he cared to recall the possession.
He could not think of the others without feeling a chilly aversion
to the memories creep over him.

Now he had lost Ingunn, and when he thought of the last night
before she died, he knew it was his own fault that he had lost her
entirely. He was well aware of what had befallen him. When he
was plunged in the most helpless distress and sorrow, about to
lose his only trusty companion in life, God, his Saviour Himself,
had met him with outstretched hands to help. And had he but had
the courage to grasp those open, pierced hands, he and his wife
would not now have been parted. Had he but had the courage
to stand by the resolve he had taken at that meeting with his God
—whatever might have been his lot in this world, whether pilgrimage or the headsman's sword—in a mysterious way he would
have been united with the dead woman, more intimately and
closely than friend can be united with friend while both are alive
on earth.

But once again his courage had failed him. He had stood looking on when God came and took Ingunn, carried her away alone.

And he was left behind as a man is left sitting on the beach
when his ship has sailed away from him.

And to bide here at home in Hestviken after that—it was the
same as waiting for the days and nights to pass by in an endless
train, one like another.

No, he would not turn away the Richardsons' offer, that was
sure.

From out of the darkness came the boy's wide-awake voice:
"The Danes, Father—they lie out in the English Sea and seize our
ships, I have heard."

"The English Sea is wide, Eirik, and our vessel is small.—Best
that you stay at home this year, for all that."

"I meant it not so—" Olav could hear that the lad sat up in his bed. "I meant—I had such a mind to prove my manhood," he whispered in bashful supplication.

"Lie down and go to sleep now, Eirik," said Olav.

"For I am no longer a little boy—"

"Then you should have wit enough to let folk sleep in peace. Be quiet now."

His father's voice sounded weary, only weary but not angry, thought Eirik. He curled himself up and lay still. But sleep was impossible.

He would be allowed to go, he believed that firmly—so firmly that when he had lain for a while thinking of the voyage, he felt quite sure of it. He was certain that they would fall in with Danish ships. They have a much higher freeboard than ours usually have, so at the first onset it might look bad enough. But then he calls out that all hands are to run to the lee side and hold their shields over their heads, and then, when all their enemies have leaped on board, they come forward and attack them. His father singles out the enemy captain—he looks like that friend of Father's they met in Tunsberg once: a stout, broad man with red hair and a full red face, little blue eyes, and a big mouth crammed with long yellow horse's teeth.—Then Eirik flings his shield at the stranger's feet, so that he slips on the wet floor-boards and the blow does not reach his father—yes, it does, but his father takes no heed of the wound. The Dane stumbles and his hauberk slips aside so as to expose his throat for an instant; at the same moment Eirik plies his short sword as though it were a dagger. Now the Danes try to escape on board their own ship. The ships' sides creak and give as they crash against one another in the seaway, and while the men hang sprawling, with axes and boathooks fixed in the high, overhanging side of the Danish vessel, the Norwegians lay on them with sword and spear. "Methinks 'tis no more than fair," says his father, "that Eirik, my son, should take the captain's arms—but if ye will have it otherwise, I offer to redeem your shares from this booty." But all the men agree: "Nay, 'tis Eirik that laid low this champion single-handed, and we have saved the ship through his readiness."

"Are you the young Norse squire, Eirik Olavsson from Hestviken?"—for the tale has spread all over London town. And one day when the governor of the castle rides abroad, he meets him. The White Tower is the name of London's castle; it is built of white marble. And one day when he has gone up to have a sight of it—this castle is even greater and more magnificent than Tunsberghus, and the rock on which it stands is much higher—the governor comes riding down the steep path with all his men, and some of them whisper to their lord, pointing to the lad from Norway—

Nay, stay behind in London when his father goes home, that he will not, after all. Not even in play can Eirik imagine his father leaving him and going back to Hestviken, and the life here taking its wonted course, but without him. In his heart Eirik harbours an everlasting dread; even if of late he has been able to lull it to sleep, he goes warily, fearing to awake it—what if one day he should find out that he is not the rightful heir to Hestviken? Even if he lies here weaving his own story from odds and ends that he has heard—the house-carls' tales of the wars in Denmark, the wonderful sagas of old Aasmund Ruga—the boy does not forget his secret dread: if he should be renounced by his father and lose Hestviken. Then let him rather play at something else—at strangers who make a landing here in the creek; his father is not at home, he himself must be the one to urge on the house-folk to defend the place, he must rouse the countryside—

But in any case his father shall soon have proof of what stuff there is in this son of his. He shall have something to surprise him, his father. Then maybe he will give up walking as one asleep, taking no heed of Eirik when they are together.

But the next day Olav set Eirik to bring home firewood for the summer, and his father said he was to have it all brought in today. The snow still lay over the fields here on the south side of the creek, but tomorrow most of it might well be gone.

The going was good early in the morning. Anki loaded one sledge while Eirik drove home the other. But as the day wore on, it grew very warm, and even before the hour of nones Eirik was driving through sheer mud a great part of the way.

Eirik spread snow along the track, but it turned at once to slush. Olav went higher up and spread snow on the fields there; he called down to the boy to drive round under the trees. But this was many times farther, around all the fields—and Eirik made as though he had not heard.

When Olav looked down again, the load of wood had stuck fast at the bottom of the slope leading to the yard. Eirik heaved off billets, making the rocks ring; then he went forward, jerked the bridle and shouted, but the horse stood still. "Will you come up, you lazy devil!"—and back went Eirik, dragging at the reins. Then he threw off more wood.

The sledge was stuck in a clay-pit at the bottom of the rock under the old barn, where the road from Kverndal turned up toward the yard. The sun had not yet reached this spot, so the rock was covered with ice, but water trickled over the surface. Eirik took hold of the back of the sledge and tried to wriggle it loose. But the horse did not move. The boy strained at it all he could, stretching to his full length over the ground; then he lost his foothold in the miry clay, dropped on his hands and knees, and some billets of wood slid off the load and hit him on the back—and there was his father standing on the balk of the field beside him. Fear at the sight of him gave Eirik such a shock that he was on the verge of tears; he plunged forward, tore at the reins, and belaboured the horse with them: the horse floundered, threw its head about, but did not move from the spot. "Will you come up, foul jade!" Quite beside himself, seeing that his father did nothing but stand and look on, Eirik struck at the horse with his clenched fist, on the cheeks, on the muzzle. Olav leaped down from the balk and came toward him, threateningly.

Then the horse put its forefeet on the frozen surface, slid, and looked as if it would come down on its knees. But at last it got a foothold, came up to the collar—the sledge with its lightened load came free—and dashed at a brisk pace up the slope.

On reaching the yard Eirik turned and shouted back to his father, with tears in his voice: "Ah, you might have lent us a hand—why should you stand there and do nothing but glare!"

A flush spread slowly over Olav's forehead. He said nothing. Now that the boy shouted it at him, he did not know how it had been—but he *had* simply stood and glared, without ever a thought that he might give Eirik a hand. A queer, uncomfortable feeling came over Olav—it was not the first time either. Of late it had happened to him several times to wake up, as it were, and find himself standing idly by—simply staring without a thought of bestirring himself and doing the thing that lay to his hand.

Up by the woodpile he heard Eirik talking kindly and caressingly to the horse. Olav had seen this before—such was the lad's

way with both man and beast: one moment he was beside himself
with sudden passion, the next all gentleness, imploring forgiveness.
With a grimace of repugnance Olav turned away and walked up
again across the fields.

The Richardsons returned to Oslo, and Eirik guessed that his
father had made a bargain with them. But now he dared not ask
whether he would be allowed to go too. What deterred him was
that not even this last misbehaviour of his had sufficed to drive his
father out of his sinister silence. When Olav suddenly appeared
beside the sledge, Eirik had been so sure that now he would be
given a thrashing—he winced already under his father's hard hand.
But afterwards he felt it as a terrible disappointment that nothing
had happened. Blows, curses, the most savage threats he would
have accepted—and returned, inwardly, at any rate—and felt it
as a relief, if only it put an end to this baneful uncertainty—not
knowing what to make of his father.

Olav would sit of an evening staring straight at Eirik—and the
boy could not tell whether his father were looking at him or
through him at the wall, so queerly far-away were his eyes. Eirik
grew red and unsteady beneath this gaze which he could not read.
Sometimes Olav noticed his uneasiness: "What is it with you,
Eirik?" There was a shadow of suspicion in his voice. Eirik found
no answer. But it might chance that he collected himself, seized
upon something that had happened during the day, and poured
out his story, usually of how much work he had performed or of
some remarkable thing that had befallen him—when he came to
speak of it to his father, everything became far more important
than he had guessed at first. Most commonly it fell out that long
before Eirik had finished he found that his father was no longer
listening—he had glided back into his own thoughts. But the worst
was when his father finally gave the faintest of smiles and said
quietly and coolly: "Great deeds are common when you are
abroad." Or "Ay, you are a stout fellow, Eirik—one need only ask
yourself to find that out."

Yet Eirik did his best, when talking to his father, to remember
everything as it had happened and to say nothing beyond that.
But when his tongue was set going, it came so difficult to him—
before he knew it he was relating an incident as it might have

happened, or as he thought it ought to have happened. Another thing was that the house-folk egged him on to tell everything in the way that was most amusing to listen to. They knew as well as Eirik that he tricked out his truthful tales with a few trimmings, but they agreed with him that so it ought to be, and not one of them betrayed a knowledge that Eirik was apt to tell a little more than the truth. It was only his father who was so cross and dull of apprehension and always required to be told everything so baldly and exactly.

But one day his father should be forced to say it in earnest—that Eirik was a brave fellow. Of that he was resolved.

For that matter, Eirik now gave a good account of himself, for his age, both on the farm and in a boat. He had not much strength in his arms, was slender and lightly built, but tough and tenacious, so long as he did not trifle away his time and forget to do what he had been set to. But, for all that, the house-carls were glad to have Eirik working with them—he was of a kindly and cheerful humour so long as no one provoked him, but then he was quick to anger. He had also a fine, clear voice for all kinds of catches and decoy songs and working-chants.

This spring both Tore and Arnketil spoke to the master about him, praising his industry and handiness. Olav nodded, but seemed not to see the expectant look on the boy's face. And much as Eirik strove to please his father and serve him—well, sometimes Olav did remember to thank him. And at other times he appeared quite unaware of it when Eirik gave him such help as he could; he accepted it without looking at the boy or giving him so much as a nod.

Then Eirik's anger flared up. He turned over in his mind something he would do simply to vex his father—*then* maybe he would remember to chastise him at any rate. But when it came to the point he did not dare—for that would end all chance of his going on the voyage to England.

In the week after Whitsunday, Olav Audunsson sailed up to Oslo, and ten days later the Richardsons' little hoy lay alongside the quay at Hestviken. The freight that Olav was to take was soon loaded, though he had charged himself with some trifles for Baard Paalsson of Skikkjustad; skins and pig-iron. Apart from this,

Olav had not been able to get hold of any goods in the country round at this unfavourable time of year. The very next day Olav's boats towed the hoy out of the creek; they came out into the fiord and hoisted sail. It was a bright, calm morning of early summer.

Eirik had been on board, helping to stow the cargo and talking to the men. There was not a strip of plank or boarding, not a block or a rope's end, that he had not pried into and handled.

Toward evening the boy sat on the lookout rock gazing after the little craft, which was now sinking out of view far away to the south. He went down to the quay, cast off his own boat, and rowed away under the Bull.

Some way up the headland there was a green ledge, and in the middle of it lay some great rocks. On the biggest of these grew three firs; Eirik called it the King. One could crawl in between these rocks; underneath the King there was a little hollow like a cave, and here he had a hiding-place.

On this side of the Bull there was only one place where one could land from a boat and climb up by a cleft in the rock. Otherwise one had to row round to the north side, or else up to the head of the creek. And toward the water this ledge ended in a sheer drop. Eirik had thought many a time that if a man were surrounded by his enemies up on that ledge, he could leap out, swim a long way under water, and save himself, before the others found the path down to their boat.

But this evening he was so sad and heavy of heart that there was no solace in the thought of these things. He crept into his cave and took out his possessions, but felt none of the old thrill and joy of ownership when he sat with them in his lap. He had not had them out more than once before this year—and then he had overhauled his treasures with the same intense delight as of yore.

There were two wooden boxes, turned on the lathe. The little one he had used for collecting rosin in summer, but now it held nothing but some scraps of little birds' eggs that he had kept because they were redder than most. In the other box he had the bones of a strange fish. It had been caught in the nets one day, several years ago; neither his father nor the boatmen had seen the like of it before, and so Olav ordered them to throw it into the sea—it looked likely to be poisonous. But Eirik saw that it had fallen between the piles of the old pier; when the men had left the waterside he rowed out and fished it up. There was no knowing whether it was dangerous to keep its bones, or whether there might be some hidden virtue in them; therefore he had always counted them very valuable. Until now—and now even he thought they were only trash.

He also had a leather bag full of smooth and barbed flints. Under an overhanging crag above the mouth of the stream in Kverndal he found plenty of these in the gravel, but he only kept the finest, those that looked like arrow-heads. His father said they *were* arrow-heads—the Lapps had used such things in heathen times, long before the Norsemen came and settled Norway. But Eirik thought there might well be something queer about them—perhaps they were thunderbolts. He had also found a bone fish-hook up there one time—a fine hook, with barbs and an eye for the line. He had thought of using it some day, when the fish would not bite; then the others would marvel at him, pulling up fish by the heap when no one else had any. But now he had lost that hook.

For all that, his dearest possession was the horse. It was roughly whittled from the root of a tree, and was not much bigger than his hand. Eirik did not know where it had come from—he had brought it with him from the place where he was fostered as a child, he believed; and he had a notion that it had been found under a rock, beneath which mound-folk dwelt—it was a gift from them. He had given away his childish toys long ago, for he saw that he was too big to play with such things without disgracing himself. But the horse seemed to be more than a toy, so he kept it up here under the King Rock.

Eirik knelt on the ground looking at the horse. It was dark and worn; one of its hind legs was so short that it stood on three, and it had an eye on only one side of its head, which stood out, a knot that had been cut away. It gave it such a weird look.

He took it up and placed it on the flat white stone that belonged to it. With closed eyes he walked backwards three times withershins about this altar, crooning softly the while:

"*Sun sinks in the sea, carrion cumbers the foreshore,*
    Down go we to our doom, Fakse my fair one. . . ."

But having accomplished this, he did not care to make the sign of the cross backwards—that was sinful, and foolish besides. He had a misgiving that the whole game had always been foolish.

He could never really have expected to see it turn into a copper
horse with a silver bridle. But he had believed in a way that one
day something wonderful must happen, after he had sung that
ugly spell over it.

Jörund Rypa would think it a foolish game. He was always
afraid that Jörund might come upon him while he was thus employed. It was not very likely—Jörund had kinsfolk who lived
far up the parish and sometimes he came to stay with them, but
it was scarcely to be imagined that he would show himself out
here on the farthest rocks of Hestviken. Nevertheless Eirik was
always afraid Jörund might come upon him. He felt in himself
that Jörund would make nothing of it, would only think he was
faddling here like a little child—and he could well believe that
Jörund would bear the tale of it and make mock of him. Yet
Jörund Rypa was, of all the lads of his own age Eirik had met,
the only one of whom he wished to make a friend. But Jörund
had not been in the neighbourhood for more than a year now—
his home was in the east, by Eyjavatn.

Eirik sat with his hands clasped about his knees and his chin
resting on them, gazing over at the manor.

It was now flooded by the evening sun, and the creek below
was still as glass, so that it could not be seen where the land came
to an end and the reflection began in the deep shadows under the
foreshore, but below the quay with its sheds another quay stood
on its head in the water, and deep down in the creek he saw the
image of the sun-gilt rocks on the hill and the row of turf roofs,
already slightly yellowed by the sun, and the meadows and all
the fair strips of plough-land where the corn was now coming up
finely, and evenly—but across this mirrored Hestviken a bright
wavy streak was drawn by the current.

The constant sound of bells from the wood under the Horse
Crag came nearer. Ragna was calling the cows home: the herd
came in sight at the gate at the brow of the wood. The line of
roan and dappled cows moved forward along the edge of the top
field.

Again a breath of distasteful memory crossed the boy's mind.
Just before his father went to Oslo he had sent him on an errand
to Saltviken. Up on the hill he had met the cattle, and then he
had gone and stuffed the cow-bell full of moss—not for any reason, it had just occurred to him to do it. But Jon, the herdsman,

had gone on about it and complained to the master when he came home in the evening. And once more the devastating thing happened that his father was moved neither to wrath nor to laughter by his prank; he only muttered something about child's tricks and looked unconcerned.

There went Liv up the path from the quay—she had been to the shed again, with Anki no doubt. Eirik moved uneasily. His body was hot and tingling, he felt guilty and ashamed. Though indeed *he* had done nothing wrong—he could not help it if she said such things to him, and it only made him angry and ashamed when she tried to take hold of him and hug him in the dark. What did she want of him? He was not yet grown up, and she had men enough without him, the ugly trollop.

But he could not get it out of his thoughts, for he guessed that she hung about his father too. And then it all came back to him, all the evil he had had in his mind when he found out about his father and Torhild Björnsdatter—his dread and his despair, not knowing whether he were sure of his right to his father and to Hestviken, and a miry flood of foul and evil thoughts and visions, and a mortal hatred that made his cheeks go white and cold when he thought of how he hated.

His father's fits of silence, which lasted from morning to night, the tired, drawn look of his mouth, of his eyes with their thin, filmy lids—even the way he rose to his feet after a rest, to go back to his work, as though laboriously collecting his thoughts from far away—all this filled the child's mind with insecurity. He guessed that he was living under the same roof with a pain of such a kind that it must strike him with terror if he ever saw it laid bare. And he hated, he raged against anything in the world that prevented him from ever having peace and happy days. And at the same time the boy could see that his father was still a handsome man, and no old man. The house-folk openly discussed what maidens and widows might be reckoned a fit match, both in the parish itself and in the neighbouring districts—little joy as Olav had had of his wife for many years, they doubted not he would marry again as soon as might be.

Had not this Liv been such a loathsome creature, it were almost better—for his father could never *marry* her. Many men were content to keep a leman in their house. But then he recalled the time when Torhild was here. No, his father must *not* bring any strange woman to dwell at Hestviken—he would not have anyone going about here, keeping the stores and dealing out the food, whispering in his father's ear at night, asking a boon or giving a word of advice, making mischief for him and Cecilia with their father, and filling the place with her own brood the while.

From here not much more was seen of the houses of Hestviken than the row of turf roofs on the slope under the crag. The shadow crept higher and higher up the hill, but the sun still shone on the roofs and the black cliff behind, with green foliage brightening the crevices. Up on the back of the Horse the red trunks of the firs were still ablaze.

All at once the tears burst from his eyes. His love of the manor smarted like homesickness; his grief at his father's leaving him was overwhelming. The relish had gone out of all his former joys. Eirik gave himself up entirely, he lay on the ground weeping so that the tears ran down.

There was a rustling sound on the edge of the cliff above him. The boy started up, burning with shame. A sheep thrust out its black face among the bushes—there was a white gleam of sheep behind it. Eirik scrambled up and chased them away. A good thing it was not men. Or Jörund—

Slowly he came down again. There stood his wooden horse, a wretched little toy. He snatched it up, ran forward to the brink, and threw it over.

It was now just dark enough under the cliff to prevent his seeing what became of it—whether it landed on the rocks below or in the water. For an instant he stood as though spellbound—now he had done it! Then he turned and ran, sobbing with remorse. He slid, leaped, tumbled almost, down the steep path in the cleft, to where his boat lay.

Eirik reached it and cast off. "Oh nay, I must find the copper horse again"—so intent was he that the faint gurgling of the water against the bottom of the boat troubled him. As noiselessly as he could, he poled and rowed along under the cliff, staring and listening intently in the shadows. *There* was something black floating among the rocks—he raked it toward him with an oar. No, it was only a stick of wood. And there—no. What if he searched all over the beach tomorrow—it was so small.

"Dear, holy Mary, help me, let me find the copper horse! I will give my three pennies to Helga with the tooth, next time she comes.—*Ave Maria, gratia plena Dominus tecum—*"

There it was! On the other side of the boat, a little way out. It was almost a miracle that it had not drifted in among the stones of the beach, and then he would never have found it. The boy drew a deep breath of happiness when he held the wooden horse in his wet hand. Now that it was so late he dared not go up again and hide it in the cave; he stuffed it into the folds of his coat.

Then he seized the oars and rowed briskly across to the other shore.

The quay was deserted when he came ashore. In the wood above, the thrush was singing—Eirik had to stop and listen to it. Then he went at a run up the path to the houses, he was so beside himself with happiness. And every now and then he had to stop to listen to the song of the birds.

All was still at the manor. As the lad opened the house door the thought struck him: now he was to lie alone in this house the whole summer. He had slept alone there now and then for a few nights, when his father was from home, and never been afraid, but now he felt his flesh creep a little.

The smoke-vent was not closed. Some food was left for him on the bare, clean-swept hearth. But the room had a cheerless look in the pale twilight. Eirik made haste to close the door leading to the black hole of the closet. He would close the outer door too, before sitting down to his food. But on coming to the doorway he could not help staying a moment to listen—how the birds sang tonight!

Out on the meadow a dark shadow stirred. Eirik whistled softly —the dog dashed up, but stopped a little way off, wagging his tail and not daring to come nearer. Eirik coaxed and coaxed—"Come along, King Ring—what have you been doing now?" The rascal was a most mischievous beast; his life had long been threatened daily both by Olav and by the servants, but none had yet had the enterprise to make an end of him.

At last King Ring took courage and slipped through the door, crouching down and rubbing his head against the boy's calf. Eirik hastened to bolt the door, and as he stooped in the darkness, the dog nearly knocked him down as he whimpered affectionately and licked his face with his hot tongue.

Sitting on the edge of the hearth, he ate cold porridge and sour milk and shared the wind-dried meat with the dog. Now his only thought was that it would be fine to have the living-room to himself this summer.

He hid the copper horse under the pillow in his bed. King Ring jumped up and lay down over his feet.

"—And when the ogress comes in and gropes about in the dark for this Christian man, he whistles for his white bear—"

Eirik drew his legs up closer under him and thought it all over again from the beginning. There is a man—and this man is himself, as it might be—who has wandered all day through wild forests; late in the evening he comes to a house. It is deserted, but he finds food and a bed prepared, and he goes to rest. In the course of the night he hears a great noise, and in comes an ogress —she is so tall that she reaches to the roof-beams and as broad as she is high. And she sniffs and scents the blood of a Christian and gropes and searches, for she wants to take the man and roast him on the fire. But then he whistles for his dog—

Sleep began to creep over Eirik; his thoughts were confused. He took it up again—through wild forests all day long, he and the white bear—and then there came in an ogress—first they came to a great house in the depth of the forest—he saw it all as large as life, the little clearing and the empty house.—Then sleep overcame him and quenched all visions.

2

CALMS and contrary winds delayed the *Reindeer's* voyage southward along the shore, and only on the twelfth day after their departure from Hestviken were the men able to stand out to sea. But once in open sea they had a good breeze and by the third morning Olav made a landfall on a high, mountainous coast that he took to be Scotland. He had heard that there was war between the English and the Scottish Kings; therefore he chose to bear off to sea again. They stood off and on for the best part of a day, and then the wind became more northerly. Now the men put on their shirts of mail and steel caps, for the southern sea between England and Flanders was never peaceful and safe for trading voyagers.

Since his life had been spent far up country until he was grown up, there was always something adventurous about the sea and a sea-voyage for Olav Audunsson; and though his body was tired out, his heart felt wonderfully fresh and rested. He had watched through the long, grey summer nights, always with mind and senses calmly alert, directed toward sea and sky—it was as though he were sailing away from the very memories of endless wakeful nights, when he had lain imprisoned at the bottom of a dark bed in the pitch-dark cave of the closet. They sank beneath the horizon at his back like the very coast from which he had steered. The weather had been fair almost all the time—the steady wind whistled in the rigging and bellied out the sail; the long, heaving ocean waves lifted the little hoy. For an instant it seemed to hesitate and think about it before plunging into the hollow—then a foaming at the bows, a little flying spray, a glimpse of grey-green water along the gunwale, the full note of the ocean as it raised its waves and drove one before another—the three big waves that came again and again after a certain interval. Clouds covered the whole vault of heaven, pale grey, drifting unhurriedly across the sky, now and again a pale gleam of sunshine falling on the sloping wet deck. Toward evening the weather often cleared a little; over on the horizon there was a glitter of sunlight on the sea. Then the bank of clouds closed in, reddened by the sunset behind them.

His sleep in the daytime refreshed him through and through, lying in a barrel, with the fur lining of his cloak wrapped warmly about his cheeks. The rushing of the waves, the sighing and creaking of the ship's timbers, the cries of the crew, rattling and heavy steps on deck—all these sounds reached him as he lay feeling the vessel lifting under him, gliding and sinking. Under the wide vault of daylight, where wind and wave flowed freely, filling his head with a loud, monotonous roar, he could fall asleep as easily as a child.

He felt young; it was as though the wind and the sea had washed and scoured him to this sensitiveness of body and soul—that afternoon when at last he stood on the vessel's poop as she was borne by wind and tide up the London river. The land on both banks was low and green—marshy meadows, cornfields on the rising ground, thick forest farther off on low hills undulating one behind another, till the farthest were lost in the pale blue haze of distance. Feeble gleams of sunlight broke through bright rifts in the clouds; somewhere in the west a cluster of pale rays fell upon the ground, saturated with moisture: the sun was drinking up rain.

It was not unlike Denmark. But Olav had never scanned those coasts, from which his mother had once come, with the same joyful expectation as he now felt. And England was much more populous. Innumerable towers and spires of great churches showed up inland above the woods. And they had sailed past many strong houses, built of white stone, enclosed by walls and watchtowers.

And when one of the men in the bows called out that now they could see the town, Olav leaped down and ran forward under the sail.

Through the light mist ahead he could make out towers and pinnacles, an innumerable multitude close together. And the darker grey streak that lay low down over the river, that must be the famous London Bridge. Olav forgot all else and gazed ahead.

Torodd Richardson came up to him. He had been talking to the pilot whom they had taken aboard at the mouth of the river. That was London's castle, the mighty fortress with four towers and a surrounding wall rising straight out of the water—that was the White Tower itself. And the long ridge of a leaden roof they saw on this side of it was St. Katherine's Church. The highest of all the spires on the rising ground was St. Paul's.

It was nevertheless the sight of the bridge that impressed Olav most deeply, for it was like nothing else that he had seen. It was the greatest marvel—built on huge arches that stood in the bed of the stream; what was more, it was of stone, and there were houses upon the bridge all the way. South of the river stood St. Olav's Church, said Torodd, and thither they must go to mass tomorrow; perchance they would meet fellow countrymen there. In former days, when the Norwegians sailed their own merchandise to London town, this had been their church. Nowadays they seldom came so far south. The *Reindeer* was the only vessel that had sailed hither from Oslo this year, but there might be men from Trondheim or Björgvin in town.

Olav listened in a way to the other's talk while gazing and waiting—he knew not for what.

. . .

They were late in going ashore next morning. The sun was already up when the six men from the *Reindeer* crossed London Bridge.

It gave Olav a queer feeling to think that this narrow street between the clothiers' shops lay over a broad river. The tide rushed upstream in a wave that was sucked out to sea again: he had noticed it in the little haven where they had put in the night before; there was more difference between ebb and flood here than at home in Hestviken. But men had been able to build up these heavy pillars of stone in the midst of the rapid current and throw a bridge over it. The thought made him strangely happy.

In many places the street was so narrow that only a little strip of sky could be seen between the houses. But farther along the bridge there was a break in the row of houses, so that wagons might pass each other. The Norwegians went out to the parapet to look down into the river.

The sun was above the woods in the east, and the air was filled with a bright haze; the sunlight glimmered in snow-white patches on the stream. The water ran through the arches with a rapid, steady roar; it was strange to see this strong stone wall rising straight out of the river. Unconsciously Olav raised his head and looked back at the town. Behind the thin mist, towers and spires shone in the morning sun. And all at once an immense flock of pigeons flew up from some place within there, circled about in a great ring, and turned, with the sun shining on their white and sea-blue wings.

A rowboat worked its way up against the stream, the sun glistening on the blades of the oars, twelve or fourteen pairs. It was not quite like any craft Olav had seen before, but it reminded him of a longship. Olav would have liked to stay and watch it go under the bridge, but Galfrid reminded him that the morning was far spent and mass would soon be over in all the churches.

There was not much traffic on the bridge so late in the day. But now they had to step into a shop door to make way for a company that came toward them: in front went a tall, large-limbed old man with an iron-shod staff in his hand and an armorial device embroidered on the bosom of his cloak. After him came two young maidens in trailing gowns, bearing their trains over their arms and holding books and rosaries; they wore wreaths of flowers in their fair, flowing hair and were beautiful as the morning, both of them. They were followed by an old serving-woman and two young pages, who carried the damsels' cloaks, and one of them had in his arms a lap-dog that yelped and jingled the bells on its collar.

Meanwhile a young man had appeared in the shop behind them; he chattered and tried to show his wares—took hold of Olav's coat and held before him a particoloured surcoat, half yellow and half blue. But when he found that the strangers were in no mind to bargain—or did not understand his speech—he pulled a face and laughed scornfully.

On the battlements over the southern gate of the bridge were some human heads stuck on stakes. On arriving in the open space beyond, Olav and his companions stopped to look at this. Immediately a little humpbacked old woman hobbled forward on crutches; after her came a young boy who crept on boards under his hands and knees—he had no feet. They pointed and chattered. Torodd Richardson was the only one of the party who knew a little of the language of the country; he interpreted for the others: the four nearest heads were those of great lords from the north country, rebels.

Olav Audunsson nodded in serious approval. There was nothing gruesome in this sight. He looked up, thoughtfully. The sun shone upon bare, greyish-yellow skulls, the morning breeze faintly stirred some tufts of hair. The flesh had rotted away, or the crows had pecked off what they could—there was not food for a bird left on any of the heads. A strange peace was upon these noseless faces that stared straight into the sun with unblinking eye-sockets. They looked iridescent, striped with black and greenish mould, but calm.

Olav had never before seen the heads of executed men close at hand. Often enough he had sailed past the Wheel Rock at Sigvalda, but had never landed on it. And the gallows hill outside Oslo lay in a quarter he had never had occasion to visit; nor had there ever been anything to take him thither, for it had never chanced that any was to be hanged when he was in the town.

But there was no horror in this sight, nothing that cried shame and dishonour over the dead. They looked like men of valour on guard over the gateway, waiting patiently for something, with faces turned toward the sun and the fresh morning breeze.

Olav was the first who remembered to make the sign of the cross; half-aloud he began to pray:

"*Pater noster qui es in cælis, sanctificetur nomen Tuum, adveniat regnum Tuum—*"

"*Opera manuum Tuarum, Domine, ne despicias,*" the beggars took up the response, and said it together with his shipmates.

"*Requiem æternam dona eis, Domine, et lux perpetua luceat eis.*"

Olav and Galfrid gave alms to the beggars, and then they hobbled off, this way and that. The thought struck Olav that these were the first words he had understood of folks' speech in this country—the prayer for the souls of the beheaded men.

The portreeve's officers had assigned the *Reindeer* to an anchorage west of the bridge—a little square-shaped dock at the riverside. None but small vessels lay there and most of them seemed to be English. The water was turbid and muddy; at low water the slimy bank was exposed. But the harbour itself was well compassed about on three sides with a quay and warehouses; the upper story was supported on pillars, so that the place resembled a cloister in a convent. These quays were astir all day long; more than a score of men were regularly employed in loading and unloading goods and in ferrying folk across the river. Torodd had found out that they had better not use the ship's boat to take them to and from the shore; the ferrymen did not like it, and it was foolish to set them against one. So they made a bargain with one of them that he should row the *Reindeer's* men ashore and back every day and have five English pence a week for it. It was dear—but it had not taken Olav long to perceive that he was unlikely to reap any great profit from this English voyage.

Oaken timber, furs, and hides they had here in abundance—there was no need to carry such things over the English Sea, and not much was to be got for fish at this time of the year. The otter and marten skins and Baard's iron were the only wares he was able to sell with any profit. It vexed him somewhat that he had known so little of how things were in the outside world. But he did not regret the voyage.

Nor had he any need to feel ashamed in the presence of the Richardsons—they were no shrewder merchants than he. But their chief business in this voyage was not trade. It was their brother, the Minorite friar, who had moved them to go. When he was in England some years ago he had found a kinsman, a rich priest in the west country, and this man had taken so kindly to his sister's grandson that he promised to give the Minorites of Oslo a great quantity of costly books and mass vestments at his death. News had been brought last year that the priest was dead, and now the Richardsons were to see to taking up the heritage; the Franciscans' house here in London would help them and send men with them into the west. At the same time their brother had obtained for them the charge of buying silk yarn, gold wire, flax, and velvet in England, both for the convent of nuns in Oslo and for the Queen's household.

The Richardsons were to lodge with their kinsmen here in London, a man named Hamo, who was by craft an armourer. Olav was also bidden there as a guest. But in the narrow street where Hamo's house lay there were smithies in every yard, and in the alleys about were taverns and stews—noise in the daytime and racket and shouting all night. Moreover he would have to give great gifts to everyone in the house at his departure. So Olav chose rather to stay on board with a young lad and an old man whom folk called Tomas Tabor, because in wintertime he went round in Oslo playing the tabor at banquets. The other two mariners stayed with the Richardsons up in the town.—Another thing was that Olav thought he slept so well under the open sky. It often rained at night, so that the water streamed in upon them where they lay under the poop, but in spite of that he preferred it to sharing a warm bed with a strange bedfellow.

Every morning early the waterman fetched him and one of his companions and set them ashore. By his second day in town Olav had already found out that the preaching friars had a great convent here, and thither he went to mass—St. Olav's was so far out of the way, and he was not very eager to meet fellow countrymen either. They followed the river westward through a narrow street that ran behind the warehouses; here was a rank, raw smell in the cold depth between the lofty gabled houses. At last they came to a little green space among heaps of stones and rubble, beside which grew bushes and flowers; the town wall had here been pulled down and moved out farther to the westward to give the Dominicans room to build. The convent lay close up to the new wall, and the church was still in building—it's outer walls stood naked and unadorned. But it was exceedingly fair within, built with pointed arches and a very lofty roof with crossed ribs. The morning light poured in full and clear through the lofty, narrow windows, which were not yet filled with pictured glass.

Olav sought out a place so near to the altar that he could hear the words of the priest saying mass. The Latin had a somewhat different sound from that of Norwegians, but not so much so that he could not recognize the passages proper to the saint of the day:

Me exspectaverunt peccatores, ut perderent me: testimonia tua, Domine, intellexi: omnis consummationis vidi finem: latum mandatum tuum nimis. Beati immaculati in via: qui ambulant in lege Domini—[2]

This was the office for a virgin martyr; but they also sing *Beati immaculati* over little children when they are carried to the grave. With hands clasped over his breast brooch and his chin resting on them Olav stood gazing at the priest's red chasuble. The gospel that followed had once been taught him by Asbjörn All-fat.

In illo tempore: Dixit Jesus discipulis suis parabolam hanc: Similie est regnum cælorum thesauro abscondito in agro: quem qui invenit homo, abscondit, et præ gaudio illius vadit, et vendit universa quæ habet, et emit agrum illum—[3]

He was always reminded of Arnvid Finnsson when he was in this church. The priest before the altar became as it were Arnvid —though when he turned toward the people he bore no resemblance to Arnvid, who had never attained to his heart's desire, of being ordained priest.—*Et vendit universa quæ habet, et emit agrum illum—*ay, that must be what Arnvid had meant by the counsel he gave him, when they met for the last time.

Another morning they celebrated the memory of a saint whose name Olav had never heard before—he must have been an Englishman. But this was a martyr too:

In illo tempore: Dixit Jesus discipulis suis: Nolite arbitrari, quia pacem venerim mittere in terram: Non veni pacem mittere, sed gladium—[4]

*Gladium—*Olav had always thought that word sounded so finely. And he saw that it could not be otherwise: when God Himself descended into the world of men and appeared as a man among men, it had to be, not peace, but a sword. For God could

[2] Psalm cxix, 95, 96, 1.   [4] St. Matthew, x, 34.
[3] St. Matthew, xiii, 44.

not intend to be as a sorcerer who puts man's will to sleep; He
must needs come with a war-cry: for or against Me! God's peace
—that must be like the peace that comes when the raging of the
storm is past and the fight has been fought out—as indeed Saint
John the Evangelist had seen in his visions; Bishop Torfinn had
spoken of it.

In these early morning hours, when he knelt here during mass,
the memories of his mornings in the church at Hamar were so
near and living—though it had been winter then and dark outside,
when he accompanied Asbjörn All-fat to the northern gallery.
Asbjörn said his mass there at the altar of Saint Michael. It was so
cold that he could see the priest's breath as a white vapour against
the red flames of the two candles on the altar. No others ever
came up there—and sometimes they were so early that the scholars
were still asleep; therefore Asbjörn had taught him to serve as
acolyte at the mass. When Olav did not remember to answer at
once, Asbjörn whispered the first words of the response; with
scarcely perceptible nods and pointings he signed to the young
man to move the books or bring the ampullæ and the holy water.

His heart had been filled to the brim with a deep, solemn joy
when he was permitted thus to assist at the sacred act, the eternal
sacrifice, which was here carried out on the border between night
and day. Here, in the secret chamber at dawn, he had felt safely
in harbour—after his long, rough voyage through the tempest of
his own and other men's uncurbed passions. He had pretended to
be careless of the storm—but he had been so young; in secret he
trembled with weariness. And he had not come through unsoiled:
his heart was surely as turbid as the tarn north in the woods, when
on the melting of the snows all the grey and rapid streams had
emptied themselves into it. And no sooner had it cleared a little
after the flood than the spruce forest round its banks came out
and powdered the brown bog-water with yellow. But here at the
foot of the altar he felt the Spirit of God as a cleansing wind—the
mawkish pollen was blown away: once more his life would be
bright and open as the tarn, reflecting the sheer blue and the sun
and the clouds on their passage across the sky.

"Lord, Lord—'tis long ago! I am no more a young man. But
even in autumn, when the ice has already begun to form around
the rocks, and the tarn is choked with withered reeds and green
scum—even then Thou canst send a wind that breaks up the half-

formed ice and sweeps the surface clean so that it lies still and bright and blue for a while—before winter comes and imprisons it in ice."

These thoughts were scarcely formed, but the images haunted Olav as he knelt with bowed head and a corner of his cloak held up before his face. Everything was present to his memory, nothing would he attempt to deny. Nevertheless he was calm, full of confidence.

Now the little mass bell rang; the priest bowed low over the altar table, kneeling. Now he rose again, holding aloft in his hands the sacred body of our Lord, wrapt in the humble garment of the bread.

Olav looked up and worshipped: "My Lord and my God!"

Whether he would or would not, never could his heart cease to love God, he now knew. Whatever he might do and however he might try to drown the voice that made complaint in his inmost being: "Lord, Thou knowest that I love Thee!"

Nor had he forgotten that here he was, a traitor and a fugitive from God's host. For years he had done wrong, and never because he knew no better. But yet he did not now feel the gnawing pain of a sore conscience, which had tormented him so long, whenever he prayed or appeared to pray. Now every prayer he uttered was like kneeling down and quenching his thirst at a fountain.

Behind him in space and time he recalled all the years at Hestviken as a period of sickness—the memory of one long fever. The pain and ache had come from within, all the evil, all the nightmare visions had been bred within himself. Now it was as though the door were thrown open, light and refreshing coolness flowed in upon him from without.

He now felt whole again. The sea, the breezes, the nights on watch with senses directed outward, had washed away the close and fusty heat and cleansed him of his scalded sensitiveness.

It was not that he now thought less of his sin, but that he himself bulked far less in his own eyes. While he was brooding at home in Hestviken, silent and despairing over the loss of his soul, it had seemed to him there was so much he must throw overboard if he would find peace with God—*his* honour, *his* welfare, *his* life perhaps—these had been such great things. But now that he was in a place where he saw more of the glories and riches of this world than he had believed could be collected in one spot—now all that he called his own suddenly appeared to him so little—a man ought to be able to fling this from him as lightly as he would hang up his harp on the wall, when the trumpet summoned him to arms.

By God, there would always be men enough left upon earth. But each man's *soul*—that was a thing no man could take hold of, weigh and measure by the standards current among men. And in the end God collects all souls and weighs them with a weight that is His secret.

So he listened in calm meditation to the only voice that spoke to him in a tongue he understood—here in the foreign land, where all other voices shouted at him as though there were a wall between him and them. The voice of the Church was the same that he had listened to in his childhood and youth and manhood. *He* had changed—his aims and his thoughts and his speech, as he grew from one age into another—but the Church changed neither speech nor doctrine; she spoke to him in the holy mass as she had spoken to him when he was a little boy, not understanding many words, but nevertheless taking in much by looking on, as the child takes in its mother by following her looks and gestures, before it understands the spoken word. And he knew that if he journeyed to the uttermost limits of Christian men's habitation—folks' form and speech and customs might indeed be strange and incomprehensible to him, but everywhere, when he found a church and entered it, he would be welcomed by the same voice that had spoken to him when he was a child; with open hands the Church would offer him the same sacraments that she had nourished him with in his youth, and that he had rejected and misused.

And Olav felt like a man who has come home to his mother—from distant voyages that have brought him more of wounds and losses than of honour and profit. And now he sits alone with her, listening to her plain, reasonable speech and hearing her wise counsel: "If thou hast been the loser in every conflict thou hast essayed, be yet assured that not even the most hapless man has lost the fight that has not yet been fought."

Outside, the morning sun shone so fairly upon the little green before the church—this summer it scarcely rained but at night. After mass Olav and his companion strolled northward through the streets that led up to St. Paul's churchyard.

The houses here were much higher than in Oslo and they were

built of timber, with daubing between and boarded gables. But here and there the rows of houses were broken by strong stone halls surrounded by walls; watchmen with sword in hand stood at the gates. A green courtyard could be seen within, where men-at-arms exercised themselves in archery and games of ball.

There were trading booths along the walls of the churchyard, but if anyone stopped for a moment to look at the wares, a man instantly appeared to pounce upon the customer. Such was never the custom in Oslo—except among the Germans of Mickle Yard, where it was young women who stopped to look. But otherwise a man might go in everywhere, look around the shop, turn over and handle everything that was exposed for sale—the owner feigned not to see, scarce looked up from his work as he answered any question that was put to him. But here the prentices ran out into the street after folk. And here was a vast deal of noise and shouting.

The church bells rang incessantly above their heads—bells here and bells there, the deep booming of great bells and the busy tinkling of little chimes. Then for a while all the bells began to peal together in an immense chorus of resonance. With the conventual churches and all the small parish churches Olav thought there must be far more than half a hundred churches in London. At least ten of them were as great as the Halvard Church in Oslo; St. Paul's was greater than any other church he had seen.

In the east by the town wall stood the convent of the Franciscans, and in the open place before it the corn market was held. Huge wagons with teams of oxen and great heavy-limbed horses made the market-place and the streets about it difficult to move in. Olav and Tomas Tabor walked about for hours looking at this fair show of wealth. Even now in the middle of summer the great bulging sacks stood ranged along the pavement—untied, so as to show the good golden corn. The dust from it hung over the place like a light mist. The cooing of a multitude of pigeons was heard as an undertone through the din and the hum of voices.

The town wall was also worth looking at closely, with its strong towers and barbicans before the gates. There were prisoners in some of the gate towers, and they let down little baskets from the loop-holes, so that people might give them alms. The guards at all the gates were picked men, excellently clothed and armed.

The convent bells rang for the last mass; the sun was now high and it began to feel warm. Olav and his companion were sweating: they wore shirts of mail under their tunics; the Richardsons had told them they must always do so here. The soil, fed with the offal of human habitation for hundreds of years, gasped out its stench, but from the gardens behind the houses, enclosed by stone fences or convent walls, was wafted the sweet scent of elders and roses, the hot, spicy breath of pinks and celery. And now the smell of food, roast and boiled, poured out of open doors—it was getting on for dinner-time. The two strangers increased their pace through the lanes leading down to the river; they felt the suck of hunger under their ribs.

Black swarms of crows and jackdaws whose nests were in the church towers swooped down as soon as any offal was thrown out. There was a sickening stench from the blood that ran out of the slaughterhouses, making the gutter in the middle of the street run red. But when they came into the street of the brewers they were met by the sweet steam rising from the warm grains that were thrown out, and they had to drive off the pigs that were gobbling them, before they could pass. It was good to feel hungry and to buy bread on the way, two smooth, round, golden-brown loaves.

The ale-keg lay waiting for them in the ferryman's boat; he had offered to fetch the ale for them every morning and would not take pay for it beyond what was agreed. But then he took toll of the keg. Olav and the men swore a little and laughed a little when they shook it after coming aboard.

They brought their sheepskins out on deck into the sunshine, and produced from their chests butter, dried meat, and cheese. Olav made the sign of the cross on the loaves with his knife and divided them. Then they flung themselves down on their sleeping-bags and ate and drank in silence, for they were both hungry and thirsty. The ale was excellent. And then this new-baked bread that they ate every day over here—they agreed that there was no need to waste money on fresh meat in the taverns when they had that.

Olav got on well with his two shipmates; they were men of few words, both of them. A good thing that chatterer Sigurd Mund, as they called him, had gone with Galfrid.

After the meal Olav and Leif stretched themselves on their bags. Tomas Tabor sat down to play on a little pipe he had bought in the town. The thin tone of it, rising three notes, trilling down again, and leaping about the scale, the same over and over again, sounded, as Olav lay half-asleep, like a little maid at play, climbing about a stairway—at times he could plainly see Cecilia.

Toward evening Olav took the ship's boat and rowed on the river. The finest of all views of the town was from the water; there was a movement on the stream like that of a great highway. From the stately houses on the Strand, west of the city, came great barges, flying swiftly along under ten or twelve pairs of oars; across the water came the music of minstrels and pipers playing to the lords and ladies on board.

A little lower down, the walls of a castle rose out of the river, with strong water-gates and a wharf outside, and lofty gabled halls behind—*Domus Teutonicorum*. Olav fixed his eyes on the castle as he drifted past in his little boat. It booted little for folk of other lands to contend with these merchants of Almaine; bitterly he reflected that no doubt the day would come when they would found their hanse on Oslo wharves too. But it was a fair house, this of theirs, as everything that bears witness of strength is fair in its way.

He turned and rowed up against the stream. Now he passed the south-western water-tower of the town wall and could see the whole western sweep of the wall from the outside, with the towers and barbicans before the gates. Soon the roofs of the Knights Templars' *præceptorium* appeared above the trees.

Olav had never been out there, but Galfrid said he ought to go on a Friday morning. Then they carried out into the field an immense red cross, and while a priest preached to the people, the knights stood around, clad in mail with drawn swords in their hands, the points raised to heaven; they stood as though cast in bronze. And their priest must be the most powerful of preachers, for the people wept and sobbed, both men and women.

Olav's thoughts were busied, half toying, with this monastery of warriors. He had heard that the Pope had given their Grand Prior the same right of loosing and binding as he had himself. Before a man was admitted to the brotherhood he had to confess all the sins he had committed in his life, both atoned and unatoned—and of the severe penance he had to undergo the world heard no more than it hears of what is done in purgatory. They had strange

customs, folk said—he who would enter their ranks was compelled
to strip naked and lie thus for a night in an open grave in the floor
of the church, as a sign that he was dead to all his former life.

He had seen the Templars ride through London more than
once; they were clad in chain armour from the throat to the soles
of their feet, with a red cross on their white tunic, which they
wore over the shirt of mail, and on their white mantle; their great
battle-maces also bore the sign of the cross. He had heard of the
warrior monks before, but never seen them.

Then there were the anchorites. There were so many of them
here in London; some dwelt in cells within the town wall and
some in little houses that were built against a church with an opening in the wall between, so that the hermit might see the altar
and the ciborium that held the body of the Lord. Some had a
lay brother or a lay sister to do their errands for them, but many,
both men and women, had caused themselves to be walled up,
that they might share the lot of the most wretched prisoners. One
of them dwelt in the wall close to a dungeon—till the day of his
death he was to live there in a cold, black hole into which the
water dripped, in his own stench and in his sour and mouldy rags;
he was crippled and paralysed with rheumatism. And this man's
life had been distinguished by great holiness even as a child and
while he was living as a monk in his convent. When men who
were to suffer punishment were led past the orifice of his cell, the
anchorite cried out: "Be merciful, as your Father in heaven is
merciful!"

Of late years Olav's thoughts had now and then been drawn
toward the monastic life—whether it might be the end of his difficulties if he adopted it. But not for a moment had he believed it
in earnest. Whatever might be God's will with him, he was surely
not called to be a monk. Of that he had the most certain sign—for
it was not the hardships of the monastic life that he shrank from.
On the contrary, to let fall from his shoulders all that a monk is
bound to renounce, to submit to the discipline of the rule—for
this he had often longed. Nevertheless no man was fit for this
unless God gave him special grace thereto. But now Olav had
roamed long enough as an outlaw on the borders of the realm of
God's grace to perceive that when once a man of his own will sur-
renders himself to God and accepts what is laid upon him, God's
power over him is without limit. And in the long, sleepless nights

he had often thought: "Now they are going into the choir in their convents, men and women, standing up to serve their Lord with praise, prayer, and meditation, like guards about a sleeping camp." But it was all the things that were included in the rules for the relief and repose of man's frail nature that *he* could not think of without distaste: the brotherly life, the hours of converse, when a monk has to show humility and gentleness toward his fellows, whether he like them or not, whether he be minded to speak or be silent; to have to go out among strangers or to serve in the guest-house when the prior bade him, even if he would rather be alone. He had seen that this was beyond the power of many monks, who were otherwise good and pious men; they grew sour and cross with strangers, quarrelsome among themselves. But this was a sign that these men were not fitted for the monastic life. "One may carve Christ's image as fairly in fir as in lime," Bishop Torfinn had once said to Arnvid, on his expressing a wish that he could be as calm and good-humored as Asbjörn All-fat; "but never have I heard that He turned fir into lime, like enough because it would be a useless miracle. With God's grace you may become as good a man as Asbjörn, but I trow He will not give you All-fat's temper, for all that."

But now he saw that the life of a monk had other paths than those he knew at home in Norway. There were paths also for those who were not fitted to associate with strange brethren. Warfare with the discipline of the convent behind that of the warrior, like a hair shirt under the coat of mail—in the Holy Land the Templars' hosts had been cut down many a time to the last man. In the Carthusians' monasteries each monk lived in a little house by himself; they met only in church. And now he had seen some other monks, the Maturines—their white habit resembled that of the preaching friars, but they bore a red and blue cross on their breasts. They collected alms, wherewith to cross the sea and redeem Christian men from slavery among the Saracens. And when they had no more money, the youngest and strongest of these monks gave themselves in exchange for sick and weary prisoners.

It had not yet come to any fixed purpose with Olav, but it made him thoughtful. The world had widened to his vision, and he now saw that that other world which stretched its curtain over the earth from one end to the other was without bounds. And now, when he saw himself standing beneath this immense vault, he felt

so small and so lonely and so *free*. What mattered it if a franklin
from the Oslo fiord never came home again? He might be stabbed
any evening on the quays here—they might be plundered and
slain by pirates on the Flanders side this autumn, they might be
wrecked on the coast of Norway—every man who put to sea on
a trading voyage knew that such things might easily happen, and
none stayed at home on that account. Strange that he could have
thought it so great a matter, as he tramped over his land and
splashed about his creek, that he should rule the manor—indifferently well—if he had to murder his own soul to do it.

That might yet be while *she* was alive. But now—Arne's daughters and their husbands would take charge of the children and of
the estate if he sent home a message this autumn that he would
not return.

London's church bells rang—time to put out fires. Olav rowed
downstream again. He put in at a little wharf just below the western water tower. The old man who took his boat was so thickly
covered with beard and dirt that he seemed overgrown with moss.
Olav exchanged a few words with him—he had picked up a little
English now. Then he made his way through the lanes, where
children ran and shouted and refused to obey their mothers who
called them in, up to the Dominicans' church.

He said the evening prayers and a *De profundis* for his dead,
and then found himself a seat on some steps that led to a door in
the wall. With his chin in his hands he waited till the monks
should come into the choir and sing complin.

The lofty windows darkened and grew dense; dusk collected
under the vaulting and filled the aisles. A single votive candle
burned before one of the side altars, but up in the choir the
golden lamp alone hovered like a star in the twilight. Outside the
open doors the fading daylight paled in a grey mist. Folk came
strolling in to hear evensong; the echo of their chattering whispers
murmured incessantly through the lofty pillared church; their
footsteps rang softly on the stone flooring. Then came the hushed
but penetrating beat of many footfalls in the choir, the clatter of
seats being turned up; the tiny flames of the candles were lighted
on the monks' desks, throwing their faint gleam on the rows of
white-clad men standing up in the carved stalls. And down in the
body of the church there was a rustle of people rising and drawing nearer, while a hard, clear, man's voice began to intone and

was answered by the chant of more than half a hundred throats, the first short sentences and responses—till the whole male choir raised the song of David on sustained, monotonous waves of sound.

Olav sat down again when the psalm began. Now and again he sank into a half-doze—woke up as his head dropped—then the veil of sleep wound about him again and his thoughts became entangled in it. Till he grew wide awake at the notes of *Salve Regina* and the sound of the procession descending from the choir. The people moved forward into the nave as the train of white and black monks advanced, singing:

"Et Jesum, benedictum fructum ventris tui, nobis post hoc exsilium ostende. O clemens, o pia, o dulcis Virgo Maria!"

Olav strode quickly down toward the wharf; it was dusk outside now, bats flitted like flakes of soot in the darkness. He must be aboard the *Reindeer* before it was quite dark—the other evening the river watch had called to him from their boat. To his very marrow he felt the good this evening service had done him. It was the same as he had heard in Hamar, in Oslo, in Danish and Swedish ports—in good and evil days he had always attended evensong, wherever he found a convent of the preaching friars. He had also heard the singing of nuns one evening here in London—for the first time in his life. He had never chanced to enter the church of a women's convent before, but Tomas Tabor had taken him one evening to a nunnery. Marvellously pure it had been to listen to—but nevertheless it did not stir the depths of him in the same way. The clear, sharp, women's voices floated like long golden streaks of cloud on the horizon between earth and heaven. But they did not raise themselves above the world over which the veil of darkness was falling as did the song of praise from a choir of men on guard against the approach of night.

Tomas Tabor appeared at the gunwale as Olav came alongside. Now it was dark already, he complained, and Leif had not yet come—likely enough he would stay ashore again tonight, and tomorrow he would make the same excuse, that he could not get a boat in time. Olav swung himself over the gunwale.

"You must refuse him shore leave, Olav! He cannot be so steady as we thought him, Leif!"

"It seems so." Olav shrugged his shoulders and gave a little snorting laugh. The men walked aft and crept in under the poop.

"I trow that serving-wench out at Southwark has clean be-witched him."

They snuggled into their bags and ate a morsel of bread as they lay.

" 'Twill end in the boy getting a knife between his shoulder-blades. That place is the haunt of the worst ruffians and ribalds."

"Oh, Leif can take care of himself—"

"He is quick with the knife, he too. You must do so, Olav, you must forbid him to go ashore alone."

"The lad is old enough; I cannot herd him."

"God mend us, Master Olav—we ourselves were scarce so wise or heedful that it made any matter, at seventeen years—"

Olav swallowed the last mouthful of bread. After a while he answered:

"Nay, nay. If he cannot come back on board betimes, he must not have leave. And he should have had his fill of playing now, enough to last him a good while."

Presently: "I think we shall have rain again," said old Tomas.

"Ay—it sounds like it," said Olav sleepily.

The shower drummed on the poop above them and splashed on the boards; the hiss of raindrops could be heard on the surface of the river. The men shuffled in under cover, as far as they could come, and fell asleep, while the summer shower passed over the town.

Torodd and Galfrid were tarrying in the west country, it seemed—perhaps they had not found it so easy to get their hands on the heritage of Dom John. Olav was as well pleased one way as the other—and the days went by, one like another.

3

ONE EVENING Olav had been sitting half-asleep in his corner of the church. When he heard the scraping of feet in the choir, he stood up and went forward into the nave.

Right opposite on the women's side was a statue raised against one of the pillars, of the Virgin with the Child in her arms and the crescent moon under her feet. This evening a thick wax candle was burning before the image; just beneath it knelt a young woman. The moment Olav looked at her, she turned her face his way.

And now his breath went from him and he lost all sense of himself and where he was—but this was Ingunn, she was kneeling there, not five paces from him.

Then he recalled the time and place and that she was dead, and he knew not what to believe. It felt as if the heart within him stood still and quivered; he knew not whether it was fear or joy that made him powerless, whether he was looking on one dead—

The narrow face with the straight nose and long, weak chin —the shadow of the eyelashes on the clear cheeks. The hollows of the temples were darkened by a wave of golden-brown hair; a transparent veil fell from the crown of the head in long folds over the weak and sloping shoulders.

Even as he drank in the first vision of her charm, Olav saw that perhaps this was not she—but that two persons could be so like one another! So slender and delicate from the waist down to the knees, such long, thin hands—she held a book before her, and her lips moved slightly—now she turned the leaf. She knelt on a cushion of red silk.

A sobering sense crept over him that it was not she after all. As when one wakes from a heavy sleep and recognizes one thing after another in the room where one is, realizing that the rest was a dream—so now he realized little by little.

His poor darling, she had not been able to read a book. Nor had she ever had such clothes. As he looked on the rich dress of the strange woman, a bitter compassion with Ingunn stirred within him—there was never anyone to give *her* such apparel. He remembered her as she had been all the years at Hestviken, in bad health and robbed of her youth and charm, poor and unkempt in the coarse, rustic folds of her homespun kirtle. *She* should have been like this one, kneeling on her silken cushion, rosy-cheeked, fresh and slim; her mantle spread far over the stone slabs, and it was of some rich, dark stuff; her kirtle was cut so low that her bosom and arms showed through the thin golden-yellow silk of her shift. Half-hidden in the folds at her throat gleamed a great rosary— some of its beads were of the color of red wine and sparkled as her bosom rose and fell. She was quite young. She looked as Ingunn had looked as she knelt in the church at Hamar, childlike and fair under her woman's coif.

The strange woman must have felt his continual stare—now she looked up at him. Again Olav felt his heart give a start: she had the same great, dark eyes too, and the uncertain, hesitating, side-long glance—just as Ingunn used to look up at those she met for the first time. She had never looked at *him* in this way—and a vague and obscure feeling stirred in the man's mind that he had been cheated of something, because Ingunn had never looked upon *him* for the first time.

The young wife looked down at her book again; her cheeks had flushed, her eyelids quivered uneasily. Olav guessed that he annoyed her with his staring, so he tried to desist. But he could think of nothing but her presence—every moment he had to glance across at her. Once he met a stolen look from her, shy and inquisitive. Quickly she dropped her eyes again.

The procession came down from the choir, and the sprinkling of holy water recalled him wholly to his senses. But truly it was a strange thing that here in London he should chance to see a woman who was so like his dead wife. And young enough to be her daughter.

He remembered that he had not yet said his evening prayers, knelt down and said them, but without thinking of what he was whispering. Then he saw that she was coming this way—she swept past so close to him that her cloak brushed against his. When he rose to his feet, she was standing beside him, with her back turned. She had laid her hand on the shoulder of a man who was still kneeling. Behind her stood an old serving-woman in a hooded cloak, carrying her mistress's cushion under her arm.

The man stood up; Olav guessed he must be the strange woman's husband. Olav knew him well by sight, for he came to this church nearly every day. He was blind. He was young, and always very richly clad, and he would not have been ugly but for the great scar over his eyebrows and his dead eyes. The left one seemed quite gone—the eyelid clung to the empty socket—but the right eye bulged out, showing a strip under the lid, and this was grey and darkly veined as pebbles sometimes are. His face was pale and swollen like that of a prisoner—he looked as if he sat too long indoors; his small and shapely mouth was drawn down at the corners, tired and slack; his black, curly hair fell forward over his forehead in moist strands. He was of middle height and well-knit, but somewhat inclined to fatness.

Olav stood outside the church door and watched them: the blind man kept his hand on his wife's shoulder as he walked, and after them came the serving-woman and a page. They went northward along the street.

That night Olav could not fall asleep. As he lay he felt the slight rocking of the vessel in the stream and heard the sound of the water underneath her—and through his mind the memories came floating—of Ingunn, when they were young. Sometimes they gathered speed, came faster, wove themselves into visions. He thought he had opened his arms to receive her—and started up, wide awake—felt that he was bathed in sweat, with a strange faintness in all his limbs.

It was too hot in his barrel; he crawled out and went forward on deck. It was dripping wet with dew; the sky was clear tonight above the everlasting light mists that floated over the river and the marshy banks. A few great stars shone moistly through the haze. The water gurgled as it ran among the piles of the wharf. A man was rowing somewhere out in the darkness.

Olav seated himself on the chest of arms in the bow. Bending forward over the gunwale, he gazed out into the night. The outline of the woods in the south showed black against the dark sky. A dog barked far away. Dreams and memories continued to course through him; it was their youth that rose from the dead and appeared to him. All the years since then, his outlawry, the time of disaster that came and shattered all his prospects, all the after-years when he had tried to bear his own burden and hers too as well as he could—they seemed to drift past him, out of sight, as he headed back against the stream.

At last he started up—he had fallen asleep on the chest, and now he was chilled all through. Now he would surely be able to sleep if he crept in again and lay down. Outside, the day was already dawning.

He grunted when Tomas Tabor came and waked him. Today Tomas could take Leif with him to mass; then he would stay aboard.

In the course of the afternoon Olav made ready to row ashore. It was warm now in the daytime; he could not bear his haqueton under his kirtle, the one he had brought with him was so heavy, of thick canvas padded with wool. There could be no great danger in going undefended—as yet he had had no quarrel thrust upon him in the town—and it made him so bulky and awkward. Olav girded himself with a short, broad sword before putting on his kirtle, which was split over the left hip so that one could easily get at a concealed weapon. It was a rich kirtle, reaching to the feet, of black French cloth with green embroidery, light enough for warm weather. Ingunn had made it for him many years ago. At that time he had much more need of suitable working-clothes; not often had he had use for this handsome garment, but it was finely sewed and finished. Olav chose a brown, hoodless cloak bordered with marten's fur and a black, narrow-brimmed felt hat with silver chains about the crown. He pressed it down, so that his greying silvery-golden hair waved out under the brim on every side. But—though he would not admit it to himself—when he took the pains, he still looked a fair and manly man, and few would have guessed that he was as old as seven and thirty winters.

He rowed straight in to the town and strolled through the streets and alleys. But as soon as the bells began to ring for vespers, he made straight for the church of the Dominicans. Just after him came the blind man and his wife and their two servants.

Olav had now forbidden Leif to leave the ship after nones; instead he sent him ashore with Tomas Tabor every other morning. In this way he himself could only attend mass every other day, but it would be too bad if the young man met with a mischance out there in Southwark. And it would bring trouble on them all if one of their ship's company came to any harm ashore.

The blind man came to mass at the convent church every morning and on most days to complin as well. She was always there at vespers and sometimes with her husband at evensong.

Olav did not know who these folks might be or where they lived, nor did he ever think to find it out. It was only that a change had come about in his mind: all the thoughts that had been habitual with him for years, all the daily doings and cares and all that belonged to his life as a grown man had been flooded by a fountain that had sprung up in him. It was beyond his own control—in all these years, when he had thought of his youthful memories, he had not recalled them in this way. Now they were not things of the past—he walked in the midst of them; it was as though everything was to happen now for the first time. Or it was as when one lies between sleep and waking, knowing that one's dreams are dreams, but seeking to hold them fast, struggling not to be wholly awake. And every day he came hither to see this blind man's wife, for at the sight of her these clear, dreamlike memories flowed more freely and abundantly; the image of the rich young wife became one with the sweet, frail shadow of the young Ingunn.

And she was no longer angry with him for looking at her—she vouchsafed him this, he had noticed. One evening he entered the church, walking fast, and bent the knee as he passed the high altar. The scabbard of the sword he wore under his kirtle struck the pavement hard, driving the hilt against his chin. He must have cut a ridiculous figure—and when he looked round at her, he saw that she was bursting with suppressed laughter. Olav turned red as fire with anger. But after a while, when he looked round again, he met her eyes, and then she smiled at him—and then he had to smile too, though he was both vexed and angry. After that he kept an eye on her; she followed her book diligently, but all the time little secret smiles played like gleams across her lovely face.

After the service he stood outside the church as she came out, leading her husband. She saw him, bowed slightly—Olav did not know whether it should betoken a greeting or not, but before he had time to reflect, he had bowed in return, with his hand on his breast. Afterwards he was vexed with himself—if only he had known whether she had meant to greet him or not!

The next day he took his station outside the church door at the time folk began to come to vespers. She came, with her usual company; Olav bowed—but she made as though she did not see him and went in. Then he was angry and ashamed and would not look over to where she was; he tried to join in the singing and not think of other things. But presently he felt that *she* was look-ing at him—and as he met the glance of her great dark eyes, she smiled, a bright and gentle smile that was like sunshine.

And after that they exchanged glances and smiles as though they had been old acquaintances, though they had never said a word to each other, and Olav did not know so much as her name.

.   .   .

Olav never thought that his shipmates must have remarked the change that had come over him. He was not himself aware that he had put a distance between him and the two seamen. Until now they had lived together as companions and equals; that Olav was the master of Hestviken, and Tomas a minstrel in Oslo in winter-time, while Leif was the son of a widow who served in the house of the armourer—this difference was so familiar and obvious that it concerned them no more than that Olav was fair and middle-aged, while Tomas was old and grey, and Leif a boy, red-haired and freckled. But now Olav moved among them without being aware that he scarce noticed them—as the young son of a lord instinctively and without premeditation puts off his childhood's familiarity with the serving-men of the manor from the day he first divines the path that lies before him and feels that he is des-tined for another lot than theirs.

Each time Olav was going into the town he put on his long kirtle; he shaved himself regularly and one evening he went to a haircutter. But the others made as though they did not see such things, and Olav never thought whether they saw it or not. He was not himself aware that he had become as it were another man and was acting more as became a lad of twenty than a landowner of wellnigh two-score years.

Torodd and Galfrid had returned to London and it could not be very long before they would be ready for the homeward voy-age. Olav thought of it with a twinge of reluctance; he did not feel that he was ready to leave England, and his vague thoughts of letting them go home without him stirred within him. The idea he favoured most was that of entering an order, the Maturines for choice, and setting out for the lands of the paynims.—But he was not yet ready for that. Just at this time it was as though he had grown deaf and dumb to the voice that had spoken so powerfully to him—but that should not be for long. Only there was something else that he must think out first—he was not very clear about it. But he had already known as it were a fore-taste of the peace that results when a man has surrendered him-self to God. So he knew that he would make that surrender in the end.

Two young Englishmen had bespoken a passage in the *Rein-deer*—they wished to make a pilgrimage to St. Olav in Nidaros.

They were good seamen both of them; so the Richardsons had no need of him as a shipman.

And now the summer was already far spent.

Three weeks had gone by since he saw the strange woman for the first time. One evening she did not come to evensong. As Olav left the church after the service, someone caught him by the mantle. He turned round—it was her servant, the old woman in the hooded cloak. She said something—he did not understand a word. And yet he knew. He nodded silently and followed the old nurse.

Olav had never been outside Ludgate before. He remembered as he crossed the drawbridge that in an hour the curfew bell would ring, and then they closed the gates, and he wore no armour under his kirtle and no other weapon than the little sword he had hidden in its folds. But even these thoughts were not able to raise their heads above the frenzy that flooded his soul.

Here under the western wall ran a little stream that came in from the country and flowed into the Thames, foul and stinking with the refuse that was thrown into it over the city wall. There were but few buildings before this gate, and the ground was marshy along the banks of the brook. But a few steps and they were on a path that led through the swamp. There were little ponds, shining white, and beds of rushes and brushwood on both sides. The low land farther out was dotted with farms and groves and church towers, and the sky, arching wide overhead, was covered with fleecy clouds, streaked with yellow from the setting sun behind.

The path brought them back to the little stream. The woman said something and pointed to a cluster of houses beyond the meadows. Olav saw the gables of a stone-built mansion among trees and the roofs of outhouses. But they did not approach the place on the side where the stone hall stood; they followed a paling over which hung green thorn bushes, and Olav could smell that the cattle-yard was inside. Then along the bulging wall of a long mud house with a thatched roof. There was a gate in the wall, and the woman unlocked a little wicket in one side of it. A strong, rank smell of pigs met his nostrils, and between the outhouses the passage into which they came was so miry that he walked almost ankle-deep in greasy, black slush.

They went across a little field in which linen was laid out to bleach, and the woman let Olav into a garden through a gate in a wattled fence.

The grass was already bedewed under the apple trees, and in the cool air floated the scent of fruit trees and dill and celery and of flowers whose names he did not know, but all seemed bathed and cooled by the evening air. Here in the garden the daylight had already begun to fade.

The woman led Olav to a corner of the herbary, where bushes grew in a ring; she said something. He guessed that he was to wait here, while she left him and was lost among the apple trees.

Close by grew a cluster of tall white lilies that shone in the gathering dusk and breathed out their heavy, over-sweet scent. Then he saw that the lilies stood at the entrance to an arbour which was half-hidden among the bushes. Olav went a few steps toward it and looked in. Just inside the entrance hung a wicker birdcage; there was a bird in it and it hopped silently up and down between two perches. Within the arbour he saw that there was a bed prepared.

His heart hammered and hammered in his breast; he stood motionless. A moth fluttered against his face, making him start.

There she came across the grass among the fruit trees; she walked with bent head, holding up her light gown before her with one hand. Her cloak was thrown back over her slender shoulders, and Olav saw that she wore nothing but the thin yellow undergarment—with a gasp and a thrill of happiness he knew that in a moment he would clasp her tender, pliant body under the thin silk.

She bore a silver goblet in the other hand. Now she stood straight before him, bending her head yet deeper. Then she raised the cup and drank to him. Olav accepted it and drank—there was wine in it, so sweet as to be mawkish.

He handed her back the cup. The young woman paused for a moment with it in her hand; then she let it fall on the grass. And now she raised her face and looked into his. The great eyes, the wide nostrils, and the half-open mouth were like chasms of darkness in the pale oval. Olav took a step forward and threw his arms about the slender, silk-clad wife.

She sank into his embrace, with her ice-cold fingers clasped

about his neck. Olav bent the crown of her head to his lips; first
of all he would drink in the scent of her—and found with a shock
of aversion that she smelt of unguent, a luscious, oily scent.
Nevertheless he kissed her on the hair, but the mawkish smell of
her ointment filled his senses with repugnance, as though he had
been deceived; he had thirsted for a breath of young hair and skin.

Unconsciously he turned his head away. He knew well enough
that rich ladies used such perfumes to anoint themselves with, but
he disliked it. Although he felt how she clung to him in abandonment, him who for years had not held a woman in his embrace,
yet as he stood there with his arms full of her, his senses were
cooled by the thought that this was an unknown.

No, this was not she—and it was as though he heard a cry coming from somewhere without; a voice that he heard not with
his bodily ears called to him, aloud and wild with fear, trying to
warn him. From somewhere, from the ground under his feet, he
thought, the cry came—Ingunn, he knew, the real Ingunn, was
striving to come to his aid. He could tell that *she* was in the utmost distress; in bonds of powerlessness or sin she was fighting to
be heard by him through the darkness that parted them.

The woman hung upon him with her arms clasped about his
neck and her head buried in his shoulder. Olav was still holding
her, listening, as he gazed over her head, feeling his own desire,
not quenched, but as it were dissolved in foam, far away from
this one. Ingunn called to him, she was afraid he would not understand that this stranger was one who had borrowed her shape,
seeking to drag him under.—"No, no, Ingunn, I hear you, I am
coming—"

He strained all his senses to catch clearly this ringing cry of distress which did not reach his bodily ears, even as he did not see
with his bodily eyes the form that struggled beneath folds of
gloom. Now it grew fainter—

Olav gently loosened the strange woman's hands from his neck
and drew back from her a little. She followed, and now she looked
up—his head swam as he met her timid, gentle, animal look. She
was so like that he was sick with desire to kiss the living lips,
though he knew it was a stranger who looked at him beseechingly
and cravingly from the depths of those eyes that were so terribly
like. But he felt as if he must use his utmost force to tear himself

away from her; it was like the temptation of his worst nights, when he could not help thinking of the fiord—of plunging into its waters and being free of it all.

"No—Ingunn, I hear you. Help, Mary!"

As he gave way, she threw herself into his arms, like a wave striking a ship's bows, and unconsciously he raised himself on his toes as he shook himself free of her. The touch of her long, white hands was the last he felt. He turned and walked quickly away.

Behind him he heard a low, long-drawn whine—and then cries, howls of scorn and rage. He swung himself over the fence—his kirtle caught in it a moment. "Now they will come after me," thought Olav; "she will call her servants now—" He ran across the bleaching-field and between some cattle-sheds and reached the palisade. It was twice the height of a man, at least.

How he got over he did not know, as he stood outside in a little dry field among haystacks—he had a feeling that he had pushed something against the fence, and instantly he seemed to recall having done the same once before—made his escape over a fence.

"That was that." He had said it aloud, standing ready to run, as he listened whether any sound came from within the enclosure. He was on a different side of the mansion from that to which the woman had brought him. Olav heard nothing; then he ran straight across the fields, taking the nearest way to cover.

Passing through the grave, he found a track that led by some mud cabins and down to the marshes about a little river. He did not know exactly where it was—it was down in a valley, but he followed the path along the river, thinking meanwhile that now the gates would be shut, darkness was falling fast. He could not enter the town, and could scarcely reach the *Reindeer* tonight. Well, there was no help for it. He passed his hand over his forehead and noticed that he had lost his hat. Well, well, so be it.— Here was a plank bridge, and when he came up the slope on the other side, he could see the light town walls and the high, pale watchtowers in the dusk. He continued to follow the ill-marked path across the fields to the northward—down toward the Thames the land seemed to be all swamp.

How far and for how long he had walked he did not know, but he thought he must be somewhere to the north of the town. Pools of water shone here and there in the darkness, and from some place came the baying and howling of great deep-voiced hounds.

Olav knew that the townsmen's hunt had its kennels somewhere out in the country. But it had an ugly sound in the dark.

To the left of the path he made out a piece of rising ground on which tall trees grew—there was a faint glimmer of dead leaves underneath them. Olav's senses grasped, without his being aware of it, that the ground here would be as good and dry as he could expect to find. He went up the slope—the brambles caught and tore his clothes. Then he came on something like a suitable hollow and lay down, wrapping his cloak about him as well as he could.

Now he felt that he was bathed in sweat, soaked and bemired almost to the waste, both kirtle and hose. Olav drew his sword and lay on his side, holding it under him. He fell asleep at once.

He woke in pitch-darkness, choking with horror, and thought he had cried out. Struggling with the tangle of his dream, he knew not where he was—he lay on the bare ground, and around him was a blackness that stirred and flickered, and he was wet and icy cold, and his heart was ready to break with despair and remorse and guilty feeling. He was lying in withered leaves.

Then memories dawned on him—of his adventure and of his dream, interwoven. At the same time as he recalled how he had come to be lying out in the woods, he remembered his dream too, and slowly the horror ebbed away—even now it seemed gruesome to recall it, but it was only a dream. And he had not done it, no, not even in his dream could he remember that *he* had done anything to the young child. That three-edged dagger of his he had not even brought with him on the voyage; it lay at home in his chest.

He had thought he stood by a bed—in the dark, and in a forest, as it seemed—a bed that was full of withered, wet, and earthy leaves, and half buried in the leaves lay a naked human body. The leaves covered it to the waist and covered the upper part of the face. He was not sure whether it was a boy or a girl, but he thought it was a little girl—the smooth, childish breast was so white and looked so soft—and under the left pap there was a triangular wound, as if someone had thrust in one of those daggers with a three-cornered blade up to the hilt. A little blood had oozed from the lowest lip of the wound—but it was one of those ugly, silent wounds which hardly bleed at all—the blood runs inward, suffocating the heart.

And the mortal horror of it had been that he had thought this was his work, and he was not able to bear it.—He tried to take the dead child up in his arms; he must bring her back to life. Yet he could not remember having dreamed that he thrust the dagger into the child. And it was but a dream.

A wind was blowing, with a sighing in the tree-tops and a rustling of leaves. He lay shivering and tried to distinguish things about him in the dark. A little animal was stirring among the dry leaves. His dream still troubled him; and he could not guess what it might mean—he had never wronged any *woman* that he knew of, save Torhild; but this was a little girl. He remembered plainly the face of the dead child among the leaves: the chin was short and broad, the lips full, the hair dark and reaching no farther than the shoulders. He could not recall having known any child like her.

It could not be Cecilia, his fair-haired child. A warm feeling of relief went through him: there could be no danger threatening her.

But his thoughts would not leave the dream. It was either a sorcery of the evil powers or a warning that he was unable to interpret—as yet. And he thought of that adventure in the garden the evening before—was that real or glamour? She had been so like Ingunn that it could not be true—and he had felt that Ingunn herself was there, quite near him, wailing in the fires of sorrow and impotence. And all at once he saw it—*if* she had not been able to make him hear, if she had been forced to witness it, in the place where she was, bound with fetters of gloom and death and powerlessness—that he yielded himself to the pixy or whatever she was—

It was as though something went to pieces within him. Sorrow and tenderness flowed over, hot as blood, and filled his being, thawed and relaxed every fibre—*so* near had he been to working her destruction—after he had striven, all the years she had lived, to sustain her as well as he could.

Then it flashed on him that he had called on Mary for help—and he wondered at it; for it was years since he had asked anything of *her*. It had seemed that he must think himself above seeking help there, when he wilfully defied her Son. He had said his Ave as he had been wont to do from childhood, in order to show her such honour as was her due, but never with the thought of gaining anything. And now he had called upon her, as a lost child calls for its mother.

Olav turned over on his other side and settled himself with his face buried in his arm so as to shut out the darkness. *Salve Regina, mater misericordiæ*—he would repeat the anthem over and over again until he fell asleep and had no other thought in his mind. "Ay, Mary, now I will come and pray for grace with our Lord."

By turns he slept awhile, woke again, slept, and tossed in a riot of disconnected dream-visions, and over them all was a vague horror—each time he awoke with a stab of pain at the heart. But each time he settled himself again, summoning all his will to the same end: the prayer that was to be his shield that night.

And then at last he woke and felt that the sun was shining and that he was rested. And there still lingered in his mind the after-taste of a morning dream, giving sweetness and security beyond compare.

He was penetrated all through by the raw cold of the ground, but he lay still, gazing about him in the woodland, where the dew glistened blue and white in the brightness of the morning. The drops lay thick on every blade of grass. The bushes with the dark, hard, spiked leaves shone like burnished steel. A blue haze lay among the trees, round which the ivy twined its green curtain. And the dream ran on in his mind like the soft and milky morning light.

He had thought he lay in a woman's lap, with his head against her heart, and from his feeling of deep sweetness, free from desire, he knew who she was, and said it: Mother! He did not recall the look of her face—did not recall it now—but in his dream he thought he had recognized her, though he had been but a tiny witless infant when she died.

Arnvid had also been dimly present once in his dream, in a long, white garment—the habit of his order, no doubt—and Arnvid had spoken to his mother; but they had talked as it were over his head, as though he had been a child in swaddling-clothes that his mother held in her lap. Bishop Torfinn he had also seen. Their figures were all illumined as clouds are by the sun behind them, but this refulgence did not shine upon him; and he knew that it was not the sun, but a knowledge, or a vision, that was theirs; but he had it not, he only saw the reflection of it in them.

A little church bell began to tinkle not far away. Olav got to

his feet, stiff with cold. He was in a sorry state, with kirtle rent
and soiled. He brushed and picked off leaves and litter. If he had
only had a cloak with a hood to it—he took it off and carried it
over his arm; thus his going hatless would be less noticed.

Olav followed the sound of the bell; the path led down along
the edge of the beechwood. On rounding the corner he looked
involuntarily to the westward—but instantly thought it would be
of little use to look for *that* manor-house: it would scarce be
there today. The little church where the bell was ringing stood
on a mound on the other side of a brook. He made for it, sure
that there he would find the solution of all that baffled him.

It was a bare and poor little house and the air was musty and
raw within; Olav guessed that mass was not often said here, and
the mass that was now being celebrated was for the benefit of the
ten or twelve poorly clad men who stood near the altar with a
banner in their midst—it was no doubt some little brotherhood
and this was their feast-day. The men had made themselves trim
according to their means. But the priest's chasuble was threadbare,
the deacon and the choirboys seemed listless and comported themselves without grace or dignity, while the priest hurried through
the service, as though his only thought was to get it over.

Any message to himself he could not find, other than that he
stood there, poor and a stranger, among these poor men who
took part with him in the perfunctory office. It became clearer
to him than before, how little a middle-aged man counts for in
this world when he is stripped of all the added worth that goods
and kindred bring. And he would learn this more and more
thoroughly the farther he strayed from his home—he saw that
now.

He had learned it once before, he remembered—in his youth, in
the years when he was an outlaw. A clear, cool bitterness seized
upon him. Was it for this he had come home, and was it for this
he had dwelt all those years with his only dear one as in a dark
house—that God should now lead him out, lock the door behind
him, and send him roaming again?

He *saw* his manor, as in a vision—more clearly than he had ever
seen it with his eyes. The wharf and the sheds with the water of
the fiord lapping about the piles, the long row of sun-scorched
turf roofs and dun gables up on the hillside and the wall of the
Horse Crag behind, his cornfields among bare grey and reddish

rocks, the hills around, grey and weather-worn, with wind-bent firs toward the fiord, meadows inland along the valley, and then the forest. The domain was not so great but that he had seen greater, but it was *his;* from here his fathers before him had gone out into the world, and hither they had returned. If all else in his life had turned out otherwise than he had expected, he had won back his patrimony and maintained it; he would leave behind no less than he had received. There were boats now, great and small, by the wharves; there were fields and meadows that he had cleared anew on the mossy, alder-grown land toward Kverndal.

The poor men advanced to the altar in a body. Now he saw the image on their banner: Jesus bending under the cross, and a man walking behind and helping to bear it, Simon the Cyrenian. So it was a guild of porters. A deacon made a sign to Olav, thinking he belonged to the fellowship. Olav shook his head and knelt down where he had been standing, by the door.

And in the poor vesture of the host our Lord descended and gave Himself to His poor friends—he was the only one present who dared not to go forward to the table. For years he had known that when he needs must go, at Easter, he went as Judas went to the Last Supper. As a child he had never been able to understand that Judas dared, for he must have known that God knew what he had done. Now he himself was in the same case as Judas Iscariot: he moved among his even Christians, and they reckoned him a good Christian, even as the apostles had reckoned Judas their fellow as they sat down with him at table that evening. And his only thought had been that in the midst of the company he was alone with Him who knew of his betrayal.

Such a man had he become. Yet his spirit had once been as a young field, full of the good corn that had been sown in it: the heritage of his ancestors, loyal men and unafraid, who did not cast their eyes backward after their lost happiness so long as they could keep their honour bright. But he had so ordered his life that now it had become as the lost fields he had found when he came home to Hestviken, overgrown with weeds and scrub.

Olav looked up. On the wall opposite there was painted a picture of our Lord sitting at the marriage feast in Cana. And near to Him stood Mary; she motioned with her hand to the servants, while her eyes looked straight into those of the man kneeling by the door:

"Whatsoever He saith unto you, do it!"

Olav knew not whether he had heard the words from without or within himself.

"Then clear me, Lord, as the husbandman clears his field with fire and with sickle—take back Thine inheritance, that it may bear increase for Thee!"

Once again he saw Hestviken as in a magic vision. A vision of a grey sea, flecked with silver over the glittering waves, and beyond it the coast sinking in a blue-grey mist. And he saw himself, so puny and alone, as a man standing on a rock in the outermost belt of skerries. In solitude he waited for Him who walks upon the glittering waves as a husbandman walks over his fields, and checks the storm as a man checks his horse. And the man on the skerry was free, so free as none can conceive, save him who has been stifled in the darkness through the long night of deadly sin.

Among the torch-bearing acolytes the priest advanced along the line of poor workmen. Each time he took a host from the ciborium Olav prayed softly: "Thou rich Christ, have mercy upon me!" Thou rich Christ—never till now had he reflected why men called God so. Now he knew it. "Lord, I am not worthy that Thou shouldst enter in under my roof, I am poor and naked, I own nothing wherewith to do Thee honour; but Thou enterest into an empty house, Lord, and fillest Thy creature with blessings.

"Then it may be that Thou wilt take me into Thy service again. Am I too old to learn to read and sing Thy praises? Then I am surely young and strong enough to be sold in exchange for an outworn slave in the land of the blacks."

He became aware of someone tapping on the wall close beside him. A half-grown boy was chipping off plaster with the key and seemed impatient to lock up. The church was empty. Olav rose to his feet and went out.

Down through the fields they passed, the brotherhood, the priest and his assistants. The blue silken banner showed up against the yellowing wheat. The boy locked the church door and darted after them. Olav followed slowly, bareheaded in the sunshine.

The ship's boat was gone when he reached the landing-place in the west of the town; he had to go on to the hithe where they lay and find a ferryman. He laughed on seeing Olav, and said something. Olav guessed the meaning, if not the words, joined in the laugh, and shook his head. He was strangely cheerful and light-hearted—as though in face of a new departure.

On board he found the Richardsons. Olav saw that they had been talking about him—and they looked at him with sly merriment, coming home so late in the day, ragged and without his hat. But they ignored it, and so did Olav.

The Richardsons had come to get the others to join them in a pilgrimage. There was a sanctuary somewhere in the woods north of London, with a miraculous image of our Lady; this had once been hidden in a hollow oak when the vikings were harrying the land, and found again in that place. Tomorrow was the feast-day.

Olav was glad. He had already thought that from tomorrow he would attend a church of Mary; he cared no more to think of the Dominicans' church.

4

In the afternoon of the next day Olav stood on the green outside the place of pilgrimage—he was looking for his companions.

In the yellow rays of the declining sun the dust hung like a mist over the trampled grass—the place swarmed with folk who were now taking their departure. An immense cross came swaying along, carried in the midst of a body of men in penitential garments; they sang the litany as they marched, stirring up fresh clouds of dust with their feet. For a long time the notes of their singing floated after them like a streak through the drone of voices and the thunder of hoofs, the plaintive whining of fiddles, and the sombre throbbing of harps.

The beechwood surrounded the place like a wall, and the foliage shone with a dull gleam in the sunshine against the blue-grey sky—it was a hot day. At the bottom of the slope a fair was being held in a meadow by the stream: the smoke of bonfires rose above the copsewood; oxen and sheep were being roasted whole down there, and the shrill cries of the vendors cleft the hum and uproar of folk who were now beginning to be drunken and frolicsome.

A few people were still moving in and out of the church; but that morning the men from the *Reindeer* had barely been able to press their way in to the mass, and they had seen nothing, so

packed was the great church. And it had taken a long time to elbow their way into the chapel where stood our Lady of the Oak.
At least a hundred candles were burning in there, like a wall of
living flame; the shrine gleamed with gold and silver. The image
was black as pitch, the face was long, stiff, and hard under the
golden crown, and the child peeping out under the mantle of
gold brocade was like the stump of a root. But it was very ancient
and venerable. There was no time to say any long prayer within
the sanctuary, such was the press of folk.

Afterwards, when they were to share their provisions, they had
bought cider—it was mighty good and their heads were a little
mazed with it. Then they lost one another in the crowd down in
the fair-field. Olav and Tomas had kept together longest, but then
Tomas would stand listening to a minstrel so long that at last Olav
was tired of waiting and went on. Now he stood at the edge of
the forest looking out, if he could see any of his companions in
the swarm that drifted hither and thither on the green.

He felt within his kirtle for the packages he was carrying over
his belt. They were gifts that he would send home—a last greeting.
Embroidered velvet gloves for Signe and Una, a rosary of corals
and gold beads for Cecilia, a dagger for Eirik. Though Eirik
would now inherit all his arms—except Kinfetch; he must remember to send a message home that the axe was to descend in
Cecilia's branch of the family.

The thought was like stirring up a wasps' nest. He turned away
from it, looked about him; no, he could see none of his company.

From somewhere in the wood behind him he heard singing; it
sounded like ballads. Olav turned and followed the woodland
path—if they were dancing he would be certain to find Galfrid in
any case, and Leif.

After a while he came to a great open space in the forest. Upon
this plain stood a band of dancers, getting their breath; people lay
on the grass under the trees, eating and drinking. A little child
ran toward Olav, stumbled, and fell. Olav picked up the little boy,
who was howling, and tried to comfort him. He stood looking
about him with the child on his arm, when a stout, good-looking
young woman came running up. Olav smiled faintly and shook
his head at her flood of words. With a sudden gesture he pressed
the boy to him and kissed him before handing him to the mother.
It was like taking farewell of something.

The dancers formed a ring again—they were only men, who went arm in arm and broke into a wild and stirring tune. Olav went forward, forcing his way through the crowd looking on.

The strange, resounding, and provocative dance inflamed him through and through: it was fighting they sang of, and it seemed like something he had heard before—his heart stirred as the grave-mould stirs over a dead man who wakes and struggles to come out—and when he saw the look on the faces of those around him, his excitement grew. Old men stood leaning forward, beating time with their heads, glowing with passion. Big, portly matrons listened with hard faces, as though the song had to do with disasters they themselves had suffered. Even Olav felt that he knew something of it, but could not come at what it was—

—And all at once he had it! The river, Glaana, rushed down in flood, cold in the shadows, while the sun still blazed on the pinnacles of the keep—the castle stood on a little island, cleaving the stream. And he stood in the water-meadow watching the Earl's retainers, the lads from the Cinque Ports, as they danced and sang of the battle between English and Scots. *That* was the song, by God!

Memories that he had never recalled for years rushed up from the depths within him, like prisoners from a dungeon. A stream of rapid visions—furious hand-to-hand fighting, torchlight flickering over wild sword-play in a narrow gateway that sloped away into darkness—and then he was in a boat, rowing in the pale evening light outside the island walls of Stockholm, and facing him in the stern sat the Earl, short and broad as the door of a loft, invincibly strong and shaggy and warm as a he-bear, bright in his crimson velvet cloak, with his clear amber eyes laughing at war and adventure—oh, Lord Alf, Lord Alf, my liege!

The chain of dancers surged past him, and there was no end to the wild, ringing song. The men hung together, hooked arm in arm, leaning backward with their shoulders, and the chain swayed; the fiery faces of the singers could be seen through the clouds of dust each time they leaped high and stamped hard as they came down. Then a sudden jerk to the right all round the ring, and back they came charging toward the left.—His memories still sped through Olav's mind: of men with whom he had been friends in a cool and pleasant fashion, each man for himself within the iron shell of his coat of mail, but covering one another with shield and sword. Oh, to hell with all women, they cling all too closely to a man! The glare of flames among the dark timber gables of a city street. And himself, a lad of twenty, fully armed, standing in a doorway—a young serving-maid, whose name he had forgotten, seeking to drag him in and hide him. He laughed, snatched a kiss and tore himself away, rushed up the street, sword in hand, to where he heard the trumpets of the Danish King's men—and he was wild with an angry fear lest the Earl's men should let themselves be driven down to their ships without attempting resistance.

Olav's hands clenched upon the borders of his cloak—his spirit was in a violent uproar: to think that he could forget all this! And now it came back, his vision of the manor on the hill above the creek, but strangely paled and faded now; it was fraught with memories of ill health and contention with a dense, grey, overmastering force, and of a sick woman who crushed the youth and manhood out of him and who grew ever paler and more faded in spite of sucking his strength dry. And, with a sudden break, whatever feelings these memories had brought him hitherto—they now sickened and revolted him—Jesus! had he not been as one bewitched—or thrust into hell?

The song ended in a resounding roar and the thud of half a hundred feet that struck the ground at once. Olav drew a deep breath.

The ring of dancers broke up and the crowd of onlookers scattered. Olav moved about, uncertain what to do with himself. Then he ran against someone—looked at him and saw that it was the blind man from the church of the preaching friars.

For a moment they stood and stared at each other—so it seemed to Olav: the wan, sightless face, contracted with misfortune or bitterness, seemed all agaze. Olav's only thought was that he had been clumsy. Then a change came over the stranger's face, as though awakening from an evil dream. A smile broke out on it as he felt before him with his hands and spoke a few words.

"*Cognovis me?*" whispered Olav doubtfully.

The stranger—he was not much more than a lad, Olav now saw —replied at once in the same language, but he spoke it so quickly and fluently that Olav did not understand a word.

"*Non capio bene latinum,*" muttered Olav awkwardly.

The other smiled courteously and began again more slowly, in fewer words. Olav grasped so much: that he was parted from his company, and now he asked Olav to lead him somewhere—to the church. With hesitation Olav accepted the young man's proffered hand and felt with aversion how clammy it was. Then he let the other take his arm and led him toward the path by which he had come.

The young man tried to enter into conversation—in Latin, English, and French, a little of each. Olav understood him to say that he knew him from the Dominicans' church.

"*Non es—*" he sought the word for "blind." He stole a look at the other's ruined eyes. No, he must be stone-blind. A shock went through him—then someone had pointed him out to the man. "*Non es cæcis?*" The tension filled him with something like joy. Now he must be on guard.

It was dark in the forest; cautiously Olav led the blind man over roots and stones in the path—watching intently for any sign of men lurking in the undergrowth. And it had chanced unluckily that he had the stranger's left arm locked in his right—or had the other managed it of set purpose? Olav was ashamed to change now. But he kept an eye on the man's sword-hand.

He was waiting all the time for the flash of a dagger—or for someone to burst out of the thicket—and the way could not have been so long as he went to the sports green, nor the path so narrow—and dark it was here in the wood. But to the blind man's questions he replied calmly that his name was Olav; he was a Norseman and a merchant. He would have told him too where he lay with his ship—it were well that the man should know he had no thought of hiding—but when he tried to explain it, he could not make himself clear in the foreign tongue.

And all at once they were out of the wood. Olav led the blind man up toward the church, which now gleamed faintly in the fading light. And a dull, oppressive fear came over Olav—it was not with dagger or armed men the stranger would attack him. But into the church with this man he would not go!

Then a serving-man came running down toward them and called out on seeing his master. The latter at once dropped Olav's arm, took him by the hand, and thanked him for his help. Olav was dumb with surprise. The young knight turned to his man, laid a hand on his shoulder, and allowed himself to be led away, as he turned once more and greeted Olav with a parting "*Vale!*"

Olav stood still; it was now so incomprehensible that he felt almost disappointed. He followed the stranger with his eyes. Before the gate of the little priory by the church a company was getting into the saddle. And in a little while they came riding past him.

There were several men of rank in velvet, with gold chains on their breasts; they had excellent horses and costly gear. The blind man rode on a black stallion, which was led by a page. The serving-men who followed were armed and equipped for a journey, and in the rear came several horses laden with merchandise. Olav guessed they had come from far away.

And now it dawned on him that the blind man must have been away from home for some days. So she, the wife, had sent for him while she was alone.—He recalled the arbour in the secret corner of the garden, the young woman who came with perfumed hair, naked under her thin silken robe—neither pixy nor phantom as he had made himself believe—only an unfaithful wife.

In a surge of passion Olav felt as if he himself were the man betrayed. His rage was red and hot as lust—he could have seized and killed her with his bare hands. And he was dazed the while by a strange, unreal feeling—this had happened to him once before.

Then the rush of blood ebbed back, the red mist faded from his eyes. He felt the ground under his feet once more and saw everything about him with a strange distinctness. The beeches were bathed in a pale, subdued light, and the sky above was whitish, with a few bright shreds of cloud; the grey stones of the church flushed faintly in the afterglow. The place was now almost deserted, and a scent of dew and dust arose from the trampled grass. And Olav saw the cold, clear truth of it: that this game in which he had here been involved—he had taken part in it once before. But this time he was himself the thief.

He took the front of his cloak in both hands, as though he would tear off his bonds. But from the innermost chambers of his soul—now that at last he had been forced to open a crack of the door—the darkness spoke to him, a voice without words. This was the *meaning* of what had lately befallen him. Another man's wife had been offered to him, so that he had but to reach out his hand to take her. And he himself had had no other thought— until that cry had warned him, from heaven or from purgatory.

Had he not been *snatched* away, as a child is snatched from the
fire by its mother, he himself would now have been a wedded
woman's paramour.

Olav began to walk swiftly, as though he would escape from
these thoughts. He strode across the fair-field. Embers still glowed
upon the ground in the increasing dusk; in one place a fire was
burning brightly. Many people still lingered here, and all seemed
drunken. Olav walked on rapidly; he entered another wood by a
well-marked path that led downhill.

In a kind of desperate resentment he struggled to drown the
voice—"in the devil's name, I did not *touch* the woman. I have
behaved like a fool, making eyes at an English bitch, because I
thought she was like my wife." And he might well be angry, at
his age, for being caught in the woman's snares—"but I had no
such thought in my mind, and did I not make off at once, when I
saw what she would with me?" And that the blind man had
known him could hardly be a miracle; for he had often seen that
blind men—beggars and aged folk—seemed to see with their whole
body: they had the scent and hearing of dogs.

But all his striving to drown the voice within him was of no
avail—*he* had violated no man's honour indeed, but he had not regarded it in this way as he led the blind man through the wood;
then he had been sure that the other sought his life, and justly.
And again he knew that he had been guilty in accompanying the
strange lady's messenger—or an old, drowned guilt had floated up
into the daylight.

As he hastened down the wooded path in the growing darkness, over stock and stone and bog-hole, sure of foot as a sleep-
walker, it was borne in upon him that this darkness into which he
hurried farther and farther was his own inner self, and presently
he would have entered its deepest and darkest secret chamber.
Soon he would be driven in, with his back against the last wall;
but he knew withal that he would fight and defend himself to the
utmost. And he understood—

First God had spoken to him face to face—that was in the night
when he was to lose Ingunn. In that hour, when he was forsaken
by his only friend, God had spoken to him from the forsakenness
of the cross. In that night, when his grief was such that he could
have sweated blood, God had appeared to him, bedewed with the
blood of the death agony and the scourging and the nails and the

thorns, and He had spoken to him as friend to friend: "O all ye that pass by, behold and see if there be any sorrow like unto my sorrow!" And he had seen his own sin and sorrow as a bleeding gash upon those shoulders. Yet he had not been strong enough to come.

And God had spoken to him a second time. He had spoken to him in His holy Church, as soon as Olav was so far healed of grief's fever that he could compose himself and listen to calm words. Yet he had voluntarily delayed on the road—nor was he any longer sure that he had obeyed the call. Unless—

But now this last thing had befallen him, so that he was forced to see what manner of man he was and what was his sin.

All at once he stood as it were outside and looked upon himself—as one stands behind a fence and looks at a man labouring in a barren, weed-grown field.

The man toils about a bramblebush, trying to clear it away, and tears his flesh and his clothes on it. But the weeds, the coarse and noxious growth of tares and thistles, he seems not to see. Yet it is not the bramble that has choked all the good seed in his corn-field: it may bulk large as it stands in full bloom, but it does not seed and scatter everywhere; one may clear it out once for all if one will take the trouble. And there it stands flowering, rank in its unprofitable beauty, and no one will *despise* it.

He had only been willing to acknowledge his great sins. For indeed they were blood-red transgressions against the laws that prevail in the kingdom of heaven. That he had always known, but at the same time he had known that among men it was accounted otherwise. And according to the law that held good among the men with whom his birth entitled him to rank himself, he had done no more than his duty—vindicated his right and his wife's honour.

Even if it came out, this thing that he had done in secret, the murder, the dastard's deed—it was not so sure that his memory would be tarnished with dishonour, even if his head had paid the penalty on the block. Not *one* man of all those he reckoned as his equals would judge him to be a dastard—if they knew all. Olav saw now that this knowledge had lain somewhere far back in his soul, always.

Young as he had been, he could not escape doing wrong, since his fate was tangled in the coil of other men's wrongs and mis-

fortunes. But all the evil that followed was due to the attempted
betrayal of him and Ingunn by those who should have defended
the two children's rights. Up to the last and worst evil, his false
confessions, the sacrilege that burned his mouth and heart—foot
by foot he had been driven to all this, since he had had to take his
own and his foster-sister's cause into his own hands, and as a raw
youth he had grasped it mistakenly.

He had never before thought it out clearly in this way, but
within himself he had always known, in the midst of his distress,
that God, the all-seeing, saw this much more clearly than he did—
that his greatest sins were the sins of others no less than of himself.
And inextricably bound up with the burden of his own misdeeds
he bore the burden of others.

So he had bowed low and smitten his breast when the deacon
said the Confiteor in the mass; he was willing to confess: "not one
of these men standing about me is guilty of such black misdeeds
as I." In the mirror of God's justice he saw himself sunken so
much deeper than these others, as the reflection of the oak in a
pond sinks deeper than that of the undergrowth around it. And
even in a human view he must have seen himself standing like an
oak above the brushwood.

But in this unearthly light which now shone into his darkness,
what he had secretly wished to preserve from God's hand appeared to him at last: the pride of the sinner, which is even harder
to break than the self-righteousness of the righteous.—"Be it as
it may, I am innocent of the sins of a mean man."

Twice had Jesus Christ spoken to him out of the sweetness of
His mercy—and he had shrunk away like a timid hound. Twice
had the Voice spoken: "Behold, who I am, behold the depth of
my love!" Now it said to him: "See then who *thou* art. See that
thou art no greater a sinner than other men. See that thou art as
small a sinner!"

The sword sank into the most hidden roots of his being and
pierced him. *Non veni pacem mittere, sed gladium. Qui invenit
animam suam, perdet illam, et qui perdiderit animam suam propter
me, inveniet eam.* Olav saw that these words were truth, such as
he had never dreamed of before, and when he understood their
meaning, it was like sinking beneath the ice-cold waters of the
very ocean.

He laughed with pain as he ran through the dark forest.

He had behaved as though he were afraid of losing his life—
he who had long been so tired of life that if it had not been for
Ingunn's sake he could never have borne it for a day. He would
not go back to it—he lost nothing if he now chose obedience,
poverty, chastity, nay, the lot of a slave and a martyr's death at
last, for all that he must renounce he counted nothing worth, but
what lay before him promised gains beyond measure—adventures
and travels in distant lands, and at the last peace and God's forgiveness, and admission to the ranks of His soldiers again.

But now he tardily understood that then he must choose, not
between God and this or that upon earth, not even his worldly
life, but between God and himself.

The path brought him to an open glade; it led high up along
a slope, where the trees had been cut. Above him he now saw a
wide stretch of the sky, dark and strewn with stars. Below him
lay a little valley, he could see that he was looking down over the
tops of trees; a sound of running water came from somewhere in
the darkness.

Unconsciously he slackened his pace. The light, cooling breeze
fanned his cheek; Olav wiped the sweat from his forehead. And,
feeling that he was walking on high ground with open, airy space
about him on every side, he had a sudden instinct that he was
being led out into the wilderness; he walked here all alone in
a foreign land and knew not whither he was going. Here was
no familiar place or thing that might help him to escape seeing
what he would not see; folks' speech, which he did not understand, could not break in and drown the Voice that he would
shun.

Olav halted abruptly. He seemed to absorb strength from the
gloom around and from the raw, cold earth under his feet, so that
he felt his ego swell and grow in black defiance: "Why dost Thou
deal thus with me? Other men have done worse—and more con-
temptible—deeds. But Thou dost not drive them from home and
peace and persecute them, as Thou drivest and persecutest me."

The voice that replied seemed to dwell in the very stillness under the wide, star-strewn heaven and the forest that rustled faintly
in the night breeze and the hushed murmur of the brook in the
valley.

"Because thou dost yet love Me, I seek after thee. Because thou dost long for Me, I persecute thee. I drive thee out because thou dost call upon Me, even as thou fliest from Me."

The path descended steeply, leading into the thick of the woods. Olav stopped again, threw himself down at the entrance of the dark gap that penetrated the foliage, and sat with his head buried in his arms.

Visions came swarming upon him without his being able to hinder them. Once he complained aloud. Was it to see this that he had been brought back to the very starting-point, his youth? In secret he had been proud of his youth: "After all, I was overborne by force, I was compelled to stand alone, none helped me—whatever I have done or left undone, was not the sin of an ignoble man."

Was there none who helped him? Now he descried a little light low down, a lantern stood on the floor in a dark stable, and there were two young men. He recognized the face of Arnvid Finnsson, stricken and perplexed—it was he himself who had wounded his friend with a lie. Ay, *that* sin was his own and none other's. Now he saw that this was surely the first sin he had committed deliberately and wilfully: when he cast his guilt upon the shoulders of his friend, who, he knew, never refused to take up another's burden.

"No!" He whispered it breathlessly. This he would not have—let it be good for monk and priest, but *he* would not be imprisoned in this cell of self-knowledge they talked of; let it be their concern alone to watch the mirror that reflects God's light and man's darkness.

But he could not protect himself—the light that shines in darkness continued to burn, and in it he saw the thousand things that he had wilfully forgotten.

Had none helped him? They had helped him, those of whom he had asked help, Arnvid and the good Bishop, Lord Torfinn. They were the men he had loved and looked up to as his superiors—of his inferiors he had never asked anything. But of the friendship of these two he had availed himself as fully and eagerly as any of his inferiors had availed themselves of him. The difference was merely that *he* had never thought of calling any man his friend and equal who came to him as a suppliant. Out of a pity that was both proud and lukewarm he had given his gifts.

But the men who took *him* under their protection when he came
to them in his need had received him as a younger brother.—
Humiliation overwhelmed Olav like a landslide—he was painfully
crushed beneath the rocks.

"Nay, God, I will not have this. Ingunn, help me," he prayed
in his distress; "you must bear witness for me—Ingunn, I was never
false to you?"

Again he felt with overpowering clearness how near she was
now. Death only hid her form, like a darkness. But he heard her
answer close beside him, out of a sorrow so deep that it made
the living seem like children who lacked understanding:

"I witness for you, Olav, and every soul to whom you have
shown pity witnesses for you of your good deeds. They are many,
Olav—you were designed to render abundantly to God. But your
deeds have become as withered stalks of corn, tainted in root and
ear—they have so long been choked by the tares."

He *saw* them before him, sick and wan, ears that bore no corn
to ripeness. His inmost will had driven them on—that will which
God had given him for ruling and protecting. But this will had
been overpowered by whims and desires and perversity and unwise impulses, as vassal kings overpower their rightful sovereign
lord. He had been sustained by the secret pride that his sins in
any case were not those of cowardice and ignominy. And now
he saw that these great sins were a load that he had allowed others
to put upon him, because he had never been strong enough to
admit it when he had taken a false step through weakness and
cowardice and thoughtlessness.

By tricks and by honest dealing, by a little lying and a little
truth combined, he had gained advantage for himself from the
few men he had met in the world whom he had reckoned good
enough to call his friends, to love and respect. He had never dared
to tell them the truth about his own conduct, because he wished to
have their respect—and because he needed their help. He stood in
debt to his friends—he who had always looked down with pity on
every debt-burdened wretch.

It was not true, that which he had said to Bishop Torfinn, and
to all his friends, so often that he himself had almost forgotten
what was the truth. It was a lie that he had asserted his right to
his betrothed merely because miscreants sought to take away their

rights. Oh no, he had not been a strong-willed, resourceful grown man who took Ingunn and made her his, reckoning that, if there is dispute about a thing, he is best placed who has that thing in his possession. The truth was otherwise, humiliating—and at the same moment he was bathed in the sweetness of all these memories of his youthful love, now that at last they leaped up, naked, from beneath all the lies under which he had tried to hide them. He had been but a boy in those days at Frettastein, and he had had no thought of either right or wrong when he took to himself his young bride, dazed and wild with desire to possess her full sweetness and charm. He had thought no more than a child who grasps for everything it wants, without heeding, as it runs forward, whether it may fall.

Behind his closed eyelids he saw a cleft in a scree; under the rocks at the bottom of it ran a beck; red rosebay waved on the face of the precipice. Before him walked Ingunn: he saw her long, supple back in the red kirtle; she was plaiting her thick, dark-yellow hair, and he thought her so fair that he followed her as one bewitched. Before them the firs stood erect on the rocky cliff, and by the pale-blue radiance of the summer air he could see that the hillside dropped sheer beyond. He walked behind and looked at her, with mind and senses filled with secret memories of their meetings in her bower at night, with pride in being the master of her loveliness. And when they came to the end of the glen, where the lake lay far below under the dark, wooded heights —there was a little grassy slope between great shivering aspens— he ran up, embraced her from behind, and turned her face toward his own. Hers was pale, bedewed with warmth; as soon as he took her in his arms he felt that she grew weak and trembled in her everlasting animal docility.—This was before he knew that Stein-finn was to die, and before he had ever suspected that any man could hold their betrothal to be aught but a binding, irrevocable bargain.

In all these years he had never dared fully to recall to mind how it had been to feel nothing but the youth within him and all the world's beauty in a young maid. His longing caught him by the throat and made his eyes burn in their sockets.

Olav rose from the ground and let his arms drop. He gazed out at the patch of starry sky, black velvet powdered with gold, that lay above this unknown country in which he had lost himself. Unconsciously he caught a whiff of smoke from a fire somewhere in the night.

He divined that now he had wellnigh unravelled the whole skein of his life's misfortunes to the end of the thread. "Cleanse thou me from secret faults, O Lord," he had learned in his morning prayers—in all these years, when he recalled that psalm, he must have thought upon his own evil deeds. Now he saw that what he had tried to conceal, from both God and men, was that he might have gone astray from weakness, from childish thoughtlessness and blind desire—*that* he had sought to deny at any cost: even if he should take upon himself the guilt of far worse deeds, charge himself with a burden of sorrow so heavy that it broke him down, then rather that. If only it might look as if he had acted with premeditation and accepted his sorrows knowingly and of his own free will.

"—And preserve thy servant from the power of strangers: let them not have dominion over me; so shall I remain unspotted—" "Let me not submit to my enemies," he had meant. And then it had been nothing but his own sheer nature that kept him from submitting to his enemies, he would not bend to men for whom he had no respect or who opposed him; to such he had always shown his stubborn obstinacy and his mute, cold defiance. It was toward his friends he was weak and submissive, even to falseness and dissembling; it was when he first became aware of his love for his child bride that his whole being was inflamed and bent aside from uprightness, melting and leaning over like a heated candle.— *That* should have been the object of his prayers: courage, so that he dared acknowledge his blushing; strength, so that he ventured to act rightly and speak the truth without heeding the judgment of those he loved.

But in all these years he had believed himself to be a hard and stubborn, steadfast man; he had himself chosen the bitter lot of Cain, and he had chosen it of necessity, since he was to be the master and protector of the frail, weak-minded wife to whom he had been bound as a child.—And yet he had had to do violence to himself many a time before he could act as a hard man—gag the voice of his own conscience: do we not know how ready a man is to do wrong blindly when friendship and love are at stake, when joy and pleasure call?—He had said to himself he was play-

ing for a high stake—and he had not been playing, he had merely
shuffled the draughtsmen like a witless child. He had not *chosen*
the lot of Cain; he himself had never known *when* he made a
choice.

Olav clenched his teeth; it was as though another had pronounced this judgment upon him, and he would still defend himself, deny it. But the memory of that evening in the garden came
back to him: old as he was, it required no more than a false air of
youth, and he let himself be carried away, ran to grasp at the first
shadow that played before his eyes. True, he had not thought of
sinning—he had thought of nothing. As for the blind lad at whose
side he had heard mass day after day, he had not remembered his
existence.

His mouth filled with water—as in his boyhood when he
chanced to see anything that was alive with maggots.

Weak, hasty, short-sighted, sleek-skinned, and spiritually yet a
babe—a man of near forty winters—Olav laughed despairingly. No,
that judgment he would not accept.

In a fleeting vision he recalled the dream of his former night in
the woods: a bed of leaves in the midst of the darkness, a naked
white body lying in it, the slain child—as he had seen in pictures
of a deathbed: the soul leaving the dying man's mouth in the likeness of a little child, and angels and devils contending for it.

He trembled in extreme terror. Again the feeling came over him
that he had had as a child on seeing maggots. And in the wild horror that seized him now that he saw what he had concealed from
himself beneath his manifest sins, the temptation awoke—simply
to throw more leaves over the murdered child, hide it completely,
and fly.

And as though the words were spoken without him he heard:
childish, soft, heedless—such a character he would scarcely be
given by the neighbours at home. Weak—he? The memories
roused by the fever of the dance returned, and now they seemed
like a troop hastening to his succour. He could not judge his whole
conduct as a grown man by the headlong follies he had committed
on finding himself, a lad bereft of kinsfolk, charged with a cause
that called for great resourcefulness if a full-grown man were to
bring it to an honourable issue. Nor by the years he had spent at
Hestviken, tied to a wife who was able neither to live nor to die.
He had always been different in those periods of his life when he

had been able to act with free hands. Surely he need not call himself white-livered and soft-hearted for disliking his uncle Barnim's fatuous and useless cruelty. Nor weak because it went against the grain to slay Teit; it was, as that youth himself had said, far too like hunting flies with a falcon. Had he not been just as brave, just as eager for the sword-play, as the boldest among the Earl's men—a trusty comrade, well liked by his fellows, a friend with most, not too good a friend with any, loyal to defend his neighbour, cautious whom he trusted—? "God, my lot might have been so cast that I could lead a man's life, perform manly deeds like my forefathers, achieve my meed of honourable exploits—Thou didst set me where I had to fight with sickness and misfortunes black as hell, till I felt myself sink to the knees in mire. Does it make me a coward if I know myself that I was oft afraid, though no man saw me flinch?

"Did I run blindly after my own desires when I renounced pardon, manor, and wife at the moment when all were within my reach, for the sake of following my banished lord in his outlawry?"

But at the bare thought of the Earl his heart began to quiver with the old, ardent loyalty—oh, nay! If at any time he had blindly followed his own desires, it was when he rejoined the Earl. At that time he had *forgotten* Ingunn almost—he knew he was bound to her; never would he abandon his claim that their relation that autumn had been a lawful one, the consummation of an agreed marriage; but he had not remembered his love for his wife. Of his affection for Earl Alf he had never spoken to a soul—fate had given him a woman for his only trusty friend, and how should *she* be able to grasp anything of a squire's affection for his lord?

Olav drew himself up in agitation. About him loomed the trees; black and immensely high, they hid from him the starry heaven. He had a feeling that he was in flight, carrying himself off as booty into the woods. Here the path dropped so steeply that every moment he was in danger of falling headlong—it was dark as a badger's hole under the huge masses of foliage, and the track was full of big stones and twisted roots. Olav guessed that he must have left the broad, beaten path that he had followed at first. This gave him a strange feeling of relief—now he was forced to have a care of his feet, and he had to think of where he was, and whether perhaps he might reach some habitation where he could obtain a lodging for the night. In this country one could not enter the first house one came to along the road and ask for shelter, as at home

Once, when he had to stop to empty his shoes of all the earth he had got in them, he came across the same smell of smoke as he had noticed before when he sat on the ridge. It must be the smoke of a watch-fire—'twas not likely that folk would keep the hearth-fire burning in any house so late at night. So it seemed there were men abroad in the wood. Olav took his sword out of the slit in his kirtle and let it hang in readiness. With his wonted caution he tried if it were loose in the scabbard and then walked on, slowly and quietly, holding it in his left hand.

The path swung out round a sort of promontory where the slope of the valley was bare of trees. Right under him, farther down, he saw a fire burning among the brushwood.

The discovery filled him with unreflecting joy; none could tell what sort of men might frequent this place. But Olav rejoiced at the prospect of meeting no matter whom, if only he might escape from solitude.

Now he saw the flame through the trees, heard the crackling of the fire. It lighted up a little clearing under the wooded slope on the farther side of the river, casting a red reflection on the black, running water. Between him and the fire he made out the dark forms of two men and heard voices.

The path led down to a little plank bridge and across to the meadow. The men lying about the fire did not hear his approach as they had just thrown an armful of dry faggots into the blaze. They were three young fellows—dressed as men of the people, none of the worst sort, seemingly. So he called to them.

They started up. Olav held his cloak wrapped about him with his left hand. As he stepped into the light of the fire it struck him that it would have been just as wise if he had first taken off the two gold rings with gleaming stones that he wore on that hand, but now it was too late. He greeted the men and asked, as well as he could, if this was the way to London.

As far as he could make out from their answer, it was not—the men pointed in the direction of the stream and over the hill. It was evident that the road to town ran on the high ground toward the south-west, but the men thought he would not be able to find it in the dark and he had better stay with them till daylight. Olav

nodded and thanked them. Then they threw him some armfuls of
leafy boughs they had cut. Olav spread them out and lay down by
the fire.

It did him good—now he felt that he was ready to drop with
tiredness and hollow with hunger; he had eaten no more than
once that day, and that was many hours ago. So he wished these
strangers would offer him something, but they did not; it seemed
they had eaten their supper. Now they tied up the mouths of their
bags again and stretched themselves on their beds of leaves, two
of them. The third was to sit and watch. So Olav did not care to
ask for food.

They lay chatting for a while, as well as they could. The men
were from the west—nor was their speech like that of the London
folk, Olav heard. To their questions he replied that he had been
to the pilgrims' church, he had lost his companions, he was a
Norseman. But the conversation flagged. Then one of them began
to snore, and soon after, Olav also fell asleep.

It was still night when he awoke, but the darkness seemed to
have thinned; dawn was not far off. He had slept heavily and
dreamlessly, but cold and hunger waked him. The fire had almost
gone out, and the watchman seemed to be asleep.

Olav got up noiselessly and went down toward the river. At
any rate he would have a drink of water. He knelt down and filled
his hand—then he was on his feet again with a bound: he felt that
someone was behind him. No time to draw his sword—he flung
himself upon the man and felt the knife slash his cheek; it was
lucky he did not get it in his eye. But he had got a good hold of
the other and gripped his head under his arm, so that the man's
cries were half-stifled. "The knife," thought Olav, but could not
let go; so he raised his knee and drove it into the fellow's ribs,
scarcely noticing that he got a stab in the thigh as he tried to
wrest the knife away. But this gave the stranger a chance to close
with Olav; and, locked together, they rocked and wrestled in the
darkness, each trying to throw the other into the river. The man's
smell and the firm, hot hug of a flesh-and-blood opponent filled
Olav with a deep sense of voluptuous joy. He put forth all his
strength—it was like pressing back the iron-bound gates of a castle
against the assaults of the enemy.

Now he heard that the others were on their feet. At that moment he got a hold and succeeded in throwing his adversary; his

body crashed into the bushes. Olav drew his sword and ran to meet the other two, with never a thought that he was running into danger and not away—there they were! In the dark he knocked aside a weapon—an axe, no doubt—struck and felt that he got home, and well; there was a cry and something fell in a heap. His second blow found nothing but the empty air, and he ran on. The plank bridge was too far, so he took a run and leaped out into the stream.

He splashed a stroke or two, then found bottom. When he stood up, the water came to his middle, but the bottom was muddy and he sank into it. Then he got hold of something—overhanging branches and then a root; the turf broke away under his knee; mould and gravel or whatever it was rolled down into the water. A moment later he was standing on the other bank. They were howling and roaring yonder.

Olav threw off his drenched cloak and wound it about his left arm, broke into the thicket, and forced his way through the undergrowth, with his bare sword in his right hand. Only now did he notice that he had cut it in wresting the knife from the first robber; the blood poured from it. Now and then he stopped a moment to listen—they must be on the plank bridge now. It seemed they had no great heart to pursue him; perhaps they guessed it was too uncertain in the dark and the thick underwood—a cursed wood it was, nothing but thorns and brambles.

Olav made his way on up the slope protecting his face as well as he could with the cloak about his left arm.

Arrived on the high ground, he presently came upon a broad road that seemed to lead down the valley. The sky was growing lighter now and the stars were fewer and paler, the woods swelled darkly against the first signs of dawn.

Again he stood and listened—he heard nothing of any men now, no sound but the tiny rustling of some small animal low on the ground among fallen leaves; here were tall trees, beeches. Olav walked on, more slowly, and now he felt the whole weight of his soaking kirtle beating heavily against him as he walked—ay, he was wet from top to toe, and as soon as he had gone a little way at an even pace he began to shiver in his clothes, which clung to him, cold as ice.

It did him good in a way. Vaguely and with a strange indifference he remembered the rushing stream of inward experiences that had carried him along from evening till darkest midnight—what had afterwards befallen him, his fight with the robbers and his flight through the thorn thicket, seemed to have placed an enormous distance between him and his hours of revelation. It was clear to him that he had not seen these visions with any faculty that dwelt within himself; a light had poured in upon him from without; and it was clear to him that he had called troops to his succour against this power, and help from that quarter where a man never seeks it in vain when he would defend himself against the truth—that help had surely been given him. He knew too that if at that moment he had had the power to see clearly and understand fully what it was that he had done—understand not only with the head, but also with the heart—then he must have been a desperate man. But he felt nothing but relief, and the cold from his clinging wet clothes wrapped itself around him and made him calm, as one puts out a fire with wet sails.

He wiped his face and found that it was scratched by the thorns, and bleeding, and blood was running down the inner side of his right thigh. After a while he was going lame, but kept on walking—it was as though he could not check his pace. So he walked and walked, stupid at times with sleep.

A mist rose from all low-lying lands on the approach of morning; all at once the fog surrounded him, dense and white, hiding the blue of heaven and putting out the last of the stars. Olav had been walking half-asleep for some time and stumbling now and again in the deep ruts that scored the turf of the road. Now he was wide awake for a moment.

Within the moist and muffling fog the trees loomed huge, beyond their natural size. Through Olav's tired brain there flashed a last glimpse of that world of visions to which he had been admitted and from which he had fled. In an instant it was gone again.

The grass was soaked with dew, bent down and grey all over. The road led through a forest of great ancient oaks, and in the thick undergrowth every bush was wreathed in cobwebs, which were coated with dewdrops. Olav shivered as he stood—and when he moved on again, he felt his right leg heavy and painful and his hose stiff with blood.

After a while he came out into a field, where red-dappled cattle were grazing in the fog. Olav called to the old man who was herding them, but received no answer that he could understand. Again a while, and he was in a little village street, and now he could ask his way, so that he reached London just as the sun was breaking through and all the bells of the city were ringing. He entered by one of the gates on the east side—he had gone a great way round out in the country. Olav looked neither to the right nor to the left; half-asleep he limped through the town, ragged, bespattered, and torn about the face. Down at the hithe he found a waterman to take him off to his ship.

The others had come home the evening before. They seemed to be glad when Olav came aboard. He told them he had been surrounded by some men who tried to rob him, in the forest, but he had cut his way out in the darkness, and after that he had lost himself. Not much more was said about it. But when Galfrid was helping him and washing away the clotted blood, and Leif came with a bucket of water, the lad could not contain himself.

"So it was you, Olav, not I, that came home at last with a hole in his skin," he said with a sly smile.

"Ay, one never knows—" Olav shrugged his shoulders.

Galfrid bound up his hand and bandaged his thigh. The other scratches were nothing.

Olav stayed on board for the most part, during the week they lay by Thames-side. Then they sailed home.

5

OLAV sailed home down the Oslo Fiord one morning with a fresh northerly breeze; it was a day of blue sky and sparkling sunshine, and the fiord lay dark, flecked with white foam. Every tree on the wooded slopes of the shore was bright and glorious; the wind tore the first yellow leaves from the tops of the birches. The surf creamed white over every skerry and around every islet with its yellow, sun-scorched grass among grey rocks—Olav thought the very spray that sprinkled him felt good and homely, different from the empty sea. Once more he sat steering his own boat; long enough had he been away from all that was his. All was well at Hestviken, said Arnketil.

Olav called to Eirik forward, who had stood up and was about
to fall over the thwart as the boat dipped into the trough of a
wave.

It was marvellous how the boy had grown. Eirik had come up
to the town with Arnketil to fetch the master home, but Olav had
had little leisure to talk to them, the few days he had to stay in
Oslo, and moreover Eirik worried him with all the questions he
asked about his voyage to England. Olav himself was not very
well pleased with the way it had turned out; the profits were wellnigh swallowed up by the expenses, and he would rather have had
no more talk of it. With some surprise Olav had remarked that
Eirik offered to answer back, with sullen disrespect—evidently it
had not been good for the lad to pass the whole summer with no
one over him to keep him in order. But now, as he sailed home by
the familiar channel, with Haa Isle and Hougsvik Sound ahead, he
was more inclined to forget the boy's ill manners and to be
friendly with him. So when Eirik came straddling aft and took his
seat on the thwart facing his father, Olav nodded. Eirik burst
into the story of a murder that had been done in the parish on the
eve of St. James [5]—and he himself had had leave to ride with
Baard of Skikkjustad to the Thing. Olav nodded unconcernedly—
he knew neither the slain man nor the slayer; they were strangers
who had served on one of the farms in the forest tract to the
north.

And Beauty had had two calves, Eirik went on.

"That was news!" Olav gave a little laugh.

And Ragna had two sons on the eve of St. Cnut [6]—

"That was not so well," Olav commented with a smile. " 'Tis
many children—and she is left alone with them." Ragna, the dairy-
woman, had been left a widow at the new year, and she had a
daughter already.

But Cecilia had done her best to make them fewer, said Eirik
mirthfully, Cecilia was so fond of the little twins. And one day
when Ragna was out, Cecilia had gone in to them, and then she
had stuffed the mouth of one of them full of ferns to quiet him.
It had almost cost the babe his life.

Olav shook his head with a little laugh.

His dogs rushed hither and thither along the quay, barking and
whining with delight as the boat came alongside. Then he stood

[5] St. James's Day is July 25.   [6] St. Cnut's Day is July 10.

on his own wharf, shook hands with his own people, while the dogs jumped noisily about him, snapping their teeth and licking him in the face.

Liv pushed Cecilia forward. The child was dressed in a faded and outgrown red kirtle, but it shone in the sunlight, and her hair surrounded the white little face like a floating, radiant cloud. She looked healthy, though her skin was so white—it seemed but cold as grass and flowers are cold—and her immense eyes were a very pale blue-grey, or greenish like sea-water. She looked up at her father's face rather like a stranger, when he bent over her and spoke to her. Then Olav took his daughter's hand and led her as he walked toward the manor with the dogs around him and his household in the rear.

He took the path up hill by the side of the "good acre." The corn was ripe, it made a good show, and Olav felt strangely relieved: there were not many weeds among it this year. It was as though his life were connected in a mysterious way with the crop of this field. But it ought to have been cut ere now, the gales had damaged it somewhat.

"They say you have brought great gifts for me, Father," whispered Cecilia, and these were the first words the child had spoken.

"Ah, if they say that, it must be so," replied her father with a smile.

In the evening he sat in his high seat, with hands resting on the smooth-worn heads carved on its posts, and neck leaning against the old tapestry that covered the logs of the wall. In his thoughts he went over all the things he had seen to and arranged in the course of the day, while his glances idly followed the flickering light of the hearthfire on the smoke-stained walls of the hall.

He was filled with a vague well-being and something like a hope of the future. It did not shape itself as a thought—but for the first time the husband realized without pain that *she* was gone. The very emptiness felt like the physical peace that sets in, when the wound is healed, after the amputation of a diseased and aching limb. Olav was himself scarcely aware of it, but he had lost the desire of thinking of Ingunn since that evening in the strange woman's garden. The shameful memory of that adventure had in a way infected those memories that lay beneath it.

Liv came in, swung aside the pot and its hanger, and made up the fire. Inconceivably ugly, thought Olav; inconceivable that the men cared to touch her—and yet they *had* done so, it seemed—

"You are late with supper for us tonight, Liv," he said, and the maid giggled with pleasure, as she always did if her master but addressed a word to her.

The door stood wide open for the sake of the draught; from outside came the sound of iron-shod heels on the rock. Then Cecilia's fair head appeared in the shadow of the anteroom door. Olav kept his eyes fixed on her as she climbed over the threshold. She went up to the hearth—the glow lighted up her red frock and fair hair, as she picked up a few grains that had fallen on the hearthstone and put them in her mouth.

"Come hither, Cecilia," Olav called quietly.

The child came and stood by his side.

"Have you put away my rosary, Father?"

"I have so." Olav reached out for her, trying to take her on his knee. But she slipped away from him, back to the fire.

The groats were bubbling and popping in the steaming pot. Olav looked forward to a meal of porridge and ale—hot food he had not tasted since he left home.

He took a turn in the yard before going to bed. The wind had dropped toward night, the fiord sighed back and forth in the shoal water under the hill. It was dark outside and the stars twinkled brightly; not unlikely there would be rime-frost toward morning. Olav walked up to the cattle-sheds. There was a muffled beating against the stable wall—he waited outside for a moment, then opened the door and went in. He went up to Ran, the mare, and spoke a few words to her—taking deep breaths of the warm, acrid smell of the stable.

Up behind the barn he paused again, listening to the faint autumnal murmur of the stream down in the valley and looking at the stars that blazed over the top of the black wooded ridge. To the westward he made out a faint whiteness along the beach where the sea broke against the rocks. Up the valley the ripening cornfields showed under the shroud of darkness.

God! he thought for an instant, looking at a great star that blazed just above the tops of the firs opposite. He recalled that starry night in England when he had been held fast and addressed by a Voice that no man can remember if he has chosen not to hear. He had chosen, and now it was as though he had fled and hidden himself, creeping beneath the corn that stood pale and ripe in the darkness; he stole down to the raw, cold fields and hid himself there.

It was true enough what they said of Hestviken, that it was a strangely dead place. Old folk said it was Olav Half-priest who had driven away all the elves and underground beings—save one— and that one he could not cope with. No one knew exactly what kind of being it was; its usual haunt was by the bridge over the mouth of the stream, and it appeared in the likeness of an immense badger with only three legs; it did neither good nor harm. Olav vaguely wished now that there had been more life about the manor.

Then he walked slowly down to the house again and went to bed.

Just as he was falling asleep a thought occurred to him—Liv. What if the people of the parish should take it into their heads that it was *he*? The thought made him wide awake and burning hot—he had always had such a violent loathing of the stumpy, toad-like, loose-living wench, and now he felt he would give he knew not what rather than that any soul should believe he had resorted to her foul couch. This time he would have to see to getting her married and away from the manor—Arnketil might be the likeliest to take her. Olav lay awake a long time, tormented by this sickening uneasiness.

Next day he spoke to Liv. The maid wriggled this way and that and tittered foolishly, but at last she agreed that the child was most likely Arnketil's. At first she seemed but middling glad when Olav said he would help them to marry. But then she changed her tone, was full of thanks and promises—he guessed she thought that now she and Arnketil were to be set over the servants of the manor. He told her curtly that such was not his intention; he would help them to set up house for themselves.

But how he was to manage this, Olav himself did not know; he could not turn out any of his tenants. Only Rundmyr stood empty.

Olav had carried on the farm there for Torhild Björnsdatter and her brothers and sisters ever since the maid came to Hestviken. One after another most of the fields had been left fallow,

for he saw no means of manuring them; Olav used the land for
hay, and the houses stood empty. Now and then the elder sons of
Björn and Gudrid stayed there for a few weeks—they took after
their mother, were unsteady and reputed untrustworthy. Egil, the
eldest, was now over twenty; ever since Olav had abused his half-
sister he had hung about Hestviken when he was in need of help—
demanded this and that as though it were his due. He hinted that
he was the son of a good man and therefore it would cost Olav
dear to atone for the shame he had brought upon the family. Olav
put up with it, though at the time he had paid fines in full to the
brothers and made good provision for Torhild and the child—but
Egil was certainly never under his half-sister's roof. Olav saw here
another advantage in buying Rundmyr: he would no more have
Egil idling about the neighbourhood.

But when Olav was alone with Arnketil, he somehow did not
bring himself to speak of the matter. The man was a picture of
poverty and simplicity: tall and scraggy, with loose-hung limbs,
and his head, far too small, was set upon a long, thin, sinewy neck
with a huge and prominent Adam's apple. It was impossible to
tell his age from his begrimed and sallow face, but he could not
be more than five or six years above a score, for he had not been
fully grown when he first took service with Olav. So stupid was
Arnketil that he must have lacked something of his full wits;
nevertheless he was in his way a useful workman, and he had always served Olav faithfully—until he had taken up with this Liv,
for she taught him both lying and pilfering; though the girl was
scarcely more than half-witted herself, she was remarkably cunning in such things. So Olav thought it was a pity of the poor
body and said nothing to him about his marriage.

But a day or two later Olav came in to supper tired and wet,
and Liv was bearing round the bowls of food—since she had taken
on herself the duties of mistress the table was seldom set up.
Eirik had seated himself a long way down the bench by the side
of Arnketil. There was some joke that amused those two so that
they had to keep their eyes fixed on the cups they held in their
laps; even then they spirted with sudden laughter now and again.
Olav glanced angrily at them once or twice. At last the fun was
too much for Eirik; he fell forward and the porridge spirted from
nose and mouth with his bursts of laughter. Then Arnketil could
not contain himself either; he laughed, swallowed a mouthful the

wrong way, coughed and laughed, and coughed again so that the
tears ran down his cheeks, and then Eirik laughed quite uncon-
trollably.

Olav turned round sharply. At that Eirik jumped up and darted
from the room, roaring with laughter, while Arnketil dropped his
porridge-bowl on the floor and let himself go, and Liv stood
sniggering foolishly without even knowing what this unseemly
merriment was about.

After supper Olav took Arnketil outside and told him his intentions about the marriage with Liv. Arnketil answered compliantly
and seemed well pleased. Again Olav felt pity for him—God
alone knew what sort of house this pair would keep at Rundmyr.
But they would have to make the best of it now—help they could
be given, if they needed it.

At night Olav lay pondering—whether he should let them stay
at the manor after all. But then he thought—no. Liv had managed
the house wretchedly enough while she was alone; if these two
were to stay here, with their children, a cow or two, goats, and
sheep, it would make far too much trouble. For he could not send
away Ragna and her three children; she was an honest woman,
widow of an upright man. And she brought luck with the cattle,
so it seemed.

In the afternoon of the next day Olav took the lightest skiff and
rowed across the fiord.

It was a longer walk over the hills than he remembered. Now
and then he halted, uncertain whether he was on the right path,
but he would not ask his way.

The day was calm, with a heavy, leaden sky, but now the eye
of the sun pierced the clouds, lighting up the dark-green firs and
giving a strange richness to the colours of the birch groves against
the thick grey air. The yellow leaves of the aspens rustled gently;
their foliage was already much thinned up here on the high
ground, and the path was brightened by fallen leaves. A raw
breath rose from the ground under the trees, as always in autumn,
even when it was dry.

At last Olav recognized where he was. Beyond a great bog,
with tufts of red heather and white bog-cotton around its pools,
lay the farm to which Auken had belonged. Through an opening
in the forest he came to a gate and saw the yellow timbers of the

newly built houses standing on a rocky piece of ground, with small fields below, in which the corn stood in stooks.

The path ran by the edge of the cornfield, past some great heaps of stones. It turned a corner, and straight before him Olav saw a child, a boy of two with pale-yellow hair that curled over the neck. He was crawling among the stones and plucking wild raspberries; on hearing someone approach he turned round. The boy had been thrust into a pair of leather hose that were far too big for him, so that the thongs were crossed over and under his shoulders, and his homespun shirt hung out before and behind, looking ridiculous. But in spite of that he was a singularly handsome child.

Olav stood still, and the boy looked up at him, till his little berry-stained face puckered with coming tears. Olav looked about him, and now he caught sight of Torhild—she raised her head among the yellow corn in the field. She looked this way, then put down her sickle, took off the coif that had slipped down about her neck, and bound it tightly over her hair. She was dressed as Olav had always been used to seeing her when she was at work, in a grey homespun shift reaching to the ankles and held in at the waist with a woven belt. Her bare feet were thrust into rough shoes. She looked neither younger nor older than she had seemed in all the years Olav had known her, but as she came toward him with sickle in hand he thought her handsome, so stròng and stalwart and upright was her gait.

They greeted one another in silence.

Torhild said: "This was unlooked-for—are you abroad in these parts today?"

"Ay, I had business on this side."

Torhild laid the sickle on a stone, bent over the boy, and lifted him up in her arms.

"He looks so queer," she said, as though excusing herself; "but we are so thick with snakes up here—I dare not let him go barefoot."

Together they walked up toward the houses.

On entering the living-room Torhild bade him sit down. "Maybe you are thirsty?" She fetched a bowl of ale, with a head of froth on it, and drank to him. "I am brewing now for Michaelmas."

As he sat there, Olav recognized the faint and delicate scent of withered garlands that Torhild had always been used to hang up indoors in summer to keep away vermin. Meanwhile Torhild had passed behind the foot of the bed: she slipped a green kirtle over her working-dress and put on the belt with copper mounts which she wore on the minor holidays. Then she sat down to dress the boy, asking the while after the folk at Hestviken, how Eirik and Cecilia were thriving, and what was the state of the crops.

Olav replied that he had been out of the country this summer.

"Ay, so I have heard. You have been on a long voyage too. And it was to be expected—that you should wish to see something of the world, now you are a free man."

Torhild set food before her guest, and while he ate she stood aside with the boy on her arm.

Once Olav could not help saying, as he looked around: "He is big for his age, the boy—two winters old?"

"Folk say he is big." The mother bent her head and stroked her cheek against the child's. But now the boy began to kick and struggle, he wanted to get down, and she put him on the floor. He went up to the strange man and stood for a moment looking at him. But then he remembered something more important, stumped away to a corner, and sat down to play with a toy.

Olav bade Torhild be seated: " 'Tis with you I have come to speak." She took the dish of food and set it aside. Then she sat down on the edge of the hearth facing him, looking down with her hands in her lap as she listened to Olav's proposal.

"As to this I must consult with my brothers," she answered when Olav had finished. " 'Tis so that you may rightly look to me to meet your wishes in this matter; you may look for that with all of us. But I wonder, Olav, if it be wise of you to lodge such folk as Anki and Liv in a cabin so near to your house."

"I have thought of that myself. You mean, they are somewhat uncertain. But from year's end to year's end 'twill not be more but that I can bear the loss without being brought to beggary. And I can see no other way to deal with them."

Torhild then promised that she would advise her brothers to consent.

Afterwards they went out to look over the place. Torhild took her milking-pail—she had two cows and a fine heifer grazing just outside the fence in the wood. While she was milking, Olav stood leaning on the fence and looking at her; they exchanged a few

words about the cattle and the weather and such things. The boy
Björn came up and tried to climb on the fence so that he could
see his mother; Olav took hold of him and helped him up; he kept
hold of him while he and Torhild talked as before.

From out of the wood came three half-grown children with a
sledge-load of dry leaves; the two boys pulled and the girl
pushed behind. They were Kaare and Rannveig, Torhild's youngest half-brother and sister. Olav gave the children good-evening;
they had been reared at Hestviken.

The third was a tall, thin, fair-skinned boy with lank hair and
a long, low chin; he had a foolish look, but Torhild said he was
very useful to her. "He is my foreman, is Ketil." He had been
found by the cross on the highway north of here fourteen years
before, as a new-born child, and the old people, who took him in
for the love of God, were now dead; thus he came to be at Auken.

They walked back toward the houses, and Olav declared that
such fine corn as this of Auken he had not seen anywhere that
year.

"Then I must send you a box of seed-corn, Olav," said Torhild
with a little smile. "If you will accept such a gift from me."

"Thanks, but that is too much."

The children sat at their meal when they entered the house.
Torhild told them they must sleep in the byre tonight: "—for we
have a guest from far away."

They went out at once, and Torhild took out of her chest a
pillow and two coverlets woven with stars, with which to deck
the bed.

"You must not trouble yourself for my sake," said Olav in a
low tone. "I must needs return to Hestviken tonight."

Torhild stood with her back to him. She was silent for a moment; then she said:

"The path down to the shore is none too easy. And it will soon
be dark."

"Ay. Maybe it were better not to stay much longer—"

"No. If it is so, that you must cross the fiord tonight—then
surely you must go now."

Olav stood up, took his cloak and his spear. He came forward
and gave Torhild his hand, bidding her farewell.

"There is a shorter road here—I can go with you."

Torhild lifted the child from the floor, where he was rattling

some stones in a wooden cup, and laid him in the bed. Then she
went out with Olav.

The curious dark-blue colour of the day had faded to grey twilight and a few drops of rain were falling; but when Olav bade
her go in again, Torhild answered that the wet would come to
nothing. She walked before him southward across the fields to the
beck that divided Auken from the main farm. On coming to the
manor lands she waited for him and they walked side by side
along the edge of a field that had been cut and lay pale with
stubble under the grey sky.

"Whom have you taken, then, instead of Liv," asked Torhild,
"to keep house for you at Hestviken this winter?"

"Nay, I have had no time to look about for anyone yet," said
Olav. "But I dare say I shall find somebody."

Torhild was silent for a few paces. Then she said—and seemed
a little short of breath: "Olav—what woman—of those you know
—think you best fitted for this post?"

He said nothing.

Then she repeated more plainly: "Who, think you, would be
most zealous for your welfare and serve you to the best of her
powers, more faithfully than all other women?"

Olav replied hoarsely: "I know that, as you know."

They walked on in silence; then he said: "But you see it well
enough too. It would scarce be long before— I will not ask you to
return to such a—dishonourable lot."

Torhild said in a low voice: "I would gladly accept such a lot
—with you, Olav."

Again they walked a little way in silence.

Then Olav said with warmth: "No. I will not have you suffer
more ills for my sake than I have already put upon you. And you
are best off here at Auken, you and the boy. I have seen enough
today to know that you will hold your own here, Torhild."

"No doubt of that." He could hear she was smiling. "I am not
ungrateful, Olav. But I know not—had it not been for her lying
there sick and palsied, whom we had wronged—I know not
whether I should have reckoned myself badly off that last winter
I was at Hestviken."

Olav shook his head. A moment later they came to a gate at the
brow of the wood.

"Now you cannot go wrong," said Torhild. "By this path it is much easier to find your way to the hard than by the path you came."

She held out her hand and bade him farewell.

Olav looked at the woman—in the last rays of daylight he dimly saw the fair oval of her face and the upright carriage of her high-bosomed figure; for aught one saw, she might have been quite young. Far below under the woods the fiord lay dark and lifeless under the heavy, autumnal sky; the farther shore was merged in the blackness of the raincloud.

With a thrill of desire he thought of taking her. Within the forest the fallen leaves showed up against the dark, rounded cushions of the heather; up at the house the hearth would be glowing cosily—the boy lying asleep. The thought of his homeward journey filled him with repugnance.

He knew that she was waiting as she stood there.

Then he quietly bade her farewell, turned, and went rapidly down the hill.

From time to time he stopped and was lost in thought on his way through the woods. It was quite dark when he came to the shore. He found the place where his boat was drawn up on the beach, was about to push it into the water, but paused, leaning against the boat, gazing into the night and listening.

Olav could not tell what had prompted him to leave Torhild— but he had had no choice. It was raining, he noticed all at once; he had not known when it began, but now there was a hiss of rain-drops in the water of the fiord, a dripping and rustling in the foliage behind him.

As he stood there in the darkness, letting himself be soaked by the autumn rain, he felt to the roots of his being that he was bound to live alone, just as firmly as if he had bound himself by a monastic vow—only that it seemed as though his own will had had nothing to do with it. It *was* to be so, whether he would or would not. His life had now become like a journey in a trackless wilderness; he saw neither path nor trail, and he had to find his way alone.

He got the boat out; the scraping of the keel over the sand and the little hollow sounds as he put out the oars roused him. The rain still poured down. Now and again he looked over his shoulder at the other black coast, to see that he was not drifting too far down.

Torhild—he felt his heart contract at the thought of her. But it was a shame—the station to which her father had brought his daughter. Had not Björn Egilsson played away all his possessions, then married that Gudrid, begotten all those children to grow up as servants and vagabonds— As he rowed Olav worked himself up into indignation against Björn, who had left his daughter in such a case. From her birth and ancestry Torhild had had a right to look for a good and honourable marriage.

Olav was half-aware of a reversal of his own standpoint. When faced by a misfortune, he had never before tried to shuffle out of his share of the blame; he had never before been afraid to bear his own part and more, if a weaker sought to lay his burden on his shoulders. Now he was himself seeking someone to whom he could transfer the blame for wrongs of his own doing.

IN THE WILDERNESS

PART TWO

THE WILDERNESS

THE WILDERNESS

I

ᛖARLY in the spring, the year after Olav Audunsson's foreign
voyage, a Thing was held at Haugsvik one morning, and
Eirik was allowed to attend it with his father. But as they
were going home, it fell out that the Rynjul folk went in Olav's
boat, and Eirik was to follow in another craft.

Not till late in the afternoon did he come—in a little sailboat
that was laden to the water's edge with half-grown lads. Ragna
came in to her master and said that as many of the boys came from
far up the parish, they might well want food and drink before
setting out inland. Yes, said Olav.

The lads made their way indoors and Olav replied to their
greetings with a nod. Then he went out, for he felt disturbed by
all these strange children who hung about the benches looking ill
at ease.

He was standing by the stable door when the band of youth
came out again. But they did not seem to think there was any
hurry about leaving; they stayed about the yard, nosing here and
there among the houses, two or three together, prying and looking
about them; others kept together in a bunch, chattering and laughing and bickering in a mild way; but it was all play and good
humour.

Olav stayed where he was, for he had no desire to mix with
this throng. It was cold, now the sun was down, and the sharp
young voices carried far in the still spring evening.

Snow was still lying under the north walls of the houses, and
presently the lads took to snowballing. Olav paid no great attention to them, but there was one who showed up among the other
lads; he was the tallest of the company and handsome in a way,
red and white like milk and blood, with long, smooth straw-
coloured hair. Eirik kept close to this lad and helped him.

But after a while Olav saw that all the other boys had joined in
attacking Eirik; they belaboured him with snowballs and barred

his way to the drift, so that he had none to throw back. The tall
lad stood looking on.

Then Eirik made a dash between the byres. The hollow behind
the outhouses was still full of snow. Eirik jumped into it and
began making snowballs, which he hurled at the crowd of his pur-
suers. And now Olav stepped behind the outhouses to see what
would happen.

Eirik shook off the first enemies who leaped down on him;
plunging through the crust so that he sank to the middle in the
wet snow, he pulled himself out of the hollow and onto a ledge of
the rock behind. From there he sent fistful after fistful of turf and
loose stones at the heads of his assailants, who replied with snowballs. There was a great shouting at this—evidently the game was
about to take an angry turn.

A snowball caught Eirik in the eye, making him duck and put
up his hand. At that moment the tall fair boy who had stood aloof
jumped up and threw his arms round Eirik. He flung him head-
foremost into the snowdrift, and all the other boys threw themselves on him and ducked him in the filthy snow, yelling and
laughing the while, as Eirik howled with rage, half-stifled under
the heap.

Olav came a few steps nearer—the tall fair boy caught sight of
him and said something to the others. They got up at once.

Eirik got onto his feet; he was bleeding at the mouth, and he
turned to the tall boy, shrieking frantically:

"A dirty clown you are—call yourself a man! I—I helped you—"
he was crying with rage.

Olav noticed that the tall fair boy looked strangely foolish now,
as he blinked and turned away from Eirik's father. But all the
other lads made haste to get out of the hollow. Olav followed
slowly; on reaching the yard he saw the whole band of them up
by the barn making for the east. They had neither taken leave nor
thanked him for his hospitality.

Eirik stood just behind his father. He was still panting as he
pressed a snowball, now against his swollen eye, now to his bleeding lip.

"Who was he, that fair lad?" asked Olav.

"Jörund Rypa." Eirik snuffled and swallowed; he was staring
at the band as they disappeared in the darkness toward Kverndal.

"Jörund? Have they that name anywhere hereabouts?"

Eirik replied that Jörund came from a great farm to the east-ward, by Eyjavatn, but he had an aunt who was married at Tjer-naas and kinsfolk at Randaberg; he was often there.

Olav shook his head unconcernedly; he knew little of these folk and had never spoken with them.

After supper the men sat in the hall; they had brought in some saddlery and implements to put in order for the spring work of the farm. Once on waking from his own thoughts Olav heard his house-carls laughing and sneering, while Eirik poured out an impetuous tale:

"—when they came and set on me all at the same time, what could I do? Do you think I could not have thrown every single one of them, if we had met on level ground?"

"Oh, ay, surely. You would have done that."

"And I kept them off me a long time—"

"But then you had such help from that brave foster-brother of yours, Eirik," laughed one of the men.

Eirik was instantly silenced. Olav saw that the boy's lips quivered; he was pressing back the tears and trying to look unconcerned.

Olav felt with latent anger that there was something wrong in this—that the house-carls dared to taunt and slight the son of the house while his father was by. Eirik was no longer a little boy. So he put down what he had in his hands, stretched himself, and yawned:

"Nay, men—'tis already late. Time to go to rest."

When father and son were left alone in the hall, Olav came and stood before Eirik. The lad sat on the bench weeping quietly.

"You must have done with this now, Eirik—this childish boast-ing—so that the serving-folk think they may make a fool of you."

As the boy made no answer, but simply sat there struggling with his tears, Olav went on, rather more harshly:

"And you ought to be ashamed to cry because you got a beating!"

Eirik snuffled once or twice. "I am not crying because I got a beating!"

"What are you crying for, then?"

"Jörund—" Eirik swallowed. "We had promised each other

loyal fellowship for life—we took the oath of blood-brotherhood
last autumn and—"

"What nonsense is this?" asked his father rather scornfully.

Eirik explained with sudden eagerness. They had met at church
one Sunday in the autumn, and then Eirik had spoken of something he had lately heard: that it was a custom in old days for
friends to bind themselves by an oath of blood-brotherhood.
Jörund was willing. But every time they got so far as lifting the
strip of turf on the points of their spears, it broke to pieces, and
at last Jörund lost patience—and then Sira Hallbjörn came out,
and he was very wroth when he saw all the holes they had dug in
his calf paddock.

Olav shook his head in despair. "What folly!"

Eirik was standing with one foot on the hearth, close to the
glowing embers, and a cloud of steam came from his shoe. The
boy looked so melancholy with his tall, weedy body, his long
neck, and the dark, curly head bent down—everything about
Eirik was young and slight. Olav had a sudden desire to show the
boy a kindness.

"Do not scorch your shoe—'twill be hard as a board tomorrow."
Olav handed him a pair of his own shoes. "You may have the loan
of these tomorrow—stuff straw in your own, so they may dry
slowly."

Eirik thanked him cheerfully, and Olav began to pull off his
clothes. Presently the boy cried out with a laugh:

"Father, I have outgrown your shoes now—look here."

It was true. Ah yes, his own feet were unusually small. And
Eirik looked like being large-limbed.

Olav lay long awake; the thought of Eirik galled and troubled
him.

In these last years—nay, ever since his relations with Torhild
Björnsdatter took that unfortunate turn—he had shunned the boy,
almost without premeditation. Eirik *was* there, but the less he
thought of it, the better.

But this last winter it had seemed as if Eirik sought to thrust
himself on his father's attention. At first Olav believed this was
the result of the lad's having run loose a whole summer without
any man's hand over him; now he must quickly find some means
of quelling these loud-voiced ways that the boy had got into. But

Olav was startled to see, with great surprise and little joy, that he
was no longer able to relegate Eirik to that outer sphere of his
father's life to which the lad had so long been banished. It was
clear that he would have to devote more care to the boy's training, cordially as he disliked the thought. He saw all the lad's faults
and failings, and things could not go on as now—when their inferiors showed openly that they, too, saw them. Eirik had now
reached an age when it was only seemly that he should mix with
other men in his father's company. But then Olav would have to
see that the lad was shown the respect due to their position.

But Eirik himself had little sense of how to behave himself. At
home he mixed with the servants of the house: one day he was
their familiar, childish and fatuous; the next he put on a proud and
lofty air—but the folk only made fun of this before the boy's very
eyes.

The worst thing, however, was that he haunted Rundmyr early
and late. The place had become a vile den since Liv and Arnketil
had gone there. Egil and Vilgard, his younger brother, were also
housed there now, and they brought in others of the like sort. It
came to Olav's ears that Eirik had actually joined in dicing with
folk who came in from the highways, all kinds of vagabonds, both
men and women. He took the lad to task for it, chiding him
sharply. Then to Olav's unspeakable surprise Eirik turned in-
solent and answered back. Olav simply took hold of the boy's
neck, forced his head down, and flung him aside—but he liked
doing it no better, as he felt how weakly and as it were dis-
jointedly the lad collapsed under his hand. And the expression of
Eirik's eyes, at once cowed and malicious, aroused violent repugnance in Olav, though at the same time he felt pity for the
weakling.

There was another matter that troubled Olav tonight. He had
guessed well enough what Una had in her mind when she came
down to the boats on leaving the Thing and asked him to take
her with him. And he had been right—when they came ashore she
had contrived to be alone with him by the boathouses. Then she
told him in plain words: there were now other suitors for Disa
Erlandsdatter. But both she and Torgrim would rather that Olav
won the bride.

Olav thought he had given no very definite reply, but now he
could no longer avoid making them a plain answer. And doubtless

it would lead to some cooling of friendship between him and his kinsfolk when he showed so little appreciation: he saw clearly enough how kindly they had meant it when they as good as offered him Torgrim's rich cousin in marriage. And assuredly the whole neighbourhood had heard of the matter. Olav saw now that he ought to have let them know long ago that he did not wish to marry again.

They had every right to complain that he had rewarded their loyal spirit of kinship with disdain. Since he had been a widower there had been a revival of intercourse between him and his kinswomen, the daughters of Arne, and their husbands. And now too he remarked that his neighbours seemed to smooth the way for him; did he wish it, he could now come forward and resume the position that the master of Hestviken ought to occupy in the district. Together with his kinsmen by marriage at Skikkjustad and Rynjul he could acquire both power and honour in the hundred. And he liked both Torgrim and Baard—ay, Baard he liked better than most men.

It was the daughters of Arne and their husbands who stood in the background and induced people—those who had their boats and boathouses on his beach—to come forward and suggest that all the old questions that had been left undecided, as to the rights to the different estates, his share in the catches of fish, and such matters, might just as well be settled now. There were many things that Olav had let drift for years, because he felt lonely and overburdened. And his neighbours and others, who had been wont to make the lower road down to the creek, keeping away from the manor on the hill, now found occasion to visit his house and enjoyed such hospitality as had been shown in former days at Hestviken. Perhaps it was not unnatural—it had been reasonable enough that folk kept away from the house so long as its mistress lay there sick and disabled.

But now Olav was offered an opportunity of retrieving—ay, he might just as well be frank about it—he could now recover all it had cost him to be Steinfinn Toresson's foster-son and Ingunn's bridegroom. But he *would* not!

Disa was rich, of good family; her first marriage had added to her repute, and she had inherited Roaldstad and its wealth from her two little sons who had been drowned a year or two before in the breaking up of the ice. Her age agreed with his—some thirty

years. And if she was not a lady of surpassing beauty, she was far
from ugly, a shapely, kind, healthy, and cheerful woman. Never
again would he be offered so good a match. If he did not grasp
at her with both hands, it would be deemed by all that he did not
desire his own welfare. And he liked the young widow, the little
he had seen of her.

But he would not marry Disa Erlandsdatter. It was not the
same as when he refused Torhild; that he had done under com-
pulsion, he knew not of what. From time to time desire came upon
him when he thought of Torhild—he longed to embrace her
great wholesome body as a man bleeding to death longs to quench
his thirst. And he would be sick with impatience to place everything in her capable hands when he himself had to wrestle with
matters that properly came under the care of the mistress of the
house. He had renounced her because he felt he must, whether he
desired her for himself or not.

But at the thought of Disa dwelling here at Hestviken, meeting
him at his own door, of his having to listen to all that she said and
and answer her—no, then he knew he would not—not if she
brought him all the gold there was in Norway. He shuddered
with aversion at the thought of having her sleeping here between
himself and the wall through the long, sleepless nights. At such
times he could not possibly bear to have an entirely strange
woman close to him. Torhild—if she had been sleeping by his side
now, he knew that whether asleep or awake her loyal heart would
be full of care for his welfare; he would not feel ashamed with
her, were his mind never so restless.

So it was: he often thought it hard that an instinct which he did
not himself understand forbade him to fetch home the lowly Torhild and resume his concubinage with her. But his whole being rebelled if he did but call to mind that his best and most faithful
friends sought to have him married to the rich and virtuous widow
of Svein of Roaldstad.

He remembered having once thought that in the end it might
turn out that his life would shape itself after the manner of this—
happiness. When it began to dawn on him that Ingunn was not
destined for a long life. At that time he had thrust such thoughts
from him as infidelity. But then she *was* here, she was his wife,
and behind every grey and evil day and every fresh misfortune,
every fresh drop of bitterness that fell into his cup, he had known

that he would rather have the life he had, with Ingunn, than any other lot without her.

But now she was gone. And it would cost him but a word to acquire Roaldstad and wealth, a healthy and capable wife, heirs to all they might possess in common, a firm alliance with the kinsfolk whom he liked, a powerful position in the district. And then Olav felt that rather than have all this happiness he would *die*.

The brightness had passed from Ingunn's memory since that adventure in London; it was as though he could no longer keep her distinct from the other. All seemed blind, unthinking, bestially stupid—that she had frittered away the happiness of both, that he himself had strayed from every path he should have followed, till he now felt as though his own soul were nothing but a little grey, hardened stone.

Since that night after the pilgrimage all the thoughts he had struggled with seemed to have turned to stones. He remembered them and knew them in a way—as the lad in the fairy tale recognized his friends in the pillar-stones outside the giant's castle. But they left him dull and cold. He knew that in this new calm that had come upon him he was a poorer man than before, when he had lived in fear and pain: beneath every stab of remorse and every longing for peace there had been something that was much greater and stronger than his fear: he loved Him from whom he fled, and even to the end he had secretly hoped that the hour would come when he could fly no more. Sooner or later, he must have thought, he would be reconciled with God—without its being left to him to choose. But he had been forced to choose and choose again. And so long had he chosen himself that he had lost even his love of God. But therewithal the fire and strength seemed to have gone out of his love for all else he had held dear in this world.

God, Jesus Christ, Mary—once he had only had to think upon these words for his heart to glow with fervour within him. Now it mattered nothing to him whether he said his prayers in church or at home, morning and evening, if others were by and it was the time, or whether he omitted to pray when alone. But this new indifference was as much poorer than his old torment as a heap of ashes is poorer than a blazing fire.

But Ingunn—were her memory never so faded and burned out, he would not cast it out to make room for new possessions. And as his life was now, he would neither own nor bring into it this happiness he was offered.

Olav Half-priest had once told him of Hvitserk's howe, the largest of the mounds here by the brow of the wood. It was before the Christian faith had come to the land; the race of Inggjald then possessed Hestviken, that stock of which his grandfather's grandmother had come, and the name of the chief was Aale Hvitserk. He had been a famous viking, but now he was in extreme old age. Then his enemies burned his homestead of Hestviken—this was the first of the three burnings that had laid the manor in ashes. Aale's sons cleared the site and had timber brought to build the houses anew, but Aale let his house-carls cast up a barrow, and on the day they set about dragging off the charred beams of Aale's hall, the old man went into the mound and bade his thralls close up the earthen house with stones.

Olav Audunsson remembered that he had shaken his head when his old namesake told him this tale—but at the same time he had thought him a doughty fellow, that same old heathen.

Now he lay in the darkness smiling a little at this thought. He had taken good heed not to speak of it to any priest, but he offered a Yule cup to the spirit of the mound and carried out a bowl of ale on the eve of other great festivals. Even Arnvid did so at his own home—'twas no great sin, said he, if one did but go quietly about it, without asking anything of the dead in return. Now maybe he ought to be more mindful of his offerings—like enough he would meet with his heathen ancestor in the end.

2

It had chanced, while Olav was in England, that Eirik had received full assurance that he was true-born.

He had had to go up to Rynjul one day with a packload—cups and vessels that Olav had borrowed for his wife's funeral feast. Now they had a very snappish little bitch tied up in the yard there, and that day she had slipped out of her thong, dashed up, and bitten Eirik in the leg as he came in between the houses. Eirik kicked the bitch so that she rolled over on the grass howling. Torgrim rushed out of a door in a great rage:

"—afraid of a little dog like that—and kicking at a bitch—none but a child of bawdry such as you would do the like!"

Eirik had come into the hall, and Una was counting over her vessels; then the lad burst out:

"Una—those words that Torgrim said—are they *true*?"

"Are what true?" she repeated from among her wooden cups.

"Child of bawdry—that is the same as whoreson, is it not, Una?" whispered Eirik dolefully.

"Yes—why?" She looked up and saw the lad standing there, pale as bast, his narrow young face stricken with despair. "Holy Mary—what ails you, Eirik?"

"*Am* I that? Answer me truly, Una mine!"

Una Arnesdatter stood speechless.

"Ay, I guessed it long ago," whispered Eirik.

"*What* did you guess? Are you not ashamed—to say such a thing of your father—and your mother, who lies under the sod? Help us, what have you taken into your head now again!"

"You must have heard him say it, Torgrim—Father himself called me bastard once."

"You may be sure," said Una more gently, "neither of the two would have called you such bad names if you had been so indeed. Surely you have wit enough to see that 'twas only the word of an angry man."

"Then *was* Mother married to Father?" asked Eirik.

"You have no need to ask that. Olav kept the poor woman in good and honourable state so long as she lived. You can have seen naught else."

"He took the keys from her and gave them to his leman," muttered Eirik. "That was a year and more ere Mother lost her health."

"Say no more of that, boy." Una turned red with indignation. "You do not understand it. I will speak no ill of your mother, poor soul that she was—'twas not *her* fault that her kinsmen dealt falsely by Olav, still less that she was as she was, sickly and feeble-minded. None could expect a man to be well pleased with such a marriage as fell to the lot of our kinsman. Scarce had the Stein-finnssons got the rich heir into their power when they bound the little boy in bonds of betrothal to one of their own children; and then they cheated him of all he should have received with his bride; never has Olav had help or honour of that alliance, but he was forced to take the ailing woman, for they had trapped him into her bed ere he was fully grown."

Una talked thus for a good while and said what she thought of Olav's married life. She was faithful to her own kin and fond of Olav as though he had been her brother; but though she had always been helpful and kind to his wife, she had had but a moderate liking for Ingunn, and in her heart she had called her a worm.

Together with Eirik's first sense of boundless relief on knowing that none could drive him away from Hestviken, there came a smouldering indignation against his father. He might have spared himself these years of anxious insecurity—but it was his father's fault: so barefaced had he been in his evil life with that cursed jade Torhild that it was only natural Eirik should fear the worst. Wrong, wrong, wrong had his mother suffered under her own roof.

Eirik spent that summer at Hestviken. Every corner of the old walls, every crack in the smooth-worn, reddish-grey rocks had a face that met his loving glances with a look of gentle kindness. The strip of seaweed under his own rocks looked different from seaweed elsewhere. No other wharves or boats smelt so good as theirs. When he took up the oars in his own boat or put out his nets, his whole body was filled with delight—*he* owned them! He caressed every animal he met that was theirs. Eirik took an ear of barley and laid it on his wrist over the pulse so that it crawled up under the sleeve—this old child's game had become a sort of magic ceremony: it was *his* corn. He need no longer be afraid as he lived and moved among all these things—they would never vanish away out of his hands.

Eirik's memory of his mother had quickly faded. In her last years, when she never left her bed, she had already passed out of the boy's world; after her death he had soon ceased to think of her. Now that he was so indignant with his father, he felt an added resentment on his mother's behalf; his affection for her awakened, he often longed for her. He had been so fond of her as long as she was well and he could be with her—and his father had treated her so harshly and cruelly.

But it only needed a friendly word from Olav, and Eirik forgot all his bitterness. Afterwards he remembered it and was angry at his own weakness. But no sooner did the man show him the least indulgence, no sooner did Eirik see but a shadow of the pale, frozen smile on his father's lips as he spoke to him, than the son became insensible to all but his abject adoration of his father.

A short time after Olav's return from England, Eirik heard the rumours that he was to marry Disa Erlandsdatter. Up at Rundmyr they gossiped freely about everything.

Eirik's temper rebelled again. He would not have a stepmother. He would not hear of joint heirs in Hestviken. No strangers should come, bringing new customs or anything new. All should be his and Cecilia's, the manor and the wharf and the woods on the Bull and along the back of the Horse Crag, Kverndal and Saltviken. He knew every path there, he had his own places, outlooks, and hidden grassy hollows among the grey rocks toward the sea; his habit was to go there, simply to sit there alone rejoicing vaguely and obscurely in the possession of these hiding-places. The hunting in the forest, the sealing, the fishery, all this would one day be in his control. But the last and inmost thought, which always made him mad with passion—for he knew he had no power to hinder its coming to pass—was that one day another might come between him and his father. He even spun long fabulous dreams of the deed that would one day make him his father's favourite.

The seal-hunting wellnigh failed that year. And Olav lost a good new six-oared boat out in the skerries; the painter was cut one night, whether it was the work of an enemy or someone had stolen the boat. So Olav came home from sea in a gloomy temper, even for him.

Some days after, he had business that took him inland, and Eirik was to accompany him as far as the church; it was a Wednesday in the ember days, and Sira Hallbjörn insisted that all who could should attend church in the ember days.

The frost fog was thick that morning and left a film of ice on rocks and woodwork. Olav stood outside the stable door, while Eirik led out the horses and was about to saddle them. Olav was standing there, sleepy and dazed and fasting, when suddenly he turned to his son and said hotly:

"Will you not rub the bit before you put it in the horse's mouth
—in this searing cold?"

" 'Tis not cold," replied Eirik sullenly. " 'Tis only the raw
weather that feels cold."

"Hold your tongue! Will you teach me to judge of the weather?
If you had that scorching cold iron in your own jaws—"

Eirik snatched an iron rod that was stuck in the stable wall and
bit on it. His father pulled it from him and flung it on the rock.

"You see—you are bleeding!"

" 'Twas not that it scorched me—you tore my mouth."

"Be silent," said Olav curtly, "and have done now."

About midday some of the church folk sat in the priest's house
taking a bite of the food they had brought, before setting out for
home. The wound at the corner of Eirik's mouth began to bleed
again, and he told some of the other lads how he had got it; but he
said it was his father who had taken the bit and forced it into his
jaws.

Then he noticed that the silence which followed was heavy
with scorn.

At last a boy said: "Shame on you, Eirik—do you let your father
make a jade of you?"

Eirik look around, hesitating. He had meant to boast of what
had befallen him. When he noticed the scorn on the others' faces,
something seemed to shrivel up within him. So he would make
up for it.

"No. But indeed it were useless for me to stand up against him,"
he said, warming with excitement. "I can tell you, I pulled off the
halter and struck at him. But he has the strength of a troll, my
father. One time, while he was with the Earl, they made wagers,
how big a load he could lift. Father put his shoulders under the
bench and raised himself till he stood upright. Eight men sat on
that bench."

He was met with icy silence.

"Then says the Earl: 'If you can lift the table-top Olav Audunsson, it shall be yours, with all the silver that stands upon it.' My
father took the table and lifted it at arm's length."

" 'Tis almost like the story you told us last year, Sira Hallbjörn,"
said a young girl, with a giggle; "of that Christian knight who was
a captive with the Saracen earl—what was his name?" There was
a hearty laugh from some of the grown people.

Sira Hallbjörn was sitting apart on his bed. That day he was neither surly nor frolicsome; he seemed rather dull. He looked coldly at the maid.

"You remember, Sira Hallbjörn—at my brother's wedding?"

"I know no such story. Your memory is at fault."

But a little later, when folk were breaking up, the priest came abruptly behind Eirik Olavsson and took him firmly by the arm:

"What is your meaning with such talk—do you tell lies of your father?"

"Nay, I lied not, Sira," Eirik answered coolly.

"You lied." Sira Hallbjörn gave him a blow under the ear. "And now you lie to your parish priest. The Devil is in you, I believe. Be off with you now!"

At dusk Olav Audunsson rode up to the priest's door. He would not go in, he said, it was too late. Sitting in the saddle he handed Sira Hallbjörn the casket of letters and turned to ride away at once. Sira Hallbjörn came out and walked at his side as Olav rode at a foot's pace between the fences.

"Master Olav," said the priest hotly, "you should not suffer your son to assort with those folk you have thought fit to set up at Rundmyr. 'Twill do the boy no good, what he learns there."

Olav knew not what to reply to this. As he said nothing, the priest continued, repeating what Eirik had said of his father: "—he makes himself a mockery in the eyes of the whole parish, your son, by lying in this fashion—and lying so foolishly." Meanwhile they had come to the crossroads, and the priest laid his hand on Olav's bridle and held it as he looked up into the other's face. There was still a glimmer of daylight within the mist that was gathering again—Olav saw with surprise that the priest seemed greatly agitated.

"I cannot guess why Eirik should say that." Olav told him what had taken place between him and his son that morning.

"Ay, so goes it when the young have bad masters."

Olav frowned and puckered his lips in a sort of smile, but made no answer. Eirik hardly needed a master to teach him lying—that talent he was surely born with.

"Had any wise man counselled my father as I now counsel you," said Sira Hallbjörn, "then he had taken me away from the house where I was fostered after my mother died. I was a pious child while I was with her—she had vowed me to God while I was yet unborn. But then Father sent me to a foster-father, and he was of Lappish race—"

"Do there dwell Lapps in Valdres?" asked Olav; he felt he ought to say something.

The priest nodded. "I saw many a strange thing as I grew up, Olav. They are the most excellent hunters, the Lapps—and divers creatures are abroad in the mountains, both beasts and men—and others. Since then it goes ill with me to live elsewhere. I yearned not to return thither during the years I was in foreign lands, resorting to one school after another. But these folk hereabouts—they provoke me so that I lose patience—"

"So it seems." Olav could not forbear to smile a little mockingly.

"Ay," said the priest hotly. " 'Tis not good to dwell in these parts. You have no friends here either, Olav."

"So it seems," said Olav again. "But I know not if it be because — Maybe folk are no different here than elsewhere."

"Have you ever taken part in hunting reindeer?" asked Sira Hallbjörn abruptly—"at the old deer-pits among the fells? Have you seen the reindeer herd on the move—many thousand deer?"

"Nay," said Olav. "I have never seen a living reindeer."

"Bear me company some time"—there was almost an entreaty in the priest's voice, so eager was he—"when I go home to visit my brothers."

"I thank you, Sira Hallbjörn. Should the occasion suit, I would gladly bear you company one day."

They took leave of each other. The priest said once more:

"But keep Eirik from Rundmyr. If not, they will trick the lad into a share of their stealings—or father some wench's brat on him, before he is two years older. And you would be ill served with that, both of you, Olav."

Olav thought deeply over his talk with the priest as he rode down in the dark. He felt something like disappointment. Not that he had any quarrel with his parish priest—on the contrary; he was one of the few men in the district who had not yet been in conflict with him. But he too had thought there was some secret about Sira Hallbjörn—and then his being exiled, as it were, to this parish, outside all the positions and dignities to which he might be entitled by his high birth and his learning. So Olav had half expected that one day something or other would come to light about him. And now it seemed nothing but this, that Hallbjörn Erlingsson thrived ill down here in the lowlands and found it hard to be friends with their people, being headstrong and whimsical as fell-dwellers often are. No doubt it was little to his liking to have the quiet charge of a parish church and be at the call of any who had need of his ministrations.

Formerly Olav had instinctively sought the company of such men as he felt to be pure of heart and faithful toward God. Without thinking of it he had shunned the black sheep when he met them. Now he felt just as much at his ease among men who were less strict—who had the name, in any case, of being not too strict with themselves, though for aught he cared they might judge others strictly. In a way he was not displeased at heart to find some fault or other in a man, especially if it were a priest or a monk. Nor did he ever inquire into rumours now; he held his peace when the talk was of such things, but lent an ear, and that no longer with repugnance or sensitiveness.

He thought too of what Sira Hallbjörn had said about Eirik and it vexed him. But he did not care to speak to the boy about it —much better seem to know nothing. But he would have to forbid the boy haunting Rundmyr.

And he did so. But Eirik did not obey. Olav came to hear of it. Sometimes he spoke harshly to his son about it, but at other times he let it pass, as though he did not know Eirik had been there.

He had acted foolishly in letting Anki and Liv have Rundmyr. If they would only keep to what was his—that he could afford to wink at—but now there were murmurs abroad, folk found that there were light fingers at Rundmyr. At last Olav had to take Arnketil to task about it: "Meseems you two might live awhile on what you pick up at Hestviken." The man promised to mend his ways—but Olav was not so sure that the promise was worth much.

And now it might be difficult to be rid of them. When Arnketil came and asked him to hold their babe at the font, he had not the heart to refuse the poor simple man. Moreover he thought that if he agreed to be godfather to the boy, no one could suspect him of commerce with the mother. It never entered Olav's mind that, so far as he knew, no one had had such a thought; it was only himself who feared folk might hit upon this. There had been a hint of it when she had her first child—but then he was common talk over the matter of Torhild, and there are always those who are ready to make a man blacker than he is. But by accepting the god-child, he had now bound himself to support its parents.

To Eirik, Arnketil had been in some sort as a foster-father, so it was not easy to part the lad entirely from him. And Liv came out to Hestviken with her babe on her back—stayed there the whole day, dealing out good advice to the serving-women and talking of how everything had been done when she was in charge.

Torhild had turned out right in saying he acted unwisely in housing such people so near to the manor. Olav thought of it with a dull bitterness: that he could be so placed that he could not bring in Torhild and profit by her sensible advice.

It was a vexation to Olav that Eirik forced himself thus upon his notice and his thoughts. And again and again he came upon this incomprehensible mendacity. Each time it was like a riddle to Olav. He had told lies himself, hard and cold enough to split rocks—he had not forgotten that—but then he had known why he lied; he had lied because he was forced to it. But Eirik lied and lied, and his father could never espy anything that looked like a plausible reason—he did not lie for gain and he seldom lied for concealment. Olav had seen that, though he had not been so care-ful to note how seldom Eirik attempted to deny or to lie if he were asked a straight question: the lad was quite ready to confess even his worst misdeeds; falteringly, blushing and blinking, he said how it was, if he were asked. So it was almost as though Eirik made up these lying stories of his because it amused him—incompre-hensible as such a thing seemed to Olav.

Year in and year out Olav's feelings for the child had swung between a vague longing to be able to like this young being who had been placed in his power—and dislike of this stranger who was as a thorn buried in his flesh. Now at last they were coming to rest for good. There were times when Eirik's incomprehensible and positively high-spirited mendacity aroused hatred in Olav's heart: as though the very lie he had taken upon himself as a yoke were incarnate in Eirik's person, mocking him in the smile of the fairy-like, brown-eyed boy.

Nevertheless there were other times when it was not so.

This second summer after his wife's death Olav had to attend the Eidsiva Thing. He was short-handed now at Hestviken and could not easily take any man from his work. So it came about that Eirik was to ride with his father.

Olav had little mind to this long journey, nor had he any great desire to meet his brother-in-law. He had not been north of Oslo in all the thirteen years since he had brought home Ingunn, except that one time when he fetched Eirik, and then it had been winter.

Now he took the summer road northward through Raumarike. It was fine, sunny weather, but warm for travelling in the middle of the day. So they found a suitable place near the road; Eirik unsaddled the horses and hobbled them. After their meal Olav and Eirik stretched themselves on the ground. The lad fell asleep at once.

Olav lay with his head on his saddle, gazing before him through the tissue of grass. The meadow was golden yellow with buttercups, flower upon flower, and round the little brown watercourse below were silvery tufts of bog-cotton. Beyond the brook blazed a mass of red campion in the shade of the alders. He looked at the flowers as though they were old acquaintances he had met again after an interval of years: it was true he noticed at home too when this grass or that came out, taking auguries from it of how the summer would turn out. But here as he lay idly watching the flowers blooming on land of which he knew not the owner, it was different—bringing back to him in some measure the tracts in which he had spent his youth.

Great silver-grey clouds shining at the verge welled up over the fir-tops and spread quietly and with wonderful swiftness over the whole warm blue sky—down on the ground not a breath stirred. Now they came over and put out the sunshine. Olav drew his cloak over his face because of the midges and slept.

In the course of the afternoon they came out of a forest and saw a great manor lying before them under the sinking sun. It looked like some great man's seat there on the top of its mound, with a little white stone church to the north of the group of houses, and the meadows surrounding it on every side. Eirik cried out with joy, so grand it seemed to him. Olav made no reply to his exclamation.

The bridle-path led up the hill and straight through the manor. This was no less imposing when one came up to it, with countless

houses, new and old, in two rows by the side of the way, and
every sign of activity and habitation.

When they had come down into the valley and were riding by
the bank of a river, Olav asked Eirik: "Know you what that
manor is called, Eirik?"

"Nay?" asked the boy eagerly.

"That was Dyfrin."

"Was it!" After a while Eirik said in a hushed voice, with strong
emotion: "*We* should have been there, if we had our rights—is it
not so, Father?"

"So it is." Olav rode in silence for a few moments. Then he
asked with a sort of smile: "Which of the two manors do you like
best, Eirik—Dyfrin or Hestviken?"

"Hestviken," answered Eirik warmly, without hesitation.

"Dyfrin is more than twice as large—you could see that?"

"No matter. At Dyfrin they have not the sea either—or wharves
or boats. But 'tis galling to call to mind the injustice. Methinks a
man who worked so much injustice to the landholders of the
country as that Sverre—he could not be fitted to be king—"

"Some injustice must be done by every man who will gain his
cause," replied Olav.

Eirik wished to hear of the old traditions—of Torgils Fivil and
his sons and of the widow whom King Sverre gave to one of his
men. Olav replied to his questions. But then they saw the road
lying before them across a sandy plain, level and easy, and Olav
urged on the horses; with that their talk came to an end.

Hallvard Steinfinnsson gave a hearty welcome both to his
brother-in-law and to his nephew. With the passing of years
Hallvard had grown very like his father, Olav saw, and he also
resembled Steinfinn in his ways; he was merry, open-handed and
not over-wise. He had the eldest son of Tora and Haakon Gautsson with him at the Thing. Eirik had looked forward with great
joy to meeting his mother's kindred, but though they were so
friendly to him, Eirik seemed unusually shy, and he kept close to
his father at all times and places while the Thing lasted.

Quite unexpectedly Olav met his kinsmen from Tveit in Soleyar
at the gathering: Gudbrand and Jon Helgessons with two sons
and a son-in-law. Olav had met the men of Tveit only once be-

fore—at the time he was engaged in discharging the fines for the
slaying of Einar Kolbeinsson, and then he had thought they gave
themselves little trouble for a young kinsman. Now they were
getting on in years, both he and the Helgessons, and it seemed
late to take up the ties of kinship. But he exchanged words with
them when they met. And on one of the last days of the gathering,
when Hallvard had asked Olav to come and drink with him at
his inn, he found the men of Tveit there; Hallvard had fetched
them in to show courtesy to his brother-in-law.

Hallvard lodged in the same house Steinfinn had used when he
came to the Thing. Olav could not recall it; he was not sure that
this hall they now sat drinking in was the same in which they
had betrothed him to Ingunn. Apart from that he remembered
everything so clearly—Ingunn and Steinfinn and his own father
—ay, he scarce remembered his father apart from that evening—
and many of the guests' faces he could recall as though it were
yesterday.

Olav was very taciturn the whole evening, but the others paid
no heed to that; they drank, and at last they seemed entirely to
forget that he sat there. But what chiefly occupied Olav's attention was Eirik—he kept so quiet and was utterly unlike himself as
they were used to seeing him at home.

The lad sat on the outer bench together with the younger ones
from Tveit. Olav looked at him: old feelings, by no means unfriendly, were strangely revived in him—during the journey Eirik
had not chanced to do anything that might irritate his father. He
sat there very quiet and well-mannered, talking easily in low tones
with Knut and Joar. The dark-skinned, sharp-featured boyish face
was beginning to put on a maturer look: the forehead was high
and narrow under the shock of black hair, the nose was high
and thin, hooked, or rather indented, from the very root down
to the bridge; the mouth was prominent, with a pronounced curve
in the upper jaw; when listening he was apt to show something of
his front teeth, and they were very white; the two midmost were
very slightly crossed. Nevertheless his face was far from ugly:
he had a fine complexion, red-cheeked and browned by the sun,
the lips bright red, the eyes unusually large and pale brown, so
light that they made one think of amber, or bog-water in sunlight. Olav felt, as a fleeting quiver through his mind, that here
he sat in company with his own kinsmen and brother-in-law, and

he found little to say to them. And underneath the honest, open
ties that bound him to the others, the ties of blood and of the law,
he was joined to this slender, swarthy lad who sat like a stranger
among the fair, red Tveit boys—he knew not himself how in-
dissolubly.

Hallvard had wine, and so it was near midnight before the
guests broke up. It was a half hour's walk down to the booth
where Olav lay, and at the parting of the roads he stood awhile
talking to some men who were going the other way. Then he
walked on quickly with Eirik. The night was mild and so light
that the moon seemed quite pale and faint. When they had gone
some distance they heard the men of Tveit before them on the
road—they were drunken and noisy, and Olav had no desire for
their company. So he turned out of the path with Eirik; they
strolled along the hillside, which was covered with great rocks
and juniper and other bushes; a few dun horses grazed among the
tussocks in the moonlight.

They came out on some little crags, and beneath them lay a
great bog, which would be tiresome to go round; so Olav sat
down to let the Tveit folk get ahead. But now it sounded as if
they had come to a halt on the path just below here—they made
no move, and Gudbrand vomited with loud retching, while the
others formed a ring and made sport of him. Eirik lay on his
stomach on the close-cropped grass, laughing quietly and mimick-
ing to his father the words and noises that came up from below.

"Look at the moon, Father," said Eirik. The half-moon was
near its setting now, floating on its back above the tree-tops in
the west, with a few thin strips of golden cloud lying under it.
Near it was a great star blazing alone in the pale blue sky.

"Ay," said Olav. "We shall have wind."

"It looks like a ship," said Eirik, laughing quietly at his own
idea, "sailing on the sea—and the big star is like a dog running
after the ship."

"Nay, Eirik"—Olav could not help smiling—"how can a dog run
after a ship that sails on the sea?"

"Oh yes," said the boy eagerly, "they have left it behind—and
now it runs along the shore, in and out among the headlands,
barking and howling after the boat."

The boy's words reminded Olav of something—he had once
heard or dreamed something like this about a dog that ran along

the shore wailing after a ship that sailed away—a dog, or a man, that had been left behind.

He looked down at the lad's upturned face—quite pale it seemed in the twilight, and the wide-open eyes were dark in the shadow. It was as though the man in moving had tightened the invisible bond between them.

"Of the noise of cats' treading and the beards of women and the roots of the rocks and the breath of the fishes and the spittle of the birds—" it was a rigmarole he had known as a child, of someone who had forged a chain, and it was more pliant than silk and bound faster than fetters of steel—a wild beast was to stay bound in it till doomsday.

It was quiet down on the road. "Come," said Olav, and unconsciously he let his hand drop on the boy's shoulder, kept it there a moment.

They went down and found the path again. Of the Tveit folk they saw no more and reached without delay the booth where Olav had hired night quarters for them.

The bed was exceedingly narrow. Eirik fell asleep at once, and very soon he turned over in his sleep, so that he almost lay on top of his father.

In the narrow, uncomfortable couch, with the darkness around thick with the smell of men, Olav lay feeling the pressure of Eirik's thin, slender body, the warm scent of his skin and hair—without distaste, with an unreasoning sense of pity. Though only God and His blessed Mother could tell why he should have compassion on Eirik. He knew of nothing to make him pity his son, but it was as though the lad's very youth made him soft-hearted—though that is a fault one soon grows out of, thought Olav.

Olav got no proper sleep, but lay, as it were, rolling back and forth between sleep and waking like a piece of driftwood on the beach. But after an hour or two, when he heard some men moving in the other rooms, Olav gently withdrew from beside the sleeping lad and went out to see to the horses himself. He had not the heart to wake the boy.

3

THE FRIENDSHIP that had grown up between Olav Audunsson and his kinsfolk at Rynjul and Skikkjustad was declining again. Una had gone so far, that day in the spring when he sailed her home, that they could not honourably carry the matter farther. And Olav made no move. So they avoided each other. But that the people of Rynjul resented it Olav was well aware.

How his conduct was interpreted by his neighbours he had a chance of hearing one day when he met Sira Hallbjörn down on the wharf. The priest burst out in his abrupt way:

"A great gull you were, Olav, to take up again with that Torhild woman—she coaxed you into buying her wretched cot and, worse than that, you let her spoil a good marriage for you."

"What idle talk is this?" Olav's face turned red as fire. "I ask counsel of no one, either in buying land or taking a wife—in such things I do as I *will*."

"Pooh! You think so, I can well believe. You thought, no doubt, you had your will with her when she did as she willed. Torhild Björnsdatter is the wiser of you two. Beware now, Olav, that she make not another halter for you of her girdle."

Olav replied angrily: "Howbeit, this can be no concern of yours, Sira Hallbjörn, so long as I have not lain with her again. Belike I may take counsel where I will—I have not begged it of you!"

He turned his back and leaped down into his boat.

But afterwards a raging desire for Torhild flared up in him again—day and night, day and night. Simply to take her to him in defiance. If folk were resolved to meddle with his affairs, then let them have something to meddle with. And Björn—he had banned the child's memory, driven back his thoughts whenever they would go that way. Now it came upon him—was it worth the trouble? So many a thing had gone amiss with him, should he not after all take what good there was to take?

Waking and sleeping, he dreamed of his son. But behind the image of the little fair-skinned boy he saw the other fair child—Cecilia. For her sake he must stand firm and deny himself that which he desired. It would not be good for her to grow up in a

house of which her father's leman was mistress. Not yet had he
wrecked Cecilia's future, and he would not do so either.

Olav saw little of his daughter now. If she ran out into the yard
to play and her father stopped to speak to her, Cecilia had scarce
time to answer him. At night she slept with Ragna in Torhild's
old house. But Ragna was only a poor serving-woman, unfitted to
rear the daughter of a man of Olav's condition when the maid
grew a little older. Moreover Ragna had all the household duties
to perform and her own three children to herd. The eldest lay
outside the house door all day long, drivelling and snoring and
rocking his great head—the poor child lacked something of his
wits—but the year-old twins were lively as kittens and could be
seen creeping and crawling everywhere in the yard and across
the thresholds.

Olav was at his wits' end to know what to do with this daughter, to have her brought up in seemly fashion. Maybe *this* would
have been easier if he had married Disa—though one never knows
with any woman how she will turn out as a stepmother.

And there was this Liv hanging about the place early and late—
Cecilia clung to her—she remembered no mother else.

Then quite unexpectedly a way appeared out of these difficulties, it seemed to Olav. One day two townsmen from Tunsberg came to him with a message that Asger Magnusson lay dying
in the Premonstratensian convent in their town and would speak
with him. Olav had nothing special to do that day, and the wind
was fair; so he sailed over at once.

It seemed strange to him that they should thus come up again
in his life, one after another, the men he had known in his youth
and for years had wellnigh forgotten. It was almost as if he had
come out of the fairy hill—and as they say of those whom the fairies have carried off, so it was with him; he felt a stranger among
these men and cared little for them one way or the other. Not that
there had ever been any warmth of feeling between him and Hallvard Steinfinnsson or the men of Tveit. Asger in any case had been
his friend: they were distantly related to each other, and when he
was in Denmark he and Asger had associated not a little, though
they had never had much to say to each other—this friendship
was the only tie that had not broken of those he had formed in
his days of outlawry. Apart from this the years with his uncle

at Vikings' Bay seemed to Olav like a half-forgotten dream. But
Asger had come hither to Norway with the banished Danish
lords, and so they had been brothers-in-arms on the raids against
Denmark. At the thought of those war summers Olav's heart rejoiced—he longed to see his comrade again. He caught himself
feeling thus as he stood at the steering-oar keeping an eye on the
familiar sea-marks. Asger was surely not so near dying as the
townsmen said, 'twould not be like him.

But next morning after mass when he was taken to the upper
chamber where the Dane lay abed, he saw at once that death
could not be far off. Asger's great broad face was greenish grey
beneath his red beard, and his powerful, rather hoarse voice had
shrunk to a broken wheeze. And he said as much himself as soon
as he saw his friend: " 'Tis all over with me now, Olav."

On a chest under the little dormer in the gable sat an old woman
and a little girl. The woman stood up and gave her hand to Olav
when he greeted her. Her appearance was such as to cause some
wonder in Olav: she was a good head taller than he, broad-
shouldered, thin and erect in her black weeds; outside her coif
she wore a dark-blue widow's veil. The narrow face, white as
bone, must once have been passing fair: her great blue eyes still
shone beneath bushy, iron-grey brows, and the ridge of her fine
hooked nose was glossy as ivory. But her cheeks were furrowed
with long wrinkles and she had strong tufts of grey hair at the
corners of her mouth. She was the mother of Asger's wife, and
her name was Mærta Birgersdatter. Olav had never before heard
of any living woman being called Mærta, but this one looked as
though she brought no shame on her patroness, the good lady of
Bethany.

She went out at once, and Olav seated himself on the edge of
his friend's bed. Asger was now an outlaw both in Norway and
in Denmark; he had had the misfortune to slay a rich man in his
home district of Hising, where his wife had brought him an estate.
And the slain man was a friend both of King Haakon and of
Count Jacob. Nevertheless he had fled hither to Tunsberg; he was
well known of old in the convent here, and so sick was he that
they might well let him rest in peace while treating for his atonement, or die in sanctuary. For the Abbot maintained that this convent had right of asylum, though it was doubtful if this had ever
been confirmed. But whatever might be the upshot of this, there

was his mother-in-law and his child; would Olav take them in? Olav said yes at once and gave Asger his hand on it.

He had heard at the time that Asger had made a good marriage in the south. But now Asger told him that his wife had died three years before, and he himself had been broken in health of late years, after he had been shipwrecked one winter; he had suffered some inward hurt and since then he had been spitting blood and had little joy of his food.

"And yet you were not so broken but that you cut down Sir Paal in his shirt of mail?" asked Olav, and could not resist smiling.

Asger laughed and coughed weakly. No— It was the mother-in-law, Olav guessed, who had been most helpful in drawing Asger into these quarrels—ay, she looked to be the right one for that, and Asger had never been wont to sing small either. But the man was used to the ups and downs of fortune, and now he took his ill luck calmly. But his child's future seemed to weigh heavily on the father's mind.

Olav turned his eyes to the little girl sitting on the chest; he held out a hand to her. "Come hither, Bothild, my foster-daughter-to-be—shall we talk together, you and I?"

The child sat still as a mouse, and when the strange man spoke to her, she dropped her eyelids—she had thick black lashes. She was a little bigger than Cecilia—six winters old, her father said.

Olav saw that she was a most comely child—though she resembled Asger. She had the same broad face as he, a low, broad forehead, eyes far apart, and a short, square chin, but her skin was bright and clear, her forehead white as milk under the smooth, auburn hair that lay in two heavy plaits over her chest. When she looked up at Olav for an instant her eyes were a pure sky-blue. The lay brother who came up with Olav had given her a big apple, and there she sat clasping it untasted with both hands—she looked so still and timid, as though she understood how friendless and forlorn she was in the world.

Olav had never liked the smell of apples—it seemed to him mawkish or musty—and now it was mingled with the smell of sickness and bed-straw and fusty woollen garments. And the sight of the child's motionless grief stirred up a flood of vague tenderness and pain in Olav's breast. Memories of all the defenceless children he had seen in the course of his life, of mortal wounds inflicted on the weak and helpless, and every thought he had had of his own children, if they should be orphaned, of the child whose father he was, but over whom he could never have a father's right—all this passed through his mind like a stream of shadows. He went over to where the little maid was sitting and caressed her soft, cool cheek.

"Will you not look at me, Bothild? I mean you well. I have a daughter at home, Cecilia—you are to be foster-sisters and live together. How will that please you?"

Without a sound Bothild slid down off the chest and slipped under Olav's arm. She was away to her father's couch, nestled up to him, and took his hand in both hers.

"I will be with you, dear Father mine," she said miserably.

Olav picked up her apple from the floor and gave it to her.

Asger Magnusson opened his little bright-blue eyes wide, as though in great pain; his voice was feeble with helplessness:

"You must not take it amiss, kinsman Olav. I have given this daughter of mine her way more than was good for her." He put his arm about her and clasped the child's dark little head against his shoulder. "You must not think ill of her for this."

"Nay, nay." Olav sat on the bedstead and turned his eyes away. He felt quite abashed with pity for them both.

About a month later Olav received a message that Asger Magnusson was dead, but it was not till after Yule that he could sail down and fetch the old woman and the child. The Abbot told Olav that the dead man's goods had been seized, but doubtless Mærta Birgersdatter had saved no small store of movables in that great chest of hers. Since Asger when living had always proved himself a friend of the monks, the Abbot offered, if Olav would rather escape the charge of the poor child, to give him a letter to the lady Groa in Oslo, asking if she would take Bothild for the love of God—the little maid seemed well fitted to be a nun, for she was quiet and gentle, a winning child. Olav thanked him, but said he had promised the dead man to be to Bothild in the place of a father.

As Olav left the Abbot's chamber he ran straight on the child—she was on her knees in the gallery playing chuckie-stones. The weather was bitter and boisterous, sleet and snow blew in under the roof of the gallery; so Olav spoke to her, bidding her get up. Bothild did not answer, but obeyed at once. Olav took her by the

hand; it was icy cold, and he rubbed her hands between his. He
had occasion to go down to his boat, and he asked if she would go
with him. Bothild nodded, and he led her down.

Her little hand lay so submissively within his that it made him
fond: if he took Cecilia's it slipped away again at once; she could
never walk quietly by the side of a grown person. But he could
not get a word out of his foster-daughter beyond a faint yes
and no.

He took Bothild with him back to the guest-chamber, and as
he sat down by the fire to dry himself, he drew Bothild up on his
knee. She settled herself there, leaning her head against his breast;
such a sweet scent came from her hair. Olav lifted up her face and
kissed her on the mouth—felt the living movement of the soft
childish lips—she kissed him back. A warm, melting thrill went
through him.

Eirik had often been ready to sit on his knees when he was
small, but Cecilia always wanted to get down as soon as he had
picked her up. And if it chanced that he tried to kiss his little
daughter, he noticed that Cecilia did not like it.

For the last year Olav had slept in the hearth-room, in the bed
that had been his marriage-bed. He slept better than he had done
for many years, but even now he often lay long awake. At such
times it was pleasanter to lie here than in the closet; there the daylight never penetrated, so that its air was always chillingly sour and
musty, and there was always a cold, raw smell of oil and food that
they stored in there during the winter. The great room smelt of
men and smoke; even at night a hint of cosiness seemed to be
given off by the hearth, where live embers were hidden beneath
the ashes. A piece had been broken off the cover of the smoke-
vent one night when it was blowing, and Olav had not yet had a
new one made. When the moon shone he could see a corner of
light on the parchment pane of the vent, and he could watch the
dawn. Olav liked that.

Now he moved back into the closet; Mærta and the children
were to have the south bed in the hearth-room.

Olav had expected Cecilia to scream and make a great to-do
when she was told she was to sleep with the strangers instead of
with Ragna, as she had been accustomed. But it turned out otherwise. He had come in to Hestviken late in the day, having taken

three days on the voyage from Tunsberg, as he had met with bad
weather and run for shelter. Bothild was more dead than alive
when Olav carried her up to the houses—she sat the whole evening on the stool where he had first put her down, feeling as if
she were still in the boat. Folk tramped in an out, carrying one
thing and another, and meanwhile Cecilia Olavsdatter hovered
about the strange little maid, and her big bright eyes were all
agaze under the tumble of flaxen curls.

No sooner had Mærta laid the poor exhausted little thing under
the bedclothes, and Olav said that now Cecilia must go and lie
down by her foster-sister, than she pulled off all her clothes in a
twinkling and jumped up into the bed. Soon after, Mærta came
with a pillow; she took hold of Bothild, who was already asleep,
to put it under her head. Instantly Cecilia threw her arm around
the strange child:

"You shall not touch her! This is *my* sister!"

It was a jest among folk in the countryside that now at last
Olav Audunnsson had got a heritage from his rich kinsmen in
Denmark: he had inherited a mother-in-law. They soon found a
name to call her by and dubbed her the Lady Mærta.

Olav got on well with the new mistress of his house. He was
spared further trouble with such matters as did not rightly come
under his control, and she seemed to be kind to Cecilia.

Galfrid Richardson owed Olav some money, and now he asked
him to accept in payment a handsome, well-trained falcon—Galfrid had bought her in the spring of an Icelander, but he himself
had little skill in hawking and wished to be rid of the bird. Olav
knew of old that it was difficult to mew these birds at Hestviken
so that they kept in good condition over the winter; nor had he
any horse now that would serve for hawking. Nevertheless he
could not control his desire to own this fine bird. He rode out
with her a few mornings, before the snow came. Most days he
got only black game, but once or twice it happened that he had
the luck to see the falcon hunt kites. When he came home,
warmed and cheered by the fine sight of the struggle in the air,
Eirik had the benefit of his father's good humour. When the boy
talked of catching young hawks in the spring and taming them
for hunting, Olav laughed a little—it was not so easy for an unpractised hand, but he had known something of it in his youth and

he promised to help Eirik as well as he could. It was the lad's
work to change the sand and keep the bird's cage clean. His
father taught him how to handle the falcon, to slip on the hood
and fasten the jesses on the legs. The man and the boy became
good friends over this bird.

Then the kites left the country, and the snow came. Olav had
set up a perch for the falcon within the closet and hung up some
old blankets for a curtain. At night, when the walls were rough
with rime and the coverlet over him was frosted with his breath,
he lay listening for any movement of the falcon. He was anxious
lest she might fare badly and be useless in the spring. Every day
he examined her shanks and castings, watched whether she fed.
He was still strangely happy in the possession of this treasure, so
proud and wild and yet so frail and easily spoilt. He loved to feel
the weight of her on his wrist; he carried her into the light and
looked at her fine markings, the greyish bands and pale brown
spots that showed in her white plumage. At night, when all smells
were deadened by the cold, he thought nevertheless he could
catch the rank scent of the bird of prey, and then he looked forward with longing to the spring, as he had not done since—he
knew not when.

The deer had left the district after the last two winters, when
wolves were rife.

As the new year wore on, Olav remarked several times that
there was dissension in the house because Eirik set himself against
Lady Mærta. Olav was very angry, for now he wished for peace
—he corrected the boy with harsh words, but this seemed not to
make him any better. Olav took it for granted that Eirik was to
blame—so courteous a woman as Mærta Birgersdatter could hardly
have expected the son of the Master of Hestviken to be so rude
and childish an oaf.

Until now Eirik had never paid much attention to his little
sister's doings. But on the other hand he had never been used to
tease her; if now and then he turned to Cecilia, it would be to
show her kindness and help her in her games. Now that too was
changed; he was constantly in the way of the two little maids,
provoking them and amusing himself by making Cecilia as savage
as a young hawk. The other little girl simply shrank into a corner,
dumb with misery.

One evening Olav came in from outside; he stayed in the ante-room awhile, getting out a chest of arrow-shafts and feathers—he intended to spend the evening making ready some arrows for fowling. He moved noiselessly, as had been his habit in all the years when he had had so much on his mind—he had come to hate noise.

He heard the children in the great room, Eirik and Cecilia—he was laughing and she was angry. Olav looked in. Cecilia was sitting before the hearth on the little three-legged stool that was her own. Tore, the old house-carl, had made it for her. She sat clutching the stool with both hands under the seat and her feet braced against the floor. Her mouth was slightly puckered and her eyes were round and staring; they were almost as blue in the whites as in the light pupils—she looked like a white, blue-eyed kitten crouching for a spring. Behind her stood Eirik. He put his foot under the stool and rocked it a little. Cecilia resisted with all her weight.

Olav came into the room for a lantern. Eirik left his sister, but no sooner was his father back in the anteroom than he began again. He dangled a red hair-ribbon—dropped it into the straw that covered the floor. Cecilia was to be quick and snatch it first, but Eirik was quicker still; roaring with laughter, he dropped astride on her stool.

His sister darted at him and seized his hair with both hands. She pulled it without making a sound; Eirik laughed and swung her this way and that, so that she fell into the hearth, put out her hands, and got hold of a log that still had some heat in it. Then she set up a howl and turned furiously on her brother, spitting at him so that it dribbled down on her little chin.

Olav came in, seized Eirik's hand roughly, and pulled it aside—the boy had got Cecilia by the hair when she tried to bite him. Her father lifted her up in his arms.

"So you pull little girls by the hair, I see."

"*She* pulled mine first."

"Nay, did she?"

Eirik turned red as blood. Cecilia remembered that she had burned her hand, and burst into a pitiable fit of crying. Olav comforted her, found some candle-grease, and smeared the burned place. Bothild came out of her corner and stood looking on.

Olav enjoyed being able to sit awhile with Cecilia in his arms and the other little girl at his knee. Eirik he pretended not to see. But when Lady Mærta and Ragna came in with the food and Mærta asked what was the matter, Olav answered: "Nothing."

Then Cecilia looked up from her father's breast. "Must not Eirik give me my horse now, Father?"

"Surely he shall give you your horse."

" 'Tis not her horse," said Eirik, red as fire again.

Then Mærta put in a word: "I gave the children a little wooden horse I found in Eirik's bed when we changed the straw for Yule. And now they have been quarreling over it for twelve weeks."

Olav smiled mockingly. "Is that wooden horse such a treasure, Eirik, that you will not let your sister have it?"

"Yes," replied Eirik defiantly. "Mother carved it for me when I was a child."

"Then you must let Eirik have it," said Olav. "Wooden horses I will give you, as many as you wish."

Later, after supper, Eirik came and asked if he might help his father with the arrows. Olav said he could. Once when Eirik could not get the feathers to sit straight, Olav paused in his work and looked at him.

"I cannot say you are very handy, Eirik."

This was not true; Eirik was deft and quick, it was only a fault in the wood of this shaft, which made the groove for the feathers too shallow.

One afternoon some days later father and son were down at the waterside salting auks. Olav flayed the birds; Eirik cut out the breasts, laid them in the kegs, and salted them. Now and then Olav dried his hands on the lappet of his coat; Eirik was tempted to do the same, but the salt stung his chapped and swollen hands so sharply that it was too painful even to touch the coarse woollen garment.

The south wind howled and beat against the wall of the shed; now and then a shower of rain poured down. Underneath the floor the waves splashed and gurgled, grinding the flakes of ice and breaking them against the rock. It was turning to foul weather. Eirik felt intensely happy at being allowed to stay here in the shed alone with his father and help him.

.   .   .

King Haakon came from the border round by the north to
Tunsberg just after Easter. It was then rumoured in the country
about the fiord that the peace with the Danish King was to hold
for two years more. Folk were glad of this, for the first tidings
that had come from the Kings' meeting there said that in the
spring King Haakon would ravage Denmark with a greater war
fleet than ever before.

But Olav felt no gladness when he began the work of spring.
It was wearisome to look forward to a whole summer at Hestviken. He did not ponder why the days should seem much more
dreary now, when at last he was rid of the lingering torment of a
wife who was always sick. In those days time had hung heavily on
him; now it went swiftly, though his mind was now filled with a
never ceasing impatience. It was as though he had sold his soul
and been cheated of the payment.

It was not in order to busy himself about this farm here on the
hill by the creek—to sail out with his fishing-boats, to dig the
ground, to visit the mill and go out to Saltviken—it was not for
this he had finally silenced the voice that had urged and called to
him so long. The secret spiritual conflict that for twelve years
had been his whole life was like a web, woven by himself and
One other. And he had acted like a woman who cuts down the
tapestry from her loom, rolls it up, and hides it in a locked chest.
To Olav it seemed as if he had thrown the key into the sea.

But he had not done so in order to have these calm days, wear-
ingly alike, in its place. He had forgotten his doings in England
and all the thoughts he had had there, better than he would have
believed it possible for a man to forget such things. Nevertheless
a dim memory flickered forth of that which had turned the scale:
the song of the retainers and the salt, sweet taste of blood it
brought back from his own brisk youth of outlawry, and he remembered the joy of grappling with foes of flesh and blood, foot-
pads who used the knife in the darkness of the woods. It was as
though these had been the bribes he was offered—no great matters,
but enough to turn the scale in the hour when he was tempted to
turn away from God for good and all, since it was so hard to return to the banner of his rightful Lord for a man who had become
a traitor and a runaway. Thirty pieces of silver are not so great a
sum as to have tempted Judas, had it not been for that bag of our

Lord's travelling-resources for which he would have had to account.

And at times the thought came over Olav this spring— He stood under the pale and boundless arch of the evening sky, still faintly yellow over the ridge on the western side of the fiord; the surface of the water beneath him loomed grey and restless, wrapped in an indefinite gloom where the darkness was gathering about the shores. Olav washed the rough dirt from him in the tub before the house door. Whatever he might turn his hand to, every day's work began and ended in his toiling up and down the familiar paths to the yard, creeping into his house, creeping to his rest within the closet. For an instant there came over him a temptation to do like Judas—he had such a hellish loathing of going in to the others.

Early in the winter, when the talk was of war, Olav had said that this year he would take Eirik with him on board. And so long as all men thought the fleet would sail, Eirik had been busy looking over all the things he was to take with him and exercising himself in the use of his weapons. But when the word came that peace was not to be broken, Eirik was yet busier, and now his talk was that if and if and if— It galled Olav every time he heard the lad's boasting.

Another thing that annoyed Olav was that Eirik was continually humming and singing. It had not mattered so much while Eirik was a child, he had had such a clear, sweet voice. But now that his voice was breaking he still sang as before; it did not sound well.

One noontide in the haymaking Olav sent Eirik home to the houses to fetch a rope. Time went on and on. A thunderstorm broke on the heights over Hudrheimsland; it was coming this way, the men worked hard to bring the dry hay under a rock shelter, and Olav grew angrier and angrier as he carried great armfuls of hay. He ran up to the farm.

In the yard stood Cecilia playing ball. She threw the ball against the wall of the storehouse and caught it in one hand; the other little free hand mimicked the action more feebly. Every time she threw the ball she tossed her fair head charmingly. Bothild sat on the ground looking on.

All at once Eirik leaped in between his sister and the wall and caught the ball. He ran backwards across the yard, throwing the ball into the air and catching it, Cecilia following and trying to get it back. Sometimes Eirik pretended to throw it to her. "Catch it, catch it—" and then he tricked her. Suddenly he threw it over the roof of the house.

Then he caught sight of his father. He picked up the ropes, which he had flung down on the rock, and handed them to Olav.

"Could you not find some that were rottener?"

"Nay, these are not rotten, Father," said Eirik confidently.

Olav put his foot in the hank, gave a tug, and threw away the broken ropes. Eirik was crossing over to the storehouse, when his father ordered him sharply: "Find your sister's ball and give it to her." He went himself to find a fresh rope.

In the storehouse all was in confusion; Olav hung everything in its place before he went out. He was making a loop in the new rope when he heard a disturbance in the dairy.

It was Mærta, who had given the little girls some curds and cream to taste; but Eirik forced himself in and wanted to taste the curds too. Mærta took hold of him and pushed him out.

Eirik shouted angrily: "You behave as if you were mistress here—'tis not *your* curds."

Mærta took no notice of him, but Cecilia made a grimace at her brother, finger in mouth.

Eirik was furious and shouted louder: "'Tis not yours, I say, nothing is yours here in *our* house—even if my father allows you food and lodging, you and the brat you have with you—"

Then Olav was at his side.

"That is no courteous speech, Eirik. You must beg pardon of your foster-mother for it."

Eirik was obstinate and defiant; he turned red.

Olav flared up wrathfully: "Beg Mærta's pardon—kiss the lady's hand and do as I bid."

A flash of lightning cleft the black darkness over the fiord. Olav counted under his breath as he waited for the thunderclap. The peal rolled away among the hills.

"Be quick now, do as I tell you, and then come out to the hay." Eirik did not move.

Olav let the leather thong run between his fingers; coldly and quietly he said: "'Tis an age since you felt my hand on you, Eirik. But do now as I tell you, else you shall taste this." He gave the rope a little shake.

Eirik bent down on one knee and rapidly kissed Mærta Birgers-datter's hand. But at that instant Olav felt he could not bear to see the lad's miserable face.

The father took the coil of rope and set off at a run for the fields. He did not even look round to see whether the boy fol-lowed him. Abundantly as Eirik had deserved the humiliation, Olav hated having to force the lad thus on his knees before a stranger; he hated Eirik for it.

4

YET father and son got on together in a way for another year and more.

Then came Advent in the following winter, and they were kill-ing meat for Yule.

Arnketil and Liv came out to Hestviken in the pitch-dark early morning; the man was to be butcher, his wife to help the women with puddings and the like.

It had snowed the week before, enough to whiten the fields, but with the new moon came mild weather, and that morning, as Olav came out into the yard, the fog was so thick that they could scarce find their way between the houses. Olav told the men they must rope the pig before they drove the toughness out of it—if it escaped them in this fog, it might not be easy to catch it again.

Olav stood on the doorstone, watching the torches lighting up the thick sea-mist; a moment later they only showed as faint red gleams in the downy grey darkness and then vanished. But soon after, he heard cries and roars and the squealing of the pig, and men came running over the smooth rocks of the yard. Something dashed past him in the dark, and Olav guessed it was the pig. He tried to jump in the way of it, but it was gone in the dense gloom, making eastward across the fields.

After it came the men with torches and brands through the mist, dark forms swathed in darkness. Olav ran on with them. Arnketil and Eirik stooped as they ran, lighting up the pig's tracks in the snow. Olav halted by the barn, and old Tore told him how it had happened. Eirik was to have held the pig, while Arnketil got on its back to ride it tender, and then he had let go.

One of the pigs that were not for slaughter had got loose at the same time. So this pig's flesh was to be effectually worked into softness before they stuck it. They could hear it through the fog.

Olav knew of old that Eirik was always squeamish on pig-killing days—but nobody *likes* them. And the lad was still as clumsy as ever when he had to lend a hand with a beast; it made things no better when he tried to conceal his shrinking with un-becoming flippancy and foolish jesting.

The house-carls came back. They did not think they could catch the pigs again until the fog lifted, and they cursed over the waste of time.

But an hour later Arnketil and Eirik returned with the pig—it had run itself into a drift of thawing snow. Olav went indoors again and lay down on the bench—it was the custom that the master of the house should keep away from pig-killing and only show himself in the yard when he brought out the ale-bowl for the refreshment of the butchers. He lay listening to the pig's shrieks—it was quite preposterous the time it took today before the life was out of it.

It was already daylight outside, stiff with grey fog, when Olav went across with Arnketil to the cook-house. On the snow out-side it lay the pig's carcass split in two.

Under the cook-house wall stood Eirik and little Aasta, the youngest of the serving-maids; they were washing themselves in the water-butt, laughing and splashing each other. Eirik was not aware of his father for the fog; he made a dash at the girl and tried to dry his hands on her clothes—his conduct was not very seemly. Aasta screamed, but laughed still more and made no great struggle to escape the lad's forwardness, and Eirik made free with his hands under her kirtle.

The next instant Olav had him by the neck and flung him aside. Eirik had a glimpse of his father's face, grey and wild with fury —then he got a blow of his fist on the jaw which made him reel, his father caught him again, shook him, and hurled him back-wards, so that he fell at full length in the snow.

"Be off, you foul trollop," said Olav to Aasta—she was standing there awkwardly. The girl slipped away. "Stand up!"—he gave Eirik a push with his foot.

Eirik rose to his feet and stood dazed before his father.

Olav said in a low voice, shaking with rage: "Do you think you can behave thus in your father's house—you and your bitch—in broad daylight, before folks' eyes—like a dog!"

Eirik turned red as fire. He too began to tremble with rage. " 'Tis not true—'twas only—jesting." His anger brought him to the verge of tears, and then he shouted: "May I not touch one of the maids here without you must needs think—that I shall deal with her as you did with Torhild?"

He raised his arms to fend off the blow—Olav threw him and was over him. He crushed the boy with his knees as he lay in the miry, blood-stained snow. He did not desist as long as he felt any sign of resistance in the body beneath him. Eirik lay limply, with his face half buried in the snow, as Olav stood up and left him.

Old Tore had stood watching Olav punishing his son. Now he knelt down in the dirty slush and tended the unconscious lad.

Later in the day they found the other pig that Eirik had allowed to escape in the early morning. It lay in the hollow behind the outhouses in a pool of slush, dead. Olav shrugged his shoulders when they came and reported the mischance. He clenched his teeth: he had *not* chastised Eirik too severely that morning.

No one saw any more of Eirik that day—nor was it noticed, so busy was the household. It was only old Tore who had seen Olav strike Eirik. The other house-folk remarked no doubt that there was discord once more between father and son, but that happened so often.

But at dusk, when Olav came in from outside, there was one standing in the anteroom; he followed the master into the empty hall and closed the door behind him. It was Eirik. A few logs were burning on the hearth—in the uncertain flicker Olav could see that the lad's face was bruised and swollen.

Olav seated himself on the bench. On the table lay a bannock and a tasty sausage, smoking hot. The man took a bite of the food, chewed and ate slowly—but Eirik stood erect and silent in the shadows.

"What will you?" asked his father at last, reluctantly.

"I wonder if you yourself believed what you said—" Eirik began, so calmly and naturally that his father wondered at him—and then felt a chill of remote misgiving: never had he heard the boy speak in this way. "If you think it so ill of me to trifle with the young maid—then you are not very reasonable, Father. But you are seldom reasonable or just with me."

Olav pushed away his food. He sat upright on the bench—a feeling of tension clutched at his heart. Then a cold clearness of vision came upon him, like acknowledging a defeat: Eirik was surely right.

The son paused for a moment. Then he spoke as before: "It is almost as though you had taken a hatred to me, Father."

But as the man on the bench still sat motionless, Eirik went on, more hotly, more like his usual self: "The way you treat us, one would almost think you had taken a hatred to your own children! You grant your son no honour and no authority—you keep me as a child—and I am in my sixteenth winter!" His voice had broken now, turning to a scream.

"I can see that *you* think so," said his father. And presently he added, with a touch of scorn: "Nevertheless you are very young, Eirik, to judge of your own worth."

Eirik turned and went out.

Eirik had already crept under the skins in his bed—so it appeared—when Olav came in that night to go to rest. The little girls were already asleep in the south bed, Mærta was still busy in the cook-house. But the next morning when the lady went to wake Eirik, she found nothing but a bundle underneath the coverlet.

Sticks and straw tumbled out when she took hold of the old cloak. Mærta was angry—she thought the boy had done this to make a fool of her. Olav stood by and saw it—for a moment he felt alarmed—absurdly, as he saw at once. He turned away in annoyance: what wretched child's tricks! The boy had not been in his bed that night, he wished to show he was offended; but such nonsense as this bundle! Then it struck the man: surely he had never gone to Aasta, to defy him? Ah, if that were so, he should have a beating he had never dreamed of.

He would ask no questions. But by the afternoon it was clear to the whole household that Eirik was not at the manor.

None of the boats was missing, and his horse stood in the stable. There was the same thick, wet fog again today—it was vain to search for the boy, nor could Olav spare any men to send out. But he wondered whither Eirik had betaken himself—to Rynjul or Skikkjustad or perhaps to that Jörund Rypa?

At night the wind got up from the south and it began to rain. In the course of the day the fields were all a mirror of ice, the air was filled with a roaring blast from sea and woods.

As yet Olav had not uttered a word to his house-folk about the matter. Lady Mærta tried to speak of it, but Olav cut her short.

Now and again anxiety dragged at him. The boy could not have taken it so that he—surely he had not fallen over somewhere in the night and the fog? Thoughts crowded upon him, which he strove to drive away. It was unlikely.

He found occasion to see to the boats—took courage and looked under the sheds and the quay, went round the shore of the bay— all the while saying to himself: "Eirik is surely at Rynjul"—he had always been Una's favourite.

On Sunday he met both the Rynjul folk and those of Skikk-justad at church. After mass he fell into talk with Jörund Rypa's kinsmen. He saw at once that they knew nothing of Eirik's flight.

He went over to the parsonage. Several people had been in there to speak with the priest, and mass had been late that day, for the roads were almost impassable after the bad weather. Sira Hallbjörn had not yet tasted bite nor sup—he was pale about the nose from his long fast.

Olav told him his son had run away.

"Ay, 'twas not too soon," said the priest.

His ancient housekeeper came limping in with the dish of porridge; the men moved forward and took their places at the table. The priest and the deacon said grace, Olav stood silently waiting at the door. With a mute gesture Sira Hallbjörn invited him to sit down with them and break his fast.

Olav thanked him, but said he must go home. But he asked the priest to come to the outer door with him—he had three words to say to him. Sira Hallbjörn went out reluctantly.

"You know nothing of Eirik, do you, Sira? You have heard no rumour of where he is gone?"

"I—?"

Olav went out, angry. His horse stood outside in the rain, hanging its head; the water poured off its mane, running in streams among the darkened strands. It fell in a sheet from the cloak he had laid over the saddle and the horse's quarters when he put it on.

On the way he looked in at Rundmyr and questioned Anki and

Liv closely, making no concealment. They denied all knowledge of the matter, and Olav saw that they spoke the truth for once.

In the evening he asked Aasta—swallowed his pride and questioned the young serving-maid: "You can surely tell me, Aasta, whither Eirik has made off—since you two were such good friends?"

The girl turned red and tears came into her eyes. She timidly shook her head.

"But he came and said farewell to you, did he not, before he took himself off?"

Aasta broke into sobs. "There was no tie of friendship between me and Eirik, Master Olav." Eirik had only jested a little with her once or twice; Eirik was good-natured, wanton, but kind. On seeing her master's little crooked smile she wept outright and swore most solemnly that she never forgot the teachings of her honest parents, her honour and good name were without stain or blemish.

"Ay, if you let the young lads handle you as I saw that morning, you will soon find yourself without either the one or the other," said Olav sternly. "Now go and cry outside."

Then there was nothing left but to peer into his own despair. All day long Olav cudgelled his brains to find some credible explanation—what *could* Eirik have done? He had gone away in his great hooded cloak, his sword and spear he had taken with him. A little gold pin in the band of his shirt and a great brooch in the bosom of his jerkin, these and his finger-ring with a red agate he always wore; had he made for the town he might have provided himself with a lodging by selling one of these trinkets. He might have gone to Claus Wiephart or to the armourer's—or to one of the monasteries. Or, if he had been able to get carried across the fiord, to Tunsberg—likely enough the lad might have taken it into his head to seek his fortune where so many lords were passing to and fro. Between whiles Olav tried to fan into flame his first indignation at Eirik's flight.

But at night he lay awake—and then his thoughts would only dwell on what might have *happened* to Eirik. He might have lost his way in the fog that night, have fallen over the cliff somewhere. For the son of Hestviken manor was well enough known to many —it was incredible that he could disappear as if he had sunk into the ground or— Carried off, spirited away, spellbound by the

powers of evil—now Olav called to mind all the stories Eirik had
told as a child, about his intercourse with the folk of that world.
There might have been some truth in it after all, even if he made
up a deal of it. Or if he had been out on the fiord the second day
after he ran from home—many boats' crews had not been heard of
since that day. Nor were the roads inland so safe but that it might
be dangerous for a young lad, well dressed and armed, with
jewels on him, to travel alone. Northward, in the forests about
Gerdarud, there were reports of robbers.—Or, or— For all that,
Olav knew not a little of Eirik's fickle nature; he turned to melancholy as suddenly as to sport and dalliance. But he could not
surely have taken his correction so much to heart as to throw
himself into the fiord—

"Ingunn, Ingunn, Ingunn mine—help me, where is the boy?

"Jesus, Mary—where *is* Eirik?"

Olav rose on his knees in the bed with his head in his clasped
hands. He leaned his forehead against the foot of the bed. "Not
for myself do I pray for mercy. Holy Mary, I taught the boy
these prayers myself when he was a child—be mindful of that
now!"

But that was an age ago—he did not know whether Eirik remembered anything of them now. It was an age since he had
thought of teaching the children anything of that sort. Cecilia
never a word—that he had left to Mærta. It had come to this, that
he *could* not and *dared* not. But, God, God! *they* must not suffer
for it. He prayed God to take Eirik under His protection, he
prayed God's Mother for his son, he prayed Saint Olav and Saint
Eirik, as he had never been wont to pray.

Sometimes it made him a little calmer. For himself he cared not
now, but for the young lad, Ingunn's son—

He never thought of Cecilia thus—that she was Ingunn's daughter as much as his.

He could not prevent the servants from talking of Eirik's flight.
He himself said hardly anything, but he listened stiffly and intently—whether the others might have heard some news.

The southerly weather held. A draught of wind whistled
through the church on Christmas Eve, levelling the flames of the
candles in the lustrous choir whenever the storm came down with
full force—the vault above was darkened, and then the heavy

doors shook and the window-shutters rattled—as if the spirits of
the tempest flung themselves with all their might against every barrier in their fury to thwart the sacred ceremony that was pro-
ceeding in the choir. There was a howling and piping about the
corners of the building, a vast droning in the ash trees on the
ancient burial mounds beyond the churchyard fence. Through
the roaring dissonance of the storm the singing of the mass
sounded strangely still and strong—like the smooth streak of a
current in the midst of a rough sea.

The moment the silver bells chimed and the congregation knelt,
while *Sanctus, sanctus, sanctus* resounded from the choir, it fell
still. The candle-flames recovered themselves and gleamed erect;
the painted images on the whitened walls of the chancel seemed
to spring forth, shining in their blue and yellow and rust-red
colours. Sira Hallbjörn's tall form, clad in pure white linen with
the golden chasuble, appeared like that of an angel, descended
straight from the heavenly visions of Saint John—a bearer of good
tidings and a herald of God's judgment.

Then came a fresh gust of wind, crashing and roaring against
the walls; the choir was plunged in gloom as the priest bent over
the paten, whispering. The tolling of the bell in the ridge-turret
over the people's heads was drowned in the raging of the storm.

When the congregation rose to its feet after the *Agnus Dei*,
Olav Audunnsson remained sunk on his knees. Baard Paalsson
from Skikkjustad, who stood by his side, bent down, trying to
look into his face in the darkness.

"Are you sick, Olav?"

Olav shook his head and stood up.

After mass Olav and Baard struggled side by side across the
green to the tithe barn. The great lantern under the roof swayed
hither and thither. Everywhere in the shadows they descried the
forms of folk who lay in the straw to take a short rest before the
Mass of the Shepherds.

Olav unhooked his cloak and shook the rain from it.

"Are you sick?" asked Baard again. "You are pale as a ghost."

"No," said Olav. He went in and lay down in the straw, where
some men moved closer to make room for the two.

"Nay, but I thought it," said Baard, "since you were not with
Eirik. I saw how pale you turned tonight, and I thought maybe

you had been unwell. Gunnar and Arne spoke of it; they thought
it strange that you let your son travel thus alone, with only a
token—"

"What mean you?" Olav managed to say.

Baard made no answer—he could not follow.

"Gunnar and Arne—is it Arne of Haugsvik you speak of?" As
Baard said nothing, Olav resumed, as unconcernedly as he could:
" 'Twas not with my consent that Eirik left home—nor *against*
my will either. He deemed he was old enough to shift for himself
now—so I thought, let him try it. Then he took the road for
Oslo," Olav ventured at a hazard. "He came through safe and
well?" he asked when he received no answer.

Yes, he came through safe and well, replied Baard sleepily—it
was the day of the storm. And he had been in good heart, said
Arne, when the lad parted from them. But out at Haugsvik, when
he came and asked for a place in their boat, he had told them there
was an agreement between Olav and one of the great lords in the
town that Eirik should enter his service in order to learn the trade
of war and courtly ways. Nay, who his new lord was to be, Eirik
had refused to say—that was his way, always such an air of
secrecy.

Olav lay with his hands clasped under his cloak. "God, my God,
I thank Thee—Mary, most clement, most kind, what shall I do to
show my gratitude?" Memories of burned out thoughts stirred
like ashes driven off by a puff of wind. Nay, that was all over—
but he would give something to her poor, a cow to Inga, who
had the leper son.

But as he rode homeward after the morning mass, in pouring
rain—the wind had dropped now—his anger revived. Such conduct he had never heard of indeed—and there had been the usual
bragging and romancing out at Haugsvik, he could guess.—A
token, it occurred to Olav; what could that token be?—surely he
had never taken something, his seal or seal-ring, for instance—run
away from home as a thief?

He sat leaning over the table, silent and gloomy, scarcely noticing his house-carls, who fell on the steaming dish of meat. Now
and then he recollected himself sufficiently to raise the ale-bowl,
drink to them, and let it go round.

Afterwards he went in and turned over his store of treasures. But nothing was missing.

His wrath came and went in waves, died down and gave place to uneasiness. Eirik had made his way to Oslo—more than that he did not know as yet—and there was no saying what he might fall into there. There was no help for it, he would have to go and find out about his son, ill as it suited him to leave home at this time.

At last, on Twelfth Day, Olav met with a farmer up the parish who had spoken with Eirik in the town. He had been in to Nonneseter at Yule—the convent owned a share in the farm he occupied—and there he had come upon Eirik in the guests' refectory. He sat waiting while his master, Sir Ragnvald Torvaldsson, had speech with the Abbess.

The day after, Olav sailed in to Oslo. Inside the Sigvalda Rocks the fiord was frozen over. A great number of boats had been left at the edge of the ice, and there was not a horse to borrow at any of the farms about. So Olav let old Tore stay with their boat while he walked alone across the ice to the town.

He found Tomas Tabor and sent him out to the old royal castle at the river-mouth—Sir Ragnvald had custody of the place. But Eirik did not come to his father's inn the first day; the evening of the second day was wearing on and still Olav sat there waiting.

The travellers, as many as were at home, lay under the skins in their sleeping-places—it was cold. The hostess sat dozing by the hearth, huge in her sheepskin wraps; she was only waiting till it was time to rake over the fire and bar the door. Olav sat on his bed, with his hands hanging over his knees; his legs were like ice from the cold of the floor, and he was dull with waiting.

The woman got up to tend the two lanterns that hung at each end of the long hall of the inn. "Will you not go to bed, master?"

Then there was a knock at the door. It was Eirik.

Olav went a few steps to meet him and gave him his hand in greeting. They happened to come together just under the lantern. In a way the father must have noticed before now that Eirik had grown taller than himself and that shadows of dark down had begun to appear about his mouth, but never before had he been wholly aware of the change—Eirik was grown up. He was well dressed—wearing a plain steel cap, and under it a dark blue woollen hood that framed the narrow, swarthy face, making it seem yet narrower. His long cloak was brown and of good stuff; under it he was clad in a tight leather jerkin and he wore a sword at his belt, in token that he was now one of his lord's men-at-arms. Long iron spurs jingled as he walked.

"You will not get me back with you to Hestviken, Father," he said as soon as Olav let go his hand.

"I had not thought to do so either," replied Olav. "If you have taken service with a lord, you must know that I would not have you run from it before your time." To the hostess, who came up and asked whether she should bring drink for him and his guest, he replied yes, the best German beer.

"Nay," said Olav as they seated themselves on his bed; "I would have liked it better if you had spoken to me before you made off —but it is useless to talk of that now."

Eirik blushed slightly and asked with embarrassment: "You have business that brings you here, then?"

"My business is to give you what you need—you shall be provided as befits *my* son when you go out into the world." Olav pulled out of the bed a bag of clothes, a good battle-axe, and the blade of a thrusting-spear. Then he handed his son a purse: "Here are four marks of silver in good, old money. It is my will that you get yourself a horse as soon as you can—that you may be held of more account. It ill befits a man-at-arms to ride his master's horses like a serving-man of villein birth. More than that you shall not have of me, Eirik, so long as you stay abroad. You have chosen to be master of your own conduct—so be it then, and let it be such that you win honour thereby."

Eirik rose and thanked his father with a kiss of the hand. It gave him a warm thrill that his father spoke to him as a grown man; it was not often his father had addressed so long a speech to him. And yet there was a shade of disappointment—that this meeting did not turn out as he had pictured it to himself ever since Tomas Tabor brought him Olav's message: he had expected his father to be greatly angered, to threaten and command him to return; and then he would have made answer— But it seemed his father had taken his flight very calmly and had no thought at all of bringing him home again.

"Thanks, I am not hungry—" but, for all that, Eirik helped himself from his father's box of victuals and took a good draught as often as Olav offered him the tankard. At heart he very soon felt quite proud—it was an uncommon and almost a solemn occasion to be sitting here eating and drinking with his father at an inn and asking for the news from home—two grown-up men together.

"But how did you find out that I was here in Oslo, with Sir Ragnvald?"

Olav smiled his little pinched smile. "Oh—I find out most of what I *will* know, Eirik. When you have come to my age, perhaps you will have got so much wisdom as not to let men see all that you know."

Eirik turned red as flame—memories of all kinds of secret misdeeds, great and small, in the whole of his young life hovered through his mind and gave him a moment's insecurity. His father noticed it and smiled as before. But he went on talking calmly, gave his son good advice as to how he should conduct himself, now he was in a knight's service, spoke a little of his own youth.

The last of the guests came into the inn. The curfew rang from the church towers, and Eirik said he must go.

"I think to go home again tomorrow about midday—maybe I shall not see you again before that?" asked his father.

Eirik did not think he could come.

"Nay, nay." Olav went to the door with him. "Keep yourself well and in honour, Eirik. May God Himself and His blessed Mother be your protection." He kissed the young man on both cheeks and gave a little nod, as Eirik seemed to pause at the door —the lad had such a strange feeling at this solemn farewell, with the kisses of his father's hard, thin lips on his face.

Olav had business with Claus Wiephart next day, and the German accompanied him down across the common. Due south the sun's disk shone through the light frost-fog, gilding the surface of the ice. "Fine weather, Olav."

They turned into a narrow street between warehouses, which led to a strip of beach among the quays; from there the ice could be reached. From the common behind them came the noise of a band of horsemen, clanking of arms and harness. Olav and Claus had to cling to the walls as the troop thundered into the lane and rode past. At its head rode a short, thickset knight—Olav knew Sir Ragnvald Torvaldsson by sight. His men followed, one by one, for the lane was narrow. One of the horses was near being squeezed between two others, there was some confusion in the rank, and one or two horses reared. Olav saw Eirik among the rest; he sat erect and easy in the saddle—but he did not see his father, he had enough to do to manage his horse, which seemed very fresh. He laughed and called to the man ahead of him in the crowd of steaming animals.

"But—was not that your son?" asked Claus Wiephart.

"It was."

"Ay, time flies. Ere one is aware of it, one is an old man. How old are you now, Master Olav?"

"Forty winters."

"Then you are younger than you look, after all. Is it not four winters since Ingunn died? You are yet too young to let your beard grow—and to sleep wifeless on a winter's night."

"You will see, I will shave off my beard yet, Claus—and a wife I will get me too, if so be that such is my lot." Olav gave a little laugh.

Claus bade him farewell and went back to his warehouse. Olav walked out on the ice, where a path was marked on the gleaming, coppery surface. He saw the band of horsemen far ahead—they were making across the creek toward Akersnes, where the massive walls of King Haakon's new castle rose in the fine frosty mist.

Again he felt the thought of Eirik like a cord that drew his heart together—but now it was like envy, of the other's youth.

5

THE NEXT three years passed much more rapidly—time whirled away like smoke with Olav.

He had settled down. This was a life that Olav Audunsson had never before experienced. In his heart he felt its quietude as emptiness or as a loss. But if he had been asked what he *thought* of his life now, he must have answered that he was well content.

His affairs prospered in these years, and he bought some shares in farms in the neighbouring parishes—Olav never changed in this respect, that he put more faith in the land than in the sea. And he had better luck with his farming than ever before. When he first came to Hestviken, full of zest and courage, he lacked experience—and since then he had always been tied.

Nevertheless it must be said that there had always been prosperity at Hestviken. But now, under Mærta Birgersdatter's control, it was more noticeable. There was no longer any trouble with the serving-folk. The old ones stayed on—the foreman, old Tore, went about his work, quiet and cool-headed; Svein, the herdsman, Jon and Bodvar, the house-carls, remained unmarried all three; Ragna lived in Torhild's house with her children and was dairywoman, Aasta had put aside all wantonness and still enjoyed her honour and good name. Besides these there was a young lad and a half-grown maid. They went somewhat short of merriment and jollity at the manor, but these folk lived well; the mistress was just and fairly open-handed. Pauper couples who were maintained in the homesteads of the parish were glad when their turn came to Hestviken.

The master of the house said little, and there was no denying he depressed the folk around him; but this was only until they got to know him, his servants said—one grew accustomed to him. Olav was not badly liked by his household. He left Lady Mærta a free hand and was glad to take her advice in those matters which came under himself. The footing between them was almost as if she had been his mother—a very masterful mother, and he a compliant son.

Even at the hovel, Rundmyr, things were quiet. Mærta Birgersdatter had reduced Arnketil and Liv to order. He had become rather hunchbacked, wrinkled, and dried up; she was ever yeasty and exuberant—a child appeared in the cot every year toward spring. Some trifles were always missed—food, wool, or tow—when Liv had been about at Hestviken; but it had become a sort of right that she might take without asking leave, so long as she kept within bounds. Elsewhere she never pilfered now, except from Una at Rynjul. Arnketil had given up stealing since Mærta surprised him one evening; he was in one of the storehouses struggling to strike a light. "No need for a light here, Anki—I think you know the way."

The two little maids were growing; their beauty was noised abroad. They were now old enough to be present at feasts and

gatherings—which were but few, for Olav held intercourse with
none but the circle of nearest neighbours, who visited each other
year after year. But the people of the parish saw the Hestvik maids
at church. Olav Audunsson rode up first, and Bothild Asgersdatter
sat behind on his horse with her arms round his waist—for Cecilia
rode with old Tore; that was his right, and if they took *that* from
him, he would not stay at the manor another day, he threatened
jokingly. The two children were always richly and handsomely
dressed when they came to mass—Lady Mærta gave them kirtles
of dyed cloth, with gaily embroidered edges, and she bound their
flowing hair with silken ribbons worked with gold.

In everyday life Olav did not see much of his daughters. He
had built a women's house by the side of the old hearth-room
house—Mærta thought that the women ought to have a house of
their own, where they could work with their looms, their sewing,
and the like: Cecilia and Bothild must now learn to use their hands.

The new house was a fine one: Bodvar was a skilful wood-
carver, and he decorated it with much handsome ornament. It was
not every month that Olav set foot inside the door of it.

But although he saw so little of the children, a pale, wintry
sunshine fell upon his spirit from the two fair young lives that
were growing up so near to his own frozen life.

It looked as if Lady Mærta had succeeded in taming Cecilia's
hot temper—or she had grown out of it as she got more sense.
Headstrong she was still, but she had acquired a calmer, rather
sulky way. The house-folk laughed when the child gave a short,
sharp answer—she was so like her father, they said, but they
thought it became her well. She was so fair to look upon that,
whatever she said or did, folk thought it suited her.

She liked Lady Mærta, that was easily seen, though Cecilia gave
little sign of it in words or loving behaviour. In the same way she
showed her affection for old Tore, for Ragna and her children—
a tacit, steady loyalty through thick and thin. Only toward her
foster-sister, Bothild, did she show a different, gentler and softer
way; so far as could be judged by the manner of this calm, reticent little girl, she loved Bothild better than anyone in the world.
But all at Hestviken took pains to be gentle and kind to Bothild—
she still seemed a little forlorn; there was something about her
that seemed to ask them to deal tenderly and cautiously with her.
Even Olav showed his fondness for his foster-daughter more than

his affection for his own daughter. If some chance prompting led him to fondle the children, it was Bothild whose hair he stroked or whose cheek he patted—as though it came easier with her, as she brightened up with joy at the slightest caress. If the children came down to the waterside to meet him or accompanied him out into the fields, it was Bothild he took by the hand and led, for he saw she liked it. She looked up at him at every word they exchanged, and her blue eyes were so demure beneath her thick auburn hair. Cecilia's bright, pale eyes looked the world straight in the face, wide awake; there was an air about her whole compact little figure which said she could quite well walk alone. She was his own child, Olav bore his love for his daughter within him as a safely locked treasure that he had no need to look to. His kindness for his foster-daughter he could much more easily pay out in small coin, as occasion arose.

There was not a thing about Cecilia Olavsdatter to recall her mother. The last shadow of a memory of Ingunn Steinfinnsdatter's vain and hapless life seemed to have vanished from her home. Sira Hallbjörn remarked this one day when he had come to ask for a passage in Olav's boat:

"I wonder if there be any in the countryside who remembers your wife but you."

He caught sight of Olav's face as soon as he had said it. Instinctively he turned his own away, as when he was hearing a confession.

"But you remember her," said Olav after a pause, almost inaudibly.

"You know, 'tis not many days since I last said a mass for her—it came into my mind just now—I remember all the years I saw her lying in the bed there— I had thought to see you, though, at the mass for the dead," said the priest.

"I had forgot it was that day—until the evening. Oh no," Olav added after a moment; "there cannot be many who remember her now."

One evening early in the spring some men had come into the house at Hestviken—they were folk from within the parish who had their landing-place on Olav's shore. They had come by water from a feast higher up the fiord, and the drink was still in them.

Olav and old Tore were sitting together, mending some gear; the other men had not yet come in, and the women were in the outhouses. Only the little girls were playing on the bench. Then Olav sent Tore to fetch ale for the guests, and for a while the talk went peaceably, about the wedding and such matters.

In the course of it one of the men said to Olav: "That Torhild you had a child by when she was here, she was at the feast too. She bade us bring greetings to Hestviken."

Olav thanked them and asked how things were with her.

Well, said the men; she enjoyed great respect in the neighbourhood and she was prospering. She had done so well with Auken that folk now called the place Torhildrud.

Old Tore asked eagerly for more news of Torhild Björnsdatter; he had always liked her so well. Then they talked for a time of her way of keeping house.

Olav listened, but took no part in the conversation, except to ask: "Had she the boy with her at the feast?"

The men said yes, he was a handsome boy, fair and strong—"no need to ask who is his father."

But as the men stirred up the remnant of drink that was in them, they grew first fuddled, and soon after two of them began to quarrel and threaten each other. At last Olav had to ask them to keep the peace or go out.

At that moment the two men came to grips. The little girls jumped onto Olav's clothes-chest and stood there. Then one of the men caught sight of them, turned that way, and tried to make game of them.

Olav got up, upsetting all he had on his lap onto the floor—he was going to part the two who were fighting. At the same moment the third man caught hold of the girls. Olav saw Bothild shrink away, with a little helpless whine of terror. Something flashed in Cecilia's hand—the child had drawn her little knife and struck at the man. Olav took him by the shoulders, put his knee to the small of his back, and forced him to the floor. Tore now came to his master's aid and opened the door. Olav took the stranger by the shoulders and middle and heaved him out through the anteroom into the yard. Then he ran back to deal with the others.

With many a crash against walls and doorposts, with roars and oaths, but no very hard struggle, Olaf and Tore got the room cleared of the strangers and the door bolted. They raged and bellowed out in the yard, kicked at the outer door and banged on the walls. Olav and Tore listened, laughing and panting as they put their clothes straight; they too had got some knocks, either from the drunken men's fists and heels or from striking against the walls of the dark anteroom.

Smiling, Olav turned to the children. Cecilia's round, milk-white face was still contorted with fury; there was a pale-green flash in her eyes. But Bothild was clinging to the wall, trembling so that her teeth chattered. When Olav touched her, she burst into a fit of weeping so terrible that her foster-father was quite alarmed. He drew her toward him, had to sit down and hold her in his arms while he tried to comfort her like a little child—though she was no longer a little girl, he felt, she was growing up now, thin and long of limb—twelve winters she must be. He stroked her head with its long plaits, telling her not to be afraid—though he knew of old it was of little use; she was always taken thus when folk came to blows and she was by, even though no one thought of doing anything to her. Whenever the bawling and battering outside grew louder, a twitching went through the girl's delicate frame.

Then Olav gently pushed her away, got up, and went out. At the same moment the house-carls entered the yard, and the strangers took flight.

Later, as they sat at table, and Cecilia was about to cut herself a slice of cheese, one of the house-carls cried with a laugh: " Your knife is bloody, Cecilia!"

Bothild set up a screech, but now Olav and the men could not help laughing at her timidity. They were enlivened by the little tussle earlier in the evening, and now they sat at their ease over the table with good ale and food and a brisk fire on the hearth.

Cecilia spat on her knife and wiped it on the inside of her kirtle, then she cut herself a good piece of cheese and laid it between two slices of bread—not a word did she utter.

Olav laughed.

"May I see that knife of yours—'twas a feeble defence that, my daughter!"

"Then give me a better knife, Father!" said the maid.

"That I will," replied her father, gaily as before.

After supper Olav fetched in the little iron-bound coffer in

which he kept his treasures. The girls hung over his shoulders as
he searched in it—not many times had the children been allowed
to see what their father kept therein. They uttered a cry and asked
a question as each thing was brought to light, and Olav, who was
in a good humour this evening, let them handle the jewels and try
them on. At the bottom lay four handsome daggers—Olav never
wore them.

Cecilia snatched the longest. "Will you give me this one,
Father?" She drew it out of its sheath.

It was a foreign weapon with a three-cornered blade, the handle
and sheath finely ornamented with gilt rings. Olav took it from
her, looked at it a moment.

"That is no woman's knife, Cecilia—'tis only fit to strike down
a foe. This you will find more useful—" he handed her a big Norwegian knife with a broad, strong blade and a handle of carved
walrus tusk.

"I would rather have the other," said the maid.

Olav considered a moment. " 'Tis not often you ask anything of
me—take it then." He took up her thick flaxen plait—it lay in coils,
so curly was Cecilia's hair. "You should not have been the *daughter* of this house, Cecilia, that is sure."

Olav heard tidings of Eirik once in a while. And as he grew accustomed to the boy's absence, the thought sometimes came to
him: perhaps Eirik would never come home. And it might happen
that he thought that were best. He must surely receive something
in return for having sold his soul. If the fraud were wiped out, so
that his race and his heritage were not falsified—then it seemed to
him it would be somewhat easier to face death and judgment. His
own life he had thrown away—by his own fault; he thought of it
with a strange, clear composure—it almost gave him a kind of
chilly joy to recognize that the injustice was his, God was just.
He had never been able to understand how any man could find
consolation in blaming or cursing God. And he himself was only
one man; his fate could be no such great matter. He felt it a good
thing to know that the world was safe in the hands of the gentle
Christ, however many men might rise in revolt.

Cecilia's happiness—that he believed in firmly.

The same year, about midsummer, Baard of Skikkjustad and
Signe Arnesdatter married off their eldest daughter. The bride-

groom lived in the neighbouring parish, and Olav Audunsson was one of those who brought the bride home to his house, for he was her godfather.

A good godfather he had not been; he had paid little heed to the maiden—her name was Helga. She was of plain and modest appearance and had little to say for herself, by all accounts; but on her wedding-day she was fair to look upon.

At first Baard had refused to hear of this marriage; he had had many matters in dispute with the bridegroom—who was much older than Helga. But at the mid-Lent Thing this year an atonement had been made between the men and so Baard betrothed his daughter to Hoskold Jonsson.

Olav was strangely moved at the sight of the young bride—Helga Baardsdatter was so changed that she seemed to have taken on a new semblance. Others of the wedding guests had felt the same, he found—they spoke of it as they sat together on the evening of the third day of the feast in a little house apart, where quarters had been assigned to the older and more esteemed guests who attended the wedding. Olav had been placed high up, next after Torgrim of Rynjul, the husband of the bride's aunt; facing him sat Sira Hallbjörn in the highest seat.

From Hoskold and Helga the talk shifted to other women who had been notably fair and merry brides—or good and staunch housewives. The old men always thought that none of those now living could bear to be set beside the women they remembered in their youth.

Sira Hallbjörn leaned over the table, drawing lines with the spilt ale. He had been out of humour all through the wedding, tired and taciturn. This seemed to weary him.

"Do you mean to sit here all night prating of these dead women? While they lived, their husbands were as sick of them as are most men, I'll warrant. Methinks that fair companion of Olav Audunsson's is better worth possessing than all the rest together." He laughed weakly, being somewhat gone in drink. "Tell me, friend Olav, will you sell me that fair mistress of yours?"

Olav straightened himself abruptly, red and angry—he could not guess what the priest was aiming at. Torgrim of Rynjul did not see it either; he asked:

"What mean you, Sira?"

Sira Hallbjörn laughed as before, stretched behind Torgrim's back, and passed his hand over the blade of Olav's axe, which hung behind his seat. "She it is I mean—" he let his hand fall on Olav's shoulder.

Olav shook it off with a laugh of displeasure. "No, priest— lately you would have my falcon—and this axe is not—"

The axe Kinfetch rang—everyone present heard it. Its deep notes sang out through the room and slowly died away.

Sira Halbjörn leaped up and seized the axe. "Is she one of those that sing, your axe, Olav?" he asked excitedly.

"So 'tis said. But I thought she had lost her voice long ago— from old age." He took the axe from the priest and hung it back on the wall.

The men fell into a discussion, whether the axe had sung of itself or whether it was owing to Sira Hallbjörn's touching it.

Olav and the priest had looked each other in the eyes an instant —then they both laughed, alike uncheerful. It was as though they had discovered a bond between them—that the heart of neither was in this merriment.

Olav took his leave of the bridal gathering the same evening, but told his men they might stay till the next day and escort Mærta Birgersdatter and the children home.

The sky was covered high up by a thin veil of cloud. Under the colourless vault of the summer night the farms loomed grey with uncut meadows and strips of pale-green corn, as Olav rode along the path that ran through the belt of copse skirting the home fields. The world was asleep but for the harsh note of the corn-crake somewhere in the meadow.

He reached the hamlet by the church, and the horse moved more freely, eager for home. The church stood on a little height with its stone walls shining faintly and its shingle roof rising above the little window-slits. Olav turned his horse into the track that led to the church green. The stillness of night seemed to press upon him like a living thing, as the sound of the horse's hoofs was deadened in the rough grass.

By the churchyard wall lay some ancient burial mounds; the largest came right up to the fence, so that the old ash trees that surmounted it cast their shade beyond it. Olav dismounted and tied his horse to a rail near the gate of the churchyard. He must have no steel on him, he remembered—he took off his belt and laid it on the ground together with his axe. Then he went forward to the biggest of the mounds.

The very sound of dry twigs breaking under his footsteps—there was a thick carpet of them under the ash trees—gave him a chill feeling that raised the hair on his head. He walked over the mound, down to the churchyard wall, and mounted it. Within, the gravestones lay sunken in the summer growth of grass, which reached to the wall of the church. Olav gazed till black specks seemed to float before his eyes, and his heart beat so that he had a taste of blood in his mouth. But the feeling of dizziness was only as though the world swam around him; within himself there was calm, an undisturbed core. Nevertheless he involuntarily closed his eyes at the sound of his own voice, as he called clearly and firmly:

"Ingunn Steinfinnsdatter—arise!"

His horse out on the green gave a start, he could hear. He dared not turn and look that way; his eyes were fixed on the church wall, where he descried the gravestone close by the women's door. Cold and stiff in the cheeks with pallor, he called again:

"Ingunn Steinfinnsdatter—arise!
"Ingunn Steinfinnsdatter—arise!"

Again he had closed his eyes, but he *saw* it—the grey stone slowly lifting, the white figure of the dead rising up and shaking the mould from her grave-clothes.

He bent his head back, drew breath, and opened his eyes. There was nothing to be seen but the grey, mild night. Olav stared—as though this was more incredible than aught else. But the churchyard lay there asleep, with the sunken stones half-hidden by the long grass, right up to the grey wall of the church.

At last he turned, walked back across the mound, down to his horse. As he untied the reins he saw that the dun noticed something; he stood with his head raised, nostrils distended, laid back his ears, and started twice as Olav lay his hand on him—but Olav could see nothing. Then he got into the saddle and gave the horse his head—the swift pace did him good; the pressure of the air and the thud of hoofs overcame the sinister silence.

It was morning when he reached Hestviken; the clouds were faintly tinged with pink. When Olav had stabled his horse he went out on the rock to look at the weather—from habit. A little breeze before sunrise darkened the water of the fiord.

The living-room was empty and deserted. Olav went into the
closet, flung himself on the bed without undressing. But as soon
as he had closed his eyes, he started up, wide awake. He stared at
the grey opening into the larger room—but there was no one.

Thoughts rose in him like bitter waters. She had once *promised*
—if the dead may visit the living.

But now she was infinitely farther from him than before—the
first year, nay, the first summer after her death he had felt how
near she was yet, in the darkness that concealed them from each
other. Now they had come so far asunder that she no longer heard
him when he called.

As he lay, the solitude about him turned little by little to a kind
of vision. He was up on a bare and rocky mountain-top, where
some heather grew and the rocks were grey with lichen. Beneath
him on every side lay forest, grey with rime, and in the hollows
were pale bogs with frozen water-holes, but far away the grey,
closed sky was merged in low, dark-blue ridges. He tried to send
a cry out yonder, but knew it was useless. The vision faded slowly
into a dreamless gloom of sleep, and he did not wake till Ragna
came in at breakfast-time; she had wondered greatly, she said,
when she heard from Svein that his horse stood in the stable, but
not the others'.

6

IT chanced several times that autumn that Olav saw smoke on the
high ground above Hudrheimsland. He paused in his work to
watch it. It must be there that Torhildrud lay, as near as he could
guess.

There came some gleaming blue sunny days, when the very roar
of the waves against the rocks seemed permeated with light and
wind. Yellow leaves flew brightly in the air, and space itself was
widened, from the dark-blue, foam-flecked surface of the fiord
up to the bright, wind-swept vault, where little shreds of white
cloud raced along, infinitely high. And one day about nones Olav
went down, took one of the smallest boats, and sailed across alone.

Today it was like a sport to lie sailing over the flowing translu-
cent waves. The spray that wetted him through was gleaming

white. The sky was so high up that he felt lost in this little boat among the waves, and every time the boat rose on the crest, he saw that the land on the other side had come nearer, plainer to the sight. He was almost in the mood of his boyhood, when he had run away from Frettastein to play in the woods.

On coming ashore he walked rapidly up the path to the hills. The wooded slopes here were already thinned; yellow leaves whirled and drifted, flying past him like showers of glittering light, dancing over the path. The rushing wind filled Olav with well-being.

Now his only wonder was that he had not thought of this years ago: he ought to have come over to see her, find out how she and the boy were doing. Not but what he could be sure she would hold her own, capable woman that she was. But he ought to have offered to help her, if she would accept his help—seeing that he was the father of her son.

He himself did not understand why it had once seemed so impossible to meet Torhild—as though their meeting could only breed new difficulties. For they were no longer young, either of them—but he had never thought of that before.

He came to the gate at the edge of the wood, followed the path between the cairns. There was much more plough-land now —stubble fields. She seemed to have harvested all her crops.

Olav looked forward, but without excitement, to seeing her again, and Björn.

A dog began to bark within the house. The door opened—the dog came rushing toward him, yelping. Behind it Torhild stooped in the doorway, looking out.

He could not interpret the expression of her face, but it was somehow quite different from what he had expected. She accepted his hand rather half-heartedly.

"Are *you* abroad—over here?"

"Ay—think you that so strange?"

"Oh, nay. There may well be reason in it too," said Torhild quietly.

She invited the man in, bade him be seated, offered a bowl of milk—"ale I have none." Then she knelt down by the hearth, blew life into the embers, and made up a fire. "You must be wet and cold—will you not sit closer?"

Olav thanked her and seated himself on the stool she had pulled

forward—for that matter, he had walked himself dry. "But warm
your feet now," suggested Torhild.

From the bed came a faint sound of whimpering—an infant, he
could hear. Torhild gave a rapid glance over her shoulder, but
took no further notice; she hung a pot over the fire and poured
milk into it. Meanwhile their talk was of the wind and the fine
weather; it dragged somewhat with both of them.

"Björn is not at home?" asked Olav.

"No, he went with Ketil—they were to take a cow to the manor
here."

"Ay, it has been told me how much you have increased your
estate. You must have not a few head of cattle, since you till so
many acres?"

"We have four that give milk and three young heifers—" The
infant screamed louder and louder while Torhild was telling Olav
of her cattle.

"*He* seems to be in great distress, though," said Olav with a
smile. He was about to ask whose child it was, but remembered
Ranveig, Torhild's young sister, and checked himself.

"It is a little girl," said Torhild, suddenly getting up. "I shall
have to quiet her." With a rapid gesture she parted the folds of
her kirtle and drew out one full, blue-veined breast.

Olav looked at her, his mouth half-open with astonishment.
Then he bowed his head—his forehead grew hot, a blush spread
over the man's face. He felt he could not look at her, had to keep
his eyes firmly fixed on the floor. *That* was the only thing he
had never once thought of, that it might turn out thus!

Torhild had seated herself on the step of the bed, with the child
at her breast. Olav felt that she was looking at him; and he was
angry with himself that he could not cease blushing. They sat thus
for a good while, saying nothing. Then all at once Torhild spoke,
quietly and in a clear voice:

"I would rather you said your business now, Olav—then I will
answer you as well as I can."

"Business—I have no other business than that I thought—I would
ask after Björn—see him and hear how he does—and you—"

Torhild answered, as though weighing every word she uttered:
"I see right well, Olav, that you may think—that it was not for
this you gave me the farm here—I was given Auken that I might
support myself and the child over here. But as I told you, the

work here is now double what it was when I came. And I hold it
better to have a man here to help one than that I should carry on
the farm alone with hired servants. Then you must bear in mind, I
am now so old—Björn cannot have *many* brothers and sisters.
Perhaps no more than this one—" she bent her face caressingly
over the sucking child and pressed it to her.

As Olav was still silent, Torhild resumed with more warmth:
"I considered it last year, before I gave him his answer—whether
I should go over to Hestviken and speak to you of the matter.
But then methought it was long since I had heard from you. But
I see that you may think I have acted otherwise than was in your
mind when you gave me house and land—though there never
passed a word between us that I was not to marry."

Olav shook his head. "I knew not that you were married."

" 'Twill soon be a year ago," said Torhild shortly.

Olav rose, went up and gave her his hand. "Then I must wish
you good luck." She shook his hand, but did not look up from the
child. " 'Tis a daughter you have got—what is her name?"

"Borgny, after my own mother." Torhild took the child from
her breast, gathered together the kirtle over her bosom, dried the
little one's mouth with the back of her hand, and turned her face
to Olav.

"A fair child." Olav felt he must say so. Out of the tiny red face
the dark eyes, wondering, as is the way of infants, seemed to meet
his. Then they slowly closed; she was asleep. Torhild remained
sitting with her in her lap.

Olav thought that now she would surely tell him something of
the man she had taken in here to be her husband. But she did not.

"Your brothers," Olav then asked, "were they at one with you
in this?"

"You know, they have been used to that from childhood—if
only I have them under my eyes, they listen to me."

Olav thought in that case she might have done better to keep
at least one of them here, but all he said was: "Nay, 'tis like
enough you should deem there was need of a man here now."

"Ay, as matters stood, I *had* to marry Ketil—he would not stay
here longer on other terms. And had I not had his help all these
years—he has done more than a man's work at Auken since he
grew up. If I had let the lad go—hired another labourer—I could
not be sure that he would not come to me one day with the same

demand. So it was fairer to let Ketil take me and share the good
fortune that is so largely due to him."

Olav made no reply. Then she said again:

"You remember Ketil? You saw him when you were here
last?"

"Nay?"

"Ay, he was not fully grown then—"

It dawned on Olav: a half-grown lad with a foolish face—a
foundling—who had been with Torhild at that time. Flushing
deeply, without looking at her, the man asked: "Is *he* the one you
have taken to be to my son in the place of a father?"

"Yes," said Torhild in a hard voice.

"Nay, I have never claimed to order your doings." Olav
shrugged his shoulders. "And Björn?" he asked. "But maybe he is
too young to have a say in this?"

"Oh no. He has known Ketil as far back as he can remember.—
Here they come." Her pale, large-featured face softened and lit
up in a little smile.

The door flew open—it led straight into the open air—and a gust
of wind brought in the sound of young, laughing voices, a child's
and a young man's. The smoke in the room swirled blue in the
daylight. The boy had a windmill in his hand; he ran straight to
his mother, beaming and shouting with joy. The man followed
him, tall and fair; he said something as with a laugh he pushed
back his ruffled yellow hair and wiped his face. Then they both
caught sight of the guest.

Olav saw that Ketil knew him. He checked himself, became
more reserved in his manner, and looked confused.

Torhild's husband was tall, rather loosely built, with big labourer's hands, which hung dangling to his knees, but his face was
childish and rather foolish, with the long, low chin covered with
fair stubble. Yellow, shaggy hair hung over his forehead. For all
that, he was far from ugly.

Torhild got up and laid the child in the bed, saw to the pot.
She signed to Ketil that he was to take his place in the master's
seat. He did so.

The boy had remained standing by his mother. He was not tall
for his age, but was close-knit, shapely, and strongly built. Olav
saw that Björn took after the Hestvik race—curly hair, pale as bog-
cotton, large eyes, clear as water, set rather far apart under fair,

straight brows. His skin was white as milk, with a few little dark freckles over the root of the nose. He stood coolly surveying the stranger.

Torhild spoke to her husband, asking how he had fared in his errand at the neighbouring manor. Then they talked awhile of the weather and the crops; she tried to draw both the men into the conversation, but to little purpose. Then a young woman came in—one of the neighbors who came to help Torhild in the dairy; Torhild had not yet been churched after her childbed. Torhild asked whether Olav had a mind to go out with Ketil and look round the farm.

Björn went with them. He took his stepfather by the hand, and while the men went round the little farm, indoors and out, the boy grew talkative—he agreed with everything his stepfather said or added something to it. Hitherto they had borrowed a horse, said Ketil, but if their luck held a few years more—

"You must know, Ketil," said Olav, "that if Torhild thinks I ought to do something more for her—"

"I know she does not," Ketil interrupted. And Olav, meeting his eyes, saw that the young man did not always look such a fool. "We have shifted well enough for ourselves all these years."

They had eaten their porridge, and Olav said he must think of going down to his boat. Then he called Björn and bade him come over to him.

The boy came and stood before Olav, looking at him with the cool, watchful expression in his handsome, sullen young face.

"Do you know who I am, Björn?" asked Olav.

"Ay, I guess that you are that Olav of Hestviken who is my father."

Olav had drawn a gold ring from his finger. "Then you will accept this ring, Björn—a gift from your father?"

The boy looked at his mother and then at his stepfather. As they both nodded, he replied: "I will, Olav—I thank you for the gift!"

He tried the ring on, looked at it a moment; then he went over to his mother and asked her to keep it.

Olav took his leave soon after. He asked Torhild to go outside with him. It was dusk, and the wind had increased. The violent

gusts bent the bare rowan trees so that their branches scored the
chilly green of the clear sky, but thick masses of cloud were advancing from the south.

Torhild said: "Will you sail home against this wind?—we can
house you tonight."

Olav said he must go in spite of it. He threw the flap of his
cloak over his shoulder. "Since you are now married and have a
child in wedlock—might it not be as well that Björn came over to
live with me?"

He could not hear the answer for the wind, and repeated his
own words.

"You must not ask me that, Olav."

"Why not? I shall not marry again—and I shall bring the boy
up as befits my son."

"No. You too have true-born children. I will not have Björn
go where he will be reckoned an inferior. Better to be the first
at Torhildrud than the last at Hestviken."

"Eirik has not been home now for four years. We seldom hear
news of him, and 'tis uncertain when he will come back."

"I know it. But there is Cecilia—and that foster-daughter of
yours, and your kinswoman, Lady Mærta. Then you know that
the name my brothers bear in those parts is not such as to bring
the boy more honour."

"You are well instructed about my affairs," said Olav sharply.

"Such things are noised abroad, Olav, of a man in your station."

Then Olav bade her farewell and left her.

He tried to shake it from him as he walked down through the
darkness and the storm. It was unreasonable to be so angry. Torhild had a perfect right to marry. But that was the only thing he
never thought could happen.

It was true that she might need a master on her farm, and true
what she said, that if she let Ketil go, the next foreman she took
might make the same demand. But that she should choose this
foundling of all others— He recalled Ketil's face, childishly young
and fair, a tall, powerful lad—hand in hand with the boy, merry
and playful both. The last time he took leave of her—it must be
seven years ago now—it had been Torhild's wish that *he* should
take her back.—No, he would not harbour such thoughts; it was
servile to think basely of any, without certain knowledge.

Björn. It must be bitter as death for a man to lose such a son, if he had had one.

The roar of the surf filled the whole air—through the gathering darkness the breakers rolled, alive and white. The packed stones of the little pier were battered and ground together with a dull booming by the waves that broke over them. Olav stood for a moment looking out—the wind had shifted due south. For all he had to do at home, he might just as well have stayed at Torhildrud till the morrow.

He had never thought of taking up with her again—but still his anger seethed within him whenever he recalled what he had seen up there. He was so wrought up that it surprised himself.

He had known all the time that she should never more be *his* —but he had nevertheless had some sense of ownership, in knowing that she was there—

The seas broke right over him as he went out on the little pier, where his boat lay rocking on the lee side.

7

THE FROST came early that year. Week after week the weather held, calm and cold, with brazen dawns over dark ridges; the fields were grey with rime, lakes and bogs frozen hard. On clear days the fiord was dark blue and ruffled; then the light breeze died away, and the surface seemed to expand as it turned grey under the frosty mist that came and settled, raw and biting, on the country about Folden. One day the sky was sullen; there was a scent of snow in the air. In the course of the day a few hard little flakes began to fall; the snow grew thicker, rustling down with a faint, dry sound—toward evening it fell in great flakes.

It snowed for a couple of days, one evening the south wind got up, and then there was driving snow.

They had gone to rest early at Hestviken that night—it was two days before Lucy Mass.[1] Olav was waked by a thundering at the outer door; he heard one of the house-carls get up and go out. It often happened in such weather that people of the neigh-

[1] December 13.

bourhood, coming ashore late, asked lodging for the night at Hestviken, so he lay down again; was sleepily aware of folk coming into the room; someone stirred the embers, rekindled a flame. Then he was wholly roused by hearing his name called. Before his bed stood Torhild Björnsdatter with a lighted splinter of pine; the snow lay white on her hood and the shoulders of her mantle.

Olav raised himself on his elbow:

"In God's name—are you here! Is it Björn?" he asked hastily.

" 'Tis not to do with Björn. But Duke Eirik crossed Lake Vann today—with five hundred horsemen, they say. He will be bound for Oslo, to greet his father-in-law and return him thanks." [2]

"Where have you heard this news?"

Torhild thrust her torch into a crack of the wall and sat on the side of his bed as she talked. Her brothers had had a share in a fishing-boat this autumn, and now she had been with them out to Tesal, to her mother's kinsfolk there. Thither some yeoman had come that morning, who had fled before the Swedes—they were ravaging the country, plundering both goods and cattle.

"God have mercy on the country people," said Olav. "They cannot secure their cattle in the woods either, in wintertime."

"Hestviken lies out of the way," replied Torhild; "yet I have thought, Olav, it were safer for your little maids and for the women on our side of the fiord. They say there are German mercenaries with the Duke. So I bade Egil to put in here to Hestviken, I would offer to take them home with me."

"You are faithful to me and mine, Torhild," said Olav gently. "And thoughtful."

"I was well off while I was with you—and Cecilia is sister to my son. But what will you do yourself, Olav?"

"Carry the news northward to Galaby."

Torhild went into the hearth-room to the house-folk. When Olav came out to the others, he was dressed in a short homespun coat, which showed the leather hauberk underneath, long woolen breeches swathed about the calves; on his head he wore an Eng-

---

[2] Duke Eirik was the brother of King Birger of Sweden, son of King Magnus Ladulas, and grandson of the great Earl Birger. Eirik had been betrothed in 1302 to Princess Ingebjörg, the little daughter of King Haakon V of Norway. His ambition was to make himself master of the three Scandinavian kingdoms, and as one of the steps to this end he seized his brother Birger and threw him into prison. Eirik's invasion of Norway, here described, took place in 1308.

lish helmet with cheek-pieces and gorget. He carried his shield and the axe Kinfetch in his hands. Torhild looked at him.

"Think you Reidulf would try to raise the yeomen to resistance?"

"That would be no bad plan," said Olav. "There is both the Hole and Aurebæk Dale—narrow defiles between screes, where the horsemen cannot move to either side. The Duke must have thought he could trust to the black frost's holding till the change of moon at least, but these snowdrifts will delay his march."

Mærta Birgersdatter said she would stay at the manor. If the Swedes came, it was not impossible that she might find kinsfolk and friends from the border country among them: "and then it might be of use that I speak with them—that they deal gently with your property. I owe you so much, Olav, that I would fain do you a service in return, if I can."

"Think not of *that*," said Olav deprecatingly. It troubled him vaguely that these poor women came and wished to show their gratitude for the little he had done for their welfare—as though it reminded him of old and half-forgotten things: of One who had stretched out His hands to help him, but *he* had turned away, ungratefully.

He bade Bodvar arm himself to go with him northward, and went out to the storehouse together with old Tore. They put up some sacks of food, for Olav thought that Torhild could not possibly bear the cost of feeding so many mouths for an indefinite time. While busy with this he chanced to knock down his skis, which stood in the store. He had used them little since he came south—folk hereabout had given up ski-running a generation ago. Now it occurred to Olav that they might be useful: the road from the shore up to Galaby must be well covered with fresh snow.

Together with his men he carried the sacks aboard the Björnssons' vessel; she was not so very small, there were seven men in her. While they were engaged, in the darkness and the driving snow, in stowing sacks and boxes, the light of the lantern fell on a big bundle that lay near the mast, well covered over, among barrels and other goods. Wrapped in rugs and skins, Torhild's children lay asleep; Olav had a glimpse of the boy's fair head.

The herring-boat put off from the pier, and Olav stood awhile listening for her after the night had swallowed her up. The gloom and the flying snow surrounded him like a tent on every side. He

could feel the hill behind him and the homestead under the steep
black wall of the Horse Crag in the black night, and before him
the pitch-black water swirled below the edge of the pier, the
teeming snowflakes sank into it and were gone. He stood there
with Bodvar and a strange lad who had been on board the fishing-
boat; on seeing the master was armed, he had begged leave to join
him.—All at once an unruly joy surged up in Olav—as though he
were released from fetters; it was dark behind and dark before,
and here he stood all alone with two armed men, utter strangers,
and he knew naught of what the morrow might bring.

Bodvar leaped down into the boat and began to bale her out.

It was toward midnight when the three men from Hestviken
reached Galaby. Through the driving snow they caught the smell
of smoke beating down from the louver, and on reaching the door
Olav heard that folk were still up in the hall—drunken men who
were bawling and singing. He had to hammer on the door for
some time before at last it was opened. He who opened it was a
tall, thin man—he gave a low cry of surprise as Olav and his companions entered. Olav recognized Sira Hallbjörn.

"Are you come with a message of war, Olav—or why are you
helm-clad, you and your men?"

"You seem to be a soothsayer, priest."

Olav looked across the room—two torches stood burning on the
long table, and the eight or nine men who sat around it or lay
sprawling over the board were drunken, all of them. Olav knew
most of them—they were landholders from his or the next parish.
Reidulf Jonsson, the Warden's deputy, had slipped down between
the high seat and the table as far as his stomach would let him; his
big head with its brown beard had sunk upon his chest. It was the
youngest of his brothers who sat on the floor singing, with his legs
stretched out into the straw and his head in the lap of another
young lad who sat astride the outer bench, twanging on a little
harp. The priest alone was almost sober. Sira Hallbjörn suffered
from the same defect as Olav Audunsson: God's gifts did not bite
on him; he was just as thin, no matter what he ate, and just as sad,
drink as he might.

He stood tense and erect, listening to Olav's tidings. Olav had
not remarked before that the priest's red hair had become strongly
streaked with grey of late, and his narrow, bony, and freckled face

was aged and wrinkled now. But he was still clean-shaven, like Olav himself—such had been the usage in their young days.

It was not many of the franklins that they could rouse to sufficient clarity to make it worth while taking counsel with them. They had come to Galaby for the settlement of a suit. "Baard, your kinswoman's husband, went home early," said the priest; "and ill it was that he did so. He was the man we had most need of as leader—Reidulf is little worth."

Olav said they must first send a messenger in all haste to the town, to the captain of Akershus—"but sooth to say, I have more mind to stay with you here—if you hold with me that it will be a great shame on us if we let the Duke march through Aurebæk Dale without trying whether perchance we may give him some trouble."

"Fifty men should be able to hold the pass a day long against an army," said the priest. "And the townsmen will gain time—if we gain no more."

Young Ragnvald was sober enough by now to take things in pretty clearly. He offered to ride in at once. The priest got out writing-materials; meanwhile Olav and some of the others went to the servants' room to wake the men there.

The snow had abated a little as the body of franklins made their way toward the church town, but every trace of the road was drifted over. The priest and some of the others rode; so they soon went ahead of the rest, who had to tramp on foot in the snow-drifts. Olav glided quietly and lightly on skis by the side of the horsemen; now and again he had to stop and wait for them. He was standing at the edge of a little clearing, when Sira Hallbjorn appeared out of the darkness. The priest reined in his steaming horse, leaned over to Olav:

"I have been thinking: we are two men here who can run on skis—what if we struck southward tonight and scouted?"

Olav said he had thought the same.

At the parsonage they came into a pitch-dark, ice-cold house —Sira Hallbjörn had been from home since break of day, and his house-folk were in bed. At long last he managed to strike fire and light candles. To Olav it seemed many days since he took boat at Hestviken; the night had been hard and long, the sail up the fiord, then on skis and into one strange homestead after another—it had all taken time. From within the closet Sira Hallbjörn called: would he not rest awhile before they set out?—but Olav said they could not afford to waste time. He packed in his scrip some frozen bread and meat and a ball of butter that the priest's servant brought him—remembered that he had left home without food or money, thinking he should be back before they took the field. But the very fact that he was now headed straight for warfare gave him an easy feeling.

Sira Hallbjörn stepped out. He wore a smooth, old-fashioned iron helmet with a big, hinged visor and a pitch-black canvas hauberk over the priest's blue frock, which he had kilted up; his sword hung in a leather baldric over his shoulder. In his hand he held a longbow such as the English and the men of Telemark use; the arrows rattled in their quiver on his back.

Olav could not resist saying, with a little smile: "You are arrayed to sing a man's requiem now, father!"

A tremor seemed to pass over the other's sharp, long-nosed face:

"*Tempus occidendi, et tempus sanandi*—you told me once, they taught you something of the scripture when you were at Hamar in your youth. Did he teach you that saying, the stubborn Lord Torfinn?"

"No. But so much do I know, that I think I can tell the meaning. A time to kill and a time to heal?"

The priest nodded; he bent his bow and strung it. "'*Tempus belli et tempus pacis.*' Solomon wrote that in the book that is called Ecclesiastes—'tis one of the bravest books in scripture. But take off your armour, Olav—'twill be heavy to run in."

Olav removed his surcoat and took off his hauberk. It was of elk's hide with thin iron plates about the waist to protect his vitals. As he folded it and tied the thongs he asked: "Are there more such sayings in the book you named—of war?"

" '*Laudavi magis mortuos quam viventes. Et feliciorem utroque judicavi, qui necdum natus est, nec vidit malo quæ sub sole fiunt*' —such are his words."

Olav shook his head: "That was too learned for me!"

" 'I praised the dead which are already dead more than the living which are yet alive. Yea, better is he than both they, which hath not yet been born, nor seeth the evil work that is done under the sun.' "

"Is such the wisdom of Solomon?" Olav slung the bundle of armour on his back, and the two men went out. Now it was snowing again so that the night flickered about them. "He must have said that because he sat too safely there in his castle of Zion and his days were too full of ease," said Olav, laughing quietly. Sira Hallbjörn laughed too as he ran and was swallowed up by the darkness; he had to go and find his skis.

They had the driving snow right in their faces across the fields and Olav had to exert himself so as not to lose the other's dark shadow in the flurry. Sira Hallbjörn went forward with long, supple strokes; the points of his skis sank deep in the heavy snow at each sweep. In the blind night he aimed blindly at gap after gap in the fences, where the gates were in summer. Olav wiped his face now and then and his helmet, on which the snow lay melting, sending streams of water down his neck, but he could not stop for an instant if he was to keep up with his companion.

Within the forest it was better. *Where* they were going Olav no longer knew, but the other seemed as sure as ever. Sometimes the firs stood so thick that their skis scraped the bare ground when they ducked under the snow-laden boughs. Olav recalled what he had heard said of the priest—that he was not afraid to hunt in another man's wood—but none cared to speak of it; Sira Hallbjörn raised strife enough without that. Likely enough it was true; the priest went forward as though he knew every turn of the way in spite of the darkness and the snow.

Once Olav recognized where he was—they had entered a narrow track with a steep wall of bare rock to the east of it and loose stones at the bottom, so Olav was afraid the skin underneath his skis would be cut to pieces, as they struck the bare rock so often. There was a faint gurgle of water underneath the snow. The weather had cleared; high up above the defile strips of black sky peeped out between light clouds, and a star twinkled. Folk shunned this pass after dusk:—any evening the troll's hound might be heard barking among the crags. Involuntarily Olav hailed the other under his breath.

"Are you afraid, master?" asked the priest with a little laugh as Olav came up to him. "Not even the troll will turn out his tike tonight."

"Not afraid either." Olav lifted off his helmet and let it hang on his back. "Only my head itches so; I am in such a sweat."

Sira Hallbjörn waited till the other was ready, then he set off again.

They went side by side over a flat white surface darkened by patches of water—it was oozing up now in the thaw. Sira Hallbjörn stopped for a moment, leaning on his staff and getting his breath.

"You are tired now, Olav?"

Above their heads the clouds were parting more and more, showing deep rifts of blackness and a few stars faintly shining. A deep sigh went through the snow-covered forest around the lake, and here and there the branches let fall their burden with a low gasping and rustling sound.

"Oh, nay. I feel I am not so good a ski-runner as I was in my youth."

"You are not used to finding your way at nighttime?"

"I went once from Hamar town to Miklebö in Elfardal—I have made that journey many times—but once I did the half of it by night and found my way—I knew not where I was going."

"Were you alone?" asked the priest.

Olav said: "I had company—half the way—with a young lad. But he was untried—had little skill at ski-running."

But Sira Hallbjörn asked no more. They stayed awhile longer to regain their breath, then the priest flung himself forward and they were off again. They plunged into the woods again and followed a watercourse—Olav had to go in the other's tracks, and they ran on and on. In a way he was pleased that the priest had asked no questions—and he felt it to be a good thing that he was beginning to be tired; more and more his body moved of itself. When he was gliding downhill he felt his heart beating less violently, and the breeze was cooling to his overheated body. A little shock of anger ran through him every time a branch caught in the load on his back and gave him a bath of wet snow.

He did not know how long they had been going, but at last the night began to fade away. It was in the grey light of early morning, with a sky again heavy with snow, that Sira Hallbjörn and Olav passed along the top of an enclosed field that sloped down to a cluster of farms in a plain. Olav was broad awake all at once— every yard was full of people, men in steel caps, armed with long

swords, their horses close at hand. And thick black smoke rolled
up from every roof—on one farm farther south a great bonfire
was burning out in the yard.

Sira Hallbjörn stood watching, sniffing at the scent of smoke.
Then he made for the alder thicket, creeping down gently and
spying out. Olav followed, excited and wide awake.

They came to a rail fence. Before them a great white field
sloped down toward the outhouses of the nearest farm. In front
of the byre some armed men stood round two countrymen who
were holding and flaying a slaughtered beast. Olav and the priest
watched for a while.

"I declare!" Sira Hallbjörn laughed angrily. "They have forced
him, Sigurd himself, to hold the beast, and 'tis his son that flays it."

Olav knew where he was now—these farms lay south and east
of Kambshorn. The village was surrounded by forest, which
divided it from the district to the east toward Jalund Sound. Olav
advanced a little farther along the fence while he considered
which way they ought to take in order to reach the more populous
district under cover of the woods, so that they might have a sight
of the Duke's main force.

Then he heard the twang of a bow-string behind him. He saw
the arrow fly and bury itself in the snow behind one of the men
who watched the flaying. Sira Hallbjörn knelt down on one ski
and picked up another of the arrows that he had stuck in the snow
before him. Olav turned abruptly and dashed uphill toward him.
At the same moment the first bolt whizzed past him into the
thicket, shaking the snow from the branches. The men by the
houses rushed out into the field, but sank deep in the new snow.
Then one of them fell. Sira Hallbjörn had shot a second arrow,
but now he leaped up, and he and Olav fled together uphill over
the pasture. One or two more bolts came whistling after them, but
it was vain for the Swedes to give chase to the two ski-runners.

They halted a moment and listened—in a white clearing within
the forest, where a few old barns stood.

"You shot unwisely, Sira Hallbjörn," said Olav with vexation.

"I have hit a longer mark ere now," said Sira Hallbjörn coldly;
"but I sprained my thumb last night, so my first arrow went
wide."

"It is not that I meant," said Olav impatiently. "But now we
shall have small profit of our scouting—we have seen no more

than we knew already. And 'tis most likely they will take revenge on the poor folk of these farms—"

Sira Hallbjörn's face flushed deeply with anger, the veins stood out like cords on his temples; but he received Olav's words in silence. And so they went on.

They now made for the highway, and early in the day they reached the southernmost farms of Saana parish. The folk here had already had news of the trouble, and as they came farther north they heard the church bells ringing. By the bridge north of the church they came upon a great body of countrymen, eager for news.

It was very mild and the sky hung low and grey over the level country, but the ice on the river was safe under the covering snow, so it would be useless to try to check the Swedes at the bridge. Moreover, many of the folk from here had taken their cattle with them eastward into the forest tract of Gardar; it lay well out of the way.

Sira Hallbjörn urged the men to go with him and join the countrymen farther north, all those able to bear arms. But it was easy to see that the people of Saana parish thought things were well as they were: they expected the invaders to march straight through their district without doing them great damage. And they even seemed not to wish that the Swedes would be thrown back—if they had the hostile army pouring over them, smarting under a defeat, it would be worse than all. "The rich townsmen, merchants and clerks, are better able to pay ransom than we."

Olav saw the priest was so angry that it would be imprudent to let him have a hearing. So he himself stepped forward and spoke:

"Good friends and kinsmen, see you not that if Duke Eirik get possession of the castle of Akershus, we shall have this hard master over us all for we know not how long, till the spring at least, and then he will fleece us all to the skin. He has with him three hundred German horsemen—we all know what that means—and he owes them pay. Much better were it that we meet him now and see if we can make him change his mind."

Someone suggested that surely King Haakon must come home now and defend the country.

"The King has his hands full with defending the border by the river. We franklins here about Folden had a name in old time of being peace-lovers, so long as we were left in peace. Do you not remember how our forefathers danced more than once with their enemies on the ice outside Oslo?"

"They did not carry off the victory in that dance, Olav Audunsson," a man interrupted. "Know you not that?"

"They gained by it in the long run, for all that, Erling—'tis always worst in the end for him who dare not defend himself. And so thickly peopled is the country hereabout that we should be men enough to bring the Duke to another mind."

The end was that Paal Kurt of Husaby and the sons of Bergljot from Tegneby promised to follow with as many men as they could raise. Sira Hallbjörn and Olav then went on.

"Knew you not," asked the priest, "that the King sailed to Björgvin before Martinmas? Sir Helge and Count Jacob have charge of the new castle on Baagaholm with few men—"

"Better to let them think hereabout that they have our army at their back."

"Where have you heard that the Duke owes the Germans pay?" he asked again.

"Never have I heard aught else of dukes and mercenaries—" Olav gave a little laugh. "*Tempus bellus*, was it not so you said?"

"*Tempus belli*," Sira Hallbjörn corrected him, and laughed too.

Arrived in their own country, they heard that Baard of Skikkjustad and Reidulf, when he was sober again, had given up the plan of meeting the invaders in the Aurebæk Dale and had gone forward with more than eighty men to join the men of Aas; they had taken up arms. Folk judged that with the snow in this state the Duke could not advance farther the first day than Kraakastad or Skeidis, and so the country levies would wait for him a little to the northward, where the road runs under a little ridge, having on its eastern side some bogs that never freeze till after midwinter, as they are full of springs; there they thought they could decoy the horsemen out into the morass. Olav was not very familiar with the country inland, but the priest muttered and shook his head when he heard of this plan.

They reached the place as it grew dark. In a little hollow on the ridge the watchmen had made a fire. The scouts made their report, as they had agreed upon it—they both thought it useless to say that they had seen a little of the hostile army. They took off their boots and hung them on poles by the fire, threw themselves down on beds of pine branches close to the crackling logs, where some men had set up a sort of tent of blankets and cloaks, and fell asleep, dead-tired both of them.

It was not yet full daylight when Olav was aroused as they broke camp. He snatched his boots from the pole above the embers; they were toasted hard, but gratefully warm, for he was chilled all through. He pulled on his hauberk over his coat and ran, axe in hand, to the brow of the ridge.

Below him the rock sloped smooth and steep for thrice the height of a man to the narrow road that skirted the bog. Farther on, it swung onto the high ground. The slope was not very steep, and the weak point of the position was that at the top of the pass there was level and open ground on both sides—mossy ground with scattered trees. Up here lay the men of Aas and Saana, a hundred or more. On the edge of the ridge stacks of timber had been built.

From below, the muffled rumble of the advancing body could be heard already, and the splashing of horses' hoofs in the slushy road—he made out the leading horsemen to the southward; they could ride three abreast here. Out on the bog dark clumps of men could be seen running, where the ground was hard; they were the yeomen who had lain at the little farms under the brow of the wood in that direction. At that moment came the first shower of arrows and javelins, but most of the men on the bog had aimed too high, so that their shots flew over the heads of the horsemen and struck the cliff—one fell in the heather about the feet of those standing on the ridge.

"Too soon besides," said Baard of Skikkjustad with an oath—he was standing just in front of Olav.

For all that, there was confusion in the ranks of the horsemen on the road below; some of the horses reared or tried to break out to the side. Those who rode in the van reined theirs in; there were shouts to those behind and answering shouts. Then the leaders spurred their horses; it looked as if they would ride on without heeding the body of men on the bog. Great pools of water had formed during the night, disclosing the danger of attempting to pursue the attackers on horseback—nay, but some of them were leaping out of the saddle, they would try a bout after all.

So far as Olav could judge in the grey dawn, the mounted troop
was about an old hundred in number. They pressed on from the
rear; some horsemen were forced out to the edge of the bog. And
now the leaders had reached the top of the pass; there they were
met by the country levies, who received them with spears, axes,
and swords, and now the shots from the men in the bog began to
take effect—some riderless and wounded horses screamed and
neighed and caused confusion as they tried to break out of the
ranks, and the cries of wounded men rose above the clash of arms
in the pass.

Down in the road a loud young voice called out above the
tumult—a tall, erect man in knight's armour held in his horse and
called for a hearing. When the noise of the battle died down a
little the men on the ridge could hear that the knight was Norwegian. They could make out most of what he shouted to the
countrymen in the pass. In the stillness that followed Olav noticed that it had begun to rain.

The Norwegian knight called out that Duke Eirik had not come
to wage war on the people of the country, unless they attacked
him first. It was King Haakon who had broken treaties and agreements both with the Duke and with the Danish King, so now they
might expect another raid on that land when summer came; and
he had made a pact with King Birger and would lead Norwegian
forces out of the country to support the Swedish beggar King
who wronged his own brothers. King Haakon had foully betrayed the man he had lately embraced as his son-in-law—and the
Duke sought no other aim here in Norway than to come to speech
with the King, but so basely had King Haakon outraged his own
knighthood, and so harshly and presumptuously did he rule in
Norway's realm, that Duke Eirik had found support with many
good and noble Norwegian lords, and they looked to it that the
people of the land would back their demand for a settlement.

"That is Sir Lodin Sighvatsson," said Sira Hallbjörn, "Bjarne-
fostre—a fox and a traitor like his uncle."

"Let go now," cried Baard along the line, and the men on the
ridge hurled down the piles of timber and stones. There was a
smell of scorched rock as the falling mass thundered over the
troop of horsemen below. Among the mass of tumbled logs Olav
saw horses' legs kicking in the air as the animals rolled; there were
neighs, cries, and shouts in the confusion and men struggled to

get out of the saddle and onto their feet—the road was a-crawl as when boys drop stones into a cup full of earthworms. Then he ran with the others along the edge of the rock and rushed out at the top of the pass, where the first troop of yeomen was now hard pressed and some men lay on the ground—and several of the horsemen had already hacked their way through, turned their horses, and attacked the Norwegians in the rear.

Olav had flung his shield over his back and wielded his axe in both hands, fighting among the steaming bodies of horses, while flakes of foam showered over him from the muzzles of the neighing and rearing animals. He seized hold of a bridle, warding off as he did so the rider's spiked mace with the head of his axe, pulled the horse down to its knees, and struck at the man so that he reeled to one side. Olav ran on past the overthrown horse and rider, and several of his own men followed him. He received a blow on the helmet which staggered him, but it glanced off and he kept his feet, fighting, feeling that this was an unequal struggle, men on foot with horsemen against them before and behind—the place was ill chosen. Now the Swedes broke through to the moor east of the road, where the opposing force was thin. Above the din of strokes and the noise of battle he heard a voice from there, shouting to the men to stand firm; it was that leader of the men of Aas whom he did not know. He could not see much on either side for the cheek-pieces of his helmet, but he realized that more and more of the enemy were riding round to the east over the moor—now the hottest part of the struggle was over there, and behind him his comrades were fighting with their backs to him and the others who received the advancing enemy. They had the bulk of the hostile force at their back now: the franklins' effort had collapsed, he saw that, and he yelled with the full force of his lungs, plying his axe like a madman. He guessed that the yeomen on the moor to the left of him were taking to flight, but the little band in the pass who were now fighting back to back, with mounted foes both above and below them, defended themselves with the frenzy of despair—no falling back, no falling back! sang the blows of their axes.

Then he saw down the road under the ridge a long line of advancing horsemen armed with lances; in the wretched grey light there was a gleam of wet on their steel caps and shoulder-plates, on the horses' armour—further resistance was useless.

He managed somehow to hack his way through to the steep
side of the road, hooked his axe into a crevice, and got up. Before
and after him his comrades climbed, scrambled, and ran—most
of them had succeeded in getting up. A little way up the height
he stopped and looked back. On the other side of the road the
greater part of the country levies were in flight across the moor,
pursued by horsemen, and they disappeared into the pine woods.

In the road, which was now much cut up, horses and men lay
here and there, dark forms in the mud; some moved and some lay
still, and on came the Duke's main force of steel-clad, heavily
armed warriors, tramping and jingling—and the rain was now
pouring down. Then Olav ran on along the wooded ridge.

Olav was making his way over a field, where some small houses
lay, down by a brook. Before him he saw a man reeling as he ran;
now he fell and lay still. Olav stopped as he came up to the man,
lifted him, and turned him over. It was Baard's son-in-law, the
bridegroom of last summer, he saw. Hoskold Jonsson pushed him
away as though in stupor and sat half-upright, leaning on one
hand, with drooping head; then he turned round and dropped
down on his other side—like a child when one tries to wake him,
Olav thought, turning over in his bed and going to sleep again.
The snow was bloody about Hoskold. Olav gently raised the
other and with some difficulty hoisted him onto his shoulders. It
was heavy labour to trudge with him on his back through melting
snow over the rough ground, but he got him into one of the
houses and laid him down in a little room where two old women
sat. Afterwards he could not remember what he had said to the
women or they to him as he ran on in the tracks of some others,
together with three men who had joined him by this hut. Now
for the first time he noticed that he must have received a blow or
a kick in the plate that covered his loins; it had made a dent that
plagued him as he walked.

After a while he came up to a high, rock-strewn moor, where
a number of the fugitives had halted. He flung himself down in
the heather, leaning against the trunk of a spruce, and took some
food—several of the men had bags of provisions and shared with
the others. Baard was there and Sira Hallbjörn and four or five
more whom he knew—in all, a band of something over twenty
men had collected.

One of the men gave a shout, ran forward to a knoll, and looked

out. Others followed him. From here a corner of Skeidis parish
could be seen to the south. Beyond the forest a column of thick,
black smoke rose up and spread itself in the heavy air. It was
Hestbæk that was burning, said the men who hailed from that
part. A little farther to the eastward they saw more smoke—the
Duke's men must be taking revenge for the attack.

"You are sore stricken, Baard," said Olav in a low voice. Arne
of Hestbæk, Baard's father-in-law and Olav's kinsman, was still
alive, active and hearty in his old age. And now Olav had to tell
Baard of his son-in-law, whom he had left behind, badly wounded,
in one of the little crofts under the hill.

But Baard, the silent, good-natured franklin, only gave an angry
laugh.

It was raining fast with a faint, rustling sound in the melting
snow. The country where the farms were now blazing was
ringed in by a thick, dark sky, which lay low on the black woods
that closed the view. The men had crept in under the thickest
trees, chewing food and sucking at lumps of snow as they talked
together.

Now they could all see that an unsuitable place had been chosen
for the attack. Aurebæk Dale would have been much better, with
the narrow bridle-path between screes in the glen. But those
whose homes lay nearest the forest there would have been loath
to provoke the hostile army before it had left their district behind. Then it was said that the stacks of timber should have been
saved till the mail-clad horsemen came up—and one man asked
why the scouts had not reported that the force contained such a
troop. Olav had just been thinking that had they known that, then
—but it was Sira Hallbjörn's fault, so let him reply. But the priest
said merely that these mercenaries must have lain at farms farther
south than he and Olav Audunsson had been able to penetrate.
The men cursed a little, others swore roundly: sure enough the
Duke himself had been with that troop.

Then there was talk of what should be the next step. Most of
the men were inclined to make for home and see how it fared
with their farms.

Then Sira Hallbjörn spoke up: " 'Tis not to be thought that the
Duke will be suffered to plant himself in Oslo without any trying
to disturb him. If he sits down before the castle of Aker—he will
scarce take *that* so soon; Munan Baardsson is neither a fool nor a

coward, and he has a good following with him. It seems to me, then, that the best we can do is to make our way eastward to Eyjavatn and thence up to Sudrheim. Haftor, the King's son-in-law, and his brothers are brisk lads and the right ones to lead, if there be a levy. Haftor, I know, will scarce weep so sorely if he lose the chance of calling Duke Eirik brother-in-law—at Sudrheim they were but middling glad when the King betrothed to him the Lady Agnes's little sister."

Some young lads came climbing up from the wood, supporting among them an elderly yeoman who was bleeding like a pig. While some men, the priest among them, were tending the wounded man, one of the lads asked for Olav Audunsson of Hest-viken—was he here? At first Olav did not recognize the young man, but then he saw it was the lad who had leaped ashore from the Björnssons' fishing-boat and had gone with him to Galaby. Now the boy asked what Olav purposed to do and whether he might join with him. Olav said he might indeed, but he had not brought more with him than what he stood up in, and he for his part would follow Sira Hallbjörn's advice and betake himself to the Jonssons of Sudrheim, to see whether the men of Raumarike would try to drive the Duke out.

The stranger said that was to his mind. His name was Aslak and he was a son of Gunnar of Ytre Dal in Rumudal, but he had three brothers older than himself, and so his parents desired that he should enter a monastery. He had now been for three years, since he was thirteen, with the white friars at Tunsberg, for Father Sigurd Knutsson was his uncle. But he was not made for a monk —indeed, most of the time he had spent on one of the convent's farms at Andabu, and now he had leave of his uncle to return home.

"So when I heard of the raid and they spoke on board of putting in to Hestviken, and I saw you were in war-harness—uncle had spoken of you—you and he are friends, I think."

"Did Father Sigurd speak of *me*?" asked Olav, rather incredulously. "I have seen him, when I had occasion to go thither, but never have we exchanged many words—I cannot guess why he should speak of me."

"He said you were a bold man and had fared much in foreign lands—he told me you were fostered in his home country, at Frettastein, and had made your marriage there."

Olav made no answer to this. He never liked to hear of his young days or to meet with men from the Upplands who knew of him from that time. That Father Sigurd of the Premonstratensian convent had kinsfolk in that part of the country he had never known. But this seemed not to be worth a thought now. He asked Aslak where he had been during the fight in the pass and let the lad talk, but said little himself. He was rather tired too, and wet to the skin; he now felt his head aching from the blow he had had on his helmet, and his boots had rubbed the skin off his feet.

Soon after midday the party on the hill broke up. Most of them were going home—among them Baard of Skikkjustad; he wished to see to his son-in-law. But eleven men started eastward, led by one from Skeidis parish, who was to guide them through the forests to Eyjavatn. There were Sira Hallbjörn and Olav Audunsson, Markus and Simon, sons of Alf of Berg, and a stalwart young franklin whom Olav did not know; the rest were house-carls, and then there was this lad Aslak.

Within the forest a few more men joined the company, and there was talk of the fight; but none knew anything certain as to how many of the country levies had fallen or how many men the Duke had lost. One party of the horsemen had turned back, plundered and burned some farms, but they had not given themselves time to range far afield.

Soon all talking ceased. The little company tramped in single file up and down the woodland, over and around low pine-clad heights, in thick wet heather and sodden snow—on the tarns the slush was ankle-deep above the ice. And the rain poured and poured from a grey sky. At dusk they reached houses and cultivation; before them lay the lake, Eyjavatn, a wide grey surface under the darkening, rainy sky.

No one here had heard the least news of the troubles, and the people of the manor, where they asked shelter for the night, sent a messenger at once to the knight at Ormberg; war arrows were sent out and men went up to light the beacon. By next day they had assembled a band of over eighty men, who marched northward across the slushy surface of the lake on foot, on horseback, and in sledges.

8

THE FRANKLINS from outside were lodged at farms up and down the parish and lay there during the feast of Yule. In most places they were well received—the Raumrikings had a right good mind to march upon Oslo and give Duke Eirik a taste of their steel. But Sira Hallbjörn was invited to stay at Sudrheim—he was distantly related to Sir Jon Raud—and so the latter asked Olav Audunsson also to be his guest during Yule.

He occupied the manor with his youngest son, Ivar; the two others, Sir Haftor, the King's son-in-law, and Sir Tore, speaker of the Thing, were with the King at Björgvin. Sira Hallbjörn and Olav were assigned a bed in a fine house apart, where the two unmarried sons lived, and Sir Jon had suitable clothes sent out to them.

Not for years had Olav kept Yule with so cheerful a heart. Messengers left the manor and came home with news: Sir Jon had his scouts abroad. The King's young kinsman, Munan Baardsson at Akershus, had received tidings of the raid in good time. The castle was undermanned, so he could not venture a sally, but he had beaten off the first attack. After that the Duke sat down before the castle, but the long-continued rain forced him to break camp in the swampy ground about Aker and retire upon the town of Oslo. There he kept Yule in the old royal palace on the riverbank, dubbed his Norwegian friends knights, and held a tournament—though it was said he had got an ague in the camp, so that he was often sick. He exacted a ransom from the country districts, nor did the townsmen go free, though he dealt somewhat more gently with them. The folk at Sudrheim laughed rather maliciously when they heard of it, for there had been no bounds to the affection the men of Oslo showed Duke Eirik before, when he visited the town as King Haakon's son-in-law to be. The Duke's army numbered three hundred German horsemen and a hundred and fifty Swedish men-at-arms, and his Norwegian adherents had among them a little over an old hundred of men, most of them armed after the fashion of squires.

Sir Jon Raud of Sudrheim was not so very old, but he was in bad health, so it fell upon his son, Ivar Jonsson, to lead the country levies, and he was courageous, prudent, and well liked by the people—but he was very young, just one and twenty. They kept their Yule feast at Sudrheim as usual, and here Olav met several men and women with whom he could claim distant kinship, going back to the time when his forefathers were in possession of Dyfrin. He was also related to the men of Sudrheim, it turned out.

"How can it be, Olav," asked Sir Jon one day, "that you have never cared to serve the King? 'Tis not right that a man of such good birth, substance, and courtly breeding should have no place among his bodyguard."

"I have served King Haakon when he called out the levies," replied Olav; "but you must know, sir, I was Alf Erlingsson's liegeman in my youth, and I swore by God and by my patron saint, when I heard the Earl had died in banishment, that never would I swear any other allegiance on the hilt of my sword, and least of all to the man who made him an outlaw."

"Then you are more loyal than most men," said Sir Jon, with a little sigh. He himself had known that Earl well, and after this he often talked with Olav of the gentle Lord Alf; and Olav felt he had not been drawn so near to his own youth and the time when he was free and light of heart—ay, not since he came home to Norway.

Sira Hallbjörn too was like another man, a sociable and kindly companion. He was in the war heart and soul and took part in all the Sudrheim men's plans. It was clearly far easier for him to mix with worldly lords and knights than with priests and countrymen. Sometimes he and Olav went hunting with young Ivar and his friends, when the weather suited. On the holy-days he said mass in the church, to the great joy of the people, for he carried himself nobly at the altar and had a clear and powerful voice, whether in speaking or singing—but the parish priest here was a bungler, and Sir Jon's chaplain was so old that he was in second childhood. He could still say mass, but he no longer knew people rightly; he often took Ivar to be Sir Jon, who had been his foster-son in his youth.

Sir Haftor's young wife, Lady Agnes Haakonsdatter, was at home at Sudrheim, as she was expecting her second child. There was already a son, and no doubt his kinsfolk had their plans for that boy, should the little Lady Ingebjörg die without heirs.

What Olav had heard of the lady's mother, King Haakon's

leman, had always moved him strangely, though most folk made
a scornful jest of her. She was a yeoman's daughter from the
fiords, and she had been Queen Ingebjörg's bath-house maid. One
day when she had made the bath too hot, her mistress had struck
her so fiercely that she left the bath-house bleeding and in tears,
and there she was met by the King's young son, Duke Haakon.
He spoke to the maid and asked why she was weeping so. Fair to
look upon she was not, and she was much older than he, by a score
of years at least; but before the year was out she had a child by
the King's son. The Queen was sore displeased, but the Duke
would not part from his leman, and when he took up his residence
in Oslo, he gave her a manor in the hundred of Bergheim. Of the
children he had with her, only Lady Agnes grew up. When he
was to marry the German princess, he took his base-born daughter into his own house, but sent her mother to the convent of
Reins; there she became a nun some years later. A pious and virtuous woman she had always been, and kind to the poor—but in
the King's bodyguard they all thought she was ill chosen to be a
royal leman, being small and pale, modest and shy with strangers;
it was said she had often begged her lord to show mercy to such
as deserved severe punishment. Lady Agnes took after her
mother; she was small and wan, without charm, hard to talk to,
but a gentle lady.

One day as Olav was sitting alone in the house, seeing to his
weapons, a woman came in and went along the beds, lifting the
coverlets and feeling the pillows. When she came into the light,
Olav saw that it was Lady Agnes herself. He stood up and bowed,
and when she came and gave him her hand, he dropped on one
knee before the King's daughter and kissed her hand, thinking the
while that she was more like a worn-out cottar's wife who was
forced to keep up her toil until the very hour when she would be
brought to bed.

"I wish to see if our guests are honourably housed here," said
Lady Agnes. She sank upon a stool, and Olav stood before her
with bowed head and a hand laid upon his breast; he thanked her,
they lived well here in every way.

"You men from Folden can know but little of how it has fared
with your homes?" the lady asked.

No, said Olav; they had heard no news from thence since they
took the field.

"Then you have not had a joyful Yule?"

Olav could not help laughing a little—he had never drunk so good a Yule, he answered.

"But you know not whether your manor be standing or lie in ashes?"

"Hestviken has thrice lain in ashes, my lady," replied Olav as before. "If 'tis burned now for the fourth time, then I must even do as my fathers: take such fortune as God sends me and build it up anew."

"And what of your kinsfolk?" asked Lady Agnes.

"My son is with Sir Ragnvald on the border, and my daughters are with friends on the west side of the fiord, so I need not distress myself for them."

"Then you have no wife alive?"

"No, lady, this is the eighth winter since she died."

"Ah yes, then it must be easier for you, Olav, than for many men. One hears so many tales—the poor country folk in the south, God help them!"

"Amen, lady—but if He will, they will not have long to wait either, ere they be helped and avenged. Ill it is that we have not your lord with us, but Ivar has good will enough—"

"Oh, I know not," the lady sighed. "I cannot say I grieve so sorely either that Sir Haftor is away. Yeomen against German mercenaries—'tis an unequal struggle, even though the yeomen have numbers. And yet it is sad for me that my lord is absent from me at this time."

Olav looked down at the little wife; he thought her condescension somewhat uncalled-for and her words ill suited to a King's daughter, but he felt sorry for her. She had fine brown eyes like those of a hind, but other beauty there was none in her.

Nevertheless it was with a strangely keen pity that he heard, one morning a few days later, that now Lady Agnes lay in the pains of childbirth, and the ladies who were about her knew not how it might fare with her. Sir Jon and his kinsmen wandered about with gloomy looks, but what they must chiefly have feared was that if Lady Agnes should die, the strongest tie would be broken that bound Haftor Jonsson to the King, and if the child were lost, it would be one arrow less in their quiver.

But in the course of the evening a message came that Lady

Agnes had been delivered of a fine big son, and then there was
joy: Sir Jon ordered in mead and wine, and the men drank to the
welfare of the new-born babe. The grandfather had the elder boy,
the year-old Jon, brought in, whom his kinsmen called the Junker
among themselves—he was hailed and passed from man to man,
and the franklins drank till they were under the table, like men,
as Ivar said.

Next day the new-born son was christened by Sira Hallbjörn—
Magnus he was called. The guests at the manor joined the kinsfolk
with their offerings, and in the evening they held the christening
ale with great merriment, but Olav could not but think of the
young mother, whom all seemed to forget—one of her ladies had
said she was very sick, lay wandering in a fever and wailing that
Sir Haftor did not come in to her they could not make her understand that he was in Björgvin.

But two days before St. Hilary there came word in the evening
to Sudrheim that a levy of over two thousand men, from Lier and
Ringerike, was marching on Oslo. The state of affairs in the town
was that Duke Eirik had been dangerously ill during the holy-
days, but now he was better and, for joy of that, his friends would
keep the last day of Yule with wassailing. The men of Lier had
had news of this, and they thought to fall upon the town that
night.

Ivar Jonsson and his friends held a council at once, and next
morning they set out with a body of over three hundred men, but
the rest of the Raumrikings, who dwelt farther to the north and
west, were to follow as quickly as they could: Ivar was afraid
the men of Lier might forestall him and reap all the glory.

The men from Folden now mustered about fifty, and Olav
Audunsson was their leader. It was he who had raised the yeomen
for the first attack on the Swedes, and it was he who had sent
warning betimes to the captain of Akershus. He himself had
thought nothing of this till now, nor had he been among the
leaders in the fight on the Oslo road; but here at Sudrheim he
won credit for it, and it seemed to come about of itself that he
was held to be the man of greatest mark among his company, the
master of the ancient chieftains' seat of Hestviken and Alf Erlingsson's liegeman in days gone by. And here he himself thought it
natural—as it should be, beyond that it concerned him no more.

The other three subordinate chiefs were much younger men, nearer in age to Ivar Jonsson.

As it was falling dark they reached the village of Tveit, below the Gellir ridge, and here they learned that the Duke had set guards at Hofvin Spital, at Sinsen, and at Aker by the church, but only a few men at each place, for it happened luckily that all these houses on the highroads belonged to Nonneseter, and the Abbess, Lady Groa Guttormsdatter, had protested with heavy threats against any injury being done to her dependants—nor would the Duke care to break peace with the masculine nun more than there was need. Everywhere in the ravaged districts the sisters' tenants had been let off more lightly than other farmers, whether owners or tenants; those who held their land of the Crown or of the nobles had fared worst. Sira Hallbjörn laughed when he heard it: there was no love lost between him and the Lady Abbess, for he had disputes of his own with her, but he too saw the humour of this. The priest accompanied Ivar in arms and armour.

After consultation with some of those who lived in the neighbourhood it was decided that the Raumrikings should move up into the forest before daybreak and conceal themselves there till the next evening. Then they would advance along the river Alna, surprise the guards at Hofvin on the way, and fall upon the town above Martestokker, at the same time as the men of Lier entered it from the west by way of the convent of nuns. The latter body would have to pass round by Aker church and over Frysja bridge, as the ice on the Bjaarvik was unsafe, and the lower reach of the Frysja was not yet frozen over.[3] Up here on the high ground it had frozen a little, and there was enough snow to enable the messengers sent westward by Ivar Jonsson to use their skis, if they kept to the roads and fields.

---

[3] This river (now called the Akers-elv) runs through some of the eastern quarters of the modern town of Oslo (Christiania). Its course lay some little distance to the north-west of ancient Oslo, cutting off the town, by land, from the fortress of Akershus, to the north of which was a marsh (where the city of Christiania was afterwards built). By water (or ice) the distance between mediæval Oslo and Akershus was comparatively short, across the Björvik (Bjaarvik), a small inlet at the head of the fiord. Akershus was newly built at the time of this story; the old royal castle of Oslo, which had been handed over to the Governor of the town and the clergy of St. Mary's, stood on the opposite shore of the Björvik, at the mouth of the little river Alna, which runs at the foot of the hill of Eikaberg.

They settled themselves in the farms of Tveit, Ivar and his captains, intending to rest there till near daylight. But shortly before
midnight the door of the house was suddenly flung open, and in
came one of the farmers with whom they had spoken earlier in
the evening, accompanied by an old woman, his mother.

She lived in the town with her married daughter, and they kept
an alehouse in a yard near the palace. The Duke's men had
had word that a strong body of country levies was marching on
Oslo from the west, and therefore they were making ready to
attempt a storming of Akershus castle in the morning. The
woman had watched her chance of slipping out of the town and
bringing the message; for in Oslo it was whispered among the
townsmen that the lords of Sudrheim were also engaged in raising men from the Upplands, but the Swedes believed nothing of
this.

"There'll be another dance then, for the last day of Yule," said
Sira Hallbjörn.

Now it was hard to know what course the Raumrikings should
follow. Then Sira Hallbjörn demanded a hearing and said there
were no more than two counsels to choose between: "—and
neither is of the best. One is, that we set off at once and go west,
the same way that our messengers went; cross the river by San-
dakrar, fall on the guards at Aker farm, and then we must hold
Frysja bridge tomorrow until the Lidungs [4] come up—if we can.
Should the Duke have the luck to take Akershus, he can prepare
a bloody bath for the yeomen's army coming from the west and
buy his peace with King Haakon at whatever price he himself
may offer—he and his Norse friends.—The other counsel is that we
turn home again, up to Raumarike, and wash down our shame
with the last of the Yule barrels at Sudrheim."

Young Ivar and his captains discussed the priest's counsel. It
would be fighting on unequal terms, three hundred men, and of
those not more than seven and forty mounted and armed after
the manner of horsemen, the rest yeomen on foot, against the
Duke's mercenaries and well-trained men-at-arms.

"What say you, Olav Audunsson?" asked Ivar. "You are the
oldest and most experienced."

"I say the priest is right. There are but two courses open.
Neither is good—but the first plan seems to me not so bad after

4 Men of Lier (near Drammen).

all. If we cannot hold the bridge, we can break it down and take refuge in Akershus."

Sira Hallbjörn reminded them that it was of great moment to prevent the Duke's getting possession of the castle. They must make ready to break down the bridge, as Olav said, and they had the church of Aker and the churchyard in their rear; that was a good position to defend if the enemy got part of his men across; and if they were driven back from the churchyard, they would have to take refuge in the church—that they could hold till the army from the west came up.

"Do you yourself believe what you said?" asked Olav as he and the priest were arming—"that the Lidungs can cut their way through to the church if the mounted troops reach the heights west of the Frysja?"

Sira Hallbjörn shook his head. "But we cannot return home without having ventured a brush. And it may cost the country dear, if Duke Eirik is to hold Akershus and treat for peace with his father-in-law that was to be—"

"Nay, that is so. Methinks this business has been somewhat brainlessly undertaken. But Ivar is young; 'tis worse to be heartless than brainless, and the heart is good enough both in him and in the men—no lack of fighting spirit."

"No.—Do you remember last summer at the wedding—when your axe sang? Now we shall soon see whether the warning was for you or for me."

"I have never heard that such weapons rang save for their own kin. But as things are shaping here, it looks most likely that it may mean both of us," said Olav with a little laugh; and Sira Hallbjörn laughed too—"Ay, it looks so indeed."

There was no moon, and the sky was strewn with stars. The snow was not deep enough to hinder the advance seriously; and now it was freezing a little. Olav Audunsson and Sira Hallbjörn rode at the head of the Folden troop—it was the last in the line. Olav and the priest had borrowed horses from Sudrheim, but Olav said he would fight on foot, for he was more used to that.

"If this frost hold a few days," said the priest, "the Duke will be able to bring mail-clad horsemen across Bjaarvik."

"Ay, we are late in moving," said Olav; "and lucky if we be not too late."

"At Sudrheim they would stay for the christening ale—and be sure these men from the west have had weddings and funerals and Yule barrels that must be emptied. But maybe we can yet drive back the Duke—as a repentant sinner drives off the Devil at his last gasp."

Olav said nothing. He looked before him, where the host of constellations descended to the dark line of the wooded ridge. It was strange to think he should have suffered so much all these years on account of *one* dead man, have pondered so sadly upon death and all that came after—but when it came to war and fighting, all such thoughts flew away and were as nothing. And so, no doubt, it is always and for every man.

Their guide could not find the ford over the river where the advanced guard had crossed; they had to go right up to a kind of pool, where boats lay. This delayed the Folden troop so much that it was already growing light as they came down again by a path that ran through the alder brakes on the right bank. The sky stretched above them wide and light, yellow as sulphur down toward the eastern hills, as they sighted the tower of Aker church above the trees, and below them, on the farther side of the Frysja, they saw the roofs of Fors, white with snow against the white ground. At the head of the fiord a mist lay over Akershus and the town, spread out in a thin sheet, above which rose the towers of Hallvard's Church and the gables of the old royal castle.

It looked more hopeful at the bridge than Olav had imagined —he had not passed this way since the King had built wooden towers at the bridgeheads. They were bigger than he had thought. The eastern one, on the Oslo side, was so much lower that the men on the western tower could shoot over it at an army advancing against Akersnes from the east.

Nor had Ivar been idle: his men were engaged in hoisting up stones and missiles into the barbicans, and in the middle of the bridge, where it rose highest, they were building a breastwork— some men were pulling down a few small cottages near the bridge, dragging out the logs and doors, while others loaded sledges with stones on the hillside and others again drove them down. So the men of Folden found work to do at once. From the Raumrikings they learned that the guards at Aker farm had been overpowered and cut down or made prisoner. Sira Hallbjörn at once secured two of the crossbows that Ivar had taken from the Swedes, for

himself and Olav Audunsson—they both shot just as well with
these weapons as with the longbow.

The day was already so far advanced that the Norwegians were
saying that either the widow at Tveit had been doting, or the
Swedes had given up the attack on the castle. The south-western
sky was already afire above the forest on the Eikaberg ridge—
the sun was just rising—when they heard the muffled beat of
kettledrums just below at the brow of the wood under Fors. Their
own work had been so noisy, and the falling water roared so
under the bridge, that they had not heard the sound of advancing
troops before. Now the rumble of many hoofs and the clanging
of mail-clad men and horses rose and rolled toward them together
with the undertone of drums.

The yeomen had been seen. A storming-ladder swung up above
the bushes and shot down again: they were trying whether it
worked in the grooves.

Olav flung his shield onto his back and dashed across the bridge
with fourteen others, climbing over the obstacle in the middle.
He had offered to take his stand in the foremost tower and had
picked his party of young, strong lads who had a brisk look, to
his thinking.

A boy came with them, bearing a banner—Olav knew his face
from the streets of Oslo, but knew not who he was or how he
had come here—and Olav answered, laughing: ay, let them set it
up. It was a yellow banner with an image of Saint Olav on it—
they had taken it out of the church; no doubt it belonged to a
guild in Oslo.

The sun's disk shone in splendour over the top of the ridge as he
stood on the flat roof of the barbican and saw and heard the enemy
breaking out of the brushwood beyond the fields. The long mail-
clad ranks advancing with a faint jingling and a subdued glitter in
the cold shadows upon the white ground, the bright patches of
the banners, the scaling-ladders and battering-rams that they carried—and now a horn rang out, and short cries were heard—Olav
felt his heart beat fast: it was a hostile troop, but no matter, his joy
at the sight ran down him like a deep draught of cold, strong ale.

He cried the watchword, at the same moment raising his shield
aslant without thinking—old habits revived of themselves in every
joint of his body. Simultaneously with the whirring of the two

small catapults he had on his tower came the first shower of arrows and bolts from the western tower over their heads.

The men on the eastern barbican crouched down with their shields over their heads and looked out through the loopholes. Some horses had fallen, breaking the ranks and causing confusion.

"Have they only four ladders?" cried Olav to his neighbour, the boy from Oslo.

"They lost some under Akersnes."

A volley from the hostile army came flying, striking the wall of the barbican, rattling on the bridge behind them, but only a few shots fell on the roof, and none took effect. With exultant jeers the Norwegians picked them up. Now the ground thundered with heavily armoured horses. A troop of them were trotting toward the gate; they bore an iron-shod pole among them.

"What kind of playthings are these they use—do they think to take Akershus with the like of that?"

"You know they cannot bring their great battering-rams by this road," the Oslo boy roared back, "across the hill. They have reckoned on the frost—"

"Then they have been almost as bull-headed as our Ivar."

They shot the Swedes' own bolts back at the troop—they fell harmless on their defensive armour—set their shoulders to the pole, and raised the cauldron of boiling water up to the top of the parapet. As the first blow of the ram crashed against the gate, making the whole tower shake, the Norwegians emptied the cauldron upon the men below.

The shrieks of scalded men and horses, the thud of hoofs, and the jingling of armour were drowned almost at once in the din of a fresh troop that came up and thrust aside the sprawling mass of the first. "Go slow," shouted Olav to his men; "reserve your stones—" They had not too many of them and had to try to shoot straight down so as to prevent the attackers as long as possible from taking up the ram their comrades had dropped when the water came down on them. Meanwhile bolts and arrows from the archers in front rained down on their shields, and from the rear the shots of the Raumrikings in the western tower flew over their heads.

Olav saw one horseman who had been pressed too far out to the right—his horse slipped under him. Brought down on its

haunches, it slid down the riverbank. Its shrill neighing rose above
the din and the roar of the waterfall as it was carried into the dark,
rushing water, with its rider hanging in the stirrup. The steep
bank was covered with ice underneath the snow on both sides of
the foot of the tower, and this was of great assistance to the Norwegians: the enemy could not send so many men at a time against
the gate, and so far they had not succeeded in bringing up ladders.
But it could not be long delayed.

A shout reached him from the bridge—eight or nine men were
lifting baskets of stones over the breastwork and dragging them
along. It had occurred to Ivar Jonsson that missiles might soon run
short in the foremost barbican—thoughtless the young man was
not. Olav's heart laughed with joy within him. Ivar had withdrawn his men from the breastwork and stood waiting with them
in the western barbican, and this was right: it could not be very
long before the Swedes broke down the eastern gate and reached
the bridge. Ivar had had the parapet of the bridge thrown down
at each end of the obstacle.

They had just had time to hoist up the baskets of stones when
the first scaling-ladder fell against the parapet. So now it was the
turn of the axes. It was a good thing he had brought up the
basket-bearers, thought Olav, otherwise he would have been short
of men for this work. Man after man they hurled down as they
swarmed up the ladders. One or two of his own lay low, and the
boards of the floor were bloody—but so was the snow at the foot
of the tower—what snow there was left.

They could not hold the tower for long. Olav glanced up at the
sun—the fight had scarce lasted half an hour.

Now the gate gave way beneath them with a crash, and it felt
as if the whole tower staggered. Olav ran to the other side and
looked down to see how things were going. The yeomen had
dashed forward and manned the breastwork, Ivar in the midst of
them. The horsemen could only advance two-abreast. The blows
of the yeomen's maces and axes and the clash of swords rose above
cries and the tramping of horses—for a while this might go well.
More of the mounted troop, horse and man together, had gone
down in the torrent; now the Swedes were sending footmen onto
the bridge.

Sira Hallbjörn he saw on the top of the breastwork, slashing
with his great two-handed sword; the priest fought like a devil.

Olav threw away the fragments of his shield; there were only splinters left between the iron bands. He grasped Kinfetch in both hands and turned to where the ladder had been, but now it was gone; it hung on a jutting rock in the hollow sheet of ice over the torrent, and they were bringing up another. Behind him his men thrust down the enemies who were trying to mount the inside ladder to the roof—they ought to have drawn it up.

Now Ivar and his men sprang over the breastwork and advanced over the bridge. They cleared it in a moment—for that time. And the Swedes drew back across the fields, out of bow-shot.

Olav lifted off his helmet to cool himself a moment. There was refreshment too in the stillness, with the roar of the torrent, which had been drowned by the fighting. And now he found it was not only sweat that had made his clothes stick to him, for his elk's-hide hauberk was slit just over the body-plate, and bloody, but the scratch he had got was not a deep one, by the feeling.

A morion appeared in the opening—Sira Hallbjörn was climbing up the ladder.

"How many of you are alive? Go back now, you, and we fresh men will receive the next shock."

"There is not much here to receive a shock with, Sira Hallbjörn."

They saw men coming across the fields from the houses of Fors; they were carrying something.

"They will try to set fire to the barbican," said Olav. "We must hold out as long as we can."

"Ivar has placed combustibles within the breastwork," said the priest.

"Then it will end in the bridge being burned. After that they can stand on either bank and sing staves against each other," laughed Olav. "And then the issue will be better than we had looked for."

In the fields in front the horns sounded the assembly. Olav stooped and picked up the yellow Olav banner, which had been torn down, and set it up again—it was now stained with blood.

"Now we must show them what we can do with the crossbow, Sira Hallbjörn!"

The horsemen came on in close array, and in their rear followed men with fire-cauldrons, pots of pitch, and faggots. A bolt from Sira Hallbjörn's bow was so truly aimed that one of the fire-pots dropped on the ground and turned over.

Ivar Jonsson and his men had propped up the doors and wreckage in the gateway. They stood behind with long spears, clubs, and cudgels with scythe-blades, and in their rear the bridge was filled with men, waiting to go forward as those in the front rank fell.

The third attack thundered against the gate and the shaking walls of the barbican. Once more Ivar Jonsson and his yeomen succeeded in beating back the assault, and the sullen little fire that smouldered at the base of the tower was put out by the men on the roof with the cauldron of water from the cold fireplace in the tower—no one had managed to keep the fire in.

Again the Swedes withdrew a little way, and the noise died down. From the barbican they could see the leaders ride round the ranks and come together for a consultation. Then all at once the priest cried: "Look!"

Olav turned and looked where the other pointed.

"Ay, now we can make an end and sing *Nunc dimittis*," said Sira Hallbjörn.

Teams of horses broke through the copsewood yonder—they drew the great catapults and heavy siege engines.

Ivar Jonsson ordered the horn to be blown. He stood on the bridge and called up to the men on the barbicans—his silken surcoat hung in strips outside his harness. They could do no more now but retire and see if they could break down the bridge after them.

Then came the sound of a horn from the hill behind them—in notes that answered Ivar's. A bright, resonant ribbon unwound itself in the blue and white light of the winter day. Olav turned round—up behind the churchyard fence the morning sun flashed on a close array of spear-points.

The shouts of joy from the little force about the bridge were met by a fresh blast of the horns. This was an ancient call—folk named it the Andvaka strain or King Sverre's dance. Little as Olav Audunsson was minded to praise old King Sverre, there was yet no tune he would so gladly have heard in this hour.

Sira Hallbjörn had laid hold of Olav's arm—the priest's hand was bloody. Olav saw with surprise that the other's cheeks were ashy white, his face was distorted in a wild luxury of pain:

"That is *our* horn! My father's, I mean—I should know it above all others. Then they must be here, my brothers—Finn or Eystein."

And as the horn sounded anew the Andvaka strain, Sira Hallbjörn joined in, singing in his fine and powerful voice the ancient stave that went to that tune:

> "*Cattle die,*
> *kinsmen die,*
> *last dies the man himself;*
> *one thing I know*
> *that never dies:*
> *the fame of each man dead!*" [5]

They took it up and sang with him, all those who knew the stave, while the Raumrikings tore down the obstacle before the first mounted troop—there were at any rate fifty men on horseback, armed after the fashion of the King's men. They rode across the bridge, and after them swarmed the footmen, country folk, but most of them handsomely armed. Olav saw Sira Hallbjörn running out into the fields by the side of a high brown horse, holding on to the saddle-bow—the man who rode it wore a closed helm and a fluttering blue silken surcoat over his armour.

What the new-comers meant to do he could not rightly guess; it looked as if they would try to drive back the enemy in open fight out in the fields. They had already surrounded the body of Swedes who were on their way to the bridge, and with the knights who led them at their head, the men from the west were now advancing, far off, against the main body who stood by the siege engines at the brow of the wood.

Ivar Jonsson had mounted the barbican with Markus of Lautin, one of his captains.

"Can they do that—drive back German mercenaries with a rabble of peasants—then anything may happen!"

"There must be two thousand of them at least," said Olav. They continued to pour down the hill below the church and across the bridge.

"And not one in twenty can get back over the bridge if they are beaten," said Markus.

[5] These lines are from the Eddic poem called "The Guest's Wisdom." The speaker is Odin.

The attack of the Norwegian knights had already broken down —two of them were dragged from their horses and carried away as prisoners. But the Lidungs simply went on—if one body was thrown back, another troop dashed forward. Time after time the German mercenaries rode into the mass, trampled them down, and used their lances, but the Norwegians ran in upon them from the other side, hammering at men and horses with clubs and axes, cutting and thrusting with hafted scythe-blades and spears. They had pressed up to the edge of the wood in great numbers and managed to hold the enemy there, so that his catapults were of little use against them; but neither could the men in the barbicans support the Lidungs to any extent—they were fighting out of bow-shot.

Before the bridge all was quiet. A few horses and men lay stretched in the brown and bloody slush, and one of the horses moved and struck out with its hoofs now and then. A young lad came walking toward the bridge, supporting his right arm, from which the blood dripped, in his left, and he jogged homeward with a curiously peaceful, solitary air, as though he were carrying something he had been out to buy.

But now the first groups of yeomen were being driven back over the lands of Fors. Olav grasped his crossbow; as he put his foot in the stirrup and drew it, he noticed for the first time that his body was stiff with tiredness.

Once more the flying Lidungs rallied in the fields, and once more the enemy rode forward. At that moment something struck Olav on the right cheek-piece of his helmet—there was a crash inside his head, and he fell backward into Ivar's arms. For a moment everything went round. When he stood up again and took his bow, he felt his mouth full of blood and pulpy flesh; he spat out blood and splinters of teeth and shot again with his crossbow.

Now the Lidungs had retreated so far that the Swedes could reach them with their catapults; stones and other missiles fell among the knots of men, and the first fugitives began to make, some for the bridge, others for the forest to the northward. Olav had stopped using his bow; he stood gazing intently at the conclusion of the fight, while all the time, without thinking, he had to feel with his tongue the sharp edge of steel that had penetrated his cheek and the broken molar in his upper jaw. But soon his tongue grew stiff and swollen and the wound filled his whole mouth like a bloody sponge. But he gave little attention to it as he watched the fight drawing to its end.

The horn of the Valdres knight sounded the assembly, untiringly, and once more the main body of the western men formed up just below the barbican. The Raumrikings in the towers had now been relieved by fresh men with bags and quivers full of bolts and stones. Olav tried to speak to those who had come up and stood around him, but it was no more than a blob-blob-blob and a croaking in the throat, with all the blood and spittle that filled his mouth. He could scarcely believe his eyes, but the Swedes were not advancing; it looked as if they were about to retire into the woods—had they' had enough of the game?

Awhile after, he walked back across the bridge, as in a dream, so heavy was his head—amid the stream of strangers who were returning. But he had bethought him of his axe before going down from the tower; as in a dream he remembered striding over dead bodies that lay inside the barbican at the bottom of the ladder, and as in a dream he heard the shouts of the men who manned the towers, making ready to defend them again, if there were need. He had to make way for two men who were carrying a third by the shoulders and knees. Drowsily he noticed that the planks of the bridge were dark and slippery with blood, and he turned a little giddy at the sight of the black water that rushed under the bridge and thundered over the fall.

When he had come a little way up the hill toward Aker church he stopped and laid down his axe—he wanted to take off the helmet that pressed so painfully on his head, and it was horrible with this splintered steel among the torn and tender flesh of his mouth. A man stopped and helped him with it. The sweat burst out anew all over his sweat-drenched body, and the tears came into his eyes, before the other had got the helmet off him, and his cheek was gashed worse than before. The stranger offered to take him under his arm, but Olav shook his head, tried to laugh, but could not, for his face had grown so stiff and seemed enormous. Then the other picked up the axe and the helmet and gave them to him, said something, with a laugh, and went on. Olav tried to wipe away some of the blood that trickled down his neck, it made him so disgustingly wet underneath his clothes.

The sun was now high in the heavens, he noticed; it was past midday and had turned to the clearest and finest of winter days.

The tree-tops round the church shone against the blue sky as
though it were springtime, but the light hurt his eyes.

He came up to a farm on the hill and went into one of the
houses. It was packed full of men, but he saw none he knew. Several spoke to him when they saw his shattered face, but he could
not get out a word. Some of them made room so that he could
sit on the floor in front of a bench, and one who sat on the bench
took his head in his lap, and then weariness overcame him. He did
not really sleep, for the pains in his head increased, as though
tearing out his very skull, and he felt himself growing chilled and
numb, but he sank into a sort of lethargy.

Once he was roused from it—a bulky, elderly woman had told
of him. A half-grown girl with solemn, staring eyes stood by,
holding a bowl from which steam rose, and the woman dipped a
towel, which was now stained brown, and washed the blood from
his face and neck with lukewarm water. Dizzy and impatient with
fatigue and pain, he had to submit to be helped up, so that he
could sit on the bench—gazing the while with longing at the great
blaze on the hearth, for he was shivering. The woman and a man
stripped away his elkskin hauberk, peeled off his jerkin and shirt,
which stuck fast to the skin; naked to the middle, he sat shivering
as they washed him and tended his wound, a cut reaching upward
to below the left nipple; and then they drew on his clothes again,
which were now soaking wet.

He staggered to his feet and tried to go and sit by the fire, but
a woman who was like Torhild took him by the arm and led him
to a bed that had been made on the floor. When once he had lain
down, it was good indeed to stretch out his limbs and lean his
back and neck against the big sacks of hay. She who looked like
Torhild spread a thin coverlet over him and offered him a warm
drink, but he could not take much into his mouth and it was too
painful to swallow. But soon he felt the warmth of the rug, and of
a big, black-bearded man against whom he was lying, and the
warmth was an unspeakable relief, though his head felt as if it
would burst with pain.

After a while he was again roused from his doze; they wanted
him to go out with them. He went. It was almost dark outside,
the southern sky a greenish yellow; great white stars were shining
in the frosty evening. Up by the church great red bonfires were
burning, around which moved black figures—the stables and the

church barn were crowded with men. The main door of the church stood wide open, and he saw that many candles were lighted in the choir, a flood of song welled out, but his companion led him past, to a group of houses.

He came into a room where many men were assembled—he recognized Ivar Jonsson and one or two from home. Some of them were busy about a bench, and on it lay a naked corpse they were washing. Olav stepped up and saw that it was Sira Hallbjörn.

He lay on his back, long and white, with his arms hanging down so that the hands rested on the clay floor with the palms upward. The left arm was broken, so that the bones protruded above the elbow. They were just washing the blood out of his grizzled red hair, and there was a faint crackling of broken bone—the skull had been shattered above the left temple. Beside the bench stood a bucket of steaming red water.

Ivar Jonsson came up to Olav. He told him in a whisper that they had found the priest's body in a thicket of briers close up to where the Swedes' catapults had been posted—half-naked and plundered: his arms were missing, as was his seal-ring and the gilt Agnus Dei that Olav remembered Sira Hallbjörn always wore about his neck.

His brother, the knight Finn Erlingsson, was among those the Swedes had taken prisoner, but his sons, Eindride and Erling, were here, Ivar went on to tell him. Olav looked at the two slight red-haired lads who stood by their uncle's body, and nodded. Ivar was still talking—there had been Lidungs, Ringerikings, and men from Modheim parish among the levies, and a little band from Valdres led by Sir Finn.

The dead man's face was grey and calm as a stone image. The men who stood by were discussing what the scars could be that the priest carried on his body: the left shoulder and upper arm were scored as though the flesh had been torn, and on the left pectoral muscle were four deep little pits; from there a silver-white furrow ran down across the stomach. But the scars were old, so it was hard to say what kind of wild beast he had been at grips with.

Olav knelt down together with some others, but his wound and his whole head ached so that he could say no prayer. When he rose to his feet they had dressed the corpse and moved it to the bier. Now Sira Hallbjörn lay like a priest, dressed in an alb and

an old chasuble, with sandals on his feet and a pewter chalice between his clasped hands: some of the priests of Aker church had
provided what was fitting for their dead brother.

Olav accompanied the bier as it was carried down to the church;
several other biers were already standing before the chancel arch.
But he had not the strength to stay and hear the vigil. The man
who had accompanied him to the mortuary chamber took him
under the arm and led him back to the farm where he had found
shelter; it was Little Aker, the other told him.

Bodily pain was a wholly new experience for Olav Audunsson.
Wounds and scratches he had known many a time, with smarting
and fever, but they had always been such as he counted for nothing—flesh wounds that healed rapidly and cleanly.

But this wound in his face was downright torture: a racking and
shooting pain in his skull and an intolerable aching in the jawbone and in the root of the broken tooth. But worst of all was the
loathsomeness of it—his mouth was always filled with the foul
taste of matter from the wound.

Now and again he had high fever, and then it was as if the bed
he lay in rose up and up and his body felt flat as an empty bladder,
while something round and heavy that had been inside his head
rolled down over him, and visions hovered along the ridge of his
brows—creatures that were neither beast nor man, faces that he
recognized without knowing who they were. In particular there
was a beggar without feet who darted along at a terrible pace on
boards fixed to his hands and knees; it tormented him more than
anything when that vision came.

One night he saw Ingunn—she stood a little off the ground
against the wall at the foot of his bed and leaned forward over
him, so that her light-brown hair swept over her thin bare arms
and fell forward like a mantle. He thought she was clad in nothing but a shift, which was embroidered at the neck with little
green flowers, so that all the little coloured spots danced before
his eyes. Olav raised his hands to keep her from coming nearer,
for just in those days his wound was angry and stank foully; but
she sank down upon him like a wave of warmth and sweetness, he
was flooded as it were with the goodness of her—then he lost his
senses, fell into a kind of swoon.

In the morning he was able to spit out a whole mass of matter and splinters that had worked out of his jaw; the woman who tended him could wash the wound fairly clean, and he felt better. He was weak and cold, and as he could only lie on the left side, it felt as if the bones were coming through the flesh there, so tender was it. At the same time he was famished; he had hardly been able to swallow anything of what they brought and tried to make him drink.

They had been to see him almost every day, one or another of his companions-in-arms, but he had not been fit to pay much attention to what they told him. But this morning came Ivar Jonsson himself and some more; they could scarce conceal their exultation. The Duke had withdrawn from Oslo at daybreak; it was clear he had lost his relish for trying his teeth on the walls of the castle of Aker, sick as he was himself, and with three thousand men of the country levies posted on the high ground. And Munan Baardsson had received reinforcements and was thought to have put the castle in excellent posture of defence.

The Duke had not lost much above half a hundred men in the fight at Frysja bridge; of the yeomen two hundred had fallen, and many had got wounds great and small. But it seemed Duke Eirik thought this might be enough; he had looked for no opposition at all, counting rather that the greater part of the Norwegian nobles would be so discontented with King Haakon that they would make common cause with him.

After his friends had left him, Olav lay feeling how his whole being was now permeated by the pent-up joy and confidence that had lain in the depths of his soul all these long days while his body was one mass of pain and fetid humours and burning fever. In spite of all, this joy had lived within him the whole time like a glow on the hearth of a ruinous house. No pain could take from him the joy of having had the chance to stand up and act and fight for his home and his native soil against the strangers who poured over it. Even if it had availed nothing, that could not have undone the joy it gave him that they *had* risen in defence, he and his fellows in the countryside. But now that it *had* availed, he lay here feeling his tortured body as but a thin and passing scab on sound, healing flesh.

He was glad, deeply and cordially glad, as he had not been since he was young. During all his long years at home, while it seemed as if his life had so shaped itself that in other men's eyes he had

nothing to complain of—had he not prosperity, health, and peace?
—it had been with him in secret as though the snakes were striking
and tearing at his heart, as in the image of Gunnar on the door of
the closet at home. In his soul he had fought without hope, harried
by a terrible dread, against powers that were not of flesh and
blood.

He saw now it was not his suffering that destroyed the happiness of his life—a man may be happier while he suffers than when
his days are good. And sufferings that are of some *avail*, they are
like the spear-points that raise the shield on which the young
king's son sits when his subjects do him homage.

Some days later Claus Wiephart came with a sledge. He proposed that Olav Audunsson should move down to his house and
submit himself to his leechcraft. Olav said yes to this—he could not
in any case stay longer at Little Aker. Claus tortured and plagued
him sorely at first, wrenched out the stump of his tooth, picked
out splinters of bone, cut and burned at the wound. Olav bore it
all with patience; nothing made any impression on this strange,
quiet joy of having fought and seen that it was of use. Not the
thought that Claus would surely see to it that he was well paid for
the cure, nor all that he heard of the Swedes harrying the countryside as they withdrew from the realm. He could get no word of
how things were at Hestviken—whether the manor had been
burned—but this touched him little. Had he had women and children at home, it would have been otherwise.

The grass was green in Claus Wiephart's garden, and great yellow buds were bursting on the trees, when at last Olav could make
ready for the homeward journey. The wound was now almost
healed and the skin had grown again on his cheek. The day before
he was to leave he asked Claus's leman if she would lend him her
mirror. He sat with it awhile, breathed on the bright disk of
brass, wiped it, and looked again at his own face.

His light hair had turned all grey, its curls were lank and lifeless, and his square, clean-cut face was furrowed and faded. The
right side was spoiled, the cheek so sunken that the whole face was
awry, and the great red scar had an ugly look; the mouth was also
drawn down a little on that side.

In a way Olaf Audunsson had always been aware that he was an
unusually handsome man. Not that it had made him vain, and in

his youth it had annoyed him if anyone spoke of it or if the
women let him see that they would be glad to have dealings with
him because he was so bright and fair. In an obscure fashion he
had felt that his physical grace was itself a part of the tie of flesh
and blood that bound him to Ingunn—since he had not yet been
fully grown when they were mated. But it had been an element
in his knowledge of himself that he was, once for all, a well-
favoured man, rather short than tall, but strong and faultlessly
built, without an unhealthy spot in his whole close-knit, shapely
frame, fair and bright of hair and skin and eyes, as befitted the
race from which he was sprung.

It was something of a humiliation that now this was past and
gone, but he took it patiently, as a judgment, that now he must
think himself old. Nor was he so many years from the half-
hundred, so he must needs bow to it.

And so he came home to Hestviken one fine spring day, to
green meadows and bursting leaves in the groves. The houses
were standing, but all of them were empty—the Swedes had cut
down and carried off all they found. In the byre stood a cow and
a heifer that Lady Mærta had bought of Torhild Björnsdatter
when she fetched home the children and the serving-maids.

But Mærta Birgersdatter was just as calm as was her wont, and
Olav was just as calm as she, and they sat and talked together in
the evening. But Olav said very little, for he spoke rather thickly,
from the wound in his mouth, and it shamed him to talk. He was
glad that the children *had* been fetched—Torhild Björnsdatter
was the only one he was loath should see him, now that he was
thus marred.

THE SON AVENGER

PART ONE

WINTER

WINTER

I

ONE evening in late autumn Olav Audunsson went down to his sheds at the waterside to see that all was made fast and well closed. It had been blowing hard during the day and the tide was high, and now on the approach of night the wind was rising. Going out on the pier, he saw that a little sailboat had put in under its lee. There was only one man in the boat, and so Olav went up to see if the stranger might need a hand.

"Now luck is with me," said the new-comer, shaking the water from his clothes, while Olav took charge of his arms and wiped the worst of the wet from them. "My wish was to speak with you alone, Olav, as soon as might be; and here you come yourself to meet me."

He talked as if they had known each other of old, and Olav thought he had seen this young lad before, but could not put a name to him—his face was fair and bold-featured, with a delicate, thin-lipped mouth; a little spoiled by the bulging, pale-blue eyes, but in spite of that he was good-looking. The hair clung to his forehead under the waxed linen hat from which the water poured, but it could be seen that it had a reddish tinge. The stranger was tall and well grown.

Olav took the man into one of the sheds and bade him declare his errand.

"Ay, 'tis best I say how it is, master; I have had the mischance to slay a man, and no atonement has yet been made—the case may drag on. And so I could think of no better way than to put myself in your hands: I know you for a man who will not refuse to hide me while my kinsmen make terms on my behalf."

Olav was silent. It had become a far more risky matter to harbour outlaws of late years since the country had grown quieter and King Haakon enforced the laws more strictly. But on the other hand he could not send the young man away—the fiord was white with foam, and night was already falling.

"Where did this thing happen?" he asked. "And what manner of man was it you slew?"

" 'Twas at home, and the man was Hallvard Bratte, the Warden's nephew."

"At home—where may that be?" asked Olav rather impatiently.

"I see—you do not know me," said the young man, seeming hurt. "Although I was with you as your trusty comrade both in the fight by Skeidis church and at Frysja bridge—"

"Ah, yes—now I mind me where I have seen you before—Aslak Gunnarsson from Yttre Dal. But you have grown much since that time, Aslak, 'tis nigh four years ago."

Aslak went on with his tale. The way of it was that Aslak's father had given summer pasturage to some cows for the lady Signe, Hallvard Bratte's sister, and two of these had been struck down by the bear. When the dalesmen came back to Hamar with the lady's cattle, she had been very unreasonable, and so one word had led to another. At last Hallvard, the lady's brother, who was standing by, had uttered words of Gunnar of Yttre Dal to which Aslak could not listen with patience. He had got away after the slaying, had ridden south, and first sought refuge with the White Friars at Tunsberg. But on coming to the convent he learned that his kinsman Prior Sigurd was lately dead, and he quickly guessed that the monks were loath to give him shelter: they had been compelled to abandon their claim that the right of asylum enjoyed by the convent of Mariskog also applied to the house of their order in Tunsberg. The Abbot said he might indeed repair to Mariskog, but it was becoming somewhat too common for King Haakon's enemies to take sanctuary there, and Aslak had remarked that the monks were a little uneasy, since the King no longer looked with favour on this monastery which possessed the right of asylum. That being so, Aslak had no great mind to betake himself thither: "and then I bethought me of you, Olav. A man without fear I know you to be, and one that is wont to do as he thinks fit. You yourself have roamed as an outlaw in your youth—so I thought you would not refuse me help."

Olav was not more favourably disposed to hide the manslayer by what he had just heard—that the lad was from the Upplands and seemed to know more about Olav's youth in that part of the country than Olav cared to be reminded of; *how* much it was not easy to guess. Until now he had believed that folk in the north had long ago forgotten him and his affairs, it was so many years now since he had shown himself in those regions. Eirik had been there awhile two years ago and had visited Steinfinn Haaksonsson at Berg; Olav had not been pleased when he heard of it, nor did he grieve overmuch when it came to his ears that the cousins had fallen out a few months later, so that Eirik had not stayed long in the Upplands. But as for refusing to receive Aslak Gunnarsson, there could be no question of that.

So he said they had better go up to the houses; Aslak must need some warm food and dry clothes.

At any rate, thought Olav as he helped to carry the other's gear, it was a lucky thing that nobody at home would try to ferret out who their guest was. Since Lady Mærta's death in the spring, Bothild Asgersdatter and Cecilia managed his house, and the two young maids were so well brought up that they never troubled their father with unnecessary questions.

Aslak Gunnarsson settled down at Hestviken. It had not been Olav's intention that he should remain there, but he could not bring himself to say anything about the matter, and when spring came Aslak was still there, bearing himself in every way as if he belonged to the household. They called him Jon Toresson—it was Olav who hit upon this name, from which no one could guess who he was.

Otherwise Olav was quite willing to admit that Aslak, or Jon, was a most agreeable house-mate, and he had a way of making himself useful. He was strong and industrious, incredibly handy besides—an excellent worker in both wood and iron, and he always found something to occupy him. Olav himself had never been more than a moderately skilful craftsman; he could accomplish all that was needed about the farm, but not such things as required special cunning or deftness of hand and a delicate eye. And since he had lost Bodvar, the house-carl who fell at Frysja bridge, he had not had a man who was practised in such crafts. And then Aslak was always cheerful and of good humour; he had a fine voice for singing, but above all he could whistle so sweetly and truly that it was a pleasure to hear him—he almost always whistled at his work. He could read a little too, so Olav got him to look at some of the writings he had concerning his estates and privileges—there were one or two matters about which he could not trust his memory.

Withal Aslak was quiet in his ways, so that he did not too roughly disturb the muffled tone that prevailed at Hestviken.

Life at the manor was calm and still. Little was said among the household, and all spoke low: the master's silence lay like a damper on all these people who had lived with him so long—they were for the most part the same. Nevertheless the life of Hestviken seemed to have taken on a brighter hue since Mærta Birgersdatter's sharp voice was hushed and her keen eyes closed. The two young foster-sisters, who now shared the duties of housewife between them, were the most demure and courteous maids a man could see; yet there was a youthful joy and brightness about them, they were so fair and so well beloved of all.

Bothild Asgersdatter was now in her eighteenth year, quick and capable beyond her age, and not strong in health, blithe and gentle at home, but very shy among strangers.

As to Cecilia Olavsdatter, no one ever thought of putting it down to bashfulness or timidity that she was so retiring in folks' company: she looked everyone straight in the face with her clear, cool, pale-grey eyes. Olav's young daughter was as taciturn as her father, and just as fair-skinned as he had been in his youth. The shining, flaxen hair lay in soft curls about the girl's head when she wore it loose on holy-days; her complexion was white as the kernel of a nut, and her skin seemed so firm and close that sun and wind made little impression on it, and the full young lips were pink as the pale brier-rose. She was short for her fifteen years, and rather broadly built, but round and shapely, with small hands and feet, but strong of hand and sure of foot. It was rarely that Cecilia Olavsdatter smiled, and her laugh was rarer yet; but she had never been heard to weep. In her actions she was kind with her own people and charitable to the poor and sick, but rather sullen and short-spoken in her manner.

The foster-sisters were always good friends and of one mind; they seemed to be bound together in intimate affection.

The Hestvik maids were never abroad, except to the annual feastings within Olav's own circle of friends; otherwise they were not to be seen at such meetings as were frequented by young people. But they went to mass every Sunday and holy-day unless

the weather was very bad. And then they were so handsomely
dressed and adorned that no other woman had better clothes or
heavier silver belts and buckles than Olav's maids—both were
called so among the folk—and they rode, one on each side of their
father, on good, well-groomed horses with newly clipped hog-
manes.

Olav's heart was filled with deep and silent joy as he walked up
the church with his daughters. Their coloured mantles of foreign
cloth trailed after them; through the thin church veils shimmered
the maidens' unbound hair, Bothild's smooth and copper-brown,
Cecilia's silky mane bright as silver. He stood during the mass and
never once looked over to the women's side; nevertheless it was
as though all his thoughts were centred on their presence in that
place.

He no longer thought of himself and his own affairs; he was
now an old man, it seemed to him, had made his choice of what
was to become of him. But, for that very reason, all that he might
yet achieve ere evening fell upon him had but one object: to
brighten the lives of these two children. How their future would
shape itself—of this he scarcely thought; it would surely fall out
for the best. In course of time he would marry them off, and it
would be a strange man indeed who would not bear such treasures
safely through the world when once he had had the good fortune
to win them. But still he had time enough to look about him—they
were yet so very young, both of them.

There was Eirik. But it was as though the figure of Eirik had
faded into unreality in Olav's mind; he seldom gave him a thought.
He had not seen him since that day at Oslo. Olav had been away
from home the only time Eirik had visited Hestviken since—it
would be four years ago this summer, and then his father had
gone with Ivar Jonsson on the campaign in Sweden, where that
brave young leader fell. And it had grown almost to a certainty in
Olav's mind that Eirik would never possess Hestviken after him—
that sin God had taken from him; the false heir was not to take
over the old manor. God Himself would defend Cecilia's rights.

Then there came a morning in early summer. Olav and one of
his men were down on the beach by the pier, busy hanging up
some nets. The weather was as fine as could be. The sunlight lay
in great white flakes on the sea; around the bay, fields and mead-

ows shone with a wealth of green, and the leaves of the alders were dark already with their summer hue, while the firs had long, fresh shoots.

Cecilia knelt on the sun-baked rock by the pier with a heap of bright, floundering fish beside her. In the morning sun the girl's old rusty-brown everyday frock was quite resplendent; her thick, fair plaits hung over her shoulders—they were not very long, and her hair was so curly that the plaits escaped from the red ribbons that bound them. Her knife flashed as she raised it and tried the edge against her finger.

It gave a sound of summer and mild weather in the morning stillness as Aslak loaded his boat. The water splashed and gurgled as he moved about and arranged the goods he was to take with him—Olav had sent him on an errand south to Saltviken.

"Jon!" called Cecilia softly. The man looked up—Olav saw his healthy young face light up in a quiet smile. As the girl beckoned to him with her knife, he drew the boat up to her along the edge of the pier; she was now standing on the rock.

She wanted him to sharpen the knife for her. She sat down as he did so, looking out across the water, with her hands resting in her lap. They were not talking together, that Olav could see—but when he had finished and took his place in the boat again, the same quiet, warm smile played across Aslak's face. And as Cecilia went back to her work, a reflection as it were of the same smile lay upon her fair features.

She began to clean the fish. As Aslak rowed past the rock, he dropped the oars for a stroke and waved his hand to the maid. And Cecilia raised a hand slightly in reply. Then she bent over her work again with a furtive little smile.

Olav stared—it had given him a shock: something was passing before his eyes of which he had had no suspicion.

Cecilia threw the cleaned fish into the bucket and straightened herself a moment. She turned her lovely white face up toward the sun and sat with closed eyes. And the smile that spread over the child's stubborn little face was like nothing her father had ever seen before; it beamed with a sweet and secret joy—no fairer sight had Olav seen in his life.

Afterwards he tried to shake it off. Go and take a fancy to a man who lived here at Hestviken as a servant; nay, his daughter could never do that. She could not even have known who this Jon Toresson was.

Nevertheless Olav determined to be rid of Aslak as soon as might be. The lad was now free to remain in the country; during the past winter he had received news through the monks of Tunsberg that the ban of outlawry had been removed. So now there was no reason for Olav's keeping him longer than he had use for his services.

But a week went by ere Olav found occasion to broach the matter to Aslak. Covertly he kept an eye on the two young people; but he could see no sign that they were closer friends with each other than with the rest of the household. He comforted himself with the thought that he had been mistaken that morning by the pier.

—Until the Saturday evening, when Olav and the men were to go to the bath-house, but the women would wash themselves in the cook-house; they had been preparing juniper water. Olav and the men were crossing the yard when Cecilia called to Aslak from the cook-house door.

It struck her father that she knew their guest's real name.

Aslak went over to the maid, took from her two pails, and dashed past Olav. In the golden afternoon sunshine he ran light-footed down the meadow to the spring. He was a big man, slight and loose of limb, handsome and cheerful; his curly, reddish hair shone gaily in the evening sun.

Olav stood still. Now Cecilia appeared again at the cook-house door. She had put off her kirtle and stood in her blue undergarment, which fell about her in rich folds down to her little bare feet as she stood warming one with the other, for the stone was cold in the shadow. While waiting for the water she let down her plaits, shook out her hair, and combed it, so that it waved about her face and arms.

Aslak came up with the pails of water. The two young people exchanged a few words, which Olav could not hear, but again Cecilia's face beamed with that new and lovely light. And Aslak was smiling as he left her.

On Monday evening Olav went out to the smithy and spoke to Aslak:

"Your mind will be set toward home, Aslak, now that your atonement is made. And I think perchance you would do well to profit by the fine weather while it lasts—you reckon it a four days' journey, do you not?"

Aslak laid down what he had in his hands and looked at the older man. "I have thought the same myself, Olav, that I would go home ere long. If I shall not be leaving you in the lurch—will you then let me go before the haymaking?"

"You may be sure I will. 'Tis not my wish that you stay here as my serving-man, now that you no longer need my harbouring."

"No, no," said Aslak; "I am not that sort of man either. You know well that I will stay as long as you have use for me."

Olav shook his head. Aslak removed some scythe-blades he had been sharpening; he seemed somewhat agitated. Then he turned and faced Olav. He had a serious look: the fellow *was* handsome, his bold-featured, ruddy face was frank and honest; it was remarkable how little it was spoiled by the prominent eyes.

"If I were to come back, Olav, so soon as my father or my eldest brother can make ready to accompany me south—you can guess what it is I would have my kinsmen ask of you?"

Olav made no reply.

Aslak went on: "You can guess what our business would be with you? How would you receive us, and what answer might my father expect of you?"

"If your meaning is what I believe it to be," said Olav very low and indistinctly, "then I will tell you that you shall not trouble your kinsmen to make the long journey for naught."

Aslak gave a little start.

"Can you say that so surely, Olav—before you have heard what conditions we could offer you? 'Tis true, you might find a richer son-in-law, but you might also find a poorer. And the richest men are seldom those of best birth or repute—as times are now—unless you should look for them among those knights and nobles with whom you yourself have not cared to associate in all the time you have dwelt here at Hestviken. I come of such good kin, so old in all its branches, that I may claim on that score to be a match for your daughter, and there are not many men in Heidmark who enjoy such honour as my father."

Olav shrugged his shoulders slightly. He could not find an answer to this, offhand; it was not quite clear to his mind *why* he would not at any price marry Cecilia to a man from the Upplands.

"There is this too," said Aslak again; "it may be a good enough thing to marry one's child to wealth, but this avails little if the son-in-law be such a one as knows not how to husband his estate and improve his position. I think I may promise you this: in my hands it shall not decrease, if God do grant me health and save us from great misfortunes. Ay, now I have been with you more than half a year, and you know me."

"I say naught else but that I like you, Aslak—but that is not reason enough for giving away one's only daughter to the first man who asks for her. I know little more of you than that you have many brothers and sisters, and you yourself have said that Gunnar's lot is not an easy one—though indeed I have never heard aught but good of your house, the little I have heard of it. But 'tis another matter that, young as you are, you have already been the death of a man—and it was as an outlaw you came hither to me"— Olav felt a strange relief in every reason he found for refusing the lad. "Moreover it seems to me you are far too young to think of marriage without having asked the advice of your kinsfolk."

"I have repented and atoned for my sin," said Aslak; "and as to my having slain a man so early in life—that surely is the more reason for thinking I have learned to command myself better, so that I shall not fall into the like another time, unless I be strongly provoked. But you should be the last man to blame me for that, Olav Audunsson; nor can *you* rightly deem me too young to seek a bride. For I am full nineteen winters old—you were fifteen or sixteen, I have heard, when you took a wife by force and cut down her cousin who sought to deny her to you."

"The one case is not like the other, Aslak." Olav succeeded in speaking quite coolly. "The maid whom I took to myself was affianced to me and I to her; there was a legally binding act between her father and my father while we were yet of tender age, and afterwards her kinsmen tried to set at naught the rights of us two fatherless children. *You* will lose neither honour nor rights if you fail to win the first young maid you have cast your eyes upon, without your kinsmen so much as knowing what you have in mind.

"No, no," said Olav hotly; "your father shall never have leave to say of me that I received you when you came hither, a friendless outlaw, and then treated with you, a young lad under age, for the hand of my daughter, without even knowing whether your kinsfolk were minded to ally themselves with my house."

"You know yourself," replied Aslak coolly, " 'tis not likely my father woud be loath to see me wed the daughter of Olav Audunsson of Hestviken. I know not what you mean! Is it on account of those rumours that were abroad concerning you at the time when your marriage with Ingunn Steinfinnsdatter was at issue? So much water has flowed into the fiord since then that no man cares any more what you did or left undone in your young days—for since that time you have lived peaceably for more than twenty years and have won renown for honourable conduct in both' peace and war."

Olav felt his heart beating with terrible force. But he broke off, cold as ice: "That is well and good, Aslak—but 'tis vain for you to say more on this subject. For Cecilia I have other designs."

"Of that she knows nothing!" exclaimed Aslak hotly.

"Is it so"—Olav felt relieved at being given just cause for breaking out in anger—"that you have made bold to woo my daughter behind my back?"

"You surely do not believe that of me. Not one word have I spoken to Cecilia with which you could have found fault. But that I like her she has seen; and I have seen that she likes me—neither of us can help that, such things cannot be hid. If you would listen to us, Olav, Cecilia would give her consent without sorrow—so much I have guessed."

Olav said: "Nor will it bring so much sorrow upon either of you if I refuse to listen to your suit. The maid is but a child—and you are not so old either."

"Say you so! You yourself and her mother held fast to each other for ten years or more and would not suffer her kinsmen to part the love that was between you—I have heard you spoken of it at home, Olav, as patterns of loyalty in love!"

Olav was silent a moment. The boy's words went strangely to his heart—while at the same time he was yet more unshakably determined that he would never have Cecilia married to a man from that part of the country. Then he replied in a low and faltering voice:

"That was different, Aslak—I had a *right* to her. And we had grown up together like two berries on a twig—loved each other as brother and sister from early childhood. You two, Cecilia and you, have known each other for one winter, and there is no compact between you. So it cannot be so great a grief to either of you if you now must part."

Aslak flushed deeply. He stood for a moment with bowed head, his hand on his breast, his fingers plucking at his brooch.

"For your daughter *I* cannot answer," he then said shortly. "I—" He shrugged his shoulders, then turned on his heel and went out.

Next day he was already prepared for the road. He took it with a good grace, thanked Olav in well-chosen words for the help and friendship he had shown, and bade him farewell. He went round and took leave of all his fellows. Privily Olav kept an anxious watch on the two young people when they said farewell to each other. But they took it well: they did not look at each other, and their hands dropped with a strange slackness after they had joined them; otherwise there was no sign, for one who did not know.

Then Aslak rode away from Hestviken.

Olav continually watched his daughter in secret. But Cecilia was like her usual self, and her father tried to make himself believe that she did not regret Aslak—not much, anyway. And she was only fifteen.—Fifteen had been Ingunn's age. But that was different altogether.

He had nothing to regret. The youngest son from Yttre Dal— Cecilia Olavsdatter of Hestviken might well look for a better match than that. It was natural that she should like Aslak; she had seen so few young men, and the boy had winning ways; but she would forget him sure enough when she met others.

It had made a stir in Olav's mind, an insufferable welter of conflicting emotions, to find that there were still folk in the north who remembered his and Ingunn's love and talked about it. As a pattern.— And rumours—he knew not what sort of rumours they might be. He had believed them both forgotten in those parts, both himself and her. Here none remembered Ingunn save himself alone, and he no longer remembered her so well that he thought of her often; it was only that he knew of all that had been, that he was aware of the origin of all that had befallen him.

Sin and sorrow and shame, and, beneath it all, the memories of a sweetness which might well up as water wells up over the ice

and flood his whole soul whenever a break was made in the crust
of his peace of mind.—And there in the north all this lived among
folk as a legend, true or false. Not for anything in the world
would he resume fellowship with men who perhaps talked behind
his back of his youth's adventures.

And this merely for a young maid's fancy, which she would
surely have forgotten ere a year was out, if only none reminded
her of it. Was he to return alive to such a purgatory for the sake
of two children's childishness? Never would he consent.

2

A MONTH later Eirik Olavsson came home to Hestviken. He had
sent word in advance that he was bringing with him a friend,
Jörund Kolbeinsson from Gunnarsby, and he begged his father
to receive the guest kindly.

The sun-warmed air of the valley was charged with the scent
of hay and of lime blossoms as Eirik rode down by the side of the
Hestvik stream. At Rundmyr the hay was still lying in swaths,
dark and already somewhat spoiled, in the little meadows; around
the poor homestead stood the forest, deep and still, drinking in
the sunlight. Anki came out when he heard the horseman, shading
his eyes with his hand, and then he broke into a run, with his thin
neck stretched out, his back bent, swinging his overlong arms.
After him came the whole flock of half-naked, barelegged children, and last of all waddled Liv herself, carrying her last baby in
her arms and with the next one already under her shift; she was
so marked with age that with her chinless face she looked like a
plucked hen.

Eirik stayed in the saddle, so that they might have a good sight
of him. But when the first greetings were over, he had to dismount, and Anki looked his horse over and felt him, while Liv
sang the praises of Eirik and his companion. He had to go back to
the hut with them.

The very smell within, sour and putrid as it was, seemed grateful and familiar. The round mud hut, with no walls and a pointed
roof like a tent, was divided into two raised floors with a passage
between, and this passage was wet like a ditch of stinking mud:

one had to sit with legs drawn up. The dark hole was full of a litter of rubbish. Eirik's memories were of all that was strange and lawless: here he had lain listening, all ears, to vagabonds' tales of a life that lurked, darkly and secretly, like the slime of Liv's floor, beyond the pale of law-abiding, workaday men, in bothies and caves in summertime, on the fringe of the great farms—the life of husbandmen, townsmen, priests, as seen from the beggar's pallet. He heard of smuggling in wares banned by the King, of robbery and of secret arts, of illicit intercourse between men and women who kept company for a while and then parted, of St. Olav's feast and the consecration of churches, and of sheer heathendom, sacred stones and trees. Here he had won in gaming a silver-mounted knife, which he gave away, for he dared not keep it. And over there in the corner they had once found a dead child— the mother had overlain it in the night, and then she had simply gone her way. Liv had got rid of the corpse. Eirik had been sick with suspense—what if his father came to hear that such a thing had happened in a croft that belonged to Hestviken! It was a dire thought, but at the same time there was solace in it! It would be a sort of redress for his miserable, everlasting rebuffs—his father ought just to know what things he dared to see and hear and do at Rundmyr. As yet his father knew nothing of his defying him in this way. Even when he first misconducted himself with a woman it was more to avenge himself on his father than for anything else. Afterwards he had been sick with shame and fright when he had to creep home in the dark and steal from the storehouse the piece of meat he had promised her; and he knew not which was the stronger, his remorse or a kind of joy that he had ventured to do a thing at which his father would be beside himself with wrath— if he knew of it.

Eirik picked the flies out of the old wooden bowl and drank. The milk was villainously sour and acrid, but it had the familiar taste that was proper to Liv's cabin. After that he sat with his knees drawn up and his hands clasped about them, listening to the talk of Anki and Liv: ay, they were well off, now that Cecilia and Bothild ruled the house; nay, Olav himself never had a hand in it, either when Mærta refused them or when his daughter gave. In-terwoven with their talk came news of deaths and births and feast-ings throughout the countryside, of Hestviken and the ravages of the Swedes, so far as these things had affected their life.

Eirik listened to them with half an ear. Rather sleepily he allowed his memories to drift through his mind, wondering with a faint smile what was to come now. He had buffeted about the world so long that he felt old and invulnerable. Outside the door the sun shone upon rock and mossy meadow; lower down the bog-holes glistened among the osier thickets, and behind him rose the dark wall of the spruce forest. It was *his* land and *his* forest, the cabin here was his, and these people were his: his heart warmed toward them in all their wretchedness of body and soul. He would be good to them, for they had been true to him when he was a child.

Jörund Rypa called to him from outside—he lay taking his ease in the grass, had refused to enter the foul hut. Anki and Liv and their whole flock of children followed at Eirik's heels as he came out.

The millstream trickled, narrow and shrunken, among the rocks. Eirik recognized pool after pool where he used to take trout. The sheeny green flies that darted hither and thither under the overhanging foliage might have been the same as of old, and the same tufts of setwall and clusters of bluebells were to be found as he remembered them. He rode past one meadow after another; in some places the haycocks were still out. The scent was overpowering; screes and bluffs were covered with lime trees that clung fast to the cliff with their honey-coloured bunches of blossom showing beneath the dark overlapping leaves. Where a tongue of the forest intruded on the bridle-path, the shingles-grass [1] carpeted the whole ground with little pale-pink bells.

There was the little overhanging rock under which he had found thunderbolts lying in the sand—Lapps' arrows his father had called them. He forded the stream near its mouth and rode out of the thicket, and there lay the old creek before him, glittering in the sun. On the north the Bull rose with the reflection of the water like a luminous net on its rusty, smooth-worn cliff; on the south side the land sloped upward, meadows already cut and bright, waving cornfields under the steep black wall of the Horse, and against the blue summer sky the roofs of the manor showed up on the knee of the hill, below the crag. Smoke whirled above the roofs up there; outside there was a glimpse of the fiord, dark

[1] *Linnæa borealis*—reputed to be a cure for shingles.

blue in the fair-weather breeze. Every stone of the path and every straw in the fields was his and he loved it.

There stood the bath-house, a little apart, and the great barn above it. He rode up the steep little bend that was so hard to get round with a loaded sledge when there was no snow on the ground. And now the horses' hoofs were striking against the bare rock of the courtyard.

From the door of the living-room came his father, followed by his sister. His father was in holiday dress, a green kirtle reaching to the feet with a silver belt about his waist; he went to meet his son, erect and dignified. He was freshly shaved and combed, and about his square-cut, stone-grey face with its bloodshot, pale-blue eyes, a wealth of hair lay curled. It was now quite grey, with pale-yellow strands floating here and there in the softly waving locks. Eirik had always pictured to himself God the Father Almighty in his father's likeness.

He was the handsomest and manliest man in the world. He was that still, though his head had grown grey and the right side of his face seemed driven in and the cheek was wrinkled and furrowed all over by the great scar. The two young men sprang from their horses; Eirik took his father's outstretched hand and kissed it.

Then Olav greeted Jörund and bade him welcome.

Cecilia came forward. She bore the old drinking-horn in both hands, and she too was in festival attire with her flowing hair bright about her grave little face. She stood there in doubt, looking from one young man to the other, when her father gave a nod: she must offer it first to the son of the house.

A wave as of the final, perfect joy came over Eirik—this was his sister! Young and erect, fair and fresh and pure as the noble damsels he had never been able to approach—here was one, the fairest, the brightest of all high-born maids, meeting him at the door of his home; and she was his own sister.

"Our guest first, sister mine," said Eirik joyfully, and Cecilia greeted Jörund and drank to him.

Indoors a fire had been lighted on the hearth; the flame played palely in the sunshine that made its way through the smoke-vent and turned the smoke blue under the rafters. The floor was thickly strewn with leaves and flowers; on the northern bed, which had been Eirik's when he was a boy, a new red and yellow coverlet had been spread over the skins. The table was laid as for a banquet, and on each side of Olav's high seat were set the two silver-mounted griffin's claws from which he and Jörund were to drink; never before had Eirik been allowed to drink from these horns.

After sunset they sat on the lookout rock, the three young people. Eirik lay in the heather, in a little dry hollow among the rocks; his sister sat higher up, straight in the back, with her little, short hands folded in her lap. With quiet delight Eirik listened to her talk—she was sparing of words and judicious beyond her years.

It was dead calm; the ripples gently licked the base of the cliff. The sky was perfectly clear but for some strips of red-tinged cloud down in the south-west. A flood of light from the fiord and the pale vault of heaven shone upon his sister's white face, as she turned it upward to see if any stars were visible tonight.

Jörund sat a little apart. He too was unusually silent this evening; he listened to the others' talk and looked at Cecilia.

Nay, said Cecilia, it was on Bothild that most of the household duties fell, Bothild was a far better housewife. And she had left everything in such good order that it was easy for Cecilia to work single-handed for a time. 'Twas always so that Signe Arnesdatter took one of them with her when she went to visit her married children, and this time it was Bothild who was to go—nay, she would not be home for a good while yet; Helga did not expect to be brought to bed before St. Margaret's Mass [2] or thereabouts, and Signe always made a long stay with that daughter.

Nay, Bothild was not yet betrothed, but no doubt their father would soon look about for a husband for her. And Bothild might well look to make a good match; she had inherited not a few chattels from her aunt, and Olav would add to her dowry, and with her gifts and her goodness, and her beauty—ah, beauty! There were not many maidens hereabout who were so fair as Bothild Asgersdatter, so said all the countryside. Her hair was fine as silk, and so long and thick "she can scarce comb it herself; I do that for her; we are wont to plait each other's hair."

Eirik lay smiling to himself from pure joy. He rejoiced too that Jörund could see what his ancestral home was like: a great manor and a house of gentlefolk, maintained in lordly fashion—but after the old usage; the houses were small and old, here were no new-

[2] July 20.

fangled courtiers' ways, but it was the more dignified on that account. Such things might be suitable for the new families who had risen from a poor estate, but there was no need of them here at Hestviken; Olav Audunsson and his children had no need of ostentation.

Eirik saw his father come out of the stable in the yard below. Olav stopped, looked up at the rock where the young people were sitting, but went indoors without calling to them or saying anything.

Cecilia, however, rose at once. "I am sure Father thinks 'tis time we go in and go to bed. And you may well be tired too, brother."

Eirik awoke next morning to the sound of bells and lowing—leaped up, into his clothes, and out.

The sun had just risen above the ridge in the north-east; it shone in splendour upon the green that clung fast to the clefts of the rock. Outside, the sea lay bright and smooth as a mirror; over the meadows at the entrance to the valley lay long shadows of trees and bushes in the morning sunlight.

The feeble warmth of the beams was grateful in the early coolness. Eirik came out in time to see the last of the cattle disappear into the woods. Cecilia stood by the gate, fastening the hasp of withy and calling to the herdsmen. Now she came back, walking along the high balk of the cornfield, for she was barefooted and the path was muddy. She was dressed like a working-woman, in an old blue smock she had kilted up to her knees, and her feet were red with cold in the dewy grass.

"Are *you* up already?" she greeted her brother. Ay, she was always early up: "the first morning hours are the busiest." There was a smell of the byre about her, and her white arms were soiled from milking; the wrists were as round as if they had been turned in a lathe. The two stiff plaits that hung over her bosom were short and thick, and ruffled in the knots, so curly was her hair.

Cecilia had to go off to the bleaching-ground; Eirik sat on the step of the barn and watched her laying out her linen. She went into the dairy and spoke to Ragna, and he stood at the door meanwhile—she was so brisk and prompt in all that she did.

Her brother followed at her heels, sitting on the threshold of the women's house while she washed herself in the water-butt outside and rinsed her feet. She stepped past him over the threshold and called from within: would he come in and see the room?

The women's bower was the largest room in the manor; with its walls of fresh yellow logs it was much finer than the dark hall, and its furniture was richly carved; the beam from which the pot hung over the hearth ended in a wild, gaping horse's head. Along the wall stood weaving-frames, reels of yarn, and chests; over the crossbeams hung folded blankets and cushions for the benches. Cecilia, who had now put on shoes and stockings, took down the best of them to show him.

From a carved box his sister fetched a stone jar and a little silver goblet, filled it, and drank to her brother.

"Father gave us this last year—we were to have it, he said, in case one day we might have to receive a guest. And now you are the first."

"Thanks! It was good wine too."

"But strong? We were all drunken on it one evening last autumn, Bothild and I and the maids." She looked up at her brother with a bashful little laugh, as though unused to tell strangers of her own affairs. "There was one whose name was Yngvild, she is not here any more; 'twas she who thought of it—we danced in here. There were to be games on the green by the shore to the northward, and they would have had us with them when they came down to take boat, Gaute Sigurdsson and Jon Tasall and a few more; but Father said no, though there were two from Rynjul among them—'twas of no use. Yngvild was angry; she said Father kept us stricter than Lady Groa keeps the children who are sent to her convent to be taught. So she persuaded us to lay aside our sewing, and we danced in here, and then we drank of the wine that was meant for our guests."

"What said Father to that?" Eirik smiled. He felt nothing beyond his bright new-born love for this sweet young sister. Every word she spoke and every gesture she made filled his soul with joy.

"Father? He said nothing, as you may well guess. But two days after, he came and ordered us to move into the hall and sleep in the upper chamber there; 'twas too unsafe for young maids to sleep alone in a bower that lay so near the shore. Until then we had lived here night and day. And next time Yngvild offered to oppose him, he answered that 'twas best she went home to her own father, for belike she would obey him."

"Is he so strict with you, Father?"

Cecilia had put on her kirtle; it was red, handsomely embroidered. She fastened her belt about her and hung on its scissors and knife, purse and bunch of keys. The little barefooted dairymaid was now a fine young franklin's daughter.

"Strict he is, in that he holds so firmly to customs and manners as they were observed in old time—we may not open our mouths or move our eyes when strangers are present. But he bears us goodwill withal." She took out of her chest and spread on the bed a sleeveless, low-necked kirtle of brown velvet, embroidered with rings and crosses of yellow silk. The long-sleeved shift that belonged to it was of red silk and had gilt hooks to fasten it over the bosom. "Such dresses he gave both to Bothild and me—'twas after he had refused us leave to go into Oslo to see the damsels' wedding with the Swedish dukes. Meseems 'tis high time we came to town one day—to the fair or to Halvard's Vigil. But father will not have it."

"Have you never been up to Oslo?"

Cecilia shook her head and wrapped her finery in its covering of homespun cloth. "God knows when we shall have a chance to wear these trappings."

"That will come when we are to drink your betrothal ale."

Cecilia's face changed in an instant; she turned to her chest and put away her finery. "I know naught of that."

The beauty and charm of his sister went to Eirik's head like a slight intoxication. He did not know how it was he had never thought of *her* in all these years; had he done so, he would surely have kept himself from one thing and another, from drinking and gaming, brawling, wenching, and debauchery. He regretted now that he had had so little thought of curbing himself—he had never thought of it—had yielded to every temptation and obeyed the fancy of the moment. Thus he had been carried away by what soon became habit, and he got the reputation of being a man of immoral ways, one who haunted taverns and worse places. Nor was this reputation undeserved. But the result was that he enjoyed no more respect than other hired servants, a man-at-arms in his lord's retinue.

Now that it was too late, he saw that he ought to have followed his father's advice; then he could have asserted himself so that

none would ever forget he was the son of Olav of Hestviken. If
he had kept himself more from dice and ale-houses, bought himself clothes and arms instead, kept his own horse—and then he
should have stayed indoors, in the company of older men of good
report, sat still and modestly listened to their talk. Then he might
also have been received in the ladies' hall, where high-born damsels
sat; he might have borne them company to the dance and to mass.

He had kept himself a stranger to all such women, dreaming of
them, in pale, harmless dreams. But he was too shy in their presence, and far too lazy and irresolute to compel himself to break
with his evil habits.

Yet in a way he did not *believe* they were so pure and grand
as he liked to *think* they were. Jörund told a different tale, and he
was just as welcome in their bower as in other places. And Jörund
used to say that he dallied with them freely and boldly. There
was only one thing they were afraid of, he sneered—short of that
they liked a man to handle them somewhat rudely.

This was one of the things Eirik disliked in his friend—that he
could speak thus of the damsels of his own estate. It took away
Eirik's desire to try his fortune there—he did not realize that he
was unwilling to hazard his own good opinion of good women.
There were plenty of the other sort for other uses.

But the truth was that every maid would gladly have married
Jörund—he never let people forget who he was: one of the sons
of Gunnarsby, and that he had only taken service in a lord's retinue
in order to see something of the world before settling down at
home on his own estate. His morals were no better than Eirik
Olavsson's, he was no more squeamish in the choice of those he
drank with, and at the sight of dice and gaming-tables he went
clean mad—but luck was with him more often than not. Nevertheless no one ever forgot that Jörund was no less a man than any
of the King's body-guard, for all that he had chosen to serve a lord
whose followers enjoyed a freer life.—But then it was true that
Jörund had not left home at enmity with his kinsfolk.

At the bottom of Eirik's mind lay the thought that one day he
would break with this retainer's life. One day he would return to
his ancestral home, be reconciled to his father, recover his position
as the heir of Hestviken. And then no doubt it would be time to
marry—it would be for his father to find a suitable bride for him.

. . .

Eirik had been on a ride round the parish, had visited his kinswoman Una Arnesdatter and met others of his acquaintance. In the evening Eirik mentioned at home that on the next day there would be dancing on the green by the shore to the northward, where young people from north and south were sometimes wont to assemble.

"Cecilia may go with us to the games, may she not?"

Olav answered: "They are unused to taking part in such gatherings, the children here. Nor can we stay up so late at home on a Saturday evening—we have a long way to church."

Eirik protested: there were many other houses that lay just as far from the church, and they could rest when they came home from mass. Olav muttered something—a refusal—and made as though he did not notice that Cecilia was looking at him.

Jörund guessed it was of no use to pursue this subject with the master of the house and took up another. But a little later Eirik asked suddenly:

"What was that, Father, that I heard from Una? She said you had that Aslak Gunnarsson from Yttre Dal here last winter—he called himself by another name, and you kept him hid, so that the Sheriff never knew you were harbouring an outlaw."

"Did he not?" said Olav with a faint smile.

"One cannot say your father hid him so well as that," said old Tore laughing. "Reidulf is not fond of trouble. And since the winter of the Swedish broil I trow he is more afraid of Olav disturbing him than minded to disturb Olav."

"Nevertheless it was unmanly to fling himself upon strangers in such a case," said Eirik. "But those red-polls of Yttre Dal are like that—proud in spite of their poverty, but ready to accept help where they can find it, when they are hard pressed. I met his brother, that time I was in the Upplands, a haughty and ungracious fellow he was—"

"Then Aslak is not like him," said one of the house-carls warmly; "we were all fond of him." At this Olav interrupted the man, sent him out for something, and began to talk to Tore about a horse that had some boils under its mane.

Olav had gone down to the waterside before going to rest. As he came back he saw Cecilia standing on the lookout rock. Her father went up to her.

"You must come in now, Cecilia—'tis late."

The girl turned round to him. In the pale gleam of the summer night her father saw that her face was discomposed—the stubborn features were slackened in irresolution. But she said nothing and followed him obediently down to the houses.

Next morning, when Cecilia brought in the food, Olav said to his daughter: "You know, if you have a mind to go with them for once and listen to the dancing, I will not deny you—now that you can have your brother's company."

Cecilia looked at him rather doubtfully.

"But perhaps you have no mind to go—?"

"Oh, yes. Gladly would I be there for once," said Cecilia.

The thin new moon floated in summer whiteness in the rosy grey of the sky above Hudrheimsland as Olav rowed round the foot of the Bull. A reflection of daylight still rested on the rocky wall of the promontory. Olav rowed with cautious strokes in the evening stillness. He put in at a little cove where there was a strip of sand, drew up the boat, and made his way up through the wooded cleft in the rock.

He had bow and arrows with him, and he stole along quietly. On reaching the height, where the trees thinned out and the moss-grown rocks sloped down to the Otter Stone, he paused for a moment, but then resumed his way northward into the forest. After a while the sound of singing came up to him and the smell of smoke.

As he came out on a little knoll, he saw the fire blazing far below; beneath him he had the bay with the clear curve of its sandy beach, and higher up between the flat rocks lay the dancing-green, burned yellow by the summer sun. Around the great bonfire the chain moved in a ring, black against the flames; the dancers' feet drummed on the dry ground, and their song rang sweetly in the still evening air. Olav could not catch the words, for he did not know this ballad by heart, but he recognized the tune and knew that it was the lay of Charlemagne and Roland. The one who sang for them had a deep, warm voice; Olav wondered if it might be Eirik—he had always been singing when he was a boy. They were too far off for Olav to recognize any of the dancers in the twilight. Some were sitting down to rest outside the circle.

Olav stretched himself on the crisp bog-moss, which still felt

warm from the heat of the sun. The ballads were wafted up to
him, and the sound of the tramping in time to the song:

It was dum-dum dumdelideia
dum-dum dumdelidei—

Now and again he heard the crackling sound of the fire, and,
far below, the fiord murmured and lapped against the rocks. The
moon had gone down long ago; above him the summer night grew
dark. Nor were there many stars out tonight—it was already a
little past midsummer.

At last the man rose, picked up his bow and arrows, and walked
quietly back, down through the forest.

He lay in his bed within the dark closet, dozing and losing himself in a web of vague dreams, but every time he was on the point
of falling asleep, he woke up with a start. Each time it was nothing, only a feeling that he had been waked by something from
without. But there was no one in the hearth-room, and it was
growing lighter and lighter—they had forgotten to close the
smoke-vent.

At last he heard them in the yard—they were taking leave of
the other young people who were going farther inland. Then his
own folk came in. From the closet Olav could hear them talking
and yawning as the men took off their footgear. Cecilia had not
gone up; once or twice she gave a little laugh.

" 'Tis morning already," her father heard her say. "In three
hours we must ride away to church. 'Tis not worth while to go up
to the loft—I think I will lie down in here."

There was a slight creaking in the south bed as she got up into
it, then came the louder sound of the men getting into the other.
A few words passed between them. Cecilia's voice grew faint with
sleepiness, then she left off answering, and soon after, one of the
men began to snore.

Olav got up after a while; he would go into the hearth-room and
close the vent. In the north bed he saw the heads of the young
men; they had rolled the coverlet about them.

Cecilia was asleep in the other bed; she lay right on her back,
her delicate, flower-like face showed white among the masses of
loosened hair. Olav was reminded of her mother, who had lain

thus, in the same bed, year after year, flung down like a corpse, paralysed to the waist, slowly withering to death.

But the sleeping child was radiant with health. She was white in the face, but it was fresh and round as pearls; a little stubborn and self-willed she looked, even when asleep, and the long, pale lashes cast a shadow on the rounded cheeks. The short, straight nose and the broad curve of the chin betokened obstinacy or steadfastness—one could not say which it was at her age.

One of the hands hung down over the side of the bed—it looked uncomfortable. Olav cautiously raised it and laid it on her bosom. Her breasts were rounded firmly and delicately under the red woollen gown, making a wide gape at the opening and showing an embroidered kerchief under the silver lacing. She had outgrown this gown in the sleeves too—they did not reach nearly to her wrists.

Olav stood looking at his daughter till he felt himself shivering in the chilly morning air with only a cloak about him. He bent down and made the sign of the cross over her. Then he picked up the little red shoes; they were dark with wet from the water in the bottom of the boat—her father set them on the edge of the cold hearth.

3

EIRIK and Jörund went much abroad to feastings and merrymakings and often Cecilia was with them; Olav had nothing to say to it.

The two friends were handsome men; at any rate they made a handsome pair when they went about together; they brought life and gaiety with them, and they were well liked. When folk met Olav they said he might feel honoured in his son.

Now that he had stopped growing, Eirik was very tall, long and big of limb, but shapely, narrow in the hips and thin about the waist, though the upper part of his body seemed somewhat too broad and heavy—he had grown so broad-shouldered that he stooped a little, so that folk said in jest that he was rather top-heavy—but his head was small in comparison.

He had grown very dark of hair and complexion, and he had

a long, narrow face; his features were not so handsome: the nose
hooked, or rather indented, first between the eyes, and then another dent over the bridge; the mouth was so big and the upper
jaw so sharply curved that his great white teeth made one think
of a horse's mouth; the long, flat chin lacked roundness. But he
had such matchless eyes, said folk—Eirik's eyes were large and
light brown and seemed full of an inner light. And then he had
youth, so that he passed for a handsome young man, even if his
features might have been better.

Jörund Rypa was such as most call handsome, tall and well
grown, with smooth flaxen hair, blue eyes, a ruddy face, and a
large, rather pointed nose, a fresh, rather thick-lipped mouth. He
was quiet and retiring enough among the neighbours here—Eirik
was far more winning in his ways. So the one was thought handsome because he was lively, and the other's good looks were held
to excuse his being somewhat indolent or haughty.

It was this subdued manner of Jörund's that made Olav like him,
so long as he was in the room with him. But if he chanced to
think of Jörund Rypa when he no longer had him before his eyes,
Olav felt a profound, obscure ill will toward his son's friend.

With unreasonable clarity he recalled an ugly little act he had
seen this man do when he was a boy—one day when he and some
other lads were snowballing here in the yard; Jörund had then
behaved disloyally to Eirik. It was a small thing to lay so much
stress on, a child's trick during a children's game; but at the time
it had revolted Olav like the blackest treason, and the impression
had remained with him, so that he could not think of Jörund
without antipathy.

But when he was in Jörund's company this feeling vanished
almost entirely—he could see the injustice of laying a long-past
boyish trick to the charge of this grown man. Jörund conducted
himself becomingly, was quiet in his manner, looked folk frankly
in the face, and never spoke without need. Olav saw therefore that
he was unjust in thinking of the young man as though there were
something underhand about him, for there *was* nothing underhand
about Jörund Rypa, either in his speech or in his face or in his eyes.

One day Olav chanced to hear a scrap of talk between brother
and sister. He was busy in the smithy when Eirik came to the
door with Cecilia. They stopped outside.

"—every maid would be glad to be married to Jörund Kolbeins-son," said Eirik.

"Then 'twill not be hard for him to find a match."

"But how comes it, sister, that *you* like not Jörund?"

"I never said that I like him not," replied Cecilia.

"You said so but now, when I asked you."

" 'Tis not to say I like him *not*"—there was a laugh in Cecilia's voice—"if I answer no when you ask me do I *like* your friend!"

"But is it not one and the same thing? If you do not like him, then surely you like him *not*?"

"No, 'tis *not* the same!" The girl was laughing now; Olav heard her run on down the field. Eirik opened the door and came in, smiling at his sister's words.

This new, exhilarating fondness for his sister filled Eirik's heart entirely. It was as though all his childhood's unrequited affection for his father, his anxious and burning passion for Hestviken, had dissolved in the sunny warmth and peaceful well-being of these summer days; the evil in it ran away, and the good was left behind, remoulded as a warm and golden joy in this little sister's winning brightness and pert girlish charm. He followed her about at home, he had to have her with him whenever he went abroad, he lavished gifts on her—the best jewels and clothes he possessed, which he had never thought to part with.

He rejoiced in everything wherever he went over his father's land—his love for this land, which was to be always his, was increased by a vague memory of his strange thought, as a child, that he might lose it in the end. It was the same as with Hestviken itself when the sun returned after a long spell of bad weather: never did the fields and the manor gleam with so bright a glance as then.

It was almost the same with his love for his father. It had been the groundwork of Eirik's whole life that no man in the world was like his father; the only change was that he no longer *thought* about it. He no longer took it to heart that his father was taciturn and could by no means be called a man of good cheer—they were now friends in spite of that. Eirik did not see that it harmed any-one if his father was gloomy and cross; he himself had now grown out of the shadow that Olav cast around him.

He took his ease and disported himself in the glory of his own youth. His sister had grown into a winsome maid; he could share his joy in life with her. He had his best friend with him, and the three together enjoyed the happiness that each day brought.

Thus it was that he had already half formed the thought that Jörund spoke one evening when the two were out fishing in the fiord.

"I have been thinking, Eirik—what if we two bound our friendship in a closer tie? Think you Olav would receive it well if I let my kinsfolk ask for the hand of your sister?"

"You know right well," replied Eirik gladly, "Father could but esteem so good an offer—and I know none to whom I would so gladly see her given, dear as I hold her; never would I advise her betrothal to a lesser man than you. And Father sets great store by my advice—" No sooner had he said it than Eirik believed his own words.

From that time it was a settled matter in Eirik's mind that Jörund and he were to be brothers-in-law. And unconsciously he began from that moment to regard his friend in a slightly different light.

It escaped him altogether that, though he had loved Jörund Rypa ever since he first knew him as a child, it was nevertheless true that he had never entirely liked him, nor had he ever trusted Jörund so well as not to have a care—how far he might venture with him. Unsure as Eirik himself had been in everything, he was drawn to the other boy, who was so unshakably sure. But all the time he had known that what made Jörund so secure was that he was firmly resolved to keep himself safe, at whatever cost to others. Jörund Rypa would neither blink nor waver if it came to leaving a friend in the lurch. Jörund's was not a timid nature, nor was he afraid of how folk might judge him.

But this power of Jörund's of being sufficient to himself had clean bewitched Eirik when they were boys. And when Jörund Rypa turned up in Ragnvald Torvaldsson's following, Eirik had pressed himself upon him, claiming the right to call himself Jörund's best friend from childhood. There was no one in the company with whom he was better friends than another in spite of all his efforts to please his comrades; they liked him well enough—he was ready to do them a turn, brave, a daredevil in many ways, though in other things he would show himself strangely and unexpectedly petty-minded. But they laughed a little at him too—he was altogether too credulous for them, and he made too great demands on plain folk's credulity when he told a story.

Jörund accepted the position of Eirik's best friend, and Eirik did not haggle about the price; in the course of time he had had more than once to serve as a cat's-paw to Jörund. But Jörund affected complete ignorance when Eirik took the blame for the other's wrongdoing, and at the sight of his friend's innocent, blue-eyed look Eirik himself believed in Jörund's good faith—it would be unworthy to think otherwise. He was so good-natured in his ways, was Jörund, with his genial voice and his prompt smile, when Eirik talked nonsense to him. Careless he was in many ways, to the downright alarm of Eirik—for Eirik himself was scrupulous in the performance of his duty, though he was too short of memory to do it well always, and he was hurt at any disparaging word of his conduct. Jörund knew how to take care of himself better than Eirik liked or would have admitted to be the case; Jörund spoke of women in coarser terms than Eirik could have brought himself to use even of the loose wenches who were all he yet knew. But in spite of all this, Eirik loved Jörund.

In this way they had now kept fellowship for several years. Now and again they had been parted, for Eirik from time to time would take himself off and seek service with another lord; but it always ended in his coming back to Sir Ragnvald, with whom Jörund stayed.

There was but one thing about his friend which Eirik could never put up with, and that was Jörund's singing. Jörund comported himself well in a dance, and he had a powerful voice, so that he often led the dance; that was his pride. But he did not sing true. Eirik himself had a fine ear for music, and his singing voice was not so full as his friend's, but warm and soft—and when Jörund broke into a ballad, Eirik felt quite sick with shame on his friend's behalf.

The very next day Eirik told Olav that Jörund seemed to have thoughts of Cecilia. The two men were walking together across the ridge to Saltviken.

Olav listened to his son in silence and walked on without answering.

"You may be sure," Eirik went on, "that Jörund is a man who is attended by good fortune. And you must have heard a good report of the house of Gunnarsby—"

"I know they are called rich." Olav walked a few paces in silence. "Have you been there—at Gunnarsby?"

At once it struck Eirik that this was a thing Jörund might well have done—asked him to bear him company some time or other when he went home to see his kinsfolk. It gave him a little pang: "It never happened that I was able, when Jörund wished to have me home with him."

"What do *you* think of the man *himself*?" asked Olav. "Is he such a one that you would deem Cecilia and her welfare safe in his hands?"

Involuntarily the old disquietude returned, vague and distant. But he had thought all this over, Jörund's faults were such as a man may lay aside when he sets up house; and if they were to be brothers-in-law they must be loyal to each other. So Eirik answered yes, and began to sing Jörund's praises loudly—cool-headed he was, good-natured, cheerful, mettlesome—his father had seen that for himself.

"Ay, I have seen naught but good in him." Olav heaved a sigh. They walked on in silence. Then the father said:

"I shall speak with Baard—ask what he knows. Baard must be able to find out about these folks; he has kinsmen of his own in that part. Till then I look to hear no more said of the matter. Jörund is our guest and he must know enough of good manners not to bring forward his suit again before his brothers can take it up."

"You may be sure of that." Eirik was at once mortally afraid lest Jörund should upset the whole plan, if he gave any hint of it in speaking to his father, who insisted so strictly that all should proceed in seemly fashion. Or that he might scare away Cecilia if he approached her with the rather rough and aggressive good humour with which Eirik had seen him win the favour of other maids. But Cecilia would not like such ways, he saw that at once; she had been brought up by this father and she had far too much of both pride and modesty. He would have to speak of this to Jörund.

· · ·

The day before Laurence-mass,[3] Eirik had been on an errand up the fiord. It was a dead calm as he rowed homeward—in the north and east heat clouds with gleaming edges surged up over the hills; their reflection darkened the pale blue of the fiord and gave the water a leaden hue, while the patches of sunlight beyond were bright as silver. Eirik rowed fast—he had his best coat on and was trying to be home before the storm burst. It was warm; the sun scorched him, and the reflection on the water dazzled his eyes.

He looked over his shoulder—down in the south the sky was clear and blue, and the sea was all aglitter. Hestviken lay in sunshine—the fields of ripe corn and those which had been already cut, where the corn stood in shooks among the stubble, showed white amidst all the green. Eirik thought he would have to see to getting in all that was nearly dry, in any case—his father and Tore were not at home. He remembered storms that had threshed out the sheaves over the ground.

The sky was blue-black over toward Oslo, and the thunder rolled far away—it looked as if perhaps the storm would pass farther north. From the quay Eirik took the path by the side of the "good acre"; he leaped the fence, felt the sheaves and tore off a handful of the white barley, rubbed it between his hands and stuffed the sweet grains into his mouth. Then he heard someone singing above, on the lookout rock—a soft, veiled female voice. It could not be Cecilia, she had no voice for singing.

Eirik went up to see. On the rock lay a strange young woman; she lay with her back to him, and her face turned toward the sea. Her heavy tresses, dark with wet, were spread over the rock to dry. As she lay resting at full length on her side, with one hip raised, there was something about her that stirred Eirik's senses, so that he came to a standstill, as though he had taken the wrong track.

In indolent repose the woman lay humming to herself as she gazed into the sunlight over the fiord. Then it struck Eirik who she must be. He came toward her.

On hearing footsteps on the rock she turned and rose on her knees. Eirik saw that her figure was full in all its outlines, but without firmness, as though overripe for a young maid, and when she rose to her feet, her movements were heavy and lacked elasticity. She flushed deeply as she looked up at him with a hesitating,

[3] August 10.

evasive look of her great dark eyes, while her hands struggled to throw her heavy, dark hair back over her shoulders.

Eirik went up to her and gave her his hand.

"Have you come home now, Bothild? Welcome!"

She did not return the pressure of his hand, but withdrew hers quickly and shyly; she stood with bent head, looking down, and her voice was toneless and veiled.

Eirik himself felt confused and heavy at heart because he had been so suddenly disquieted at the sight of this girl—her doubtful attitude, her drooping head, and her hushed voice were enough to warn him that the days of their innocent and carefree life together were gone. Bothild's startled air as she stood with her shoulders rounded, full-bosomed and broad of hip, the strong scent of her hair, wet with sea-water—it seemed as though both his conscience and hers were already darkened.

They said a few words about her journey and then spoke of the weather, which looked so threatening. Eirik told her he meant to get in what he could of the corn before the storm burst. Bothild whispered yes—if it did not come before, they would have it at night. Now and then there was a faint blink of lightning far to the north, followed by a distant rumble.

Eirik stole glances at her as they walked side by side toward the manor. She was tall, but did not hold herself erect; her hair was very thick and long, but seemed stiff now from the sea-water. But her face was fair, round, and white, with red roses in her cheeks; she had a broad forehead, smooth and white; black, curved eyebrows; and her dark-blue eyes looked up with a covert, side-long glance under thick white lashes; her mouth was big, her chin small and round as an apple. Once she smiled at something he said, and then he saw that she had small short teeth with gaps between them, like a child's milk teeth, and she showed her gums as she smiled—he felt he would like to take and kiss her, but roughly, without kindness.

He got in all the corn off the "good acre" that afternoon; the storm passed round to the north over the fiord, but did not reach Hestviken. It was already dark outside and distant lightnings flashed in the evening sky; between the claps of thunder the still-ness of the fiord seemed uncannily hushed beneath the cliffs in the close evening air of late summer. The men went indoors. Bothild brought in supper, hanging her head, as in all she did. But it was easy to see that Cecilia was delighted to have her foster-sister back again. This added to the touch of hostility that was part of Eirik's uneasy feeling toward Bothild; she was not a seemly play-mate for his sister, he thought—a woman who excited his desire in this way.

In the course of the night he was awakened by the crash of thunder; now the rain was pouring down: it drummed dully on the turf of the roof, ran off and splashed on the rocky floor of the yard, streamed over the foliage of the trees. From one corner of the smoke-vent it ran down into the room. The vivid flashes lighted up chinks in the wall at the end of the house; the logs were no longer weather-tight after the long drought. And clap after clap of thunder crashed and rattled right above the houses.

Eirik remembered Bothild the moment he woke—now she would be lying in the loft above the closet. Jörund slept like a stone on the inside of the bed, against the wall; Eirik lay outside. He was tempted to get up and go to the ladder—call up to hear if the girls were also awake; perhaps they would be frightened by the storm. But he lay where he was.

He tried to think of other things—of the fields farther up the valley, and the corn that stood there ready for the sickle; how would it fare in this weather? He could not remember that he had noticed Bothild Asgersdatter when he was last at home, the year of the Swedish troubles—it must be three years ago now. Cecilia was only a child at that time, his father was with Ivar Jonsson in Sweden, Bothild was helping her aunt in the housework; both the girls did so. He had not seen much of them, nor had he heeded them greatly.

He could not tell what had put it into his head that Bothild was not a pure maiden like Cecilia.

4

For Eirik there was an end of the peaceful home life and the pure, innocent summer days. They were now a company of four young people—for it never occurred to Cecilia to go anywhere without her sister. But to Eirik's fevered senses it seemed that Bothild clung

to the younger girl. She was always a little in the rear, dropping
behind with her indolent tongue and voluptuous gestures and her
everlasting shy and stolen sidelong glances—it was at himself they
were aimed, and he felt them as if she had touched him with her
hand; but as soon as he looked at her, her eyes were turned away.
It roused a kind of fury in the man—that she would never leave
him in peace. He was ashamed of his own thoughts—here he was
at home, with his father and his sister, but through Bothild's fault
he was harried and beset with desire.

He felt inclined to deal harshly and cruelly with her when he
got her in his power—to send her away from him in tears and
overcome. It was a senseless whim, this spiteful prompting which
sprang from an unknown depth in his soul—the blind and witless
caprice of a master who is angry with a slave because he is irritated by the slave's frightened looks and humble efforts to conceal his sorrow.

For it was of a thrall she reminded him, a woman captive. Even
the two thick plaits she wore hanging over her full, rather flaccid
bosom made him think of chains; they reached nearly to her knees,
and their weight seemed to force her head forward and give her
a stoop in walking. And Bothild's hair was not black and stiff as
he had thought at first, when he saw it wet; it had a soft brown
hue, with a tinge of red, and went well with her red and white
complexion and her dark-blue eyes. But not even her fairness
sufficed to soften Eirik's mind toward her.

He scarcely spoke to her—it was only in his thoughts, all this
of Bothild. To do anything to a woman who lived in his father's
house was not to be thought of. Besides, he was afraid of his father; now that the peace and purity within him had been bemired,
his childhood's dread of his father was also reawakened in full
force.

Either Olav and Cecilia were ignorant that anything was passing
in secret between Eirik and Bothild Asgersdatter, or they mis-
interpreted what they saw—thought that the two disliked each
other, or were shy of each other. In any case neither the father
nor the sister showed any sign that they thought about the matter.

Jörund had quickly guessed what was wrong with Eirik, but
he contented himself with hinting at it once or twice in jest.

"I cannot make out," he said one day, with the sneering smile that Eirik disliked, "why you have such a mighty fancy to her. She sweats so."

Another time he said—it was one evening after they were in bed: "'Tis a great pity you cannot have her for a leman, since Olav is her guardian—and she cannot be rich enough for you to think of marrying her!"

Eirik was silent, overwhelmed with agitation. Marry *her*—she was the last woman in the world he would take to wife! 'Twas not *thus* he had thought of Bothild.

Jörund made ready for his departure—he was to be home for the Nativity of Mary.[4] Baard of Skikkjustad had made inquiries about Jörund. He must be reckoned a good match, said Baard. There was wealth at Gunnarsby, and Gunhild Rypa's sons might look to inherit more; Kolbein had been like a chief in those parts and a man held in honour. The sons who were now in possession of the manor were not so well liked, but what folk had to say of them was for the most part such envious talk as is always heard when rich men stand on their rights. The two elder brothers were married to daughters of high-born men of good repute—"so I will not seek to dissuade you from listening to them, if in other ways you hold Jörund to be worthy your alliance," said Baard to Olav.

Olav then let fall a few words to Eirik: if Jörund was so minded, and his kinsmen would consider the matter, there would be no harm in discussing it.

When it came to the point, Eirik was a little dispirited. He did not know why, but now he thought all at once that there was no such hurry in getting Cecilia married. She was not much more than a child, his good little sister.

One morning Cecilia said to her father that now she and Bothild must move out and sleep in the women's house awhile—they had to repair the winter clothing for the folk of the manor and they would be working till late at night.

Before Eirik went to bed that evening, he took out the clothes he was to wear next morning on the fiord—Olav and the house-carls were going out after mackerel at dawn. Then he saw that the woollen shirt he meant to put on was ragged at the elbows. Eirik took the shirt and went out to ask his sister to mend it—the

4 September 8.

maids were still up, he had heard, as he went by their door just now.

It was pitch-dark in the anteroom. On the other side of the thin boarding he heard his sister clattering with chests and boxes; she called to Bothild to open, as Eirik knocked at the door of the room.

Then the door was opened, and the room was light behind her. The dark female figure in the doorway seemed to collapse with fright when she saw who stood outside. In her toneless whisper she said that Cecilia was busy turning out the clothes: "I will sew this for you." She put out her hand for the shirt.

"Come hither," Eirik bade her in a low voice, and seized her by the wrist. With a little gasp as of fear the girl obeyed: she bent her head under the lintel and let him draw her out into the anteroom. Instantly he took her in his arms and thrust her against the wall, pressed her close and searched with his lips for her face in the dark, came upon her plaits and found the soft, ice-cold rounding of her cheek. With his kisses he nailed her head, which struggled to be free, against the wall.

"Come with me," he whispered; "come out with me—"

She gulped with terror, he heard her teeth chattering and her soft, cold hands struggled in vain; she tried to defend herself, but had no strength. Eirik took both her hands in one of his and pressed them, as though he would squeeze the blood out under the roots of her nails. So terrified was she that Eirik scarcely knew whether she understood a word of his wild and shameless whispering—

Then Olav called through the outer door. They had not heard him coming. He called for Cecilia. Eirik let go of Bothild—he himself was trembling—as Cecilia came to the inner door.

"Are you two *here*?" she asked in surprise, and then spoke past them: "What is it, Father?"

Olav asked for the little bucket he had brought up the week before to be cleaned.

"Inga has surely forgotten it—I will find another for you, Father."

She went back for a lantern and came out again. "Have you been quarrelling?" she asked, half smiling, as the light fell on the faces of the two in the anteroom. Then she ran off.

Eirik heard the sound of his father's iron-shod heels die away on the rocks of the yard. He had caught a glimpse of Bothild's face, deadly pale, as she slunk through the door of the room. Now he went and looked in.

She was crouching on her knees over a chest of clothes, her head sunk in her clasped hands. It made him furious to see her kneeling thus—as though in prayer.

"Stand up," he said, and his voice was rude and harsh, "before Cecilia comes. Do you wish *her* to find out about this?" Then he went out.

As he went down to the waterside at dawn next morning, he saw her in front of him, carrying a great box. When he reached the boat, she had taken it on board and was just returning over the gangplank. Eirik put out a hand to help her. As he touched her for a moment, her body shrank up and he saw she was dead-white in the face, but under her eyes there were deep black rings. But she often had those, it struck him—no doubt that was why her eyes looked so big.

But scarcely had Eirik stepped aboard when Olav came and told him he had better stay ashore. It might be they would stay out two days, and he half expected Reidulf, the Sheriff, to come on the morrow about a case. Olav gave Eirik orders as to what he should say and do if the Sheriff came.

Eirik stood watching the boat till it was lost in the morning mist. He could just see across the creek—the leaves of the little trees in the crevices of the rock were yellow already—he had scarcely noticed it, but here was autumn well on the way. He listened for the sound of oars in the mist; the little craft could still be seen, like a shadow. Eirik shivered a little—it was chilly—he turned to go up to the houses.

As he passed the shed he heard someone within. Instantly he halted and listened, stiff and tense—could it be she?

He stole up to the door and peeped in. Bothild stood with her back to him, taking dried fish out of a bundle. In two bounds he was upon her, throwing his arms about her from behind. He felt her body give way, as though every bone in it were dissolved; she hung powerless over his arms, which were crossed below her bosom. Then he flung her from him, so that she fell on the floor. Eirik ran to the door and barred it.

As he turned, she stood up and faced him, erect, with face

aflame. "What are you doing!" Her eyes were big and black as coal. "You act like a—you are not acting like a *man*—oh!" Bothild gave one scream, loud and shrill, and then her tears gushed out.

A chill gust passed over Eirik—the sight of the girl's anger sobered him at once. But her tears plunged him headlong into a fresh tumult—he was bewildered by a sense of shame and misfortune, and her weeping frightened him.

"Do not weep so—" he muttered in his agitation.

But Bothild continued to sob, so that the tears poured down her distorted features. Once she threw her hands before her face, but the next moment she let them drop heavily again.

"What have I *done* to you?" she cried; "what sort of man are you become?"

"Bothild!" Eirik begged, miserably. "You surely cannot think I meant it in earnest—'twas only jesting."

"Jesting!" Flashing with anger, she looked him full in the eyes. "Is that what *you* call jesting?" Then her tears got the better of her again. She wept so that she had to sit down—sank down on a chest and turned her face from him. With her forehead leaned against the wall, she now wept more quietly, in bitter lamentation.

Eirik stood still. He could not find a word to say.

At long last Bothild half turned round to him again; she heaved a long, quaking sigh. "Ah me! It was not this I had looked for, when you came home to us again."

"When I came home?" asked Eirik weakly.

"We thought you would surely come home again one day," she said almost scornfully. "We often spoke of it, Cecilia and I—" Now she was weeping again.

"Do not weep so," Eirik begged at last.

Bothild got up, passed her hands over her tear-stained face.

"Open the door for me," she bade him curtly.

Eirik did so, but did not move from the doorway.

"Stand aside," she said as before. "Let me out now!"

Eirik stepped aside. Bothild went out past him. Eirik did not move—his surprise felt like a gleam of light within him, faint at first, then growing stronger and stronger. Now he was utterly unable to understand how he could have treated her as he had done.

A little way up the hill he overtook Bothild. She stood holding dewy leaves to her tear-stained cheeks and red eyes. As he stopped before her, she charged him, with looking round: "Go—" He hesitated. Bothild said impatiently: "Go now—I cannot show myself like this, all tears—you must see that!"

Eirik made no reply, walked on.

He could not understand what had gone wrong with him. The moment the defenceless maid had turned to resist, it was as though a devil had gone from him. He was bewildered and ashamed, but not deeply, for already his own evil thoughts appeared to him unreal—nothing but an ugly dream.

The sun shone brilliantly in the course of the day and it was warm as summer. Eirik and the house-carl who was left at home were busy on the newly broken ground under the woods. Eirik worked hard—he always did so when once he had taken anything in hand. But at the same time he was deep in thought—Bothild was in his mind the whole time. He could not forget her quivering rage and her bitter tears. And now for the first time he realized what she had said: she and Cecilia had often spoken of his coming home.

A lingering, painful shame pierced him at the thought. Had these two poor little maids waited here all this time for their brother? Bothild must have expected that he would look on her as another sister.

The rude and turbulent thoughts he had conceived of her lay dead at the bottom of his soul like the dried mud left by a flooded stream. And as new and tender green struggles up through the hardened grey slime, so did new thoughts of Bothild shoot up in him unceasingly.

That day he did not see her again till he came in to supper. She busied herself gently, holding her fair head bent as usual under the weight of her plaits, but the cowed and secret air that had been upon her and had provoked him to evil and sensual thoughts was now gone. She was merely a gentle young housewife going calmly about her duties.

Even her beauty now stirred him in another way: now he saw nothing but sweetness and gentleness in her rounded, red and white face, dignity in her languid movements and in the fullness of her form.

. . .

The Sheriff did not come next day, and by noon on the following day he was not yet there. An hour or two later Eirik went
down to get a bite of food. As he came out with a piece of bread
in his hand he heard Inga calling to Bothild, who was sitting outside by the north wall of the house, toward the sea. He went
thither—she sat in the sunshine, sewing the shirt he had given her
that evening.

She looked up for a moment as he came, but there was none of
the anxious, clinging look in her glance now. Bothild bent over
her sewing again; she looked melancholy, but calm and sweet.

Eirik stood there, leaning against the corner of the house. When
he had eaten his bread and she had neither spoken nor looked up
again, he had to break the silence himself.

"Are you still angry with me, Bothild?"

"Angry—" she repeated in a low voice, and went on sewing in
silence for a while. "I hardly know myself *what* I am, Eirik—for
I cannot understand it. Nay, I cannot understand why you should
treat me thus!"

Eirik was at a loss. For as he was about to reply that he had believed she was trying to allure him, he saw that he must not say
such a thing—it would make the matter far worse.

"I can promise you now," he said softly, with a little sigh, "I
shall not hurt you again."

Bothild let her sewing drop into her lap and slowly turned up
her face toward him. And now Eirik was moved by it in quite a
new way: the round, white face with the two bright roses in
the cheeks, the dark, thoughtful eyes, the fine mouth, which
seemed small when she was distressed. Now his only desire was to
pat her cheek, to pass his hand tenderly and kindly over the long,
white curve of her throat—he felt he wished her well with so
warm a heart.

"Is it for my aunt's sake," she asked him earnestly, "that you
were so—spiteful toward me?"

Eirik seized upon this eagerly. "Yes—but now I cannot understand how I could think you were like Mærta—"

"Even so, my aunt never desired aught else than Olav's welfare," said Bothild meekly. "She would ever bid me be mindful
of how great were the thanks we owed your father—God must
reward him, we cannot. And I too wish him naught but well—I
am not greedy of authority, Eirik, but consult Cecilia in all I do."

Eirik felt a thrill of intense joy and relief. God be thanked for her innocence—she believed no more than that he was bad to her because he was jealous on his sister's account, or would avenge himself on her for the old ogress, her aunt—beyond that she had no thought. She firmly believed he had only meant to humiliate her.

He had heard sounds of horsemen coming down from Kverndal, and now he thought he must go and see who was coming. So there was no help for it, he had to tear himself away.

The horsemen were already in the court. They were Ragnvald Jonsson, the Sheriff's young brother from Galaby, and Gaute Sigurdsson, whom folk called Virvir; Eirik had often met them in the two months he had spent at home. He called to Bothild, and she appeared at the corner of the house.

"Heh!" said Ragnvald with a laugh. "So you were not alone! Then our coming is untimely, I fear."

"Are you sewing that shirt for Eirik, Bothild?" Gaute Virvir rallied her.

And now she hung her head again, and her eyes hovered this way and that. She hurried away, as though she would avoid them.

Ragnvald and the other had come by land, for they had had business up in the church town, and they were not altogether unrefreshed, so Eirik guessed it would be well to settle the matter in hand ere they went to table. The sisters had spread the cloth and laid the table when they returned from the upper chamber, and by that time the guests were hungry and not a little thirsty. While the men ate and drank, the two young maids sat in another part of the room. Ragnvald tried conclusions with Cecilia the whole time, and Cecilia gave him sharp and snappish answers; but Eirik could see that this word-play amused her—he had remarked the same thing before, his sister was ready enough for a wrangle. But Bothild had relapsed into her diffidence and shyness and seemed utterly miserable when Gaute teased her about a certain Einar from Tegneby whom she was supposed to have met in the summer, while staying with Signe Arnesdatter at her daughter's house. Eirik did not like to hear her teased about another man, and he did not like her looking as though she had a bad conscience.

Ragnvald and Gaute delayed their leave-taking for some while after sundown. Then they would have Eirik and the maids to bear them company a part of the way.

"Nay, I dare not go with you, Ragnvald," said Cecilia Olavsdatter; "I might meet with the same misfortune as befell Tora
Paalsdatter—you jested with her so long that she put out her jaw
with yawning. It may be Father and the men will soon come in, I
cannot leave the houses. But you, Bothild, might go up to Liv,
since Eirik can bring you back."

So the four set off. Ragnvald and Gaute let their horses walk in
front, the three young men chatted together, and Bothild followed
a little way behind with her box and her bundle. Dusk was already
falling; a thin white mist lay over the pale autumnal fields, and the
orange glow in the sky faded and turned to rust-red. A bitter,
withered scent hung about the alder thicket along the river, and
the path was wet with the dew from falling leaves.

At Rundmyr Bothild left the path; before the men were aware
of it the dark, bent figure was already darting across the fields.
Eirik would have gone on with the others, but they begged him
with a laugh not to give himself the trouble. Then they mounted
their horses.

"Bitter cold to sport in the grove with one's lady fair," said
Ragnvald laughing. "But I dare say you cannot choose your own
time, you two—with the old man always about you down yonder."

"Good night," they both cried. "Beware, Eirik, lest the trolls
snatch away your ladylove tonight!"

Eirik stood listening to the beat of their horses' hoofs as the
two rode away into the dusk. Then he turned and went up to the
cabin.

There was a good fire burning on the hearth by the door, and a
candle stood in an iron clip by Liv's couch on one of the raised
floors. Bothild sat at the mother's feet swathing the child. On the
other side sat Anki and the six older children, eating the food
Cecilia had sent; the savoury smell of a boiling pot of meat almost
overcame the wonted evil odour of the hut. Comfort and uncon-
cern in the midst of poverty met Eirik as he entered, ducking his
head, from the raw autumn evening outside.

He sat for a while talking to Anki, while Bothild tended the
child—she dawdled over it till Eirik grew impatient: now she
must come, 'twas already black night outside.

They went, he in front and she behind, across the Rundmyr
fields, which showed faintly grey in the darkness, and down to the
bridle path through the woods. They walked by the side of the

river, which rippled and gurgled very softly among the bushes;
there was hardly any water in it that autumn.

Now and again Eirik heard that she was hanging behind; then
he stopped and waited till she came up. And every time he had
to halt and wait like this in the dark under the trees, his evil will
seemed to grow more irresistible.

At last, when he had halted thus, she did not come. Eirik held
his breath as he went back, treading as noiselessly as he could.
He ran against her in the dark; as he took hold of her shoulder he
felt she was trembling like one sick of a fever.

"What is it?" His pulses were throbbing so that he could hardly
command his voice.

"I can go no farther," she whispered miserably.

"Then we must rest awhile." He took her in his arms and drew
her to the edge of the road, where there was a little clearing
among the trees. " 'Tis your own wish!" he muttered threateningly.

Instantly Bothild tore herself away from him. It was a moment
before Eirik recovered himself—he heard her flying footfalls on
the path ahead, ran after her; then came a dull thud—Eirik nearly
stumbled over the prostrate body. He knelt beside her—she had
fallen face forward. Eirik took hold of her, put his hand over her
mouth, and felt it wet with a scalding stream that came bubbling
out. At first he did not know what it was; disgust and rage boiled
up in him—was the bitch lying there vomiting! Then with a shock
of horror he knew that it was blood.

He turned her on her back, knelt in the mire of the path, and
supported her against his chest. It was so dark that he could only
just make out the pale round of her face and the dark flood that
poured in pulse-beats from her mouth.

"Bothild—what is it—have you hurt yourself so badly?"

He could get no answer, but beneath his hand he felt the girl's
heart throbbing as fast as his own. In vain he begged, time after
time: "Can you not answer, Bothild—Bothild, have you hurt
yourself?"

At last he had to lay her down. He tore his way through the
bushes; stones scattered and gravel crunched under his feet as he
floundered in the darkness, searching for a pool in the river-bed
where he could fill his hat. The water oozed through the felt

crown; he had but a few drops when he found her again, and dashed them over her. And now he could smell the blood; his own clothes were drenched with blood, and he felt sick with horror and disgust. And Bothild lay silent as though she were dead· already.

Then he saw there was nothing else to be done—he lifted her up in his arms. He was forced to get her home; but heavy she was, as she hung lifeless in his embrace. That little distance, over stocks and stones in pitch-darkness, was as long as eternity. And he himself was worn out inwardly—with the wild desire that was shattered on this terrible mystery.

After an age, it seemed to him, he reached the manor with his burden. He managed to open the door of the women's house, found his way to the bed and laid her on it. Then he went out in search of help—Cecilia, where was she?

In the living-room—as he came in he saw his father and the three boatmen were sitting at the table over their porridge. His sister and the serving-maid were hanging up clothes by the hearth.

"Bothild is sick, I think—"

Cecilia turned sharply—saw her brother standing there, just in the firelight, with blood on his face, and hands as though they had been plunged in blood. With a loud groan she dropped the garment she was hanging on the bar, darted past him and out of the door.

But Olav too had leaped up. He sprang over the table and out after his daughter.

And the men had risen and came out into the room.

"Jesus, Mary!" old Tore wailed, "Jesus, Mary—has it come upon her again?"

Inga, the serving-maid, sighed as one who knew: "What else could we look for?—'tis ever thus with the wasting sickness, it will not give up its hold, when it has fastened on a young body. I have thought this the whole time—for Bothild, poor thing, there is no hope of cure."

"Cecilia will take this sorely to heart," said one of the men. "Olav too—they love her as their own flesh and blood."

"Far too red and white," said Tore; "I was sure of it—no long life was in store for her. Like a stranger she was here—little use was it that Olav had masses sung for her and was a father to her."

Eirik had sunk on the beggar's bench by the door. Without knowing it he had hidden his face in his arms. It was as though veil after veil was being drawn from before his eyes. The wasting sickness, they said, she had had these blood vomits before—she had been sick the whole time, and no one had said a word to him of it. The whole time, while he had had such thoughts of her, had played his cruel game with her, she had been a sick child.

Such were his thoughts when someone took him by the shoulder.

"How did it come about—that she was stricken so sorely?" Olav had spoken in a low voice. Eirik looked up. His father seemed already to have forgotten his question. He gazed vacantly before him, in bitter grief. Eirik could not bear to look at him more than an instant.

Now Cecilia came in. The house-folk swarmed about her with their questions. The maid merely shook her head—her face seemed compressed; she would not weep. In haste she took out of her chest a little box and was going out again.

"I will watch with you tonight," said Olav in a low voice.

His daughter paused and nodded. Olav took her in his arms and held her face against his breast a moment. Then he went out with her.

Eirik was outside the door of the women's house but dared not go in. He thought of that other evening, when he stood with her between the doors—he had not guessed it was a sick woman.

Inga came out after something. It was ill with Bothild, she replied to Eirik's question. The smell of blood from his own clothes wellnigh choked him.

He went in and to bed. He had not guessed that she was sick— and now he began to understand what had lain behind her strange manner—till he was afraid and resisted and would not be forced to see it all. Beware lest the troll snatch away your ladylove, they had said—Ragnvald, or was it Gaute?

He had fancied she was not as she should be, pure and unde-filed. But he had never dreamed that he who had defiled her was Death.

Cecilia came into the room with red eyes next morning. Nay, Bothild had slept but little, she answered—nay, she had not spoken

either, seemed to have no strength for that—she must have lost
more blood this time than ever before.

Cecilia took the clothes that her brother had worn the evening
before. "I will take charge of these and have them washed clean."

" 'Twill be best for me to take myself away now," said Eirik
doubtfully —"back to Sir Ragnvald—since you have sickness in
the house—"

"Is there any need for that?" asked Cecilia in surprise.

Eirik said the same to his father when he met him later in the
day. Olav gave a start—looked at Eirik so strangely that the young
man felt all his old fear of his father awakening. What if *he* had
guessed—or Bothild had said something to him. Eirik turned red,
and was furious with his father for causing him to blush. Olav answered not a word, but went out.

Two days later Eirik was ready for the road.

He wished to set out early in the day; so he had to go and visit
Bothild—he must bid her farewell before he left the manor.

She lay with red roses in her cheeks, but when he came near the
bed, he saw that her face had sunk in, especially under the eyes.
She had been holding a rosary in her hands; now she hid it hastily
under the coverlet. Eirik felt a choking pang of grief as he saw it.

The sharp and acrid odour of sweat that had inflamed him so—
oh, now he knew what it meant; in the wasting sickness they sweat
so profusely, for it devours them with the heat within. And that
little cough of hers which had vexed him so—

He stood still, resting both hands on the hilt of his sword. He
found it impossible to say anything—if he were to ask her forgiveness, there would be no end to it. Rather would he have
thrown himself on his knees, laid his head on her sick bosom.

"You must not believe worse things of me than— My intent was
not so evil as it must have seemed. With all my faults I am not
such as you believe me now."

The sick girl lay looking at him with great dark eyes.

"You must tell me, Bothild—can you forgive me?"

"Yes," was all she answered. Eirik waited yet a little while.

Then he went right up to the bed, took her hand—it was cold
and clammy.

"Fare you well, then." He ventured so far as to stroke her cheek

—but her face was hot as fire. "God give you health again—that you may be well when we next meet."

"Farewell, Eirik. God be with you."

His father and sister went with him no farther than to the barn. Alone he had to ride from home. And he could not shake off his heaviness—he felt like one who rode away an outlaw and accursed.

5

Bothild lay abed through the autumn. It was up and down with her.

Olav watched his young daughter moving about, silent and serious, divided between her sick sister and all the household work of the great manor. She was brave and loyal, Cecilia. Her father saw that her heart was oppressed with sorrow and anxiety; she was often not far from tears, but she would not give up—capable and diligent, she performed the work they had shared between them.

Then Olav said that Cecilia must sleep at night. He himself would watch by the sick girl.

The cough and the fever left Bothild little sleep—on her worst nights Olav sat by her bedside. For the first time in his life Olav found himself regretting that he had no practice in such things as pass the time—he knew no games, he could not sing, nor tell tales. And to speak to his foster-daughter of death and of heaven was not in his power.

He had not felt the silence as a burden when he watched over his wife. Between him and Ingunn there had been a life—of childish games and youthful joys and sorrow and shame, and love stronger than death; the silence between them had been a living one, with a murmur like that of the sea. But this child was both known and unknown to her foster-father; all he had seen of her was that she had grown up in his house, grown fair and winsome so that it was a delight to look upon her; he had taken such care of her as he could—and now she was dying as a young tree withers and dies.

She had let him feel, more plainly than the other children, that she needed his protection; that made it all the more bitter for him now to *know* that she must die. Though he knew it would have been even worse, had it been his own daughter that lay here.

So he sat in the log chair between the hearth and the bed, nodding and dozing, got up and supported the sick girl when the fits of coughing came, drew the bedspread up to her chin lest she should take cold, bathed in perspiration as she was, held the dipper to her lips as she drank, and then went back to his seat.

He was tired, and he was heavy at heart—and yet he felt that this sorrow dwelt in his soul as a stranger in an empty house—only an echo and a shadow of the sorrow he had borne for his mate. That had been so much worse, and yet it had been a thousand times better when she was parted from him, like the tearing asunder of living bonds of flesh and blood—than now, when he sat waiting for the frail and slender bond between him and this stranger's child to be dissolved.

She had spat blood more than once—not so much as that evening when she fell sick on the way home from Rundmyr. But it was easy to see that she was going downhill, and rapidly.

One morning at the beginning of Advent she had another severe fit of coughing and brought up blood. As the day went on, Olav saw that she was now very weak. She fell asleep at evening; her father stayed up. And when Bothild woke again about midnight, and he had settled her so that she lay comfortably, he said what he thought he *must* say:

"When daylight comes, my Bothild, 'twill be best I fetch a priest to you."

"Oh, no, oh, no—" she clutched the man's arm with both hands in an agony of supplication; "oh, no, say not so! Foster-father, do you think I am going to die?"

No other thought had ever crossed Olav's mind but that the child herself must have known this long ago.

"Child, child," he said, hushing her, "why should you not die? You are young and good—why need you fear death? God's holy angels will meet you and lead you before God's high seat, to join the blessed virgins to whom it is given to follow the Lamb of God eternally—"

But the tears welled forth under Bothild's sunken eyelids. "I am not ready to die, foster-father—all I long for is to live on here in this world. I am *afraid* to die!"

"Afraid you must not be. 'Tis better to dwell in heaven and follow Mary as the least of her handmaids than if you possessed the whole round ball of earth and had command of all that is in it."

"You say that because you are a righteous man and a good Christian," said Bothild, weeping.

"So folk believe me to be," replied Olav, greatly agitated. "Daughter, my dear one, I am not so; God knows what I am. And yet, Bothild—I could tell you such things of God's mercy, of His patience with our sins and of the love that our Lord shows us in His five holy wounds, in His bloody stripes and blows— Years have now gone by since I myself turned aside from that path, and my own path is overgrown with weeds and wild bushes— Could I but tell you what I myself once saw and learned—it is the worse for me that I dared not live in the way I know to be right—foster-daughter, I know that you ought to be glad to die now, ere you have acquired a greater share of guilt in our Lord's death and wounds—"

Bothild looked at her foster-father in terrified wonder. But then she began to weep again. "Sins I may have to answer for, though I be young—"

"You will tell them tomorrow to Sira Eyvind and then you may rest with an easy mind—"

Olav seated himself on the side of the bed, holding Bothild's hand in his; she was weeping quietly and miserably.

"The Christmas feast is better kept in heaven," he said softly.

"You may fetch him, then," she whispered at last, utterly broken, and then she wept again.

Next day Olav fetched the priest. Bothild was shriven, and when it was done she sent for her foster-father and sister and the whole household, begged their forgiveness if she had offended them, wittingly or unwittingly. Then Sira Eyvind gave her extreme unction and the bread of parting.

After the priest had ridden away, Olav went in and sat by the dying girl.

"Now, my Bothild, you will soon be gathered to your father. And then you must beg my friend Asger to forgive me for not keeping my word to him so well as I ought—the word I gave him on the day when I received you at his hands and promised to be to

you as a father. Do you remember that day?—you sat outside the
door of the room where your father lay, it was raining and snowing; you were blue with cold. A good, obedient child you have
always been, foster-daughter—God grant you may not have
cause to complain too bitterly of me when you come before the
judgment-seat."

"Toward me you were ever the most loving father." She paused
awhile, then whispered as though she feared to broach this other
subject: "Would you were never harder toward any other—"

"What mean you?" asked her father rather coldly.

"Eirik," said Bothild very softly. "Toward him meseems you
were often hard."

"I trow not," replied Olav, dismissing the matter. "I know not
that I have been stricter with Eirik than there was need."

Bothild was silent for some moments. Then she summoned up
courage:

"There is Cecilia too, Father. I would wish that you do not give
her to Jörund Kolbeinsson, if this be too grievously against her
will."

"Is it so?" Olav asked reluctantly after a moment.

"She liked Aslak better," whispered her sister.

To that Olav made no answer.

"I had not thought to force Cecilia," he said at last. "I will not
marry her to a man she is loath to take. But I cannot promise
therefore to give her to any man on whom her fancy may light,
if I have reason to count him no good match for her."

Olav's tone was such that the sick girl dared say no more of the
subject.

It vexed Olav that his foster-daughter had spoken of these
things. Eirik's departure from Hestviken had been too like a flight
for Olav not to wonder at it. And there was one thing and another
that he had seen—his suspicions were dawning. Only Olav would
not admit them. No, such a thing one ought not to believe of any
man, nor of Eirik either: that he could engage in clandestine commerce with a young maid who was under his own father's protection, his foster-sister. It was true that foster-brothers and sisters
—but that of himself and Ingunn was another matter; they had
been called an affianced pair from childhood; that it grew to love
between them, that they even forgot themselves in each other's

arms—that was bound to come when there was none to take care of them and lead them aright, as inevitably as that two young saplings growing side by side should blend their twigs and leaves into *one* crown of foliage. Neither Eirik nor Bothild had ever been told of such plans in their case. It was true that he had *thought* of it at times: if it turned out that Eirik came home, and that Cecilia would not inherit Hestviken after him—then he might marry her, who was scarcely less dear to him than his own daughter, to Eirik. It might be a sort of consolation that the new race would be her children. But these had been but the vaguest thoughts, he had spoken of them to none; so far as he recalled he had only given Bothild's youth and poverty as his reasons when he let Ragnvald of Galaby know that he not be at the trouble of sending his suitors for her.

Then there was that about Cecilia. No word had come from Jörund's kinsmen, and in his heart Olav was bitterly offended; 'twas not good manners that Jörund should first feel his way in a matter of this kind, and when he was told he might try his luck, should do no more. In secret Olav was angry both with Jörund and with Eirik, who was to blame in this.

That affair of Aslak was not worth further thought. He could see no sign that Cecilia thought any more of their guest.

But nevertheless Olav was disturbed in mind. He was by no means so sure that there had not been something between Eirik and Bothild of which he knew nothing—he could not tell *what* it had been. A feeling of uncertainty stole in upon him during the long nights of watching.

Cecilia— Folk said it was always thus: if a woman has bastards, the same fate will befall her daughters as far as the third generation. Ingebjörg Jonsdatter, Ingunn— 'Twas monstrous to think of such a thing with Cecilia, cool and chaste as the day at dawn: unthinkable that any man could decoy that steadfast child from the right way. There was nothing about her to remind him of her grandmother's ardent waywardness or her mother's defenceless weakness. But God, my God! can one human ever answer for another in such things? He had only to think of himself—

In any case he would be glad when the day came that he had Cecilia married and safely disposed of—he knew that now.

* * *

In the evening, as he sat with the sick girl, Bothild asked a question about her father—a little thing she thought perhaps Olav would know.

It had never occurred to Olav to speak of his friend to that friend's daughter. He was now surprised to find that Bothild had faithfully remembered her father all these years. Olav was glad that at last he had found a subject on which he could talk to the sick girl. Now one youthful memory after another came up—as far back as the time he was in Denmark with his uncle. Indeed, there was a great deal he could tell Bothild about Asger Magnusson and the kinsfolk they had in common.

"How near akin are we then, Eirik and I—and Cecilia?" asked Bothild after a while.

Olav unravelled the relationship. It was very distant. But to Eirik, of course, Bothild was not related at all, he thought to himself.

Surely she could never have asked that in order to find out whether there were kinship within the prohibited degrees?—for she must now have reconciled herself to the thought of death.

Never again did he bring himself to speak as he had spoken that night when for the first time he had seen that the poor child was unwilling to die—of the kingdom of God and Christ's love and of the paths he had once followed but had allowed to become grass-grown.

Then, ten nights before Yule, Bothild Agersdatter died in the arms of her foster-sister.

Sir Ragnvald Torvaldsson spent that winter at his manor near Konungahella. He was a little surprised when Eirik Olavsson returned, since, for all he knew, the lad this time had meant to leave his service for good. But he received the young man well—he was used by now to Eirik's fitfulness and love of change; but the man was brave, loyal and active when on duty, and Sir Ragnvald liked his ways.

So Eirik was given his old place in Sir Ragnvald's hall; and then he went about among his old comrades like a man who has been bewitched. There was neither song nor sport in Eirik that winter.

The more he struggled to tear himself out of his own thoughts, the worse it was—he was like a fish in the net: the more he tossed and floundered to be free, the faster he was caught.

If he tried to think of the first happy, innocent days at home with Jörund and Cecilia, their gaiety and summer work at the beloved manor, it only aggravated his pain: he himself had destroyed all this for ever. The sorrowing figure of Bothild came before him—the frightened child whom he had betrayed and profaned and hunted like a wolf, though he loved her—she was the first and only one he had loved.

He did not understand how he could have acted thus to her. It was not like him— But he had an obscure feeling that some ancient evil met him wherever he went at Hestviken last summer, welling up from the ground and the water and the old houses and from Liv's cabin—as the black water oozes up in a man's footsteps as he passes over marshy ground. And like the fumes of stagnant, putrid bog-water it had made him feverish and light-headed.

But now there was an end of *that*—to Hestviken he could never return. Now he was an outlaw, exiled from his home. For now his father must have heard all. And the thought of meeting his father after this, of being called to account by him—that terrified Eirik much more than the thought of doomsday.

In vain, in vain that Bothild held him dear. He knew now that she did so, and she had been waiting for him all these years while he was abroad in the world. It was her timid, faithful, waiting love that he had seen in those humble glances, in her helpless submission, when they were together. And now he had wasted it all.

At times he tried to take heart of grace. In the first place it was not *true* that he had profaned and betrayed his beloved. For he had never *done* her any ill—and surely thought is free in this world. He had behaved rudely and discourteously more than once—'twas bad enough, but no worse than that.

It availed nothing that he said such things to himself. That evening in the doorway of the women's house, the horror of that night in the wood—these were not to be surmounted. He could not shake off the feeling that much more had happened than he knew to be the actual fact. And it was like sinking into an abyss of horror.

And then came the temptation to make an end of it. To set his sword-hilt against a stone and aim the point at his heart; then the cold steel might quench the burning anguish in his breast. It was

toward Yule that this thought haunted him; he had no peace, day
or night—it must be such a relief to take one's life.

But one morning in the new year he awoke in a mood so
changed that it seemed a mist had been blown away. It had suddenly become incomprehensible to himself that he could have had
such thoughts.

Bothild, his poor sweet wife—was she to wait in vain! Of course
she was waiting now for him to come back to her. He had been
cruel and bad toward her—but he had not outraged her, God be
praised! And when they parted—they had parted as friends; he
had promised to come back to her.

His father—he could not understand how he had been so mortally afraid of him. Was he not a grown man? If his father wished
to fly into a rage, then let him! Besides, why should Bothild have
said anything to his father? Nothing had taken place between him
and her that would give her ground for complaining to her foster-
father. What if he had taken her in his arms rather roughly once
or twice, given her a kiss—no maid need be distressed at that!

Cecilia had said that their father would seek out a good marriage for Bothild—he loved Bothild as though she were his own
child. And even if he should deem her not rich enough to be his
daughter-in-law—Eirik would make his father change his mind!

It was glorious winter weather, the snow gleamed in the sunshine, and the sky was as blue as if spring were on the way. As
he went about, Eirik hummed or sang aloud. And in the evening,
when he accompanied his lord to his bedchamber, he asked to be
relieved of his service. To Sir Ragnvald's question what it was
this time, Eirik replied that he had received word that he was to
come home and be married.

Sir Ragnvald had drunk freely and was in good humour; he
rallied the young man and drew him out, and Eirik told him a tale:

It was his foster-sister—daughter of that Asger Magnusson who
had gotten Eirikstad by his marriage with Knuthild Holgeirsdatter
—Sir Ragnvald knew this story and how he had slain Paal Galt and
been made an outlaw. Well, Olav of Hestviken had taken to himself both the old she-bear and the little maid—Olav and Asger had
been brothers-in-arms. Now she was grown up, fair and bonny,

a mirror for all women, but possessed of neither land nor rich kinsfolk; so Olav would not hear of the marriage. 'Twas for that Eirik had returned to Sir Ragnvald in the autumn—he would give his father time to change his mind, for he had declared they should not see him at Hestviken again until his father was willing to give him Bothild. And Olav knew from of old that Eirik was not one to give in.—And now his father was well on in years; he found it hard to cope single-handed with the whole charge of the manor; he needed his son at home. So he had sent a message: Eirik must come home; he should have Bothild to wife, and now his father wished it to take place as soon as might be—no doubt the betrothal would be held at once and the wedding as soon as the fast was at an end. Ay, truly, said Eirik, he had received the message yesterday at church; a man from Maastrand who had been with the Minorites, and he had spoken to him after mass. Some of the folk from his home parish were always engaged in the herring fishery at Maastrand. Therefore he would fain go at once; he could then accompany this man as far as Maastrand and get a passage home in one of the fishing-boats.

Sir Ragnvald wished him joy and gave him as a parting gift the horse Eirik was wont to ride, with saddle and harness, and a red cloak with a hooded cape of black silk.

No later than the next day but one Eirik rode northward; he was bound for Maastrand. It did not trouble him that the story he had told Sir Ragnvald was untrue; but it was a fact that fisherfolk from near his home were often to be found there in winter, so he was sure to meet with some who could take him up to Folden.[5]

The fishing was in full swing, and besides, Eirik wished to take his horse on board with him, for now he had the idea of giving it to Bothild as a bridal gift. So more than a week went by before he could get a passage—with some men from Drafn who had been at Maastrand selling salt.

They had rough weather on the voyage along the coast, and when they came to Stavern the traders had to put in to shore and lie there. Folden was full of drift-ice to the northward, and long stretches were frozen over; there was no crossing the fiord either by boat or on horseback.

[5] The Oslo Fiord.

Eirik's impatience had increased hourly during the whole voyage. Bothild, Bothild, ran constantly in his mind; he imagined her waiting for him at home in Hestviken. There was none to whom he could pour out his cares.—Or else they were sitting in the women's house, she and Cecilia, spinning and sewing, and talking of him. He could see her face and her eyes as she stepped into the room—when it had been cried over the whole manor that Eirik had come home. And when he thought how he would hold her in his arms, the first moment they were alone together, every drop of blood in him thrilled and laughed in joyful longing; his evil mood was only recalled as a spell from which he had been set free. Now she too had been set free from sorrow and sickness, and they would live together in joy and amity all the days of their life. He doubted not that his father would yield, when first he had had time to growl and show his black looks. But when he saw that his son would *not* give in—!

So Eirik Olavsson saddled his horse and took the road northward along the western shore of Folden. At Tunsberg folk said the same: 'twas useless to attempt to cross the fiord to Hestviken. So he rode on. Right up into the hundred of Skogheim he had to go; the head of the Oslo Fiord was firmly frozen over. Eirik had no time to go round by the town; he turned his horse southward.

It was afternoon as he rode through the church town at home. There he met Ragnvald Jonsson with a loaded sledge; they stopped and greeted each other. Eirik asked whether Ragnvald had been out at Hestviken lately.

"Not since the funeral ale," said Ragnvald.

As Eirik made no reply, Ragnvald thought he must break the silence:

"I have not spoken with your father or Cecilia since—I have not seen them elsewhere than at church. 'Twas a heavy sorrow for them—though not unlooked for; but she was young and good, God rest her soul! He could not have made a fairer funeral ale if it had been for his own child—and he spoke handsomely over the bier, did Olav, as she was borne out of the house."

"I knew not that my sister was dead—"

Eirik was motionless, gazing before him. Ragnvald felt ill at ease, for he guessed that this was a great blow. Then he gathered up the reins and urged on his horse.

"Nay, if I am to reach home ere dark— Farewell, Eirik, we shall meet again if you mean to stay at home awhile."

Eirik came to where he could see the little houses of Rundmyr snowed under beyond the white expanse. A shudder of disgust and sickly fear assailed his stricken soul.

The endless grey frost-fog from the fiord grew denser over the smoke-coloured clouds in the west, behind which the sun had gone down. There was so little depth of snow that stones and roots showed bare in the track under the alders; dark bristles left from the summer's meadowsweet and yellow, withered grass bordered the path beside the frozen stream.

Light, bare, and open the woods were now. But somewhere upon this very path it had happened—and Eirik vividly recalled the rank and clammy darkness of the autumn night as a night of wickedness in which they two had been imprisoned.

It was growing dark as he rode into the yard at home. Olav himself was out of doors. He went to meet the stranger; on recognizing his son he gave him a surprised but friendly greeting: "Is it you—?"

His father's close-knit figure, not very tall, looked broad and bulky in his sheepskin coat; he was bareheaded. In the dusk Eirik could just make out his hair and face, grey all over, the clear-cut features gashed and drawn in on one side. Eirik did not know whether his despair grew worse or better at the sight of the other. A kind of hope sprang up in him that he might find help in his father, but he checked it as one checks a hound on the leash: so many a time he had hoped in vain of Olav.

Then came old Tore, greeted him and took his horse. Olav bade his son go in.

6

OLAV and Eirik lived but moderately well together for the rest of the winter.

Eirik knew no peace. He could not bear Hestviken; he had forgotten what his father was like in daily life—silent, with a far-off look in his eyes; if one spoke to him it was often like calling over hill and dale. And then it might happen that Eirik felt his father staring at him, and Eirik could never be sure whether his father

was looking at him or whether he glared like this without knowing it. Eirik could not stand him. And his sister was always so
quiet and distant.

So Eirik went about among their neighbours, and when he came
home he had usually been drinking. Olav knew that the men
whose company the lad sought were fit for nothing but drinking
and gaming; immoral in other ways they were too. Most of them
were younger sons on the great manors, such as stayed at home
and refused to do what might be held the work of a servant. But
Olav said nothing to Eirik about the company he kept—he ignored
him.

It was Ragnvald Jonsson, the Sheriff's brother, who had now
become Eirik's best friend. At first Eirik had associated with
Ragnvald because in a vague way he hoped or expected that the
other would tell him more, since it was from his lips that he had
first heard of Bothild's death. Even if Ragnvald had not known
his sisters very well, he had nevertheless seen more of them than
most other young men thereabout.

Later, as the torment gnawed and gnawed at Eirik's soul, there
arose within him a morbid desire to question his friend: had rumours ever been abroad concerning Bothild? By degrees he had
been ground down to such a depth of misery that he believed
it would be easier to live if he could hear that she had had a name
for being light or wanton. For it was more than he could bear,
if he had shed innocent blood.

But no one ever spoke of Bothild Asgersdatter. And at last he
swallowed his shame, one night when he slept at Galaby and
shared a bed with Ragnvald.

Eirik then asked his friend: "What meant you by what you
said, that day you were out at Hestviken last autumn? Of Bothild?"

"I cannot recall that I said anything—"

"Oh, yes. You spoke of her, so lightly—"

"Are you out of your wits—I spoke lightly of your sister?"

"She was only my foster-sister. Your words made me think that
maybe Bothild was no more steadfast than that folk deemed she
might let herself be tempted by a man—"

"He would have to turn himself into a bird, like the knight in
the ballad, the man who would tempt one of Olav's daughters, so
well are they herded! I think you are out of your wits, Eirik!

Maybe I said a word or two in jest—now you speak of it, I believe I remember. To tell the truth, I myself liked Bothild so well that I got Reidulf to make inquiry of Ólav one time. But the answer he was given was such that we could only suppose Ólav had chosen her to be your bride" Ragnvald gave a little laugh—"unless he meant to take her himself, old as he is."

Some days later, when Olav and Eirik were alone in the great room, Eirik asked suddenly: "Father—is it true what folk say in the parish—that you were to marry Bothild?"

Olav looked up sharply from the thongs he was plaiting into a rope. He *looked* at his son for a moment, then went on with his work, said nothing.

Eirik insisted, almost pleading: "I have been told it for sure—"

"I wonder," said Olav quietly, "*what* thing you could be told that was too foolish for you to believe it!"

Eirik whispered: "You—or I. They say that, from the way you spoke of her, they could only deem you to have chosen her to be mistress here at Hestviken one day."

Again Olav looked up. Still he made no answer, but Eirik saw the changing expression in the elder man's ravaged face—surprise, or pain, or both.

"Father—is it true—was it your purpose that Bothild and I should possess this house in common?"

"It may be," Olav said in a low voice, "I had purposed something of the sort. That it would be for the good of the manor—after my time—that you took a wife whom I knew to be well fitted and not idle, when the time came for you to be master—"

"Had we but known that!" Eirik smote his hands together, clasped them. "Had we but known that! But we both thought you would never hear of such a thing—since she was a poor orphan, without kinsfolk, without a foot of land—'twas vain to think of it—"

Olav leaned forward, resting his elbows on his knees and letting his hands hang down.

"Then you spoke of this?" he asked at last, quietly, without looking up.

"We spoke of it that last evening, on the way home from Rundmyr."

"Ah, well," sighed Olav after a long pause. "But she had been

sick ere that. So God alone knows how it would have turned out."
．They sat in silence for a while.

"'Tis not easy either, for a woman," said Olav in a low and
earnest voice, "if she be weak in health—to have the charge of a
great house like this, to take part in her husband's cares and counsels, to bear maybe one child after another, though she be weary
and sick. I saw that with your mother, Eirik—her lot was a hard
one here—"

Eirik rose and stood before his father. "That may be, Father.
But now I have lost all desire to deal with the things of this world.
So now I mean to betake myself to a convent."

Olav raised his head—stared at the young man in astonishment.

Eirik said: "I feel, Father, this is a heavy blow to you. You have
but one son to be your heir, and he is to be a monk. But you must
not oppose me in this!"

"Oppose you— But it comes unlooked for."

At that moment Eirik was aware that it had come unlooked for
upon himself. He had not thought of it until the instant he uttered
the words. But then God Himself must have put them in his
mouth.

"After the holy days I had purposed to go in to Oslo, to speak
with the guardian."

"Is it to *them* you will go—to the begging friars?"

Eirik nodded.

"Do others know of this—do they await you at the convent?"

Eirik shook his head.

"Then you must give me time—to think the matter over," said
Olav.

Eirik nodded. They said no more to each other, and soon after
Cecilia came in with the maids.

No sooner had Olav gone into the closet than Eirik threw himself down before the crucifix. His state of mind was that of a man
who has lost his way in bogs and wastes and suddenly comes upon
a firm path—and he prayed as a man astray hurries toward the
haunts of men. It seemed to him almost a miracle—never before in
all his days had he thought for a single instant of entering a convent—and the longer he prayed, the more clearly he seemed to
see the path before him and the lighter it grew about him.

He did not think even now of what the words meant, any more

than he did when he repeated them morning and evening and every time he entered a church. But they bore his soul up like a stream, and he floated upon it on and on toward new scenes.

Little had he learned of the Christian religion, and of that little he no longer remembered much. But as he now tried to call forth what he had once known—of our Lord's life and death, the story of Mary, the words of the Prophets and the songs of David, the prayers of the mass—he felt as though he had come into a noble gallery where massive, fairly carven chests and coffers stood in every corner. He himself was now the young heir, who had entered for the first time with the keys in his hand. Full of impatient zeal, he was scarce able to await the hour when he might unlock and possess and handle all the hidden treasures of the faith.

Perhaps it would be his lot to be made a priest—he was no slower at learning than other men, so he must be able to achieve this. Eirik had a vision of a man standing before an altar; garbed in fine linen and gold embroidery he lifted up his hands to receive heaven's deepest mystery, incomprehensibly united with Christ Himself in the miracle of the mass. It was as though the angel of the Lord had seized him by the hair, raised him out of his wonted world, placed him there—as he remembered to have heard of one of the wise men of the Jews: he went out into the fields with his porridge-bowl to bring food to his mowers, when the angel of the Lord came, seized him by the hair, and carried him away to Babylon.

They would be astonished, the brethren of Konungahella, when they heard that Eirik Olavsson had entered their order—little had either they or he dreamed that one day he would be a barefoot friar! Now he recalled that this had also come to him as an inspiration, without his having to think or choose—to the Minorites of Oslo he was to go. And in this too he was satisfied with God's choice. He had always made his confession to the Minorites, both in Oslo and in Konungahella—folk said they prayed far more for their penitents than did the secular priests. Though he had seldom made up his mind to be shriven more than once a year, before Easter—he had dealt unwarily with his soul, he saw that now. But he had always liked these brethren, and looked forward to seeing their joy when he came and asked to be admitted to their company.

Olav lay awake. And as he strove to see clearly in the welter
of thoughts to which his son's words had given rise, he heard the
hurried whispering stream of words—Pater, Ave, Credo, Laudate
Dominum. The young voice rose and fell, the words ran faster or
slower, as the stream ebbed and flowed in Eirik's mind.

The lad had lighted a candle when he went to his prayers. It
was so placed that Olav could not see it from where he lay, but
beyond the open door the room swam in a soft golden light.

Olav's heart was oppressed. Yet he said to himself that it was
a great godsend if Eirik so utterly unexpectedly and of his own
accord had now found a call for the monastic life. A godsend for
the lad himself, a godsend for Cecilia. And he would be freed
from the rankling thought of the bastard heir whom he had falsely
brought into his kindred.

Great as was the injustice he had committed in giving out another man's child for his own, had he *not* done so, but let the boy
stay where his mother had hidden him away in the wilds—then
indeed Eirik's lot would never have been other than that of a poor
man's child. That too would have been an injustice—on *her* part.
Now he would be a servant of God—and he might bring the convent a rich dower; if he wished to bestow on it the whole of his
mother's inheritance, Olav would not oppose it. Then *that* sin
would be undone. And this child of her misfortune would be
made a life dedicated to the glory of God and many men's profit;
for in times such as these, when so many seemed indifferent, un-
charitable, and froward in their attitude to God, it was good and
salutary to see a young man of Eirik's condition give up all for the
sake of the kingdom of heaven. And now he might be an aid to
his mother, maybe. Perhaps to him too—

Nevertheless his father's heart was heavy.

He could not rid himself of the thought of what Eirik had said
of a marriage with Bothild. An unwise match it would have been
—Olav was not sure whether he would have consented to it. But
he could not help thinking of the grief of the two young people
—of all the nights he had watched beside his foster-daughter. Had
the child had this sorrow upon her as she lay there? It almost made
him wish they had spoken to him. And yet the sickness must have
had a good hold on her—'twould only have been the misery of
Ingunn over again. And Eirik had been vouchsafed a better lot.
It was better as it was.

But, but, but— Often as he had thought it would be better if
Eirik never returned to Hestviken—intensely as the lad's ways had
often irritated him, rousing him a thousand times to wrath, contempt, perplexity in his dealings with this strange bird he had taken
into his nest—there had been so much else blended with these feelings while he had under his protection the offspring of that disaster which had wrecked his own and Ingunn's lives. He had taken
charge of Eirik since the lad was a child, had cared for him as
he grew up into a man. And now that he was to relinquish his
charge, it was as though the young man had been his own son.

The voice within was hushed, but the candle was still burning—
and now and again he heard a sound of snoring. Olav got up and
looked into the room. Eirik was still on his knees, sunk forward
on a chest with his head buried in his arms. The lighted candle
stood just by his elbow. It might easily have been overturned into
the straw.

His father took hold of Eirik and aroused him as gently as he
could. Barely half-awake, his dreamy eyes heavy with sleep, Eirik
undressed without a sound, lay down on his bed, and fell asleep at
once. Like a child he had been, as in a deep torpor he obediently
did as his father told him.

Olav blew out the light, pinched the wick between wet fingers,
and stole quietly back to the closet. Lying awake in the dark, he
resumed the contest with his unreasoning heart.

7

ONE evening in the following week, as Eirik was at his prayers—
and now it seemed to him an immemorial custom that when the
rest of the household had gone to rest he abandoned himself every
night to hours of praying—he was aroused by a sharp whisper:

"Eirik—?"

He turned. Halfway down the ladder that led to the room
above the closet and anteroom the white form of his sister appeared.

Eirik broke off abruptly with "*In nomine—*" and crossed him-

self, as though throwing a cloak about him. Then he sprang up
and went to her.

"Do I keep you awake, Cecilia?"

"Yes—I am afraid you will fall asleep and forget the candle. You
have done so many times—and yesternight I had to come down
and put it out, for Father was asleep too."

The girl was shivering with cold in her thin nightdress. Eirik
stood before her, looking up at her bright form: he thought she
was like an angel, and he bowed his head forward, breathing affectionately on the bare toes, red with cold, that protruded below
the long ample garment, clinging to the step of the ladder.

"Go up now, Cecilia, and lie down," he said gaily. And there
came upon him a desire to speak with his sister of all the new
thoughts that filled him. "Then I will come up to you anon."

He slipped in under her coverlet, crooked an arm around the
head of the bed, and began, in an eager voice:

"Now you shall hear news that will surprise you, Cecilia—I am
to go into a monastery."

"Ay, that I have heard."

Eirik checked himself, taken aback.

"You have heard it! Has father told you?"

"No, Ragna told me."

Ragna, the dairy-woman. Ah yes, he had chanced to mention
it to her too. It dawned on Eirik that he had already mentioned it
to not a few. But Ragna had always shown him kindness, and so
he had said to her that when he was a monk he would pray specially for her eldest child, the sick girl. Ragna's three children had
all been such good friends with Eirik last summer.

"Ah—" said Eirik. "Have you never thought the like, Cecilia—
have you never been minded to become a nun and serve Mary
maid?"

"No," said Cecilia. It sounded like a lock shutting with a snap,
and Eirik was silenced.

"Nay, nay," he said meekly after a moment, "nor did this
thought come to me of myself—'twas sent me by God's mercy."

"This came upon you rather suddenly?" asked Cecilia with
hesitation.

"Yes," replied Eirik gleefully. "Like a knock at the door by
night and a voice calling on me to rise and go out. Like you, I

had never thought upon such things before. And so it may be with you too, sister."

"I know not," said Cecilia quietly. "I cannot think it. But 'twill be stilled here now," she whispered, and all at once her voice sounded pitifully small and weak. "First I lost Bothild—and now you are going from us—"

Eirik lay still, struck by his sister's words. He had almost forgotten their summer in all that had followed after; he seemed to have travelled a long way from the memory of Bothild in these last days. But now he called to mind how she had been wont to sleep by Cecilia's side, where he was now lying. All his memories, suddenly released, filled him with melancholy beyond bounds. He could not utter a word.

"Are you weeping?" he asked at last, as Cecilia did not break the silence either.

"No," replied his sister as curtly as before.

. Ay, now Bothild slept under the sod, and his feet were set upon a path that led far away from all this. But Cecilia, she would be left here, lonely as a bird when all its fellows have flown, alone with her sad and silent father.

"Have you heard no more of Jörund this winter?" it occurred to him to ask.

"We have not." He could hear by her voice that she was in a ferment.

"That is strange. He let me suppose he would be here some time this winter."

Cecilia gave a start; she turned abruptly to the wall. Eirik noticed that the girl was trembling. He raised himself on his elbow, leaning over his sister.

"What ails you?" he asked anxiously.

"Nothing ails me," she whispered, half choking. "I do not ask how it is with Jörund Kolbeinsson. *I* have not set my mind on him."

Eirik said doubtfully: "I cannot make this out. You speak as if you were angry with him."

"Angry?" She flung herself round again, facing her brother. "Maybe I am. For I am not wont to hear such speech from a man as Jörund used to me. And I gave him such answer that he—that he— I am unused to put up with a slight."

"Now you must tell me how this is," Eirik begged her quietly.

"Nay, I know not—maybe it counts for little among folk nowadays, and 'tis only I, a home-bred maid, who deem that the word of a noble damsel is worth so high a price. But he came to me in the women's house, the evening before he was to ride away. And then he said—ay, he let me know that he would come back together with his kinsmen and sue for me. Then he asked if this was against my will. To that I said no. He also asked leave to kiss me," she whispered almost inaudibly. "Again I did not refuse him. God knows I would rather have been left unkissed. God knows I had not set my mind on him. But his speech was such that I could but think it was Father's wish—and yours. And so I would not set myself against it. At that time I thought so well of Jörund that I believed he might be better than most others. Since I can clearly see that Father is little minded to let me have a say in my own marriage. But Jörund, I ween, counts a word and a kiss for little worth."

With a sudden impulse Eirik bent over his sister and kissed her on her lips. Then he lay down quietly again.

"Maybe Jörund could not decide for himself," he said, finding an excuse on the spur of the moment. "Maybe his kinsmen had already treated of another marriage for him, without his knowing it."

"Then he should not have spoken," replied Cecilia angrily—"if he knew not whether he were bought or sold."

"That may be so. But—ay, he spoke to me of this matter as though it lay very near his heart—that he got you to wife, I mean. But you know, he had to go home and consult his brothers—"

"Then do they think we are not good enough for Jörund?"

Eirik did not know what to say. His sister had reason to be angry. And now he seemed to remember speaking of this to Jörund, and Jörund had promised him not to say anything of the matter to Cecilia before he came as a suitor. But he could guess that Jörund might easily forget that promise, Cecilia being so fair and sweet. So he took her hand, laid it on his breast, and stroked it, while he fell back upon the first excuse he had tried to offer for his friend:

"They must have designed another marriage for him, without his knowing it."

Cecilia did not answer. Eirik lay patting her hand—but now he found he was getting very sleepy. She must be already asleep.

Once more Eirik bent over her, cautiously kissed his young sister, then stole out of the bed and down. He was already on the ladder when the chilly little voice asked in the darkness above:

"You will say no more prayers tonight, will you?"

"No," replied Eirik feelingly; "now I will go to rest."

"Then you will put out the light?"

Eirik did so. He lay in bed feeling angry with Jörund for having shown his sister and all of them so little respect. But at the same time he had in some sort conceived an aversion for the thought of giving Cecilia to Jörund. This one week of his conversion had altered his view of many things. He now thought of his whole life since he had run away from home with repugnance, nay, with sorrow. He repented his sins, that was well enough—but beyond that he wished, now that his life was to be consecrated to God, that it had been less defiled.

But Jörund, to whom no such call had come—of him no man could require that he should be better than other men. And Jörund was no *worse*. But Cecilia—she was so *good*.

Olav had not meant very much by it when he hinted that he had no very great esteem for the order of the Minorites. He had grown somewhat tired of them, like many other folk in the neighbourhood, in Sira Hallbjörn's time—because the priest constantly had them at his house. The Grey Friars had long been at strife with the cathedral chapter and the priests of Oslo, but it was not certain that the brethren had been chiefly to blame for the quarrel. And there had been some ugly talk of one of the Minorites and Eldrid Bersesdatter of the Ness—but there had always been ugly talk about Eldrid, ever since her father gave the reluctant maid to old Harald Jonsson, though no one could give clear proof of it; she was barren as the sole of an old shoe. She was moreover the daughter of a nephew of old Sira Benedikt and a second cousin of the daughters of Arne, but her kinsfolk never spoke of her; she had quite dropped out of good company. The young friar, Brother Gunnar, who had been too often with her at the Ness, had been sent out of the country, to a school of learning, it was said.

The only men of the order whom Olav knew something of were the Richardsons' brother, Edvin the painter, and Brother Stevne, who used to come out to Hestviken once a year, in Lent— he had done so ever since he attended Ingunn in her hour of death.

Olav did not like Brother Stevne's appearance: he was a little
crook-backed man with a face like a bad fairy; one intuitively expected him to wag his long, flexible nose. But Olav had never
heard or seen anything but good of the man.

And as Eirik seemed so fixed in his desire to enter this order,
his father was quite willing to give him to the Minorites with a
fitting endowment.

Olav gave much thought to the question of Eirik's birth. But
he had never heard of dispensation for bastard birth being denied
to any man who was otherwise well suited to be a monk or priest.
And he had already burdened his conscience with so much that
he might well add this to the load—hold his peace about his secret.
This burden had grown into his flesh and into his soul—he felt it
was beyond his power to rid himself of it.

Eirik felt his father's changed attitude toward him as part of his
new happiness. Although Olav had not much more to say to his
son than usual, Eirik was aware of the new warmth with which he
was met whenever he was in the elder man's company. Most of
the sayings and preaching of pious men that Eirik had heard of
late years had gone in at one ear and out at the other, but now one
thing and another recurred to his memory. "Seek ye first the kingdom of God and His righteousness, then shall all other good things
be added unto you"—something like this Christ had once said to
His disciples, he had heard. Eirik remembered it now. All his life
he thought there was one thing he had desired more than all else
in the world: to force his father to acknowledge him with loving
pride. Now, when he was about to renounce all the good things of
this world in order to win heaven, he received as a parting gift
that for which he had begged from his childhood's days.

So it was only the thought of his sister that caused Eirik uneasiness. He said to himself that after all none but his father and
sister could have thought of taking this matter of Jörund's suit so
seriously, calling it an affront and a broken promise. For nowadays
folk were not so scrupulous about every word spoken at random—
he himself had never been so. But now it seemed to him that his
father was right—life would be much better if folk were more
prone to keep their word.

· · ·

One day when Olav and Eirik were down on the beach engaged in tarring a boat, and Cecilia had brought them their afternoon meal, her brother said, after she had gone:

" 'Twill be lonely for her when I have left."

"Maybe." Olav followed the girl with a thoughtful look as she went up the hill.

Eirik said: "That is the only care on my mind, that I must go away before her future is assured."

"I think you may leave me to deal with that." Olav's lips twitched with the little crooked smile that had been so habitual to him of old when answering his son. "For many years we have seen no sign that you troubled yourself about your sister's welfare."

"Nay, nay. But I had to see the world first, like other men. And I knew she was safe in your care."

"Think you that is no longer good enough?"

Eirik paused, pressing the scraping-iron against the boat's side and looking down.

"You know, Father, you begin to grow old, so—" Eirik stole an embarrassed glance at his father. Olav's mien was now cold and unfriendly. Nevertheless he went on: "My sister is not so cheerful and easy in her mind as she should be—at her age."

Olav could not forbear, though he was loath to put the question. "Has she complained—to you?" he asked suspiciously.

It was Aslak he had in his mind. But Eirik answered:

"I think she marvels that she has heard no more of Jörund."

Olav went savagely at the work he was doing, but said nothing.

"Have you had no message from them?" asked Eirik at last.

"Does she *know* that Jörund—? If I remember aright, I bade you tell your friend that I enjoined him not to give the child any hint of the matter till it had advanced much farther. I call it unmanly and little consonant with honour if he has spoken to so young a maid ere his kinsmen and I have come to an agreement."

Olav's tone was so disdainful that something of Eirik's old feeling of comradeship with Jörund was awakened.

"*Spoken* he has not, for sure. But when two young people have a kindness for one another, 'tis not easily hidden, so that the one knows not the other's mind—"

Olav worked on in silence.

Jörund!" he exclaimed all at once, so gruffly and scornfully

that Eirik dared not ask another question when his father relapsed
into silence.

It was not one year since Aslak had used the same words—such
things could not be hidden. Then he had kept an eye on his daughter, fearing she might regret Aslak too deeply. But he might safely
have spared himself that. It was well she had not taken it so sadly
but that she could now think of Jörund—so she would surely get
over this fresh sorrow. And indeed she was little more than a child.
—But, for all that, Olav felt it as a disappointment that his daughter
could be so quick to forget.

Eirik wished to sail up to the convent before Easter—he could
find no peace in his soul till he was admitted to the monastic life.

It had been Olav's intention to accompany his son. But he fell
sick. He had got an inward hurt in the fight at Frysja bridge; he
had taken little heed of it at the time, but ever and anon it showed
itself in a bloody flux and vomiting. This time he had to take to his
bed. But Eirik could not wait. So he promised to send his father
word in good time, when the day was appointed for him to take
the habit.

On the morning of his departure he went into the closet to take
leave of his father. He knelt beside the bed and asked his father's
blessing.

Olav said: "One thing I will ask of you, Eirik—that you learn
the office for the dead and say it each week for your mother's
soul and for your father."

"That I promise. To the best of my power I shall pray for my
mother and for you."

In a low voice Olav answered: "For your father you must pray.
But you are not to utter my name."

Deeply moved by his father's humility, Eirik kissed his hand.

Eirik Olavsson was received most affectionately by the Minorites. And so eager was he that he could not wait till after the holy-
days; he began at once to seek instruction of the brethren regarding his new life, accompanied them to the choir, and took part in
the singing as far as he could.

But in the week after Easter he went to the guardian and said
he had a friend of whom he would take leave before he renounced
the world. And he wished to ride thither at once; then perhaps

there might still be time for him to take the habit on St. Eirik's Day,[6] as had been proposed.

Éirik had become convinced that his sister's agitation, on the night when he had talked to her, must be due to a feeling of love for Jörund. And now at any rate he would see whether he could render his beloved sister a service before he took his vows—in any case he would try to find out how the land lay.

At Gunnarsby he was well received, but Jörund was somewhat reserved. But when Eirik told him that he was to enter a convent and had come hither to bid his friend good-bye, both Jörund and his brothers seemed mightily surprised.

Two nights before Eirik was to leave, he and Jörund went out together to find a haunt of wood grouse. As they walked through the wood Jörund Rypa said to his friend:

"Howbeit, Eirik, it seems to me you should wait awhile and prove yourself ere you give up Hestviken and all the good things of this world."

He could hear by Eirik's voice that he was smiling in the darkness. "Why so? What should it avail, think you, that I proved myself, when I know this has not come from myself? You would not have me let Him wait who has called me?"

"This too you must lay aside," said Jörund as if in jest, nudging the bow that Eirik carried. "You were always a keen hunter, Eirik."

"I change it for a bow that shoots higher."

"Ay, so it is, no doubt. But will you not wait till we have time to speak with your father of that matter you know of—put in a word for me with Olav and Cecilia?"

Eirik could scarcely conceal his joy. And now Jörund said he had been uneasy the whole winter with longing for Cecilia. But he had waited because there had been a talk that Steinar and Brynhild should move to Norderheim, and he would rather the young Cecilia were spared having to dwell under the same roof with Brynhild, who was a shrew. But now that matter was in order.

Éirik nevertheless held to his purpose and left at the time he had appointed with the guardian. He gave Jörund a brooch to take to Cecilia as a token.

6 May 18.

8

OLAV AUDUNSSON had barely risen from his bed after his sickness when the brothers from Gunnarsby came riding to visit him.

Olav received them well. He did not think his guests would notice that he was still unwell and could take little food—and his spirit was also weary within him: he found it hard to come to a decision as to what answer he should make, when the strangers set forth their errand.

In his anger with this Jörund Rypa, who had first lured him into giving a half-promise and then allowed three quarters of a year to go by without making a sign, Olav had thought: nay, he did not like the fellow, he did not trust him farther than he could see him; Cecilia might find ten husbands that were better than Jörund. But now these Rypungs had come, and he could not deny that they were courtly and well-born men. Aake, the eldest, was married to Lucia Toresdatter from Leikvin, and Steinar to Brynhild Bergsdatter from Hof in Lautin—so it was difficult for him to find any pretext, if he was to reject Jörund's suit. He had no other reason than his unwillingness to say yes.

So he sent a message privily to Baard of Skikkjustad and made a tryst with him at a place within his forest, not far from the manor.

Baard came and repeated all that he knew of the Gunnarsby folk.

The old oaks showed their tiny new leaves, reddish brown against the mild blue sky, and the grass sprouted up through the pale crust of withered leaves wherever the sun could reach it. Around the great embedded rocks that gathered its rays bloomed greater clusters of violets. Olav had stretched himself on the ground, and Baard, who sat watching his friend, thought he looked as if he might well be fey. He was grey and sunken in the face, his eyes as pale as milk and water, and yellow in the whites, the fine silvery sheen of his hair and stubbly beard was as it were tarnished. Then said Baard:

"You know, kinsman, Torgrim and I will protect Cecilia and her estate as well as we are able, if it should happen that she were left alone. But now all you possess will be hers, since Eirik is to enter a convent. And, after all, a husband takes better care of an estate than any other—"

Olav nodded.

He knew it. However good may be the intentions of a child's guardians, an estate fares best in the hands of an owner. If Jörund got Cecilia to wife, they would move out to Hestviken as soon as he died or grew too old to have sole charge; already there dwelt two married sons at Gunnarsby. Without a doubt it was the rumour that the son and heir was to become a monk that had induced the brothers to bring forward their suit at this time. But since the two young people had conceived a love for each other so long ago as last summer, as Eirik said, then Jörund would scarcely love her less now, when he was to get the manor with her. And all the Rypungs had the name of being active and prudent husbandmen, said Baard.

Olav himself had thought the child might be left alone before they were aware of it; he had been very low this spring. True, Cecilia would be in good hands with Baard and Signe, and, young as she was, she had good sense enough. But nevertheless her father was ridden by a kind of anxiety—what was it she might take after —her mother, and himself, God mend him—

"Then you advise me to it, I perceive," said Olav in a low voice.

"Mm—not that either," replied Baard. "But as matters stand now, with Eirik away, I will not *dissuade* you from it either, Olav!"

So when Aake Kolbeinsson brought forward the brothers' errand, Olav listened to him graciously and showed himself well disposed. The final agreement was that the betrothal feast should be held at Hestviken on the eve of St. Columba, and the bride should be brought to Gunnarsby four days before St. Laurence.[7]

Olav Audunsson had not been inside the church of the Minorite convent since the building was finished.

It was a bright and fresh May morning, and spring had come early this year, so that the wild cherry stood in full bloom by the roadside as Olav went up the hill from the wharf to the convent. He was early abroad—the bells were only beginning to ring in the steeple as he stepped upon the green before the church. Their

[7] St. Columba's Day is June 9; St. Laurence's August 10.

sonorous pealing right above his head sent a cold thrill down his back.

Within the church the sunlight entered the windows aslant like broad beams, in which the dust-motes danced. Olav threw a rapid glance around him, but it was not at all as he remembered the Franciscans' church—from that evening—dark and cold and desolate, still in disorder from the building, with the gaping chancel arch and black night beyond. Now the choir was flooded with light of many colours; the windows were already filled with stained glass; images were painted on the whitewash of the walls, and the high altar was very richly and handsomely adorned. Behind it, farther up the choir, he had a glimpse of the brown-frocked brethren standing in their stalls, they were already at their prayers.

By the wall to the left of the arch, where he remembered the strangely living crucifix had been placed, were now two small side altars with tapestries on the wall behind them. It was no doubt the same crucifix that now stood on the rood-beam, but it had a different look by daylight.

The church was still almost empty, so Olav seated himself on the bench near the door to wait for the time of mass. Idly he looked about him—'twas true, as folk said, the barefoot friars' church was now a fair one. Above him the bells were calling, and the guests flowed in, more and more of them. His own party came, Baard in his bravest array, Anki and Tore in the new clothes he had given them for the journey to town. They knelt awhile; when they rose Olav went forward with them toward the choir arch. Signe and Una were already kneeling at the head of the women's side, with Cecilia between them. The young girl was closely veiled. The church began to fill—it always drew many folk when a novice was to take the habit.

A monk came in with the long candlestick and lighted the tapers on the altar, and most of those who stood at the upper end of the nave knelt down. Olav felt ill at ease standing up, the mark of all eyes, so he too knelt and covered his face with a corner of his cloak. The soft coolness of the silk felt unfamiliar, for of late years he had not often worn his festival attire.

From habit he began to mumble the prayers, because he found himself on his knees—he always did so when custom and good manners demanded that he should seem to be praying. At the

same time there was a sort of purpose in it: he passed for a pious
Christian, and he *wished* to pass for one. He would keep his
apostasy hidden as a secret of his heart; openly he would not be
numbered with those who scorned or defied God. It was not their
victory or success he desired; even as he was, he knew that he
desired Christ's victory and honour—as a leader, outlawed in a
foreign land, may secretly rejoice over the victories of his countrymen, secretly hope for the success of the banner under which
he himself may never fight again.

But he knew too that these words which flowed from his lips
were like seed-corn in which the germinating power had been
killed, and he scattered them abroad nevertheless, because he did
not wish his neighbours to know of his poverty.

But now, when he called to mind that next winter he would be
alone at Hestviken, he could no longer steel himself against the
soundlessness and emptiness within by the thought that he was
working for others, all those whose welfare depended on his
effort. It would be a gain to Cecilia, Olav saw that well enough,
if her husband could take over without delay all that she was to
bring him. And Eirik was gone, and Bothild was gone—

Then he would be left alone with his own soul, as a captive in
the deepest dungeon is left alone with the corpse of his fellow
prisoner.

Olav felt that these thoughts had brought him into a whirlpool; with desperate rapidity he was being sucked under. A sort
of dizziness at the vision of the loneliness that would now prevail
at Hestviken; then a stillness, as though he had sunk to the bottom
of a sea, a clear and motionless abyss of darkness, and then the
certainty that even in this abyss he was not alone. When everything on which he had been able to fix his thoughts was plucked
out of his reach, he would again be alone with the Living One
Himself, from whom he had sought to fly away and hide.

God, my God, hast Thou pursued me up into the sky and down
into the depths of the sea? Once he had found himself face to face
with God under the vault of pale-blue winter night—when he
lost the other half of his life. Now, when he was losing all that he
had tried to put in her place, he was forced to feel that God's eyes
were looking upon him as though out of a forest of weed in the
dark depths of the sea.

What if the seed-corn he had thought dead were not dead after all, what if the murdered child stirred on its bed of withered leaves and awakened?

Olav knew not whether there were more of terror or of hope in it; but in the vision that again overwhelmed him he saw that he had never been afraid to bear terror and pains when he believed he could save a life from being wasted or ruined. The only thing he had always been afraid of was to see a life brought to destruction, rot away. And with marvellous clearness he saw on a sudden that the same instinct that had forced him to take care of all who came in his way would now force him to be mindful of his own soul. That a man should love his even Christian as himself he had always heard and seen to be right, and the more one could follow that precept, the better. But as when a painted window is lighted up by the sun, so that one can distinguish the images in it, so did he perceive in a flash the meaning of God's command, clear and straightforward, that a man must also love himself.

He was aroused by a hand on his shoulder. One of the monks signed to him to move forward—Olav had not noticed how far the mass had progressed, but the priest was already at *Orate, fratres*—and now he saw Eirik; he had not remarked his son's coming.

But there under the choir arch lay Eirik, with his hands extended on either side, his forehead touching the pavement. His dark-red velvet cloak covered the kneeling figure, spreading out over the grey stones of the floor, and below it could be seen the outline of his sword; for today, when he was to offer himself and all that he owned to God, Eirik alone of all men was permitted to bear arms in God's house.

Olav stood up and advanced the few steps, then knelt in his place at the young man's left side. And at the last his affection for this son burst all bonds. It was his own son he was giving away today.—Olav hid his face again in the folds of his cloak.

His daughter he had promised—her he was to give away to a man whom he trusted no more than halfway, to all that was uncertain and transitory in this world; but for that reason it seemed to him that he was not taking his hand entirely from Cecilia; he might yet be compelled to intervene in her destiny. But Eirik was to be given to God, to what is firmer than all rocks, more certain than death and judgment—this was complete severance, for all time, for eternity, it might be.

"My son, my son, who is to make amends for my failure—"

Olav was too absorbed to follow the mass—he was aware of nothing around him until he heard the voice just above his head. The guardian stood in the centre under the arch; before him Eirik now knelt upright and erect, his young face turned upward, his cloak thrown back, so that the brooches and the bridegroom's chain flashed on his silken jerkin. Eirik was clad entirely in red, for his garments were to be offered to the altar, and they had most need of a new set of red vestments.

Olav heard Eirik say the responses—loudly and clearly so that he was heard over the whole church. Some women at the back wept aloud—but there are always some women who do that, Olav tried to persuade himself, so as not to be unmanned.—Eirik was of full age, so Olav was not called upon to answer.

He saw Eirik raised to his feet by the hand of the guardian. His spurs jingled faintly as the young man followed the monk up to the high altar. Olav saw the bundle of coarse, ashy-grey homespun that lay on the altar—the novice's habit was being blessed. Now it was given to Eirik, who took it and clasped it to his breast.

The contracting pain in his throat became unbearable—and Olav felt his burning eyes dimmed with tears. He drew his cloak before his face again. When he looked up once more, Eirik was gone.

Olav rose and went back to his place by Baard's side. He took in nothing of the prayers and lessons that followed. They had sung the *Veni Creator* to the end without his hearing it.

And at last they came back. Olav thought he did not know this young monk. The fine, narrow skull shone smooth and newly shaven above the black fringe of close-cropped hair, and was it Eirik's dark and mobile face that was now so changed, pale as bast beneath the brown complexion? His great yellow eyes blazed like stars. He looked even taller and broader in the shoulders in the grey frock with the knotted rope around his slender waist. Below the edge of the frock Olav saw his son's feet naked in the sandals.

For a moment Eirik stood still, beaming. Then he turned, passed round the choir, was greeted by his new brethren with the kiss of peace. When his father looked up again, the last of the monks were disappearing through the door leading to the convent.

Outside the church Olav met with his company. One after another they took him by the hand, wishing him joy of his son. Several of the townsmen who knew Olav Audunsson came up and greeted him.

The daughters of Arne were wiping their tear-stained faces with the flaps of their coifs. Cecilia wore her veil down—she had certainly never raised it once while in church.

"What think you of this, my daughter?" Olav asked her as they went round to the guest-house; they had all been bidden to break their fast there.

" 'Tis well," the maid said simply.

Oh, nay, but then 'twas true she had seen so little of her brother for many years, thought Olav.

9

OLAV had spared nothing in making his daughter's betrothal feast, and folk who had been present spoke well of it afterwards. Laughter and merriment were always somewhat rare at Olav Audunsson's banquets, but all was done in a handsome and worthy manner.

Signe and Una stayed on with two of their daughters and some serving-maids, and now there was a busy time at Hestviken. Cecilia's rich dowry was to be inspected and to receive its last touches, and festival garments were to be prepared for those of his household whom Olav was to take with him on the bridal journey.

One morning Signe came and said to Olav that now they must look through those things which the child was to inherit from her mother.

Ingunn Steinfinnsdatter's bridal chest had stood during all these years in the closet where Olav slept; he had never answered when anyone had suggested removing it to the storehouse. So when he and old Tore carried it into the light, the women were afraid that the stuffs might have suffered damage. Olav had indeed kept it resting on the ends of two beams, but the air of the closet was always so raw.

Olav saw that Cecilia was filled with expectation, though she appeared as calm as usual. His daughter had never set eyes on the goods she was to inherit from her mother; the chest had not been opened since the days Olav took his wife's grave-clothes out of it.

Olav gave the key to Signe. But the women could not cope with the lock—he had to do it himself. Then he stood by and looked at what they took out of the chest.

The first thing that met his eyes was a folded cloth of reddish-brown wool. A glimpse of the wrong side was enough: they had used it in his childhood at Frettastein, when they hung the walls of the hall. It was embroidered with the New Jerusalem and saints adoring the Lamb, according to the vision of Saint John. Above and below the images there were borders of vines, with beasts and hunters between.

The women shook it out, and there fell from it a shower of dried flowers that had been put in to guard against moth. It had taken no hurt.

"But beautiful you cannot call it," said Una; "it must be old as the hills." The saints were stumpy and broad and all the men had beards. "This cannot be anything for Cecilia to take to Gunnarsby?"

" 'Tis only laid over for a covering." Olav took the tapestry, rolled it up, and laid it on the bench behind him.

Piece by piece the things were lifted into the daylight and shaken out, making the bystanders sneeze with the herbs and spices that filled the air. Cushions and tapestries, kirtles and mantles, chaperons of velvet and Flemish cloth, shifts with embroidered fronts of silk and linen, and many vests to which the skirts had not been attached.

"Deft with her hands was Ingunn," said Una, handing one of these vests to Cecilia. "Have you ever seen such fine sewing?"

Cecilia fingered the costly piece: it was of white silk, embroidered in black and gold thread at the wrists and neck. "Nay, I have never seen the like. Mother had great skill!"

Her father nodded—he had no wish to enter the conversation. But in fact it was not Ingunn who had sewed this shirt body; he had bought it when he was in Stockholm with the Earl, of a man who said it came from Micklegarth.[8] Ingunn had never finished it for wear.

The women took out the carved coffer and spread the jewels over the table—finger-rings fastened together with a ribbon,

[8] Constantinople.

brooches white and gilt, but blackened and tarnished for want of use, a decayed leather belt studded with plates of chased metal. A ring-brooch of pure gold, which he himself had given her; he had inherited it of his father. Around the ring was inscribed the Angel's Greeting and "*Amor vincit omnia.*" Then Signe handed Olav a faded band of green velvet, thickly set with gilt roses—Ingunn's bridal garland, the symbol of inviolate maidenhood and gentle birth.

"I wonder that you did not give this to Cecilia for her betrothal," said Signe.

"The other garland that I gave her is better," replied Olav, turning the matter aside. "This one weighs scarce the half of it."

The women brought forward into the light a kirtle of green silk, woven with golden flowers and birds. Down to the waist it was fairly close-fitting, but wide below and exceedingly long. All the women broke into exclamations of delight at the beautiful stuff —'twas great pity that they must cut it shorter, if Cecilia was to wear it at her bridal.

Olav remembered that Ingunn had had to lift it as she went round the table pouring wine—she had caught her foot in it as they ran hand in hand across the wet courtyard that summer night—and in the dark bower he had felt the soft silk about her slender body as a part of the lawless sweetness of the adventure. His heart grew hot within him at the thought that that man should embrace his daughter in this very garb.

" 'Twould be a shame to cut up and spoil such costly silk," he said. "Cecilia is not so old but that she may grow taller yet—her mother was a tall woman. Better to let this gown lie by a few years longer."

Olav had arranged with Aake Kolbeinsson that he was to visit Gunnarsby before the haymaking, in order to become acquainted with the home of the Rypungs before he brought his daughter thither. He went by way of Oslo, taking a number of jewels and vessels to the goldsmith—Cecilia would have to bring a share of such into the estate, but there was such good store at Hestviken that he needed only to have some of the old vessels remade. His daughter's marriage entailed expense enough without his having to buy new silver for her dowry.

The last day he was in the town he went out into the fields and heard vespers in the Minorites' church. After the service he went to the gate and asked leave to speak with his son.

Brother Eirik came down to the gate—again Olav gave a start on seeing the young monk, he was so unlike his old self. He had already acquired the monastic air, but in such a way that it suited *him*. At home Eirik had never seemed to know how to bear himself—now he was too noisy and now too abrupt, now too courteous and now too rude; but however he might be, there was too much effort in all he did. Now he seemed to have learned to comport himself calmly, and he talked as though he had thought of what he was to say.

He had little time, he said—'twas this sickness that was rife, they had it here too. Father Einar said it came from the water; it turned rotten in the heat. So now he and Brother Arne were busy in the garden. But he would ask leave to bring his father thither, so that they might talk as he worked.

It was cool in the shade of the great birches, and the grass grew high and rank under the drip from the hollowed logs that carried a stream from Eikaberg down to the convent garden. Olav sat taking his ease as he watched the two young friars in grey frocks watering rows of beans and beds of celery. In the flower-beds beyond, a rose bloomed already here and there, and round about them yellow lilies swayed, and some blue flowers the name of which Olav did not know.

Now and then as Eirik went to the water-butt he said a few words to his father. Father Einar, the master of the novices, had already begun teaching him to read in a book and to write; it came easy to him.

In one thing and another Olav recognized his son as of old—he had always had such a strong belief in himself when he was to do anything, before he had really set about it. But Eirik had not been here more than six weeks, and already Olav could see a great change in him. He sat there letting his affection for Eirik thaw and warm his heart: after all, he had always been fond of this child in a way, and it was good to feel that this battered and crippled affection might now be suffered to grow healthy and strong.

At Gunnarsby Olav was received with such marks of friendship and honour by the Kolbeinssons that he could not help liking the place.

The manor was a fair one and a great, and lying as it did on the

sunny slope above a little lake, with broad acres and meadows
about it and many new and well-built houses, it might well support three brothers in lordly fashion. Here the household was
ordered more after the custom of the new nobles—as was to be
expected with young masters and a greater range of husbandry.
Between the masters themselves and the labourers in farmyard
and workyard a crowd of serving-men and maids passed to and
fro—some of these were poor kinsfolk of the Rypungs.

Olav had seen none of the women of Gunnarsby before now.
Gunhild Rypa, the mother of the Kolbeinssons, was infirm and in
her dotage. So Cecilia would have no mother-in-law above her.
Aake's and Steinar's wives had just been brought to bed, both of
them, when the betrothal feast was held at Hestviken. Olav liked
them least of all the folk of Gunnarsby. Brynhild had a hard look,
but Lucia was far too mild—she promised Olav that Cecilia should
have milk to wash in and wine to drink, as the saying goes. Olav
smiled to himself—Cecilia would be able to hold her own with
them well enough; his child lacked neither wit nor will, and she
bore herself in just as courtly a fashion as these two knights'
daughters. Moreover, it was only natural that these brothers'
wives should be glad to see the youngest of the family marry a
franklin's daughter; then he could leave Gunnarsby with wife and
children, when the time came.

So Olav was not ill pleased with what he had seen, when he
rode from Gunnarsby.

The summer heat held on day after day. Toward nones the sky
was often overcast—a dark-blue wall, flecked with flame-coloured
clouds, rose above the wooded ridges; within the blue darkness
gleamed distant lightnings, as when a candle is moved within a
tent, and the thunder rolled faintly far up the country. Sometimes
a shred of cloud brought a scud of rain over the dried-up fields,
but the storm that was to clear the air was long in coming. And
every evening it cleared up, and every morning dawned with a
hazy blue sky that heralded a hot day.

And broiling hot it was even in the middle of the morning, the
day Olav and Tore rode home through the woods that divide the
districts of Eyjavatn and Folden. And toward nones, as they were
riding high up on a hillside, the thunder-clouds again rolled up in
the north and east, casting shadows over the sun-drenched woods,

and darkening the tarns scattered over the pale bogs that stretched everywhere on the lower land.

The path led across some mountain pastures at the top of the ridge, and here they would unsaddle their horses and rest a few hours. Outside one of the sæters they found a young woman sitting and spinning, while she kept an eye on a caldron that hung over a fire close by. When she saw that the new-comers were peaceful wayfarers, she was overjoyed at having guests; she pressed upon them both fresh milk and curds to take on their journey. After they had talked awhile it came out that old Tore had known some kinsfolk of her master. So they two sat and talked, while Olav went down toward the brook they heard murmuring in the wood near by—he would look for a cool place where he could lie down and sleep.

He had to go some way down; up near the sæters the banks were trodden into mire round the watering-places, and the ants swarmed on the moss where he had first flung himself down under the firs. But then he came to a little patch of dry, close-cropped grass, thyme, and ground ivy, and there he stretched himself at the edge of the wood.

He was not so sleepy—lay looking up at the great dark, silver-bordered clouds that drifted over the tree-tops, causing a succession of shadows and sharp yellow sunlight. The thunder muttered far away, and at the bottom of the slope the brook swirled and gurgled among great stones.

On the other side of the stream the wood rose steeply to the rounded summit, but right opposite to him was a scree, where masses of red-flowered willow-herb grew among the stones. And all at once it flashed on Olav that he had been here once before—he recognized the scree and the cascade of flowers and these black clouds silently rising, and the murmur of the brook and the distant thunder—all had been present before.

Then the mirage vanished as suddenly as it had come. The place looked like any other watercourse in a wood. Olav lay down again, dozed with eyes half-open to the sunshine, and breathed in the scent of herbs that floated about him and made him sleepy.

Then all at once he was roused, broad awake, by a little whirring sound—before he had time to grasp what it was, a shadow flitted past him as swiftly as the shadow of a bird in flight. He opened his eyes, looked about him, and was aware of Ingunn standing in the scree on the other side of the brook among the red flowers.

Olav felt no surprise—as he rose on his knees he saw in a flash every detail he afterwards called to mind. A gust of warm wind passed through the wood at that moment, and the tall red tufts of flowers waved, the trees leaned over with a yielding droop of their tops and a soughing in their branches, but her mantle of flowing light-brown hair never stirred. She stood motionless, with her long, pale hands crossed on her bosom. Her white face was also perfectly motionless; she gazed at him with a strange, beseeching look in her great, wide eyes. Although he was so far away, he could see that her skin was pale and as it were bedewed —as it always was when she felt the heat.

It did not occur to him to marvel that he saw her as she had been at the time when they were newly grown up. It did not occur to him that he was of any age either, as he rose and ran toward the vision. Time seemed to be no more.

As he crossed the brook she stretched out her hands toward him —he could not tell whether it was to receive him or forbid him to come nearer. But now he could read a great dread in her snow-white face.

Then a stone slipped under his foot. Olav fell on his knee, and behind him there was a splash in the water. When he raised his head again, the vision was gone, but the tall swaying willow-herbs scattered over the scree stirred as though someone had fled that way.

For a moment he remained as he had fallen, on one knee, trying to collect himself. Then it came upon him, a wave of blood that seemed ready to burst his heart and his brain—and the scree was whirling upward, while dark patches fell one by one before his eyes, and he sank forward in a swoon.

He was roused by spots of rain—the first he saw was that the stones were thickly splashed, but not all wet; he saw there was blood on the stones where he had lain, and he felt his face stiffened and wet with blood. He saw the grey trail of the shower as it swept up the course of the stream, while the wood was whitened by a gust that reversed the leaves.

Olav stood up, feeling as if all the marrow had been taken from his bones. He had a terrible pain in the head—not from the fall, but from within—and in the heart, as he realized that she had

been here and was gone, and that the vision had been a revelation
of other times than these, times that he believed to have gone by
more than a generation ago. Body and soul were rent with a pain
unlike any other he had known, and he thought: "This is Death."

Then the fit of pain passed over; he got back his breath and
shook himself under the pouring rain. As he leaped back across
the brook, he found he was trembling and weak all over.

The rain streamed down as Olav a moment later hurried across
the pasture. Tore and the woman were peeping out through the
door of the shed. "What have you *done* to yourself, Olav?" asked
the house-carl in surprise.

Olav had forgotten the blood on his face. He answered that he
had run his forehead against the trunk of a fir. He flung himself
down on the couch at the far end of the sæter hut and lay prone
with his hands before his face, trying to get to the bottom of this.
The other two stood at the door looking out at the rain.

The sun was shining again, and the woodland gleamed, green
and blue and fine after its bath, as Olav and Tore rode on in the
afternoon. Olav was deep in thought. But at the bottom of his
soul, deeper than doubt and disquietude, lay joy. He had seen
that death had not yet parted him from her, and that his own
youth was living somewhere in time and space, in spite of all he
had done to kill it.

They did not reach Hestviken till night. Olav helped Tore with
the horses—they put them in the stable, in case there might be
another thunderstorm during the night. Then a strange thing happened as Olav reached over to pat the colt that stood in the stall
next his saddle-horse: the animal plunged, making a great clatter,
shied and backed. When Olav in surprise was going up to it, the
colt went quite wild.

"It seems the horse is afraid of you!" said Tore.

Olav had to leave its stall; he said nothing.

He fell asleep as soon as he lay down. In the morning his memory of the vision was half faded, or as though it had happened
long ago. But as he was about to dress, he went to the door of the
closet to look over his shirt—he was afraid he had got ticks from
the sæter. Then he saw with the corner of his eye that he was
bleeding behind the shoulder—there was the mark of a bite. As he
looked at it fresh blood oozed out of the little tooth-marks.

Once more the choking, bursting pain returned in his head and heart, and Olav had to clutch the doorpost until he had mastered the thought that this inconceivable thing was true—however it might have come about.

He had had a little scar there. Ingunn had bitten him once in wantonness—one night when he had been with her in her bower at Frettastein. It was an age since he had thought of it, for the mark had almost faded out with the years, and it was so far back on his shoulder that he could not see it without turning his head. But now the blood trickled red and fresh from the little pits left by her teeth.

1 0

OLAV went about like a sleepwalker in his own house, while the daughters of Arne and his kinsfolk and friends made ready for the great bridal journey. His whole mind was turned inward, upon the memory of his vision. He had to think out what it might betoken, that she had come back thus.

The scar on his shoulder continued to bleed in the mornings. He felt nothing of it at other times, but if his thoughts ever strayed for a while from his meeting with his dead wife, it recalled itself to his mind by a little pricking or smarting.

His past now seemed so far behind him that he no longer knew what was true memory and what was dream. But he thought he remembered that she had said that night, laughing, that she would mark her own with a bite. And had she now come to remind him of that?

Now he would soon be left alone again. All that he thought he could never part with would soon have slipped out of his hands. Soon he would be as alone in the world and as free as when he bound himself to his child bride.

It was a long and weary road he had travelled since their young days. And when he thought of it, the time they had lived their life together as man and wife here in Hestviken was but the smallest part of it: for twelve years they had dwelt together, but the years of his outlawry in his youth had been near ten, and now it was over thirteen years since she died. Never before had he chanced to think about it—the time they had been suffered to live together as married folk had really been short. It had appeared to him that they had belonged to each other as long as he could remember, and this did not cease with her death. It was only when his own life began to dry up and wither, as a tree grows old, hollow, and decayed, with fewer and fewer branches that burst into leaf in spring, that he had ceased to feel they were bound together, in a far deeper sense than he had ever been able to see; but the brief years in which they had been suffered to enjoy each other's love, at Frettastein that autumn and the first years here at Hestviken, had been but the visible sign of the mysterious relation between them.

And had it now been vouchsafed her to fulfil her promise and come to him—the living to the dying—and had she been permitted to renew the mark she had put on him in wild girlish wantonness, then it must have been in order to remind him that the bond between them was not yet broken, that their pact still held, and that she could still claim him for her own.

If that were so, they could not be parted, unless God's judgment parted them as far asunder as heaven and hell—when finally they had become as unlike each other as the free and blest spirits in God's presence are unlike the Devil's fettered thralls.

Another thing he saw, though he knew not how it came about that he could see it: that souls have no age. Sin and grace fashion them and give them shape, but not as years and labour and sickness mark the bodily husk. Ingunn's ravaged body and his own weatherbeaten, war-scarred frame were but as hard-worn garments; that was what the makers of images meant when they painted souls as naked little children, the angels and devils taking each their own as they issue from the mouths of the dying. Old age does not survive death; but the blest and the lost shall receive their everlasting destiny in the full force and wakefulness of youth. And that too they had been taught by Brother Vegard—in eternity all are ever young.

There were fifty in the company, with house-carls and serving-women, when Cecilia Olavsdatter's bridal progress set out from Hestviken. With pack-horses and cattle it was a brave train passing through the countryside. Olav looked at it well pleased: as his neighbours reckoned such things, he had prospered of late years. Since the Swedish troubles he had enjoyed honour in the district;

all knew that he might have had power there, had he cared to use
it; wealth he had, and his children had turned out so as to bring
him joy and honour. To no man had he made complaint in the
hard years, and none had seen him puffed up in the days of prosperity—*this* world had never been able to prevail against him.

So now he must follow the course that his heart had prompted
all these years—fall at the feet of Christ crucified and confess that
he had lived the whole time secretly at war with God and now
knelt before Him, vanquished.

What might afterwards befall him he could not tell. 'Twas unlikely any man would care now to drag forth into the light his
manslaughter of long ago. That was only a sting he had pressed
into his own flesh—it had worked out again long since and was forgotten, but the wound had spread and consumed him.

The likeliest penance to be imposed on him would be to make
a pilgrimage that might last until his death, old as he now was.
And he thought upon it with an easy heart, at the very moment
when he surveyed the marks of his prosperity—he would gladly
leave it all, suffer hands and feet to be fettered, wander as a peni-
tent pilgrim from sanctuary to sanctuary, begging his food—

But every time he thought of Eirik a thrill of anxiety went
through him. His son was only present to his mind as he knelt
before the choir of the convent church, erect and radiant in his
bridegroom's attire. Eirik had given himself to God, without fear
and without self-seeking. And as he came forward in the frock of
a barefoot friar to bid the world farewell—in the eyes of his father,
who dared now give free play at last to his love for his son, all the
brightness of the scene was centred on Eirik's narrow, shining
crown.

To him he would now say: "I am not your true father—your
father's slayer I am."

If Eirik raised him up after *that*—then all would be well.

How Cecilia would take it was a question to which he gave little
thought.

The wedding at Gunnarsby passed off bravely; it brought honour both to the Rypungs and to Olav. Cecilia Olavsdatter was so
fair a bride that she shed a radiance about her when she appeared
with the golden crown upon her loose and frizzly flaxen hair.

It struck Olav next morning, when he saw the young wife

attired with the linen coif—her hair had been the fairest thing about Cecilia, and now that it was hidden away, she seemed much smaller, so pale and light-eyed was she, and short of stature. But the place was strange to her, she was unused to her condition—no doubt she would be brighter when she was used to the married state and to Gunnarsby. Jörund seemed mightily pleased with his bride.

The sixth day of the wedding—Olav was to take his departure the day after—the Kolbeinssons showed him and some of his nearest kin the jewels that their mother owned and that they would one day share among them. She had a great treasure, Gunhild Rypa, and many beautiful things.

The Kolbeinssons and the young wives of Aake and Steinar grew very animated after a while. And again it came upon Olav that he did not altogether *like* these folks. It struck him as immodest and unmannerly that they could not handle the valuables in a calmer and more dignified way—their voices jerked up and down, now loud and sharp, and the next moment smirking and bland, as they watched each other with greedy and suspicious glances. " 'Twill scarcely be an amicable division of the inheritance when the mother is gone," thought Olav. That at least they had not failed in, the gentlefolk among whom he had been fostered, nor himself either—not letting it be seen that either loss or gain disturbed their serenity.

He chanced to look at his daughter. She stood silently by her husband's side. Olav read in her eyes that her thoughts were the same as his, and he felt a little sting as he recalled that tomorrow he was to ride away and leave her behind with these folks.

In the evening he went out strolling with his daughter on a path that led down to the lake. He himself had asked her to go with him—he wished to find out how she was doing in her new home. But Cecilia said nothing about that, and Olav could not bring himself to ask any questions.

Only when they were going up toward the manor again did the man say: "Now thus it is, Cecilia—you know that the day will come, mayhap sooner than any of us looks for it, when you will return to Hestviken, and then all will be yours. Bear that in mind if it should chance now and again that you feel a longing for your home at first."

"God grant you a long life, Father," the bride hastened to say.

"Have you never spoken of it with Jörund—that he should move
to Hestviken in your lifetime?" she then asked.

Olav had never thought of this, so he remained silent. There
was no great comfort in the thought: he did not believe he would
care to live under the same roof as his son-in-law. So he merely
answered:

"Likely enough when you have been some time here at Gunnarsby you will be unwilling to leave the place. Here you have
young people in the house"—he meant to say something of young
women of her own age, but shrank, when it came to the point,
from reckoning Cecilia's sisters-in-law as an advantage—"wide
lands and many neighbours. And you will be free to go abroad
and will have much at your command."

To this Cecilia made no reply.

Next morning Olav left the table before the other guests; there
were many who were to ride homeward in his company, so he
thought he ought to see to the saddling and packing of the horses.
When he came out on the steps of the barn—where their saddles
and harness had been stored—he heard Cecilia's voice within; she
was talking to old Tore. His daughter said:

"To think that you are to be parted from me—can you not come
hither and dwell with us at Gunnarsby? Brynhild and Lucia have
their own henchmen and waiting-women; they can scarce grudge
me a man who can tend my horses and serve me."

"God forgive us, Cecilia"—the old man laughed—"could you
not find a man who is even worse fitted to be a lady's henchman
at Gunnarsby?"

Olav could not help smiling at the thought. Tore was a strange
figure, he was so huge and broad in the chest and shoulders, but
his legs were short and crooked, he had a round head with long
grey hair hanging stiffly about it, his face was covered with little
wrinkles, red and fleshy, and his eyes were dull as those of a
boiled fish. He was strong as a giant and chose the hardest work,
a man of few words and one to be trusted; one could not call his
manner discourteous, but he was sufficient to himself and could
never have learned such meekness as the servants at Gunnarsby
had to practise—and now his age was three score years and more.

"I should be so *kind* to you!" Cecilia begged.

"You are as good as gold, I know that. But now I have served your father twenty years and more, and if the truth be told, 'twould be harder for Olav to get on without me at Hestviken than the man himself can guess, or anyone else."

" 'Twill be hard for me to do without you. No friend have I had so faithful as you, since I was so small that you let me ride on your back."

"When I am too old for aught else," said old Tore with a laugh, "I will come and be nurse to your children, Cecilia."

"Ay, will you promise that?"

Olav went in. Cecilia was sitting on the old house-carl's knees and had put her arm round his neck; she looked into his ugly face like a child begging for something.

Olav nodded to the two. "You are unhappy at parting from Tore, I can see."

Cecilia had risen hastily, and now her face was as calm and stubborn as usual.

"I have asked Tore, Father, if he would come and live with us here at Gunnarsby."

" 'Tis not sure, Cecilia, that it would go well with him here—old folk are ill matched with new customs."

Tore agreed with his master.

In going eastward the bridal progress had been compelled to follow the best roads there were, but on the homeward journey Olav, together with some of the guests who wished to travel rapidly, took the same short cut through the forest as he had ridden in returning from Gunnarsby the first time.

They rested at the same sæter as before. And while his companions lay and took their ease in the meadow above, Olav stole from them and walked down by the bank of the stream.

The sun was shining, and nothing was changed—only the willow-herb was pale and flowerless; it had begun to shed its seed, which drifted like silvery down in the breeze. Olav stood for a while gazing over at the scree, but today he could see nothing strange.

For the first time it occurred to him that his vision might have been a phantom—or something else: "*a negotio perambulante in tenebris, ab incursu et dæmonio meridiano.*" Thus in the evening prayer one asks for help against the thing that walketh in dark-

ness, and against the assaults of evil spirits at noonday. And in
truth he had often felt that just in the stillness of the noonday
heat there are many things abroad that one cannot see.

Or what if it had been she, but with some other purpose—to beg
him take good heed, ere he gave away their only child—

Then Olav shook it from him. He would hold to what he had
believed at first.

Coming through the church town Olav was told that there had
been a fire at Hestviken. The great old barn to the east of the
manor and the haystacks had been burned down.

It had begun in the forest away on the north side of the inlet—
fishermen had made a fire over on the Bull—and then it had caught
the heather, and the fir forest was burned up, but the flames were
checked at the cleft that runs inland and is overgrown with lime
and hazel. But for a while the wind had blown from the north,
and sparks had fallen on the roofed haystacks outside the barn;
then hay and barn had gone up in a blaze—for a time the houses
beyond had been in danger.

It was strange how unhomely it had made the place look,
thought Olav, as he stood next morning looking over toward the
Bull—with the stumps of trees that stood out, jagged, blackened,
and scorched red, or lay fallen on the burned moss. A thick band
of charcoal and soot floated along the beach all the way.

The barn was the only building at Hestviken that belonged to
the great days of the manor, so Olav was sorry to lose it. And now
they would be in sore straits for fodder in the coming winter.

He had now to think of rebuilding and of getting in what
might serve for fodder. Then came the seal-hunting and the fishing season. Olav had his hands full with one thing and another
throughout the autumn and winter. His house-folk remarked that
he gave unusual care to all that he did that winter. To Tore he had
dropped hints that led the men to suppose he was minded to make
another journey in foreign lands next summer, and perhaps he intended that Jörund Kolbeinsson should come to Hestviken with
his wife.

Olav was happier at home than he had been in all the years he
had been there. He liked the loneliness and he liked the busy activity, for he felt it to be a preparation for departure. He even got

to like the view of the Bull's neck with the burned wood when
he was used to it, especially after the autumn storms had cleared
it and snow had fallen. It had a more open look.

That winter Einar and Valgard, the sons of Björn, Torhild's
brothers, were away north in Haugsvik. Olav had often wished
he could hear something of his son, the young Björn, and of the
boy's mother. Now he sent off Tore, for he knew Einar and his
brother well from of old.

Tore came back and was able to tell him that Björn had left
home last spring: he wished to go out into the world and try his
fortune. His uncles said he had gone away to learn the trade of a
blacksmith—from childhood he had been more cunning with his
hands than most lads—he had talked of going to a man in the
Dovre Fell of whom folk said that his mother was a giant's daughter—but maybe that was not true; he was accounted a most excellent smith. With him Björn Olavsson would take service.

Torhild and Ketil prospered; there were three children born
to them: a daughter and then a son and daughter who were twins.
Nay, Björn had parted from his parents in all kindness, and his
mother had bestowed on him saddle and horse and all he needed
for the journey, in such noble sort for their condition that folk
had called her overweening.

Olav had little to say to Tore's report, for over this son he had
never had any rights.

I I

Next year, in the early summer, Olav put up a new barn and had
it roofed by the time of bearing in the hay. He and his house-folk
were busy haymaking in the meadows down by the mouth of the
river—it was an afternoon a few days before Margaretmass [9]—
when a strange man came up to him among the hay-cocks, gave
him greeting, and said:

"I have a message for you, Olav, which is such that I may not
tarry in the telling. Will you go with me a little apart, so that we
may speak—alone?"

[9] June 10.

Olav did so, and when they came a little way from the others, the man said:

"I come from Gunnarsby. Your daughter is in travail of child-birth and in great jeopardy; it were well if you could come to her and that as swiftly as your swiftest horse can bring you."

"Is it so," asked Olav, "that they deem her life to be at stake?"

"There is peril of it," replied the other.

Olav ran back to the field, found Ragna and Tore, and told them how matters stood. He bade Tore bring Brunsvein from the paddock and Ragna fetch food; then he went down to the stranger and asked him to go with him to the house. As they went, Olav asked, of a sudden:

"But where have you your horse, man?"

"Nay, I have walked from Gunnarsby."

"Have you walked?" Olav looked at his guest suspiciously. He was a man in the thirties, looked like any other serving-man—Olav could not call to mind having seen him before, but that was noth-ing to go by, since they had so many folk about them at Gun-narsby; he had a trustworthy look. "Did Jörund send you hither with such a message and gave you no horse?"

"To tell the truth, Olav, 'twas not the Rypungs that sent me. But Cecilia helped me once when I was in bad straits, and then I vowed to God and Saint Halvard I would repay her if it were ever in my power. I thought I had a chance to do so now—if it be given her to see you and speak with you, before she may die—"

Olav was somewhat easier in his mind as he thought that perhaps his daughter was not in such a bad way after all, since it was neither her husband nor his brothers' wives who had dispatched the messenger. There seemed to be something strange about the whole affair, but however it might be, he was glad to have been told of his daughter's sickness, and he would ride to Gunnarsby at once. He asked no more questions of the stranger—Finn was his name—but on arriving at the manor gave orders that he should be well housed and cared for, and when he had taken his rest, they were to lend him a horse for his homeward journey.

An hour later Olav was in the saddle and stretched Brunsvein to the utmost—this was the swiftest colt in his stable, but he did not usually ride him himself, as he was not so handsome to look at as Bay Roland, his own saddle-horse. On reaching Skeidis parish he stayed for a few hours with his kinsfolk at Hestbæk and gave

Brunsvein a rest, but Olav mounted again long before sunrise, and late in the day he came to Gunnarsby.

But there he was told at once that Cecilia was doing well; she had given birth to a fine and healthy son; this was already a day and a half ago. No, Mistress Lucia replied to his questions, Cecilia had not had so hard a travail, she had been in no more peril of her life than any other young wife. Olav saw plainly that they were greatly surprised at his coming, and he was no more than moderately welcome at Gunnarsby this time. There was something behind this—he could not guess what—but so as not to betray this Finn he replied, when Lucia asked him where he had heard of Cecilia's illness, that he had met some folk at church who had kindred in these parts; they had told him that his daughter who was married at Gunnarsby last summer might expect a child about the time of Margaretmass.

"Ay, but 'twas not expected before Marymass [1]—" Mistress Lucia broke off in confusion, as though she had said too much, and there was an odd look on the faces of the others. Brynhild said the young wife had been sore afraid all the time she had been with child; maybe she had talked of it, saying she was afraid of this too, that it might come before its time—

It was strangely unlike Cecilia to be afraid, thought her father. But with women one can never know, and after all a man was no judge of these things. He could only be glad that Cecilia was doing well, and since he was here, he was glad too that he would see his daughter again.

It was fairly dark in the upper chamber where Cecilia lay, when Lucia took Olav up to see her in the evening. It rejoiced Olav to see that his daughter was glad he had come; she said that all was well with her now, and she was doing well in every way. The room in which they had laid her was spacious and richly bedight, and there was no lack of neighbours' wives and serving-maids to attend to her and her child.

Jörund spoke very lovingly to his wife and seemed exceedingly proud that he too had a son. And the women loudly praised the child. Olav took it in his arms when they handed it to him, looked at it—this was the little lad who would one day take his place at Hestviken, if God should suffer him to grow into a man—but he

[1] Assumption, B.V.M.—August 15.

had always thought that new-born babes were ugly little monsters to look at, all except Cecilia; she had been fair from the first day of her life.

Next morning Olav sat with his daughter again; they talked for the most part of those they knew at home. It was very little Cecilia had to say of how she liked her new home—only that there was far more bustle here than at Hestviken, and the folk of Gunnarsby were much abroad to feastings and the like—this had been a burden to her of late; but now, to be sure, she would stay more at home, as she had a child at the breast.

"Ay," said her father, "but a little lad like this will grow quickly, and soon you will be free again."

" 'Twas not of that I thought," replied the young wife hastily. "I must take after you, Father—I like best to live where there is no such crowd."

Her last word struck her father as strangely scornful; he was about to correct the child, bid her enjoy her youth while she had it.

At that moment one of the neighbours' wives came with the babe, to lay it to its mother's breast. Cecilia wore only a little vest covering her bosom and arms; as the woman raised her on the pillows, her father had a glimpse of her naked body about the waist, and he saw that her side was all black and blue. At the same time the sun shone in on the bed—there were snatches of brightness between the clouds—and he noticed that her face also bore marks, as of blows.

"Have you hurt yourself?" her father asked after the strange woman had gone.

"Yes, I fell and bruised myself," said Cecilia. "That is what made him come before his time."

Olav thought it so far well that a mishap of this sort had caused it—he had been afraid she might have inherited her mother's infirmity; and no doubt it was this fall that had made her uneasy.

"So then it was you thought of sending this Finn for me?"

Cecilia was silent for moment, as though reflecting:

"I did not ask him to go either—but perhaps he thought he owed me gratitude. And then maybe he took it into his head to repay me thus—when he heard I had fallen and hurt myself—"

"I wonder, though," said Olav, "whether he be yet returned—

have you heard? He was to borrow a horse of ours, so I could take it back with me."

"Finn will take good care that you have the horse back. But to tell the truth, Father, I do not think we shall see him at Gunnarsby. They are stricter with their servants here than we are wont to be, and as Finn ran off from here without asking leave—"

"Did he so?"

Cecilia nodded. "I wish I knew," she said, "what he will do with himself now. He has been a trusty man to me."

"Perhaps you wish me to take him into my service at Hestviken?" Olav asked.

Cecilia was silent for a moment, looking down at the child at her breast.

"Nay, *that* I wish not at all," she then said in her curt little voice.

Next day the boy was baptized, and Olav intended to return home on the day after. But in the evening, as he was about to bid his daughter good-night, he chanced to be alone with her for a moment. Then he made up his mind to ask her.

"Tell me now, Cecilia, while we are alone—have you aught on your mind that you would fain tell me?"

"No, I have not," said the young wife firmly. Seeing that her father looked disappointed, she gave him her hand. "But, for all that, I am glad you came, Father!"

On the morrow Olav set out for home. He had left the parish itself behind him and was now riding uphill by the bank of a little stream, on both sides of which were small farmsteads in the midst of green meadows. He was deep in thought when his horse gave a sudden start—a man had risen abruptly from beneath some bushes at the edge of the bridle-path. It was that Finn.

They exchanged greetings. But as the man said nothing, Olav thought he must.

"It turned out not so ill as you foretold, my friend," he said kindly. "My daughter is now in good case, and yesterday we christened Kolbein Jörundsson."

"Ay, so I have heard."

"Are you on your way down to Gunnarsby?" asked Olav.

"Nay, I am bound southward," said the man. He had slept at one of the little farms yonder, where he was known.

Olav reflected that it was this Finn who had brought him the

news of his grandson's birth, so to speak. He said so and thanked
him for it. He had brought with him ten English florins [2] that he
had had by him since his voyage to England—to make a suitable
altar-offering if there should be need of such. He now took out
the two he had left and gave them to Finn.

The man accepted them, hesitating a little. Then he stood looking at Olav, and Olav sat looking down at him. Neither of them
spoke. At last Olav said he must be getting on. "Maybe we are
going the same way?"

They were, said the man. So Olav made Brunsvein go at a
foot's pace, and Finn walked at his side, and not a sound was heard
but the gurgling of the brook in its turf banks and the horse's
hoofs when they struck a stone, and the faint summery murmur
in the tree-tops; and the sun beat down, gleaming upon the foliage
—and both men kept silence.

Once Olav asked if the other had had the loan of a horse from
Hestviken, and Finn answered no, he had preferred to walk. After
a while Olav asked whether Finn was from these parts, and Finn
answered no, he came from Ness in Raumarike. With that their
talk came to an end.

When they had journeyed together for an hour or more Finn
said he must turn aside here—he pointed along a little path that
led up a hill. So Olav thanked him for his company, and Finn
thanked in return and was gone into the wood.

Afterwards Olav regretted that he had not tried to find out
something. But he had shrunk from cross-questioning his daughter's serving-man.—So he rode on at a brisker pace.

Olav had had to promise that he would look in again at Hestbæk on his way home. And this time they did not let him go so
soon—it was six years since he had last been to see his kinsfolk
here, said Arne, "and 'twill surely be six years ere you come again
—and then I shall be under the sod."

Arne Torgilsson was now over eighty winters old, but his age
sat none too heavily on him. He was like his father, Torgils Foulbeard, as he might have been had he not lost his wits; Arne was
rather a small man, but handsome and well built; his hair and beard
were white as bog-cotton, and his florid cheeks and sea-blue eyes
showed brightly in the midst of all this whiteness. Torgunn, his

[2] A gold coin worth six shillings and eightpence.

youngest daughter, carried on the farm together with her sons; she had been widowed many years already.

Arne gave a grunt when Olav told him that Cecilia had borne a son.

"Then 'twill be the same as here—none but a daughter's son to succeed you at Hestviken! To me God would not grant a son, in spite of my prayers and vows—you had one, and he has turned barefoot friar. You, Olav, who are so rich and have always stood so well with the priests, could you not have sent to Rome and been given dispensation? Then you might have married Torgunn and carried on the Fivil race [3] in our old home."

"Could you not have thought of that before, kinsman," said Olav with a laugh, "ere Torgunn and I were old folk?"

Olav had to stay at Hestbæk till the third day. It was near sunset when he came riding out to Hestviken. The sky was full of clouds, which shone and blazed and cast red and yellow reflections in the waters of the fiord. The rays of the sinking sun shot out aslant, and the long shadows fell fitfully across the meadows, so that Olav could not distinguish plainly who it was that came toward him through the fields; but there was something both familiar and strange in the tall, broad-shouldered figure, and the cut of his dress had a courtly air ill suited to the place. By the man's side walked a gigantic he-goat, black as coal, with a huge pair of horns.

Then Olav saw that it was Eirik—Eirik who came to meet him in a particoloured jerkin, half red and half yellow, so short and tight that Olav thought it unseemly; he had a leather belt about his waist, with a long dagger, a knife, and a pouch hanging from it. The dark, curly hair had not yet grown so long as to hide the tonsure. Olav could not quite rid himself of his first impression, something devilish in the vision that presented itself, even when he had recognized the goat as their own old he-goat.

Olav reined in his horse. Eirik ran forward the last few steps, laid his hand on his father's saddle-bow, and asked, looking up at him:

"Father—is she dead?"

"Cecilia? Nay, she is well." In silence they continued to look

[3] *Fivil* means bog-cotton, alluding to the fair hair and complexion of the Hestviken family. See *The Snake Pit*, p. 338.

at each other, Eirik growing ever redder and more distressed. But
there was no help for it, he had to speak out himself:

"I have come home, Father," he said in a tone of supplication.
"As you see."

"I do see," Olav jerked at the reins, so that Eirik had to stand
aside, but he walked beside his father's horse up to the houses.

Olav dismounted in the yard, replying to Tore's and Ragna's
questions concerning Cecilia. Then he turned to the house door,
where Eirik stood outside, waiting. The son followed his father
in. Olav flung off his cloak, laid aside his arms; not till then did he
turn to Eirik.

"Where have you come from?"

"You know that well," said Eirik in a low voice. "I left home—
the convent, I mean—yestermorn—had the loan of a boat from
Galfrid—"

"Have you lost heart for the cloistered life?" Or—have the friars
sent you away? Have you done amiss, so that they will not have
you?" asked Olav harshly.

Eirik was crimson in the face; a quiver as of pain passed over
his features. But he answered very meekly: "The brethren thought
I was not intended for the life. For you know, Father—'tis for that
one has the year of probation—and my year was up two months
ago. I was loath to part from my brethren; they let me stay awhile
longer. But then they told me they believed I was not meant for
a monk—I could better serve God if I lived in the world."

"You were to live in the world and serve God?" There was icy
scorn in his father's voice. "Little must those brethren know you!"

He saw that his son shrank a little. But then Eirik answered as
meekly as before: "Nay, Father—my brethren know me best of all
—my father, Brother Einar, and the guardian. I shall not forget
what they have taught me. Think not I am come home to take
up that—iniquitous—life I led before. I—I—they have adopted me
as their brother—as a brother *ab extra*. And you yourself know
best that a man may live in the world and yet be mindful of his
Redeemer and serve Him."

Olav stood looking at the young man in silence.

"What is this for—what garb is this?"

Eirik blushed again, all cramped and pinched in the ridiculous
finery that was too tight and skimpy in every way.

"They gave it me in the convent," he said humbly. "They had

received it as a gift, and they all agreed to give it to me—that I
might avoid falling into debt in the town for clothes to go home
in."

"Ah."

Then Ragna came in with the food, and the household followed
her to take their meal. Olav talked with his folk, but said no more
to Eirik—scarce looked at him.

When the meal was ended Olav had ale and mead brought in
—bade his house-folk drink to the welfare of Kolbein Jörundsson.
Eirik accepted the horn, drank to his nephew's honour, and let it
go further. But next time it came round to him, he let it pass, and
soon after he stole quietly out of doors.

He must be gone to say his hours, said Ragna with feeling—he
kept his hours and wore a great rosary round his neck underneath
his jerkin.

It only stirred Olav to deeper scorn and anger when he heard it.

I 2

OLAV's exasperation had settled on him, as it were, at first sight
of his newly returned son. He had accustomed himself to think
of Eirik as though he were already half a saint, and utterly unlooked-for his son came strolling toward him across the fields at
home, ridiculously tricked out, with a stinking black he-goat as
companion.

And then came the thought of all the difficulties that Eirik's
fickleness would bring in its train. A settlement with these barefoot friars he must have too. According to their rule he thought
they could not accept any endowment from the men who sought
admission to their fraternity, so all that they had received when
Eirik went to the convent had been given as alms; Olav could not
demand its return. But if they tried to claim anything of what he
had promised them when Eirik became a monk, then—! Olav was
now angry with the whole crew of them; first they had strength-
ened Eirik in his purpose as much as they could, and then—if indeed he could place any reliance on what Eirik himself said—they
had supported him again when he began to have scruples and to
doubt his calling to the monastic life.

But there was something worse than this. It was Eirik's determination to forsake the world that had induced Jörund Rypa to
come forward with his suit—it was impossible to doubt that. And
in spite of all, Olav was not so sure—not even after his last journey
to Gunnarsby—that Cecilia's happiness was fully assured among
the Rypungs. If, then, they were justified in thinking that her kinsmen had not dealt quite honestly by them—

Olav said something of this to Eirik one day. He saw that it
made his son unhappy.

"But 'tis not unheard of," replied Eirik meekly, "for a novice
to be found unfitted to live according to the Rule."

Olav made no reply to this. What Eirik said was true, but then
most of those who entered the cloister became monks and nuns
in due time, and Eirik had been so zealous when he took the habit
last year, and he had formed his determination to become a monk
without persuasion or pressure from anyone.

" 'Tis not sure either that I shall ever marry," he then said.

"Is it not? Do you think then to take up your old evil courses
again?"

Eirik turned red as fire. But he answered calmly and mildly:
"But you, Father, you have lived as becomes a Christian man in
all these years since our mother died—although you have neither
married again nor taken to yourself a leman."

"I?" exclaimed Olav, revolted. "I was a man well on in years.
And not even in my youth was I known in the stews or in the
haunts of dicers—"

Still Eirik spoke composedly: "I promised Father Einar, when
I parted from him, that I would keep myself from dicing and
overmuch drinking. Will you not believe, Father, that I have
learned *something* good and profitable in this year I have dwelt
under Saint Franciscus's roof and prayed every day in the presence of God Himself in the mystery of His holiest sanctuary?"

"Ah, well," muttered Olav, somewhat ashamed. "Time will
show, Eirik—how long you hold to *these* resolutions."

"You should not say such things!" Eirik sprang up and went
out.

But it seemed only to increase Olav's irritation that Eirik to all
appearance had now turned pious and meek. He never allowed
himself to be goaded into an angry answer, he neither boasted nor

told fabulous stories. His father kept him so strictly now that Eirik owned nothing he could call his own. Olav himself had always been a generous giver of alms, but none of his gifts to the poor and sick were allowed to pass through Eirik's hands. Eirik devised a means, however: he rendered many charitable services to his house-mates and to folk who passed through, showing thereby his humility and goodwill. That too was a vexation to his father, and it vexed him every time he noticed that Eirik withdrew himself apart, went down among the rocks by the waterside or into one of the outhouses to say his prayers alone. He told his beads daily and said the little hours of our Lady, most of which he now knew. By degrees Olav discovered that Eirik had set up little crosses here and there on the outskirts of the manor, in the places he frequented for saying his prayers.

In the course of the autumn a rumour came to Olav's ears that Eirik Olavsson had forsaken his convent because he felt a call to a yet stricter life of penitence. It was said to be his intention to build himself a cell in the churchyard and become an anchorite. The like had never been known in the parish before, so there was great talk among the folk—some made a mock of it, but others thought it must be a great blessing to the countryside. At last Olav guessed that in one way or another Eirik himself must have originated these rumours, and so he took his son to task. Eirik was thrown into dire confusion—and it was the first time since his return from the convent that his father had seen him falter and blink his eyes. But his answer was that he had never said he himself would turn anchorite; he had only spoken of something that had been read aloud in the refectory last winter, a book that was called *Vitæ Patrum*.

One day Eirik came to Olav and asked if he might bring the eldest of the Rundmyr children to Hestviken. The boy had become a cripple after an illness at the age of seven; when they laid him on the ground outside in summer he could just push himself about a little with his arms; he scarcely had the power of speech either. Before his sickness he had been a lively, handsome child— he bore no resemblance either to Liv or to Anki, but to a young and merry, red-haired and brown-eyed house-carl who had been at Hestviken the winter before those two were married. But that did not detract from Anki's paternal pride, and even now, when the boy was in this state, both Anki and Liv said they would rather lose all their other children than this one. But though they loved him so, and though they always received such abundant doles from Hestviken that they ought not to have suffered want, the sick child was covered with sores and lice and likely to rot away in his own uncleanliness. His parents did not neglect him, they stuffed him with the best morsels, but they could not cope with the filth.

Olav did not see how he could say no to Eirik's request, for the child was his godson and was called Olav after him. So he merely said that Eirik was not to bring him into the house until he could rid him of his lice and keep his sores so clean that they did not stink too foully. Eirik then kept Olav Livsson in the barn until the cold set in, but then they had to let him lie in the living-room. By this time Eirik had got him tolerably clean, and the boy had learned to swing himself along a few steps with a pair of crutches. In the course of the winter he acquired sense enough to be able to perform a little light work, such as soaking withies and deer sinews, or planing rough wooden implements. He also learned to speak better, but he was still a stammerer and tongue-tied. However, there were many drawbacks to having him in the house. Not that the house-folk were ever unfriendly with him; and if once in a while Olav Audunsson took notice of his godson, it was always in the way of kindness—as far as that went, Olav was not displeased that the poor creature was now looked after like a Christian child—but when he was vexed at the trouble the sick boy caused them, Eirik was made to feel his father's ill humour.

As yet Olav knew nothing of how the folk at Gunnarsby had taken the news that the son of Hestviken had returned. But he was a prey to misgivings whenever he thought of it, and it was never long absent from his mind.

In late autumn Olav found time to make a journey to Oslo, and while there he visited the Minorite convent. But he soon saw that he would be told nothing there of the reason for Eirik's defection. It was clear that the friars reckoned this as one of the convent's domestic affairs, and the silence of the cloister was as a wall. They had nothing but good to say of Eirik: they had grown devotedly attached to their young brother, but since it had been made clear both to himself and to them that God desired to lead this soul by other paths than that of the monastic life, then—

"Was it after the beating he gave that peasant at Tveit that you were clear about this?" asked Olav.

He had heard of this through Claus Wiephart. A pious widow at one of the farms of Tveit had sent word to the convent that she would give them some homespun cloth and victuals. Brother Stevne was to fetch the gifts and took Brother Eirik with him; he was to help carry them home. But when they were ready to leave, each with his load on his back, the widow's only son came home, and he had less love for the beggar monks than his mother, so he covered the two friars with abuse—till Brother Eirik could command himself no longer, flung down his sack, sprang upon the peasant, and dealt him a blow on the jaw that felled him to the ground. True, Brother Stevne had remonstrated with him on the spot, and Eirik had humbled himself before the peasant; at home in the convent, too, he had doubtless had to do penance— the barefoot friars would be ill served by a revival of the memories of their former combativeness. But the incident was talked of far and wide.

So Olav had thought to hit the mark with this. But the guardian never winced. Nay, said he, they could not send away a novice on account of a false step of that kind, if he showed true repentance of his sin. Eirik had made no attempt to excuse his hot temper, but had submitted to his penance in such a way that he might be called a pattern of obedience.

Eirik's father smiled incredulously.

Then at last the guardian told him—Eirik had come hither because he believed himself called to be a priest. But since there was a hindrance to this—

"Hindrance?" Olav turned suddenly red in the face. "Who has said, father, that there was any hindrance?"

"Such is the commandment of Holy Church, Olav. No man who has a blemish on body or limbs may serve before the altar. So with his maimed hand Eirik cannot—"

Olav said nothing. He had forgotten that Eirik lacked two joints of the little finger of his left hand. His first thought had been of Eirik's birth.

The guardian resumed, and now he spoke rapidly and with full assurance: Eirik had sought admittance to their order because he believed that God had called him to be a priest. But since God never gives a man a call that he cannot follow, it was clear that

Eirik Olavsson had been mistaken in this. But that placed the matter at once on a different footing. During the remainder of his year of probation Eirik had striven to ascertain whether he were chosen to serve God in the cloister as a lay brother; but in the end they had all been certain that it was not so.

With that Olav had to be satisfied. The brethren said nothing of the gifts they had received when Eirik came to them, but on the other hand they were silent as to what had been promised them later. So these questions were never broached.

But Olav Audunsson parted from the Minorites in but indifferent kindness. And after that time he always spoke of these friars with ill will. And since in all else he was known to be a pious man and one so well disposed to cloister folk and priests that not even Sira Hallbjörn Erlingsson had been able to quarrel with him, folk deemed that he must have just cause to complain of the barefoot friars' conduct in this matter.

It was true that the first thing to shake Eirik's determination was the knowledge that he could not be ordained priest.

He had thrown himself into the new life with such burning zeal that the master of the novices, Brother Einar, had rather to restrain him. Many of the monks were wont to stay behind in church after matins in order to pray til prime. Eirik forthwith asked leave to do this every morning, and Brother Einar had to order him to go back to the dormitory and lie down again.

Eirik himself thought he needed no more sleep than a bird on the bough. Were he never so tired when called to matins, the first breath of the cool air of the summer night which met him as he came into the cloister garth was enough to make him wide awake. To enter the cold, dark church was almost as it had felt when, as a child, he plunged into the sea for a swim. During matins the lofty vaulted building grew lighter and lighter. At midsummer the first rays of the morning sun swept clear over the hills behind Aker as the brethren left the choir and crossed the green courtyard to return to their dormitory.

But two mornings in the week he was given leave to stay behind in church after matins. As he knelt in prayer the images in the choir windows became clearer, the colours began to shine—then the sun fired the glass, and the reds and yellows glowed and sparkled, till the whole choir was filled with unearthly light and

warmth from the many-coloured sunbeams that splashed the paint-
ings on the walls and the altar cross and the candlesticks with
flecks of blue and violet and gold. When the brethren returned to
say· prime, every corner of the church was filled with sunshine
and reflected sunshine—and then came the sound of footsteps in
the nave, echoing in the vault, as folk came in to hear mass.

Every time he was to join in the singing he felt the same surge
of joy: he looked forward every day to singing during mass, he
looked forward to Sundays and feast-days, for then they sang the
hours as well; he looked forward to all masses for the dead, for
then he joined in singing the vigil the evening before. He had always rejoiced in his own beautiful voice. Now he thought of
how he was turning this precious gift to account, and in holy awe
he set himself to learn to use it in singing God's praises. He was
then reminded of a verse, one of the first he had learned in this
house: "*Eructavit cor meum verbum bonum: dico ego opera mea
Regi.*" [4] Eirik often chose the whole of the psalm that opens with
these words as a theme for reflection when he was allowed to stay
behind in the church; he did not yet know it word for word, but
there were riches enough in what he had learned.

The first image that had presented itself to him when he gave
himself over to prayer—when his Christianity appeared to him as
an upper chamber full of locked chests that he had never thought
of unlocking—remained with him. Every day new keys were
placed in his hands, and he saw that a man's life in this world is
never long enough to permit him to lay his hands on more than a
tiny fragment of the treasures that lie hidden in the secret stores
of the faith.

One day a book on paradise had been read out in the refectory.
Eirik recalled this chapter next morning as he knelt in the choir
and thought upon Gethsemane. He saw paradise before his eyes:
a garden like their own, where the hard fruit now clustered
thickly on the trees, while pot-herbs teemed on the rich mould of
the beds, and the flowers were beginning to bloom along the walls.
Thus had God planted and sown it for a possession for the first
human pair. One tree alone He had forbidden them to touch, but
that made them ready to believe the serpent, when he tempted
them and said this tree was the most excellent of all—and immediately they fell to plundering it. It was this garden that God gave

[4] Psalm xlv, 1.

to the race of man as an earnest. But in Gethsemane the lean and dried-up branches of the olives straggled in the moonlight—in the convent they had some branches of olive trees that had been brought from the castle where their father, Saint Franciscus, was born; they were coarse and ugly, with hard and shrivelled leaves. Thus had men planted their garden, to receive God in it when He came down to visit them and redeem them from sin. Among these bitter, withered bushes He had lain upon His face, sweating blood, as He saw at the bottom of the chalice all the evil that the race of Adam and Eve had committed and shall commit from the dawn of the ages until the Day of Judgment. All the blood that had been spilt, all the robbery and murder and false swearing and deceit and lewdness and betrayal were in the chalice, and all this He was now to take upon Himself and atone for—and over by the gate lay His disciples asleep, but on the path from the castle Judas is already at hand, leading the servants of the high priest and the soldiers of Pilate with torches and with swords and staves to bind and smite and slay God.

There was no one else in the church that morning. Eirik crept forward on his knees to the tabernacle, loosed his clothes, and let them fall to his waist. Then he took the knotted rope he wore as a girdle and scourged himself with it till it was red with blood.

During the day he was sent out into the garden to weed. The sun was broiling hot. At first his back did not feel very sore, but by degrees, as he lay crawling among the beds and the coarse frock grew fast to the raw flesh, was torn away again and rubbed the wounds, and the sun beat straight down on him, it was like a burning fire across his shoulder-blades. But the pain filled him with a deep and humble bliss, for he thought it must feel almost like this to have a cross resting on one's back—and then he felt his own unworthiness, and it made him so humble that he could have cast himself down with his face in the mould. For the first time he began rightly to understand the meaning of all penitential exercises and all self-discipline—that such things were not an end, but the means: the body required to be chastened and taught obedience as one trains a horse; and he had a glimpse of the paths that are opened to the soul as it makes itself master of the flesh.

But when he spoke to Father Einar of this in his next confession, his master said seriously that these were matters in which a newcomer might easily go astray, and he ordered the novice not to impose discipline on himself another time except after consultation with him.

The whole forenoon until dinner-time they were at work in the cloisters, all those of the brethren who were at home. Only the church and the east wing—the chapter-house and the scriptorium—were yet built of stone, with a paved colonnade outside. To the west and south of the garth stood timber houses, with a cloister walk of timber. In the stone cloisters sat those brethren who read or wrote, but outside the south wing old Brother Arnstein Antonius had his loom, and there stood Brother Sigvard and Brother Johannes at their lathe and bench. In these forenoon hours Brother Eirik had his place beside Brother Hubert, an old German monk who had been an inmate of this house since its foundation. He was to teach the novice booklore and Latin, and for the sake of quiet they sat in the inmost corner of the cloister, close beside the church door.

There was only one other young brother in the convent that summer, Brother Arne, but he had been there since his seventh year, when his father, Brother Sveinke, had taken the habit; the mother with two daughters had entered the nunnery of Gimsöy, and the elder of these sisters had already died, at the age of eighteen, in odour of sanctity. Brother Arne was but seventeen years old, but already an accomplished clerk, so Eirik had to take his lessons alone, and he showed such aptitude that both his teacher and the master of the novices were astonished. And then there came a day when Eirik again had filled the tablet, and his writing was so fair and firm on the green wax that Brother Hubert had to show it to some of the others, before it was all smoothed out again: "Great pity is it that Brother Eirik should bear such blemish that he cannot be made a priest."

This was the first cloud of weeping that passed across Eirik's bright summer sky. He had been so small when he lost that finger that he had never felt the want of it, and it had never crossed his mind that it might debar him from the service of the altar. The novice-master remarked that the young man took it deeply to heart, so he spoke to him about it, bidding him bear in mind that it was a far greater aid toward perfection to suffer patiently the trials that were laid upon him than if he himself sought out never so many afflictions of his own devising. And there was just as great need of his being a good clerk if he was to be a lay brother; their father, Saint Franciscus, had never wished to be other than a layman, and in the beginning he had intended to found his order as a company wholly of lay brothers.

Eirik listened meekly to the novice-master's speech and never spoke of the matter again, but for long after he was in deep dejection. And then autumn came on.

There was no more to be done in the garden. The pease-straw lay tangled on the grey, frost-gripped beds, and the fallen leaves under the fruit trees were whitened with rime. The monks had long ago taken to their little lanterns when they went to matins in the church. Quitting the scrap of warmth that was to be found under the thin coverlets of his couch, he had to pass through the cold dormitory and down into the cloister, where the raw frost-fog stung his nose and crept icily up his naked calves. Thick as wool the wintry mist lay on the convent; as soon as one entered it, it seemed to force its way in and dim the little lantern. But inside the church it was colder than cold.

Eirik was so cold that he thought his brain froze to a lump inside his skull. He did not grasp a word of the prayers he said during the office, for he was too cold to be able to think of their meaning. The fog forced its way even into the church; the candles by the choir stalls shone in a mist, and the friars' breath poured from their mouths like white smoke. But the nave was lost in outer darkness.

He now shuddered at the thought of the mornings when he had leave to stay behind after matins for private prayer. Stiff with cold he knelt with his eyes firmly fixed on the little lamp that shone before the tabernacle. Behind him he felt the body of the church, dark and empty, with the tombstones in the floor. Just outside the choir arch lay Sira Hallbjörn—and Eirik could not rid himself of the thought: what if the dead priest should appear to him one morning? If he were to turn round now and see Sira Hallbjörn standing behind him with the blood pouring down from his shattered skull over his pale, bony face, the chasuble in which he had been laid all besprinkled with blood—

Now and then he heard a low murmur from one or other of the brethren who had stayed behind as he had. But for the most part they knelt in perfect silence. They had led this life year after year, winter and summer, and now neither the marvellous glory of the summer mornings nor the dismal horror of the winter nights seemed to move them any longer.

He tried to keep a hold on himself with all his thoughts centred on the tabernacle. But even that mystery now inspired him with terror rather than consolation—that God had suffered Himself to be imprisoned in that little painted tower of wood and *was* there. Wide awake, in bodily substance, spirit and soul, he filled the church, looked into his own sinful heart and saw his drooping courage, saw all that stirred in the hearts of all—and in the omnipotence of his Godhead watched over the whole of this wintry land, filling every space: the icy convent—and the town and the fiord and the homesteads along the frozen shores—and Hestviken, Rundmyr, Konungahella—all the places he could think of. In summer, when he knelt here and felt the full sweetness of being able to speak with God so near, it had been joy upon joy to know that from the bodily presence of God in the sacrament he went out in His invisible presence wherever he might be—in the sunshine that filled the cloisters outside, baked the soil of the garden so that the young shoots expanded from morn till eve, poured down through the foliage—while the town fiord and the islands outside and the woodlands round about lay wrapped in heat haze. But now that winter had the world in its clutch, there was nothing but desolation—as though he divined the mighty, soundless struggle between Christ and Satan, life and death at grips. All things of sight and sense became lifeless trifles rocking to and fro amid the furious encounter.

He would not ask to be released from these hours of watching to keep which he himself had begged leave. But as time went on, Brother Einar remarked that Eirik no longer had any profit of them, and so he bade the young man go back to bed after matins each morning for a while.

But Eirik found it hard to fall asleep again. He could not get any warmth on his narrow couch with only one sack of straw under him and two thin blankets. Another effect of the cold was that he was late in falling asleep at night, so that he was always tired and short of sleep; and often what kept him awake in the morning was simply his dread of having to get up again for prime. And if by chance he got a little warmth in bed, the chilblains on his fingers and toes began to burn and itch intolerably.

He himself was in despair over his lack of spirit and tried to
summon up courage: had he not been through much that was far
harder, and without caring a scrap! He tried to think of rides in
storm and driving snow, when at times he had scarce been able to
see his horse's head. Or in a boat in wintertime—that night last
year, just after he had come home, when they sailed to Tunsberg
and a storm sprang up. Right ahead of them in the darkness was
a loud booming amid the howl and roar of the stormy night—the
white wall that seemed alive there must be the Hangman's Reef,
and they were drifting straight onto it; with every wave that
lifted their boat high into the air he thought the breakers came
nearer. Everything on them had been sheeted with ice when at
last, late in the morning, they were able to slip into shelter somewhere a long way south—he had thought that Knut, one of
Ragna's sons, would not come through with his life. And had he
now grown so soft that he whimpered at the itching of his chilblains, he who more than once had ripped the boots from his
frozen feet, who had been used to feel the sea-salt bite into the
raw flesh of his hands—

But such hardships were part of the day's work, and one took
them as they came. And afterwards—if life were not in danger—
there was the sweet delight of coming under a roof, thawing out
one's frozen carcass, eating and drinking one's fill, creeping in
under the skin coverlets somewhere or other, two or three men
in a bed to keep each other warm, and sleeping like a log. And
there was always a raciness in it: one never knew how things
would turn out or what the next day might bring.

But here it was a choice made for one's whole life—after each
summer's warmth and joy of heart one was faced by the winter,
and one had to shiver one's way through it, watching, praying,
fasting, from Holy Cross Day to Easter, so stiff with cold that
neither the hours of rest on the hard bed nor the brief warmth of
the refectory gave more than a breath of relief. One had just not
to think of it, take the days as they came, for there would be no
change until God sent warmth into the air again.

And Eirik discerned where the true sacrifice and severity of
the monastic life lay: that a man had to will it himself and will it
once for all, renounce playing with fortune and choose a life
from which the unexpected was barred and where all was willed
in advance. The submission of one's will was itself an act of will.

But then he thought he must give up—*that* was more than he could do!

At last he had to tell Father Einar how it was with him. The monk answered that a man's destiny must be thought to follow him even into the convent, or, to speak more justly, God might send him much that was unlooked-for, sickness or journeys abroad, for example. Eirik must pay for strength to overcome this temptation.

And Eirik prayed. But he knew himself that from deep within him, below the place in which he found the words of his prayer, a voice was pleading: "Show me not this grace for which I pray! Send me home!"

At times he thought, perhaps it was just in this that the Devil showed his profoundest cunning—in never tempting him with anything that pertained to the profligate life of his young days. He hated the thought of it and hated his old self. Even if he had to return to the world, at any rate he could never be like that again.

It was the memory of Hestviken that broke through and overwhelmed him, as he lay at night remembering, remembering with all his body and all his senses. No place in the world had just the same smell as their own beach; their corn when it stood in shooks and when there had been a frost at night was different from the corn of other fields—as he lay he thought he could catch the scent of their own haycocks and of the limes on the cliffs around the bay. Behind his closed eyelids floated visions of the land from which he had cut himself off: the sedgy paths up in Kverndal, the little dry mound where he found Lapp arrowheads, every crack in the rocks at home, the black wall of the Horse behind the houses, and the reddish, rounded side of the Bull rising from the sea, the surf at its foot, fresh and white on blue, sunny days, but on autumn evenings it sent out a lowing in the darkness, and through the night one could glimpse the dancing breakers and flying white foam.

Most of the calves that were born at Hestviken were brindled and usually had white markings—a heart on the forehead or patches of white on the sides or white feet. He remembered the look of them as they grazed on the salt pasture of the great level meadow by the shore at Saltviken and on the slopes where the wood had been cut down for burning charcoal. But the great junipers were left, dark and bushy. The salt-pans he remembered, and the homestead a little way inland, with its houses falling into ruin; only one was kept in repair so that the salt-boilers and mowers might sleep in it. His father left the farm to hay and pasture, but Eirik himself had always thought that when his time came he would take it up again—it might be much better for corn than the head manor at Hestviken.

And this that called and allured his very body and blood, this was no sin—this too was an honourable and Christian life. Generation after generation of men had lived at Hestviken who showed God reverence and obeyed His commandments; their hand had been open to the poor and to strangers, they had had both the power and the will to defend widows and the rights of lesser men —had been the first to fly to arms when the peace of the countryside was threatened by enemies from within or without the realm. If it fell to Jörund Rypa to possess the manor after his father, then much would be changed from the old ways—he knew his brother-in-law well enough for that. And what of himself, who all his life had had but one thought, of when one day he should be master of Hestviken?

Nor did he seem to be able to make any progress with his reading and writing now. Besides, he was now not the only novice under Brother Hubert; early in the autumn the son of a poor cottar from Eiker had taken the habit. Much then had to be repeated which Eirik had already learned, and the new lessons dragged, for this Brother Torbjörn was very dull of apprehension.

Little by little the novice-master, Brother Einar, began to lose faith in Eirik Olavsson's calling for the cloister. He had grown fond of the young man, doubting not that it was God Himself who had roused him and brought him from thoughtlessness to reflection. Eirik's early fervour, his zeal to submit himself to the rule of the order—this had been far more than a whim.

But now in the first place there was the fact that he had been driven to the convent gate by grief over a woman—even though there were much else besides. But it was the experience of the novice-master that those who surrendered their love to God because they had been disappointed of their desires in this world seldom made the best monks. And what had been the actual rela-

tion between Eirik and this foster-sister of his he could not tell;
now the man said that nothing sinful had taken place, and he was
afraid it was the Devil who had tempted him to think it worse
than it was in order to frighten him into the convent without a
true calling for it—in which case he would be a bad monk and a
sure prey of the Evil One. Brother Einar had indeed corrected
him severely for speaking thus: the Devil has no more power over
a man than God permits and the man himself gives him, and he
cannot rob God's household of its servants unless they themselves
open the door to him. But there was something in what Eirik
said; the novice-master perceived that Eirik was never wittingly
untruthful, but it was clear that the man himself did not remember
the real circumstances of the case. And he had seen the same many
times before. Eirik had difficulty in remembering anything in such
a way that he could tell the story of it twice alike. But if this was
a fault in men of any condition, it was a grave fault in a monk.

And Eirik was of a variable disposition and no doubt would
always be so. Brother Einar had seen enough and more than
enough of such natures, and it was ever a misfortune for a convent
to admit a brother who always longed for change—always desired for himself another office or other work than that to which
he had been assigned, or yearned to be removed to another house,
until he had tried all the convents of his order in three or four
realms. Had not Brother Edvin Richardson been a sore trial to
the fraternity, pious and pure-hearted man as he was, with the
spirit of unrest that dwelt within him? In his case, indeed, there
was a sort of remedy for his roving disposition—he had such fame
as a painter of images that he was sent for from all parts, where
folk would have him come and work for them. But a restless spirit
such as his was likely to infect a whole convent. Brother Einar
himself had been a Black Friar among the Benedictines of Björgvin for ten years ere he received a call to join a stricter order, and
he had now been a Minorite friar for more than thirty winters;
but still he held that without weighty reason a monk ought not
to abandon the convent where he first took the vow.

With the spring Eirik's affection for his convent was revived
—but at the same time his longing for Hestviken grew stronger,
and now he was utterly unhappy, for no path seemed open to
him, and however much he prayed and disciplined himself, he

was still torn in two directions by his longing. When therefore his trial year was at an end, it was so ordered that he was to delay his profession until the autumn, when the other two novices, Brother Arne and Brother Torbjörn, would take the vow. Then it was that he forgot himself and struck that peasant of Tveit to the ground. Had it been himself that this loon affronted, he believed he could have borne it now. But it was the house that he loved even more fervently, now that he had half decided to leave it, and the brethren of whom he was fond, and the habit of the order, which he had striven to wear honourably and well. He humbled himself before the man at the first word from Brother Stevne, he humbled himself at home in the chapter-house—but nevertheless it was this that finally turned the scale.

But on the day when all the brethren went to Brother Bjarnvard, the barber, to have their crowns shaved, and he was not to go with them—that gave him a pang. And the morning when he was once more dressed in hose and shoes, with the red and yellow jerkin, far too tight for him, and the belt and knife about his waist, he broke down altogether—he wept as he knelt in church, wept from shame and remorse, wished he had chosen to remain. But he knew in himself that now he would have regretted it, whichever choice he had made.

The brethren took an affectionate leave of him, promising him their prayers—for he would still belong to their fellowship as a brother *ab extra.* Then he walked down toward the quay, feeling naked and ashamed in his unwonted dress, and shrinking from the eyes of everyone in the armourers' yard. And his heart was ready to break with grief as he set sail and steered out among the islands, alone in the little boat that Galfrid had lent him.

But when he had passed through the Haaöy sound and come far enough to see the familiar places along the shore—no, then he had no more regrets. And when he saw the white surf at the foot of the Bull as he rounded the promontory and stood inshore—no, he had no more regrets.

And as he walked up from the waterside, bare and empty-handed—the sea breeze sporting before him, making the corn of the "good acre" sway like flames, with the sun gleaming on its silky beards—Eirik felt inclined to leap the fence and stroke the barley that the wind was lashing.

•   •   •

His father's coldness did him more good than harm. It cost him
an effort to go about his daily life here at home in such different
guise from his former self. But that he was not suffered without
a struggle to live as he deemed to be right and worthy of a Christian man, that reassured him: he had chosen aright. He had not
fled from the convent to return to his old thoughtless and idle life
—there was yet a third way, and he had found it; it put fresh heart
into him every day to feel that it was not always easy to follow it.

So the winter went by without Eirik's showing the least sign
of lukewarmness.

About a week before Easter, Olav and Eirik went together up
to Galaby. Late in the afternoon, when the matters he had come
about were settled and Olav sat at table drinking with the Sheriff
and some others of the elder franklins, there was a noise in the
courtyard; the door burst open and a boy called to the men within
that Eirik Olavsson lay outside and had surely got his death-hurt.

Olav sprang up and ran out. Over by the stable a group of men
stood surrounding one who lay on his side in the snow, which
was red with his blood; his right hand still grasped his dagger.
Eirik lay in a swoon. Olav and another man carried him in, laid
him on a bed, and attended to his wounds. He had been stabbed
with a knife in the back and again in front near the collar-bone;
his face bore marks of blows. They were ugly wounds, but need
not be fatal unless the mischief was in it. While his father was
tending him, Eirik opened his eyes.

"Could you curb your manhood no longer?" asked Olav, but
not unkindly—he was smiling a little.

Eirik's eyelids dropped again.

Olav then heard how this had come about. It was two house-
carls who had fallen out as they were saddling the horses—they
seemed to have been old enemies—and it had come to blows; their
arms had been left indoors since the sitting of the court, so they
took to their knives. When Eirik had tried to come between them,
they had both turned on him, and then he drew his dagger, but
only to defend himself; neither of the house-carls had received
more than a few scratches. Now they lay bound in a cellar.

Eirik came to his senses for a while early in the night; he whispered that if this proved his bane, he did not wish a charge to be

made against the poor men, but he forgave them as he hoped God would forgive him.

To this Olav made no answer. Neither he nor Reidulf meant to spare the men if Eirik's wounds should take a bad turn. But all went well; Reidulf had sent for an old man who could stanch blood and was a good leech. A week later Olav was able to move his son to Hestviken, and there he himself and Ragna tended the wounded man so well that Eirik was on his feet again before Whit Sunday.

After this, peace was re-established between father and son. But while he lay sick Eirik had dropped out of the way of saying his hours and all his other practices; on getting up he did indeed resume them, but either kept them less strictly than before or concealed them better from his house-mates. And if Olav came upon him while he said his paternosters, or noticed that Eirik imposed on himself any kind of self-discipline, his son was sure to hear of it later in the day.

" 'Tis a good thing, Eirik," his father said with a quiet laugh, "that we have seen your hand still knows its way to your dagger. Else it would not be well for the rest of us to dwell under the same roof with so pious a man as you have grown."

Eirik turned red. It hurt him that his father should talk in this way, but Olav said it so good-humouredly, and he had never been able to resist his father when he showed him the smallest speck of kindness.

13

EIRIK lay awake in bed one morning at Gunnarsby. Jörund was putting on his clothes in another corner of the room. Cecilia came in from outside with something and exchanged a few words with her husband. Then he said:

"Will you not speak to your brother of that matter we talked of?"

"No. I have told you I will not."

Jörund muttered something in anger. Then he followed his wife out.

Eirik got up and dressed himself. When he came out Cecilia

was sitting on the earthen bench outside the house with her son in her lap. The child crawled over his mother and wanted to be caressed; Cecilia pressed the boy to her, but looked as if she were thinking of other things. Eirik greeted his sister and stood looking down at her.

"What did Jörund wish you to say to me?"

"Since you heard that"—Cecilia glanced up with her clear, cool look—"you must also have heard my answer."

"Was it about my leaving the convent?" asked Eirik. "Has that made it worse for you here at Gunnarsby?"

"Oh—'tis not that alone." Her eyes still rested on her brother's tall and handsome figure as he stood before her with the morning sun shining on the brown locks of his bent head. He was dressed in a dark-red gown that reached to the knees and fitted his broad shoulders well, a leather belt with silver buckle about his slim waist. *She* liked him better thus—it had revolted her to see her lively, handsome brother in the frock of a barefoot friar; never could she believe that was a life for Eirik. "There is much else—"

Eirik said: "Even with a sister's portion in Hestviken, Jörund will get more with you than his brothers got with their wives. Brynhild has four brothers, and Lucia's father had to make dear amends to the King for the foolish game he played when the Duke lay before Akershus."

Cecilia nodded. "Jörund knows that—they all know it. But that makes it no easier for Jörund now—we live here, the youngest of this crowded household, and we must bow to the others in everything."

"Is it Mistress Brynhild?" asked Eirik.

"Brynhild I like best. She says what she means. But true it is that she and Jörund have never been friends. And Aake and Lucia do not like me."

Eirik looked down at the young mother. He had guessed this during his stay here—neither Jörund nor Cecilia had an easy lot.

"Tell me withal what Jörund wished you to say to me," he asked her. "Tell me," he repeated, as his sister blushed but would not answer.

Suddenly, with a movement of impatience, Cecilia set the babbling child down on the ground. The infant rolled over and made ready to scream—Eirik took him up on his arm.

"Ay, 'twill be no longer than to Clement's mass [5]—and then I shall have another one like this." Cecilia drew two or three deep breaths. "I cannot deny—I would give much if I could be spared giving birth to the child here in the hands of these brothers' wives. Even if Hestviken is to be yours—could we not live there together? He and Aake, they could never *bear* each other. Jörund has wished this ever since we were married. He begged me—'twas one of the first nights we slept together—he begged me ask Father if we might take up our abode with him. But if he could wish that —if he would rather dwell with Father, who is so glum and hard to get on with, than with his brothers—then 'twould be all the easier one day when Father is gone and you are the master—you and he have been fast friends so long."

"Is it your wish," asked Eirik, as Cecilia had to stop and take breath, "that I speak with Father—ask him if you may come out to us by autumn?"

"Yes," said Cecilia, and blushed again.

Eirik handed her the child, which was struggling to get back to its mother. Then he turned and went to find Jörund.

All that forenoon the two friends were together on the outskirts of the manor; they walked hither and thither, sat or lay on the ground, and Jörund talked without ceasing. He swore that he had not taken it amiss when he heard Eirik was not to be a monk after all; *he* at least had never forgotten that probation was probation—but Aake and Steinar and their wives had uttered words that provoked Cecilia to retort—and Eirik knew well enough how stubborn and unbending she was when she thought differently from others. She often did so here, and it generally happened that there was some truth in what she said. But it *was* unbearable for them to stay here—the dissension between him and his brothers had become ten times worse since he had married Cecilia. But if they came to Hestviken, he was sure he could live happily with her. Then he began to talk of the table silver in Cecilia's dowry— Aake's wife had found out from Magnus, the goldsmith of Oslo, that this was the old silver that Olav had brought out at the betrothal feast; Olav had had it refashioned, but that, they declared, was cheating his son-in-law of the heritage—and Cecilia had given them an answer.

[5] November 23.

Eirik's head reeled with listening to Jörund's complaints when at last they returned to the manor.

As Eirik rode homeward he was determined that his father must yield, though it might be difficult to obtain the old man's consent. What happened was the only thing he had not looked for: Olav said yes without hesitating. So Jörund and Cecilia moved to Hestviken that autumn. They were given the women's house to live in.

Soon after, Cecilia gave birth to her second son. He was called Torgils—by mistake: the boy came into the world half-suffocated, and the women fetched in Eirik to baptize him in emergency. In his hurry he gave the child the first family name he could think of. Olav was angry—the boy ought to have been called Audun after his father and his little dead son, and he had no wish to have Foulbeard's name perpetuated in the family—though the man's own offspring had used it and two of Arne Torgilsson's daughters had named children after their grandfather.

One day Eirik said to his father: "Could you not be less curt of speech with Jörund? He thinks you like him not."

"No, I cannot," said Olav gruffly. Then he added, already a little more graciously: "Jörund can hardly expect me to treat him as if he were still our guest, now that he has taken up his abode here."

Olav had reached a point where he was no longer able to keep up his ill will toward Eirik. The young man had compelled a certain respect from his father: he was now in his second year at home, and the change that had come over him since his stay in the convent still lasted. Olav noticed that Eirik always tried to do what was right and had achieved a mastery over himself that Olav would have sworn Eirik could never attain. His father felt something like shame when he recalled that at first he seemed to have expected and almost wished that Eirik would relapse into his old bad ways.

Without any design on their part, without their even being clearly aware of it, they drew more closely together, all these people who for so long had formed *one* household. Since Jörund Rypa's coming they felt that they had grown into unity, and he was a stranger.

He idled among the houses, as though out of place—doing nothing. Nor had he a hand for any of the work that was to be

done at this manor. He went out in the morning, stood at the
stable door and watched his man grooming the horses that were
his; if the weather was not too bitter he sauntered down to the
pier, stood there awhile looking out and spitting into the sea. He
had been out with the boats a few times, but then he would go no
more. Then he lay dozing on the bench in his own house—there
was so little sleep to be had at night with the two children, he
complained. When Olav and Eirik came in with the boatmen—
this was in the fishing season—he turned into the old house and
sat there; but the men were tired and hungry and had no thought
of beguiling the time for Jörund Rypa. When the season for
catching auks came on he revived somewhat and went out with
the others—but then they had a week of tearing northerly gales,
and that put an end to it.

The others saw little of Cecilia; she spent her time in the
women's house or with the maids in the cook-house and outhouses.

There was great shortage of fodder in Hestviken that year, as
they had Jörund's beasts as well as their own, and they had had to
make use of an old byre that had been in a tumbledown state as
long as any could remember. It was mended in some sort, but the
starving animals suffered horribly in it. Cecilia would come out in
tears when she had been feeding the cattle there. Not often had
anyone seen her weep for what might befall folk, but one evening
as she came from the byre and met Eirik in the outer room, she
threw her arms about his neck in the darkness.

"Eirik—you who pray so much to God, can you not pray that
spring may come early this year?"

"I do so, you know it well."

After Olav had gone to bed that evening, Eirik went to him in
the closet and told his father what he had been thinking—that
they should take up the farm in Saltviken again. Olav thought
they had more profit of the land, using it as they did now, for
pasture and hay, than if they let it out at rent. Eirik replied that
he did not mean they should take a tenant there, but should carry
on the farm with men from here: "if Jörund is to keep ten cows
and four horses here at Hestviken, then we ourselves must raise
far less stock than before, or move some of it out."

At last he got a kind of consent out of his father. Eirik took
with him Knut and Svein, Ragna's young sons, and rowed south
only a couple of days later with two boatloads of fencing. They

spent a whole week there, making ready what they could. No sooner was the frost out of the ground than he set off again, this time with some of the cattle; and before Halvard's mass [6] Eirik had fenced in most of what had been the home fields, with bush fencing if with nothing else. In time even his father would have to grant he was right—this could be made a good farm.

Olav Audunsson himself had been in to Oslo for the winter fair. And as usual he had made some bargains, which were to be completed by Halvard's mass. He would now send Eirik in to the town, and Eirik asked Jörund to go with him.

The brothers-in-law stayed in the town a couple of days over the feast; they had met acquaintances, and in the evenings they drank in one house or another. Eirik had a care of himself—he would not enter any of the places where formerly he had been too well known; this was one of the reasons he had asked Jörund to accompany him: if he was with a married man it seemed more natural that he should refuse to go to the common inns and confine himself to the halls of the guilds and the townsmen's houses. Another reason was that he guessed Jörund was weary to death of Hestviken.

The evening before St. Eirik's Day [7] they both came home late to the armourers' yard and they were in drink, so that Eirik overslept next morning. On that day at any rate he had meant full surely to hear mass among his own brethren—he had not succeeded in reaching the convent since the first day he was in town —but once more it was too late. The masses were now over in all the churches except St. Halvard's; he would have to go there, and to the Minorites' for vespers.

But as he prayed during the mass, the thought came to him that he would ask at the convent for some cuttings of the great cherry tree below the hill. Near the houses in Saltviken was a hollow beside a sunny ledge of rock, just the place where fruit trees might thrive. There were many places at Hestviken too, but his father had laughed at him when he proposed it: this was no knightly manor, that they should plant rose gardens or pleasances. But Eirik already thought of Saltviken as his own manor.

When he came back to their lodging he heard from Galfrid that Jörund had gone out with some men who lived in Brand's Yard. He went after him and found his brother-in-law in a house

at the far end of this yard, in company with some men who kept
cocks there. First they watched the cockfight, and then they
went into an upper chamber and drank. After a while some
women came in—one of them, called Gyda Honeycake, Eirik had
known in old days. She seated herself on his knees, and he drank
with her, fondled the wench too a little, thinking all the time that
the wisest thing he could do was to go his way, but feeling
ashamed because of the other men. Then the dice-box was brought
out. Eirik had no desire for gaming, since he had promised to keep
himself from such things—but it was not always possible. At the
same time he was shy of refusing before the others. There happened to be a man there, one whom Eirik did not know, who said
he cared not to throw dice, but was there anyone who would
play chess? Here he was freed from two temptations at one stroke,
since he could not play chess with Mistress Honeycake in his lap;
so Eirik declared himself willing and set the girl down, not without a secret regret at being rid of her. But the stranger, Helge,
was so good a chess-player that Eirik soon forgot all else in the
game. He would have liked to stay away from vespers too, but
when the bells began to ring he remembered the cherry trees, and
now he had set his heart on them. So he took his leave. Jörund
stayed on. Eirik saw that he was already far gone in drink; he
himself had been sobered by his zeal for the game as soon as he
had found how skilful an opponent he had. Jörund was playing
wildly, but Eirik gave little thought to that: the man was always
lucky at dice; besides, he was married now, he could surely take
care of himself.

And it had already passed out of his mind when he stood once
more in his own church and joined in the singing of *Ave Maris
Stella* and the Magnificat. After the service several of the brethren
came down to him and he went with them into the convent; now
he had to talk with them all, and soon the hour of the evening
meal arrived. The end was that Eirik was to sleep in the guest-
chamber that night; next morning after mass they could take up
those shoots for him. The fruit trees were far advanced, but Father
Einar thought that if the shoots were well wrapped in moss and
birchbark and he sailed straight back to Saltviken and planted
them that evening, they would take root.

Eirik was in church for complin and slept in the guest-chamber,
and in the light spring night he was roused by the monk who came

with his hood drawn over his head and whispered: *"Benedicamus Domino."* And he went to matins, and back to bed again, and to mass. Then for the first time he remembered the purse with the money he had received for his father—it lay at the bottom of his bed in the Richardsons' house—but surely it was safe enough there.

When once the brethren had procured the cherry-tree cuttings for him, they found many another thing to give him from their garden. Eirik carried the whole load down to the boat, got hold of an old sail, and wrapped his cuttings to keep them from the sun. It was high noon ere he returned to the armourers'. There he was told that Jörund had come in for a moment the evening before, but he had not been home that night.

Eirik walked into the town to seek out his brother-in-law. In Brand's Yard he met Helge, and from him he heard that late in the evening he had gone with Jörund Rypa to a house where no man would have liked to find his sister's husband. He was still sitting there when Helge left. Eirik asked Helge to go thither with him, but when they came to the house they were told that Jörund had gone home a little while before. So Eirik went back to their lodging.

There he found Jörund, engaged in packing their belongings. He looked somewhat the worse for wear. Eirik could not bring himself to say a word. He put together the last of their baggage. When he felt in his bed for the purse, it was gone.

"I have taken charge of that," said Jörund. "I could not tell how long you would be taken up with those brethren of yours—"

Eirik turned sharply on his brother-in-law. But then he swallowed the answer that was on the tip of his tongue. 'Twas bad enough as it was—would be made no better by talking.

So they went down to the boat. During the sail they did not exchange an unnecessary word. Eirik was glad enough they had none of the house-folk with them, so Cecilia would not hear of her husband's doings.

After supper that evening Eirik gave his father an account of how he had discharged his business. "Jörund has the purse with the money on him."

Jörund Rypa stood up. "Dear father-in-law of mine—sooth to say, I have not the money here. It fell out that I met a man who made a claim on me—I was in his debt for a mark and a half of silver—a dalesman it was, the man who sold me Greylag, but he had gone home when I had the money for him—so now I borrowed this money of yours, to be rid of the old debt."

Olav stared at his son-in-law till Jörund was out of countenance.

"Ay, we were throwing dice too—I am so used to having luck with me in my play; I had looked to win enough to pay this Simon what I owed him. But here is this stoup, which is worth much more than the silver I borrowed of you—" Jörund took a handsome little cup from the folds of his kirtle and placed it on the table before his father-in-law. "You must take this—"

Olav seized the cup, crushed it in his hand, then flung it right in the face of Jörund Rypa.

"I have not asked for your stoup. My silver I will have—neither more nor less!"

Eirik had leaped up. For a second he saw something in Jörund's face—and he was chilled through with fear—this should not have happened!

Jörund looked down at the twisted cup that lay before him. Then he put his foot on it and trod it flat.

"Take your stoup," said Olav, so that his son-in-law obeyed. Then Jörund went out.

Eirik and Olav stood in silence without looking at each other. Then the father asked in a low, angry voice:

"And you—were you gaming too?"

Eirik shook his head. "He must have done this the last evening we were in Oslo. We went each our own way. He went to one of his kinsmen, and I was with the brethren, stayed there the night."

"Did you know no better," asked Olav cuttingly, "than to lie out there playing with your rosary—when you had *him* with you? *You* ought to know your friend. 'Tis an ill thing to set a sheep to herd a fox."

Eirik stood in silence. ("For all that, you should not have done it, Father"—but he dared not say it.)

Eirik could not fall asleep that night. He ought not to have left Jörund—his father was right there, more than he knew himself; for he did not know what sort of company it was he had left Jörund in. He might have tried to get Jörund to church with him, but he had shrunk from that; he had wished to be left in peace with those friends of his for whom he had a different kind of affection from that he felt for Jörund.

For all that, his father should not have done it—flung the stoup in his face and treated him as a thief. Eirik gave a low groan—Jörund would never forget this against his father. And if they were now to live together here— He had a feeling that foreboded, he knew not what disasters.

Then he bethought him of what he had lying in the shed at the waterside, wrapped in a ragged sail. He must have it in the ground as soon as might be, both Father Einar and Brother Hubert had told him that. Eirik would just as soon avoid meeting either his father or Jörund or Cecilia on the morrow. He got up and stole quietly out.

The fiord lay pale and calm in the spring night, which was already turning to dawn. The gently heaving swell licked at the yellow band of seaweed under the rocks, the gulls sat on the surface like white spots—now and then one rose and flew out. But in the pine forest that filled every hollow of the mossy grey hills along the shore, the song of birds awoke little by little. The pale-grey clouds in the south were tinged with red and the north-eastern sky turned to orange as he rowed along the broad, curving, white sandy beach of Saltviken. Inland was a great plain, poor pasture, with a few alders that the salt-boilers had spared, and huge old junipers, in shape like gigantic spearheads. Eirik rowed past; he had a mind to look at the nets that he usually had lying out off some rocks in the south of the bay—whether the boys had seen to them while he was from home. As he rowed back again, a score of fish lay floundering in the bottom of the boat.

The houses stood a little way from the beach, half-hidden from the sea behind a low ridge of rust-coloured rock that looked like the back of a gigantic whale. Inland the soil was broken by more such whale-backs as it sloped up to the edge of the forest.

As he passed the door of his house, Eirik heard his dogs—they knew of his coming. He let them out, received their joyful welcome. But the boys, his house-carls as he called them, slept heavily —Knut and Svein in one of the beds and Olav Livsson on the bench. Eirik had moved him hither, for he could see that his beadsman was irksome to them at Hestviken; he would serve in any case to mend their clothes while they lay out here with no woman's help.

But he had to shut up the dogs again while he was planting— they would scratch up the seedlings as fast as he put them in. He had almost finished his work when he heard the boys going to the

byre. The sun had already been up some time; the fiord and the
land on the other side lay bathed in the fresh, pale morning light.
When the lads had brought out the cows and let them into the
fenced field that he meant to sow with corn next year, his task
was done.

He went down, greeted them, and gave orders about the fish.
Then he threw his muddy garments to Olav Livsson, took a deep
draught of the warm morning milk, and flung himself into his bed,
feeling that now he would sleep on till evening.

14

EIRIK spent most of his time at Saltviken that summer. It seemed
as if he had transferred all his affection for his ancestral home to
this place; he no longer felt happy at Hestviken, and when he was
compelled to stay there for some days, he simply longed to get
back to the deserted manor and thought of what he would next
turn his hand to there.

His father gave him angry words for it: "Soon you will be of
no more use to me than my son-in-law."

"Ay, he can be no great help to you."

Olav laughed wrathfully.

Eirik worked hard to have the outhouses put in such state that
some men could stay here next winter with half a score of cattle.
He had only the two young lads and the cripple with him, but
he made shift with them. Olav had two salters in the bay that summer, and they lay up at the manor.

At last, when Eirik had made an end of haymaking, Olav came
over one day to see how it went with the salt-pans. He found
fault with the appearance of the yard—a litter of building-materials
and chips. The house itself was what one might expect where five
men and a helpless cripple had their abode without a woman to
look after them. He muttered disapproval of the ugly withered
bush fences right up among the houses—and he wanted Eirik at
home now, to help in the haymaking. He had little to say as Eirik
went round with him, showing him what he had done and telling
him what more he meant to do. But as they walked down to the
boat, Olav halted a moment.

"You were right, Eirik. This farm here can be made much better than I thought. I see now that what you have done is well done."

Eirik turned red with joy. He said with a little smile: "Do you know, Father, this is the first time so long as we have known each other that you have acknowledged me right?"

Olav answered thoughtfully: "I am not sure of that. Did I not approve you when you would enter the convent? When you ran from home, desiring to go out into the world and try your fortune—I call naught else to mind but that I owned you right in that too, abeit I liked not your leaving me in that manner. And had you spoken to me of Bothild—maybe I had not refused you there either."

Eirik held his peace, in confusion. He saw that what his father said was true—but he knew that it was not the *whole* truth.

"Have you put the convent quite out of your thoughts?"

It was not easy to answer this. In a way he always looked back on that life with regret—and sometimes he had thought that when the farm at Saltviken was fully restored— If he could have taken his vows forthwith, he believed he would have done so. But he knew that he would have to go through the novitiate once more, and he could not support another whole year in which to make his choice.

"You are inconstant, my son," said Olav in a low voice as they walked on; "and I wonder whether there may not come a day when you will no longer have a mind to stay at Saltviken."

Eirik spat out the juniper berries he had been chewing. But then he checked himself and did not answer his father. Inconstant— Father Einar had said the same. It was strange—

"Since you have no more thought of the convent," said Olav, " 'twill soon be time for you to marry."

As Eirik made no reply, Olav pursued: "You are eight and twenty winters old, Eirik; 'tis well time. And I am over the half-hundred—at my age no man can tell if he will be above ground next year. I would fain know what will become of Hestviken when I am gone."

"Cecilia has two fine sons," said Eirik.

"Two and a half, I fear," said Olav curtly. "Ay, they are goodly babes, I hear the women say. But mouse-eared—like their father."

Eirik said: "Have you thought of any—? With whom you would have me married, I mean."

"Berse of Eiken has a daughter—"

"Gunhild? But there is enmity between you and Berse?"

"No worse but that we might be friends again." Olav smiled faintly. "If he could win the heir of Hestviken for a son-in-law, why—"

They had no more talk as Eirik rowed homeward in the summer evening. Only when they were at the quayside his father said:

"Then old Tore will have to be at Saltviken this winter with the cattle you will have there."

"Tore? But can you spare him here?"

"Better him than you." Olav paused a moment. "I should be loath to live here alone with Jörund." Eirik saw that it cost his father a good deal to say it.

Next day during the after-dinner rest Eirik went in to his sister. As she rose, Eirik saw that she was indeed as his father had said. It did not show much in her, except that she seemed to have difficulty in stooping—and at once it struck her brother that nothing seemed to change Cecilia: she only became unbending and stiff in the back.

She fetched flagon and cup and set them before him; then she sat down again to her sewing. The ale had stood; it was so flat that Eirik only drank so as not to offend his sister.

He scarce knew what to talk to her about. She sat perfectly straight, holding her sewing up close to her face; her fine pale mouth seemed hardened into a firm, straight line, and her cheeks had fallen in so that the powerful cheek-bones and the square chin appeared prominent. He saw that her bright eyes had lost their lustre; they were like little pale-grey pebbles on the beach.

Kolbein, her elder boy, came stumping in with something he had found—a strip of bark—laid it on his mother's knee. She said thanks, seriously, but shook her head when he wanted to climb into her lap; she was busy sewing.

Then he picked up his piece of bark and carried it over to Eirik. Eirik lifted up the boy and played with him; he had always got on well with children. Kolbein was fat and lusty—Eirik passed his fingers through the child's fair, moist hair. It was true, he had mouse's ears; but still, it shocked him that the boy's own grand-father should say so. It had never occurred to him that Jörund's ears were like that—he wore his hair so that they were hidden. It was a sign that thralls' blood had found its way into a family, folk said.

Eirik had a mind to ask Cecilia about Gunhild Bersesdatter—they were of the same age—but did not bring himself to do so. He had seen Gunhild at church many times, but could not remember clearly how she looked—neither fair nor foul, he thought, and with red hair.

He wished his sister would take her children on her lap, laugh and play with them, boast of them as he had heard other young wives do. But Cecilia did no such thing. She cared for them well, but without a smile or a jest. She spoke to Jörund and of Jörund —the little he had heard her say—as a good wife should. But always with the same cool gravity. He would rather she had made complaint—for he knew that if she had anything to complain of, it was not Cecilia's way to do so. He was uneasy on Jörund's account and—not by such methods would she be able to keep Jörund kind and in good humour, and if Jörund was now at enmity with their father too—

His brother-in-law came in at that moment, greeted Eirik, and poured himself out a drink of ale.

"Where is Magnhild?—bid her fetch us fresh ale!"

"I know not where Magnhild is." Cecilia put down her sewing, took the flagon, and went out.

"Has he sent for you to help with the hay?" Jörund stretched himself. "Ah, I have not stirred a hand—I'll not do it till Olav offers amends for the insult he put upon me in the spring."

In the evening Eirik asked his father: "Has Jörund restored to you the silver he borrowed in the spring?"

Olav snorted scornfully, did not even answer.

On Sunday, as the Hestviken folk were leaving church after mass, Torgrim of Rynjul came up to them.

"Una says you might give your young folk leave today, Olav —'tis so long since she spoke with Eirik, she says."

"With all my heart—" Olav swung himself into the saddle. He and the servants rode off.

As Eirik gave his hand to Una Arnesdatter he saw that Gunhild
was standing close by with the Rynjul children. She was just un-
hooking her cloak, which she handed with her veil to Torgrim's
son. " 'Tis so warm today," she said to the boy. Her voice was
bright and good—Eirik liked it.

He stole a glance at her while Una was greeting Jörund and
Cecilia. She was not red-haired, as he had thought—her plaits were
ash-coloured, but she had the fine red-and-white freckled complexion that often goes with red hair, and her skin shone like silk.
She was tall, straight, and slender—and her reddish-brown habit
fitted closely to the body, down to the silver belt about her hips;
below that it fell in rich folds, which lay on the grass about her
feet. The sleeves of her kirtle almost touched the ground and
were split to the elbow, showing the ruffled sleeves of her pale-
blue shift.

She looked no different from so many other healthy women of
good birth who have been brought up free from care—her face
was oval and full, her nose straight and rather thick at the tip, her
eyes grey. But Eirik looked at this maid who was intended for
him and began already to distinguish her from among all other
women. Torgrim and Una must be privy to the matter, he
guessed.

So when they were to ride away, Eirik lifted Gunhild Bersesdatter into the saddle. She thanked him frankly and kindly, looked
down into his narrow, swarthy face, saw that the man's great
yellow eyes were of rare beauty, and then she smiled very faintly
and thanked him once more as she took the reins.

He had no chance of talking to her while they were together at
Rynjul, but the fact that she *was* there seemed to fill the whole
day for him. In the course of the evening the young people of the
house, Astrid and Torgils and Elin, wished to start a game.

At first Eirik would not join them, he was so much older than
Una's children and their friends; and he had usually held aloof
from games and dancing since he came home. But he was fond of
dancing—and his young kinswomen were bent upon having him
sing for them. When he came into the chain, Astrid dropped
Gunhild's hand and reached out for his. So it came about that he
was placed between the two young maids.

The sun was about to set, and in the warm yellow glow the
shadows of the dancers fell far across the grass. The song rang

out finely in the peaceful summer evening, and Eirik felt the joyful intoxication of hearing his own good voice. All the time he felt Gunhild's hand lying in his—it was warm and slightly moist, and it sent a current of sweetness and goodness through his whole body. He looked forward to each turn, when the chain swung the other way; then he was brushed by her waving sleeves and the folds of her kirtle.

Once, when the dancers stopped to take breath, he chanced to look where Cecilia was sitting with Una watching the young folks' game. His sister had wrapped herself closely in her blue mantle; her face showed yellow as bone against the white folds of her linen coif. Games and dancing were over for her, and she was a little younger than Gunhild. Eirik dropped Astrid's hand and went over to the two married women.

He stretched himself on the grass at their feet, turned his face up toward Una as he talked. Soon after, the young people followed him; the rest went back at once, but Gunhild sat down by Cecilia, and the two talked together in low tones. Eirik heard her fresh voice behind him as the younger ones danced and sang on the green and he himself chatted to Una.

The brother and sister broke up as darkness was falling. Torgrim said that Jörund had ridden away some time ago, saying he had business somewhere. When they entered the forest, Eirik dismounted and walked, leading his sister's horse. He ought not to have stayed so long at Rynjul, he was thinking—it was not prudent for her to be out after dark.

At Rundmyr he took the little path that ran by the upper edge of the bog; he had a message for Arnketil and dared not leave Cecilia, but thought perhaps he might see someone outside. Just as they were below the slope on which the houses stood, the door opened—the light of the fire shone out—and some folks came out, men and women; he could hear by their voices that they were vagabonds.

But among the crowd he caught sight of a particoloured kirtle that he thought he recognized. He had sold Jörund the clothes the Minorites had given him at parting; they fitted his brother-in-law. Eirik was perturbed—did Jörund go to Rundmyr now! Hot about the ears, he recalled all he had himself told Jörund in old days of his adventures there—making them more wonderful than they were. But he had a vague feeling that if Jörund sought diversion there, worse things might be looked for. Though he had never accounted to himself for it, he knew the coldness of the other's nature well enough to be sure that if Jörund wallowed in the mire, there was nothing in him that could be mirrored in the puddles and lend them lustre.

Cecilia had seen nothing, thank God—she sat facing the other way.

Arrived at home, Eirik put up the horses in the stable, where the stalls were now all empty in the summer night. Then he seated himself on a chest that stood by the door—he would be there when Jörund came, try to get the man in without waking Cecilia.

Gunhild, Gunhild—she glided in and out of his thoughts the whole time. His hands had scarcely approached a woman since he left the convent. For more than three years he had kept a guard on himself, in deeds, in words, in thoughts. When he had been tempted of the devil, the world, and his own flesh, he had fought.

Now he was set free to look at one, to think of one. He was free to recall what it had been like to take her and lift her into the saddle, to recall her hand, which he had held in his—a sweetness and a promise of more, more—

Beneath the memory of these last serious years, when he had trained his will and learned to use it against himself, floated the shadowy memories of his youth, the embraces of venal wenches and dreams of high-born maids—dreams that he dared not jeopardize by frequenting any such. And Bothild—to think of her directly he never dared, but the shame and the horror and the pain of what she had betokened in his life lay dissolved and precipitated within him and had coloured all the currents that had passed through his mind in these last years.

Now the bright image of Gunhild Bersesdatter began to take shape against this dark-purple background. He had already abandoned himself to loving her.

It was past midnight and yet Jörund had not come. Eirik sat and waited, grew anxious on his brother-in-law's account, thought of Gunhild, and was happy.

Then he awoke and saw that he had slept a long time; it was light outside. He looked out—up by the fence was Jörund's handsome dun saddle-horse; and in the shed outside, his saddle and bridle hung in their places. So in any case he could not have been very drunk.

His father did not allude to the matter until about a week later. "Have you thought over that of which we spoke lately? About a marriage for you?"
"It shall be as you desire, Father."

A day or two later Eirik again found occasion to visit Rynjul. Gunhild was still there. Not many words did he exchange with her, but she sat with Una while he was talking to his kinswoman.

Berse of Eiken was a cousin of Arne of Hestbæk, the father-in-law of Baard and Torgrim. But he and Torgrim of Rynjul had been estranged for many years—Torgrim was hot-headed and loose of tongue; in general folk paid little heed to his outbursts, for he was generous and the last man to bear a grudge, but Berse would not put up with an uncivil word, for he was mighty jealous of what he called his dignity. Olav Audunsson had also fallen out with him at one time: the two had been chosen as umpires in a dispute, but were unable to agree; and Olav had expressed his opinion in terms that were sharper than Berse considered becoming to his dignity.

Eirik had never before given a thought to this ill feeling among the three old men. But now, when the women had left the room, he asked Torgrim: "Are you kinsmen now reconciled—since the daughter from Eiken is here as a guest?"

Torgrim laughed and drank to Eirik. "Ay, I have shown the old man I dared be his enemy seven years. But, God's death, I'll now show him I am bolder yet—I dare be friends with him other seven years, if need be. But so long he cannot look to live—he is seventy winters old, all of that. And Gunhild takes after her mother—which is well for her." He nodded to Eirik.

So Eirik saw that Torgrim was the one who was to take the first steps toward the contract.

Some days after Bartholomew's mass [8] Una came out to Hestviken to visit Cecilia; with her she had her two young daughters and Gunhild Bersesdatter.

[8] August 24.

All the young people were sitting in the ladies' house with the women, when Una said to Cecilia that her first business was to offer to foster Torgils this winter: "since you are to have another child ere he is a year old, 'twill be too much for you, and now I have a foster-mother for him; Ingrid bore her child yestereven, and it was dead, poor young wife. She would gladly take your Torgils and give him the breast."

"Nay, nay—I will not send my son from me."

Then Jörund said: "Rather should you thank Mistress Una. You need your night's rest now, Cecilia, and maybe Torgils would be less sickly if he had a change of mothers."

Una said Jörund was right. Then she began to speak of Ingrid's misfortune. She had been Una's maid for many years and almost like a foster-daughter at Rynjul; from there she was married a year ago to a good and brave man who served with Gunhild's uncle, Guttorm of Draumtorp in Skeidis parish. Guttorm and his wife had been to a wedding in Raumarike, and they had with them a sack of valuables that had been lent for the wedding feast. In the forest by Gerdarud they had been surrounded by robbers—the master and his three house-carls had defended themselves well, but Jon, Ingrid's husband, died of his wounds a little later. The widow was almost out of her mind from grief, and one night she ran away from Draumtorp; alone with a little lad whom she had got to go with her, she came on foot to Rynjul.

They sat talking for a while of the robberies and ambushes that were reported in many parts of the country round Oslo. But then Una sent the young people out; she would speak a little with Cecilia privately.

Again Eirik felt that twinge of pity that his sister must be left, faded and cheerless, with the elder woman, while all the rest went out into the open air, where the sunlight flickered on the rocks, and the fiord gleamed brightly under the fair-weather breeze.

Astrid and Elin, they were as fair as their mother had been in her youth, sixteen and fourteen years, no more. Elin had carried Torgils out, defending herself laughingly against her sister, who also wanted to carry him—he was a fine, fair-haired little child, but pale and weak of limb. "You will have four foster-mothers when you come to Rynjul," laughed little Elin, pressing the babe closely to her.

"You have never been out here before?" Eirik asked Gunhild as they stood side by side watching the two young girls struggling for the child.

"No. I think I would fain go down and look at the sea."

"Perhaps you would like me to row you?" Eirik ventured to ask.

"That I would indeed."

They had lost sight of Jörund, so Eirik was alone in the boat with the three girls. Gunhild sat forward in the bow, raised against the blue sky, and her bright, slender figure was a little indistinct with the light behind her, but her movements were graceful when she turned and looked about her. On the thwart facing him sat the two young sisters: Astrid, who talked and laughed, and Elin, with the little child who had fallen asleep on her bosom; now and again she wrapped her cloak more closely about him and then drew it aside and peeped at the boy. Eirik would have liked to row far enough to give them a sight of Saltviken, but there was not time for that.

"Hestviken looks best from the water," said Gunhild as they walked up from the pier.

"But to live by the fiord—maybe you would not care for that?"

"Oh, yes, I think I should like it very well," said Gunhild, and again Eirik thought her voice frank and kind.

"Then you would not say no to a suitor—merely because he would bring you out to these parts?" He thought to himself it was awkwardly put.

"Oh, no—" Gunhild gave a little smile. "Not if there were no worse things to be said of him."

"What, then? That he—that you would have to live in the house with his married brother or sister, for instance?"

Gunhild shook her head.

"A maid who has had a stepmother since she was twelve," she said seriously, "has had time to learn to adapt herself. So I trow that would not scare me, if I liked the man in other ways."

"I would I knew," whispered Eirik—"if you think you could come to like me?"

Gunhild answered in a clear voice, smiling as she spoke: "I have never heard aught else of you, Eirik, but that you were a kindly man."

"So it would not grieve you if my father could be agreed with Berse?"

At this she laughed. "No! How should I take it into my head to grieve if Father were agreed with an enemy?"

Then Eirik laughed too.

That evening he ventured to lean his breast slightly against her knee when he lifted her into the saddle.

"I wonder when I shall see you again?"

"I cannot tell. I am to go home tomorrow."

Cecilia and Eirik accompanied their guests a little way across the fields. Little Torgils was asleep, well wrapped up, in Una's spacious lap. Before they parted his mother held up her arms. "Let me have him a moment, Una!" She kissed the boy, cautiously so as not to wake him. "I know well that you will have as good a care of him as I myself—"

Slowly the brother and sister walked back to the manor.

"But 'tis surely best that Una have charge of him this winter," he said soothingly.

"Ay, 'tis so; I know it. But—"

Eirik was wishing he could have taken her in his arms—or could have done something that would make her happy. It cut him to the soul that she should not be happy, now that he was. After the agitations of his talk with Gunhild he was quite unusually happy.

When he came into the room, his father sat there eating—he had not yet taken off either hat or cloak. Eirik paused for a moment.

"Father—cannot you be reconciled with Jörund? 'Twill be unbearable for Cecilia if you two go about here and never say a word to each other."

"Has *she* begged you to ask this of me?"

"Cecilia? Can you think of such a thing! But you must see—"

"Hm. She does not speak to me either, more than she can help. She takes Jörund's part, I believe. And maybe 'tis better so— We must wait awhile, Eirik, see how it goes. I have no great mind to be the first to hold out my hand. 'Tis not that I cannot forgive an enemy—but Jörund. If I do it *once*—yield to him when he is in the wrong—then I fear 'twill not be long ere he venture the same again."

So it was of no use. Nor was what his father said untrue. He would have to wait.

Not long after, Eirik saw Berse at a Thing in Haugsvik.

He was a giant in stature and bulky of body, with a mass of silvery hair and beard, his features large and handsome, but he was marked and blind of one eye from smallpox. He sat by himself on the raised seat; in his rich kirtle he seemed to have the bosom of an old woman, and his belly rolled out upon his knees. Olav and Torgrim sat on the side bench, and for the first time it struck Eirik that after all there was a great difference between seventy years and fifty. His father looked small beside Berse, but in spite of his white hair and scarred face he seemed young and elastic, straight and well-knit. But Torgrim with his lean and loose-hung frame and shock of brown and grey-streaked hair around his lively, angular face appeared to Eirik almost like a man of his own age. Then Olav called Eirik forward.

Eirik stood before Berse, answered with respectful courtesy to the words the old man addressed to him with the utmost gravity and dignity. Then Berse made a sign that he might go.

And well it was, thought Eirik. Out in the courtyard he came upon Ragnvald Jonsson.

"What makes you grin like that?" asked Ragnvald in surprise.

Eirik gave his friend a slap between the shoulders that made him gasp; then he could contain himself no longer; he burst out laughing so that he had to hold on to Ragnvald.

As they rowed homeward Olav asked: "What think you of Berse of Eiken, my son?"

Eirik bit his lip and struggled to look serious.

Olav said: "You know, 'tis a good old stock, many gallant men —great wealth there is, too. And the maid takes after her mother; Helga was a brave woman. In every bargain there is something one would wish to alter. And here there is Berse—"

On seeing his father smile, he dared to laugh too.

"But he is as old as the hills, is Berse, and 'tis a far cry from Eiken to Hestviken."

"Ay, Gunhild said the same."

"Have you spoken with Gunhild?" asked his father rather sharply.

"But little. We said a few words when she came out to us with Una. She let me know that she thought it pleasant by the fiord, and that Eiken lay far up the country."

"Ah, well. But beware of acting unwisely, Eirik—better have no more speech with her till all be in order. Berse will come—of

that we may be sure—but we must let him come at his own pace,
give him time to get his breath. 'Tis more seemly thus, you understand."

They looked at each other and laughed.

About Michaelmas it was cold for some days; the ground was
covered with rime and all the pools were frozen over, now and
again a snow-squall swept across. Then there was mild weather
again; the hills were blue-black, splashed with yellow foliage, the
blue fiord sparkled in the sunlight. The meadows along the shore
were green with after-grass among white stubble-fields; there was
light in all the groves, where yellow leaves shivered down and the
alders alone still showed a faded green in their tops.

Eirik had come sailing in from Saltviken one morning. The
weather was so fine that he stayed a moment outside the house
door. The brindled cattle grazing in the green meadow were still
fat from summer pasture, many fine beasts among them. They
could well take five or six out to Saltviken.

He caught sight of Cecilia on the steps of the storehouse that
had been assigned to Jörund for his use. She carried in her arms a
heavy load of fur cloaks and other garments. Eirik called to her,
ran up, and took it all from her.

"I thought I ought to mend our winter clothing ere I am
brought to bed—the cold may soon set in in earnest." She turned
toward the door of the loft.

"If there is more to come, take it out—I will come up and carry
it for you."

Eirik came back, ran up the stairway whistling, and entered the
loft. The sun shone in at the open door on his sister as she knelt
by a chest. In one leap Eirik was beside her.

"Cecilia! Are you sick?"

"Nay—" She uttered a loud shriek of pain; she had flung down
the lid of the chest so suddenly that it caught her fingers.

Eirik raised the lid slightly—saw a glimpse of what lay within.
Then he put his arm about his sister's waist and supported her
to a seat. He took her crushed hand and fingered it charily, to
see if it were damaged. She panted and panted, wearily and
painfully.

"Is there more you would have me carry down for you?" He
flung the chest wide open.

Cecilia sent him one anxious glance. He saw she was trying to rise, but had not the strength.

"Jörund chooses a strange place to keep his silver."

He found his own hands shaking as he took one piece after another out of the homespun cloth: a great silver tankard in which lay a lump of silver that had been melted down, two smaller cups.

"I have not seen these things before?"

"Nor I either," whispered Cecilia. Then she collected herself. "This must be something he has brought lately."

Eirik nodded in spite of himself.

Cecilia went on in desperate eagerness: "He has always thought his brothers had dealt unfairly by him—twice when they divided an inheritance. That is why Jörund thinks he can never get silver enough. They set more store by such treasures at Gunnarsby than — So Jörund will always buy all he can."

Eirik nodded again. Jörund had been like a hawk after silver —though often enough he lost it again in play. But never had he thought it could lead to such a thing as—as what he was afraid of; though to be sure he knew nothing as yet.

He took up the clothes that Cecilia had dropped beside the chest and gave his sister his hand. She was trembling all over.

"Erik—in God's name—what will you do?"

"Speak to Jörund. Have no fear, Cecilia," he begged her.

Her brother helped her down the stairway, took her into the house, and laid her on her bed.

"Shall I find Magnhild for you?"

Cecilia shook her head.

"Is it not imprudent that you be left alone now?"

"No, I can well be alone."

Out in the yard Kolbein ran straight into his legs. Eirik picked up his nephew; with the child in his arms he went back to the women's house and put his head in at the door.

"Kolli wants to go to his mother, he says—may he come in?"

"I would rather be alone."

He played with the boy, sang to him, and sought to allay the dread in his own heart. Till he saw Jörund's boat outside; then he carried Kolbein in to the women in the cook-house. Eirik was

waiting by the fence of the "good acre" as Jörund came up from
the sea.

"You have come home?"

"Yes, I came this morning. I shall have to stay here awhile.
There is a thing I must speak with you about." They walked
together across the yard. "We can go up into your loft."

Jörund backed away from him. Eirik looked the other in the
face till he succeeded in holding the shifting eyes a moment.

"Remember, Jörund, I have been your friend since our young
days—many a time ere this have I rescued you from a tight corner.
And now we are in the same boat; your welfare is ours. And if
you have behaved foolishly, your misfortune will be my sister's
and ours.—Nay, you can go first," he said when they came to
the stairway.

Jörund took his hand from the hilt of his dagger and obeyed.
On entering the loft Eirik went straight to the chest and
opened it.

"What have you been doing in my chest?"

"Nothing. Cecilia came to look for some clothes and I helped
her to carry them down."

"Cecilia—!"

"Ay. But she was not the cause of this—I believe God Himself
so ordered it that we might be rescued from this danger. And if
you mean to make Cecilia suffer for this, you may go straightway
and be shriven."

"Do you threaten me?"

"I do."

"Do you think I am afraid of you? A holy hound like you—
turn the other cheek if a man smite you under the ear—"

"True, I have curbed myself at times these last years when I
was provoked. But you know very well, in old days I was never
slow to take up a quarrel—unlike you. You never had cause to
fear me—but I know well you are none of the bravest."

"Where have you left your piety today?" Jörund tried to sneer.

"Have no care for that. We have to speak of what is to be done
with this silver."

"The silver I have bought—"

"Ay, so I thought. You have bought it of the folk you met at
Rundmyr on the evening of Suscipimus Deus Sunday?"

"I should have remembered they are your thralls"—Jörund flared up; "and of course you would keep the nest for your own with all that are in it of thieves and whores—"

"Be quiet now," said Eirik calmly. " 'Tis true you ought to have remembered that these folk are faithful to us, and if you are such a gull as to believe all the tales I once told you for entertainment's sake—how could I tell you were so credulous; 'tis not like you. But it so happened that I was riding past and saw you come out with someone— They have said nothing; I advise you to remember that! Was it the thieves themselves, or was it their fences?" he brought himself to ask.

"It was a woman," said Jörund curtly.

Did you think that bride had inherited the silver she carried along the road?—but he kept the question to himself.

"I have thought of a way, Jörund. We will bury these things in the ground by Rundmyr. And then we must find them again when they have lain there awhile, and bring them to Guttorm at Draumtorp."

"I have bought them," said Jörund angrily.

"I will give you Agnar in exchange"—he instantly regretted that he had not thought of something else; Jörund was not always good to his horses. "I wager he is worth more than you gave that woman," he said rather scornfully. "Cannot you see, man, 'tis your own honour and welfare that you have to save by this?" he went on earnestly. "What use have you of silver that you must keep hidden?"

He wrapped the treasure in the cloth again, put it under his cloak, carried it down, and hid it in his bed.

In the course of the afternoon, when he had seen Jörund go out, he slipped into the women's house to hear how it was with Cecilia.

She sat sewing at some of the things he had brought down for her in the morning. Eirik was afraid to ask the question, but at last he said nevertheless:

"Has Jörund spoken to you of what we talked of this morning?"

"Yes. I must thank you, Eirik, for giving him your help. He says he cannot guess how he could be so thoughtless as to let them trick him into taking these things. But in sooth it was because he wished to restore to Father what he owed him."

"That must be a lie," thought her brother. He leaned over her and stroked her wimpled head once or twice as she bent over her sewing.

In the evening, as he and his father were going to bed, Eirik said:

"Now I have a boon to ask of you, Father, and 'tis the same I asked before—be reconciled with Jörund!"

"I have already given you my answer."

"Yes. But now I say to you—this is worse for Cecilia than you think. For the love of God who died for us all—grant what I ask of you this time!"

Olav looked at his son, but made no answer.

"Ay, there is yet more I would ask of you. When Cecilia is over her churching—let her rule here as mistress of the whole manor!"

"What say you! When you yourself are to bring a wife into the house at John's mass! 'Twill leave but a short space for Cecilia to wear the keys."

"Oh, I know not.—I had thought that Gunhild and I might be at Saltviken most of the time."

"No, Eirik! Saltviken is far too small for the daughter of Eiken."

"I am not sure of that. One day Hestviken will be ours in any case—and then we shall be thought no less of for having kept to its desert and dependent manor for some years."

"I told you," said Olav slowly, "last time we spoke of these things—I believe Jörund is a dangerous man to give in to, when he is in the wrong."

"Father!" Eirik rose, stood facing Olav, and spoke with vehement insistence. "I beg this of you, with all my power! Think of our mother! Have you ever felt pity for her, in the years when she lay here broken and powerless—and you must have—did you ever rue it that you made her lot more grievous—Father, Christ knows I do not speak thus to accuse you, I know your own lot was hard enough—I know you would not have taken her, but they forced the marriage upon you, ere you were grown up. But even if you did not love her, you must have pitied her; do not then so order it that Cecilia's lot must be as hard as Mother's!"

Olav had listened to his son—with an expression that bewildered Eirik.

"What has put this into your head? That I did not love your mother?" The strange smile that spread over the man's whole face reminded his son, as it died away, of rings that spread over a sheet of water. "I did so. And for her sake I will do as you ask."

When Eirik had gone to bed—he lay on the silver and thought he would rather have had a nest of vipers in his bed-straw—his father came to the door of the closet.

"Will you stay at home now?"

"I thought I would sail across tomorrow with Tore—give him directions there. Then I could come back on the second or third day."

"That were well."

In the midst of all the misery on which he lay brooding it suddenly occurred to Eirik: things had so shaped themselves that he now counted for not a little at Hestviken. And he was not sorry at the thought. And by John's mass, his father had said. He lay sleepless that night, in a fever of dread and disgust over the affairs of others, in a fever of joy over his own.

About midnight he stole out and made his way up toward Rundmyr. He found the hiding-place he had in mind, buried the Draumtorp silver there. On coming home he waked Tore, and when Olav came out in the grey dawn, they had loaded the boats and were ready to sail.

At Saltviken they were met by Olav Livsson. With his two crutches and his thin, dangling limbs the cripple made one think of a huge creeping spider. But his face was handsome, narrow and refined, with great brown eyes. Eirik remembered with disgust Jörund's asking whether he were father to the lad. When Eirik laughingly replied that he must have been but twelve or thirteen at the time, Jörund smiled slyly—"Well?" Eirik could not make out how he had ever liked Jörund Rypa. But he had been fond of him, for all that.

He had a busy day. Out here he had to lend a hand with everything. The dead leaves were still stacked outside, but now they were dry; the good, bitter-sweet scent of them carried a long way. In the spring, when they had dung enough and could take up more cornfields, the ugly bush fences should be replaced by rails. He went to look at his cherry trees too—there was no fruit on them, nor could that be expected, but only four of the ten trees were dead, and two of the rosebushes were alive. He plucked a sprig of mint, crushed it between his fingers, and smelled it. Some fine, blue-green leaves had also come up—they must be the herb that Brother Hubert called aquilegia; no doubt there had been some of its seed in the mould about the roots. There would be great bright-blue flowers on it—had Gunhild ever seen the like before? She would be surprised when she saw that he even had a garden to his manor.

Before he fell asleep that night, the thought came to him that from here it was not nearly so far up to Eiken as from Hestviken. And next morning he saddled the bay and rode inland.

He had never before seen Eiken except at a distance—no high-road passed near it. Now he turned his horse into a side-track that led in the direction of the manor.

It stood secluded on a hill that came down in a tongue between two converging watercourses, close under a dark wooded height.

Eirik rode up and past it. There was no one about among the houses; the manor lay as though deserted below its wood, with many houses, and beyond them stood great oaks with browned leaves against the sky.

Above the manor the road led upward into the forest. The weather was fine and it amused Eirik to ride thus into the unknown; he had a mind to see whither this track might lead—whether perhaps he might come out on a height, from whence he could have a view of this part of the country—it was unfamiliar to him.

He came upon some great slabs of rock where the forest was thin, the firs broken at the top by wind or weight of snow. Heather and moss grew thick over the ground, and among the rocks were patches of bog with dying, hoary trees and gnarled and yellow birches around tarns that mirrored the blue sky.

Up here, in the shadows, all was white with rime, and a few little snowflakes in the bog showed that a shower had passed over the forest. But now the sky was clear and blue, scored by white fine-weather clouds, and the sun shone on the autumnal woods. Eirik let his horse get its breath, sitting at his ease and thinking of nothing—when there came a call from beyond the bog, a loud, clear woman's voice. She was calling a goat, cried something, a name it must have been, in a sad and plaintive tone; then came the call again.

Eirik listened intently. Then he crossed himself—if this was other than human, it would have no power over him against his will. But indeed it might be someone from Eiken.

The calling came nearer. Now he could hear: "Blaalin, Blaalin," she was calling. Now he caught sight of a woman clad in green; she came out upon the stony ground on this side of the tarn, stopped by some yellow stunted birches.

Now she had seen that a strange horseman had appeared on the mountain—she stopped, hesitating. Then he turned his horse and, taking up her luring tone, he called her name in a voice that rang: "Gunhild, Gunhild—" and rode toward her.

"Have I frightened you?" he cried when he was near enough for her to know him.

She came forward to meet him, still hesitating a little. "Are you *here*? On this side?"

"Ay, I had business—" He checked himself. Of all his good resolutions, the most difficult to keep was that he must always speak the truth instead of saying the first thing that occurred to him. "I had a mind to look around here for once. I have never been east of the Kambshorn road."

Her kirtle was green edged with red, but simple in cut as a serving-woman's working-shift: the sleeves did not reach the wrist, and it was so short that her ankles showed; she wore coarse shoes that were black with wet and besmeared with bog mire. Dry twigs and leaves were caught in her dress and in her plaits, which were half-undone. Eirik thought she looked younger and as it were nearer in this simple dress.

"But—is it not rash of you, Gunhild, to roam the woods thus alone?" He knew there were many bears on the hills hereabout—and mountain-folk too, 'twas said.

Gunhild looked up into his face; he saw that she had been afraid. "My goat did not come home last night—one that I have had from a kid."

"Then shall I join you in the search?" The goat had been taken by a wild beast, he thought, but it might be they would find a trace—

"Thanks, will you? Then perhaps it were best you turned your **horse** into the paddock by our summer byre—'tis just here."

"But you will come too? I like not your being alone here in the forest."

He carried the bridle on his arm, and she walked at his side. They still kept a few young cattle and goats up here, she said, and when her father and stepmother set out from home two days ago, she had come up hither to see how it went. Yesterday morning Blaalin had given but little milk; she had thought nothing of it, but since then the herdsman said she had walked so strangely, almost as if she were drunken—and then she did not come home with the rest at evening. And Gunhild had scarcely been able to sleep for uneasiness—Blaalin, poor creature, lying out in the open. Eirik swallowed her every word—she spoke to him as if they had been friends a great while.

The path ended in a meadow, where some old black houses were falling to pieces. Since he had repaired the old houses at Saltviken, Eirik could never see a ruinous building without thinking of what he would have done with it—so also here. Building was now become his favourite occupation.

"But we ought rather to go over to the other side, Gunhild—the wind was from the south-west last night."

Gunhild did not know that—the goat always goes against the wind.

So they set off in the other direction. They kept within sight and sound of each other and answered each other's calls the whole time.

The fine, loud notes resounded in the clear autumn weather. Eirik ran over crunching dry moss, down the face of screes, where the bracken was shrivelled and the wild raspberry still bore blood-red fruit, but its leaves lay fallen among the stones, showing their silvery undersides. He leaped into swamps, so that the mud splashed and his spear-shaft sank deep when he wanted to support himself on it; he came upon frozen ground where the thin ice broke under his feet at every step, into thick spruce forest, where he lost sight of her. Then he called:

"Are you, are you, are you there, Gunhild, Gunhild, Gunhild, my Gunhild—"

And she called back to him: "Are you, are you, are you there, Eirik, Eirik, Eirik—"

He could tell by her voice that she had forgotten her sorrow in the sport, and he leaped with joy and let his pure and flexible voice ring out under the blue sky. Once they came to a place where the echo answered so plainly that they stayed shouting and singing at the rock and forgot all else.

They were walking on a slope where great trees lay over-thrown by the wind, with shreds of mossy soil clinging to their roots, and among them the cranberry shone red. They walked in sight of each other—when she gathered up her kirtle in both hands and ran slantingly toward him, leaping and climbing over stocks and stones. At the same moment he too heard the feeble, piteous cry—he too ran in the direction of the sound. They met by the little pit—within it the rime lay thick upon moss and with-ered leaves—and there they found the little black-saddled goat. She lay with her legs stretched out and her neck turned back; there was not much life in the poor creature. But Gunhild flung herself down and got the goat halfway up in her arms, fondling it and talking to it the while.

Eirik lifted Blaalin out of the pit and carried it, and Gunhild took his light spear and walked at his side. It would have been better to kill the poor beast, which was nearly dead already—and the goat was a heavy burden after a while. But he was too glad of the chance of walking thus with her to say anything of this; every moment Gunhild had to caress Blaalin in his arms.

At last they found their way back to the summer byre. Eirik fetched a truss of hay for her to strew under Blaalin, and she had found an old ragged coverlet to spread over the goat.

Then she said: "But you must come in, Eirik, and rest. I have naught else to offer you than goat's milk and a slice of cheese."

"Did you sleep here last night?" he asked in a low voice—they entered a little dark hut where the daylight crept in between the logs. The hearth was a hole in the floor, and the couch a pallet of cleft logs with hay and a few blankets spread on top. So she was not proud—gentle she was and full of care for all that was in her charge, faithful and diligent. Eirik looked at her, full of tenderness and wonder, as he sat on the edge of her poor couch and drank the smoky goat's-milk.

He made up the fire for her, and she put the kettle on. While she waited for the milk to be ready for curdling, they sat side by side on the pallet, chatting together like old friends. Till Gun-hild said all at once—and turned red as she spoke:

"I wonder, Eirik—the dairywoman may come back soon—she might think it strange that I have a guest in the hut."

Eirik rose rather reluctantly. "But go with me across the paddock, Gunhild, if you can leave the kettle."

He took his horse and led it through the gate into the forest. Then they must needs part.

"You have soot on your hand—" he held it between both his. They stood looking at each other, smiling slightly. She·made no resistance when he drew her close to him, and so he threw his arm about the girl and kissed her on the mouth.

She let him do it; then he kissed her all over her face, pressing her tightly against him—till he felt her struggle.

"Eirik—now you must let me go."

"Oh, no—?"

"Yes—let go!"

He let her go. "Are you angry now, Gunhild?"

"Oh, I know not." So he drew her toward him again. She flung her arms about his neck an instant. "But now you must go—nay, nay, what are you doing?"

He had thrust a hand down under the neck of her kirtle and pressed it for a moment against her smooth breast. Half laughing and half embarrassed she pushed him from her, and fished up the hard, cold thing he had slipped under her dress.

"Nay, Eirik—you must take this back—so great a gift I may not take from you yet." She held out the gold brooch he had taken out of his shirt.

"Oh, yes." He swung himself into the saddle; when she came up, gave him his spear with one hand, and tried to force the brooch on him with the other, he bent down and once more brushed her smooth, cool forehead with his lips. "You are to have it—you must keep it till you can wear it!"

Then he let his horse go. Time after time he turned and nodded to her. When he saw her for the last time, as the path turned down into the thicket, Gunhild raised her hand and waved to him.

Eirik smiled to himself, laughed quietly now and then, as he rode back toward the fiord. At intervals he hummed the notes of the call, but very low, and he dared not sing her name aloud. This was the happiest day he had known.

15

On the last Sunday but one before Advent, Cecilia Olavsdatter held her churching, and when they came home to Hestviken her father gave her the keys of his stores in the sight of the whole household, asking her to be pleased to take upon herself the duties of mistress of Hestviken.

Olav and Jörund now spoke to each other—not very much, but at any rate Olav was not unfriendly toward his son-in-law. And he had visited Cecilia several times to see this last child of hers; the folk of the place thought he must be glad there was once more an Audun at Hestviken. And indeed it was a fine big child. Cecilia was pale and thin, but seemed in good health—she took charge of the house as a capable wife, and the old serving-folk, who had known her from a child, were eager to comply with the behests of their young mistress and loved her little sons.

Eirik's joy was such that not one of these quiet people in this quiet household could fail to be cheered by it—though he himself was calm enough at this time. Since that day in the forest he had spoken only once with Gunhild—at church—and then he did no more than ask after Blaalin—Blaalin was dead.

But Olav had told him that now Torgrim had received Berse's answer; they had his leave to come and speak with him of the matter after the last day of Yule—he held it unbecoming to conclude a bargain of this nature during Advent or in the holy-days. The betrothal ale might then take place before Lent, and if Olav Audunsson desired the wedding to be held so soon as the early summer, Berse would not oppose it, seeing that Eirik was not so young and Gunhild had already completed her twentieth year.

And Una said both she and Signe would so order it that he could meet Gunhild Bersesdatter at Yuletide: "for you two ought to hold some converse ere you be bound together in betrothal—since it is now agreed you are to wed Gunhild."

He was troubled enough in his mind over what he had buried in the ground at Rundmyr. That hiding-place was known to others besides him. True, he had long ago forbidden Arnketil to harbour dishonest folk, but here was proof that at Rundmyr they held his commands but lightly. And Jörund had challenged

him more than once, demanding to know what he had done with
the treasure. Eirik put him off, reminding him that he had bought
the silver of him for the price of a good horse, and saying that it
lay in a spot that it was unsafe to visit even in broad daylight.
Moreover, he tried every means of keeping Jörund in good humour—took him out hunting and in his boat and found pretexts
for making visits to all the houses where he had friends or kinsfolk. It was no longer quite to his mind to roam about so much,
but he saw that the quiet life at Hestviken was dangerous for Jörund: the man was as full of humours as a bull, and if he turned
vicious, Eirik was afraid Cecilia would suffer for it.

But he himself was too happy to let any of this take a real hold
of him. When he brought Gunhild out hither, he thought that in
some way the others' troubles and difficulties would also grow
less. She brought such gladness with her.

Then one morning, a fortnight before Yule, when Eirik came
out into the yard he saw that a thin coat of snow lay on the
ground. The morning moon shone like a bright speck behind the
drifting mist, promising a heavier fall. Eirik made up his mind
that today he would take up the silver again; otherwise the snow
might force him to wait he knew not how long, and he yearned
to be rid of it.

He asked Jörund to go out hunting with him during the day,
and when the two came home at dark Eirik had killed a fox and
carried with him a little bundle in an earthy homespun cloth.

He did not know whether to tell his father of it or not. But he
had no desire to lie more than he could help in this wretched
affair. And he was afraid it would trouble and distress Cecilia if
there were once more talk of this silver—she had enough hard
work in any case, making ready for Yule, and at night she had
little rest, for the infant child.

So he merely said to his father that Jörund had business north
in the next parish and he had promised to accompany his brother-
in-law. Then they rode to Draumtorp.

They arrived there at evening, and Eirik was ill pleased when
he heard that Berse of Eiken was there with two of his sons, Gunhild's own brothers. It had increased his indignation over the
affair from the first that Guttorm of Draumtorp was her uncle.
But that he should be compelled to utter his lying tale in the

hearing of those who were soon to be his brothers-in-law, that was a thing he had not looked for.

But it went well. When Eirik had once made a beginning, he told a smooth and credible story of his fox-hunt and of his dog that had stuck fast in an earth and of the find they had made, which Jörund and he at once had thought might be a part of the Draumtorp treasure.

Guttorm was glad to get back some of his silver, so Eirik and Jörund were given the best of welcomes. The attack in the Gerdarud forest was then discussed at great length. The brothers-in-law from Hestviken listened to the old men and replied no more than there was need—this seemed to please Berse; he grew very friendly; he even jested with Eirik, saying mayhap they would be better acquainted in time—and in the end Eirik was vouchsafed the honour of escorting Berse to bed. Now that he was rid of his ugly secret, Eirik's mood soon became light and gay, and he had drunk all he needed, so it was with a right merry heart he helped his father-in-law that was to be. Even when he was overwhelmed by the frailty of his nature, this old Berse contrived somehow to preserve his dignity in the midst of his throes.

Guttorm of Draumtorp had a long talk with Eirik next morning. He seemed to be a wise and sober man. He spoke of Berse, calling to mind that the old man had been honoured for many years as the franklins' leader, and with every right; he had been a generous, brave, and shrewd man in his younger days. Now in truth he had grown somewhat odd with age—and his young wife, the third, whom he had married when he was already sixty winters old, had no little sway over him, though he would not allow it. And his children by the first wife had brought great sorrow upon him. The son, Benedikt, had blamed his father for his sister's misfortune, and he had ridden from Eiken in anger; Berse never saw him again, for he fell the year after in Denmark. But Eldrid did not die, 'twas not so well.

"But all the children he had by Helga, my sister, are good and virtuous folk, Eirik—and now I am glad Gunhild shall make so good a marriage."

Eirik guessed from this that all the maid's kinsfolk knew of the agreement; her younger brothers, Torleif and Kaare, also greeted him as one who was soon to be their brother-in-law.

Guttorm had once met Olav Audunsson at Hestbæk, and in

taking leave he bade Eirik bring greetings to his father. So when
Eirik came home he had to say he had been at Draumtorp and
to tell Olav of the finding of the silver. Olav was angry when he
heard that such things had been found in his woods. Eirik replied
that he had already reproved Anki and Liv and that he would not
fail to keep a watch in future, but he begged his father to spare
them this time.

At Yule Eirik met the folk from Eiken, and now they greeted
him in such wise that all could see what was in the wind. When
they rode to church from Skikkjustad on the eighth day of Yule,
in driving rain on a road slippery with ice, Berse bade Eirik ride
beside Gunhild and keep an eye on her horse; and at Rynjul they
were allowed to sit by themselves over the chessboard a whole
evening. It was a strange game, for Gunhild was as stupid as could
be at this play, but this too became her well in Eirik's eyes—he had
never before played chess with any woman but his sister, and she
played better than most men.

That same evening Olav of Hestviken and Berse of Eiken
spoke long together in another house on the manor—though it
was a holy-day—and kinsmen and friends on both sides were
present. Afterwards Olav told Eirik of the agreement they had
come to regarding the bride's portion; Olav was to come to Eiken
on the eve of St. Agnes [9] with his son and his witnesses, and next
day Eirik Olavsson was to betroth Gunhild Bersesdatter with ring
and gifts.

On the following morning Gunhild was sent home together
with her stepmother and her eldest, married brother, but Berse
stayed behind at Rynjul with his two younger sons. It was the
finest, clearest winter weather, and so Eirik proposed that they
should ride into the town, as many as were minded to see the
great procession when the King visited the Church of St. Mary on
the day of Epiphany—for it was reported that King Haakon was
in Oslo.

All the young men wished to go—Berse's sons, young Torgils
Torgrimsson and his cousin, Sigmund Baardsson from Skikkjustad. Then said Torgrim himself, the master of the house, that he
might have a mind to go. "What think you, Olav, shall we two
join company with the young folk for once?"

Olav laughed and shook his head. He must be thinking rather

[9] January 20.

of returning home. "Long enough has Cecilia been left alone at Hestviken."

Then Berse himself spoke up. He had served in King Eirik's body-guard and afterwards in King Haakon's, and now he would do his King a last homage and would take his place in the procession.

Thus they made slow progress, and when they came to the town it was so late that Eirik could not go to his convent and seek lodging there, as had been his intention, but followed the rest of the company to a yard where Guttorm's son-in-law owned a house.

Late as it was, the upper room into which they came was full of men, and the tables were full of food and drink. The men flocked about Guttorm to tell him the great news that was over the whole town: three nights ago the men of Aker had descended on the den of those miscreants who so long had made the forests around Oslo unsafe. Last autumn the ruffians had fallen upon a little farm in a clearing by Elivaag, where two brothers dwelt with their wives and a young sister; they had plundered the place and slaughtered the cattle, ravished the women, who were alone at home—but one of the robbers seemed to have liked the young girl so well that he had visited her since. She received him with a show of kindness and at last coaxed him into telling her where was the robber stronghold, and so her brothers had gathered the peasants and led them thither; six of the robbers had been slain or burned in their house, but four men and one woman lay in the dungeon of the old royal castle waiting to receive the reward of their misdeeds on the rock of execution. The girl had claimed as her meed to be allowed to hold her ravisher's hair clear of the headsman's axe.

At long last, when the men had said their say and drunk their fill, all came to bed. Eirik lay on the outside in a bed with Jörund Rypa and Kaare Bersesson; they two fell asleep at once, but he lay awake, in a torment of dismay, trying to tell himself that he need not be afraid, ere he knew whether there were aught to be afraid of.

He took the rosary from his neck and held it in his hands. But in all these years he had never been wont to pray *for* anything— he had only prayed in order to feel that God was there and that he could speak to Him, but he had been content with all that fell to him from God's hand. Ah, yes, he had prayed for Cecilia. But now he knew not what he might do—if what he had done were wrong, then he could not well pray God to help him conceal the truth, if it were meant to come to light.

He stood down by the castle quay, caught in the press of people, so that he could scarce see anything of the procession—listening to folks' talk around him. It seemed impossible they could speak of aught but the robbers.

The church was full of folk, so there was no room to kneel down, and he could not follow the mass, for his heart was in too great a tumult. But he stayed behind when the church began to empty. Then he saw that he had been standing close to a side altar, and on the wall beside it was painted Mary with her attendant virgins: Margaret, Lucy, Cecilia, Barbara, Agatha; last of the band stood Agnes with her lamb. She was to have been the witness of his plighting his troth to Gunhild; he had been glad of that, for he had had a special affection for this young and childlike martyr ever since he had heard her legend. So he approached her with a prayer: "Pray for me for what is best." He grew calmer on the instant; it was as though he had taken counsel with a little sister.

Someone touched him on the shoulder, and he rose at once—it was Guttorm of Draumtorp. Eirik had expected this, it seemed to him. They went out of the church together, but as they stood outside the porch looking up the street, Guttorm said suddenly:

"We may just as well talk inside. Something has come up of which I thought I would fain speak with you in private, Eirik Olavsson. Maybe you guess what it is?"

Eirik looked at the other, but made no reply.

"I wish to hear," said Guttorm, "if aught else had come to light about my silver, the rest of it. So we went out to the castle this morning between matins and mass—Berse was bound thither in any case, and so I went with him. Sir Tore then had the prisoners brought up into the hall, so that we might question them."

Eirik pressed his hat between his hands, but answered nothing. Now they were standing by the same side altar—and on the wall above him he saw the painting of the holy virgins; lithe and slender in their bright kirtles they stood in a ring about their Queen, smiling upon the King's Son in her lap. Eirik was reminded of the verse: *Ego mater pulchræ dilectionis, et timoris, et agnitionis, et sanctæ spei*,[1] and of the response: *Deo gratias*.

Guttorm scratched his head.

"Sooth to say, Eirik—it mislikes me to have to speak of these things— And I am thinking—could you not say it yourself?"

"I—?"

"You can guess I questioned them closely of that hiding-place of theirs out in the Hestvik woods." He looked searchingly at the young man who stood with a calm, white face looking down at the floor. "For, to be brief, it would seem that as you found my silver, you knew where to look?"

Eirik nodded slightly.

"I have got you back your silver, Guttorm," he said quietly. "Can you not be content with that?"

"Is it true that you had bought it?"

"Yes. But you will hardly think I bought it of any unknown," he went on, in a more lively tone. "The place where—where I got wind of this affair—is the dwelling of poor and ignorant folk —the man was like a foster-father to me when I was a boy. They have little wit—and all kinds of beggars and the like frequent their cot, some of our own beadsmen among them, good folk, such as have served in our boats, all kinds of vagabonds besides. Guttorm—could you not forbear to look more closely into this matter, be content that I have borne the cost of getting back your goods—and leave me to sit in judgment at home over my own folk?"

"No, Eirik—'tis useless that you try to give out that it was one of your folk—"

Eirik broke in: "In God's name, if you know more, then you must know that I have special grounds for dealing with the matter as I have done—secretly."

"That may be so." Guttorm paused awhile, turning over something in his mind. "You know not if there be more of my silver to be found up there?"

"No.—I have given no thought to that. I cannot believe it either—but if you will, you could come out to us when the snow is gone, I will gladly help you to make search."

Guttorm looked at the young man sharply—he himself red-

[1] "I am the mother of fair love, and fear, and knowledge, and holy hope." Ecclesiasticus, xxiv, 18.

dened as he spoke. "Better we make an end of it," he then said.
"Jörund Rypa says there were four cups—the great tankard and
four small ones—"

Eirik looked at Guttorm, bewildered. The lump of silver, he
thought; then it was Jörund himself who had melted down some
of the booty—this grew worse and worse. He shook his head.

"I have seen it in no other shape than as it was when I gave it
to you. So I know not who has melted down your silver cups."

"There should be four cups and the lump of silver, says he,"
Guttorm rejoined in a low voice.

Eirik stared—slowly a blush crept over his pale face.

"Then Jörund's memory is at fault."

"That horse you gave him in exchange," asked Guttorm warily
—"that was worth more than the silver you brought me—'twas
the one he rode yesterday?"

"Since you know *who* it was," said Eirik hotly, "can you suppose I was minded to haggle over the price?"

Guttorm was silent for a few moments. Then he asked slowly:
"Then you know of no more than the silver that I received back
from you? You give me your answer here, where we stand, and
I take your word for it."

Involuntarily Eirik looked up at the wall—it flashed through
his mind that he had heard of pictures that found a voice: Mary
herself and her Son had witnessed from painted lips and mouths of
stone that the truth might be made manifest. But no change came
over the gentle faces under the golden crowns, and the holy virgins stood motionless, showing forth the wheels and the swords
that had once torn their bodies asunder.

"No. I know naught of more," he said simply.

Guttorm held out his hand. As Eirik made no move to take it,
he seized the young man's, pressed it hard.

"I believe you, I say. But that I had to get this affair straightened out—you cannot bear me ill will for that?"

"No. You had to do it—"

" 'Tis cold standing here," said Guttorm. "Come, let us go out."

Outside, the smoke whirled up from all the white roofs—it was
mild, the sun shone, and the sky was blue. The thin coat of fresh
snow that had fallen during the night had been trodden down, so
that the street was slippery. "I shall have to take your arm," said
Guttorm.

Eirik could utter nothing in reply. He saw what the elder man meant, but it was bitter to have to swallow such amends when he had been forced to put up with so immense and undeserved an insult. Arm in arm the two walked up West Street. In the square outside St. Halvard's Church Guttorm met some men he knew; he leaned heavily on Eirik's arm while he spoke to them. Eirik stood dumb as a post. But when they reached the house by Holy Cross Church, where they were lodged, he said to Guttorm:

"Ere we go in—*I* would fain ask you of one or two matters."

"That is fair enough."

They had passed behind the yards, where the river ran between clay banks. Eirik bade Guttorm tell him what had passed in the hall of the castle that morning, and who had been present.

Guttorm said Berse had been there with both his sons, Torgrim from Rynjul and Jörund Rypa, himself and his son-in-law Karl. Of the castle folk none had been present but Sir Tore and the men-at-arms who brought in the prisoners.

None of these had taken part in the attack on Guttorm and his company—the robbers either had been killed or had left the band before this winter. But the woman had been ready to make known what had become of the Draumtorp silver; she had sold it to that man who stood there, Jörund Rypa. The two had known each other of old. Then Jörund had straightway confirmed her words, but said that Aasa had declared to him it was her heritage, which she had just fetched from home, and he had believed her, for he knew that she came of good family. He bought the silver of her because she said she would then see about leaving her man—married they were not—and she would amend her life.

To this the woman had replied that nothing had been said of where the silver came from, nor had she seen any sign that night of Jörund's zeal for the improvement of her morals.

Then Jörund said that she was lying, and he had never a thought but that she had inherited the silver from Aasmund of Haugseter. So much was true, that she was this man's daughter, but she had fallen into evil courses and had run from home. It was only when Jörund had shown Eirik his purchase that his brother-in-law had hinted it might be stolen goods. Thereupon Jörund would keep it no longer, but Eirik offered to buy it of him for the black gelding he was now riding—and there was a great tankard, four smaller cups, and a lump of melted silver. But afterwards, when winter

was come, Eirik had said he dared not keep it any longer—since
he was now to marry Guttorm's niece, he thought it safest to
restore it to the master of Draumtorp ere the betrothal took
place.

Eirik stood inertly leaning his back against the fence. The
snow-covered fields across the river sparkled so that it hurt his
eyes with the glare of blue and white—and if he looked down,
where the river ran dark between its snow-clad banks of clay,
he turned giddy. A raging headache had come upon him all at
once.

"What said Berse?" asked Eirik.

"Berse—oh, you may well guess. But tell me, Eirik, what manner of man is this brother-in-law of yours, Jörund Rypa?"

"You must have heard of the Rypungs of Gunnarsby. He and
I were friends for many years—"

"Are you no longer so? It struck me, when he spoke of how
you had no thought of giving me back the silver until there was
talk of coming affinity between us—you know, he need not have
said that; 'twould have been more natural if he had *not* said that
of his wife's brother. Unless he purposed thereby to *prevent* your
marriage with Gunhild—?"

Eirik looked at the other a moment.

"It is hard to believe such a thing—" he whispered feebly. Then
he straightened his shoulders, shook himself slightly, and flung
his cloak about him. "But now I will go and find Berse," he said
briskly.

Guttorm put out a hand as though to detain him. "One thing
you cannot fail to see, Eirik—that which we had in mind for you
and Gunhild, there can be naught of that now?"

"But you will speak on my behalf, Guttorm," asked the young
man eagerly—"tell Berse you believe I am an honourable man?"

"That I will do, be sure of that. But there is—the other, Eirik.
So surely as we believe you to be true men, you and your father
and all your kinsmen beside, even so must we fear all the more
to be linked in affinity with that one—"

Eirik stared at Guttorm—he had turned white about the mouth
like a sick man.

"I will find Berse, for all that," he said, and began to walk
rapidly back toward the street.

•   •   •

But when they came back to their lodging they were told that
Berse had ridden away with all his company. And Jörund had
left immediately after. It was Torgrim of Rynjul who had taken
Eirik's part, said Karl, Guttorm's son-in-law; but when Berse
utterly refused to believe that Eirik was as innocent as the babe
unborn, Torgrim had flown into a rage, saying 'twas an ill thing
Berse had been given no wits, for now he had great need of some
—and so the old man had swept out of the house in great wrath.
Torgrim's parley with Jörund had ended in the franklin's seizing
a cowhide whip that lay there and striking Jörund across the
face with it—

"And would God and Saint Olav had guided my hand so that
I had found a spear instead and run him through," Torgrim be-
wailed when they spoke of it.

Then he turned his wrath upon Eirik, who had made no answer
to this outburst. "You sit there moping like a big-bellied bride—
or like an archangel that has had his wings stripped of feathers
by the devils! Better be off at once to the friars and beg them to
give you back your frock! Then Jörund will have got what he
sought!"

Karl whistled—Guttorm looked up sharply.

But Eirik replied calmly: "Whatever may befall—'twill not be
in *that* way that I go back to the convent—if I go."

It was Torgrim who said they ought to ride away at once—
acquaint Olav with the turn of events. "You are an upright man,
Guttorm, so you will come with us." Guttorm promised.

"It had been better if you had asked counsel of your father,"
said Guttorm to Eirik as they rode across the ice of the Botnfiord,
"or ever you came to this!"

"You who know him," replied Eirik hotly, "how think you
Father would have taken it? 'Twould have been unbearable for
us all to live together at Hestviken thereafter. God help my sister
and her children now—"

A little way from Draumtorp one of Guttorm's house-carls
met them; he announced that Berse had arrived and demanded
speech with the master ere he rode farther on the way to Eiken.

"Let him wait," said Torgrim, and Guttorm answered that he
would return home next day.

. . .

It was dark when they came out to Hestviken. As the company rode up to the door of the house, Eirik saw that someone stood up on the lookout rock, black against the last green light on the horizon. As his father came down toward them Eirik was reminded of One who was haled from one judge to another—"I have not strength to bear it, God, my God, help me to have strength!"

It was so dark that they could not see the expression on Olav's face when he came, but Torgrim had leaped from his horse and ran toward him.

"Has he come home, this Jörund, and what has he said?"

"Not a word that I believe," Olav answered scornfully. "But come in!"

It was dark in the great room; only a little red eye glowed on the hearth. But then a light appeared in the anteroom—Cecilia Olavsdatter entered, bearing a candlestick with a lighted candle in each hand. Eirik stood by the door, leaning on his sword, still in his travelling-cloak. "This is the worst," he thought as he saw his sister's stony face. She set the candles on the table, knelt by the hearth, and began to feed the embers with bark and chips of fir, while Olav greeted Guttorm.

"These men will surely sleep here tonight?" she asked when she had made up the fire; "and will you talk together first or wait till you have supped?"

"In God's name, let us say out what has to be said," cried Torgrim.

At a nod from her father she turned to the door. At the same moment Jörund appeared and came forward into the light. He looked around at the new-comers.

"Eirik has mustered a troop, I see—of his friends, young and old. Now we shall hear his tale—and we all know he was ever good at making up a fable to beguile the time, so I look for naught else but that you will believe him, you, Olav, and all his kinsmen. I have no such gift, so I know I shall be the loser—I cannot devise a more likely tale, when the truth sounds unlikely."

Behind them they heard a crash—Cecilia had barred the door. Now she stepped forward and placed herself by her husband's side.

"Then 'tis best I begin and tell what I know—since it was I who found the silver, and it was my fault that my brother was mixed up in our affairs."

Jörund turned upon her furiously. "You witness against your own husband—"

—and Eirik was at his sister's other side: "Nay, Cecilia—you are not to say anything—"

Cecilia pushed both men away.

"I witness what is true—thereby we are all best served," she said calmly, "you too, Jörund! But first I beg you all to be silent on this matter, as you hope the angels on the Day of Judgment may be silent on those of your sins which you would be most loath to hear cried aloud at the summoning of souls!"

"We shall do what we can, mistress," said Guttorm, "that this evil business may be kept close." The others agreed.

Then she told of the finding of the silver.

Torgrim asked: "Are you certain there was no more in the chest than these three cups?"

"Ay, for I had taken all out—the cloak I sought for lay at the bottom. But now I must go and attend to my duties—you must be both hungry and thirsty, since you have ridden so far to-day."

Jörund turned and would have gone out with his wife. Olav said: "Nay, Jörund, wait awhile—we have not yet had our say on this matter."

Cecilia turned in the doorway. "Remember, Father, what I have said to you—Jörund was taught full young that he could not depend on his own nearest kinsmen. Ill it is that it has turned out so that he now believes you and Eirik to be among his enemies, and he thought he had something to avenge."

"And a swingeing vengeance he took!" Torgrim cut in.

"You too, kinsman, may have helped to give my husband the belief that all here wished him ill. 'Tis not easy for a stranger to know how little you mean of all you say when the rage is upon you."

It was an uncomfortable meal—the men ate and drank all the good things that Cecilia and her maids set before them, in silence for the most part. Olav had scarcely spoken—not a word did he address to Eirik, and Eirik and Jörund sat there silent as stones. Cecilia stayed in the room, going round herself and filling the cups. But when the maids had carried out the meats, and more ale was brought in, the mistress of the house turned to Guttorm:

"I have a boon to ask of you, Guttorm, and a great one it is, but there is none other I can turn to—my kinsman Torgrim would stand me in no good stead. Will you ride with me to Eiken tomorrow? I will speak with Berse himself."

"Berse is at Draumtorp under my roof, mistress."

"Then let me ride home with you. Sigmund Baardsson here will do me the kindness to come with us and bring me back."

"I ride with Guttorm myself tomorrow," said Olav.

"So much the better—"

"Nay," said her father; "we cannot take you with us, my daughter. It was never our custom at Hestviken to let women speak for men."

Eirik stole out a little while after his sister had left the room. He found her in the cook-house—she had just put out the fire and was leaving. Eirik took her in his arms. "Cecilia!"

She stood still for a moment, with her hands on her brother's shoulders. Then she freed herself.

"I must lock up here, Eirik—'tis time I go in to bed."

"Can you not sleep—in the upper chamber?" he asked eagerly. "Cecilia—you cannot go in—lie by *him* tonight!"

"I must," she replied with a sort of laugh. "You have little sense, all of you. Could you not leave Jörund in peace?" she said hotly. "I know not if I can quiet him, but— Remember, I have three children by him."

Eirik silently pressed her to him.

"I am not afraid," said Cecilia in a little dry, frozen voice, and tore herself away.

Torgrim with the two young lads, Torgils and Sigmund, rode homeward next morning, as soon as they had broken their fast. Then Olav sent out word that they were to saddle the horses for Guttorm and him. Eirik brought the men their cloaks and arms. Guttorm went out first; as Olav was following, his son entreated him:

"Father—!"

Olav looked up into the young man's white, despairing face.

"You must remember, Father—it was not I who cast my eyes upon her—Gunhild. It was you two, you and Berse, you wished it. We knew, both of us, when we met, what was your will— that we should take kindly to each other. Remember that, when you speak to her father—"

Olav shook his head. "What you have in mind, Eirik—can never be."

"Oh, yes!" He clasped his hands vehemently. "Now all the countryside knows there is to be feasting at Agnes's mass. Will you gain anything by it, you and he, if you set all the folk talking, when it comes to naught—? Think of that, Father, if you will think of nothing else! Be not too harsh when you speak with Berse—"

"It is a great thing you ask of me, Eirik," said Olav quietly.

"And we have great things at stake—"

"If I can, I will think about it," said Olav as before.

"'Tis not much you promise," muttered Eirik.

"To none other would I promise so much, my son." Olav went out, and Eirik followed.

Guttorm was already in the saddle. Eirik came forward to hold his father's horse while he mounted; at that moment Cecilia came out of the door of the women's house. She was dressed in her dark, fur-trimmed hooded cloak. She carried her infant in her arms, and Kolbein walked by her side, holding his mother's cloak.

"Will you saddle Brunsvein for me, Eirik?" she asked. "My grey is lame of one hind leg, I saw this morning. I shall but take the children up to Ragna—"

"Nay, Cecilia," said Olav. "I have told you, you cannot do this."

"I must, Father. It touches me more nearly than any other of you. If Berse will not listen to you—to me he *must*, as he is a Christian man—when I plead for my husband and my three young sons."

Olav stood and looked at his daughter.

Then said Guttorm, as he sat on his horse: "I believe the woman is right. Let your daughter ride with us; I think she knows best."

"You have not strength enough, Cecilia." Her father went up close to her. "In this cold. And 'tis not certain we can reach home this evening. It may be I must stay the night at Hestbæk. 'Twill be bad for you with milk in your breast—"

"Oh, yes, I have the strength—" with a fleeting smile she took her children over to Ragna's house, and Eirik turned into the stable.

As they rode into the forest by the mouth of the stream, Eirik moved toward the women's house. His heart beat fast at the thought of meeting his brother-in-law; even now it seemed he had no right to judge Jörund's actions—the man was Cecilia's husband, and so long as they were all alive, he was one of them.

At that moment he chanced to recall that it was here in this anteroom he had stood with Bothild that evening. He had half forgotten it—the man he had been in those days of madness, when his only wish was to hurt that poor child, had become a stranger to his new self.

Suddenly, like gleam after gleam of summer lightning, there flashed across Eirik's soul—all the forgiveness and all the gifts he had received in these last years. And even if it were now his lot to forfeit his happiness in this world, that did not diminish the value of what God had done for him: never more could he become as he had been when he persecuted her—he realized in wonder how his raw and immature nature had ripened to hard grain. And as he opened the inner door he felt a burning compassion for Jörund's perfidy.

The moment he crossed the threshold, Jörund struck at him—Eirik fell back a step, so that the blow fell on the door. In another instant he dashed in, seized his brother-in-law round the waist and arms; he wrenched the sword from him and flung it across the floor. Jörund had been hiding behind the door.

"Stop it now, Jörund—you have done yourself harm enough, man!" The other stood panting and scowling, and for the first time Eirik saw clearly what a change had come over Jörund of late years—he was bloated in both face and body, slack of feature, with eyes closed up, and it seemed he could not look folk in the face. Eirik shuddered—then he crossed the room, picked up the sword and handed it to his brother-in-law. "You have done enough folly—do not make it worse. You were ever too fond of your own life—you can scarce have reflected ere you risked it to be revenged on me. If you think you have cause to seek vengeance, you will hardly pay such a price for it."

"I forestalled you, for all that," scoffed Jörund Rypa; "do you think I could not guess what you had in mind? I heard you lurking here outside the door—"

"As you see, I am unarmed—but better sit down."

Jörund shot a queer, hesitating glance at his brother-in-law. Then he raised his sword threateningly. Eirik smiled faintly and shook his head.

"I could cut you down on the spot—and fly to the woods—"

"That may be. But 'twill be hard to support life in the woods at this season—for one who is a stranger hereabouts. 'Tis not so sure either that you would get so far. Maybe you would not escape from the manor—"

"Am I guarded like a prisoner?" shouted Jörund. Eirik saw that his eyes looked like a hunted rat's.

"Oh, no. But it might make some noise—the men are outside—"

Jörund threw away his sword, crossed the room, and flung himself on his bed. He lay leaning on his elbow, staring at Eirik. "What *have* you come for, then?"

"To tell you," replied Eirik, "that you will not be rid of me in this way—if that is what you intend. Whatever I do or do not, you must surely see—Father is an old man, Cecilia has no other near kinsman but me. So long as your conduct is such as to make me fear she has no happy life with you, there is small chance I shall go off and be a monk!"

"Cecilia is a whore!" said Jörund viciously.

"Beware of saying that again!" replied Eirik, still calm. "I believe the Evil One has taken away your wits—" No sooner had he said it than he was afraid—Jörund's look was such that one could believe it to be true.

"I am not Kolbein's father," roared Jörund; "I have it from her own lips! I begged her to tell me I was so—not a word did I get out of her in answer!"

"You could scarce expect an honourable woman to answer such a question." He felt sick with horror and disgust. Then Jörund began to howl like a dog, howled and howled—then broke into sobs and tears, while the words poured bubbling from his mouth: all had treated him faithlessly, his brothers, their wives, every friend and kinsman he had in the world, Cecilia and Olav and all here—Eirik scarcely understood one word in ten.

"Do you trust *none*, Jörund?" asked Eirik when the other paused for a moment in his rage.

In answer Jörund gave a yell as if he had been kicked.

"Jörund," said Eirik impressively, "your wife has gone to beg Berse of Eiken hold his peace about this affair, so that your good name may be saved. She will not find it easy to plead to him—I fear you know that better than any of us. Never a word of complaint has she uttered to us her kinsfolk. You will be well advised

to believe what I tell you—in our family we have never been wont
to deal in guile or treachery; we may have enough to answer for
without that, but we have always had a name for keeping our
word—"

Jörund Rypa buried his head in the bedclothes, weeping and
gasping for breath. Then, quite suddenly, he began to snore. Eirik
was afraid he might be taken sick—tried to turn him so that he lay
more comfortably. The eyes in Jörund's red and swollen face
half-opened for a moment, but closed again at once—it was sleep.

Eirik sat for a while by his bedside, but Jörund slept on. So he
stole out, with a mind uneasy and oppressed.

An hour before nones Eirik came out, dressed for a journey.
He looked into the women's house—Jörund filled the room with
his snoring. Then he went to the stable, led out the bay, and
saddled him.

The sun was so low that its rays tinged the fields and the
snow-covered woods behind the manor with red and gold when
Eirik came in view of Eiken. He asked leave to put up his horse
at a little farm by the highroad. He must venture it, even if it
came to Berse's ears.

He went on foot across the fields up to the manor, past the road
that led to the houses. The sun had now set and the white ground
had turned to a greyish blue, but the sky was orange, with a few
golden clouds floating down in the south, and up in the vault some
stars peeped out already.

The road he had taken when he was last here, up to the ridge,
had been lately used—there were sledge-tracks and wisps of hay
along it. For some distance it followed the fence that divided the
farm from the forest. He waded up to the fence and stood there
scanning the houses. It struck him as an evil omen: he had never
been received here.

He waited, uncertain whether to go down and ask if he might
speak with Gunhild. Then a door opened—a woman and a man
and a dog came out.

In a low voice Eirik gave the call—the same they had used last
autumn. *She* started, the dog set up a bark and darted up to him,
the man after.

"Is it you, Kaare?" cried Eirik.

Kaare Bersesson came up to him. "Are *you* here?"

"Yes. Will you ask your sister if I may speak with her? I will wait in the road here."

It had already grown much darker—the sunset had faded to yellow and pale green and there were many more stars. She came up, wrapped in a long, hooded cloak; her brother and the dog were with her.

"You must let Gunhild and me be alone awhile, Kaare," said Eirik. His sister said something to the boy, who turned back again, followed by his dog.

Then he came forward and took her in his arms. She burst into tears. "What is this, Eirik? I know not what to make of it."

He held her close and felt miserable—he was so little used to women's tears. But after a while he released the girl and began, quite calmly, to tell the whole story, of which she had heard something from her brothers.

Gunhild had checked her tears. "Nay, *that* I knew—what they said could not be true, my brothers do not believe it either. But what does he aim at, Jörund Rypa?"

Eirik told her something of Jörund's strange fancies and how he thought they were plotting against him at Hestviken—"but this is what I wanted to say to you, Gunhild. I had thought —I make bold to think you will not oppose my wish—that the compact between us be carried out?"

"I think I have let you see that—perhaps more than I ought." She withdrew herself when he tried to take her in his arms again, but let him hold her hand.

"There will be nothing of it at Agnes's mass. We must wait, that is sure. But I cannot but think that when your father has well considered it, he must see that this marriage is so desirable in every other way that—"

Gunhild squeezed his hand. "I hope we may not have to wait too long," she said in a timid little voice, which sent a thrill of joy through the man. " 'Tis not good to live with a stepmother when one is a grown maid. And I have had this trust in you ever since we first met—*you* will be good to her who is to live with you!"

Then she could not prevent his clasping her in his arms once more.

"There is one thing besides that I would say to you," he went on after a moment. "You know there was a time when I desired to be a monk—I was over a year in the convent. So I know some-

thing of church law and such matters. Should it go so hard with
us that Berse brings forward another suitor, then know that a
marriage is no marriage after God's ordinance and the law of the
Church unless you yourself have consented thereto. If you dare
to hold fast and refuse to say yes, they cannot force you—and it
is the bishop's duty to take you under his protection, if you make
complaint to him."

"Nay, force me to take one I will not have!" said Gunhild impulsively. "Rather will I fly from home—rather will I seek refuge
with Eldrid, my sister—"

It flashed upon Eirik: no, not that in any case. His Gunhild,
pure and proud, in company with that old— In seven parishes
there was not a woman who bore an uglier name than Eldrid
Bersesdatter. That must never be.—But all he said was:

" 'Twill not be so ill as that—I only thought, *if* it should drag
on so long that there should be talk of another marriage. God
bless you, Gunhild—it cannot be that your steadfastness will be
put to so hard a proof."

"I am cold," she said after a pause; she was shivering and treading the ground.

"Come—I will wrap my cloak about you." He drew her to a
pile of logs that lay by the wayside, seated himself, and took her
on his knees. "Are you still cold?" he whispered.

"My feet are like ice—"

He took hold of her under the knees, lifted her so that she lay
huddled in his embrace, wrapped his cloak about her feet. He felt
the whole weight of her young, healthy body against his, she
filled his arms so well, and his face sought her soft, cold cheek
inside the fur-bordered hood. And he felt his own youth and vi-
tality, and that they two were warmed with the warmth of their
blood in the chilly freshness of the winter night.

A little frightened by his firm grasp and the heat of his kisses,
she struggled to reach the ground. "Eirik—I dare not stay out
longer—"

So he had to let her down at last—trembling and panting a little
from the violence of his last embrace. He went with her as far
as the entrance to the manor.

"It may be long ere we meet again—?"

Gunhild gave him her hand. "Be not afraid, Eirik—they shall
not bear me down!"

"May Christ and Mary Virgin bless you—if only I am sure of that, we shall find a way!"

It was already dark and a thousand stars were shining as he hurried down toward the highroad. Piercingly cold, so that the snow cried under his feet—the Milky Way spread so brightly across the black, starry vault. But the cold was good—it gave him a feeling of his own strength and warmth.

They were about to go to rest at the little homestead when he came and took out his horse. And the night was far spent when he reached Hestviken. He looked in upon Jörund—it was icy cold in the women's house, the fire had died on the hearth. Eirik listened to the sleeper's breathing—went to his own house, lighted a lantern, came back and looked at his brother-in-law. Jörund looked as if he had not moved, but his sleep seemed healthier now.

Eirik spread the coverlet over him, collected some skins and blankets, and made a bed for himself on the bench. He pulled the boots from his feet, stiffened with cold, took off his belt, wrapped himself in his frozen cloak, and soon fell asleep.

He did not wake till Jörund shook him. "Will you not come and eat?"

Eirik sat bolt-upright. Jörund was quite different today—quiet and shy, and his voice was very gentle. When they had broken their fast, Jörund asked, avoiding the other's eyes:

"Tell me—Eirik—is it true that—did I try to come at you—did we come to blows yesterday?"

"Can you not recall what we spoke of yesterday?" asked Eirik seriously.

"I know not rightly—whether I was dreaming or not. Sometimes my head aches so intolerably that I remember nothing afterwards—".

"Are you better today?"

"My head still pains me—but not in the same way."

And as soon as they had finished their meal he went back to bed and fell asleep again. Eirik went in several times to look at him.

About midday Olav and Cecilia returned. Eirik went out and met them. He searched his father's face—Olav seemed not to see him, gave him no greeting, but dismounted and went straight into his own house without looking to one side or the other.

Eirik accompanied Cecilia to Ragna's house. When she had laid

Audun to her swelling breast she gave a little sigh of relief. Eirik
picked up her cloak, which had fallen on the floor.

"You are waiting to hear how we have sped?" She looked
down at the infant's head. "We might have fared better—but we
might also have fared worse. Berse promised to hold his peace. But
I will not conceal from you he said things to us— Ay, Father—
Father curbed himself in a way. But I wish—I wish he had been
spared this—now that he is an old man too. You had better not go
near him."

"I must—" Eirik stroked his sister's cheek. "You seem to think I
have less courage than you have, Cecilia," he said mournfully.

"I know not." She moved the babe to her other breast. "There
may be some things that a man can do better than a woman. And
others that a man cannot do so well—"

But when he came into the great room, Olav still sat there in his
travelling-clothes, with his hands on the hilt of his sword and his
chin resting on them. He threw a fleeting glance at Eirik, but said
nothing; and so Eirik did not venture to speak.

16

So it went by, another winter—one day after another. Not a word
had Olav ever uttered about his meeting with Berse at Draumtorp,
and Erik took good heed not to ask him questions. Indeed, they
seldom spoke to each other; their footing was the same as it had
been when he was a boy: his father sat and stared, and Eirik did
not know whether the man was looking at him or through him at
something else; if he had to speak to Olav about anything, it
seemed as if his father only listened to him with half an ear, and
a breath of ill will and unfriendliness smote him in the presence
of the old man. Eirik remembered that in former days his father's
manner had nearly driven him frantic. Now he thought: God
knows, perhaps even then he had had a secret burden on his soul.
And he felt that his affection for his father had grown firmer of
late years, like all else within him—had, as it were, solidified into
pith.

It was bad for Cecilia and Jörund that he should be so unsociable, but there was no helping it.

As far as he could, Eirik associated with the young married couple in the women's house. He had given up pondering over his brother-in-law's behaviour—was inclined to think the man must have been unsettled in his mind during the autumn and winter, and now he seemed to be rid of his venom for this time. All through the latter part of the winter Jörund Rypa was in good humour, chatty and cheerful, like his old self. He played with his children, showed affection for his wife—sometimes in a way that made Eirik blush; nor could he help thinking that Cecilia disliked it too, but she did not betray herself. She discharged her share of the household duties with the greatest diligence, and Eirik saw that the house-folk would have been ready to go through fire for their young mistress. Cecilia could even force her father to rouse himself, when she wished to consult him.

Never did Eirik see a sign that Jörund gave a thought to what had happened at Yuletide, or troubled himself about what rumours it had given rise to. There was talk among the neighbours, Erik could tell that, but no one hinted anything to him. This too he knew: had it been two poor men who had been involved in a case of receiving stolen goods, they would not have escaped without being branded for life, at the very least. But they were the sons of Gunnarsby and Hestviken, and their kinsmen were Baard of Skikkjustad, who was one of the mightiest men of the countryside, especially since he had married off all his four daughters so wisely, and Torgrim of Rynjul, who could say and do as he pleased—most men liked him, for all that, and bore with his rough tongue; even he who was the victim of it could console himself that tomorrow another would be made to feel it.

Eirik acknowledged the truth of all that had been said by the holy fathers—the judgment of men, worldly prosperity, and all such things now seemed so small in his eyes that he could only wonder how anyone cared to strive so hard for them as they did —with pain and grief, with cunning, treachery, and violence. Had it not been for Gunhild and the love that was between them, had it not been that Cecilia and Jörund needed his support, he would gladly have let all else go, and today rather than tomorrow. But he was now beginning to see the meaning of being in the world and not of the world—he felt there was nothing more that could subdue his innermost freedom and peace of mind.

One day early in spring Eirik accompanied his sister up to

Rynjul; she wished to see her child that was being brought up
there. He sat with Una in her weaving-room, watching Cecilia as
she led her son across the floor—Torgils Jörundsson had learned
to walk since his mother saw him last. Then Torgrim came in.

After a while the master of the house said: "You may have
heard, Eirik, that Gunhild has a new suitor?" He mentioned a
man whom Eirik did not know even by name, one from Agder.
"Berse will not learn wisdom by experience. He had his way
with Eldrid's marriage, and it turned out as it did. In spite of that
he means to sell Gunhild into the hands of another old troll."

Brother and sister rode homeward in the twilight; beyond the
thick tangle of the alders' foliage the first great stars were shining
in the clear sky. It was a mild evening—the raw scent of earth
rose from the bare brown surface, and the birds sang in every
grove. They had ridden a long while in silence when the sister
said:

"Eirik—that news that Torgrim brought you of Gunhild. It is
our fault that you are to lose her."

"Gunhild will not submit to be forced," said Eirik.

"Forced—there are so many ways," answered Cecilia.

After a pause Eirik said: "Since we have begun to speak of such
things—and do not answer if you are unwilling—has Jörund ever
troubled you with his suspicions that everyone is against him?"

"How have you found that out?" she asked with warmth.

"That time last winter—when he seemed beside himself, accused
everyone—you did not escape either—"

"Oh, I am partly to blame for it myself," said Cecilia. "I was
so young then. I knew no better than to provoke him by my silence and provoke him by what I said."

Young, thought Eirik—"she is not so old as Gunhild."

Cecilia said after a while: "I acted wrongly, too, I doubt not.
The others were going to a feast; I refused to go with them.
Chiefly because I was so far gone with Kolbein at that time—
but I knew too that they had a guest in that house, one whom I
was not minded to meet. But in the evening he came to Gunnarsby, and I went out nevertheless and spoke to him by the gate.
Nay, we said not a word that Jörund himself might not have
heard—that is not *his* way. But Jörund came to hear of it, and he
knew the man had known me at Hestviken—You know him not.—
Then I was stubborn—and Jörund lost his temper. He has never

done such a thing since—it gave him a fright when Father came. Indeed Jörund is a reasonable man between these fits of his."

"But it can never be a sin," thought Eirik, "if I urge Gunhild to resist—"

Some days later Eirik went down to Saltviken. All through the winter he had looked forward to doing the spring work on his farm. Now he set about it, but at the same time his thoughts wandered to other things. He could not get over what he had guessed from his sister's words—even that insult had been offered Cecilia, who had certainly never let any man touch her even when she was a child. And then there was the thought of Gunhild.

It was the finest of weather every day. Now the manure was spread and dug in on his new dark-soiled cornfields, blending its good warm smell with the acrid scent of growing grass in the meadows. Where the soil was thin over the rocks, the pansies already showed blue. The first shoots on the trees shone bright as pale-green flames against the sunlight—little green leaves had appeared already. The boughs of his cherry trees were pearly with buds; here and there a branch beside the sun-warmed rock had burst into white blossom. In the midday rest Eirik went down to the bay, undressed, and swam out. The water was still cold, but otherwise it was like summer down here on the beach.

The day he had finished sowing he stopped work at nones and changed his clothes—he kept a blue kirtle here, so that he might go to church without passing round by Hestviken. Then he rode inland toward Eiken.

There had been a flock of children at the homestead where he had put up his horse when he was last in these parts. He now made his way thither, found a half-grown girl who was washing clothes in the brook. He took out some small silver coins and asked if she would go an errand for him.

"Then run away to Eiken, see if you can speak with Gunhild alone. You are to ask her if she has any message for the owner of this token."

He took out of his bosom an embroidered shirt-sleeve; Gunhild had given it him at Yule when they were togther at Rynjul, and promised him its fellow for Easter.

He lay on the grass above the little farm. The woman came up and began to talk to him; from her he learned that Berse and

his wife were not at home; they had gone southward down the
fiord a week before, but the place was being made ready to receive guests on the return of the master and mistress. So it was
a good thing after all that he had made his way hither, he thought.

At sunset the little girl came running down the road. Eirik
went to meet her; she handed him back the token:

"Gunhild bade me bring greetings and say you are to ask the
owner of this token to ride to the Ness with all speed and wait
there; he shall there be given all he is to receive according to the
covenant."

Eirik stared at the child—this took his breath away. Never could
he have imagined it.

Eirik rode southward as the shades of evening gradually deepened to a pale-grey spring night and the birds sang jubilantly all
through the forest. It was cool and good to ride at this late hour,
and he had never been afraid to travel by night.

And, to be sure, he was glad. But at the same time he was not
a little dismayed. That Gunhild should make good so wild a
threat—could any man have thought it!

He saw quite clearly that now they would both be placed in
a difficult position. If it became known whither Gunhild had betaken herself and that they had been there together, the worst
would certainly be said. He must take her away from her sister's
house as quickly as he could. But where could they seek refuge?

The law was even as he had said—it was a bishop's duty to defend women against forced marriages—but very few bishops were
ever called upon to fulfil this duty, even when their rule was a
long one. He knew pretty well how welcome Gunhild Bersesdatter would be made in the Bishop's castle or with the strict
Lady Groa at Nonneseter if she were sent thither. Ask any of his
father's friends in the town or in his home parish to receive a
woman whom he had carried off by force, that was impossible.
Torgrim and Una would do it no doubt—but he could not drag
them into such difficulties. And Rynjul was too near both to
Eiken and to Hestviken. For his own father would scarcely be
better pleased with this than hers.

The best plan he could think of was to take her to his kinsfolk
in the Upplands. He had not parted in friendship from Steinfinn
Haakonsson of Berg, but he knew enough of his cousin to be

sure that if he sought his support in such a case as this, he would
find a loyal kinsman in Steinfinn.

This plan involved difficulties enough and—the way was long;
they might be pursued, and then in God's name the encounter
could scarcely pass off without an exchange of blows. But if they
had a start, and travelled by unfrequented paths— There was more
than that—he knew it well enough as he rode here in the spring
night and breathed the acrid scent of growing leaves and grass
and felt the warmth of his own sound youthful body. Already he
had visions of the chances he would have of kissing his fair bride
and clasping her in his arms as they rode together unattended for
five or six days and nights, through forests and remote country
districts. But it was well he was old enough to know that he must
be on his guard. What would be said of them he knew; but she
must know it too, and yet she had chosen to accept this hazard.
But to be forced to weep over a secret sorrow of his causing—he
would not bring that on Gunhild.

His heart failed him at the memory of thoughts he had once
had—no, in Jesu name, Bothild was enough.

It was clear he would have been wiser to have sent her back a
message that she must not think of keeping so ill-considered a
promise. But that would surely have offended her. And what kind
of man would he have to be who should be capable of such pru-
dence?

If at least he knew where this Ness was to be found! Somewhere on the border between Saana and Garda parishes. He had
ridden past it once with old Tore, when he was a lad—one saw
the homestead on the farther side of a lake. Now he did not even
know if he were on the right road—he was in the depth of the
forest, where patches of snow gleamed here and there and the
birches had not yet burst into leaf and the cold ground breathed
the raw scent of early spring from the musty slime that covers
the ground as soon as the snow recedes. It was already past midnight, and the song of birds, which had been silent awhile, began
to be heard again, but the notes of the night-birds were not yet
hushed, the night-raven croaked—and in some bogs that he had
passed the capercailye was calling. Eirik was sleepy—and the bay
was tired and a little lame.

He leaped from the saddle and led his horse down a steep descent, where the water streamed over the path, past some small

farms—and soon he came out on a broader road. A little farther
on, this road led past a little lake.

The black forest surrounded the whole piece of water except
on the north side, where a solitary homestead stood on a point
of land that jutted out into the lake. A mist was rising from the
surface of the water and from the marshy meadows around the
homestead, so that only its green roof showed above the haze.
From the head of the lake a track branched from the road across
the marsh. Eirik rode along it—the worst bog-holes were bridged
with logs; the birches were dripping wet, with a strong and bitter
scent of bursting leaves. He passed many places that had once
been meadow, where young green fir trees had sprung up. The
dawn was now so far advanced that the sky was white and the
surface of the water like steel between the driving mists. In the
field before the homestead the grass was already high and lush,
grey with moisture in the thick air, and here too birch and alder
were almost in leaf.

He could not wake folk in a strange place at this time of the
morning, but he saw a little barn standing at the edge of the wood.
He turned his horse loose outside, went in and lay down in the
empty barn.

When he awoke, the sun was shining in through every crack
of the logs. Outside the open door all was gleaming green and
gold in the sunlight, and in the doorway stood a woman holding
the bay by the forelock. Eirik sprang up, shook out his wrinkled
cloak, went forward and greeted her:

"Can you tell me, mistress, if this house be the Ness, where
Eldred Bersesdatter lives?"

As he spoke he was sure that this must be Eldrid: she was
dressed like a working-woman and looked like—he knew not
what, but not like a woman of the people.

She was not very tall—not so tall as Gunhild, and thin, broader
across the shoulders than across the narrow, scanty, mannish hips,
and she held herself straight as a wand. Her brown, weatherbeaten
face looked as if the flesh had been scraped from under the skin
—the forehead was smooth, as were the strongly arched cheek-
bones and the fine, straight nose. But the longer Eirik looked at
this ravaged and aging woman, the more clearly he saw that she
must once have been beautiful—so beautiful that not one of all the
fair women he had seen could compare with Eldrid.

"I am Eldrid of the Ness—have you an errand to me?"

"I have—one that will seem strange to you, I fear." Then he told her who he was.

"Are you a son of Olav Audunsson of Hestviken?" Her voice too was beautiful, rich and ringing. "You are not like your father. I remember him—he came home to these parts the year before I disappeared from—"

She asked him to go up with her to the houses, and Eirik saw that the place looked well, now the sun was shining; trees and meadow were nearly as far advanced as at home. But it was strangely deserted and lonely—and shut off, with the dark forest behind it, which was beginning to invade the old meadow-land, and the narrow lake in front, where the reflection of the high wooded slope on the south side darkened half the surface even on a bright May morning like this.

The ness on which the houses stood was almost cut off from the shore, by a neck of land so low that the water came over the grass on both sides. In flood-time it came right across, Eldrid told him.

"Then you must use a boat?"

"Boat?" Eldrid laughed mockingly. "We have naught to take us abroad, we who live here."

The houses lay irregularly on the little mound, according as there had been room to build them. They were small and might have been kept in better repair. A bent old woman with her coif drawn low over her surly eyes glanced at the two as they went past.

The walls of the dwelling-house were only three logs high; there was a penthouse of upright timbers which formed a sort of anteroom, and only a single room within. Instead of the central hearth there was a fireplace by the door, and the wall in that corner was covered with slabs of stone and daubed with clay; at each end of the other long wall was an untidy bed. Other furniture there was none, but on the bench that ran round the walls all kinds of cups and platters, garments and pots and a butter-churn were piled in confusion.

Eldrid cleared a seat for him at the end of the room. "You must be hungry."

He was—now he remembered that since he rode from home the day before at noon he had tasted nothing but a drink of milk

at the cottage by Eiken. So he relished what Eldrid set before
him on the bench: curds, oaten bread, and old cheese. Then he
had to come out with his message:

"I come from your sister, Eldrid—from Gunhild of Eiken—"

"My sister!" Eldrid gave him a strange look. Then she took a
spindle from the jumple on the bench, thrust it into her belt, and
began to spin. "That sister of mine whom you name I have
neither seen nor heard from until now. And I wonder who can
have spoken to her of me. Not her parents, I trow. What would
she, then—Gunhild, my sister?"

"She begs you to save her. They will give her to an old man,
a widower, whom she has never seen. And now she thinks—perhaps you will take pity on her. There is none other in the world
from whom she may look for kindness."

Eldrid looked at him with a shadow of a smile on her brown
and broken lips. "Hm. And you—maybe you are he whom she
would have?"

"It was agreed that I should be betrothed to Gunhild last
winter. But then her father broke with us."

"And maybe it was too late?" said Eldrid as before.

Eirik guessed her meaning; he was annoyed with himself for
turning red, but replied in an even tone: "Ay—so long as we
thought we had only to wait a year or so, and the old people
would have made up their differences—we should have been content. But if Berse will once more give his young hind to an old
buck, he will find it is too late, he shall not so dispose of Gunhild. She will not submit, and I will not suffer that man to get
her."

"But what help do you look to me for?" asked Eldrid. "Shall
I go to Berse and invoke a curse on him?"

Eirik had sat and watched her. Although she looked as if she
had been dried over many fires, there was still something fine
about her; her hair was not wholly hidden by the stiff coif: it
was dark, streaked with grey, and a lock of it fell with a strange
charm over the broad, smooth forehead, across which ran two
sharp furrows. Hollow as her cheeks were, he had never seen
anything more beautiful than the rounding of her jawbone
and the curve of her chin. The eyes were deeply sunk in their
great sockets, and there were many wrinkles about them,
but they were large, dark, and grey. Her mouth, however, was

brown and scaly, with a deep red crack through the underlip. And the hands that span were red and cracked and knotted with gout.

Yet he could not believe that everything he had heard about her was true. And even if she had erred—gravely—they must first have wronged her cruelly. And however that might be, it was a pitiable sight to see this fair and high-born woman, banished and aging, dwelling in so miserable a cabin.

Then he began and told her the whole story of his courtship from beginning to end.

"So it was she who sent you hither?"

"Yes."

"And you expect her to keep her word and come hither?"

"Yes. But if you will tell us of a place where we can find lodging till she be rested, we will gladly betake ourselves thither, if you would rather have it so."

"If I am afraid to have to do with this affair, you mean?" Eldrid laughed. "Rather will Gunhild be afraid, when she comes from Eiken and sees how her sister lives."

"She will think as I do," said Eirik quietly. "It should not be so. And it must be mended."

"Do you seek to tempt me with a reward?" asked Eldrid mockingly.

"I know not if you will call it a reward if I do what I can to see my sister-in-law righted. I have heard that your brother tried, but he fell—"

Eldrid let her hands sink into her lap. But then she said: "You seem to have no fear of defiling yourself, Eirik, if you touch pitch. But if you purpose ever to be reconciled with Berse, you must throw over both that brother-in-law of yours who deals in stolen goods and the sister-in-law who is a whore. Ay, Berse was the first of all men who called me by that name, and he told no lie of his best friend's wife. Better that no man hear of it, if it should come about that you lie with your young bride at the Ness any night."

"I thought to ask one other boon of you," said Erik. "I will ask you to show Gunhild such kindness as to ride north in our company. None will think it of you that you sold your young sister to dishonour."

Slowly Eldrid's face flushed red. But then she laughed. "I should have to ride my grey bull then—I have no horse!"

"The bay will carry both Gunhild and me," said Eirik imperturbably, "till we get one for you on the way."

Eldrid only laughed again.

"Must you do your spring husbandry here without a horse?" asked Eirik after a while. "Or do you borrow one of your neighbours?"

"I have mattock and spade," replied Eldrid shortly. "And basket and pannier."

Now he was told that she lived here alone with the old hag he had seen, a palsied old man who was her kinsman—she had taken him in because he was Berse's enemy—and a half-grown lad who herded for her and helped with whatever there might be.

"But then we must seize the opportunity while I am here with my horse," said Eirik. And when she would not hear of it, he laughed and said she must take it as if she had a brother come to the house. Then he jumped up and ran out.

When she came out awhile after, she found him down in the cornfield, where only a little work had been done in one corner. He had dragged out an old plough and was engaged in putting it in order so that he could harness the bay to it. His long cloak and his blue holy-day kirtle lay on the ground, and Eirik stood in nothing but a red homespun shirt, short breeches, long hose, and riding-boots.

"Are you going to plough in those boots?" asked Eldrid.

"No, if you could lend me something else to wear on my feet, it would be better."

"How old are you, Eirik Olavsson?" asked Eldrid.

"Oh—I am not young—nine and twenty."

"One would not think you were nineteen."

"When I was nineteen," replied Eirik with a laugh, "I was far wiser—as folks reckon."

Late in the afternoon Eirik said he would ride northward—to see if anyone were in sight.

"How did you think she would come hither?" asked Eldrid.

Eirik said he did not know—perhaps she had someone at the manor who was faithful to her.

"I believe you think she will come!" Then she said: "It will be late ere you come back?"

No, said Eirik, the bay was tired—"but I can go into the barn and lie there, as I lay last night."

"No," said Eldrid curtly; " 'tis not often we have guests here, but since you are come, I will not suffer that you be treated otherwise than is fitting. I shall make ready the outer bed for you and leave the door unbolted."

It was nevertheless later than he had thought when he returned. A white mist was rising from the water and the bog as he rode across from the end of the lake; all was still· at the homestead. Eirik stole in quietly. The room was dark and warm; he guessed that Eldrid was in bed.

He had not said his hours since prime, so he knelt at the foot of the bed and prayed—seven paternosters for each of the lesser hours, fifteen for vespers, and seven for complin. The last he said for her who gave him hospitality: he had seen something of her loneliness, and he swore that if it were in his power he would better her condition.

He had taken off his outer garments and was climbing into bed when Eldrid's voice came from the far corner:

"I have left milk and food for you on the hearth—you played truant from your supper."

"Thanks, I am not hungry. 'Twas ill of me to wake you."

"Is it your practice every evening—to pray so long?" she asked again.

"Yes. But I have told you, I had as lief sleep in the barn. Then I shall not disturb you with my practices."

She gave a little laugh. "Nay, you may freely keep your practices for me."

The days went by. When Eirik thought of Hestviken and Saltviken and of his people there, it all seemed strangely far away and long ago. He wondered at times what they could think had become of him. And he wondered a little how Gunhild would contrive to come hither. Now it would soon be a week—

But he felt it was as it should be, that he was living here at this strange and lonely homestead in the depth of the dark forest. Every morning when he came out, the ness lay like an island in a sea of white mist, and above it rose the hills, dark with firs. Then

came the sun and drove away the mist, and all day long it shone
on these awakening fields, the corn that she had sown before he
came was already green, and the leaves grew denser in the thickets,
and the grass in the meadow was long and glossy. He determined
to do all the work for her that he could find—and there was
enough to put one's hand to here. Her poverty astonished him—she
had scarcely any meal in the house, and of her cows three gave
no milk and the other two but little, though they were in better
condition than most cows in springtime—she had pasture for
many more cattle than she owned. Most of her sheep had been
taken by wild beasts the year before, and her corn had frozen;
houses and implements were as might be expected in a place
where there was no man and no horse to bring in materials of any
sort. To make up for the shortage of food she had nets in the lake
and snares in the woods, and Eirik undertook to look after both
for her.

It dawned on Eirik that this place had a strangely familiar air—
as though he had once lived here, long ago. It was the first home
he could remember that now came back to him—it was long since
he had thought of it, but now it stood forth; that too had been a
place far out of the way and deep in the forest, but he did not
recall any water. And Eldrid became merged in a strange way
with a dream he had had when a child—of a woman in a blue
mantle, half human and half bird; he had been afraid of her, but
she was beautiful too, and he had called her Leman, for he was so
small he knew not the meaning of that word, but he thought it
was something that flew. Ay, he had confused this dream vision
with his mother—he knew not how it was, but now it came over
him that the Ness was like that first place he remembered in the
world, and Eldrid reminded him of Leman in his dream.

But every evening he rode out along the road by which he had
come, to meet Gunhild, and back he came across the marshes,
when evening had deepened to grey spring night and the white
mist from lake and meadows was rising about Eldrid's farm.

On the seventh day it clouded over—there had been some showers, but toward evening the sun gleamed fitfully over the Ness.
Eirik was sawing up some logs that lay on the woodpile—from
where he stood he could see Eldrid at the door of the byre; she
was calling in her cows. Last of all came the little shaggy grey
bull, splashing through the mire. Eldrid waited for its coming,

laid her hands on its cheeks, and leaned her forehead caressingly against the bull's head.

Eirik went in to put on his kirtle and cloak. There was food left for him on the step of his bed—she took care now that he had something before he rode out. He did not hear anyone coming until the horses were just outside the house; then he started up and ran to the outer door.

Outside, where drops of rain now glittered in the sunlight, two men had dismounted from their horses. The second one, a young lad, swung himself back into the saddle, took his master's horse by the bridle, and rode off into the fields; but the first was a tall, elderly man of fine presence; it was Guttorm from Draumtorp, and he hurried in out of the rain.

"'Tis wellnigh more than I had looked for," he said as he stepped into Eldrid's house, "that you should be here!"

Eirik had turned white in the face. "Have you come!"

"Ay, it is I who have come. Gunhild has yet so much kindness for you—though God knows how you deserved it!—that she turned to me and neither to her father nor her brothers. You may well suppose they would not have met you without drawn swords in their hands."

"I should have liked that better." Involuntarily Eirik's hand went to his sword-hilt.

"Silence with such talk! Can you expect we should think much of your manhood—do you call it manly to try to entice the child out of her kinsmen's keeping—to such a den as this?"

"This is her sister's house—"

"Did you think Gunhild would submit to be ruled by you, because she is sister to Eldrid? But they are not daughters of the same mother—"

"Can you not say what you have to say, Guttorm, without abusing a woman?"

"You may be right, there. Not many words are needed either. Gunhild bade me give you back this—that says enough, I think."

Eirik took what Guttorm handed him, scarcely looking at it. Then he let the gold brooch drop and it fell at his feet.

Guttorm spoke again, sadly: "Ay, it made me angry to hear this, Eirik Olavsson—never would I have thought such a thing of the son of so upright a franklin as Olav is. I took you for an hon-

ourable man—I believed you on your bare word, though appear-
ances were against you."

"You do not so now?"

"We will not speak of that," replied Guttorm hotly. "I have
delivered my message and now I will go. How would you have
me judge your conduct toward my niece?" he flared up; "you
have lain in wait by the fence like a barn-door thief, decoyed the
child out to you late at night, visited her at the sæter and sat with
her alone in the hut as if she were a hireling—you hear, she had
to make a clean breast of how she came by your brooch. And because she is innocent and childlike, you thought you could decoy
her to you—hither!"

"Will you not greet the mistress of the house, man!" cried Eirik
furiously.

Eldrid had gone in, clad as she came from the byre. Calmly and
proudly she returned Guttorm's greeting.

"You have received a message from my sister, Eirik?" she
asked gently.

"Yes, I have brought him a message."

"But so far as I understood you, Master Guttorm, this sister of
mine has told you it was Eirik's device that they should seek
refuge with me? Eirik told me it was Gunhild who prayed him
to come hither, saying she would follow—"

"Said he *that!*"

Eirik himself replied; he was pale even to the lips: "Yes."

"Shame on you, then!" Guttorm spat.

Eldrid spoke. "So said Eirik—and that he purposed, as soon as
she was rested, to take her away to his rich kinsfolk in the Upplands, give the maid into their charge, until he might be reconciled with Berse. I believe he too thought that Gunhild had chosen
unwisely when she appointed this as their trysting-place."

"Gunhild has heard nothing of his rich kinsfolk in the Upplands, so far as I know. But 'tis not amiss if he has since thought
better of his design."

Eirik said, calmly and earnestly: "Does it seem so strange to
you, Guttorm—'tis known to every soul in the parishes hereabout
that Berse sold his eldest daughter to—to—Jephthah's daughter in
Jewry had a better bargain than the mistress here. I had conceived
a love for Gunhild—and I know she liked me well. When there-

fore I came to hear that Berse had allotted the same fate to her—would give her to a hideous ancient who had already worn out one wife at least—"

"What stuff is this?" Guttorm interrupted angrily; "old—he is a year or two older than yourself, a courteous and goodly man. Ay, he was married ere he was of age, but Mistress Hillebjörg lived but a year or two—"

"Was it when she heard this of her new bridegroom," asked Eldrid, "that my sister gave up her sinful project and took counsel of you?"

"No," replied Guttorm reluctantly, dropping his voice. "I got wind that the child meditated a mischief. But since she has seen Sir Magnus she must needs admit that her father has sought to provide well for her in every way.—But enough said of this. Good night."

"Nay, tarry awhile, master—" Eldrid followed Guttorm out.

In a few moments she came back; Eirik had not moved.

"Nay, he would neither rest nor take food," she said. She looked up at the tall, dark man, who loomed huge in the dim light of the room. "Now I trow 'twill be long ere you believe a woman's word again?" she asked, with something like mockery.

Eirik turned from her and went out.

It was now raining quietly and steadily, and the growing scent of spring seemed even heavier in the wet evening. Eirik thought that now he could only leave this place—but he felt so strangely weak and empty, almost as when he had been stabbed with knives up at Haugsvik and came near bleeding to death. He wandered along a path through the meadow, down toward the lake. He thought of taking the boat and rowing somewhere.

Then Eldrid came running after him in great haste and seized him by the arm. "Eirik—where are you going? Man, you do not think to drown yourself for such foolishness as this!"

"No, no." He shook her hand off. "I had not thought of that."

"Come up now," Eldrid begged him. "Do not go moping here in the rain."

Eirik looked at her; then, rather unwillingly, he went back with the woman.

She had heaped fuel on the fire—the light of the flames played over the walls and roof in the low room with the heavy beams under which a grown man could not stand upright, except under the roof-tree. Eirik drank a little of the milk she offered him, absently thinking it was not so ill to have the fireplace in the corner, as here—the rain did not fall into the fire when the smoke-vent was open as now.

"Let us go to rest," Eldrid then said. "You need no more ride out at night."

Eirik undressed, so far as was his habit. But then he remained sitting on the bench at the foot of his bed, with his arm around the carved horse's head, staring at the embers that shrank together in the fireplace. Eldrid already lay under the skins in her bed. "Lie down now," she bade him more than once, and Eirik answered: "Yes," but stayed where he was.

Then she sprang out again and came over to him, barefooted, in her coarse, dark under-kirtle. She seized him by the shoulders, forced him to sit upright, so sharply that his neck struck against the log of the wall.

"Do not sit staring like this!" she said impatiently. "You have not a little to learn yet, Eirik!"

"Learn—" He took hold of her wrist. "Shall I learn of you maybe?"

She looked down into his distorted face. Her nostrils expanded and her eyes grew wide. "Oh, ay—I could teach you much—"

Then he pulled her down to him, crushed her broken lips with kisses.

17

EVER since he was at the convent Eirik had been used to wake at the time when the brethren rose to go to matins. And he did the same now, when he slept in Eldrid's arms.

Now the caller passed through the dormitory whispering "*Benedicamus Domino*," and the friars answered softly: "*Deo gratias*," as they slipped from their pallets. He himself had been one of those who filed quietly down into the bright choir to sing the hymn of praise at daybreak; he himself had knelt and prayed from the first faint streak of dawn until the sun ruled in all its power and all men had gone to their labour. And now he had strayed hither, and what this woman had taught him was such that he had felt a blast of the heat of hell.—And yet, he thought, with a strange rigour of pain, what had befallen him was a destiny that had been laid on him from his birth, and now it was accomplished. More and more clearly he felt the familiarity of this forest wilderness: it had all been in his dream—even the little cornfield with the withered bush fence about it; in his dream he had ridden the bay, when Leman came flying on her broad blue wings, plucked him from his horse, and flung herself upon him with the wild, hot caresses that terrified him. Ay, now she had him under her wings, had beak and claws in him, struck at his heart and drank his life-blood.

He knew of no return. This time he could not tear himself away from Leman and fly as in his dream—he had no strength for that now. Of the women he had possessed, she was the first he loved—and the first who had desired *him* and not a penny in reward. And then—to ride away from her one day and leave her alone, deserted and in want, that he could never bring himself to do.

And in the midst of his misfortune it dawned upon him—this was not the end. He had been drawn down into evil before, but he had been saved, his feet had been set on the firm rock and he had been made a freer man than before. And He who had saved him then would save him again. From his destiny no man can fly, but above his destiny is God. And so in what had befallen him it could not have been designed that Leman should strike her beak into his heart and drink him dry and empty, but he began to think he might be called to set free Leman from her semblance.

It had lasted for more than a week. He continued to work for Eldrid in the daytime, and he had become acquainted with his three house-mates, the hag, the herdboy, and Holgeir, Eldrid's old kinsman. They seemed not to be surprised—folk were not likely to be surprised at anything with Eldrid. Nor was he himself surprised, somehow—all that lay between his childhood in the forest and the present, when the forest had recaptured him, seemed like a dream.

Once or twice he had taken bow and arrows—the house was well furnished with arms; when he asked Eldrid who was their owner, she merely answered: "I." Then he went hunting.

He came home toward noon on the tenth day after Guttorm's visit to the Ness, bringing Eldrid two wood-grouse. Then he asked her abruptly, with no beating about the bush:

"Will you marry me, Eldrid?"

Eldrid gave a little laugh. "No, I will not."

"Why not?"

"Do you know how many men I have had?" she asked mockingly.

"Scarce so many, I warrant, as that Mary of Magdala."

"Ho, ho! Is that your aim? You may spare yourself the trouble, Eirik. A monk too I have had—when I made him go the way I would, he was the worst of all."

"Ay, that is likely enough," said Eirik. "Since he had broken a holy vow. But none can say that of me—it must be held that Gunhild has released me from all oaths and promises."

Eldrid had dropped her work and stood staring at her young lover.

"Well, how had you thought this would end?" asked Eirik.

"Oh—some I drove away when I grew tired of them—others were tired of me first and went of themselves. Which it will be with you I have not yet thought."

"Eldrid," said Eirik, "I have seen it in your eyes, every time I took the bow and went into the woods, you were afraid I would not come back."

She stared at him, red and speechless. But then she broke out:

"Afraid! Ay, 'tis true—and think you I am afraid to be afraid? Did you know—I learned what it is to be afraid while you were yet sucking your mother's breasts—afraid!" Eldrid's great eyes flashed. "Take yourself off, little lad, when you will, and go back to saying your hours and creeping to the cross and doing penance—not for me! I prayed, the day I rode as a bride to Harald's house—the storm came upon us on the way, I prayed God to send his lightning and save me. I prayed Mary Virgin—to take me in her keeping—I too was a virgin of fourteen years as she was when the angel visited her. I prayed her send the angel with the flaming sword and save me. It had struck the great ash in Castle Cleft, we saw the marks of the lightning in the grass as we rode up; but there was no mercy for me. And you talk to me of being afraid—" She stalked hither and thither in the little room.

"*You* say 'afraid' to me—I think 'twould scare you from your wits were I to tell you all the vengeance I took upon Harald, with his own house-carls, before his eyes, while he lay palsied and speechless. That might have been enough—the rest I have regretted; maybe 'twas stupid, not worth the pains—after Harald was dead and his children had driven me out and I dwelt at Sigurdstad wasting myself and my estate—but I rejoice whenever I recall Harald, as he lay there babbling and glaring—"

Eldrid stood facing Eirik, with a sneer on her dry, brown lips. "Go! You are afraid of *me* now—milksop, puny creature that you are—your face is grey and white as a flock of wool!"

Eirik shook his head. "I am not afraid." He smiled faintly. "And I mean to stay here and be married to you."

Some evenings later, when old Holgeir was with them in the room, Eirik said to him:

"I have asked Eldrid if she will marry me. She is a widow and can dispose of herself, but 'twere better she acted in accord with one of her kinsmen. Therefore I now ask you."

Holgeir answered that if Eirik would make him a promise in the presence of witnesses that he should remain here in the same condition, even if Eldrid took a husband, he would give his consent. To this Eirik agreed.

When Holgeir had gone out he turned to Eldrid. "Say yes, you too—'twill be tiresome for both you and me to be talking for ever of the same thing."

Eldrid replied hotly: "You are like the witless beasts, Eirik, like a horse or a steer; 'tis vain to try to save them from the fire—they run straight back into the flames."

"May I take that for consent?" asked Eirik with a little laugh. "Take it for what you will!"

Then he sold to Holgeir the little silver chain with a cross on it which he had worn round his neck under his clothes since he was a boy, and bought meal and malt. Eldrid brewed and baked and they killed a calf; she made preparations for the betrothal feast with a gloomy air and strange words, but every time he held her in his arms he knew why she was thus—it was because he now had power over her: she still thought this marriage was madness, but she could not lose him.

One night she asked him: "What will you do with me when you go back home to Hestviken?"

" 'Tis not sure it will ever be ours to dwell there, so long as Father lives," said Eirik. "But you have had a greater manor than that under you ere now."

She was so thin when he pressed her to him that it made him think of grouse he had sometimes shot—they had once been winged, but had lived on and supported themselves in a fashion long after.

Just before marrying, then, Eirik invited the neighbours to a feast, and then he went off to the parish priest at Saana church. Eirik had lent Holgeir the bay, and himself walked behind with the two peasants from the little farms up in the woods.

Holgeir was spokesman. Eirik gave his name and his father's name and his home parish. Sira Jon promised to publish the banns of marriage in lawful manner and he also promised to come to the betrothal feast.

It was held three days before Knut's mass [2] and all went well. Eirik betrothed Eldrid with his ring; for surety's sake he turned his words so as to say: "I take you to wife," so that he might be sure the marriage was now made, since he had already lived with the woman. Eldrid used the same form of words in her response.

Sira Jon then said some prayers, blessed them with holy water, blessed the company and the food. The feast passed off right well. The poor peasants who were witnesses seemed to have known but little of their neighbour ere now, but they made good cheer at her table. The priest was allotted the high seat; now that he and his two assistants had removed their white vestments he grew very talkative and very cheerful. He was himself the son of a poor peasant of the neighbouring parish, and he had often been at the Ness in his childhood, for it was of his aunt's husband that Benedikt Bersesson had bought the farm for his sister. He boasted greatly of what the Ness had been in those days and gave Eirik good advice as to what he ought to do now that he was to be master here, at the same time enjoining him to show gratitude to God for having been raised to such prosperity.

It dawned on Eirik that the priest took him to be a man of naught who had taken service here and was now to get a farm

2 July 10.

and a wife who came of great folk, though she was somewhat the worse for wear. All the guests thought the same—they had seen him working here in a rough frock that Eldrid had made for him and shoes of rawhide that he had made for himself. None but Eldrid and Holgeir knew more of him than that. This roused all his old love of giving play to his fancy—he grew very free and said not a word that might lead any of them to suspect the truth, but talked and behaved as though he were a poor serving-man who was now being received into the ranks of landowners.

The priest said among other things that nowhere in the land was better fish to be found than in this lake, especially the perch. Eirik promised to render his fishing-tithes well and duly, and said that if one day he caught some fine perch in his nets he would bring the priest a little present.

The banns had been called twice for Eirik and Eldrid. But one morning during the week before the third time of asking, Eirik had a great catch of fine fish in his nets, and so he thought he would now fulfil his promise to the priest and bring him some fresh fish for the fast-day. He strung the biggest of the perch together, took his horse, and rode off.

But no sooner had he entered the door of the priest's house than Sira Jon came at him, looking as if the eyes would start from his head; he took the string of fish and flung it away, as though it were a string of vipers:

"Man of ill omen—you have befooled me abominably and made sport of me—so you are none other than the only son of Olav Audunsson of Hestviken!" He waved his hands in dismay.

"Nay, Sira, have I befooled you? I told you my name and my father's name and where I came from—"

"Ay, Eirik and Olav—there are many of those names. Then I send word to your parish priest, to know if you were unmarried and in no affinity to the woman—and this is what I hear!"

"Ay, but you cannot possibly have heard of any lawful hindrance?"

"His only son besides, and heir to an estate—and you will be married to Eldrid Bersesdatter!"

"Ay," smiled Eirik, "since I hold myself to be an equal mate for her."

At this Sira Jon exclaimed that never in this world would he

say their bridal mass, nor would he publish the banns the third
time.

"That you have no right to refuse us, Sira!"

"Right—ay, I know you have had your nose inside a convent
and have smelled at the books they had there—you may complain
to Dean Peter or to the Bishop, if you dare!"

All that Eirik could say was of no avail—that he had long been
of full age and that Eldrid was a widow and had betrothed herself
to him by the counsel of a kinsman, and that their cohabitation
was already binding marriage by the law of the Church and could
not be dissolved without mortal sin; and since neither Olav nor
Berse were sheep of his flock, he could not see why the priest was
so afraid of them. It was all of no use, even when he tried to tempt
Sira Jon, promising to remember him when once he was master of
Hestviken.

So nothing came of the wedding. Eirik cared little—since Eldrid seemed not to take it to heart. What had been done was
enough to satisfy the law of God, according to which they were
husband and wife; and what view the law of the land might take
of their cohabitation mattered little, as yet anyway.

But his talk with the priest had nevertheless forced him to remember that there was a world outside the Ness on Longwater.
And one day in the course of the autumn he told his wife that he
would have to ride home and see his father.

The morning he set out, Eldrid accompanied him a little way
across the marshes.

"Do not look at me like that," he said with an embarrassed
smile as they parted. "I shall be home again by the evening of the
third day at the latest, but it may well be I shall come sooner."

It was past midday when he came out by the river-mouth and
saw once more the bay and the fiord outside and the rust-coloured
rocks by the shore. He had ridden through the fields. They had
finished cutting the corn here, and the cattle were loose in the
paddocks. He knew every beast, and he knew every foot of
ground; there was not a bush or a heap of stones or a tussock in
the meadow that he had not gone round with scythe and bill-
hook. And yet he did not feel at home here any longer, in the
way he was at home at the Ness, at the farm where he was always
coming upon corners that were unknown to him, on the lake, to

the farther end of which he had never yet rowed, in the woods around, where he was always striking tracks that led he knew not whither—and yet wherever he went he had the feeling that here he had been born and brought up, that he had seen it all before, either when he was a child, or in his dreams.

As his horse's hoofs struck the rocks of the yard, Ragna came to the door of the cook-house. She cried aloud and ran toward him. Then others of the house-folk came out and swarmed about him, and last came Cecilia with a little child on her arm. It gave Eirik a shock to realize that it was Audun and that he had not grown much since he last saw him. It was not yet a year since that day in the storehouse loft.

Then he saw his father come to the door of the house. Olav stood there a moment, looked at his son, then turned in again.

Eirik kissed his silent sister on the lips. "I will come in to you, when I have spoken with Father."

He followed Olav into the living-room. His father sat in his seat. Eirik remained standing by the door with his hat in his hands.

"I have come home, Father—"

"Ay, I am growing used to that now."

"Nay, Father, I know you have good reason to chide me for leaving home without warning and staying away so long—"

Olav interrupted him: "A vagabond you are, and never will there be aught of you but a vagabond and a bird of passage. I make no complaint—'tis your nature. A fool I was to believe time after time that each new whimsy would last. I believed you when you said you would be a monk, I believed you when you said you would live at Saltviken and restore the farm there, I believed you when you thought you had set your heart on Gunhild Bersesdatter—But one thing I did not believe of you—that you would take so paltry a revenge on Berse. As when you went off and debauched his daughter, who was so situated that you knew no man would defend her—"

"I am married to Eldrid, Father."

As his father made no reply, Eirik said again: "I thought you had heard that—since our priest had to make inquiry about me here in my own parish—"

"I heard of it. But I thought you would act according to your wont, as like as not—as when you were to take your vows in the convent. But it falls worst on yourself. God knows how you will carry it on the day when you begin to feel galled by a bond that cannot be broken."

Eirik stood still, looking at his father. Again he seemed to be wondering—all that his father said was true enough, and yet he knew that the truth was otherwise.

"I do not blame her," said Olav bitterly. "I would not have done what Berse did—given away a fair young child to an oldster who had buried two wives already—and an ugly sight he was with the big white bumps on his skull grinning out of his tousled hair, and never have I heard that he did a kindness to man or woman. Maybe other wives would have transgressed as much as Eldrid, had they not lacked the courage.

"And naturally she was ready to marry you, if she could bring it about. For all that, I will not have such a woman established in your mother's seat here or taking precedence of your sister here at Hestviken—not while I am master. When I am dead or unfit to have control, then you may come back, and then it may be more honourable that you bring with you the wife you have chosen rather than thrust her into a corner—if you have not done so already before that time comes. But till then you two must keep away from my domains."

"As you will, Father."

"Nay, I do not mean it so," said Olav curtly, "that I would drive you from home. You may stay here as long as you wish—I suppose you will fetch such things as are yours, visit kinsfolk and friends. I will not deny you that. Nor that you come hither to visit your sister—but you must come alone. But *dwell* here you shall not again in my time. I am tired of this; no sooner do we think you are settled somewhere than we have you back—and when we think you mean to stay at home, of a sudden you are gone.—But put off your cloak now," said his father, as he would speak to any other guest, "and take your rest."

Cecilia had ordered food and ale to be brought to her house for her brother. Jörund had gone to Gunnarsby to see his brothers, she said. They talked together, first of her children—all three were thriving—and then of the manor and the summer and of folk they knew, but not of his affairs.

Eirik asked whether Jörund and their father were on better terms now.

"They are not at enmity," replied the wife. She turned red. "He has begun to do more on the farm—Jörund has not had his baleful headache so much this summer. Father talks of moving out to Saltviken," she added, "letting Jörund have charge here."

Eirik lifted Kolbein onto his knees. "You know," he said quietly, "my wife has never had a child—and now she is not so young either. I had it in my mind to tell you this—so you may know, you and Jörund, if you are now to take over all the work here—'tis most likely that this little lad will one day have Hestviken after me."

"Eirik—that you could undo yourself thus!" said Cecilia in a horrified whisper.

"It is not as you think," replied Eirik; and what shocked his sister most was that she could not read the expression in his eyes, but it was not one of sorrow or remorse.

Eirik took his departure late in the afternoon of the third day. He had packed a saddle-bag with such of his things as he needed most; more he would have sent after him, for he was to ride home alone and he could lead no pack-horse with him—there was no fodder for more than one horse at the Ness. But Gisti, one of his old dogs, he would have with him; it had followed its master's heels wherever he went these three days, jumping up at him whenever he snapped his fingers. He was glad, for he felt the want of a dog at the Ness.

Cecilia wished to ride with him part of the way; she could then see to her child at Rynjul at the same time.

His father said farewell to Eirik in the yard. They parted kindly, but Eirik knew that from now he was a stranger here.

Brother and sister rode inland together; Knut Ragnason, who was now Cecilia's henchman, followed at a little distance. As they passed Rundmyr, Eirik asked Cecilia to take care of Olav Livsson, the sick lad: "He is fit to do a little woman's work." Cecilia promised.

They came to where the road branched off to Rynjul. Eirik did not wish to go and meet his kinsfolk there; so they took leave of each other. He had dismounted. His sister laid her hand on his head, forced it sharply into her lap.

"Eirik, Eirik," she whispered despairingly, " 'tis as though they would draw you back to elf-land!"

Eirik gently freed himself. "What fancies! I am content with the lot that has fallen to me."

It was dark when he reached the end of the lake. The Ness stood out black against the pale surface of the water. He made out a figure walking toward him on the road. Eirik leaped from his horse.

"Here am I, Eldrid."

She did not take his hand; he heard her breathing heavily, and then she burst into tears. She sat down at the edge of the road, bent double in the dark, and wept convulsively. Eirik stood still, leaning against his horse, and waited. At last he went over, took her by the hand and raised her.

"Now you must weep no more, Eldrid!"

Then they walked together across the marshes, home to the farm. The bay walked in front and Eirik's dog followed at his heels.

"I have made ready no food," she said when they had entered her house. "I had done so yestereve—you remember you said maybe you would be home so soon. But it made me so sick to see it standing there useless. Now I will go and fetch—"

Eirik watched his wife go with pensive eyes.

As he supped and afterwards unpacked his saddle-bag, they spoke some words of his journey. Eirik said that his father had not received him too badly. But it had been agreed that he was not to move home to Hestviken at present.

No sooner had Eldrid come to bed than she began to weep again. And she wept on and on—she wept under her husband's caresses, she fell asleep with her face against his shoulder and sobbed in her sleep, and woke and wept again. Eirik lay still and let her weep her fill.

"Would I had died," she lamented once, "ere you met me!"

"You must not say such a thing," he begged her earnestly. "You must not wish you had died while you hated God and all men."

"Yes! Rather that than that you should lie here, cast out from your heritage and kin."

"You are she who was set apart for me from the first. From here I am come, and hither I was to return."

Then he told her his dream of the bird-woman, Leman.

But next morning, when Eirik came in to his meal, Eldrid asked dryly: "Did you hear aught of that sister of mine, Gunhild—what has become of her?"

Eirik looked up.

"Nay," he said, taken by surprise; "that I clean forgot to ask!"

1 8

OLAV moved out to Saltviken.

The work afloat had to be done from Hestviken; here was no other quay than the little boat-pier of piled stones, no boathouse or warehouse, but only the little sheds by the salt-pans. And it would be a great piece of work to make a harbour in the open and shallow bay. Saltviken could be made a good corn-growing farm. Eirik had been right there.

Olav sailed up to Hestviken, went on board his own boats, spoke with Cecilia on dark winter mornings on the quay, but did not go up to the manor. Yet he knew that his son-in-law let fly abuse of the old kelpie that haunted the beach.

He knew that his daughter's husband could not cope with any of the things that had been placed in his charge. He had to depend on his old tried folk and on Cecilia. But it had come to this, that he thought himself obliged to pretend a trust in Jörund Rypa even though he had none.

What folk said of it all—it was clear that he himself was the last who would hear that. But it could not possibly be any secret that he had chosen ill in choosing a husband for his daughter. And as to Eirik's conduct, Jörund had let him hear what all thought of it: he had meant to take revenge on Berse—and a dastard's revenge—so he only got his deserts when he found out that the old adulteress was too sly and that he was the one who was caught.

Olav was wearied to death of everything. This turmoil in which he had been caught up, when he had had to swallow Berse's insults—and he had controlled himself, for Eirik's sake he had controlled himself more than he believed possible—and then Eirik behaved like a hothead, without a thought of honour or of aught but his own caprices—when at last this turmoil had calmed down, Olav felt that now he cared for nothing more. Now it was all one to him.

But he would not give up, for all that; he would have to continue the fight against disgrace and misfortune. He would stake all the respect he had won in the country round against his neighbours' judgment of Cecilia's husband, affect to think that Jörund was worth his salt and that his shield was untarnished. And at the same time, while living at the deserted manor, he tried secretly to keep an eye on everything, to direct and advise—whether Jörund liked it or not. It might well be that thus he might bring about better times for Cecilia and her children. Now that he could play the master at Hestviken, Jörund had found friends; they were not the best men of the neighbourhood, and he himself was quarrelsome and unamiable—with luck he might come by a few inches of cold steel.

And Eirik, who had acted in such a way that there was no excuse for his conduct—he must be banned from home. And it was better so—would he might never have to look on this creature again while he lived. He should have foreseen it, that time when he came home and found Ingunn with calamity incarnate in her womb—that he would be haunted by this spectre throughout his life and never find peace: he had hated him, despised him, hardened his heart against him, wished him dead—and longed for him, believed in him when the other deceived him, wished him well as soon as he had allowed himself to be deceived—this stranger had been more his own than the children whose father he was. Time after time he had believed that the curse was turned to—well, to something else—the bastard to a son of whom he was fond—and then the changeling had always swung to the right-about—and he himself was left deluded, the victim of scorn—and of what was worse and smarted more keenly.

But now it was finished. And well it was.

Yet ever and anon he caught himself thinking of Eirik. He longed to tell Eirik what was in his mind, without restraint. He longed to see him.

Time seemed long to him out at Saltviken a whole winter. He

lived there alone with Knut Ragnason and the young wife the lad had lately married.

One day in spring Galfrid Richardson came unexpectedly to Saltviken to see him. In the evening he told Olav his business.

There was a man who sought the hand of Galfrid's youngest daughter, Alis, and Galfrid himself was willing enough to have the man for a son-in-law, but he wished to speak to Olav first: "For it is that Björn, the son of Torhild of Torhildsrud—so 'tis you who are his father."

Olav answered he had gotten this son while his wife was yet alive, so he had no right over the man, but if Björn needed help to establish himself, he would not refuse—

'Twas not so meant, said Galfrid; he only sought to know whether Olav had anything to say against the marriage. Björn was doing well, and his mother and stepfather were now prosperous. He had become acquainted with the young man last autumn, when Björn hired the smithy in their yard. He was to make the ironwork for the new doors of St. Laurence's Church; it was some of the knights of the King's body-guard who made this gift to the church. Björn had acquitted himself of the task in such fashion that one of the knights would have him forge two branched candlesticks and an iron-bound coffer for the chapel of ease that stood on his manor. But when Björn brought these things to Sir Arne and claimed his reward, the knight deemed it too high and would chaffer. Björn made answer that if Sir Arne could not afford to give what the smith claimed, he could afford to present the knight with both coffer and candlesticks; but he held that none other than himself could judge what his work was worth. Then Sir Arne gave him the sum he claimed. Now Björn Olavsson had bought himself the houses he needed in the old Gullbringen Yard—Olav knew it, next below Fluga Yard, between Sigrid's Yard and the river.[3]

After this, Olav had a strong desire to see Björn once more. At Margaret's mass [4] he found that he had business in the town. And on Sunday, when he came from mass in St. Halvard's, he went

[3] That is, the little river Alna, on the bank of which stood the ancient town of Oslo.

[4] June 10.

down toward the yards that lay at the bottom of the slope, by the river bank. Gullbringen was the largest, and it had three court-yards, one beyond the other.

The houses around the innermost yard stood on the very bank of the Alna. There was a smithy, a stable with lofts, and a fine stone house. A great rosebush grew against the wall of the dwelling; beside it stood a young man and two women, who bent down and smelled the roses. Olav recognized the young slender one with the long auburn plaits; she was Alis Galfridsdatter, he had seen her at her father's house. The other was one of her married sisters.

Alis had seen him; she whispered something to the young man. Then she turned and went, giving Olav Audunsson a shy greeting as she slipped past. She had a fine, healthy, freckled face, wore a rose in her bosom, and carried roses in her hand.

The man came up slowly and greeted Olav: "Have we such great honour?"

His smile was boyishly self-confident—he must be twenty now, thought his father.

"I had a mind to see you again—"

"And indeed 'tis long since the last time. And the years seem to have dealt hardly with you—you are grown old, Olav Audunsson! But go in—"

So he sat on the bench in the smith's house, and in the corner opposite sat the man who was his only son.

The lad was handsome—as he himself had been in his youth—a good deal bigger in stature, but not so shapely and well-knit. But he had the same fair complexion, the bright silvery sheen of hair and eyebrows, the white skin, and the clear grey eyes rather far apart.

Olav soon found that it was no easy matter to converse with Björn—he had nothing to say to him. His mother, his stepfather, his brothers and sisters, they were all well and prosperous; and so was Björn himself. His house declared plainly enough that the young man held his own.

"You are young to be a householder and practise your craft as your own master?"

"Oh, I have stood on my own feet since I was fifteen."

Olav said he would fain see proofs of Björn's skill—he had heard it greatly praised. Björn replied that he had nothing here which was worth showing: "but you can go up to Laurence's Spital and look at the ironwork on the south door of the church and the three candelabra that hang in the nave. They are the best I have wrought till now. I have no leisure today or I would have gone with you—"

"Is it true," asked Olav with a little laugh, "that the master of whom you learned your craft is of giant race?"

"He told me naught of that. And I never ask folk uninvited questions." This was meant for a reproof, his father saw, and he was inclined to smile. Never had he seen a man so heartily self-sufficient as this lad.

"But a good smith he was—none better in Norway," said Björn. He went across to a chest, came back, and handed Olav a lock and key for a coffer. "This I wrought while I was with him. The locks I make now are more cunning. If you like it, you may have it, Olav."

Olav thanked him and praised the work.

"'Tis not from your father's family you have this skill," he said tentatively. "We were never good handicraftsmen in our race."

"My father's family I know not at all," replied Björn in a clear voice.

"And that you resent?" said Olav in the same tone.

Björn looked him straight in the eyes, with his pert young smile. "Nay, Olav, that I do not. You begat me—and I say you did well in that. And have you done no more for me since—then I hold you have done me no ill there."

Olav looked at his son—wondered whether the boy knew what he was saying, or were these words put into his mouth?

Björn got up and went to the shelf over the door. "But you must think I am inhospitable." He filled the cup and drank to his father: "Hail to you, Olav Audunsson! It cheers my heart none the less to know you have sat on my bench for once."

Olav accepted the drink, with a little smile. "I cannot say your looks betray it, Björn!" It was wine, and good wine.

"Ay, but I mean it—and I wish you to have a token to remind you of it." Again he went to the chest. This time it was a brooch, fairly large and gilt all over; in the centre was an image of Mary with the Child, and around it a wreath of bosses, each of which bore an angel's face.

"Nay, Björn—that is far too great a gift, I will not have it!"

"Yes, take it now. Do you not remember I had a gold ring of you once?"

"Is it that you wish to quit scores with me, then?"

"No, no, not that either. I may tell you, Olav, 'tis with that ring I shall plight my troth to Álís Galfridsdatter at Clement's Church door on the eve of Laurence's mass."

" 'Twill be honoured, then."

As Björn went with him to the door, Olav asked: "Your mother —she is well content with your choice of a wife?"

"Mother—" For the first time Björn's smile was purely gay, with no challenge in it. "Mother is content with me, whatever I do."

"That is well," replied Olav. "Then I know that you have always done what is right and manly."

They pressed each other's hand at parting and Olav went.

Olav walked over toward his inn, half smiling. He might rest content with this Björn. Young and overconfident—but they were faults that life mends in a man—and God grant the lad might lose little of himself in the mending. So that the man might fulfil the promise of the boy, when once he was full-fledged.

What Björn had said was true—he might have done more for this son of his. Other men treated such matters differently—had their bastards brought up in their own homes or in those of their friends. He had indeed given the mother her farm, but Björn seemed to count that for nothing—and true it was, she owed her prosperity to herself and that husband. And if Torhild had not married, perhaps he and Björn would have seen more of each other. Although the true reason was that he felt he could not bear to look a son constantly in the face whom he had no power to bring into the family and set in his place—and so all else he could do was nothing worth.

And whatever the lad had meant in saying it, there was truth in his words: that, if he had done nothing for Björn but beget him, he had thereby done him no ill. The son who stood outside the family and would not call him father—he was also outside the family misfortune.

19

FOR the third time Eirik brought in the corn frozen and half-ripe.
It froze down here by the lake earlier than anywhere else in the
country round. It was not so great a disaster either—they could
always make gruel from it, and grain for malt and bread they
could buy. Meat and fish were the foods they had in plenty, and
in Lent it was all to the good if they had to go a little hungry.

He smiled when he thought of the first year's Lent. He kept
the fast as had been his custom since he was in the convent, drank
nothing but water once a day, and put a piece of ice in his mouth
if he was too thirsty at other times. At night he slept on a sack
of straw in the porch. He did not ask what Eldrid did. But one
morning when he came in he saw her lying on the floor—she was
still asleep. Then she said that she lay there every night, after he
had gone out to rest, and as she saw that he went barefoot in his
shoes, she did the same.

"You must not, for you are not used to it."

Eldrid said she had been shriven every year in Lent and had
received *corpus Domini* on Easter Day—but she had only done so
to avoid being cited.

"It is well that you have left such evil ways," said her husband.

"Nay, I made a vow that night I waited for you on the road—
when you had been out to Hestviken."

"Then they did some good, the foolish thoughts you had. But
I had told you I should be home again the third evening."

"Had you not kept your word," said Eldrid, "I know not what
would have become of me."

"God help you, Eldrid—but you ought to know better than
most, that no man is worth much as he is in himself."

"You are not like other folk."

"Oh, but I am. In most things I have not been better than my
fellows, and in some I have been worse."

But he had never spoken Bothild's name to his wife.

Now he knew the lake from end to end, and the woods around,
the paths and the wastes. There was not much to be done on the

little farm, so he had ample time to roam about to his heart's content. When he found, the first winter, that Eldrid had skis—they made it easier for her to move about among the outhouses, so long as she had no horse—he too had to make himself a pair. When he had accustomed himself to the use of them he liked this mode of travelling so well that he ran on skis oftener than he rode. There were times when he was out from morning to evening; often he did not come home till late at night—until it chanced that there was some piece of work or other that he could postpone no longer. Then he would find a host of other things that it might be well to get done, and for a while he would not leave the houses, had scarce time to swallow his food and none at all to rest; in the evenings he sat by the fire with knife and chisel, awl and sinews, and worked, while Eldrid sewed and span, as silent as her husband.

They never talked much together, beyond what the work required. They knew not much more of each other's earlier life than they had known when they met. But he felt that her life had gone up in his, she drifted with him as a boat drifts with the stream, and both were content it should be so.

He had been two years at the Ness when Brother Stefan came to preach at Saana church for a few days in Ascension week. On the last day Eirik persuaded him to come home to the Ness and stay the night there, and the next morning he accompanied Brother Stefan by a short road through the forest into the next parish.

They sat talking for a long time on a ridge, whence they had a view of tarns and forest, but never a homestead under the broad sky, and Eirik's dogs lay in the moss at his feet. Eirik cleared his mind to Brother Stefan of all that he had not been able to bring out in confession, because it had not to do with sin or grace, but with the All in which all things move and have their being.

While they were talking thus, Brother Stefan said he counted it a gain that Eldrid was no longer bound in thraldom by her own hate. "But it will not be your lot to live all your days here at the Ness—have you thought of how it will be when one day you two move out to Hestviken?"

"No," replied Eirik. "It must be as God pleases—*if* we ever

come there. Father may live to see eighty years. Moreover,
Eldrid is a discerning woman, and open to reason. The finest and
most promising foal may be spoilt by cruelty and foolish treatment."

"You must not liken a Christian soul to an unreasoning beast,"
said Brother Stefan.

"That old Ragnhild you saw at our house—she told me—
Harald Jonsson once bound Eldrid to the post of the loft ere
he rode from home; he would have her stand there till her feet
swelled so that she could bear no more—if he could make his
wife so meek that she would show him kindness. Ragnhild set her
free the second night and tended her—she was sixteen at that time,
Eldrid. She had been Harald's leman, and he sent her away when
he wedded Eldrid, but afterwards he took her back to Borg; she
was to help him break in Eldrid—this Ragnhild."

They sat in silence for a while, both of them.

Brother Stefan said they had grieved, all the brethren, when
they heard the course Eirik had taken: Brother Arne had vowed
to scourge himself every Thursday evening so that the blood
flowed about his feet, till he heard his brother had repented.

Brother Arne, who had been the companion of his novitiate,
was the one for whom Eirik cared most of all in the convent—
he was but a young lad and had been with the Minorites from a
child. Eirik now bade Brother Stefan take Arne his greeting and
his thanks.

When they came down into the neighbouring parish, at the
first fence about a green field Eirik said farewell to his friend.
Brother Stefan gave him his blessing; then the monk went on
toward the village, and the solitary hunter, with his bow over his
shoulder and his hounds at his side, turned back to climb the hill
again.

That summer went by at the Ness, and most of another winter.
In Candlemas week there was severe cold. Eirik was up on the
hill in the daytime, felling timber; but one night he woke to find
Eldrid trembling by his side. She said she had fallen into the spring
that day, as she was fetching water for the byre, and thought
she must now be too old to go about in ice-covered clothes. Eirik
then found out that the old serving-woman, Ragnhild, had a way
of being out of temper with her mistress at times, and then she

shut herself up in Holgeir's cabin till the mood passed off. While it lasted Eldrid herself did all the work of the farmyard; they had no herdsman in winter.

Soon after she grew hot as coals all over, had some bad fits of coughing, and then began to be light-headed, wailing and muttering and throwing herself hither and thither. For some days she lay grievously sick. The first evening she began to be better, on seeing her husband come in with the milk, she asked after Ragnhild. Eirik laughed and said the old hag's wrath had fallen on them both—none knew why—so she still sat in her corner, and he had seen to her duties.

"Nay, Eirik, this is too bad—milking and cleaning byres is no work for a man."

"Who milks in the monasteries, think you?" asked Eirik with a laugh.

Next day came Gaute Virvir, Eirik's old friend from home. He had had business in the neighbourhood and so bethought him that he would visit the Ness. He found Eirik occupied in feeding the cows. Eirik gave his guest such welcome as he could, his wife being sick. Gaute had just had judgment given against him in the matter of an estate, so he was in a gloomy mood and the news he gave of his neighbours at home was told with a sad mien, like a tale of disaster. Olav still dwelt at Saltviken, and Cecilia's last child had died just after baptism, and Gunhild Bersesdatter was now Sir Magnus's wife and dwelt in the Lady Ingebjörg's bower —the knight was one of the Duchess's liegemen.

Eirik thought that, all in all, the tidings he had from home were not bad. It was hard on Cecilia that she had lost a child. But it seemed they managed just as well without him; his father and Cecilia together had the whole charge of the manor, he could guess, and Jörund was allowed to play the master—so doubtless he had become more tractable.

Three summers he had lived here, and soon the third winter would have gone by—Eirik was thinking of this one evening as he stood at the outer door looking out into the blue-grey dusk. The whole ness, which faced the sun, was brown and bare of snow; the eaves dripped a little; this evening was so mild that no icicles hung from them. In the forest the snow still lay deep, but the surface of the lake was black with melting ice, and along the shore the evening sky was mirrored in clear water—which had grown broader since the day before.

Then he became aware of something black moving over the ice down by the end of the lake—it looked like two figures, and they had dismounted and were leading their horses. Eirik ran toward them—he must stop them, bring them in to land at the only place where the ice could be called anything like safe. As he ran down, calling to them to stay where they were, he wondered a little who they might be—there was no other house but the Ness on the whole lake, so they must be bound thither.

As he hurried across the flat among the glassy pools of water, he saw that one of them must be a woman. But not till he had come close to them did he recognize Cecilia.

"In God's name, let me help you ashore. Take the horses, Svein, and I will lead Cecilia."

He thought he could see in the dim light that there was something wrong with her, wondered whether it was only fear when she saw how unsafe the ice was, or whether it was something else as well.

When they reached land, Eirik said: "You can find the way now, Svein. My wife will be asleep already, but you must go in and wake her, tell her who is coming." He took Cecilia's horse. "You must mount, Cecilia—the snow is knee-deep here across the marshes."

Then she threw her arms about her brother's neck and clung to him, and he could feel how she was trembling.

"I am come to beg you go back with me," she said in despair. "It has come to such a pass that I can bear no more." She gave a violent shudder. "I cannot bear to look upon Jörund again."

Eirik pressed her to him. " 'Tis best you come indoors first," he said; "take off your wet garments. For it must be a long tale you have to tell, I am afraid."

"The end of it is," said Cecilia, as she released her brother, "that yesterday he struck Olav, Anki's son, so that the lad died this morning. Then I bade Svein saddle my horse—"

Eirik stood aghast:

"The cripple! Can such things *be!*—What have you done with your children?" he asked abruptly.

"Tore has them. But he has never done aught to the children—

I charged them at home," she went on, as he led her horse along
the shore, "to send no word of this to Father. I dare not—till you
are there. You are the only one who can help us—perchance."

Eldrid met them at the door of the house. Eirik could see afar
off that she had swathed her head in her long, snow-white
church-coif. She gave Cecilia her hand and bade her welcome.

Indoors Eldrid had stirred up the fire on the hearth; she led
Cecilia to the warmest seat on the bench, took her wet cloak, and
thrust a pillow behind her guest's back.

"You must be tired, Eirik's sister—you have ridden all the way
from Hestviken in this heavy going, your man says."

Eirik saw that his sister looked about her with wondering eyes
—the room was tidy and snug, even if it were small and low, and
the beds were well provided with bedclothes and skin coverlets
—and then she looked up at her brother's wife. Eldrid had not
aged in these three years, and in her kirtle of dark colours, with
the white linen headdress falling low over her back, she looked
like a fine elderly woman.

"I think, Cecilia, you had better go to bed at once, wet and cold
as you are—and I will bring your supper." She took the young
wife to their own bed, knelt down, and drew off her footgear.
"Your feet are like ice—you must take the coverlet from the other
bed, Eirik, and warm it; then I can wrap it about your sister."

Cecilia sat clutching the edge of the bed with both hands; the
tears now ran down her cheeks as she wept almost without a
sound; and when Eldrid had wound the warm skin coverlet about
her legs and laid her down, she turned to the wall and buried her
face in the pillows. She lay thus till her sister-in-law came with
the food.

"Now you must come out with me, you—Svein was your name,
was it not? I shall go to Holgeir's house and sleep with Ragnhild
tonight, Eirik—I think your sister would fain speak with you
alone, you have not seen each other for so long."

With that Eldrid bade them good-night and went out.

Cecilia ate and drank.

"Shame on Gaute—he has put it about all over the countryside
that you go in rags, half-naked, and live like the meanest cottar,
and your wife is so infirm she must ever take to her bed—"

"Then Gaute is a worse tattler than I am myself," said Eirik.

"Had I known the truth of your condition," replied Cecilia, "I am not sure I should have come hither to complain of my trouble. I thought you could not be worse off than you were."

"Then it was well that Gaute spread his tale."

But when he had taken away the empty cups and seated himself on the bed by his sister, while the embers fell together in the fireplace, he felt a dread of what he was about to hear.

Between whiles Jörund had been tractable and kind, said Cecilia. But he scented covert injuries and distrust of himself in all that their father and the old serving-folk said and did, and it was often hard for her to intervene. Then there were Anki and Liv—he had conceived a hatred for them since that unfortunate affair, and he would have them out of Rundmyr. Olav said he would not hear of it—then Jörund was beside himself, made the most incredible accusations against their father, said it was known to the whole countryside why he kept such a den of thieves close beside his manor, but now they should go or he would set fire to the whole nest. This happened last autumn, while she still lay in after her little daughter who died—her father had come over to see her. Shortly after, it came out that Gudrun from Rundmyr, who had been helping at Hestviken during the summer, had not returned to her parents as she had left them, and Jörund had offered money to Svein Ragnason and several other men to take the blame on themselves. "I have never told Jörund of it," said Cecilia, "but I went up thither one day lately—Anki takes it much to heart, for Gudrun is not ill-looking; her at any rate he had thought to marry off, and she is but fourteen, so the poor child could scarce help herself."

But Jörund had gone quite wild when he got to know it. And for Olav, the cripple, he had always had a loathing. And yestermorn Olav had been in the fields with the children—he was cutting willow pipes for them—when Kolbein came running home; the boy cried and said his father had come upon them, so angry, had snatched Olav's crutches from him and struck him with them.

Cecilia had dashed out. There lay Olav, with the blood running from his nose and mouth. "I said to Jörund what first came into my head." But Jörund was like a raging bull and not like a reasonable being. Then Svein and Halstein came up, and he let her go. They carried Olav Livsson in to Ragna, and Cecilia had sat by him all night, but in the morning he died.

At last Cecilia fell asleep, and Eirik went and lay down in the farther bed.

He had no doubt that Jörund was distracted at times—he ought to be watched, perhaps put in bonds. And Cecilia could not live with him any longer. Either she must move out to Saltviken with her children, or he himself must go thither and take his brother-in-law with him, while his father returned home to Hestviken and stayed there with Cecilia—that he must decide when he had seen how things were on the spot.

Next morning at daybreak Eldrid stole in to change into her working-dress. Eirik said he would have to ride over to Hestviken that day—"and I fear it may be some while ere I come home to you."

"Ay, so I thought."

Cecilia insisted on riding back with Eirik, though both he and Eldrid begged her to stay at the Ness till her brother sent for her.

Not much was said between them on the journey; the roads were in a bad state, and Eirik could see too that Cecilia already repented of having said so much as she had.

When they came to Rundmyr, Eirik asked his sister and Svein to wait in the old houses that stood by the roadside; he would go on to Anki and Liv. He knew not what he should say to the poor folk. As he hurried on foot along the familiar path over the bog, he recalled how here he had played with fire, blinded by childish anger against his father, filled with a vain desire to make himself acquainted with all that was evil—and he himself had come off free, in a way, while those who had less sense and less guilt lay writhing, burned beyond help.

Two sheep were in the tussocky field, seeking what pasture there might be; they ran off as he came up. The door of the cottage was barred, and there was no answer to his knocking. And the little byre was open and deserted. Eirik's anger was kindled—had Jörund driven them out after all?

As they rode into the yard at the manor, the house-folk appeared from every door. They collected about Eirik as he sat on his horse, looked up at him, grave and anxious. But no one said anything, until Tore came forward and held the bay while Eirik dismounted.

"You have not come too soon either, Eirik!"

To that he could answer nothing. Then he asked: "Where is Jörund?"

At first there was none who answered; then someone murmured that he must be indoors; but at last a half-grown lad whispered fearfully—Jörund had gone down to the waterside awhile ago, he had seen—

As the men were about to follow him, Eirik forbade them, and to Svein, who handed him an axe, he said: "I have my sword, as you see—but I look not to have use for it."

He did not take the road, but went down the hill below the front of the dwelling-house. Between the spur on which the manor was built and the waterside there were only a few small scraps of arable land; the rest was rocky knolls and scrub, briers and juniper. Eirik crept along stealthily so that the madman should not see him coming. But as he went down he could not help seeing how much farther advanced the spring was out here by the sea; everywhere fresh green appeared among the withered grass in the crevices of rock, there were great red shoots on the brier bushes, and the goats that picked their way on the hillside had already recovered from the winter. And outside, the fiord gleamed in the afternoon sunshine.

He saw no one on the quay. But as soon as his steps were heard on the planks, a man dashed out from behind a shed, flew past him, bent almost double, and leaped straight into a boat that lay alongside. Eirik did not stop to think, but ran after him and jumped into the boat in his turn, just as Jörund had cast off. They both stood up in the boat. Jörund seized an oar and struck at his brother-in-law, and in an instant the boat capsized.

As soon as they were in the water the other flung his arms about Eirik; he guessed that Jörund was trying to hold him under —he had swallowed a mass of water, and his cloak and sword and heavy boots hindered him; he was dizzy and choking already. But in spite of that he was more used to falling into the sea than Jörund; he contrived to free himself from the other's hold and get his head above water. They were not far from the shore; he reached the slippery seaweed, clambered up, and sat down on the rock.

Eirik spat out the sea-water, took off his dripping cloak, and shook himself, so that the water splashed inside his boots.

"Can you get ashore by yourself?" he called out as he saw Jörund's head above water. "Or shall I come and help you?"

Then Jörund scrambled in; Eirik gave him a hand and pulled
him onto the rock. There they stood, with the water pouring
from them.

"I believe your madness is half feigning," said Eirik. "Do you
think thus to escape from your misdeeds more lightly?"

Jörund sent him the ugly look, like a scared rat, that Eirik had
seen before, and it made him wince inwardly.

"Anyhow, you failed again to take my life," said Jörund scornfully. As Eirik made no answer, his brother-in-law went on:
"I knew very well you have hated me and planned revenge and
sought my life all these years. Ever since that night at Baagahus,
when you had drunk your wits away and struck at Brynjulf Tistill
—and I saved you from the dungeon!"

It came back hazily to Eirik—an old memory of some half-forgotten brawl in the castle. They had both been mixed up in it, he
and Jörund, but he it was who had to pay the penalty, and Jörund had got off free.

"Let us go up now," he said impatiently; "we are standing here
like a pair of wet dogs."

"And since I found out what you meant by having such folk
settled at Rundmyr—and I can guess 'twas irksome for you and
your father that you were not suffered to pursue this noble trade
in peace—"

Eirik had drawn his sword and was drying it as best he could
with heather and tufts of grass. "If you do not go home, I will
baste you with the flat of this!"

"More likely you will run it through me, now you have me
unarmed." But he began to move.

Eirik did not know what to think: whether Jörund himself believed all this or was only feigning.

The house-folk in the yard stared at these two as they walked
up, all wet. Eirik bade one of them tell Cecilia that they must
have dry clothes. Then he followed Jörund, who went toward the
great room; as he came in he saw that they must be living here
now. He hung up his sword and seated himself, opposite Jörund;
and there they sat in silence.

But when in a little while Cecilia came in with her arms full of clothes, Jörund looked up with an ugly smile at his young wife. "Have *you* time to give *me* a thought? I did not think you could tear yourself from the corpse of your bold paramour, the six-legs that I chastised yesterday."

"Nay, Jörund," said Erik below his breath, but with a shake in his voice, "if you are never so mad—you can still go too far. That you could raise your hand against a poor cripple—"

" 'Tis her way to have a fancy for cripples, this wife of mine." Again he smiled, that horrid, imbecile smile. "The first one she played the whore with, he was a limping cripple too—"

A sudden change came over Cecilia's face; there was an icy green glint in her great bright eyes. Instinctively Eirik sprang to his sister's side.

"I saw it myself," the man went on, "the halting misshapen wretch—and she big with my own child—"

Cecilia's cold voice was sharp as a knife: "If you thought you saw aught unseemly—how was it you did not come forward till this halting cripple was so far away that he could not defend me when you trampled me underfoot?"

Eirik seized his sister by the arm. "Come out!" In a flash he had seen the depth of Cecilia's hatred of her husband, and he was afraid.

"Nay, I cannot bear the touch of Jörund's clothes," he said, when they had come into Ragna's house. "There are some old things of mine in the chest above in the loft.—Did you not once learn of Mærta," he asked as she turned to fetch his clothes, "how to brew draughts that send a man to sleep? Better mix something of the sort in his ale tonight. I will go over and find Father this very evening; and I am afraid to leave this house unless I can be sure that he is fast asleep."

When he had changed into some of his old clothes, he went up into the loft in which they had laid Olav Livsson on straw. There were two candles burning by the dead man's head, and he was wrapped in a good linen cloth. Eirik uncovered the face only: that too bore black marks of ill usage, but the narrow white features were peaceful, as though the lad had fallen asleep. Under the winding-sheet the body looked ungainly in its length, with its thin, withered limbs.

Eirik kissed the ice-cold forehead, knelt beside the bier, and recited the prayers and the litany for the dead; and those of the household who sat there murmured the responses: "*Ora pro nobis*" and "*Te rogamus, audi nos.*"

Afterwards he spoke in a low tone with the house-folk. They had not dared to send word to the priest, but they themselves had sat by the corpse the night before, and they promised to take turns at watching tonight as well. Eirik said that he would make provision for the funeral when he came back on the morrow, but now he must go out to Saltviken and speak with Olav. They had heard nothing of Arnketil and Liv; the houses at Rundmyr had stood empty since yestermorn, so they must have fled with all their flock from terror of Jörund, for he had threatened them with fire and murder.

He had asked Halstein to take supper in to Jörund and stay with him till he fell asleep—Halstein was a big, strong man. Now Eirik looked into the room before going down to the boat. Jörund was asleep. The door of the house could be locked from the outside; Eirik gave the key to Halstein and bade him bring Jörund his breakfast betimes in the morning.

When he landed in Saltviken it was already dusk. Nothing was left of the sunset but some copper-red edges below the grey clouds that lay over the west country. The sea was dark, crisped by the evening breeze, and broke against the faintly gleaming curve of the beach with the low rippling murmur he knew so well.

The gravel crunched under his feet and the wind whistled in the bent grass; on the scanty strip of pasture with its tall junipers lay some bullocks. Ah, he had not set foot here since the day he rode out to seek Gunhild. And now there was not a thing in his life that he had forgotten so completely as Gunhild.

He had expected the folk to be in bed at the farm, but as he came up between the fences he saw a dark figure standing by the gate—his father.

"It is I, Father"—instinctively he wished to forestall the old man, so he spoke hurriedly: "I come from Hestviken; it has come to such a pass there that Cecilia thought we must all take counsel what is to be done; she sent for me."

"It has long been so," said Olav. "But of you we heard never a word. It can hardly be worse now than it has been all this time, when you felt no call to see how things were at your own home."

But it was his father himself who had forbidden him to come. His youthful anger reverberated in Eirik: could his father never be fair and just toward him? But he controlled himself—to justify his actions would only make bad worse.

"I never heard other than good tidings—but you may be right; one can never trust hearsay."

Knut and Signe slept in the living-room, said Olav—they would have to go into the upper chamber, where his own bed was. It was dark as the grave in the room above, and Eirik stumbled and ran against things that lay scattered about. And in the darkness, with the door ajar to the spring night, they sat and talked together. Eirik told of what had happened at Hestviken and what was in his own mind: "Cecilia cannot live with Jörund after this."

"No, that must fall to you and your wife. And 'twill be a merry life at Hestviken when you three share it."

The bitter scorn in the voice that came out of the darkness put an end to Eirik's patience. "There has never been a merry life at Hestviken, Father. You wore down Mother—I know not whether of set purpose or not. Since then you have done all in your power to wear us down, till we were of the same mind, Cecilia and I— that anything was better than to dwell in the same house with you. Remember that, when she comes to live here—and be like a Christian man and not like a mountain troll to her children—even if they have mouse's ears."

"Would to God I had never seen you!" came in his father's voice, shaking with passion. "Would to Christ and our Lady I had let you stay where you were, at the back of beyond!"

"That was in other hands than yours—I came whither I was meant to come. But for that I say it would have been as well for me to have stayed there—and for you too: in one way or another it seems you were fated to deal unjustly with every child you have begotten."

"You I have not begotten! You are not my son!"

"Shame on you!" Eirik sprang up in his wrath. "What is this strain that is in such men as you and Jörund? When the world goes against you, you cry shame upon your own wives with infamous words—"

He heard Olav breathing hard in the darkness and restrained himself.

"But this is an ill season for us to take up our old quarrels, Father—and I beg you forgive me if I spoke too hotly. But you might spare Mother your insults"—he was on the point of firing up, but checked himself again. "Let us to bed now, Father—best that we set out for Hestviken as soon as it is day."

With that he rolled himself up on the bench. Sleep was impossible—his mind was in a whirl: the long day's ride, and Jörund, and his struggle with the madman in the water, and the dead lad in the loft, the deserted cottage at Rundmyr, and Cecilia—the sudden distortion of her pale features into the very face of naked hate, the icy glint in her deep clear eyes. Fear for his sister made him shudder—never could Cecilia stray on those false paths that Eldrid had followed, but it dawned upon him that hate knows many roads, and they all lead to the same goal at last.

Then he recalled his father's words—and he recalled his childhood's terror of one day being driven out as a bastard. Could it be that there had been some reason for his fear, that he had once heard words of which he had forgotten all but the fright they gave him—that his father had suspected his poor mother, persecuted her, as Jörund persecuted Cecilia, as he himself had persecuted a woman to death with shameful suspicions?

A longing for his home at the Ness came over him, an irresistible temptation to take flight. But thither he could never more return, he knew that. But at the same time he knew that if he and Eldrid were forced back into this foretaste of hell, he had a wife on whom he could rely. Never had he put so secure a trust in any human being as in her, whose soul had breasted torrents unbearable.

His father was not sleeping either, he felt sure. And now his anger gave way to pity for the old man.

Olav waked him—just as he had fallen asleep, he thought. The sun rose as they rounded the Horse. Then Olav broke the silence:

"When we come up," he said, "I must ride inland at once—Svein and I. They cannot be left out in the woods with all their children and Gudrun. I must get Anki and Liv back to Rundmyr first of all—you will herd Jörund meanwhile. He shall be made to pay the full penalty for the lad he slew and for their daughter whom he has debauched. Then, I think, next time his wit is about to fly from him, he will remember to catch it by the tail."

As Eirik held the boat against the pier for his father to step out, he heard Olav say: "What is afoot, Halstein?"

The house-carl looked strange and pale. He waited till Eirik had joined his father.

"Jörund is dead this night, Olav," he said in a low voice.

After a pause Olav asked: "Is it—?"

"The wound is from a dagger. Straight in the breast. More I know not."

"He was wild and out of his wits," said Eirik hastily. "God have mercy on his soul—he cannot have been in his right mind when he did it."

The house-carl gave him a look but made no answer.

Father and son went together into the living-room, Halstein followed them. He had not touched the body. Jörund lay in the south bed—his great naked body with the left leg and arm and shoulder hanging out, the head bent to one side: it looked as if he had tried to get up. There was a wound in the left breast below the nipple, and blood, but not very much, on the white skin, clinging to the tuft of curly hair. On the bench by the bedside still stood the food that Halstein had brought in when he found him.

Eirik was almost as pale as the dead man: in his father's face he read nothing but the same hate as he had seen in the eyes of Jörund's wife. This had been his friend—the thought of the other's derangement and ignominy and miserable death broke his heart as he lifted the ice-cold body and disposed it with the head on the pillow; he tried to close the dead eyes and press together the nostrils.

Olav raised the coverlet, felt about the body. "Where is the dagger?"

The wound was three-cornered, as though made by one of those foreign daggers with a triangular blade; it was clean, and of such size that the weapon must have been thrust in with force right up to the hilt.

Halstein crossed the room quietly and barred the door.

"I must say what has to be said—you are the next friends of the dead man—and it was I who was to answer for him. But when Eirik gave me the key yestereven, I knew not there was another way into this house—"

"Another way—" Father and son said it together.

"When I came in this morning," whispered the house-carl, pointing to the north bed, which had been Eirik's when he lived at home, "it was all tumbled in a mess of straw and bedclothes, half across the floor, and the hatch was not quite closed, for some straw was caught in it."

The two stood stiff and speechless. The north-western corner of the house did not rest upon the rock, but upon a wall of masonry, and when Olav Ribbung built it after the fire, in the time of the Birchlegs, he had made a postern here toward the sea, with a hatch leading to it from the bottom of the north bed. In Olav Audunsson's time this secret passage had never been used, but it was certainly known to the oldest members of the household, and Eirik himself had sometimes tried it when a boy.

He saw his father was leaning his hand on the table, stooping lower and lower—it looked as if the old man would fall forward in a heap. Eirik took hold of him—Olav half raised his head, and the grey, scarred old face looked as ancient as sin; the mouth was open, but the eyes were close shut. He raised one hand, gently pushed Eirik aside, and went toward the bed, swaying like a blind man.

He bared the breast of the corpse again, fingered the wound, and pushed aside some bloody hair that clung to one of its corners. Then he felt again all over the bed, searching for the dagger.

When he turned round, his son saw that the sweat ran down his forehead below the soft white hair. He looked hither and thither as though at a loss.

"Father?" said Eirik inquiringly, seized with anxiety—but he could not guess what this was.

Olav was moving away, with a strange padding gait, like an animal caught in a pitfall.

"Father," said Eirik again, "we must go and find Cecilia."

Olav supported himself against the doorpost of the closet, which was carved with the figure of Gunnar:

"Go you— I shall come—"

"We must make fast the door," replied Eirik in a low voice, "till we have collected men to view the corpse." He saw the terror in his father's eyes. "Remember, his brothers must be fetched."

Olav gave one loud groan. Then he went out, following his son.

· · ·

When they entered the women's house, the widow sat crouching in the farthest corner of the room. Ragna, the old serving-woman, was with her. Cecilia shrank yet closer to the wall, staring at the men with eyes that were wild with terror.

Eirik went forward to embrace her. She resisted:

"Have you seen him?" she whispered.

Eirik nodded, and took her in his arms in spite of her efforts; she was trembling as though seized with spasms. Then he lifted her up like a child, carried her to the bed, and laid her on it. And the father stood watching the two with the same look on his face, which seemed to have been struck inhuman.

Cecilia lay trembling. Little by little her convulsions ceased and she lay still, but her eyes were just as wild and staring as before. Her father had seated himself on the bench; as though absently he still held his old barbed axe between his knees, with his hands resting on its head.

After a while Eirik went out. He called together the men and gave them orders: one was to ride first to Rynjul for Torgrim and Una, then to summon men hither, neighbours who could view the corpse; another he sent up to the churchtown to ask the priest to come at evening and keep vigil over the two bodies. The slain and the slayer—for he would have to persuade Sira Magne that Jörund might be given Christian burial—the deed was done in madness. The message to Gunnarsby he could send on the morrow.

It was some time before he had given his men all instructions. Then it struck him that he must try to make Cecilia take something, if it were-but a drink of milk. He went in with the maid who carried the bowl. His sister still lay with staring eyes, and his father sat as before.

She put her lips to the bowl, but pushed it away at once. "I cannot—'twill make me sick—"

Eirik seated himself on the edge of the bed. The serving-women had gone out.

"Sister!" said Eirik all at once. "If you could but weep!"

"Ah—if I could," she replied tonelessly.

At that her father raised his head. "Would I could help you to *that*! Would I could help you to it ere it be too late! Better you were burned alive at the stake than that you should fare as I have fared! Never believe you will benefit your children by holding your peace and hardening your heart and soul. Eirik spoke more truly than he knew when he said it had been better for you to live with a mountain troll who devours Christian children than with me!"

The son and the daughter stared at him, uncomprehending.

"I too was young then," Olav went on; "not many years older than you are now, Cecilia. And 'twas not so grave a thing as this. My deed—I know not if it were a crime; myself I thought to have right on my side. But I concealed it. At first I thought, when the time came that I *could* do so, I would make confession, repent, and purge my sin. Now the time for that is long past. It has corrupted me, and all that I have touched and taken in my hands has been tainted with my corruption."

Still Cecilia did not understand, but Eirik:

"Jesus Christ—Father!" he whispered, pale about the mouth.

"Now I *cannot* repent," said Olav firmly. "The light that I once had has been taken from me—my repentance is now as the sight of a man whose eyes have been put out. But now I will make my confession nevertheless; Cecilia—you and I will go together, and one fate shall fall upon us both."

Then she understood. She sat up in the bed with a start.

"I!—Think you that I—!" Her voice was wild and sharp.

Eirik had leaped up and stood in front of his sister. "Father—stop!"

"Then the same fate can fall upon us both," Olav repeated. "If you must flee the country, we will go together."

"With you!" His daughter shuddered. "Rather will I do as Jörund has done!"

Olav asked: "That foreign dagger you had of me once, when you were a little maid—where have you that, Cecilia?"

"In my coffer." She stepped out of bed, went across the room to her chest; her brother saw that she was now trembling again, but her mouth was hard set and her eyes flashed. She took from the chest a little coffer and turned out on the bench all that was in it—brooches and chains, a little coral rosary, several knives.

"It is not here. Perhaps Jörund took it," she said; her teeth were chattering.

"We can go in and search once more," said Olav quietly.

"No!" she shrank back.

"Dare you go in to him with me?"

"No—" Cecilia bowed her head. "I must not look upon a corpse, as I am now," she whispered almost inaudibly.

"If you are innocent, it can hurt neither you nor it."

Her whole body seemed to give way. Her father went on:

"If you are innocent, then go in with me, lay your hand on his breast—"

"No." She shrieked: "I *will* not—"

"Monster!"

Eirik sprang to his sister's side.

As Olav took his daughter by the wrist, she started back, tried to tear herself free, but slipped and fell. She lay on her knees with bent head, struggling with the other hand to loosen her father's grip. To Eirik it looked as if he dragged her over the floor.

Then he seized Kinfetch, rushed at his father with the axe raised in both hands. Olav saw it, let go his daughter—and, straightening himself, he raised his forehead to the blow—

But she too had seen it, flung herself against her brother's hip; Eirik stumbled, and the steel rang upon the stone curb of the hearth.

"Eirik!" Cecilia's piercing cry reached him.

He looked into his father's bloodshot eyes and felt that they gave him his death: it was not hate, it was not anger, it was not the wild and tense excitement of a while ago. He knew not what it was—these were the eyes of a man who came from a land that has never been seen by the living.

The axe fell from his hand. He flung his hands before his face, staggered to the bench and dropped upon it, sat half turned to the wall, with his head hidden in his arms.

He heard that one went out at the door, and at the same moment Cecilia lightly touched his shoulder.

"Eirik—how could you!" She looked as if she could not bear much more. "He is our father—"

"Yes." He moaned faintly without looking up. "I know it. The Lord have mercy on us. I know it."

Then he raised his face to her for a moment. "I know it. I would have killed him. I would. My father."

She broke into violent sobbing and threw herself down beside him. With her face pressed against her brother's dark hair Cecilia wept and wept, till he drew her down into his embrace and,

clinging to each other, they wept with terror at the life in which
they were entrapped.

But at last Eirik pushed her from him. "I must go and find
him."

As he went out, she followed, took him by the hand, and
squeezed it—they went together like two children scared out of
their wits. Outside the door of the great house he hesitated a moment; then they went slowly on, hand in hand, as though seeking
their way in a wilderness. When they had reached the end of the
houses, they looked down and saw Olav just rowing away from
the pier.

"Eirik—what will he do?" she whispered.

He shook his head. "I know not."

"Eirik," she whispered again, "could you grasp what he meant
—what has he done?"

Again he shook his head. "I know not—"

Their father was rowing northward round the Bull. Then the
two turned and went slowly back to the houses. Outside the door
of the great house Eirik paused.

"He shall not lie there alone like a heathen dog. I will go in to
him—"

Cecilia caught her brother's arm in a close embrace.

"Then I will go with you. I am not afraid if you are with me—"

Cecilia felt that a shock ran through her brother's frame—a
strange look came into his face—he too must have doubted. But
she would not admit the thought. So brother and sister went in
together to the dead man.

20

Olav had never rowed up to Oslo before. Now and again he
rested on his oars for a while; the water gurgled underneath the
drifting boat. The fiord was calm today, and there was not a craft
to be seen.

A light mist had floated up from the south, turning water and
sky to grey; the wooded hills grew dark, and the new green of
oak and ash made feathery patches against the blue-black firs.
Olav plied his oars again.

The flaming terror that had caught his spirit had now burned itself out; he was tired and drab within. He was now on the way to do the thing from which his whole life had been a flight, and this time he knew he would do it; he knew this as surely as he had known all the other times that he would flee from it as soon as he saw a way out. But his soul was grey and cold as a corpse.

He had heard a thousand times that God's mercy is without bounds, and in secret he had relied on this: what he fled from was always there, waiting for him when he took courage to turn, since it was all that was outside time and change: God's arms spread out on the cross, ready to enfold him, grace streaming from the five wounds, the drooping head that looked down over all creation, watching and waiting, surrounded by Mary and all the saints with prayers that rose like incense from an unquenchable censer. His servants were ever ready with power to unlock his fetters; the Bread of Life was ever upon the altar. God was without bounds.

But he himself was not, he saw that now. It was too late, after all. The bounds that were in himself had set and hardened into stone—like the stones folk had shown him here and there about the country which had once been living beasts and men.

Now he *could* no longer repent. There was no longer any love of God within him, nor any longing to find his way back; now he would rather have gone on and on away from God, everlastingly. That was hell. That was the realm of eternal torment, he knew it, but the home of torment had become his home.

The game was played out, and now he might indeed confess and do the penance imposed by the Bishop—it would be of no avail. Absolution cannot absolve him who has no repentance within him. He had lost his faith of a Christian—though he knew that what he had once believed was all that is and was and shall be, and he himself was what was not; but so many times had he chosen himself, and that which was naught, that he had lost sight and sense for that which was Life.

But for Cecilia's sake he would do it nevertheless. He had learned to know his daughter in these last years; and now it seemed as if he had been long aware that she might end by doing a deed like this. He ought to have acted before.

Eirik had something of this in him; he saw that now. He had hated as a travesty of himself the changeling's mendacity, hated

his lax nature, hated him for never being able to carry through
any of the intentions he had formed. Ah, yes, he had married
that adulteress. Eirik too had done that. And he had loved Eirik,
who lied and boasted and followed every fancy and turned again
from every path he had set out on—loved this incubus that he had
got on his back, this goblin that had sucked blood of him till they
were as father and son after the flesh. The murdered man's son
had avenged his father as secretly as he himself had slain Teit.

He thought he had seen all this in a flash when Eirik rushed
at him with the axe lifted to strike and he had held up his head to
the blow—with something akin to joy he had seen the end coming. Then the axe had been turned aside in the hand of the son
avenger.

And he knew that this had happened for Cecilia's sake. *How* it
was to benefit his daughter he could not tell. But she was young—
she had a long life before her in which to be hardened and die,
if she did as he had done. He saw the horror of what he wished
to bring about—and he thought of the three little sons who would
grow up as children of a mother who had killed their father. But
worse still that they should grow up under her hands while she
carried such a secret within her. In one way or another he knew
it would be the saving of them all if he now laid at Cecilia's feet
the corpse he had dragged about so long: Behold—and take good
heed, ere it be too late for you to do the like.

The afternoon was far spent when he rowed westward along
the quays of the townsmen: Claus Wiephart's quay with his warehouse—where he was wont to land—the quay of Mickle Yard, of
Clement's Church, Jon's quay—on to that of the Bishop's palace.
And he gave a cold and snappish answer when a young fellow
came down and called out to him discourteously that he must
not put in there with his boat. Olav replied that he intended to
tie up his boat here, and that he had business in the Bishop's castle
—as he spoke he remembered that neither in clothes nor in person
was he fit for a visit to town, and it vexed him as he crossed the
green.

Half an hour later he stood in the narrow square between the
Bishop's palace and the wall of Halvard's churchyard.

The Bishop was at the point of death. None had time to listen
to him or answer his questions—folk hurried hither and thither
in the palace: the Lord Helge's sickness had come upon him so

suddenly, and with the Easter festival at hand. True, tomorrow was Palm Sunday, he had forgotten that.

He had never thought that *this* could happen—that when at last he was ready to throw down his arms, there would be no one to receive his surrender. And now he felt that his deathlike calm was nothing but extreme suspense, for now he was cold and trembling—and in despair at being forced to take the plunge once more; this postponement seemed to him unbearable.

Olav knew not what to do with himself. The mist had condensed into a fine drizzle. The great stone buildings around the square—the wall of the Bishop's palace and the churchyard fence and the mighty mass of the cathedral with its heavy towers and leaden roof glistening in the rain—loomed even greater in the dark weather. But the bursting poplars that reached over the churchyard wall seemed to curl up their new and fragrant leaves, and the grass grew luxuriantly among the cobblestones of the pavement.

He could not face going out to Claus, sitting and listening to the merchant's chat. Nor to the armourer's either. He had only been in Oslo once since Galfrid's daughter was married to Björn. They had one child—unless there were more since—but it was as though he scarcely dared to hear of this grandson of his; if he had been a leper he could not have been more afraid of thrusting himself into Björn's life.

A church bell began to ring close by with loud clangour—it was from St. Olav's Convent; the tower rose from the end of the churchyard wall. At that moment two preaching friars came round the corner; with their heads well shrouded in their hoods they hurried homeward to shelter from the rough weather, their black capes fluttering away from the white frocks. Olav watched them go; the short one must be old Brother Hjalm, but he would hardly know him now, it was so many years since he had set foot in their convent.

Olav followed the same way; he could at any rate go into St. Olav's Church and so pass the time. Afterwards he would have to think of a place to spend the night, where he would not be forced to speak of what had happened at home in Hestviken.

In the church door he was met by a great sandy dog that came rushing toward him, followed by the lay brother who had chased it out; they nearly ran into each other. "Nay, is it you, Olav Audunsson?" said the monk joyfully. "We have not seen you here since— But you are come to look for Father Finn, I can guess— ay, he will be glad to meet you—such a good friend of his father you were, I mind me. Ay, now he is preaching to the townsmen, the sermon that he gave us in Latin this morning—" the talkative lay brother nodded and slipped through the side door into the choir.

It dawned on Olav that the tall, middle-aged monk who stood on the steps of the choir preaching—he must be the second son of Arnvid Finnsson. The last time he saw Finn he was a pupil in the school at Hamar. Now the close-cropped hair that bordered the monk's shining scalp was silvery grey, the narrow, weather-beaten face marked with wrinkles.

He did not resemble his father—none of Arnvid's sons had done so; they were handsome, as he had heard their mother was. Father Finn was erect and thin; he stood very still as he preached, clad in white, with the heavy black cape over his shoulders; he had a fine, clear, and gentle voice:

"—but that part which lay buried in the earth is to remind us of God's invisible power and hidden counsel. That part may be likened to the root of the cross; unseen by the eyes of men, it bears the trunk of the cross, its branches, and its precious fruit. Such tokens are given us that we may be able to hold it fast in our minds that our salvation has sprung from the root, which is God's unseen counsel.

"But what availeth it us, good brethren, to interpret in words the token of the cross if we do not show in our works that we have interpreted aright the words of our Lord: 'He that taketh not his cross and followeth after Me is not worthy of Me'? He taketh up his cross and followeth in His footsteps who feareth not to suffer pains and hardships for love of God and his even Christian and his own soul. We may bear the cross in two ways, with our body or with our soul—"

It was a *sermo crucis*, such as was usually preached in the conventual churches during Lent. Olav looked about him—it was long since he had been in this church. The nave was long and narrow and somewhat gloomy now that no candles were lighted; the windows were darkened by the great ash trees of Halvard's churchyard and the mass of the cathedral beyond. There were not many folk either—under the misrule of the last Prior the convent of St. Olav had lost much of its ancient reputation.

Father Finn Arnvidsson's sermon was intended in the first place for the brethren of the order, Olav could understand; he had so much to say about penance and discipline:

"—in this way every man must beware of himself, for here lurketh the danger which is inward pride: causing us to look down on those of our brethren who are less able to bear fasting, watching, frost, and scourging. We cannot render like again to our Lord for the pain He suffered, scourging for scourging, wound for wound—in chastising our own body we must take good heed lest we deem ourselves to be vying with Him. But if others offer to scourge us, to wound or use us despitefully and deliver us into the hands of the tormentors, then must we bear such things with gladness, remembering that we are thereby vouchsafed an honour of which we are unworthy."

A scud of rain lashed the windows of the church; Olav heard that a wind had sprung up.—A thought had dawned within him—should he tell Finn Arnvidsson what it was that had brought him to Oslo? Although his case was such that he could make no valid confession to any other than the Bishop, unless he were at the point of death—he might say to Finn that he was here to confess an old blood-guiltiness, a secret slaying committed at the very time of their last parting, when Finn was yet a boy; he remembered now that he had bidden the lad farewell outside the schoolhouse on the day of his setting out for Miklebö. That would be the same as breaking down the bridge behind him.

"We bear our cross in the spirit when our heart is grieved for the sins and sorrows of other men, as Saint Paul maketh mention: 'Who is weak, and I am not weak?' saith he; 'who is offended, and I burn not?' Good brethren, it is not for us to wonder whether the Lord hath laid it upon us to bear the sins and sorrows of others or to atone for the transgressions of our brethren, though He hath made all atonement for us all. But when we are tempted to ask why then must we atone, we ought to remember that He bears heaven and earth as an orb in His hand, but He deigned to lay aside the royal robe of His omnipotence and array Himself in the poor kirtle of Adam. He fainted by the way as He bore the cross out of Jorsalborg, that a great boon might be bestowed upon Simon of Cyrene, in that he was held worthy to help his God and bear the cross with Him. Blessed above all other men who have lived upon earth was this countryman. But it is given to all of us to taste of Simon's blessedness, when God calleth us unworthy sinners out of the multitude standing by the wayside to watch the passage of the cross, and biddeth us share its burden with Him—"

No sooner was the sermon over than the old lay brother who had recognized Olav came back. Bustling and loquacious, he led the way to the parlour; now he would go and tell Father Finn.

It was a little square room with a groined vault; a narrow pointed door stood open to the cloister. Olav went and stood in the doorway, watching the rain, which was now pouring down upon the bare green carpet of the cloister garth; the rain came in under the arcade, sending up splashes from the stone-paved floor. A strong south-westerly gale had set in, and well it was; this early spring had made him uneasy—it was not to be relied on so long as no rain came to carry away the snow in the woods.

The heavy black clouds that came drifting over the sky made the evening dark for the time of year, and there was a pale and shifting glimmer in the air from all the wet leaden roofs. A soughing came from the great ash trees, whose tops, tufted with blossom, towered above the ridge of the church roof; the wind whistled and shrieked in the windlass of the well in the middle of the grass plot. Then the bells of Halvard's Church began, with a hollow booming, the shrill little bell of the convent church joined in, and soon all the church bells in town were ringing.

Behind the pillars on the other side of the garth came a white monk—Father Finn Arnvidsson walked briskly toward him with outstretched hand. "Hail to you, Olav Audunsson—'twas a kindly thought to come and seek me out!"

They sat in the parlour—they had not seen each other since the one was a boy and the other a young man. That was more than thirty years ago.

Olav asked after Finn's brothers and after his kinsfolk, the Steinfinnssons and Haakon Gautsson's children from Berg. Finn replied that he could give no tidings that were new: he had lately come to Norway from a journey in foreign lands which had lasted two years, and before that he had been subprior in Nidaros, but now he was to go home to his convent at Hamar.

"But now it is almost the hour of complin. Shall you be in town for a time?"

Olav said he did not know. "My son-in-law is lately dead—"

"Where do you lodge—nay, surely you have a house of your own here in Oslo?"

When he heard that Olav had not yet secured a lodging for the night, Father Finn thought that he might sleep there. The guest-house was full, but there were some guests' cells in the upper story —he would go and ask the Prior:

"I have many things to set in order in these days, ere I set out for home, but I would gladly have more speech with you—you were my father's best friend. And it will be easier to find occasion for converse if you dwell under this roof."

Olav sat in the guest-chamber eating his evening porridge. There was no other in the room but a sick man who lay in one of the beds, groaning in his sleep; the other guests had gone over to the church to hear the singing. Olav pushed the bowl from him, leaned the back of his head against the wall, and stared into the light of the candle; from the church came the notes of the choir, and outside the rain splashed and the wind howled.

Then came the sound of footsteps on the flags of the cloister— the monks returning from church. And a young lay brother with a lantern in his hand stood in the doorway and signed to him: now silence would reign here till after early mass next morning.

The lay brother went before him up a creaking stair and along a passage, opened a door, and set the lantern on the floor of the cell.

It was a tiny room with grey stone walls. There was a narrow sleeping-bench against one wall, and a desk with a kneeling-rail and a crucifix under a little bow-window, which was closed by a shutter with a parchment pane. The shutter shook and rattled in the wind. Olav opened it and looked out into the stormy spring night—over the shining wet roof that covered the cloister, down upon the green garth with the well and the windlass, which creaked with every gust. It was so long since he had been in a room as high up as this that he felt as though imprisoned in a tower.

He took off his outer garments and lay down on the bench.

Sleep he could not; he lay listening to every sound from the blustering and rainy night outside.

The night before, he had lain at Saltviken—knowing nothing of Cecilia's mad deed. 'Twas no longer ago than that. As he tried to gather up in his memory all that had happened since he met Eirik by the fence late in the evening, the hurry of events seemed like a headlong plunge. He had come to the end of the road and over the edge.

His thoughts went to the words Finn had spoken of Simon of Cyrene—had he been thinking of his father? Arnvid had been a man who suffered himself to be called out of the crowd to succour anyone who was driven past to his doom. And it must have been for this reason that he had always held Arnvid to be more than other men. Arnvid was so stout-hearted that he was not afraid to bend his back if any man would lay his cross upon him. He had not been afraid to follow so closely in his Lord's footsteps that he had his share of folk's spitting and abuse.

Had he himself been as fearless as Arnvid, then he would have proclaimed the slaying of Teit at the first house he came to. And he had condemned Ingunn to hide her child far away in the wilderness, deprived of rights, of name, of kindred—till he saw that the wrong she had done was breaking her down, and he tried to mend one injustice with another. He should have defended the boy's right from the first—the right to be called Ingunn Steinfinnsdatter's son, though a bastard, to be his mother's heir and to look to his mother's husband for support and protection. Had he been as Arnvid, he would only have asked what was right; would have been man enough to live with a seduced wife, to honour her to whom he had plighted his troth before God, and to love her to whom he had given his affection since he had the wit to prefer one person to another.

Nay, he might have had the courage to hearken to his own conscience when it pleaded for Teit: "the fool knows not what he has done, he is naught but a witless whelp as you yourself were when you went to your bridal bed ere you were out of your nonage.

"But, the sin once committed, he would in any case have had the courage to stand by it: while I cleared myself by lying of the injury I did my foster-father, when I was young and wild and thoughtless; but the man who was so thoughtless as to injure me, him I struck down. For I thought I could not live if another had stained my honour and I let it go unavenged. I thought it easier to live besmirched if I myself had stained my honour—so long as none knew of the stain. For such a cause as this I turned Judas against my Lord, armed me with the hardest sins, if but they might be hard enough to weigh upon my weakness like an armour."

Such fear had he had of the judgment of men—he who had believed himself indifferent to what folk might think of him. For he did not desire to wield a chieftain's power over them, nor to be a rich man among them, if he should use craft and suppleness to gain riches, nor friendship with any man whom he could not like outright, nor such good fortune as makes a man fat and lazy—he had only desired to stand among them as the oak stands above the brushwood.

And he saw that such was the lot intended for him. God had given him as a heritage from loyal, brave, and pious forefathers that which He has promised to the offspring of the righteous: a mind and a heart that hated cruelty, that feared not luckless days, that faced any foe undaunted—only those he loved could scare him into anything.

"God, my God, who lovest us all, who loved me—whom I once loved; had I chosen Thee, I should have chosen my deepest love."

He saw that in a way he had had a right to judge of himself as he did—he had only forgotten that he held all that was good in him as a vassal holds his fief under the sovereignty of the King. And he had rebelled, had broken his faith and laid waste his land.

He *should* have grown as the oak, patient and spreading, with light and shelter for all who sought its wide embrace. Such was his destiny, nor had he been able to grow otherwise—his inward hurt had only cankered the pith in him, so that he had become hollow and withered and barren. Not one had he been able to protect to any purpose: from Ingunn herself down to such as Anki and Liv and their children, he had tried to act as a providence for them, and it had been in vain. He had wasted his wealth in the struggle with his rightful Lord—but as a man who is born open-handed, generous even with stolen goods, he had taken in all who came to his door—though all he offered was a beggar's feast and a mumper's wedding.

Simon of Cyrene—now he recalled that the image of this man

had been shown to him once before, many years ago in England;
then he had seen in a dream his own soul wounded to death, and
he had been compelled to stand outside the band of poor men
who went forward to receive the body of the Lord.

How, he wondered, would he have felt on Easter morn, that
countryman from Cyrene, if he had refused when they would
have him bear the cross, if he had slipped away and hidden himself in the crowd of those who mocked?

He too had had children—Alexander and Rufus were their
names. He had once heard what became of these sons of Simon,
saints and crowned martyrs.

Olav still lay awake when he heard the distant singing from
the church. As he listened to the strains of matins, drowned now
and then by gusts of wind, he fell asleep.

Morning was far advanced when he awoke. There was singing
again—they were blessing the palms, he knew, and then would
come the procession round the church. Olav still lay abed—once
more he was assailed by bitter regret, that he had left home in the
clothes he stood in. When at last he came down in his coarse old
everyday clothes and heavy boots, the service was already far
advanced; the words rang out from the choir:

"Passio Domini nostri Jesu Christi secundum Matthœum." [5]

From where he stood he could not see the priests who were
singing. And today was the long lesson, so he could not follow
it from memory, but only knew some fragments. Wrapped in
his old brown cloak he stood far back by the door, and as the
clear and powerful male voice intoned the gospel, rising and falling and rising again, he was carried along past words and names
he recognized—*Pascha*—*tradetur ut crucifigatur*—*Caiaphas*—bea-
cons that told him where they were now. Jesus and the disciples
were in Bethany, in *domo Simonis leprosi*, and sat at meat; now
Mary of Magdala came in at the door, bearing a box of ointment,
that she might pour out the most precious thing she could find
before God. And the voice of Judas snarled at the woman with
miserly scorn.

Then another voice, fuller and richer, answered with the

[5] On Palm Sunday the 26th and 27th chapters of St. Matthew's gospel are
sung (on Tuesday in Holy Week the story of the Passion according to St.
Mark, on Wednesday according to St. Luke, and on Good Friday according to St. John).

Master's own words as He took Mary under His protection and praised her loving-kindness.

Olav waited for the words he knew, the words that were branded upon his heart with red-hot irons—would they not come soon? They were not so far away. Ah, now they were coming— now He was sending the disciples into the city to make ready the supper. Now—

His heart beat against his chest as though it would burst as the great, rich voice pealed from the choir:

"*Amen dico vobis, quia unus vestrum me traditurus est—*"

The voice of the Evangelist followed with a short strophe, and then the whole chorus of disciples broke in, harsh and agitated:

"*Numquid ego sum, Domine?*"

Olav felt the sweat break out over his whole body as the voice of Christ rang out. And then they came, the words that were burned into his heart:

"*Væ autem homini illi, per quem Filius hominis tradetur: Bonum erat ei si natus non fuisset homo ille.*"

The evangelist sang: "*Respondens autem Judas qui tradidit eum, dixit*"—and the loud voice of Judas followed:

"*Numquid ego sum, Rabbi?*"

The voice of Christ replied: "*Tu dixisti.*"

Olav had bowed his head upon his breast and thrown the flap of his cloak over his shoulder, hiding half his face. The coarse homespun smelt of stable and boat and fish. Among the crowd in festival attire he alone was unprepared.

Words that he knew flowed on in the chant. Now they were going to the Mount of Olives—but Olav seemed to be watching from afar: as Judas stood somewhere in the city, spying after them. Now he was thrust out, now all his companions knew what had only been known to God and himself when he came in and sat at supper with the others.

The visions floated farther and farther into the darkness. Among the trees God Himself falls upon His face: *Tristis est anima mea usque ad mortem*— But the disciples are asleep and take no heed. From a gate in the city wall come the watchmen with torches and flashing spears, while Judas goes before and shows the way. Saint Peter leaps up out of his sleep; in the boldness of youth he snatches his sword from the sheath to fling himself between his Master and His enemies—lays about him like a fool, strikes off a servant's ear—and when he sees that they are overpowered and hears the calm answer of the Lord, to him incomprehensible, he throws down his sword and runs away; they all run, all the disciples who but a while ago promised so stoutly. Christ is left standing alone, holds out His hands unresisting, lets them bind Him—passing comprehension. But who has seen that part of the cross which was in the ground, who knows the root of the cross—?

Round about Olav men and women stole a chance of sitting or kneeling awhile—there was no end to it, this hateful arraignment by men of their Maker, the voice of the people in shrill chorus: "*Crucifigatur!*" And again: "*Crucifigatur!*" The long road out of the city up to the hill of Calvary, the horror of the crucifixion—and the reviling, which did not cease even there.

After the last loud cry from the cross, when He gave up the ghost, the singing stopped abruptly and the congregation sank on its knees, as though struck down by this dead silence.

Strangely quiet it sounded when the Evangelist's voice began again, assuming now the customary Sunday tone, and sang the narrative of the grave and of the Pharisees' timid consultation with Pilate.

The mass followed upon the gospel as though out of a gate—manifesting again the vast and awful mysteries of man's deceit and God's mercy. It was Holy Week advancing upon mankind, Maundy Thursday and Good Friday; Saint Mark and Saint Luke and Saint John would each in turn bear witness. And Easter Day on the far side of this week of evil seemed infinitely distant.

When Olav came to the guest-house, he found it so crowded with folk that he hesitated to go in. Two lay brothers hurried forward with steaming dishes, followed by two more with cans of ale: it was past midday and the good folk of the inn were pale and pinched about the nose and hungry as wolves.

One of the lay brothers was the same young man who had conducted him to the guest's cell the evening before. As soon as he saw Olav he took him in hand, made room, and pushed him into the place of honour—the franklin was a friend of the Prior of Hamar. He tried to force food and drink on Olav, but Olav could get nothing down.

As soon as decency allowed, he rose from the table, went up

to his cell, and lay on his bed. He fell asleep at once and slept till the young lay brother woke him: "Now Father Finn has time—"

When Olav came down into the parlour, where Finn Arnvidsson sat waiting, there were several others in the room: two young monks, so much alike that Olav guessed them to be twins, sat there with a woman, their mother, and some young maids. The whole band of kinsfolk had the same fiery-red hair and freckled complexion, upturned noses, and pale-blue eyes; their talk was of news from home—Olav heard it with half an ear while he listened to what Father Finn told him of his father's last years.

Olav sat with eyes cast down; his hands clutched and clutched at his dagger, he pulled it half out of its sheath and thrust it back again. Then he cut short the other in the middle of his calm and quiet narration:

"Ay, Finn—your father knew something of that which I am now to tell you. He counselled me, before he died, to do that for which I am now come." Without thinking, Olav rose to his feet and stood erect, and as he raised his voice the company on the opposite bench ceased their talk and listened to him:

"I once slew a man in my youth and I have never confessed it. Arnvid, your father, knew of it, but at that time, I would not do what he begged of me—confess my blood-guiltiness and purge my sin by penance. But this that lately happened in my home—my son-in-law has been killed in his sleep and we know not who did it—this drove me hither to seek the Bishop. I knew not that *you* were in Oslo."

Finn Arnvidsson had also risen. They stood looking each other in the face. Then Father Finn slipped away to the other company, who stood staring, and whispered a few words to the two young monks. A moment later all the red-haired folk were out of the room, and Olav stood alone with Arnvid's son.

The monk laid his hands on his shoulders.

"God be praised," he said warmly.

"Did your father speak to you of this?" asked Olav, looking up into the other's face. Finn was a much taller man.

"No. But now I understand much better one thing and another with which he charged me—that I should say a Miserere daily for all men who are burdened with an unshriven sin, for instance--and other things besides. God be praised that you have

now resolved to do this.—But you should not have spoken of it in
the hearing of those strange women."

"I am not sure that I had said it to you if we two had been
alone. But now I have broken down all bridges behind me." Olav
smiled faintly.

The monk stared at him a moment. Then he nodded in silence.

"Now that the lord Helge is at the point of death," said Olav,
"and none can tell me who acts in his stead—whether official or
penitentiary or what he may be called—"

"I myself will find that out tomorrow, Olav."

"But now I will go. I would rather be alone now—"

"Yes indeed. I understand."

They took each other firmly by the hand. Olav went up, lay
down on his bed, and fell asleep at once. He slept till the young
lay brother came up with his supper. Olav ate and lay down again.
God, my God, how good it is to have thrown down all bridges
behind one!

When he came down into the cloisters next morning, on his
way to church, Finn Arnvidsson came toward him.

"Olav—know you not that so long as you have not confessed
this sin in lawful manner, you must not enter the church? I remind you of this, for, you know, you will only have more to
answer for if you set at naught the interdict—"

Olav stopped, overwhelmed. Assuredly he knew it—he was
banned just as wholly as if excommunication had been pronounced on him in church. But so long had he defied the ban,
stealing in where he had no right to be and committing sacrilege,
that at last he had forgotten.—He answered nothing, turned back
and walked down the cloister.

Father Finn followed him, took him by the arm. "You must remember, Olav—ay, you know Latin, I think?"

"A little I know—"

"You must remember these words of Saint Ambrose: '*Novit
omnia Deus, sed exspectat vocem tuam, non ut puniat sed ut
ignoscat.* God knows all things, but He waits to hear your voice,
not to chastise, but to forgive.'"

Olav nodded.

On coming to his cell he threw himself on his knees at the little
desk with the crucifix.

Assuredly he had known it—but he had forgotten. This was the first thing he would have to bear—that he must stay outside the church door. He saw that it was there he had sought nourishment during all these years—as the outlawed Danish lords had lived by making descents on their own land.

He took the crucifix from the desk and kissed the image of the King.

"Lord—I am not worthy that Thou shouldst take pity on my repentance and show me grace!"

He had made his confession mentally so many times, the whole chain of his life's sins—from the time when his pride was young and childishly thin-skinned; he had faced the men on whom his boy's heart was set with white lies and petty deceit that they might think him a man. In the beginning it had meant no more than that he was afraid they might smile if they found that he was only a young, hot-headed, obstinate and weak-spirited lad, while he wished to be taken for one who was resourceful, prudent, and strong. But he had carried this playing with truth to such length that he became a secret slayer, perjured and sacrilegious; link by link he had wrought his fetters, stone by stone he had built his own dungeon. Till it had come to this: that every time his thoughtless daring sprang up, the fetters held it back, and every time his heart would fly out to meet all who called it forth, it beat its wings against the stone walls and fell back.

Repent—now he saw that life would not be granted him long enough to see fully all of which he had to repent. If he had chosen loyalty to his Chieftain and been able to bear such burdens as he need never have repented taking on his shoulders— He could not repent having opened his door to everyone who craved shelter by his hearth, and never could he sufficiently repent that he had so acted toward himself that it was to a man full of leprosy that he let them in.

Nothing could be undone. Cecilia sat out at Hestviken with the body of the husband she had slain; the three fair-haired, mouse-eared boys stood about her, the fourth child lay under her heart, and she, their mother, had killed their father.

How could he have been deaf to his own heart, which told him: trust not a man who was false to his friend as a boy? So long had he strayed in shadows that he could not believe his own eyes —Jörund was not a fit husband for his only child. And afterwards he had done nothing—although he felt now that he must have known something might happen. This husband whom his daughter defended in word and deed, true as the sword is true to its master—he would be sure to try her patience once too often, and then Cecilia would turn against him. He remembered what she was like as a child: a dogged little spitfire, with her sharp bright eyes under a shock of flaxen hair. How could *he* believe Cecilia would change her nature, even if she were tamed and tutored by life? One can tame both bear and hawk; it does not make domestic animals of them.

Now it was too late, and he could only pray God to help him. Pride and presumption it would be if he now prayed God to use him as His instrument. For him it only remained to sever himself from the company of men—a lonely pilgrimage of penance. And to be thankful it was granted him to do it.

To take Cecilia with him was not in *his* power. Rather follow Jörund than go with him, she had said. So be it; perhaps she would think otherwise when she heard what he had done.

This was the first bitter cup he had to drain—to see that his conversion came too late in the evening for him to hope that God would send him back into the fray as His man. His work in the world was ended, and he could not undo it. He had rejected the glorious task of Simon of Cyrene; now he could only humble himself sorrowfully before the cross.

Olav took the crucifix in his hand again, stood looking at it. Somewhere, beyond the long week of pain and conflict, bided the Easter morn, and beyond death and purgatory it would be given even to him to see the glorious victory of the Cross. But here on earth it would never be his to see the radiance of a standard under which he might fight with the powers that were given him at his birth.

Olav looked up from the desk and turned half round as the door opened. It was Finn Arnvidsson who entered. His speech was dry and strangely cool—Olav guessed he was trying to conceal his emotion.

The monk said he came straight from St. Halvard's Church, where he had spoken with Master Sigurd Eindridson, who was delegate during Bishop Helge's illness to confess homicides. And he would hear Olav's confession in the sacristy after mass.

"So you have a day in which to prepare yourself. I too shall watch tonight, and pray that you may make a good confession. But remember that you are an old man, Olav—lie down and take your rest when you can watch no longer. It is of no use to constrain your body more than it can bear."

Olav compressed his lips. But it was true—he was old; even on his bodily strength he could rely no longer. Arnvid's son knelt by his side and remained on his knees a long while with his face in his hands. Then he rose silently and went out.

The hours went by. Now and again Olav caught sounds from outside—footsteps in the paved cloister as they fetched water from the well. The rain continued to splash on the roof and pour off it, gusts of wind beat upon the house, with a roar in the tree-tops, a creaking and crashing everywhere—then the blast died down for a while. The bells told him how the day was passing; the distant singing from the church showed how the life of the convent followed its wonted way.

A day and a night—the time of waiting seemed unbearably long. He held the crucifix in his hand and looked at it from time to time—but it seemed to him that his prayers fell from his lips as withered leaves flutter down from the trees in autumn. Was it so hard to wait?—but He had been kept waiting thirty years. From the beginning of time until the last day, God waited for mankind.

At dusk the young lay brother came, bringing him food—Olav saw that the man guessed something of what was afoot. He drank up the water and ate a little bread. Then he knelt down again and waited.

Night fell outside, the house grew silent, only the rain continued to pour down, the wind rose and fell. Once he went to the window and looked out. In an upper window of the opposite wing a faint light glowed through a little pane. There was one man who watched with him tonight.

As morning advanced on the next day it looked as if the southerly weather would soon have spent itself for this time. There were short fine intervals and once the sun peeped out strongly enough to be reflected from the wet roofs.

Olav sprang up as Finn Arnvidsson appeared at the door. He

took his hat, threw his cloak about him, and followed the monk down the narrow stairway that led to the cloister.

From the parlour someone came flying toward them in great haste—a tall man in a dark-red cloak with the hood drawn over his head. He was as wet as he could be. It was Eirik.

"Father! Cecilia is innocent—" He greeted as though absently the preaching friar who stood by his father's side. "Ay, Father, there is so much I have to tell you—but this comes first—she is innocent!"

Olav stared at his son—slowly he turned crimson in the face.

"God be praised—thanks be to God—" His voice became unsteady. "Are you *sure?*—You are not to tell me this now if later I am to hear—for I cannot bear it a second time—"

"They have found the man who killed him, Father. It was Anki. The poor wretches were so frightened that they ran away with their children and all they possessed, hid themselves in the woods by Kaldbæk. But late in the evening of Sunday, Anki came down to Rynjul and asked Una to go with him to Gudrun. Poor child, she was already dead when Una came. Then she sent a message home, and Torgrim came over himself with the men who were to carry the bodies to the village. Then they found both the dagger and Jörund's brooch in the bog-hole under Gudrun. Arnketil denied nothing—seemed rather to be glad it had come out, says Torgrim—they were to know that his children were not left unavenged."

Olav swayed so strangely as he stood; a stifled rattling sound came from his lips, and they had turned blue—the whole face was blue. Then he fell, like a tree that is blown down.

Eirik threw himself down beside the strange monk, who was already loosening the clothes at the neck, raising the shoulders in his arms. His father's face was dark, the whites of the eyes showed yellow and bloodshot under the lids, the breathing was stertorous. Eirik could not read the look in the monk's face—despair or horror that he fought to repress—but it added to the son's fear.

"Is he dying—?"

"No," said the other hastily. "Help me to take hold, so we can carry him in."

THE SON AVENGER

PART TWO

THE SON AVENGER

THE SON AVENGER

I

MIDSUMMER was gone before Eirik was able to visit his home at the Ness.

Across the bogs the sunshine blazed on the shining leaves of the osiers, and the new blades of grass were agleam in the little tussocky meadows. The lake reflected the woods on the other side and the warm blue sky and the clouds, which were already turning to gold—it was the end of the day.

As he approached the gate of the paddock a scent of new-mown hay was wafted toward him. Eirik dismounted, but paused for a moment before opening the gate: the days of the evening sun were yellow as gold, and the cluster of little houses on the ness threw long shadows over the meadow, where Eldrid and old Ragnhild were spreading hay.

His wife had seen him; she put down her rake and came to meet him. She walked lightly and erect, barelegged in her working-clothes. Erik thought once more that he knew nothing finer than Eldrid's forehead above the great eye-sockets and the rounding of the cheek, though the face was brown as wood, the skin drawn tight over the bones, and she had deep furrows right across her brow, many wrinkles about the great eyes, and cracks in her rough lips.

Never had he felt so intensely that here was the home he would have chosen; he liked best to dwell in the forests. This was the last time he would come *home* to this place. But it was not that he thought with any regret of the destiny that was now bearing him away from here. At one time he had loved Hestviken so that it sent a tremor through mind and sense if he did but come near anything that belonged to his home. Now he loved Hestviken because the manor needed him, the old folk looked to him and expected him to take control as master; he was the brother who was to care for Cecilia and her children, and he was the son, bound to stay by the old man who lived on, stricken and swathed in his dumbness and mysterious calamity as in a cloak of darkness.

Man and wife gave each other their hands in greeting, but their manner was the same as if Eirik had ridden from home the day before. Eldrid asked how his sister fared now, and Eirik answered: well. And Olav? There was no change, said Eirik.

As soon as he saw that it would be long ere he himself could come home, Eirik had sent Svein Ragnason over to the Ness. The young man had told Eldrid all he knew of what had taken place at Hestviken in the spring, and it did not occur to Eirik to tell his wife any more or even to inquire how much she had heard.

He lay awake that night and felt how securely Eldrid slept in his arm. He was glad he should be at home for a while in their own house, before they had to move out to Hestviken and live in the same house as his father. He remembered full well that their life together had begun in a flame of passion, when they had rushed into each other's arms as though each would devour and suck the other dry. A change had come over them by degrees, and now they lived together as if the hunger and thirst of both were appeased. Eldrid was the first human being he had known with whom he felt so safe that he could hold his peace. It had been so from the very first days, before they were married—nay, from the days when he was a new-comer here and never had a thought that she was to be his. Not even then had he been tempted to talk wildly and at random or to assert himself noisily when he was in Eldrid's company.

These were not new thoughts—he simply felt that with her he had enjoyed silence, calm like that of the forest, and freedom. The bond that bound him to her was the first to which he had submitted without feeling the strain.

He had seen Gunhild again at church, one day in spring. Ay, surely, she was fair—like a bell-cow with her jingling jewels, honest and capable she looked. But they had not been suited to each other after all. He was thankful to have got a wife of whom he would not tire.

He did not reflect upon what Eldrid might have found in him. He saw her calm demeanour, watched her sleeping securely by his side, and that was enough for him.

He and Svein mowed the grass on the marshes during the next few days; at evening he rowed out with Eldrid and set the nets. During the midday rest he lay on the green by the wall of the house, and most of the household did the same. Eirik listened to

the two old folk and chatted with them. Holgeir seemed well
pleased that he and Eldrid were leaving the place. When Svein
married and came hither, Holgeir would be more of a man at the
Ness, being the mistress's kinsman. Eldrid wished to take Ragnhild with her; the woman was in two minds about it: now she
would go with her mistress, now she would not. Young Svein
slept with his cap over his eyes. Eldrid sat a little apart, mending
a garment or spinning.

Eirik said to her one day when they were alone: " 'Tis no easy
lot I have in store for you at Hestviken, Eldrid. There you will
find much that is not well."

But he said nothing of what the difficulties were. It was long
since Eirik had thought of speaking to anyone of the difficulties
that might await him. Perhaps he had never done so, but formerly
he had tried to deaden his own feelings with talk and with
fussing about other things. Now he had taught himself the calm-
ness with which one must go to work if one would unravel a knot.

It was terrible to see his father in such a state, but he dared not
show that he felt it—dared not even show him special care or
affection: in the man's present plight this would only add to his
torment.

Olav had been almost entirely paralysed in one side when he
came to himself. Little by little he recovered sufficiently to be
able to walk, but he was bent quite over on the left side; he could
just move his arm, but could not control it, and the scarred and
ravaged face was now quite distorted and awry. When he tried
to speak, it was almost impossible to catch a word; his lips only
gave out a babbling. But now he no longer tried.

One day, about a month after Eirik had brought him home to
Hestviken, he made signs that he wished to be shaved of the
ragged white beard that had grown over his face. Apart from
that, Eirik saw how it hurt Olav to be obliged to accept help;
he was always making impotent attempts to do without it. But
he made an ugly mess of his beard when eating—that was the
reason.

As far as Eirik could tell, his father's understanding was not
darkened. Perhaps it would have been easier if it had been.

When Olav lay sick at Oslo, Father Finn Arnvidsson had said
he would give him extreme unction and the viaticum if his life
were in danger—he had proved his will to confess his hidden sin.

But if he was destined to recover and live on for a time with the seal of this secret doom upon his lips, then let no man venture to think there are limits to God's mercy or that he can fathom God's mysterious counsel. As a king receives his faithless liegeman back into his friendship, but bids him dwell awhile without the court until he be sent for—so must Olav await with manly patience a sign from our Lord.

Eirik had lodged with his own brethren during the last days at Oslo. There he made his confession to Brother Stefan and took counsel with him. And next morning, when he went forward and received *corpus Domini*, he prayed:

"O God, Thou who art King of kings and eternal Love. No king of this world, be he never so hard, refuses a son who would ransom his father; rather will he take the son as his father's hostage. Lord, look not upon my sins, but look upon Thy Son's sacred wounds and have compassion upon my poverty, that my offer may find favour in Thy sight, so that I may do such penance in his stead as my father should have done."

Brother Stefan said that he too must wait for a sign.

One of the greatest difficulties was that Cecilia could scarcely bear to look at her father—and Eirik guessed that affection had little part in the horror she felt for him.

None could fail to see that Cecilia had rallied and grown younger again since her husband was no more. She had grown so fair in these three months of widowhood—it was as though she had been stifled in a dungeon and were now set free. What she had said when her father would force her to lay her hand on the corpse was not true. And well it was not, thought Eirik; it would have been dreadful had it been so with her, after the ugly death that came upon Jörund.

She was a faithful mother to her two little sons. The second boy, Torgils, was still at Rynjul, where the old people would not let him go. Kolbein was now six and Audun three winters old. They were handsome and healthy children, obeyed their mother like lambs and held her in high honour; but among the folk of the manor they were full of sport and high spirits, and when they came to know their uncle, they followed at his heels wherever he went. They were not at all afraid of their grandfather, Eirik saw—they scarcely noticed him.

Early in the autumn Eirik came again to the Ness, and this time it was to bring his wife home to Hestviken.

There was a diversity of opinions among folk when Eldrid Bersesdatter came back to the country where she had lived in her youth and took her place as mistress of one of the greatest manors. But for the most part they thought it was well. True, she had done much that was ill, but that was very long ago; it was right that she should be taken out of the humble cot in which she had lived for fifteen years and restored to such condition as became her birth. Her kinswomen, the daughters of Arne and their families, received her, Una and Torgrim cordially, Baard and Signe more coolly, but in very seemly fashion.

She was still a handsome woman and carried herself so well when she mixed among folk that those who were old enough to recall Eldrid's beauty at the time she was given to old Harald Jonsson revived the memory of that marriage. And many there were who could tell tales of her evil courses when she was mistress of Borg and later at Sigurdstad in a different way. Now she was an elderly woman, nearing the half-hundred. But she and Eirik were not so ill matched a pair to look at, for all that.

He was so big and bony that he began early to look more than his age. Tall and broad-shouldered, he stooped a little with his bulky chest and long, powerful limbs, and his back was rounded by hard work. His thin and narrow face, with its indented nose and prominent jaw, was brown, tanned, and furrowed; though no one would have called him ugly, it was not easy to see that he had once passed for a comely youth. Only the great light-brown eyes were unusually handsome; but his dark and curly hair was strongly marked with grey.

With the passing of years Eirik Olavsson had grown very like his father, folk said—not so much in outward appearance; the tall, dark, rather loose-limbed man had indeed remarkably little in common with the father, who had been so fair-complexioned, shapely, and well-knit. But folk could clearly recognize the father's nature in the son.

Like him, Eirik was taciturn; they were all so in that family. As Olav in his time could stand quite motionless by the hour together on the lookout rock or leaning over the fence of a cornfield, so the son now stood gazing in the same places. But he was a much

more capable master of Hestviken than Olav had been. Not that
the father's management had been other than careful and wise;
the family estate had not shrunk in his time. But with the son
everything went with more life and spirit, and success attended
him. The manor of Saltviken, which had been left untenanted in
Olav Half-priest's time, had been reclaimed, and he had helped
the young folk whom he had established at Rundmyr to clear the
land around.

He had brought Liv and her remaining children south to a
house in Saltviken. It was indeed a better abode than the woman
was used to; nevertheless she was loath to leave her cot. But Eirik
said it was better that Anki's children should live farther from
Hestviken when Jörund's sons grew up.

Anki had seized a chance of escaping from the men who were
to carry him bound to the Warden. In the first two years rumours
were heard from time to time that the murderer had appeared,
now here, now there, on the outskirts of the parish and in the
neighboring country; he must have a haunt somewhere in the
forests. And when Liv had a child a year and a half after the dis-
appearance of her husband, she gave out that he was the father—
he had looked in at home a few times.

In the third spring after Jörund's death three men of the parish
were taking a short cut through the woods on the way to Gardar.
Close to the Black Tarn they found in a scree the remains of a
corpse, badly mangled by beasts. But one leg in a boot had been
caught fast among some stones. The men then searched the forest
around, seeking for traces of the dead man's hiding-place, for they
guessed him to be a robber. And, sure enough, they found a little
way up the hill a kind of hut built on a ledge of rock. It looked
as if the man had not been so badly off there; the couch was well
covered with clothes and a great food-box stood there, still half
full of food.

Now, there was one of the men who thought he had seen that
box before—the low, flat carving of interlacing vines looked like
the work of Eirik Olavsson of Hestviken, and there were runes
cut on the pin that held the lid in place. One of the men was
scholar enough to make out what was written: it was "*Eirekr.*"
Then it occurred to them that they had seen Eirik of Hestviken

wearing boots that were patched in just the same way as the one the corpse had on.

They got Arnketil's remains up to the village, and the murderer was laid in earth just outside the churchyard wall. Then they carried what they had found to Hestviken and told Eirik the news: "The thrall was true to his nature, a thief to the last."

"Anki did not steal these things," said Eirik. He fixed his great, clear eyes on the peasant who had spoken. "Thrall or thief, he avenged son and daughter in such way as he was able. And it is for God to judge how great was his sin."

No one sought to find out more. If Eirik Olavsson had secretly helped the slayer of his brother-in-law, that must be his affair. The Hestvik men had always shielded their dependants—even when they were in the wrong. It came out afterwards that he had caused masses to be said for Anki—ay, the dead man might well need that.

They had always been good Christians there and open-handed with alms. Olav had been generous while he was master, and Eirik was the same. But Olav always seemed to listen to the woes of poor folk with but half an ear and in helping them looked as if he were thinking hard of something else. Eirik said loans must be given with a laugh, and gifts with a joyful countenance. Though he was not much more of a talker than his father, one could see that he listened to what folk said; there was nothing oppressive in his silence. In every way he was more friendly than the old man had been.

The day after these men had been with him Eirik rowed south to Saltviken; he wished to give Liv the news himself.

Before setting out for home he went up to the manor to find Cecilia. He knew that she had not yet held her churching, and she still kept to the same upper chamber where she had sat with her father on the night when she had fetched him home from the Ness.

The spring sun shone in through the three small bayed loopholes and fell straight upon the woman's coifed head; she sat on a low chest, bent over the sucking child. When her brother came in at the door, she looked up and smiled in greeting. But her eyes went back at once to the new-born boy at her breast—she looked young and thoughtful and happy. Her face had grown rounder, but her eyes were clear and her lips had recovered their bright-red hue.

She listened calmly to her brother's account of Arnketil's death. "Ay, that was bound to be the end," she said sorrowfully, "since he never *would* follow your advice and take himself away from here."

Then she asked after Kolbein and Audun and Eldrid, also after her father. But all the time she was looking down at the child who now lay full-fed and asleep in her lap. Eirik was strangely moved to see this mild and blissful animal-look in the young mother's eyes; she had never been like this when she sat with her other children.

She was fond of them. She had made clothes for them and sent them across during the winter, with a message that when she was over her childbed they might come and visit their mother. But he guessed it was something new with this little Gunnar. Him she had borne under a cheerful heart.

Una came in with ale and food for the guest. She had grown older and more portly, but was as cheerful and active as ever. She went over to Cecilia, had to look at the child—it half opened its eyes, and at once the two women were delightedly busy over the little thing.

Una took the boy in her arms and brought him over; Eirik must take a good look at him. She unswathed the back of the little head: was it not finely shaped?

"Ay, 'tis a goodly child," said Eirik. "But he has red hair," he laughed teasingly.

Cecilia looked up, her cheeks flushed deeply, and her brother saw she was on the point of flying into a rage. But then she laughed too. "Certainly he has red hair. 'Tis as I say—my Gunnar has every fine thing you can think of." She came over and took back the child.

Eirik said he could not wait till Aslak came home: "but give him my greeting!"

Cecilia Olavsdatter had not been a widow more than a year when a suitor announced himself; it was Ragnvald Jonsson, the friend of Olav's youth. He had been out and tried his fortune at Hestviken before, when the two young maids were there; first it was Bothild Asgersdatter he would have, and then Cecilia. Nothing came of it; then he took a wife who brought him an estate at the head of the fiord, and there he dwelt now, a widower with two little daughters.

Cecilia was not unwilling—she had known Ragnvald from childhood, and he was upright, kind, and a fine man to look at— even if there were many wiser than he. And Eirik could see no cause to refuse him if Cecilia herself desired this marriage.

He guessed it was a little hard for his sister to have to share her authority with Eldrid. The two women liked each other; they associated without friction. But the fact was that Cecilia had held sway as mistress of her father's manor for the greater part of her grown-up life, and now Eldrid had to take precedence of her; she was so much older, and she was his wife. But he doubted not that Cecilia longed above all to escape from the proximity of her father.

When Eirik laid Ragnvald's suit before Olav and gave his own opinion, his father nodded assent. So he and Ragnvald came to terms. The betrothal ale was to take place during the summer.

At Botolph's mass [1] Cecilia herself went into Oslo to make purchases for the feast. But on the evening of her return Eirik saw, as soon as his sister stood up in the boat, that something had happened. "What is it?" he asked as he helped her onto the quay.

"That I will tell you later."

Change after change came over Cecilia's face, usually so unruffled—she seemed to be listening, with a youthful, faraway look in her eyes; then her features contracted in mournful brooding.

Eirik was about to see his father to his bed; Eldrid was already bending down to loose her shoestring when Cecilia came in upon them.

"Stay awhile, Father—there is a matter I would fain have disposed of this evening, so I beg you will listen to me now. Nay, do not go, Eldrid—I wish you to hear it too. It is that I cannot marry Ragnvald."

"You cannot!" Eirik turned round to his sister. "He has our word already, Cecilia!"

"I know it, but he must release us." She looked at her father, and he looked at her with his one ice-blue, bloodshot eye; the other was half closed by the palsied lid.

[1] June 17.

"You remember Aslak Gunnarsson, Father; Jon Toresson he called himself the winter he was with us. I met him in the town; he had heard that I was now a widow, and he was on his way hither. He has not married. And now I have promised myself to him."

Eirik saw that his father was attacked by the spasms which sometimes occurred in the dead side of his face and the palsied arm.

"You have promised yourself to two men—"He checked himself and said quietly: "It is far too late to speak of this tonight. Wait till tomorrow."

"There is no need of much speaking. 'Tis true that I have promised myself to two men. But only one can have me. And that will be Aslak."

"But Father and I have given our word to *one* man. We did so with your consent. And we will not break our word."

"*Once* I have been married on the advice of you two." The green flash that came into her eyes seemed no more than a reflection, but it reminded Eirik of the time when he had believed his sister capable of killing her husband. "I shall never give Ragnvald my troth. And if you will not betroth me to Aslak, I shall go northward with him in spite of you."

"You must not say such things, Cecilia—you have three sons."

"Ay, I have thought of that. But they must stay with you—they are your heirs. What say you, Eldrid?" She turned to her brother's wife.

"I say that no good can come of breaking one's word. But 'tis not good either to marry against one's will. You ought to wait awhile—"

"Aslak and I have waited long enough. What say you, Father?" Think you not we have waited long enough now?"

Olav nodded.

"Father!" exclaimed Eirik. "Do I understand you rightly—do you wish us to withdraw from the bargain with Ragnvald?"

Olav laid his sound hand heavily on his son's arm and nodded again.

"Ah, if that is the way of it, then— You are the master, Father."

Not much more was said of the matter. Eirik had to ride to Ragnvald and tell him of the turn it had taken. At first Ragnvald was very wroth, but before long he said it was all one about the marriage. "If Cecilia has made up her mind to a thing, I am loath to be the one who should try to force her away from her purpose."

So it was not Ragnvald who came out to Hestviken at St. Olav's vigil,[2] but Aslak Gunnarsson. As the guest dismounted and came toward him, Eirik saw that Aslak halted a little. The brother felt a slight shock, of aversion, or he knew not what.

They were betrothed in the course of the autumn, and the wedding was held at Hestviken in the following spring; by that time Jörund had been dead two years. Aslak had no home of his own, but lodged with his brothers at Yttre Dal. He bought up horses from the districts where the farmers carried on the breeding of foals, sold them in Oslo and along the border; he was now a man of substance and owned shares in many farms in the Upplands, but liked none of them so well that he would live there. So it was arranged that he and Cecilia should live at Hestviken.

Eirik and Aslak lived together in amity and concord. The new brother-in-law was prudent and upright, an active and companionable man—Eirik saw that. But it could never grow into any warm friendship between the two men, they both knew that. And when Aslak and Cecilia had been married over half a year, Aslak came and said he thought they might as well move to Saltviken —for in any case he or Eirik must constantly be there to see to the work of the farm, and here at Hestviken they were already so many, and now that Cecilia was with child—

Eirik guessed that the two would be glad to enjoy their happiness in a place where they would not be reminded of all the past mischances, and where Cecilia could be mistress in her own house and need not have her father before her eyes. So he and Aslak were soon agreed.

Eirik thought of all this as he came down from the upper chamber and remembered his sister's face as she sat bending over the child she had had by Aslak. And he remembered the day in late autumn when they moved out hither; he had sailed them round himself. It was raining heavily, and the road between the fences was under water in places; Aslak lifted up his wife and carried her right up to the manor, though her feet were already as wet as they could be and the man was lame—though not so badly. And he remem-

2 July 28.

bered the blaze of anger in Cecilia's eyes when he once happened
to mention Aslak's defect: "He got it fighting one against five; at
last a man threw him from behind so that he broke his leg."

He did not believe there had been a shadow of truth in Jörund's
talk. It was not like her—nor like Aslak either. With this man his
sister was in good hands, and the manor was in good hands. He
would have liked to go up to the stream and look at the mill Aslak
was building—he was tired of carrying his corn round to Hestviken by boat, he said. But he felt he never had any desire to seek
out his brother-in-law, though they were always good friends
when they met. He liked Aslak and thought well of him, but
there was no help for it.

He had said to Eldrid one day: "I know not what it is, but when
I am in company with Aslak it always comes over me that the
man finds life irksome."

"That is likely enough," said his wife with a kind of smile. "But
I do not believe he finds it so irksome as you do."

Eirik looked at her in surprise: "No! You are right there," he
replied with a laugh.

He went over to the cherry orchard and looked at it. The first
cuttings he had planted were now trees with trunks as thick as a
child's arm, and glossy bark; ground shoots had come up all about
them. The little plantation was full of yellow buds ready to burst.
In time there would be a whole grove here as in the convent
garden.

He rowed homeward in the course of the afternoon. On the
shore, before one rounds the point of the lookout crag, there is
a little strip of sandy beach below the rust-red rocks. Eirik saw
that his father stood there with his little bow; he was struggling
with it once more, trying if he could train himself to use his half-
palsied arm and hand. It hurt Eirik anew whenever he saw that
Olav *could* not give up—again and again he attempted to conquer
his disability.

He lived in continual anxiety for his father when the stricken
old man was wandering out alone. Far away over the high ground
to the south he dragged himself; the housefolk had seen him sitting there looking down into Saltviken. But when Eirik asked if
he should sail him out thither one day so that he could have a
sight of the manor, Olav shook his head. Round the whole bay he

walked, up Kverndal or along the ridge of the Bull. He might
easily fall over the edge or have another stroke, lie there and
perish. But Eirik dared not send anyone after him to keep an eye
on the old man—he had seen that nothing would distress his father
more. And he must be left to go his way—he could not possibly
endure to sit ever indoors or drag his crippled body about among
the houses of the manor.

Not a day passed but Eirik renewed his prayer to be allowed to
bear the penance in his father's stead. And each time he felt it
with a deeper thrill—disablement, helplessness, inactivity—it made
him afraid. For he knew a man cannot feel it otherwise than as a
humiliation—a more bitter shame than being a bastard. Never before had he seen so clearly that of all vainglory the sweetest is that
which springs from pride in one's bodily strength and perfect
health.

But none other than Eldrid guessed that he laid upon himself
penitential exercises; he had to use such measure that none might
observe any change in him in his daily work. Then his wife said
to him one day:

"Now all is otherwise than when we first met, Eirik. Then we
were driven on by such desires as are kindled by hate and anger
and scorn. I will speak no more of it now, but you must know
that I am willing, whenever you wish that our life together shall
come to an end."

"You must consider well, Eldrid," said her husband quietly.
"What you have in mind would be a good issue, but not unless
we are both agreed on it."

2

ANOTHER winter went by, and then came the spring—early that
year. As soon as the ground began to be clear of snow, Olav's unrest came upon him again; he wandered abroad early and late,
though he no longer went so far as before. From the manor they
constantly saw the dark, bent, and crooked figure moving slowly
against the sky on the sun-baked rocks by the shore or under the
brow of the wood beyond the fields. He often went to the river-
mouth, where the Kverndal stream falls into the bay. A little way

from the beach there was a stretch of dry sward below an over-hanging crag—Eirik had haunted the place, digging for Lapps' arrows, when he was a boy. There they often found Olav sitting.

It had become the custom for Eldrid to go out and fetch him home to meals. From her first coming to Hestviken Olav had met his son's wife with a lingering shadow of the quiet and charming courtesy that had become him so well in his younger years—whenever he was willing or remembered to show it. Eldrid had slipped into the life of the manor much more easily than, for instance, Aslak, and Eirik guessed that Olav liked his wife. By degrees it had come about that Olav seemed less worried at accepting help from the mistress of the house than from anyone else.

Olav was taking his usual walk across the fields one fine morning. Along the high balks the pale grass of the year before lay crushed, but the bright new blades had come up so well in the last few days that soon they would cover the old. Every time Olav had to stand still for a moment, he stared at it, unseeing—the dark spines of withered meadowsweet and angelica were surrounded at the roots with thick wreaths of new crisped leaves. He leaned heavily on the spear that he used as a staff. He had grown used to the pains in his legs, till he felt them without a thought; his sound leg ached in the joints and was always tender and tired, but the half-dead one was full of a dull pricking and shooting.

The trees at the edge of the wood were breaking into leaf, but some of them were already quite green. Every year it was the same trees that came out first—earliest of all hereabout was the young wild cherry that grew at the foot of Hvitserk's mound up in the great field. Today he noticed all at once that it had grown into an old and ample tree, spreading wide its summer foliage.

Birds winged their way among the thickets; their piping and chirping came from the wood. Some osiers down by the river were yellow as gold with blossom, and their scent hung in the air, mild and over-sweet.

Olav crossed the bridge, struggled up the hill to his seat under the rock. Then he heard that at the bottom of the slope a band of children were bathing in the sea. He dragged himself farther, stood behind a clump of bursting alders, and looked down at the youngsters.

The same stretch of dry sward ran here between small rocks up to the wood on the flank of the Bull. Here the bay was shallow, with a bottom of fine light clay, so that the water had a milky look about the naked bodies of the children who splashed and played in it. Kolbein was one of them—he knew his grandson's straw-coloured mop of hair. The boy was now ten, so thin that the bones of his chest showed plainly, and his joints were knotted like growing glades of grass. The others were the children of the new foreman who had succeeded old Tore, and some no doubt belonged to the new folk Eirik had taken in at Rundmyr.

Kolbein was swimming a race with another boy—blowing and kicking far too much, thought the old man. Right up on the edge of dry seaweed toddled a little one—it was the foreman's youngest, a boy, he saw, the little tot that grubbed about in the courtyard at home every day. Now and then he gave an angry yell, for the rocks pricked his feet, but no one turned round to look at him, and so he managed to get along by himself. His sister, who must have been in charge of the little ones, sat on a big rock far out in the water, and before her a tall, handsome boy stood in the water up to his middle. Those two were older than the rest, perhaps twelve or thirteen. The girl took the mussels that the boy opened and handed to her—she was white and fair, her.bosom slightly rounded already; her dark hair dangled down her back.

All at once it seemed it could not be half a hundred years since they had been the two biggest of the band of children who played about the tarn in the forest to the north of Frettastein. It was more like a dream he had dreamed, and not so long ago.

The fat little boy had come right up to the grassy slope. Solemnly straddling, with stomach thrust out, he came along—and at that instant Olav descried, just in front of where he stood and right in the child's path, a great adder sunning itself on some stones. He went forword—instinctively he walked more steadily as he hurried to where the snake lay. But as he was about to thrust at it with his spear, it raised its head, hissed, and struck at the flashing steel—then glided in under the stones.

The little child had set up a howl. When Olav looked back, the children stood at the edge of the water staring, while the big sister dashed toward them, splashing the water all about her.

Awhile after, as he lay beneath the crag, the children came walking past along the path hidden by the bushes; they were on the way home. The big sister was leading the little boy by the hand, hauling him after her, as she chatted to her friend:

"Nay, afraid of him we are not. Mother says we have but to make the sign of the cross when we see him, then he cannot harm us. But an ugly sight he is, Olav the bad. He has been like that since he stood before the church door in Oslo to take his oath upon the book—a false oath it was, and then he was *struck* so. His left hand is *black!*"

Instinctively Olav looked at his palsied hand—black it was not, nor does one make an oath with the left hand. It was surely nothing but child's talk. Although—could children have made up that about the oath, and the name—Olav the bad?

The sign, the sign that he waited for—he watched for it everywhere, in odd or even. In the games of a band of children and the words of a little girl—

In the evening he saw the child again; she was walking with her mother and one of the serving-women toward the break of the woods, and they carried pails and pans, were going to the summer byre. No, there was nothing in her now that recalled Ingunn. He had never noticed before what they called her—Reidun, said her mother.

When Reidun found that he was looking at her, she seemed confused and furtively crossed herself.

Olav had slept but a short space, he thought, when he was awakened by the sharp pain under his ribs—but tonight it was worse than ever before, and he was cold too; an icy chill had lodged between his shoulder-blades, and when he breathed, it seemed to run over, making the cold sweat trickle down his body —his hands and feet were as cold as clammy stones.

He must have lain too long on the grass today, he decided, old wreck that he was.

Then came a sudden wave of heat—hotter and hotter till his head and body were aglow, but his limbs were still as cold as lead. The heat seemed to stream from the great lump of pain that lay embedded in his body at the edge of the chest; it was as though he had a red-hot stone there, and the stinging pains that shot out from it, up into his lungs and through his entrails, filled his whole frame with torment. A ceaseless flight of sparks went on within him; now the rain of sparks reached his head and flew around within his skull; the skin outside was all acreep; now he *saw* the sparks, they swarmed in the darkness, which turned round and round, and the couch beneath him turned, but the ball of pain under his chest was in a ferment, so that he trembled with the effort not to groan aloud, and the sweat ran off him in streams. Till the qualms forced their way upward, dilated chest and throat, filled his mouth with blood and loathsomeness, and then the surge of rusty blood burst the dam of his clenched teeth.

It gave relief as soon as the vomiting was over. He lay relaxed, feeling the pains ebbing back to their source, and now it hurt him in a clean and honest way, like a wound. He was now shivering with cold too, between the sweat-drenched bedclothes, but that did him good. If only he had been able to wipe away the blood that he lay in—it smelt so foully.

Then all at once he was on a path that led through a gap with screes on both sides and spruce firs growing in the crevices. Beyond the gap he saw water far below; it was grey weather, the land on the other side was shrouded in mist—and he knew the place again; he was at home on the shore of Lake Mjösen, and as he walked he seemed to see himself, at sixteen, clear and distinct as a raw lad in the coolness of his youthful health.

Now he saw that Ingunn was walking a little in front of him —in her old red kirtle; her heavy light-brown plaits fell half-loosened down her slender back. He began to walk faster; she sauntered ahead without hurrying, but press on as he might, he did not gain on her—it was still just as far between them.

He carried a spear on his shoulder—it was one he had hafted for her, with a red shaft and a short point, but after he had given it her, he had always to carry it for her. It had grown so heavy— heavier and heavier it grew, till his shoulder ached and he was bent double—and Ingunn walked there before him, and he could not come up with her.

Then they came down to the shore, walked along a bay. There was a beach of fine white sand with a dark edge licked by the waves, and the waters of the lake were grey. He still saw Ingunn far away, and the spear he carried on his shoulder weighed him down, and in his chest he had a smarting wound from which the blood gushed out—he saw it run down upon the sand, which sucked it up with a thousand greedy little mouths.

Olav awoke in pitch-darkness, knew that he had cried out. He

heard someone tumble out of bed in the room beyond and strike
a light. Soon after, Eirik appeared in the doorway with a burning
torch in his hand, naked in his cloak, with the flaps of it tied about
his waist.

"Are you sick, Father?"

Eldrid appeared behind her husband. They threw the light on
him.

"He has thrown up again." Eldrid found a rag, wiped him and
the bed, while Eirik raised his body. He was heavy with sleep and
went clumsily about it, so that Olav could not repress a low
groan: the sparks of pain began to whirl within him again.

" 'Tis all blood and clotted gore."

"He has been in a sweat. Better lay more over him." Eldrid
fetched a skin coverlet.

"Shall I carry you in, Father—to the other bed?"

Olav rolled his head in refusal—he lay powerless among the
pillows.

"Then I must lie in here—it were unwise to leave him alone tonight," said Eirik to his wife.

Olav rolled his head again, raised his sound hand deprecatingly.

The two went back and lay down. Again Olav's pains receded
to their centre fairly quickly; after he had lain motionless awhile,
it was no longer so bad. If only they had thought to give him a
drink of something— And it was hot with this coverlet—Olav
pushed it onto the floor.

Otherwise he did not suffer so much now; only for the pain that
was lodged under his ribs and seemed to swell over his chest with
every breath he took. Presently he thought his body was like an
old craft that lay half sunken on the beach, and every wave that
lifted it loosened the planks more and more from the timbers, and
his spirit was like a bird sitting on a floor-board awash within the
rotten boat, and when the board came clear and floated off, the
bird would fly away. But after a while the tide lapped him to
sleep.

His thirst awoke him—he was not so much in pain now as feeling ill, and he himself was afflicted by the close, cold smell of age
and death about him. He could not remember if he had dreamed
or what, but he had come out of his sleep with a feeling that
within the worn and tortured old body that now wrestled with
Death, he himself was a young prisoner.

At the foot of the bed was a loop-hole in the wall, closed with a wooden shutter. Olav lay tormented by thirst and shortness of breath and thought he would get up and open it. Two or three times he raised himself slightly, but as soon as he moved he felt that the pains were making ready to rush upon him.

Then he did it in spite of them—one wrench and he was on his knees at the foot of the bed. Flung forward over the bedstead he lay waiting till the excruciating throes aroused by the sudden movement had raged their fill.

A fresh whirl of pain sparkled over him as he took hold of the pin of the shutter and pulled it toward him. It was stiff—Olav clenched his teeth, swallowed his cries, as the red-hot devils raged within him, but then he sank back against the horse's head of the bedpost with the pin in his hand; it seemed the hardest pull he had given in his life, and the tears poured down over his ravaged face as he breathed the morning air that blew in upon him. Outside it was light, a white morning, and the birds were awakening.

He swung himself out of bed and staggered to his clothes. In a way he was himself aware that he was only a mortally sick old man struggling with a hand and a half to hitch on some wraps in a dark room, and it hurt him so much when he moved that tears and sweat ran off him, and he ground his teeth lest he might howl aloud and wake them in the outer room. But at the same time he felt that within him was himself, engaged in breaking through a ring of foes, trying to ride them down—memories of all the fights in which he had borne arms loomed before him as presaging dreams—but now it was earnest, and he struggled furiously to force his quaking limbs into obedience.

Groping along the wall, he came out into the great room, found his way to the door of the anteroom, and opened it. From there he reached the outer door and accomplished that. Then he stood on the icy doorstone, barefoot in cloak and kirtle. The morning air blew into him and filled his aching chest; it hurt, but more than that, it did him good.

He looked up at the cliff that rose behind the roofs of the outhouses, with green grass and bushes clinging to its crevices, and every leaf was still and waiting; the fir forest above waited motionless against the white morning sky.

The fiord he could not see, but he heard it moving gently at the foot of the rocks, and the murmur of the wavelets over the shingle. He must see the water once more.

Supporting himself with his hand on the logs of the wall, he made his way along the line of houses and stood leaning against the corner of the last in the row. The path leading to the water-side wound lonely and deserted by the side of the "good acre's" brown carpet, which crept into the shelter of the lookout rock; the corn was sprouting thickly with green needles. Down below, where the path came to an end, the sheds leaned listening over the sea, which swirled with a faint splash about their piles.

Olav let go his hold of the corner of the men's house. Swaying, he walked on without support. A little way up the lookout rock he climbed, but then sank down and lay in a little hollow, where the dry, sun-scorched turf made him a bed.

The immense bright vault above him and the fiord far below and the woods of the shore began to warm as the day breathed forth its colours. Birds were awake in woods and groves. From where he lay he saw a bird sitting on a young spruce on the ridge, a black dot against the yellow dawn; he could see it swelling and contracting like the beats of a little heart; the clear flute-like notes welled out of it like a living source above all the little sleepy twitterings round about, but it was answered from the darkness of the wood. The troops of clouds up in the sky were flushing, and he began to grow impatient of his waiting.

He saw that all about him waited with him. The sea that splashed against the rocks, rowan and birch that had found foot-hold in the crevices and stood there with leaves still half curled up—now and again they quivered impatiently, but then they grew calm. The stone to which his face was turned waited, gazing at the light from sky and sea.

From the depths of his memory words floated up—the morning song that he had once known. All the trees of the forest shall rejoice before the face of the Lord, for He comes to judge the world with righteousness, the waves shall clap their hands.—He saw that now they were waiting, the trees that grew upon the rocks of his manor, all that sprouted and grew on the land of his fathers, the waves that followed one another into the bay—all were waiting to see judgment passed upon their faithless and unprofitable master. It was as though the earth were waiting every

hour of the day, but it was in the quiver of dawn that the fair
and defrauded earth breathed out so that one heard it—sorrowful
and merciless as a deflowered maid it waited to be given justice
against men, who went in, one by one, to be judged. Every hour
and every moment judgment was given; it was the watchword
that one day cried to another and one night whispered to the next.
All else that God had created sang the hymn of praise—*Benedicite
omnia opera domini Domino*—he too had known it when he was
young. But those whom He had set to be captains and lords of
the earth forsook God and fought with one another, betraying
God and betraying their fellows.

The bird in the tree-top on the ridge still poured out its stream
of notes—and he too had been given his life in fief, and authority
had been his, the rich Christ had placed the standard in his hand
and hung the sword over his shoulder and set the ring upon his
hand.—And he had not defended the standard and had stained the
sword with dishonour and forgotten what the ring should have
called to mind—he must stand forth and could not declare one
deed that he had performed from full and unbroken loyalty, nor
could he point to one work that he could call well done.—Lord,
rebuke me not in thine anger, neither condemn me in thy justice.

Above him he saw the whole vault of heaven full of white
clouds, they stood thick as an immense flock of lambs, but they
were folk. They were white and shone with a light that was
within them and filled them as sunshine fills the clouds. Slowly
gliding, they moved high above him, looking down on him—he
recognized his mother and certain of the others too, Ingunn was
there—

It was the sunrise, he knew that—but it was like a writing. Thus
he had stared at the fine pattern of letters on smooth white vellum,
until all at once he knew a word—that time when Arnvid tried to
teach him to read writing.

Then the very rays from the source of light broke out and
poured down over him. For an instant he stared with open eyes
straight into the eye of the sun, tried even, wild with love and
longing, to gaze yet deeper into God. He sank back in red fire, all
about him was a living blaze, and he knew that now the prison
tower that he had built around him was burning. But salved by
the glance that surrounded him, he would walk out unharmed

over the glowing embers of his burned house, into the Vision that is eternal bliss, and the fire that burned him was not so ardent as his longing.

Eirik found his father lying in a swoon far up the hill when he went out in the morning, alarmed at the old man's absence. He carried him in and put him to bed.

Death could not be far away, he saw. Olav's hair was parted in strands, his cheeks had fallen in, and he was white about the nose, but he seemed free from pain. Eirik sent messages—for the priest, for the old people at Rynjul, and to Saltviken. The messenger was to tell his sister that this time she *must* come—Cecilia had not set foot in Hestviken since she moved out with Aslak a year and a half ago, and whenever Eirik had asked her to come and see her father she had excused herself.

They were gathered about him within the closet, his kinsfolk and household, when Sira Magne entered in alb and stole and recited:

"*Pax huic domui,*"

and the acolyte who bore the crucifix gave the response:

"*Et omnibus habitantibus in ea.*"

Kolbein and Torgils were allowed to hold the candles. They stood looking intently at their grandfather, who was about to die. The children had always known that there was something sombre and mysterious about the old man who dragged himself around on the outskirts of their life, crooked and shrunken and speechless, but at ordinary times they had not thought much about him. Now they took no notice of the molten wax that ran down on their fingers as they stared at him; in the soft light of the candles the waves of smooth white hair showed brightly against the brown pillows, Eldrid had combed him so finely. The grey face with its scarred cheek, one eyelid half closed and the mouth drawn awry, but clear and unmarred on the other side, was like the head of one of the statues in the doorway of St. Mary's Church, for that too was shattered on the left side.

Quivering with excitement, the boys watched to see if anything would happen, if any change would come over the old man's ruined face when the priest absolved him of his sins in God's name. Beside the standing figure of the priest knelt Uncle Eirik, motionless as a statue; he kept his grizzled head bent, and in his hands, which were hidden by a cloth of fine linen, he held the manor's best silver cup with six little tufts of snow-white wool. In a clear voice he said the responses together with the acolyte; the boys understood nothing of the prayers, but remembered to bow their heads whenever they heard the name of Jesus or *Gloria Patri.*

Then came the questions in Norse to the dying man, who had not been able to make any confession; at each act of repentance, faith, hope, and love the dying man smote his breast and made a bowing motion with his head. In his one living eye, which reflected the flame of the candle, the boys looked into a world of which they could form no idea, but the shattered half of the face was not made whole, as they had almost expected. Afterwards the priest and their uncle said the *Kyrie,* and Sira Magne read out of his book a long, long prayer and called their grandfather by name, Olavus, while Eirik lowered his head yet deeper, and behind them they were weeping, Una loudest of all.

Eirik's forehead nearly touched the floor as the acolyte said the *Confiteor*—they knew that, and then came the absolution, *misereatur* and *indulgentiam.*

They had never before seen a dying person anointed, and their eyes followed the priest's fingers as he took the tufts of wool one by one out of the cup in Eirik's hands, moistened with oil and smeared the sign of the cross over their grandfather's eyes and ears, nose and mouth, and the backs of his hands. Last of all Eirik, otherwise remaining motionless, raised with one hand the blanket from the dying man's feet; thus with the chrism of mercy were blotted out all the sins he had committed with sight and senses, with word and hand, and every step he had taken from the right way.

And now the children waited with a sore longing for it to be over, for they were tired of standing still and holding the candles, and Eirik's back and shoulders kept moving as though he wept, and his voice was husky as he said the responses.

In the afternoon they were out in the courtyard; they knew they must not play any game, for Sira Magne was to come back at evening and bring *corpus Domini* for their grandfather. But after a while they forgot themselves and made a good deal of noise—it was not so often that Kolbein and Audun saw their brother Torgils, and then they had to discuss with the foreman's children the wonderful thing they had seen that morning. Reidun had been in the closet with the rest, and she had seen that the black hand of Olav turned white when the priest anointed it, and Kolbein and Torgils agreed—they saw it turn lighter, at any rate.

Then they were sent for to the women's house; the old people from Rynjul were resting there, and their little red-haired brother, Gunnar, had learned to walk since the big children had last been at Saltviken. Audun remembered that this was the first time Gunnar had been here, so they took him out into the yard. Till Aslak came and told them to be quiet.

Eirik and Cecilia sat alone in the old house. The smoke-vent was open, and the evening sun shone down and gave colour to the thin column of smoke that rose from the last dying embers. Higher up, the trailing smoke began to curl and wave, then it spread out under the roof in a light cloud. The two sat watching the play of the smoke, and from outside came the sound of boys' shrill voices and little feet running on the rock.

Presently the son got up, went into the closet, and looked at the sick man.

"He is asleep now," he said as he came back. And after a moment: "When he wakes, you would speak with him alone awhile, I doubt not?"

"Speak with him is more than any can do now, Eirik."

"Say to him what you have on your mind—"

"We have already bidden him farewell, all of us. What more is there to say?"

"Cecilia," said Eirik, dropping his voice, "can you think that Father has not noticed it?—in all these four years you tried not to see him. If he came into the room where you were, you left it if you could.—Nay, I have not forgotten that he did you grave injury that time—"

"That I forgave him long ago," said Cecilia quickly. " 'Tis not that. But can you not understand, brother—if it was gruesome for you and Eldrid to have him before you here neither alive nor dead, then it must have been worse yet for me, when you remember all that happened before his life came to such a close."

"Do you remember *I* raised the axe against him?—and God knows 'twas not my fault I did not kill my father. Judge, then, if it has been a light matter for me to see him in this state for four years—I who remember how he was of old—the noblest man I have set eyes on, the goodliest and the most generous."

"So you say now, Eirik. I remember naught else but enmity between you—in all the years since you were a little lad, until the day you turned your back on home and took a wife without asking his counsel. Never could you endure to live here with us; as often as you came home you went away again almost at once —and for that you blamed Father; you said he was the most unreasonable of men. And in that I thought you were not so far wrong—unreasonable he often was with you, and hard to live with for all of us. But I tell you—I have forgiven him with all my heart, as a Christian woman should."

"It is well that you have forgiven him as a Christian woman should"—Eirik could not help smiling faintly—"but do you not think that is little enough between daughter and father?"

All at once Cecilia's eyes filled with tears. "I *have* been a good, obedient daughter, Eirik. None of you knew Jörund rightly. God rest his soul—but I have wondered many a time that I did not do what Father believed I had done. I think it was no sin in me that I was not minded to stay here and have him before my eyes as he haunted this place like a ghost of all the torment that was worse than being broken on the wheel—when at last it had been given me to share my lot with Aslak and I could say, I too, I am glad to be alive! Above all, since I do not believe Father has longed to see me more than I have longed for him!"

"That you cannot tell! 'Tis true that Father was harsh and silent at times—but judge him by his deeds, Cecilia. I warrant you never saw a man who acted more nobly and as becomes a Christian in all he did. The first to hold out two full hands to the poor, the first to open his door to widows and whosoever craved his protection—methinks your Aslak could bear witness to that: 'twas not so safe then, in the days of old King Haakon's power, to harbour an outlawed manslayer. You have no right, you and he, to bear a grudge because Father did not give him you as well, as soon as the boy cried for you! Have you heard that Father ever won a penny of goods or a foot of land by dishonest dealing or oppression of an even Christian? Not the veriest scoundrel in the countryside has ever dared to utter a word that could stain Father's fame or honour. But if any, man or woman, were in such case that his name and fame were cast as carrion to the birds of prey—then, if Father could say nothing to silence evil tongues, he held his peace. An ill word fell ever to the ground if it came to Father's door—unless one of us others took it up and flew with it. Have you forgotten that Father was the first man to take up arms and rouse the yeomen to resistance when the Duke's army scoured the country, and the last to come home to a plundered manor, wounded and unrewarded by his King?

"God help me, Cecilia—I have no right to chide you; you have been a better daughter than I a son—I rendered him naught but disobedience and a fool's defiance. I had no more wisdom than to be vexed when I thought we were aggrieved by his silence and severity. Though not many times did he chastise me as I deserved —on you he can never have laid a correcting hand. I ought to have known better—"

Eirik raised his left hand a little, looked down at the stump of the little finger.

"I remember when Father had to cut it off. I was so small, I did not see that my life was in danger if it were not taken off at once. When I saw the red-hot iron I was so beside myself with fear that I ran hither and thither about the room, bellowing and kicking in my struggles, so Father had to seize me forcibly. Do you think he tried to soothe me with sweet words? He spoke harshly to me, did Father, but when that was of no use he took the red-hot iron and pressed it into his own flesh to put heart into me."

The son hid his face in his hands, uttering stifled sobs. But presently he looked up again:

"God forgive us both, sister mine—never did we recognize what a man our father was. But you will find it true, as you grow older: the best inheritance he leaves your sons is the memory of his good name—that is God's reward to the descendants of an upright man."

Cecilia sat with bent head; her cheeks had reddened and her expression was unusually mild.

"You are right, brother—Father was more of a man than we guessed. And yet," she whispered after a moment, "for half his lifetime he bore the guilt of an unshriven slaying—and when he would make amends for it at last, God took judgment into his own hand."

"We may not inquire into such things," replied Eirik in **an** earnest whisper—"God's hidden counsels. But never will I believe it fell upon him because Father's sin was worse than most men's. Mayhap it was done to show forth an example—the rest of us take so little heed of our misdeeds. And God made choice of father to do full penance, since He knew his heart—stronger and more faithful than we poor wretches who would not be able to swallow one drop of His justice."

Cecilia said in a low tone: "Aslak has heard something—at home in the Hamar country. There was some talk about Mother, that time she was young, about a clerk or a pupil in the school. He disappeared, and some thought that Father might have had a finger in it—"

"Are you not ashamed?" whispered Eirik indignantly. "Do you and Aslak pay heed to folks' gossip about your parents—?"

"You yourself have said he was hard on her."

"I was only a child when she died—what I thought of the things I saw counts for nothing. Perhaps that was what weighed most heavily on him—to endure his marriage with patience. They were so unlike, and she was ailing from her youth. God must judge between the two. Without sin no man goes through life."

Eirik rose, took a few paces toward the door of the closet, and came back to his sister. "It may be as well that I tell you now— I had meant to announce it to you and Aslak at the funeral ale. When Father is committed to the earth, I shall go back to the convent. So that all he leaves behind him will be yours—except that which Eldrid and I will give for the repose of his soul."

Cecilia was silent a long while.

"Is Eldrid at one with you in this?" she asked at last, a little incredulously.

"Yes. She goes to Gimsöy. Whether she will take the veil I know not—she knows not yet herself. But she will take the vow of chastity and dwell there."

"Is it for Father's soul you do this?" asked his sister again.

"Ay, and for my own." And for Jörund. And for you and your children. For all of us who are rebellious and defiant, when God lays a heavy burden upon us, and who forget Him wholly or in part when He showers His bounties upon us.—This he left unsaid.

"Have you told him this?"

"No. Father was never a man to care much for words and promises. Time enough for him to see it after he is dead."

A moment later Cecilia started up—they heard Gunnar screaming outside in the courtyard. His mother hurried out. Eirik went into the closet to the sick man. In the dim light he saw that Olav lay with one eye open—he was hot and his breath was laboured, but Eirik guessed that he was conscious—and wondered whether the old man had heard anything; he looked at him so strangely—

Olav had lain awake and had heard sentence passed on his own life by the mouth of his son. Meanwhile an image hovered before his vision—it was the frenzy of fever, but not so violent that he did not know it for what it was. He saw a cornfield, overgrown with tares and thistles, willow-herb and brambles—the weeds flaunted their red and yellow flowers in the sun, and the corn was so choked by them that none could tell that the ground had been sown. But out in the field there walked *one*—sometimes he thought it was his guardian angel, but sometimes it was Eirik—a friend who did not ask whether the dying man had done him wrong, but thought only of gathering up the poor ears of corn that he could save among the thistles. It should not have been so, his life should have been like a cornfield swaying clean and bright and ready for the sickle. But one there was who had been able to find a handful of good corn and would lay it in the balance—

Kolbein came to the door and eagerly announced that now they could see Sira Magne's roan horse down by the bridge. Eirik lighted the candles, gave one to the boy, and they went out.

The crag that rose behind the line of outhouses seemed to stand out vaster and more immovable now that it was bathed in the late yellow sunlight. The firs shone with their hard red trunks and branches washed light after the winter's snow, and above was the burning blue vault of heaven. Eirik thought that never before had he seen so plainly how infinitely deep was the ocean of sky, and against this depth the firm rock was more rock and the firs were more intensely firs than he had ever guessed before. The wakeful Eye that watched over all rested upon every single one of the midges that danced before him in the air and knew every pulse-beat in his body. And in the likeness of the bread He came, borne by the priest on the great horse that was now mounting the hill by the barn, to give Himself as food for His own.

The groom who led the horse rang the little silver bell; the house-folk had come out and were kneeling in the yard. Cecilia had her little son in her arms, Aslak and the boys by her side.

Kolbein and Eirik knelt before the door of the house with their candles, whose flames were almost invisible in the sunshine. Eirik knew that the fire that now consumed him was destined to die down, to hide beneath the ashes, to blaze up again in bright flames, but never would it be quenched within him.

At the funeral feast for Olav Audunsson, Eirik announced his and his wife's determination, and at midsummer he and Eldrid had made division of their estate. He accompanied her to Gimsöy, and thence he went straight to Oslo and resumed the habit of the order in the Minorite convent. The ceremony was a quiet one this time, on a weekday morning during one of the first masses. No others of his family were in church than Aslak Gunnarsson and Cecilia. This time his sister seemed less opposed to her brother's turning monk.

Aslak and his wife husbanded the Hestvik estate so well that all Olav's grandchildren were abundantly provided for—Cecilia had three sons and three daughters by her second husband. Of Jörund's sons, Kolbein and Audun turned out well; Torgils was a wild lad, but he was drowned at an early age.

Eirik always impressed it upon the youths, when they visited him at the convent, that their worldly prosperity was a reward for their grandfather's pious and manly life, and he could quote many sayings from Scripture to this effect. The boys were fond of him and had great respect for him; they had never known him except as a barefoot friar. And he was a pious friar, diligent in tending the sick, whether in body or soul; book-learning he also acquired with years, and he was the convent's gardener most of his time. But his nephews knew from what they heard among the neighbours that in his youth Eirik had a name for being somewhat wild. Cecilia never spoke to her children of her brother's former life.

Olav's fame among men was not so lustrous as Eirik would fain have made it—all the young folk knew that well. A bold warrior he had been and a good, honest franklin, but odd and unsociable, a joyless companion in a joyful gathering.

The great pestilence came and made riddance in the family, but it was still numerous after the sickness had passed. Its ravages were not so severe in the south as in the north country. In the Minorite convent of Oslo not much more than the half of the brethren died, but in the house of the order at Nidaros only two monks were left. It was therefore decided that Brother Eirik Olavsson and three young friars from Oslo should be transferred thither. Eirik was then threescore years old, strong and hale, though he had always treated himself with great rigour. But the friars were exposed to violent storms in crossing the mountains, and a few days after he had arrived at his new convent Eirik expired in the arms of his brethren.

When W. A. Dwiggins planned the typographic scheme for KRISTIN LAVRANSDATTER *in 1935 he prepared a "designer's note." Inasmuch as the typography of* THE MASTER OF HESTVIKEN *follows Dwiggins's original scheme for* KRISTIN LAVRANSDATTER, *that note is reproduced below.*

DESIGNER'S NOTE

A PAGE of "old style" type (Linotype *Janson*) furnished with a running-title of "modern face." Quite irregular. For what reason? To be perverse, and shock the typographically pure? No. The purpose is to cut the running-head quite away from the text—to put the two parts of the page in two different regions of historic time almost—as though you had the old chronicle complete in a compact type sympathetic to the narrative, and added the running-title notations in script for your own convenience. To keep the story moving at its own pace, in its own atmosphere, without interference from merely *indexing* details. Whether or not the project is a success the reader will have to say. He will see that the flourished blackletter initials aim to contribute a faint tinge of old time.

W. A. DWIGGINS

Quality PLUME Paperbacks for Your Bookshelf

All prices higher in Canada.

†Not available in Canada.

To order, use the convenient coupon on the next page.